Frank Herbert (1920-1986), who created *Dune*, spent his early life in the Pacific Northwest of America. He was a journalist, photographer, political s⟩⟩⟩⟩⟨ and radio news commentator. Though h⟩⟩ ⟩ *Dune* he was also the author of sev⟩⟩⟩⟩⟩⟩⟩ science fiction ⟩⟩⟩⟩⟩ ⟩⟩⟩⟩⟩⟩g *The Green Brain*, *The Dragon in the Sea*, *The White Plague*, *Destination: Void* and *The Dosadi Experiment*. When Frank Herbert died in 1986 his saga remained uncompleted but he left thousands of pages of notes including historical backgrounds and plot ideas. Some of this material has now been published in *The Road to Dune*. Brian Herbert and Kevin J. Anderson told the story of the years immediately before *Dune* began in *Prelude to Dune* and *Legends of Dune* and in stories published in *The Road to Dune*.

Brian Herbert, Frank Herbert's son, is a widely-published *New York Times* bestselling science fiction author in his own right. As well as being the co-author of the *Prelude to Dune* sequence, he has created his own worlds, including the highly acclaimed novels *Sudanna, Sudanna*, *The Race for God* and *Prisoners of Arionn*. He has also written *Dreamer of Dune*, a comprehensive biography of Frank Herbert.

Kevin J. Anderson, his co-author, has written an ambitious space-opera series, *The Saga of Seven Suns*, as well as numerous world-wide bestselling novels based on the universes of *Star Wars* and *The X-Files*. He has been a *Sunday Times* number one bestseller and in 1998 established the Guinness World Record for 'Largest Single-Author Book Signing'. His critically acclaimed original no⟩⟩⟩ ⟩⟩⟩⟩est aw⟩⟩

The Dune Novels

FRANK HERBERT
THE DUNE NOVELS
Dune
Dune Messiah
Children of Dune
God Emperor of Dune
Heretics of Dune
Chapterhouse: Dune

FRANK HERBERT, BRIAN HERBERT AND
KEVIN J. ANDERSON
The Road to Dune

BRIAN HERBERT AND KEVIN J. ANDERSON
LEGENDS OF DUNE
The Butlerian Jihad
The Machine Crusade
The Battle of Corrin

PRELUDE TO DUNE
House Atreides
House Harkonnen
House Corrino

Hunters of Dune
Sandworms of Dune

BRIAN HERBERT &
KEVIN J. ANDERSON

Sandworms of Dune

Based on an outline by Frank Herbert

HODDER

First published in Great Britain in 2007 by Hodder & Stoughton
An Hachette Livre UK Company

First published in paperback in 2008

7

A CIP catalogue record for this title is available
from the British Library

ISBN 978 0 340 83752 8

Typeset in Plantin Light by Palimpsest Book Production Limited,
Grangemouth, Stirlingshire

Printed and bound by
CPI Mackays, Chatham ME5 8TD

Hodder and Stoughton policy is to use papers that are natural,
renewable and recyclable products and made from wood
grown in sustainable forests. The logging and manufacturing
processes are expected to conform to the environmental
regulations of the country of origin.

Hodder & Stoughton Ltd
338 Euston Road
London NW1 3BH

www.hodder.co.uk

We can never overstate the appreciation we owe to the genius who created this incredible series. Once again, this book is for Frank Herbert, a man of wondrous and important ideas, who has been our mentor as we continue to write new stories in his fantastic Dune universe. Sandworms of Dune *is the chronological grand finale that he envisioned, and we are pleased to finally bring it to his millions of loyal fans.*

ACKNOWLEDGMENTS

As with all of our previous Dune novels, we have depended on the efforts of a great many people to make the manuscript as good as possible. We would like to thank Pat LoBrutto, Tom Doherty, and Paul Stevens and Tor Books; Carolyn Caughey at Hodder & Stoughton; Catherine Sidor, Louis Moesta, and Diane Jones at WordFire, Inc; Penny Merritt, Kim Herbert, and Byron Merritt at Herbert Properties LLC; and Mike Anderson at the dunenovels.com website, as well as Dr Attila Torkos, who worked on fact-checking and consistency.

In addition, we have had many supporters of the new Dune novels, including John Silbersack, Robert Gottlieb, and Claire Roberts at Trident Media Group; Richard Rubinstein, Mike Messina, John Harrison, and Emily Austin-Bruns at New Amsterdam Entertainment; Ron Merritt, David Merritt, Julie Herbert, Robert Merritt, Margaux Herbert, and Theresa Shackelford at Herbert Properties LLC.

And as always, these books would not exist without the unending help and support from our wives, Janet Herbert and Rebecca Moesta Anderson.

Soon after the Honored Matres careened into the Old Empire, the Bene Gesserit Sisterhood learned to hate and fear them. The intruders used their terrible Obliterator weapons to destroy Bene Gesserit and Tleilaxu planets, Richeses with its vast industries and weapon shops, even Rakis itself.

But in order to survive the even greater Enemy that pursued them, the Honored Matres desperately needed knowledge that only the Sisterhood possessed. To obtain it, they struck like angry vipers, lashing out with extreme violence.

After the Battle of Junction, the two opposing groups were forcibly united into a New Sisterhood, but the factions continued to wrestle for control and dominance. Such a waste of time, talent, and blood! The real threat came from outside, but we continued to fight the wrong enemy.

– MOTHER COMMANDER MURBELLA,
address to the New Sisterhood

Two people drift in a lifeboat on an uncharted sea. One says, 'There! I see an island. Our best chance is to go ashore, build a shelter, and await rescue.' The other says, 'No, we must go farther out to sea and hope to find the shipping lanes. That is our best chance.' Unable to agree, the two fight, the lifeboat capsizes, and they drown.

This is the nature of humanity. Even if only two people are left in the entire universe, they will come to represent opposing factions.

– *The Bene Gesserit Acolytes' Handbook*

In re-creating particular gholas, we reweave the fabric of history. Once more, Paul Muad'Dib walks among us, with his beloved Chani, his mother the Lady Jessica, and his son Leto II, the God Emperor of Dune. The presence of Suk doctor Wellington Yueh, whose treachery brought a great house to its knees, is at once disturbing and comforting. Also with us are the warrior-Mentat Thufir Hawat, the Fremen Naib Stilgar, and the great planetologist Liet-Kynes. Consider the possibilities!

Such genius constitutes a formidable army. We will need that brilliance, because we face an opponent more terrible, than we ever imagined.

— DUNCAN IDAHO,
Memories of More Than a Mentat

I have waited and planned and built my strength for fifteen thousand years. I have evolved. It is time.

— OMNIUS

SANDWORMS OF DUNE

Twenty-One Years After

Escape from Chapterhouse

So many people I knew in the past are not yet reborn. I still miss them, even though I do not remember them. The axlotl tanks will soon remedy that.

— LADY JESSICA,
the ghola

Aboard the wandering no-ship *Ithaca*, Jessica witnessed the birth of her daughter, but only as an observer. Just fourteen years old, she and many others crowded the medical center, while two Bene Gesserit Suk doctors in the adjacent creche prepared to extract the tiny girl child from an axlotl tank.

'Alia,' one of the female doctors murmured.

This was not truly Jessica's daughter, but a ghola grown from preserved cells. None of the young gholas on the no-ship were 'themselves' yet. They had regained none of their memories, none of their pasts.

Something tried to surface at the back of her mind, and though she worried at it like a loose tooth, Jessica could not remember the first time Alia had been born. In the archives, she had read and reread the legendary accounts generated by Muad'Dib's biographers. But she couldn't *remember*.

All she had were images from her studies: *A dry and*

dusty sietch on Arrakis, surrounded by Fremen. Jessica and her son Paul had been on the run, taken in by the desert tribe. Duke Leto was dead, murdered by Harkonnens. Pregnant, Jessica had drunk the Water of Life, forever changing the fetus inside her. From the moment of her birth, the original Alia had been different from all other babies, filled with ancient wisdom and madness, able to tap into Other Memory without having gone through the Spice Agony. Abomination!

That had been another Alia. Another time and another way.

Now Jessica stood beside her ghola 'son' Paul, who was chronologically a year older than she. Paul waited with his beloved Fremen mate Chani and the nine-year-old ghola of a boy who had in turn been *their* son, Leto II. In a prior shuffle of lives, this had been Jessica's family.

The Bene Gesserit order had resurrected these figures from history to help fight against the terrible Outside Enemy that hunted them. They had Thufir Hawat, the planetologist Liet-Kynes, the Fremen leader Stilgar, and even the notorious Dr Yueh. Now, after almost a decade of hiatus in the ghola program, Alia had joined the group. Others would come soon; the three remaining axlotl tanks were already pregnant with new children: Gurney Halleck, Serena Butler, Xavier Harkonnen.

Duncan Idaho gave Jessica a quizzical look. Eternal Duncan, with all of his memories restored from all of his prior lives . . . She wondered what he thought of this new ghola baby, a bubble of the past rising up to the present. Long ago, the first ghola of Duncan had been Alia's consort . . .

CONCEALING HIS AGE well, Duncan was a full-grown man with dark wiry hair. He looked exactly like the hero shown in so many archival records, from the time of Muad'Dib, through the God Emperor's thirty-five-century reign, to now, another fifteen centuries later.

Breathless and late, the old Rabbi bustled into the birthing chamber accompanied by twelve-year-old Wellington Yueh. Young Yueh's forehead did not bear the diamond tattoo of the famous Suk School. The bearded Rabbi seemed to think he could save the gangly young man from repeating the terrible crimes he had committed in his prior life.

At the moment the Rabbi looked angry, as he invariably did whenever he came near the axlotl tanks. Since the Bene Gesserit doctors ignored him, the old man vented his displeasure on Sheeana. 'After years of sanity, you have done it again! When will you learn to stop taunting God?'

After receiving an ominous prescient dream, Sheeana had declared a temporary moratorium on the ghola project that had been her passion from its inception. But their recent ordeal on the planet of the Handlers and their near capture by the Enemy hunters had forced Sheeana to reassess that decision. The wealth of historical and tactical experience the reawakened gholas could offer might be the greatest weapon the no-ship possessed. Sheeana had decided to take the risk.

Perhaps we will be saved by Alia one day, Jessica thought. *Or by one of the other gholas . . .*

Tempting fate, Sheeana had performed an experiment on this unborn ghola in an effort to make it more like *the* Alia. Estimating the point in the pregnancy when the original Jessica had consumed the Water of Life, Sheeana had instructed Bene Gesserit Suk doctors to flood the axlotl tank with a near-fatal spice overdose. Saturating the fetus. *Trying* to re-create an Abomination.

Jessica had been horrified to learn of it – too late, when she could do nothing about it. How would the spice affect that innocent baby? A melange overdose was different from undergoing the Agony.

One of the Suk doctors told the Rabbi to stay out of the birthing creche. Scowling, the old man held up a trembling hand, as if making a blessing on the pale flesh of the axlotl tank. 'You witches think these tanks are no longer women, no longer human – but this is still Rebecca. She remains a child of my flock.'

'Rebecca fulfilled a vital need.' Sheeana said. 'All of the volunteers knew exactly what they were doing. She accepted her responsibility. Why can't you?'

The Rabbi turned in exasperation toward the young man at his side. 'Speak to them, Yueh. Maybe they will listen to you.'

Jessica thought the sallow young ghola seemed more intrigued than incensed about the tanks. 'As a Suk doctor,' he said, 'I delivered many children. But never like this. At least I don't think so. With my ghola memories still locked away, I get confused sometimes.'

'And Rebecca is human – not just some biological machine to produce melange and a brood of gholas. You have to see that.' The Rabbi's voice grew in volume.

Yueh shrugged. 'Because I was born in the same fashion, I cannot be entirely objective. If my memories were restored, maybe I'd agree with you.'

'You don't need original memories to think! You can *think*, can't you?'

'The baby is ready,' one of the doctors interrupted. 'We must decant it now.' She turned impatiently to the Rabbi. 'Let us do our work – or the tank could be harmed as well.'

With a sound of disgust, the Rabbi shouldered his way from the birthing creche. Yueh remained behind, continuing to watch.

One of the Suk women tied off the umbilical cord from the fleshy tank. Her shorter colleague cut the purplish-red whip; then she wiped off the slick infant and lifted little Alia into the air. The child let out a loud and immediate cry, as if she had been impatient to be born. Jessica sighed in relief at the healthy sound, which told her the girl was not an Abomination this time. The original newborn Alia had purportedly looked upon the world with the eyes and intelligence of a full adult. This baby's crying sounded normal. But it stopped abruptly.

While one doctor tended the now-sagging axlotl tank, the other dried the infant and wrapped her in a blanket. Unable to help feeling a tug at her heart, Jessica wanted to reach out and hold the baby, but resisted the urge. Would Alia suddenly start speaking, uttering voices from Other Memory? Instead, the baby looked around the medical center, without seeming to focus.

Others would care for Alia, not unlike the way Bene Gesserit sisters took baby girls under their collective wing. The first Jessica, born under the close scrutiny of breeding mistresses, had never known a mother in the traditional sense. Nor would this Jessica, nor Alia, nor any of the other experimental ghola babies. The new daughter would be raised communally in an improvised society, more an object of scientific curiosity than love.

'What an odd family we all are,' Jessica whispered.

> *Humans are never capable of complete accuracy. Despite all the knowledge and experiences we have absorbed from countless Face Dancer 'ambassadors,' we are left with a confused picture. Nonetheless, the flawed accounts of human history provide amusing insights into the delusions of mankind.*
>
> — ERASMUS,
> Records and Analyses, Backup 242

In spite of a decades-long effort, the thinking machines had not yet captured the no-ship and its precious cargo. That did not, however, stop the computer evermind from launching his vast extermination fleet against the rest of humanity.

Duncan Idaho continued to elude Omnius and Erasmus, who repeatedly cast their sparkling tachyon net into the nothingness, searching for their quarry. The no-ship's veiling capability normally prevented it from being seen, but from time to time the pursuers caught glimpses, as of something concealed behind shrubbery. At first the hunt had been a challenge, but now the evermind was growing frustrated.

'You have lost the ship again,' Omnius boomed through wall speakers in the central, cathedral-like chamber in the technological metropolis of Synchrony.

'Inaccurate. I must first find it before I can lose it.' Erasmus tried to sound carefree as he shifted his flowmental skin, reverting from his guise as a kindly old woman to the more familiar appearance of a platinum-surfaced robot.

Like overarching tree trunks, metal spires towered above Erasmus to form a vaulted dome within the machine cathedral. Photons glittered from the activated skins of the pillars, bathing his new laboratory in light. He had even installed a glowing fountain that bubbled with lava – a useless decoration, but the robot often indulged his carefully cultivated artistic sensibilities. 'Do not be impatient. Remember the mathematical projections. Everything is nicely predetermined.'

'Your mathematical projections could be myths, like any prophecy. How do I know they are correct?'

'Because I have said they are correct.'

With the launch of the machine fleet, the long-foretold Kralizec had begun, at last. Kralizec . . . Armageddon . . . the Battle at the End of the Universe . . . Ragnarok . . . Azrafel . . . the End Times . . . the Cloud Darkness. It was a time of fundamental change, of the entire universe shifting on its cosmic axis. Human legends had predicted such a cataclysmic event since the dawn of civilization. Indeed, they had already been through several iterations of similar cataclysms: the Butlerian Jihad itself, the jihad of Paul Muad'Dib, the reign of the Tyrant Leto II. By manipulating computer projections, and thus creating expectations in the mind of Omnius, Erasmus had succeeded in initiating the events that would bring about another fundamental shift. Prophecy and reality – the order of things really didn't matter.

Like an arrow, all of Erasmus's infinitely complex calculations, running trillions of data points through the most sophisticated routines, pointed to one result: The final Kwisatz Haderach – whoever that was – would determine the course of events at the end of Kralizec. The projection also revealed that the Kwisatz Haderach was on the no-ship, so Omnius naturally wanted such a force fighting on his side. Ergo, the thinking machines needed to capture that ship. The first to exert control over the final Kwisatz Haderach would win.

Erasmus didn't fully understand exactly what the superhuman might do when he was located and seized. Though the robot was a longtime student of mankind, he was still a thinking machine, while the Kwisatz Haderach was not. The new Face Dancers, who had long infiltrated humanity and brought vital information back to the Synchronized Empire, fell somewhere in between, like hybrid biological machines. He and Omnius had both absorbed so many of the lives stolen by the Face Dancers that sometimes they forgot who they were. The original Tleilaxu Masters had not foreseen the significance of what they had helped create.

The independent robot knew he still had to keep Omnius under control, though. 'We have time. You have a galaxy to conquer before we need the Kwisatz Haderach aboard that ship.'

'I am glad I did not wait for you to succeed.'

For centuries Omnius had been building his invincible force. Using traditional but supremely efficient lightspeed engines, the millions and millions of machine vessels now swept forward and spread out, conquering one star system at a time. The evermind could have made use of the surrogate mathematical navigation systems, which his Face Dancers had 'given' to the Spacing Guild, but one element of the Holtzman technology simply remained too incomprehensible. Something indefinably human was required to travel through foldspace, an intangible 'leap of faith.' The evermind would never admit that the bizarre technology actually made him . . . nervous.

Following a flurry of test skirmishes, the wall of robotic battleships had encountered and swiftly destroyed fringe outpost worlds settled by humans. Vanguard drones mapped out the planets ahead and distributed deadly biological plagues that Erasmus had developed; by the time the actual machine fleet arrived at a target world, military action was often unnecessary against a dying population. Each combat engagement, even clashes with isolated groups of Honored Matres, was equally decisive.

To keep himself occupied, the independent robot reviewed the streams of data sent back to him. This was the part he enjoyed best. A buzzing watcheye flitted in front of him, and he brushed it away. 'If you allow me to concentrate, Omnius, I may find some way to speed up our progress against the humans.'

'How do I know you will not make another mistake?'

'Because you have confidence in my abilities.'

The watcheye flitted away.

While the machine fleet crushed one human planet after another, Erasmus issued additional instructions for the invader robots. As the infected humans lay writhing, their pores, machine scouts be winnowed from the random lives that Face Dancers had assimilated.

With all the fresh data flowing in, Erasmus had the luxury of becoming a scientist again, as he had been long ago. The pursuit of scientific truth had always been his true reason for existence. Now the flood was greater than ever before. Glad to possess so much new information, so much undigested data, he gorged his elaborate mind on raw facts and histories.

After the supposed destruction of thinking machines more than fifteen millennia earlier, the fecund humans had spread, building civilizations and destroying them. Erasmus was intrigued by how, after the Battle of Corrin, the Butler family had founded an empire and ruled it under the name of Corrino for ten thousand years, with a few gaps and interregnums, only to be overthrown by a fanatical leader named Muad'Dib.

Paul Atreides. The first Kwisatz Haderach.

A more fundamental change, however, had come from his son Leto II, called the God Emperor or Tyrant. Another Kwisatz Haderach – a unique hybrid of man and sandworm that had imposed a draconian rule for thirty-five hundred years. After his assassination, human civilization fragmented. Fleeing to the far reaches of the galaxy in the Scattering, people became hardened by their privations until the worst sort of humans – Honored Matres – had blundered into the burgeoning machine empire . . .

Another flitting watcheye scanned the same records Erasmus was reading. Omnius spoke through resonating plates in the walls. 'I find thei͟r̲ ͟ fact – to b̲e̲ ͟ ͟ himself from the stacks of historical files. 'Their histories show how they view themselves and the universe around them. Obviously, these humans need someone to take firm control again.'

Why is religion important? Because logic alone does not compel a person to make great sacrifices. Given sufficient religious fervor, however, people will throw themselves against impossible odds and consider themselves blessed for doing so.

– MISSIONARIA PROTECTIVA,
First Primer

Two male workers appeared at the door of Murbella's coldly ostentatious council chambers during a tense meeting. Using suspensor clamps, they hauled a large, motionless robot between them. 'Mother Commander? You asked for this to be delivered here.'

The combat machine was built from blue and black metal, reinforced with struts and overlapping armor. Its conical head contained a suite of sensors and targeting arrays, and four engine-driven arms were wrapped with cables and augmented with weapons. Damaged during a recent skirmish, the fighting robot had dark smears across its bulky torso where high-energy blasts had knocked out its internal processors. The robotic thing was shut down, dead, defeated. But even deactivated, it was cause for nightmares.

Murbella's advisors, startled out of their discussions

and arguments, stared at the big machine. All of the gathered women wore the plain black unitard of the New Sisterhood, following a code of homogenized dress that allowed no indication of their origins as either Bene Gesserit or Honored Matre.

Murbella gestured to the intimidated-looking workers. 'Bring that thing inside where we can see it every time we talk about the Enemy. It will do us good to be reminded of the adversary we're up against.'

Even with the suspensor clamps, the men sweated as they wrestled the machine into the room. Murbella strode to the bulky combat robot and stared with defiance up into its dull optic sensors. She glanced proudly at her daughter. 'Bashar Idaho brought this specimen back from the battle at Duvalle.'

'It should be sent to the scrap heap. Or shot into space,' said Kiria, a hard-edged former Honored Matre. 'What if it still has passive spy programming?'

'It's been thoroughly purged,' said Janess Idaho. As the newly appointed commandant of the Sisterhood's military forces, she had become a very pragmatic young woman.

'A trophy, Mother Commander?' asked Laera, a dark-skinned Reverend Mother who often quietly supported Murbella. 'Or a prisoner of war?'

'This is the only one our armies found intact. We blew up four machine ships before we retreated and let them destroy the planet behind us. They had already turned their plagues loose on Ronto and Pital, leaving no survivors. Total population losses number in the billions.'

Duvalle, Ronto, and Pital were just the latest casualties as the machine army continued its forward march through the outlying systems. Because of the distances involved and the sheer might of the attacking ships, reports were sketchy and often outdated. Refugees and couriers surged away from battle zones, heading inward from the fringes of the Scattering.

Murbella turned her back on the deactivated robot and faced the Sisters. 'Knowing that a tempest approaches, we have the option of simply evacuating – abandoning everything we have. That is the Honored Matre way.'

Some of the Sisters flinched at the comment. Long ago, Honored Matres had chosen to run from the Enemy, pillaging on their way out, hoping to stay one step ahead of the storm. To them, the Old Empire had been no more than a crude barricade to be thrown up against the Enemy; they had simply hoped it would last long enough for them to get away.

'Or, we can board up our windows, strengthen our walls, and ride it out. And hope we survive.'

'This is no mere storm, Mother Commander,' said Laera. 'The repercussions are already being felt. Refugees fleeing the battlefront are overwhelming the support systems of second-wave worlds, all of which are preparing for evacuation as well. The people won't stand and fight.'

'Like waterlogged rats crowding to the corner of a sinking raft,' Kiria muttered.

'Says the Honored Matre, who did exactly the same,' Janess said from the end of the table, then tried to cover her comment by loudly sipping her spice coffee. Kiria glared at her.

'A shadow deep in our Honored Matre past,' Murbella said. 'Through hubris, and a violent predisposition to strike first and understand later, the whores caused all these problems.' By digging deep into her mind and history, she had been the first to remember how her long-dead sisters had stupidly provoked the thinking machines.

Kiria was indignant, clearly still associating herself with the Honored Matres. Murbella found it disturbing. 'You yourself revealed why the Honored Matres are what they are, Mother Commander. Descended from tortured Tleilaxu females, rogue Reverend Mothers, and a few Fish Speakers. They had every right to be vengeful.'

'They had no right to be stupid!' Murbella snapped. 'A painful past did not give them the right to lash out against anything they encountered. They couldn't salve their conscience by pretending they knew what they were doing when they attacked a machine outpost and stole weapons they didn't understand.' She smiled slightly. 'If anything, I can relate to – though not approve of – their revenge against the Tleilaxu worlds. In Other Memory I know what the Tleilaxu did to my ancestors . . . I *remember* being one of their vile axlotl tanks. But make no mistake, that kind of provocative and poorly planned violence has caused immeasurable trouble for the human race. And now look what we face!'

'How can we strengthen ourselves against this storm, Mother Commander?' The question came from ancient Accadia, a Reverend Mother who lived in the Chapter-house Archives. Accadia hardly ever slept and rarely allowed sunlight to touch her parchment skin. 'What defenses do we have?' The hulking combat robot seemed to mock them from the corner of the room, where the men had left it.

'We have the weapon of religion. Especially *Sheeana*.'

'Sheeana is of no use to us!' Janess said. 'Her followers believe she died on Rakis decades ago.'

The priests on Rakis had once made much of the girl

who could command sandworms. The Bene Gesserit had created a grassroots religion around Sheeana, and the annihilation of Dune had only served the Sisterhood's greater purpose. After her supposed death, the rescued girl was isolated on Chapterhouse, so that one day she might 'return from the grave' to great fanfare. But the real Sheeana had escaped with Duncan on the no-ship more than twenty years ago.

'It's not necessary for us to have *her*, specifically. Simply find Sisters who resemble her and apply any necessary makeup and facial modifications.' Murbella tapped fingers against her lips. 'Yes, we shall begin with twelve new Sheeanas. Disperse them to the refugee worlds, since the displaced survivors will be our most impressionable recruits. The resurrected Sheeana will seem to appear everywhere at once – a messiah, a visionary, a leader.'

Laera spoke in an eminently reasonable voice. 'Genetic tests will prove that these impostors are not Sheeana. Your plan will backfire once people see we have tried to trick them.'

Kiria had already thought of the obvious solution. 'We can have Bene Gesserit doctors – Suk doctors – perform the tests . . . and lie for us.'

'Also, don't underestimate the greatest advantage we have.' Murbella held out her hand like a mendicant asking for alms. 'The people *want* to believe. For thousands of years, our Missionaria Protectiva wove religious beliefs among populations. Now we must use those techniques not just for our own protection, but as a functional weapon, a means of influencing armies. No longer passive and protective, but an active force. A Missionaria *Aggressiva*.'

The other women, especially Kiria, seemed to like the

idea. Accadia scowled down at her Ridulian crystal sheets, as if trying to find profound answers written in the dense characters.

Murbella flashed a defiant look at the combat robot. 'The twelve Sheeanas will carry spice from our stockpiles. Each will distribute extravagant amounts of melange as she makes her pronouncements. She will say that Shaitan told her in a dream that spice would flow again soon. Though Rakis was burned as lifeless as Sodom and Gomorrah, many new Dunes will appear elsewhere. Sheeana will promise them this.' Years ago, groups of Reverend Mothers had been sent out on a secret Scattering, taking ships and all-important sandtrout to seed additional planets and create more desert worlds for the sandworms.

'False prophets and sightings of the messiah. It's been done before.' Kiria sounded bored. 'Explain how this will benefit us.'

Murbella shot her a calculated smile. 'We take advantage of the superstitions that will run rampant. People believe they must endure a time of tribulation, a cycle as old as the most ancient religions, long before the First Great Movement or the Zensunni Hajj. So, we tailor that belief to our own uses. The thinking machines are the great evil we have to defeat before humanity can reap its reward.'

Turning to the aged mistress of the Archives, she said, 'Accadia, read everything you can find about the Butlerian Jihad and how Serena Butler led her forces. The same for Paul Muad'Dib. We could even say that the Tyrant began to prepare us for this. Study his writings and take sections out of context to support our message, so the people will be convinced that this final universal conflict has been foretold all along: *Kralizec*. If they believe in the prophecies, they'll continue to fight long after any rational hope should be dashed.'

She motioned for the women to go about their tasks. 'In the meantime, I have set up a meeting with the Ixians and the Guild. Since Richese is destroyed, I'll demand that they devote their manufacturing capabilities to our war effort. We need every scrap of resistance the human race can muster.'

As she was leaving, Accadia asked, 'And what if those old prophecies prove to be correct? What if these truly are the End Times?'

'Then our efforts are all the more justified. And we still fight. It's all we can do.' Facing the robot, Murbella spoke to it as if the machine mind could still hear her. 'And that's how we will defeat you.'

In the enormous Guild Heighliner, no passengers ever guessed what the Navigator and his captive Tleilaxu Master were doing right under their noses.

By holding melange supplies for ransom, the Bene Gesserit witches had backed the Spacing Guild into a corner and forced them to choose drastic alternatives. Facing extinction from spice starvation, the Navigator faction urged Waff to greater speed to complete his task. The Tleilaxu Master felt the need for haste as well, since he was facing extinction himself, though for different reasons.

Turning his back on the observation lens, Waff surreptitiously consumed another dose of melange. The cinnamony powder had been provided strictly for scientific purposes. He touched the burning substance to his lips and tongue, closed his eyes in ecstasy. Such a small quantity – only a taste – was enough to buy a house on a colony world these days! The Tleilaxu man felt energy rush back into his ailing body. Edrik would not begrudge him this bit of melange to help him think straight.

Normally, Tleilaxu Masters lived from body to body in a chain of ghola immortality. They had learned patience and long-term planning from the Great Belief. Had not God's Messenger himself lived for three and a half millennia? But forbidden techniques had accelerated this Waff's growth in the axlotl tank. The cells in his body burned through his existence like flames through a forest, sweeping him from infancy to childhood to maturity, in only a few years. Waff's memory restoration had been imperfect, bringing back only fragments of his past life and knowledge.

Escaping the Honored Matres, Waff had been forced to take refuge with the Navigator faction. Since Edrik and his fellows had financed his ghola resurrection in the first place, why not beg them for sanctuary? Though the little man did not remember how to create melange with axlotl tanks, he claimed he could do the impossible – bring back the supposedly extinct sandworms. A much more spectacular and necessary solution.

In the isolated Heighliner laboratory, Edrik had provided all of the research tools, technical equipment, and genetic raw material he could possibly need. Waff did as the Navigators demanded. Bringing back the magnificent worms that had been exterminated on Rakis offered the simultaneous possibilities of manufacturing spice, and of restoring his Prophet.

I must do this! Failure is not an option.

With his accelerated maturity, Waff would be at his peak – the best health, the sharpest mind – for only a short while longer. Before he began the inevitable rapid degeneration, he had much to accomplish. The tremendous responsibility prodded at him.

Focus, focus!

He climbed onto a stool and peered into a plaz-walled containment tank full of sand from Rakis itself. *Dune.* Because of the planet's religious significance, pilgrims who could not afford the interplanetary passage contented themselves with relics, fragments of stone chipped from the ruins of Muad'Dib's original palace or scraps of spice cloth embroidered with the sayings of Leto II. Even the poorest of devout followers wanted a sample of Rakian sand, so that they could dust their fingertips and imagine themselves closer to the Divided God. The Navigators had acquired hundreds of cubic meters of authentic Rakian sand. Though it was doubtful that the origin of the grains would have any effect on the sandworm tests, Waff preferred to remove any stray variables.

He leaned over the open tank, filled his mouth with saliva, and let a long droplet splatter onto the soft sand. Like piranhas in an aquarium, shapes stirred beneath the surface, swirling to seize the invading moisture. In another place long ago, spitting – sharing one's personal water – had been a sign of respect among the Fremen. Waff used it to bring sandtrout to the surface.

Little makers. Sandtrout specimens, far more precious even than the sand of Dune.

Years ago, the Guild had intercepted a secret Bene Gesserit ship carrying sandtrout in its hold. When the witches aboard refused to explain their mission, they were all killed, their sandtrout seized, and Chapterhouse had been none the wiser.

Learning that the Guild possessed some of the immature sandworm vectors, Waff demanded them for his work. Though he could not remember how to create melange in an axlotl tank, this experiment had much greater potential. By resurrecting the worms, he could not only bring back spice, but the Prophet himself!

Unafraid of the sandtrout, he reached into the aquarium with a small hand. Grabbing one of the leathery creatures by its fringe, he pulled it flopping out of the sand. Sensing the moisture in Waff's perspiration, the sandtrout wrapped itself around his fingers, palm, and knuckles. He poked and prodded the soft surface, reshaping the edges.

'Little sandtrout, what secrets do you have for me?' He formed a fist, and the creature flowed around it to form a jellylike glove. He could feel his skin drying out.

Carrying the sandtrout, Waff went to a clean research table and set out a wide, deep pan. He tried to unwrap the sandtrout from his knuckles, but each time he moved the membrane it flowed back onto his skin. Feeling the desiccation in his hand now, he poured a beaker of fresh water into the bottom of the pan. The sandtrout, attracted by a larger supply, quickly plopped into it.

Water was deadly poison to sandworms, but not to the younger sandtrout, the larval stage of the worms. The early vector had a fundamentally different biochemistry before it underwent the metamorphosis into its mature form. A paradox. How could one stage in the life cycle be so ravenously drawn to water, while a later phase was killed by it?

Flexing his fingers to recover from the unnatural dryness, Waff was fascinated as the specimen engulfed the water. The larva instinctively hoarded moisture to create a perfectly dry environment for the adult. From previous-life memories that did remain within him, he knew of ancient Tleilaxu experiments to move and control worms. Standard attempts to transplant full-grown worms onto dry planets always failed. Even the most extreme offworld landscapes still had too much moisture to support such a fragile – fragile? – life-form as the sandworms.

Now, though, he had a different idea. Instead of changing the *worlds* to accommodate sandworms, perhaps he could alter the worms themselves in their immature stage, help them adapt. The Tleilaxu understood the Language of God, and their genius for genetics had achieved the impossible many times. Had not Leto II been God's Prophet? It was Waff's duty to bring Him back.

The concept and chromosomal mechanics seemed simple. At some point in the sandtrout's development, a trigger changed the creature's chemical response toward a substance as simple as water. If he could only find that trigger and block it, the sandtrout should continue to mature, but without such a deathly aversion to liquid water. Now that would be a true miracle!

But if one prevented a caterpillar from spinning a cocoon, would it still transform into a great moth? He would have to be very careful, indeed.

If he understood what the witches had done on Chapterhouse, they had discovered a way to release sandtrout into a planetary environment – the Bene Gesserit homeworld. Once there, the sandtrout reproduced and began an unstoppable process to destroy (remake?) the whole ecosystem. From a lush planet to an arid wasteland. They would eventually turn the world into a total desert, where the sandworms could survive and be reborn.

More questions continued to follow, one after another. Why were the fleeing Bene Gesserit Sisters carrying sandtrout samples aboard their refugee ships? Were they trying to distribute them to other worlds, and thereby create more desert planets? Habitats for more worms?

Such a plan would require a huge concerted effort, take decades to come to fruition, and kill off the native life on a planet. Inefficient.

Waff had a much more immediate solution. If he could develop a breed of sandworm that tolerated water, even thrived around it, the creatures could be transplanted onto innumerable worlds where they could grow swiftly and multiply! The worms would not need to reconstruct a whole planetary environment before they began to produce melange. That alone would save decades that Waff simply did not have. His modified worms would provide all the spice the Guild Navigators could ever desire – and serve Waff's purposes as well.

Help me, Prophet!

The sandtrout specimen had absorbed all the water in the pan and now gradually moved about the base and sides, exploring the boundaries. Waff brought research tools and chemicals to the laboratory table – his alcohols, acids, and flames, his deep sample extractors.

The first cut was the hardest. Then he began to work on the shapeless, squirming creature to pry loose its genetic secrets in any way he could.

He had the best DNA analyzers and genetic sequencers the Guild could obtain . . . and they were very good, indeed. The sandtrout took a long time to die, but Waff was certain the Prophet wouldn't mind.

A stench seeps from my pores. The foul odor of extinction.

– SCYTALE,

the last known Tleilaxu Master

The small, gray-skinned child looked worriedly at his older but identical counterpart. 'This is a restricted area. The Bashar will be very angry with us.'

The older Scytale scowled, disappointed that a child with such a magnificent destiny could be so timid. 'These people have no authority to impose their rules on me – either version of me!' Despite years of preparation, instruction, and insistence, Scytale knew that the ghola boy still did not grasp who he was. The Tleilaxu Master coughed and winced, unable to minimize his physical problems. 'You must awaken your genetic memories before it is too late!'

The child followed his older self down the dim corridor of the no-ship, but his steps were too shaky to be furtive. Occasionally the degenerating Scytale needed support from his twelve-year-old 'son.' Each day, each lesson, should bring the younger one closer to the tipping point at which his embedded memories would cascade free. Then, finally, old Scytale could allow himself to die.

Years ago, he had been forced to offer his only

bargaining chip – his secret stash of valuable cellular material – to bribe the witches. Scytale resented being put in such a position, but in return for the raw makings of heroes from the past for the witches' own purposes, Sheeana had agreed to let him use the axlotl tanks to grow a new version of himself. He hoped it wasn't too late.

For years now, every sentence, every day increased pressure on the younger Scytale. His 'father,' a victim of planned cellular obsolescence, doubted he had another year before collapsing completely. Unless the boy received his memories soon, *very soon*, all the knowledge of the Tleilaxu would be lost. Old Scytale winced at the dire prospect, which hurt him far more than any physical pain.

They reached one of the vacant lower levels, where a testing chamber had gone unnoticed in the empty expanses of the ship. 'I will use this powindah teaching equipment to show you how God meant for the Tleilaxu to live.' The walls were smooth and curved, the glow-panels tuned to a dull orange. The room seemed to be full of gestating wombs, round, flaccid, mindless – the way women were supposed to serve a truly civilized society.

Scytale smiled at the sight, while the boy stared around with dark eyes. 'Axlotl tanks. So many of them! Where did they all come from?'

'Unfortunately they are merely holographic projections.' The high-quality simulation included mock tank sounds, as well as the odors of chemicals, disinfectants, and medicinals.

As Scytale stood surrounded by the glorious images, his heart ached to see the home he missed so much, a home now utterly destroyed. Years ago, before he was allowed to set foot again in sacred Bandalong, Scytale and all Tleilaxu had always undergone a lengthy cleansing process. Ever since the Honored Matres had forced him to flee with only his life and a few bargaining chips, he had tried to observe the rituals and practices as much as possible – and had vigorously taught them to the young ghola – but there were limitations. Scytale had not felt sufficiently clean in a long time. But he knew that God would understand.

'This is how a typical breeding chamber used to look. Study it. Absorb it. Remind yourself of how things were, how they should be. I created these images from my own memories, and those same memories are within you. Find them.'

Scytale had said the same thing again and again, hammering it into the child. His younger version was a good student, very intelligent, and knew all the information by rote learning, but the boy didn't know it in his soul.

Sheeana and the other witches didn't grasp the immensity of the crisis he faced, or perhaps they didn't care. The Bene Gesserits understood little about the nuances of restoring a ghola's memories, could not recognize the moment when a ghola was perfectly ready . . . but Scytale might not have the luxury of waiting. The child was certainly old enough. He should awaken! Soon the boy would be the only Tleilaxu left, with no one to wake his memories.

As he surveyed the rows of breeding vats, the junior Scytale's face filled with awe and intimidation. The boy was drinking it all in. Good. 'That tank in the second row is the one that gave birth to me,' he said. 'The Sisterhood called her Rebecca.'

'The tank has no name. It is not a person and never was. Even when it could speak, it was only a female. We Tleilaxu never name our tanks, nor the females that preceded them.'

Expanding the image, he allowed the walls to disappear into a projection of a vast breeding house with tank after tank after tank; outside were the spires and streets of Bandalong. These visual cues should have been sufficient, but Scytale wished he could have added other sensory details, the female reproductive smells, the feel of the sunlight of home, the comforting knowledge of countless Tleilaxu filling the streets, the buildings, the temples.

He felt achingly lonely.

'I should not still be alive and standing before you. It offends me to be old and in pain, with my body malfunctioning. The kehl of true Masters should have euthanized me long ago and let me live on in a fresh ghola body. But these are not proper times.'

'These are not proper times,' the boy repeated, backing through one of the detailed holo-images. 'You have to do things you would not otherwise tolerate. You must use heroic means to stay alive long enough to awaken me, and I promise you, with all my heart, that I will become *Scytale*. Before it is too late.'

The process of awakening a ghola was neither simple nor swift. Year after year, Scytale had applied pressures, reminders, mental twists to this boy. Each lesson and each demand built, like a pebble added to the pile, higher and higher, and sooner or later he would add enough to that unstable mound to trigger an avalanche. And only God and his Prophet could know which small stone of memory would cause that barrier to come crashing down.

The boy watched the flickering moods cross his mentor's face. Not knowing what else to do, he quoted a comforting lesson from his catechism. 'When one is faced with an impossible choice, one must always choose the path of the Great Belief. God guides those who wish to be led.'

The very thought seemed to consume Scytale's last energy, and he slumped into a nearby chair in the simulation room, trying to recover his strength. When the ghola hurried to his side, Scytale stroked the dark hair of his alternate self. 'You are young, perhaps too young.'

The boy placed a comforting hand on the old man's shoulder. 'I will try – I promise. I'll work as hard as I can.' He squeezed his eyes shut and seemed to push, as if wrestling with the intangible walls inside his brain. At last, perspiring heavily, he gave up the effort.

The elder Scytale felt despondent. He had already used all the techniques he knew to push this ghola to the brink. Crisis, paradox, unrelenting desperation. But he felt it more than the boy did. Clinical knowledge was simply insufficient.

The witches had used some sort of sexual twisting to bring back the Bashar Miles Teg when his ghola was only ten years old, and Scytale's successor was already two years past that mark. But he could not bear the thought of the Bene Gesserit women using their unclean bodies to break this boy. Scytale had already sacrificed so much, selling most of his soul for a glimmer of hope for his race's future. The Prophet Himself would turn his back on Scytale in disgust. Not that!

Scytale placed his head in his hands. 'You are a flawed ghola. I should have thrown away your fetus and started anew twelve years ago!'

The boy's voice was rough, like torn fiber. 'I will concentrate, and push my memories out of my cells!'

The Tleilaxu Master felt a weary sadness weighing him down. 'It is an instinctive process, not an intellectual one. It must come to you. If your memories don't return, then you are of no use to me. Why should I let you live?'

The boy was visibly struggling, but Scytale saw no flash of awe and relief, no sudden flood of a lifetime's experiences. Both Tleilaxu reeked of failure. With each passing moment, Scytale felt more and more of himself dying.

The fate of our race depends on the actions of an unlikely collection of misfits.
– from a Bene Gesserit study on the human condition

In his second life, Baron Vladimir Harkonnen had done well for himself. At only seventeen, the awakened ghola already commanded a large castle filled with antique relics and a retinue of servants to satisfy his every whim. Better yet, it was Castle Caladan, the seat of House Atreides. He sat upon a high throne of fused black jewels, gazing around a large audience chamber as attendants went about their duties. Pomp and grandeur, all the trappings a Harkonnen deserved.

Despite appearances, though, the ghola Baron had very little real power, and he knew it. The Face Dancer myriad had created him for a specific purpose and, despite his reawakened memories, managed to keep him on a tight leash. Too many important questions remained unanswered, and too much was out of his control. He didn't like that.

The Face Dancers seemed much more interested in their young ghola of Paul Atreides – the one they called 'Paolo.' He was their real prize. Their leader Khrone said that this planet and the restored castle existed for the sole purpose of triggering Paolo's memories. The Baron was just a means to an end, of secondary importance in the 'Kwisatz Haderach matter.'

He resented the Atreides brat for it. The boy was only eight and still had much to learn from his mentor, though the Baron hadn't yet determined what the Face Dancers really wanted.

'Prepare him and raise him. See that he is primed for his destiny,' Khrone had said. 'There is a certain need he must fulfill.'

A certain need. But *what* need?

You are his grandfather, said the annoying voice of Alia inside the Baron's head. *Take good care of him.* The little girl taunted him incessantly. From the moment his memories were restored, she had been there waiting for him in his mind. Her voice still contained a childhood lisp, exactly as she had sounded when she'd killed him with the poisoned needle of the gom jabbar.

'I'd rather take care of you, little Abomination!' he yelled. 'Wring your neck, twist your head – once, twice, three times! Make your delicate little skull pop right off! Ha!'

But it's your own skull, dear Baron.

He clamped his hands against his temples. 'Leave me alone!'

Seeing no one else in the room with their master, the servants looked at him uneasily. The Baron fumed and slumped back in his glittering black chair. Having embarrassed and angered him, the Alia voice whispered his name tauntingly one more time and faded away.

Just then, a jaunty and self-important Paolo strode into the chamber, followed by an entourage of androgynous Face Dancers who acted as his protectors. The child

carried an air of overconfidence that the Baron found at once fascinating and disconcerting.

Baron Vladimir Harkonnen and this other Paul Atreides were inextricably meshed, simultaneously drawn together and repelled, like two powerful magnets. After the Baron's memories had been restored and he understood enough of who he was, Paolo had been brought to Caladan and handed over to the Baron's tender care ... with dire warnings should any harm befall him.

From his high black chair, the Baron glared down at the cocky youth. What made Paolo so special? What was the 'Kwisatz Haderach matter'? What did the Atreides know?

For some time, Paolo had been sensitive, thoughtful, even caring; he had a stubborn streak of innate goodness that the Baron had been working diligently to eradicate. Given time, and enough harsh training, he was sure he could cure even the honorable core of an Atreides. That would prime Paolo for his destiny, all right! Though the boy still struggled with his actions occasionally, he had made considerable progress.

Paolo came to an impertinent halt in front of the dais. One of the androgynous Face Dancers placed an antique handgun into the boy's hand.

Angrily, the Baron leaned forward for a better view. 'Is that gun from my personal collection? I told you to stay out of those things.'

'This is a relic of House Atreides, so I'm entitled to use it. A disk gun, once carried by my sister Alia, according to the label.'

The Baron shifted on his throne, nervous to have the loaded weapon so close to him.

'It's just a woman's gun.'

Inside the thick black armrests the Baron had secreted his own weapons, any one of which could easily turn the boy into a wet smear – hmm, fresh material for growing another ghola, he thought. 'Even so, it's a valuable relic, and I don't want it damaged by a reckless child.'

'I won't damage it.' Paolo seemed pensive. 'I respect artifacts that my ancestors used.'

Anxious to keep the boy from thinking too much, he stood. 'Shall we take it outside, then, Paolo? Why don't we see how it works?' The Baron gave him an avuncular pat on the shoulder. 'And afterward we can kill something with our bare hands, like we did to the mongrel hounds and ferrets.'

Paolo seemed uncertain. 'Maybe another day.'

Nevertheless, the Baron hurried him out of the throne room. 'Let's get rid of those noisy gulls around the midden piles. Have I mentioned how much you remind me of Feyd? Lovely Feyd.'

'More than once.'

Watched over by Face Dancers, they spent the next two hours at the castle's trash heap, taking turns shooting the raucous birds with the disk gun. Oblivious to the danger, the gulls swooped and shrieked at one another, fighting over morsels of rain-splattered garbage. Paolo took a shot, then the Baron. Despite its antiquity, the gun was quite accurate. Each spinning, microthin disk chopped a bird into bloody meat and dislodged feathers. Then the surviving gulls squabbled over the fresh gobbets.

Between them, they killed fourteen birds, although the Baron did not do nearly as well as the child, who had quite an aptitude for cool marksmanship. As the Baron raised the disk gun and aimed carefully, the girl's annoying voice rang in his head again. *That's not my gun, you know.*

He took the shot and missed by a wide margin. Alia giggled.

'What do you mean it's not yours?' He ignored Paolo's puzzled stare as the boy took the weapon for his turn.

It's a fake. I never had a disk gun like that.

'Leave me alone.'

'Who are you talking to?' Paolo asked.

After reaching into a pocket the Baron offered several capsules of orange melange substitute to Paolo, who obediently took them. He grabbed the weapon back from the boy. 'Don't be ridiculous. The antiquities dealer provided a certificate of authenticity and documentation when he sold the weapon to me.'

Grandfather, you shouldn't be so easily fooled! My own gun shot larger disks. This is a cheap imitation and doesn't even have the maker's initials on the barrel, like the original.

He studied the carved ornamental handle, turned the gun toward his face, then looked at the short barrel. No initials. 'And what about my other things, the objects supposedly owned by Jessica and Duke Leto?'

Some are real, some are not. I'll let you find out which are which. Knowing the nobleman's penchant for buying historical artifacts, the dealer would return to Caladan soon. No one made a fool of the Baron! The Baron ghola decided the next meeting would not be quite so cordial. He would ask a few incisive questions. Alia's voice faded away, and he was glad to have a moment of peace inside his head.

Paolo had consumed two of the orange capsules, and as the melange substitute took hold, the boy dropped to his knees and stared beatifically into the sky. 'I see a great victory in my future! I'm holding a knife that drips with blood. I'm standing over my enemy . . . over myself.' He

frowned, then beamed again, yelling, 'I *am* the Kwisatz
Haderach!' Then Paolo let out a bloodcurdling scream.
'No . . . now, I see myself dying on the floor, bleeding to
death. But how can this be, if I am the Kwisatz Haderach?
How can this be?'

The nearest Face Dancer grew animated. 'We were
instructed to watch for signs of prescience. We must notify
Khrone immediately.'

Prescience? the Baron thought. *Or insanity?*

Inside his mind, the presence of Alia laughed.

DAYS LATER, THE Baron strolled along the top of the cliff
and gazed out to sea. Caladan did not yet have the lovely,
grimy industrial capacity of his beloved Giedi Prime, but
at least he'd paved over the gardens in the vicinity of the
castle. The Baron hated flowers with their eye-straining
colors and sickening odors. He much preferred the
perfume of factory smoke. He had great ambitions of
turning Caladan into another Giedi Prime. The march of
progress was more important than any esoteric plans the
Face Dancers had for young Paolo.

On the lowest level of the restored castle, where other
great houses would have prepared chambers for 'policy
enforcement activities,' House Atreides had instead used
the space for food storage rooms, a wine cellar, and an
emergency shelter. Being a more traditional nobleman,
the Baron had installed dungeons, interrogation rooms,
and a well-equipped torture chamber. He also had a party
room on that level, where he often took young boys from
the fishing village.

*You can't remove the marks of House Atreides with such
cosmetic changes, Grandfather,* said the pestering voice of
Alia. *I preferred the old castle.*

'Shut up, devil child! You were never here in life, either.'

Oh, I visited my ancestral home when my mother lived here, when Muad'Dib was Emperor and his jihad splashed blood across the star systems. Don't you remember, Grandfather? Or weren't you inside my head then?

'I wish you weren't inside mine. I was born before you! I can't possibly have your memories inside me. You're an Abomination!'

Alia chuckled in a particularly disconcerting way. *Yes, Grandfather. I'm that, and much more. Perhaps that's why I have the power to be inside you. Or, perhaps you are just flawed – completely mad. Have you considered the possibility that you might be imagining me? That's what everyone else thinks.*

Servants hurried by, glancing fearfully at him. Just then the Baron saw a groundcar negotiating the steep road from the spaceport. 'Ah, here is our guest.' Despite Alia's intrusion, he expected this to be an entertaining day.

After the groundcar pulled up, a tall man stepped out of the rear compartment and made his way past statues of great Harkonnens that the Baron had erected in the past year. A suspensor platform floated behind the antiquities dealer, carrying his wares.

What do you plan to do with him, Grandfather?

'You know damned well what I'm going to do.' High on the wall above, the Baron rubbed his hands together in gleeful anticipation. 'Make yourself useful for a change, Abomination.' Alia giggled, but it sounded as if she was laughing *at* him.

The Baron hurried down as a haunted-looking house servant escorted the visitor inside. Shay Vendee was an antiquities dealer, always pleased to meet with one of his best customers. As he strolled in with his goods trailing behind him, his round face shone as radiantly as a small red sun.

The Baron greeted him with a moist handshake, clasping with both hands and holding on a little too long, squeezing a bit too hard.

The merchant extricated himself from his customer's grip. 'You'll marvel at what I've brought, Baron – amazing what turns up with a little digging.' He opened one of the cases on the suspensor platform. 'I saved these treasures especially for you.'

The Baron brushed a speck off one of the jeweled rings on his fingers. 'First I have something to show you, my dear Mr Vendee. My new wine cellar. I am quite proud of it.'

A look of surprise. 'Are the Danian vineyards operating again?'

'I have other sources.'

After the dealer disengaged his suspensor platform, the Baron led him down a wide rock staircase into increasing gloom. Oblivious to the danger, Vendee chattered cordially. 'Caladan wines used to be quite famous, and deservedly so. In fact, I heard a rumor that a cache was found on the ruins of Kaitain, bottles perfectly preserved in a nullentropy vault. The nullentropy field prevented the wine from aging and mellowing – in this case for thousands of years – but even so, the vintage must be quite extraordinary. Would you like me to see if I can acquire a bottle or two for you?'

The Baron stopped at the bottom of the dim stairs and peered with spider-black eyes at his guest. 'So long as you can provide the appropriate documentation. I wouldn't want to be duped into buying anything fake.'

Vendee wore a look of horror. 'Of course not, Baron Harkonnen!'

Finally, they passed through a narrow corridor illuminated by smoking oil lamps. Glowglobes were too efficient and harsh for the Baron's taste. He loved the dank, gritty smell of the air; it almost masked the other odors.

'Here we are!' The Baron pushed open a heavy wooden door and led the way into his fully stocked torture chamber. It had the traditional accoutrements: racks, masks, electrified chairs, and a strappado, by which a subject could be alternately hoisted into the air and dropped. 'This is one of my new playrooms. My pride and joy.'

Vendee's eyes opened wide in alarm. 'I thought you said we were going to your wine cellar.'

'Why, over there, my good man.' With a good-natured expression, the Baron pointed to a table from which loose straps hung. A wine bottle and two glasses sat on top. He poured red wine into both glasses and handed one to his increasingly agitated guest.

Vendee glanced around, nervously eyeing the red stains on the table and rock floor. Spilled wine? 'I have just made a long journey, and I'm tired. Maybe we should go back up to the main rooms. You will be absolutely delighted with the new items I've brought. Quite valuable relics, I assure you.'

The Baron fingered one of the straps on the table. 'There is another matter, first.' He narrowed his eyes. From a side door a sunken-eyed boy marched in, carrying what looked like two ornate old weapons, disk handguns of ancient manufacture.

'Do these look familiar? Examine them carefully.'

Vendee held one weapon to examine it. 'Oh, yes. The antique gun of Alia Atreides. Used by her own hands.'

'So you said.' Taking the other handgun from the serving boy, the Baron said to Vendee, 'You sold me a fake. I happen to know that the gun you hold is not the original weapon used by Alia.'

'I have a reputation for integrity, Baron. If anyone has told you otherwise, they are lying.'

'Unfortunately for you, my source is beyond reproach.'

You are lucky to have me inside you to point out your mistakes, Alia said. *If you believe I am real.*

Indignantly, Vendee placed the gun on the table and turned to leave. He only made it halfway to the door.

The Baron pulled the trigger of his own weapon, and a large, spinning disk shot out and hit the dealer squarely in the back of his neck, decapitating him. Swiftly, smoothly. The Baron was sure it hadn't hurt a bit.

'Good shot, eh?' The Baron grinned at the serving boy.

The servant did not flinch at the murder. 'Will that be all you desire from me, sir?'

'You don't expect me to clean up this mess myself, do you?'

'No, my Lord. I will get right to it.'

'Then wash yourself afterward.' The Baron looked him over. 'We'll have even more fun this afternoon.' Meanwhile, he went back upstairs to study what the antique dealer had brought with him.

Once, I was born of a natural mother, and then reborn many times as a ghola. Considering the millennia over which the Bene Gesserit, the Tleilaxu, and others have meddled with the gene pool, I wonder – are any of us truly natural anymore?

– ship's log, entry of
DUNCAN IDAHO

Today, Gurney Halleck would be born again. Paul Atreides had looked forward to this during the months-long gestation process. Since the recent birth of his sister Alia, the waiting had become nearly unbearable. But in a matter of hours, Gurney would be removed from the axlotl tank. The famed Gurney Halleck!

In his studies under Proctor Superior Garimi, Paul had read much about the troubadour warrior, had seen images of the man and heard recordings of his songs. But he wanted to know the real Gurney, his friend, mentor, and protector from an epic time. Someday, though their ages were topsy-turvy now, the two would remember how close their friendship had been.

Paul couldn't keep the grin off his face as he rushed to get ready. Whistling an old Atreides song that he'd learned from Gurney's recorded collection, he stepped into the corridor, and Chani emerged from her own quarters to join him. Two years his junior, the thirteen-year-old was whip-thin and fast, soft-spoken and beautiful, only a preview of the woman she would become again. Knowing their destinies, she and Paul were already inseparable. He took her hand, and the pair happily hurried toward the medical center.

He wondered if Gurney would be an ugly baby, or if he had only become a rolling lump of a man after being battered by the Harkonnens. He hoped the Gurney ghola would have a natural skill with the baliset, too. Paul was confident that the no-ship's stores could re-create one of the antique musical instruments. Maybe the two of them could play music together.

Others would be there for the new birth: his 'mother' Jessica, Thufir Hawat, and almost certainly Duncan Idaho. Gurney had many friends aboard. No one on the ship had known Xavier Harkonnen or Serena Butler, the other two gholas who would be decanted today, but they were legends from the Butlerian Jihad. Each ghola, according to Sheeana, had a role to play, and any one of them – or all of them together – might be the key to defeating the Enemy.

Aside from the ghola children, many other boys and girls had been born over the years of the *Ithaca*'s long flight. The Sisters bred with male Bene Gesserit workers who had also escaped from Chapterhouse; they understood the need to increase their population and prepare a solid foundation for a new colony, if the no-ship ever found a suitable planet to settle. The Rabbi's group of Jewish refugees, who had also married and begun families, still waited for a new home to fulfill their long quest. The no-ship was so vast, and the population aboard still so far below its capacity, that there was no real concern about running short on resources. Not yet.

As Paul and Chani approached the main birthing creche, four female proctors ran toward them down the hall, urgently calling for any qualified Suk doctor. 'They're dead! All three of them.'

Paul's heart stuttered. At fifteen, he was already training in some of the skills that had once made him the historical leader known as Muad'Dib. Summoning all the steel he could put into his voice, he demanded that the second proctor stop. 'Explain yourself!'

The Bene Gesserit blurted, surprised into her answer. 'Three axlotl tanks, three gholas. Sabotage – and murder. Someone destroyed them.'

Paul and Chani rushed toward the medical center. Duncan and Sheeana were already in the doorway looking shaken. Inside the chamber, three axlotl tanks had been ripped from their life-support mechanisms and lay in puddles of burned flesh and spilled liquid. Someone had used an incinerating beam and corrosives to destroy not only the life-support machinery, but the core flesh of the tanks and the unborn gholas.

Gurney Halleck. Xavier Harkonnen. Serena Butler. All lost. And the tanks, which had once been living women.

Duncan looked at Paul, articulating the real horror here. 'We have a saboteur aboard. Someone who wishes to harm the ghola project – or maybe *all* of us.'

'But why now?' Paul asked. 'The ship has been fleeing for two decades, and the ghola project began years ago. What changed?'

'Maybe someone was afraid of Gurney,' Sheeana suggested. 'Or Xavier Harkonnen, or Serena Butler.'

Paul saw that the other three axlotl tanks in the creche

had not been harmed, including the one that had recently given birth to the spice-saturated Alia.

Standing by Gurney's tank, he saw the dead, half-born baby among the burned and dissolved folds of flesh. Nauseated, he knelt to touch the few wisps of blond hair. 'Poor Gurney.'

As Duncan helped Paul to his feet, Sheeana said in a coldly businesslike voice, 'We still have the cellular material. We can grow replacements for all of them.' Paul could sense her deep fury, barely controlled by her strict Bene Gesserit training. 'We will need more axlotl tanks. I'll send out a call for volunteers.'

The ghola of Thufir Hawat entered and stared in disbelief at what had happened, his face an ashen mask. After the ordeal on the planet of the Handlers, he and Miles Teg had bonded closely; Thufir now helped the Bashar with security and defenses aboard the ship. The fourteen-year-old struggled to sound authoritative. 'We will find out who did this.'

'Scan the security images,' Sheeana said. 'The killer can't hide.'

Thufir looked embarrassed, as well as angry and so very young. 'I already checked. The security imagers were deactivated, intentionally, but there must be other evidence.'

'All of us were attacked, not just these axlotl tanks.' Duncan's anger was plain as he turned toward young Thufir. 'The Bashar has cited several previous incidents that he believes may be sabotage.'

'Those were never proved,' Thufir said. 'They could have been mechanical breakdowns, systems fatigue, natural failures.'

Paul's voice was ice as he took a last, lingering look at

the infant that would have been Gurney Halleck. 'This was no natural failure.'

Then Paul's legs went suddenly rubbery. Dizziness rose around him, and his consciousness blurred. As Chani rushed to grab him, he reeled, lost his footing, and hit his head hard on the deck. For a moment blackness enveloped him, a gloom that brightened into a frightening vision. Paul Atreides had seen it before, but he didn't know if it was memory or prescience.

He saw himself lying on the floor in a spacious, unknown place. A knife wound deep inside him sucked out his life. A mortal wound. His life's blood poured onto the floor, and his vision turned to dark static. Gazing up, he saw his own young face looking back at him, laughing. 'I have killed you!'

Chani was shaking him, shouting into his ear. 'Usul! Usul, look at me!'

He felt the touch of her hand on his own, and when his vision cleared he saw another concerned face. For a moment he thought it was Gurney Halleck, complete with an inkvine scar on his jawline, the glass-splinter eyes, the wispy blond hair.

The image shifted, and he realized it was the black-haired Duncan Idaho. Another old friend and guardian. 'Will you protect me from danger, Duncan?' Paul's voice hitched. 'As you vowed to do when I was a child? Gurney is no longer able.'

'Yes, Master Paul. Always.'

The Honored Matres clearly devised their own name for themselves, for no one else would ever apply the term 'honor' after seeing their cowardly, self-serving actions. Most people have a very different way of referring to those women.

— MOTHER COMMANDER MURBELLA,
assessment of past and present strengths

Weapons and battleships were as important as air and food during these supposed End Times. Murbella knew she would have to change the way she approached the problem, but she had never expected such resistance from her own Sisterhood.

With both anger and disdain, Kiria cried, 'You offer them Obliterators, Mother Commander? We can't just hand over such destructive weapons to Ix.'

She had no patience for this. 'Who else will build them for us? Holding secrets among ourselves only benefits the Enemy. You know as well as I do that only the Ixians can decipher the technology and manufacture great quantities for the coming war. Therefore, Ix must have full access. There is no other answer.'

Many worlds were building their own gigantic fleets, armoring every ship they could find, working on new weapon designs, but nothing had so far proved even remotely effective against the Enemy. The technology of the thinking machines was unsurpassed. But with a supply of new Obliterators, Murbella could turn the machines' own destructive power against them.

After snatching the weapons from fringe machine outposts centuries ago, the Honored Matres could have formed an impenetrable line and hurled Obliterators at the oncoming Enemy. If they had stood together for the common good, they could have prevented this whole problem. Instead, those Honored Matres had fled.

Thinking about the hidden history she had excavated from deep within Other Memory, Murbella continued to be annoyed at those ancestors. They had taken the weapons, used them without understanding them, and depleted most of their stockpiles in their petty revenge against the hated Tleilaxu. Yes, many generations earlier the Tleilaxu had tormented their females, and the Honored Matres had good reason to direct vengeful violence against them.

But such a waste!

Because the Honored Matres had been so profligate in using the planet-roasting weapons against any world that offended them, only a few Obliterators remained intact. Recently, when cracking down on the rebel Honored Matre strongholds, Murbella had expected to unearth greater stockpiles. But they had found nothing. Had someone else stolen the weapons? The Guild perhaps, under their original pretext of helping the Honored Matres? Or had the whores truly used them all, holding nothing in reserve?

Now the human race had insufficient weapons left to stand against the real Enemy. The Obliterators were as incomprehensible as any device Tio Holtzman had ever created for folding space, and the women had never known how to create more. For the sake of humanity, she hoped the Ixians could do so.

Times of extremis demand extreme actions.

Under her orders, the members of the united Sisterhood now removed the powerful weapons from their no-ships, battle cruisers, and infiltration vessels. She would take them to Ix herself. Murbella cut off continued arguments as she marched with a small entourage toward the Chapterhouse spaceport.

'But Mother Commander, at least negotiate patent protections,' Laera said, a flush showing even on her dark skin. 'Impose restrictions so that the technology does not become widespread.' She was one of the most businesslike Reverend Mothers, filling much of Bellonda's old role. 'Proliferation amongst planetary warlords could result in the devastation of the largest star systems. CHOAM alone, working with Ix, could wreak—'

Murbella cut her off with a disgusted noise. 'I have no interest in who may or may not benefit commercially *after we win this war*. If the Ixians help us achieve victory, they are entitled to profit.' She rubbed her chin thoughtfully as she looked up at the ramp of her small, fast lighter. 'We'll let the planetary warlords deal with their own problems.'

You play with feelings as a child plays with toys. I know why your Sisterhood does not value emotions: You cannot value what you do not understand!

– DUNCAN IDAHO,
letter submitted to Reverend Mother Bellonda

Sheeana used an authoritative tone, just short of Voice. '"Respect for the truth comes close to being the basis for all morality." And I want the truth from you. *Now.*'

Garimi raised her eyebrows and said calmly, 'A quote from Duke Leto Atreides to bolster the interrogation? Shall we bring in blazing lights and a Truthsayer?'

'My Truthsense is sufficient. I have always known you well enough to read you.'

The shock waves from the appalling crime in the birthing center rippled through the no-ship. The slaughter of unborn gholas, the destruction of three axlotl tanks – tanks created from volunteer *Sisters*! – went beyond anything Sheeana had expected from even her most vehement detractors. Her suspicions had naturally turned toward the outspoken leader of the ultraconservative faction.

Inside an interior conference chamber whose doors

were sealed, Sheeana stood like a stern schoolteacher, facing nine of the most prominent dissenters. These women had opposed the ghola project since its inception, disagreeing even more vehemently after Sheeana's decision to restart the work.

Under the blistering scrutiny, Garimi stared back, while her supporters were openly hostile – especially the squat Stuka. 'Why would I damage an axlotl tank? It makes no sense.'

Within her mind, among the lives in Other Memory, she heard the now-familiar voice of the ancient Serena Butler, sounding horrified. *Killing a child!* Serena was an odd visitor in Other Memory, a woman whose ancient thoughts should not have traveled down the corridors of the generations, and yet she had been with Sheeana for years now.

'You have shown a previous willingness to kill ghola children.' Sheeana finally sat down.

Garimi fought to control her trembling. 'I attempted to save us before Leto could become a threat, before he could become the Tyrant again. That was all, and I failed. My reasons were well known, and I stand by them. Why would I go to such extremes now? What do I care about Halleck? Or old General Xavier Harkonnen? Even Serena Butler is so far buried in our past that she's little more than the smoke of a legend. Why would I bother with them when the worst gholas – Paul Muad'Dib, Leto II, the fallen Lady Jessica, and Alia the Abomination – already walk among us?' Garimi made a disgusted rumble in her throat. 'Your suspicions offend me.'

'And the evidence offends *me.*'

'Despite our disagreements, we are all Sisters,' Garimi insisted.

At first the fleeing Bene Gesserits had had a common cause, a shared goal. But in a matter of months after their escape from Chapterhouse the divisions had begun, power struggles, command questions, a bifurcation of visions. Duncan and Sheeana focused on escaping from the outside Enemy, while Garimi wanted to found a new Keep and train a fresh Bene Gesserit population according to established ways.

How have we changed so dramatically? How did the divisions get so deep?

Sheeana gazed from face to face, looking for indications of guilt, particularly in the eyes. Short, curly-haired Stuka had a line of moisture on her upper lip, one of the indicators of nervousness. But she detected no hatred there, no loathing sufficient to have sparked an act of such brutality. With dismay, she had no choice but to conclude that the perpetrator was not here.

'Then I need your help. The person standing next to any of us could be a saboteur. We must interview everyone. Gather our qualified Truthsayers, and use the last stores of the truthtrance drug.' Sheeana rubbed her temples, already dreading the huge task. 'Please leave me alone, so I can meditate.'

After the nine dissenters departed, Sheeana stood alone, her eyes half closed. The population aboard the *Ithaca* had grown, spread out in the no-ship over the years. Even she wasn't sure how many children were aboard, but she could easily find out. Or so she presumed.

She murmured to Other Memory, 'So, Serena Butler – was your murderer in the room? If not them, then who could it be?'

Serena's voice interjected, full of sadness. *A liar can hide behind barricades, but all barricades eventually fall.*

*You will have other opportunities to discover the murderer.
There is sure to be more sabotage.*

THE TRUTHSAYERS TESTED each other first.

Twenty-eight qualified Reverend Mothers were gathered
from Garimi's followers and from the general population
of Sisters. The women did not protest their innocence or
complain about the suspicions cast upon them. Instead,
they accepted mutual questioning.

Sheeana observed coolly as the women formed triads,
two individuals acting as interrogators, the third as the
subject. As soon as each subject passed the rigorous
questioning, the roles switched, so that everyone was
questioned. One by one, the Truthsayers created an ever-
growing pool of reliable investigators. Everyone passed
the test.

Once the Truthsayers had confirmed each other,
Sheeana allowed them to question her. Garimi and her
dissident Sisters also faced the challenges and proved
their innocence, as did Sheeana's staunch followers. All
of them.

Next, with a Truthsayer named Calissa beside her,
Sheeana stood before a stiff-backed Duncan Idaho. The
very thought of Duncan being a murderer and a saboteur struck her as absurd. Sheeana wouldn't have believed
it of anyone on board, and yet three axlotl tanks and three
ghola children had been butchered.

But Duncan . . . Standing so close to him, smelling his
perspiration, feeling him somehow fill the room with his
presence, summoned dangerous memories in her. She
had used her own sexual bonding skills to break him free
of Murbella. Despite their backgrounds, both knew there
had been more to that passionate encounter than just a

necessary task. Duncan had been uneasy around her ever since, afraid of what he might succumb to.

But in this situation there was neither romance nor sexual tension, only accusations. 'Duncan Idaho, do you know how to bypass the security imagers in the medical center?'

He looked past her, not blinking. 'That is within my capabilities.'

'Did you commit this terrible act and cover your tracks?'

Now his gaze met hers. 'No.'

'Did you have any reason to prevent Gurney Halleck, Serena Butler, or Xavier Harkonnen from being born?'

'I did not.'

Now that Duncan faced her and a Truthsayer, Sheeana could have asked him questions about their personal relationship to witness his reaction. He would not be able to lie to her or pretend. But she feared his answers. She didn't dare ask.

'He speaks the truth,' said Calissa. 'He's not our saboteur.'

Duncan remained in the room when Bashar Miles Teg came for questioning. Calissa displayed images of the horrific scene from the birthing chamber. 'Are you in any way responsible for this, Miles Teg?'

The Bashar stared at the images, looked up at her, turned his gaze to Duncan. 'Yes.'

Sheeana was so startled that she struggled to think of another question.

'How so?' Duncan asked.

'I am responsible for security aboard this no-ship. Clearly, I failed in my duty. If I had done a better job, this atrocity never would have occurred.' He glanced at the troubled Calissa. 'Since you asked me in the presence of a Truthsayer, I couldn't lie.'

'Very well, Miles. But that isn't what we meant. Did you commit this sabotage or authorize it? Do you know anything about it?'

'No,' he answered emphatically.

Dozens of private chambers were set up, where the interrogations could continue unabated. They asked every one of the ghola children, from Paul Atreides all the way to nine-year-old Leto II, and the Truthsayers detected no criminal falsehoods.

Then the Rabbi and all of the Jews.

And every other passenger aboard the no-ship.

Nothing. Not a single person seemed to be connected with the murderous incident. Duncan and Teg used their Mentat skills to check and recheck the lists of people aboard, yet they could find no errors. No one had evaded questioning.

Sitting across from Sheeana in the otherwise empty interrogation room, Duncan steepled his fingers. 'There are two possibilities. Either the saboteur is capable of deceiving a Truthsayer . . . or someone we don't know about is hiding aboard the *Ithaca.*'

IN WELL ORGANIZED teams, the Bene Gesserit blocked off, then sectioned the no-ship's decks, methodically moving from cabin to cabin and chamber to chamber. But it was a formidable task. The *Ithaca* was the size of a small city, more than a kilometer long and hundreds of decks high, each filled with passages, chambers, and hidden doors.

While trying to guess how someone else might have sneaked aboard, unknown to them, Duncan remembered discovering the mummified remains of Bene Gesserit captives the Honored Matres had tortured to death. That sealed chamber of horrors had gone undetected during the whole time Duncan had been held prisoner inside the ship on the Chapterhouse landing field.

Could someone else – an unknown Honored Matre, perhaps? – have remained hidden aboard for all that time? More than thirty years! It did not seem possible, but the vessel had thousands of work bays, living quarters, corridors, and storage lockers.

Another possibility: During the escape from the planet of the Handlers, several Face Dancers had crashed small fighters into the no-ship's hull. Mangled bodies had been pulled from the wreckage of those ships . . . but could it all have been a ruse? What if some had actually survived those kamikaze crashes and slipped away? Perhaps one or more Face Dancers were lurking in the untraveled passages of the no-ship, looking for ways to strike.

If so, it was imperative to find them.

Teg had already installed hundreds more surveillance imagers at strategic locations, but that was only a stopgap measure at best. The *Ithaca* was so large that even the best security equipment had thousands of blind spots, and there simply weren't enough personnel to monitor the imagers already in place. It was an impossible task.

Still, they tried.

As Duncan accompanied a group of five searchers, he was reminded of a beating party marching through the tall grass on a big game hunt. He wondered if they would scare a deadly lion out from somewhere in the vastness of the vessel.

Deck after deck was searched, but even with a dozen teams, a complete inspection from the topmost deck to the lowest cargo hold would take a great deal of time, and in the limited searches they conducted, they found nothing. Duncan was exhausted and stressed.

And the murderer – or murderers – remained aboard.

Only two options are before us now: defend ourselves or surrender to the Enemy. But if any of you believes that surrender is a viable option, then we have already lost.

— BASHAR MILES TEG,

speech given before the Pellikor Engagement

Leaving the Obliterators on Ix for the fabricators to study and duplicate, Murbella traveled next to the main Guild shipyards on Junction.

Administrator Rentel Gorus, with long, pale hair and milky eyes, led Murbella among the construction bays, suspensor cranes, conveyors, and assemblers, all of them teeming with workers. The buildings were tall and blocky, the streets serviceable rather than beautiful. Everything on Junction was done on a breathtaking scale. Great lifters hauled components up to the skeletons of gigantic ships, assembling one vessel after another. The air held the bitter tang of hot metal, the chemical residues from welding mismatched components into huge vessels.

Gorus seemed overly proud. 'As you can see, we have the facilities you request, Mother Commander, provided the price is right.'

'The price will be right.' With the New Sisterhood's wealth in melange and soostones, Murbella could meet virtually any demand for payment. 'We'll pay you well for every ship you create, every vessel that can be placed into battle, every craft that can stand against the thinking machine army. The end of our civilization is at hand if we don't defeat the thinking machines.'

Gorus did not seem intimidated. 'Every side in every war believes their conflict is crucial to history. But most often those are delusionary and needlessly alarmist thoughts. This war may be over before you have to resort to such measures.'

She scowled. 'I don't know what you mean.'

'There are other ways to solve the problem. We know that outside forces are sweeping in to many planetary systems. But what do they *want*? To what will they concede? We believe such discussions are worth pursuing.' He blinked his milky eyes.

'What sort of trick is the Guild trying to play on us this time?'

'No trick, just sensibility. Regardless of politics, commerce must continue. Wartime desperation inspires technological innovation, but peace promotes profitability in the long run. Trade will go on, no matter who wins the conflict.'

Heighliners had long been the luxury ships of the universe; now Murbella forced the Spacing Guild to devote their shipyards to creating the tools of war. For centuries the Guild's commercial fleet had been stable, and demand for trade steadily increased as people returned from the Scattering. Now, however, with Omnius's fleet wiping out whole populations and sending refugees in panicked flight back into the heart of the Old Empire, CHOAM and the Guild were in turmoil.

A hot wind from the assembly bays blew in Murbella's

face, burning her nostrils with the acrid smoke of waste chemicals. A shiver coursed down her spine.

'Our common enemy must be rational,' Gorus continued. 'We have therefore dispatched emissaries and negotiators out to the war zone. We will find the thinking machines and make our proposal. The Guild would prefer to continue its commerce regardless of the outcome of this disagreement.'

Murbella gasped. 'Are you insane? Omnius seeks the extermination of all humanity. That includes you.'

'You overstate your case, Mother Commander. Some of our emissaries will, I believe, achieve our goal.'

In the background, blasts of steam curled up from the stone smokestacks. She ignored the noise and the smell. 'You are a consummate fool, Administrator Gorus. Thinking machines do not follow the rules you assume.'

'Be that as it may, we feel obligated to try.'

'And what is the result so far?'

'Acceptable losses. Our first emissaries have disappeared, but we will continue the effort. We plan for all eventualities – even disaster.' Casually, he led her out onto a broad, open field under the half-assembled hulk of a huge ship. 'Thus, we are comfortable with extending certain beneficial terms to the New Sisterhood. You have always been a valued customer, but the order you submitted is massive. Even under wartime conditions, you have asked for more ships than we are able to provide.'

'Then offer your workers more incentive.'

'Ahh, Mother Commander, but will you provide enough incentive to *us*?'

She bristled. 'How can you think solely of profits when the fate of the human race is at stake?'

'Profits determine all our fates.' The Administrator

gestured casually, as if to encompass the huge assembly of the ships around him.

'We'll pay what you demand, and the Guild Bank will offer us loans if necessary. We need those ships, Gorus.'

He smiled coolly. 'Your credit is good, but we must address another problem. We do not have enough Guild Navigators to man so many new ships. All of the vessels we build for you will have to be equipped with Ixian mathematical compilers, rather than traditional Navigators. Is that acceptable?'

'Provided the ships function as we require, I have no objection. We don't have time to develop and train another population of Navigators.'

Obviously pleased, Gorus rubbed his hands together. 'Of late, Navigators have proven somewhat intractable, due to the shortage of spice – a shortage which your Sisterhood created, Mother Commander. It is because of you that we had to look for alternatives to Navigators.'

'I have no fondness for Navigators, or for your obscene profits. I don't care how the Guild accomplishes it, but we need those ships.'

'Of course, Mother Commander, and we shall provide what you wish.'

'That is precisely the answer I need.'

What is the advantage of prescience if it serves only to reveal our own downfall?

— NAVIGATOR EDRIK,
message to the Oracle of Time

The Guild bureaucrats had the audacity to call Edrik's Heighliner back to the shipyards on Junction. Staring ahead with his milky eyes, Administrator Gorus blithely announced that the Heighliner would be fitted with one of the new Ixian mathematical compilers. 'Our spice supply line is undependable. We must be certain each vessel can operate safely if its Navigator fails.'

Over the past two years, more and more Guildships had been outfitted with the hated artificial controls. Mathematical compilers! No simple engine or tool could adequately complete the phenomenally complex projections that a Navigator performed. Edrik and his fellows had evolved through immersion in spice, their prescient vision strengthened through the power of melange. There could be no mechanical substitute.

Nevertheless, Edrik had no choice but to accept a team of qualified and arrogant Ixian workers who shuttled up from the Junction shipyards. The tight-lipped men boarded the Heighliner under the watchful eyes of the

Guild, with their smug expressions, compiler machines, and dangerous curiosity.

In his tank, Edrik was concerned that they would snoop around under the pretext of completing their installation. The Navigator faction could not risk these men finding Waff's laboratory, the genetically altered sandtrout, and the small mutated worms he was producing in his tanks. The Tleilaxu man claimed to be making excellent progress, and his work must remain a secret.

Therefore, when the Ixian installers were all safely aboard, Edrik simply folded space, informing no one in the shipyards where he was going. He carried his empty Heighliner far out into an isolated wasteland between solar systems, and there ejected the disbelieving Ixians, along with their accursed navigation machines, out into the cold vacuum.

Problem solved.

His acts would be discovered eventually, but that could not be avoided. Edrik was a Navigator. Mere human Administrators had no hold over him.

Edrik suspected that the devious Administrator and his faction saw the melange crisis as an opportunity to shift the Guild's burden away from problematic Navigators; they did not really want a new source of spice. Gorus was now an absolute ally, if not a puppet, of the Ixians. Edrik had seen the economic projections and knew that the Administrators considered navigation machines to be more cost-effective than Navigators – and more easily controlled.

With the Ixians and their machines happily ejected, Edrik knew it was time to call another meeting with his fellow Navigators; they needed to receive fresh guidance from the Oracle of Time. Because Junction and several other Guild planets were already compromised by Gorus and his cronies, Edrik chose a place that no one but Navigators could find.

Once they had been shown how, they could fold their Guildships deep into another dimension, a nontraditional universe where the Oracle occasionally went on personal, incomprehensible explorations.

Ignited by the light of seven newborn stars, the cosmic gases swirling around his giant ship seemed inflamed. The nebula shone pink and green and blue, depending on which window of the spectrum Edrik chose to look through. The misty curtains put on a spectacular show, a great whirlpool of ionized gases – and a perfect place to hide.

When the ships gathered, the Navigators were in quite an uproar, and their numbers were less than Edrik had hoped. So far, four hundred Heighliners had been decommissioned, their parts salvaged to construct new no-ships that relied on artificial guidance systems. Seventeen Navigators had died horribly, their tanks emptied. Edrik learned that six of his fellows had likewise murdered the Ixian engineers rather than allow them to install mathematical compilers. Four Navigators had simply disconnected the machines, and the onboard Ixian teams failed to realize that their vaunted systems were no longer functional.

'We require melange,' he transmitted. 'By the grace of spice, we see through folded space.'

'But the Sisterhood has denied it to us,' one of the other Navigators said.

'They have spice. They spend spice. But they do not give it to us.'

'The witches give it to the Guild for ships . . . but the

Administrators have cut us off. We are betrayed by our own.'

'They control the spice.'

'But they do not control us,' Edrik insisted. 'If we find our own source of spice, we will not need the Administrators. This is for the survival of Navigators, not simply for commerce. We have struggled with this problem for years. The Tleilaxu ghola has finally come up with a solution.'

'A new source of spice? Has it been proven?'

'Is anything fully proven? If this goes well, we can destroy the corrupt old Spacing Guild and supercede them.'

'We must speak to the Oracle.'

Edrik waved his tiny, misshapen hands. 'The Oracle already knows our problem.'

'The Oracle has not deigned to help us,' said another.

'The Oracle has her own reasons.'

Drifting in his tank, Edrik acknowledged their conundrum. 'I have spoken to her myself, but perhaps all of us together can urge her to respond. Let us summon the Oracle.'

Using their spice-enhanced minds, the numerous Navigators shot a message arrow through the folds of space. Edrik knew they had no way to coerce the Oracle of Time – or the Oracle Infinity, as she was sometimes called – to respond, but he sensed her presence, and her deep uneasiness.

With a silent flash, a trapdoor opened in the vacuum, and the ancient container arrived. It was not quite a ship, for the Oracle could travel anywhere she wished, mentally folding space without the help of Holtzman engines.

Even in that small and nonthreatening enclosure, Edrik

knew full well the power and immensity of that highly advanced mind. As a human, Norma Cenva had first discovered the connection between spice and prescience. She had developed the technology of folding space, had created the incomprehensible equations that Tio Holtzman had taken as his own.

Though the Oracle used no known transmitting device, her words were loud and implacable in their minds. 'Your concerns are parochial. I must find the wayward no-ship. I must determine where Duncan Idaho has taken it, before the Enemy intercepts it.'

The Oracle often chose her own esoteric goals without explaining them. One of the Navigators asked, 'Why is the no-ship so important, Oracle?'

'Because the Enemy wishes to have it. Our great foe is Omnius – except that he is as changed from his former computer evermind as I am evolved from the human I once was. The machines have completed their high-order projections. The evermind knows he must have the Kwisatz Haderach, just as I know the Enemy must *not* have him.' The Oracle let the silence hang in space like a hole, before she added a stinging rebuke. 'Your appetite for spice is not the priority. I must find the ship.'

Abruptly discontinuing the debate, she winked out again and vanished into her own place in an alternate universe.

Edrik and the gathered Navigators were shocked by her response. Navigators were dying, spice was dwindling away to nothing, Administrators were trying to overthrow the Guild – and the Oracle simply wanted to find a lost ship?

Twenty-Two Years After

Escape from Chapterhouse

These new Face Dancers cannot be detected by DNA analysis or any other form of cellular scrutiny. As far as we know, only a Tleilaxu Master can tell the difference.
— Bene Gesserit report on human mutation

Though the Ixian specialists had studied the Obliterators for half a year, they still hadn't given the Sisterhood an answer. Murbella brooded in her offices on Chapterhouse, waiting. The news seemed to worsen with each passing day.

She received regular updates on the depredations of the thinking-machine fleet. The powerful Enemy ships moved inexorably through the fringe systems like a crashing tidal wave, drowning world after world. Another ten planets evacuated or contaminated by plagues, another ten lost, and more refugees flooded into the Old Empire.

A network of Sisters met with any refugee ships that came from the battleground systems. Taking statements from groups of survivors, they compiled an exhaustive three-dimensional map of the movements of the machine fleet. The pattern seeped like a bloodstain through the galaxy.

In a single desperate stand, nineteen Sisterhood no-ships expended their last three Obliterators to destroy a whole battle group of oncoming machine ships and temporarily prevent the annihilation of one human-inhabited system. In the end, though, even that devastation amounted to only a brief delay; the machine fleet came back with greater strength and crushed the world after all, killing every inhabitant. With the last Obliterators gone, the New Sisterhood was woefully underdefended.

Unless the Ixians could help. *What was taking them so long?*

Finally, a lone Ixian engineer came to Chapterhouse to deliver his news. When he said he would speak to no one but the Mother Commander herself, escorts brought him to the main Keep. Waiting on her imposing throne in front of the dust-streaked, segmented window, Murbella could respect the man for bypassing bureaucracy and getting to the core of the matter.

The engineer's face was bland and unmemorable, his brown hair closely cropped, his demeanor unassuming. He had a peculiar, unpleasant odor about him, perhaps from chemical residue or the machinery of Ix's underground fabrication plants. He bowed perfunctorily and stepped in front of her. 'Our best engineers and scientists have deconstructed and analyzed the sample Obliterators you provided.'

Murbella leaned forward, giving him her full attention. 'And you can reproduce them?'

'Better than that, Mother Commander.' His confident smile held no warmth at all, was simply an imitation of a facial expression. 'Our fabricators understand the underlying concept of the weapon, and are able to concentrate its destructive power. Previously, it required several Honored Matre battleships deploying multiple Obliterators to kill a planet. With our enhanced weapon a single ship can launch enough firepower to do what was done to

Rakis.' He gave a perfunctory shrug. 'Imagine what such an energy release would do to Enemy battleships.'

Murbella tried to conceal her delight. 'We need as many as you can produce. Instruct your factories to begin work on these weapons immediately.' She kept her voice hard, letting her impatience seep through. 'But why did you need to see me in person, when you could easily have sent a message with this information?' Her lips quirked. 'Do you require a pat on the back? Shall I give you my applause? There, you have it.'

The Ixian engineer remained bland. 'Before we begin, Mother Commander, there is the matter of payment. Chief Fabricator Sen has instructed me to inform you that Ix must be compensated if we are to pull our profitable manufacturing centers off-line in order to create these Obliterators for your war.'

'My war? All humans must share the burden of the cost.'

'Unfortunately, we disagree. The only payment we will accept is spice. And the only source of spice is your New Sisterhood.'

'We have other ways to pay you.' Murbella tried to conceal her alarm. She wasn't sure their fledgling spice operations could supply the necessary amount. And why would Ix care about spice, in particular? Sisterhood accounts in Guild banks could be drained; CHOAM could be convinced to supply important commodities; and soostones were more valuable than ever, especially since the recent turmoil on Buzzell.

When she offered these alternatives, though, the Ixian fabricator shook his head. 'I have no flexibility in these negotiations, Mother Commander. It must be melange. No other coin will do.'

She ground her teeth, but had no patience for further delay. 'Spice it is, then. Get started.'

DEPARTING FROM CHAPTERHOUSE, Khrone the Face Dancer felt content. The New Sisterhood had bowed to his demands, as he had known they would. Back on Ix, he had the ear of the Chief Fabricator, and Face Dancer replacements already controlled all key Ixian manufacturing centers.

Khrone found it ironic to demand payment in spice, since Ix had devoted so much technological effort into installing navigation machines in Guildships. Thanks to the mathematical compilers, melange was basically obsolete when it came to folding space, and the Navigators were fading swiftly.

But by insisting on such a huge payment in spice alone, and then hoarding the commodity, Khrone would remove a large amount of it from the market, making it even rarer. That, in turn, would force more and more ships to convert to the Ixian navigation compilers, because the Guild could not support the melange needs of their Navigators. Before long, with no way of supporting their own Navigators, the whole Spacing Guild would fall under Khrone's control. He had worked it all out in exquisite detail.

In the meantime, he and his disguised workers would make it look as if they were providing everything the Sisterhood demanded. Let them fight useless battles while the real war was already won, right under their noses! Mother Commander Murbella would be quite satisfied – up until the moment a curtain of darkness fell on humankind. Permanently.

*Every man makes errors. When a security chief makes
them, though, there are consequences. People die.*

— THUFIR HAWAT,
the original

The Bashar and his protégé marched down the corridors
toward the no-ship's life-support center. 'I am deeply
ashamed, Thufir. It has been almost a year, and I am
incapable of finding a blatant saboteur and murderer.'

The young Hawat looked up at him, clearly idolizing
the military genius. 'We have a limited pool of suspects,
and a discrete area in which he – or she – could hide.
We've done everything possible, Bashar.'

'And yet the saboteur is here, somewhere.' Teg did not
slow his pace. 'Therefore, we have not done everything
possible, because we still haven't found the person responsible. The fact that there have been no further murders
does not mean we can let down our guard. I am convinced
our saboteur is still among us.'

The *Ithaca* was constantly being searched and monitored. Additional surveillance imagers had been installed,
but the culprit seemed to have an affinity for hiding. Teg
suspected that the work of the saboteur went well beyond
the murder of the gholas and the axlotl tanks. In recent

months, many ship's systems had inexplicably failed – too many to be caused by random events and natural breakdowns. 'Our adversary is still at work.'

The Thufir ghola raised his smooth chin in a display of pride. He was strong and gangly with a heavy brow; he had let his hair grow shaggy. 'Then you and I will find him.'

Teg smiled at Thufir. 'As soon as you regain his memories and experience as a warrior Mentat and Master of Assassins, you will be a formidable ally.'

'I'm formidable now.' Thufir had already proved his worth during the tense escape from the Handlers, risking his own life to help the Rabbi get away from Face Dancers in league with the Enemy. Teg believed the young ghola had the potential to do much more.

Varying his pattern, he insisted on an exhausting round of daily security inspections while he left Duncan Idaho on the navigation bridge, ever vigilant for the Enemy's glowing net.

The *Ithaca* continued to wander in empty space. At first, their voyage had simply been to get away from the Enemy hunters. Duncan had been forced to remain hidden behind the ship's veiling no-field, since the old man and woman seemed to want him in particular. Now, after more than two decades, the population aboard had increased, and children were growing up and being taught necessary skills without ever having set foot on a planetary surface.

Despite all the worlds settled during the Scattering, habitable systems seemed sparse indeed. For the first time, Teg wondered how many ships of refugees fleeing from the Famine Times had simply died without ever finding their destination. The *Ithaca* had no Guild Navigator; only pure chance brought them within range of planets. So far, they had encountered only two places that might have supported a new colony: one Honored Matre world that had been completely wiped out by Enemy plagues, and the planet of the insidious Handlers.

Nevertheless, with its recyclers, greenhouses, and algae tanks, the aging *Ithaca* should have been able to sustain the present number of passengers for centuries, if necessary. They – and their successors – could effectively stay onboard forever and never stop running. *Is that our fate?* Teg asked himself. But because of leakages, losses, and 'accidents,' the passengers had cause for concern. Sooner or later, they would need to replenish their reserves.

Thinking of resources, the Bashar took a side corridor to the fermentation bins and adjacent algae-growth tanks. Grown in the vaulted, humid chamber, the biomass provided raw material for the food-manufacturing units. A prime vulnerability.

As he opened a hatch, Teg caught the rich, marshy smell of compost and algae. They climbed metal steps to a catwalk and looked down into the cylindrical vat filled with hairy green slime. The stinking wet mass of fecund algae digested anything organic, growing large amounts of edible, rather unpalatable, material that could be converted into better-flavored foods. Ceiling fans whirred, drawing the odorous air upward through filters and into the intricate set of ducts that acted as the no-ship's circulatory system. After taking samples and testing the chemical balance of the tanks, Teg concluded that everything was in order. No sign of sabotage since his last inspection.

The serious young man tagged along beside him. 'I

am not a Mentat yet, sir, but I have been giving the sabotage problem a great deal of thought.'

With raised eyebrows Teg turned to his protégé. 'And do you have a first-order approximation?'

'I have an idea.' Thufir did not try to conceal his anger. 'I suggest you have a long talk with the Yueh ghola. Perhaps he knows more than he has admitted.'

'Yueh is only thirteen. He does not have his memories back.'

'Maybe the weakness is in his blood. Bashar, we know that *someone* committed the sabotage.' The young man sounded disappointed in himself for allowing it to happen. 'Even the real Thufir Hawat didn't find the traitor in House Atreides before he betrayed us to the Harkonnens. That traitor was Yueh.'

'I'll keep it in mind.'

Back in the corridors again, the two passed a sick-looking old Scytale and his clone emerging from their quarters. Because they isolated themselves and lived with odd traditions and behavior, the Tleilaxu were natural suspects, but Teg had found no evidence against them. In fact, he believed the real saboteur would be careful to blend in perfectly and draw no attention at all. It was the only way he could have remained hidden for so long.

Two pregnant women passed by them in the corridor, chatting as they continued on their way. Both were part of Sheeana's conventional breeding program to maintain the population of the Sisterhood, providing an adequate genetic base should the splinter group ever find a place to settle.

Finally, Teg and Thufir reached the cavernous, humming engine chamber, and entered the large aft compartment through a round doorway. Apparently safe but lost again since their last passage through foldspace, the *Ithaca* drifted, though Duncan insisted on keeping the Holtzman engines ready at all times.

Thick clearplaz separated the Bashar and Thufir from a trio of power plants that fed the machines. Walkways laced the outside of an explosion-proof plaz chamber that contained the side-by-side engines. The two stared up at the giant mechanisms that could fold space. A true miracle of technology. All of the readings remained within nominal range. Again, no sign of sabotage.

'We're still missing something,' he mused. 'I can feel it.'

Once before, at the end of the Battle of Junction, Teg had failed to see the terrible and deadly 'Weapon' that the Honored Matres had held in reserve. That mistake had nearly lost him the entire war. He considered their situation now. *What deadly device will I fail to see this time?*

Humanity has a great genetic compass that constantly guides us onward. Our task is to keep it always pointed in the right direction.

> — REVEREND MOTHER ANGELOU,
> famed breeding mistress

Wellington Yueh had a powerful need to be forgiven. The blank spot in his mind was filled with guilt. He was just a ghola and only thirteen, but he knew he had done terrible things. His own history clung to him like tar to his shoe.

In his first life, he had broken his Suk conditioning. He had failed his wife Wanna by allowing the Harkonnens to use her as a pawn and had betrayed Duke Leto, bringing about the Atreides downfall on Arrakis.

After studying records of his prior existence, learning in painful detail what he had done, Yueh tried to find solace in considering the Orange Catholic Bible, along with other ancient religions, sects, philosophies, and interpretations that had developed over the millennia. The oft-repeated doctrine of Original Sin – so unfair! – was a particular thorn in his side. Yueh could have made a coward's excuse that he couldn't remember and there-fore didn't deserve blame, but that was not the path to redemption. He had to turn elsewhere.

Jessica was the only one who could forgive him.

The eight ghola children in Sheeana's project had been raised and trained together. Because of their individual personalities they had formed personal bonds and friendships. Even before they knew the history that should tear them apart, Yueh had tried to be a friend to Jessica.

He had read the journals and instructional writings of the original Lady Jessica, bound concubine to the Duke Leto Atreides. She'd also been a Reverend Mother, an exile, the mother of Muad'Dib, and the grandmother of the Tyrant. That long-dead Jessica had been a strong woman, a role model despite how the Bene Gesserit reviled her for her flaw, her weakness. *Love.*

Together, the gholas now faced a far greater enemy than the Harkonnens. When Jessica's memories were finally awakened, would the shared threat be sufficient to keep her from wanting to murder him? He had read her own words, as written down by Princess Irulan, expressing her poignant agony of grief: 'Yueh! Yueh! Yueh! A million deaths were not enough for Yueh!'

Yes, she was the only one who could offer him any hope of forgiveness. With a clean slate and an open heart, he prayed that it was possible for him to lead an honorable life this time.

Jessica often occupied herself in the main conservatory, tending the plants that served as a supplemental food source for the hundreds aboard. She had an affinity for the greenhouse work and was happy to be around the fertile dirt, the misting irrigators, the fleshy green leaves, and sweet-scented flowers. With her bronze hair and oval face, noble and young, she looked exquisitely beautiful. How she and Duke Leto must have loved each other long ago . . . until Yueh destroyed it all.

Jessica looked up from the flowers and lush herbs to focus haunted eyes on Yueh.

He said, 'Do you mind the company?'

'Not yours. It's refreshing to be with someone who doesn't blame me for things I don't remember doing.'

'I hope you'll grant me the same consideration, my Lady.'

'Please don't call me that, Wellington. At least not yet. I can't be the Lady Jessica until I . . . well, until I become the Lady Jessica.'

He tried to guess the reasons for her gloomy mood. 'Has Garimi been haranguing you again?'

'Some Bene Gesserits won't forgive me for having gone against the strict commands of the Sisterhood, for betraying their breeding program.' She seemed to be reciting something she had read. 'The consequences of that brought down an empire and subjected the human race to thousands of years of tyrannical rule and many more centuries of privation.' She let out a bitter laugh. 'In fact, if your actions had actually resulted in the death of Paul and me, maybe Bene Gesserit histories would describe you as a hero.'

'I am no hero, Jessica.' To his credit, the original Yueh had given her and Paul the means to survive in the desert after the Harkonnens stormed Arrakeen. He had facilitated their escape, but was that enough for redemption? Could it possibly be?

She moved on, smelling the flowers, checking the moist soil. She had a habit of running her fingertips along the leaves, touching the undersides.

Yueh followed her as she walked through a small grove of dwarf citrus trees. Overhead, the segmented panes of the filtered windows showed only distant starlight and no nearby sun. 'If they hate us so much, why did the Sisters bring us back?'

Her expression was one of bitter amusement. 'Bene Gesserits have a terrible habit, Wellington: Even if they know a hook is hidden inside the juicy worm, they'll still bite. They always think they can avoid traps that get the rest of us.'

'But you're a Bene Gesserit yourself.'

'Not anymore . . . or not yet.'

Yueh touched his own smooth, unmarked forehead. 'We're starting over, Jessica. Blank slates. Look at me. The first Yueh broke his Suk conditioning – but *I* was born without the diamond tattoo. Entirely unblemished.'

'Maybe that means some things can be erased.'

'*Can* they? We gholas were raised for one purpose: to become who we once were. But are we anyone in our own right? Or are gholas simply tools, temporary tenants living in houses on borrowed time until the rightful owners return? What if we don't want those old lives? Is it right for Sheeana and the others to force them upon us? What about *us* as we are right now?'

Abruptly the gridwork of interlocking solar panes overhead seemed to glow brighter, as if the system had absorbed a wash of outside energy. The rows of densely arranged plants inside the greenhouse chamber became more defined, as if his eyes had suddenly become much more sensitive. Overlaying the whole chamber he saw a complex mesh of thin iridescent lines, resolving and focusing.

Something was happening – something Yueh had never experienced before. The lines became visible all around them, like fine netting that drifted through the air itself. They crackled with energy.

'Jessica, what is this? Do you see it?'

'A web . . . a net.' She caught her breath. 'It's what Duncan Idaho claims to see!'

Yueh's heart lurched. *The hunters?*

A loud security klaxon went off, accompanied by Duncan's voice. 'Prepare for activation of Holtzman engines!'

Whenever the no-ship folded space, unguided by a Navigator, they risked a disaster. Until now, Duncan's warnings had been unsupported by outside witnesses, though the Handlers had proved that the threat from the mysterious Enemy was real.

From the ship's corridors, Yueh heard the shouts of people running to emergency stations. The gossamer stranglehold grew brighter and more powerful, surrounding and infiltrating the whole ship. Surely, everyone could see this!

He felt a shudder through the deck, a disorientation and a *slipping* as the immense ship folded space. Staring through the conservatory dome, he saw star systems, swirling shapes and colors . . . as if the contents of the universe had been placed in a mixing bowl and stirred.

Suddenly the *Ithaca* cruised along elsewhere, far from the snares. Duncan's calm voice came over the intercom. 'We are safe again, for the moment.'

'Why did we see the net now and never before?' Jessica asked.

Yueh rubbed his chin, his thoughts in turmoil. 'Perhaps the Enemy is using a different sort of net – a stronger one. Or maybe they are testing new ways of tracking and snaring us.'

We must never voice doubt. We must believe utterly that
we can win this struggle against our Enemy. But in my
darkest times alone in my quarters, I always wonder: Is
this truly faith, or is it mere foolishness?

> – MOTHER COMMANDER MURBELLA,
> private Chapterhouse Archives

When Murbella's small Missionaria Aggressiva council gathered again, the meeting was tense. In the past year, the Sisterhood had sent seven Sheeana surrogates to refugee camps in order to rally the fighters. The counterfeit Sheeanas had their work cut out for them, convincing fanatics to stand firm in the face of certain defeat.

The seemingly unstoppable Enemy warships proliferated like the heads of a hydra; no matter how many vessels the humans destroyed, more and more appeared. Given millennia to prepare for his final conquest, Omnius had left nothing to chance. The dots on the star charts showed one planet after another falling under the onslaught of thinking machines.

Murbella sat in a hard and uncomfortable seat at the end of the table; most of the others selected furry chair-dogs. At the head of the table, Bashar Janess Idaho waited at attention, ready to deliver her report.

'I have news.'

'Good or bad?' Murbella dreaded the answer.

'Judge for yourself.'

Her daughter looked haggard, weary, and considerably older than her years. Having undergone the Spice Agony and extensive Bene Gesserit training, Janess had the ability to slow her body's changes, not for the sake of appearances, but to keep herself strong and limber. The constant fighting required it. Even so, the unending crisis was taking its toll. Murbella noticed a scar on her daughter's left cheek and a burn mark on her arm.

The female Bashar's words were unemotional, but Murbella could feel the turmoil in her clipped voice. 'Even before the first Enemy battleships were seen in the Jhibraith system, the machines sent scout probes to disseminate plagues. The people of Jhibraith had already called for an evacuation, but once the first signs of disease appeared, the Guild turned their ships around and refused to come closer. One Heighliner had to be quarantined. Fortunately, the plague was contained within seven isolated frigates inside its hold. All passengers aboard those frigates died, but the rest were saved.'

'What about the planet itself?' Murbella asked.

'The plague spread rapidly across all continents. As expected. The current viral strains are far worse than anything previously encountered, more deadly than even the legendary plagues during the Butlerian Jihad.'

Laera skimmed a Ridulian crystal sheet in front of her. 'Jhibraith has a population of three hundred twenty-eight million.'

'Not anymore,' said Kiria.

Janess locked her fingers together, as if to draw strength from her own grip. 'One of our Sheeana surrogates was on Jhibraith. As soon as the Guild quarantined the planet, the faux Sheeana rose to her calling and spoke to crowd after crowd as the plague spread. They knew they would all die. They knew the thinking machine forces were on their way. But she convinced them that if they must die, they should die as heroes.'

'But if the Guildships had already departed, how could they fight?' Kiria sounded skeptical. 'By throwing pebbles?'

'Jhibraith had its own in-system frigates, cargo vessels, and transport runners, none of them equipped with Holtzman engines or no-fields. As the disease cut people down, survivors raced to create a homegrown military force that might stand against Omnius. The people had to work faster than the epidemic killed them off.' She forced her lips into a cold, hard smile as she continued her report.

'Our false Sheeana was like a demon herself. I know for a fact that she went five days without sleeping, for the records show she appeared again and again at different cities and factories, rallying the citizenry, forcing them to crawl to their assembly stations if necessary. Nobody bothered with quarantines, since everyone was already infected. As people died in the factories, their bodies were dragged out to mass burial pits and huge bonfires. Others took their places at workstations.

'Even when the Enemy fleet surrounded the world, people did not pause. Then our Sheeana disappeared.' Janess looked around the table, lowered her voice. 'Afterward, I learned from a coded Bene Gesserit signal that our surrogate contracted the disease, and died from it.'

Murbella was startled. '*Died?* How can that be? Any Reverend Mother knows how to fight off infection.'

'That requires great concentration and significant physical resources. Our Sheeana had depleted her reserves. If she'd rested for a day or two, she might have rallied her strength and driven off the disease. But she kept going and going, using up whatever energy reserves she had. Knowing Jhibraith was doomed, that the invading machine armies would destroy her if the plague did not, Sheeana never slackened in her efforts.'

Old Accadia nodded. 'She had pushed the people into a fanatical fervor. No doubt she realized that if they saw her weakened and dying, they would lose their resolve. She was wise to remove herself from public view.'

Janess's thin smile showed true admiration. 'As soon as her symptoms began to manifest, Sheeana delivered one last grand speech, telling them she would now ascend to heaven. Then she isolated herself and died alone so that no one could see the horrific plague take its toll on her.'

'A marvelous and brave story for the archival histories.' Accadia pursed her withered lips. 'Her sacrifice will not be forgotten.'

'If anyone still studies the histories after this,' Kiria mumbled.

'And what of the subsequent fight on Jhibraith?' Murbella asked. 'Did the people defend themselves?'

'When the Enemy came, the people fought like ancient berserkers, to the last man and woman. Nothing could stop them. They met the Enemy fleet with ship after ship flown by grandfathers, teenagers, mothers, husbands, and even criminals released from detention centers. All fought and died bravely. Their sheer ferocity drove back the machines. Even with no defined military force, the people of Jhibraith destroyed more than a thousand Enemy vessels.'

Reality forced ice into Murbella's voice. 'My enthusiasm is tempered by the knowledge that even after losing a thousand vessels, the thinking machines have countless others to throw against us.'

'Still, if all planets fought like that, there might be a chance for humankind to survive,' Janess pointed out. 'The species would be preserved.'

Choosing her moment to pounce, Kiria peeled crystal sheets from another set of reports, then propped an image projector in the center of the table. The chairdog shifted subtly and compliantly to accommodate her movements. 'This new report shows why we can't count on all planets. We are being attacked by a rot from within, as well as the outside fleet.'

Murbella frowned. 'Where did you get this?'

'Sources.' Wearing a smug expression, the former Honored Matre activated the projector. 'While we face the thinking machines head-on, a more devious opponent undermines us from within.'

The image resolved to show a mob scene. 'This is Belos IV, but such occurrences have been documented elsewhere. Sparked by helplessness in the face of the approaching Enemy fleet, brushfire wars and political struggles are starting on planet after planet. People are afraid. When their leaders don't tell them what they want to hear, they riot, overthrow their prime ministers, and prop others in their place. More often than not, they depose the new leaders as well.'

'We know this.' Murbella looked at Janess, who remained rigidly at attention at the front of the table. She wished her daughter would sit down. On the images, the citizens of Belos IV had risen up against their governor, who had advocated surrender to the oncoming thinking machines. 'Obviously, the people didn't want to hear such a message. Why is this relevant?'

Kiria jabbed a sharp-nailed finger at the image. 'Observe!'

When the crowd attacked the middle-aged leader, he fought remarkably well, using skills and speed rarely demonstrated by any bureaucrat. While Murbella watched, she decided the governor must have acquired some sort of special training. His combat methods were unusual and effective, but the mob far outnumbered him. They dragged him through the streets to the balcony of the governor's palace and threw him off onto the flagstones far below. As he lay still, the howling, cheering mob backed away. The images drew in closer. The dead governor shifted and paled. His face became sunken and scarecrowish, somehow unformed. A Face Dancer!

'We always suspected the new Face Dancers had questionable loyalties. They allied themselves with Honored Matres and turned against the old Tleilaxu. We found them among the rebel whores on Gammu and Tleilax, and now it appears that the threat is even worse than we suspected. Listen to the governor's words. He advocated surrender to the thinking machines. Who are the Face Dancers really working for?'

Murbella reached the obvious conclusion and dragged her sharp gaze like a serrated knife across the other Sisters. 'The new Face Dancers are puppets of Omnius, and have infiltrated our populace. They are far superior to the old ones, able to resist almost any Bene Gesserit technique. We always wondered how the Lost Tleilaxu could have created them, when their skills were so inferior to those the old Masters demonstrated. It did not seem possible.'

Laera said coldly, 'It is possible if the thinking machines helped to create them, then sent them back among Tleilaxu returning from the Scattering.'

'A first wave of scouts and infiltrators.' Kiria nodded. 'How far have they spread? Could there be Face Dancers among *us*, undetected by Truthsayers?'

Accadia scowled. 'A frightening thought, if we have no way of exposing these new Face Dancers. From what I can tell, their mimicry is perfect.'

'Nothing is perfect,' Murbella said. 'Even thinking machines have flaws.'

Without humor, Kiria said, 'Oh, we can identify them easily enough. Kill them, and Face Dancers revert to their blank state.'

'So you suggest we simply kill everyone?'

'That's what the Enemy intends to do anyway.'

Restless, Murbella stood up. She could remain here on Chapterhouse with the other anxious Sisters, receive reports for another year, listen to summaries, and plot the advance of the thinking machines on a map, as if it were some kind of war game. Meanwhile, the Ixian engineers struggled to build weapons equivalent to the Obliterators, and the Guild shipyards worked to produce thousands of ships, all of them equipped with mathematical compilers.

But the crisis went far beyond internal politics and power struggles. She decided to go out there herself and travel among the worlds on the edge of the war zone, not as Mother Commander, but as a keen observer. She would let a council of Reverend Mothers run the everyday activities here on Chapterhouse, dealing with bureaucratic matters and doling out spice rations to the Guild in order to ensure their cooperation.

When Murbella announced her intent, Laera cried,

'Mother Commander, that's not possible. We need you here – there's so much to do!'

'I represent more than the New Sisterhood. Since no one else will step up to the plate, I am responsible for the whole human race.' She sighed. 'Somebody has to be.'

Our no-ship holds many secrets, yes, but not nearly the number we hold inside ourselves.

> – LETO II,
> the ghola

Leto II and Thufir Hawat had never known each other in their original lifetimes. To them, that was not a disadvantage. It left them free to form a friendship without any expectations or preconceptions.

Nine-year-old Leto hurried ahead, down the corridor. 'Come with me, Thufir. Now that nobody's watching, I can show you a special place.'

'Another one? Do you spend all your days exploring instead of studying?'

'If you're going to be deputy chief of security, you need to know everything about the *Ithaca*. Maybe we'll find your saboteur down here.' Leto turned sharply right, dropped into a small emergency lift, then paused at a dim, lower deck, where everything seemed larger and darker. He led Thufir to a sealed hatch that was posted with warnings and restrictions in half a dozen languages. Despite the locks, he opened it with barely a pause.

Thufir looked puzzled, even a little offended. 'How did you bypass security so easily?'

'This ship is old, and systems break down all the time. Nobody even knows this one failed.' He ducked into the low passageway.

The tunnel on the other side was a whistling, cool air channel. Up ahead the roaring grew louder, and the wind became powerful. Thufir sniffed. 'Where does it go?'

'To an air-exchange filtration system.' The passages were smooth and curving – like worm tunnels. A shiver brushed across Leto's skin, perhaps from a memory of when he had been joined with numerous sandtrout, from when he was the God Emperor of Dune, the Tyrant . . .

The two reached the central recyclers where large fans drove the air through thick curtains of filter mats, scrubbing out particulates and purifying the atmosphere. Breezes tugged at the boys' hair. Ahead, sheets of filtration material blocked further passage. The lungs of the ship, replenishing and redistributing oxygen.

Recently, Thufir had begun to mark his lips with a cranberry-red stain. As the pair stood in the bowels of the ship, listening to the roaring wind, Leto finally asked, 'Why do you do that to your mouth?'

Self-consciously, the fourteen-year-old rubbed his lips. 'My original used the sapho drug, which made stains like these. The Bashar wants me to live the part. He says he's preparing to awaken my memories.' Thufir didn't sound entirely pleased with the situation. 'Sheeana has been talking about forcing me to remember. She has some special technique to trigger a ghola's awakening.'

'Aren't you excited at the prospect? Thufir Hawat was a great man.'

The other boy remained preoccupied and troubled. 'It's not that, Leto. I really don't want my memories back, but Sheeana and the Bashar have their minds made up.'

'That's why you were created.' Leto was baffled. 'Why wouldn't you want your past life? The Master of Assassins would not be afraid of the ordeal.'

'I'm not afraid. I'd just rather be the person I choose to become, and not emerge fully formed. I don't feel I've earned it.'

'Trust me, they'll make you earn it, once you become the real Thufir again.'

'I *am* the real Thufir! Or do you doubt that, too?'

Thinking of the restless worm that crouched inside him, aware of all the atrocious things he would soon remember, Leto understood completely.

> *By following the same beliefs and making the same decisions, one wears Life's path into a circular rut, going nowhere, accomplishing nothing, making no progress. With God's help, though, we can turn a sharp corner in the circle and achieve enlightenment.*
>
> – The Cant of the Shariat

At last Waff was ready to release his new worms, and Buzzell was a convenient ocean planet on Edrik's standard trade route. A perfect test bed.

The giant vessel carried merchants who traded in soostones. Earlier, when Honored Matres had conquered Buzzell and killed most of the exiled Reverend Mothers, the whores had taken the soostone wealth for themselves. Since then, few of the aquatic gems had been traded on the galactic market, which made their value skyrocket. Now that the New Sisterhood had recaptured Buzzell, soostone production was up again. The witches ran tightly regimented operations there and kept smugglers at bay, thus maintaining stable but high prices for the stones. With mercenary armies to protect them, CHOAM merchants began to sell large quantities of the gems, reaping profits before a glut drove prices down again. A temporary market fluctuation.

Though pretty and desirable, soostones were not *necessary*. Melange, on the other hand, was vital – as the Navigators well knew. Waff knew that his experiments would eventually produce far more wealth than these undersea baubles could ever represent. Soon, if his expectations were met, Buzzell would be home to something far more interesting than baubles . . .

The Heighliner appeared above the liquid sapphire world, where tiny islands dotted the expansive ocean. Buzzell's oceans were deep and fertile, a large zone where the genetically altered worms would thrive, provided they survived their initial baptism.

The Tleilaxu Master paced the cold metal floor of his laboratory chamber. Soon, Edrik would inform him that the commercial lighters and cargo transports had disembarked for the island outposts. Once they were safely gone, Waff could begin his real work on Buzzell without being observed.

Inside the lab, the smell of salt, iodine, and cinnamon had replaced harsh chemical odors. Waff's test tanks were full of murky green water, rich with algae and plankton. Once turned loose in the oceans, the modified worms would have to find their own sources of nourishment, but Waff was sure they could adapt. God would make it all possible.

Serpentine forms swam about in the tanks looking like ringed eels. Their ridges were an iridescent blue-green, showing a soft pink membrane between segments, a surrogate set of gills that absorbed oxygen from the water. Their mouths were round like those of lampreys. Though they had no eyes, the new seaworms could navigate using water vibrations in much the way that Rakian worms had been attracted by tremors in the dunes. Using carefully mapped models from sandtrout chromosomes, Waff knew that these creatures had the same internal metabolic reactions as a traditional sandworm.

Therefore, they should still produce spice, but Waff didn't know what kind of spice, or how it would be harvested. He stepped back, interlocking his grayish fingers. That wasn't his problem or concern. He had done as Edrik commanded. He only wanted the worms back.

It had taken more than a year out of his accelerated lifetime, but if Waff succeeded in resurrecting God's messengers, his destiny would be complete. Even if the little man never received another ghola lifetime, he would have earned his place beside God in the highest levels of Heaven.

Under proper conditions, sandtrout specimens reproduced swiftly. From them, he had adapted nearly a hundred seaworms, most of which he would deposit in the oceans of Buzzell. For a new species to survive, especially in an unfamiliar environment, the creatures faced quite a challenge, and Waff fully expected that many of his test specimens would die. Maybe most of them. But he was also convinced that some would live – enough to establish a foothold.

Waff stood on his tiptoes, pressing his face to the tank. 'If you are in there, Prophet, I will soon give you a whole new domain.'

Five Guild assistants entered the lab without knocking. When Waff turned abruptly, the seaworms sensed his movement. With a thump, fleshy heads struck the reinforced tank walls. Startled again, Waff turned the other direction.

'Passengers have disembarked for Buzzell,' said one of the gray-clothed men. 'Navigator Edrik has commanded us to follow your instructions.'

The five all had oddly distorted heads, swollen brows, and asymmetric facial features. Any Tleilaxu Master could have repaired genetic flaws so that their descendants would be more physically attractive. But that would serve no purpose, and Waff had no interest in cosmetics.

He gestured to the tanks as the Guildsmen sealed them for transport. 'Exercise extreme care. Those creatures are worth more than all your lives.'

The reticent assistants installed handles on the crowded tanks and began lugging them along the curving halls of the Heighliner. Knowing he had only four hours to complete his task before the passenger shuttles returned, Waff urged them to hurry.

Because of the schism in the Guild between Navigators and Administrators, some people might not wish him to create this new avenue for spice production. The Ixians, the New Sisterhood, even the bureaucratic faction of the Guild might all work together, or separately, to assassinate him. Waff didn't know how or why these particular five Guildsmen had been chosen to assist him. If he expressed any misgivings about them, Waff knew that the Navigator would not hesitate to have all five killed, just to keep his Tleilaxu researcher happy. As the troupe walked to a small transport craft, Waff decided that was exactly what he would do. Get rid of these men, these witnesses. Afterward.

The sample tanks were loaded aboard the small transport. Waff did not usually leave the safe confines of the Heighliner, but he insisted on accompanying the crew down to the open sea. It was his experiment, and he wanted to be there in person to make sure the worms were released properly. He didn't trust the five Guildsmen to be sufficiently competent or attentive.

Then his suspicions ran deeper. What was to stop these men from flying off in the ship, revealing – or selling! – the seaworms to one of the opposing factions? Could they be perfectly loyal to Edrik? Waff saw danger everywhere.

As the transport dropped out of the cargo bay, Waff wished belatedly that he had demanded additional body-guards, or at least a sufficiently powerful hand-weapon for himself. Whom could he really trust?

Using technological apparatus connected to their throats, the silent Guildsmen communicated with each other electronically, transmitting brain signals without voicing words. He knew they could speak aloud – why would they be so secretive? Perhaps they were plotting against him. Waff looked at the immense Heighliner far overhead and wished fervently for this to be over.

The small transport descended into the cloudy skies, fighting choppy air currents. Waff felt ill. Finally, they broke through the moisture layers, and the oceans below sprawled out to every horizon. On charts displayed across the cockpit screens, Waff searched for a temperate zone where he could deposit the test worms, a place where the seas were rich with plankton and fish. It would give the creatures the greatest chance for survival.

He indicated a line of rocks not far from the Sisterhood's main island base and the center of their soostone-harvesting operations. '*There*. Safe, and close enough to monitor the worms.' He smiled, already imagining the first panicked reports of eyewitnesses. 'Any rumors or wild stories should be interesting.'

The Guildsmen nodded, all business. The transport ship flew low over the waves and hovered above the gentle swells. The lower cargo hatch opened, and Waff went down to observe the emptying of the tanks. He smelled the raw salt air, the tang of floating kelp, the wet breezes that whipped across the sea. A squall was about to begin.

Using the handles, two of the silent Guildsmen brought the first tank to the opening, released the plaz cover sheet, and spilled the water and writhing seaworms into the freedom of the waiting waves.

The serpentine creatures burst out like frantic snakes. Once they plunged into the green water, they streaked away. Waff watched their ridged bodies undulating, then diving and disappearing. They seemed joyous in their newfound freedom, glad to have a large world without plaz boundaries.

Brusquely, he gestured to the Guildsmen, telling them to release the rest of the worms, emptying all of the aquariums. Waff had kept one crowded tank of specimens aboard the Heighliner, and he could always create more.

As he stood by the open hatch, he suddenly shuddered, realizing his vulnerability. Now that he had turned the worms loose, would Edrik even require his services anymore? The Tleilaxu man feared the silent assistants might shove him overboard and leave him floating kilometers from the nearest speck of land. Warily, he backed deeper into the cargo hold and gripped a ridged wall strut.

But the Guildsmen made no move against him. They performed their work exactly as he told them to, and precisely as the Navigator had specified. Perhaps Waff was fearful only because he intended to have these men killed. He naturally suspected they would think the same about him.

Waff anticipated the seaworms would thrive here. The environment was conducive to their growth and reproduction. The worms would mark their territory, and when they grew large enough they would become leviathans of the deep. A fitting form for the Prophet.

The transport's cargo doors sealed again with a low hiss, and the Guild pilot flew away. Waff and his party would arrive back at the Heighliner well before the merchant vessels returned with their loads of soostones. No one would be the wiser.

The Tleilaxu Master glanced through the cockpit's plaz port to see the waves receding. He saw no sign of the seaworms, but he knew they were down there somewhere.

He let out a contented sigh, confident that his Prophet would come back.

It is the principle of the ticking time bomb, a strategy of aggression that has long been part of human violence. Thus we have inserted our 'time bombs' into the cells of gholas, activating specific behaviors at precise moments of our choosing.

– from *The Secret Manual of Tleilaxu Masters*

The no-ship had its own time, its own cycles. Most of the people were asleep, except for off-shift watches and maintenance crews. The decks were quiet, the glowpanels dimmed. In the shadowy chamber that held the axlotl tanks, the Rabbi paced back and forth, murmuring Talmudic prayers.

On a surveillance screen Sheeana observed the old man carefully, always alert to prevent any new incident of sabotage. When the saboteur had killed the three gholas and axlotl tanks, he or she had shut down the security imagers, but Bashar Teg had made sure that was no longer possible. Everything was under observation. As a former Suk doctor, the Rabbi had access to the medical center; he often spent time with what remained of the woman he'd known as Rebecca.

Though the old man had answered all questions the Truthsayers asked him, he still hadn't earned her trust.

Despite her best efforts, the saboteur and murderer remained at large. And the recent appearance of the glowing net had brought the Enemy too close, reminding the passengers of the very real threat. Everyone onboard had seen it. Their danger remained unabated.

Three relatively new axlotl tanks rested on their platforms; volunteers had come forward to answer Sheeana's call, exactly as she had expected. All three new tanks were currently producing liquid-form melange that dripped into small collecting vials, but she had begun preparations to implant one of the wombs with cells from Scytale's nullentropy tube. A new embryo to bring back yet another figure from the past. She refused to let the sabotage deflect her ghola project.

The Rabbi stood before the new tanks, his tense body exhibiting clear markers of loathing and disgust. He spoke to the fleshy mound. 'I hate you. Unnatural, ungodly.'

After watching the old man carefully, Sheeana left the monitor screens and entered the medical center, gliding up behind him. 'Is it honorable to hate the helpless, Rabbi? Those women are no longer aware, no longer human. Why despise them?'

He whirled, lights reflecting on his polished spectacles. 'Stop spying on me. I wish time alone to pray for Rebecca's soul.' Rebecca had been his personal favorite, willing to pit her intellect against his; the old man had never forgiven her for volunteering to become a tank.

'Even you need to be watched, Rabbi.'

Anger flushed his leathery skin. 'You and your witches should have heeded the warnings and ceased your grotesque experiments. If only the Honored Matres had managed to get rid of Scytale when they destroyed all

Tleilaxu worlds, then his hateful knowledge of tanks and gholas would have been lost.'

'The Honored Matres also hunted down your people, Rabbi. You and the Tleilaxu share the same enemy.'

'But it is not the same at all. We have been unfairly persecuted throughout history, while the Tleilaxu merely received their just desserts. Their own Face Dancers turned on them, from what I understand.' He took a step away from the fleshy mound, from the chemical and biological odors that wafted from the tanks. 'I can hardly recall what Rebecca once looked like, before she became this *thing*.'

Sheeana searched for the memories, and asked the voices within to assist her. This time they did, and she found what she wanted, like accessing old archival images. The woman had looked elegant in her brown robe and braided hair. She'd worn contact lenses to conceal the blue eyes of her spice addiction . . .

With a bitter expression, the Rabbi placed a hand on Rebecca's exposed flesh. A tear ran down his cheek. He muttered the same thing each time he visited her. A litany for him. 'You witches did this to her, made her into a monster.'

'She's not a monster, not even a martyr.' She tapped her own forehead. 'Rebecca's thoughts and memories are in here and inside many other Sisters. Shared with us all. Rebecca did what was necessary, and so will we.'

'By making more gholas? Will it never end?'

'You are concerned about a pebble in your shoe, while we seek to avoid the rockslide. Sooner or later, we will no longer be able to run from the Enemy. We'll need the ingenuity and special talents of these gholas, in particular those capable of becoming another Kwisatz

Haderach. But we must handle the genetic material carefully, nurturing and developing it in the proper order, at the proper pace.' She strolled to one of the new tanks, a fresh young woman whose form had not yet deteriorated into unrecognizability.

As she stood there, a troubling thought refused to leave her mind, no matter how much she tried to push it away. An absurd line of reasoning, but all day long it had been percolating. *What if my own abilities could be equivalent to those of a Kwisatz Haderach? I already have a natural ability to control the great worms. I have the Atreides genes, and centuries of the Sisterhood's perfected knowledge to draw upon. Would I dare?*

She felt voices surfacing from within; one rose above the others. The ancient Reverend Mother Gaius Helen Mohiam, repeating something that she once said so long ago to a young Paul Atreides: 'Yet, there's a place where no Truthsayer can see. We are repelled by it, terrorized. It is said a man will come one day and find in the gift of the drug his inward eye. He will look where we cannot – into both feminine and masculine pasts . . . the one who can be many places at once . . . ' The old crone's voice drifted away, without giving Sheeana any advice, one way or the other.

With a sneer, the Rabbi interrupted her thoughts. 'And you trust that old Tleilaxu to help you, when he's desperate to achieve his own goals before dying? Scytale hid those cells for so many years. How many of them contain dangerous secrets? You've already discovered Face Dancer cells among the samples. How many of your ghola abominations are traps laid by the Tleilaxu?'

She gazed at him dispassionately, knowing that no

argument would ever sway him. The Rabbi made the sign of the evil eye, and fled.

DUNCAN ENCOUNTERED SHEEANA in an empty corridor, in the dimness of the artificial night. The no-ship's recyclers and life-support systems kept the air comfortably cool, but upon seeing her alone like this Duncan felt a flush of heat.

Sheeana's large eyes fixed on him like a weapon's targeting system. Feeling a tingle like static electricity on his skin, he cursed his body for being so easily tempted. Even now, three years after Sheeana had broken the debilitating chains of Murbella's love, the two of them still found themselves drawn irresistibly into unexpected bouts of sex as frenetic as any he and Murbella had ever shared.

Duncan preferred to manage the circumstances of their casual meetings, always trying to make certain that others were present, that he had safe guardrails to prevent him from falling off a dangerous cliff. He did not like to be out of control: That had already happened too many times.

He and Sheeana had surrendered to each other like terrified people huddling in a bombed-out battle zone. She had cauterized him to cure his debility and stolen him from Murbella, yet he felt like a casualty of war.

Now as he saw Sheeana's expression flicker, Duncan thought she felt the same sense of vertigo and disorientation. She tried to sound reserved and rational. 'It is better if we don't do this. We have too many concerns, too many risks. Another regenerator system has just failed. The saboteur—'

'You're right. We should not.' His voice was hoarse, but they had already started down a path with ever-increasing consequences. Duncan took a hesitant step forward. The muted corridor lights reflected off the no-ship's metal walls. 'We shouldn't do this,' he said again.

Desire swept like a wave over both of them. As a Mentat he could observe and assess, concluding that what they were doing was simply a reaffirmation of humanity. When they touched fingertips, lips, and skin, both of them were lost . . .

Later, they rested on tangled sheets in Sheeana's quarters. The air carried a moist muskiness. Duncan lay sated with his fingers laced in his wiry dark hair. He was confused and disappointed in himself. 'You've taken away too much of my control.'

Sheeana raised her eyebrows in the dim light, showing amusement. Her breath was warm and close to his ear. 'Oh? And Murbella did not?' When Duncan turned away and did not answer, she chuckled. 'You're feeling guilty! You think you've betrayed her somehow. But how many female imprinters did you train back on Chapterhouse?'

He answered the question in his own way. 'Murbella and I were trapped together, and no part of our relationship was voluntary. We had a mutual addiction, two people brought to a stalemate. That isn't love or tenderness. For Murbella – for all of you witches – our love-making was supposed to be "just business." But I still had feelings for her, dammit! It isn't a matter of whether or not I should.

'But you – you were like a violent detoxification of my system. The Agony served the same purpose for Murbella, breaking her bond to me.' He reached out and cupped Sheeana's chin. 'This cannot happen again.'

Now she looked even more amused. 'I agree that it should not . . . but it will anyway.'

'You're a loaded weapon, a full Bene Gesserit. Every time we make love, you could easily let yourself get pregnant. Isn't that what the Sisterhood would demand? You could carry my child whenever you allow yourself to do so.'

'True. But I haven't. We are far from Chapterhouse, and I make my own decisions now.' Sheeana pulled him back to her.

*Scientists see sandworms as specimens, while the Fremen
see them as their god. But the worms devour anyone who
tries to gather information. How am I supposed to work
under such conditions?*

> — IMPERIAL PLANETOLOGIST PARDOT KYNES,
> ancient records

Sheeana stood in the high observation gallery where she
and Garimi had once gone to discuss the future of their
journey. The kilometer-long great hold was large enough
to offer the illusion of freedom, though much too small
for a brood of sandworms. The seven creatures were
growing but remained stunted, waiting for the promised
arid land. They had been waiting a long time, perhaps
too long.

More than two decades ago, Sheeana had brought the
small worms aboard the no-ship, stealing them from the
growing desert band on Chapterhouse. She had always
intended to transplant them to another world, far from the
Honored Matres and safe from the Enemy. For years, the
worms had zigzagged endlessly in the sand-filled confines
of the hold, as lost as everyone else on the *Ithaca* . . .

She wondered if the no-ship would ever find a planet
where they could stop, where the Sisters could establish

a new and orthodox Chapterhouse, rather than the mongrel organization that made concessions to the ways of the Honored Matres. If the ship simply fled for generations and generations, it would be impossible to find a perfect world for the sandworms, for Garimi and her conservative Bene Gesserits, for the Rabbi and his Jews.

She recalled searching Other Memory for advice the evening before. For a while, there had been no response. Then Serena Butler, the ancient leader of the Jihad, came to her just as Sheeana drifted off to sleep in her quarters. Long-dead Serena told of her experiences being lost and overwhelmed by an endless war, forced to guide vast populations when she herself didn't know where to go.

'But you found your way, Serena. You did what you had to do. You did what humanity needed.'

And so will you, Sheeana.

Now, seeing the sandworms ripple the sand far below, Sheeana could sense their feelings in an indefinable way, and they could sense hers. Did they dream of endless, dry dunes in which to stake their territory? The largest of the worms, nearly forty meters long with a maw large enough to swallow three people abreast, was clearly dominant. Sheeana had given that one a name: Monarch.

The seven worms pointed their eyeless faces toward her, displaying crystalline teeth. The smaller ones burrowed into the shallow sand, leaving only Monarch, who seemed to be summoning Sheeana. She stared at the dominant worm, trying to understand what it wanted. The connection between them began to burn inside her, calling her.

Sheeana descended to the sand-filled cargo hold. Stepping out onto churned dunes, she strode directly toward the worm, unafraid. She had faced the creatures many times before and had nothing to fear from this one.

Monarch towered over her. Putting her hands on her hips, Sheeana looked up, and waited. In the heady days on Rakis, she had learned to dance on the sands and control the behemoths, but she had always known she could do more. When she was ready.

The worm seemed to be playing upon her need for understanding. She was the girl who could communicate with the beasts, who could control and understand them. And now, in order to see her own future, she had to go farther. Literally and metaphorically. It was what Monarch wanted. Dangerous and frightening, the creature exhaled a stink of inner furnaces and pure melange.

'So, now what do we do, you and I? Are you Shaitan, or just an impostor?'

The restless worm seemed to know exactly what she had in mind. Instead of rolling its body toward her so she could climb its rings to ride, Monarch faced her with its round maw open. Each milky-white tooth in a mouth the size of a cave opening was long enough to be used as a crysknife. Sheeana did not tremble.

The sandworm laid its head on the soft dunes directly in front of her. Tempting her to a symbolic journey, like Jonah and the whale? Sheeana wrestled with her fears, but knew what she must do – not as a charlatan's perform-ance, for she doubted anyone was watching her, but because it was necessary for her own understanding.

Monarch lay waiting for her, mouth agape. The worm itself became a secret doorway, luring her like a dangerous lover. Sheeana stepped past the portcullis of crysknife teeth and knelt inside the gullet, inhaling the rank cinnamon odor. Dizzy and nauseated, she could barely breathe. The sandworm did not move. Willingly, she worked her way deeper inside, offering herself, though convinced that her sacrifice would not be accepted. It wasn't what the worm wanted from her.

Without looking back, she crawled farther down the throat into dry, dark warmth. Monarch did not twitch. Sheeana kept going, felt her breathing slow. Deeper and deeper she went, and soon guessed that she had gone at least half the length of the prone worm. Without the friction heat sparked by roaming endless deserts, the worm's gullet was no longer a furnace. Her eyes became accustomed to what she realized was not total darkness, but was instead an eerie illumination that seemed more the product of another sense in her own mind than traditional eyesight. She could dimly see the rough, membranous surface around her, and as she proceeded, the undigested odor of melange precursors grew stronger, more concentrated.

Finally she reached a fleshy chamber that might have been Monarch's stomach, but without digestive acids. How did the captive sandworms survive? The odor of spice was more intense here than she had ever experienced – so much so that an ordinary person would have suffocated.

But I am no ordinary person.

Sheeana lay there, absorbing the warmth, letting the intense melange seep into every pore in her body, feeling Monarch's dim consciousness merge into hers. She inhaled deeply and felt a great, cosmic sense of calm, like being in the womb of the Great Mother of the Universe.

Unexpectedly, with the unusual visitor deep in its gullet, the sandworm dove into the artificial desert and began to move through it; taking her on a strange journey. As if connected directly with Monarch's nervous system,

Sheeana could see *through* the eyeless worm to its companions beneath the sand. Working together, the seven sandworms were forming small veins of spice in the cargo hold.

Preparing.

Sheeana lost track of time and thought again of Leto II, whose pearl of awareness was now inside this beast and all of the others in the hold. She wondered where she fit into this paranormal realm. As the God Emperor's queen? As the female part of the godhead? Or as something else entirely, an entity she could not begin to imagine?

The worms all carried secrets, and Sheeana understood how much the ghola children were like that as well. They each held a treasure greater than spice within their cells: their past memories and lives. Paul and Chani, Jessica, Yueh, Leto II. Even Thufir Hawat, Stilgar, Liet-Kynes . . . and now baby Alia. Each had a crucial role to play, but only if they could remember who they were.

She saw each image, but not in her own imagination. The sandworms knew what those lost figures contained. An urgency rushed toward her like a desert wind. Time, and with it their chances for survival, was slipping away too quickly. She envisioned a succession of the possible gholas, all primed like weapons, but blurred as to what each could do.

She could not wait for the Enemy. She had to act now.

The worm resurfaced, and after moving along the sands, it jolted to a stop. Inside, Sheeana caught her balance. Then, by constricting its membranous interior, the creature gently pushed her back out. She crawled from the mouth and tumbled onto the sands.

Dust and grit clung to the film coating her body. Monarch nudged her, like a mother bird urging a chick to go out on its own. Caught up in disorienting visions, she struggled and dropped to her knees on the dry sand. The faces of the ghola children wavered around her, dissolving into bright lights. *Awaken!*

She lay gasping for breath, her body and clothing drenched in spice essence. Beside Sheeana, the big worm turned, burrowed back into the shallow sand, and disappeared from view.

Reeking and reeling, Sheeana made her way back toward the cargo-hold doors, but she kept losing her footing and falling. She had to reach the ghola children . . . The worm had given her an important message, something that seeped into her consciousness like a wordless form of Other Memory. In moments, she was left with an overwhelming certainty of what she had to do.

After being scrubbed and showered to rid her of a spice reek so strong that even the Sisters who assisted her covered their mouths and noses, Sheeana slept for two days in deep and disturbing dreams.

When she finally emerged and found Duncan Idaho and Miles Teg on the navigation bridge, she made her announcement. 'The gholas are all old enough. Even Leto II is the same age as when I restored the Bashar.' The smell of melange was heavy on Sheeana's breath. 'It's time to awaken them all.'

Duncan turned his back on the observation window where he stood. 'Triggering the process isn't like activating a subroutine or working through a bout of temporary amnesia. You can't just issue a memo and order it done.'

'The ghola children have always known that we would demand this of them,' she said. 'Without their past memories, without their genius, they are of no more value to us than any other children.'

The Bashar nodded slowly. 'To recall a ghola's past life is an experience that destroys and recreates the psyche. There are numerous proven methods, some more painful than others, but none are easy. You can't awaken the children all at once. Each critical event must be tailored to the individual. A horrible, mind-shattering crisis.' Teg's face showed echoes of pain. 'You thought you were using a humane awakening method with me, Sheeana . . . when I was only a ten-year-old child.'

Though Duncan, too, seemed uneasy at the prospect, he stepped down from the observation window and walked toward Sheeana. 'She's right, Miles. We created those gholas for a purpose, and right now they're all like unloaded guns. We need to load our gholas – our unique weapons. The Enemy's net is stronger now, and it nearly snared us again. We all saw it. Next time, we may not be able to slip away.'

'We've waited long enough.' Sheeana's voice was hard, brooking no argument.

'Some gholas may be more challenging than others.' Teg's eyes narrowed. 'You may lose some to madness. Are you prepared for that?'

'I have gone through the Spice Agony, as have all Reverend Mothers on this ship. We survived the unbearable pain.'

'I have the memories of my old life,' Teg said. 'Of wars and atrocities, and enduring unbearable torture. Somehow the bad details are much more vivid than the pleasant ones, but nothing is worse than the awakening.'

Sheeana waved her hand. 'Throughout history, men and women have had a monopoly on their own kinds of pain, each thinking theirs is the worst.' She smiled grimly.

'We will start with the least valuable ghola, of course. In case something goes wrong.'

WELLINGTON YUEH WAS summoned to stand before the Bene Gesserits in one of the no-ship's council chambers. The gangly teenager had a pointed chin and pinched lips. Already buried within his face were hints of the familiar chiseled features and broad forehead – the despised visage that had become synonymous with the word *traitor* for thousands of years in galactic reference works.

The young man was nervous, fidgeting. Sheeana drew herself to her full height and stepped closer. He flinched at her intimidating presence, but somehow found the courage to stand where he was. 'You summoned me, Reverend Mother. How may I assist?'

'By awakening your memories. Tomorrow you will be the first of our subjects to undergo the trigger.'

Yueh's yellowish face paled. 'But I'm not ready!'

'That is why we have given you a full day to prepare.' Proctor Superior Garimi's tongue was sharp, as usual.

Although Garimi had never embraced the project, she now wanted to see its culmination. Sheeana knew what she was thinking: If the awakening process failed, Garimi intended to prevent any further gholas from being grown; if the awakening succeeded, she would insist that the program had fulfilled its goal and could be discontinued. She knew that Sheeana, still intrigued by all those cells in the Tleilaxu's nullentropy capsule, was planning further ghola experiments.

Yueh's legs were locked. He seemed close to fainting and grasped a nearby chair to steady himself. 'Sisters, I don't want to have my memories back. I am not the man you think you resurrected, but a new person – my own person. The old Wellington Yueh was tormented in so many ways. Even though he was in part *me*, how can I forgive him for what he did?'

Garimi made a dismissive gesture. 'Nevertheless, we brought you back for one purpose only. Don't expect sympathy from us. You have a task to perform.'

After the proctors took the distraught young man away, Sheeana looked at Garimi and two other senior Sisters – Calissa and Elyen – who had observed the discussion. 'I will use the sexual method on him, the same one that worked on the ghola of the Bashar. It is the best technique we know.'

Elyen said, 'Your sexual imprinting unlocked the Bashar's memories only because it precipitated a crisis in him. Teg's mother had armed him against sexual imprinting. It wasn't your technique that stirred up his past, but his sheer resistance to it.'

'Indeed. So for each of our gholas we'll tailor an individualized agony that leverages their own fears and weaknesses.'

'How can sex break Yueh the way it broke the Bashar?' Garimi asked.

'Not the sex itself, but Yueh's resistance to it. He's terrified of remembering his past. If he believes we know how to unlock his memories, he'll fight us with everything he has. As he fights, I will apply my most potent procedures, and he'll spiral over the brink into complete madness.'

Garimi shrugged. 'If it doesn't work, we have other ways.'

THE ROOM WAS dim and the shadows cloying, which made Yueh's terror more palpable. The chamber was devoid of furniture except for a padded mat on the floor, like those that the ghola children used during physical training sessions.

The witches had not explained what to expect. The young man knew from his studies that the process of regaining one's past was painful. He was not a strong man, nor was he particularly brave. Even so, the prospect of pain did not petrify him nearly so much as the dread of remembering.

The door slid open with a gentle hiss of lubricated metal gliding in its tracks. From the corridor, blinding light flowed in, much brighter than the glowpanels in his cell. It silhouetted a woman's figure – Sheeana? He turned to face her and could see only her outline, the sensual curves of her body no longer masked by flowing robes. When the door sealed behind her, his eyes adjusted to the more comfortable illumination.

When he saw that Sheeana was completely unclothed, his fear increased. 'What is this?' His voice, torn by nervousness, came out as a squeak.

She stepped closer. 'You will disrobe now.'

Barely a teenager, Yueh swallowed. 'Not until you explain what is going to happen to me.'

She used the hurricane force of Bene Gesserit Voice. '*You will disrobe now!*'

In a spasmodic reaction, his arms and legs jerking, he tore off his clothes. Sheeana inspected him, running her eyes up and down his thin, naked body like a hawk assessing its prey. Yueh got the impression that she found him inadequate.

'Don't hurt me,' he pleaded, and hated himself for saying it.

'Of course it will hurt, but the pain won't be anything *I* inflict upon you.' She touched his shoulder. He felt an almost electric shock, but he was transfixed, unable to move. 'Your own memories will do that.'

'I don't want them back. I'll fight you.'

'Fight all you wish. It will do you no good. We know how to awaken you.'

Yueh closed his eyes and gritted his teeth. He tried to turn away, but she grasped his arms to hold him still, then released her grip and began touching him. The delicate strokings felt like the line of heat left by a lighted match down his arm and across his chest. 'Your memories are stored within your cells. In order to awaken them, I must awaken your body.' She stroked him, and he shuddered, unable to draw away. 'I shall teach your nerve endings to do things they've forgotten how to do.' Another jolt, and he gasped.

She touched him again, and his knees buckled, exactly as she wanted. Sheeana pushed him toward the mat on the floor. 'I need to wrench you into the full awareness of every chromosome in every cell.'

'No.' The word sounded incredibly weak to him.

As she pressed herself against him, letting warm skin ignite his perspiration, Yueh tunneled backward into himself, trying to flee. From all he had learned of his past, he found one thing with which to anchor his bravery. *Wanna!* His beloved Bene Gesserit wife, the weak link in his long chain of betrayals, and the strongest link in his original lifetime.

The evil Harkonnens had known that Wanna would be the key to breaking his Suk conditioning, and it had only worked – could only have worked – because Yueh loved her with all his heart. Bene Gesserits were not supposed to succumb to love, but he knew that she must have reciprocated.

He thought of her pictures in the archives, of all he had learned about her in his researches. 'Oh, Wanna.' He yearned for her in his mind, tried to latch onto her as a lifeline.

Sheeana stroked his waist, trailed her fingers lower and climbed on top of him. Yueh's muscles were completely out of his control. He couldn't move. Her lips vibrated against the skin of his shoulder, his neck. Sheeana was a skilled sexual imprinter. Her body was a weapon, and he was the target.

A flood of sensations nearly drove the archival image of Wanna from his mind, but Yueh fought against what Sheeana was making him feel. Instead, he focused on what he might have done in Wanna's loving embrace. *Wanna.*

As the rhythm of their lovemaking increased, real memories intruded on the information he had obtained through research. Yueh recalled those terrible moments after his wife had been seized by the Harkonnens, and saw images of the loathsome fat Baron, his thuggish nephew Rabban, the viper Feyd-Rautha, and the Mentat Piter de Vries, who had a laugh that sounded like vinegar.

Weak, helpless, and infuriated, he had been forced to watch them torture Wanna inside an isolated chamber. She was a Bene Gesserit; she could block her pain, could deflect her body's responses. But Yueh could not so easily shunt such things aside, no matter how hard he tried.

In his nightmare memory the Baron laughed, a rumbling basso sound. 'See the little chamber she's in, Doctor? A toy with some very interesting possibilities.' As the men watched the groggy and disoriented Wanna, she stood on weak knees, but upside-down within the booth. 'We can convert gravity into a thing that depends entirely on perspective.'

Rabban chuckled, a harsh release of noise. He operated artificial gravity controls in the small room, and
suddenly Wanna fell with a thud to the floor. She managed
to tuck her head and shoulders just enough to avoid
breaking her neck. With the speed and fluidity of a serpent,
Piter de Vries scurried forward carrying a pain amplifier.
At the last moment, Rabban snatched it out of the Twisted
Mentat's hands and applied it to Wanna's throat himself.
She writhed with a jagged spasm of agony.

'Stop! Stop, I beg you!' Yueh cried.

'Oh, Doctor, Doctor – you know it can't possibly be
that easy . . .' In the vision, the Baron folded his pudgy
arms across his chest.

Rabban twisted the gravity controls again, and Wanna
was thrown like a limp doll from wall to wall, smashing
into the sides of the chamber. 'When one is too lovely,
something must be done to correct that condition.'

My beautiful Wanna!

The memories were so vivid now, far more detailed
than anything he had read in the Archives section. No
mere documentation could have provided such precise
clarity . . .

In a different, newly unlocked compartment of his
brain, he lived another memory. He was artificially paralyzed, forced to watch during one of the Baron's drunken
parties while Piter played a sparking pain amplifier over
Wanna's suspended body. Each flash provoked a twitching
response of agony from her. The other guests laughed at
her pain and at his helpless misery.

When he was freed from his paralysis, Yueh trembled,
drooled, and struggled. The Baron stood over him, a huge
grin on his bloated face. He handed Yueh a projectile
pistol. 'As a Suk doctor, you should do everything possible

to stop a patient from feeling pain. You know how to stop Wanna's pain, Doctor.'

Unable to break his conditioning, Yueh shuddered and spasmed. He wanted nothing more than to do as the Baron demanded. 'I . . . can't!'

'Of course you can. Choose a guest, any guest. I don't care which. See how amused they are by our little game?' Grasping Yueh's shaking wrists, he helped the doctor point his projectile weapon around the room. 'But don't try any tricks, or we will make the torment last a great deal longer!'

He wished he could put Wanna out of her misery, killing her instead of letting the Harkonnens have their perverted fun. He saw her eyes, the spark of pain and hope, but Rabban stopped him. 'Focus, Doctor. No mistakes.'

Through blurred vision he made out numerous targets, and tried to concentrate on one, a tottering old nobleman, a semuta addict. That one had lived a long life, undoubtedly with considerable debauchery. But for a Suk doctor to kill—

He fired.

Overwhelmed by the horrific scene now playing out in his head, Yueh paid no further attention to Sheeana's ministrations. His body was drenched with sweat, but less from sexual exertion than from the extreme psychological distress. He saw Sheeana appraising him. The memories were so clear to him that his entire body felt like a raw wound: Wanna in agony and the sharp, broken-crystal pain of how his Suk conditioning had been thwarted. It had happened *thousands* of years ago!

The years before that watershed occurrence, and the years afterward, extended outward, filling his mind, now fresh and hungry. As the relentless memories returned, so did more anguish and guilt, accompanied by a disgust with himself.

Yueh felt as if he was about to vomit. Tears poured down his cheeks.

In the training room, Sheeana studied the wet streaks clinically. 'You're weeping. Does that mean you've successfully regained your memories?'

'I have them back.' His voice was husky and sounded infinitely old. 'And damn you witches to hell for it.'

We have so little trouble finding enemies because violence is an innate part of human nature. Our greatest challenge, then, is to choose the most significant enemy, for we cannot hope to fight them all.

— BASHAR MILES TEG,
military assessment delivered to the Bene Gesserit

After she departed from Chapterhouse, Murbella traveled to the battle lines. That was where the Mother Commander belonged. Posing as nothing more important than an inspector for the New Sisterhood, Murbella arrived at Oculiat, one of the systems that lay directly in the path of the advancing thinking-machine fleet.

Once, Oculiat had been at the far edges of inhabited space, a jumping-off point for the Scattering after the Tyrant's death. Objectively, this sparsely populated world had little significance, just another target on the vast cosmic map. But for Murbella, Oculiat represented a genuine psychological blow: When this world fell to the machines, the Enemy would be encroaching into the *Old Empire* itself, not just into a distant and unknown place that had been omitted from old star maps.

Until the Ixians delivered their Obliterators and the Guild provided all the ships she had demanded, the Mother

Commander had no way to stop, or even slow, the thinking machines.

Under a hazy sky illuminated by watery yellow sunlight, Murbella stepped out of her ship. The landing field seemed deserted, as if no one tended the spaceport any longer. As if they were not even watching for the Enemy.

When she made her way to the frantic crowds in the central city, though, she saw that the inhabitants had already found their own enemy. A mob surrounded the main administration building where government officials had barricaded themselves. The locals had put their leaders under siege, screaming for blood or divine intervention. *Preferably blood.*

Murbella knew the raw power that their fear generated, but it was clearly not channeled properly. The people of Oculiat – and all desperate worlds facing the oncoming Enemy – needed guidance from the Sisterhood. They were an already-charged weapon that must be aimed. Instead, they were out of control. She saw what was happening and rushed forward, but stopped short of throwing herself headlong into the mob.

They would tear her limb from limb, and they would do it for Sheeana.

The random appearances and sermons of the 'resurrected Sheeana' had prepared billions of people to fight. The Sheeanas had kindled the anger and fervor of populations, so that the Sisterhood could manipulate that raw power for their own purposes. Once unleashed, however, such fanaticism became a chaotic force. Knowing they were unlikely to survive against the oncoming machines, the men and women threw themselves into violence, seeking any sort of enemy they could get their hands on . . . even among their own people.

'Face Dancers!' someone shouted. Murbella pushed her way closer to the center of action, knocked aside flailing arms and fists, and cuffed someone on the side of the head. But even stunned, the wild and embold-ened people surged onward. 'Face Dancers! They've been manipulating us all along – selling us out to the Enemy.'

Those who recognized the Mother Commander's Bene Gesserit unitard backed away; others, either oblivious or too angry to care, were not swayed until she used Voice. Bombarded by the irresistible command, they staggered away. Just one person against the multitude, Murbella strode toward the colonnaded doorways of the government center, which the people saw as their target. She used Voice again but could not stop them all in their tracks. The shouting and accusatory shrieks rose and fell like a thunderstorm.

As she fought her way to the front of the barricade, several of the foremost mob members noticed her uniform and let out a long cheer. 'A Reverend Mother is here to support us!'

'Kill the Face Dancers! Kill them all!'

'For Sheeana!'

Murbella grabbed an elderly woman who had been yelling along with the others. 'How do you know they're Face Dancers?'

'We *know*. Think about their decisions, listen to their speeches. It's obvious they are traitors.' Murbella didn't believe that Face Dancers would be quite so obvious that common rabble could detect the faint subtleties. But the mob was convinced.

Six huffing men ran by, carrying a heavy plasteel pole that they proceeded to use as a battering ram. Inside the capitol building, terrified officials had piled obstructions against the doors and windows. Thrown stones shattered the ornamental plaz, but the crowd couldn't break in so easily. Bars and heavy objects blocked the way.

Wielded with the strength of panic and hysteria, the battering ram pounded the thick doors, tearing hinges loose and splintering wood. In moments, a wave of human bodies pushed forward.

Murbella called out. 'Wait! Why not prove they're Face Dancers before you kill anyone—'

The old woman shoved past, eager to get to the officials. She stepped on Murbella's foot, heard her shouted cautions, then turned to her with a narrowed gaze like a serpent's. 'Why do you hesitate, Reverend Mother? Help us capture the traitors. Or are you a Face Dancer yourself?'

Murbella's Honored Matre reflexes came to the fore, and her hand snapped out, cutting into the woman's neck with a blow that rendered her unconscious. She had not meant to kill the woman, but as her accuser fell to the steps a dozen people surged forward, trampling her to death.

Heart pounding, Murbella pressed against the wall to avoid the brunt of the stampede. If the cry had been taken up – 'Face Dancer! Face Dancer!' – with fingers pointing at her, the crowd would have killed her without thinking. Even with superior fighting abilities, Murbella could never fend off so many.

She backed up farther and took shelter behind the tall statue of a long-forgotten hero of the Famine Times, shielding herself with its plastone bulk. The screaming mob would crush many of its own members to get into the government building.

She could hear cries inside, a discharge of weapons, and small explosions. Some of the trapped officials must have been carrying personal protection. Murbella waited, knowing it would be over soon . . .

The bloody attack burned itself out in half an hour. The mob found and killed all twenty government officials suspected of being enemy Face Dancers. Then, still not sated in their thirst for blood, they turned against any of their own members who had not shown sufficient murderous fervor, until most of the violence drained away into guilty exhaustion . . .

Standing tall, Mother Commander Murbella entered the building, where she surveyed the smashed windows, display cases, and artwork. Jubilant murderers dragged bodies onto the polished tiled floor of the main legislative gallery. Almost thirty men and women were dead, some shot with projectile weapons, others beaten to death, many with such violence that their genders were hardly recognizable. The corpses on the polished stone floor wore expressions of horror and shock.

One of the bodies among the bloody mess was indeed a Face Dancer.

'We were right! You see, Reverend Mother.' A man pointed at the dead shape-shifter. 'We were infiltrated, but we rooted out the enemy and killed it.'

Murbella looked around, at all of the innocent humans murdered to discover one Face Dancer. What was the economy of bloodshed? She tried to assess it coolly. How much damage could that one Face Dancer have caused, exposing vulnerabilities to the oncoming Enemy forces? All of those lives? Yes, and more, she had to admit.

From their elation it was obvious that the people of Oculiat considered their uprising a victory, and Murbella

could not dispute that. But if this wave of insane vigilant-
ism continued, would all governments topple? Even on
Chapterhouse? Then who would organize the people to
defend themselves?

*Weak minds are gullible. The weaker the thought processes,
the more ridiculous the notions they will believe. Strong
minds, like mine, can turn that to an advantage.*

— BARON VLADIMIR HARKONNEN,
original recordings

Despite being unarmed, the Baron sneered into the face
of the red-eyed mongrel hound. The growling animal
moved toward him on the flagstoned floor, baring its
sharp fangs, ready to spring.

Fortunately, the Baron had killed the feral creature with
a poison dart gun some time ago, and this stuffed mechanical version merely followed a programmed reenactment.
The simulacrum went motionless when he gave it a hand
signal. An amusing toy.

Nine-year-old Paolo moved around the trophy
chamber, admiring the wild animals on display. The Baron
had dragged the boy out on many hunts in the pristine
wilderness of Caladan, so that he could witness the killing
firsthand. It was good for his development and education.

Rabban had always enjoyed such things, but Paolo
had originally been reluctant to engage in the slaughter.
Maybe it was some flaw in the genetics. However, the

Baron was gradually breaking down his resistance. With vigorous training and a system of rewards and punishments (plenty of the latter), the Baron had almost managed to squash the core of innate goodness in this ghola of Paul Atreides.

Weathersats had predicted constant rain and wind for the rest of the week. The Baron had looked forward to going out on a fresh hunt, but the cold and wet would have made for a miserable expedition. He and Paolo were trapped inside the castle. The two had formed a remarkable bond. House Atreides and House Harkonnen – how ironic! But though Paolo was a clone of the hated Duke's son, raised properly he was turning out more like a Harkonnen.

He is your grandson, after all, the internal voice of Alia nagged at him.

Overcoming an urge to shout back at her, the Baron watched four workmen with suspensors hoist an immense stuffed mastaphont onto a viewing stand. Yet another nearly extinct creature, this ferocious beast had charged at them across a field last autumn, slashing with its serrated horns. But the Baron, Paolo, and half a dozen guards had opened fire with lasguns, cutting disks, and poison flechettes, mangling the creature before it finally fell. What an exciting hunt that had been!

Paolo looked at the animated creatures on stands. 'Instead of going outside to the wilderness, let's go hunting in here. We can pretend they're not already dead. Then we don't have to worry about getting wet and cold.'

The Baron looked out at the stormy skies, wondering if the weather was the real reason for Paolo's reluctance. 'I don't mind pain, but personal discomfort is another matter entirely.' He looked around, assessing possibilities for damage. And grinned. 'You're absolutely right, my boy!' It pleased him to hear how deep his own voice was becoming.

They ordered servants to bring a selection of lasguns, dart pistols, swords, and knives for their next ersatz adventure. When the mechanical systems were activated, the dead animals went into a frenzy all over the trophy room. The two hunters took cover, imagined their danger, and shot the mechanical creatures off of their stands, chopping through prosthetic bones, stuffing, and preserved flesh. Last of all, they activated the huge mastaphont and watched it stomp over the debris. Finally catching it in a crossfire of lasgun blasts, they amputated its legs. The beast crashed to the floor, its automatic servos writhing.

The Baron found the violence to be eminently satisfying, and even Paolo seemed to warm to the activity. Afterward, the brave hunters surveyed the damage and laughed as they marched out into the corridor. The Baron spotted three workmen, who looked as if they wanted to become invisible. 'Get back in there and clean things up!'

You always make a mess of things, don't you, Grandfather?

The Baron pressed his hands against his head. 'Shut up, damn you!' Alia began humming repetitive singsong tunes, designed to drive him mad, no doubt. When a bewildered Paolo pestered him with questions, the Baron slapped him away. 'Leave me alone! You're as bad as your sister!'

Confused and startled, Paolo ran off.

The girl's grating voice vibrated in his mind until he couldn't stand it. He hurried out of the castle. Barely able to see where he was going, the Baron bumped into one of the blocky Harkonnen statues and rushed toward the sea cliff. 'I'll hurl myself over the edge – I swear it, Abomination – unless you leave me alone!'

He got all the way to the windy, rocky brink, before the Alia voice at last faded into sweet silence. The Baron dropped to his knees on the high stone walkway, looking with delicious vertigo over the tremendous drop-off. Maybe he should just do it anyway, and fall to the wet black rocks and churning waves. If the damned Face Dancers needed him so badly, they could just grow another ghola, and maybe that one wouldn't be so flawed. The Baron Harkonnen would be back!

He felt a hand on his shoulder. Gathering his remaining shreds of dignity, he looked up to see a pug-nosed Face Dancer staring at him. Though all shape-shifters looked exactly the same to him, he somehow knew this one was Khrone. 'What do you want?'

Officiously, the Face Dancer said, 'You and Paolo will depart Caladan and never return. The great war is proceeding, and the evermind has decided that he needs the Kwisatz Haderach close to him. Omnius wants you to complete the boy's preparation under his direct supervision in the heart of the machine empire. You will depart for Synchrony as soon as a ship is ready.'

The Baron flicked his gaze past the Face Dancer to Paolo, who crouched by a Harkonnen statue, close enough to eavesdrop on the conversation. He chuckled to himself, for this boy was as persistent as Piter de Vries! As soon as he realized he was discovered, Paolo scampered forward. 'Is he talking about me?'

'Discuss Paolo's destiny with him on the way,' Khrone said to the Baron. 'Do more than explain it. Make the boy *believe*.'

'Paolo is inclined to believe anything that reinforces

his delusions of grandeur,' the Baron said, ignoring the boy. 'So, this Kwisatz Haderach business is . . . real?'

Even though the Face Dancers had finally explained the truth to him, the idea still sounded preposterous. He was not convinced that this young ghola could be so important in the grand scheme of things.

Khrone looked ghastly in his blank state. Shadows around his eyes darkened as his displeasure became evident. 'I believe it, and so does Omnius. Who are you to question?'

Believe it, dear Grandfather, said the annoying voice. *By his very genes, Paul Atreides has the potential to be greater than you will ever be, in any incarnation.*

The Baron refused to reply, either aloud or in his own thoughts. Ignoring the Abomination often made her shut up.

And now they were going to Synchrony, the home of Omnius. He looked forward to seeing the thinking-machine empire. New challenges, new opportunities.

In spite of the sum of his first life's memories, the stories of the evil thinking machines and the Butlerian Jihad were too distant to seem relevant. Though he harbored considerable resentment toward the Face Dancers, he was glad to be on the side of greater strength.

Later, during the shuttle ride to orbit, the Baron gazed down at the coastline, the villages, the new smokestacks and strip-mined areas of Caladan. In his excitement, Paolo bustled from window to window. 'Will we have a long journey?'

'I'm not a pilot. How should I know? The thinking machines must be very far away, otherwise humans would have known about them long before now.'

'What will happen when we get there?'

'Ask a Face Dancer.'

'They won't talk to me.'

'Then ask Omnius when you see him. In the meantime, amuse yourself.'

Paolo sat down beside him in the passenger compartment and began sampling packets of syrupy packaged food. 'I'm special, you know. They've been grooming me, watching over me carefully. What exactly is a Kwisatz Haderach, anyway?' He wiped his mouth with the back of a hand.

'Don't crawl into their delusions, boy. There is no such thing as a Kwisatz Haderach. A myth, a legend, something with a hundred vague explanations in as many prophecies. The entire Bene Gesserit breeding program is utter nonsense.' He recalled from deep memories that he had been part of that breeding program himself, forced to impregnate the vile witch Mohiam. He had humiliated her during the act, but in retaliation the hag had transmitted the debilitating disease that had made him bloated and fat.

'It can't be nonsense. I have visions, especially when I take spice tablets. I see it again and again. I've got a bloody knife in my hand, and I'm victorious. I see myself rushing to take my prize – melange, but more than melange. I also see myself lying on the floor, bleeding to death. Which one is right? It's so confusing!'

'Shut up and take a nap.'

They docked with an unmarked ship high above Caladan. It bore no markings of the Guild and carried no Navigator. Wide hangar doors opened, drawing the shuttle up and inside. Silvery figures moved within the cold, airless landing bay, guiding the small vessel into a docking cradle. Robots – demons from ancient history!

Ah, so, at least part of Khrone's wild tale might be true.

The Baron smiled at the boy staring out the windows. 'You and I are about to undertake an interesting journey, Paolo.'

A sheathed dagger is useless in a fight. A maula pistol without projectiles is no more than a club. And a ghola without his memories is merely flesh.

— PAUL ATREIDES,
secret ghola journals

Now that the ghola of Dr Yueh had his memories restored, Paul Atreides knew he had to attempt more innovative measures to awaken himself. Paul was the oldest of the ghola children, the one with (presumably) the greatest potential, but Sheeana and the Bene Gesserit observers had chosen Yueh as a test case. Unlike the Suk doctor, however, Paul actually wanted his past back. He longed to remember his life and love with Chani, his childhood with Duke Leto and Lady Jessica, his friendships with Gurney Halleck and Duncan Idaho.

But Paul continued to be haunted by prescient memory-visions of his own double death. And he was growing impatient.

How could the passengers aboard the no-ship think there was still time for caution? Only a few months ago, they had again narrowly escaped the Enemy's net, brighter and stronger than ever before. Of great concern, the saboteur still had not been caught. Though the saboteur had done nothing else as dramatic as the murder of the three axlotl tanks and unborn gholas, the danger remained.

Paul knew the *Ithaca* needed him, and he was tired of being just a ghola. He had an idea to attempt, one that was both desperate and dangerous, but he didn't hesitate. His real memories hovered like a mirage just beyond the heat-shimmered horizon.

With faithful Chani beside him, he stood outside the hatch that led into the great sand-filled hold. He had told no one else what he intended to do. Over the past two years, security had been tightened as much as the Bashar and an eager Thufir Hawat could manage, but no one guarded the entrance to the cargo hold. The seven sand-worms were considered sufficiently dangerous to act as their own watchdogs. Only Sheeana could safely go among the large creatures, and the last time she had done so, even she had been briefly swallowed up.

Paul gazed at Chani's beautiful elfin face and her thick, dark red hair. Even without prior knowledge, without knowing his destiny was to be with her, he would have found the Fremen girl strikingly attractive. In turn, she ran a methodical eye over his body, his special new suit, his tools. 'You look like a real Fremen warrior, Usul.'

After studying records and working with a fabrication station in the engineering levels, Chani had fashioned an authentic stillsuit for him – probably the first one manufactured in centuries – and provided him with a rope, maker hooks, and spreaders. The unusual tools felt oddly familiar in his grasp. According to legend, Muad'Dib had summoned a dangerous monster for his first worm ride. These creatures in the hold, though stunted by their captivity, were still behemoths.

The hatch opened, and he and Chani stepped into the

artificial desert. When the flinty odors and arid heat struck him, he said, 'Stay here, where it's safe. I have to do this alone, or it won't be effective. If I face the worm and ride it, that may jar my memories.'

Chani did not try to stop him. She understood the need as well as he did.

He climbed up the first rise, leaving footprints in the sand, then raised both hands and shouted, 'Shai-Hulud! I have come for you!' In this confined space, he did not need a thumper to summon the worms.

A quality in the air changed. He sensed a stirring in the shallow dunes and saw seven serpentlike shapes coming toward him. Instead of running away, he sprinted toward them, selecting a place where he could set up his approach and mount one. His heart pounded. His throat was dry despite the stillsuit mask covering his mouth and nose.

Paul had reviewed holofilms to study Fremen sandriding techniques. Intellectually he knew what to do, just as – intellectually – he knew the factual details of his past. But a theoretical understanding was far different from actual experience. It occurred to him now, as he stood small and vulnerable on the sand, that the most effective form of learning was in the actual doing, which ensured a more thorough comprehension than he could derive from dusty archives.

I shall learn well, he thought, letting fear wash past him.

The nearest worm surged toward him with a rushing sound of scattered sand. The sheer size of the worms grew more incomprehensible as they approached, cresting the dunes.

Infusing his heart with courage, Paul forced himself

to face this challenge. He held up his hook and spreader and crouched for the first leap. The noise of the monsters' approach was so loud that at first he did not hear the woman shouting. From the corner of his eye, he saw Sheeana bounding across the dunes, throwing herself in front of him. The largest worm exploded through the dust and reared up, its gigantic round mouth glittering with crystalline teeth.

Sheeana held up her hands and shouted, 'Stop, Shaitan!'

The worm hesitated, and quested from side to side with its fleshy head as if confused.

'Stop! This one is not for you.' She placed a firm hand on the chest of Paul's stillsuit and pushed him behind her. 'He is not for you, Monarch.'

As if sulking, the largest worm backed away, keeping its eyeless head turned toward them. 'Get back to the hatch, foolish boy,' Sheeana hissed at Paul, using just enough Voice to make his legs respond before he could think.

Duncan Idaho was also there at the hatchway, glowering. Chani looked both fearful and relieved.

Sheeana marched Paul back toward the waiting observers. 'That worm would have destroyed you!'

'I'm an Atreides. Shouldn't I be able to control them like you can?'

'That isn't a theory I intend to test with you. You are too important to us. Of all the gholas, if *you* foolishly throw your life away, what are we to do?'

'But if you protect me too much, you'll never get what you need. Riding a worm would have brought my memories back, I'm sure of it.'

'You restored Yueh,' Chani pointed out to Sheeana. 'Why not Usul? He's older.'

'Yueh was expendable, and we weren't sure of what we were doing. We have already developed specific plans for awakening Liet-Kynes and Stilgar, and if we succeed with them, others may follow – including Thufir Hawat and you, Chani. One day, Paul Atreides will get his chance. But only after we are certain.'

'What if we don't have the time?' Paul walked away from them, brushing sand and dust from his new still-suit.

DUNCAN AWOKE TO a loud signal at the door to his quarters. His initial thought was that Sheeana had come to him again, despite their mutual reservations. He slid aside the door, ready for an argument.

Paul stood there wearing a replica of an Atreides military uniform, which evoked instant respect and loyalty from Duncan. The young man had dressed that way on purpose. Right now, the ghola Paul was almost exactly the same age as the original had been when Arrakeen had fallen to the devious Harkonnens, when the first Duncan had died defending him and his mother.

'Duncan, you say you were my close friend. You say you knew Paul Atreides. Help me now.' Grasping an ornately carved ivory hilt, the young man drew a blue-white crystalline dagger from a sheath at his waist.

Duncan stared in amazement. 'A cryknife? It looks . . . Is it real?'

'Chani made it from a worm tooth Sheeana found in the cargo hold.'

In wonder, Duncan touched his fingers to the blade, noting how tough and sharp it was. He drew his thumb along the edge, intentionally cutting himself. He let a single drop of blood fall onto the milky-white dagger.

'According to ancient tradition, a crysknife must never be drawn unless it tastes blood.'

'I know.' Paul was clearly troubled as he took the weapon back and returned it to its sheath. After hesitating, he blurted out what he had come to say. 'Why won't the Bene Gesserits awaken me, Duncan? You need me. Everyone on this no-ship needs me.'

'Yes, young Master Paul. We do need you, but we need you *alive.*'

'You need my abilities, as soon as possible. I was the Kwisatz Haderach, and this ghola has the same genetics. Imagine how I could help.'

'The Kwisatz Haderach . . .' Duncan sighed and sat down on his bed. 'The Sisterhood spent centuries creating him, but at the same time they were terrified of him. He can supposedly bridge space and time, seeing the future and the past, places even a Reverend Mother dares not look. Through brute force or guile he can forge a union between the most diverse of factions. It's a grab bag of tremendous powers.'

'Whatever those powers are, Duncan, I need them. And for that I require my memories. Convince Sheeana to try me next.'

'She will do what she will do, at a time of her choosing. You overestimate the influence I have among the Sisters.'

'But what if the Enemy's net ensnares us completely? What if the Kwisatz Haderach is your only hope?'

'Leto II was a Kwisatz Haderach, as well, though neither you nor your son turned out exactly the way the Bene Gesserit intended. The Sisters are very afraid of anyone who manifests unusual powers.' He laughed. 'After the Scattering, when the Sisterhood brought the great Duncan Idaho back, some of them even accused *me* of being a

Kwisatz Haderach. They killed eleven of my gholas, either by Bene Gesserit heretics or Tleilaxu schemers.'

'But why don't they want these powers? I thought—'

'Oh, they want the powers, Paul, but only under carefully controlled conditions.' His heart went out to the young man, who looked so lost and desperate.

'I can't do anything without my past, Duncan. Help me retrieve it! You lived through part of it with me. You remember.'

'Oh, I remember you very well,' Duncan laced his hands behind his head and leaned back. 'I remember your christening on Caladan after you were nearly killed by Imperial intrigues as an infant. I remember how Duke Leto's whole family was put at risk in the War of Assassins. I was given the great honor of taking you to safety, and you and I went to the wilds of Caladan. We stayed with your exiled grandmother Helena, and we hid among the Caladan primitives. That was when you and I became so close. Yes, I remember it very well.'

'I don't,' Paul said with a sigh.

Duncan seemed caught in a loop of his past lives. Caladan . . . Dune . . . the Harkonnens . . . Alia . . . Hayt. 'Do you know what you're asking me, about your memories, about your life? The Tleilaxu created my first ghola as an assassination tool. They manipulated me because I was your friend. They knew you could not turn me away, even though you saw the trap.'

'I wouldn't have turned you away, Duncan.'

'I had the knife raised against you, ready to strike, but in the last instant, I collided with myself. The programmed assassin Hayt became the loyal Duncan Idaho. You can't imagine the agony!' He pointed a stern finger at the young man. 'Restoring your past will require a similar crisis.'

Paul squared his jaw. 'I'm prepared for it. I'm not afraid of pain.'

Wrinkling his brow, Duncan said, 'You're too content, young Paul, because your Chani grounds you. She makes you stable and happy – and that's a severe drawback. In contrast, look at Yueh. He fought against remembering with every fiber of his being, and that's what broke him. But you . . . what fulcrum can they use on you, Paul Atreides?'

'We'll just have to find something.'

'Are you really ready to accept it?' Duncan leaned forward, offering no mercy. 'What if the only way you can have your past restored is that you must *lose* Chani? What if she has to die bleeding in your arms, before you can remember?'

More than anything, I need my father to know I did not fail. I do not want him to die thinking I was unworthy of his genes.

— THE SCYTALE GHOLA,
no-ship security interview

It must be built according to precise standards,' insisted the old Tleilaxu. His voice cracked. '*Precise* standards!'

'I will take care of it, Father.' The ghola, only thirteen, tended the degenerating Master who sat in a stiff armchair. Old Scytale refused to lie down until a traditional bier for his body was built. He intentionally kept his austere living quarters locked to keep others away. He had no desire to be interrupted or harassed during his dying days.

The Tleilaxu Master's organs, joints, and skin had begun to fail in increasingly problematic ways. It reminded him of how the no-ship itself seemed to be breaking down, its systems failing as air leaked into space, water was inexplicably lost, food stores went missing. Some of the more paranoid refugees saw sabotage in every flickering glowpanel, and many turned their suspicious eyes toward the Tleilaxu. It was another reason for him to grumble. At least he would soon be gone.

'I thought you said my bier was already being built. It cannot be rushed.'

The teenager bowed his head. 'Do not worry. I am following the strict laws of the Shariat.'

'Show it to me, then.'

'Your own bier? But that is meant to carry your body only after you . . . after you . . .'

Old Scytale glowered with his dark eyes. 'Purge those useless emotions! You have become too involved in this process. It is shameful.'

'Am I not supposed to care about you, Father? I see your pain—'

'Stop calling me Father. Think of me as *yourself*. Once you become me, I will not be dead. No need for weeping. Each of our incarnations is disposable, so long as the memory train continues uninterrupted.'

Young Scytale tried to regain his composure. 'You are still a father to me, no matter what memories are buried inside me. Will I stop feeling these emotions when my old life is restored?'

'Of course. At that glorious moment you will understand the truth – and your obligations.' Scytale grabbed the young man by his shirt and pulled his face close. 'Where are your memories? What if I were to die tomorrow?'

Old Scytale knew death was imminent, but he had dramatized his infirmity in an attempt to shock his replacement. The premature construction of the bier was yet another attempt to provoke a crisis. If only the two of them could be back on Tleilax, where full immersion in the holy traditions of the Great Belief would be enough to trigger even the most stubborn of gholas. Here onboard a godless no-ship, the difficulties seemed insurmountable.

'This should never have taken so long.'

'I have failed you.'

The rheumy eyes flashed. 'You are not only failing me, you are failing your people. If you do not awaken, our whole race – our entire history and all the knowledge in my mind – will vanish from the universe. Do you want to be responsible for that? I refuse to believe God has turned His back on us entirely. Our fate, lamentably, depends upon you.'

The ghola looked crestfallen, as if an unsupportable weight rested on his shoulders. 'I am doing all I can to achieve that goal, *Father*.' He said the word deliberately. 'And until I succeed, you must do all you can to remain alive.'

He's finally showing a little strength, Scytale thought, bitterly. *But it's not enough.*

DAYS LATER, THE ghola stood by his father's deathbed, his *own* deathbed. He felt as if he were having an out-of-body experience, watching his life slip away moment by moment. It gave the boy an oddly disconnected feeling.

Since emerging from the axlotl tank, Scytale had loved only one person: himself . . . both his older self and the self he was going to be. The degenerating man had provided cells from his own body, cells that held all his memories and experiences, all the knowledge of the Tleilaxu.

But he hadn't provided the key to unlock them. No matter how hard the young ghola strained, his memories obstinately refused to emerge. He clutched the old man's hand. 'Not yet, Father. I've tried and tried.'

With near-sightless eyes, old Scytale glared at his counterpart. 'Why do you . . . disappoint me so?'

Yueh had been restored to his past life, and two other gholas – Stilgar and Liet-Kynes – were even now being raked over the mental coals. How could mere witches succeed where a Tleilaxu Master failed? Bene Gesserits should never have been so adept at triggering the avalanche of experiences. If Scytale could not do it, the Tleilaxu would be relegated to the dustbins of history.

The old man on the bed coughed and wheezed, while the younger leaned close, tears trickling down his cheeks. Old Scytale spat blood. His disappointment and utter despair were palpable.

An insistent signal at the door announced the arrival of two Suk doctors. The bespectacled Rabbi was obviously repulsed by his duties, while young Yueh still appeared to be shaken by the recent return of his memories. Scytale could see in their eyes that they both knew the older Master would perish very soon.

Among the witches there were other Suk practitioners, but Scytale had insisted on being tended only by the Rabbi, and only when absolutely necessary. They were all unclean powindah, but at least the Rabbi wasn't a disgusting *female*. Or, perhaps Scytale should choose Wellington Yueh over the old Jew. The old Tleilaxu Master had to accept certain medical examinations, if only to keep himself alive until his 'son' reawakened.

Scytale lifted his head. 'Go away! We are praying.'

'Do you think I like tending to gholas? To filthy Tleilaxu? Do you think I *want* to be here? You can both die, for all I care!'

Yueh, though, moved forward with a medical kit, easing the younger Scytale aside to check the dying man's vital signs. Behind Yueh the Rabbi squinted through his spectacles with vulture eyes. 'It won't be long now.'

Such an odd old holy man, young Scytale thought. Even compared to the smells of disinfectant, medicine, and sickness, he'd always had an odd smell about him.

Sounding compassionate, Yueh said, 'There isn't much we can do.'

Gasping for air, old Scytale croaked out, 'A Tleilaxu Master should not be so weak and decrepit. It is . . . unseemly.'

His youthful counterpart tried again to trigger the flow of memories, to squeeze them into his brain by sheer force of will, as he had attempted to do countless times before. The essential past must be in there somewhere, buried deep. But he felt no tickle of possibilities, no glimmer of success. *What if they are not there at all?* What if something had gone terribly wrong? His pulse pounded as the panic began to rise. Not much time. Never enough time.

He tried to cut off the thought. The body provided a wealth of cellular material. They could create more Scytale gholas, try again and again if necessary. But if his own memories had failed to resurface, why should an identical ghola have any better luck without the guidance of the original?

I am the only one who knew the Master so intimately.

He wanted to shake Yueh, demand to know how he had managed to remember his past. Tears were in full flow now, falling onto the old man's hand, but Scytale knew they were inadequate. His father's chest spasmed in an almost imperceptible death rattle. The life-support equipment hummed with more intensity, and the instrument readings fluctuated.

'He's slipped into a coma,' Yueh reported.

The Rabbi nodded. Like an executioner announcing his plans, he said, 'Too weak. He's going to die now.'

Scytale's heart sank. 'He has given up on me.' His father would never know if he succeeded now; he would perish wondering and worrying. The last great calamity in a long line of disasters that had befallen the Tleilaxu race.

He gripped the old man's hand. So cold, too cold. He felt the life ebbing. *I have failed!*

As if felled by a stunner, Scytale dropped to his knees at the bedside. In his crashing despair, he knew with absolute certainly that he could never resurrect the recalcitrant memories. Not alone. *Lost! Forever lost! Everything that comprised the great Tleilaxu race.* He could not bear the magnitude of this disaster. The reality of his defeat sliced like shattered glass into his heart.

Abruptly, the Tleilaxu youth felt something changing inside, followed by an explosion between his temples. He cried out from the excruciating pain. At first he thought he was dying himself, but instead of being swallowed in blackness, he felt new thoughts burning like wildfire across his consciousness. Memories streamed past in a blur, but Scytale locked onto each one, absorbing it again and reprocessing it into the synapses of his brain. The precious memories returned to where they had always belonged.

His father's death had opened the barriers. At last Scytale retrieved what he was supposed to know, the critical data bank of a Tleilaxu Master, all the ancient secrets of his race.

Instilled with pride and a new sense of dignity, he rose to his feet. Wiping away warm tears, he looked down at the discarded copy of himself on the bed. It was nothing more than a withered husk. He no longer needed that old man.

These ghola children contain old souls that are not unlike the voices in a Reverend Mother's Other Memory. The challenge is to access and exploit these old souls.

– ship's log, entry of
DUNCAN IDAHO

In the gangly body of a teenager, filled with the memories of a long life and the shame of things he had done, Wellington Yueh walked with painstaking slowness. Each step brought him closer to the moment he had been dreading. The skin of his brow burned where a diamond tattoo should have been; at least he no longer displayed that lie.

Yueh knew that if he ever intended to make this life different from his error-prone past, he must confront the terrible things he had done.

Here, thousands of years later and on the other side of the universe, House Atreides lived all around him: Paul Atreides, Lady Jessica, Duncan Idaho, Thufir Hawat. At least Duke Leto had not been resurrected as a ghola. Not yet. Yueh didn't think he could bear to look into the eyes of the man he had betrayed.

Facing Jessica would be tough enough.

Walking ponderously toward her quarters, Yueh heard

voices ahead, a child's giggle and a woman's rebuke. Suddenly little Alia toddled out of one doorway and ducked into another, followed by a scolding proctor. The two-year-old was extremely precocious, with a hint of the genius that the first Alia had been; the spice saturation in the axlotl tank had altered her somewhat, but she didn't possess the complete Other Memory of her predecessor. The proctor followed and sealed the door behind them. Neither of them had glanced at Yueh.

Alia was the most recent ghola to be born; the program had been stalled since the horrific murder of the three tanks and unborn children. *At least that is one crime I do not have on my conscience.* But the Bene Gesserits would soon begin the program again. They were already discussing which cells to implant in the new axlotl tanks. Irulan? Emperor Shaddam himself? Count Fenring . . . or someone far worse? Yueh shuddered at the thought. He feared that the witches had gone beyond true need and now were just toying with lives, letting their infernal curiosity sidestep all caution.

He paused in front of Jessica's quarters, steeling himself, *I will face my fear.* Wasn't that part of the Litany the witches so often quoted? In their present incarnations as gholas, Jessica and Yueh had been close enough to think of themselves as friends. But since becoming Dr Wellington Yueh again, everything was different.

Now I have a second chance, he thought. *But my road to redemption is long, and the incline very steep.*

Jessica opened her door at his signal. 'Oh hello, Wellington. My grandson and I were just reading a holo-book about Paul's younger years, one of those tomes Princess Irulan was always writing.' She invited him inside, where he saw Leto II sitting cross-legged on the carpeted floor. Leto was a loner, though he frequently spent time with his 'grandmother.'

Yueh twitched nervously when she closed the door behind them, as if to seal his doom and prevent escape. He kept his eyes down, and after a deep sigh he said, 'I wish to apologize to you, my Lady. Though I know you can never forgive me.'

Jessica placed an arm on his shoulder. 'We've been through this. You can't bear the blame for things that were done so long ago. It wasn't really you.'

'Yes it was, because I remember it all now! We gholas were created for one purpose, and we must accept the consequences.'

Jessica looked at him impatiently. 'We all know what you did, Wellington. I accepted that and forgave you long ago.'

'But will you do it again after you *remember*? One day those vaults will be opened in your mind, the terrible old wounds. We've got to face the guilt our predecessors left for us, or we'll be consumed by things we never did.'

'It's uncharted territory for all of us, but I suspect we each have plenty of things to atone for.' She tried to console him, but he didn't feel he deserved it.

Leto paused the filmbook and looked up with an eerie intelligence in his eyes. 'Well, I'm only going to take responsibility for what I do in *this* life.'

Jessica reached out to touch Yueh's face gently. 'I can't understand what you went through, what you're still going through. I'll know soon enough, I suppose. But you should think about what you would *like* to be, not what you're afraid of being.'

She made it sound so simple, but despite his best

efforts, he had been twisted before. 'What if I do something bad in this lifetime, too?'

Jessica's expression hardened. 'Then no one can help you.'

You think your eyes are open, yet you do not see.
                        – Bene Gesserit admonishment

Water crashed against the black reef on Buzzell, sending up a veil of spray. Mother Commander Murbella stood with the once-disgraced Sister at the edge of the cove, watching Phibians frolic in deep water. The amphibious creatures swam together, slick and smooth-skinned, diving under the combers and then bursting to the surface again.

'They love their new freedom,' Corysta said.

Like dolphins in an ancient Earth sea, Murbella thought, admiring their forms. Human . . . and yet dramatically not so.

'I'm more interested in seeing them harvest soostones.' She turned her face into the salty wind. Gray clouds were gathering, but the air remained warm and humid. 'Our debts in this war are staggering. Our credit is stretched beyond its limits, and some of our most vital suppliers will accept nothing but hard currency – like soostones.'

In the months since leaving Oculiat, the Mother Commander had traveled from planet to planet, studying humanity's defenses. Realizing their great peril, local kings, presidents, and warlords provided independent battleships to add to the newly constructed Guild vessels being released by the Junction shipyards. Every government and cluster of allied worlds scrambled to invent or acquire new armaments to use against the Enemy, but so far nothing had proved effective. The Ixians were still testing the Obliterator weapons, which had proved to be more difficult to manufacture than expected. Murbella continued to demand more work, more material and sacrifices. It wouldn't be enough.

And the war continued. Plagues spread. Machine fleets destroyed every human-inhabited world they encountered. Near the edge of one of the main combat zones, three more Sheeana surrogates rallied the people caught between a hammer and an anvil, but to no avail. So far, since the beginning of Omnius's march across space, Murbella could not claim a single clear victory.

In her bleakest moments the odds seemed poor and the obstacles insurmountable. Millennia ago, the fighters of the Butlerian Jihad had faced another impossible situation, and humankind had won only by accepting an appalling cost. They had unleashed countless atomic weapons that not only destroyed thinking machines, but also trillions of human beings who had been held in slavery. The Pyrrhic victory had left a horrendous stain on the human soul.

And now, even after that monumental sacrifice, Omnius was back, like a noxious weed whose roots had never been destroyed. Gauging the progress of the thinking machines, in the next year or two the human race would be forced into a climactic showdown.

Once the Ixian industrialists delivered their long-awaited Obliterators, all the collected militaries from planet after planet would draw a line in space. As far as she was concerned, that opportunity could not come soon enough.

'Our soostone shipments have increased every month for the past two years.' As she spoke, Corysta did not remove her gaze from the frolicking aquatic creatures. 'The Phibians are more productive, now that the Honored Matres have stopped torturing them. And they never used to play like that before. They consider the seas of Buzzell their home instead of their prison.'

Corysta, a former Breeding Mother exiled here for the crime of trying to keep her own baby, had become a stalwart monitor of soostone harvests. She oversaw the grading, cleaning, and packaging of the pearlescent gems, which were delivered regularly to CHOAM intermediaries.

'Even so, we need more soostones.'

'I'll speak with the Phibians, Mother Commander. I'll explain that our need is great, that the Enemy draws near. For me, they might work harder.' Corysta's smile was strangely unreadable. 'I'll ask it as a favor.'

'And that will work?'

The other Sister shrugged. The Phibians leapt high into the air and dove back into the water, while Corysta waved to them, laughing. They seemed to know she was watching them. Sunlight glinted on the water. Were these Phibians putting on a special performance?

Quite suddenly, something large and serpentine emerged from the depths near the splashing creatures. An eyeless head rose above the waves, its round mouth flashing crystalline teeth. The head quested around, fin-edged gill flaps sensing vibrations, like a sea serpent from ancient legends.

Murbella caught her breath. To her amazement it

resembled a sandworm from Rakis, though only about ten meters long – and with adaptations that enabled it to live in the water. Impossible! A seaworm?

Corysta ran frantically down the rocks and waded into the surf. The Phibians had already seen the monster and tried to swim away. The worm darted toward them, spray glistening from its greenish rings.

Two more of the long, sinuous monsters appeared from the deep water and circled around the Phibians. The aquatic people clustered in a defensive formation; one male with a scar on his forehead drew a wide, flat-bladed knife used for scoring cholisters on the ocean floor. The other Phibians brandished their own weapons, which were laughable against a sea serpent.

Knee-deep in waves, Corysta slipped on the algae-slick rocks. Murbella ran after her, fixated on what she saw in the water. 'What are those creatures?'

'Monsters! I have never seen them before.'

The scarred male Phibian emitted a loud vibrating sound and slapped one webbed hand on the water with a sharp crack. The clustered Phibians bolted like a startled school of fish, several diving underwater, others swimming briskly across the waves.

Though they had no eyes, the swimming worms knew where the Phibians were. With a blur and a flick of long serpentine bodies, they pursued the aquatic workers, driving them toward the rocky shore.

Murbella and Corysta watched the largest worm lunge and grab one of the Phibians, scooping him down into the wet gullet. The other worms attacked like a group of frenzied sharks.

Murbella waded out to grab Corysta's shoulder, preventing her from swimming farther into the churning water. They were both helpless to prevent the violence. 'My Sea Child,' Corysta moaned.

The seaworms thrashed and splashed as they fed. Bloody waves lapped against Murbella's legs, and she dragged the sobbing Corysta back to shore.

A planet is not merely an item for study. Rather it is a tool, perhaps even a weapon, with which we can make our mark on the galaxy.

— LIET-KYNES,
the original

Now that Stilgar and Liet had their ghola memories back, they had become the no-ship's experts on extreme recycling, making the most of their reduced resources. The *Ithaca*'s life-support systems had been designed by geniuses out in the Scattering, descendants of those who had survived the horrific Famine Times. The highly efficient technology could serve passengers and crew for long periods, even in the face of the increasing population. But not in the face of deliberate sabotage.

Tall and lean, with the body of a youth and the aged eyes of a naib, Stilgar looked ready to embark on a desert journey. He and Liet-Kynes had been bound at first by common interests and more recently by their awakened pasts. Liet refused to talk about the crisis through which Sheeana had broken him – it was a matter too private even for close friends.

For himself, Stilgar couldn't forget what the witches had done to him. To the very depths of his being he was a desert man of Arrakis. Watched over by Proctor Superior Garimi, he had read of his history as a young commando against the Harkonnens, later as naib, and then as a supporter of Muad'Dib. But to trigger his ghola memories, the Sisters had tried to *drown* him.

At a water-filled recycling reservoir, Sheeana and Garimi had tied weights around his ankles. Stilgar fought, but the witches were more than a match for him. 'What have I done? Why are you doing this to me?'

'Find your past,' Sheeana said, 'or die.'

'Without your memories you are useless, and better off drowned,' Garimi said. They dumped him into the pool.

Unable to free himself from the weights on his ankles, Stilgar had quickly sunk. He had struggled mightily, but the water was everywhere, more oppressive than the thickest dust cloud. Trying desperately to peer upward, he made out only the vague wavering shapes of the two women up there. Neither lifted a hand to help him.

His lungs screamed, and blackness closed in around his eyesight. Stilgar thrashed violently and grew weaker every second. He was starving for breath. He wanted to cry out – *needed* to – but there was no air. Exhaled bubbles roared out of his open mouth. When it was more than unbearable, he inhaled a huge gulp into his lungs, flooding his air passages. He couldn't see any way out of the tank—

—and suddenly it was no longer a tank, but a wide, deep river, which he realized was on one of the planets where he had fought in Muad'Dib's jihad. He had marched with a regiment of Caladan soldiers and they had needed to ford the river. The water had been deeper than anyone anticipated, and all of them went under. His companions, who had been born swimming, thought nothing of it, even laughed as they made their way to shore. But Stilgar was dragged beneath the surface. He reached up, clutching for air. He had inhaled water then, too, and nearly drowned—

Finally, Sheeana dragged Stilgar out of the tank and pumped his lungs. A disapproving Suk doctor scolded her and Garimi as she revived the young ghola. They rolled him over, and he vomited up sour mouthfuls of water. He was barely able to rise to his knees.

When he turned his glare on Sheeana, he was more than an eleven-year-old boy. He was Naib Stilgar.

Later, when he saw Liet restored as well, Stilgar was afraid to ask what terrible ordeal his friend had been forced to endure . . .

Now the two headed for the great hold to see the sandworms, as they had done many times before. The high observation chamber was one of their favorite places, especially now. The tremendous worms called up strong and atavistic feelings in them.

As they approached, Stilgar breathed in the comforting scent of warm, dry air with the distinct odors of worms and cinnamon. He smiled briefly in a passing nostalgia, before his face creased in a frown. 'I should not be smelling that.'

Liet picked up his pace. 'That environment has to be carefully controlled. If the seals are leaking, then moisture could penetrate the hold.' Yet another breakdown, after so many others!

Rushing into the equipment chamber, they found young Thufir Hawat supervising repair operations. Two Bene Gesserit Sisters and Levi, one of the refugee Jews, worked to install sheets of replacement plaz. They applied thick sealants around the windows high above the sand-filled cargo hold. Thufir was scowling.

Stilgar strode forward, his demeanor intimidating. The task of monitoring the sandworms and the recycling systems was generally reserved for himself and Liet. 'Why are you here, Hawat?'

Thufir showed surprise at the coldly accusatory tone of the Fremen's voice. 'Someone poured acid on the seals. The corrosive destroyed not only the sealant, but part of the plaz and the wallplates as well.'

'We patched it in time,' said Levi. 'We also found a timed device that would have emptied one of our water reservoirs into the hold, flooding it.'

Stilgar trembled with rage. 'That would have killed the worms!'

'I checked those systems myself, only two days ago,' Liet said. 'This is no simple breakdown.'

'No,' Thufir agreed. 'Our saboteur is at work again.'

While Stilgar ran his gaze suspiciously over the gathered people, Liet hurried to the instrument consoles to check the desert environment. 'There appears to be no permanent damage. The readings are still within the creatures' tolerance range. Scrubbers should bring the air back to desired levels in short order.'

Stilgar took special care to inspect the new seals, found them adequate. He and Liet exchanged looks that said they had to be suspicious of everyone onboard. *Except for each other*, Stilgar decided.

Long ago, when he and Liet had first known each other, the two had shared many adventures fighting the nefarious Harkonnens. Like his father, Liet had led a double life, delivering grand dreams to the desert people while acting as Imperial Planetologist and Judge of the Change. Liet was also the father of Chani. While the Fremen girl's ghola did not remember him yet, he remembered her, and he looked at Chani with a strange, age-worn love.

Bothered by the acrid odors of acid and sealant, Stilgar turned grimly away from the observation window. 'From now on, I sleep here. I will not let Shai-Hulud die, not while I still breathe.'

'I'm working with the Bashar. There must be some kind of a trail, so we only need to find it. The corrosive was acquired from secure stores, so there may be finger-prints or genetic traces.' Thufir's lips were not stained red with sapho, his skin not grizzled, his eyes not weary with age and experiences, as in the famous old portraits. 'Perhaps the imagers captured the saboteur sneaking to the observation deck. Once I catch him, we can all rest more easily.'

'No,' Stilgar said. 'Even then, I would not let my guard down.'

IN A SUDDEN resurgence, the maddening sabotage continued in myriad ways and at random points around the huge ship, setting everyone's nerves on edge. The Bene Gesserits remained vigilant and wary, while the Rabbi preached to a growing number of followers about spies and murderers lurking among them.

Duncan studied the readings, ran projections. Again, he wondered if one or more of the Face Dancer Handlers might still be aboard, having escaped the wreckage of a crashed ship. Where else could the sabo-teur be hiding? After years of searching, Duncan and Teg had run out of ideas. How could this enemy elude surveillance imagers, Truthsayer interrogations, and vigorous searches? In a few suspicious incidents, a blurry form could be seen moving in restricted areas, but even enhancement could not sharpen the facial features to recognizability.

The saboteur seemed to know exactly where and when to strike. An endless succession of little breakdowns and small accidents, each taking its toll, ran the ship's company to exhaustion.

One time, imagers detected what appeared to be a man as he moved furtively down a corridor near a bank of oxygen-scrubber units and air-circulating machines. Dressed in dark clothing and a tight-fitting hood that covered most of his face, he carried a long silver knife and a pry bar, and his body leaned forward against the heavy air flow. Then, like liquid flowing around a corner, the man slipped into the central recirculation chamber, where great fans blasted air through a system of arteries in the no-ship, pushing it through thick curtains of matted fibers coated with biogels to remove impurities.

With sudden fury, the unidentifiable saboteur slashed and hacked at the porous filter mats, ripping them from their frames and destroying their ability to purify air. After completing this mayhem, the saboteur turned to flee. Not a single frame of the imagers showed the face; it wasn't even absolutely clear whether the hooded vandal was male or female. By the time security personnel rushed into the area, the saboteur had vanished into the howling, recirculated wind.

Duncan did not need to whisper the obvious answer. *Face Dancer.* He studied all records of the kamikaze ships from the Handlers, noting where they had crashed into the hull and how the bodies aboard had been confirmed dead and disposed of. One of the shape-shifting Handlers must have crawled out of the flaming wreckage.

Even worse, there might be more than one.

THE AIR SMELLED moist and foul, like seaweed and sewage. Duncan stood on the mist-slickened catwalk above one of the largest algae tanks. The entire vat was dying. *Poisoned.*

Standing next to him, gripping the catwalk rail with a white-knuckled hand, Teg frowned at the chemical analyses displayed on his datapad. 'Heavy metals, potent toxins, a list of deadly chemicals that even this stuff can't digest.' He pulled up a dripping handful of the once-fecund green substance. The goop was brownish now, breaking down.

'The saboteur is trying to destroy our food supply,' Duncan said.

'Our air, too.'

'To what end? To kill us, it appears.'

'Or simply to make us helpless.'

Duncan glared at the vat, feeling angry and violated. 'Get work crews to drain and scrub the tank. Decontaminate as quickly as possible. Then harvest starter material from other tanks to fertilize the biomass. We've got to stabilize it before something else goes wrong.'

DUNCAN WAS ALONE on the navigation bridge when the next disaster occurred. Over the years the passengers had learned to ignore the faint vibrations of the no-ship's movement. Now, though, an abrupt lurch and an obvious deflection in course nearly threw him out of his chair.

He called for Teg and Thufir, then scrambled over the

controls, scanning empty space around them. He feared they might have run into a piece of space debris or some gravitational anomaly. But he found no evidence of impact, no obstacles in their vicinity. The *Ithaca* was obviously yawing, and he struggled to steady it using the numerous smaller engines distributed around the hull. This slowed the spinning of the ship, but did not entirely stop it.

As the immense vessel continued to turn, he saw a glittering silver path like a scarf of mist, spewing from the stem. One of the no-ship's three primary water reservoirs had been dumped – intentionally. The great swath of water had been ejected with enough force to push the *Ithaca* off course. The evacuated water shifted the ship's ballast and sent them into a spin. The loss of angular momentum made their situation worsen as more and more water poured away, like a comet's tail behind them. The ship's reserves!

Working feverishly at the controls, Duncan overrode the reservoir hatch, praying all the while that the mysterious saboteur had merely opened the door to space, rather than using one of the deadly mines locked away in the armory.

Teg burst onto the navigation bridge just as Duncan managed to close the cargo doors and reestablish containment. The Bashar bent over the screens, his young but seasoned face creased in concern. 'That was enough water to supply us for a year!' His gray-eyed gaze flitted around nervously.

Pacing the deck, Duncan stared out at the misty veil of dispersed water. 'We can retrieve some of it. Scoop it up as ice, and when I fully stabilize our spin—'

But as he looked at the smear of lost water spreading

out against the starry backdrop, he saw other lines appear, sparkling multicolored threads drawing together and enclosing the no-ship like a spider's web. The Enemy's net! Again it was bright enough for Teg to see it, too. 'Damn it! Not now!'

Lunging into the pilot's seat, Duncan activated the Holtzman engines. With one or more saboteurs aboard, the engines themselves could have been rigged to explode, but he had no choice. He forced the enigmatic machines to fold space well before he could think about what course to take. The no-ship, still spinning, lurched off to another place.

They survived.

Afterward, Duncan looked at Teg and sighed. 'We couldn't have retrieved much of the expelled water anyway.'

Even the ship's sophisticated recyclers had their limits, and now the actions of the saboteur had driven them – intentionally – toward an inescapable conclusion. After many years of constant flight, the no-ship's provisions had to be replenished as soon as an acceptable planet could be located. Not an easy task in a huge galaxy, encompassing vast distances. They had found nothing suitable in years. Not since the planet of the Handlers.

But Duncan knew that would not be their only problem. When they found a place, they would be forced to expose themselves – again.

Synchrony is more than a machine, more than a metropolis; it is an extension of the evermind itself. It constantly shifts and morphs into different configurations. At first I believed this effect was for defense, but there seems to be another force at work, a surprising creative spark. These machines are exceedingly odd.

— BARON VLADIMIR HARKONNEN,
the ghola

The metropolis before them was beautiful in an industrial and metallic way: sharp angles, smooth curves, and a great deal of energy as structures moved and flashed like a perfectly tuned machine. Angular buildings and windowless towers covered every square meter of ground. The Baron saw no offensive greenery, no gaudy flowers or landscaping, not a leaf, blossom, or blade of grass.

Synchrony was a bustling symbol of productivity – along with concomitant profits and political power, if thinking machines ever figured out how to pay attention to such things. Maybe Vladimir Harkonnen would show Omnius how it was done.

After the long journey from Caladan, the Baron and Paolo rode a tram to the shifting center of the machine city. The Atreides ghola peered out through the curved windows, his eyes wide and hungry. They were crowded in the tram with an escort of eight Face Dancers. The Baron had never understood how the shape-shifters were connected with Omnius and the new Synchronized Empire. The elevated car shot along an unseen charge path high above the ground, whizzing like a bullet between the perpetually shifting buildings.

As they went deeper into the city, huge edifices moved up, down, and sideways like pistons, threatening to crush the streaking tram. When the half-alive buildings swayed like robotic seaweed, he noticed that the Face Dancers inside the tram moved in unison, wearing placid smiles on their cadaverous faces, as if they were part of a choreographed presentation.

Like a needle threading a complex maze of holes, the tram sped toward an immense spire that rose out of the center of the city like a spike thrust up from the netherworld. Finally, the car came to a clicking stop in a spectacular central square.

Anxious to see, Paolo squirmed and pushed his way out the door. Even with uncertainty and fear gnawing at his gut, the Baron marveled at the numerous fires burning at specific geometric points around the spire, each with a human tied to a stake, martyr-fashion. Obviously, in their conquest of world after world, the thinking-machine fleet had taken experimental subjects. He found the extravagance breathtaking. These machines certainly showed a lot of potential and even uncanny imagination.

He thought of the huge thinking-machine fleet out in space, as it methodically plowed deeper into human-settled territory. From what Khrone had explained, when the machines finally obtained a pet Kwisatz Haderach, Omnius believed he would be fulfilling the terms of the mechanical prophecy, making it impossible to fail. The Baron found it amusing how the thinking machines viewed everything as an absolute. After fifteen thousand years, they should know better.

Paolo had let himself be caught up in a megalo-maniacal whirlwind. The Baron's job was to feed those delusions, always keeping in mind that he was in a dangerous situation himself and needed to keep his wits and focus. Unsure whether personal glory or ignomin-ious death lay ahead, the Baron was repeatedly reminded that he was merely a catalyst for Paolo. *Secondary impor-tance indeed!*

Emerging from the back of his mind, Alia interrupted him, insisting that the machines would discard him when he had fulfilled his purpose. When he sputtered internally in protest, she screeched over him: *You're going to get us killed, Grandfather! Think back to your first life – you weren't always such a gullible fool!*

The Baron shook his head briskly, wishing he could get her out of his mind. Maybe his Alia tormentor was the result of a tumor pressing upon a cognitive center of his brain. The malignant little Abomination was deeply entrenched in his skull. Maybe a robot surgeon could cut her out . . .

The Face Dancers led him and his young ward across a platform and down a set of stairs to the square. Giddy, Paolo ran ahead and did a brief dance of joy. 'Is this all mine? Where is my throne room?' He looked back at the Baron. 'Don't worry – I'll find a place for you in my court. You have been good to me.' Was that a scrap of leftover Atreides honor? The Baron scowled.

The Face Dancers nudged the Baron into a lift tube, while allowing Paolo to enter unassisted. Instead of climbing to the apex of the tower as the Baron expected, however, the lift plunged in free fall toward the bowels of hell. Swallowing the impulse to scream, he said, 'If you're really the Kwisatz Haderach, Paolo, perhaps you should learn to use your powers . . . *immediately.*'

The boy shrugged dumbly, showing little recognition of the peril they were in.

As soon as the lift settled to a smooth stop, the walls melted away around them to reveal an immense, underground chamber. Here, as outside, nothing remained stationary. Rotating walls and a clearplaz floor left the Baron dizzy and disoriented, as if the two humans stood in a vault of space.

A mist rose and congealed in the shape of a large man, a faceless, ghostlike figure. The foggy form, nearly twice the height of a grown man, stopped in front of them and moved its arms to make a swirl of icy air that smelled of metal and oil. Within the countenance, two glowing eyes became apparent. From a misty mouth, a deep voice said, 'So, this is our Kwisatz Haderach.'

Paolo lifted his chin and recited what the Baron had told him, with considerable passion. 'I'll be the one who can see all places and all things simultaneously, the one who will lead the multitudes. I am the shortening of the way, the rescuer, the messiah, the one spoken of in countless legends.'

Words flowed from the fog. 'You have a charismatic presence that I find fascinating. Humans exhibit an irresistible compulsion to follow physically attractive, charming leaders. Properly harnessed, you could be an effective and destructive tool for us.' The fog creature laughed, swirling the cold wind around him. Then his otherworldly eyes riveted on the Baron. 'You will see that the boy cooperates.'

'Yes, of course. Are you Omnius?'

'I speak for the evermind.' The fogginess shifted as the mist flowed into itself and resolved into the gleaming metallic shape of a polished robot with an exaggerated but menacing smile molded onto his face. 'For the sake of convenience, I call myself Erasmus.'

The walls of the chamber shifted like a kaleidoscope to reveal hundreds of angular combat robots stationed around the perimeter like strange beetles. Their metal eyes glittered in the same hostile fashion.

'Perhaps I will question you now. Or later? Indecision is a very human thing, you know. We have all the time in the world.' The smile on the robot's platinum face had locked into place. 'I so love your clichés.'

Twenty-Three Years After

Escape from Chapterhouse

Even with a Navigator's incredible mental advancement,
I cannot forget the fundamental thread that ties us to the
rest of humanity: the old emotion of hope.

— NAVIGATOR EDRIK,
unacknowledged message to the Oracle of Time

The four specialized Guild craft were shaped like hornets, sleek sensor-studded ships that skimmed low over the waves of Buzzell. Scan eyes pointed down at the water, searching for movement. From the lead ship Waff peered through the spray-specked plaz windows, hoping to catch a glimpse of seaworms. The Tleilaxu's excitement and anticipation were palpable. Worms were down there somewhere. *Growing.*

He had released the creatures just over a year ago, and judging from the flurry of rumors the Guild had picked up, the seaworms must have thrived. None of the Bene Gesserit witches on the rocky islands understood where the serpentine creatures had come from. Now, Waff thought with a thrill, it was time to reap the harvest he had sown. He couldn't wait to see them, to know that he had accomplished his holy mission.

The sky was overcast, with patches of fog lying low over the sea. At regular intervals, the scanning crews dropped sonic pulsers into the water. The throbbing signals would map the movements of large underwater denizens, and theoretically attract the seaworms just as Fremen thumpers had once attracted the huge monsters on old Rakis. Near Waff in the cockpit, five silent Guildsmen monitored the equipment while separate, smaller hunting platforms circled lower, keeping pace with the hornets. Periodically the platforms went back to check the points where the pulsers had been dropped.

The leviathans of the deep from the ancient scriptures were more than just God's judgment on powindah unbelievers. This was the return of the Prophet, God's Messenger resurrected from the ashes of Rakis, in an adaptive new form.

The initial sightings of the beasts had occurred within six months. At first the tales told by the amphibious soostone harvesters had been met with disbelief, until the seaworms attacked in full view of island settlements. According to eyewitness accounts – and Bene Gesserits were well trained in accurate observation – the monstrous things had grown far larger than Waff had predicted. Truly, a sign from God that his work was blessed!

So long as they were fed, the worms continued to grow and multiply. Seaworms apparently preferred to eat the large cholisters that produced soostones, tearing into beds tended by Phibians. The aquatic people had rallied to drive away the sea monsters, but they had failed.

Waff smiled. Of course they had failed. One could not change a path that God had laid down.

The angry witches had led hunting parties, taking boats out onto the waters, guided by vengeful Phibians. They begged Chapterhouse for weapons to kill the seaworms. But with Enemy forces attacking hundreds of fringe worlds, and the industries of Junction and Ix consuming most of the New Sisterhood's resources, they were stretched far too thin.

The Bene Gesserits needed soostone wealth to build and replenish their armies faster than the Enemy could destroy them, but if the seaworms produced what Waff hoped, the creatures would be worth far more than any gem. Soon, there would be multiple sources of spice, including a new and more potent form. Waff could transplant the creatures to any ocean planet, where they could thrive without reconfiguring an entire ecosystem. Considering their current monopoly on melange, that would not make the Sisterhood happy.

The pilot circled the lead hornet ship. Guild assistants stared fixedly at monitors. 'Picking up shadows at various depths. Numerous tracks. We are close.'

Waff moved eagerly to the other side of the craft and stared down at the choppy waves. Pulse beacons continued to emit siren songs, and hunting platforms flitted alongside. 'Be ready to move as soon as you detect a worm. I want to see one. Let me know when you have a sighting.'

Down in the water, he noticed two slick-skinned Phibians, who seemed curious about the pulse beacons and the flurry of activity. One raised a webbed hand in an incomprehensible signal as the hornet ships and hunting platforms streaked overhead.

'Seaworm surfacing,' announced one of the Guildsmen. 'Target acquired.'

The little Tleilaxu rushed forward to the cockpit. Below, a long, dark shape appeared in the water, breaching like a great whale. 'We must capture and kill it. That is the only way to see what's inside.'

'Yes,' said the Guildsman. Waff narrowed his eyes,

never able to understand these people. Was the man agreeing with him, or simply acknowledging the orders? This time he didn't care.

Waff glanced at the projected map, noting that their search had taken them to one of the inhabited rocky islands. Once he verified the success of the new worms, there would be no need to continue keeping secrets. The witches could do nothing about the seaworms, nor what they produced. They could not stop his work. Today, after his team captured a specimen and confirmed the results of his experiments, the truth would be obvious.

We will show the witches what lies beneath the waves, and let them draw their own conclusions.

The lead hornet craft slowed, its engines buzzing. The moment the seaworm emerged from the waves, ringed and glistening, Waff's hunters fired a fusillade of supersonic harpoons from their hovering platforms. The barbed tips hit the beast before it could realize its danger and submerge. Spear points caught in the soft rings, anchoring themselves as the worm thrashed and writhed. Waff felt joy, as well as a twinge of sympathetic pain. From behind the lead craft, three other hornet ships shot more harpoons into the trapped creature, pulling back on hyperfilament cables.

'Don't damage it too much!' Waff intended to kill the thing anyway – a necessary sacrifice in the name of the Prophet – but if the carcass and internal organs were too mangled, his dissection would be more difficult.

The group of hornet craft went into hover mode above the waves, their cables taut and straining as the seaworm thrashed. Milky fluid oozed into the water, dissipating before the Tleilaxu researcher could order one of the Guildsmen to collect samples. Other seaworms circled their struggling brother like hungry sharks.

The worm was twenty meters long – a tremendous rate of growth for such a short time. He was impressed. If the creatures were reproducing as rapidly as they were growing, the oceans of Buzzell would soon be teeming with them! He couldn't ask for more.

The wounded beast quickly tired. Engines humming with the strain, the Guild vessels began to drag the feebly struggling worm toward the nearest reef, which was barely visible in the wispy fog banks. The small hunting platforms returned to the hornet ships, docking inside their cramped cargo holds.

The island was one of the main Sisterhood outposts for soostone processing, complete with barracks, warehouses, and a flattened spaceport capable of handling small ships. *Let the witches see this!*

Flying in formation, the hornet ships towed the captive worm to shore. In the water below, at least twenty Phibians appeared carrying crude spears and tridents – as if they thought they could pose a threat to the giant creatures! Shouting curses and threats, the Phibians attacked the tangled worm, stabbing and cutting.

Annoyed at the interference, Waff turned to his Guildsmen. 'Drive them away!' Using small cannons mounted on the deck of the lead hornet ship, Guildsmen took potshots at the Phibians, killing two. The others dove underwater. At first they left the bloody corpses bobbing in the waves, but a number of the Phibians returned moments later. When they attempted to retrieve their fallen comrades, a second seaworm streaked in and devoured the bodies.

The droning hum of the hornet ships attracted a crowd of women on the docks as the sluggish prize was dragged into the village harbor. Dark-clad Sisters left their barracks, perhaps thinking that smugglers or CHOAM representatives had arrived. From the recent depredations of the seaworms, most soostone operations had stalled. Sorting bins and packaging lines were silent and unmanned.

His chest swelled with pride, Waff jumped down from the ramp onto the metal and stone wharf as the Guildsmen hoisted the ringed creature onto the main dock. Its narrow tail drooped into the water. Exhausted from its struggles and oozing fluids from the harpoon wounds, the captive worm thrashed one more time, expending the last of its energy. Though Waff and his servants had conquered and subdued the worm, he still felt impressed to be so close to the magnificent creature.

Seven curious Phibians floated by the dock pilings, staring upward. In their bubbling, hissing voices, they mumbled in awe.

Waff stood triumphantly before the large, dripping thing. Slime trickled from the dead seaworm onto the dock, and a gush of milky-gray fluid flowed from its mouth. The long sharp teeth were very fine, like needles. Rather than reeking of fish, the seaworm had a distinct sharp-sweet odor with a hint of pungent cinnamon.

Perfect!

Women came forward to confront Waff. 'We've never captured and killed a seaworm before,' said a Sister in a brown dress who introduced herself as Corysta. She seemed delighted to see the leviathan dead. 'They have caused great havoc in the seas.'

'And they will continue to do so. Learn to adapt your operations.' Waff perfunctorily turned from her to issue instructions to his crew, then told Corysta and the other Bene Gesserits to stay back. 'We are on strict Guild business. Do not attempt to interfere.'

Though dead, the seaworm twitched as nerve impulses continued to fire. Waff ordered the Guildsmen to lash down the carcass, so that he could dissect it without interruption. The Guild assistants brought him a lascutter, a superfine shigawire saw, spreaders, and shovels.

Setting the lascutter to full power and holding it in both hands, Waff swept sideways in a broad arc and sliced the seaworm open, so that the round, dripping segments flopped apart. Guildsmen hurried forward with spreaders to pull open the wound and expose the internal structure. Waff reveled in the gore. The Prophet must be so pleased with him.

In preparation, he had already killed and autopsied two of the original small specimens in his laboratory, so he knew the creatures' basic arrangement of organs. The worm was a biologically simple creature, and working on this larger scale made the process easier. Water and slime oozed onto the dock, splattering Waff. Under other circumstances he might have been disgusted, but this was the sacred essence of his Prophet. The Tleilaxu man sniffed more deeply, and there – a definite undertone to the smell – he caught the vital, pungent aroma of pure melange. No doubt about it.

Waff buried his arms up to his shoulders in the organs, feeling around, identifying specific structures by their shapes and textures. Guild assistants used wide scoops to shovel offal onto the dock. Witches and Phibians watched in fascination, but Waff paid little attention to them.

Ignoring the obviously confused and impotent Sisters, he laser-cut deeper into the worm, sliced along its length and rummaged through the stinking debris, until finally a large bluish-purple lump of soft liver-like material spilled out. Waff stepped back for a breath, then leaned closer, poking and prodding with his fingers. He made a cut with the lasknife at its lowest setting.

A rich oily-cinnamon odor boiled out, so thick it could be seen as fumes. Waff reeled dizzily. The intensity of the melange nearly bowled him over. 'Spice! The creature is saturated with melange! Extremely concentrated spice.'

The Sisters looked at each other and came closer with curious expressions. 'Spice? The seaworms produce *spice*?' The Guildsmen stood close to Waff and his dripping prize, blocking the Bene Gesserits.

'The seaworms destroyed our soostone beds!' another woman shouted.

Waff stared them down. 'These creatures may have destroyed one economy on Buzzell, but they created an even more important one.' His assistants picked up the large, melange-saturated organ and carried it back to the nearest hornet ship. Waff would have to test the substance thoroughly, but he already felt confident in what he would find.

Up in the orbiting Heighliner, Edrik the Navigator would be pleased.

Dripping with slime and seawater, Waff hurried back to the ship.

Some see spice as a blessing, others as a curse. To everyone,
however, it is a necessity.

– PLANETOLOGIST PARDOT KYNES,
Original Arrakis Notebooks

After her long and exhausting journey across the Old
Empire, from the planets preparing for battle, to the Guild
shipyards, to the soostone operations on Buzzell, Mother
Commander Murbella returned to Chapterhouse with
renewed determination. Since she had been gone for many
months, her quarters in the Keep now looked like a
stranger's rooms. Harried acolytes and male workers
scurried to unload her belongings from her ship.

After a polite knock on the door, an acolyte stepped
in. The young woman had short brown hair and a furtive
smile. 'Mother Commander, Archives sent these updated
charts. They were supposed to be waiting for you upon
your arrival.' She held out thin maps with finely detailed
lines, then drew back, startled, when she noticed the
hulking combat robot, deactivated but still standing in the
corner of the room like a war trophy.

'Thank you. Don't mind the machine – it is as dead
as they will all soon be.' Murbella took the reports from
the girl's hands. With a second glance, she realized the

young woman was her own daughter Gianne, her last child with Duncan Idaho. Another daughter, Tanidia, also raised by the New Sisterhood, had been shipped off to work among the Missionaria.

Do Gianne or Tanidia even know who their parents are? Years ago she had made the choice to tell Janess of her parentage, and the young woman had thrown herself into the study and understanding of her famous father. But Murbella had let her other two daughters be raised among the Bene Gesserit in the more traditional way. She doubted they knew how special they were.

Gianne seemed hesitant, as if hoping the Mother Commander would ask her for something else. Though she knew the answer, on impulse Murbella asked, 'How old are you, Gianne?'

The girl seemed startled that she knew her name. 'Why, twenty-three, Mother Commander.'

'And you have not yet undergone the Agony.' It was not a question. Occasionally, the Mother Commander had been tempted to use her position to interfere with the girl's training, but had not done so. A Bene Gesserit was not supposed to show such weakness.

The young woman seemed ashamed. 'The proctors suggest that I would benefit from more focus and concentration.'

'Then devote yourself to that. We need every Reverend Mother we can find.' She glanced at the ominous combat robot. 'The war has worsened.'

MURBELLA REALIZED SHE could not rest, could not waste the time. She demanded to see her advisors, Kiria, Janess, Laera, and Accadia. The women arrived, expecting a meeting, but Murbella herded them out of the Keep.

'Prepare a 'thopter. We leave immediately for the desert belt.'

Carrying a stack of reports, Laera did not react well to the news. 'But Mother Commander, you've been gone so long. Many documents await your attention. You have to make decisions, give proper—'

'I decide the priorities.'

Kiria, looking scornful, bit her words back when she noted the Mother Commander's complete seriousness. They all crowded aboard an empty ornithopter, then waited for the tedious takeoff preparations. Murbella wouldn't sit still for a moment. 'If I don't get a pilot, I'll fly this damned thing myself.' A young male pilot was quickly brought to her.

As the 'thopter took off, she finally turned to her advisors and explained, 'The Guild demands an exorbitant payment for all the warships we have under construction. Ix already accepts payments only in melange, and now that soostones from Buzzell are no longer economically viable, everything hinges on spice. That is our only coin significant enough to appease the Guild.'

'Appease them?' Kiria snapped. 'What madness is this? We should conquer them and force them to produce the weapons and vessels we need. Are we the only ones who understand the threat? Thinking machines are coming!'

Janess was astonished by the other woman's suggestion. 'Attacking the Guild would create open civil warfare at a time when we can least afford it.'

'Do we have enough resources to spend on these ships?' asked Laera. 'Our credit has already been strained past its limits with the Guild Bank.'

'We all face a common enemy,' old Accadia said. 'Surely, the Guild and Ix would be willing—'

Murbella clenched her hands. 'This has nothing to do with altruism or greed. Despite the best intentions, resources and raw materials do not appear like rainbows after a storm. Populations must be fed, ships must be fueled, energy must be produced and expended. Money is only a symbol, but economics is the engine that drives the whole machine. The piper must be paid.'

The 'thopter raced across the sky, buffeted by dry winds and blown dust long before they saw the desert. Murbella gazed out the curved window, sure that dunes had not extended this far across the continent the last time she'd visited the desert. It was a spreading *anti*flood, total dryness sweeping outward in waves. At the heart of the desert, the worms grew and reproduced, keeping the cycle going in a perpetually increasing spiral.

The Mother Commander turned to the woman behind her. 'Laera, I require a complete assessment of our spice-harvesting operations. I need to know numbers. How many long tons of melange do we gather? How much do we have in our stockpiles, and how much is available for export?'

'We produce enough to meet our needs, Mother Commander. Our investment continues to go into expanding the operations, but our expenditures have increased dramatically.'

Kiria muttered a bitter comment about the Ixians and their endless bills.

'We may need to bring in outside workers,' Janess pointed out. 'These obstacles can be overcome.'

The 'thopter swooped toward a chimney-plume of dust and sand thrown up by a harvester. Around it, like wolves circling a wounded animal, several sandworms approached the vibrations. Already the operations were beginning to wrap up, with miners rushing and carryalls hovering to snatch the heavy machinery away as soon as worms ventured too close.

Murbella said, 'Squeeze the desert, wring out every gram of spice.'

'Beast Rabban was given the same task long ago, during the days of Muad'Dib,' said Accadia. 'And he failed in a spectacular fashion.'

'Rabban did not have the Sisterhood behind him.' She could see Laera, Janess, and Kiria all making silent mental calculations. How many workers could be diverted to the desert zone? How many off-planet prospectors and treasure hunters could they allow on Chapterhouse? And how much spice would be enough to keep Guild and Ixian engineers producing the desperately needed ships and weapons?

The male pilot, having been silent until now, said, 'While we are out here, Mother Commander, shall I take you to our desert research station? The planetology crew is studying the sandworm cycle, the spread of desert, and the parameters necessary for the most effective spice harvest.'

'"Understanding is required before success is possible,"' Laera said, quoting directly from the old Orange Catholic Bible.

'Yes, let me inspect this station. Research is necessary, but in times like these it must be *practical* research. We have no time for frivolous studies concocted by the whim of an offworld scientist.'

The pilot banked the 'thopter and accelerated far out into the open desert. On the horizon, a lumpy, black ridge showed a reef of buried rock, a safe bastion where worms could not go.

Shakkad Station had been named after Shakkad the Wise, a ruler from days before the Butlerian Jihad. Nearly lost in the mists of legend, Shakkad's chemist had been the first man in history to recognize the geriatric properties of melange. Now, far from Chapterhouse Keep or any outside interference, a group of fifty scientists, Sisters, and their support staff lived and worked. They set up weather-testing devices, traveled out onto the dunes to measure chemical changes during spice blows and monitor the growth and movement of sandworms.

When the 'thopter settled onto a flat cliff outcropping that served as a makeshift landing pad, a group of scientists came out to meet them. Dusty and windblown, a survey team was just returning from the edges of the desert where they had set out sampling poles and weather-testing instruments. They wore stillsuits, exact reproductions of those once used by the Fremen.

A majority of the scientists at Shakkad Station were men, and several of the older ones had made brief expeditions to charred Rakis itself. Three decades had passed since the ecological destruction of the desert planet, and by now few experts could claim firsthand knowledge of the sandworms or original conditions on Dune.

'How may we assist you, Mother Commander?' asked the station manager, an offworlder who pushed dusty protective goggles up onto his forehead. The man's owlish eyes had already begun to turn a faint blue. Spice had been in his diet every day since his arrival at the outpost. His body gave off an unpleasant sour odor, as if he had taken his assignment in the waterless belt with particular seriousness, even to the point of foregoing regular bathing.

'Assist us by getting more melange,' Murbella answered bluntly.

'Do your teams have everything they need?' Laera asked. 'Do you require additional supplies or workers?'

'No, no. We just want solitude and the freedom to work. Oh, and time.'

'I can give you the first two. But time is a commodity none of us has.'

We can conquer our enemy, of course, but is it worthwhile to achieve victory without understanding the flaws of our opponent? Such an analysis is the most interesting part.

— ERASMUS,
Laboratory Notebooks

The machine-based cathedral on Synchrony was a mere manifestation of what the rest of the galaxy might become. Omnius was pleased at the progress the thinking-machine fleet had made in the past few years, conquering one system after another, but Erasmus knew that so much more remained to do.

The voice of Omnius boomed much louder than necessary, as he sometimes liked to do. 'The New Sisterhood offers the strongest resistance to us, but I know how to defeat them. Scouts have verified the secret location of Chapterhouse, and I have already dispatched plague probes there. Those women will soon be extinct.' Omnius sounded quite bored. 'Shall I display the map of star systems, so you know just how many we have encountered and conquered? Not a single failure.'

Displays jabbed into Erasmus's mind, regardless of whether he wanted to see them or not. In bygone days the independent robot had been able to decide what he wanted to download from the evermind, and what he didn't. Increasingly, however, Omnius had found ways to override the robot's decision-making abilities, forcing data into his internal systems, sliding it past multiple firewalls.

'Those are mere symbolic victories,' Erasmus said, intentionally shifting to his disguise of the wrinkled old woman in gardening clothes. 'I am pleased that we have made it to the edge of the Old Empire, but we still have not won this war. I have spent millennia studying these stubborn, resourceful humans. Do not assume victory until we actually have it in our hands. Remember what happened last time.'

Omnius's snort of disbelief echoed through the entire city of Synchrony. 'We are by definition better than flawed humanity.' From a thousand watcheyes, he looked down upon Erasmus and his matronly disguise. 'Why do you persist in wearing that embarrassing shape? It makes you look weak.'

'My physical body does not determine my strength. My mind makes me what I am.'

'I am not interested in your mind either. I simply wish to win this war. I must win. I *need* to win. Where is the no-ship? Where is my Kwisatz Haderach?'

'You sound as demanding as Baron Harkonnen. Are you unconsciously imitating him?'

'You gave me the mathematical projections, Erasmus. Where is the superhuman? Answer me.'

The robot chuckled. 'You already have Paolo.'

'Your prophecy also guaranteed a Kwisatz Haderach aboard the no-ship. I want both versions – redundancy to assure victory. And I do not want the humans to have one. I must control them both.'

'We will find the no-ship. We already know there are

many intriguing things aboard, including a Tleilaxu Master. He may be the only one left alive, and I would very much like to speak with him – as would you. The Master needs to see how all those Face Dancers have shaped us, built us, so that we could become closer to gods. Closer than humans, at any rate.'

'We will keep sending out our net. And we will find that ship.'

All around the city, in a dramatic statement of the ever-mind's impatience, towering buildings collapsed, full metal structures fell in upon themselves. Hearing the thundering sounds and feeling the floor shake beneath him, the independent robot was not impressed. Too many times he had witnessed such overblown theatrics. Omnius certainly enjoyed running the show, for better and often for worse, though Erasmus continually tried to control the ever-mind's excesses. The future depended on it – the future that Erasmus had ordained.

He dug through the projections that he'd digested from trillions of datapoints. All of his results were colored to fit precisely the prophecies he had formulated himself. Omnius believed them all. The gullible evermind relied too much on filtered information, and the robot played him well.

Given the proper parameters, Erasmus was absolutely certain the millennia ahead would turn out properly.

Those who see do not always understand. Those who claim
to understand can be the blindest of all.

– the Oracle of Time

What remained of Norma Cenva's ancient corporeal form
was confined inside a chamber that had been built and
modified around her during thousands of years. But her
mind knew no physical boundaries. She was only tenu-
ously connected to flesh, a biological generator of pure
thought. The Oracle of Time.

Her mental links to the fabric of the universe gave her
the ability to travel anywhere along infinite possibilities.
She could see the future and the past, but not always
with perfect clarity. Her brain was such that she could
touch the Infinite and almost – almost – comprehend it.

Her nemesis, the evermind, had laid down a vast electronic network throughout the fabric of space, a complex
tachyon road map that most people could not see. Omnius
used it as a net to sift for his prey, but so far he had not
managed to snare the no-ship.

Long ago, Norma had created the precursor to the
Guild as a means of fighting the thinking machines. Since
that time, the Guild had taken on a life of its own, growing
away from her while she stretched herself farther into the

cosmos. Politics between planets, power struggles between the Navigator faction and the human Administrators, monopolies on valuable commodities such as soostones, Ixian technologies, or melange – such problems did not concern her.

Keeping watch over mankind required an investment of her mental currency. She felt the turmoil in civilization, knew the great schism in the Guild. She would have chastised the Administrators for creating such a crisis, if she could only remember how to speak to such small people. Norma found it exhausting to talk in simple enough terms to make herself comprehensible even to her advanced Navigators. She had to make them understand the true Enemy, so that they could shoulder the burden of fighting.

If the Oracle of Time did not attend to grander priorities, no one else would. No one else in the universe could possibly do it. With her prescience, she grasped what was most important: *Find the lost no-ship.* The final Kwisatz Haderach was aboard, and Kralizec's black cloud had already released its torrents. But Omnius was searching for the same thing and might get to it first.

She had felt the recent struggles between the Bene Gesserits and the Honored Matres. Before that she had witnessed the original Scattering and Famine Times, as well as the extended life and traumatic death of the God Emperor. But all of those events were little more than background noise.

Find the no-ship.

As she had always foreseen and feared, the unrelenting foe had come back. No matter what guise the thinking machines now wore, regardless of how much they had changed, the Enemy was still the Enemy.

And Kralizec is well under way.

While her prescience flowed outward and inward, ripples of time eddied around her, making accurate predictions difficult. She encountered a vortex, a random, powerful factor that could change the outcome in uncounted ways: a Kwisatz Haderach, a person as anomalous as Norma Cenva herself, a wildcard variable.

Omnius wanted to guide and control that special human. The evermind and his Face Dancers had sought the no-ship for years, but so far Duncan Idaho had eluded capture. Even the Oracle had been unable to find him again.

Norma had done her best to thwart the Enemy every step of the way. She had saved the no-ship, hoping to protect the people onboard, but she had lost contact afterward. Something on the ship was more effective than a no-field at blinding her search. She could only hope the thinking machines were as blind.

The Oracle's search continued, her thoughts reeling out in delicate probes. Alas, the vessel simply *was not there*. In some mysterious manner, the passengers hid it from her . . . assuming it had not been destroyed.

Though her prescience was not clear, Norma realized that time was growing shorter and shorter, for everyone. The crux point had to occur soon. Thus, she needed to gather her allies. The foolish Administrators had reconfigured many of their great ships, installing artificial controls – like thinking machines! – so that she could no longer call upon them through her paranormal means. But she could still command a thousand of her loyal Navigators. She would make them ready for battle, the final battle.

As soon as she found the no-ship . . .

The Oracle of Time expanded her mind, casting her thoughts into the void like a fisherman, until the neural ache was incredible. She pushed harder than ever, stretching her boundaries beyond anything she had previously attempted. No price of pain could be too great. She knew full well the consequences of failure.

All around her, a vast clock ticked.

There must be a place where we can find a home, where we can be safe and rest. The Bene Gesserit sent out so many Sisters on their own Scattering before the Honored Matres came. Are they all lost, as well?

— SHEEANA,
confidential no-ship journals

Flying ever onward, the *Ithaca* reeled from the recent spate of damage. And the saboteur continued to elude them. *What more can we do to track him down?* Even Duncan's most thorough Mentat projections offered no new suggestions.

Miles Teg and Thufir Hawat once again dispatched teams to inspect, and even ransack, the quarters of all passengers, hoping to find incriminating evidence. The Rabbi and his people complained about purported violations of their privacy, but Sheeana demanded their full cooperation. To the extent possible, Teg had been closing down sections of the immense vessel with electronic barricades, but the clever saboteur was able to get through anyway.

Assuming no further incidents, with the life-support, air-recirculation, and food-growth systems crippled, the passengers could not last more than a few months without stopping somewhere to replenish the stores. But it had been years since they had found another suitable world.

Duncan wondered: *Is someone trying to destroy us . . . or drive us to a particular place?*

With no starmaps or reliable guidance, he tried to use his uncanny prescience one more time. Another big gamble. Activating the Holtzman engines and closing his eyes, Duncan folded space again, spinning the cosmic roulette wheel—

And the no-ship emerged, intact but still lost, at the perimeter of a star system. A yellow sun with a necklace of worlds, including a terrestrial planet that orbited at the appropriate distance to support life. Possibly habitable, certainly with oxygen and water that the *Ithaca* could take aboard. A chance . . .

Others had gathered on the navigation bridge by the time the no-ship approached the uncharted world. Sheeana got down to business. 'What do we have here? Breathable air? Food? A place to live?'

Gazing through the observation window, Duncan was pleased at what he saw. 'The instruments say yes. I suggest we send a team immediately.'

'Resupply is not good enough,' Garimi said, her tone gruff. 'It never was. We should consider remaining here, if this is the kind of world we've been looking for.'

'We considered that at the planet of the Handlers, too,' Sheeana said.

'If the saboteur drove us here, we need to be very cautious,' Duncan said. 'I know it was a random fold-space jump, but I'm still troubled. Our pursuers cast a wide net. I would not be quick to dismiss the possibility that this place is a trap.'

'Or our salvation,' Garimi suggested.

'We'll have to see for ourselves,' Teg said. Working with the bridge controls, he displayed high-resolution images on the wide screens. 'Plentiful oxygen and vegetation, especially at the higher latitudes away from the equator. Clear signs of habitation, small villages, mid-sized cities, mostly far to the north. Large-scale meteorological scans show that the climate is in upheaval.' He pointed to storm patterns, swaths of dying forests and plains, large lakes and inland seas shriveling into dust bowls. 'Very few clouds in the equatorial latitudes. Minimal atmospheric moisture.'

Stilgar and Liet-Kynes, always fascinated with new worlds, joined the group on the high deck. Kynes drew a quick breath. 'It's turning into a wasteland down there. An artificial desert!'

'I've seen this before.' Sheeana studied a clear brown band like a knife slash across what had apparently been a lushly forested continent. 'It's like Chapterhouse.'

'Could this be one of Odrade's seed planets?' Stuka asked, from her usual position at Garimi's side. 'Did they bring sandtrout here and disperse them? Will we find our Sisters down on that planet?'

'Untainted Sisters,' Garimi said with a gleam in her eyes.

'Quite possibly,' Sheeana said. 'We'll have to go down there. This looks like more than a place to replenish our resources.'

'A new colony.' Stuka's excitement was infectious. 'This could be the world we've been looking for, a site to reestablish Chapterhouse. A new Dune!'

Duncan nodded. 'We cannot pass up an opportunity like this. My instincts brought us here for a reason.'

Are we the last ones left alive? What if the Enemy has destroyed the rest of mankind by now, back in the Old Empire . . . back with Murbella? In that case, it is imperative that we establish as many colonies as possible.

— DUNCAN IDAHO,
no-ship logs

Keeping themselves hidden from the planet's inhabitants, several teams of efficient Bene Gesserits launched a major effort to restock the no-ship with necessary air, water, and chemicals. They sent out mining ships, air scoops, water-purification tankers. That was the *Ithaca*'s immediate priority.

Stilgar and Liet-Kynes insisted on going down to inspect the growing desert band. Seeing the passion on the faces of the two awakened gholas, neither Teg nor Duncan could deny the request. Everyone was guardedly optimistic about finding a welcoming landscape here, and Sheeana wondered if this might be a place where she could release her seven captive sandworms. Although Duncan could not leave the veiling of the no-ship, because then he would be exposed to the Enemy searchers, he had no cause to prevent the others from finding a home at last. Perhaps this would be it.

Bashar Teg piloted the lighter down to the surface himself, accompanied by Sheeana and an eager Stuka, who had long wanted to establish a new Bene Gesserit center, rather than just drift aimlessly in space. Garimi had let her staunch supporter make the first foray, while she formulated plans with her ultraconservative Sisters aboard the no-ship. Stilgar and Liet were most eager just to set foot on the desert – a real desert with open skies and endless sands.

Teg flew directly toward the ravaged arid zone, where an ecological battle was taking place. If this was indeed one of Odrade's seed planets, the Bashar knew how voracious sandtrout would seal away a planet's water, drop by drop. Environmental checks and balances would fight back with shifting weather patterns; animals would migrate to still-untouched regions; stranded plant life would struggle to adapt, and mostly fail. Reproducing sandtrout could act much faster than a world could adapt.

Sheeana and Stuka stared through the lighter's plaz viewing windows, seeing the spreading desert as a success, a triumph of Odrade's Scattering. To the exquisitely prudent Bene Gesserit, even the ruin of an entire ecosystem was an 'acceptable casualty' if it created a new Dune.

'The change is happening so swiftly,' Liet-Kynes said, his voice tinged with awe.

'Surely, Shai-Hulud is already here,' Stilgar added.

Stuka echoed words that Garimi had said time and again. 'This world will be a new Chapterhouse. The hardships will mean nothing to us.'

With the detailed information in their archives, the people aboard the *Ithaca* had all the expertise they needed to establish a new place to live. *Yes, a colony.* Teg rather liked the sound of the word, because it represented the hope of a better future.

Teg knew, however, that Duncan could never stop running, unless he chose to face the Enemy directly. The mysterious old man and woman were still after him with their sinister net, or after something on the no-ship, maybe the vessel itself.

The lighter descended with a rough roar through the china-blue sky. In the middle of the abrupt desert band, dunes stretched as far as he could see. Sunlight reflected from the sands into bone-dry air, and thermal currents jostled the ship from side to side. Teg wrestled with the guidance systems.

In the back, Stilgar chuckled. 'Just like riding a sand-worm.'

Cruising over the middle of the widening desert belt, Liet-Kynes pointed at a rusty-red splash that marked an eruption from beneath the surface. 'Spice blow! No mistaking the color or pattern.' He gave a wry smile to his friend Stilgar. 'I died on one of those. Damn the Harkonnens for leaving me to die!'

Mounds rippled and stirred the top layer of sand, but they did not emerge into open air. 'If those are worms, they are smaller than the ones in our hold,' Stilgar said.

'But still impressive,' Liet added.

'They have had less time to mature,' Sheeana pointed out. 'Mother Superior Odrade did not send volunteers on her Scattering until after the desertification of Chapterhouse was well under way. And we do not know how long the wandering Sisters took to get here.'

Below, obvious lines marked the rapid expansion of

the sandy wasteland, like ripples on a pond. At the fringes were die-off perimeters, places where all vegetation had perished and the dirt had become blowing dust. The encroaching desert had created ghost forests and inundated villages.

Flying low, searching with uneasy anticipation, Teg discovered half-buried rooftops, the pinnacles of once proud buildings drowned under the spreading desert. In one shocking glimpse, he saw a high dock and part of a capsized boat that sat atop a blistering dune.

'I look forward to seeing our Bene Gesserit Sisters.' Stuka sounded eager. 'Obviously they succeeded here in their mission.'

'I expect they will welcome us,' Sheeana admitted.

After seeing the city drowned in sand, Teg did not think the original inhabitants of this planet would have appreciated what the refugee Sisters had done.

As the lighter followed the northern edge of the desert, the scanners picked out small huts and tents erected just beyond the sand's reach. Teg wondered how often the nomadic villages were required to move. If the arid zone expanded as rapidly as it had on Chapterhouse, this world would be losing thousands of acres every day – and accelerating as sandtrout continued to steal precious water.

'Set down at one of those settlements, Bashar,' Sheeana said to him. 'Any of our lost Sisters could be here on the edge of the dunes to monitor the progress.'

'I long to feel real sand under my boots again,' Stilgar muttered.

'It's all so fascinating,' Liet said.

As Teg circled above one of the nomadic villages, people ran out and pointed up at them. Sheeana and

Stuka pressed excitedly against the plaz windows, searching for distinctive dark Bene Gesserit robes, but they saw none.

A formation of rocks towered over the village, a bulwark offering shelter against blowing sand and dust. People, waving, stood atop the pinnacles, but Teg could not determine if the gestures were friendly or threatening.

'See, they cover their heads and faces with cloths and filters,' Liet said. 'The increased aridity forces them to adapt. In order to live here on the edge of the dry dunes, they are already learning to conserve bodily moisture.'

'We could teach them how to make real stillsuits,' Stilgar said with a smile. 'It has been a long time since I wore a decent one. I spent a dozen years aboard that ship, drowning my lungs with moisture. I can't wait to taste dry air again!'

Teg found an open landing area and brought the lighter down. He felt unaccountably troubled as the natives scurried toward them. 'Those are obviously nomadic camps. Why wouldn't they move inland, to where the climate is more hospitable?'

'People adapt,' Sheeana said.

'But why would they have to? Yes, the desert belt is growing, but there are still plenty of wide forests, even cities not far from here. Those people could outrun the spreading dunes for generations to come. Yet they stubbornly remain here.'

Before the hatch opened to let in a breath of parched air, the nomads encircled the craft. Sheeana and Stuka, both wearing traditional dark robes from Chapterhouse so that their refugee Sisters would recognize them, boldly led the way. Teg followed with Stilgar and Liet.

'We are Bene Gesserit,' Sheeana called to the people

in universal Galach. 'Are any of our Sisters among you?' Shielding her eyes against the brightness, she searched the few weathered female faces she saw, but got no response.

'Perhaps another village would be best,' Teg suggested in a whisper. His tactical senses were alert.

'Not yet.'

An elderly man drew closer, pushing a filter mask away from his face. 'You ask for Bene Gesserits? Here on Qelso?' Though coarse, his accent was understandable. Despite his age, he appeared to be healthy and energetic.

Taking the lead, Stuka stepped ahead of Sheeana. 'The ones who wore black robes, like ours. Where are they?'

'All dead.' The old man's eyes flashed.

Stuka's suspicion came too late. Moving like a striking snake, the man hurled a hidden knife from his sleeve, with deadly accuracy. At an unseen signal the rest of the throng rushed forward.

Stuka plucked clumsily at the blade that protruded from her chest but could not make her fingers work. Crumpling to her knees, she tumbled sideways off the lighter's ramp.

Sheeana was already moving, retreating. Teg shouted for Liet and Stilgar to get back inside the ship as he drew one of the stun weapons he had brought from the no-ship's armory. A large rock struck Stilgar in the head, and Liet helped his young friend, trying to drag him back into the lighter. Teg fired a swath of silvery energy, making part of the dusty mob collapse, but more knives and stones clattered at them.

Frenzied people rushed the ramp from all sides, jumping at Teg. Many hands grabbed his wrist before he could fire again, and someone ripped the stunner out of his grip. More took hold of Liet by the shoulders, pulling him away.

Sheeana fought with a whirlwind of blows from her repertoire of Bene Gesserit fighting techniques. Soon a crowd of fallen attackers lay around her.

With a roar, Teg prepared to lurch into his hyperaccelerated metabolism, with which he could easily dodge blows and weapons, but a silvery beam from his own stunner gushed out like tinkling rain, dropping the Bashar, and then Sheeana.

IN SHORT ORDER the villagers bound the hands of their four prisoners with strong cords. Though badly beaten, Teg regained consciousness and saw that Liet and Stilgar were tied together. Stuka's body lay near the ramp while the attackers ransacked the lighter for equipment and hauled things off.

A group of men lifted Stuka's body. The old man retrieved his knife, yanking it from the dead woman's chest and wiping it on her robe with an expression of revulsion. He glowered at the corpse and spat, then marched toward the prisoners. Looking at the three young men, he shook his head in disapproval. 'I did not introduce myself. You may call me Var.'

Defiantly, Sheeana glared up at him. 'Why have you done this to us? You said you knew of the Bene Gesserit order.'

Var's face contorted, as if he had hoped to avoid speaking to her. He leaned close to Sheeana. 'Yes, we know the Bene Gesserit. They came here years ago and delivered their demon creatures to our world. An experiment, they said. An experiment? Look what they did to our beautiful land! It is becoming nothing more than useless sand.' He held his knife, considered Sheeana for a long moment, then sheathed it. 'When we finally real-ized what those women were doing, we killed them all, but too late. Our planet is dying now, and we will fight to protect what's left of it.'

The first law of commercial viability is to recognize a need and meet it. When acceptable needs do not present themselves, a good businessman creates them in any way possible.

— CHOAM primary commercial directive

When yet another Navigator died in his tank, few of the Spacing Guild's Administrators mourned the loss. The giant Heighliner was simply brought back to the Junction shipyards to be refit with one of the Ixian mathematical compilers. It was considered progress.

After long years of practice, Khrone easily concealed his pleasure at the sight. So far every aspect of the wide-reaching plan had proceeded as expected, one domino falling after another. Posing in his familiar disguise as an Ixian inspection engineer, the leader of the Face Dancer myriad waited on a high, copper-floored platform. He observed the clamorous shipyards, while warm breezes and industrial fumes drifted around him.

Nearby, the human administrator Rentel Gorus was not quite as proficient at covering his satisfaction. He blinked his milky eyes and looked up toward the piloting bay of the ancient, decommissioned ship. 'Ardrae was one of the oldest remaining Navigators in our commercial fleet. Even with his spice supplies drastically cut, he clung to life much longer than we expected.'

A plump CHOAM representative said, 'Navigators! Now that these drains on our resources are disappearing one by one, Guild profits should increase significantly.'

Without prompting from his master, the Mentat assistant recited, 'Knowing the lifetime of that Navigator, and considering the quantities of melange required to institute his initial mutation and conversion, I have calculated the total amount of spice consumed during his service to the Guild. With fluctuating prices based on the relative glut during the Tleilaxu years and recent skyrocketing costs due to severe shortages, the Guild could have bought three full-sized Heighliners, complete with no-field capabilities, for the same cost in spice.'

The CHOAM man muttered in disgust, while Khrone remained silent. He found it most effective simply to listen and observe. Humans could be counted on to draw their own conclusions (often erroneous ones) so long as they were pointed in the proper direction.

Savoring his secrets, Khrone thought of the numerous ambassadors the Guild had sent to the front, attempting to negotiate nonaggression treaties with the thinking machines, hoping to declare themselves neutral for the survival of the Guild. But many of those emissaries had been Khrone's Face Dancer plants, who intentionally achieved no success. Others – the human ones – never returned from the encounters.

With Richese conveniently obliterated by rebel Honored Matres (secretly guided by Khrone's Face Dancers), humans had no choice but to turn to Ix and the Guild in order to obtain the technological items they required. The Junction shipyards had always been immense complexes for constructing huge interstellar ships.

Murbella's defensive fleet was growing with remarkable speed, but Khrone knew that even these efforts would not be very effective against the sheer size and scope of Omnius's military, which had been thousands of years in the making. The fabrication facilities of Ix (also controlled by Face Dancers) were still delaying the development and modification of the Obliterator weapons upon which the Sisterhood's defense relied. And since every new Guildship was controlled by an Ixian mathematical compiler rather than a Navigator, the Mother Commander and her allies would have many surprises in store.

'We will build more ships to make up for the obsolescence of the Navigators,' Administrator Gorus promised. 'Our contract with the New Sisterhood seems infinite. We have never had so much business.'

'And yet interplanetary trade is down drastically.' The CHOAM representative nodded to both Khrone and Gorus. 'How is the Sisterhood to pay for these expensive ships and armaments?'

'They have met their obligations with an increased flow of melange,' Gorus said.

Khrone finally nudged the conversation where he wished it to go. 'Why not accept payment in horses or petroleum or some other outdated and useless substance? If your Navigators are dying and your ships function perfectly well with Ixian mathematical compilers, the Guild no longer needs melange. What good is it to you?'

'Indeed, its value is greatly diminished. Over the past quarter century, following the destruction of Rakis, the Tleilaxu worlds, and so much more, those who could afford spice recreationally have dwindled to a tiny number.' The CHOAM representative glanced at his Mentat, who nodded in agreement. 'Chapterhouse might have a monopoly on melange, but by their very iron grip, by decreasing the amount of spice available for popular consumption, they have strangled their own market. Few people really *need* it anymore. Now that they have learned to live without spice, will they be so keen to reacquire their addictions?'

'Probably,' Gorus said. 'You need only drop the price, and we'd have a stampede of customers.'

'The witches still control Buzzell,' the Mentat pointed out. 'They have other ways to pay.'

The CHOAM man disdainfully raised his eyebrows. He made very expressive noises without words. 'Luxury items during war? Not a good economic investment.'

'Providing soostones is no longer easy for them either,' Gorus pointed out, 'since sea monsters are destroying the shell beds and attacking their harvesters.'

Khrone listened intently. His own spies had brought back disturbing, but intriguing, reports about strange happenings on Buzzell, and a possible secret Navigator project centered there. He had demanded more information.

Khrone watched while jawlike machinery on a large crane pried open the pilot's bay on the gigantic decommissioned Heighliner. Heavy suspensor lifters strained and groaned as they pulled out the Navigator's thick-walled plaz tank. During the slow, clumsy extraction, the tank caught on the edge of the hole in the Heighliner's structure. A hull plate broke off and spun downward, striking the side of the Heighliner and ricocheting with a shower of sparks, then tumbling until it finally slammed into the ground far below.

Wisps of orange spice gas escaped from the Navigator's

chamber, stray exhaust vapors leaking into the atmosphere. Only a decade or so ago, such a quantity of wasted spice gas would have been enough to buy an Imperial palace. Now the CHOAM representative and Administrator Gorus watched it dissipate without comment. Gorus spoke into a tiny microphone at his collar. 'Deposit the tank in front of us. I wish to stare at it.'

The crane raised the thick-walled chamber, swung it away from the hulk of the Heighliner, and brought it over to the observation platform. Suspensors lowered the container gently to the copper-floored deck, where it settled with a distressingly heavy thump. Spice gas continued to vent from the chink in the thick plaz.

The melange vapors smelled strangely flat and metallic, telling Khrone that the Navigator had inhaled and exhaled them until very little spice potency remained. At a curt direction from the milky-eyed Administrator, silent Guild workers unsealed a cap on the tank, causing the remainder of the spice to blast out in a death rattle.

As the polluting gas drained, the murky clouds swirled and thinned, revealing a silhouetted form slumped inside. Khrone had seen Navigators before, of course, but this one was flaccid, gray-skinned, and very dead. The bulbous head and small eyes, webbed hands, soft amphibious-looking skin gave the thing the appearance of a large, misshapen fetus. Ardrae had died days earlier, starved for melange. Though the Guild now had plenty of spice in their stockpiles, Administrator Gorus had cut off the Navigators' supplies some time ago.

'Behold, a dead Navigator. A sight few will ever see again.'

'How many still survive among your Guildships?' Khrone asked.

Gorus seemed evasive. 'Among the ships still in our inventory, only thirteen Navigators remain alive. We are on a death watch for them.'

'What do you mean the ships "still in your inventory"?' the CHOAM man asked.

Gorus hesitated, then admitted, 'There were some still flown by Navigators, vessels that we had not yet managed to equip with mathematical compilers. They have . . . how shall I say this? Over the past few months they have disappeared.'

'*Disappeared*? How many Heighliners? Each ship is hugely expensive!'

'I do not have precise numbers.'

The CHOAM man had a hard voice. 'Give us your best estimate.'

'Five hundred, perhaps a thousand.'

'*A thousand*?'

At his side, the Mentat held his silence, but he appeared as upset and startled as the CHOAM representative.

Trying to demonstrate control over the situation, Gorus said in an almost dismissive tone, 'When starved for spice, the Navigators grow desperate. It's not surprising that they take irrational action.'

Khrone himself was concerned, but he didn't show it. These disappearances sounded like a widespread conspiracy involving a Navigator faction, something he had not expected. 'Do you have any idea where they might have gone?'

The Guild Administrator feigned nonchalance. 'It doesn't matter. They will run out of spice and die. Look at these shipyards and see how many vessels we are creating every day. Before long, we'll make up for the loss of those outdated ships and obsolete Navigators.

Have no fear. After so many years of bondage to a single substance, the Guild is making a good business decision.'

'Thanks to your partners from Ix,' Khrone pointed out.

'Yes, thanks to Ix.'

Following a lull, the noise of the shipyards became very loud. Welders went to work, and heavy machinery lifted curved components into place. A cargo hauler half a kilometer wide brought in two sets of Holtzman engines. The men continued to watch the magnificent activities for a long time in silence. None of them even looked again at the pathetic dead Navigator in his tank.

Humanity has many profound beliefs. Chief among them is the concept of Home.

> – Bene Gesserit Archives,
> *Analyses of Motivating Factors*

The next time Edrik's Heighliner went to Buzzell on a run, the vessel left the planet carrying something vastly more important than soostones.

Hidden on the sealed laboratory decks was a package of the uniquely powerful substance extracted from the slaughtered seaworm's strange, dense organ. With extravagant optimism, Waff had named it 'ultraspice.' Tests proved that the potency went beyond that of any spice ever recorded. This remarkable substance would change everything for the Navigator faction.

The Tleilaxu Master also understood the importance of his achievement, and meant to use it to his advantage. Without being summoned, he pushed past Guild security forces and made his way to the restricted levels reserved for the Navigator. Officiously ignoring all challenges, Waff opened thick doors until he stood before the plaz-walled tank that held Edrik in his expensive bath of spice gas. Having succeeded in restoring at least one breed of worms, Waff was no longer a sycophant. He could make brash demands of his own.

Waff's shortened ghola life span didn't give him much time to meet his critical goals, thus making him increasingly desperate. He was already well past his physical prime, and now his body was in a rapid plunge to degeneration and death. He probably had no more than a year or so left.

Full of rigid defiance, Waff stood before Edrik's tank and said, 'Now that my altered seaworms are capable of creating spice in a form accessible by Guild Navigators, I want you to take me to Rakis.' He no longer had anything to lose, and everything to gamble. He crossed his thin arms over his chest in triumph.

Swimming slowly, Edrik drifted close to the plaz wall. The swirls of orange gas were hypnotic. 'The new melange has not been proved in practice.'

'No matter. Its chemistry has been proved.'

Edrik's voice grew louder through the speakers. 'I am troubled. In its original form, melange has complexities that cannot be revealed in any laboratory analysis.'

'You worry unnecessarily,' Waff said. 'Seaworm spice is more potent than anything you have ever consumed. Try it yourself, if you do not believe me.'

'You are in no position to make demands.'

'No one else could have accomplished what I did. Buzzell will be your new source of melange. Seaworm hunters will harvest more ultraspice than you can possibly use, and Navigators will no longer be dependent upon the Bene Gesserit witches or the black market. Even if the Sisters decide to harvest the seaworms and try to create another monopoly, you can ignore them. By changing the *worms*, instead of the planet, we can place them anywhere. I have given you the road to freedom.'

Waff snorted, raised his voice. 'Now I demand my payment.'

'We kept you alive after the Honored Matres were overthrown on Tleilax. Is that not sufficient compensation?'

With a conciliatory sigh, the Tleilaxu ghola held his hands out. 'What I ask will cost you little and gain you much honor, a blessing from God.'

The Navigator wore a look of displeasure on his distorted face. 'What do you desire, little man?'

'I repeat: Take me to Rakis.'

'Absurd. The world is dead.' Edrik's words were flat.

'Rakis is where my last body perished, so consider it a pilgrimage.' He continued in a rush, saying more than he had intended. 'In my laboratory I created more small worms from the remaining sandtrout specimens. I have strengthened them, made them capable of surviving in the harshest environment. I can repopulate Rakis and bring back the Prophet—' He abruptly fell silent.

At the first rumors that the seaworms were thriving, Waff had turned his efforts to the last few sandtrout in his original stock. Sculpting worm chromosomes for survival in a comfortable ocean environment had been a challenge; much more difficult, though, was the task of toughening the monsters to survive out in the blasted wastelands of Rakis. But Waff did not turn his back on difficulty. All along, his goal had been to bring the sandworms back where they belonged. *God's Messenger must return to Dune.*

He studied Edrik, who stroked with webbed hands as he considered the request. 'Our Oracle recently sent us a message, calling upon Navigators to leave the Guild and join her in a great battle. That must be my priority now.'

'I implore you, take me to Rakis.' As if to remind Waff of his imminent mortality, a twinge of pain shot through his chest and down his spine. He needed all his effort not to show the anguish of dying, the misery of failure. He had so little time remaining. 'Is that so much to ask? Grant me this one favor at the end of my life.'

'That is all you wish to do? *Die* there?'

'I will spend my last energies on my sandworm specimens. Perhaps there is a way of reintroducing them to Rakis and regenerating the ecological systems. Think of it: If I succeed, you will have yet another source of melange.'

'You will not be pleased with what you find there. Even with moisture recycling, shelters, and equipment, survival on Rakis is more difficult than it has ever been. Your expectations are unrealistic. Nothing useful remains.'

Waff tried unsuccessfully to keep desperation out of his voice. 'Rakis is my home, my spiritual compass.'

Edrik thought it over, then said, 'I can fold space to Rakis, but I cannot promise to return. The Oracle has called me.'

'I will remain there as long as necessary. God will provide for me.'

Waff rushed back to his private research levels. Intending to stay on the desert planet, undoubtedly for the rest of his life, he requisitioned all the supplies and equipment he might need for years, allowing him to be entirely self-sufficient on that bleak and lifeless world. After placing the order, he looked at his tanks where the new armored sandworms writhed, eager to be released.

Rakis . . . Dune . . . was his destiny. He felt in his heart that God had summoned him there, and if Waff perished on the planet . . . then so be it. He felt a warm, soothing wave of contentment. He understood his place in the universe.

THE BLACKENED, FAINTLY coppery ball appeared in the Heighliner's private viewing plates. Waff had been so anxious gathering his things that he hadn't even felt the activation of the Holtzman engines, the folding of space.

Edrik surprised him by offering additional supplies and a small team of loyal Guild assistants to help with the labor of setting up a camp and administering the experiments. Perhaps he wanted his own people on hand to see if the Tleilaxu man succeeded again with his worms. Waff didn't mind, so long as they stayed out of the way.

Without introducing himself to the silent members of his new team, Waff directed the transfer of his armored sandworm specimens from the isolated lab, his self-erecting shelters and his equipment, everything they would need for survival on the charred world.

One of the silent, smooth-faced Guild assistants piloted the lighter. Before they reached the dead surface of Dune, the Heighliner had already drifted out of orbit. Edrik was anxious to be on his way to answer the Oracle's call, carrying its cargo of ultraspice and the tidings of new hope for all Navigators.

Waff, though, had eyes only for the blistered, lifeless landscape of the legendary world.

Bacteria are like tiny machines, notable for their effects on larger biological systems. In a similar way, humans behave as disease organisms among planetary systems, and should be studied as such.

– ERASMUS,
Laboratory Notebooks

When the virulent plague reached Chapterhouse, the first cases appeared among the male workers. Seven men were struck down so swiftly that their dying expressions showed more surprise than pain.

In the Great Hall where younger Sisters dined, the disease also spread. The virus was so insidious that the most contagious period occurred a full day before any symptoms manifested; thus, the epidemic had already sunk its claws into those most vulnerable before the New Sisterhood even knew a threat existed.

Hundreds perished within the first three days, more than a thousand by the end of the week; after ten days, the victims were beyond counting. Support staff, teachers, visitors, offworld merchants, cooks and kitchen help, even failed Reverend Mothers – all fell like stalks of wheat under the Grim Reaper's scythe.

Murbella called upon her senior advisers to develop

an immediate plan, but from prior epidemics on other embattled planets they knew that precautionary measures and quarantines would do no good. The conference room doors were securely locked, because younger Sisters and acolytes could not be allowed to know the strategies being discussed here.

'Survival of the Sisterhood is our primary purpose, even as the rest of Chapterhouse dies around us.' Murbella felt sickened to think of all the unprepared acolytes, spice-harvesting teams in the dune belt,transport drivers, architects and construction workers, weather planners, greenhouse gardeners, cleaners, bankers, artists, archive workers, pilots, technicians,and medical assistants. All the underpinnings of Chapterhouse itself.

Laera attempted to sound objective, but her voice cracked. 'Reverend Mothers have the precise cellular control needed to fight this disease on its own battle-ground. We can use our bodily defenses to drive away the plague.'

'In other words, anyone who hasn't gone through the Spice Agony will die,' Kiria said. 'Like the Honored Matres did. That was why we pursued you Bene Gesserits in the first place, to learn how to protect ourselves from the epidemic.'

'Can we use the blood of Bene Gesserit survivors to create a vaccine?' Murbella asked.

Laera shook her head. 'Reverend Mothers drive out disease organisms, cell by cell. There are no antibodies we can share with others.'

'It is not even as simple as that,' Accadia rasped. 'A Reverend Mother can channel her inner biological defenses only if she has the energy to do so, and if she has the time and ability to concentrate on herself. But this plague forces us to turn our energies to tend the most unfortunate victims.'

'If you make that mistake, you'll die, just like our Sheeana surrogate on Jhibraith,' Kiria said with the undertone of a sneer in her voice. 'We Reverend Mothers will have to take care of ourselves and no one else. The others have no chance anyway. We need to accept that.'

Murbella already felt the beginnings of exhaustion, but her nervous anxiety made her pace the sealed council room. She had to think. What could be done against such a minute, lethal enemy? *Only Reverend Mothers will survive* . . . She spoke firmly to her advisors, 'Find every acolyte who is close to being ready for the Agony. Do we have enough Water of Life?'

'For all of them?' cried Laera.

'For every single one. Any Sister who has the slightest chance of survival. Give all of them the poison and hope they can convert it and survive the Agony. Only then will they be able to fight off the plague.'

'Many will die in the attempt,' warned Laera.

'Or *all* of them will die from the plague. Even if most of the candidates succumb to the Agony, it's an improvement.' She did not wince. Her own daughter Rinya had perished that way, many years ago.

Smiling slightly with her wrinkled lips, Accadia nodded. 'A Bene Gesserit would rather die from the Agony than from a sickness spread by our Enemy. It is a gesture of defiance rather than surrender.'

'See that it is done.'

IN THE DEATH houses she turned a deaf ear to the moans of the sick and dying. The Chapterhouse doctors had drugs and potent analgesics, and the Bene Gesserit acolytes had been taught how to block off pain. Even so, the misery of the plague was enough to break the deepest conditioning.

Murbella hated to see the Sisters unable to control their suffering. It shamed her, not for their weakness but because she had been unable to prevent this from happening in the first place.

She went to where lines of makeshift beds held young acolytes, most of them terrified, some of them determined. The room smelled of rancid cinnamon – harsh instead of pleasant. With her brow furrowed and eyes intent, the Mother Commander watched two stony-faced Reverend Mothers carry out a stretcher bearing the sheet-wrapped body of a young woman.

'Another one failed the Agony?'

The Reverend Mothers nodded. 'Sixty-one today. They are dying as fast as from the plague.'

'And how many successes?'

'Forty-three.'

'Forty-three that will live to fight the Enemy.'

Like a mother hen, Murbella walked up and down the line of beds, observing the plague-stricken Sisters, some sleeping quietly with new bodily awareness, others writhing in deep comas from which it was uncertain they would ever find their way back.

At the end of the row, a teenage girl lay with frightened eyes. She propped herself up in bed on trembling arms. She met Murbella's gaze, and even in her extreme sickness the girl's eyes glimmered. 'Mother Commander,' she said hoarsely.

Murbella moved closer to the young one. 'What is your name?'

'Baleth.'

'Are you waiting to undergo the Agony?'

'I'm waiting to die, Mother Commander. I was brought here to take the Water of Life, but before it could be administered the symptoms of the disease manifested themselves. I'll be dead before the end of the day.' She sounded very brave.

'So they will not give you the Water of Life, then? You won't even attempt the Agony?'

Baleth lowered her chin. 'They say I will not survive it.'

'And you believe them? Aren't you strong enough to try?'

'I am strong enough to *try*, Mother Commander.'

'Then I'd rather you died trying, instead of giving up.' As she looked down at Baleth, she was poignantly reminded of Rinya . . . eager and confident, so like Duncan. But her daughter hadn't been ready after all, and she had died on the table.

I should have delayed her. Because of my need to prove myself, I pushed Rinya. I should have waited . . .

And Murbella's youngest daughter Gianne – what had happened to her? The Mother Commander had kept herself apart from the young woman's day-to-day activities, letting the Sisterhood raise her. But in this time of crisis, she decided to ask someone, Laera perhaps, to track her down.

Right now, Baleth seemed to show hope, looking with fervid eyes toward the Mother Commander. Murbella ordered the Suk doctors to attend to her immediately. 'Time is shorter for this one than for the others.'

From the doctors' skeptical expressions, Murbella could see they considered this a waste of the valuable Water of Life, but she stood firm. Baleth accepted the viscid draught, took a last look at her Mother Commander, and gulped the toxic substance. She lay back, closed her eyes, and began her fight . . .

It did not last long. Baleth died in a valiant attempt, but Murbella could feel no guilt about it. The Sisterhood must never stop fighting.

THOUGH MELANGE WAS rare and precious, rarer still was the Water of Life.

By the fourth day of Murbella's desperate plan, it became apparent that Chapterhouse's supplies would not be sufficient. Sister after Sister consumed the poison, and many perished while struggling to convert the deadly toxin in their cells, trying to change their bodies.

The Mother Commander tasked her advisors to study the exact amount of poison necessary to trigger the Agony. Some Reverend Mothers suggested diluting the substance, but if they didn't give enough to be fatal, and thus effective, the entire experiment would fail.

Dozens more Sisters died. More than 60 percent of those who took the poison.

Kiria offered a hard but coldly logical solution. 'Assess each candidate, and dole out the Water of Life only to those most likely to succeed. We can't gamble foolishly. Each dose we give to a woman who fails is wasted. We must discriminate.'

Murbella disagreed. 'None of them has a chance unless they undergo the Agony. The whole point of this operation is to give it to everyone – and the most fit will survive.'

The women stood amidst the bedlam of the dormitory rooms in the sick houses that had been converted from any building large enough to accommodate beds.

Four lifeless bodies were carried past them by exhausted-looking Reverend Mothers. They had run out of sheets, so the corpses were uncovered, their faces twisted in a display of the incalculable pain they had suffered.

Ignoring the dead, Murbella knelt beside the bed of one young woman who survived. She had to look at the casualty total from a different perspective. If they were *all* destined to die, it was a fruitless exercise to count those who perished. In that light, the only relevant number was the tally of those who did recover. The victories.

'If we don't have enough Water of Life, use other poisons.' Murbella got wearily to her feet, ignoring the smells, the sounds. 'The Bene Gesserit may have determined that the Water of Life is most effective at forcing the Agony, but long ago the Sisters used other deadly chemicals – anything that would push the body into an absolute crisis.' She perused the young students, these girls who had hoped one day to grow up to become Reverend Mothers. Now each of them had one chance, and one chance only. 'Poison them one way or another. Poison them all. If they survive, they belong here.'

A courier ran up to her, one of the younger Sisters who had recently survived the transformation. 'Mother Commander! You are needed immediately in Archives.'

Murbella turned. 'Has Accadia found something?'

'No, Mother Commander. She . . . you have to see for yourself.' The younger woman swallowed. 'And *hurry.*'

The ancient woman did not have the strength to leave

her office. Accadia sat surrounded by wire spool readers and stacks of data-dense crystal sheets. She sprawled back in her large chair, breathing heavily, barely able to move. The old woman's rheumy eyes flickered open. 'So, you've come . . . in time.'

Murbella looked at the archivist, appalled. Accadia, too, had the plague. 'But you are a Reverend Mother! You can fight this.'

'I am old and tired. I used the last of my stamina to compile our records and projections, to map out the spread of this disease. Maybe we can prevent it on other worlds.'

'Doubtful. The Enemy distributes the virus wherever they consider it strategic.' Already she had made up her mind to have several other Reverend Mothers Share with Accadia. Her extensive memories and knowledge must not be lost.

Accadia struggled to sit up in the chair. 'Mother Commander, don't be so focused on the epidemic that you fail to see its consequences.' She began coughing. Blotches had appeared all over her skin, the advanced stages of the disease. 'This plague is a mere foray, a test attack. On many planets it is sufficient, but the Enemy must know the Sisterhood well enough by now to be sure we can fight this, at least to a point. After they soften us up, they'll attack by other means.'

Murbella felt cold inside. 'If thinking machines destroy the New Sisterhood, then the remaining fragments of humanity will have no chance of resisting them. We are the most important hurdle Omnius has to overcome.'

'So you finally understand the implications?' The old woman grasped the Mother Commander's hand to make sure she understood. 'This planet has always been hidden, but now the thinking machines must know the location of Chapterhouse. I would wager that their space fleet is already on its way.'

One man's dream is another's nightmare.

– a saying of Ancient Kaitain

After dragging Stuka's body away, the nomads separated Sheeana and Teg from Stilgar and Liet-Kynes. Apparently they saw the two boys – twelve and thirteen – as no threat, not knowing that both were deadly Fremen fighters, whose clear memories held many raids against the Harkonnens.

Teg recognized the strategy. 'The old leader wants to interrogate our young ones first.' Var and his hard-bitten comrades would assume the youths would be easily intimidated, not capable of resisting difficult questioning.

Teg and Sheeana were taken to a holding tent made of a tough, weather-worn polymer. The structure was an odd mixture of primitive design and sophisticated technology, made for serviceability and ease of transport. The guard closed the flap but remained outside.

The windowless tent was just an empty enclosure, devoid of blankets, cushions, or tools of any kind. Teg paced in a small circle, then sat beside her on the packed dirt. Digging with his fingers, he quickly found a couple of sharp pebbles.

With Mentat clarity, he assessed their options. 'When we do not return or report in,' he said in a low voice, 'we can expect Duncan to send another party down. He will be prepared. It sounds trite, but rescue will come.' He knew that these nomads would crumble easily against a direct military assault. 'Duncan is wise, and I trained him well. He will know what to do.'

Sheeana stared at the door as if in meditative trance. 'Duncan has lived hundreds of lives and remembers them all, Miles. I doubt you taught him anything new.'

Teg gripped one of the pebbles, and it seemed to aid his concentration. Even in an empty tent, he saw a thousand possible avenues of escape. He and Sheeana could easily break out, kill the guard, and fight their way back to the lighter. Teg might not even need to take advantage of his accelerated speed. 'These people are no match for me, or for you. But I will not leave Stilgar and Liet behind.'

'Ah, the loyal Bashar.'

'I wouldn't leave you, either. However, I fear that these people have disabled our ship, which would certainly tangle our escape plans. I heard them ransacking it.'

Sheeana continued to stare at the shadowy wall of the tent. 'Miles, I'm not so concerned about the possibility of escape as I am curious to learn why they kept us alive. Especially me, if what they said about the Sisterhood is true. They have good reason to hate me.'

Teg tried to imagine the incredible exodus and reorganization of populations on this planet. Within years, all the inhabitants of the towns and cities would have seen the sands strangling their croplands, killing their orchards, creeping closer and closer to the city boundaries. They would have pulled away from the desert zone like people fleeing a slowly advancing fire.

Var's nomads, though . . . were they scavengers and misfits? Outcasts from the larger population centers? Why insist on staying at the threshold of the advancing desert, where they would have to uproot their settlement and retreat constantly? To what purpose?

These were technologically capable people, and Qelso clearly must have been settled long ago during the Scattering. They had their own groundcars and low-altitude flyers, fast ships to take them back and forth across the dunes. If they weren't outright exiles, perhaps Var's people replenished their supplies in the distant northern cities.

Teg and Sheeana hardly spoke for hours as they listened to the muffled sounds outside, the dry wind pushing and tugging at the tent, the *scritch* of blowing sand. Everything seemed to be comprised of movement outside: The people sent out parties, marched back and forth, set machinery to work.

As Teg listened to the noises, he catalogued them in his mind, building a picture of the operations. He heard a pounding drill that bored a well shaft, followed by a pump dispensing water into small cisterns. Each time, after only a brief gush of liquid, the flow dwindled to less than a trickle and stopped. He knew that such problems, caused by sandtrout, had been the bane of drilling operations on Arrakis. Water existed in deep enough strata, but it was blocked off by the voracious little Makers. Like platelets at the site of a wound, sandtrout would swiftly seal off the leak. As he listened to the resigned complaints of these people, Teg realized that they were familiar with the routine.

When night fell, a dusty young man entered the tent through the flap held open by the guard. He delivered a small meal of hard bread and dried fruit, as well as gamey-tasting white meat. The two captives also received carefully measured rations of water.

Sheeana looked at her sealed cup. 'They are learning the fundamentals of extreme conservation. They begin to understand what their world will become.' Obviously despising her Bene Gesserit robes, the young man glared at her and departed without a word.

Throughout the dark night, Teg remained awake, listening, trying to plan. The lack of activity was maddening, but he advised patience rather than rash action. They had heard nothing from Liet or Stilgar, and he feared the two young men might already be dead, like Stuka. Had they been killed during interrogation?

Sheeana sat beside him, in a heightened state of alertness. Her eyes were bright even in the tent shadows. As far as Teg could tell, the guard outside never stepped away from his position, never even moved. The people continued to send out parties and skimmer ships throughout the night, as if the camp were the staging area for a war effort.

At dawn, old Var came up to the tent, spoke briskly with the guard, and pulled the flap aside. Sheeana rose to a half crouch, ready to spring; Teg tensed, also prepared for a fight.

The nomad leader glared at Sheeana. 'You and your witches are not forgiven for what you have done to Qelso. You never will be. But Liet-Kynes and Stilgar have convinced us to keep you alive, at least as long as we can learn from you.'

The weathered leader brought the pair out into the bright sunlight. The wind flung stinging sand into their eyes. All around the settlement, trees had already died. The blowing dunes had encroached another few feet past the prominent rock outcroppings during the night. Each breath was crackling dry, even in the relative coolness of the morning.

'You put the other Bene Gesserits to death,' Sheeana said, 'and killed our companion Stuka. Am I next?'

'No. Because I said I would keep you alive.'

The weathered man led them through the settlement. Workers were already disassembling large warehouse tents to move them farther from the edge of the sand. A heavy groundcar rumbled by, full of crates. A bloated flyer circled and landed near the smooth sand. Some kind of tanker?

Var led them to a large central building made from sectional metal walls and a conical roof. Inside, a long table was cluttered with charts. Reports were fastened to the walls, and one entire wall displayed a polymer-paper map, a high-resolution topographic projection of the entire continent. Mark after mark showed the steady growth of the desert belt.

Men sat around the table sharing reports and raising their voices in a tumult of conversation. Stilgar and Liet-Kynes, both dressed in dusty shipsuits, waved a greeting at the other two prisoners. The young men seemed pleased and relaxed.

As he scanned the setup, it was obvious to Teg that Stilgar and Liet had spent the whole previous day in the command tent. The old leader positioned himself between them, leaving Teg and Sheeana to stand.

Var pounded on the table, interrupting the cacophony.

Everyone stopped talking, impatiently it seemed, and stared at him. 'We have listened to our new friends describe what our world is sure to become. We've all heard legends of long-lost Dune, where water is more precious than blood.' His face had a pinched look. 'If we fail and the worms take over, our planet will become valuable only by the standards of outsiders.'

One of the men snarled at Sheeana, 'Damned Bene Gesserits!' The others glared at her as well, and she met their disapproval squarely, without comment.

Liet and Stilgar seemed to be in their element. Teg recalled the Bene Gesserit discussions over the original ghola project, how the long-forgotten abilities of those historical personages might become relevant again. Here was a perfect example. This duo of prominent survivors from the old days of Arrakis certainly knew how to deal with the crisis these people now faced.

The grizzled leader raised his hands, and his voice sounded as dry as the air. 'After the death of the Tyrant long ago, my people fled into the Scattering. When they reached Qelso, they thought they had found Eden. It was a paradise for fifteen hundred years afterward.'

The men glowered at Sheeana. Var explained how the refugees had established a thriving society, built cities, planted crops, mined for metals and minerals. They had no wish to overextend themselves or go searching for other lost brothers who had escaped during the Famine Times.

'Then a few decades ago everything changed. Visitors came, Bene Gesserits. At first we welcomed them, glad to have news from the outside. We offered them a new home. They became our guests. But the ingrates raped our entire planet, and now it is dying.'

Another man clenched his hands into fists as he picked up the story. 'The sandtrout multiplied out of control. Huge forests and vast plains died within years – only a few years! Great fires started in the wastelands, and weather patterns changed, turning much of our world into a dust bowl.'

Teg spoke up, using his command voice. 'If Liet and Stilgar told you about our no-ship and its mission, then you know we don't carry sandtrout and we have no intention of harming your world. We stopped here only to replenish vital supplies.'

'In fact, we fled the heart of the Bene Gesserit order because we disagreed with the policies and leadership,' Sheeana added.

'You have seven large sandworms in your hold,' Var accused.

'Yes, and we will not release them here.'

Liet-Kynes spoke quietly, as if lecturing children. 'As we already told you, once it has begun, the desertification process is a chain reaction. The sandtrout have no natural enemies, and their encysting of water is so swift that nothing can adapt quickly enough to fight against them.'

'Nevertheless, we will fight,' Var said. 'You see how simply we live in this camp. We have given up everything to stay here.'

'But why?' Sheeana asked. 'Even as the desert spreads, you have many years to prepare.'

'Prepare? Do you mean surrender? You may call it a hopeless fight, but it is still a *fight*. If we cannot stop the desert, we will at least slow it. We'll battle the worms and the sands.' The men at the table muttered. 'No matter what you say, we will try to hinder the desert's progress in every way. We kill sandtrout, we hunt the new worms.' Var stood up, and the others followed suit. 'We are commandos sworn to slow the death of our world.'

The desert still calls me. It sings in my blood like a love song.

— LIET-KYNES,
Planetology: New Treatises

Early the next morning, Var led his group of dusty, determined fighters to a landing zone of fire-baked pavement. 'Today, my new friends, we'll show you how to kill a worm. Maybe two.'

'Shai-Hulud,' Stilgar said with great uneasiness. 'Fremen used to worship the great worms.'

'Fremen depended upon the worms and the spice,' Liet replied quietly. 'These people do not.'

'With each demon we eliminate, we give our planet a little more time to survive.' Var stared out into the desert as if his hatred could drive back the sands. Stilgar followed the man's gaze across the deeply shadowed dunes, trying to imagine the landscape in front of him as lush and green.

The sun was just rising over an escarpment, glinting off the silvery hull of an old low-altitude flyer parked on an area of pounded gravel and flash-fused cement. Var's people did not bother with permanent landing strips or spaceport zones, which would only be swallowed up by the spreading dunes.

Despite the protests of the two young men, Sheeana and Teg were forced to remain behind in the camp as hostages, watched suspiciously. Liet and Stilgar had been accepted on the hunt because of their invaluable knowledge of the desert. Today, they would demonstrate their skills.

Var's commandos clambered into the heavily used craft. It had obviously weathered countless storms, rough flights, and incomplete maintenance; its hull was scuffed and scraped. The interior smelled of oil and sweat, and the seats were stone-hard, with only bars or straps for the passengers to hold onto.

Stilgar felt comfortable enough among the twenty weathered, grim men. To his trained eye, the commandos had a look of edgy anticipation, but they were too soft in the flesh for the adaptations they would soon face. With the rapid climate shift, even living in their nomadic camps at the fringe of the sand, these people remained unaware of the desert's true harshness. They would have to learn swiftly enough to face the escalating hardships. He and his friend could teach them – if they would listen.

Liet took his seat beside Stilgar and spoke to Var's men with genuine enthusiasm. 'Right now, Qelso's air still contains enough moisture that truly dramatic measures aren't required. Soon, though, you will need to be careful not to waste so much as a thimbleful of water.'

'We already live under the strictest conservation,' one man said, as if Liet had insulted him.

'Oh? You don't recycle your sweat, respiration, or urine. You still import water from the higher latitudes, where it is readily available. Many regions on Qelso are still able to grow crops, and people live a fairly normal life.'

'It will get worse,' Stilgar agreed. 'Your people have

much hardening to do before the planet reaches its new equilibrium. This is the first day of your new field training.'

The men muttered uncertainly at hearing such words from two seeming boys, but Liet sounded optimistic. 'It is not so bad. We can teach you how to make stillsuits, how to conserve every breath, every sweat droplet. Your fighting instincts are admirable, but useless against sand-worms. You must learn to survive among the behemoths that will eventually take control of your world. It is a necessary shift in attitude.'

'The Fremen did so for a long time.' Stilgar seated himself beside his friend. 'It was an honorable way of life.'

The fighters held onto straps and spread their feet for balance, preparing for takeoff. 'That is what lies in store for us? Drinking recycled sweat and piss? Living in sealed chambers?'

'Only if we fail,' old Var said. 'I choose to believe we still have a chance, no matter how naïve that sounds.' He closed the ship's hatch and strapped himself into the creaking pilot seat. 'So, if that doesn't sound pleasant to you, then we'd better stop the desert from gaining more of a foothold.'

The flyer lifted from the dry camp and swung out over the ghost forests and hummocks of fresh dunes that were swallowing the remnants of grasslands. The engine sput-tered periodically as they flew southeast to a region where sandworms had been sighted. The craft seemed like a sluggish bumblebee, its tanks overloaded and heavy.

'We will stop the moving sands,' one young commando said.

'Next you will try to stop the wind.' Stilgar grabbed a dangling strap as a thermal updraft shook the craft. 'In a few short years, your planet will be sand and rock. Do you expect a miracle to turn the desert back?'

'We'll create that miracle for ourselves,' Var answered, and his team murmured in agreement.

They flew across the wilderness of dunes, far past the point where they could see anything but buttery tan from horizon to horizon. Stilgar tapped a finger against the scratched windowplaz and shouted against the engine noise. 'See the desert for what it is – not a place to fear and loathe, but a great engine to power an empire.'

Liet added, 'Already, small worms in the desert belt have created priceless amounts of melange just waiting to be mined. How have you survived for so long without spice?'

'We haven't needed spice for fifteen hundred years, not since we came to Qelso,' Var called from the cockpit. 'When you do not have a thing, you learn to live without it, or you don't live.'

'We don't give a damn about spice,' one of the commandos said. 'I'd rather give a damn about trees and crops and fat herds.'

Var continued, 'Our first settlers brought a great deal of spice from far away, and three generations fought addiction until the supplies were gone. Then what? We were forced to survive without it – and we have. Why should we open ourselves to that monstrous dependency again? My people are better off without it.'

'If used carefully, melange has important qualities,' Liet said. 'Health, life extension, the possibility of prescience. And it's a valuable commodity to sell, should you ever reconnect with CHOAM and the rest of mankind. As Qelso dries up, you may need offworld supplies for your basic needs.'

If anyone survives the outside Enemy, Stilgar thought to himself, recalling the ever-present threat of capture by the shimmering net. But these people were much more concerned with their own local enemies, fighting the desert, trying to stop the unstoppable.

He remembered the great dreams of Pardot Kynes, Liet's father. Pardot had done the calculations and determined that the Fremen could turn Dune into a garden, but only after generations of intense effort. According to the histories, Arrakis had indeed become green and verdant for a time, before the new worms reclaimed it, and brought the desert back. The planet seemed unable to achieve a balance.

The battered craft flew low, its engines droning. Stilgar wondered if the noise of their passage would attract worms, but as he stared down at the hypnotic, oceanic dunes, he saw only a couple of patches of rust-colored sand that indicated fresh spice blows.

'Dropping signal vibrators,' Var called, while throbbing canisters – the equivalent of ancient thumpers – tumbled out of the small bays below the cockpit. 'That should bring at least one of them.'

With a puff of sand and dust the thumpers plunged into the dunes and sent out droning signals. After circling back to make certain the devices were operating properly, Var selected two more spots within a radius of five kilometers. Stilgar could not determine why the craft still felt overloaded.

As they cruised in search of a worm, Stilgar described his legendary days on Dune, how he and Paul Muad'Dib had led a ragtag Fremen army to victory against far superior forces. 'We used desert power. That is what you can learn from us. Once you see we are not your enemies, we can learn much from each other.'

Under Stilgar's firm hand, these people could come to understand their possibilities. With the awakening of the populace would come the awakening of the planet, with plantings and green zones to keep the desert under control. Perhaps they could succeed, if they could just find – and maintain – an equilibrium.

Stilgar remembered something Liet's father had said to him once. *Extremes invariably lead to disaster. Only through balance can we fully harvest the fruits of nature.* He leaned closer to the craft's observation windows and saw a familiar wrinkling of the sand, ripples of deep movement disturbing the smooth dunes. 'Wormsign!'

'Prepare for our first encounter of the day.' A grin wrinkled Var's grizzled face as he turned away from the cockpit. 'The shipment that came in last night brought us enough water for two targets – but we need to find them.'

Water! The heavy ship was carrying water.

The men shifted position, heading toward gunnery hatches and hoses mounted on the sides of the stripped-down flyer. The pilot banked back toward the first cluster of thumpers.

As the commandos prepared to strike, Stilgar mused about the strange turnabout. Pardot Kynes had spoken of the need to understand ecological consequences, that humans were stewards of the land, and never owners. *We must do a thing on Arrakis never before attempted for an entire planet. We must use man as a constructive ecological force – inserting adapted terraform life: a plant here, an animal there, a man in that place – to transform the water cycle, to build a new kind of landscape.*

The battle today was the opposite. Stilgar and Liet would help fight to prevent the desert from swallowing all of Qelso.

Through the nearest window Stilgar saw a mound in motion, a bucking sandworm drawn toward the thumper. Liet crowded close beside him, and said, 'I estimate it at forty meters. Larger than Sheeana's worms in our hold.'

'These have grown in the open desert,' Stilgar said. 'Shai-Hulud wants this planet.'

'Not if I can help it,' Var said. But as if to defy him, directly below the flyer an immense head surfaced and quested around, trying to track the conflicting sources of vibrations.

Long tubes protruded from the front and rear of the flyer. The commandos gripped their gun mountings, nozzles that could be turned and aimed. The flyer swooped low. 'Fire when ready, but conserve what you can. The water's deadly enough.'

The fighters shot high-pressure streams from their hoses, blasting the sandworm below. The drenching bursts were more effective than artillery shells.

Taken by surprise, the creature writhed and twisted its round head back and forth, convulsing. Hard ring segments split apart to reveal softer pink flesh between, and water burned like acid into the vulnerable parts. The worm rolled on the wet sand, in obvious agony.

'They are killing Shai-Hulud,' Stilgar said, sickened.

Liet was also stunned, but said, 'These people have to defend themselves.'

'That's enough! It is dead – or soon will be,' Var shouted. The small force reluctantly shut off their hoses, looking with hatred upon the dying worm. Unable to dig deep enough to escape the poisonous moisture, the mortally wounded creature continued to squirm as the flyer circled over its death throes. Finally the beast gave a great final shudder and stopped moving.

Stilgar nodded, his expression still grim. 'There are necessities to life in the desert, hard decisions to be made.' He had to accept the clear fact that this worm did not belong here on Qelso. No sandworm did. On the way back to the settlement, they encountered a second worm, drawn by the vibrations of their flyer's engines. The commandos emptied their water reservoirs, and the second worm perished even more quickly.

Liet and Stilgar sat together in uncomfortable silence, wrapped up in what they had seen and the fight they had agreed to join. 'Even though she doesn't have her memories back yet,' Liet said, 'I'm glad my daughter Chani did not see this.'

Though the mood of the fighters was upbeat aboard the flyer, the two young men, remembering Arrakis, murmured Fremen prayers. Stilgar was still contemplating what they had seen and done when Var yelled a strangled-sounding alarm.

Suddenly strange ships swarmed around them.

You see only harshness, devastation, and ugliness. That is because you have no faith. Around me I see a potential paradise, for Rakis is the birthplace of my beloved Prophet.

— WAFF of the Tleilaxu

When he first glimpsed Rakis, the bleak ruins brought dismay to Waff's heart. But when Edrik's Heighliner deposited him and his small team of Guild assistants there, he experienced the joy of setting foot on the desert planet again. He could feel the holy calling deep inside his bones.

In his previous lifetime he had stood on these sands, face to face with the Prophet. With Sheeana and Reverend Mother Odrade, he had ridden a great worm out to the ruins of Sietch Tabr. His ghola memories were corrupted and uncertain, riddled with annoying gaps. Waff could not recall his final moments as the whores closed in around the desert planet, deploying their awful Obliterators. Had he run for hopeless shelter, looking behind him like Lot's wife for a last glimpse of the doomed city? Had he seen explosions and walls of flame searing the sky, sweeping toward him?

But the cells of another Waff ghola had been grown in an axlotl tank in Bandalong as part of the usual process.

The secret council of the kehl had planned for the serial immortality of all Tleilaxu Masters long before anyone had heard of Honored Matres. The next thing he knew, Waff was awakened to his past life during a grand guignol stage show as the brutal women murdered one of his twins after another until just one of them – him – reached a sufficiently desperate crisis to break through the ghola barrier and reveal his past. Some of it, at least.

But not until now had Waff actually seen the Armageddon that the whores had wrought on this sacred world.

The ecosystem of Rakis had been fundamentally destroyed. Half of the atmosphere was burned away, the ground sterilized, most life forms dead – from the microscopic sandplankton all the way up to the giant sandworms. It made the old Dune seem comfortable by comparison.

The sky was a dark purple, touched with an underburn of orange. As their ship circled, searching for a spot less hellish than others, Waff studied a panel of atmospheric readings. The moisture content was abnormally high. At some point in its geologic history, Arrakis had possessed open water, but sandtrout had sealed it all away. During the bombardment, underground rivers and seas must have been vaporized as they were released from aquifers.

The Honored Matres' horrific weapons had not only turned the soft dunes to a baked moonscape, they had also thrown up great clouds of dust that had not settled entirely out of the atmosphere, even decades later. The Coriolis storms would be worse than ever before.

He and his team would likely have to wear special bodily protection and supplemental breather masks; their small dwelling huts would need to be sealed and pressurized. Waff didn't mind. Was that so different from

wearing a stillsuit? By degrees, perhaps, but not fundamentally harder.

His lighter circled over the remains of a sprawling
metropolis that had been called Arrakeen in the days of
Muad'Dib, then the Festival City of Onn during the reign
of the God Emperor, and later – after Leto II's death –
the moated city of Keen. No longer concerned about
secrecy, now that the seaworms had successfully taken
hold on Buzzell, Waff was happy to have four assistants
help him with the hard work he was sure to face on this
Obliterator-blasted planet.

Studying the surface, he discerned lumpy geometric
shapes that had once been angled streets and tall buildings. Surprisingly, in the dimness of seared daylight, he
also spotted numerous artificial illumination sources and
a few dark structures of recent construction. 'There seems
to be a camp down there. Who else would come to Rakis?
What could they possibly want here?'

'The same as us,' said the Guildsman. 'Spice.'

He shook his head. 'Too little here anymore, at least
until we bring back the worms. No one else has that skill.'

'Pilgrims perhaps? There may still be those who make
a hajj,' a second assistant said. Waff knew that a dizzying
mishmash of religious splinter groups and cults had
sprung from Rakis.

'More likely,' suggested a third Guildsman, 'they are
treasure hunters.'

Waff quoted quietly from the Cant of the Shariat:
' "When greed and desperation are coupled, men accomplish superhuman feats – though for the wrong reasons." '

He considered choosing a different place for their base
camp, then accepted the idea that joining resources with
the strangers might help them all last longer in the harsh

environment. No one knew when – or if – Edrik might be coming back for them, or how long the sandworm work would take, or how much longer Waff himself would last. He planned to be here for the remainder of his days.

After the lighter landed unannounced at the edge of the camp, the Guildsmen waited for instructions from Waff. The Tleilaxu man settled goggles over his eyes to protect against the caustic wind, and emerged. For long journeys outside, he might have to wear a supplemental oxygen mask, but the Rakian atmosphere was surprisingly breathable.

Six tall and dirty men faced him from the encampment. They wore rags wrapped around their heads, carried knives and antique maula pistols. Their eyes were redveined, their skin rough and cracked. The foremost man had shaggy black hair, a square chest, and a rock-hard potbelly. 'You are fortunate that I'm curious about why you are here. Otherwise, we would've shot you out of the sky.'

Waff held up his hands. 'We are no threat to you, whoever you are.'

Five men leveled their maula pistols, and the other slashed the air with his knife. 'We have claimed Rakis for ourselves. All spice here is ours.'

'You've claimed a whole planet?'

'Yes, the whole damned planet.' The first man tossed back his dark hair. 'I'm Guriff, and these are my prospectors. There's damned little spice left in the burned crust, and it's ours.'

'Then you may have it.' Waff performed a perfunctory bow. 'We have other interests, as geological investigators and archaeologists. We wish to take readings and run tests to determine the extent of damage to the ecosystem.' The four Guild assistants waited beside him in complete silence.

Guriff laughed loudly and heartily. 'There isn't much of an ecosystem left here.'

'Then where does breathable oxygen come from?' He knew that Liet-Kynes had asked that question in the ancient days, curious because the planet had neither widespread plant life nor volcanoes to generate an atmosphere.

The man just stared. Obviously, he had not thought about this. 'Do I look like a planetologist to you? Go ahead and look into it, but don't expect any help from us. Here on Rakis, you are self-sufficient or you die.'

The Tleilaxu man raised his eyebrows. 'And what if we wish to share some of our spice coffee with you, as a token of friendship? I understand that water is more easily obtainable than in the old days.'

Guriff glanced at his prospectors, then said, 'We're happy to accept your hospitality, but we have no intention of reciprocating.'

'Nonetheless, our offer stands.'

INSIDE GURIFF'S DUSTY hut, Waff used his own supplies of melange (left over from his sandworm experiments) to brew coffee. Guriff didn't have a desperate shortage of water in his camp, though his dwelling smelled of long-unwashed bodies and the savory sweetness of a drug smoke that Waff could not identify.

At his command, the four Guildsmen erected the shelters brought down from the Heighliner, setting up armored sleeping tents and laboratory enclosures. Waff saw no reason to assist them. He was a Tleilaxu Master after all, and these were his workers, so he would allow them to perform their tasks.

While they drank a second pot of spice coffee, Guriff grew more relaxed. He didn't trust the diminutive Tleilaxu, but he didn't seem to trust anyone. He took pains to say he harbored no particular hatred toward Waff's race, and that his scavengers held no grudges against others of low social position. Guriff cared only about Rakis.

'All that melted sand and plascrete. By chipping away the upper crust of glass, we were able to get down to the foundations of the sturdier buildings in Keen.' Guriff produced a hand-drawn chart. 'Scraping out buried treasure. We found what we think is the original Bene Gesserit Keep – a few heavily barricaded bomb shelters filled with skeletons.' He smiled. 'We also uncovered the extravagant temple built by the Priests of the Divided God. It was so huge we couldn't miss it. Full of trinkets, but still not enough to pay for our effort. CHOAM is expecting us to find something much more extraordinary, though they seem happy enough to sell containers of "genuine Rakian sand" to gullible fools.'

Waff didn't reply. Edrik and the Navigators had obtained such Rakian sand for him to use in his original experiments.

'But we've got a lot more digging to do. Keen was a big city.'

In his previous life, Waff had seen those structures before they were destroyed. He knew the ostentation that the deluded Priests placed in all the rooms and towers (as if God cared about such gaudiness!). Guriff and his men would indeed find plenty of treasure there. But the wrong kind.

'The Priesthood's temple had collapsed worse than most other large buildings. Maybe it was a direct target of the Honored Matre attack.' The prospector smiled with thick lips. 'But deep in the sublevels beneath the temple, we did find chests of stored solaris and hoarded melange. A worthwhile haul. More than we expected, but not so much. We're after something bigger. The Tyrant buried a huge spice hoard deep in the southern polar regions – I'm sure of it.'

Waff made a skeptical sound as he sipped spice coffee. 'No one has been able to find that treasure for fifteen hundred years.'

Guriff held up a finger, noticed a hangnail, and chewed on it. 'Still, the bombardment may have churned up the crust enough to reveal the mother lode. And, thanks be to the gods – there are no worms left to torment us.'

Waff made a noncommittal sound. *Not yet.*

WITHOUT BOTHERING TO sleep, knowing his time was short, the Tleilaxu man began to make preparations to continue his work. His Guild companions seemed confident that the Navigator would eventually return, though Waff wasn't so sure. He was here on Rakis, and this gave him great pleasure.

While the Guild assistants finished connecting the generators and sealed the prefab shelters, the Tleilaxu researcher went back aboard the near-empty lighter. In the cargo hold he smiled paternally at his magnificent specimens. The armored worms were small but ferocious. They looked ready to tackle a dead world. *Their* world.

Ages ago, the Fremen had been able to summon and ride sandworms, but those original creatures had died out when Leto II's terraforming operations had turned Arrakis into a garden world with green plants, flowing rivers, and moisture from the sky. Such an environment was fatal to sandworms. But when the God Emperor was assassinated and his body fissioned into sandtrout, the whole process of desertification began anew. The freshly spawned worms became far more vicious than their predecessors, tackling the huge challenge of recreating the Dune That Once Was.

Waff now faced a challenge many times more difficult. His modified creatures were armored to resist the most severe environment, with mouths and head ridges powerful enough to crack through the vitrified dunes. They could dig deep beneath the black surface; they could grow and reproduce – even here.

He stood before the dusty holding tank in which the worms churned. Each specimen was about two meters in length. And strong.

Sensing his presence, the creatures twitched restlessly. Waff looked outside to where the sky had turned the deep purple-brown of dusk. Storms swirled gritty dust through the atmosphere. 'Be patient, my pets,' he said. 'Soon I will release you.'

We are naïve to think that we control a precious commodity. Only through guile and eternal wariness do we keep it out of the hands of our competitors.

– Spacing Guild internal report

Edrik moved his Heighliner away from the ruins of Rakis, no longer concerned with the Tleilaxu Master. Waff had served his purpose.

More important, the Oracle of Time had summoned all surviving Navigators, and Edrik would give them joyous news. With the seaworms obviously thriving on Buzzell, there would be plenty of ultraspice for the taking. The unusual concentrated form might even be superior to the original spice: a frighteningly potent melange to keep Navigators alive without the meddling, greedy Administrator faction or the witches of Chapterhouse.

Freedom!

It had amused him to see Waff taking his worm samples to Rakis, hoping to establish a new spice cycle. Edrik didn't think the little researcher could do much there, but an alternative source of melange would be a bonus. But even without that, never again would the Navigators be strangled by power games. The four Guildsmen whom Edrik had sent to accompany Waff were spies and would secretly report everything the Tleilaxu achieved.

Inside his tank, Edrik smiled to himself, pleased that he had thought of all eventualities. With the first package of Buzzell ultraspice safely stored in his security chamber, the Navigator guided his Heighliner out into the emptiness of space. Even the Oracle would congratulate him for this remarkable news.

Before he could travel toward his scheduled rendezvous, however, the emptiness rippled around him. When Edrik studied the distortions, he realized what they were. Moments later, scores of Guildships appeared like buckshot in space, winking through foldspace and emerging forward and back, above and below, to surround his Heighliner completely.

Edrik transmitted on a band that only fellow Navigators should have received. 'Explain your presence.'

But none of the imposing newcomers answered. Studying the glyphs and cartouches on the sides of the enormous hulls, he realized that these were new Guildships, guided by Ixian mathematical compilers.

The computer-controlled vessels closed in. Sensing the threat, Edrik transmitted with greater alarm, 'What is your justification?'

The other Guildships formed a smothering blanket around his Heighliner. The silence of the great vessels was more intimidating than any voiced ultimatum. Their proximity distorted his Holtzman fields, preventing him from folding space.

Finally a voice spoke, flat and dull in timbre, yet unnervingly confident. 'We require your cargo of seaworm spice. We will board your ship for inspection.'

Edrik assessed these enemies, his mind racing through

a labyrinth of possibilities. The ships appeared to belong to the Administrator faction. They functioned with Ixian devices, so they had no need for Navigators or melange. Why then would they want to confiscate the ultraspice? To prevent Navigators from having it? To ensure the Guild's complete reliance on Ixian navigation machines?

Or could this be another foe entirely? Were these ships flown by CHOAM pirates hoping to seize a valuable new asset? Witches from Chapterhouse wanting to force continued dependence on the Sisterhood's melange?

But how would any outsiders know about the ultraspice?

While Edrik's Heighliner hung helpless in space, small interdiction ships emerged from the surrounding Guild vessels. He had no choice but to allow boarders onto his ship.

Though Edrik did not recognize him, a man wearing appropriate Guild insignia marched along the decks and ascended to the restricted level, brushing aside all security barriers. Six well-muscled men accompanied him. The leader smiled condescendingly when he stood before the Navigator's tank and looked into it. 'Your new spice has fascinating possibilities. We require it from you.'

Edrik boomed from within his chamber, intentionally amplifying the speaker system. 'Go to Buzzell and obtain your own.'

'This is not a request,' said the man, his face bland. 'We have learned the intensity of this substance and believe it to be a remedy for our difficult situation. We will take it to the heart of the thinking-machine empire.'

Thinking machines? What did the Administrator faction have to do with the Enemy? 'You may not have it,' Edrik repeated, as if he had any say in the matter.

The bland-faced Guildsman gestured to his burly bodyguards, and they withdrew iron-tipped hammers from their slick gray robes. The leader gave them a calm, matter-of-fact nod.

Panicked, Edrik swam backward in his tank, but he had nowhere to go. The muscular bodyguards did not care that he was inside the container or that exposure to the air would kill him. With thick arms, they swung their heavy sledges and smashed the thick plaz walls.

Jagged cracks split out in starburst patterns, and concentrated orange spice gas whistled out through the breaches. The guards did not react to the melange streaming into their faces, though the concentration should have made a normal human reel. Their bland-faced leader watched like a man smelling an approaching storm while Edrik's atmosphere drained out.

When the air pressure was no longer sufficient to buoy him, the Navigator collapsed to the floor of his tank. Weakly, he raised his webbed hands and demanded answers in a voice that was little more than a gasp. The Guildsman and his companions offered no explanations.

Withering and twitching, Edrik lay on the floor. He extended a rubbery arm and tried to crawl, but with all the spice gas draining away, the air was too thin. He could no longer breathe, could hardly move. Even so, the Navigator was slow to die.

The bland-faced man stepped closer to the shattered wall, and his features metamorphosed. Khrone said to his Face Dancer companions, 'Take the concentrated spice. With this substance, Omnius will awaken his Kwisatz Haderach.'

The others departed to search the decks and soon uncovered the hoard of modified melange. When the disguised guards returned to the interdiction ships, Khrone held one of the heavy packages in his arms. He inhaled deeply. 'Excellent. Remove all of our people from this Heighliner. When we are safe, destroy the ship and everyone aboard it.'

He looked coolly down at the dying Edrik. Only a few rusty curls of gas continued to ooze from cracks in the tank. 'You have served your purpose, Navigator. Take solace in that.' The Face Dancer strutted away.

Edrik continued to heave great breaths, but barely a scent of melange remained. By the time the computer-controlled Guildships got into formation in space, he could barely keep from slumping into unconsciousness.

The opposing vessels opened fire. Edrik's Heighliner exploded before he could utter a curse.

There is an art to legend-telling, and an art to living the legend.

— a saying of Ancient Kaitain

The *Ithaca*'s replenishing operations had taken place in the still-rich northern latitudes, far from any visible population centers. Garimi managed the complex process with dozens of flying craft from the hangar decks, leaving Duncan on the command bridge. He felt trapped there, unable to leave because of the protective veil that the no-ship usually afforded him. He hated having to remain behind while others did the risky work . . . and he didn't even know what the old man and woman wanted from him.

He had no idea what was going on back in the Old Empire, with Murbella and Chapterhouse. He knew only that the Enemy was still searching for him – and he was still hiding, as he had been for decades. Was this truly the best way to fight, the best way to defend humanity? He had been adrift for as long as the *Ithaca*, and of late, the waters of uncertainty seemed deeper than ever.

It had been two days now without word from Teg or Sheeana and their team. If their group was simply meeting with the natives, someone should have checked in by now.

Duncan feared another trap like the one they had encountered on the planet of the Handlers.

Miles Teg had been his mentor and his student, and Sheeana . . . ah, Sheeana. They had been lovers and sexual opponents. She had cured him and saved him, so of course he cared for her. He had tried to protect himself by denying it, but she hadn't believed him, and he hadn't believed himself. Both knew they had a bond unlike any other, different from the one he and Murbella had imposed upon one another.

As he studied the landscape below, it seemed to call to him. Many cities were discernible in the northern and southern forested latitudes. He felt he should be down there facing any possible dangers with the others, not stuck aboard the *Ithaca*, forced to remain safe and out of sight.

How long am I supposed to wait?

When he was Swordmaster of House Atreides he would never have hesitated. If it had been young Paul Atreides under threat, Duncan would have leapt in to fight for him, ignoring the intangible threat of the old man and woman. As the witches said in their oft-quoted Litany, *I will face my fear.* And it was about time he did so.

He closed his eyes, not wanting to see the spreading desert that looked like a seeping knife wound across the continent. 'I will not ignore this.' Duncan summoned Thufir Hawat as well as Garimi, who had recently returned to the no-ship with all of her flying craft after reloading the *Ithaca's* stores.

Duncan stood when they arrived. 'We are going to rescue the landing party,' he announced, 'and we're going to do it now. I don't know what kind of military force those people have down there, but we'll stand against it if the Bashar is in trouble.'

Thufir's eyes brightened and his face flushed. 'I'll pilot one of the ships.'

Duncan remained stern. 'No, you will follow my orders.'

Garimi was taken aback by Duncan's bold comment, but nodded as she heard him rebuke Thufir. 'Do you have instructions for us before we depart? Shall I command the mission?'

'No – I will do it personally.' Before either could argue with him, Duncan strode toward the lift, and they were forced to follow him. 'I'm sick of hiding. My plan has been to run and remain unobtrusive, staying one step ahead of that strange net. But in doing so, I've left too much of myself behind. I am *Duncan Idaho*.' He raised his voice as they entered the lift. 'I was Swordmaster of House Atreides and consort of St Alia of the Knife. I acted as advisor and companion to the God Emperor. If the Enemy is out there, I won't leave the rest of humanity to face it themselves. If Sheeana and the Bashar need my help, then I'm going to help.'

Thufir stiffened, then allowed himself a pleased smile. 'You should have left the *Ithaca* long ago, Duncan. I don't see what you've accomplished by staying here. The no-field hasn't exactly offered perfect protection.'

Garimi seemed pleased by Duncan's attitude. 'My recovery teams took a good look at that planet down there, and it seems a fine place to settle. Does that mean you'll stop opposing my efforts and let us form a colony at last?'

The lift doors closed, and the group began to drop toward the hangar decks where the many ships were being refueled. 'That remains to be seen.'

TEG BIDED HIS time in the camp long after Stilgar and Liet flew off into the early morning. By now, Duncan would certainly have drawn the obvious conclusions.

'Do you think they'll kill us, after all?' Sheeana's tone was surprisingly matter-of-fact, as if she had accepted the inevitable.

'Maybe just you. You're the one they blame.' He spoke without humor. Though they were allowed to sit on the ground outside, their captors still watched them closely.

She sipped from a small cup of water that had been provided. 'Is that a joke?'

'A distraction.' Teg glanced up at the sky. 'We have to trust Duncan to decide on the correct response.'

'Maybe he thinks we can handle this ourselves. Duncan has great confidence in our independent abilities.'

'As do I. Should it become necessary, I could slaughter every one of these people.' He chose the word intentionally. *Slaughter.* As he had done with the Honored Matres in their fortress on Gammu. 'And it would take me no longer than the blink of an eye. You know it.'

Sheeana had seen him move against the Handlers, helping her, Thufir, and the Rabbi escape, and she had also seen how much that brief burst of energy had drained him. 'Yes, I know, Miles. And I pray it doesn't become necessary.'

Off in the distance they heard the whining drone of the small flyer returning from the desert. Teg's sharply attuned ears recognized its sputtering engine sound. The villagers gathered at the packed landing zone, anxious to receive the hunting party. First, two specks appeared in the sky, flying low; then they were joined by many more dots, like a dispersed flock of migrating birds. The drone grew to a roar.

Teg shaded his eyes, identifying many of the flying craft. 'Mining shuttles and lighters from the no-ship. So this is how Duncan plans to rescue us. He's trying to impress them. It appears he sent everything we have.'

'We certainly have superior firepower. Duncan could have taken the direct method and rescued us by force of arms.'

Watching the ships come closer, Teg smiled. 'He's smarter than that. Like me, he wants to avoid bloodshed, especially in a conflict he doesn't entirely understand.' *Did I teach him that lesson, or did he teach me?* As the Bashar reflected on their past lives, he didn't know the answer.

More than forty craft landed together in a flat, open space at the outskirts of the village. They weren't war vessels or armored attack ships, though some had defensive weapons. The Bashar stepped with Sheeana away from the tents, to face the largest mining shuttle. No one tried to stop them; the people were too awed by what they saw.

It surprised Teg to see Duncan Idaho himself march down the ramp of the lead craft, wearing his traditional House Atreides uniform, complete with polished boots and the starburst insignia of his rank. If the Qelsans had been gone from the Old Empire for fifteen centuries, they weren't likely to recognize any of the symbols, but Teg thought the uniform gave his friend a distinguished aura of command, and undoubtedly provided self-assurance.

Duncan swept his gaze across the confused villagers, finally spotting Teg and Sheeana. The relief on his face was obvious as he made his way to them. 'You're still alive. And unhurt?'

'Stuka isn't,' Sheeana said with an edge of bitterness.

'You shouldn't have left the no-ship,' Teg said. 'You're vulnerable now, visible to the searchers and their wide net.'

'Let them find me.' Duncan appeared stony, as if he had reached an inescapable conclusion. 'This endless chase and hiding accomplishes nothing. I can't defeat the Enemy unless I confront them.'

Sheeana glanced nervously at the sky, as if expecting the old man and woman to appear suddenly. 'Garimi could have led the attack, or even Thufir. Instead, you let yourself be swayed by your emotions.'

'I factored them in when I made my correct decision.' Duncan's face flushed, as if he were hiding the real answer, and he rushed ahead with an explanation. 'By commline, I spoke with Stilgar and Liet-Kynes aboard the flyer. We intercepted them out in the desert, so I have some inkling of what's going on here. I know how they killed Stuka – and why.'

'And you're surprised to see me alive?' Sheeana asked. 'Grateful, too, I hope.'

Teg interrupted. 'The death of Stuka was a tragic over-reaction. These people made assumptions about us.'

Nodding, Duncan said, 'Yes, Miles. And if I had made an overzealous response with superior firepower, that would have caused many more deaths and a much greater tragedy. In one of my earlier lives I might have done exactly that, but I only needed to think about what you would have done.'

Stilgar and Liet emerged with the commandos from the tanker. The two young gholas displayed a hardness to them now, and new life behind their eyes. The Fremen naib and the planetologist had found something on Qelso that reenergized them and transported them to other times.

Teg understood what all the gholas had gone through since recovering their memories. They had been sheltered and comfortable aboard the *Ithaca*, forced to content themselves with reading about their pasts and watching the sandworms in the cargo hold, as if they were specimens in a zoo. But these gholas could remember the real Arrakis. The lives of Stilgar and Kynes had not been safer or more comfortable in the tumultuous old days, but there had been a certain sharp definition to who they were.

Others continued to emerge from the landed vessels: Thufir, Garimi and more than a dozen Sisters, muscular male Bene Gesserit workers, second-generation children born aboard the no-ship setting foot on a real planet for the very first time in their lives. Five of the Rabbi's followers stood in bright sunlight, looking around in wonder at the landscape, at the open spaces. Presently the old man himself emerged, blinking his bespectacled, owlish eyes.

Var looked admiringly at the mining shuttles and lighters, at his new companions Stilgar and Liet. He raised his chin. Apparently, Duncan had also spoken with the village leader at length during their flight back from the desert. 'Duncan Idaho, you know what trials we face here, what we've been driven to do. We are the only ones who'll stand against the death of this planet. We did not bring the desert here. You have no right to condemn us.'

'I didn't condemn you for your struggle, but I can't condone what you did to our companion. Years ago, Bene Gesserit visitors to your world acted without considering the consequences of what they were doing to you. And now it appears you have done the same thing.'

The old leader shook his head. His eyes burned with anger and righteousness. 'We killed the witches responsible for depositing sandtrout here. Finding another witch, we killed her too.'

Duncan abruptly cut off what was sure to be a pointless argument. 'We will take our friends and leave you. I'll let you have your fruitless fight against a desert you can't defeat.'

Teg and Sheeana stepped forward, anxious to leave this place. Liet and Stilgar, though, held back and looked at each other. The latter squared his shoulders and said, 'Duncan, Bashar . . . Liet and I are having second thoughts. This is the desert – not *our* desert, but closer than anything we have yet encountered as gholas. We were brought back to life for a purpose. The skills from our past lives can be vital resources in a place like this.'

Liet-Kynes picked up the speech as if he and Stilgar had rehearsed what they were going to say. 'Look around. Can you imagine a world where our talents are more desperately needed? We are trained as fighters against impossible odds. We're used to desert combat. As a planetologist, I know the best ways to control the spread of the dunes, and I understand more about the sandworm cycle than most people.'

Stilgar added, his passion rising, 'We can show these fighters how to build sietches in the harshest desert. We can teach them to make real stillsuits. One day, perhaps, we shall even ride the great worms again.' His voice cracked. 'No one can stop the desert, but we can keep the people alive. The rest of you go back to the no-ship, but the Qelsans need us here.'

Sheeana stopped at the hatch of the nearest ship, clearly displeased. 'That is not possible. We need you, and all of the gholas, aboard the *Ithaca*. Each one of you was created, raised, and trained to assist us against the Enemy.'

'But no one knows how, Sheeana,' Duncan pointed out, moved by what the two young men had said. 'None of you can say for certain why we need Stilgar and Liet. And what exactly is our fight?'

'We are not your tools or game pieces.' Stilgar crossed his arms over his chest. 'We are human beings with free will, regardless of how we might have been created. I never asked to serve the Bene Gesserit witches.'

Liet stood by his friend. 'This is what we want to do, and who's to say it isn't our destiny? We could save a planet, or at least its population. Isn't that an important enough goal?'

Teg understood the dilemma all too well. These two had found a connection they could hold onto, a battle they could fight that did indeed require their specific abilities. He himself had been created as a pawn, and he'd been forced to play that role. 'Let them go, Sheeana. You have enough experimental subjects on the ship.'

Thufir Hawat came up to the Bashar, relieved to see his mentor safe. He shot a disturbed glance toward Sheeana. 'Is that all we are to them, Bashar? Experimental subjects?'

'In a certain sense. And now we must go back to our cage.' He was anxious to leave this dying planet before other problems arose.

'Not so fast,' the old Rabbi said, stepping forward. 'My people are not, and never have been, part of your reckless flight across space. We've always wanted a world to settle. Compared to metal decks and small chambers, this planet looks good enough.'

'Qelso is dying,' Sheeana said. The Rabbi and his hardworking companions simply shrugged.

Var scowled, as did some of the nomadic villagers nearest him. 'We do not need any further drain on our resources. You are welcome here only if you intend to fight back against the desert.'

Isaac, one of the strong Jewish men, nodded. 'If we decide to stay here, we will fight and work. Our people are no strangers to surviving when the rest of the universe is pitted against us.'

No matter where I go, no matter what I leave behind, my past is always with me, like a shadow.

– DUNCAN IDAHO,
no-ship logs

Liet-Kynes and Stilgar returned briefly to the *Ithaca* to retrieve informational archives and some of the equipment they would need to monitor Qelso's changing climate. Liet even converted several spare sensor buoys into orbital weathersats, which the no-ship deployed.

He said his goodbyes to the other ghola children who had been raised with him – Paul Atreides, Jessica, Leto II. And Chani, his own daughter. With a surge of emotion, Liet grasped the hand of the young woman, who was physically almost three years older than he. He smiled at her. 'Chani, someday you will remember me as I was on Arrakis – busy in the sietches, working as the Imperial Planetologist or the Judge of the Change, carrying on my father's dream for the Fremen and for Dune.'

Her expression was intense, as if she struggled to grasp some faint flicker of memory as she listened to him. Releasing her hand, he touched her forehead, her dark red hair. 'Maybe I was a strong leader, but I'm afraid I wasn't much of a father. So I must tell you, before I go, that I love you. Then *and* now. When you remember me, remember all we shared.'

'I will. If I remembered everything now, I'd probably want to go with you back to the desert. And so would Usul.'

Beside them, Paul shook his head. 'My place is here. Our fight is bigger than one desert.'

Stilgar took his friend's arm, urging Liet to hurry. 'This planet is large enough for us. I feel in my soul that this is why Liet and I have been brought back, whether or not Sheeana realizes it. Perhaps someday, no matter how it appears now, we will all see that this is part of the greater battle.'

Meanwhile, the Rabbi spoke to his fifty-two enthusiastic followers at their stations on the no-ship. Isaac and Levi had taken over many of the old man's duties, and at his signal they directed the Jews to gather their possessions and bring prefabricated shelters from the *Ithaca's* vast storage chambers. Soon, all of them had shuttled down to the surface, where they disembarked and began unloading the landed cargo ships under Isaac's direction.

On the ground Var strode through the activity, marshalling his followers. He ran a covetous eye over several of the craft that Duncan had brought down during his show of force. 'Those mining shuttles would be a great help to us for carrying supplies and water across the continent.'

Sheeana shook her head. 'Those ships belong to the *Ithaca*. We may need them.'

Var glowered at her. 'Small enough compensation for causing the death of an entire world, I'd say.'

'I didn't contribute to the death of your world. You, however, killed Stuka in cold blood, before—'

Quickly, Teg went into Mentat mode, mentally inventorying the supplies and equipment they carried aboard the no-ship. To Sheeana, he murmured, 'Although we had no part in the damage done to this world, we did resupply our ship here, and many of our people are staying behind as settlers. A token payment is not unreasonable.' When she nodded, Teg turned to Var. 'We can spare two shuttles. No more.'

'And two desert experts,' Liet piped up. 'Stilgar and me.'

'Not to mention a willing and hardy workforce. You'll be glad to have the Jews here.' Teg had noticed how industrious the Rabbi's people were. He expected they would do well on this planet, even as the climate turned harsher. Someday, however, they might decide that Qelso wasn't their promised land after all.

NOT SURPRISINGLY, GARIMI and her conservative followers also wanted to leave the no-ship permanently. More than a hundred of the Sisters asked to be released from the *Ithaca* to settle on Qelso, even with its ever-growing desert. There, they planned to establish the foundation for their new order. Back on the no-ship, Garimi announced their choice to Sheeana more as a courtesy than a matter for discussion.

But the people of Qelso would hear none of that. They met the Sisters' landed shuttle with drawn weapons. Var stood with his arms crossed over his chest. 'We accept Liet-Kynes and Stilgar among us, as well as the Jews. But no Bene Gesserit witch is welcome here.'

'No witches!' other Qelsans cried, their expressions suddenly murderous. 'If we find them, we kill them.'

Having accompanied them for a farewell, Sheeana tried

to speak on Garimi's behalf. 'We could take them to the other side of the continent. You would never know about their settlement. I promise, they'll cause you no trouble.'

But the incensed Qelsans were not inclined to listen, and Var spoke again. 'Your kind act only for the benefit of the Sisterhood. We welcomed them once, to our deep and lasting regret. Now Qelsans act for the benefit of Qelso. No member of your Sisterhood is welcome here. Short of violence, I cannot be more clear than that.'

Sending up a puff of dust with every step, the Rabbi trudged past tents and portable buildings toward the shuttle. He wiped sweat from his brow and came to stand before Teg and Sheeana, looking uneasily from one to the other. 'I think my people will be happy here, by the grace of God.' He kicked at the dry dirt with his shoe. 'We were meant to have ground under our feet.'

'You look disturbed, Rabbi,' Sheeana noted.

'Not disturbed. Sad.' To Teg he appeared crestfallen, and his watery old eyes seemed redder than usual, as if from crying. 'I will not be with them. I cannot leave the no-ship.'

Black-bearded Isaac draped a consoling arm around the elderly man's shoulders. 'This will be the new Israel for us, Rabbi, under my leadership. Won't you reconsider?'

'Why aren't you staying with your people?' Teg asked.

The Rabbi lowered his gaze, and tears dropped on the hardscrabble ground. 'I have a higher obligation to one of my followers whom I failed.'

Isaac explained to Sheeana and Teg in a soft voice, 'He wishes to remain with Rebecca. Though she is an axlotl tank now, he refuses to leave her.'

'I shall watch over her for all my remaining days. My

followers will be in good hands here. Isaac and Levi are their future, while I am their past.'

The rest of the Jews surrounded the Rabbi, saying their goodbyes and wishing him well. Then the weeping old man joined Teg, Sheeana, and the others on the waiting shuttle, which took them back up to the no-ship.

Twenty-Four Years After

Escape from Chapterhouse

We are wounded, but undefeated. We are hurt, but can endure great pain. We are driven to the end of our civilization and our history – but we remain human.

– MOTHER COMMANDER MURBELLA,
address to the survivors of Chapterhouse

As the epidemic burned itself out, the survivors – all of them Reverend Mothers – struggled to hold the Sisterhood together. No vaccines, immunity treatments, diets, or quarantines had any effect as the general populace died.

It required only three days for Murbella's heart to turn to stone. Around her, she watched thousands of promising young acolytes perish, diligent students who had not yet learned enough to become Reverend Mothers. Every one of them died either from the plague or from the Agony that was rushed upon them.

Kiria slipped into her former Honored Matre viciousness. On many occasions she argued vehemently that it was a waste of time to care for anyone who had contracted the plague. 'Our resources are better spent on more important things, on activities that have some chance of success!'

Murbella could not dispute her logic, though she did not agree with the opinion. 'We're not thinking machines. We are humans, and we will care for humans.'

It was a sad irony that as more and more of the population died, fewer Reverend Mothers were needed to tend the remaining sick. Gradually, those women were able to turn to other crucial activities.

From a nearly empty chamber in the Keep, Murbella peered through the broad, arched window segments behind her throne chair. Chapterhouse had once been a bustling administrative complex, the pulsing heart of the New Sisterhood. Before the plague struck, Mother Commander Murbella had been in charge of hundreds of defensive measures, monitoring the constant progress of the Enemy fleet, dealing with the Ixians, the Guild, refugees and warlords, anyone who could fight on her side.

Far away, she could see the brown hills and dying orchards, but what concerned her was the eerie, unnatural silence of the city itself. The dormitories and support buildings, the nearby spaceport field, the markets, gardens, and dwindling herds . . . all should have been tended by a population of hundreds of thousands. Sadly, most normal activity around the Keep and the city had halted. Far too few remained alive to cover even the most basic work. The world itself was virtually vacant, with all hope dashed in a matter of days. So shockingly sudden!

The air in the surrounding city was heavy with the stench of death and burning. Black smoke rose from dozens of bonfires – not funeral pyres, for Murbella had other ways to dispose of the bodies, but simply the incineration of contaminated garments and other materials, including infected medical supplies.

In an admittedly petty moment, Murbella had summoned two exhausted Reverend Mothers. Telling them to bring suspensor clamps, she had ordered them to remove the deactivated combat robot from her private chambers. Though the hated machine had not moved in years, she had begun to feel that it was mocking her. 'Take this thing away and destroy it. I abhor everything it symbolizes.' The obedient women seemed relieved to follow her orders.

The Mother Commander issued her next instructions. 'Release our melange stockpiles and distribute spice to all survivors.' Every healthy woman was dedicated to tending the remaining sick, though it was a hopeless task. The surviving Reverend Mothers were utterly exhausted, having worked without rest for days. Even with the bodily control taught by the Sisterhood, they were hard-pressed to continue. But melange could help keep them going.

Long ago in the time of the Butlerian Jihad the palliative properties of melange had been an effective measure against the horrific machine plagues. This time she didn't expect spice to cure anyone who had already contracted the disease, but at least it would help the surviving Reverend Mothers perform the daunting work required of them. Though Murbella desperately needed every gram of spice to pay the Guild and the Ixians, her Sisters needed it more. If the unified Sisterhood died on Chapterhouse, who would lead the fight for humanity?

One more cost among so many. But if we don't spend it now, we will never buy victory. 'Do it. Distribute whatever is necessary.'

As her orders were being carried out, she made calculations and realized to her dismay that there weren't enough Reverend Mothers left alive to deplete the Sisterhood's hoarded spice anyway . . .

Her entire support staff had been stripped away, and she felt isolated. Murbella had already imposed austerity measures, severely cut back services, and eliminated every extraneous activity. Even though most of the Reverend Mothers had survived the plague, it was not certain they would survive the aftermath.

She summoned those who were Mentats and ordered them to assess the vital work and create an emergency plan of operations, using personnel who were best qualified for the essential tasks. Where could they possibly get the workforce necessary to maintain Chapterhouse, rebuild, and continue the fight? Maybe they could convince some of the desperate refugees from devastated planets to come here, once the last vestiges of plague died out.

Murbella grew tired of simply recovering. Chapterhouse was only a tiny battlefield on the vast galactic canvas of the climactic war. The greatest threat still remained out there, as the oncoming Enemy fleet struck planet after planet, driving refugees like frantic animals before a forest fire. The battle at the end of the universe.

Kralizec . . .

A Reverend Mother came running up to her with a report. The woman, barely more than a girl, was one of those who had been forced to attempt the Agony long before she should have, but she had survived. Her eyes bore a faint bluish tinge now, a color that would grow deeper as she continued to consume melange. Her gaze had a stunned, haunted look that penetrated to the depths of her soul.

'Your hourly report, Mother Commander.' She handed Murbella a stack of Ridulian crystal sheets on which names were printed in columns.

In a cold and businesslike fashion, her advisors had at first provided her with simple numbers and summaries, but Murbella demanded actual names. Each person who died from the plague was a *person*, and each worker and acolyte on Chapterhouse was a soldier lost in the cause against the Enemy. She would not dishonor them by boiling them down to mere numbers and totals. Duncan Idaho would never have condoned such a thing.

'Four more of them were Face Dancers,' the messenger said.

Murbella clenched her jaws. 'Who?' When the woman spoke the names, Murbella barely knew them, unobtrusive Sisters who called no attention to themselves . . . exactly as Face Dancer spies would do. So far sixteen of the shape-shifters had turned up among the plague victims. She had always suspected that even the New Sisterhood had been infiltrated, and now she had proof. But, in an irony the thinking machines could not possibly grasp, the Face Dancers were also susceptible to the horrible epidemic. They died just as easily as anyone else.

'Keep their bodies for dissection and analysis, along with the others. If nothing else, maybe we can learn something that will allow us to detect them among us.'

The young woman waited while Murbella scanned the long list of names. She felt a cold whisper run down her spine as an entry in the third column of one sheet caught her eye. She felt as if she had been struck a heavy blow.

Gianne.

Her own daughter, her youngest child by Duncan Idaho. For years the girl had delayed passing through the Agony, never reaching the point where she was ready for the ordeal. Gianne had shown great promise, but that was not nearly enough. Though she had not demonstrated herself to be ready, the girl – among thousands of others – had been forced to take the poison early, the only chance of surviving.

Murbella reeled in shock. She should have been at Gianne's side, but in the chaos no one had told the Mother Commander when her daughter would be given the Water of Life. Most Sisters did not even realize that Gianne was her daughter. The frantic, exhausted helpers would not have known. With her priorities set in true Bene Gesserit fashion, Murbella had tended to her official duties and had gone without sleep for several days in succession.

I should have been there to support her and help, even if I could only watch over her as she died.

Yet no one had informed her. No one had known that Gianne was special.

I should have thought to check on her, but I put it off, made assumptions.

With so many events crashing around her, Murbella had misplaced her own daughter's life. First Rinya, and now Gianne, both lost to the perilous Agony. Only two other daughters remained: Janess was off at the battle-front fighting thinking machines, while her sister Tanidia, not knowing the identity of her parents, had been sent to join the Missionaria. Though both of them faced risks, they might at least avoid contracting the horrific plague.

'Two of my children dead,' she said aloud, though the messenger did not understand. 'Oh, what would Duncan think of me?' Murbella set the report aside. She closed her eyes for a moment, drew a deep breath, and straightened herself. Pointing to the name on the list of victims she said, 'Take me to her.'

The messenger glanced down, ran a quick assessment. 'The bodies in that column have been hauled off to the spaceport. 'Thopter loads of them are taking off right now.'

'Hurry. I must try to see her.' Murbella rushed out of the hall, glancing back to be certain the young woman was right behind her. Though the Mother Commander felt disturbingly numb, she had to do this.

They took a groundcar to the nearby spaceport, where the fluttering hum of 'thopters droned. On the way, the young Reverend Mother activated her commline, and in a quiet voice requested information. She then directed the driver of the car to take a particular access road.

On all of the spaceport landing pads, large cargo 'thopters were being loaded with the dead, and were lifting off as soon as they were full. In normal, better times when Bene Gesserits died, they would be buried in the thriving orchards or gardens. The bodies would decompose and provide nourishment and fertilizer. Now they piled up so fast that even large cargo ships could barely keep up with removing them.

The young assistant directed the driver to a specific grid in the landing zone, where a dark green 'thopter was being loaded by workers. Bundle after bundle of bodies went into the large hold. 'She has to be in that one, Mother Commander. Would you . . . would you like them to unload so that you can find and identify her?'

As the two women stepped out of the groundcar, Murbella felt stunned, but tried to steel herself. 'Not necessary. It is only her body, not *her*. Just the same, I'll allow myself enough sentimentality to accompany her out to the dunes.' Leaving the young Reverend Mother to tend to other duties, Murbella climbed into the 'thopter and sat next to the female pilot.

'My daughter is aboard,' Murbella said. Then she grew silent, and stared glumly out the window.

A vibrating shudder passed through the 'thopter as it took off with jets and flapping wings. It would take them half an hour or so to get out to the desert zone, an hour the Mother Commander could ill afford to be away from the Keep. But it was time she desperately needed . . .

Even the best of the Sisterhood who had undergone the most arduous testing were dismayed by the very real and material tragedy – but not to the point of total surrender. Bene Gesserit teachings showed them how to control base emotions, how to act for the greater good and see the overall picture. Upon watching almost 90 percent of a planet's population fall within a few days, however, the magnitude of the disaster – the *extermination* – was breaking down even the strongest barriers in many Sisters. It was up to Murbella to maintain the morale of the survivors.

The thinking machines have found a cruel and effective way to destroy our human weapons, but we are not so easily disarmed!

'Mother Commander, we have arrived,' the pilot said, her clipped words loud enough to be heard over the thrum of the wings.

Murbella opened her eyes to see clean desert, tan eddies of sand and dust curling from stray breezes. It seemed pristine and untouched, no matter how much human debris the Sisterhood dumped there. She saw other 'thopters circling in the sky, descending over the dunes and opening cargo doors to expel loads . . . hundreds of black-wrapped bodies in each aircraft. The dead Sisters tumbled out onto the sand like charred cordwood.

Natural elements would dispose of them far more efficiently than huge funeral pyres could. The aridity would desiccate them, and scouring sandstorms would wear them down to bones. In many cases, the worms would simply devour them. A sort of purity.

Their 'thopter hovered over a small basin. Large swells

of dunes swept up on either side, while dust kicked up by the 'thopter wings swirled around them. The pilot worked her controls, and the bottom doors opened with a weary groan. Bodies tumbled out, wrapped in fabric. They were stiff, their features covered, but to Murbella they were still individuals. One of those unidentified shapes was her own little girl . . . born just before Murbella underwent the Agony herself, just before she lost Duncan forever.

She didn't delude herself into thinking that if she had been at her daughter's side she might have helped Gianne survive. Passing through the Spice Agony was solely an individual's battle, but Murbella wished she could have been there.

The bodies spilled unceremoniously onto soft sand. Below, she could see serpentine shapes stirring – two big worms drawn by 'thopter vibrations or the thumps of falling bodies. The creatures scooped up and devoured the human shapes, then plunged back beneath the sand.

The pilot lifted the 'thopter high enough to swing around, so that Murbella could look down and observe the horrible feeding frenzy. Touching the commline in her ear, the pilot received a message, then offered a faint smile to Murbella. 'Mother Commander, there is some good news, at least.'

After seeing the last unmarked body vanish below, Murbella wasn't in the mood for any sort of cheering up, but she waited.

'One of our deep-desert research settlements has survived. Shakkad Station. They were far enough out in the sand and had no contact with the Keep. Somehow they avoided the touch of the virus.'

Murbella remembered the tiny group of offworld

scientists and helpers. 'I isolated them myself so they could work. I want them to stay completely cut off – no contact whatsoever! If a single one of us goes near, we could contaminate them.'

'Shakkad Station doesn't have enough supplies to last long,' the pilot said. 'Perhaps we could arrange a package drop-off.'

'No, nothing! We can't take the chance of contamination.' She thought of those people as living at the center of a deadly minefield. But once the epidemic passed, perhaps these few could survive. Only a handful. 'If they run out of food, they should increase their consumption of melange. They can find enough to survive for at least a little while. Even if some of them starve, it's better than having every single one succumb to this damned epidemic.'

The pilot did not disagree. As she stared out into the desert, Murbella realized what she and her Sisters had become. She muttered aloud, her words drowned by the thrum of engines. 'We are the new Fremen, and this whole besieged galaxy is our desert.'

The 'thopter soared away, heading back toward the Keep, leaving the worms to their feast.

Hatred breeds in the fertile ground of life itself.

                                    – ancient saying

The no-ship had flown away from the turmoil of the planet Qelso, leaving behind some of their people, some of their hopes and possibilities. On that world Duncan had taken a great risk, daring to leave the no-ship for the first time in decades. Had he revealed his presence? Would the Enemy be able to find him now, seizing upon that clue? It was possible.

Though he had decided not to cower and hide, Duncan did not intend to bring possible destruction to all the innocent people on this planet. He would make another jump, cover his tracks. And so the *Ithaca* had risked another unguided plunge through folded space.

That was three months ago.

Through a thick plaz viewport, Scytale had watched Qelso dwindle, then suddenly vanish into blankness. He had never been allowed to set foot off the ship. Judging by what he had seen, he would have been happy to settle on that world, in spite of its spreading desert.

Although he had his memories back, Scytale found that a part of him missed his father, his predecessor, himself. His mind now contained everything he needed. But he wanted more.

With this new body, the Tleilaxu Master should have another century before cumulative genetic errors caused him to break down again. Enough time to solve many problems. But when another hundred years were gone, he would still be the last Tleilaxu Master, the only remaining keeper of the Great Belief. Unless he could use the cells of the Council of Masters stored in his nullentropy capsule. Someday, maybe the witches would allow him to employ the axlotl tanks for the purpose the Tleilaxu had intended them.

Back at Qelso, he had agonized over whether to remain there and create a new homeland for the Tleilaxu. Could he build the proper laboratories and equipment? Recruit followers from among the people there? Should he have taken that gamble? Young Scytale had studied the scriptures, meditated long and hard, and finally decided against staying behind – the same decision the Rabbi had reached. On Qelso, he wasn't likely ever to have access to the axlotl technology he needed. His decision was perfectly logical.

The Rabbi's recent misery and anger, however, was not so easily explained. No one had forced him into his choice. Ever since the ship left the planet and its spreading deserts, the old man had been marching up and down the corridors, spreading dissent like poison. He was the only one of his kind left aboard. Just like Scytale.

The aged holy man ate with the other refugees, grumbling about how harshly he was treated and how difficult it must be for his people to establish a new Zion without his guidance. Garimi and her hardliners, having been forcibly turned away from the planet, had expressed no sympathy for his grievances.

Watching it all, Scytale concluded that the Rabbi was the sort of person who placed external blame in order to position himself as a martyr. Since he would not leave the axlotl tank that had once been Rebecca, he could cling to his hatred of the Bene Gesserit order, faulting them instead of his own bad choices.

Well, Scytale thought, there was certainly enough hatred to go around.

IN HIS PRIVATE quarters, Wellington Yueh studied his mirror reflection – the sallow face, dark lips, and pointed chin. The narrow visage was younger than the one his memories told him to expect, but still recognizable. Since regaining his memories, he had let his black hair grow out until he had enough at the back to bind in an improvised Suk School ring.

Yet he did not fully accept himself. There was one more critical step to take.

In his hand he held an indelible scriber filled with dark ink that would leave a permanent stain. Not exactly a tattoo, and without any implant or attendant deep Imperial Conditioning, but close enough. His hands were steady, his strokes confident.

I am a Suk doctor, a surgeon. I can draw a simple geometric shape.

A diamond, prominent on his forehead, perfectly centered. Without hesitation, he drew another stroke, connected the lines, and filled in the skin of his brow. When he was finished, he examined himself again. Wellington Yueh looked back at him from the mirror, Suk doctor and personal physician to House Vernius and then House Atreides.

The Traitor.

He set the scriber aside, dressed in a clean doctor's smock, and headed for the medical center. Like the old Rabbi, he was as qualified as any Bene Gesserit doctor to monitor patients and tend the axlotl tanks.

Recently, Sheeana had begun growing another ghola as part of her program, using cells from the Tleilaxu Master's nullentropy tube. Now that Stilgar and Liet-Kynes were gone, she had felt justified in taking that step. Clinging to security, she refused to identify the child gestating in the axlotl tank.

The Bene Gesserits still claimed to need the gholas, though they could not clearly explain why. Their success in restoring the memories of previous lives in Yueh, Stilgar, and Liet-Kynes had not led to similar accomplishments with the other gholas yet. Some of the witches, especially Proctor Superior Garimi, continued to voice grave reservations about bringing back Jessica and Leto II, because of their past crimes. So they had tried to awaken Thufir Hawat next.

Yueh did not know what the witches had done in attempting to break down Hawat's walls, but it had backfired on them. Instead of awakening, Hawat had fallen into convulsions. The old Rabbi had been present and rushed to attend the seventeen-year-old ghola, pushing the Sisters away and scolding them for the foolish risks they had taken.

But Yueh, like Scytale, already had his old knowledge. He was no longer a child, no longer waiting to *become* something. One day, he mustered his courage and implored Sheeana to put him to work. 'You witches forced me to remember my old life. I begged you not to, but you insisted on awakening me. Along with my memories and my guilt, came useful skills. Let me act as a Suk doctor again.'

At first he wasn't sure the Bene Gesserits would agree, especially considering the constant threat from the unknown saboteur – but when Garimi automatically objected, Sheeana decided to support him. He was granted permission to make rounds in the medical center, so long as he remained under surveillance.

At the entrance to the main axlotl chamber, two security women scanned Yueh carefully, then waved him through. Neither of them remarked on the new diamond-shaped stain on his forehead. He wondered if anyone still remembered what that mark had once symbolized.

In preoccupied silence, Yueh went about his inspections of the healthy axlotl tanks. Several produced melange for the ship's stockpiles, but one was obviously pregnant. This unnamed ghola baby would gestate under much tighter security. Yueh was convinced that the child would not be another attempt at Gurney Halleck, Xavier Harkonnen, or Serena Butler. Nor would it be a duplicate of Liet-Kynes or Stilgar. No, Sheeana would experiment with someone else – someone she believed could dramatically help the *Ithaca*.

Knowing Sheeana's impetuous nature, Yueh feared who the baby might be. The Sisters were not immune to making poor choices (as they had proved by bringing *him* back!). He couldn't believe any of the women had imagined he might be a savior or a hero, yet he had been one of their first experiments. Judging from this, what if the witches were curious to study nefarious personalities from the dark pages of history? Emperor Shaddam? Count Fenring? Beast Rabban? Even the despised Baron Harkonnen himself? Yueh could imagine Sheeana's excuses already. She would no doubt insist that even the worst personalities had the potential to provide invaluable information.

What snakes will they set loose among us? he wondered.

In the main medical center away from the tanks, he found the old Rabbi grumbling as he assembled a portable medical kit. Since refusing to remain behind on Qelso with his people, he lingered for hours at a time over the tank that he called Rebecca. Though he despised what had been done to her, he seemed relieved that she hadn't been the one implanted with the new ghola.

Reluctant to have the Rabbi hover too long near the axlotl tanks, the Sisters gave him duties to keep him busy. 'I am going to run Scytale through a battery of tests,' the old man huffed to Yueh, starting to retreat from the medical center. 'Sheeana wants him checked out – again.'

'I can do that for you, Rabbi. My duties here are light.'

'No. Sticking needles into the Tleilaxu is one of my few pleasures these days.' His gaze fixed on Yueh's new diamond mark, but he did not comment on it. 'Walk with me.' The Rabbi took Yueh's arm in a tight grip and led him into the corridors, away from the hovering Bene Gesserits. When they were far enough away for him to feel safe, the old man leaned closer, speaking in a conspiratorial tone. 'I am certain Scytale is the saboteur, though I have not found evidence yet. First the old one, and now his ghola replacement. They are all the same. With his memories restored, the young Scytale continues his insidious work to destroy our ship. Who can trust a Tleilaxu?'

Who can trust anyone? Yueh thought. 'Why would he want to harm the ship?'

'We know he has some dirty scheme. Ask yourself why he would store Face Dancer cells in his nullentropy tube, along with all the others – yours included. Why would he need them? Isn't that suspicious enough for you?'

'Those cells were confiscated and secured by Sheeana. No one has had access to them.'

'Can you be sure of that? Maybe he wants to kill us all so he can restore an army of Face Dancers for himself.' The Rabbi shook his head. Behind the spectacles, his reddened eyes were angry. 'And that isn't all. The witches have their own schemes. Why do you suppose they won't reveal the identity of the new ghola baby? Does even Duncan Idaho know who is growing in that *tank*?' He craned his neck, glanced over his shoulder back toward the medical center, watching out for surveillance imagers. 'But you can find out.'

Yueh was perplexed, and curious, but he didn't tell the Rabbi that he had been having some of the same doubts. 'How? They won't tell me either.'

'But they don't watch you like they watch me! The witches are afraid I'm going to do something to hinder their program, but now that you have your memories, you're their trusted little ghola.' The Rabbi slipped him a small sealed polymer disk, with a dab of filmy substance in the center. 'You have access to the scanners. These are cell samples from the pregnant tank in there. Nobody saw me obtain them, but I dare not run the analysis myself.'

Yueh surreptitiously pocketed the disk. 'Do I really want to know?'

'Can you afford not to? I leave it to you.' The Rabbi slipped away, muttering. Carrying his portable medical kit, he trudged off to the Tleilaxu's cabin.

The sample weighed heavily in Yueh's pocket. Why would the Sisters keep the new ghola's identity secret? What were they up to?

It took several hours for him to find an opportunity

to slip into one of the no-ship's small lab chambers. As a Suk doctor, he had permission to use the facilities. Even so, he worked as swiftly as possible, running the small sample from the axlotl tank through a DNA catalog. He compared the cells from the growing ghola with the identifications that had been run years ago, when the Sisters first assessed the material in Scytale's nullentropy capsule.

Yueh found a match fairly quickly, and when he learned the answer, he physically recoiled. 'Impossible! They would not dare!' But in his heart, as he remembered the torment Sheeana had used to awaken his memories, he didn't doubt the witches would do anything. Now he understood why Sheeana refused to reveal the identity of the ghola.

Even so, the choice itself made no sense. The Sisters had numerous other options. Better ones. Why not try again to bring back Gurney Halleck? Or Ghanima, as a companion for poor Leto II? For what purpose could they possibly need – he shuddered – *Piter de Vries?*

Because Bene Gesserits liked to play with dangerous toys, resurrecting people to serve as chess pieces in their great game. He knew the sort of questions they would pursue, just to satisfy their infernal curiosity. Was the genetic makeup of Piter de Vries corrupt, or was he evil because he had been Twisted by the Tleilaxu? Who better to think like an Enemy than a Harkonnen? Was there any evidence to suggest that a new Piter de Vries would turn out evil, as before, if he were not exposed to the corruptive influence of the Baron?

He could picture Sheeana giving him a condescending frown. 'We need another Mentat. You, of all people, Wellington Yueh, should not hold the past crimes of a ghola's old life against him.'

He still did not believe it. He squeezed his eyes shut, and even the fake diamond tattoo on his forehead seemed to burn. He remembered being forced to watch Wanna endure her endless torture at the hands of the vile Mentat. And the man thrusting a knife deep into his back, grinding the blade. *Piter de Vries!*

He still felt the sharp steel ripping into his organs, a mortal wound, one of the very last memories of his first life. Piter's laugh reverberated, along with the screams of Wanna in the agony chamber . . . and Yueh unable to help her.

Piter de Vries?

Yueh reeled, barely able to absorb the information. He could not allow a monster like that to be reborn.

DAYS LATER, YUEH entered the medical center, and walked toward the single pregnant tank. This was just an innocent baby at the moment. Even if it was de Vries, this ghola child had committed none of the crimes of the original.

But he will! He is twisted, evil, malicious. The Sisters would raise him and insist on triggering his memories. Then he would be back!

Yet Yueh was trapped by his own previous logic. If the Piter ghola – in fact, *all* the gholas – were unable to escape the chains of fate, wouldn't it be the same for Yueh? Was Yueh therefore destined to betray them all? Would he be doomed to make another terrible mistake – or must he sacrifice everything to prevent one? He had thought about consulting Jessica, but he decided against it. This was his burden, his decision.

Using the Rabbi's sample, he had run the genetic scan privately and seen the result. He had to act alone. Though he was himself a Suk doctor, trained and conditioned to save lives, sometimes the death of one monster was required to save many innocents.

Piter de Vries!

Indirectly he had caused de Vries's death the first time around, by giving the poison-gas tooth to Duke Leto, who bit down on it in the Mentat's presence. Yueh had failed in so many ways, caused so much pain and disappointment. Even Wanna would have hated what he'd done to himself, and to the Atreides.

Now, though – a second life, a second chance. Wellington Yueh could make things right. Each of the resurrected ghola children supposedly had a great purpose. He was convinced that this was his.

The handmade black diamond staining his brow added to the burden as Yueh wrestled with his decision. In his restored memories, he saw with clarity when he had become an actual Suk doctor, when he passed through an entire Inner School regimen of Imperial Conditioning and took the formal oath. '"A Suk shall not take human life."'

And yet, Yueh's oath had been subverted, thanks to the Harkonnens. Thanks to *Piter de Vries*. What irony that the breaking of his Suk pledge now allowed him to destroy the very man who had broken that conditioning! He had the freedom to kill.

Yueh already had the instrument of death in the pocket of his smock. His plans were in place, and he would take no chances. Since surveillance imagers still monitored the med center and its axlotl tanks, Yueh could not do this in secret, as the real saboteur had. Once he acted, everyone aboard the *Ithaca* would know who had killed the de Vries ghola. And he would face the consequences.

Perspiration formed on his brow as he crossed the room. With the sharp-eyed Bene Gesserit guard watching him, he could not delay, or the damned witches might detect his uneasiness, his nervous movements. Bringing out his device, Yueh turned a dial as if to recalibrate it, then inserted its probe into the pregnant tank, as he would do in taking a biological sample. Thus he easily administered a lethal dosage of fast-acting poison. So far, no one suspected a thing.

There. Done. Fittingly, de Vries had been an expert in cleverly concocted poisons. And no antidote was available for this toxin; Yueh had seen to that. In a matter of hours, the unborn de Vries would shrivel up and die. Along with the tank, unfortunately. But that could not be avoided. A necessary sacrifice.

Leaving the chamber, he smiled grimly and quickened his pace. By tomorrow, there would be no hiding. Thufir Hawat and Bashar Teg would review surveillance holos and interview the guards. They would know who had done it. Unlike the real saboteur, he could not delete the images. He would be caught.

Despite this knowledge, Yueh was content with himself for the first time since his reawakening. At last, he savored the elusive taste of redemption.

> *Send a fact-finding team to Buzzell to learn why soo-stone exports have dropped off so drastically. This lack of supply, coupled with the precipitous decline in melange production following the Chapterhouse plague, is highly suspicious, especially in light of the fact that the witches are involved in both enterprises. We have learned over the millennia not to take them at their word.*
>
> – CHOAM directive

Now that he possessed the sample of ultraspice, Khrone knew exactly what lived in the fertile seas of Buzzell. The Navigators certainly had an unexpected scheme there, releasing a new breed of melange-producing worms. He needed to go there and see for himself. The leader of the Face Dancer myriad cared little for the loss of soostone revenue, but in his guise as a CHOAM functionary, he had to feign extreme displeasure.

'Monsters?' Standing on the main dock, he gave the woman Corysta a withering glare. 'Sea serpents? Can you think of no better excuses for your incompetence?'

Khrone scowled at the sea and gathered his dark business robes about his shoulders. Out there in the water, wary Phibians swam, diving to harvest the gems from beds of cholisters, many of which had already been devoured by the hungry and growing seaworms. Armored boats patrolled the coves, though they would surely prove insignificant if one of the large creatures should decide to attack.

Reverend Mother Corysta held herself erect, surprisingly unintimidated by the faux official. 'It's no excuse, sir. No one knows where the worms came from or why they have appeared at this time. But they're real. Guild hunting ships dragged in a carcass, if you care to see it.'

'Nonsense. Such a story obviously benefits the New Sisterhood.' Ignoring her protestations, he motioned for Corysta to accompany him along a rocky shoreline path, his shoes crunching on the loose stones. Stepping in a puddle, he frowned down at his feet and kept walking. 'CHOAM suspects that you're creating a false shortage in order to drive up prices. You have financial obligations. For years now, the Sisterhood has been commissioning extremely expensive ships, weapons, and military supplies. Your losses are tremendous.'

'They're *humanity's* losses, sir.' Corysta's voice was sharp.

'And now Chapterhouse itself, brought to its knees by a plague. It appears that the Sisterhood can no longer meet its financial obligations. Thus, CHOAM no longer considers you a good credit risk.'

Corysta turned into the brisk sea wind. 'These are matters you should take up with the Mother Commander.'

'I *should*, but since she is on a quarantined planet, I can't very well call on her, can I? Your Sisterhood is falling apart as a result of external attack and internal strife.'

Women stood on plastone ramps at the water's edge to receive a tired-looking group of Phibians who carried a net filled with small, misshapen soostones.

Khrone could tell at a glance the gems were of poor quality, but at least it was part of a shipment he could seize as overdue payment. 'Are your Phibians afraid of sea monsters? Can they not go to richer beds of shell-fish?'

'They harvest what they can, sir. There are no richer beds. The monsters have eaten many of the cholisters. Our underwater crops are ravaged. And, yes, the Phibians are understandably frightened. Many of them have been slaughtered.' Corysta stared at him coldly, and Khrone appreciated the steel in her expression; he could respect it. 'We have holo-footage of that, too, if you doubt me.'

'It doesn't matter if I believe your story. I only want to know what the Sisterhood intends to do about it.' Khrone knew the women could do nothing. Eventually the seaworms would bring down the soostone economy of Buzzell, thus removing another one of the Mother Commander's bargaining chips when she desperately needed to buy allegiances and secure equipment.

Kept in the dark, the exiled Sisters did not yet under-stand the true potential of those worms. The primary chemical attributes of the new melange stolen from Buzzell would be a thousand times more effective on human nerve receptors. Oh, it would work very nicely indeed!

He wondered if the Spacing Guild was even aware of Edrik's destroyed Heighliner yet. It was possible that they weren't. So many of their Navigators had vanished anyway, what was one more? If necessary, by planting a few hints here and there, Khrone could easily blame the loss on an attack by the thinking-machine battle fleet. If nothing else, Omnius made a fine scapegoat.

The Face Dancer myriad had set their hooks every-where. The Ixians were building supposed weapons and draining the Chapterhouse coffers of spice; now the Sisterhood's soostone wealth was also disappearing. The Guild relied entirely on computerized navigation devices for their new ships, and the Navigators had no source of melange.

All enemies of the Face Dancers would fall. He would see to that. The Lost Tleilaxu and the original Masters had already been erased. The Ixians were in Khrone's pocket. Next would come the New Sisterhood, the Guild, and all of humanity. Finally, when he and his minions defeated the thinking machines, nothing would remain but the Face Dancers. And that would be enough.

Pleased with himself, Khrone marched up to the dock and yanked the net of soostones from the women trying to sort them. 'Your production has dropped off drastically, and too many CHOAM merchants have gone away empty-handed.'

Corysta hovered close behind him. 'I hope to hire mercenary hunters to track down the seaworms. It is possible that we may find something of interest – maybe something more valuable than soostones.'

So, this woman already had her suspicions about the ultraspice! 'I doubt it,' he said. Khrone took the net of rough soostones and marched back to the landing pad. Considering the vast game board, he decided it was finally time to head toward the heart of the thinking-machine empire. He would deliver the ultraspice to Omnius and let the evermind continue with his mad dream of creating and controlling his own Kwisatz Haderach.

It wouldn't help him in the end.

We believe that confession should lead to forgiveness and redemption. Usually, however, it leads only to further accusations.

— DR WELLINGTON YUEH,
encrypted entry

The axlotl chamber smelled of fetid death. Duncan could not tear his gaze away from the still, cold flesh of the tank and the clear signs of necrosis. Rage and helplessness chewed at his gut. And who would the child have been? Sheeana hadn't even told him. Those damned Bene Gesserits and their secrets!

'Touch nothing,' Teg warned. 'Get me all security images right away. We will find the saboteur this time.' One of the Sisters hurried to obtain the recordings.

Meanwhile, young Thufir cordoned off an area around the poison-ravaged tank and its unborn ghola. Mostly recovered from the memory-trigger attempt that had gone so dramatically awry, he now sternly followed the methods the Bashar had taught him. The corrosive poison had completely destroyed the growing fetus and then eaten through the wall of the womb that kept the thing alive. Somehow the tank had fallen to the floor, and yellow puddles oozed around the dead flesh.

Sheeana turned to one of her Sisters. 'Bring Jessica here. Immediately.'

Duncan gave her a sharp look. 'Why Jessica? Is she a suspect?'

'No, but she will be hurt by this. Maybe I shouldn't even tell her . . .'

Presently, Teg received a surveillance holotube from one of the Bene Gesserits. 'I will scan every second. There must be some piece of evidence pointing to the traitor among us.'

'There is no need. I killed the ghola.' A young man's voice. All of them spun to look at a grim-faced Dr Wellington Yueh. 'I had to.' Thufir moved swiftly to seize him by the arm, and Yueh did not resist. He stood firm, ready to face the questions that would be thrown at him. 'You can punish me, but I couldn't allow you to spawn another Twisted Mentat. Piter de Vries would only have caused bloodshed and pain.'

While Duncan immediately grasped the implications of Yueh's confession, Sheeana sounded perplexed. 'Piter? What are you talking about?'

Yueh didn't struggle in Thufir's firm grip. 'I witnessed his evil first-hand, and I couldn't allow you to bring him back. Ever.'

Just then, a breathless young Jessica hurried in with the three-year-old Alia in tow. Alia had intent, eager eyes, full of maturity and understanding that she should not have had. She carried a chubby doll that looked remarkably like a juvenile version of the fat Baron Harkonnen. One of its arms had almost torn loose. Leto II followed his grandmother, looking curious and worried.

Sheeana still didn't understand. 'What does Piter de Vries have to do with any of this?'

Yueh made a distasteful expression. 'Don't try to divert me with lies. I know who that ghola was.'

'That baby was not Piter de Vries.' Sheeana spoke her words in a normal tone. 'It would have been Duke Leto Atreides.'

Yueh looked as if he had been felled with an axe. 'There was no doubt – I ran a genetic comparison!'

Jessica listened from just inside the doorway, her face flickering with a rush of hope before plunging into sadness. 'My Leto?'

Yueh tried to sink to his knees, but Thufir held him upright.

'No! It can't be!'

With adult-sharp awareness, Alia tried to take her mother's hand, but Jessica pulled away from the two children to loom over the Suk doctor. 'You killed my Duke? *Again?*'

He grabbed his temples. 'It can't be. I saw the results myself. It was Piter de Vries.'

Thufir Hawat raised his chin. 'At least we have found our saboteur.'

'I would never have killed the Duke! I loved Leto—'

'And now you've murdered him twice,' Jessica said, stabbing with each icicle-sharp word. 'Leto, my Leto . . .'

Finally, Thufir's comment seemed to sink in. 'But I didn't kill the other three gholas or harm their tanks! I committed no other sabotage.'

Teg said, 'How can we believe you? This will require a great deal more investigation. I will review all evidence in light of this new information.'

Sheeana was clearly troubled, but her words surprised everyone. 'My own truthsense leads me to believe him.'

The flesh tank and unborn fetus lay on the floor,

chemically decomposing. Black streaks covered all tissue and spread into the surrounding puddle. Yueh struggled to throw himself into the poisonous corrosive, as if by doing so he could kill himself.

With an iron grip, Thufir held him away from it. 'Not quite yet, *Traitor*.'

'No good will come from any of this,' the old Rabbi said, standing at the doorway of the medical center. No one had heard him arrive.

Desperate, Yueh looked at him. 'I tested the samples you gave me – the baby was de Vries!'

The old man backed away like a startled bird. He looked indignant at the very suggestion he might have provoked the unstable young man. 'Yes, I gave you a sample I obtained from the axlotl lab. But I merely raised a question – and never suggested that you should commit murder! Murder! I am a man of God, and you are a doctor – a Suk doctor! Who would imagine . . . ?' He shook his head. His gray beard looked especially wild today. 'That tank you killed might have been Rebecca! I could never suggest such a thing.'

Everyone in the room exchanged glances, silently agreeing that Yueh must be the saboteur after all.

'It wasn't me,' he said. 'Not the other times. Why would I confess to this but deny the others? My crime is the same.'

'Not the same at all,' Jessica said in a knotted voice. 'This was my Duke . . .' She turned and left, while Yueh stared beseechingly after her.

Each human, no matter how altruistic or peaceful he seems, carries the capacity to commit tremendous violence. I find this quality particularly fascinating, especially because it can lie dormant for extended periods and then flare up. For instance, consider their traditionally docile women. When these life-givers decide instead to take lives, it is a beautiful ferocity to behold.

— ERASMUS,
Laboratory Notes

On Chapterhouse, the meeting of Reverend Mothers degenerated quickly to murderous intent.

Eyes flashing, Kiria nudged the chairdog away from her as she stood. 'Mother Commander, you have to accept certain facts. Chapterhouse is more than decimated. The Ixians still haven't produced the Obliterators they promised. We simply can't win this fight. As soon as we admit that, we can begin to make realistic plans.'

Eyes bleary, Murbella gave the former Honored Matre a level look. 'Such as?' The Mother Commander dealt with so many ongoing crises, obligations, and unsolvable problems that she could barely concentrate on the reports coming to the mostly empty Keep. The plague had passed on Chapterhouse, so everyone who was going to die was already dead. With the exception of the isolated inhabitants of the deep desert Shakkad Station, the only survivors on the planet were Reverend Mothers.

All the while, the thinking machines continued to move through space, penetrating deeper into the Old Empire – though by sending scout probes and their plagues here to Chapterhouse, they had broken their previously predictable progression. Omnius must understand the significance of the New Sisterhood; a key victory here could stop the rest of humanity's scattered fighting.

'Let's take what we need,' Kiria said, 'copy our Archives, and vanish into the great unknown to create seed colonies. The thinking machines are relentless, but we can be swift and unpredictable. For humanity's survival and the preservation of the Sisterhood, we must disperse, reproduce, and *remain alive*.' The other Reverend Mothers watched guardedly.

Anger boiled within Murbella. 'Those old attitudes have proved wrong time and again. We can't survive simply by running or by breeding faster than Omnius can kill us.'

'Many Sisters believe as I do – the ones still living, that is. You've led us now for almost a quarter of a century, and your policies have failed. Most of Chapterhouse is dead. This crisis forces us to consider new alternatives.'

'Old alternatives, you mean. There is too much work ahead of us to rehash this tired debate. Is the identification test for Face Dancer genetics ready for distribution yet? That test is critical for all key planetary governments. Our scientists have studied the cadavers for weeks, and we must send—'

'Don't change the subject, Mother Commander! If you won't make the rational decision, if you can't see we need to adapt to circumstances, then I challenge you for leadership.'

In astonishment, Laera backed away from the table, while Janess watched her mother, showing no emotion. After the plague had run its course, the female bashar had returned from the fringe battles.

Murbella allowed herself a cool smile as she faced Kiria. Her voice dripped with acid. 'I thought we finished this nonsense years ago.' She had fought off numerous challengers, killing each one. But Kiria was ready to put it to the test again. 'Choose your time and place.'

'Choose? That's just like you, Mother Commander – putting off what must be done now.' In a flash as swift as nerve impulses could travel, Kiria leapt and lashed out with one foot. Murbella spun away, her spine bending backward with a suppleness that surprised even her. The deadly edge of Kiria's foot came within a hair's breadth of her left eye. The attacker landed on her feet, poised for further combat in the council chamber. 'We can't choose a time and place for fighting. We must always be ready, always *adapt*.' She lunged forward again, both hands outstretched, fingers rigid as wooden stakes to gouge Murbella's throat.

She writhed out of the way as Kiria thrust. Before her opponent could yank her hand away, Murbella grabbed the woman's arm and added her own momentum, pulling Kiria off balance and slamming her into the council table, scattering Ridulian crystal sheets. Tumbling off, Kiria crashed into a chairdog. In angry reflex, her fist broke through the placid animal's furry hide and spilled its blood on the floor. The piece of living furniture died with only the faintest peep of alarm and pain.

Murbella sprang onto the tabletop and kicked a loose

holoprojector at her opponent. The sharp edge of the device caught Kiria on the brow, making a cut that bled profusely. The Mother Commander crouched, ready to defend herself from a frontal attack, but Kiria ducked under the table and heaved upward with her back, knocking the table over. When Murbella fell, Kiria dove over the capsized table and dropped onto the Mother Commander. She wrapped wiry hands around her throat in a primitive but effective method of assassination.

With rigid fingers, Murbella jabbed Kiria's side with enough force to fracture two ribs, but at the same time she felt the sickening snap of her own fingers breaking. Instead of withdrawing as expected, Kiria snarled in pain, raised Murbella's neck and shoulders, and slammed her head against the floor.

Murbella's ears rang, and she felt her skull crack. Fluttering black spots of unconsciousness circled her vision like tiny vultures waiting for fresh carrion. She had to stay awake, had to keep fighting. If she faded now, Kiria would kill her. And if she was defeated here, she would lose not just her life, but the Sisterhood as well. The fate of the entire human race could be decided in this moment.

Janess watched her mother with anguish, but Laera and the other Reverend Mothers were well trained and would not interfere. The unification with Honored Matres had required certain concessions from the Bene Gesserits, including the right of anyone to challenge the Mother Commander's leadership.

Kiria continued to choke her, while Murbella strained to draw a breath. Blocking the pain of her broken fingers, she clapped her palms hard against Kiria's ears. As the deafened woman reeled, Murbella gouged out her right eye with a crooked forefinger, leaving blood and jelly all over her face.

Kiria writhed away, pushing to her feet, but Murbella followed with a flurry of hand blows and kicks. Even so, her challenger was not defeated yet. Kiria hammered her heel into Murbella's sternum, then struck her abdomen with a side blow. Something ruptured inside; Murbella could feel the damage but didn't know how bad it was. Digging into her energy reserves, she drove Kiria aside with her shoulder.

The Honored Matre's lips were drawn back to expose bloody gums and teeth. Rallying, Kiria gathered all of her strength to strike, ignoring her mangled eye. But as she planted her foot, she slipped on a smear of the chairdog's blood on the smooth floor. This threw off her balance for an instant – just long enough to give Murbella the advantage. Without hesitating, the Mother Commander struck a blow so hard that her own wrist shattered – as did Kiria's neck. The challenger fell dead to the floor.

Murbella swayed, while Janess came forward, concern on her face, ready to help her mother, her superior. Murbella raised an arm. Her broken wrist flopped limply, but she banished the wince of pain from her face. 'I am capable of standing by myself.'

Some of the younger Reverend Mothers, with wide eyes and intense expressions, had backed up to the walls of the council chamber.

Murbella wanted so badly to fall beside her victim on the floor, letting the exhaustion and pain take control. But she could not allow that – not with so many Reverend Mothers observing. She could never reveal a moment of weakness, especially now.

Summoning her breath, dredging up the last sparks of

endurance, Murbella spoke in an even voice. 'I will go to my quarters now and heal.' Then, in a lower voice, 'Janess, have the kitchens send up a restorative energy drink.' She cast a dismissive glance at the dead Kiria, then raised her eyes to Janess, Laera, and the awed spectators in the hall. 'Or do any of you wish to challenge me and take advantage of my condition?' In defiance, she held up her broken wrist. No one took the offer.

Injured inside and out, Murbella had no clear memory of how she made it back to her quarters. Her progress was slow, but she accepted no aid. The other Reverend Mothers, sensing her determination, left her alone.

In her dim room, the spice drink was already waiting for her. *How long did it take me to get here?* After a single sip she could feel energy surge through her body. She murmured a thankful blessing to Janess; her daughter had made this drink extremely potent.

Leaving word that she was not to be disturbed, she sealed her door and consumed the rest of the rejuvenating beverage. It boosted the internal repairs she had already begun to make, delicately probing with her mind to judge the extent of her injuries. Finally, allowing the flood of pain to wash into her senses, Murbella carefully assessed what Kiria had done to her. The degree of internal damage frightened her. Never in any previous challenge had she come so close to losing.

Will the rest of the Reverend Mothers rally behind me – or will they start sniffing out my weaknesses again like hungry hyenas?

She could not afford to waste time and energy battling her own people. Few enough of them remained alive after the plague. What if the Sisterhood was infiltrated by Face Dancers again? Could one of them, trained in exotic fighting techniques, pose as an Honored Matre challenger and kill Murbella? What if a Face Dancer became the Mother Commander of the Sisterhood? Then all indeed would be lost.

She lay back, closed her eyes, and plunged into a healing trance. Time was of the essence. She had to regain her full strength. The forces of Omnius had located this world and would be coming soon.

Every man casts a shadow . . . some darker than others.
                                    – The Cant of the Shariat

While Yueh was under arrest and interrogation, yet another instance of sabotage occurred.

The Bene Gesserit Sisters summoned the passengers to the great auditorium for an emergency meeting. Garimi seemed particularly agitated; Duncan Idaho and Miles Teg were alert. Eyes intent, Scytale observed, always the outsider. What had happened now? *And will they blame me for it?*

Was it worse than the murder of another ghola and axlotl tank? Had someone else been killed? Had another water reservoir dumped into space, squandering the new supplies they had acquired at Qelso? Spice stockpiles contaminated? Food vats destroyed? The seven captive sandworms harmed?

The Tleilaxu man sat back, watching everyone stream in from outside corridors and take their seats in islands of friendship or shared opinions. Palpable tension radiated from them. More than two hundred gathered, most of them curious, alarmed, or frightened. Only a few proctors stayed in isolated sections with the younger children that had been born during the journey; others were old enough to be treated as adults.

The Bashar himself made the announcement. 'Explosive mines have disappeared from the sealed armory. Eight of the hundred and twelve – certainly enough to cause severe damage to this ship.'

After a brief silence, conversation returned in a riptide of whispers, gasps, and accusations.

'The mines,' Teg repeated. 'Back on Chapterhouse they were placed around this ship as a self-destruct mechanism in case Duncan or anyone else tried to steal it. Now eight of them are gone.'

Sheeana went to stand beside the Bashar. 'I deactivated those mines myself, so that this vessel could escape. They were locked securely away, but now they've disappeared.'

'If they are missing, they might have been dumped out into space . . . or planted around the ship like time bombs,' Duncan said. 'I suspect the latter, and that our saboteur has further plans.'

The Rabbi moaned loudly. 'You see? More incompetence! I should have stayed on Qelso with the rest of my people.'

'Maybe you stole the mines,' Garimi snapped.

He looked horrified. 'You dare accuse me? A holy man of my stature? First Yueh says I manipulated him to murder a ghola baby, and now you think I have stolen explosives?' Scytale saw that the frail old man could never have lifted one of the heavy mines, much less eight of them.

'Yueh has been under the constant surveillance of Thufir Hawat and myself,' Teg said. 'Even if he did kill the axlotl tank and the growing ghola, he could not have stolen the mines.'

'Unless he has an accomplice,' Garimi said, setting off another chain of muttering.

'We will discover who took them.' Sheeana cut off the squabble. 'And where they have been hidden.'

'We've heard similar promises in the past three years,' Garimi continued, with a meaningful glare at Teg and Thufir. 'But our security has been completely ineffective.'

Paul Atreides sat in one of the front rows, near Chani and Jessica. 'Are we certain the mines only disappeared recently? How often is the armory checked? Maybe Liet-Kynes or Stilgar took them for their war against the sandtrout without telling us.'

'We should evacuate this ship,' the Rabbi said. 'Find another planet, or go back to Qelso.' His voice quavered. 'If you witches hadn't . . . hadn't . . . taken Rebecca, I would be safe now with my people. We all could have settled there.'

Garimi scowled. 'Rabbi, for years you've encouraged dissent with your sniping and destructive arguments, without offering alternatives.'

'I speak the truth as I see it. The stolen mines are only the latest in a string of sabotage. My Rebecca remains alive only by chance when four other axlotl tanks have now been murdered. And who damaged the life-support systems, the water holding tanks? Who contaminated the algae vats and destroyed the air-filtration mats? Who poured acid on the seals of the observation window in the sandworm hold? There is a criminal among us, and he is growing bolder and bolder! Why don't you find him?'

Scytale remained silent and unobtrusive, listening to the debate. Everyone feared there would be more incidents of sabotage, and the stolen mines would be sufficient to cripple or destroy the great ship.

The Tleilaxu had no doubt they would eventually turn

their suspicions toward him because of his race, but he could prove his innocence. He had laboratory records, surveillance images, a solid alibi. Nevertheless, *someone* had committed the acts of sabotage.

When the exhausting meeting broke up, the Rabbi stalked past Scytale in a huff, saying he was going to go sit in a vigil beside Rebecca, 'to make certain no one else tries to kill her!' As the old man passed close, Scytale caught the Rabbi's usual faint, strange scent, a subtly different flavor in the air.

On instinct, Scytale emitted a barely audible whistle in a complicated melody that he remembered from deep in his past lives. The Rabbi ignored him and stalked away. Scytale frowned, not sure if he had noticed a brief hesitation as the old man walked past.

God is God, and life is His alone to give. If God Himself
has not the strength to survive, then we are left with nothing
but despair.

— The Cant of the Shariat

Every investigation of Rakis yielded the same result. Only
a few insignificant pockets of its ecosystem had survived.
The planet was empty and haunted, yet it seemed to
have its own will to live. Against all odds and science,
Rakis still clung to its sparse atmosphere, its gasps of
moisture.

Guriff's hard-bitten prospectors happily accepted
supplies that Waff and the Guildsmen offered as a gesture
of goodwill. Waff's primary motivation for this was to get
the men to leave him alone while he conducted his
innocuous 'geological investigations.' The prospectors
were supplied by irregular CHOAM vessels that came to
check on their work, but Guriff had no idea when the
next ship would come. The Tleilaxu Master had enough
packaged food from the Heighliner to last for years, if
his deteriorating body lasted that long.

Above all, he needed to tend to his worms.

As he'd hoped, the prospectors spent the harsh days
and nights concentrating on their own digging, hoping

to find the legendary lost hoard of the Tyrant's melange. Insulated scout cruisers braved the rugged weather, carrying sensors and probes up to the polar regions, while the men bored test holes, searching unsuccessfully for any threads of spice.

The large dropbox from Edrik's Heighliner had included a wide-bed groundcar that could roll across even the roughest terrain. When the prospectors departed, Waff called his four Guildsmen to assist him. With no curious eyes watching, they wrestled the long, sand-filled test tanks aboard his groundcar. Waff would make a pilgrimage out into the charred and glassy wasteland that had once been a sea of dunes.

'I will release the specimens myself. I don't need your assistance.' He directed the Guildsmen to return to the rigid-walled survival tents. 'Stay. and prepare our food – and make certain you follow the accepted ways.' He had given them precise instructions on the proper techniques. 'Once I free the worms, I intend to come back for a celebration.'

He did not want Guriff and his men, nor any of these untrustworthy Guild assistants, to observe such a private and holy moment. Today he would restore the Prophet to Rakis, to the planet where He belonged. Dressed in protective clothing, he keyed in coordinates and drove off with the two long aquariums in the back of his groundcar. Heading due east, he sped away into a ruddy orange dawn.

Although the landscape here was smeared, eroded, and unrecognizable, Waff knew exactly where he was going. Before coming to Rakis, he had dug up the old charts, and because the Honored Matres' Obliterators had altered even the planetary magnetic field, he had carefully recalibrated his maps from orbit. A long time ago, God's Messenger had purposefully carried him to the location of Sietch Tabr. The worms must consider it sacred, and Waff could think of no more appropriate place to turn loose the armored, augmented creatures. He drove there now.

Light from the dust-thickened sky bathed the glassy ground in eerie colors. From the tanks behind him, Waff could feel the thumping of the worms as they writhed, impatient to burst out onto the open desert. Home.

Back on the Heighliner, Waff had observed the bucking and thrashing creatures, measuring their growth in the lab. He knew the worms were dangerous, and that long confinement in small tanks sapped the creatures' strength. Even under carefully controlled conditions, he hadn't been able to replicate the optimal environment, and the specimens had weakened. Something was wrong.

But hope infused him. Now that he was actually here, all would be right again. Holy Rakis! He could only pray that this injured dune world would provide what a Tleilaxu Master could not, offering some ineffable benefit to the worms, to the Prophet.

When Waff reached the plain and saw the melted rocks, he remembered the weathered line of mountains that had sheltered the buried tomb of the Fremen city. He stopped the groundcar. A vitrified crust – rocky grains melted to glass by the blasts of incomprehensible weapons – covered what had once been open sand. But the worms would know what to do.

Behind the vehicle, Waff paused a moment to close his eyes in prayer to his God and His Prophet. Then, with a flourish, he disengaged the plaz walls of the tanks and let sand spill out. Long serpentine shapes lunged free like uncoiled springs, and dropped to the ground around the vehicle. Waff gazed in wonderment at their thick, ridged bodies, and the python fluidity of their motion.

'Go, Prophet! Reclaim your world.'

Eight worms slithered on the hard, smooth ground. *Eight*, a sacred Tleilaxu number.

The freed creatures spread out in random paths, while he watched them in awe. Waff hoped they could break through the fused sand and tunnel into softer levels below, as he had designed them to do. Each of the specimens had a tiny implanted tracer that would enable him to follow them and continue his investigations.

However, the sandworms turned and circled the vehicle, coming closer. Hunting *him*. In a moment of fear, Waff froze. They were certainly large enough to attack and kill him. 'Prophet, do not harm me. I have brought you back to Rakis. You are free to make this your kingdom once again.'

The worms raised their blunt heads, swaying back and forth. *Are they trying to send me some sort of message?* He struggled to comprehend. Could their hypnotic movements be an alien dance? Or a predatory maneuver?

He did not move. He waited.

If this landscape was too harsh for them, if the Prophet needed to consume him in order to survive, Waff was fully prepared to donate the flesh of his own deteriorating body. If this was to be the end, so be it.

Then, as if at a silent signal, the sandworms turned in unison and sped off, their flexing ridges bumping across the glassy dunes. Presently they stopped, bent their armored heads downward, and smashed into the hard surface. They broke the crust and plunged downward, tunneling into the pristine, sterilized sands. Returning to the desert! Waff's heart swelled. He knew they would survive.

As he returned to the groundcar, he realized he had tears in his eyes.

When the forces are arrayed and the final battle is engaged, the outcome may be decided in only a few moments. Remember this: By the time the first shot is fired, half the battle is already over. Victory or defeat can be determined by the preparations that are set in place weeks or even months beforehand.

— BASHAR MILES TEG,
resource allocation request to the Bene Gesserit

Chief Fabricator Shayama Sen agreed to come to Chapterhouse, but the Ixian dignitary remained aboard his ship high in orbit, far above the recovery operations. He would not risk exposure to any last vestiges of the plague, though the disease had burned itself out down there.

Murbella had to go to him to make her demands – but under the strictest quarantine conditions. Encased in her own decontamination sphere, like a laboratory specimen in a tank, she felt foolish and helpless. The Bene Gesserit sphere's outer hull – though scorched by its passage through the atmosphere on the way to orbit and then exposed to the vacuum of space – underwent additional irradiation and sterilization procedures up there. Fail-safes, redundancies. *Justified paranoia*, she admitted to herself. Although Murbella did not fault him for taking such extraordinary precautions, the Ixian nevertheless had much explaining to do.

While waiting inside her sealed chamber aboard the Guildship (which was guided by a mathematical compiler rather than a Navigator), she composed herself. Still sore and battered from her duel with Kiria, she was satisfied that her violent response to the stupid power play had been necessary. None of the other distraught Sisters would challenge her now, thus leaving her role as Mother Commander uncontested.

Once again, Murbella cursed the rebel Honored Matres and their mindless destruction of the massive shipyards and weapons shops on Richese. Had that not happened, with both Ix and Richese producing armaments, the human race could have consolidated a meaningful defense. Now that Ix was the primary industrial center, the Chief Fabricator felt he could be intractable. Shortsighted fools!

Shayama Sen marched into the large metal-walled room and took a comfortable seat facing her. He looked smug and safe, while she felt like a caged zoo animal. 'You called me away from our work, Mother Commander?'

Despite the inherent awkwardness of her position, Murbella tried to take command of the meeting. 'Chief Fabricator, you have had three years to duplicate the Obliterators we provided, but all we've received in exchange for our melange payments are reports on your tests, and promise after promise. The Enemy has destroyed more than a hundred planets, and their battleships keep coming. Chapterhouse itself was nearly eradicated by the recent plague.'

Sen bowed formally. 'We are fully aware of this, Mother Commander, and you have my condolences.' He got up and poured himself a glass of water from a pitcher, then roamed the large meeting room, flaunting his own freedom.

Anger heated her cheeks and neck. How could this man sound so calm in the face of the crumbling human civilization? 'We require the weapons you promised us – and without further delay.'

Sen tapped his circuitry-imprinted fingernails together, pondering her containment sphere with a blank stare. 'But we have not yet received full payment, and we hear your New Sisterhood is in dire financial straits. If we continue to devote all our resources to these Obliterators, and you renege—'

'The agreed-upon amount of melange is yours the moment you finish installing Obliterators in our new warships. You know this.' She didn't dare let Sen discover that she had released a great deal of stockpiled spice to help her fellow Reverend Mothers fight the plague.

'Ah, but if your spice is contaminated by the plague, of what use is it to us? How else will you pay?'

Murbella couldn't believe his blindness. 'The spice is not contaminated. We will implement any sterilization measures you require.'

'And what if that destroys its efficacy?'

'Then we will give you the original spice to decontaminate in whatever manner you see fit. Stop quibbling about nonsense when the extinction of the human race is imminent!'

Sen seemed scandalized. 'You call it nonsense? The properties of spice are complex and could be harmed by such aggressive measures. The substance is of no value to us if we cannot use it.'

'The plague organism has a short lifetime. Unless it is

transferred from host to host, the disease dies swiftly. Place the spice on an airless moon for a year if you choose to.'

'But the difficulties and the inconvenience . . . I believe these circumstances merit a renegotiation of our price.'

If the container wall had not prevented her, Murbella would have killed him for his insolence. 'Have you any idea of how much destruction the Enemy has spread?'

He pursed his lips, and said, 'Let me dispense with subtleties, Mother Commander. Honored Matres provoked this Enemy into launching its fleet against them, and in turn against the rest of us. Your association with the whores was your own folly, and the whole human race has paid for it. Ix has no quarrel with these robotic invaders. Since they evolved from ancient thinking machines, it is possible that we Ixians have more in common with *them* than with manipulative, murderous females.'

Ah. Now she was beginning to understand. Listening to the sharp voice of Odrade-within and a thousand other Reverend Mothers frantically offering advice, Murbella forced calm upon herself. It was clear that the Ixian was trying to escalate this discussion. But why? To distract her? Had he failed to make as much progress in developing the Obliterators as he claimed? Was production running behind schedule?

She selected a gambit that she hoped would shut down his blathering. 'I authorize a thirty percent increase in your spice allotment, to be put in a trust fund held in the Guild Bank of your choosing. I expect that is sufficient to make up for any inconvenience? However, payment will be contingent upon your *actual delivery* of the weaponry in our contract. The Guild has delivered our new warships. Now, where are my Obliterators?'

Shayama Sen bowed, accepting her offer and withdrawing his objections. 'Our manufactory worlds are operating at full capacity. We can begin loading Obliterators aboard your new ships immediately.'

'I'll issue the orders.' She paced within the decontamination bubble like a Laza tiger. The smells of disinfectant chemicals seeping through the air filters made her want to gag. She didn't think the chamber's replenishers were working properly. 'How do we know your weapons will perform as you promise?'

'You provided the originals, and we duplicated them precisely. If the originals functioned, then these will, too.'

'The originals *functioned*. You've seen what's left of Rakis and Richese!'

'Then you have nothing to fear.'

'From now on, I insist that we place Bene Gesserit inspectors and line supervisors in your manufactories. They will keep you accountable and guard against sabotage.'

Shayama Sen struggled with the demand, but could find no legitimate argument against it. 'Provided your women do not interfere, we shall allow them access. Is that all?'

'We also need to witness a successful test before going into battle.'

Sen smiled again. 'You would have us annihilate a world merely to prove a point? Hmm, I see Honored Matre methods persist in your New Sisterhood.' He chuckled. 'I'll give you full records of our previous tests and even arrange for a new demonstration, if you like.'

'We will review your data, Chief Fabricator. Transmit it to Chapterhouse, and arrange for a demonstration that I can see with my own eyes.'

He tapped his silicon fingernails again, an annoying nervous habit. 'Very well. I'll find a nice planetoid to blow up for your entertainment.'

Murbella pressed against the curved, transparent wall of her sphere. 'And there's one other thing I insist upon. Face Dancers have been found on many worlds, manipulating governments, weakening our defenses. Some even managed to infiltrate Chapterhouse. I need to have assurance that *you* are not a Face Dancer.'

Sen reeled backward in surprise. 'You accuse me of being an Enemy, a shape-shifter operative?'

Murbella leaned against the solid wall, regarding him coolly. His indignation did nothing to convince her. She worked the internal controls, and a small, sealed container opened near the base of the Bene Gesserit chamber. It was a sterilization bin, an autoclave and chemical bath. Steam still curled from the package as it emerged for the Chief Fabricator to take.

'This is a testing device we have developed. After analyzing Face Dancer specimens found among our dead, we ran genetic tests and developed this infallible indicator. Right now, Chief Fabricator – as I watch – you will complete this test on yourself.'

'I will *not*.' He sniffed.

'You will, or you'll receive none of our melange.'

Sen roamed again, frowning. 'What is this test? What does it do?'

'It is mostly automated.' Murbella explained the principle to him and the easy steps. 'As a bonus for you, we can allow Ix to produce these in great quantities. There are plenty of suspicious people who see Face Dancers everywhere. You could make a tidy profit selling these kits.'

Sen considered. 'You may be right.'

While Murbella observed, he went through the motions, standing close enough to her bubble that she could watch his every movement. As far as the Reverend Mothers knew, the test could not easily be foiled, and the Chief Fabricator had had no time to prepare a deception. She waited with intense interest, and was relieved when the indicators declared him fully human. Shayama Sen was not a Face Dancer.

With an irritated expression on his face, he held the chemical tab up for her to see. 'Are you satisfied now?'

'I am. And I advise you to perform this test on all of your chief engineers and team leaders. Ix is a likely target for the Enemy to infiltrate. Another reason for my Sisters to supervise your vital work for us.'

Sen looked genuinely disturbed, as if that possibility had not occurred to him. 'I concede your point, Mother Commander. I would like to see those results myself.'

'Then include them when you send your data about the Obliterator tests. In the meantime, prepare to install your weapons in all the new warships coming out of the Junction shipyards. We are about to engage in an all-out offensive against the thinking-machine fleet.'

> *Each sentient life requires a place of extreme serenity, where the mind may roam afterward in memory and to which the body longs to return.*
>
> — ERASMUS,
> contemplation notes

Now that you have been among us for more than a year, it is time to show you my special place, Paolo.' The independent robot waved a metal arm, and his majestic robes flowed around him. 'And you too, of course, Baron Harkonnen.'

The Baron scowled, his voice dripping with sarcasm. 'Your special place? I'm sure we'll be charmed by what a *robot* considers to be a special place.'

During the time that he and Paolo had lived on Synchrony, he'd lost his awe and fear of thinking machines. They seemed plodding and grandiose, full of redundancy and very little impulsivity. Since Omnius thought he needed Paolo, along with the Baron to keep Paolo in line, the two were safe enough. Even so, the Baron felt a need to show some backbone, and turn the circumstances to his own benefit.

Around the interior of the now-familiar cathedral chamber, the walls became a wash of color, as if invisible painters were hard at work. Instead of blank metal and stone surfaces, the murky shades of green and brown sharpened into highly realistic trees and birds. The oppressive ceiling opened to the sky, and peculiar synthesized music began playing. A gemgravel pathway ran through the lush garden with comfortable reclining benches at intermittent intervals. A lily pond appeared on one side.

'My contemplation garden.' Erasmus formed his artificial smile. 'I enjoy this place very much. It is special to me.'

'At least the flowers don't stink.' Paolo ripped up one of the bright chrysanthemums, sniffed it, and discarded it at the side of the path. After a year of constant training, the Baron had finally made the boy's personality into something he could be proud of.

'This is all lovely,' the Baron said drily. 'And utterly pointless.'

Be careful what you say to him, Grandfather, cautioned the Alia-voice within. *Don't get us killed today.* It was one of her continual harangues.

'Is something troubling you, Baron?' Erasmus asked. 'This should be a place of peace and contemplation.'

See what you've done! Get out of my head.

But I'm trapped here with you. You can't get rid of me. I killed you once with the gom jabbar, and I can do it again with a little careful manipulation.

'I see that you are often plagued by disturbing thoughts.' Erasmus stepped closer. 'Would you like me to open your skull and look inside? I could fix the problem.'

Be careful with me, Abomination! I just may take him up on the offer!

He forced a smile as he replied to the independent robot. 'I'm just impatient to learn exactly how we can work with Omnius. Your war against humanity has gone on for some time now, and we've been your guests for a year. When will we do what you brought us here for?'

Paolo kicked a divot into the gemgravel path. 'Yes, Erasmus. When do we get to have fun?'

'Soon enough.' The robot swirled his robes and guided his companions through the garden.

The boy had just passed his eleventh birthday and was developing into a strong young man, well-muscled and highly trained. Thanks to the Baron's constant influence, virtually all traces of the former Atreides personality had been extinguished. Erasmus himself had supervised Paolo's vigorous combat training against fighting meks, all to prime him to become the supposed Kwisatz Haderach.

But the Baron still could not fathom *why*. Why would the machines care about some obscure human religious figure from ancient history?

Erasmus motioned for them to sit on the nearest bench. The synthesized music and birdsong around them grew louder and more energetic until they became intertwined melodies. The robot's expression shifted once again, as if in reverie. 'Is it not beautiful? I composed it myself.'

'Most impressive.' The Baron despised the music as too smooth and peaceful; he preferred more cacophonous, discordant selections.

'Over the millennia, I created wondrous works of art and many illusions.' Erasmus's face and body shifted, and he became entirely human in appearance. Even the gaudy and unnecessary garments altered, until the robot stood before them again as a matronly old woman in a floral-print dress holding a small hand trowel. 'This is one of my favorites. I have perfected it over the years, drawing from more and more of the lives my Face Dancers bring me.'

With the hand trowel she dug in the simulated soil near the bench, getting rid of weeds that the Baron was sure had not been there moments earlier. A worm crawled out of the exposed, dark dirt, and the old woman sliced it in half with the trowel. The two parts of the squirming creature faded into the dirt.

A gentle undercurrent flowed in her voice, not unlike that of a grandmother telling bedtime stories to children. 'Long ago – during your original lifetime, dear Baron – a Tleilaxu researcher named Hidar Fen Ajidica created an artificial spice that he called amal. Though the substance proved to have significant defects, Ajidica consumed huge quantities of it himself, and as a result he went increasingly mad, which led to his demise.'

'Sounds like a failure,' Paolo said.

'Oh, Ajidica failed spectacularly, but he did accomplish something very important. Call it a side effect. For his special ambassadors, he created greatly improved Face Dancers, with which he intended to populate a new domain. He dispatched them into deep space as scouts, colonizers, preparers of the way. He died before he could join them. Poor foolish man.'

The old woman left her trowel stuck in the ground. When she straightened, she pressed her hand against the small of her back, as if to comfort an ache. 'The new Face Dancers located our machine empire, and Omnius allowed me to study them. I spent generations working with the shape-shifters, learning how to draw information from them. Lovely biological machines, far superior to their predecessors. Yes, they are proving to be extremely helpful in winning our final war.'

Looking around the illusory garden, the Baron saw other forms, minor workers who appeared to be human. New Face Dancers? 'So you made an alliance with them?'

The old woman pursed her lips. 'An alliance? They are servants, not our partners. Face Dancers were made to serve. To them, Omnius and I are like gods, greater Masters than the Tleilaxu ever were.' Erasmus seemed to be pondering. 'I do wish they had brought one of their Masters to me before the Honored Matres destroyed nearly all of them. The discussion could have been most enlightening.'

Paolo brought the conversation back around to a subject that interested him. 'As the final Kwisatz Haderach, I will be a god, too.'

Erasmus laughed, an old woman's cachinnation. 'Beware of megalomania, young man. It has brought down many a human – such as Hidar Fen Ajidica. Soon I expect to have a key to help you reach your potential. We need to free the god that crouches inside your body. And that requires a powerful catalyst.'

'What is it?' the young man demanded.

'I keep forgetting how impatient you humans are!' The old woman brushed off her flower-print dress. 'That is why I enjoy the Face Dancers so much. In them, I see the potential for perfecting humans. Face Dancers could be the sort of humans that even thinking machines might tolerate.'

The Baron snorted. 'Humans will never be perfect! Believe me, I've known plenty of them, and they're all disappointing in some way.' Rabban, Piter . . . even Feyd had failed him in the end.

Don't omit yourself, Grandfather. Remember, you were killed by a little girl with a poison needle. Ha ha!

Shut up! The Baron scratched nervously at the top of his head, as if to dig through flesh and bone to rip her out. She fell silent.

'I fear you may be right, Baron. Humans may not be salvageable, but we don't want Omnius to believe that, or he will destroy them all.'

'I thought you machines were already doing that,' the Baron said.

'To a certain extent. Omnius is stretching his abilities, but when we find the no-ship, I am certain he will get down to business.' The old woman dug holes in the garden and planted seedlings that simply appeared in her hands.

'What's so special about one lost ship?' the Baron asked.

'Our mathematical projections suggest that the Kwisatz Haderach is aboard.'

'But *I* am the Kwisatz Haderach!' Paolo insisted. 'You already have me.'

The old woman gave him a wry smile. 'You are our fallback plan, young man. Omnius prefers the security of redundancy. If there are two possible Kwisatz Haderachs, he wants both of them.'

His face a mask of displeasure, the Baron cracked his knuckles. 'So you think there's another ghola of Paul Atreides aboard that ship? Not likely!'

'I claim only that there is another *Kwisatz Haderach* aboard the ship. However, since we have one Paul Atreides ghola, there could certainly be another.'

*Are we on the Golden Path, or have we strayed from it?
For three and a half millennia we prayed for deliverance
from the Tyrant, but now that he is gone, have we forgotten
how to live without such stern guidance? Do we know
how to make the necessary decisions, or will we become
hopelessly lost in the wilderness and starve of our own
failings?*

— MOTHER SUPERIOR DARWI ODRADE,
Pondering My Epitaph, sealed Bene Gesserit Archives,
recorded before Battle of Junction

Highly agitated, Garimi refused to take a seat in Sheeana's
private quarters, no matter how many times it was offered.
Even the Van Gogh painting on the wall did not seem to
interest her. The stolen mines had brought long-simmering
tensions to a new, raw level. Frantic search teams had
been unable to locate any of the explosive devices. Sheeana
knew that the stern Proctor Superior had her own suspicions and her own set of people to blame.

'You and the Bashar didn't make a good bargain back
on Qelso,' Garimi said. 'Leaving all those people and
equipment, and getting nothing for ourselves!'

'We replenished all our stores.'

'What if further sabotage hits our life-support systems?

Liet-Kynes and Stilgar were the two most capable of conservation, recycling, and repairs. What if we need them to help us? Do you intend to grow new ones?'

Sheeana angered the other woman further by responding with a calm, amused smile. 'We could, but I thought you suspected all the ghola children. Yet you want Liet and Stilgar back? Besides, maybe Liet was right; maybe it's their destiny to remain on Qelso.'

'Now it's obvious that neither of them was the saboteur – though I'm still not entirely convinced about Yueh.'

Sheeana stared at the bright daubs of color that the ancient artist had swirled into an image of such power. Van Gogh was a genius. 'I took a necessary action, based on our needs and priorities.'

'Hardly! You bowed to the demands of those murderous nomads to keep all Bene Gesserits off the planet. We should have formed a new school there – and now, instead, this whole ship could explode at any moment!'

Ah, the core of what is really bothering her.

'You know very well that I would have been happy to let you and your followers settle there.' She forced a chuckle. 'But I was not willing to start a war with the people of Qelso. We can train others in the nuances of our life-support systems. This ship will survive, as it has for decades.'

Obviously in no mood to be brushed aside, Garimi said, 'Survive how? By creating another ghola to save us? That's always your solution, whether an Abomination like Alia, a traitor like Yueh or Jessica, or a Tyrant like Leto II. At least Pandora had the good sense to close her box.'

'And I want to open it wide. I want to bring back the history, especially Paul Atreides – and Thufir Hawat. We could certainly draw on the security knowledge of the Weapons Master of House Atreides.'

'Hawat failed spectacularly the last time you tried to awaken him.'

'Then we'll try again. And Chani could be an excellent fulcrum for awakening Paul. Jessica is also ripe for awakening. Even Leto II is ready.'

Garimi's eyes flashed. 'You are playing with fire, Sheeana.'

'I am forging weapons. For that, fire is necessary.' Sheeana turned, letting Garimi know that the discussion was at an end. 'I've heard your opinions often enough to memorize them. I will dine with the gholas today. Maybe they have fresh ideas.'

Incensed, the dark-haired woman followed Sheeana out of her quarters and down the corridors toward the dining hall. Unexpectedly, young Leto II stepped out of a lift tube, alone and quiet as usual. The twelve-year-old often wandered the halls of the no-ship by himself; now he looked at the two women and blinked, but did not speak to them. Such an odd, preoccupied child.

Before Sheeana could stop her, the Proctor Superior marched toward Leto, stiff and intimidating. Garimi had a fresh target for her anger and frustration. 'So, Tyrant, where is your Golden Path? Where has it led us? If you were so prescient, why didn't you warn us of the Honored Matres or the Enemy?'

'I don't know.' The boy seemed genuinely perplexed. 'I don't remember.'

Garimi studied him in disgust. 'And what if you *did* remember? Would you be the God Emperor, the greatest butcher in all of human history? Sheeana thinks you could save us, but I say the Tyrant could just as easily destroy us. That's what you're best at. I don't want you or your monstrous ego back, Leto II. Your Golden Path is a blind man's road, sunk in a swamp.'

'It is not this boy's Golden Path,' Sheeana said, taking the other woman's arm in a viselike grip. 'Leave him alone.'

Leto took a quick step, darted around them, and fled down the corridor. Garimi looked triumphantly at Sheeana, who merely regarded her as a fool, condemned by her own irrational outburst.

HIS EYES AND ears burned from the Proctor Superior's accusations, but Leto refused to allow a tear. A wise person didn't waste water trying to drown his emotions; he knew that much about old Dune. As he moved away from Sheeana and the insufferable Proctor Superior, and everyone else who thought they knew what to expect from him, the boy silently denied what Garimi had said, trying to block away what he himself knew.

I was the God Emperor, the Tyrant. I created the Golden Path . . . but with my memories locked away, I don't truly understand what it is! Despite all he had learned about his original lifetime, Leto felt like nothing more than a twelve-year-old who had never asked to be reborn.

He rode the transport tube to the deep lower decks, heading for a place where he felt more comfortable and safe. At first he considered slipping into the roaring winds of the recirculation chambers and the atmosphere-pumping ducts, but the strict security measures imposed by Bashar Teg and Leto's friend Thufir had closed off all access.

Before his unpleasant encounter with Garimi, Leto had planned to join Thufir for his regular session on the training floor. Though the other ghola boy was now seven-teen and had his security duties with the Bashar, he still frequently sparred with Leto. Despite his youth and size, Leto II was highly competitive even against a larger, stronger opponent. For the past few years they had provided quite a challenge for each other.

At the moment, though, Leto needed to be alone. He reached the bottom levels of the ship and stood at the main access door into the immense hold. The surveillance imagers would have spotted him already. He swallowed hard. He had never dared to go inside alone, though he had stared for hours through the plaz at the captive sandworms.

A pair of young guards stood in the hall, monitoring access to the cargo deck. Seeing the boy approach, they tensed. 'This is a restricted area.'

'Restricted to *me*? Do you know who I am?'

'You are Leto the Tyrant, the God Emperor,' said the young woman, as if answering a proctor's question. She was Debray, one of the Bene Gesserit daughters who had been born in space after the no-ship's escape.

'And those worms are part of me. Don't you remember your history?'

'They're dangerous,' the male guard answered. 'You shouldn't go in there.'

Leto gazed calmly at the pair. 'Yes, I should. Especially now. I need to feel the sands, smell the melange, the worms.' He narrowed his eyes. 'It could well restore my memories, as Sheeana wants.'

Debray frowned as she considered this. 'Sheeana did say that every means must be used to trigger the reawakening of the gholas.'

The male guard turned to his companion. 'Call Thufir Hawat and inform him first. This is highly irregular.'

Leto approached the heavy door. 'I just need to go inside the hatch. I won't stray far. The worms stay out in the center of the habitat, don't they?' Boldly, he used the simple controls to unseal the door. 'I know these worms. Thufir will understand. He hasn't recovered his memories either.'

Before the guards could agree on stopping him, Leto darted into the hold. The sand itself seemed to give off a crackling, staticky sound. The temperature was warm, the air so dry that his throat burned. The powerful smells of flint and cinnamon seared his nostrils. At the far end of the kilometer-long hold, the large worms moved toward him.

Just standing on the sandy surface took the boy back to a place he had studied extensively in the no-ship's library. The real Arrakis, which had changed from desert to garden during his first extended life. Now the dry heat baked his skin. He took deep, calming breaths of air redolent with the odor of melange.

Not bothering to avoid making noise, Leto strode farther out on the sand, sinking up to his ankles in the soft dunes. He ignored the shouted warnings of the guards as he trudged away from the metal wall. This was the closest thing to an open desert these worms had ever known.

Climbing the crest of a dune and gazing around to the limits of the hold, Leto imagined how magnificent Arrakis must have once been. He wished he could remember. The dune on which he stood was small compared to a real one, and the seven worms in the hold were more diminutive than their unfettered ancestors as well.

Ahead of him, the largest worm churned through sand, followed by the others. Leto felt the connection with these seven worms. It was as if the magnificent beasts sensed his mental pain and wanted to help him, even if his memories were still locked away in a ghola vault.

An unexpected release of tears flowed down Leto's cheeks – not of anger toward Garimi but of joy and awe. Tears! He could not stem the flow of moisture. Perhaps if he perished right there on the sands, his body would be absorbed into the flesh of the worms, leaving behind all his fears and expectations.

These worms were his descendants, each with a nugget of his former awareness. *We are the same.* Leto beckoned them. Although his ghola cells hadn't yet released memories of the thousands of years in his original life-time, these sandworms possessed buried memories as well. 'Are you dreaming in there? Am *I* in there?'

A hundred meters from him the worms stopped and dove back into the sand, one after the other. He sensed that their presence was not threatening, but . . . protective. They *did* know him!

From the hatch behind him, Leto heard a familiar voice calling his name. Looking back, he saw the ghola of Thufir Hawat standing on the verge, motioning him to come back to safety. 'Leto, watch out. Don't tempt the worms. You are my friend, but if one of them eats you I won't jump down its gullet to get you back!' Thufir tried to chuckle, but looked deeply anxious.

'I just need some time alone with them.' Leto sensed something moving beneath the sands. He felt no concern for his own well-being, but did not want to endanger his friend. He picked up a strong whiff, the cinnamon odor of spice.

'Leave! Now!'

Then, wrestling with his fear, Thufir ventured closer

to the young man, a few meters away. 'Suicide by worm? Is that what you're doing out here?' He glanced at the hatch behind them, apparently wondering if he could still get back to safety if necessary. Worry lines etched his features. He looked terrified for himself and for Leto, wrestling with something that ran against his instincts. Yet he still stepped forward, as if drawn to his friend.

'Thufir, stay back. You're in more danger than I am.'

The worms knew that someone else was in their realm. But they seemed far more agitated than an intruder could account for. Leto sensed a hatred, a roiling and instinctive reaction. He sprinted back to Thufir to save him. His friend seemed to be struggling with himself.

Sand erupted, and worms encircled him and Thufir. The creatures rose from the low dunes, their round and hollow faces questing this way and that for something.

'Leto, we have to go.' Thufir grabbed the boy's sleeve. His voice was husky, ragged. 'Go!'

'Thufir, they won't harm me. And I feel . . . I feel as if I could make them go away. But they are deeply disturbed. Something about . . . you?' Leto sensed something here that he didn't understand.

Simultaneously, the worms shot like battering rams toward the two young men on the dune. Thufir bolted away from Leto and lost his footing on the soft surface. Leto tried to go toward him, but the largest worm exploded up between them, scattering sand and dust. Another beast loomed on the other side of the transfixed Thufir, stretching its sinuous body into the air.

Thufir let out a shuddering, gut-wrenching scream. It didn't sound at all like the ghola friend Leto had known. It didn't even sound human.

The sandworms struck Thufir, but they did not simply

devour him. As if in vindictive anger, the largest worm slammed down on him, smashing the young man's body into the sand. The next worm reared up and rolled over the already broken Thufir Hawat. For good measure, a third worm crushed the lifeless form. Then the trio of worms backed away, as if proud of what they had done.

Leto stumbled across the sand toward the smashed body, oblivious to the threat of the worms. He slid down a churned dune, and fell to his hands and knees beside the smashed, partially buried form. 'Thufir!'

But he did not see the familiar face of his friend. The crushed features were pale and blank, the hair colorless, the expression inhuman. The black-button eyes were unfocused and dead.

In shock, Leto reeled backward.

Thufir was a Face Dancer.

Here is my mask – it looks just like yours. We cannot see what our masks look like while we are wearing them.
    – The Wheel of Deception, Tleilaxu commentary

Uproar in the hierarchy of the no-ship. Astonishment. Even Duncan Idaho could not grasp how such a thing could have happened. How long had the Face Dancer been watching them aboard the no-ship? The mangled, ugly corpse left no room for doubt.

Thufir Hawat had been a Face Dancer! How could it be him?

The original warrior Mentat had served House Atreides. Hawat had been Duncan's good and loyal friend – but not this faux version of him. In all this time, during the three years of sabotage and murder – and perhaps even longer – Duncan had not detected the Face Dancer in Hawat, nor had Bashar Teg who mentored him. Nor had the Bene Gesserit Sisters, nor any of the other ghola children. *But how?*

An even worse question hung over them, blackening Duncan's thoughts like a solar eclipse: *We have found one Face Dancer. Are there others?*

He looked at Sheeana, at the stricken Leto II, and at the two shocked guards who stared at the alien body. 'We have to keep this secret until we can account for everyone aboard the ship. We've got to watch them, find a way to test them somehow . . .'

She agreed. 'If there are any other Face Dancers aboard, we need to act before they discover what happened.' In Bene Gesserit Voice, using a tone that was the equivalent of a verbal blow, she said to the guards, '*Speak of this to no one.*'

They froze. Sheeana was already making plans to implement a crackdown and sweep of everyone on the ship. Duncan's Mentat mind raced as he tried to comprehend what could have happened, but the nagging questions defied all his attempts to impose logic.

One rose above others: *How do we even know a test will work?* Thufir had already faced interrogation by the Truthsayers, just as everyone onboard had. Somehow, these new Face Dancers could evade even the witches' truthsense.

If the young ghola had been replaced by a Face Dancer at some point, how could such a substitution have occurred without Duncan's knowledge? And when had it occurred? Had the real Thufir accidentally encountered a hidden Face Dancer in a darkened passageway? One of the secret survivors from the Handlers' suicide crashes in a long-term elaborate ruse? How else could a Face Dancer have gotten aboard the *Ithaca*?

In assuming the identity of a victim, a Face Dancer imprinted himself with a perfect copy of the original person's personality and memories, thus creating an exact duplicate. And yet, the false Thufir had risked his life for young Leto II amongst the sandworms. Why? How much of Thufir had actually been in the Face Dancer? Had there ever been a real Thufir ghola?

At first, with the Face Dancer exposed, Duncan had felt a sense of relief that the saboteur and murderer was at last revealed. But after a swift Mentat analysis, he quickly put together several instances of sabotage during which the Thufir Hawat ghola had a clear alibi. Duncan had himself been with him during some of the attacks. The next projection was incontrovertible.

There is more than one Face Dancer among us.

DUNCAN AND TEG met in a small copper-walled room designed for private meetings, blocked from all known scanning devices. Subtle indications implied that this had originally been designed as an interrogation chamber. How often had the original Honored Matres used it as such? For torture, or simply amusement?

Standing coolly at attention, Teg and Duncan faced the Reverend Mothers Sheeana, Garimi, and Elyen, who had consumed the last available doses of the truthtrance drug. All of the women were armed and highly suspicious. Sheeana said, 'Under various pretexts, we have isolated everyone aboard, using layers of observers. Most of them think we're searching for the missing explosive mines. So far, very few people know about Thufir Hawat. Other Face Dancers would not be aware that they are at risk of exposure.'

'I would have thought the entire idea absurd – until recently. Now no suspicion seems too paranoid.' Duncan locked gazes with the Bashar, and both nodded.

'My truthtrance is deeper than it has been before,' Elyen said, sounding distant.

'Perhaps we didn't ask the correct questions previously.' Garimi put her elbows on the table.

Teg said, 'Ask away, then. The sooner you clear us of

suspicion, the faster we can root out this cancer. We need a different kind of test.'

Normally a trained Bene Gesserit should have been able to uncover deception with a mere question or two, but this extraordinary inquiry lasted an hour. Because they were building a cadre of trustworthy allies, Sheeana and her Sisters needed to be thorough. And they needed to do a better job than before. The three Reverend Mothers watched for even the slightest flicker of evasion. Neither Duncan nor Teg gave them any.

'We believe you,' Garimi finally said. 'Unless you give us cause to change our minds.'

Sheeana nodded. 'Provisionally, we accept that you two are exactly who you say you are.'

Teg seemed bitterly amused. 'And Duncan and I accept you three as well. *Provisionally.*'

'Face Dancers are mimics. They can change their appearance, but they cannot change their DNA. Now that we have cell samples from the Hawat impostor, our Suk doctors should be able to develop an accurate test.'

'So we believe,' Teg said. With the loss of his protégé, the Bashar seemed fundamentally disturbed. He no longer took anything at face value.

With an iron-hard scowl, Garimi said, 'The obvious answer is that Hawat was born a Face Dancer, then carefully planted and manipulated by our Tleilaxu Master. Who would know Face Dancers better than old Scytale? We know he had the cells in his nullentropy tube. If that scenario is true, the deception went on for almost eighteen years.'

Sheeana continued, 'A Face Dancer infant could have mimicked a generic human baby from the very beginning. As he grew, he took a shape based on archival records of the young Atreides warrior-Mentat. Since no one here – not even you, Duncan – remembers the original Hawat as an adolescent, the disguise would not need to be perfect.'

Duncan knew she was right. In his original lifetime, when he'd escaped from the Harkonnens and gone to Caladan, Thufir Hawat had already been a weathered battle veteran. Duncan remembered his first real conversation with Hawat. He'd been a stable boy at Castle Caladan, working with the Salusan bulls that Old Duke Paulus loved to fight in grand spectacles. Someone had drugged the bulls into a frenzy, and young Duncan had tried to raise the alarm, but no one believed him. After Paulus was gored to death, Hawat himself had led the investigation, hauling young Duncan before a board of inquiry, since evidence indicated that he was a Harkonnen spy . . .

And now this Thufir was a Face Dancer! Duncan still had trouble wrapping his mind around the undeniable reality.

'Then all of the ghola babies could be Face Dancers,' Duncan said. 'I suggest you summon Scytale. He's now our prime suspect.'

'Or,' Teg said in a brittle voice, 'he may be our best resource. As Garimi already stated, who would know the Face Dancers better?'

When the Tleilaxu Master was brought into the copper-walled chamber, Duncan and Teg took seats at the other side of the table, part of the growing inquisition to root out the Face Dancer infiltration. Scytale appeared frightened and unsettled. The Tleilaxu ghola was fifteen years old, but he did not look like a boy. His elfin features, sharp teeth, and gray skin made him seem alien and suspicious, but Duncan realized that was only a knee-jerk response based on primitive superstitions and previous experiences.

After Scytale sat down, Elyen leaned forward. She looked the sternest of them all. 'What have you done, Tleilaxu? What is your plan? How have you tried to betray us?' She used an edge of Voice, enough to make Scytale jerk.

'I did nothing.'

'You and your genetic predecessor knew what you were growing in the axlotl tanks. We tested the cells before allowing you to create them, but you deceived us somehow with Thufir Hawat.' They showed him images of the dead Face Dancer. Duncan could see that the Tleilaxu's surprise was genuine.

'Are all of the ghola children similarly tainted?' Sheeana demanded.

'None of them are,' Scytale insisted. 'Unless they were replaced sometime *after* being decanted from the tanks.'

Elyen narrowed her gaze. 'He's telling the truth. I see none of the indicators.' Sheeana and Garimi silently consulted each other and nodded simultaneously. Then Sheeana said, 'Unless he is himself a Face Dancer.'

'Scytale isn't likely to be a Face Dancer substitute simply because so few of us trust him anyway,' Duncan pointed out. 'A Face Dancer would choose to be someone who could more easily move among us.'

'Someone like Thufir Hawat,' Teg said.

Young Scytale looked greatly disturbed. 'Those new Face Dancers were brought back from the Scattering. The Lost Tleilaxu claimed to have modified them in ways we didn't understand. Much to my dismay, I have now learned that even I can't detect one of them. Believe me, I never suspected Hawat.'

'Then how did a Face Dancer get aboard, if not grown from the Face Dancer cells in your nullentropy capsule?' Sheeana asked.

'The Face Dancer could already have been posing as one of us when we left Chapterhouse,' Duncan mused. 'How carefully did you check all of the original hundred and fifty who rushed aboard during the escape?'

Teg shook his head. 'But why wait more than two decades to strike? It makes no sense.'

'A sleeper agent, perhaps,' Sheeana suggested. 'Or, could the Face Dancer have been someone else for a long time, and only recently replaced Thufir?'

'Yes, look for a scapegoat to persecute,' Scytale said bitterly, slumping in the overlarge interrogation chair. 'Preferably a Tleilaxu.'

Sheeana had fire in her eyes. 'As a precaution, we have sealed all of the ghola children in separate rooms, where they can cause no damage if another of them is a Face Dancer. I've already directed our Suk doctors to take blood samples. They won't escape.'

Duncan wondered if her vehemence might suggest that *she* was a Face Dancer. He narrowed his eyes suspiciously and continued to watch her. He would have to watch everyone he could, at all times.

Garimi looked around at their small trusted cadre. 'I – or another of our choosing – will remain on the navigation bridge and monitor the no-ship while every single person aboard is brought into the main meeting chamber. Herd them in, account for every one, even the children. Lock the doors and test them all. One by one. Learn the truth.'

'What definitive tests can we use?' Teg asked. 'On any of us?'

Scytale piped up, 'I believe I can develop a reliable

method. Using a tissue sample from the Hawat Face Dancer, I will prepare a comparison panel. There are certain . . . techniques I could use. He is one of the new breed brought back by the Lost Tleilaxu, and he differs from the old ones. But with this sample—'

'And why should we trust you?' Garimi said. 'Your own purity hasn't yet been proven.'

Scytale wore a forlorn expression. 'You have to trust someone.'

'Do we?'

'I would allow myself to be observed by your experts at all times during the preparations.'

Duncan glanced at the Tleilaxu Master. 'Scytale's suggestion is a good one.'

'Or I can offer another option. When the Face Dancers betrayed my fellow Masters back on Tleilax and our other worlds, some of us had time to fight back. We created a toxin that specifically targets Face Dancers – a selective poison. If you grant me access to laboratory facilities, I can recreate that toxin and deploy it as a gas.'

'To what purpose?' Teg asked. Then his expression changed to one of understanding. 'Ah, to flood the *Ithaca*'s air systems. We would kill any Face Dancers who remain among us.'

'The quantities necessary to saturate our ship would be huge,' Duncan said, racing through a Mentat calculation to estimate the volume of air within the gigantic vessel, the concentration of gas that would prove lethal to the shape-shifters, the possibility of making others ill and debilitating the crew.

Garimi couldn't believe what she was hearing. 'You're suggesting we let this *Tleilaxu* release an unknown gas into our ship? They created the Face Dancers!'

Scytale answered her in a voice heavy with scorn. 'You witches fail to think. Don't you see that I myself face a dire threat? These are *new* Face Dancers, brought in from outside by the Lost Tleilaxu – our bastard stepbrothers who cooperated with the Honored Matres to annihilate all the old Masters like myself. Think! If other Face Dancers are aboard the *Ithaca*, then I am in greater personal danger than anyone else. Can't you understand that?'

'Scytale's gas must only be a last resort,' Duncan said.

Sheeana looked around the room. 'I'll let him begin work on the toxin, but I'd prefer that we identify any Face Dancer directly.'

'And interrogate it,' Garimi said.

Scytale laughed. 'You think you can interrogate a Face Dancer?'

'Never underestimate the Bene Gesserit.'

Sheeana nodded. 'Until we root out any other infiltrators, until we prove there are no more Face Dancers among us, our only safety lies in staying in large enough groups that the shape-shifters can't attack without being seen.'

'What if an overwhelming number of us are already Face Dancers?' Teg said.

'Then we're all lost.'

DURING THE LOCKDOWN, each of the ghola children was tested; Leto II submitted first. When the sandworms had turned on Thufir Hawat, somehow sensing the alien Face Dancer, Leto's shock had seemed genuine. The imagers showed him staring in disbelief at the ruined body that had reverted to its blank Face Dancer state. But Thufir had clearly placed himself in danger, voluntarily going toward Leto when he did not need to. Why would a Face Dancer put himself at risk, unless the copy was so accurate that even the friendship was real?

Leto, ghola of the Tyrant, was many extraordinary things. But he was not a Face Dancer. Scytale's genetic analysis proved it.

Paul Atreides was also found to be clean, along with Chani, Jessica, and the three-year-old Alia, who was intrigued by the needles and samples. Despite the usual suspicions surrounding him, Wellington Yueh was also who he claimed to be.

After Scytale completed the blood and cellular tests, Sheeana was still not satisfied. 'Even if we can now trust the ghola children, that means only that other Face Dancers – if there are any more – must be hidden among the rest of us.'

'Then we'll test the rest,' Garimi said. 'Or use Scytale's poison gas. I'll personally submit to any scrutiny, again and again, and I suggest we all do so.'

Scytale raised his small hands in alarm. 'This test is an intensive one. I'll need to prepare enough panels for all passengers, and that will take a great deal of time.'

'Then we will take the time,' Sheeana announced. 'Doing anything less would be foolhardy.'

Why do we find destruction so fascinating? When we see a terrible tragedy, do we think ourselves clever for having evaded it ourselves? Or is our fascination rooted in the thrill and fear of knowing we could be next?

— MOTHER SUPERIOR ODRADE,
Documentation of Consequences

Murbella and Janess – mother and daughter, Mother Commander and Supreme Bashar – orbited the dead world of Richese. They rode in an observation ship, separate from the teams of engineers, who were still leery about the burned-out plague on Chapterhouse. Though the disease had run its course, the Ixians refused to be in a confined space with Murbella and Janess, who had been exposed to it.

Nevertheless, alone in their small ship, the two women had a perfect view of the unfolding test.

More than five years earlier, rebel Honored Matre ships from Tleilax had bombarded Richese, erasing not only the entire population, but also the weapons industries and the half-constructed battle fleet that was to have been delivered to the New Sisterhood. Now that the planet was lifeless, however, Richese was a perfectly appropriate place for the Ixians to demonstrate their new Obliterator weapons.

Murbella opened the commline and spoke to the four

accompanying test ships. 'You take a smug pleasure in doing this, don't you, Chief Fabricator?'

On the screen, Shayama Sen arched his eyebrows and jerked his head back in a fine display of innocence. 'We're testing the weapon you ordered from us, Mother Commander. You asked for a demonstration, rather than taking us at our word. We must prove that our technology functions as advertised.'

'And the rivalry between Ix and Richese had nothing to do with your choice of targets?' She barely held her sarcasm in check.

'Richese is just a historical footnote, Mother Commander. Any enjoyment Ixians might have taken from our rivals' unfortunate fate has long since faded.' After a pause, Sen added, 'We admit, however, that the irony does not escape us.'

Since last visiting her high above Chapterhouse, the factory leader sounded subtly changed. Recently, when Sen had come back to deliver full records of all their tests on Ix, he had seemed surprised, even embarrassed. He had followed her suspicious suggestion and used the cellular test on all of his people, with the result that twenty-two Face Dancers had been exposed, all of them working in critical industries.

Murbella would have liked to interrogate them, maybe even apply an Ixian T-probe. But those Face Dancers who weren't immediately killed took their own lives, somehow using a machinelike suicide shutdown in their own brains. The lost opportunity angered her, but she doubted her Sisters would have learned anything from the shape-shifters anyway. Nevertheless, she was glad to have installed eight trusted inspectors to watch over the industrial progress from that point onward.

'Our delivery schedule is tight, Mother Commander, as you demanded,' Sen transmitted. 'We are arming the ships from Junction as quickly as possible. After seeing these four Obliterators successfully tested, you can't deny that our technology is reliable.'

'It seems a shame to waste such destructive power on a target that doesn't harm the true enemy,' Janess said. 'But we require proof.' Both of them had reviewed earlier films of the tests, but those could have been faked.

'I still want to see it with my own eyes,' Murbella said. 'Then we'll throw everything into a defense against the machine advance.'

'Deploying the nodes now,' transmitted one of the Ixian pilots. 'Please observe.'

Four balls of light spat from the quartet of Ixian ships, and the incandescent Obliterators spun like pinwheels toward the cracked world below. They shuddered and expanded as they descended, throwing off rippling waves that grew brighter instead of dampening.

The atmosphere of Richese had already been scorched, its forests and cities leveled in the first chain reaction. Even so, the Ixian-modified weapons found sufficient fuel to set the world ablaze all over again.

Murbella remained silent as she watched the awesome swiftness of the flame fronts. She stared without blinking until her eyes felt dry. The planet flared like an ember in a breeze. Cracks appeared across the continents; orange rifts blazed up. Finally, she spoke to her daughter, not caring that the Ixians could overhear on the open commline. 'If we deploy such a weapon in the midst of a thinking-machine battle fleet, it will wreak inconceivable havoc.'

'We might actually have a chance,' Janess said.

Shayama Sen interrupted through the speakers, 'You

assume, Mother Commander, that the thinking machines will be foolish enough to fly their ships in such a tight cluster that one weapon will suffice.'

'We know a great deal about the Enemy's battle plan and how their fleet has been advancing. They do not use foldspace engines, so they move methodically from one target to the next, step by step. With the thinking machines there are few surprises.' Murbella looked at her daughter, then back at the burning planet before snapping orders to the Ixians. 'Very well, no need to squander any more Obliterators. When we finally hurl them at machine battle-ships, that will be demonstration enough for me. I want at least ten Obliterators aboard each of our new warships. No more delays! We have waited too long already.'

'It will be done, Mother Commander,' Sen said.

Murbella chewed at her lower lip as she watched Richese continue to blaze. It wasn't like the Chief Fabricator to be so cooperative, failing to demand additional payment. Perhaps, after seeing countless worlds already destroyed, the Ixians had at last recognized their true enemy.

Face Dancers aboard.

In her quarters with little Alia and twelve-year-old Leto, Jessica felt very much like a mother again – after all these centuries. The three of them had a shared past and blood-line, but no other knowledge or memories in common. Not yet. To Jessica it seemed that they were little more than actors memorizing lines and playing roles, trying to be who they were *supposed* to be. Her body was only seventeen, but she felt much older as she comforted the two younger ones.

'What is a Face Dancer?' three-year-old Alia asked, toying with a sharp knife she kept at her side. Since the time she could walk, the girl had harbored a fascination for weapons, and she often sought permission to prac-tice with them, rather than playing with more appropriate toys. 'Are they coming to get us?'

'They're already in the ship,' Leto said, still shaken.

He could not believe that Thufir had been a Face Dancer and that he hadn't known it. 'That's why we were all tested.'

'No others have been found yet,' Jessica said. She and Thufir had been decanted in the same year. In the crèche, she had been raised with the ghola of the warrior-Mentat, and never had she noticed any change in his personality. It did not seem possible that Thufir could have been a Face Dancer from the very beginning.

The real Hawat, Master of Assassins and former weapons master of House Atreides, had been a veteran of numerous successful campaigns like Bashar Miles Teg, serving three generations of House Atreides. No wonder Sheeana and the Bene Gesserits had considered him an invaluable ally. That was why they had wanted to bring him back, and now it was obvious why their memory-triggering crisis hadn't worked. Thufir was not really Thufir, and perhaps never had been.

Now – unless clean cells were found to grow a new ghola – the people aboard the *Ithaca* would never have access to Hawat's Mentat and tactical skills. In fact, Jessica realized that after all this time, the ghola project had produced very little that could be used to help them. Only Yueh, Stilgar, and Liet-Kynes had been reawakened to their past lives, but the latter two were gone. And Yueh, while a skilled Suk doctor, was not a particularly great asset to their team.

He killed my Duke Leto – again.

With the Face Dancer threat, the missing explosive mines, and the various incidents of sabotage, the need for the gholas and their old skills had become more urgent. The remaining unawakened ghola children must have special abilities; Jessica knew they had all been brought back for a reason. Each of them. Paul, Chani, and she were all of an appropriate age; even Leto II should be old enough. Gradual, careful measures could not possibly be sufficient. Not anymore.

She sighed. If not now, then when would their historical abilities be useful? *I must have my memories back!*

Jessica could offer so much more to benefit the no-ship, if given the opportunity. She felt like a husk of a person without her original life. In her quarters, she stood up so swiftly that she startled both Alia and Leto. 'You two should return to your rooms.' Her gruff voice invited no argument. 'There's something important I have to do. These Bene Gesserits are cowards, though they don't realize it. They can no longer afford to be.'

In some ways, Sheeana was brash and impetuous, but in other ways overly cautious. Jessica knew someone, however, who would not shy away from inflicting pain upon her.

'Who are you going to see?' Leto asked.

'Garimi.'

THE HARD-LINE REVEREND MOTHER regarded her with a stony expression, then smiled slowly. 'Why should I do this? Are you mad?'

'Just pragmatic.'

'Do you have any understanding of how much this is going to hurt?'

'I am prepared for it.' She looked at Garimi's dark, curly hair, her flat and unattractive features; Jessica, by contrast, was the very ideal of classical beauty, designed by the Bene Gesserit to play the role of a seductress, a breeding mother whose features had been copied again and again for centuries after her death. 'And I know, Proctor Superior, that if anyone can inflict that pain, you are prepared to do so.'

Garimi seemed caught between amusement and uneasiness. 'I have imagined countless ways to twist the knife in you, Jessica. I have often considered how much harm your actions did to the old Sisterhood. You derailed our entire Kwisatz Haderach program, created a monster we couldn't control. After Paul, as a direct consequence of your defiance, we suffered thousands of years under the Tyrant. For what conceivable reason would I want to awaken you? You betrayed us.'

'So you say.' Garimi's words struck like hurled stones. The woman had tormented Jessica for years, as well as poor Leto II. Jessica knew all the accusations, understood how the conservative Bene Gesserit faction viewed her. But she had not previously endured the shocking depth of hatred and anger that the woman now showed toward her. 'Your own words reveal a great deal, Garimi. The *old* Sisterhood. Where are your thoughts? We are already living in the future.'

'That doesn't negate the terrible pain you caused.'

'You keep insisting that I should bear that guilt. But how can I feel it, if I don't remember? Are you content with me as a scapegoat, a whipping boy for all the imagined wrongs of the past? Sheeana wants my memories restored so that I can help us. But *you*, Garimi, should be just as eager to awaken me. Admit it – can you think of a better Bene Gesserit punishment than drowning me in the unforgivable things you say I've done to the Sisterhood? Awaken me! Make me see it for myself!'

Garimi reached out and grabbed her wrist. Instinctively, Jessica tried to pull away, but was unsuccessful. The other woman's expression hardened. 'I am going to Share with you. I'm going to give you all my thoughts and memories so that you'll *know*.' Garimi leaned closer. 'I will dump into your brain those hundreds of generations of past lives that occurred after you committed your crime, so that you can see the full scope and consequences of what you did.' She pulled Jessica up against her.

'That's not possible. Only Reverend Mothers can Share.' Jessica tried to scramble backward.

Garimi's eyes were steely. 'And you are a Reverend Mother – or you were. Therefore, one lives within you.' She clasped the back of Jessica's head, grabbed her bronze hair and yanked her closer. Garimi leaned her own forehead down, and pressed it against Jessica's. 'I can make this work. I'm strong enough. Can you imagine why I'm doing it? Perhaps the grief will be enough to paralyze you!'

Jessica fought back. 'Or it will . . . make . . . me . . . stronger.'

She'd wanted her own memories, yes – but had never offered to accept all of Garimi's experiences, or those numerous ancestors who had lived through the persecutions of the God Emperor of Dune, her own grandson. All those who had survived the Famine Times, struggling to overcome their addiction to melange, which was no longer available. The horrors of those generations had left deep scars on the human psyche.

Jessica did not want that at all. *Garimi insists that I caused it.*

She felt something inside her head and resisted, but Garimi was stronger, forcing the Sharing upon her, pouring memories, unleashing them. Hammers pounded Jessica's skull from the inside, strong enough to crack through bone and break out. She heard a snapping sound in the blackness, and wondered if Garimi had won . . .

SHAKEN, JESSICA – THE *real* Jessica, bound concubine to Duke Leto Atreides, Reverend Mother of the Bene Gesserit – looked around herself with a new wonder she had never imagined possible. Though she saw only the walls of the no-ship, she recalled how good her life had been with the Duke and with their son Paul. She remembered the shell-blue sky of Caladan, the spectacular sunrises on Arrakis.

In the end, she had beaten Garimi. Now she marched out of the angry woman's quarters, swaying and saturated with the knowledge. That flood of memories was a mixed blessing and a new burden, for she was without her beloved Duke Leto.

The sudden emptiness made her feel as if she were plunging into an endless pit. *Leto, my Leto! Why couldn't the Sisters have brought you back at the same time, like Paul and Chani? And damn you, Yueh, for taking him from me twice!*

She felt profoundly alone, her heart drained and her mind left with mere memories and knowledge. Jessica was determined to find a way to make herself useful to her Sisters once more.

Returning to her quarters, she found Alia waiting for her. Possessing a sharp intelligence far beyond her years, the girl looked her over calmly and said, 'Mother, I told Dr Yueh you would have your memories back. Now he's even more afraid of you. You could kill him with a look. I chased him and kicked him for you.'

Jessica fought back her automatic hatred of Yueh. The old Yueh. 'You mustn't do that. Especially not now.'

The Traitor had been right to fear the return of her memories, even though she had already known of his crimes and forgiven him. *But that was with my head, not with my heart.* As she stood there, Jessica's restored memories and emotions drove the dagger in deeper.

With a rush of emotion she found herself unable to keep from reaching out and hugging Alia fiercely. Then she looked upon her daughter for the very first time. 'I am your mother again.'

A test must be defined before it can be useful. What are the parameters? What is the accuracy? Too often a test does nothing more than analyze the tester herself.

        – The Bene Gesserit Acolytes' Handbook

The death of the Hawat Face Dancer couldn't be kept secret for long. Everyone was accounted for and locked away while Sheeana and her cadre of tested individuals performed a full count, isolated and approved security teams, and then guided all of the ship's inhabitants into the main meeting hall. That giant chamber could easily house hundreds of people for days, if need be, and if enough food was brought in. Meanwhile, Garimi remained up on the navigation deck, monitoring the *Ithaca* by herself.

Since all hands – at least the known ones – were sealed in the meeting hall, any hidden traitors could very well be trapped inside. In the next few days, over the course of meticulous testing, any remaining Face Dancers among them would be rooted out.

At first, the younger children born during the journey seemed to think it was a game, but they soon grew restless; the people became uncomfortable and suspicious, wondering why only a handful of individuals were allowed to come and go on mysterious assignments. And why was the horrid little Tleilaxu one of the trusted ones? Many of those aboard still viewed Scytale with open scorn, but he was accustomed to such treatment. The Tleilaxu race had always been despised and distrusted. Now who was to blame?

Working frantically over the past day, he and the Suk doctors had assembled enough analytical kits to perform a genetic comparison on every untested individual. As a backup plan, he had also created enough of his Face Dancer-specific toxic gas to fill numerous canisters, though Sheeana was not ready to approve such a hazardous experiment – not yet. They didn't trust him enough and kept the gas under their strict control.

He didn't trust them entirely, either. After all, he was a Tleilaxu Master, perhaps the last one in existence. Secretly, he put together a more startling, fail-safe test, knowing full well what he was doing. He told no one of it.

When all was ready, Scytale sat in a front row for what he expected to be an important process of revelation. He watched the uneasy Bene Gesserits, Suk doctors, archivists, and proctors. Out in the audience, Teg sat next to the Rabbi and two Bene Gesserit Sisters. The ghola children were a few rows away, each of them already proven to be untainted. Duncan Idaho waited by one of the sealed doors, and male Bene Gesserits guarded the other exit points.

While the gathered passengers waited, Sheeana spoke from the front of the meeting chamber, her words clear and uncompromising, with an edge of Voice. 'We have discovered a Face Dancer among us, and we believe there are more in this room.'

A moment of shocked silence extended uneasily as she attempted to make eye contact with every individual.

Scytale was not surprised that no one stepped forward. The old Rabbi looked simultaneously indignant and lost without the rest of his people. From the seat next to the old man, Teg told him to be patient. The Rabbi glared but did not argue.

'We have created a foolproof test.' Sheeana sounded weary even though her voice boomed. 'It will be tedious and time-consuming. But you will all submit to it.'

'I hope none of you has anything better to do.' Duncan crossed his arms over his chest and flashed a grim smile. 'The doors will remain guarded until this process is complete.'

Scytale and the Suk doctors came forward to the stage, carrying kits, syringes, and chemical swabs. 'As each one of you is cleared, our ranks of reliable allies will grow. No Face Dancer can elude this scrutiny.'

'Who was this Face Dancer you caught?' one of the Sisters asked, an undertone of anxiety in her voice. 'And why do you assume there are others among us? What is your evidence?' When Sheeana explained how the worms had killed Thufir Hawat, stunned murmurs rippled through the audience.

The Bashar called from his seat, with an edge of guilt and revulsion in his tone. 'We know that the false Thufir could not have been responsible for all the sabotage incidents we have on record. He was with me, in person, when several of the known incidents occurred.'

'How do I know you're not *all* Face Dancers?' The Rabbi rose to his feet and glared at Sheeana, the Suk doctors, and especially Scytale. 'Your behavior has never been comprehensible to me.' Teg tugged him back down.

Sheeana ignored the old man's question and pointed to the front row. 'I will take the first subject now.'

Two female Suk doctors moved forward with their kits, and Sheeana said, 'Make yourselves comfortable. This will take a while.'

For Scytale, though, this process was primarily a diversion – and even the Bene Gesserits didn't know it. Feeling trapped, any Face Dancer in the audience would be trying to find a way to escape detection. Therefore, the Tleilaxu Master had to act precipitously, before any hidden shapeshifters could make a move. Watching the large audience closely, he fingered the small device he carried.

While the slow analytical procedure was certainly reliable, Scytale had fashioned his secret plan based on what he knew of the old Face Dancers created by the original Tleilaxu Masters. He was betting that the new shapeshifters from the Scattering were similar, at least in their fundamental responses. They must have emerged from the same basic blueprint. If so, he might know how to expose them, a weak and secondary test . . . but its very unexpectedness might work in his favor.

In the center of the meeting chamber, the Suk doctors performed their first test on a submissive Sister. She extended her hand, waiting for a drop of blood to be drawn.

Without warning, Scytale activated his high-pitched whistle emitter. A shrill tone warbled up and down, intense but faint, above the range of most human hearing. The original Face Dancers had once communicated with the Tleilaxu in a coded whistling language, a secret set of programming notes burned into their neurological structures. Scytale believed the irresistible noise would make any Face Dancer lose his disguise, at least temporarily.

Suddenly, out in the tiers of seats, the old Rabbi flickered, and his body convulsed. His leathery face shifted and smoothed behind his beard. He let out a cry of surprised outrage and lunged to his feet. Now the old man was unexpectedly supple, wiry, and vicious. His face was flat with sunken eyes and a pug nose, like a bare skull made of half-melted wax.

'Face Dancer!' someone shouted.

The Rabbi became a whirlwind and threw himself against the Bene Gesserits.

Never underestimate your enemy – or your allies.

— MILES TEG,
Memoirs of an Old Commander

Due to his constant complaints, negative attitude, and frail appearance, everyone aboard had dismissed or misjudged the old Rabbi. As had Miles Teg.

In moves as swift and deadly as a lasbeam, the Face Dancer slammed the Bashar with a blow that would have shattered his skull, if it had struck squarely. Just in time, Teg recoiled with a flash of inhuman speed. It was enough to save his life, but even so, the attack stunned him.

Abruptly, the Rabbi killed two Sisters on the other side of him, then moved in a direct, murderous line toward the nearest exit, clearing the way with a flurry of deadly blows. From hidden pockets in his dark, conservative clothes, the Face Dancer withdrew a small throwing dagger for each hand. The blades were no longer than his thumbs, but he hurled them with precision. The sharp tips, undoubtedly poisoned, pierced the throats of two male Bene Gesserits who guarded the door. With barely a sound, the Rabbi shoved their dying bodies out of the way and plunged out into the corridor.

Scytale urgently scanned the crowd to make certain

that this one escaping enemy did not divert attention from any other Face Dancers hidden among those gathered in the chamber. The Tleilaxu saw no other sudden shiftings.

Sheeana shouted for others to pursue the Rabbi. 'We know who he is, but he can change his shape. Now we have to track him down.'

One of the Sisters tried to use the ship's intercom to warn Garimi, but got no response. 'It's been damaged.'

'Fix it.' Sheeana realized that the Rabbi had had sufficient time during their quarantine in this large chamber to subtly perform more sabotage.

Dr Yueh rushed to a groaning Teg and bent to check the severity of his injury; beside him, the two fallen Sisters were obviously dead. The look on the ghola doctor's face was of dismay rather than vindication. As he examined Teg, he murmured, as if trying to make sense of the situation. 'The Rabbi gave me the sample of the ghola baby's cells. He must have taken Piter de Vries's cells from storage and tricked me. He knew what I would do, how I would react.'

Duncan glanced from Yueh and Teg to Sheeana. 'The connection is obvious to me now. Thufir Hawat and the Rabbi. Why didn't I see it?'

Sheeana caught her breath as she suddenly realized the same thing. 'Both went down to the planet of the Handlers!'

Duncan nodded. 'Hawat and the Rabbi were alone together during the hunt of the Honored Matres. You all had to fight your way back to the lighter after you discovered that the Handlers were Face Dancers.'

'Of course.' Sheeana's face was grave. 'Those two came running in from the forest at the last moment. It seems they didn't escape the Handlers after all.'

'So the original Rabbi and Thufir—' Duncan began.

'Both dead long ago, replaced by Face Dancers on the planet, and their bodies discarded during the hunt.'

Finally achieving Mentat focus, Duncan jumped to the next obvious conclusion. 'Then it's been more than five years since the substitutions. Five years! In all that time, the Hawat and Rabbi duplicates must have been waiting for their opportunity, killing gholas and axlotl tanks, sabotaging our life-support systems, forcing us to stop at Qelso, where we were vulnerable to discovery by our pursuers. Did the Enemy pick up our trail there? So far, we've managed to elude the net, but now that the Face Dancers have been exposed—'

Sheeana paled. 'And what about the stolen mines? What did the Rabbi do with the explosive mines? He can set them off at any time, if he gets to them.'

Starting to recover but clearly woozy, Teg was already moving toward the door. 'That Face Dancer knows he has to seize the no-ship before we can kill him. He will head for the navigation bridge.'

'Garimi is there,' Sheeana said. 'Let's hope she can stop him.'

BY THE TIME the Face Dancer reached the navigation bridge, he had resumed his disguise as the Rabbi. He contained all the memories, experiences, and personality details of the old man, and much more. The frail and frightened-looking Rabbi burst into the chamber, startling Garimi. 'What are you doing up here?' she asked.

His eyes were wide and panicked as if he thought she could offer him protection. His spectacles had fallen off. 'Face Dancer!' he panted, staggering toward her. 'He's killing Bene Gesserits!'

Garimi spun toward the intercom panel to contact Sheeana – and the Rabbi struck. His deadly blow came close to her neck, but she sensed the movement and turned at the last possible moment. The side of his fist drove down on her shoulder instead. She slid from her chair, and the Rabbi dove at her again.

Garimi launched a kick up at him from the deck, aiming for one of the old man's knobby and uncertain knees, but he sprang away like a coiled panther. The Rabbi let out a feral yowl as Garimi leapt to her feet again and assumed a defensive stance. Her lower lip curled. 'Clever, Rabbi. Even now that I know what you are, I can hardly smell any Face Dancer stink on you.'

With a yank and a twist, the Rabbi uprooted an anchored chair and swung it at her. She ducked and reached up to grab the chair as it whistled over her head. Tearing it out of his hands, her pull was enough to knock him to the floor.

When the Rabbi rose to his feet again, he shifted his body to mimic the form of a ferocious Futar. His body bulged with muscles, his teeth became sharp and elongated, and his claws slashed the air. Garimi stumbled back to get out of his killing reach and hammered her hand down on the intercom. 'Sisters! Face Dancer on the navigation bridge!'

The Futar lunged, and his sharp, newly grown claws ripped her robes. Using wild and frantic punches intended more to hurt her foe than protect her own life, Garimi shattered his ribs. With an outraged kick that employed the full force of her heel, she smashed his left femur out of its hip socket.

But the Futar rolled as he collapsed, spun in a blur, and before she could feel a moment of victory, he snapped

Garimi's neck. She dropped with barely a sigh. In a purely spiteful gesture, he ripped out her throat before calmly reshaping his body to his blank Face Dancer state. He wiped blood from his face with one sleeve.

More broken than even his own shape-shifter abilities could easily heal, the Rabbi crawled and then limped to the *Ithaca*'s main controls. He heard running feet in the corridor, so he sealed the navigation bridge, applied emergency locks, and activated a mutiny-defense protocol.

In the years he had maintained his disguise, the Face Dancer had covertly sampled the skin cells of Duncan Idaho, Sheeana, and Bashar Miles Teg. Now his hands flowed into the proper identification prints so that the no-ship's highly secure controls responded to him. The sealed doors would stand against any intrusion. Eventually the Bene Gesserits would find a way to break in, but by that time he would have completed his mission.

His thinking-machine masters would be alerted. And they would come.

Long ago, he had studied how to operate the Holtzman engines. Estimating the coordinates as best he could, not worried about the lack of a Navigator, the Face Dancer folded space and plunged the *Ithaca* across the galaxy. The ship tumbled out into a different stellar region, not far from Omnius's advancing forces. He reconfigured the ship's comsystems and triggered a locator beacon. His superiors knew the signal.

The thinking machines would respond swiftly. Already the Face Dancer could sense the hungry, invisible tachyon net coming closer. This time there would be no escape. The no-ship would be completely trapped.

By the time Duncan, Sheeana, and Teg reached the navigation bridge, the thick hatches were sealed and locked. Impregnable. The bridge had been designed to remain secure against even an army.

Within moments, other Sisters followed, having first raced to the armory and obtained hand weapons: poisonous needle guns, stunners, and a high-powered lascutter. None of those devices would be sufficient. Rushing forward, the ghola children joined the crowd outside the sealed bridge, among them Paul, Chani, Jessica, Leto II, and young Alia.

Duncan could feel the change when the no-ship lurched through foldspace. 'He's at the controls, moving us!'

'Garimi is dead, then,' Sheeana concluded.

'The Face Dancer is going to take us directly to the Enemy,' Teg said.

'Now is the time to use Scytale's poison gas to kill the Face Dancer.' Sheeana turned to two of the Sisters standing in the corridor. 'Find the Tleilaxu and take him to our guarded cabinet. Get one of the canisters, and we will flood the air on the bridge with the gas.'

'No time for that,' Duncan said. 'We've got to get in there!'

Alia sounded eerily cool and intelligent as she announced, 'I can get inside.'

Duncan looked at the girl. To him, the echo-memories evoked by this child were unsettling. The original Duncan had never known her as a youngster – he had been killed by Sardaukar while Jessica was barely pregnant. But he did have vivid memories of an older Alia as his lover, in another life. But that was all history. Now it might as well be myth or legend.

He bent down to talk to her. 'How? There isn't much time.'

'I'm small enough.' With a flick of her eyes, the little girl indicated the narrow air-exchanger vents leading into the command deck. She was far more diminutive than even Scytale.

Sheeana was already removing the grate. 'There are baffles, filters, and bars in the way. How will you get through?'

'Give me a cutter. And a needle gun. I'll get the door open for you as soon as I can. From the inside.'

When Alia had what she needed, Duncan hoisted the girl up to where she could squirm inside the tiny tunnel. Not yet four years old, she weighed very little. Jessica stood watching, looking more mature than she had been only a few days earlier, but even seeing her 'daughter' placed into such a dangerous situation, she did not protest.

Cold and intent, the child clamped the cutter between her teeth, tucked the needle pistol into her small shirt, and began to creep through the vent. The distance between the chambers was not far, but each half meter was a battle. She exhaled, making herself as small as possible so that she could wriggle ahead.

Outside, the others began pounding on the sealed door as a distraction. They used heavy cutters that sparked and fumed, screeching through the dense, armored barricade a millimeter at a time. The Face Dancer would know they'd need hours to cut through into the navigation bridge. Alia was confident the Face Dancer would not expect an ambush from her.

She encountered the first barricade, a set of plasteel bars interwoven with a filtration grid. The dense mat was coated with neutralizing chemicals, and charged with a faint electrostatic film to scrub all drugs and poisons from the air that passed into the bridge. With the filter in place, Scytale's toxic gas would not have worked, even if they'd been able to release it.

Elbows digging into her sides, Alia took the cutter from her teeth and with jerky wrist movements sliced away the bars. Gently, she set the screen in front of her, careful not to make a noise, and crawled over it. The sharp edges scratched her chest and legs, but Alia cared nothing for the pain.

Similarly, she passed through a second grid, and then found herself at the last opening, from which she could observe the Face Dancer through the grille. His appearance flickered occasionally, sometimes reverting to the old man's shape, sometimes becoming a Futar, but primarily the Face Dancer wore a blank, skull-like visage. Even before she saw the torn body of Garimi on the deck, Alia knew not to underestimate this opponent.

With the tip of the glowing cutter, she sliced the tiny fasteners that held the last screen in place. Moving as silently as she could, she held the plate where it was and squirmed to free the needle gun from her shirt. She tensed, then drew a deep breath, waiting for the right moment.

I will have only a brief instant of surprise, so I must use it to full advantage.

The Face Dancer was working the controls, probably transmitting a signal to the mysterious Enemy, presumably more of his own kind. Every second she delayed would place the *Ithaca* in greater danger.

Suddenly the Face Dancer jerked his head up and snapped his gaze toward the grille. Somehow he had sensed her. Now, without hesitating, Alia shoved the loosened screen toward him like a projectile. He dodged out of the way, reacting just as she had expected. Still lying prone in the ventilation shaft, she extended the needle gun in front of her and fired seven times. Three of the deadly needles found their target: two in the Face Dancer's eyes, another in the artery on his neck.

He spasmed, thrashed, and fell lifeless. Wriggling out of the air shaft, Alia dropped to the floor, recovered her balance, and glanced to verify that Garimi was indeed dead, before casually walking to the door. With her nimble fingers she disarmed the internal security measures and unsealed the hatch from the inside.

Duncan and Teg stood there holding weapons, afraid of what might emerge. The little girl met them with a placid expression. 'Our Face Dancer is no longer a problem.'

Over Alia's shoulder they could see the inhuman form sprawled next to an overturned chair. Small trickles of blood leaked from the dart wounds in his eyes, and he wore a full crimson collar of blood around his neck. On the floorplates lay the mangled Garimi.

Sheeana narrowed her gaze. 'I see that you are a born killer.'

Alia was unruffled. 'So I've been told. Didn't you bring the ghola children back for our abilities? This is what I do best.'

Duncan hurried to the no-ship's controls to assess what the false Rabbi had done. He extended his senses and was dismayed to see the deadly strands of the shimmering net suddenly appear and intensify all around them. Unbreakable. The trap was bright enough, powerful enough, that everyone could see it.

Teg rushed to a scanner station. 'Duncan! Ships approaching – a lot of them! The Face Dancer has brought us right to the doorstep of the Enemy. We're tagged, and the net has locked onto us.'

'After all these years, we are caught in the strands.' Duncan swept his gaze across all of them. 'At least, we're about to find out who our Enemy really is.'

Our shared humanity should, by definition, make us allies.
In sad fact, however, our very similarities often appear to
be vast differences and insurmountable obstacles.

— MOTHER COMMANDER MURBELLA,
address to the New Sisterhood

Given the critical shortage of time, the thousands of newly
equipped Guildships could not undergo thorough shake-
downs and test runs. The mass-produced Obliterators
were loaded aboard the heavily armored vessels that had
been built at Junction as well as seventeen satellite shipyards. Crews made preparations to go to the front lines.

Fresh from conscription across hundreds of at-risk
planets, novice commanders received only minimal
training, barely sufficient to stand against the Enemy at
numerous vulnerable points as humanity tried to draw
its line in space. Murbella knew that despite their determination and bravery, and no matter how much training
and practice they received, most of the human fighters
would be annihilated.

In the months after the plague had run its course on
Chapterhouse, the Mother Commander had opened her
doors to displaced refugees from any evacuated planet. At
first they were frightened to settle on the once-quarantined

world, but then they had begun to stream in. With so few options available to them, the ragtag groups accepted the Sisterhood's offer of sanctuary in exchange for performing vital labors in the war effort. Politics and old factions had to be set aside. Now every life was devoted to preparing for the last stand against the oncoming forces of Omnius.

From Buzzell, Reverend Mother Corysta sent the incredible news that the giant seaworms wreaking havoc with soostone operations also produced a kind of spice. Murbella immediately suspected some kind of Guild experiment. It could not be a natural occurrence. Corysta suggested that the worms be hunted and harvested, but the Mother Commander could not think that far ahead. A new source of spice mattered only if the human race survived the Enemy.

Mother Commander Murbella called a grand war council for delegates of the front-line planets that were in imminent danger of attack by thinking-machine forces. Despite their indignation, every one of them had undergone cellular testing to root out hidden Face Dancers. Murbella took no chances; the insidious shape-shifters could be anywhere.

In the Keep's grand meeting room, she strode down the length of the elaccawood table to her designated seat. Using her Bene Gesserit powers of close observation, she studied those assembled, all of them driven here by desperation. Murbella tried to view these representatives in their various costumes and uniforms as military leaders, essentially generals in the last great battle for humanity. The people in this room would guide the thrown-together clusters of ships and make a thousand defiant stands. But were they the quality of heroes the human race needed?

When she turned to face the delegates, Murbella saw

the uneasiness in their eyes and smelled fear-sweat in the air. The vast Enemy fleet surged forward like a flame front across the map of the galaxy, rolling over star system after star system, heading inexorably toward Chapterhouse and the remaining worlds at the heart of the Old Empire.

After moving among the various embattled worlds and studying their preparations, Murbella had secured alliances with these planetary leaders, warlords, commercial conglomerates, and smaller units of government. Leto II's vision of the Golden Path had fragmented humanity so that they no longer followed a single charismatic leader, and now Murbella had to repair that damage. Diversity might once have been a path to survival, but unless the numerous worlds and armies could stand together against the far greater foe, they would all perish.

If the Tyrant's prescience was so formidable, how could he not have foreseen the existence of the great machine empire, no matter how far away it was? How could the God Emperor not have known that another titanic conflict awaited humankind? She felt a faint shudder. Or *had* he, and everything was playing out exactly as the Tyrant planned?

After considerable effort, she had won a critical internal battle when the various leaders agreed that the strongest defense came from a unified plan – *her* plan – rather than a hundred independent and hopeless defensive battles. To get her message across, she'd had to cut through the stubborn tentacles of various planetary bureaucracies. Nothing was easy in this war.

Feeling the burdens of her position, Murbella rapped a large spherical stone on the table, producing a loud, echoing boom that called the meeting to order. 'You all know why you're here. We must make our last stands, a thousand of them across space. Many of us will die – or *all* of us will die. There are no alternatives. The only questions are how soon we will die, and how it will happen. Do we choose to die free and fighting to the last . . . or defeated and running?'

The room resounded with a cacophony of voices, accents, and languages, though she had insisted that they all speak the common Galach tongue. She used Voice to cut through the clamor. 'The machines are coming! If we cooperate and do not retreat in the face of our foe, we just might have the means of stopping them dead in their tracks.'

She noted Guild officials and Ixian engineers in the audience. Given the short delivery schedule, some of the warship construction had been unavoidably slapdash, but her handful of Bene Gesserit inspectors and line supervisors had overseen the operations.

'Our weapons and ships are now ready, but before we proceed I have one question for all of you.' She skewered the leaders with her gaze. If she'd still been an Honored Matre, her eyes would have blazed orange. 'Do you have the resolve and courage to do what is necessary?'

'Do *you*?' bellowed a bearded man from a very small planet in a remote system.

Murbella rapped her sonic stone again. 'My New Sisterhood will bear the brunt of the initial clash against the thinking machines. We have already fought them in one star system after another, destroying many of their ships, and we survived their plagues here on Chapterhouse. But this war will never be won on individual battlefields.' She gestured, and Janess worked the controls. 'Look at this, all of you.'

Startling the assemblage, a large holographic projection appeared, filling the open space of the Keep's great meeting room with detailed maps of the galaxy's numerous solar systems. An advancing blot indicated the thinking machines' conquests, like a tidal wave drowning every system in its path. The darkness of defeat and extermination had already blackened most of the known systems in the regions of the Scattering.

'We have to focus our efforts. Because they don't use foldspace engines, the Enemy proceeds from system to system. We know their path, and therefore we can put ourselves directly in their way.' Murbella stood amidst the simulated stars and planets. Her finger darted from point to point, the glowing stars and habitable planets that lay in the Enemy's path. 'We've got to hold the line – here, and here, and everywhere! Only by combining all of our ships, commanders, and weapons can we hope to halt the Enemy.' She swept her hand through the shimmering images that were just ahead of the encroaching thinking machines. 'Any other choice would be cowardice.'

'Do you call us cowards?' the bearded man roared.

A merchant stood. 'Surely we can negotiate—'

Murbella cut him off. 'The thinking machines do not want a particular world. Nor are they searching for gems, spice, or any other goods. There is nothing we can offer them to sue for peace. They do not compromise, and will keep pursuing us no matter where we run.' She looked at the blustering man and said, 'By fleeing conflict today, you *could* survive for a time. But there'll be no escape for your children or grandchildren. The machines will slaughter them, down to the last infant. Do you value your life over theirs? Then, yes, I do call you cowards.'

Despite the murmurs in the hall, no one else spoke

out. On the giant star display, a line of tiny fireworks erupted along the interface line between the machine-conquered territories and the vulnerable human planets.

Murbella's gaze moved across the audience. 'Each of us is responsible for stopping the Enemy from crossing this line. Failure means death for the human race.'

The leader of the Face Dancer myriad arrived at Synchrony, bearing a long-anticipated gift for the ever-mind. The thinking machines still viewed Khrone as nothing more than a servant, a delivery boy.

Omnius and Erasmus never suspected that the shape-shifters might be formulating their own schemes independent of both humanity and the thinking machines. Naïve, oblivious, and so very typical. The evermind would treasure this new melange for his grandiose plans, and it would keep the machines from doubting Khrone and his Face Dancers. He intended to make the most of it.

With their brutality and arrogance, the 'old man and woman' had long ago given the new shape-shifters reasons to break their loyalty. Erasmus fancied himself reminiscent of a Face Dancer, but much more . . . and similar to a human, but greater. And like Omnius . . . but infinitely more powerful.

Khrone and the rest of the myriad had never truly

given their allegiance to the thinking machines. He saw no more reason to accept slavery under machine masters than to have accepted the domination of the original Tleilaxu who had created their predecessors so many centuries ago. Forced allies, second-class partners . . . The evermind was merely one more layer in the grand pyramid of those who *thought* they controlled the Face Dancers.

After so much effort, Khrone couldn't wait until he could drop this endless deception. He was no longer amused by the number of masks he had to wear and the complicated threads he continued to pull. Soon, though . . .

Alone, he flew his small ship directly to the heart of the modern machine empire. The location of Synchrony had been genetically programmed into all new Face Dancers, like some sort of homing beacon. As he entered the airspace over the technological metropolis, Khrone let his thoughts drift back to Ix. The fabricators and engineers had successfully completed a special demonstration at dead Richese, and now Obliterators were emerging from the production lines. Mother Commander Murbella had been impressed with the power she witnessed, and she'd been entirely convinced by the show. Fool!

But not in all things. In her prior meeting with Chief Fabricator Shayama Sen, Murbella had forced him to administer a biological test that proved he wasn't a Face Dancer. Given what had happened, Khrone was vastly relieved that he had *not* replaced the man, as he'd been tempted to do many times in the past.

Face Dancers already controlled most of the important positions on Ix, and when the Chief Fabricator blithely distributed the biological tests to all the main engineers and team leaders (never suspecting there might actually be a majority of Face Dancers among them), the myriad had been forced to act precipitously. When an indignant Sen announced the Sisterhood's suspicions, the infiltrators had finally been forced to kill him and assume his identity. They had already taken care of the troublesome Bene Gesserit line supervisors and production monitors. And so the deception continued, unmarred.

Enhanced Face Dancers quickly subsumed the last humans among the leaders of Ix. Then, working together, they contrived all the necessary tests, selected the required scapegoats, substituted convincing data, and submitted everything to Chapterhouse in accordance with Murbella's demands. All in perfect order.

After surviving the plague, the Sisterhood's leadership had forced all human protectors to finally band together against the thinking-machine fleet, to defend their race rather than simply their own worlds. The hundreds of new ships that emerged from the Junction shipyards were being loaded with enough Obliterators for a final, concerted stand against the oncoming wave of Omnius's ships. So far, the evermind's forces had encountered very little significant resistance, and now they were on their way to Chapterhouse. For the last time.

Khrone had actually been tempted to let the Reverend Mothers and their last-stand defenders succeed. Given enough functional Obliterators, they could send the machine fleet reeling. Humans and thinking machines could easily annihilate each other. However, that was simply too . . . easy. Kralizec demanded much more! This time, the fundamental shift in the universe would get rid of both rivals, leaving all the remnants of the Old Empire for the Face Dancers.

Khrone felt completely confident in the future as he landed his ship in the convoluted labyrinth of copper steeples, golden turrets, and interlocked silvery buildings. Sentient structures shifted aside to allow a place for his ship to settle. When the small vessel came to rest on a smooth quicksilver plain, Khrone stepped out, breathing air that smelled of smoke and hot metal. He did not spare a moment to look around.

The central machine world was based entirely on theatrics. He suspected the touch of Erasmus in this, though Omnius had such an overblown perception of his own importance that he no doubt wanted all machine minions to bow before him as a god – even if the ever-mind had to program them to do so.

Rectangular plates appeared on the ground, laying down an interlocked pathway that guided Khrone to his destination in the magnificent arched cathedral. Head held high, he strode along carrying his precious package, refusing to look like a supplicant summoned before his lord. Rather, Khrone was a man on a mission with important business to complete. Omnius would be pleased to have the concentrated ultraspice for use with his cloned Kwisatz Haderach . . .

Inside the ostentatious hall, the ghola of Baron Harkonnen stood with young Paolo at a nine-level pyramid chess board. Glowering, the Baron knocked over a rook on one of the top levels. 'That move is not allowed, Paolo.'

'It enabled me to win, didn't it?' Pleased with his ingenuity, the young man crossed his arms over his chest.

'By cheating.'

'It's a new rule. If we are as important as you say, we should be allowed to make up our own rules.'

A flash of anger crossed the Baron's face, and then vanished into a chuckle. 'I see your reasoning – and that you are learning.'

When Khrone stepped forward, they looked at him with identical expressions of distaste. 'Oh, it's you.' The Baron sounded entirely different from when he'd been tormented by the Face Dancers. 'I didn't think we'd be seeing you again. Bored of Caladan?'

Ignoring them, Khrone noted that the two principal thinking machines had resumed their guise of an elderly couple in gardening clothes. Why were they wearing these personas now? For the benefit of these two gholas? It wasn't as if the thinking machines were keeping secrets from anybody here. Khrone had never been able to determine a pattern in their behavior.

Perhaps it was linked to the fact that Omnius and Erasmus wanted to receive all of the lives Khrone had gathered and assimilated during his last mission among the humans. They looked forward to the sharing of their Face Dancer 'ambassadors' each time one of the far-flung representatives returned. It seemed to make them feel superior, and allowed the independent robot to feel that he belonged to the human race, somehow.

'Look, he's brought something,' Paolo pointed out. 'A present for us?'

Khrone went directly to the old man and woman. As the woman leaned toward him, her visage had a feral and hungry look. 'I think you brought more than just a package, Khrone. You haven't been back to Synchrony in some time. Show us the personas you've acquired. Every little bit adds to us, makes us greater.'

'I have had enough.' The old man turned away. 'I am beginning to find them somewhat distasteful. They are all the same.'

'How can you say that, Daniel? Every human is different, so beautifully chaotic and unpredictable.'

'Exactly what I mean. They are all confusing. And I am not Daniel, I am Omnius. Kralizec is upon us, and we have no time for further preparatory games.'

'Sometimes I still like to consider myself Marty. In many ways it's more appealing to me than the name or guise of Erasmus.' The old woman took a step closer to Khrone. The Face Dancer didn't dare flinch, though he despised what was about to happen. Her hand was gnarled, with large knuckles. It felt clawlike when she touched his forehead. She pressed harder, and Khrone shuddered, unable to block the intrusion.

Each time a Face Dancer mimicked a human shape, he sampled the original subject and acquired both a genetic trace and an imprint of the memories and persona. The thinking machines had set the shape-shifters loose into the Old Empire. Infiltrating the humans, they gathered more and more lives as they subsumed useful people and played their roles. Whenever a Face Dancer returned to the machine empire, Erasmus in particular wanted to add those lives to his vast repository of data and experience.

Out of forced subservience, Khrone and his comrades surrendered that information. But though the thinking machines could upload the various lives the Face Dancers copied, they could not take their core personas. Khrone held onto his secrets, even as he offered up all those people he had been in recent years – an Ixian engineer, a CHOAM representative, a crewman on a Guildship, a dock worker on Caladan, and many others.

When the process was finished, the old woman's hand withdrew. Her wrinkled face wore a satisfied smile. 'Oh, those were interesting ones! Omnius will certainly want to share them.'

'That remains to be seen,' the old man said.

Feeling drained, Khrone caught his breath and straightened himself. 'That is not why I came.' His voice was shamefully weak and quavering. 'I have obtained a special substance you will find invaluable for your Kwisatz Haderach project.' He held out the ultraspice package, as if offering a gift to a king, precisely as Omnius expected him to behave. The old man accepted the package, scrutinized it carefully.

The Face Dancer gave Paolo a condescending look. 'This potent form of melange is sure to unlock the prescience in any Atreides. Then you will have your Kwisatz Haderach, as I have always promised. There is no need to continue pursuing the no-ship.'

Omnius found the comment amusing. 'Strange you should say that now.'

'What do you mean?'

Beside him, the old woman grinned. 'This is a momentous day, since both of our plans have come to fruition. Our patience and foresight have paid off. Now, what shall we do with *two* Kwisatz Haderachs?'

Khrone paused, startled. 'Two of them?'

'After so many years, the no-ship has finally fallen into our trap.'

Khrone slid his surprise back into himself and went rigid. 'That is . . . most excellent.'

The old woman rubbed her hands together. 'Everything is culminating at once. It reminds me of the climactic movement in a symphony I once wrote.'

The old man began to pace around the chamber, holding the package of ultraspice in his hands. He sniffed it.

Paolo turned away from the chess game. 'You don't need another Kwisatz Haderach. You have *me*. Give me spice now!'

Erasmus shot him an indulgent smile. 'Perhaps in a little while. First we'll see what the no-ship has for us, who their Kwisatz Haderach is. It should be interesting.'

'Where is the vessel?' Khrone asked, focusing on the main question. 'Are you sure you have it?'

'Our cruisers are surrounding it even now, and our operatives aboard took steps to guarantee that it could not escape again. Your Face Dancers did a fine job, Khrone.'

Omnius interrupted, 'And, on a greater scale, our largest battleships are closing in on human defenders in their Old Empire. We will conquer Chapterhouse soon, but that is only one of many simultaneous targets.'

'It should be quite a spectacular battle.' Erasmus sounded more dry than eager.

The evermind was stern. 'Triumph will be assured as soon as the proper conditions are met, according to our mathematical prophecies. Success is imminent.'

With glee on his flowmetal face, Erasmus beamed at Paolo and the Baron. 'Two Kwisatz Haderachs are better than one!'

Time is a commodity more precious than melange. Even the wealthiest man cannot buy more minutes to put into each hour.

A gossamer net of jeweled colors closed around the *Ithaca*. The no-ship's engines strained, but could not break away. Scrambling to reassert control over the helm and drag themselves free of the strange bonds, Duncan powered up the Holtzman engines, preparing to rip a hole through the glimmering mesh. It was their only way out.

Glaring at the dead Face Dancer on the deck, Sheeana ordered two Sisters nearby, 'Remove that thing from the navigation bridge!' Within moments, the women carried away the limp and bloody shape-shifter.

Now that the net was visible to them all, Duncan focused his Mentat awareness to study the woven grid that ensnared them. He searched frantically for holes or weak spots in the powerful structure, but found nothing to suggest the slightest defect, no frayed point that might allow them to escape.

He would try brute force, then.

Years ago, he had broken free of the net by using the

Holtzman engines in ways they had never been designed to function, flying the *Ithaca* at just the proper angle and speed to penetrate the fabric of space. It had reminded him of a Swordmaster's move, using a slow blade against a personal shield.

'Accelerating now,' he said.

Teg leaned over the navigation controls, sweating. 'This is going to be close, Duncan.' The large ship pulled against the multicolored strands, tore several, and then picked up speed. 'We're breaking free!'

Duncan felt a brief moment of hope, a surge of triumph.

An explosion rocked the ship, followed by another, and another. Vibrations and shock waves rang through the hull and decks as if some titan were smashing the vessel with a great hammer. The navigation bridge shuddered.

Holding his chair, Duncan called up diagnostic maps. 'What was that? Is the Enemy firing on us?'

The detonations threw Teg to the floor, but he scrambled back to his feet and gripped the console for balance. 'The stolen mines! I think we just found them.' His words tumbled out in a rush. 'Either Thufir or the Rabbi must have set them to go off—' As if to confirm his speculation, another explosion rocked the deck, much closer than before.

The *Ithaca* reeled out of control, its engines paralyzed. The deck tilted, as artificial gravity generators were knocked offline. Duncan felt a sickening disorientation as the vessel spun off axis.

The shimmering net grew brighter, tightening like a noose.

Finally, out in the distance, Enemy ships drew into view, like hunters approaching a trap they had set. Duncan stared at the external screens. Who had pursued them for so long? Face Dancers? Some vicious, unknown race? What could be frightening enough to drive the Honored Matres back into the Old Empire?

'The bastards think they have us.' Duncan made a fist.

'Don't they?' Looking up from his status screens, the Bashar was dismayed by the severe damage indicators lighting up sections of the vessel like fireworks displays. 'The mines have ruined our most vital systems, and we're dead in space.'

Using Mentat focus, Duncan studied the panels on his command console. The intricate displays showed the strangling net all around them. He jabbed his finger toward a knot in the diagram, an area of pulsing, flickering electronic signals. At first glance the tangle seemed no different from the rest of the interconnected strands, but as he studied it, he thought he might have found a weakness. 'Look there.'

Teg feverishly bent closer. 'A loophole?'

'If only we could move!' Racking his brain, Duncan stalked back and forth in front of the controls. 'It would be quite a drunkard's dance to get through that maze – if this ship could fly at all.'

'If we all worked together, the entire crew, it would take a week to make repairs. We don't have that much time.' The Bashar gestured to the tactical screens that displayed data from the long-distance sensors. 'Enemy ships are closing in. They know they've snared us.'

Duncan accepted the grim reality. 'Holtzman engines are dead. No way to make the repairs in time, no way to escape.' He hammered his fists on a panel next to the tangled, pulsing loophole on the console's projections. 'But I know I could do it. Why won't this damned ship fly?'

Teg glanced at the sensor blips that indicated the encroaching Enemy, saw the automated damage reports streaming across the display, and knew exactly what had to be done. Only he could do it.

'I can fix the ship.' He had no time to explain. 'Be ready.' Then he simply vanished.

MILES TEG ACCELERATED his metabolism, kicking himself into the hyper-fast speed he had learned after surviving unendurable torture at the hands of the Honored Matres and their underlings. Around him, time slowed. This would be dangerous to him because of the extreme energy requirements, but he had to do it. The rapidly strobing alarm lights became a slow pulsation that seemed to take an hour for each cycle, brightening and dimming. Re-accessing the archival records of the ship's systems would take too long, but Teg had examined them before. As a Mentat he remembered everything, and now he set to work.

By himself.

Even at his accelerated speed, Teg exerted himself to run as fast as he could. On deck after deck, everyone aboard stood like statues, their expressions showing concern and confusion. Teg flashed past them to the nearest damage sites.

Where the first mine had gone off, he stared in amazement and consternation at the twisted metal, the melted craters in the machinery, the vaporized systems. Teg hurried from one explosion to the next, determining how far the damage extended and which systems were crucial for their immediate escape. The Face Dancer infiltrators had planted and hidden the eight mines well, and each detonation had resulted in a crippling blow: navigation, life-support, foldspace engines, defensive weapons.

Teg made snap decisions. His life had primed him for emergencies; on the battlefield, one could not hesitate. If Duncan couldn't manage to fly the *Ithaca* away right now, they would never again require life-support systems. He, or someone else, could fix those later. An acceptable gamble. The no-field generators were off-line.

Engines. Four of the eight mines had been set to damage the foldspace engines. The Face Dancer saboteur had deliberately flown the no-ship close to the Enemy's stronghold, and the detonations had left them crippled and stranded.

With hyper speed Teg studied, analyzed, and compiled a plan using his Mentat abilities. He inventoried spare materials, replacement components, emergency equipment. He needed to work swiftly with what he had; there was no one to help him. First, he rerouted and reprogrammed the weapons, and prepared them to launch a volley of blasts at the oncoming ships. That might grant them an extra few moments.

Teg continued to hurry. The pulsing alarm lights flickered on to off, like a sun rising and setting. Another hour gone in his own frame of reference. In real time, only a few seconds had passed since his disappearance from the bridge. Next, he turned to the engines, which were essential to their escape.

The primary linkages had been disrupted, with Holtzman catalysts shaken from their cradles, shoved out of alignment, made inoperable. Two reaction chambers were breached. An explosion had nearly broken through the hull. He stood stunned, his arms shaking, thinking he couldn't possibly fix this. But he forced such thoughts away, went back to work.

Teg's muscles trembled with exhaustion, and his lungs

burned from gasping air so fast the oxygen molecules could barely move into position.

Fixing the hull should be easy enough. Teg ran to the maintenance sectors, where he located extra plates. Since he could never make the ship's heavy-lifting machinery operate fast enough for his time-sense, he decided that suspensors would have to do. He applied the null-gravity projectors to the heavy plates and hurried with them down corridors, dodging petrified people.

With each second, the Enemy battleships were getting closer. Some of his fellow passengers were only just now learning of the mines that had been detonated. He put on another burst of speed, and the suspensor carriers kept up with him.

In a few 'hours,' according to his metabolism, and only a few moments in reality, he fixed the hull damage that could have resulted in an engine breach. Sweat poured off of Teg's body, and he was near collapse. But in spite of that utter exhaustion, he could not let himself slow down. Never before had he allowed himself to fall so deeply into a pit of burning metabolism.

Teg's body could not maintain this pace for long. But if he didn't, the ship would be captured, and they would all die. Fangs of hunger gnawed at his stomach. This would not do. He had to concentrate, had to fuel the engine of his body so that he could do what must be done.

Ravenous, not slowing from his superspeed, he raided the ship's stores, where he found energy bars and dense food wafers. He ate concentrated nutrients until he was gorged. Then, burning calories as fast as he could swallow them, Teg ran again from one disaster area to the next.

He spent subjective days at these highly focused labors;

to observers on the outside, caught in the glacial pace of normal time, only a minute or two passed.

When the task grew overwhelming, the Bashar struggled to reassess what the ship needed in order to function. What was the bare minimum of repairs that would let Duncan fly through the weakened loophole?

The exploding mines had led to a cascading series of damages. Teg nearly got lost in the details, but reminded himself of the immediate need and forced himself to skate the thin ice of possibilities.

Teg and his brave men had stolen this very vessel from Gammu more than three decades ago. Though it had performed admirably since then, the *Ithaca* had not undergone any of the usual necessary maintenance at Guild shipyards. Worn components had not been replaced; systems were breaking down from age and neglect, as well as the depredations of the saboteurs. Limited by the spare parts and materials he could find in the maintenance bays, he tried and discarded possible fixes.

Alarms continued to pulse slowly. He was moving too fast for sound waves to mean anything. In real time, there would be shrieking sirens, shouting people, conflicting orders.

Teg fixed another of the Holtzman catalyst cradles, then took the time to look at a viewer. In the image displayed between scan lines, he saw that the Enemy ships had finally arrived, massive and heavily armed . . . a full fleet of monstrous, angular things that bristled with weapons, sensor arrays, and other sharp protrusions.

Though he already felt used up, Teg knew with a sickening certainty that he needed to go even faster.

He raced to the ship's melange stores and broke the locks with a twist of his hand because he was moving so fast. He removed cakes of the dark brown compressed substance, stared at it with Mentat calculation. Considering his hypermetabolism and his body churning through its bio-chemical machinery faster than it ever had before, what was the proper dosage? How quickly would it affect him? Teg decided on three wafers – triple the maximum he had ever consumed – and gobbled them all.

As the melange rushed through his body and poured into his senses, he felt alive again, recharged and capable of accomplishing the requisite impossibilities. His muscles and nerves were on fire, and his feet left marks on the deck as he ran.

He repaired the next system in a few moments. But in that time, the Enemy battle fleet had closed in, and the no-ship still could not fly.

Teg looked down at his forearms and saw that his skin seemed to be shriveling up, as if he was consuming every drop of energy within his flesh.

Outside, the encroaching vessels launched a volley of destructive blasts. Balls of energy tumbled forward like storm clouds approaching with exquisite slowness. Those blasts would clearly render his repairs useless, maybe even destroy the ship.

In another burst of extreme speed, Teg dashed to the defensive controls. Thankfully, he had restored a few of their weapons. The *Ithaca*'s defensive systems were sluggish, but the firing controls were swift enough. With a scattershot cannonade, like a burst of celebratory fireworks, Teg returned fire. He launched beams carefully targeted to intercept and dissipate the oncoming projectiles. Once he had fired the volley, though, Teg turned his back on the weapons systems and raced to the next damaged engine.

Bashar Teg felt like a candle that had been burnt entirely down to a lump of discolored wax. Despite his best efforts, the exhausted man still saw their doom closing in.

How do we repay a man who has done the impossible?
— BASHAR ALEF BURZMALI,
A Dirge for the Soldier

On the navigation bridge, Duncan stared at the sensor projections for moments after Miles had disappeared. He knew what the Bashar must be doing.

After the internal explosions, the *Ithaca* hung dead in space, surrounded by Enemy ships that bristled with more weaponry than he had seen on an entire Harkonnen battle fleet. The mines had disabled the no-field generator, leaving the great ship visible and vulnerable in space.

After almost a quarter century of fleeing, they were caught. Maybe it was about damned time he faced the mysterious hunters. Who were his strange and invincible foes? He had only ever seen the ghostly shadows of the old man and old woman. And now . . .

On the screens before him, the discontinuity in the gossamer net shifted, almost closed, and then strayed open again, as if taunting him.

Duncan spoke aloud, more to himself than anyone else. A prayer of sorts. 'As long as we breathe, we have a chance. Our task is to identify any opportunity, however transitory or difficult it might be.'

Teg had said he would fix their systems. Duncan was aware of the Bashar's closely held abilities. For years, Teg had concealed his talent from the Bene Gesserits, who feared such manifestations as the sign of a potential Kwisatz Haderach. Now those abilities might save them all. 'Don't let us down, Miles.'

The encroaching ships fired a series of blasts at the no-ship. Duncan barely had time to shout a curse and brace for impact – when a flurry of impossibly fast and deft defensive bursts intercepted the Enemy volley. Precisely targeted, instantly fired. All shots blocked.

Duncan blinked. Who had launched the return salvo? He shook his head. The no-ship should have been incapable of even basic maneuvers or defense. A chill of delight coursed down his spine. Miles!

Suddenly, the control deck's systems began to glow; green indicator lights winked on by themselves. One after another, systems came back online. Sensing movement, Duncan snapped his head to the left.

The Bashar materialized in front of him, but it was a different Miles Teg – not the young ghola whom Duncan had raised and awakened, but a horribly drained man, as desiccated and ancient as an ambulatory mummy. Teg looked wrung out and ready to collapse. He had exerted himself through time far beyond the point where a normal man would have already died.

'Boards . . . active.' His gasping voice cost him more energy than he had left. '*Go!*'

Everything happened in an instant, as if Duncan, too, had fallen into an accelerated time frame. His first instinct was to grab his friend. Teg was dying, might already be dead. The aged Bashar could no longer hold himself upright. 'Go – damn it!' They were the last words Teg could force out of his mouth.

Thinking with Mentat clarity, Duncan whipped back to the control panels, vowing not to waste what the Bashar had done for them. *Priorities.* He reached the piloting board, where his fingers skittered like a startled spider across the controls.

Teg crumpled to the deck, arms and legs akimbo, as dead as a dried leaf, older even than the first old Bashar had been in the last moments of Rakis. *Miles!* All their years together, teaching, learning, relying on each other. Few people in all of Duncan's many lives had ever mattered so much.

He drove away his thoughts of shocked grief, but Mentat memory kept every experience clear and sharp. *Miles!* Teg was no more than an ancient husk on the floorplates. Duncan had no time for anger or tears.

The no-ship began to accelerate. He still saw how to slip out of the cruel net, but now he also had to contend with the entire fleet of Enemy ships. They had cut loose with a second volley.

The blurred crackle ahead seemed to invite them. Duncan steered toward it, moving as fast as his human reflexes could go. The no-ship ripped the stubborn strands free. 'Come on!' Duncan said, willing it to happen.

More blasts glanced across the *Ithaca's* hull, grazing the ship as it yawed and rolled. Duncan steered with all of his skill.

The Holtzman engines were hot and the diagnostic boards showed numerous errors and system failures, but none were immediately fatal faults. Duncan pushed the vessel closer and closer to the loophole. The Enemy ships couldn't head them off, couldn't move fast enough to stop them.

More of the net broke away. Duncan could see it happening.

He forced his attention back to the engines, applying acceleration far beyond what the systems normally allowed. In his frantic repairs, Teg had not bothered with the niceties of fail-safes and protective limitations. With increased velocity, they pulled free of the enclosing cordon.

'We're going to make it!' Duncan said to the fallen Bashar, as if his friend could still hear him.

A giant torpedo-shaped Enemy vessel leapt forward. No human could possibly pilot a ship so swiftly, changing directions with g-forces that would snap bones like a handful of straw in a clenched fist. Burning its engines, the attacker exhausted all of its fuel in one burst of forward motion – throwing the craft directly into their path.

With his maneuvering already hampered, Duncan could not dodge in time. The no-ship was too huge, with too much inertia. Impossibly, the suicidal Enemy vessel scraped the lower hull of the *Ithaca*, knocking it off course, damaging the engines yet again. The unexpected impact sent the no-ship spinning. The Enemy rammer tumbled and exploded, and the shock wave knocked them farther off course, out of control . . . back into the remaining strands of the net.

Duncan uttered a curse in dismay and rage.

Unable to fold space, the no-ship dropped back, its engines whining. The bridge control panels blazed red, then went dim. A small internal explosion further damaged the Holtzman engines. The *Ithaca* hung motionless in space. Again.

'I'm sorry, Bashar,' Duncan said, heartbroken. With nothing else to do, he knelt beside the husk of his friend.

A message formed on the primary screen on the bridge,

a powerful transmission from the surrounding battleships. Even in his stunned sorrow, Duncan was surprised to see the true face of the Enemy at last.

The smooth flowmetal face of a sentient machine appeared on the screen. 'You are our prisoners. Your vessel is no longer capable of independent flight. We will deliver you to the evermind Omnius.'

Thinking machines!

Duncan struggled to understand what he was seeing and hearing. Omnius? The evermind? The Enemy, posing as a kindly old couple, were really thinking machines? Impossible! Thinking machines had been outlawed for thousands of years, and the last evermind had been destroyed in the Battle of Corrin at the end of the Butlerian Jihad.

Machines? Somehow allied with the new Face Dancers?

The Enemy ships pounced like hyenas on a fresh carcass.

Some people complain of being haunted by their past. Utter nonsense! I revel in it.

— BARON VLADIMIR HARKONNEN, the ghola

Trapped by the machine fleet, the *Ithaca* was held captive with its engines damaged and weapons burned out. Duncan could do nothing but wait and mourn his dead friend. Consequences and memories roared around him. He moved methodically, relying on Mentat focus to perform even simple actions.

Sheeana was beside him on the navigation bridge. Though she prided herself in Bene Gesserit purity, holding all emotions at bay, she seemed profoundly troubled as the two of them picked up Teg's body from where it lay crumpled on the deck. Duncan couldn't believe how fragile and lightweight the Bashar's remains were. He seemed to be made of spiderwebs and sinew, dried leaves and hollow bone.

'Miles gave his life for all of us,' Duncan said.

'Two times,' she said.

Her remark made Duncan think of all the lives of his own he had given for the Atreides. In a raspy voice, he said, 'This time, the sacrifice was for nothing. Miles used up his entire life span to give us the repairs we needed, and I couldn't break us free. He shouldn't have done it.'

Sheeana fixed a hard look on him. 'He shouldn't have *tried*? We're humans. We have to try, no matter what the odds are. There are never any guarantees. Every action in life is a gamble. The Bashar fought to the last instant of his existence, because he believed there was a chance. I intend to do the same.'

Duncan looked down at the sunken, mummified face of his friend, remembering all the determination and hard training the old Bashar had given him when he was a young ghola. Sheeana was right. Even though Duncan hadn't been able to free the *Ithaca* and let them escape, he and Miles had shown the Enemy that humans were unpredictable and resilient, that they were not to be under-estimated. And it wasn't over yet. Instead of a simple capture, the thinking machines had been forced to sacrifice one of their largest battleships simply to stop them.

'We'll take him to one of the small airlocks,' he announced. Since their every movement was now dictated by the Enemy ships that dragged them along, it was point-less to remain at the controls. 'I have no intention of letting the thinking machines have him.'

The remnants of the Bashar would fly alone into the cosmos. The rest of them might be trapped, to be used in thinking-machine experiments, or for whatever reason the old man and woman had been pursuing them over the decades. But not Miles. This act would be another small victory – and enough small victories could win an entire war.

They arrived at one of the chambers, which Duncan recognized as the same airlock he had used to jettison Murbella's last possessions, items that had clung to him like cobwebs until he forced himself to let go. They placed the tragically lightweight husk of Teg's body inside the chamber and sealed it. Duncan looked through the observation port, saying his last goodbyes.

'It isn't the ceremony I would have imagined for him. Last time, the Bashar had all of Rakis for his funeral pyre. But there's no time.' Before he could have second thoughts, Duncan pushed the button that evacuated the airlock, opening the outside hatch so that the body tumbled out into the void. 'We should summon everyone aboard the ship and prepare our defenses.'

'What defenses?'

He looked at her. 'Anything we can think of.'

SHOULDERED FORWARD BY a hundred thinking-machine vessels, the battered no-ship was forced down into Synchrony, where shifting buildings moved aside to form an acceptable place for the captured craft to land. The now-visible *Ithaca* descended like a trussed wild animal, the trophy of big game hunters.

Baron Harkonnen thought it a glorious sight. From an extruded balcony in one of Omnius's capricious high towers, he studied the vessel as it descended. The no-ship's configuration was unfamiliar to him, massive but not as intimidating as he'd imagined it would be. This design was much more organic and alien-looking than huge Guild Heighliners, deadly Sardaukar craft, House Harkonnen military vessels, or his own family frigates. It seemed to be convergent evolution, eerily similar to the flow-form curves of the thinking-machine structures.

Strange ship, strange passengers.

According to initial reports from the machine scouts who had seized the no-ship, many of those aboard were gholas from his own past, annoyances resurrected from history, exactly as Erasmus had suspected – Lady Jessica, another Paul Atreides, a minor Swordmaster named Duncan Idaho, and who knew how many others? Gholas coughed up and spat out like wads of phlegm.

A keyed-up Paolo stood beside him on the balcony, facing the makeshift spaceport that waited to accommodate the new vessel. 'Will we kill them all, Grandfather? I don't want there to be another Kwisatz Haderach. I'm supposed to be the only one. I should take the ultraspice that Khrone delivered right now.'

'I would have you do it if I could, dear boy, but Omnius won't permit that. Be patient. Even if there is another version of Paul Atreides aboard that no-ship, he's probably soft and compassionate. He doesn't have the advantage of being toughened by *me*.' The Baron's full lips curled down in distaste. Paolo himself didn't realize just how much of his fundamental personality had been changed. 'You will have no trouble defeating him.'

'I have already visualized it,' Paolo replied. 'Real, prescient dreams – and now I understand what is going to happen.'

'Then you have nothing to worry about.'

The Omnius-formed buildings swayed like reeds, then embraced the battered no-ship as it landed, pulling the *Ithaca* down into a living metal cradle. The landing and lockdown process seemed interminable. Was it really necessary for so many structural braces to fold around the ship like claws? Considering the obvious damage to the engines, the captives could never find a way to launch the vessel again. However, Omnius had a penchant for doing things in a brute-force manner. The Baron could understand that.

Presently Erasmus appeared on the balcony, once again disguised as a matronly old woman. Gazing dispassionately at the robot, the Baron announced, 'I will go aboard the no-ship. I want to be the first to' – his lips quirked in a smile – 'greet our visitors.'

The old woman's eyes twinkled. 'Are you certain that would be wise, Baron? We aren't sure yet exactly who is aboard the vessel. You could be in peril if anyone recognizes you. In your past life, quite a few people were not entirely pleased with you.'

'I certainly don't intend to go unprotected! In fact, I expect *you* to provide me with full security. Some of your sentinel robots, perhaps – or better yet, an armed contingent of Face Dancers. Paolo will remain here safe, but I *will* go aboard.' He planted his hands on his hips. 'In fact, I demand it.'

Erasmus seemed amused. 'In that case, we had better give you the Face Dancers. Go aboard, Baron, and be our ambassador. I'm sure you will employ all the diplomacy the situation requires.'

*We shall face the Enemy, and die if we must die. My
strong preference, however, is to kill what we must kill.*
 — MOTHER COMMANDER MURBELLA,
transmission to human defensive forces

Ten thousand Guildships against an infinite number of
Enemy vessels.

For this confrontation, the Mother Commander had
prepared all the warlords, political leaders and other self-
proclaimed generals, as well as her ferocious Sisters –
what remained of them. Spread out across the path of
the oncoming thinking-machine forces, her human
defenders dug themselves in.

Guildsmen had been rushed in at the last minute to
help crew the numerous battleships, launching them to
their designated rendezvous points in space. The untested
military commanders were as ready as the Mother
Commander could make them. Like ghost soldiers, red-
eyed refugees from planets already ground under the
machine boot heel volunteered in droves. Each craft was
loaded with Obliterators produced by the tireless Ixian
factories.

Unfortunately, Omnius had been preparing for
centuries.

Like a force of nature, the thinking machines advanced, not dodging or changing course, without regard to the strength of planetary defenses arrayed against them. They simply rolled over anything in their path.

For Murbella's plan to work, the line of Enemy ships had to be stopped at every point, in every star system. No battleground was unimportant. She had divided her defenders into a hundred discrete groups of one hundred new Guild warships apiece. The battle groups were positioned at widely scattered but important points outside inhabited systems, ready to fend off the approaching Enemy.

As a last line of defense, Murbella's one hundred newly constructed vessels patrolled space in the vicinity of Chapterhouse, along with a number of smaller, older vessels to flesh out the military force. They knew Omnius considered this planet a primary target. Waiting for the clash, the Mother Commander thought her new ships looked magnificent, the line formidable. The fighters aboard were more confident than afraid.

By the New Sisterhood's best estimates, though, the thinking machines outnumbered them by more than a hundred to one.

To shore up their confidence, the fighters had all watched holos of the Ixian tests of the new Obliterators on dead Richese, admiring the massive destructive force contained in each of the powerful weapons. Bene Gesserit observers had monitored the Ixian production lines, and technicians had verified the complex weapons after they were installed in Murbella's fleet. She clung to the hope that this line of last stands could turn into a rout for the forces of Omnius.

More than she had for the past quarter century, the

Mother Commander wished Duncan Idaho could be at her side again, facing this final conflict with her. Feeling the loneliness of command, tempted to bow to primitive human superstition and offer up a prayer to some invisible guardian angel, she hardened herself.

This has to work!

Her great ships prowled the edge of planetary orbit, not knowing from which direction the Enemy fleet would come. Down below, the refugees who had filled temporary camps on the plague-emptied continents were anxious to evacuate from Chapterhouse, but even if there were vessels to transport them away, they had nowhere to go. Every functional craft in the sector had been commandeered to face the thinking-machine ships. It was everything the human race could rally.

'Enemy ships approaching, Mother Commander,' said Administrator Gorus, receiving a message from the sensor deck. His pale braid looked somewhat frayed, his skin whiter than usual. He had been convinced to stay aboard the main ship at the central battlefield, to stand by the new ships his factories had produced; he didn't look at all happy about it.

'Exactly on time. Exactly as expected,' Murbella said. 'Disperse our vessels into the widest possible firing spread, so we can hit the Enemy all at once, before they can react to us. Machines are adaptable, but they rarely take the unexpected into account.'

Gorus looked at her sourly. 'Are you making assumptions based on old records, Mother Commander? Extrapolating from the way Omnius reacted fifteen thousand years ago?'

'To some extent, but I trust my instincts.'

As the heavily armed machine ships approached, they

looked like a meteor shower that grew larger and larger. The monstrous vessels loomed huge – thousands of them against the Sisterhood's desperate hundred. All along the line, at a hundred other systems, she knew her defenders were facing similar odds.

'Prepare to launch Obliterators. Stop them before they get any closer to Chapterhouse.' Murbella crossed her arms over her chest. Across the commlines, each captain announced his or her readiness.

The oncoming machine ships slowed, as if curious to see what this small obstacle might be. *They will underestimate us*, Murbella thought. 'Maximize targets. Fire into close groupings of Enemy ships. Consolidate explosions.'

'Targets locked, Mother Commander,' Gorus said, his message transmitted immediately by his sensor technicians.

Murbella had to preempt the thinking machines before they could open fire. 'Launch Obliterators.' She held herself steady.

Silver sparks spat out of the launch tubes, Obliterators twirling toward the line of Enemy ships, but the glints faded. Nothing happened, though some of the heavy weapons must have struck their targets. The machine vessels seemed to be waiting for something.

She looked around. 'Confirm that the Obliterators are armed. Where are the explosions? Launch the second volley!'

Alarms began to ring. In a frenzy, Gorus ran from one station to another, shouting at the Guildsmen on the upper decks. A harried-looking Reverend Mother charged into the command center, skidding to a stop in front of Murbella. 'Our Obliterators are doing nothing. They are all useless.'

'But they were tested! Our Sisters watched the manufacturing lines. How could they be faulty?'

Then, all at once, the one hundred Chapterhouse defender ships went dead in space, their engines shutting down, lights flickering. The thrum of station-keeping thrusters faded.

'What is happening?' Gorus demanded. 'Sabotage? Were we betrayed?'

As if they had expected this all along, the machine ships closed in.

A Guildsman transmitted in a hollow voice over the speaking screen, 'The artificial navigation systems no longer respond, Administrator. We are shut out of our own controls. Our ships are . . . nonfunctional.' Emergency lights lit the decks with an eerie glow.

'Did the machines figure out how to neutralize our systems?'

Gorus turned to Murbella. 'No jamming, Mother Commander. They . . . they just don't work. None of them.'

Suddenly the machine forces were upon them, a thousand vessels that would easily overwhelm the defenders. Murbella prepared to die. Her fighters could not protect themselves, or Chapterhouse, which she had sworn to guard.

But instead of attacking, the Enemy fleet cruised slowly past the defenders, taunting them in their impotence. The machines did not bother to open fire, as if the Sisterhood's defenses weren't even worth noticing!

Far behind them, just arriving at the distant edge of the solar system, came another wave of thinking machines, closing in on Chapterhouse. The same thing must be happening everywhere, at all of her carefully staged last stands across a hundred star systems.

'They knew! The damned machines *knew* our Obliterators wouldn't work!' As if Murbella's vessels were no more than a pebble on the path, the Omnius ships flowed around them on their way to the Sisterhood's now-unprotected homeworld.

Not one of her new Guild war vessels had a living Navigator aboard; most of the Navigators and their Heighliners had disappeared. Every ship in her battle groups used Ixian mathematical compilers for guidance. Mathematical compilers! Computers ... thinking machines.

The Ixians! Now her silent curse was directed at herself for overconfidence in the new Obliterators and her own ability to predict the Enemy's tactics.

'Follow me, Administrator. I want to see these Obliterators for myself.' She grabbed Gorus's arm hard enough to leave bruises.

Guided by emergency illumination, they rushed to the weapons deck where the armaments had been installed. Inside, rack upon rack held the burnished silver eggs of the planet-melters that Ix had manufactured. A distraught Guildsman intercepted them. 'We tested the weapons, Administrator, and they were installed correctly. The firing controls are operational. We just launched dozens of Obliterators, but none of them detonated.'

'Why didn't they function?'

'Because ... because the Obliterators themselves ...'

Murbella marched over to where the man had opened one casing at random. Beneath a complicated labyrinth of circuitry and delicate components, the Obliterator charge was fused into the shell of the mechanism, making the whole thing inoperable. The weapon had been neutralized.

'It is useless, Mother Commander,' said Gorus. 'Sabotaged.'

'But I saw the tests myself. How can this be?'

'A timing mechanism may have shut everything down at a prearranged time, or the Enemy fleet might have sent out a deactivating signal. Some devious trick that we could not have anticipated.'

Murbella stood appalled, guilty of the same error she had been so certain the machines would fall victim to: She had failed to plan for the unexpected. Together, they opened another Obliterator to find it similarly fused and nonfunctional. A coldness froze her heart and spread into her bloodstream. These weapons had been built over the course of years by the Ixians, at a cost in melange that nearly bankrupted the Sisterhood. She had been duped, and her fleet had been castrated by the Ixians before the battle could even begin.

'And what about our engines?'

'They can be made to function, if we operate them without the mathematical compilers.'

'I don't give a damn about the compilers! Find a way to salvage some of the Obliterators. Are they all inactive? Every single one?'

'The only way to know, Mother Commander, is to open and inspect each of them.'

'We could just launch them all and hope a few still function.' Murbella nodded slowly. It was indeed an option. At this point, it cost them nothing. She had to find some way to fight, and she hoped her other battle groups were faring better than this . . . but she doubted it. Without functional Obliterators, every one of the planets on the front line was essentially unprotected in the face of certain destruction.

And it was all her responsibility.

Some say that survival itself can be the best revenge. For myself, I prefer something a bit more extravagant.

> – BARON VLADIMIR HARKONNEN,
> the ghola

On a whim, the Baron told the ten Face Dancers accompanying him to pose as Sardaukar from the old Imperium. He didn't know if anyone would even recognize the joke – fashions changed and history forgot such details – but it helped him present an air of command. During his original lifetime he had achieved a great victory over House Atreides with illicit Sardaukar at his side.

Leaving the restless Paolo with Erasmus, supposedly 'for his own protection,' the Baron dressed himself in a nobleman's uniform frosted with gold braids and ornate chains of office. A ceremonial poison-tipped dagger hung at his side, and a wide-beam stunner was concealed in his sleeve for easy access. Though the imitation Sardaukar were his guards and escort, he didn't particularly trust them, either. One could never be too careful.

When the Baron's entourage marched to the imprisoned no-ship, however, they could not find a door on the kilometer-long hull – a frustrating and embarrassing moment, but Omnius was not to be hindered. Guided by the evermind, parts of nearby buildings transformed into gigantic tools that tore open the hull, peeling away plates and structural girders to leave a wide gash. Brute force was easier and more direct than locating an appropriate hatch and deciphering unfamiliar controls.

With the no-ship suitably opened, the Baron and his escort ducked under low-hanging debris and sparking circuitry. Prepared for an ambush, but moving with an outward show of confidence, they made their way through the winding corridors. Several of Omnius's floating watcheyes zoomed ahead of them down the passageways to scout out and map the interior of the vessel.

The captives would surely see that surrender was their only option. What other conclusion could they draw? Unfortunately, in his original lifetime the Baron had had considerable experience with fanatics, such as the mad Fremen bands on Arrakis. It was possible that these poor wretches intended to mount a desperate, hopeless resistance until they were all slaughtered, including the purported Kwisatz Haderach among them.

Paolo would then be the only contender, and that would be that.

Inside the no-ship, they first encountered Duncan Idaho and a defiant-looking Bene Gesserit woman who identified herself as Sheeana. The two waited for the boarding party in the middle of a wide corridor. The Baron only vaguely remembered the man from the records of House Atreides: a Swordmaster of Ginaz, one of Duke Leto's most trusted fighters, killed on Arrakis while protecting Paul and Jessica in their escape. From the sneer on Idaho's face, he could tell that this ghola had his memories back, too.

'Oh ho, I see that you know me.'

Idaho didn't budge. 'I escaped from Giedi Prime as a boy, Baron. I beat Rabban on one of his hunts. I've lived many lifetimes since then. This time, I hope to watch you die with my own eyes.'

'How boldly you speak, like one of those yipping dogs Emperor Shaddam used to keep at his side: full of annoying barks and growls, yet easily stepped on.' Protected by the Face Dancer Sardaukar, he peered ahead down the hall. 'How many people do you have aboard?' He snapped. 'Bring them forward for our inspection.'

'We have already assembled,' Sheeana said. 'We're ready for you.'

The Baron sighed. 'And no doubt you've scattered commandos or snipers throughout the decks? Your personnel records will have been doctored. A childish resistance that may cause us a few headaches, but will gain you nothing. We have enough troops to mow all of you down.'

'It would be foolish for us to resist,' Sheeana said, 'at least in such obvious ways.'

The Baron scowled, and he heard the little girl's voice inside his head. *She is playing with your mind, Grandfather!*

'So are you!' he hissed to himself, startling the others.

'Five hundred more of our men are coming aboard,' said the counterfeit Sardaukar commander. 'Mobile machine sensors will scour every chamber on every deck, and we'll find anything there is to find. We will locate the Kwisatz Haderach.'

'A Kwisatz Haderach?' Idaho asked. 'Is that what the old man and woman have been looking for? On this ship? You're welcome to waste your time.'

Sheeana added harshly, 'If we had a superman aboard, you would never have been able to capture us.'

That remark disturbed the Baron. At the back of his mind he heard the maddening voice of Alia chuckling at his discomfiture. His face flushed, but he forced himself not to speak aloud. What a fool, debating with the unheard voice of an invisible tormentor! New groups came down the no-ship corridors to gather in front of him like troops for inspection.

One small-statured teenaged ghola unsettled him the most. The young man was thin and sallow-skinned, his face etched in a scowl. His eyes burned with hatred for the Baron, though he did not find the fellow at all familiar. He wondered what he had done to that one.

Look more closely, Grandfather. Surely you recognize him? He almost killed you!

I swear I will find some way to rip you out of my head!

With a neutral expression on his face, he looked again at the dour ghola, and suddenly understood the crude black diamond marked on his forehead. 'Why, it's Yueh! My dear Dr Yueh, how good to see you again. I never got a chance to tell you how much you helped the Harkonnen cause so long ago. Glad to see that I have an unexpected ally aboard this ship.'

Yueh looked skinny and ineffectual, yet the gleam in his eyes was genuinely murderous. 'I am not your ally.'

'You are a weak little worm. It was easy enough to manipulate you before – I can do it again.' The Baron was surprised that the scrawny man did not back down. This version of Yueh seemed stronger, perhaps transformed by the lessons of his ignominious past.

'You no longer have leverage over me, Baron. You have no Wanna. Even if you did, I would not repeat my earlier mistakes.' Crossing his arms over his narrow chest, he thrust his pointed chin forward.

The Baron turned abruptly from the Suk doctor as even more no-ship captives came forward. One bronze-haired young woman of about eighteen looked exactly like the lovely Lady Jessica. The way she viewed him with palpable revulsion proved that this ghola also had her memories restored. Did Jessica know she was really his own daughter? What entertaining conversations they might have!

Standing protectively beside the youthful Jessica were a younger woman dressed as a Fremen and a dark-haired young man – the perfect image of Paolo, only older. 'Why, is this young Paul? Another Paul Atreides?'

A swift slash, a mere nick from the poisoned dagger, and the rival Kwisatz Haderach would be gone. But he shuddered to think how Omnius would react to that. The Baron wanted Paolo to assume his position of power, of course, but he wasn't willing to sacrifice his own life for the boy. Though the Baron had raised and trained Paolo, he was still, after all, an *Atreides*.

'Hello, Grandfather,' Paul said. 'I remember you as being much older and fatter.' The Baron found the demeanor and tone irritating. And even worse, he felt an odd, swooning sensation . . . as if Paul had always been meant to say this, as if he had seen it in a dozen different visions.

Still, the Baron clapped his hands in mock applause. 'Isn't ghola technology marvelous? This is like an encore at the end of one of the Emperor's tedious jongleur performances. All back together again for a second run, eh?'

Paul stiffened. 'House Atreides crushed the Harkonnens into extinction long ago. I anticipate a similar outcome now.'

'Oh, ho!' Though amused, the Baron-ghola didn't step any closer. He gestured to his Sardaukar guard. 'Have a doctor and a dentist look them over before they get close to me. Pay particular attention to their teeth. Look for poison capsules.'

Having fulfilled his purpose, the Baron was about to march out of the no-ship when, among the gathered refugees, he spotted a small girl who stood quietly beside a thin boy of around twelve years, watching everything. Both had an Atreides look about them. He froze, recognizing Alia.

Not only had this bloodthirsty child jabbed him with the poison gom jabbar and haunted his thoughts, now she even stood before him! *Look, Grandfather – now we can torment you inside and out!* Her voice pierced him like ice picks in his head.

The Baron reacted, not caring about consequences. Snatching the ceremonial dagger from his hip, he grabbed the little girl by the collar and raised the blade. 'They called you Abomination!'

Alia fought like a rabid animal, but didn't scream. Her tiny feet drove with surprising power into his stomach, knocking the wind out of him. The Baron reeled, and without a second's hesitation, thrust the poisoned tip deep into her side. It went in easily. He yanked the knife back out and stabbed again, this time directly into Alia's heart.

Jessica screamed. Paul rushed forward, but too late. Duncan roared with anger and shock, and threw himself at the nearest Sardaukar guard, killing him with a bone-shattering blow to the throat. He struck a second guard, snapping his neck as well, and charged toward the Baron like a wild creature. The Baron didn't even have time to feel fear before his guards closed ranks around him, and four others held Duncan back. The rest of the faux Sardaukar raised their guns to keep the shocked captives at bay.

Regaining his composure, the Baron sneered down at the little girl dying swiftly in his grip. 'That's turnabout for killing me.' Laughing at the blood on his hands, he tossed her to the floor like a discarded doll. And inside, not a sound from his tormentor. Was she gone as well?

Murderous desperation showed on the faces of the nearby captives, making the Baron uneasy. With Face Dancer Sardaukar surrounding him protectively, he backed away smiling. The two dead soldiers had reverted to Face Dancers, and none of the captives seemed the least bit surprised. The Atreides rabble gathered around the murdered child while the Sardaukar picked up their comrades.

Sheeana stopped Duncan from lunging forward in another suicidal attack. 'One death is enough, Duncan.'

'No it's not. It is only a start.' He controlled himself with a visible effort. 'But it will have to do for now.'

The Baron laughed, and the Face Dancers hurried him away. When he looked at his escort, the shape-shifters showed disapproval at what he had done. 'What? I don't have to justify my reasons to you. At least that Abomination is gone now.'

Gone, you say? A little girl's loud titter like breaking glass inside his skull. *Gone? You can't discard me so easily! I was rooted inside your head before that ghola was ever born.* The voice grew louder. *Now I shall torment you more than ever. You leave me no choice but to serve as your conscience, Grandfather.*

The Baron marched away at a faster pace, trying to shut out her mocking presence.

The stake in a total war is total – to conquer is to save everything, to succumb is to lose everything.

                          – a warrior of Old Terra

While the thinking machines maintained a tight cordon around the no-ship, Sheeana watched Jessica carry little Alia's body away. How painful it must be for her. With her memories restored, Jessica knew intimately who Alia really was and understood her great potential. How bitterly ironic, too. St Alia of the Knife – felled by a knife.

Jessica cradled the limp child in her arms, shuddering as she fought to contain sobs. When she looked up at Sheeana, there was a cold deadliness in Jessica's eyes. Duncan stood beside Jessica, his face a mask of grim anger. 'We'll have our revenge, my Lady. So many of us despise the Baron, he can't survive for long.' Even Yueh sat coiled and dangerous, like a loaded weapon.

Paul and Chani clasped hands, drawing strength from each other. Leto II watched in silence, undoubtedly holding an avalanche of conflicting thoughts in his mind. The boy always seemed to have so much more to him, like a giant iceberg whose bulk was concealed beneath the surface. Sheeana had long suspected that he might be the most powerful of all the gholas she had created.

Jessica held her head high, finding strength within her. 'We'll take her to my quarters. Duncan, would you help me?' Dr Yueh, desperate for forgiveness, hovered close to them.

Filled with anxiety, frustration, and anger, Sheeana watched the tableau. In addition to losing the Bashar, Alia had been murdered, while three key gholas – Paul, Chani, and Leto II – remained unawakened. Stilgar and Liet-Kynes were left on Qelso, and Thufir Hawat had been a Face Dancer. Now that they were facing the Enemy and needed the ghola children to fulfill their destinies, too many of her 'weapons' were not available to her! She had only Yueh, and Jessica . . . and Scytale, if she could count on the Tleilaxu.

Exhaustion threatened to overwhelm Sheeana. They had fled for so long, carrying their plans and hopes, but never finding an end. This, though, was not at all what they had hoped for.

The quiet and distant voice of Serena Butler awakened within her again, angered by the revelation about the Enemy. She spoke from firsthand knowledge. *The evil machines have always wanted to exterminate humanity. They do not know how to forget.*

'But they were destroyed,' Sheeana said aloud.

Apparently not. Trillions of people died during the Butlerian Jihad, but even that was not enough. In the end, I was not enough.

'I am pleased to meet you finally,' said a raspy female voice. A lone old woman strolled down the no-ship's corridor, a broad grin on her wrinkled face. Despite her apparent age, she moved fluidly and had a deadly look to her.

Sheeana immediately guessed that this must be the

mysterious old woman who was their relentless hunter. 'Duncan has told us about you.'

The woman smiled in an unnerving manner, as if she could see through Sheeana to her innermost thoughts and intentions. 'You were quite a troublesome quarry. All those years wasted. Have you guessed my true identity yet?'

'You are the Enemy.'

Abruptly the crone's face, body, and clothing rippled like molten, flowing metal. At first Sheeana thought this was another Face Dancer, but the head and body took on a sheen of highly polished platinum, and the matronly clothes became a plush robe. The face was smooth, with the same smile set in radically different features. A robot.

Deep in her consciousness, Sheeana felt a tumult in Other Memory. And out of the clamor, Serena Butler's familiar voice rose to cry, *Erasmus! Destroy him!*

With great effort she shunted aside the voices in Other Memory, and said, 'You are Erasmus. The one who killed Serena Butler's child, setting off the centuries-long Jihad against thinking machines.'

'So I *am* still remembered, even after all this time.' The robot sounded pleased.

'Serena remembers you, all right. She is within me, and she hates you.'

Pure delight shone on the robot's face. 'Serena Butler herself is in there? Ah yes, I know about your Other Memory. Face Dancers have brought many of you Bene Gesserits back to us.'

Inside her, the clamor of memories returned. 'I am Serena Butler, and she is me. Though thousands of years have passed, the pain is as sharp as ever. We cannot forget what you destroyed, and what you started.'

'It was only one life – merely a baby. Logically, can't

you see how your race overreacted?' The robot sounded so reasonable.

Sheeana felt a change in the tenor and cadence of her own voice, as if her body were being taken over by a force within. 'Only one life? Merely a baby?' Serena was speaking now, thrusting herself to the forefront of the innumerable lives. Sheeana let her talk. After such a great length of time, this was *Serena's confrontation with her greatest nemesis. 'That one life led to the military defeat of your entire Synchronized Empire. The Butlerian Jihad was a Kralizec in its own right. The end of that war changed the course of the universe.'*

Erasmus seemed delighted by the comparison. 'Ah, interesting. And perhaps the end of this Kralizec will reverse that result and put thinking machines in charge again. If so, we will be much more efficient this time.'

'That is how you foresee the end of Kralizec?'

'That would be my preference. Something fundamental must change. Can I count on you to assist me?'

'Never.' Serena's projected voice was cold and implacable.

Looking at the independent robot, Sheeana understood more than ever before that she was part of something far greater and more important than one life, that she was linked to a vast continuum of female ancestry stretching into the past and – hopefully – into the future. A remarkable assemblage, but would it survive?

'There is a familiar fire in your eyes. If any part of you is indeed Serena Butler, then we must catch up on old times.' Erasmus's optic threads gleamed.

'She no longer wishes to converse with you,' Sheeana said in her own voice.

Erasmus ignored the rebuff. 'Take me to your private

quarters. A human's den reveals much about the individual personality.'

'I will not.'

The robot's voice hardened. 'Be reasonable. Or should I decapitate a few of your fellow passengers to encourage your cooperation? Ask Serena Butler inside you – she knows I will do it.'

Sheeana glared at him.

The robot continued in a calm tone, 'But a simple conversation with you in your quarters may slake my appetite for now. Wouldn't you prefer that to carnage?'

Motioning for the others to remain behind, Sheeana turned her back on the robot and walked to one of the still-functional lifts. With gliding footsteps, Erasmus followed.

In her chamber, the robot was intrigued by the preserved Van Gogh painting. *Cottages at Cordeville* was one of the oldest artifacts of human civilization. Standing rigidly, Erasmus admired the artwork. 'Ah, yes! I remember this clearly. I painted it myself.'

'It is the work of a nineteenth-century Terran artist, Vincent Van Gogh.'

'I have studied the Madman of France with great interest, but I assure you, this is actually one of the canvases I myself painted thousands of years ago. I copied the original with the utmost attention to detail.'

She wondered if he could possibly be telling the truth.

Erasmus removed the delicate painting from the wall and examined it closely, passing his metal fingertips over the thin plaz that protected the rough oil-paint surface. 'Yes, well do I remember each stroke, each whorl, each point of color. Truly, this is a work of genius.'

Sheeana caught her breath, knowing how old and

priceless it was. Unless it really was a forgery perpetrated long ago. 'The *original* was a work of genius. If this is what you say, then all you did was copy someone else's masterpiece. There can be only one original.'

His optic threads gleamed like a galaxy of stars. 'If it is the same, exactly the same, then both are works of genius. If my copy is perfect down to every single brush-stroke, does it not become a second original?'

'Van Gogh was a man of creativity and inspiration. You merely mimicked his work. You might as well call a Face Dancer a work of art.'

Erasmus smiled. 'Some of them are.'

Abruptly, with powerful hands, the robot ripped the painting and its frame into tiny pieces. As if putting a punctuation mark on the grotesque display, Erasmus whirled and stomped on the broken pieces, saying, 'Call this artistic temperament.' Moving to depart, he added, 'Omnius will summon your Kwisatz Haderach soon. We have waited a long time for this.'

The independent robot's memories of Serena were as
fresh as if the events had occurred only days ago. Serena
Butler . . . such a fascinating woman. And just as Erasmus
had survived through the millennia as a package of data
nearly destroyed and then recovered, so Serena's memories and personality lived on, somehow, in the Other
Memories of the Bene Gesserit.

This posed an intriguing question: No Bene Gesserits
could be Serena Butler's direct descendants, for Erasmus
had killed her only child. Then again, he couldn't be sure
what had happened to all of his experimental clones over
the years. He had tried many times to bring Serena back,
with no success.

Aboard this no-ship, however, the humans had grown
gholas from their past, just as his own plan had brought
back Baron Harkonnen and a version of Paul Atreides.
Erasmus knew that a nullentropy tube hidden in a Tleilaxu
Master had contained a wealth of ancient and carefully
gathered cells.

He was confident that a real Tleilaxu Master could succeed in bringing Serena back, where his own primitive experiments had failed. Erasmus and Omnius had both absorbed enough Face Dancers to have instinctive reverence for the abilities of a Master. The independent robot knew exactly where he had to go before leaving the no-ship.

Erasmus found the medical center and the axlotl chambers where the whole library of historical cells had been catalogued and stored. If Serena Butler was among them . . .

He was surprised to find a Tleilaxu already there, harried and frantic. The diminutive man had disconnected the life-support systems of the axlotl tanks. With his olfactory sensors, Erasmus noted the smells of chemicals, melange precursors, and human flesh.

He grinned. 'You must be Scytale, the Tleilaxu Master! It's been a long time.'

Scytale whirled, looking fearful at the sight of the robot.

Erasmus took a step closer, and studied the Tleilaxu's face. 'A child? What are you doing?'

The Tleilaxu drew himself up. 'I am destroying the tanks and the melange they produce. I had to surrender that knowledge as a bargaining chip. I won't let thinking machines and traitorous Face Dancers simply take it from me – from *us*.'

Erasmus showed no concern for the sabotaged axlotl tanks. 'But you appear to be very young.'

'I am a ghola. I have my memories back. I am everything that any of my previous incarnations were.'

'Of course you are. Such a marvelous process, perpetuating yourself through serial ghola lives. We machines understand such things, although we have much more efficient methods of performing data transfers and backups.' He looked intensely at the genetic library that held the potential ghola cells . . . Serena Butler . . .

Noting the robot's keen interest, the Tleilaxu sprang to stand in front of the sealed wall of specimens. 'Beware! The witches placed security sensors on these gene samples to prevent anyone from tampering with or stealing them. The library has a built-in self-destruct system.' He narrowed his dark, rodentlike eyes. If this Master was bluffing, he was doing a remarkably convincing job. 'I need only yank on a drawer, and this entire cabinet will be flooded with gamma radiation, enough to ionize every single sample.'

'Why?' The robot was perplexed. 'After the Bene Gesserit took those cells from you and used them for their own purposes? Didn't they force you to cooperate? Would you truly stand on their side?' He extended a platinum hand. 'Join us instead. I would greatly reward you for your assistance in growing one particular ghola—'

In a threatening motion, Scytale placed his small hand on one of the many cell containers. Though trembling, he seemed entirely determined. 'Yes, I would stand with them. I shall always stand *against* the thinking machines.'

'Interesting. New enemies make unexpected alliances.'

The Tleilaxu didn't move. 'In the final assessment, we're all humans – and you are not.'

Erasmus chuckled. 'And what about Face Dancers? They fall between, don't they? These aren't the shape-shifters you produced long ago, but are instead far superior biological machines that I helped create. And because of them, Omnius and I are, in effect, the greatest of all Face Dancers – among many other things.'

Scytale didn't move. 'Haven't you noticed the Face Dancers are no longer reliable?'

'Ah, but they are reliable to me.'

'Are you sure?'

The robot took a tentative step forward, testing. Scytale tensed his fingers on the handle of the sample cabinet. Erasmus amplified his voice. 'Stop!' He eased himself backward, giving the Tleilaxu Master more room. There would be plenty of time to return and test Scytale's loyalties. 'I leave you to this facility and your cellular samples.'

Erasmus had waited more than fifteen thousand years for Serena, and could continue to do so. For now, the robot had to return to the machine cathedral and prepare for the final show. The evermind was not quite so patient to achieve his ultimate goals as Erasmus was.

Come, let us eat and sing together. We will share a drink and laugh at our enemies.

– from an ancient ballad by
GURNEY HALLECK

The computer evermind sent his troops to bring Paul from the *Ithaca* to the machines' cathedral-like nexus. New-model robotic guards swarmed down the corridors like quicksilver insects. Approaching Paul, one of them said, 'Come with us to the primary cathedral.'

Chani grabbed his arm and held on, as if she too had sprouted metal hands. 'I will not let you go, Usul.'

Looking at the inhuman escorts, he said to her, 'We can't keep them from taking me.'

'Then I shall come with you.' He tried to argue with her, but she cut him off. 'I am a Fremen woman. Would you try to stop me? You might just as easily fight these machines.'

Concealing a small smile, he faced the sleek machines that clicked and flittered in front of him. 'I will accompany you without resistance, but only if Chani comes with me.'

Emerging from her quarters where Alia's body now lay on the narrow bed, Jessica placed herself between Paul and the robots. Bloodstains still marked her shipsuit. 'He is my son. I have already lost a daughter today, and cannot bear to lose him as well. I'm going with you.'

'We are here to escort Paul Atreides to the primary cathedral,' one of the robots said, its freeform face flowing like heavy rain on a Caladan window. 'There are no other restrictions.'

Paul took that as agreement. For some reason, Omnius wanted *him*, even though he did not have his memories back. All other passengers and crew were apparently extraneous baggage. Had he been the subject of the hunt from the beginning? How could that be? Had the thinking machines somehow known he would be aboard? Paul gripped Chani's hand and said to her, 'It will be over soon, in whatever manner fate decides. All along, our destinies have hurtled us toward this point, like levitating trains out of control.'

'We will face it together, my love,' Chani said. He only wished that he could recall all his years with her . . . and that she could do the same.

'What about Duncan?' he asked. 'And Sheeana?'

'We must depart now,' the robots said in unison. 'Omnius waits.'

'Duncan and Sheeana will know soon enough,' Jessica said.

Before they left, Paul made a point of taking the crysknife Chani had made for him. Like a Fremen warrior, he wore it proudly at his waist. Although the worm-tooth blade would do nothing against the thinking machines, it made him feel more like the legendary Muad'Dib – the man who defeated powerful empires. But in his mind he again saw the horrible recurring vision, the flicker of memory or prescience in which he lay on the floor in a strange place, mortally wounded – looking up at a younger version of himself who laughed in triumph.

He blinked and sought to focus on reality, not possibilities or destiny. Following the insectile robots down the corridors, he tried to tell himself he was prepared to face whatever lay in store for him.

Before the gholas could emerge from the ship through the ragged hole the machines had made, Wellington Yueh tried to push his way past the ranks of escort robots. 'Wait! I want . . . I need to go with you.' He fumbled for excuses. 'If someone gets hurt, I'm the best Suk doctor available. I can help.' He lowered his voice and pleaded, 'The Baron will be there, and he'll want to see me.'

Still wrestling with her reinjured feelings toward him, Jessica sounded harsh and bitter. 'Help? Did you help Alia?' Hearing this, Yueh looked as if she had slapped him.

'Let him come, Mother.' Paul felt resigned. 'Dr Yueh was a staunch childhood supporter and mentor to the original Paul. I won't turn down any ally or witness to whatever is about to occur.'

Following the robots, they emerged onto flowing roadways that carried them along like floating plates. Batlike fliers streaked high overhead, and mirrored watcheyes fitted about in the air, observing the group's progress from all angles. Behind them, the huge no-ship had been incorporated into the machine metropolis. Sentient metal buildings of freeform architecture had grown around the *Ithaca*'s hull like coral swallowing up an old shipwreck beneath the seas of Caladan. The buildings seemed to alter whenever the evermind had a fleeting thought.

'This whole city is alive and thinking,' Paul said. 'It's all one changeable, adapting machine.'

Under her breath, his mother quoted, '"Thou shalt not create a machine in the likeness of the human mind."'

Speakers appeared in the solid silver walls of the looming buildings, and a simulated voice mockingly repeated Jessica's words. '"Thou shalt not create a machine in the likeness of the human mind." What a quaint superstition!' The laughter sounded as if it had been recorded from somewhere else, distorted freakishly, and then played back. 'I look forward to our encounter.'

The escort robots brought them into an enormous structure with shimmering walls, curved arches, and enclosed parklike spaces. A spectacular lava fountain spouted plumes of hot, scarlet liquid into a tempered basin.

In the middle of the great cathedral hall, an elderly man and woman awaited them, dressed in loose, comfortable garments. Dwarfed by the enclosure, they certainly did not look menacing.

Paul decided not to wait for their captors to play control games. 'Why have you brought me here? What do you want?'

'I want to help the universe.' The old man stepped down the polished stone stairs. 'We are in the endgame of Kralizec, a watershed that will change the universe forever. Everything that came before will end, and everything that comes in the future will be under my guidance.'

The old woman explained. 'Consider all the chaos that has existed over the millennia of your human civilization. Such messy creatures you are! We thinking machines could have done a much neater, more efficient job. We have learned of your God Emperor Leto II, and the Scattering, and the Famine Times.'

'At least he enforced peace for thirty-five hundred years,' the old man added. 'He had the right idea.'

'My grandson,' Jessica said. 'They called him Tyrant because of the difficult decisions he made. But even he did not do as much damage as your thinking machines did during the Butlerian Jihad.'

'You cast blame too loosely. Did *we* cause the damage and destruction, or did humans like Serena Butler? That is a matter for debate.' Abruptly the old woman cast off her disguise, like a reptile shedding its dry skin. The robot's flowmetal face – male now – displayed a wide smile. 'From the beginning, machines and humans have been at odds, but only we are able to observe the long span of history, and only we can understand what must be done and find a logical way to achieve it. Is that not a valid analysis of your legendary Kralizec?'

'Only an interpretation,' Jessica said.

'The correct one, though. Right now we are involved in the necessary business of uprooting weeds in a garden – an apt metaphor. The weeds themselves do not appreciate it, and the dirt may be disturbed for some time, but in the end the garden is vastly improved. Machines and humans are but manifestations of a long-standing conflict that your ancient philosophers recorded, the battle between heart and mind.'

Omnius retained his old man form, since he had no other familiar physical manifestation. 'Back in the Old Empire, many of your people are trying to make their last stands against us. It is futile, for my Face Dancers have ensured that your weapons will not work. Even your navigation machines are under my control. Already my fleet approaches Chapterhouse.'

'Our ship has had no contact with either the Guild or

Chapterhouse since before I was born,' Paul said in a dismissive tone. He pointed to Chani, Jessica, and Yueh, all of those gholas born on the ship in flight. 'None of us has ever been in the Old Empire.'

'Then allow me to show you.' With a wave of his hand, the old man displayed a complex holo-image of stars, indicating how far his immense fleet had progressed. Paul was stunned by the scope of the conquest and devastation; he didn't think the evermind would exaggerate what the machines had done. Omnius didn't need to. Hundreds of planets had already been destroyed or enslaved.

In a soothing voice, Erasmus said, 'Fortunately, the war will soon be over.'

The old man approached Paul. 'And now that I have you, there is no question of the outcome. The mathematical projection states that the Kwisatz Haderach will change the battle at the end of the universe. Since I control you *and* the other one, we will now finish this conflict.'

Erasmus stepped forward to inspect Paul, like a scientist examining a valuable specimen. His optic threads glittered. 'We know you have the potential within your genes. The challenge lies in determining *which* Paul Atreides will be the better Kwisatz Haderach.'

Optimism may be the greatest weapon humanity possesses.
Without it, we would never attempt the impossible, which
– against all odds – occasionally succeeds.

> – MOTHER COMMANDER MURBELLA,
> speech to the gathered Sisterhood

Without Obliterators or navigation control, the human warships lay like white-bellied victims on sacrificial altars, all across the last-stand line they had drawn.

Aboard her flagship, Mother Commander Murbella shouted orders, while Guild Administrator Gorus demanded miracles from his underlings. Watching the screens on the navigation bridge, Murbella saw thinking-machine battle-ships cruise past the Sisterhood's pitiful vessels on their way to destroy Chapterhouse. Similar non-battles must be occurring at the hundred flashpoints across the front lines, key human-inhabited systems now completely vulnerable to the coup de grace. The gamble had failed, utterly.

Weighing heavily on Murbella's mind was her responsibility to humanity, the rest of the Sisterhood . . . and her long-lost Duncan. Was he still alive, and did he even remember her? It had been almost twenty-five years. Murbella had to do this – for him, for herself, or for all those who had survived thus far in the epic war.

Without letting instinctive Honored Matre rage control her actions, Murbella whirled toward Gorus. She grabbed the front of the Administrator's loose robe and shook him so that his pale braid whipped his face. 'What other weapons do your Guildships have?'

'A few projectiles, Mother Commander. Energy weapons. Standard offensive artillery – but that would be suicide! Only the Obliterators could have made it possible for our ships to deal a mortal blow against the Enemy!'

In disgust, she cast him away, so that he stumbled backward and fell to the deck. 'This is already a suicide mission! How dare you cringe now, when we have no alternative?'

'But . . . but, Mother Commander – it would waste our fleet, our lives!'

'Obviously, heroism is not your strong suit.' She turned to a meek-looking Guildsman and used the power of Bene Gesserit Voice on him for good measure. 'Prepare to launch our Obliterators. Blanket space with them. Maybe the saboteurs missed a few.'

The Guildsman operated his weapons controls, barely bothering to choose targets. He launched ten more Obliterators, then another ten. None exploded, and the machine ships kept coming.

Her voice low, Murbella said, 'Now fire all the standard projectiles we have. And once we deplete our conventional armaments, we'll use our ships as battering rams. Whatever we have.'

'But why, Mother Commander?' Gorus said. 'We should fall back and regroup. Plan some other way to fight. We must at least survive!'

'If we don't win today, we don't survive anyway. We may be out-numbered, but we can still wipe out part of the thinking-machine fleet. I will not simply abandon Chapterhouse!'

Gorus scrambled back to his feet. 'To what purpose, Mother Commander? The machines can just replace themselves.'

As they spoke, more Obliterators filled space. So far, all had turned out to be duds.

'The purpose is to show them we can still fight. It is what makes us human, what gives us significance. History shall not record that we abandoned Chapterhouse and tried to hide from the final confrontation between humanity and the thinking machines.'

'History? Who will be left to record history?'

Within three minutes of each other, six small fold-space craft raced into the battle zone over Chapterhouse, reporting from the other clusters of ships. They transmitted urgent messages and demanded new orders from the Mother Commander. 'Our Obliterators don't function!'

'All navigation systems have shut down.'

'How do we fight them now, Mother Commander?'

She answered in a strong, steady tone. 'We fight with everything we have.'

Just then, a fabulously bright flash blew across at least fifty of the Enemy vessels, vaporizing them in an expanding arc that sent a shudder through the decks of the more distant Guild vessels. Murbella gasped, then laughed. 'See! One of the Obliterators still worked! Fire the rest of them.'

To her astonishment, space around them suddenly shimmered, cracked, and disgorged hundreds of giant ships. Not human defender vessels.

At first Murbella thought that the Enemy machines had sent yet another devastating fleet, but she quickly identified the cartouche on the curved hulls. Guild Heighliners! They spilled out of foldspace from every direction, surrounding the first massive wave of thinking-machine vessels.

'Administrator, why did you hold out on us?' Murbella's voice was brittle. 'There must be a thousand ships here!'

Gorus seemed just as astonished as she was.

A female voice thrummed across the commlines that linked Murbella's defenders. 'I am the Oracle of Time, and I bring reinforcements. Mathematical compilers corrupted many Guild vessels, but my Navigators control these Heighliners.'

'Navigators?' The white-haired Administrator gasped in consternation. 'We thought they were all dead, starved for spice.'

The Oracle spoke in a powerful, lilting tone. 'And my ships – unlike those made by the traitorous fabricators of Ix – command full armaments. Our Obliterators work as designed. We took them from old Honored Matre ships and hid them away for our own defenses. We intend to use them now.'

Murbella's face flushed. She had suspected the rebel Honored Matres had possessed many more Obliterators than were found. So, the Navigators had been hiding them all along!

The Omnius invasion fleet shifted position in response to the Navigator reinforcements, but the machines could not comprehend the magnitude of the astonishing opponent they now faced. They did not react in time as the Oracle's Heighliners spewed out dazzling sunbursts in a flurry of explosions like miniature supernovas. Each incinerating burst of light vaporized entire clusters of the overly complacent Enemy vessels.

Although the machine forces scrambled to defend themselves, their response was ineffective, as if their control functions had been disconnected. The evermind had modeled his plan repeatedly, setting up contingency options for likely turns of events. But Omnius had not foreseen this.

'Thinking machines have long been my sworn enemies,' the Oracle said in her ethereal voice.

While Murbella looked on with great satisfaction, precisely targeted Obliterators wiped out countless Enemy ships. If only the Honored Matres had simply turned their stolen weapons against the thinking machines when they'd had the chance, long ago! But those women had never stood together against a common foe. Instead, they hoarded their stolen weapons and used the destructive power against each other, against rival planets. What a waste!

The overlapping detonations, each strong enough to scorch a planet, struck the front line of machine ships. A dozen Heighliners raced deeper into the Chapterhouse system to chase Enemy vessels that had already reached planetary orbit.

'We will do what we can at your other front-line planets,' the Oracle said. 'Today we hurt the Enemy.'

Almost before she could absorb what was happening around her, Murbella saw that the initial wave of thinking-machine forces had been reduced to nothing more than scattered debris. As far as she could tell, the Enemy battle-ships never got the chance to launch a single shot against the defenders of humanity.

Some of the Heighliners winked out, folding space to go to the other crippled last-stand defenders. There, they would deliver their Obliterators and speed off to further encounters with the Enemy. All across the front lines, at every flashpoint where Murbella had placed her groups of fighters, the Oracle's Navigators struck, and vanished again . . .

Murbella snapped to Administrator Gorus. 'Get me a comchannel! How do we talk to your Oracle of Time?'

Gorus was stunned by the events around him. 'One does not request an audience with the Oracle. No living person has ever initiated contact with her.'

'She just saved our lives! Let me talk with her.'

With a skeptical expression, the Administrator made a gesture toward another Guildsman. 'We can try, but I promise nothing.'

The gray-robed man fiddled with the commline until Murbella shouldered him aside. 'Oracle of Time – whoever you are! Let us join forces to eradicate the thinking machines.'

A long silence was Murbella's only response, not even static, and her heart sank. Gorus gave her a superior look, as if he had known to expect this all along. Murbella saw a second wave of thinking-machine ships race in, now that the initial attack had been thwarted. And these would not tauntingly hold their fire. 'More machines are coming—'

'For now, I must move on.' As the Oracle spoke, Heighliners began to disappear like soap bubbles popping. 'My main battle is on Synchrony.'

'Wait!' Murbella cried. 'We need you!'

'We are needed elsewhere. Kralizec will not be consummated here. At long last, I have found the no-ship that carries Duncan Idaho, and the secret location of Omnius. I must now go there to end this by destroying the evermind. Forever.'

Murbella reeled as the unexpected information hit her. The no-ship found? *Duncan was alive!*

Within moments the last of the Heighliners vanished into foldspace, leaving the Mother Commander and her ships alone to face the next wave. The thinking machines kept coming.

We have our own goals and ambitions, for good or ill. But our true destiny is decided by forces over which we have no control.

– 'The Atreides Manifesto,'
first draft (section deleted by Bene Gesserit
committee)

A door in the machines' grand cathedral flowed open like a waterfall of metal, parting to reveal two figures that stepped forward in tandem.

It had been hours since Baron Vladimir Harkonnen had murdered Alia, yet his wide lips still struggled to contain his satisfaction. His spider-black eyes glinted. Dr Yueh glared at the Baron, his personal bête noire.

Paul did not need ghola memories to recognize the Baron's companion – a lean young man, barely more than a boy, but whipcord strong with muscles tuned from constant training. The eyes were harder, the features sharper, but Paul knew the face that stared back at him from the mirror.

Beside him Chani gave a strangled cry, but the sound changed to a growl in her throat. She recognized the younger Paul, and also saw the terrible difference.

A cold sense of inexorability froze Paul's blood as

everything became clear. His prescient vision in the flesh! So, the thinking machines had grown another ghola of Paul Atreides to be their pawn, a second potential Kwisatz Haderach for their private use. Now he understood the recurring dreams of his own face laughing triumphantly, consuming spice, the peculiar image of *himself* stabbed and dying, bleeding out his life's blood on a strange floor. Just like the one on which he stood now, in this vaulted chamber.

It will be one of us . . .

'It seems we have an abundance of Atreides.' The Baron ushered his protégé forward, his hand clamped on the young man's shoulder. Almost apologetically, as if the wary audience cared, he said, 'We call this one Paolo.'

Paolo pulled away from him. 'Before long you will call me Emperor, or Kwisatz Haderach – whichever term grants me the highest respect.' Looking on, the old man and Erasmus seemed to find the whole tableau amusing.

Paul wondered how many times he had been trapped by fate, by terrible purpose. How often and in how many circumstances had he seen himself dead from a knife thrust? Now he cursed the fact that he would face this crisis as a shell of his former self, not armed with the memories and skills of his past.

Unto myself, I must be sufficient.

Snickering, the younger boy walked to where his counterpart stood stiffly at attention. Paul looked back at his mirror image without fear. Despite the age difference, they were approximately the same height, and as Paul looked into his doppelgänger's eyes, he knew he must not underestimate this 'Paolo.' The youth was a weapon as sure and deadly as the crysknife at Paul's waist.

Jessica and Chani moved protectively close to Paul,

ready to strike. His mother, with her memories restored, was a full Reverend Mother. Chani, though she did not yet have her past life, had shown considerable fighting skills in earlier practice sessions, as if she still felt Fremen blood in her veins.

Paolo's brow furrowed, his expression flickering for just a moment. Then he sneered at Jessica. 'Are you supposed to be my mother? The Lady Jessica! Well, you may be older than I am – but that doesn't make you a real mother.'

Jessica gave him a brief, shrewd appraisal. 'I know my family, regardless of the order in which they were reborn. And you are not one of them.'

Paolo crossed the chamber floor toward Chani, leering with exaggerated hauteur. 'And you . . . I know you, too. You were supposed to be the great love of my life, a Fremen girl so insignificant that history recorded little of her youth. Daughter of Liet-Kynes, weren't you? A complete nobody until you became the consort of the great Muad'Dib.'

Paul could feel her nails digging into his arm as she ignored the boy and talked to him instead. 'The Bashar's teachings were right, Usul. A ghola's worth is not intrinsic in its cells. The process can go horribly wrong – as it clearly did with this young monster.'

'It's more a matter of parenting,' the Baron said. 'Imagine how the universe would be changed if the original Muad'Dib had received different instructions in the uses of power – if *I* had raised him, as I tried to do with the lovely boy, Feyd-Rautha.'

'Enough of this,' Omnius broke in. 'My machine battleships are even now clashing with – or should I say annihilating? – the pathetic remnants of human defenses.

According to my last reports, the humans were making simultaneous stands across space. That will allow me to destroy them all at once and be done with it.'

Erasmus nodded to the humans in the cathedral chamber. 'Within a few more centuries your own warring factions would have torn your race apart anyway.'

The old man shot the independent robot an annoyed look. 'Now that I have the final Kwisatz Haderach here, all the conditions have been fulfilled. It is time to end this. There is no need to bother with grinding every inhabited world to dust.' His lips quirked in a strange smile. 'Though that would be enjoyable as well.'

Musing, Erasmus looked from Paul to Paolo. 'Although genetically identical, you two have slightly different ages, memories, and experiences. Our Paolo is technically a clone, grown from blood cells preserved on a dagger. But this other Paul Atreides – what is the origin of your cells? Where did the Tleilaxu find them?'

'I don't know,' Paul said. According to Duncan, the elderly man and woman had begun their merciless pursuit well before anyone had suggested the ghola project, before old Scytale revealed his nullentropy capsule. How could the evermind have known that Paul would reappear here? Had the machines rigged a complex game? Had the sentient machines developed an artificial but sophisticated form of *prescience*?

Erasmus made a humming sound. 'Even so, I believe you each have the potential to be the Kwisatz Haderach we need. But which of you will prove superior and achieve it?'

'It's me.' Paolo strutted around. 'We all know that.' Obviously the younger boy had been raised with a belief in his role, so that his head was filled with confidence –

though it was a confidence born of true skill, not one
arising from imagination.

'And how will that be determined?' Jessica asked,
looking at both Pauls, weighing them with her eyes.

A side door flowed open near the fountain that sprayed
molten metal, and a man in a black one-piece suit emerged
carrying an ornate bloodwood box topped with a smaller
wrapped package. He was gaunt, with bland features.

'Khrone, there you are! We have been waiting.'

'I am here, Lord Omnius.' The man glanced at the
assemblage and then, either in surrender or a flash of
independence, his unremarkable human features faded
away to reveal him as a pale and sunken-eyed Face Dancer.
Setting the box aside, he carefully unwrapped the translucent fabric of the small package to reveal a brownish-
blue paste flecked with gold spangles.

'This is a concentrated and unusually potent form of
spice.' The Face Dancer rubbed his fingertips and lifted
them to his inhuman nose, as if the smell pleased him.
'Harvested from a modified worm that grows in the oceans
of Buzzell. It will not be long before the witches understand and begin their own operations there to capture
the worms and extract the spice. At the moment, though,
I hold the only sample of this ultraspice. Its sheer power
should be sufficient to plunge the Kwisatz Haderach –
one of you – into a perfect prescient trance. You will
achieve powers that only prophecy could predict. You will
see everything, know everything, and become the key to
the culmination of Kralizec.'

Erasmus spoke, sounding almost cheery. 'After
observing how the human race has ruined things without
us around to maintain order, the universe definitely needs
changing.' The robot picked up the bloodwood box and

raised the finely etched lid. Inside lay an ornate, gold-hilted dagger, which he picked up with something like reverence. A smear of old blood remained on the blade.

Behind Paul, his mother gasped. 'I know that dagger! It's as clear and fresh in my mind as if I just saw it. Emperor Shaddam himself presented it to Duke Leto as a gift, and years later at Shaddam's trial Leto gave it back to him.'

'Oh, there is more than that.' The Baron's eyes glittered. 'I believe the Emperor gave that same dagger to my beloved nephew Feyd-Rautha for his duel with your son. Unfortunately, Feyd didn't quite succeed in that battle.'

'I love convoluted stories,' Erasmus added. 'Later still, Hasimir Fenring stabbed Emperor Muad'Dib with it and nearly killed him. So you see, this dagger has a long and checkered past.' He lifted it, letting the light of the cathedral chamber gleam off the blade. 'The perfect weapon to help us make our choice, don't you think?'

Paul drew the crysknife Chani had made for him from its sheath at his side. The hilt felt warm in his grip, the curved milky blade perfectly balanced. 'I have my own weapon.'

Paolo danced back warily, looking at the Baron, Omnius, and Erasmus, as if expecting them to leap to his aid. He snatched the gold-hilted dagger from the robot's hand and pointed the sharp tip at Paul.

'And what are they to do with these weapons?' Jessica asked, though the answer was obvious to everyone.

The robot looked at her in surprise. 'It is only appropriate that we solve this problem in a particularly human way: a duel to the death, of course! Is that not perfect?'

The worm is outside for all to see, and the worm is within me, part of me. Beware, for I am the worm. Beware!

– LETO II,
Dar-es-Balat recordings, in his voice

After Paul and his companions were taken from the no-ship, Sheeana found young Leto II in his quarters. Huddling all alone in the dark, the youth was feverish and trembling. At first she thought he was terrified at having been left behind, but she soon realized he was genuinely sick.

Seeing her, the boy forced himself to his feet. He swayed, and perspiration glistened on his brow. He looked pleadingly at her. 'Reverend Mother Sheeana! You're the only one – the only one who knows the worms.' His large, dark eyes flicked from side to side. 'Can you hear them? I can.'

She frowned. 'Hear them? I don't—'

'The *sandworms!* The worms in the hold. They're calling me, tunneling through my mind, tearing me up inside.'

Raising her hand for silence, she paused, deep in thought. All her life, Shaitan had understood her, but she had never received any actual messages from the creatures, even when she'd tried to become part of them.

But now, by extending her senses she did feel a tumultuous thrumming in her head and through the walls of the damaged no-ship. Since the *Ithaca's* capture, Sheeana had ascribed such feelings to the crushing weight of failure after their long flight. But now she began to understand. Something had been scraping through her subconscious, like dull fingernails raking across the slate of her fear. Subsonic pulses of invitation. *The sandworms.*

'We have to go to the hold,' Leto announced. 'They are calling. They . . . *I* know what to do.'

Sheeana gripped the boy's shoulders. 'What is it? What do we have to do?'

He pointed to himself. 'Something of me is *inside* the worms. Shai-Hulud is calling.'

With the no-ship safely trapped in living-metal constructions, the thinking machines paid little attention to the vessel. Apparently, they had wanted to own and control the Kwisatz Haderach . . . a goal that was not as simple as it sounded, as the Sisterhood had learned long ago. Now that he had Paul Atreides in his machine cathedral, Omnius seemed to think he possessed everything he needed. The remaining passengers were irrelevant prisoners of war.

The Bene Gesserits had planned the creation of their superman over hundreds of generations, subtly guiding bloodlines and breeding maps to produce the long-anticipated messiah. But after Paul Muad'Dib turned against them and created havoc in their carefully ordered time-line, the Sisters had vowed never to unleash another Kwisatz Haderach. But in the long-ago aftermath, Muad'Dib's twin children had been born before the damage could be fully understood. One of those twins, Leto II, had been a Kwisatz Haderach, like his father.

A key turned in Sheeana's mind, unlocking other thoughts. Perhaps in the solemn twelve-year-old Leto, the thinking machines had a blind spot! Could *he* be the final Kwisatz Haderach they sought? Had Omnius even considered the possibility that the machines might have the wrong one? Her pulse quickened. Prophecies were notorious for misdirection. Maybe Erasmus had missed the obvious! She could hear the inner voice of Serena Butler laughing at the possibility, and she allowed herself to cling to a tiny kernel of hope.

'Let's go to the cargo hold, then.' Sheeana took the boy's hand, and they hurried down the corridors and dropchutes to the lower levels.

As they approached the great doors, Sheeana heard explosive thunder from the other side. The frenzied worms charged from one end of the kilometer-long space to the other, smashing into the walls.

By the time they arrived at the access door, young Leto seemed ready to collapse. 'We have to go in,' he said, his face flushed. 'The worms . . . I need to talk with them, calm them.'

Sheeana, who had never been afraid of the sandworms before, now hesitated, worried that in their wild state they might not grant safety to her or Leto. But the boy worked the controls, and the sealed door slid aside. Hot, dry air blew onto their faces. Leto waded out and up to his knees in the soft dunes, and Sheeana hurried after him.

When Leto raised his arms and shouted, all seven worms charged toward him like snorting predators, with the largest one – Monarch – at the fore. Sheeana could feel the hot wave of their anger, their need for destruction . . . but something told her that rage was not directed at either of them. The creatures rose up from the sand and towered over the two humans.

'The thinking machines are outside the ship,' Sheeana said to Leto. 'Will the worms . . . will they fight for us?'

The boy looked forlorn. 'They will follow my path if I lay it out for them, but I can't see it yet myself!'

Looking at him, she wondered again if this boy could be the ultimate Kwisatz Haderach, the link in the chain that Omnius had overlooked. What if Paul Atreides was no more than a feint in the final duel between man and machine?

Leto shook himself, visibly bolstering his determination. 'But the prior *me*, the God Emperor, had tremendous prescience. Maybe he foresaw this as well and prepared the beasts. I . . . trust them.'

At this, the worms dipped in unison, as if bowing. Leto swayed, and they swayed with him. For a moment the walls of the hold seemed to recede, and the sand dunes flowed out to eternity. The ceiling disappeared in a vertiginous haze of dust. Suddenly, everything snapped back into focus.

Leto caught his breath and called out, 'The Golden Path is coming to meet *me*! It is time to release the worms – here, and now.'

Sheeana sensed the rightness of this and knew what to do. All systems were still programmed to obey her instructions. 'The machines deactivated the weapons and engines, but I can still open the great cargo doors.'

She and Leto hurried to the controls in the hall, where she input the commands. Machinery hummed and strained. Then, with a loud clank and a bang, a gap appeared in the long-sealed walls. From the corridor, Sheeana and the boy watched the immense lower doors slide open, like clenched teeth being pried apart.

Tons of sand spilled out in a rushing stream and propelled the sandworms, like living battering rams, into the streets of the machine capital.

Prescience reveals no absolutes, only possibilities. The surest way to know exactly what the future holds is to experience it in real time.

> – from 'Conversations with Muad'Dib' by the
> PRINCESS IRULAN

'A duel makes no sense.' The Baron frowned as he looked around the cathedral chamber. 'It is wasteful. Naturally, I am convinced my dear Paolo will defeat this upstart, but why not keep both Kwisatz Haderachs for yourself, Omnius?'

'I desire only the best one,' the evermind said.

'And we could not be certain of controlling *two* of them as they struggled for preeminence with their new powers,' Erasmus said.

'Whichever of you wins the duel will receive the ultra-spice,' Omnius announced. 'When the winner consumes it, I will have my true and final Kwisatz Haderach. I can then conclude this wasteful nonsense and begin my real work of remaking the universe.'

Chani kept one hand on Paul's arm. 'How do you know either of them is your Kwisatz Haderach?'

'You could be delusional,' Yueh said, and the boy Paolo shot him a glare.

'And why should I cooperate if I win?' Paul said, but the sickening echoes of recurring visions strangled his protest. He thought he knew what was going to happen, or some piece of it.

'Because we have faith.' The Baron, a paragon of un-holiness, laughed at his own joke, but no one else did.

Paolo drew designs in the air with the tip of his gold-hilted knife. 'I have the Emperor's dagger! You were stabbed with it once.'

'That won't happen again. This is my day of triumph.' But Paul heard the brittleness in his measured words, the vulnerability behind the bravado. He could see no way to avoid the duel, and wasn't sure he wanted to. In his mind, he drove back the troubling flashes of vision. This perverse version of himself needed to be cut out like a cancer.

The time had come. Paul gathered all of his concentration for the fight. Hardly seeing Chani, he kissed her. The wormtooth dagger she had made felt perfectly balanced in his hand. He had practiced with the crysknife on the no-ship, and he knew how to fight.

I must not fear. Fear is the mind-killer.

Young Paolo pressed his lips together in a tight smile. 'I can tell you've had the visions, too! See, we are alike in yet another aspect.'

'I've had many visions.' *I will face my fear.*

'Not like these.' His opponent's knowing smile was maddening, unnerving . . . Paul stiffened his resolve. He would not give Paolo the satisfaction of showing dread or uncertainty.

Quicksilver robots appeared and removed the human observers to the sidelines of the expansive hall. The Baron stepped back beside Khrone, his gaze flicking back and forth between young Paolo and the tempting dose of ultraspice. He licked his thick lips hungrily, as if wishing he could try some for himself.

On the smooth combat floor of the chamber, Paul stood poised a couple of meters from Paolo. His younger foe tossed the gold-hilted dagger from hand to hand and smiled at him, showing white teeth.

Calming himself, Paul summoned all the important lessons he had learned: Bene Gesserit attitudes and prana-bindu instruction, the precise muscular training and rigorous attack exercises that Duncan and the Bashar had drilled into all of the ghola children.

He spoke to his fear: *I will permit it to pass over me and through me.*

It would all culminate here. Paul felt confident that if he rose to the challenge and won, his Kwisatz Haderach powers would surface, and he would be able to go on to defeat the thinking machines. But if Paolo won . . . He didn't want to consider that possibility.

'Usul, remember your time among the Fremen,' Chani called from the side of the hall. 'Remember how they taught you to fight!'

'He remembers none of it, bitch!' Paolo slashed the Emperor's knife across the air, as if slitting an invisible throat. 'But I am fully trained, a tempered fighting machine.'

The Baron applauded, but only a little. 'No one likes a braggart, Paolo . . . unless, of course, you succeed and prove to everyone that you were merely stating facts.'

Paul refused to be controlled by his visions. *If I am the Kwisatz Haderach, I'll change the visions. I shall fight. I shall be everywhere at once.*

Young Paolo must have been thinking the same thing,

for he lunged like a viper. Startled by the abrupt beginning of the duel, Erasmus swept his plush robes aside and stepped quickly out of the way. Apparently he had intended to delineate the rules of the challenge, but Paolo wanted to make it a brawl.

Paul bent backward like a reed and let the Emperor's blade whistle past, within a centimeter of his neck. Young Paolo snickered. 'That was just practice!' He held up the dagger, showing the rust-red stains. 'I am one step ahead of you, for this knife is already blooded!'

'It's more your blood than mine,' Paul said under his breath. He drove forward with the crysknife, weaving, making the blade dance.

The younger ghola responded by mirroring Paul's movements, as if the pair had an unconscious telepathic connection. He stabbed to the side, and Paul flowed in the other direction. Was this a form of prescience, Paul wondered, subconsciously foreseeing each blow, or did the two of them know and reproduce each other's fighting styles exactly? They had entirely different training, entirely different upbringings. But still . . .

Concentrating on the duel, Paul's hearing became a fuzz of static. At first he heard encouragement, gasps, shouts of concern from his mother and Chani, but he blocked everything out. Did he have the potential to become the ultimate Kwisatz Haderach that Omnius was searching for? Did he want to be? He had read the histories, knew the bloodshed and suffering that Paul Muad'Dib and Leto II had both caused as Kwisatz Haderachs. What would the machines try to accomplish by possessing an even stronger Kwisatz Haderach? Some locked-away part of Paul already had the ability to look where no one else could – into both feminine and

masculine pasts. *What other powers lie untapped within me?*
Do I dare find out? If I win this duel, what will the thinking
machines demand of me afterward?

He felt like a gladiator on ancient Terra having to prove
himself in an arena. And he had a fatal weakness: Omnius
held Chani, Jessica, Duncan, and so many others as
hostages. If Paul got his ghola memories back, his feelings for them would be even stronger.

Obviously, that was how Omnius intended to force
Paul to cooperate, if he won this duel. His love for his
companions would only intensify, and they would suffer
because of him. Since the computer evermind had far
more patience than any human, the machines could
torture and kill these hostages with impunity, take cell
scrapings and grow new gholas. Over and over! Perhaps
Erasmus would bring back his sister Alia, his father the
Duke, or Gurney, or Thufir. Kill them, resurrect them,
and kill them again. Unless Paul Atreides, the Kwisatz
Haderach, bowed to their demands, the thinking machines
would make his life an unending hell. Or so they intended.

Now he understood the dilemma of his destiny. And
again he saw himself dying in a pool of blood. Perhaps
some things could not be changed. But if he was a true
Kwisatz Haderach, he should be able to defeat such petty
tactics.

He fought on with wild passion, driving himself into
a sweaty frenzy. Paolo kicked at him with his feet and
slashed with the Emperor's dagger. Paul dove, rolled, and
the younger ghola pounced on him. The Emperor's blade
drove down hard in what would have been a killing thrust,
but Paul slipped to the side, barely in time.

The blade slashed his sleeve, cut a thin line of blood
on his left shoulder, then clanged against the stone floor.

Paolo, his wrist jolted by the sharp impact, barely maintained a grip on the hilt.

On the polished floor, Paul swept his feet sideways, getting them under his rival and kicking upward. He did have the advantage of being physically stronger than a twelve-year-old. Paul grabbed his counterpart's wrist and pulled himself to his feet, but Paolo locked his fingers around Paul's knife arm, preventing the crysknife from stabbing down. Paul pushed, using his leverage to maneuver them both back toward the shimmering lava fountain.

'Not very . . . innovative!' The younger ghola's breath rasped as he struggled, and Paul continued to drive him back. The heat from the fountain gushed in all directions. If he knocked Paolo into the incandescent metal, would he be killing himself – or saving himself?

Paul saw his opponent clearly and could not hate the other ghola. At the core, both of them were *Paul Atreides*. Paolo was not innately evil, but had been corrupted by terrible things that had been done to him, things he had been taught, not things done of his own volition. Paul did not let his sympathy for his rival weaken him. If he did, Paolo would not hesitate to kill him and claim victory. But Paul – because he was *Paul* – would fight with every ounce of his being to save the future of humanity.

Omnius and Erasmus observed without cheering for either fighter. They would accept whichever one proved victorious. Khrone's shadowed, olive-pit eyes held no emotion at all. The Baron was scowling. Paul didn't want to look toward Chani or his mother.

The roaring lava fountain dumped heat into the air. Paul's already sweaty body became slicker. Wiry Paolo used that to his advantage, squirmed, and Paul's grip began to slip. Suddenly, at the very verge of the fountain, the younger man allowed his knees to buckle.

Paul overcompensated, which threw him off balance. He kneed his opponent in the stomach, but young Paolo had untapped reserves. When Paul raised the crysknife in his sweat-slickened grip, Paolo brought his own hand up backward, using the jeweled hilt of his dagger to smash the base of Paul's knife hand. Tendons twitched in reflexive reaction. The crysknife dropped free, clattered on the edge of the fountain, and tumbled into the molten pool.

Gone.

With the force of dominating vision, stronger than just the knowledge of his own death, Paul realized what he should have known from the beginning: *I am* not *the Kwisatz Haderach that Omnius wants. It isn't me!*

Time seemed to slow down and freeze. Was this what Bashar Teg had experienced when he accelerated himself? But Paul Atreides could move no faster than the events around him. They held him captive and squeezed in on him like the steely embrace of Death.

Wearing a venomous grin, young Paolo swung the gold-hilted dagger around in a perfect arc and, with exquisite slowness, drove the point into Paul's side. He slipped the dagger between his opponent's ribs and kept pushing, shoving the deadly point through Paul's lung and up into his heart.

Then Paolo yanked the murderous weapon free, and time resumed its normal speed. From far away, Paul heard Chani screaming.

Blood gushed from his wound, and Paul stumbled against the base of the hot fountain. It was a mortal wound; there could be no denying it. The prescient voice in his head hammered at him to no purpose. It seemed to be mocking him. *I am not the final Kwisatz Haderach!*

He slithered to the floor like a broken doll, barely saw Chani and Jessica running toward him. Jessica had Yueh by the collar and was dragging the Suk doctor over to her bleeding son.

Paul had never known that one body could contain so much blood. With fading vision, he looked up and saw Paolo prancing victoriously, holding the dripping red dagger. 'You knew I would kill you! You might as well have driven in the knife with your own hands!'

It was a perfect reproduction of his visions. He lay on the floor, dying as swiftly as his body would allow.

In the background he heard the Baron Harkonnen's boisterous laughter. The sound was intolerable, but Paul could do nothing to stop it.

Sand and worms poured out of the entrapped no-ship's hold into the carefully ordered machine metropolis. The writhing creatures plowed into the open streets like maddened Salusan bulls bursting from their pens. Beside Leto, watching the hold empty in a deafening rush, Sheeana opened her mouth, and her eyes went wide with surprise.

Through his strange connection to the worms, Leto II's mind surged outward with them into the sparkling city. Standing high above at the doorway to the immense cargo bay, he felt a wave of relief and freedom. Without a word to Sheeana, he dove into the sliding, flowing sand, following the worms in their wild exodus. He let the grit carry him, like a swimmer caught in an undertow being rapidly whisked out to sea.

'Leto! What are you doing? Stop!'

He could not have stopped to answer even if he had

wanted to. The current of flowing powder sucked him downward – exactly where he wanted to be. Leto plunged under the sand, and his lungs somehow adapted to the dust, as did all of his senses. Like a sandworm he saw without eyes, and perceived the creatures ahead of him, as if he were looking at them through clear water. This was what he had been born to do, what he had died to do, ever so long ago.

Memories reverberated in him like echoes of the past – not a visceral recollection, but greater than the knowledge he had acquired by reading the *Ithaca*'s archives. Those entries had been about another young man, another Leto II, but still himself. A thought surfaced: *My skin is not my own.* In those days, his body had been covered with interlinked sandtrout, their membranous bodies meshing with his soft flesh and nerves. They had imparted strength to him, enabling him to run like the wind.

Though still in human form, Leto II recalled some of the fantastic power, not from ghola memories but from the pearl of awareness that the original God Emperor had left within each worm descendant. *They* remembered, and Leto remembered with them.

Histories had been written by so many people who loathed him, who misunderstood what he had been forced to do. They decried the Tyrant's purported cruelty and inhumanity, his willingness to sacrifice everything for the extraordinary Golden Path. But none of the histories – not even his own testamentary journals – had recorded the joy and exuberance of a young man experiencing such unexpected and wondrous power. Leto remembered it all now.

He swam through the flow of sand to where the seven giant worms writhed, and then burst upward to break through the surface. Knowing instinctively what he had to do, Leto staggered toward the largest worm, Monarch. He caught the small part of the thrashing tail, leapt onto the hard rings, and scrambled up like a bare-footed Caladanian primitive scaling a rough-barked palm tree.

As soon as Leto touched the greatest of the seven worms, his fingers and feet seemed to acquire an unnatural adhesion. He could climb and hold on, as if he were part of the creature. And in a way, that was true. Fundamentally, he and the sandworms were one.

Sensing that Leto had joined them, all of the worms paused like enormous soldiers coming to attention. Reaching a perch atop Monarch's curved head, Leto surveyed the sprawling complex of living metal structures, and smelled the strong odor of cinnamon.

From his high vantage point, he watched the city of Synchrony as it shifted buildings into formidable barricades, trying to impede the long-confined sandworms. This was Leto's army, his living battering rams – and he would turn them loose against humanity's Enemy.

Dizzy and euphoric in the redolence of spice, Leto held onto the worm's ridges, which parted to expose the soft pink flesh underneath. He found it enticing, and his body longed for the full sensation, direct contact. Leto slid his bare hands between the ring segments, into the soft tissue membrane. There, he felt as if he was touching the nerve center of the beast itself, plunging his fingers into the neural circuitry that joined these primal creatures together. The sensation hit him like a jolt of electricity. This was where he had belonged for eternity.

At his behest, the sandworms reared higher, like angry cobras no longer interested in the soothing music of a snake charmer. Leto controlled them now. All seven of the worms went on a rampage through the machine streets, and Omnius could do nothing to stop them.

When Leto's mind merged with the largest sandworm, he felt a flood of intense sensations and recalled a similar thing that another Leto II had done thousands of years before. Again he experienced the raspy feel of fast-flowing sand beneath a long and sinuous body. He relished the exquisite dryness of old Arrakis, and knew what it had meant to be the God Emperor, the synthesis of man and sandworm. That had been the zenith of his experience. But did something even greater lie in store for him?

As a ghola child raised aboard the no-ship, Leto II was never entirely sure how the Tleilaxu had obtained his original cells. Had they been taken when he and Ghanima underwent routine medical inspections as children? If so, an awakened Leto ghola would have only the memories of a normal child, the son of Muad'Dib. What if, however, the cells in Scytale's nullentropy capsule had been stolen from the actual God Emperor in his prime? Some unlikely scraping of his enormous vermiform corpse? Or a tissue sampling by one of the devout followers who had taken the Tyrant's withered, drowned body from the bank of the Idaho River?

As Leto's mind fused with Monarch, and all of the surrounding worms, he realized that it didn't matter. This incredible joining now unlocked everything that was within his ghola body and within each nugget of awareness buried deep in the sandworms. Leto II finally became his true self again, as well as the conflicted ghola boy he had been – a loner child and an absolute emperor with the blood of trillions on his conscience. He understood in exquisite detail all his centuries of decisions, his terrible grief, and his determination.

They call me Tyrant without comprehending my kindness, the great purpose behind my actions! They don't know that I foresaw the final conflict all along.

In those last years, God Emperor Leto had strayed so far from humanity that he had forgotten innumerable marvels, especially the softening influence of love. But, as he rode Monarch now, young Leto remembered how much he had adored his twin sister Ghanima, the good times they had shared in their father's incredible palace, and how they had been slated to rule the vast empire of Muad'Dib.

Now Leto was everything he had ever been and more, enhanced by the firsthand memories of his own experiences. With his new vision, as fresh precursors of spice from the worm's body pumped through his blood, he beheld the Golden Path extending gloriously before him. But even with this remarkable revelation, he could not quite see around all the corners ahead. There were blind spots.

High atop his worm, young Leto smiled in determination, and with a single thought he sent the serpentine army forward. The leviathans charged between the great buildings, throwing themselves against reinforced barricades and breaking through. Nothing could stop them.

Hands still buried deep between the ring segments, Leto II rode with a shout of joy on his lips. He gazed forward through eyes that had suddenly become blue-within-blue, eyes that saw what others could not.

Now that I have ridden one of the sandworms and touched the immensity of its existence, I understand the awe the ancient Fremen experienced, why they considered the worms to be their god, Shai-Hulud.

— TLEILAXU MASTER WAFF,
letter to the Council of Masters in Bandalong,
dispatched immediately before the destruction of Rakis

The last pair of Waff's sandworm specimens died inside the arid terrarium.

When freeing the first test worms out in the desert, he had kept two with him at the modular laboratory for research, hoping that what he learned would improve their chances of survival. It did not go well.

Waff prayed vigorously each day, meditated on the holy texts he had brought with him, and sought guidance from God on how best to nurture the reborn Prophet. The first eight specimens were now loose, tunneling through the brittle, crusted sand like explorers on a dead world. The Tleilaxu Master hoped they had survived in the blast-zone environment.

In their final days, the last two little worms in his laboratory aquarium became sluggish, unable to process the nutrients he gave them, though the food was chemically balanced to provide the sandworms with what they needed. He wondered if the small creatures could experience despair. When they lifted their round heads above the sandy surface of the holding tank, it seemed as if they had lost their will to live.

And within a week they both perished.

Though he revered these creatures and what they represented. Waff was desperate for vital scientific information with which to better the other worms' chances of survival. Once the specimens were dead, he had little compunction against picking apart their carcasses, spreading their rings, and cutting into the internal organs. God would understand. If he himself lived long enough, Waff would begin the next phase, as soon as Edrik came back for him. *If* the Navigator ever came back, with his Heighliner and the sophisticated laboratory facilities aboard.

His own Guild assistants offered their help – persistently – but Waff preferred to work alone. Now that these men had set up their stand-alone camp, the Tleilaxu Master had no further use for them. As far as he was concerned, the Guildsmen were free to join Guriff and his treasure hunters in seeking lost spice hoards out in the wasteland.

When one of the bland Guildsmen appeared before him, demanding his attention, Waff easily lost the delicate balance of his thoughts. 'What? What is it?'

'The Heighliner should have returned by now. Something is wrong. Guild Navigators are never late.'

'He did not promise to come back. When is Guriff's next CHOAM ship due to arrive? You are welcome to depart on it.' *In fact, I encourage that.*

'The Navigator may not be concerned with you, Tleilaxu, but he made promises to *us*.'

Waff didn't care about the insult. 'Then he will return,

eventually. If nothing else, he will want to know how my new sandworms are doing.'

The Guild assistant frowned at the flayed creature spread out on the analytical table. 'Your pets do not appear to be thriving.'

'Today I will go out and monitor the specimens I released earlier. I expect to find them healthy, and stronger than ever.'

When the flustered Guildsman left, Waff changed into external protective clothing and hopped into the camp's groundcar. The locator signals showed him that the released worms had not ranged far from the ruins of Sietch Tabr. Attempting to be optimistic, he assumed they had found a habitable subterranean band and were establishing their new domain. As more and more worms grew on Rakis, they would become tillers of the soil, restoring the desert to its former glory. Sandworms, sandtrout, sandplankton, melange. The great ecological cycle would be reestablished.

Reciting ritual prayers, Waff drove across the eerie black-glass desert. His muscles trembled and his bones ached. Like the assembly lines in a war-damaged factory, his degenerating organs labored to keep him alive. Waff's flawed body could fall apart any day now, but he was not afraid. He had died already – many times, in fact.

Always before, he'd had the faith and confidence that a new ghola was being grown for him. This time, though, convinced he would not return to life, Waff was content with what he had accomplished. His legacy. The evil Honored Matres had tried to exterminate God's Messenger on Rakis, and Waff would bring Him back. What greater accomplishment could a man hope to attain in this life? In any number of lives?

Following the tracker signals, he drove away from the weathered mountains, to the dunes. Ah, the new sand-worms must have fled out into open terrain, looking for fresh sand in which to bury themselves and begin their lives anew!

Instead, what he saw horrified him.

He easily located the eight fledgling worms. Much too easily. Waff stopped the groundcar and scrambled out. The hot, thin air made him gasp, and his lungs and throat burned. He could barely see through stinging tears as he hurried forward.

His precious sandworms lay on the hard ground, barely moving. They had cracked the melted crust of the dunes and churned through the soft grainy dirt beneath, only to emerge again. And now they lay dying.

Waff knelt beside one of the weak, failing creatures. It was flaccid, grayish, barely twitching. Another had heaved itself high enough to sprawl across a broken rock, and there it lay deflated and unable to move. Waff touched it, pressed down on the hard rings. The worm hissed and flinched.

'You cannot die! You are the Prophet, and this is Rakis, your home, your holy sanctuary. You must live!' His body was wracked by a spasm of pain, as if his own life was tied to those of the sandworms. 'You can't perish, not again!'

But it seemed that the crippling damage to this world was simply too much for the worms. If even the great Prophet Himself could not endure, then these must assuredly be the End Times.

He had heard of it in ancient prophecies: Kralizec, the great battle at the end of the universe. The crux point that would change everything. Without God's Messenger, surely humanity would be lost. The final days were at hand.

Waff pressed his forehead against the dusty, dying creature's yielding surface. He had done everything he could. Maybe Rakis would never again support the behemoth worms. Maybe this was indeed the end.

From what he saw with his own eyes, he could not deny that the Prophet had truly fallen.

People strive to achieve perfection – ostensibly an honorable goal – but complete perfection is dangerous. To be imperfect, but human, is far preferable.

— MOTHER SUPERIOR DARWI ODRADE,
defense before Bene Gesserit Council

When the older and inferior Paul Atreides ghola lay dying on the floor, Paolo turned away, pleased with his victory but far more interested in his other priority. He had proved himself to Omnius and Erasmus. The special ultraspice that would unlock all of his prescient abilities was his now. It would elevate him to the next level, to his exalted destiny – as the Baron had taught him for so long. During that time, Paolo had convinced himself that this was what he wanted, brushing aside any nagging qualms or reservations.

Around the cathedral hall, quicksilver robots stood at attention, ready to attack the remaining humans should Omnius give the order. Maybe Paolo himself would decide to issue such a command, once he was in control. He could hear the pleased laughter of the Baron, the sobs of Chani and Lady Jessica. Paolo wasn't sure which sounds he enjoyed more. His greatest thrill was the clear proof of what he had always known: *I am the one!*

He was the one who would change the course of the universe and control the end of Kralizec, guiding the next age of humanity and machines. Did even the evermind know what he was about to face? Paolo allowed himself a secretive, amused smile; he would never be a mere puppet for thinking machines. Omnius would soon learn what the Bene Gesserit had long ago discovered: A Kwisatz Haderach is not to be manipulated!

Paolo slipped the bloody dagger into his waistband, strode over to the Face Dancer, and held out a hand to collect the spoils of combat. 'That spice is mine.'

Khrone smiled faintly. 'As you wish.' He extended the cinnamony paste. Not interested in savoring it, Paolo quickly consumed a whole messy mouthful, far more than he should have. He wanted what it would unlock within him, and he wanted it right away. The taste was bitter, potent, and powerful. Before the Face Dancer could withdraw the offering, Paolo grabbed more and swallowed another mouthful.

'Not so much, boy!' the Baron said. 'Don't be a glutton.'

'Who are you to talk about gluttony?' Paolo's retort drew a rumbling chuckle in response.

On the floor where he lay dying, Paul Atreides moaned. Chani looked up in despair from beside her beloved, her fingers dripping with his blood. Her face a grief-stricken mask, Jessica held her son's clenching hand. Paolo trembled. Why was it taking Paul so long just to die? He should have killed his rival more cleanly.

Kneeling over him, Dr Yueh worked feverishly to save Paul, trying to stanch the flow of blood, but the Suk doctor's deeply troubled face told the terrible story. Even his advanced medical training was insufficient. Paolo's knife strike had done all the damage it had needed to.

Those people were all irrelevant now. Mere seconds had passed when Paolo felt the potent melange burst into his bloodstream like a lasgun blast. His thoughts came faster, sharper. It was working! His mind was suffused with a certainty that outsiders might have considered hubris or megalomania. But Paolo knew it only as *Truth*.

He drew himself taller, as if he were growing physically and maturing in all ways, so that he loomed above everyone else in the chamber. His mind expanded into the cosmos. Even Omnius and Erasmus now seemed like insects to him, muddling through their grandiose, but ultimately minuscule, dreams.

As if from a great height, Paolo looked down at the Baron, the self-absorbed snake who had spent so many years dominating him, bossing him around, 'teaching' him. Suddenly the once-powerful leader of House Harkonnen seemed laughably insignificant.

The Face Dancer Khrone studied the scene, and then – with seeming uncertainty – turned toward the evermind's manifestation as an old man. Paolo saw through all of them with incredible ease.

'Let me tell you what I will do next.' In his own ears, Paolo's booming voice sounded like a god's. Even the great Omnius must tremble before him. Words flowed with the force of a cosmic Coriolis storm, rushing along on a current of ultraspice.

'I will implement my new mandate. The prophecy is true: I *will* change the universe. As the ultimate and final Kwisatz Haderach, I know my destiny – as do all of you, for your actions led to this prophecy.' He smiled. 'Even yours, Omnius!'

The false old man responded with an annoyed frown. Beside him the robot Erasmus grinned indulgently, waiting to see what the just-hatched superman would do. All of Paolo's visions of domination, conquest, and perfect control were based on prescience. He harbored no doubts in his mind. Every detail unfolded before him. The young man continued to spew pronouncements.

'Now that I have come into my true powers, there is no need for the thinking-machine fleet to obliterate the human-inhabited planets. I can control them all.' He waved a hand. 'Oh, we may have to annihilate a minor world or two to demonstrate our strength – or maybe just because we *can* – but we will keep alive the vast majority of people, as fodder.'

Paolo gasped as even more ideas flooded into his head, building momentum and power. 'Once we have swallowed up Chapterhouse, we will open the Sisterhood's breeding records. From there, we will implement my master plan of making brilliant, perfect humans, combining whatever traits I choose. Workers and thinkers, drones, engineers, and – occasionally – leaders.' He spun toward the old man. 'And *you*, Omnius, will construct a vast infrastructure for me. If we give our perfect humans too much freedom they'll mess everything up. We must eliminate the wild, troublesome genetic lines.' He snickered to himself.

'In fact, the Atreides bloodline is the most unmanageable of all, so I shall be the last Atreides. Now that I have arrived, history needs no more of us.' He glanced around, but did not see the man who came to mind. 'And all those Duncan Idahos. How tedious they've become!'

Paolo was speaking faster and faster, swept along by intoxicating spice visions. The look of confusion on even the Baron's face made the young man wonder if anyone here could comprehend him any longer. They seemed so primitive to him now. What if his own thoughts were so grand that they were beyond the understanding of the most sophisticated thinking machines? That would really be something!

He began to pace around the chamber, ignoring glares and gestures from the Baron. Gradually Paolo's motions became jerky, manic. 'Yes! The first step is to sweep away the old, mow down and dispense with the outdated and unnecessary. We must clear a path for the new and the perfect. That's a concept all thinking machines can embrace.'

Erasmus stared at him and mockingly reshaped his flowmetal face into a perfect likeness of the old man that represented Omnius. His expression reflected disbelief, as if he considered Paolo's pronouncements a joke, the rantings of a deluded child. A flare of anger rose within Paolo. This robot wasn't taking him seriously!

Paolo saw the whole canvas of the future unrolling before him, broad strokes revealed by the incredible magnifying power of ultraspice. Some of the upcoming events became razor sharp, and he discerned more specifics, intricate details. The super-potent melange was even stronger than he had imagined, and the future became intensely focused in his mind, fractal minutiae unfolding before him in an infinite, yet completely expected, pattern.

In the midst of this mindstorm, something else was unleashed from within his cells: All the memories buried there from his original life. With a roar that briefly drowned out even the other clamoring knowledge, he suddenly remembered everything about *Paul Atreides*. Though the Baron had raised Paolo and the machines had corrupted him into what they imagined would be their puppet, he was still himself at the core.

He scanned the chamber, viewing everyone from a new perspective: Jessica, dear Chani, and *himself* lying in a pool of blood, still twitching, gasping a last few breaths. Had he done that – a bizarre form of suicide? No, Omnius had forced him. But how could anyone really force a Kwisatz Haderach to do anything? Details of the fight with Paul clashed in his mind, and he squeezed his eyes shut, trying to drive back the disturbing images. He didn't want to serve Omnius. He hated the Baron Harkonnen. He could not let himself be the cause of such destruction.

He had the power to change everything. Wasn't he the ultimate Kwisatz Haderach? Thanks to the ultraspice and his own Atreides genes, Paolo now possessed a greater prescience than had ever before been possible. Not even the smallest event could slip past him.

In a glorious tableau, he knew he could see everything about the tapestry of the future. Every tiny detail, if he wanted! No unexplored terrain, no wrinkles or nuances in the topography of events to come.

Paolo paused in his restless pacing and gazed ahead, seeing beyond the walls of the grand machine cathedral, feeling overwhelmed by thoughts that no other human could begin to understand. His eyes changed to more than an intense blue-within-blue, to *black* and glassy, rippled and impenetrable like a landscape of seared dunes.

In the background, he heard the Baron's voice. 'What's the matter with you, boy? Snap out of it.'

But the visions continued to shoot at Paolo like projectiles from a repeater gun. He couldn't dodge them, could only receive them, like an invincible man standing up against ferocious firepower.

Outside in the grand machine city, he heard a tremendous commotion. Alarms rang, and quicksilver robots rushed out of the cathedral chamber to respond. Paolo knew exactly what was happening, could see it from every angle. And he knew how each action would turn out, regardless of how Omnius, the humans, or the Face Dancers tried to change it.

No longer able to move, Paolo stood staring at moments that were yet to come, everything he could influence and all that he could not. Each second sliced into a billion nanoseconds, then expanded and spread out across a billion star systems. The scope of it threatened to overwhelm him.

What is happening? he asked himself.

Only what we brought upon ourselves, whispered the voice of Paul-within.

With new eyes Paolo saw moment by unfolding moment, expanding outward from the machine city, beyond the planet, the whole scope of the Old Empire, the farthest reaches of the Scattering, and the vast thinking-machine empire.

Another nanosecond passed.

The ultraspice had given him absolutely uncontaminated revelation. He saw time folding forward and backward from the focal point of his consciousness.

Perfect prescience.

Caught in the tidal wave of his own power, Paolo began to see much more than he had ever wanted to see. He witnessed every heartbeat a thousand times over, every action of every single person – every *being* – in the entire universe. He knew how each instant would play out from now until the end of history, and in reverse, to the beginning of time.

The knowledge flooded into him, and he drowned in it.

He watched Paul Atreides in his death throes and saw

his counterpart go motionless, haloed by the crimson puddle on the floor, eyes staring into blessed oblivion.

Paolo, who had wanted to be the final Kwisatz Haderach so badly he had killed for it, now became petrified by the utter tedium of his own existence. He knew every breath and pulsepoint in the entire history and future of the universe.

Another nanosecond passed.

How could any person endure this? Paolo was trapped in a predetermined path, like a computer's infinite loop. No surprises, choices, or movement. Absolute foreknowledge rendered Paolo entirely irrelevant.

He envisioned himself sinking in slow motion to the floor and lying face up, unable to move or speak, unable even to blink his eyes. Fossilizing. Then Paolo saw the last and most terrible revelation. He was *not* the true and final Kwisatz Haderach, after all. It was not him. He would never accomplish what he had dreamed.

With spice roaring through him, the past went dark, and Paolo could only stare fixedly into the future, which he had already seen a thousand times over.

Another nanosecond passed.

One can always find a battlefield if one looks hard enough.
                                    – BASHAR MILES TEG,
                                 Memoirs of an Old Commander

Remnants of dust and sand from the emptying hold swirled out into the no-ship's corridors, but the worms were gone, and Leto II with them. Bright sunlight from the machine world shone through the gaping holes. Stunned, Sheeana listened to the sounds of the behemoths crashing through Synchrony. She longed to be with them. Those once-captive sandworms were *hers* as well.

But Leto was closer to them, a part of them, and they were part of him.

Duncan Idaho came up behind her. She turned, the smell of grit clinging to her face and clothes. 'It's Leto. He's . . . with the sandworms.'

He flashed a hard smile. 'That's something the machines won't expect. Even Miles would have been surprised.' He grasped her arm and hurried her away from the open cargo hold. 'Now we've got to do something just as dramatic for ourselves.'

'What Leto is doing will be a hard act to follow.'

Duncan paused. 'We've been running from that old man and woman for years, and I don't intend to sit here in this no-ship prison anymore. Our armory is filled with weapons stockpiled by the Honored Matres. We also have the rest of the mines that the Face Dancers didn't use to sabotage this ship. Let's take the fight outside, to them!'

She felt the steel of his determination and found her own. 'I'm ready. And we have more than two hundred people aboard trained in Bene Gesserit combat techniques.' Inside her mind, Serena Butler imparted visions of terrible combat, humans against fighting robots, incredible slaughters. But in spite of these horrors, Sheeana felt a strange exhilaration. 'It's been programmed into our genes for thousands of years. Like an eagle to a serpent, a bull to a bear, a wasp to a spider, humans and thinking machines are mortal enemies.'

AFTER DECADES OF running and many escapes from the tachyon net, this would be their final showdown. Tired of feeling helpless, the *Ithaca* captives crowded forward to the armory. All were eager to fight back, though they knew the odds were heavily against them. Duncan relished it.

The stockpile of armaments was not particularly impressive. Many of the stored weapons fired only flechettes, razor-sharp needles that would not be effective against armored combat robots. But Duncan handed out old-style lasguns, pulse launchers, and explosive projectile rifles. Demolition squads could plant the remaining mines against the foundations of thinking-machine buildings and detonate them.

The Tleilaxu Master Scytale pushed his way through the crowded corridor, trying to reach Sheeana, looking as if he had something important to say. 'Remember, we have more enemies out there than just robots. Omnius has an army of Face Dancers to stand against us.'

Duncan handed a flechette rifle to Reverend Mother Calissa, who appeared as bloodthirsty as any Honored Matre. 'This will cut down plenty of Face Dancers.'

The little man announced with a thin smile, 'I have another way to help. Even before we were captured, I began to produce the specific toxin that would target Face Dancers. I made sixty canisters of it, in case we had to saturate all the air aboard the ship. Unleash it against the Face Dancers in the city. It may make humans a little nauseated but it is lethal to any Face Dancer.'

'Our weapons could do the rest – or our bare hands,' Sheeana said, then turned to the other workers. 'Get the canisters! There's a battle outside!'

A fierce army of humans streamed out through the gaping hole torn in the *Ithaca's* hull. Sheeana led her Bene Gesserits. Reverend Mothers Calissa and Elyen guided groups through the shifting streets in search of vulnerable targets. Reverend Mothers, acolytes, male Bene Gesserits, proctors, and workers rushed out carrying weapons, many of which had never been fired before.

With a loud battle cry, a well-armed Duncan charged forward into the bizarre metropolis. In his original life-time, he had not survived long enough to join Paul Muad'Dib and his Fremen Fedaykin in bloody raids against the Harkonnens. The stakes were more desperate now, and he intended to make a difference.

The streets of Synchrony were in turmoil, the build-ings themselves pumping and writhing. Leto's sandworms had already tunneled beneath the foundations of the structures, breaking through the pliable, living metal and knocking down tall towers. Across the galaxy, Omnius's thinking-machine fleet was engaged in numerous climactic battles. Duncan thought of Murbella out there somewhere – if she was still alive – facing them, fighting them.

Combat robots swarmed the streets. They emerged from between buildings, fashioning and firing projectile weapons from their own bodies. The Bene Gesserits scrambled out of the way, finding shelter. Lasbeams cut smoking holes through the fighting machines; explosive projectiles smashed them backward into debris.

Running headlong into the fray, Duncan used his long-dormant Swordmaster skills to attack the nearest robots. He wielded a small projectile launcher as well as a vibrating sonic club that transmitted a deadly blow each time it struck a fighting machine.

From all directions, Face Dancers rallied against the humans, while combat robots turned their attention to the destructive sandworms. The first ranks of shape-shifters advanced with blank and unreadable faces, armed with machine-designed weaponry.

When the first canisters of Scytale's curling, gray-green gas landed among them, the frenzied Face Dancers did not understand what was happening. Soon they began to fall, writhing, their faces melting off their bones. Sensing the danger too late, they scrambled to retreat as Sheeana's fighters launched more poison gas into their midst.

The Bene Gesserits continued to push forward. Their demolition crews planted mines against looming buildings that could not uproot themselves in time. Powerful explosions brought down the shuddering metal towers. Sheeana rushed her teams to shelter until the thunderous collapses were over. Then they surged forward again.

Duncan decided to hang back. In the center of the city, the huge, bright cathedral drew him like a beacon, as if all the intensity of the evermind's thoughts were being channeled through it. He knew Paul Atreides was in that structure, perhaps fighting for his life, perhaps dying. Jessica was inside, as well. Compelling instincts born of memories from his first life told Duncan where he had to go. He needed to be at Paul's side in the den of the Enemy.

'Keep the machines occupied, Sheeana. Even the ever-mind can't fight on an infinite number of fronts at once.' He jerked his head toward the cathedral building. 'I'm going *there*.'

Before she could say anything, Duncan ran off.

*Enduring my own mistakes once was bad enough. Now I
am condemned to relive my past, over and over.*

— DR WELLINGTON YUEH,
interview notes taken by Sheeana

The Suk doctor, in a teenage body but with the burdens
of a very old man, knelt by the dying Paul. Although he
had administered every emergency treatment at his
disposal, he knew he could not save the young Atreides.
With specialized skill, he had halted most of the bleeding,
but now he shook his head sadly. 'It's a mortal wound. I
can only slow his death.'

Despite the betrayal in his past life, Yueh had loved
the Duke's son. In those bygone days he had been a
teacher and mentor to Paul. He had seen to it that the
boy and his mother had a chance of surviving in the
deserts of Arrakis after the Harkonnen takeover, so long
ago. Even with his full Suk knowledge restored, Yueh
didn't have the facilities to help this Paul. The knife had
penetrated the pericardium, cut into the heart. Through
sheer tenacity the young man still clung to a thread of
life, but he had already lost far too much blood. His heart
was stuttering its last few beats.

Despite the chances offered by a second lifetime, Yueh

was unable to escape his previous failures and betrayals. He had been suffering inside, wallowing in the cesspool of his past mistakes. The Sisters on the no-ship had resurrected him for some secret purpose that he had never been able to fathom. Why was he here? Certainly not to save Paul. That was out of his hands now.

On the no-ship he had tried to take action by doing what he thought was necessary and right, but he had only caused more tragedy, more pain. He had killed an unborn Duke Leto rather than another Piter de Vries. Yueh knew he had been manipulated by the Rabbi/Face Dancer, but he could not accept that as an excuse for his actions.

Chani sat on the floor at Paul's side, calling his name in an unfamiliar husky voice. Yueh sensed that something about her had changed; her eyes had a wild steeliness much different from the gaze of the sixteen-year-old girl he knew.

He realized with a start that the horror of holding Paul's bloody, dying body in her arms must have pushed her over the edge. Chani had her original memories back – just in time to experience the full magnitude of her imminent loss. Even Yueh reeled from the cruelty of it.

The Baron made despairing sounds of his own, at first confused, then angry, and now desperate. 'Paolo boy, answer me!' He crouched by the glassy-eyed young man, raging. He raised a hand as if to strike the warped copy of Paul Atreides, but Paolo didn't flinch.

From one side the independent robot Erasmus watched the whole scenario with intent curiosity, his optic threads glistening. 'Apparently, neither of the Paul Atreides gholas is the Kwisatz Haderach we expected. So much for the accuracy of our predictions.'

The moment he saw the Baron's growing confusion, Yueh knew that only one thing remained for him to do.

Struggling to regain his composure, he rose from the side of the dying Paul and made his way over to the Baron and Paolo. 'I am a Suk doctor.' His sleeves and trousers were drenched in Paul's blood. 'Perhaps I can help.'

'Eh? You?' The Baron sneered at him.

Jessica glared after the doctor, and the restored Chani looked as if she wanted to flog Yueh for leaving Paul's side. But he concentrated only on the Baron. 'Do you want me to help, or not?'

The Baron moved out of the way. 'Hurry, then, damn you!'

Going through the motions, Yueh bent and passed his hands over Paolo's face, felt the cold clamminess of the skin and the barely discernible pulse. Young Paolo sat frozen and transfixed, staring into a coma of infinite awareness and paralyzing boredom.

The Baron leaned close. 'Make him snap out of it. What is the matter with him? Answer me!'

Grabbing the Emperor's dagger from Paolo's waistband, Yueh spun in a single fluid movement. The Baron staggered back, but Yueh was quicker. He thrust the sharp tip at an angle under the hateful man's chin and rammed it all the way to the back of his skull. '*This* is my answer!'

The answer for being coerced into betraying House Atreides, for all the schemes, the pain, the resultant guilt, and most of all for what the Harkonnens had done to Wanna.

The Baron's eyes opened wide in shock. He flailed his hands and tried to speak, but could only gurgle helplessly as a crimson geyser spouted from his neck.

Spattered in blood, Yueh jerked the Emperor's dagger back out. He considered plunging it into Paolo's midsection, just to be certain he killed both of them. But he couldn't do that. Though the boy had gone wrong, this was still Paul Atreides.

The Baron collapsed onto the hard floor. All the while, the Paolo ghola continued to stare upward without blinking.

Dr Wellington Yueh allowed himself a relieved smile. At long last he had accomplished something positive and true. Finally, he had done something right. For a long moment he held the dagger, covered with the Baron's blood as well as Paul's. A potent impulse prompted him to turn the point toward himself. Yueh closed his eyes, clutched the handle of the knife, and took another deep breath.

A firm hand clasped his wrists, staying his suicide thrust. He opened his tear-filled eyes to see Jessica standing beside him. 'No, Wellington. You don't need to redeem yourself like that. Help me save Paul instead.'

'There is nothing I can do for him!'

'Don't underestimate yourself.' Her facial muscles tightened. 'Or Paul.'

Death.

Paul skirted the edge of the interior blackness, dipped briefly into infinity, and danced back out. He wavered on the balance point of his own mortality. The knife wound was deep.

Without any awareness of what was going on around him, he felt an intense coldness spreading from the tips of his fingers to the back of his head. Like a distant whisper, he could still hear the lava fountain blazing nearby. Despite the hard stone floor beneath him, Paul felt as if he were floating, his spirit drifting in and out of the universe.

His skin detected a warm, syrupy wetness. Not water. *Blood* . . . his own . . . spreading in a great pool across the floor. It filled his chest, mouth, and lungs. He could hardly breathe. With each feeble heartbeat, more of it spilled out, never to be retrieved . . .

It seemed as if he could still feel the long blade of the

Emperor's knife inside him. Now he remembered . . . In the last desperate days of Muad'Dib's jihad, the conniving Count Fenring had stabbed him. Or had that occurred at a different time? Yes, he had tasted a knife blade before.

Or maybe he was the old blind Preacher in the dusty streets of Arrakeen, stabbed by yet another knife. So many deaths for one person . . .

He couldn't see. Someone squeezed his hand, though he could barely feel it, and he heard a young woman's voice. 'Usul, I am here.' *Chani.* He remembered her most of all, and was glad she was here with him. '*I* am here,' she said. 'All of me, with all my memories, beloved. Please come back.'

Now a firmer voice yanked his attention, as if strings were attached to his mind. 'Paul, you must listen to me. Remember what I taught you.' His mother's voice. *Jessica* . . . 'Remember what the real Lady Jessica taught the real Paul Muad'Dib. I know what you are. You have the power within you. That is why you aren't dead yet.'

He found words within his throat, and they bubbled up through the blood. He was amazed at the sound of his own voice. 'Not possible . . . I'm not . . . *the* Kwisatz Haderach – the ultimate . . .' He was not the superbeing that would change the universe.

Paul's eyes flickered open, and he saw himself lying in the great machine cathedral. That part of the prescient dream had been true. He had seen Paolo laughing with victory and consuming the spice – but now Paolo himself rested on the floor like a fallen statue, frozen and mindless, gazing into infinity. The Baron lay dead, murdered with a look of disbelief and annoyance on his pasty face. So the vision was true, but all the details had not been available to him.

Some kind of commotion came from beside Omnius

and Erasmus, and Paul looked there, his gaze bleary.
Watcheyes flitted in, displaying images. The old man stood
with an impatient expression on his face. The Face Dancer
Khrone seemed unsettled. Paul could hear voices shouting.
The whole cacophony wove itself in oddly incomprehen-
sible strands through the buzzing tapestry in his head.

'Sandworms attacking like demons . . . destroying
buildings.'

'. . . a rampage . . . armies emerging from the no-ship.
A poisonous gas that kills—'

The old man said drily, 'I have dispatched combat
robots and Face Dancers to fight them, but it may not
be sufficient. The sandworms and the humans are causing
considerable damage.'

Erasmus picked up the conversation. 'Rally more Face
Dancers, Khrone. You didn't send all of them out.'

'That is a waste of my people. If we fight the humans,
their poison kills us. If we go out to battle sandworms,
we will be crushed.'

'Then you will be poisoned, or crushed,' Erasmus said
lightly. 'No need to fret. We can always create more of
you.'

The Face Dancer's features shifted and blurred, a storm
crossing his putty face. He turned and marched out of
the vaulted chamber.

Meanwhile Yueh raised Paul's head, ministering to him
with Suk medical techniques. But Paul folded his eyes
shut again and dropped backward into the pain. Again
he danced along the edge of the chasm that opened wider
and wider before him.

'Paul.' Jessica's voice was insistent. 'Remember what I
told you of the Sisterhood. Maybe you aren't the ultimate
Kwisatz Haderach that the thinking machines want, but

you *are* still a Kwisatz Haderach. You know that, and your body knows it as well. Some of your powers are the same as those of a Reverend Mother. A *Reverend Mother*, Paul!'

But he found it too difficult to concentrate on her words, or to remember . . . As he spiraled deeper and deeper into unconsciousness, her voice faded, and he could not hear or feel his heartbeat anymore. What did his mother mean?

If Jessica now remembered her past life, she also remembered the Spice Agony. Any Reverend Mother had the innate ability to shift her biochemistry, to manipulate and alter molecules within her bloodstream. It was how they selected their pregnancies, how they transmuted the poisonous Water of Life. That was why the Honored Matres had searched so furiously to find Chapterhouse – because only Reverend Mothers had the physical ability to fight off the terrible machine plagues.

Why did his mother want him to remember that?

Trapped inside the darkness, Paul felt the emptiness of his body. Completely bled out. Silent.

On Arrakis so long ago, he had undergone his own version of the Agony, the first male ever to do so success-fully. For weeks he had lain in a coma, declared dead by the Fremen, while Jessica insisted on keeping him alive. He had seen that stygian place where women could not go, and he had drawn strength from it.

Yes, Paul had that ability within him now. He was a male Bene Gesserit. He could still control his body, every cell, every muscle fiber. At last, he knew what his mother had been trying to tell him.

The pain of dying and the crisis of survival gave him the lever he needed. He stood upon his pain as a fulcrum and used it to pry open his life, his first existence – the memories of Paul Atreides, of Muad'Dib, of himself as Emperor and later as the Preacher. He followed that flood backward to his childhood and his early training with Duncan Idaho on Caladan, including how he had almost been killed as a pawn in the War of Assassins that had ensnared his father.

He remembered his family's arrival on Arrakis, a place Duke Leto knew to be a Harkonnen trap. The memories rushed past Paul: the destruction of Arrakeen, his flight into the desert with his mother, the death of the first Duncan Idaho . . . meeting the Fremen, his knife fight with Jamis, the first man he had ever killed . . . his first worm ride, creating the Fedaykin force, attacking the Harkonnens.

His past accelerated as it flowed through his mind – overthrowing Shaddam and his empire, launching his own jihad, fighting to keep the human race stable without traveling down that dark path. But he had not been able to escape political struggles, assassination attempts, the exiled Emperor Shaddam's bid for power and the pretender daughter of Feyd-Rautha and Lady Fenring . . . then Count Fenring himself had tried to kill Paul—

His body no longer felt empty, but *full* of experiences and great knowledge, full of abilities. He remembered his love for Chani and his sham marriage to Princess Irulan, as well as the first Duncan ghola named Hayt, and Chani dying while giving birth to the twins, Leto II and Ghanima. Even now, the pain of losing Chani seemed far greater than the pain he presently suffered. If he died now, in her arms, he would inflict that same anguish upon her.

He remembered wandering off into the desert, blinded from prescience . . . and surviving. Becoming the Preacher. Dying in a dusty street surrounded by a mob.

He was now everything he had once been: Paul Atreides and all the different guises he had worn, every mask of legend, every power and weakness. Most important of all, he now had the abilities of a Reverend Mother, the infinitesimal physical control. Like a beacon in the darkness, his mother had enabled him to see.

Between his last heartbeats, he searched within himself in the deep and drowning place. He found the knife wound inside his heart, saw the mortal damage, and discovered that his body's defenses were incapable of repairing the grievous injuries on their own. He needed to direct the healing process.

Although in the preceding moments he had seemed to be fading, he now sharpened himself and became part of his own heart, which was no longer beating. He saw where Paolo's blade had slashed open his right ventricle, letting blood spill out of the chamber. His aorta had been nicked, but there was no more blood for it to carry.

Paul brought the cells together and sealed them. Then, droplet by droplet, he began to draw his own blood back from the cavities of his body where it had spilled, and reabsorbed it into his tissues. He literally pulled life back into himself.

PAUL DIDN'T KNOW how long his trance lasted. It seemed as infinite as the death coma caused by touching just a drop of the poisonous Water of Life to his tongue. He became suddenly aware of Chani's grip again. Her hand was warm, and he felt his own flesh, no longer cold and shuddering.

'Usul!' He could hear Chani's faint whisper and detected the disbelief in her tone. 'Jessica, something's changed!'

'He is doing what he needs to do.'

When he finally summoned the strength to flutter his eyelids, Paul Muad'Dib Atreides rejoined the living, bringing with him both his old life and his new. In addition to those memories and abilities, he returned with a fantastic, even greater revelation . . .

Just then, a flushed and bloodied Duncan Idaho burst into the great cathedral hall, knocking sentinel robots aside. Erasmus casually gestured to allow the man to enter. Duncan's eyes went wide when he saw the bleeding Paul propped up by his mother and Chani. Dr Yueh looked astonished at the miracle before him. Duncan ran toward them.

Trying to pull together his thoughts, Paul placed the tableau around him in the context of his internal knowledge. He had learned much by dying the first time, coming back as a ghola, and nearly dying again. He had always had a phenomenal gift for prescience. Now he knew even more.

In spite of his miraculous survival and rebirth, he still was not the perfect Kwisatz Haderach, and clearly Paolo was not, either. As Paul's vision cleared, he focused on a realization that none of them had seen – not Omnius, Erasmus, Sheeana, nor any of the gholas.

'Duncan,' he said in a hoarse voice. 'Duncan, it's you!'

After hesitating for a moment, his old friend came closer, this loyal Atreides fighter who had been through the ghola process more times than any other individual in history.

'You're the one they've been looking for, Duncan. It's you.'

Even prescience has its limits. No one will ever know all the things that might have been.

             – REVEREND MOTHER DARWI ODRADE

With her arm around his shoulders, Chani rocked Paul, as she shuddered with joy and relief. Fremen prohibitions were so much a part of her that even after seeing his mortal wound and watching him come within a heartbeat of dying in her arms, she still had not shed a tear.

In the machine cathedral, Duncan wrestled with the revelation that the pale and bloodied Paul had given him. 'I . . . am the Kwisatz Haderach?'

Paul nodded weakly. 'The final one. The perfect one. The one they were looking for.'

The old-man manifestation of Omnius gave the robed form of the independent robot an accusing look. 'If this claim is correct, you were in error, Erasmus. You did not allow for the humans to twist fate yet again. You said your predictive calculations were accurate.'

The robot remained aloof, even smug. 'Only your *interpretation* of my calculations was flawed. The final Kwisatz Haderach was indeed aboard the no-ship, as I said all along. You drew the obvious conclusion that the one we sought must be Paul Atreides. When the Face Dancer found the bloody knife carrying the cells of Muad'Dib, you falsely reinforced your own conclusion.'

Duncan's mind wanted to reject what he was hearing. Even if he truly was the ultimate Kwisatz Haderach, what was he to do with the knowledge?

The old man sneered down at the frozen, useless boy Paolo and the dead Baron. 'All that work on our own clone gave us no advantage. Extremely wasteful.'

Erasmus shaped his flowmetal face into a sympathetic expression and addressed the recent arrival. 'I knew I was drawn to you for a reason, Duncan Idaho. If you really are the Kwisatz Haderach, you stand in a position to alter the course of the universe. You are a living watershed, the harbinger of change. You can choose to stop this conflict that has made enemies of humans and thinking machines for thousands of years.'

Duncan realized that Yueh, Jessica, Chani, and Paul had all played their parts, and now the focus had shifted to him.

Erasmus stepped closer to them. 'Kralizec means the end of many things, but that end need not be destructive. Just a fundamental change. Henceforth, nothing will be the same.'

'Not destructive?' Jessica raised her voice. 'You said your thinking-machine ships are attacking worlds in the Old Empire. You've already sterilized and conquered hundreds of planets!'

The robot seemed unperturbed. 'I did not say our approach was the only way, or even the best one.' The old man glowered at Erasmus as if he had been insulted.

Suddenly the sky above the great machine city was torn by multiple booms of displaced air as a thousand Guild Heighliners appeared like storm clouds. Emerging from foldspace, the fleet of huge vessels easily carried enough weaponry to level the continent.

Omnius's old man guise flickered as his concentration was wrenched by the dramatic shift. Across the city of Synchrony, robots buzzed about, fighting the sandworms that continued to rampage. Now they had to shore up defenses against the new enemy overhead.

Inside the vaulted building, Erasmus altered his form again to the kindly old woman, as if he believed this presentation more convincing and compassionate. 'I've run probabilities beyond the limits of my original calculations. I believe you have the power, Duncan Idaho – stop these Guildships from destroying us.'

'Oh, please stop prattling,' Omnius said.

Duncan looked around, crossed his arms over his chest. 'I am not afraid of the Guild and their Navigators. If I have to die to end this, I'm willing to do so.'

Yueh added bravely, 'Everyone here has died before.'

'It doesn't matter. Let them destroy Synchrony.' The old man did not seem overly disturbed. 'I am dispersed across many locations. Annihilating this entire planet, this node, will never eradicate me. I am the evermind, and I am everywhere.'

A crack sounded at the center of the wide cathedral hall. Then, with a blur and a bang of folded space, an image appeared above the bloodstained floor. The shimmering transmission appeared to be solid one moment and a staticky ghost the next. In moments, the shape clarified to a beautiful and statuesque human woman with classically perfect features. Then she shifted to become stunted and dwarfish, with a blunt, unattractive face, short arms and legs, and an overly large head. After another flicker, the image was nothing more than a disembodied face that wavered in the air. It was as if she could not remember exactly what she was supposed to look like.

Duncan immediately knew who – or what – this was. 'The Oracle of Time!'

The face swiveled to scan the people and robots in the great hall, before the image hovered closer to him. 'Duncan Idaho, I have found you. I searched for years, but your no-ship and your own . . . strangeness protected you.'

Duncan no longer questioned the bizarre storm of occurrences around him. 'Why did you come now?'

'You emerged from your no-ship only once before on the planet Qelso, but I did not follow you swiftly enough. I sensed you again when your no-ship was damaged and captured. Now, with the thinking machines attacking, I was able to trace the lines of the evermind's tachyon web and follow Omnius to you. I brought my Navigators with me.'

'What is this apparition?' the evermind demanded. 'I am Omnius. Begone from my world!'

'Once I was called Norma Cenva. Now I am exponentially more than that – far beyond anything a computer network can comprehend. I am the Oracle of Time, and I go where I please.'

In the old crone guise, Erasmus reached out like a curious child and touched, but the wrinkled hand passed through her image. 'So many of the most interesting humans are women,' he mused. The robot experimentally waved fingers through her ghostly likeness, stirring without altering it. She ignored him.

'Duncan Idaho, you have finally come to your realization. Kwisatz Haderach, I tried to protect you. Before you, Paul Muad'Dib and his son Leto the God Emperor were imperfect prophets. Even they realized their flaws. Now through a confluence in the cosmos, the nexus of all nexuses, you have become the singularity in a bold new universe, the vital point from which everything flows outward for the rest of eternity. The hopes of humankind – and much more – are distilled in you.'

Still taken aback, Duncan asked, 'But how? I don't feel that different.'

'The Kwisatz Haderach is a "shortening of the way," a figure powerful enough to force a fundamental and necessary change that alters the course of future history, not just for humanity but for thinking machines as well.'

'Yes, you have the power, Duncan Idaho.' Erasmus sounded just as encouraging as the Oracle. 'I rely on you to make the correct choice. *You* know what will benefit the universe most, and you know that thinking machines can enrich the entirety of civilization.'

Duncan marveled at the awareness of his new identity and the unfolding of his thoughts around the astounding truth. Finally, after so many attempts at life in ghola form, he knew his destiny. His mind was fully awakened.

He saw time as a great ocean stretching across the cosmos, and with his awakening powers he envisioned being able to analyze each molecule, each atom and subatomic particle. Perfect prescience would come, but not yet, not too fast or it would induce the same crippling paralysis that had befallen Paolo. Already Duncan's mind could go much faster than a Mentat's, and he sensed he could make his body move at speeds that would have astonished even the Bashar.

I am the ultimate Kwisatz Haderach. There will be no more after me.

The Oracle's image flickered, shifting her shape back to that of the beautiful woman. 'After you died the first time, Duncan Idaho – as a soldier fighting to save the

Atreides, fighting to save the first Kwisatz Haderach – the powers of the universe compelled your resurrection as a ghola, and many times afterward, over and over. The original God Emperor understood some of your destiny and played an unwitting role in bringing about this moment. The end point of his Golden Path is the beginning of something else.'

'I am linked to the Golden Path?'

'You are, but you are destined to go far beyond it.'

Paul seemed to be swiftly recovering his strength. Beside him, Jessica said to the otherworldly visitor, 'But Duncan was part of no formal breeding program! How did he develop into a Kwisatz Haderach?'

The Oracle continued, 'Duncan, with each rebirth, you came closer to completion. Instead of being developed in a breeding program, you went through a process of personal evolution. With every successive incarnation you acquired more knowledge, skills, and experience – as if a sculptor with a tiny chisel was chipping away at a large block of hard stone, slowly, ever so slowly, fashioning a perfect statue. In your one body, you manifested a tachyon evolution, a hyper-fast developmental journey that propelled you toward your destiny.'

Duncan had lived his life repeatedly for thousands of years. Not only had the Tleilaxu tinkered with his genetics to give him abilities to fight the Honored Matres, they had combined his cells so that he retained *all* of his previous lives, every one of them. With all those memories, he possessed a breadth of experience and wisdom that no one could match. This Duncan Idaho had more knowledge than the most advanced Mentat or the evermind Omnius, and more understanding of human nature than even the great Tyrant Leto II.

Duncan was the same person again and again, perfecting himself, constantly filtering out impurities, like passing through a fine mesh strainer to sift out only the best of qualities, leaving him as the One. He allowed himself a secret smile at the irony. He had succeeded only because of the meddling of the Tleilaxu, though he was certain that the Masters had never intended to create a savior for humanity.

Duncan's Mentat mind burned through the data, confirming his conclusion, knowing that the Oracle of Time must be correct. 'Truly, I am the Kwisatz Haderach!' He wished Miles Teg could have been there with him. 'And what of the great war – Kralizec?'

'We are in the midst of it now. Kralizec is not merely a war, but a point of *change*.' Her image flickered. 'And you are the culmination of it.'

'But what about the rest of humanity?' *Murbella*. 'They need to know. How will they understand what has happened?'

'My Navigators will inform them, perhaps even bring their leaders here. First, however, I need to eliminate a threat that should have been gone millennia ago. An enemy I fought ten thousand years before you were first born.'

The Oracle slid through the air toward the indignant-looking old man, Omnius. Facing him, she made her voice boom more loudly than the evermind's speakers ever had. 'I must ensure that the thinking machines can no longer harm anyone. That was my mission ages ago, when I was merely a woman, when I invented the concept of the fold-space engine, when I discovered the mind-expanding powers of melange. I shall remove you, Omnius.'

The evermind laughed, a remote old man's chuckle. The slightly stooped manifestation suddenly grew larger, looming like a giant over her image. 'You cannot remove me, for I am not a corporeal being. I am *information*, so my existence has spread anywhere the tachyon net stretches. I am everywhere.'

The female image formed a smile. 'And I am more than that. I am the Oracle of Time. Now hear my laughter.' In an eerie voice Norma Cenva chuckled long and hard, causing even the oversized Omnius to take a step backward. 'I am heard across star systems and eons, across time and space, far beyond the range of your net.'

Omnius took another step backward.

'First I crippled your fleet. Now I will rip you out like the weed that you are, and discard you.'

'Impossible—' The old man began to dissolve as he retreated into his own network.

'I will extract you – every shred of information from every node.' Her misty image became amorphous and seeped around Omnius. He nearly staggered into Erasmus, but the independent robot easily slid out of the way, his old-woman face expressing curiosity and bemusement.

'I will take you to a place where such information is no longer comprehensible, where physical laws do not apply.'

Duncan heard the evermind's voice cry out in rage, but it was muffled. In the vaulted hall, the insectile sentinel robots who tried to move forward in the service of Omnius seemed strangely disoriented and sluggish.

'There are many universes, Omnius. Duncan Idaho has visited more than one, and he knows the place of which I speak. I rescued him and his no-ship from it long ago. You, however, will never find your way back.'

Duncan considered the incomprehensible struggle before him. Indeed, when he had first stolen the no-ship from Chapterhouse, he had lurched through the fabric of space in a desperate attempt to avoid capture and had taken them to a bizarrely skewed universe. He shuddered to think of it.

'Nothing shall rescue you, Omnius.'

'Impossible!' the old man bellowed, losing his physical form and becoming no more than a spangled outline.

'Yes, impossible. Wonderfully so.'

The air in the chamber crackled with clouds of electricity that spread thinner and thinner, as the Oracle wrapped herself like a net around the iconic thinking machine. For an instant, Duncan saw Norma's face superimposed over that of the old man. The two countenances merged into one: Hers. The beautiful woman smiled, and the air filled with sparkling, hair-fine strands of electricity that she drew around her like an elegant cloak.

Then she uprooted herself from reality and vanished into the incomprehensible void, taking with her all traces of Omnius.

Forever.

You see enemies everywhere, but I see only obstacles – and I know what to do with obstacles. Either move them or crush them, so that we can be on our way.

– MOTHER COMMANDER MURBELLA,
address to the combined Sisterhood

Even after the Navigators destroyed the bulk of the Enemy fleet in a flurry of unexpected Obliterators, a second wave of machine ships advanced toward Chapterhouse.

The Oracle, upon locating Duncan Idaho and the lost no-ship, had promptly taken most of her Heighliners to Synchrony, only assigning a small percentage to aid in the defenses of other human-inhabited planets. With the outcome of those missions unknown, some or all of the other planets could still be vulnerable. One thing was certain: At Chapterhouse, Murbella and her defenders faced the remaining machine ships alone. Through it all, the Mother Commander didn't have much time to process her shock at discovering that Duncan was still alive.

Administrator Gorus groaned. 'Will they never stop?'

'No.' Murbella scowled at him for forcing her to state the obvious. 'They are thinking machines.'

High over the Bene Gesserit world, her hundred last-stand vessels hung surrounded by the debris from thousands of destroyed machine battleships. This fight had inflicted a substantial toll on the Enemy, but unfortunately it was not enough.

The new wave of Omnius vessels would not thumb their noses at the human defenders, as the first had. Murbella expected no mercy this time and didn't have much hope for the last-stand ships at other strategic points, either. The machines intended to annihilate Chapterhouse and every other world that stood in their way.

She cursed the clumsy, uncooperative Guild vessels that the Junction shipyards had produced and the worthless weapons the Ixians had supplied. She had to think of something on her own. 'I won't just let our ships sit here with their throats bared, like lambs waiting for slaughter!'

'The mathematical compilers controlled our foldspace guidance and standard—'

She shouted at Gorus. 'Rip out those damned navigation devices – we'll maneuver our vessels by hand!'

'But we will not know where we are going. We could crash!'

'Then we must crash into the Enemy, instead of each other.' She wondered if the machines would feel a need for vengeance when they saw the wreckage of the first wave. Honored Matres certainly would.

The Enemy kept coming. Murbella studied the complex tactical projections. Surely they did not need such a vast number of vessels to conquer the minimally inhabited Chapterhouse. It seemed obvious that the evermind had learned the value of intimidation and showmanship, as well as the wisdom of redundancy.

In the Heighliner control center, two Guildsmen argued

with Gorus. One claimed that disconnecting the mathematical compiler was impossible, while the other warned that it was unwise. Murbella ended the debate with the compelling power of Bene Gesserit Voice. The Guildsmen shuddered and, unable to resist her, did as she commanded.

Although the machine forces outgunned them by a substantial margin, Murbella did not flinch from what had to be done. Instead, she allowed herself to reawaken her old Honored Matre anger. This was not a time to calculate odds. It was a time to unleash every bit of destruction her people could muster. Their chances were better now than they had been when this last stand began. If they all embraced viciousness and fought like frenzied Honored Matres, they could inflict significant damage. They might still go down in flames, but if they bought sufficient time for the Oracle and her Navigators to defeat Omnius, Murbella would count it a victory. She just wished she could have seen Duncan one more time.

Murbella turned toward the broad projection plate that magnified the oncoming vessels. 'Arm all weaponry and stand ready to ram. The moment we deplete conventional armaments, our own ships will become the final weapons. A hundred of us will take out at least as many of their ships.'

Up to this point, Gorus had called her battle strategy suicidal. Now, he looked as if he might try something foolish to stop her. 'Why not negotiate with them? Would it not be preferable to surrender? We cannot stop them from destroying their targets!'

Murbella fixed her gaze on the Administrator as if he were weak prey. Even the Sisters who had started out as pure Bene Gesserits now reacted with a feral Honored Matre strength. They would never back down.

'And you base this suggestion on the success of your emissaries to the thinking machines? All those emissaries who disappeared?' Murbella's voice sizzled like hot acid. 'Administrator, if you'd like to seek another solution, I would be happy to eject you from an airlock and let you fly across the empty vacuum. As the last breath explodes out of your lungs, maybe you can gasp out your personal surrender terms. Be my guest, if you believe the thinking machines will listen to you.'

The desperate-looking Guildsman cringed. Around him, the Sisters moved to take control, ready for a final plunge.

Before Murbella could give the command, though, Janess broke in over their tight-linked channel, 'Mother Commander! Something's changed with the machine battleships. Look at them!'

Murbella examined the images on the viewing plate. The Enemy vessels no longer moved in a tight, efficient formation. They slowed and began to spread apart, as if they had no goal, like unmanned sailing ships becalmed on a vast cosmic sea.

Left suddenly leaderless.

To her amazement, the thinking-machine fleet floated listlessly in space.

Even when caught up in his own myth, Muad'Dib pointed out that greatness is only a transitory experience. For a true Kwisatz Haderach, there are no warnings against hubris, no rules or requirements to follow. He takes from all things and gives to all things, as he wishes. How could we have deluded ourselves into believing we could control such a one?

— Bene Gesserit analysis

After the Oracle vanished, Erasmus stared at the empty space in the center of the vaulted chamber, his head slightly cocked to one side. 'Omnius is gone.' His voice sounded hollow to Duncan Idaho's ears. 'No vestige of the evermind remains in the network of thinking machines.'

Duncan felt his own mind racing, expanding, absorbing new information. The terrible Enemy he had sensed for so long – the threat that the Honored Matres had provoked – was no more. By removing the evermind, uprooting it from this universe and taking it elsewhere, the Oracle had disabled the vast thinking-machine fleet, leaving it without its controlling force.

And we still remain.

Duncan didn't know exactly what had changed inside

him. Was it simply the *knowledge* of his raison d'etre? Had he always had access to this potential without realizing it? Assuming Paul was correct, something had lain dormant inside Duncan for all those years, through all of the lives – original and ghola – a latent power that had grown with each iteration of his existence. Now, like a massive genetic program, he had to figure out how to activate it.

Paul and his son Leto II had the blessing and curse of prescience. With their memories restored, each could claim to be a Kwisatz Haderach. Miles Teg had possessed his phenomenal capacity to move at a speed beyond comprehension and might conceivably have become a Kwisatz Haderach himself. The Navigators in the clustered Heighliners overhead could use their minds to see through folds of space and find safe paths for the great ships to travel. The Bene Gesserits could control their bodies, down to their very cells. All had expanded on traditional human abilities, expressing humankind's potential to exceed expectations.

As the ultimate and final Kwisatz Haderach, Duncan believed he might have the capability to do all of those things and much more, reaching the highest pinnacle of humanity. Thinking machines had never understood human potential, even though their 'mathematical projection' credited the Kwisatz Haderach with the power to end Kralizec and change the universe.

Confidence infused him, and he thought he might discover a way to make grand, epic changes . . . but not under the control of the thinking machines. Instead, Duncan would find his own way. He would be a real Kwisatz Haderach, independent as well as all-powerful.

Dispassionately, he gazed upon the old woman in her

frumpy floral-print dress and gardening apron, complete with scuffs of dirt. Her face appeared careworn, as if from nurturing people her entire life. 'Something of Omnius has vanished from me, but not all.'

Finally forsaking the old-woman disguise, Erasmus resumed the liquid-metal form of the independent robot attired in an elegant crimson and gold robe. 'I can learn much from you, Duncan Idaho. As the new god-messiah of humankind, you are the optimal specimen for me to study.'

'I am not another specimen for your laboratory analysis.' Too many others had treated him that way, in too many of his past lives.

'A mere slip of my tongue.' The robot smiled cheerily, as if attempting to veil his looming violence. 'I have long desired a perfect understanding of what it means to be human. Now it seems *you* have all the answers I so assiduously sought.'

'I recognize the myth in which I live.' Duncan recalled Paul Atreides making similar pronouncements. Paul had felt trapped by his own mythos, which had become a force beyond his control. Duncan, however, had no fear of the forces that would emerge, either for or against him.

With penetrating vision he saw through, and around, Erasmus and his minions. Across the hall he watched Paul Atreides standing unsteadily, aided by Chani and Jessica after his terrible ordeal. Paul drank from a water flagon, which he had taken from a table near the Baron's body.

Outside, the crashing of sandworms against robotic defenders had begun to subside. Though the huge creatures had not destroyed the machine cathedral, they had caused extensive damage to the city of Synchrony.

At the perimeter of the great chamber, quicksilver

robots stood attentively, the charges in their integral weapons glowing in a display of readiness. Even without the evermind, Erasmus could direct these machines to fire a deadly barrage against the humans in the vaulted room. The independent robot could attempt to kill every mortal here in a show of petulant revenge. And perhaps he would make the effort . . .

'Neither you nor your robots can make any difference here,' Duncan warned. 'All of you are far too slow.'

'Either you are over confident, or you are fully aware of what you can do.' The flowmetal smile tightened, just a little, and the bright optic threads glistened a bit more. 'Perhaps it is the latter, and perhaps not.' Somehow, Duncan knew with absolute certainty that Erasmus meant to unleash all the destructive power under his control, wreaking whatever havoc he could.

Before the robot made half a turn, Duncan was upon him with all the speed Miles Teg had shown, knocking him backward. Erasmus crashed to the floor, his weapons disabled. Was it just a test? Another experiment?

Duncan's heart pounded and his body radiated heat as he stood over the robot, but he felt exhilarated, not exhausted. He could keep fighting like this against any machines Erasmus chose to send against him. At that thought, he left the independent robot where he had fallen, dashed at hyperspeed around the circle, and battered the silvery sentinel robots with quick kicks and punches until they shattered into debris. It was so easy for him now. Before the metal pieces had finished falling to the floor, he was back, looming over Erasmus.

'I sensed your doubts as well as your intentions,' Duncan said. 'Admit it. Even as a thinking machine, you wanted more proof, didn't you?'

Lying on his back and looking upward through the hole in the dome at the thousands of huge Guild Heighliners in the sky, Erasmus said, 'Assuming you are the long-awaited superman, why don't you simply destroy me? With Omnius gone, removing me would assure the victory of humanity.'

'If the solution were that simple, a Kwisatz Haderach would not be needed to implement it.' Duncan surprised Erasmus, and himself, by reaching down and helping the robot to his feet. 'To end Kralizec and truly change the future requires more than just the annihilation of one side or the other.'

Erasmus examined his body core and his robes to ensure his appearance, then looked up with a broad smile. 'I think we just might have a meeting of the minds – something I never really achieved with Omnius.'

*When the time comes for our Great Unmasking, our foes
will be surprised by what has been disguised in front of
them since the very beginning.*

— KHRONE,
communiqué to Face Dancers

Now that the Oracle was gone, several of the Navigators'
giant Heighliners overhead folded space and disappeared
from Synchrony without explanations or farewells.

Throughout the city, sandworms continued to destroy
the living metal buildings. Because Omnius had never
allowed them autonomy, the robotic defenders were
unable to function effectively without connecting to the
evermind. The vaulted hall filled with resounding silence.

Then with a loud crash, the high doors swung open.
Dressed in black and followed by a throng of Face
Dancers, Khrone marched in from the bright machine
streets. Identical, blank-faced drones swarmed into the
room. Scytale's poison gas had killed some of the shape-
shifters, but many had avoided the battle entirely.

Out in the sprawling machine city, countless Face
Dancers had pretended to stand against the rampaging
sandworms, but secretly melted away from the barricades
the robotic soldiers had set up. Khrone had taken pleasure

in watching the worms destroy the great flowmetal buildings, smashing thousands of thinking machines. *Clearing
the way. Making our job easier.*

Khrone offered a skeletal smile as he swept forward.
'I never cease to be entertained by the erroneous deduc-
tions of those who *think* they control us.' In his mind, a
Face Dancer victory was now assured.

'Explain yourself, Khrone.' Erasmus seemed only
mildly curious.

Ignoring the humans and their dead, Khrone faced the
independent robot, who stood by Duncan Idaho. 'This
war has been in process for five thousand years. It was
never Omnius's idea, anyway.'

'Oh, our war has been building for far longer than
that,' Erasmus pointed out. 'We escaped after the Battle
of Corrin fifteen thousand years ago.'

'I'm referring to a completely different war, Erasmus
– one you never realized was taking place. From the
moment the first advanced Face Dancers were dispatched
by our creator, Hidar Fen Ajidica, we began our manipulations. When we encountered your thinking-machine
empire, we allowed you to create more and more of us.
Yet the moment Omnius let us in, the Face Dancers
became his true masters! We shared with you all the lives
we had gathered, letting you believe you were becoming
increasingly superior to us and to humans. But we Face
Dancers were in control all along.'

'There is a diagnosis for your mental condition,' Dr
Yueh said boldly. 'You have delusions of grandeur.'

Khrone's lips peeled back from blunt, perfect teeth.
'My statements, based as they are on accurate information, can hardly be called delusions.'

The amused expression on Erasmus's face did not

change. Khrone found it maddening, so he raised his voice, 'You thinking machines helped us implement our Face Dancer plans, all the while believing that we served *you*. But it was exactly the opposite. You were, in fact, *our* tools.'

'All machines began as tools,' Duncan pointed out, looking from Erasmus to the Face Dancer leader.

Khrone was not impressed. So this was the man who had revealed himself as the final Kwisatz Haderach? Nor could he understand why the independent robot was not more upset, since he prided himself on employing his artificial emotions.

Khrone continued. 'Under your guidance, Erasmus, biological facilities run by thinking machines manufactured millions of enhanced Face Dancers. At first, we ventured into human society as scouts, swiftly infiltrating the fringes of the Scattering, and then the Old Empire. We easily duped the Lost Tleilaxu into believing we were their allies. Wherever humans remained, Face Dancers quietly intruded. We lived long, and accomplished much.'

'Exactly as we instructed you to do,' Erasmus said, sounding bored with the lecture.

'Exactly as we wished to do!' Khrone snapped back. 'Face Dancers are everywhere, a hive mind more advanced than any extrasensory human linkages, more powerful than the network of Omnius. So swiftly and easily we accomplished our aims.'

'And our aims, as well,' Erasmus said.

Galled by the robot's stubborn refusal to recognize defeat, Khrone felt rage building within him. 'Over the centuries, we prepared for the day when we would implement our plan and eliminate Omnius. We never guessed that the Oracle of Time would do it for us.' He chuckled softly. 'Your empire has fallen. We have superceded all thinking machines. And now that Omnius's fleet and plagues have brought humanity to its knees, we can acti-vate our hidden Face Dancer cells – everywhere, simul-taneously. We will take control.' He planted his fists on his hips. 'It is already over for machines, and for humans.'

Behind him, all the identical Face Dancers wore blank expressions. Khrone's featureless face had been dupli-cated many times over.

'An interesting and insidious plan,' Erasmus said. 'Under other circumstances, I might applaud you for your ingenuity and duplicity.'

'Even if you could rally your robots to kill those of us on Synchrony, it would be of no use. I am reproduced everywhere.' The Face Dancer scoffed. 'Omnius thought he was seeding the universe for his own conquest, but the true seeds of his downfall were right under his mechanical nose.'

Erasmus began to laugh. It started as a chuckle that he imitated from an ages-old dataset, and he added components sifted from other recordings. The resultant sounds were quite enjoyable to himself, and he was sure they were convincing to the others.

Over his long, long lifetime, the unusual robot had expended a great deal of effort in studying humans and their emotions. Laughter particularly intrigued him. An early step, which had required centuries of deep thought, had been to understand the *concept* of humor, to learn what circumstances might elicit this strange, noisy response from a human. In the process, he had compiled a library of his favorite laughter samples. A delightful repertoire.

He played them all now through his mouth speakers,

much to the bewilderment of the Face Dancer Khrone. But Erasmus realized that not even these favorite chuckles, snickers, and guffaws were adequate to express the true hilarity that he currently felt.

'What is so funny?' Khrone demanded. 'Why are you laughing?'

'I am laughing because even you don't understand the trick that was played on you.' Erasmus chuckled again, and this time he created a unique sound that contained flavors and undertones of his best borrowed recordings. This was truly *his* individual sense of humor, something genuinely original. After such long and difficult study, Erasmus was pleased with the new comprehension he had achieved. Surely this was worth all the tribulations of Kralizec!

The independent robot turned to Duncan Idaho, who – after listening to the betrayals upon betrayals – had the faraway look of a man trying to join mismatched puzzle pieces. Erasmus knew that Duncan hadn't the faintest idea of how to achieve his full potential. Just like so many other humans! The robot would have to guide this one.

Ignoring Khrone, he spoke to Duncan. 'I am laughing because the inherent differences between humans and Face Dancers are painfully hilarious. I hold great fondness for your species – as more than specimens, more than pets. You have never ceased to astonish me. In defiance of my most careful predictions, you still manage to do the unexpected! Even when those actions work to the detriment of thinking machines, I can appreciate them for their uniqueness.'

Khrone and his contingent of Face Dancers closed in, as if expecting to mop up these few robots and humans easily. 'Your words and laughter are meaningless.'

Jessica supported a still-weak Paul, while Chani picked up the bloodied dagger that Paolo and Dr Yueh had both used. Now that she had her past memories, Chani held the weapon in the manner of a true Fremen woman, ready to defend her man.

Erasmus smiled to himself. His own confrontation with Duncan had shown only the tip of the iceberg of the Kwisatz Haderach's powers. The robot had found it terribly exciting for a few moments, placing himself at the brink of death, or at least its equivalent for a machine.

The Face Dancers would be in for quite a surprise if they thought Duncan Idaho and these other humans would be an easy conquest. But Erasmus had an even greater surprise to spring.

'What I *mean*, my dear Khrone, is that while humans can astonish me, Face Dancers are woefully predictable. It's a shame. I had hoped for something more original in your case.'

When Khrone scowled, every one of the Face Dancers in the chamber mimicked his expression, like reflections in a hall of mirrors. 'We've already won, Erasmus, Face Dancers control every foothold, and you have no place to hide from us. We will rise up across the human planets and on all machine worlds. We will look back upon the path of destruction, and only we will remain.'

'Not if I choose to stop it.' Erasmus's flowmetal face shifted into a placid, disappointed expression. 'Omnius might have been convinced that you all were our meek puppets, but I never believed as much. Who can ever trust a Face Dancer? Among humans, that saying has become a cliché. You and your counterparts did exactly what I predicted you would do. How could you not? You are what you are. It was practically programmed into you.' The robot gave a sad shake of his head.

'While you Face Dancers were laying down your schemes, sending out spies, and establishing your presence, I watched patiently. Though you thought you were hidden from Omnius, you weren't clever enough. I saw everything you did and *allowed* it to happen because I found your petty power plays amusing.'

Khrone adopted a fighting stance, as if ready to attack the robot with bare hands. 'You know nothing of our activities!'

'Now who is drawing conclusions from insufficient data? Ever since the end of the Butlerian Jihad, when Omnius and I were sent out here on our long exile to start the machine empire all over again, I was the one in control. I allowed Omnius to continue believing he ruled everything and made all the decisions, but even in his first incarnation he was a self-aggrandizing annoyance, overconfident and unconscionably stubborn. More so than most humans!' The robot swirled his plush robes. 'The evermind never learned to adapt and never bothered to face his mistakes, so I refused to let him ruin our chances again. Thus, I took control of the Face Dancer program from the moment the first of you arrived on our fringe planets.'

Khrone remained defiant, though his voice carried a slightly uncertain undertone. 'Yes, you manufactured us – and made us stronger than ever.'

'I manufactured you, and I wisely planted a fail-safe routine in each and every Face Dancer. You are biological machines, evolved and manipulated over thousands of years, according to my own exacting specifications.' Erasmus moved closer. 'A tool should never confuse itself with the hand that wields it.'

The gathered Face Dancers seemed to hold the balance of power, and Khrone did not back down. His features shifted into a monstrous, demonic mask of fury. 'Your lies cannot control us any longer. There is no fail-safe.'

Erasmus emitted a poignant sigh. 'Wrong again. This is my proof.' With a precise nod of his burnished head, he triggered the implanted shutdown virus that was genetically buried within each of the customized, 'enhanced' Face Dancers.

Like a toy discarded by a petulant child, the Face Dancer standing immediately behind Khrone crumpled lifeless to the floor, arms and legs akimbo, an expression of momentary shock animating his face before it reverted to its blank state.

Khrone stared, unable to comprehend. 'What are—'

'And this.' Erasmus nodded again. With a swift sighing thump, the throng of Face Dancers in the cathedral chamber also dropped, an army scattered in death as if mowed down by projectile fire, leaving Khrone alive to accept his utter defeat.

Then, after stretching out the moment for effect, the independent robot said, 'And *this*. Your services are no longer required.'

With his face twisted in rage and desperation, Khrone threw himself toward Erasmus – only to fall to the stone floor, as dead as the rest of his brethren.

Erasmus turned to Duncan Idaho. 'So, Kwisatz Haderach – as you see, I control fundamental parts of our intriguing game. I would not suggest my powers are as great as your own, but in this particular case, they are quite useful.'

Duncan did not show any awe. 'How far will your shutdown virus spread?'

'As far as I wish. Even though the Oracle of Time extracted Omnius from the tachyon net, the strands of that vast interconnected mesh still exist in the fabric of the universe.' Erasmus twitched his head again and sent out a signal. 'There, I just dispatched my trigger to every modified Face Dancer throughout human civilization. They are dead now. All of them. They numbered in the tens of millions, you know.'

'So many!' Jessica exclaimed.

Letting out a whistle, Paul said, 'Like a silent jihad.'

'You would never have known most of them. With memory imprints, some even believed they were human. All across what remains of your former empire, a great many people are probably quite surprised as comrades, leaders, friends, and spouses drop dead where they stand and transform into Face Dancers.' Erasmus laughed again. 'With a single thought I've eliminated our enemies. Our *common* enemy. You see, Duncan Idaho, we need not be at odds.'

Duncan shook his head, feeling oddly sickened. 'Once again, the thinking machine sees total genocide as a simple solution to a problem.'

Now Erasmus was surprised. 'Don't underestimate the Face Dancers. They were . . . evil. Yes, that is the correct word. And since each one was fundamentally part of a hive mind, they were all evil. They would have destroyed you, and they would have destroyed us.'

'We've heard that kind of propaganda before,' Jessica said. 'In fact, I've heard it cited as the primary reason why all *machines* need to be destroyed.'

Duncan looked at all the dead Face Dancers, realizing how much damage the shape-shifters had done for centuries, whether they were guided by the evermind or by their own schemes. Face Dancers had killed Garimi, sabotaged the no-ship, and caused the death of Miles Teg . . .

Looking at the robot, Duncan narrowed his eyes. 'I can't say I'm terribly sorry, but there was no honor in what you – or the Face Dancers – did here. I cannot agree with it. Don't think we are indebted to you.'

'On the contrary, it is I who owe so much to you!' Erasmus could barely contain his pleasure. 'That is exactly the way I'd hoped you would react. After thousands of years of study, I believe I finally understand honor and loyalty – especially in you, Duncan Idaho, the very embodiment of the concept. Even after an event that obviously helps your race, you still object to my tactics on a moral basis. Oh, how wonderful.'

He looked down at all the Face Dancers, the astonished and confused expression on Khrone's face. 'These creatures are the exact opposite. And my fellow machines are not loyal or honorable, either. They merely follow instructions because they are programmed to. You have shown me what I needed to know, Kwisatz Haderach. I am very much in your debt.'

Duncan stepped closer, searching for some way to access the new abilities he knew lay dormant inside him. Just knowing he was the much-anticipated Kwisatz Haderach was not enough. 'Good. Because now I want something from you.'

*A single decision, a single moment, can make the differ-
ence between victory and defeat.*

— BASHAR MILES TEG,
Memoirs of an Old Commander

'It's a trap – it must be.' Murbella stared at the vast yet
motionless Enemy fleet. The human ships were still
outnumbered hundreds to one, but the thinking machines
made no move. The Mother Commander froze, holding
her breath. She had expected to be annihilated.

But the Enemy did nothing. 'This is deeply unnerving,'
she whispered.

'All backup systems ready, as you ordered, Mother
Commander,' one of the pale young Sisters announced.
'It may be our only chance to cause some damage.'

'We should open fire!' Administrator Gorus cried.
'Destroy them while they are helpless.'

'No,' said another Sister. 'The machines are trying to
lure us from our defensive positions. It's a trick.'

Everyone on the navigation bridge stared at their dark
and quiet foe, afraid to breathe. The robot vessels just
drifted out there in the cold void.

'They have no need to trick or trap us,' Murbella finally
said. 'Look at them! They could destroy us any time they

like. It was foolish, impulsive Honored Matre violence that triggered this very war in the first place.' The Mother Commander narrowed her gaze, studying the overwhelming force of warships. Utter stillness. 'This time, I will take a moment to understand before we just open fire.'

Murbella's eyes blazed as she struggled to comprehend. She remembered when her eyes had been a hypnotic green – an alluring feature that had helped her ensnare Duncan. *Strange, the thoughts that haunt you when death waits at your door* . . .

At the time of Duncan's escape from Chapterhouse, no one had known the identity of the outside Enemy. Now, the Oracle had said Duncan was on Synchrony at the heart of the thinking-machine empire. Had he managed to get away? If Duncan was still alive, she could forgive him anything. How she longed to see him again, and hold him!

The painful silence stretched out. Another excruciating minute, followed by another. Murbella had seen the thinking-machine forces on the move from planet to planet, and the aftermath of their strikes. She had seen the plagues they disseminated and had buried her own daughter Gianne with so many others in an unmarked grave out in the Chapterhouse desert. 'No matter what the reason,' she said, 'the machines have never been so vulnerable.'

From her nearby ship, Janess gruffly acknowledged. 'If we are going to die in battle, why not take out as many of the Enemy as we can?'

Murbella had already prepared for this moment. She issued her orders, each word carrying a sharp edge. 'All right, I don't know why, but we've got an unexpected reprieve. We may be few, but we'll be like D-wolves with sharp fangs. We'll rely on our own eyes and skills.'

One of the Guildsmen who had rushed aboard the ship at the last minute reacted with alarm. He was a bald and pasty-faced man with tattoos on his scalp. 'Aiming our weapons will require precision maneuvering, Mother Commander! We can't do it without assistance.'

Murbella shot him a wilting glare. 'I'd rather rely on my eyes than on Ixian systems. I've already been deceived once today. Target the largest ships. Destroy their weapons, disable their engines, and move on to others.'

Janess transmitted to the clustered defenders, 'The wreckage of all those Enemy ships can provide cover if the machines fire back at us.'

The bald Guildsman objected again. 'Every piece of debris is a navigational hazard. No human can react fast enough. We need the Ixian devices back online, at least in a limited fashion.'

Even Gorus looked at him strangely. Suddenly, the bald Guildsman shouted, turned from his technical station, and collapsed. Near him, without a sound, another of the new crewmen dropped dead in his tracks. A third slumped over on the upper navigation deck.

Suspecting that their ships were under some kind of invisible attack from a silent, deadly weapon, the Sisters reacted quickly, trying to determine what was happening. Murbella hurried to the tattooed Guildsman, rolled him over, and watched his puttylike face shift to the blank visage of a Face Dancer.

Gorus looked around as if he finally realized how he had been betrayed. The other two fallen bodies also shifted. All Face Dancers! Murbella glared at the Administrator. 'You guaranteed me that everyone had been tested!'

'I spoke the truth! But in the rush to launch your whole fleet, someone might have been missed. And what if one or more of the testers happened to be a Face Dancer?'

She turned from him in disgust. A flurry of transmissions arrived from the other defender vessels, all reporting dead Face Dancers onboard. Amidst the jumble of comm activity, Janess's voice came in sharp and clear. 'Five Face Dancers were on my vessel, Mother Commander. All are now dead.'

Meanwhile, the listless Enemy ships continued to drift apart, though they could easily have pressed their attack on Chapterhouse and achieved victory. Murbella's thoughts spun, wrestling with yet another mystery. *Face Dancers among us, working for Omnius. But why did they drop dead?*

Not long ago, the Oracle of Time had whisked her numerous Heighliners away from this battlefield to Synchrony . . . to Duncan. Had the Oracle and her Navigators struck a blow that sent ripples through the entire Enemy fleet? Had *Duncan?* Something seemed to have shut down the thinking-machine battle fleet and all their shape-shifter spies.

Murbella indicated the dead Face Dancers sprawled near her. 'Get those monstrosities out of here.' Not bothering to hide their revulsion, several Sisters dragged the scarecrowish bodies away.

Murbella focused on the screen with such intensity that her eyes burned. The Honored Matre part of her wanted to strike and kill in a frenzy, but all of her Bene Gesserit training screamed for her to *understand* first. Something essential had changed here. Even the voices of Other Memory couldn't counsel her. Thus far, they had been mute.

Representatives of the remaining populations on Chapterhouse transmitted urgent messages, demanding reports from the front, wondering how long they might expect to survive. With no answers for them, Murbella didn't respond.

Janess transmitted a brash suggestion. 'Mother Commander . . . should we board one of the Enemy ships? It could be our best chance to discover what's happened.'

Before she could answer, space distorted again around them. Four huge Heighliners reappeared, emerging in the debris-strewn battle zone so close to the human defenders that Murbella shouted for evasive action. The Guild pilot on one of the nearby ships reacted with an exaggerated maneuver, pulling his heavy cruiser out of the way and nearly colliding with Janess's vessel. Another careened into a debris field of destroyed first-wave machine ships.

A third defender acted impulsively and opened fire on the silent thinking-machine fleet, launching a volley of explosive projectiles into the conical nose of the nearest machine battleship. Fiery eruptions burst out in a repeating pattern along the Enemy vessel's hull.

Alarms rang out, and Murbella demanded reports, wondering if the machines would respond with a massive display of force. No more caution. 'Prepare to fire! All ships, prepare to fire! Hold nothing back!'

But even thus provoked, the darkened Omnius fleet remained motionless. The Enemy vessel damaged in the impulsive barrage careened in a slow drift, still burning. Very slowly it crashed into an adjacent machine ship and caromed off, sending them both spinning.

The Enemy ships did not fire a single return shot. Murbella couldn't believe it.

In the midst of the surprise and mayhem, a Navigator's

voice sounded calm and otherworldly. 'The Oracle of Time has sent us here to locate the commander of the human forces.'

Murbella pushed her way to a commline station. 'I am Mother Commander Murbella of the New Sisterhood . . . of all humanity.'

'I have orders to escort you to Synchrony. I will now take command of your foldspace engines.'

Before her Guildsmen could scramble to their stations, the Holtzman engines hummed at a higher pitch. Murbella felt a familiar shifting sensation.

It is too simplistic to state that humans are the enemies of all thinking machines. I strive to understand these creatures, but they remain incomprehensible to me. Even so, I greatly admire them.

— ERASMUS,
private files, secure database

'You want something from me?' Erasmus seemed to find Duncan's demand amusing. 'And how will you force me to obey?'

The man's lips quirked in a faint smile. 'If you truly understand honor, robot, I won't need to. You will do what's right and pay your debt.'

Erasmus was genuinely delighted. 'What else do you wish from me? Isn't it enough that I eliminated all Face Dancers?'

'You and Omnius were responsible for far more mischief than those shape-shifters.'

'Mischief? It was rather more than mischief, wasn't it?'

'And to atone for it, there's something you need to do.' Duncan's attention was entirely focused on the robot, not on the dead Face Dancers, not on the destructive sounds of sandworms outside in the city. Paul, Chani, Jessica, and Yueh all remained quiet in the chamber, watching him.

'I am the final Kwisatz Haderach,' Duncan said, feeling the nascent abilities embedded within him all the way down to his DNA, 'yet I need to comprehend so much more. I already understand humans – maybe better than anyone else – but not thinking machines. Give me a good reason why I shouldn't just eliminate you all, now that the thinking machines are weakened. It's what the evermind would have done to us.'

'Yes, it is. And you are the final Kwisatz Haderach. The decision is yours.' Erasmus seemed to be waiting for something, his optic threads gleaming like a cluster of stars.

'And is there a way that doesn't require the annihilation of one or the other? A fundamental change in the universe – Kralizec.' Duncan stroked his chin, thinking. 'Omnius's fleet contains millions of thinking machines. They're not destroyed, but simply without guidance, correct? And I believe your empire contains hundreds of planets, many of which would never be habitable to humans.'

With his robes flowing around him, the platinum robot began to stroll through the great vaulted hall, stepping over Face Dancer corpses that lay strewn everywhere like marionettes with their strings cut. 'That is an accurate assessment. Do you want to find them all, destroy them all, hoping you never miss one? Now that they are without the evermind, it's even possible that some of the more sophisticated machines could develop independent personalities during a time of long deprivation, as I did. How confident are you in your abilities?'

Duncan followed him closely. Several times, Erasmus

glanced back at him, and made an odd series of expressions, from inquisitive scowls to tentative smiles. Did he see a bit of fear there, or was it feigned? 'You're asking me if I want victory . . . or peace.' It was not a question.

'You are the superhuman. I say it again – decide for yourself.'

'Through more lifetimes than I can count, I've learned patience.' Duncan took a long, deep breath, using an old Swordmaster technique to center his thoughts. 'I'm in a unique position to draw both sides together. Humans and machines are both battered and weakened. Do I choose extermination for one side as the solution?'

'Or recovery for both?' Erasmus stopped, and with a blank expression faced the man. 'Tell me, what precisely is that dilemma? Omnius has been ripped from the universe, and the rest of the thinking machines have no leadership. In one swift blow I have expunged the entire Face Dancer threat. I fail to see anything left to solve. Hasn't the prophecy come true?'

Duncan smiled. 'As is the case with so many prophecies, the details are vague enough to convince any gullible mind that everything was 'foretold.' The Bene Gesserit and their Missionaria Protectiva were masters at that.' He looked closely at the robot. 'And so, I think, are you.'

Erasmus seemed both surprised and impressed. 'What are you suggesting?'

'Since you were in charge of the "mathematical projections" and the "prophecies" based on them, you were in a position to write predictions however you wished. Omnius believed everything.'

'Are you saying I *made up* the prophecies?' Erasmus asked. 'Perhaps as a way to guide an evermind stubbornly intent on a narrow-minded course of action? Perhaps to bring us precisely to this juncture? A very interesting hypothesis. One worthy of a true Kwisatz Haderach.' The grin on his face seemed more genuine than ever.

Smiling coolly, Duncan said, 'As the Kwisatz Haderach, I know there are – and always will be, even as I evolve – limitations on my knowledge and my abilities.' He tapped the robot in the center of his chest. 'Answer me. Did you manipulate the prophecies?'

'Humans created countless projections and legends long before I existed. I simply adapted the ones I liked best, generated the complex calculations that would produce the desired projections, and fed them to the ever-mind. Omnius, with his usual myopia, saw only what he wanted to see. He convinced himself that in the "end" a "great change in the universe" required a "victory" for him. And for that he needed the Kwisatz Haderach. Omnius learned many things, but he learned arrogance too well.' Erasmus swirled his robes. 'No matter what the evermind or the Face Dancers thought – *I* have always been in control.'

Raising his hands, the robot gestured to the sentient metal cathedral around them, indicating the whole city of Synchrony and the rest of the thinking-machine empire. 'Our forces are not entirely leaderless. With the evermind gone, I now control the thinking machines. I have all the codes, the intricate, interlinked programming.'

Duncan had an idea that was part prescience, part intuition, and part gamble. 'Or the final Kwisatz Haderach can take control.'

'That seems a much neater solution.' An odd expression moved across the robot's flowmetal face. 'You interest me, Duncan Idaho.'

'Give me the codes and the access I need.'

'I can give you more than that – and, yes, it will require much more. A whole machine empire, millions of components. I would have to share an . . . *entirety* with you, just as my Face Dancers shared all those marvelous lives. But for a Kwisatz Haderach, that would be just the thing.'

Before the robot could laugh again, Duncan reached forward and grabbed the platinum hand that extended from the plush sleeve. 'Then do it, Erasmus.' He pressed closer, reached out his other hand and pressed it against the robot's face in a curiously intimate gesture. Prescience seemed to be guiding him.

'Duncan, this is dangerous,' Paul said. 'You know it.'

'I'm the one who's dangerous, Paul. Not the one in danger.' Duncan pulled himself to within inches of Erasmus, feeling all the possibilities roil within him. Though there were troublesome blind spots in the future, pitfalls and traps he might not be able to foresee, he felt confident.

The robot paused, as if calculating, then gripped Duncan's hand and – in a like gesture – reached out with the other to touch his face. Duncan's dark brows knitted as he experienced strange sensations. The cool metal felt alarmingly soft, and he almost had the sensation of falling into it. He extended himself, stretching his mind toward the uncharted territory of the independent robot's thoughts, just as Erasmus did the same to him. The robot's fingers elongated, spreading out over Duncan's hand like a glove. As flowmetal covered Duncan's wrist and ran up his forearm, it felt bitingly cold as Erasmus began to talk. 'I sense a growing trust between us, Duncan Idaho.'

As moments passed, Duncan couldn't tell if he was taking from the robot, or if Erasmus was surrendering what the nascent Kwisatz Haderach needed, *everything* he needed. And, though the two of them were fused, Duncan had to go further. A viscous, metallic substance covered his arm like the sandtrout that had engulfed young Leto II's body, so long ago.

I hear the clarion call of Eternity beckoning me.

> – LETO ATREIDES II,
> records from Dar-es-Balat

With the machine city heavily damaged and the ever-mind Omnius gone, the major components of Synchrony stopped moving. The buildings no longer pumped and shifted like interlocking puzzle pieces, no longer morphed into strange shapes. Like an immense broken engine, the city had ground to a complete halt, leaving many streets blocked, structures half buried or partially formed, and tramcars suspended in the air, dangling on invisible electronic wires. Grotesque Face Dancer bodies and smashed combat robots littered the streets. Columns of fire and smoke rose into the sky.

Exhausted even in victory, Sheeana stared around the city, her face filled with awe and pleasure. As she walked alone down a devastated street, she saw a young boy standing there by himself between the towering, exotic buildings. Looking wrung out but far more powerful than she had ever seen him, was the transformed boy Leto II. He had left the sandworms, having directed them off into the city, but even though he stood here in front of her, he was still part of them.

As Leto craned his neck to look up at one of the dangling tramcars, Sheeana noticed an oddness about him, a looming presence that hadn't been there before. She understood. 'You have your memories back.'

'In perfect detail. I've been reviewing them.' Leto's eyes were full of centuries, now completely blue-within-blue due to incredible spice saturation from the bodies of the sandworms he had controlled. 'I am the Tyrant. I am the God Emperor.' His voice sounded louder, yet carried a deep and abiding weariness.

'You are also Leto Atreides, brother to Ghanima, son of Muad'Dib and Chani.'

In response, he smiled as if she had lifted some of his burden. 'Yes, that too. I'm everything my predecessor was – and everything the worms are. The pearl of dreaming inside them has been broken open. He sleeps no more.'

Sheeana recalled the quiet boy aboard the no-ship. His past had been worse than anyone else's, and now that innocent boy was truly gone.

'I remember every death I caused. Every one. I remember all of my Duncans, and the reasons each died.' He looked up, then grasped her arm and pulled her back toward a twisted building that was stuck halfway out of the ground.

Seconds later, the invisible suspensor line high above snapped, and the tramcar hurtled down to smash on the street exactly where the two had been standing. Dead Face Dancers lay sprawled in the wreckage.

'I *knew* it would fall,' Leto said.

She smiled gently. 'We each have our special talents.'

The two of them climbed the high rubble of a collapsed building to get a better view of the city's wreckage.

Confused and disoriented robots milled around the smoldering piles of wreckage and broken structures, as if waiting for instructions.

'I am a Kwisatz Haderach,' Leto II said, his voice distant. 'And so was my father. But it is much different now. Did I plan for all this long ago; as part of my Golden Path?'

As if he had summoned them, four sandworms rose noisily from the churned and smashed ground and loomed over the wreckage. She heard loud grinding noises, and the remaining three worms came from other directions, knocking buildings aside, tunneling through the wreckage. Slightly larger than before, they circled Leto and Sheeana.

The largest worm, the one she had named Monarch, turned its head toward the two of them. Unafraid, Leto climbed down the remains of the building to approach the creature.

'My memories are back,' Leto said to Sheeana, stepping forward, 'but not the dreaming existence I had as the God Emperor, back when man and worm were one.' Monarch laid its head on the base of the rubble pile, as did the companion worms, like supplicants before a king. The cinnamon odor of melange filled the air from the exhalations of the beasts.

Reaching out, Leto stroked the rounded edge of Monarch's mouth. 'Shall we dream together again? Or should I let you go back to a peaceful sleep?'

Without fear, Sheeana also touched the worm, feeling the hard skin of the rings.

With a sigh, the boy added, 'I miss the people I used to know, especially Ghanima. Your ghola program didn't bring her back with me.'

'We didn't consider personal costs or consequences,' Sheeana said. 'I'm sorry.'

Tears welled in Leto's dark blue eyes. 'There are so many painful memories from before I took the sandtrout as part of me. My father refused to make the choice I did – refused to pay the price in blood for the Golden Path, but I thought I knew better. Ah, how arrogant we can be in our youth!'

In front of Leto, the largest worm lifted. Its open mouth looked like a cave full of rich spice.

'Fortunately I know how to go back into the dreaming essence of the Tyrant, the God Emperor. To the real son of Muad'Dib.' With a glance at her, he said, 'I take my last few sips of humanity.' Then he entered the towering mouth and climbed over the maw-fence of crystalline teeth.

Sheeana understood what he was doing. She had tried the same thing herself, though ineffectively. The worm engulfed Leto II, closed its mouth, and reared back. The boy was gone.

Sheeana struggled to keep her knees from buckling. She knew she would never see Leto again, though he would be with the worms eternally, merged into Monarch's flesh from the inside, becoming a pearl of awareness once more. 'Goodbye, my friend.'

But the spectacle was not finished. The other worms rose beside Monarch, and all towered over her. Sheeana stood motionless, at once horrified and fascinated. Would they devour her, too? She steeled herself for her own fate, but had no fear of it. As a young girl, after a worm had destroyed her village on Rakis, Sheeana had run wildly out into the desert and screamed at the huge creature, calling it names, insisting that it eat her.

'Well, Shaitan – do you have an appetite for me, now?'

But they did not want her. Instead, the seven worms gathered together, tumbling one upon the other, writhing like a mass of snakes. With Leto inside them now, the worms were transforming. Six worms wound themselves around the largest beast that had swallowed the boy. They twisted and twined, wrapping their sinuous bodies like vines around a tree, and then moved together.

Sheeana scrambled back up the rubble pile to keep herself safe from falling debris. The fleshy rings of the separate sandworms began to merge and metamorphose into a much larger form. The differentiation among the creatures became less distinct; the rings united, joining into one incredible sandworm: a behemoth greater even than the largest monsters from legendary Dune.

Sheeana stumbled, falling backward on the rubble but unable to tear her gaze away from the immense sandworm that towered in front of her, rippling and twining, its body stretching back hundreds of meters.

'Shai-Hulud,' she murmured, intentionally refusing to use the term *Shaitan*, just as she had always done. Truly, this was the godlike Old Man of the Desert. The dizzying odor of melange was stronger than ever.

At first she thought the leviathan would consume her after all, but the giant worm turned away and smashed down into the ground with a great thunder of noise, tunneling downward beneath the machine city.

Its new home.

A shudder of supreme pleasure ran through her. She knew the great worm would divide beneath the surface. This union between Leto II and the creatures would have a greater resistance to moisture, enabling them to survive until they could remake parts of this former machine planet into a domain of their own. One day, new sandworms would grow and thrive on this world, always lurking beneath the surface, always watching.

To defeat the humans, one option is to become like them, granting no quarter, chasing and destroying them to the last man, woman, and child. Just as they tried to do to us.

— ERASMUS,
databank on human violence

'With my curiosity, ages of existence, and understanding of both humans and machines,' Erasmus mused as he and Duncan remained joined, fused together mentally and physically, 'am I not the machine equivalent of a Kwisatz Haderach? The Shortening of the Way for thinking machines? I can be in many places at once and see a myriad of things that even Omnius never imagined.'

'You are not a Kwisatz Haderach,' Duncan said. He became aware of his comrades rushing toward him. But the liquid metal now flowed across Duncan's shoulders and face, and he felt no desire to tear himself away.

Duncan let the physical reaction between him and the robot continue. He didn't want to escape. As the new standard bearer of humankind, he needed to advance. So he opened his mind and let the data rush in.

A voice rang out in his head, louder than all the whirlwind memories and streams of data. *I can impress all of the key codes you seek, Kwisatz Haderach.Your neurons, your very DNA, form the structure of a new networked database.*

Duncan knew this was the point of no return. *Do it.*

The mental floodgates opened, filling his mind to bursting with the robot's experiences and coldly factual, regimented information. And he began to see things from that entirely alien viewpoint.

In thousands upon thousands of years of experimentation, Erasmus had struggled to understand humans. How could they remain so mysterious? The robot's incredible range of experiences made even Duncan's numerous lives seem insignificant. Visions and memories roared around the Kwisatz Haderach, and he knew it would take him much more than another lifetime just to sift through it all.

He saw Serena Butler in the flesh, along with her baby, and the startling reaction of the multitudes to what Erasmus had thought was a simple, meaningless death . . . howling humans rising up in a fight they had no chance to win. They were irrational, desperate, and in the end, victorious. Incomprehensible. Illogical. And yet, they had achieved the impossible.

For fifteen thousand years, Erasmus had longed to understand, but had lacked the fundamental revelation. Duncan could feel the robot digging around inside him, looking for the secret, not out of any need for domination and conquest, but simply to *know*.

Duncan had difficulty focusing amidst so much information. Presently he withdrew, and felt the flowmetal move the other direction, away from him – though not completely, for his internal cellular structure was forever changed.

In an epiphany, he realized that he was a new evermind, but of an entirely different sort from the original.

Erasmus had not deceived him. With eyes that extended to centillions of sensors, Duncan could see all of the Enemy ships, the fighting drones and worker robots, every cog in the awe-inspiring reborn empire.

And he could stop everything in its tracks. If he wanted to.

When Duncan returned to himself, in his relatively human body again, he looked through his own eyes around the great chamber. Erasmus stood before him, separate now and smiling with what seemed to be genuine satisfaction.

'What happened, Duncan?' Paul asked.

Duncan let out a long breath of stale air. 'Nothing I didn't initiate, Paul, but I'm here, I'm back.'

Yueh rushed up. 'Are you hurt? We thought you might be trapped in a coma like . . . like him.' He gestured toward the still-frozen Paolo.

'I'm unharmed . . . but not unchanged.' Duncan looked around the vaulted chamber, and gazed out into the vast city with a new sense of wonder. 'Erasmus shared *every-thing* with me . . . even the best parts of himself.'

'An adequate summation,' the robot said, undeniably pleased. 'When you merged into me and kept going deeper and deeper, you made yourself vulnerable. Had I wished to win the game, I could have tried to take over your mind and program you to do exactly what benefits me and thinking machines. Just as I did with the Face Dancers.'

'But I knew you wouldn't,' Duncan said.

'From prescience, or faith?' A crafty smile crept across the robot's face. 'You now have control of the thinking machines. They are yours, Kwisatz Haderach – all, including me. Now you have everything you need. With the power in your hands, you will change the universe. It is Kralizec. See? We have made the prophecy come true after all.'

Seemingly alone in the remnants of a vast empire, Erasmus walked casually around the chamber again. 'You can shut them all down permanently, if that is your preference, and eliminate thinking machines forever. Or, if you have the courage, you can do something more useful with them.'

Jessica said, 'Shut them down, Duncan. Finish it now! Think of all the trillions they've killed, all the planets they've destroyed.'

Duncan looked at his hands in wonder. 'And is that the honorable thing to do?'

Erasmus kept his voice carefully neutral, not pleading. 'For millennia I studied humans and tried to understand them . . . I even emulated them. But when was the last time humans bothered to consider what thinking machines could do? You only despise us. Your Great Convention with its terrible stricture, 'Thou shalt not make a machine in the likeness of a human mind.' Is that really what you want, Duncan? To win this ultimate war by exterminating every vestige of us . . . the way Omnius wanted to win the war by eliminating you? Didn't you hate the evermind for that fixed attitude? Do you have the same attitude yourself?'

'You have an abundance of questions,' Duncan observed.

'And it is up to you to choose the single answer. I gave you what you need.' Erasmus stood back and waited.

Duncan felt a new sense of urgency, perhaps imparted to him by Erasmus. Possibilities roiled through his head, accompanied by a riptide of consequences. With his growing awareness he saw that in order to end Kralizec, he needed to stop the eons-old schism that separated man and machine. Thinking machines had originally been created by man, but though intertwined, each side had tried repeatedly to destroy the other. He had to find a common ground between them, rather than let one dominate the other.

Duncan saw the great historical arc, a social evolution of epic proportions. Thousands of years ago, Leto II had joined himself with a great sandworm, thereby acquiring vastly greater powers for himself. Centuries later, under the guidance of Murbella, two opposing groups of women had joined forces, fusing their individual cultures into a stronger synthesized unit. Even Erasmus and Omnius had been two aspects of the same identity, creativity and logic, curiosity and rigid facts.

Duncan saw that balance was required. Human heart and machine mind. What he had received from Erasmus could become a weapon, or a tool. He had to use it properly.

I must serve as a synthesis of man and machine.

He locked gazes with Erasmus, and this time he and the robot connected without making physical contact. Somehow the Kwisatz Haderach retained a ghost image of Erasmus within himself, just as Reverend Mothers carried Other Memories inside.

Drawing a deep breath, Duncan faced the overwhelming question. 'When you and Omnius manifested yourselves as an old couple, you demonstrated the differences between you. Erasmus, while maintaining your own independence, you acquired the evermind's vast storehouse of data, the intellect, while Omnius in turn learned about *heart* from you, what it means to have human feelings – curiosity, inspiration, mystery. But even you never fully achieved all the aspects of humanity you sought.'

'But now I can. With your consent, of course.'

Duncan turned to face Paul and the others. 'After the Butlerian Jihad, human civilization went too far by completely banning artificial intelligence. But in forbidding any sort of computers, we humans denied ourselves valuable tools. That overreaction created an unstable situation. History has shown that such absolute, draconian prohibitions cannot be sustained.'

Jessica said skeptically, 'Yet eradicating computers for so many generations forced us to grow stronger and become independent. For thousands of years, humanity advanced without artificial constructions to think and decide for us.'

'As the Fremen learned to live on Arrakis,' Chani said with clear pride. 'It is a good thing.'

'Yes, but that backlash also tied our hands and prevented us from reaching other potentials. Just because a man's legs will grow stronger by walking, should we deny him a vehicle? Our memory improves through steady practice; should we therefore deny ourselves the means to write or record our thoughts?'

'No need to throw the baby out with the bathwater, to use one of your ancient clichés,' Erasmus said. 'I threw a baby off a balcony once. The consequences were extreme.'

'We didn't do without machines,' Duncan said, crystallizing his thoughts. 'We just redefined them. Mentats are humans whose minds are trained to function like those of machines. Tleilaxu Masters used female bodies as axlotl tanks – flesh machines that manufactured gholas or spice.'

When Paul looked back at him, Duncan thought that the young man's face seemed deeply old. Recovering from his past life had drained him even more than his mortal wound had. As a Kwisatz Haderach himself, as Muad'Dib, Emperor, and blind Preacher, Paul understood Duncan's dilemma better than any human present. He nodded slightly. 'No one can choose for you, Duncan.'

Duncan let his eyes take on a far-off glaze. 'We can do much, much more. I see it now. Humans and machines cooperating fully, with neither side enslaving the other. I shall stand between them, as a bridge.'

The robot responded with genuine excitement. 'Now you see, Kwisatz Haderach! You have helped me to achieve understanding along with you. You have shortened my way, too.' Erasmus's flowmetal body shifted like a mechanical version of a Face Dancer, becoming again the wrinkled body of the kindly old woman. 'My long quest is complete. At last, after thousands of years, I understand so much.' He smiled. 'In fact, there is very little that interests me anymore.'

The old woman walked over to where the still-transfixed Paolo lay, staring blankly upward. 'This failed, ruined Kwisatz Haderach is an object lesson for me. The boy paid the price of too much knowledge.' Paolo's unblinking eyes seemed to be drying out. He would probably wither away and starve to death, lost in the infinite maze of absolute prescience. 'I don't want to be bored. So I ask you, Kwisatz Haderach, help me understand something I could never truly experience, the last fascinating aspect of humanity.'

'A demand?' Duncan asked. 'Or a favor?'

'A debt of honor.' The old woman patted his sleeve with a gnarled hand. 'You now epitomize the finest qualities of man and machine. Allow me to do what only living beings can do. Guide me to my own *death*.'

Duncan had not foreseen this. 'You want to die? How can I help you do that?'

The old woman shrugged her bony shoulders. 'All your lives and deaths have made you an expert on the matter. Look inside yourself, and you'll know.'

Over the millennia since the Butlerian Jihad, Erasmus had considered distributing backup copies of himself as Omnius had done, but he had decided not to. That would have made his existence far less stimulating, and less meaningful. After all, he was an independent robot, and needed to be unique.

Duncan saw that along with all the codes and commands that controlled the host of thinking machines, he had received the life-function commands that regulated Erasmus. He could shut down the independent robot as easily as Erasmus had shut down all of the Face Dancers.

'I am curious to see what lies on the other side of the great divide between life and death.' The robot looked at Khrone and the identical shape-shifter bodies strewn on the floor of the cathedral chamber.

But it wasn't as simple as flipping a switch or sending a code. Duncan had lived and died over and over, and learned more about life and death than anyone. Did Erasmus want him to understand whether or not a robot could have a soul, now that the two of them had been inside each other's mind?

'You want me to serve as a guide,' Duncan said, 'not just an executioner.'

'A fine way to put it, my friend. I think you understand.' The old woman looked at him, and now her smile held a hint of nervousness. 'After all, Duncan Idaho, you have done this over and over again. But this is my first time.'

Duncan touched her forehead. The skin was warm and dry. 'Whenever you're ready.'

The old woman sat on the stone steps. Folding her hands in her lap, she closed her eyes. 'Do you suppose I will ever see Serena again?'

'I can't answer that.' With a mental command, Duncan activated one of the new codes he possessed. From inside his own mind, reaching down to touch his own numerous death experiences, he showed Erasmus what he knew, even if he didn't entirely comprehend it himself. He wasn't certain the ancient independent robot could follow. Erasmus would have to make his own way. He and Duncan parted, both of them traveling on utterly separate journeys.

The aged body slumped quietly on the steps, and a long sigh flowed from the old woman's lips. Her expression became utterly serene . . . and then went completely motionless, with the eyes staring straight ahead.

In death, the robot's human shape held.

Out under the burned sky of Rakis, Waff's despair took
him to a place as bleak and dry as the devastated landscape around him. On a vitrified dune nearby, only one
of his precious armored sandworms stirred with the last
flickerings of life, while the others were already dead. He
had failed his Prophet.

The cellular modifications he had made were insufficient, and he had neither sandtrout specimens, nor the
proper facilities to create additional test worms. He felt
the last grains of sand slipping through the hourglass of
his life. His body wouldn't last long enough for him to
try again with a new line of the hybrid worms, even if
he'd had the chance. Only the hope of restoring these
sandworms to Rakis had kept him from surrendering to
the damage in his accelerated ghola body, but now he
was falling apart.

Raising his fist to the sky and shouting into the dry,
caustic air, he demanded answers from God, though no

mortal had the right to do so. He hammered his hands on the hard, cracked ground and wept. His clothes were dirty, his face smeared with sooty residue. Sprawled atop what had once been magnificent dunes lay the dead worm specimens. Truly, they symbolized the end of all hope.

Rakis was forever cursed, if even the Prophet no longer wished to live there.

Then, as he huddled on the ground, Waff felt a shudder from deep beneath the surface. The resonant vibration grew stronger, and he looked up in wonder, blinking his stinging eyes. The last dying worm twitched, as if it, too, could sense something important happening.

With a thunderous crack in the thin, whistling air, a fissure raced across the glassy ground. Waff stumbled to his feet and stared at the zigzag progress of the widening split, hardly able to comprehend what he was seeing.

Widening, jagged lines appeared like fine fractures in reinforced plaz struck by a hard blow. The dunes bucked and heaved as something emerged from below.

Waff staggered backward. At his feet the last slumped sandworm stirred, as if to warn the Tleilaxu Master that it was about to end its days – and that the man, too, was about to die.

A sequence of explosions erupted like sand geysers from deep beneath the dunes. The crevices gaped wider, revealing forms stirring underground. As if in a waking dream, he saw enormous ridges crusted with stones and dust, huge behemoths rising in a cascade of sand.

Sandworms. Real sandworms – monsters of the size that used to roam the desert in the days when this world was known as Dune. A legend and a mystery reborn!

Waff stood transfixed, unable to believe, yet filled with

awe and hope rather than fear. Were these survivors of the original worms? How could they still be alive after the holocaust?

'Prophet, you have returned!' At first he saw five of the gigantic sandworms, then a dozen emerging at once. All around him the broken ground spawned more and more. Hundreds of them! The whole dead world was like an immense egg, cracking open and giving birth.

Breaking free of their underground nest, the sandworms rampaged toward the distant encampment in the rubble of Keen. Waff supposed they would swallow up Guriff and his prospectors, devouring all of the Guildsmen.

The sandworms would make Rakis their own again.

He reeled forward in ecstasy, his hands raised in joyous worship. 'My glorious Prophet, I am here!' God's Messenger was so great that Waff felt like a minuscule speck, hardly worth noticing.

His faith swelled again, and he saw that his insignificant efforts on Rakis had never mattered. Regardless of how hard he had worked with the sandtrout, trying to seed these dead dunes with enhanced worms, God had His own plans – always His own plans. He showed the way by producing a flood of life, like the wordless revelation of *s'tori*.

And Waff realized what he should have known all along, something every Tleilaxu should have understood: If each of the sandworms spawned from God Emperor Leto II's great body actually contained a pearl of the Prophet inside them – how could the *worms themselves* not have been prescient? How could they not have foreseen the coming of the Honored Matres and the impending destruction of Rakis?

He clapped his hands in glee. Of course! The great worms must have envisioned the terrible Obliterator weapons. Forewarned that the surface of Rakis would become a charred ball, some sandworms had been guided by Leto II's prescience to tunnel deep and encyst themselves protectively far beneath the sands, perhaps kilometers down. Away from the worst destruction.

This world can take care of itself, Waff thought.

Arrogant humans had always caused trouble here. When it was a pristine desert planet, Rakis was what it should have been before human pride and ambition terraformed it. The efforts of outsiders to 'improve' Dune had resulted in the apparent extinction of the great worms, until the death of Leto II brought them back. After which humans – the Honored Matres – had wiped out the ecosystem again.

Rakis had been beaten, stepped on, raped . . . but in the end, the magnificent world had saved itself. The Prophet had remained there all along and contributed mightily to the survival of Dune. Now all was as it should be, and Waff was immensely pleased.

Two giant sandworms churned toward the Tleilaxu man, who stood transfixed. Plowing through the crusted ground, the worms scooped up the flaccid carcasses of the weak test worms, devouring them as if they were mere crumbs.

Overcome by joy, Waff fell to his knees and prayed. At the last moment, he looked up into the giant mouth, with its deep, simmering flames and crystalline teeth. He smelled the spicy exhalations.

Smiling beatifically, the Tleilaxu Master lifted his face to heaven and exclaimed, 'God, my God, I am yours at last!' With the speed and fury of a crashing Guild

Heighliner, the worm descended. Waff inhaled a deep, satisfying breath of spice and closed his eyes in rapture as the monster's cavernous mouth engulfed him.

Waff became one with his Prophet.

Life is about determining what to do next, from moment to moment. I've never been afraid of making decisions.

— DUNCAN IDAHO,
A Thousand Lives

Through the broken cathedral's high dome, a preoccupied Duncan saw the sky flicker like a pattern changing in a kaleidoscope. A wealth of vessels appeared side by side, pulled along by the returning Navigator-controlled Heighliners.

Even before the signal came to him, Duncan sensed that someone very special was aboard one of the newly arrived ships. His expanded mind showed him her face, very little changed after all these years. *Murbella!* Some past part of him was terrified at the prospect of being near her again, but he was so much more than that now. He was eager to see her.

A thousand Navigator-faction Heighliners hovered over Synchrony, uncertain of their role, now that the Oracle was gone. Using his newly acquired abilities, Duncan communed with them all in a common-denominator language. The Navigators would understand him in their own way, as would the thinking machines and the humans. Duncan barely touched on his enhanced knowledge to do so.

Important changes. Necessary changes.

The human ships sent lighters down. Looking up through the dome's skylights Duncan saw the glints trailing through the sky and knew that Murbella would be with them. She would come down first, and he would see her again. Almost twenty-five years . . . a mere tick on the eternal clock, yet it had seemed an eternity all its own. He waited for her.

But the woman who entered the vaulted hall was *Sheeana*, worn and weary from her fighting out in the machine city. Her eyes were full of questions as she took in the blood on the floor, the smashed sentinel robots, the supine bodies of the Baron and glassy-eyed Paolo. Just by looking at the four young gholas Sheeana could tell that Paul and Chani had their memories back.

She noticed the motionless body of the old woman slumped on the stairs and recognized her. Speaking through Sheeana's mouth, the inner voice of Serena Butler lashed out. 'Erasmus killed my innocent – *the* innocent baby. He was the one responsible for—'

Duncan cut her off. 'I didn't hate him in the end. I think I pitied him more. It reminded me of when the God Emperor died. Erasmus was flawed, arrogant, and yet oddly innocent, guided only by insatiable curiosity . . . but he didn't know how to process what he already understood.'

Sheeana stared down, as if expecting the old woman's eyes to snap open and a clawlike hand to grab her. 'Erasmus is really dead, then?'

'Completely.'

'And Omnius?'

'Gone forever. And the thinking machines are no longer our enemies.'

'Do you control them, then? Have they been defeated?' Wonder shone on her face.

'They are allies . . . tools . . . independent partners more than slaves, and so different. We have a whole new paradigm to grapple with, and a lot of new definitions to make.'

WHEN MURBELLA AND a party of Guildsmen and Sisters were ushered into the chamber by courier drones, Duncan set all questions aside and just stared at her.

She stopped in mid-step. 'Duncan . . . you've hardly changed in more than two decades.'

He laughed at that. 'I've changed more than any instrument could measure.' All the machines in the hall, in the whole city, turned toward Duncan at the comment.

He and Murbella embraced automatically, uncertain of whether this contact would rekindle their past feelings. But each sensed the difference in the other. The river of time had carved a deep canyon between them.

As he touched Murbella, Duncan felt a bittersweet sadness to know how much damage her addictive love had done to him. Things could never be the same between them again, especially now that he was the Kwisatz Haderach. He also guided the thinking machines, but he was not their new evermind, not their new puppet master. He didn't even know how they could exist without a controlling force. They had to adapt or die, something humans had done well for millennia.

From across the room, Duncan recognized the spark in Sheeana's eyes – of genuine concern rather than jealousy; no Bene Gesserit would allow herself the weakness of jealousy. In fact, Sheeana was such a staunch Bene Gesserit that she had stolen the no-ship from Chapterhouse and fled with her refugees, rather than abide by the changes Murbella had forced on the Sisterhood.

He spoke to both women. 'We have freed ourselves from the traps we set for each other. I need you, Murbella – and you, Sheeana. And the future needs all of us more than I can express.' An infinite number of machine thoughts coursed through his mind, giving him the sudden awareness that countless human planets needed help that only he could provide.

With a thought, he dispatched the guardian robots out of the hall, marching them away as if in a military exercise. Then he stretched his mind through the empty pathways of the tachyon net, and across the universe. With his instantaneous connection to all of the human defender ships once controlled by corrupted Ixian machines, as well as the machine battleships linked to Omnius's command – *Duncan's* command, now – he summoned the vessels to the former machine planet, dragging them all simultaneously through foldspace. They would all come here, to Synchrony.

'You, Murbella, were born free, trained as an Honored Matre, and finally made into a Bene Gesserit so that you could gather the loose ends. As you were a synthesis between Honored Matre and Bene Gesserit, so I am now a fusion between free mankind and thinking machines. I stand in both domains, understanding both, creating a future where both can thrive.'

'And . . . what are you, Duncan?' Sheeana asked.

'I am both the ultimate Kwisatz Haderach and a new form of the evermind – and I am neither. I am something else.'

Alarmed, Murbella glanced at Sheeana, then back at him. 'Duncan! Thinking machines have been our mortal enemies since before the Butlerian Jihad – more than fifteen thousand years.'

'I plan to untie that Gordian knot of misunderstandings.'

'Misunderstandings! Thinking machines slaughtered trillions of human beings. The plague on Chapterhouse alone wiped out—'

'Such is the cost of inflexibility and closed-minded fanaticism. Casualties are so often unnecessary. Honored Matres and Bene Gesserits, humans and thinking machines, heart and mind. Don't our differences strengthen us rather than destroy us?' The reality-expanding wealth of information Erasmus had given him was tempered by the wisdom he had earned through numerous lifetimes. 'Our struggle has reached an end and a watershed.' He flexed his hand, and he could feel innumerable thinking machines out there listening, waiting. 'We have the power to do so much now.'

Utilizing perfect prescient and calculational knowledge, Duncan knew how to bring about an everlasting peace. With humanity and thinking machines balanced in the palm of his hand, he could control them all and seize their powers, preventing them from making further war. He could force cooperation among the Navigator-faction Heighliners, the Ixian-modified ships, and the thinking-machine fleet.

With his developing prescience, he foresaw the joint future of humankind and thinking machines – and how to implement it every step of the way. Such breathtaking power, greater than the God Emperor or Omnius combined. But power had eventually corrupted Leto II. How, then, could Duncan handle this even greater burden?

Even if Duncan Idaho acted for the most altruistic of

reasons, there were bound to be dissenters. Would he eventually be corrupted, regardless of his good intentions? Would history remember him as an even worse despot than the God Emperor?

Facing an avalanche of questions and responsibilities, Duncan vowed to use the lessons of his numerous lifetimes for the benefit and survival of the human race and thinking machines. Kralizec. Yes, the universe had indeed changed.

How terrible for a mother to bury her own daughter. There
is no greater pain, not even the Bene Gesserit Agony. Now
I have had to bury my daughter twice.

— LADY JESSICA,
Lament for Alia

Just one casualty among uncounted trillions.

Later, as Jessica gazed sadly at the cold form of her
daughter, she knew that one little girl did matter as much
as all the others. Each life had value, whether a ghola child
or a natural-born person. The titanic struggle that changed
the future of the universe, the defeat of the thinking
machines, and the survival of the human race seemed as
nothing to her. She was completely preoccupied with
preparing Alia's body for burial.

As she touched the small pale face, stroking the forehead and wispy dark hair, she remembered her daughter.
An Abomination, Alia had been called: a child born with
the full intelligence and genetic memories of a Reverend
Mother. It had come full circle now. In her original lifetime, the little girl had killed Baron Harkonnen with the
poison gom jabbar; later, as an adult and haunted by the
evil presence of the Baron, Alia had taken her own life,
throwing herself through a temple window high above

the streets of Arrakeen. Now the reborn Baron had killed the reborn Alia, before she'd ever had the opportunity to reach the potential she deserved. It was as if the two of them were forever locked in mortal combat, on a mythical scale.

A tear rolled down Jessica's cheek with the grace of a falling raindrop. She closed her eyes and realized that she had been frozen in the same position for a long moment, caught up in memories. She hadn't even heard the visitor approach her quarters.

'Is there any way I might help you, my Lady?'

'Leave me. I want to be alone.' But when she saw that it was the somber Dr Yueh, her demeanor softened. 'I'm sorry, Wellington. Yes, come in. You can help me.'

'I don't wish to intrude.'

With a wan smile she said, 'You've earned the right to be here.'

For long moments the unlikely pair stood together without speaking. Grateful just to have him there, Jessica finally said, 'Long ago when you were with us at Castle Caladan, I cared for you. You always kept your life private, and when you betrayed us, I hated you more than I thought possible.'

He hung his head. 'I would throw myself upon a knife ten thousand times if I could take back the deeds I've done and erase the pain I've caused, my Lady.'

'History can only move forward, Wellington, not backward.'

'Oh? *We've* been dredged out of the dustbins of history, haven't we?'

On old Arrakis, the Fremen had made a solemn ritual of recovering a body's water in a deathstill and sharing it among the tribe. On Caladan, the tradition had been a funeral pyre or an ocean burial. While the *Ithaca* wandered through space, their dead had been ceremoniously ejected into the void.

Using stain-free fabric from the no-ship's sheets, they wrapped Alia's small, frail body. Here in the post-Omnius machine city, however, Jessica wasn't sure how best to honor her daughter. 'We don't really have a funeral tradition anymore, so I don't know what to do.'

'We'll do what we must. The symbols don't matter, but the thought does.'

LONG AFTER THE last echoes of the battle on Synchrony had died away and survivors from the no-ship ventured out to discover the new face of the universe, Jessica and Yueh joined Paul, Chani, and Duncan in their own private funeral procession. Paul and Jessica carried the tiny wrapped body out into the streets where the sandworms had caused so much damage, where explosions in the battle against the Face Dancers had destroyed countless structures.

'Such a tiny body . . . and so much lost potential,' Paul said. 'I miss my sister terribly, even though I didn't get to know her this time as well as I would have liked.'

Duncan led the group, shunting aside his other responsibilities for the time being. 'I don't remember the original little girl, but I remember the woman. She hurt me and loved me, and I loved her passionately.'

They didn't have far to walk. Jessica had selected a particular broken tower, a slumped, thin pyramid that would serve as an appropriate grave marker. Jessica and Paul said their goodbyes during the procession, so that when they reached the collapsed structure they carried the girl inside through a lopsided trapezoidal opening, pushed debris aside to clear a space for her, and laid Alia Atreides on the smooth metal floor. Then Jessica stood over the wrapped child, saying another quiet farewell. Paul grasped his mother's hand, and she squeezed back.

After a lingering, painful silence, she turned and spoke to Duncan. 'We've done all we need to do.'

'I'll take care of the rest,' Duncan said. When they had withdrawn from the fallen pyramid, Duncan raised his hands, fingers splayed, and his face took on a distant expression. The metalform buildings around them began to tremble and sway, growing and curving. The remnants of the pyramid folded around Alia's body and reinforced the walls, drawing polished alloys from other structures. Like a magnificent crystal and quicksilver monument, the ruined spire then rose heavenward. The rapidly growing tower crackled and clanged like mechanical thunder as flowmetal streamed upward. Its curves and angles were streamlined, its polished surfaces perfectly reflective.

Duncan guided the semisentient structures with greater care and focus than the evermind ever had. When he was finished, he had created a tomb, a memorial, a work of art that would amaze anyone who looked upon it.

It left a mark on Synchrony that could never compare with the mark her daughter's loss left on Jessica's heart.

In the aftermath, the humans in Synchrony gradually began to believe that their race would survive.

When Sheeana looked at Duncan, he seemed strangely distant, though that was to be expected. Often his gaze flicked from side to side as if he were in a thousand places at once.

While Mother Commander Murbella called down lighters from her newly arrived battleships, and the Guild provided shuttles full of workers and administrators to help consolidate the strange city, Sheeana watched self-guided robots clean up remnants of the bloody duels in the cathedral chamber.

The *Ithaca*'s refugees had taken shelter inside the torn-open ship. The vessel would never fly in space again, even if Duncan forced the living-metal docking cradle to release the no-ship.

Courier drones and buzzing watcheyes, now personally directed by Duncan, led crowds of people through the broken streets, summoning them to a meeting where they would discuss the changed universe. Sheeana's renegade Bene Gesserits from the no-ship were uneasy about facing the former Honored Matre Murbella.

But the Mother Commander had grown much wiser in the intervening quarter century since the schism. Years ago, had she known of Sheeana's plan to steal the no-ship, Murbella would have killed her rival outright. Sheeana wondered what the former Honored Matre would think of all those years Duncan had pined for her. Did Murbella still love him? For that matter, had she ever?

Reverend Mothers Elyen and Calissa led a weary and uneasy crowd into the enormous cathedral hall. Guild crewmen from the ships above also entered the chamber, Administrator Gorus among them. He appeared drained, no longer in control of anything, and remained silent, following rather than leading his fellow Guildsmen.

When they had settled into a low hum of conversation approaching silence, Duncan took his place in the center of the chamber where Omnius and Erasmus had once presided over their thinking machines. He used no amplification system, yet his words resounded through the hall.

'This fate, this grand culmination of Kralizec, is what we sought for so many years.' He swept his gaze over Sheeana and the refugee Bene Gesserits. 'Your long journey is at an end, for this is the new heartland you dreamed of finding. The planet is yours now. Use the remnants of Synchrony to form an entirely new Bene Gesserit order, your base far from Chapterhouse.'

The gathered Sisters were confused and astounded. Even Sheeana had not known Duncan would propose this. 'But this is the heart of the thinking-machine empire!' cried Calissa. 'The homeworld of Omnius.'

'It's your homeworld now. Stake your claim and build your future.'

Sheeana understood. 'Duncan is exactly right. Challenges strengthen the Sisterhood. The universe has changed, and we belong here, regardless of the difficulties we may face. Even the sandworms have come to Synchrony, burrowing deep underground.' She smiled. 'They may reemerge when we least expect them. Someone has to keep an eye on the restored Tyrant.'

Beneath the hall, Sheeana thought she felt the ground trembling, as from a great behemoth moving under the foundations. Many robots had been destroyed or damaged during the sandworm attack, but thousands more of the machines remained perfectly functional. Sheeana knew that the Bene Gesserits here would have all the labor pool they could possibly desire, if the machines would work with them.

Murbella spoke up. 'I shall return to Chapterhouse. It will take some effort to spread news of the new reality.' She gazed at Sheeana. 'Don't worry. My combined Sisterhood doesn't need to be at odds with your orthodox Bene Gesserit base here. There have always been many schools, many trains of thought. In proper balance, rivalry promotes strength and innovation – so long as we can avoid the acrimony of conflict and mutual destruction.'

Sheeana knew that Duncan would go back to Chapterhouse with Murbella, at least for a time. With his guidance, Murbella would shepherd the reintroduction and integration of superior technology into a thriving society. If handled properly, Sheeana saw no reason for humans to fear cooperation with thinking machines any more than they needed to fear religion itself, or competition among Bene Gesserit elements. Any group could be dangerous if managed improperly.

Sheeana, though, would remain here. She saw no point in going back. Addressing Murbella, she said, 'Even before Honored Matres destroyed Rakis, the Bene Gesserit order made me the centerpiece of a manufactured religion. For decades I had to hide while the Missionaria spread myths about me. I let the legend continue without me. What would I achieve if I stopped it now? So I say, leave it, if the thought comforts people. My place is on this planet.'

She saw that Scytale was also in the audience. The last of the Tleilaxu Masters had, in the end, proved greatly helpful, fighting for instead of against them. 'Scytale, will you remain with us? Will you join my new order here? We can use your knowledge and genetic expertise. We are, after all, founding a colony, and we have only a few hundred people.'

'I expect others from the outside will eventually join you,' Murbella said.

The little Tleilaxu was surprised by the invitation. 'Of course I will stay. Thank you. My people have no other place now, not even sacred Bandalong.' He smiled at Sheeana. 'Perhaps at your side I can accomplish something worthwhile.'

Duncan walked among the Bene Gesserit refugees. 'You are gardeners laying down flagstones on our path of destiny. Many of us will return to worlds we once called home, but you will remain here.'

With a warm feeling toward him, Sheeana touched Duncan's arm. Though still flesh and bone, and human, she knew he was far more than that. And his words rang true. 'Thanks to you Duncan, my Sisters and I are finally home.'

Back in the Old Empire, the last Chapterhouse defenders waited, tense and alert, but nothing changed for days. The machine warships had not moved, and Bashar Janess Idaho had received no further word from the Navigator ships that had whisked the Mother Commander away. Fast scouts flitted back and forth from the hundred last-stand groupings, and the situation was the same along the entire front.

Waiting. No one knew what was happening.

Janess reacted with alarm and dismay when a large swarm of ships burst out of foldspace in all sizes and configurations. Shouting into the commline, the bashar rallied all of her functional defensive craft that remained in orbit. At first she did not recognize the configurations, but then she saw that the newly arrived cluster included smaller human and thinking-machine vessels that had been towed along by the Holtzman engines of great Guildships.

'Identify yourselves!' Janess said to the unexpected armada.

On the bridge of her large battleship, returning home, Murbella smiled at Duncan. 'That is your – *our* daughter.'

He raised his eyebrows and performed quick mental calculations. 'One of the twins?'

'Janess.' Murbella frowned slightly. 'The other one, Rinya, didn't survive the Agony. I forgot you didn't know. Tanidia, the middle one, is alive and well, assigned with the Missionaria among the refugees. But we lost Gianne, our youngest – born just before I became a Reverend Mother. She died during the Chapterhouse plague.'

Duncan steadied himself. How odd to feel a blow of genuine grief to learn of the death of two children he had never met. He hadn't even known their names until now. He tried to imagine what the young women might have been like. As Kwisatz Haderach and evermind, he could do many things . . . almost anything. But he couldn't bring back his daughters.

Duncan studied Janess's features on the screen: dark hair and round face from his own genes, a petite figure, intense eyes, and a hard expression showing she would never run from a challenge. A synthesis of himself and Murbella. He activated the commline himself. 'Bashar Janess Idaho, this is Duncan Idaho, your father. I am with the Mother Commander.'

Murbella leaned into the field of view. 'Stand down, Janess. The war is over. You have nothing to fear from us.'

Janess seemed suspicious. 'There are thinking-machine ships with you.'

'They are my ships now,' Duncan said.

The female bashar did not flinch. 'How do I know you're not Face Dancers?'

Murbella answered, 'Janess, when we stood against the thinking machines and discovered that Ixians and Face Dancers had deceived us, you and I were ready to throw away our lives in a final burst of glory. Don't be so eager to die now that we finally have hope.'

The image of Janess stared at them from the viewing plate. Duncan was proud of his daughter's caution. He said, 'We will all meet in the great hall of the Keep. A good place for us to discuss the future.' He smiled wistfully. 'I never actually saw the inside of the Keep when I was here . . . I had to remain aboard the no-ship at all times.'

Janess hesitated just a moment longer, then nodded curtly. 'We will have guards.'

Duncan already missed his no-ship comrades, but they had their own places to go now, important niches to fill. Paul and Chani would return to Arrakis, where they had always known they belonged. Jessica had chosen Caladan, and she surprised many by asking Yueh to go with her. And on Synchrony, Scytale's nullentropy capsule still contained a wealth of cells, a treasure chest of prizes.

Duncan had already decided on the first request he would make of the Tleilaxu Master. The turmoil and changes, the repercussions and adaptations would last for decades, even centuries. He would value the assistance and advice of a great man. He needed Miles Teg at his side again . . .

As the ship descended toward the main city on Chapterhouse, Duncan knew he could never think of this world as home, despite the time he'd spent there. In his genetic incarnations he had experienced many places and known innumerable people. Duncan's developing prescience, and his mental connection to decillions of eyes spread across the cosmos and linked through the evermind's tachyon net, made the entire universe his home now.

Now you begin to understand the fascinating obligation I helped you to assume, said a familiar-sounding voice in his mind. Erasmus! *I could have made it much harder on you, Kwisatz Haderach. Instead, I cooperated. This is only an echo of me, an observer. You can access me as you like. Use my knowledge like a databank. A tool. I am curious to see what you will do.*

'Are you haunting me now, like a demon?'

Consider me an advisor, but my research continues. I will always be here to guide you, and I am confident you will not let me down.

'Like the witches' Other Memory, but far bigger, and more easily accessible.'

You are here to serve both humans and thinking machines – and the future. It is all under your command.

Duncan laughed softly to himself at the friendly bantering between the two of them. Though Erasmus was in a subservient position, he still had a bit of humanlike pride, even if he was only an echo, and an advisor.

Entering the Keep, Duncan and Murbella marched into the echoing great hall, side by side. Watcheyes followed them, along with a pair of sentinel robots. The robots greatly disturbed the people who waited there, but in the future humans must learn to set aside their fears and preconceptions.

Without Omnius, the thinking-machine empire continued to function but without a unified mind or mission. Duncan would direct them, but he refused to simply continue the endless cycle of enslavement. They had potential to be more than tools or puppets, more than just a destructive force. Some of the machines were merely that, but more sophisticated robots and advisory mechanisms could grow and develop into something far superior. Erasmus himself had become independent, developing a unique personality when he was isolated from the homogenizing influence of the evermind. With so many thinking machines spread across so many planets, other prominent figures would arise if given the opportunity. If guided. If Duncan allowed them.

He had to achieve a balance.

The Mother Commander's imposing chair stood high and empty in front of a segmented window that looked out on the arid, dying landscape. Janess stood to one side, welcoming Murbella to the empty seat, with nearly a hundred of the New Sisterhood's guards standing at high alert in the chamber. Though all of the insidious Face Dancers had been exposed and killed, Janess was not letting down her guard, and Duncan felt proud of his daughter.

She bowed formally. 'Mother Commander, we are glad to have you back. Please, take your place.'

'It is no longer only my place. Duncan, your daughter has been raised in the Bene Gesserit ways, but she also made a point of learning about you. She trained herself to become the equivalent of a Ginaz Swordmaster.'

Thinking bittersweet thoughts about all he had missed, Duncan formally shook his daughter's hand and found her grip pleasingly strong. Until this moment they had been strangers who shared a bond of blood and patriotic allegiance. Their real relationship was just beginning.

Central Library

Customer name: Mr RICHARD ARNOLD

Title: Sandworms of Dune
ID: 933416863X
Due: 28/06/2024 23:59

Total items: 1
29/04/2024 16:17
Checked out: 1
Overdue: 0
Hold requests: 0
Ready for pickup: 0

Thank you for using Central Library.

Murbella had fought a long and bloody battle to combine the opposing forces of the Honored Matres and the Bene Gesserits, after which she had wrestled with the disparate groups of humanity to forge them into one whole. On an even larger scale, Duncan, through his newfound abilities, was shaping an even greater, farther reaching union.

Everything was woven together in a tighter tapestry than history had ever known, and at last Duncan grasped the extent of his newfound strength. He was not the first human in history to possess great power, and he vowed not to forget what he had learned as a pawn of the God Emperor, Leto II.

The human race would never forget the thousands of years under that terrible reign, and Duncan's comprehensive racial memory held a roadmap that showed him where the pitfalls were, thus enabling him to avoid them. The great Tyrant had suffered from a flaw he hadn't recognized. Weighed down by his sense of terrible purpose, Leto II had isolated himself from his humanity.

In contrast, Duncan clung to the knowledge that Murbella would be with him, and Sheeana, too. He could talk with his daughter Janess as well, and perhaps even his other surviving daughter, Tanidia. In addition, he had all the memories of great and loyal friends, of dozens of loves, and a succession of comrades, wives, families, joys, and beliefs.

Though he was the ultimate Kwisatz Haderach with immeasurable power, Duncan had known the best parts of being human. Life after life. He didn't need to feel alienated and worried, when he could be filled with love instead.

But his would not be a conventional kind of love. His

love needed to extend much farther, to every living person, and to thinking machines. One form of sentient life was not superior to the other. And Duncan Idaho was greater than the flesh that encompassed his body.

Epilogue

In a war, be watchful for unexpected enemies and unlikely allies.

— BASHAR MILES TEG,
final log entries

More than a year had passed on Qelso. The unnatural desert continued to spread as sandtrout reproduced and commandeered more and more of the planet's water. Though their fight seemed hopeless, Var's commandos stood against the forces that were killing their environment.

Stilgar and Liet-Kynes did their best to assist in the struggle. Both desert-bred gholas felt that their more important work was to show the natives how they could live in cooperation with the encroaching desert, rather than fight it.

During the many months since the pair had departed from the no-ship, the dry sands had extended much farther into the continental forests and plains. Var's camp had moved time after time, retreating from the oncoming dunes, and the desert kept following them. Though they had killed dozens of sandworms using water cannons and moisture bombs, Shai-Hulud was not so easily thwarted. The worms grew larger, despite all the efforts of the Qelso commandos.

With the first faint light of dawn, Liet stepped out of his rockwalled sleeping chambers and stretched. Although he and Stilgar were still teenagers, they remembered being adults once and having wives. Among the commando women on Qelso, many would accept either of them as a husband, but Liet had not yet decided when he could justify getting married and fathering children. Maybe he would have another daughter, and name her Chani . . .

No matter how much Liet-Kynes worked to remake Qelso, it would never be Dune. The fertile landscape was giving way to dry waves of sand, but it would not be the same. Eons ago, had Arrakis been fertile? Had some forgotten superior civilization transplanted sandtrout and sandworms there, much as Mother Superior Odrade had when she sent her Bene Gesserit to Qelso? Perhaps it had been the Muadru, who left mysterious symbols on rocks and cliffs, and in caves across the galaxy. Liet didn't know. His father might have been intrigued by the mystery, but Liet considered himself more practical.

Preparing for the day's work, he looked over at Stilgar, whose eyes had begun to turn blue-within-blue. For years the people here had stubbornly denied themselves the use of melange, but Stilgar called it a sacred reward from the desert, a gift from Shai-Hulud. He had small groups harvesting spice for their own uses, and Liet knew that spice was like a velvet chain – pleasant enough, until one tried to break free of it.

Two chattering and flirtatious teenage girls brought the men breakfast on a tray, knowing what Stilgar and Liet preferred for their morning meal. The girls were lovely, but so *young*. Liet knew they saw only his youthful body, not knowing how many years he carried in his mind. At times like these, he truly missed his wife Faroula, Chani's mother. But that had been so long ago . . .

Stilgar, however, remained the same. After they finished their coffee and sweet cakes, Liet stood and clapped his friend on the shoulder. 'Today we will go out into the deep dunes and plant weather devices. We need better resolution to track the desiccation patterns.'

'Why do you obsess over details? The desert is the desert. It will always be hot and dry, and here on Qelso it will keep growing.' The former naib did not see anything particularly tragic or wrong with the dying ecosystem. To Stilgar, it was the natural order of things. 'Shai-Hulud continues to build his domain no matter what you do.'

'The scientist pursues knowledge,' Liet said, and his companion had no answer for that.

Taking one of the small flyers the *Ithaca* had left behind, he had gone to the northern and as yet undamaged latitudes where the forests stood tall, the rivers flowed, and snowcaps crowned the mountains. Cities and towns still flourished in the valleys and on the hillsides, though the people knew they would all be gone before long. Var's commandos were poignantly reminded every day of how much they were missing, how much they had lost. Stilgar did not see it.

The two friends, along with a group of rugged volunteers, donned newly manufactured stillsuits and adjusted the fittings. When the commandos marched into the open desert, they walked in single file on the dunes. Liet had them practice the random stutter-step that would not attract a worm. The yellow sun grew swiftly hotter, reflecting off the granular sands, but they plodded onward, practicing their lives here. Far in the distance Liet saw the rusty-brown smear of powdery smoke that indicated a spice blow, and he thought he saw the rippling tracks of a worm moving out there.

Stilgar shouted and pointed up at the sky. The desert men instinctively clustered together in a defensive formation.

Hundreds of huge metallic ships suddenly descended, made of angular plates bristling with weapons and powered by enormous engines. The vessels looked like nothing Liet had ever seen before. Enemy ships?

For a moment he hoped the *Ithaca* had returned with them, but these were unlike the no-ship and unusual in their formation, moving in a coordinated fashion. They dropped indiscriminately onto the open desert, scattering sand and flattening dunes. Their pilots seemed oblivious to the fact that the dull vibrations would attract sandworms. As Liet stood gaping at the ships' sheer size, he had no doubt that their weapons could brush aside a worm attack as if it were no more than a nuisance.

The dusty commandos looked to the two gholas for answers. Liet had none, though, and despite the impossible odds, Stilgar appeared ready to attack, if need be.

With an ominous humming and clanking, the ships extended support struts and raised themselves on thick, powerful anchors. Then numerous doors began to open, turning loose an army of metal-skinned machines: heavy lifters, ground crushers, and excavators. Moving on treads, the lumbering self-guided behemoths crawled across the dunes. Behind them marched ranks of heavyset metal robots that smashed forward like deadly warriors . . . or were they workers? Helpers?

The commandos had only small weapons. Some of the eager ones drew their projectile launchers, dropped to their knees on the soft sand, and took aim. 'Wait!' Liet cried.

A hatch at the top of the largest landed ship opened and a pale form emerged, stepping out onto an observation platform. A human form. When the man called down to them, his voice echoed in an eerie chorus transmitted from thousands of speakerpatches on the lines of machine forces. 'Stilgar and Liet-Kynes! Don't be so quick to declare yourselves our enemies.'

'Who are you?' Stilgar shouted defiantly. 'Come down here so that we may speak to you face to face.'

'I thought you would recognize me.'

Liet did. 'It's Duncan – Duncan Idaho!'

Flanked by an honor guard of robots and accompanied by a troop of human workers wearing outfits that Liet did not recognize, Duncan came down to stand with them on the dunes. 'Liet and Stilgar, we left you here to face the onslaught of the desert. You said this was your calling.'

'It *is*,' Stilgar said.

'And the Jews? Are they here with you?'

'They formed a sietch of their own. They are thriving and happy.'

Duncan's honor guard stepped forward, women in black singlesuits and similarly garbed men who walked beside the females as equals. One of the women wore insignia and carried an air of command. He introduced her as his daughter Janess. 'I confronted the Enemy, the thinking machines, and ended the war.' He extended his hands, and all of the robot workers turned to face him. The awesome ships themselves seemed to be alive and aware of every move Duncan made. 'I have found a way to bring us all together.'

'You surrendered to thinking machines,' Stilgar said, his tone acidic.

'Not at all. I decided to show my humanity by not annihilating them. In many solar systems, they are building great things, achieving impressive works on planets inhospitable to humans. We work for the same purpose now, and I have brought them here to assist you.'

'Assist us?' one of the commandos said. 'How can they help? They're just machines.'

'They are allies. You face an insurmountable task. With as many robot crews as you require, I can help you accomplish what you need.' Duncan's dark eyes glittered, as he watched from a million eyes all at once. 'We can build a barrier against the desert, stop the sandtrout from spreading, and keep the water on a portion of the continent. Shai-Hulud will have his domain, while the rest of Qelso remains relatively unscathed. Humans can have their lives and slowly learn to adapt to the desert, but only if they choose to.'

'Impossible,' Liet said. 'How can a force of worker robots stand against the tide of the desert?'

Duncan flashed a confident smile. 'Don't underestimate them – or me. I fill the roles of both Kwisatz Haderach and Omnius. I guide all the factions of humanity and control the entire Synchronized Empire.' He shrugged, and smiled. 'Saving one planet is well within the scope of my capabilities.'

Liet couldn't believe what he was hearing. 'You can stop the desert and turn back the worms?'

'Qelso will be both desert and forest, as I am both human and machine.' At a gesture and a thought from Duncan, the massive excavating equipment rumbled out into the sand, heading toward the boundary where the dunes met the still-living landscape.

Liet and Stilgar followed Duncan, who walked ahead

of the heavy convoy. As a planetologist, a ghola, and a human being, Liet had innumerable questions. But for now, watching the machines begin their work, he decided to wait and see what the future held.

When Leto II envisioned his Golden Path, he foresaw the direction that humankind should take, but he had blind spots. He failed to see that he was not the ultimate Kwisatz Haderach.

                    – Bene Gesserit fact-finding commission

In the eleven years Jessica had been back home, she had realized more and more that some things did not add up. This planet might indeed be Caladan, or Dan, but this was not the same home she and her Duke had loved so long ago.

On a stormy evening, as she walked through the restored castle, the incongruous details finally became more than she could bear. Pausing in an upper hallway, she opened a finely carved elaccawood cabinet, an antique that some decorator had placed there. This time, she stood staring at the ornate interior, and on impulse pressed a wooden extrusion in one corner. To her surprise, a panel opened, and inside she found a small blue statuette of a griffin. Perhaps placed there by the Baron ghola, the griffin was the ancient symbol of House Harkonnen. He must have hidden it there as a clever reminder of the falseness of the castle.

As she stared at the statuette, feeling the wrongness of

the object, she considered all of her hard work since returning to Caladan. She had directed crews of local laborers to dismantle the Baron's torture devices and the Face Dancer Khrone's offensive laboratories from the underground chambers. Through it all she had worked side by side with the cleaning teams, sweating and angry as she scrubbed away every stain, every odor, every hint of the unwanted presence. But Castle Caladan still reeked with reminders. How could she make a fresh start when so much of the past – at least this awkward, out-of-focus echo of the past – hung all around her?

Behind her, moving silently, Dr Yueh said, 'Are you all right, my Lady?'

She looked at the Suk doctor. He wore an expression of deep concern on his buttery face; his dark lips turned downward as he waited for an answer.

'Everywhere I turn, I am reminded of the Baron.' She frowned at the griffin figurine in her hand. 'Some of the articles in this castle are authentic, such as that dropleaf desk with the hawk crest, but most are bad copies.'

Making up her mind, Jessica stepped to a segmented window at the end of the hall and swung it open to let in the stormy night air. In a dramatic gesture, she hurled the griffin figurine out to the crashing sea. The waves would soon erode it and break it into unrecognizable pieces. A suitable fate for the Harkonnen icon.

A cold, wet wind whispered into the hall, bringing spatters of rain. Outside, scudding clouds parted to reveal a crescent moon on the horizon, casting cold yellow light on the water.

Moments later she tore down a wall tapestry that she had never liked, and was about to throw that out the window, too, but – not wanting to spoil this beautiful planet – she instead tossed the tapestry on the floor, promising herself to cast it on the trash heap the following morning. 'Maybe I should just tear this whole place down, Wellington. Can we ever remove the taint?'

Yueh was shocked at the suggestion. 'My Lady, this is the ancestral home of House Atreides. What would Duke Leto—'

'This is a mere reconstruction, fraught with errors.' A gusting breeze blew her bronze hair away from her face.

'Maybe we waste too much time trying to recreate what we see in our old memories, my Lady. Why not build and decorate your home as you choose?'

She blinked as cold rain blew into her face, drenching her jade green dress and wetting the rug. 'I thought this place would help my Leto, give him comfort, but maybe it was more for me than for him.'

A ten-year-old boy with coal-black hair came running down the hall, his smoke gray eyes widening with excitement and alarm when he saw the open window. He was even more surprised when neither Jessica nor Yueh reacted to the blowing rain that drenched the rugs and tapestries. 'What's happening?'

'I was considering moving somewhere else, Leto. Would you like me to find us a normal home in the village? Maybe we'd be happier down there, away from this pampered life.'

'But I like this castle! It's a Duke's castle.' Jessica could not think of her Leto as a child. He wore fishing dungarees and a striped shirt, just like the ones he had worn when Jessica had first come to Caladan as a concubine purchased from the Bene Gesserit. The young nobleman had put a knife to her throat that day, a bluff . . .

Yueh smiled. 'A Duke . . . Such titles no longer mean

anything with the Imperium long gone. Do the people of Caladan even need a Duke anymore?'

Jessica's reaction was automatic, making her realize she had not thought through her notion. 'The people still need leaders, no matter what title we use. And we can be good leaders, as House Atreides has always been in the past. My Leto will be a good Duke.'

The boy's eyes glittered as he listened with rapt attention. Beyond his youthful features, Jessica could see the seeds of the man she loved. This young Atreides was among the first of a new generation of gholas produced by Scytale. The baby had been shipped to Caladan and christened there – just as the original Paul had been.

Since leaving Synchrony, Jessica and Yueh had struggled to recover here, endeavoring in the process to bring back a degree of glory to the quiet water world. The tangled threads of their initial and ghola lives made them ironic allies, two people with shared tragedies and shared pasts. Finally, though he could never have his beloved Wanna back, Yueh had found some measure of peace.

Jessica, though, knew that her true Duke waited for her. Eventually he would grow to manhood. When he got his memories back, his physical age would not matter.

Jessica's partnership with Leto would be unusual, but no stranger than the relationships of all the mismatched gholas that had grown up on the no-ship. As a Bene Gesserit, she could slow her own aging process, and with melange readily available from the operations on Chapterhouse, Buzzell, and Qelso, they could both enjoy extended lives. She would prepare Leto, and when the time was right, she would help trigger his true awakening. Miraculously, he would once again be the man she loved, with all his thoughts and memories.

She only had to wait a decade or two. As a Bene Gesserit, she could be patient.

Jessica grasped his small hand. This time there would be no political reason to prevent them from getting married, if that was what he wanted, and she wanted. It only mattered to her that they would be together again.

'Everything will be the same when you finally remember, Leto. And everything will be different.'

The future is around all of us, and it looks very much like the past.

— MOTHER SUPERIOR SHEEANA,
at the founding of the Orthodox School on Synchrony

The mangled and permanently grounded *Ithaca* had become the new headquarters building for Sheeana's splinter group. Innovative human architects in conjunction with construction robots had remodeled the large vessel into a unique and imposing headquarters. The navigation bridge, the highest deck on the no-ship, had been opened up and converted into an observation tower.

Mother Superior Sheeana stared across the breathtaking, rebuilt city of Synchrony. Dipping into her deep reservoir of memories, she drew parallels to one of the original Bene Gesserit schools on Wallach IX, which had also been founded in an urban setting. Here many of the machine spires remained, and some even moved as they had before, processing materials in automated industries.

Years ago, Duncan and the willing machines had helped her reconstruct the unusual metropolis, though he balanced his 'miraculous' work with the necessity of letting the humans achieve their own successes. He and Sheeana knew the dangers of letting people grow too soft, and he had no intention of allowing them to rely on him for things they could do for themselves. Humankind needed to solve its own problems as much as possible.

At the same time, clusters of thinking machines had begun to grow apart, given manageable goals, inhabiting niches unbearable to humans: blasted planets, frozen asteroids, empty moons. The galaxy was a vast place, and so little of it was suitable for biological life. There would be more lebensraum than any empire could possibly need.

Some of the robots had started showing traits of personalities, unique characters of their own. Duncan suggested that, in time, these could eventually become some of the greatest thinkers and philosophers history had ever known. Sheeana remained unconvinced of this, and vowed that her special trainees here would prove him wrong with their own superior achievements.

Every month fresh candidates came to join the orthodox Bene Gesserit center on Synchrony, while others joined Murbella's New Sisterhood on Chapterhouse. Surmounting early difficulties, the two orders now worked in harmony with one another. Sheeana and her stricter ways attracted a different sort of acolyte, which she knew would have pleased Garimi. Sheeana tested the applicants harshly and rejected all but the most acceptable. Far away, Murbella's order had its own attractions. In this new universe, there was plenty of room for both views.

Sheeana's conventional Bene Gesserit breeding program was in full swing now, and it warmed her heart to see so many pregnant women each day. She counted seven of them outside among the people leaving and entering the headquarters. The sight gave her confidence that her order would expand and continue into humanity's future.

Later that day, the Tleilaxu Master Scytale contacted Sheeana on the navigation bridge that had become her center of operations. Transmitting from one of his Synchrony laboratories, he actually sounded cheerful now instead of harried. 'I finished cataloguing the remaining cells and sifted out all traces of Face Dancer contamination. We must introduce some of those traits into the Bene Gesserit again.'

'After Duncan, we will breed no further Kwisatz Haderachs. It's not even a matter for discussion.' As far as she was concerned, many things did not need to occur again . . .

I merely mean to preserve our knowledge. It's like finding the seeds of long-forgotten but beautiful plants. We shouldn't just discard them.'

'Perhaps not, but we must set up strict fail-safe mechanisms.'

Scytale did not seem bothered by the restrictions Sheeana was placing on him. 'I honestly feel that the Tleilaxu race will recover their lost knowledge.' Quickly he added, 'With changes for the better, of course.'

'For the advancement of humankind,' Sheeana said.

She had never known him to work so hard. Scytale had used the cells in his nullentropy capsule to regrow gholas of the last Tleilaxu Council, and now the little ones followed him everywhere, reminding her of a mother duck trailed by ducklings.

Scytale raised the group in a manner different than was traditional for Tleilaxu males. In separate quarters, he was also raising Tleilaxu females – from newly discovered cells – though they would never be relegated to the horrific, degrading conditions their predecessors had endured. Never again would Tleilaxu females be forced to become axlotl tanks, so there would be no chance of creating another set of ferocious, vengeful enemies like the Honored Matres. In particular, Sheeana and her Sisters would monitor the council members closely, keeping watch to ensure that they did not corrupt the Tleilaxu people as they had before.

There were still axlotl tanks, of course – some women volunteered for personal reasons, while others left instructions for their bodies to be converted in the event of serious accidents. As always, the Bene Gesserits met their own needs.

After she ended the conference with Scytale, the Mother Superior gazed through the broad windows of the navigation bridge. Far away on the horizon, beyond the redefined boundaries of the gleaming city, the ground was churned and torn up, and many of the geometric structures built by Omnius lay toppled and crushed into rubble.

She adjusted one of the windows, increasing its magnification. From this vantage point she could see the new desert and one of the sandworms rising up from the debris, its eyeless head questing about. Then the creature smashed down hard, breaking part of a wall. Like huge, determined earthworms churning the soil, they had begun the process of converting the abandoned buildings into the desert they preferred.

Soon, Sheeana thought, she would go and speak to them again.

She looked down at the little girl at her side and grasped her small hand. Perhaps one day she would even take her protégée with her, the young ghola of Serena Butler.

It was never too early to start preparing Serena for her role.

The desert has a beauty I could not forget in a thousand lifetimes.

— PAUL MUAD'DIB ATREIDES

Bathed in the golden rays of sunset, two figures made their way along the crest of a dune, their steps irregular so that they did not attract the huge sandworms. The pair walked side by side, inseparable.

It was warm on Dune, but not like old times. Because of the severe damage to the environment, the weather had cooled and the atmosphere had thinned. But with the return of the worms, along with sandplankton and sandtrout bursting through the cracked shell of glassy dunes, the old planet had begun to come back. As Chani's father Liet-Kynes used to say, everything on Dune was tied together, an entire ecosystem that included the land, the available water, and the air.

And, thanks to Duncan Idaho, an extensive work force of hardened machines continued the excavation process in latitudes where the sandworms had not yet returned. Methodically, the mechanical army prepared the old sand section by section, opening the way for worms to expand their territory. Massive planting and fertilization work performed by powerful thinking-machine tractors and excavators had stabilized the seared ground, establishing a new biomatrix, while Paul's hardy settlers monitored the growth and did their own work alongside. Through his wide-reaching thoughts, Duncan made sure the thinking machines understood what Dune had once been, before outsiders meddled with its ecosystem. Misused technology had devastated the desert planet, and now technology would help bring it back.

Paul stopped a hundred meters from the nearest rock formation, where a work crew had found the ruins of an abandoned sietch. With a small group of determined settlers, he and Chani had been salvaging the Fremen habitat with their own hands. Reclaiming the old ways.

In bygone days, he had been the legendary Muad'Dib, leading a Fremen army. Now he was content to be a modern-day Fremen, a leader of 753 people who had established austere homes in the rocks, which were on the way to becoming thriving sietches.

Paul and Chani flew out regularly with survey crews. Instilled with fresh optimism, he saw the magnificent potential for Dune. Near the excavated sietch, he had discovered an underground grotto that he and his followers planned to irrigate and artificially illuminate, to support a planting project for grasses, tubers, flowers, and shrubs. Enough to support a small population of new Fremen, but not enough to shift the desert ecosystem that the new worms were recreating, year after year.

One day, he might even ride the great worms again.

Paul turned to see the pale yellow sunrise appearing over the ocean of sand. 'Dune is reawakening. Just as we are.'

Chani smiled, seeing both her beloved Usul of memory and the ghola she had grown up with. She loved each

Paul for himself. Her abdomen protruded just a little, where their growing baby was beginning to show its presence. In five months, it would be the first child born on the recently resettled planet. In her second lifetime Chani did not need to worry about Imperial schemes, hidden contraceptives, or poisoned food. Her pregnancy would be normal, and the child – or children, if they were again blessed with twins – would have great potential, without the curse of terrible purpose.

Chani, even more in touch with the weather than he was, turned her face into a cool breeze. The sunrise began to show a new richness of coppery colors from dust stirred into the air. 'We'd better get back to the sietch, Usul. A storm is brewing.' He watched her glide forward gracefully, her red hair blowing behind her. Chani sang the walking song of lovers on the sand, her words lilting beautifully and in a stutter rhythm, like the cadence of her feet:

> 'Tell me of thine eyes
> And I will tell thee of thy heart.
> Tell me of thy feet
> And I will tell thee of thy hands.
> Tell me of thy sleeping
> And I will tell thee of thy waking.
> Tell me of thy desires
> And I will tell thee of thy need.'

When they were halfway back to the rocks, the wind picked up. Blowing sand stung their faces. Paul held onto Chani, doing his best to shelter her with his own body against the abrasive wind.

'Yes, a fine storm is brewing,' she said, as they finally

reached the sietch entrance and hurried inside. 'A cleansing one.' In the low light of a glowglobe, exhilaration flushed her features.

Catching her by the arm, Paul spun her around and wiped sand from around her eyes and mouth. Then he drew her close and kissed her. Chani seemed to melt into his arms, laughing. 'So you have finally learned how to treat your wife!'

'My Sihaya,' he said as he held her, 'I have loved you for five thousand years.'

MARCEL PROUST

REMEMBRANCE
OF THINGS PAST

*"When to the sessions of sweet silent thought
I summon up remembrance of things past . . ."*

VOLUME THREE
THE CAPTIVE
THE FUGITIVE
TIME REGAINED

*Translated by C. K. Scott Moncrieff and
Terence Kilmartin; and by Andreas Mayor*

PENGUIN BOOKS

PENGUIN BOOKS

Published by the Penguin Group
Penguin Books Ltd, 27 Wrights Lane, London W8 5TZ, England
Penguin Books USA Inc., 375 Hudson Street, New York, New York 10014, USA
Penguin Books Australia Ltd, Ringwood, Victoria, Australia
Penguin Books Canada Ltd, 10 Alcorn Avenue, Toronto, Ontario, Canada M4V 3B2
Penguin Books (NZ) Ltd, 182–190 Wairau Road, Auckland 10, New Zealand

Penguin Books Ltd, Registered Offices: Harmondsworth, Middlesex, England

This translation first published in Great Britain by Chatto & Windus 1981
Published in Penguin Books 1983
Reprinted in Penguin Classics 1986
Reprinted in Penguin Books 1989

5 7 9 10 8 6 4

Printed in England by Clays Ltd, St Ives plc
Set in Garamond

CONTENTS

*

Numerals in the text refer the reader to explanatory notes while asterisks indicate the position of textual addenda. The notes and the addenda follow the text in each volume.

THE CAPTIVE

THE CAPTIVE

AT daybreak, my face still turned to the wall, and before I had seen above the big window-curtains what tone the first streaks of light assumed, I could already tell what the weather was like. The first sounds from the street had told me, according to whether they came to my ears deadened and distorted by the moisture of the atmosphere or quivering like arrows in the resonant, empty expanses of a spacious, frosty, pure morning; as soon as I heard the rumble of the first tramcar, I could tell whether it was sodden with rain or setting forth into the blue. And perhaps these sounds had themselves been forestalled by some swifter and more pervasive emanation which, stealing into my sleep, diffused in it a melancholy that seemed to presage snow or gave utterance (through the lips of a little person who occasionally reappeared there) to so many hymns to the glory of the sun that, having first of all begun to smile in my sleep, having prepared my eyes, behind their shut lids, to be dazzled, I would awake finally amid deafening strains of music. It was, in fact, principally from my bedroom that I took in the life of the outer world during this period. I know that Bloch reported that, when he called to see me in the evenings, he could hear the sound of conversation; as my mother was at Combray and he never found anybody in my room, he concluded that I was talking to myself. When, much later, he learned that Albertine had been staying with me at the time, and realised that I had concealed her presence from all my friends, he declared that he saw at last the reason why, during that phase of my life, I had always refused to go out of doors. He was wrong. His mistake was, however, perfectly excusable, for the truth, even if it is logically necessary, is not always foreseeable as a whole. People who learn some correct detail about another person's life at once draw conclusions from it which are not accurate, and see in the newly discovered fact an explanation of things that have no connexion with it whatsoever.

When I reflect now that, on our return from Balbec, Albertine had come to live in Paris under the same roof as myself, that she had abandoned the idea of going on a cruise, that she was installed in a bedroom within twenty paces of my own, at the end of the corridor, in my father's tapestried study, and that late every night, before leaving me, she used to slide her tongue between my lips like a portion of daily bread, a nourishing food that had the almost sacred character of all flesh upon which the sufferings that we have endured on its account have come in time to confer a sort of spiritual grace, what I at once call to mind in comparison is not the night that Captain de Borodino allowed me to spend in barracks, a favour which cured what was after all only a passing distemper, but the night on which my father sent Mamma to sleep in the little bed beside mine. Life, when it chooses to deliver us once more, against all expectation, from sufferings that seemed inescapable, does so in different, at times diametrically opposed conditions, so much so that it seems almost sacrilegious to note the identical nature of the consolations vouchsafed!

When Albertine had heard from Françoise that, in the darkness of my still curtained room, I was not asleep, she had no qualms about disturbing me as she performed her ablutions in her bathroom. Then, frequently, instead of waiting until later in the day, I would repair to my own bathroom, which adjoined hers and was a very agreeable place. Time was when a stage manager would spend hundreds of thousands of francs to begem with real emeralds the throne upon which a great actress would play the part of an empress. The Russian ballet has taught us that simple lighting effects, if trained upon the right spot, will beget jewels as gorgeous and more varied. This decoration, already more ethereal, is not so pleasing, however, as that which, at eight o'clock in the morning, the sun substitutes for what we were accustomed to see when we did not rise before noon. The windows of our respective bathrooms, so that their occupants might not be visible from without, were not smooth and transparent but crinkled with an artificial and old-fashioned hoar-frost. All of a sudden, the

sun would colour this muslin glass, gild it, and, gently
disclosing in my person an earlier young man whom habit had
long concealed, would intoxicate me with memories, as
though I were in the heart of the country amidst golden foliage
in which even a bird was not lacking. For I could hear Albertine ceaselessly humming:

> For melancholy
> Is but folly,
> And he who heeds it is a fool.

I was too fond of her not to be able to spare a smile for her
bad taste in music. This song had, as it happened, during the
past summer, delighted Mme Bontemps, who presently heard
people say that it was silly, with the result that, instead of
asking Albertine to sing it when she had company, she would
substitute:

> A song of farewell rises from troubled springs,

which in its turn became "an old jingle of Massenet's the
child is always dinning into our ears."

A cloud passed, blotting out the sun; I saw the prudish,
leafy screen of glass grow dim and revert to a grey monochrome.

The partition that divided our two dressing-rooms (Albertine's, identical with my own, was a bathroom which Mamma,
who had another at the opposite end of the flat, had never
used for fear of disturbing my rest) was so thin that we could
talk to each other as we washed in double privacy, carrying
on a conversation that was interrupted only by the sound of
the water, in that intimacy which is so often permitted in hotels
by the smallness and proximity of the rooms but which, in
private houses in Paris, is so rare.

On other mornings, I would remain in bed, drowsing for as
long as I chose, for orders had been given that no one was to
enter my room until I had rung the bell, an act which, owing
to the awkward position in which the electric push had been
hung above my bed, took such a time that often, tired of
feeling for it and glad to be left alone, I would lie back for

some moments and almost fall asleep again. It was not that I was wholly indifferent to Albertine's presence in the house. Her separation from her girl friends had succeeded in sparing my heart any fresh anguish. It kept it in a state of repose, in a semi-immobility which would help it to recover. But this calm which my mistress procured for me was an assuagement of suffering rather than a positive joy. Not that it did not enable me to taste many joys from which the intensity of my anguish had debarred me, but, far from my owing them to Albertine, who in any case I no longer found very pretty and with whom I was bored, with whom I was indeed clearly conscious that I was not in love, I tasted these joys on the contrary when Albertine was not with me. And so, to begin the morning, I did not send for her at once, especially if it was a fine day. For some moments, knowing that he would make me happier than Albertine, I remained closeted with the little person inside me, the melodious hymner of the rising sun, of whom I have already spoken. Of the different persons who compose our personality, it is not the most obvious that are the most essential. In myself, when ill health has succeeded in uprooting them one after another, there will still remain two or three endowed with a hardier constitution than the rest, notably a certain philosopher who is happy only when he has discovered between two works of art, between two sensations, a common element. But I have sometimes wondered whether the last of all might not be this little mannikin, very similar to another whom the optician at Combray used to set up in his shop window to forecast the weather, and who, doffing his hood when the sun shone, would put it on again if it was going to rain. I know how selfish this little mannikin is; I may be suffering from an attack of breathlessness which only the coming of rain would assuage, but he pays no heed, and, at the first drops so impatiently awaited, all his gaiety forgotten, he sullenly pulls down his hood. Conversely, I dare say that in my last agony, when all my other "selves" are dead, if a ray of sunshine steals into the room while I am drawing my last breath, the little barometric mannikin will feel a great relief, and will throw back his hood to sing: "Ah, fine weather at last!"

I would ring for Françoise. I would open the *Figaro*. I

would scan its columns and ascertain that it did not contain an article, or so-called article, which I had sent to the editor, and which was no more than a slightly revised version of the page that had recently come to light, written long ago in Dr Percepied's carriage, as I gazed at the spires of Martinville. Then I would read Mamma's letter. She found it odd, if not shocking, that a girl should be living alone with me. On the first day, at the moment of leaving Balbec, when she saw how wretched I was and was worried about leaving me by myself, my mother had perhaps been glad when she heard that Albertine was travelling with us and saw that, side by side with our own boxes (those boxes among which I had spent the night in tears in the hotel at Balbec) Albertine's too—narrow and black, having for me the appearance of coffins, and as to which I did not know whether they would bring life or death to our house—had been loaded on to the "twister." But I had never even asked myself the question, being all overjoyed, in the radiant morning, after the fear of having to remain at Balbec, that I was taking Albertine with me. But if at the start my mother had not been hostile to this proposal (speaking kindly to my friend like a mother whose son has been seriously wounded and who is grateful to the young mistress who is nursing him with loving care), she had become so now that it had been all too completely realised and the girl was prolonging her sojourn in our house, moreover in the absence of my parents. I cannot, however, say that my mother ever openly manifested this hostility to me. As in the past, when she had ceased to dare to reproach me with my nervous instability and my laziness, now she had qualms—which perhaps I did not altogether perceive or did not wish to perceive at the time— about running the risk, by offering any criticism of the girl to whom I had told her that I intended to make an offer of marriage, of casting a shadow over my life, making me in time to come less devoted to my wife, of sowing perhaps, for a season when she herself would no longer be there, the seeds of remorse at having grieved her by marrying Albertine. Mamma preferred to seem to be approving a choice which she felt herself powerless to make me reconsider. But all the people who saw her at that time have since told me that in addition to her grief at having lost her mother she had an air of constant preoccupation. This mental strife, this inward debate, had the effect of overheating my mother's brow, and she was constantly opening the windows to let in the fresh air. But she failed to come to any decision, for fear of influencing me in the wrong direction and so spoiling what she believed to be my happiness. She could not even bring herself to forbid me to keep Albertine for the time being in our house. She did not wish to appear more strict than Mme Bontemps, who was the person principally concerned, and who saw no harm in the arrangement, which greatly surprised my mother. All the same, she regretted that she had been obliged to leave us together, by departing just at that moment for Combray where she might have to remain (and did in fact remain) for many months, during which my great-aunt required her incessant attention by day and night. Everything was made easier for her down there thanks to the kindness and devotion of Legrandin who, sparing himself no pains, kept putting off his return to Paris from week to week, not that he knew my aunt at all well, but simply, first of all, because she had been his mother's friend, and also because he knew that the invalid, condemned to die, valued his attentions and could not do without him. Snobbery is a grave disease, but it is localised and so does not utterly corrupt the soul. I, on the other hand, unlike Mamma, was extremely glad of her absence at Combray, but for which I should have been afraid (being unable to tell Albertine to conceal it) of her learning of the girl's friendship with Mlle Vinteuil. This would have been to my mother an insurmountable obstacle, not merely to a marriage about which she had meanwhile begged me to say nothing definite as yet to Albertine, and the thought of which was becoming more and more intolerable to myself, but even to the latter's being allowed to stay for any length of time in the house. Failing so grave a reason, of which she was not aware, Mamma, through the dual effect of the edifying and liberating example of my grandmother, according to whom, in her admiration of George Sand, virtue consisted in nobility of soul, and of my own corrupting influence, was now indulgent towards women whose conduct she would have condemned in the past, or

even now had they been any of her own middle-class friends
in Paris or Combray, but whose large-heartedness I extolled to her
and whom she forgave much because of their affection for me.

However all this may be, and even apart from any question
of propriety, I doubt whether Mamma could have put up with
Albertine, since she had retained from Combray, from my aunt
Léonie, from all her kindred, habits of punctuality and order of
which my mistress had not the remotest conception. She
would never think of shutting a door and, by the same token,
would no more hesitate to enter a room if the door stood open
than would a dog or a cat. Her somewhat inconvenient charm
was, in fact, that of behaving in the household not so much
like a girl as like a domestic animal which comes into a room
and goes out again and is to be found wherever one least
expects to find it, and she would often—something that I
found profoundly restful—come and lie down beside me on
my bed, making a place for herself from which she never
stirred, without disturbing me as a person would have done.
She ended, however, by conforming to my hours of sleep, and
not only never attempted to enter my room but would take
care not to make a sound until I had rung my bell. It was
Françoise who impressed these rules of conduct upon her.
She was one of those Combray servants, conscious of their
master's place in the world, who feel that the least that they
can do is to see that he is treated with all the respect to which
they consider him entitled. When a stranger on leaving after a
visit gave Françoise a tip to be shared with the kitchenmaid,
he had barely slipped his coin into her hand before Françoise,
with an unparalleled display of speed, tact and energy, had
passed the word to the kitchenmaid who came forward to
thank him, not in a murmur, but openly and clearly, as Françoise had told her that she must do. The parish priest of Combray was no genius, but he also knew what was right and
proper. Under his instruction, the daughter of some Protestant
cousins of Mme Sazerat's had been converted to Catholicism,
and her family had behaved impeccably towards him. There
was a question of her marrying a young nobleman of Méséglise.
The young man's parents wrote to inquire about her in a
somewhat arrogant letter, in which they expressed contempt

for her Protestant origin. The priest replied in such a tone that the Méséglise nobleman, crushed and grovelling, wrote a second, very different letter in which he begged as the most precious favour the award of the girl's hand in marriage.

Françoise deserved no special credit for making Albertine respect my slumbers. She was imbued with the tradition. From her studied silence, or the peremptory response that she made to a proposal to enter my room, or to send in some message to me, which Albertine had expressed in all innocence, the latter realised with astonishment that she was now living in an alien world, where strange customs prevailed, governed by rules of conduct which one must never dream of infringing. She had already had a forewarning of this at Balbec, but, in Paris, made no attempt to resist, and would wait patiently every morning for the sound of my bell before venturing to make any noise.

The training that Françoise gave her was also salutary for our old servant herself, in that it gradually stilled the lamentations which, ever since our return from Balbec, she had not ceased to utter. For, just as we were boarding the train, she had remembered that she had failed to say good-bye to the housekeeper of the hotel, a mustachioed lady who looked after the bedroom floors and barely knew Françoise by sight, but had been comparatively civil to her. Françoise insisted on getting out of the train, going back to the hotel, saying good-bye to the housekeeper, and postponing her departure for Paris until the following day. Common sense, coupled with my sudden horror of Balbec, restrained me from granting her this concession, but my refusal had infected her with a morbid ill-humour which the change of air had not sufficed to cure and which lingered on in Paris. For, according to Françoise's code, as illustrated in the carvings of Saint-André-des-Champs, to wish for the death of an enemy, or even to inflict it, is not forbidden, but it is a horrible sin not to do the right thing, not to return a civility, to omit, like a regular churl, to say good-bye to the housekeeper before leaving a hotel. Throughout the journey, the continually recurring memory of her not having taken leave of this woman had dyed Françoise's cheeks with a scarlet flush that was quite alarming. And if she refused to eat or drink until we reached Paris, it was perhaps because this memory was a real "weight" on her stomach (every social class has its own pathology) even more than with the intention of punishing us.

Among the reasons which led Mamma to write me a letter every day, a letter which never failed to include some quotation from Mme de Sévigné, was the memory of my grandmother. Mamma would write to me: "Mme Sazerat gave us one of those little luncheons of which she possesses the secret and which, as your poor grandmother would have said, quoting Mme de Sévigné, deprive us of solitude without affording us company." In one of my earlier replies I was inept enough to write to Mamma: "By those quotations, your mother would recognise you at once." Which brought me, three days later, the reproof: "My poor boy, if it was to speak to me of *my mother*, your reference to Mme de Sévigné was most inappropriate. She would have answered you as she answered Mme de Grignan: 'So she was nothing to you? I had supposed that you were related.'"

By this time, I would hear my mistress leaving or returning to her room. I would ring the bell, for it was time now for Andrée to arrive with the chauffeur, Morel's friend, lent me by the Verdurins, to take Albertine out. I had spoken to the latter of the remote possibility of our marriage; but I had never made her any formal promise; she herself, from discretion, when I said to her: "I don't know, but it might perhaps be possible," had shaken her head with a melancholy smile, as much as to say "Oh, no it won't," which meant: "I'm too poor." And so, while I continued to say: "Nothing could be less certain" when speaking of plans for the future, for the present I did everything in my power to amuse her, to make her life agreeable, with perhaps the unconscious design of thereby making her wish to marry me. She herself laughed at my lavish generosity. "Andrée's mother would pull a bit of a face if she saw me turn into a rich lady like herself, what she calls a lady who has her own 'horses, carriages, pictures.' What? Did I never tell you that she says that. Oh, she's quite a type! What surprises me is that she raises pictures to the same dignity as horses and carriages."

We shall see in due course that, in spite of stupid habits of speech which she had not outgrown, Albertine had developed to an astonishing degree. This was a matter of complete indifference to me, a woman's intellectual qualities never having interested me much. Céleste's curious genius alone might perhaps appeal to me. In spite of myself, I would continue to smile for some moments, when, for instance, having ascertained that Albertine was not in my room, she accosted me with: "Heavenly deity perched on a bed!" "But why, Céleste," I would say, "why deity?" "Oh, if you suppose that you have anything in common with the mortals who make their pilgrimage on our vile earth, you are greatly mistaken!" "But why 'perched' on a bed? Can't you see that I'm lying in bed?" "You never lie. Who ever saw anybody lie like that? You've just alighted there. With your white pyjamas, and the way you twist your neck, you look for all the world like a dove."

Albertine, even in the discussion of the most trivial matters, expressed herself very differently from the little girl that she had been only a few years earlier at Balbec. She would go so far as to declare, in connection with a political incident of which she disapproved: "I consider that fearsome," and I am not sure that it was not about this time that she learned to say, when she wanted to indicate that she thought a book badly-written: "It's interesting, but really, it might have been written *by a pig*."

The rule that she must not enter my room until I had rung amused her greatly. As she had adopted our family habit of quotation, and in following it drew upon the plays in which she had acted at her convent and for which I had expressed a liking, she always compared me to Assuerus:[1]

> And death is the reward of whoso dares
> To venture in his presence unawares. . . .
> None is exempt; nor is there any whom
> Or rank or sex can save from such a doom;
> Even I myself . . .
> Like all the rest, I by this law am bound;
> And, to address him, I must first be found
> By him, or he must call me to his side.

Physically, too, she had changed. Her blue, almond-shaped eyes—now even more elongated—had altered in appearance;

they were indeed of the same colour, but seemed to have passed into a liquid state. So much so that, when she closed them, it was as though a pair of curtains had been drawn to shut out a view of the sea. It was no doubt this aspect of her person that I remembered most vividly each night on leaving her. For, quite contrarily, every morning the ripple of her hair, for instance, continued to give me the same surprise, as though it were some novelty that I had never seen before. And yet, above the smiling eyes of a girl, what could be more beautiful than that clustering coronet of black violets? The smile offers greater friendship; but the little gleaming coils of blossoming hair, more akin to the flesh of which they seem to be a transposition into tiny wavelets, are more provocative of desire.

As soon as she entered my room, she would spring on to my bed and sometimes would expatiate upon my type of intellect, would vow in a transport of sincerity that she would sooner die than leave me: this was on mornings when I had shaved before sending for her. She was one of those women who can never distinguish the cause of what they feel. The pleasure they derive from a fresh complexion they explain to themselves by the moral qualities of the man who seems to offer them a possibility of future happiness, which is capable, however, of diminishing and becoming less compelling the longer he refrains from shaving.

I would inquire where she was thinking of going.

"I believe Andrée wants to take me to the Buttes-Chaumont; I've never been there."

Of course it was impossible for me to discern among so many other words whether beneath these a falsehood lay concealed. Besides, I could trust Andrée to tell me of all the places that she visited with Albertine. At Balbec, when I had felt utterly weary of Albertine, I had made up my mind to say, untruthfully, to Andrée: "My little Andrée, if only I had met you again sooner, it's you that I would have loved! But now my heart is pledged to another. All the same, we can see a great deal of each other, for my love is causing me great unhappiness, and you will help me to find consolation." And now these same lying words had become true within the space of three weeks. Perhaps Andrée had believed in Paris that it was indeed a lie and that I was in love with her, as she would doubtless have believed at Balbec. For the truth is so variable for each of us, that other people have difficulty in recognising what it is. And as I knew that she would tell me everything that she and Albertine had done, I had asked her, and she had agreed, to come and call for Albertine almost every day. Thus I could without anxiety remain at home. Also, Andrée's privileged position as one of the girls of the little band gave me confidence that she would obtain everything I might want from Albertine. Truly, I could have said to her now in all sincerity that she would be capable of setting my mind at rest.

At the same time, my choice of Andrée (who happened to be staying in Paris, having given up her plan of returning to Balbec) as guide and companion to my mistress was prompted by what Albertine had told me of the affection that her friend had felt for me at Balbec, at a time when, on the contrary, I was afraid that I bored her; indeed, if I had known this at the time, it is perhaps with Andrée that I would have fallen in love.

"What, you never knew?" said Albertine, "but we were always joking about it. Do you mean to say you never noticed how she used to copy all your ways of talking and arguing? Especially when she'd just been with you, it was really striking. She had no need to tell us whether she had seen you. As soon as she joined us, we could tell at once. We used to look at one another and laugh. She was like a coalheaver who tries to pretend that he isn't one, although he's black all over. A miller has no need to say that he's a miller—you can see the flour all over his clothes, and the mark of the sacks he has carried on his shoulder. Andrée was just the same, she would twist her eyebrows the way you do, and stretch out her long neck, and I don't know what all. When I pick up a book that has been in your room, even if I'm reading it out of doors, I can tell at once where it's been because it still has a faint whiff of your beastly fumigations. It's only the tiniest thing—I can't really explain—but it's rather a nice thing really. Anyhow whenever anybody spoke nicely about you, seemed to think a lot of you, Andrée was in ecstasies."

Notwithstanding all this, in case there might have been some secret plan made behind my back, I would advise her to give up the Buttes-Chaumont for that day and to go instead to Saint-Cloud or somewhere else.

It was not of course, as I was well aware, that I was the least bit in love with Albertine. Love is no more perhaps than the diffusion of those eddies which, in the wake of an emotion, stir the soul. Certain such eddies had indeed stirred my soul through and through when Albertine spoke to me at Balbec about Mlle Vinteuil, but these were now stilled. I no longer loved Albertine, for I no longer felt anything of the pain I had felt in the train at Balbec on learning how Albertine had spent her adolescence, with visits perhaps to Montjouvain. I had thought about all this for long enough, and it was now healed. But from time to time certain expressions used by Albertine made me suppose—why, I cannot say—that she must in the course of her life, short as it had been, have received many compliments, many declarations, and received them with pleasure, that is to say with sensuality. Thus she would say in any connexion: "Is that true? Is it really true?" Of course, if she had said, like an Odette: "Is it really true, that thumping lie?" I should not have been disturbed, for the very absurdity of the formula would have explained itself as a stupid inanity of feminine wit. But her questioning air: "Is that true?" gave on the one hand the strange impression of a creature incapable of judging things by herself, who relies on your corroboration, as though she were not endowed with the same faculties as yourself (if you said to her: "We've been out for a whole hour," or "It's raining," she would ask: "Is that true?"). Unfortunately, on the other hand, this want of facility in judging external phenomena for herself could not be the real origin of her "Is that true? Is it really true?" It seemed rather that these words had been, from the dawn of her precocious nubility, replies to: "You know, I never saw anybody as pretty as you," or "You know I'm madly in love with you, you excite me terribly"—affirmations that were answered, with a coquettishly acquiescent modesty, by these repetitions of: "Is that true? Is it really true?" which no longer served Albertine, when in my company, save to reply by a question to some such affirmation as: "You've been asleep for more than an hour." "Is that true?"

Without feeling to the slightest degree in love with Albertine, without including in the list of my pleasures the moments that we spent together, I had nevertheless remained preoccupied with the way in which she disposed of her time; had I not, indeed, fled from Balbec in order to make certain that she could no longer meet this or that person with whom I was so afraid of her doing wrong for fun (fun at my expense, perhaps), that I had adroitly planned to sever, by my departure, all her dangerous entanglements at one blow? And Albertine had such extraordinary passivity, such a powerful faculty for forgetting, and for complying with one's wishes, that these relations had indeed been severed and the phobia that haunted me cured. But such a phobia is capable of assuming as many forms as the undefined evil that is its cause. So long as my jealousy had not been reincarnated in new people, I had enjoyed after the passing of my anguish an interval of calm. But the slightest pretext serves to revive a chronic disease, just as the slightest opportunity may enable the vice of the person who is the cause of our jealousy to be practised anew (after a lull of chastity) with different people. I had managed to separate Albertine from her accomplices, and, by so doing, to exorcise my hallucinations; if it was possible to make her forget people, to cut short her attachments, her taste for sensual pleasure was chronic too, and was perhaps only waiting for an opportunity to be given its head. Now Paris provided just as many opportunities as Balbec. In any town whatsoever, she had no need to seek, for the evil existed not in Albertine alone, but in others to whom any opportunity for pleasure is good. A glance from one, understood at once by the other, brings the two famished souls in contact. And it is easy for an astute woman to appear not to have seen, then five minutes later to join, the person who has read her glance and is waiting for her in a side street, and to make an assignation in a trice. Who will ever know? And it was so simple for Albertine to tell me, in order that she might continue these practices, that she was anxious to revisit some place on the outskirts of Paris that she had liked. And so it was enough that she should return later than usual,

that her expedition should have taken an inexplicably long
time, although it was perhaps perfectly easy to explain (without
bringing in any sensual reason), for my malady to break out
afresh, attached this time to mental pictures which were not of
Balbec, and which I would set to work, as with their predecessors, to destroy, as though the destruction of an ephemeral
cause could put an end to a congenital disease. I did not take
into account the fact that in these acts of destruction in which
I had as an accomplice, in Albertine, her faculty of changing,
her ability to forget, almost to hate, the recent object of her
love, I was sometimes causing great pain to one or other of
those unknown persons with whom she had successively
taken her pleasure, and that I was doing so in vain, for they
would be abandoned but replaced, and, parallel to the path
strewn with all the derelicts of her light-hearted infidelities,
there would continue for me another, pitiless path interrupted
only by an occasional brief respite; so that my suffering, had
I thought about it, could end only with Albertine's life or with
my own. Even in the first days after our return to Paris, not
satisfied by the information that Andrée and the chauffeur
had given me as to their expeditions with my mistress, I had
felt the environs of Paris to be as baleful as those of Balbec,
and had gone off for a few days in the country with Albertine.
But everywhere my uncertainty as to what she might be
doing was the same, the possibility that it was something
wrong as abundant, surveillance even more difficult, with the
result that I had returned with her to Paris. In leaving Balbec,
I had imagined that I was leaving Gomorrah, plucking
Albertine from it; in reality, alas, Gomorrah was disseminated
all over the world. And partly out of jealousy, partly out of
ignorance of such joys (a case which is extremely rare), I had
arranged unawares this game of hide and seek in which Alber-
time would always elude me.

I questioned her point-blank: "Oh, by the way, Albertine,
am I dreaming, or did you tell me that you knew Gilberte
Swann?" "Yes; that's to say that she spoke to me once in class,
because she had a set of the French history notes. In fact she
was very nice and lent them to me, and I gave them back to her
in class, which was the only place I ever saw her." "Is she the

kind of woman that I object to?" "Oh, not at all, quite the opposite."

But, rather than indulge in this sort of criminal investigation, I would often devote to imagining Albertine's excursions the energy that I did not employ in sharing them, and would speak to her with the enthusiasm which unfulfilled designs alone can keep intact. I expressed so keen a longing to see once again some window in the Sainte-Chapelle, so keen a regret that I was not able to go there with her alone, that she said to me lovingly: "Why, my sweet, since you seem so keen about it, make a little effort, come with us. We'll wait as long as you like until you're ready. And if you'd rather be alone with me, I'll just send Andrée home, she can come another time." But these very entreaties to me to go out added to the calm which enabled me to yield to my desire to remain indoors.

It did not occur to me that the apathy reflected in my thus delegating to Andrée or the chauffeur the task of soothing my agitation, by leaving them to keep watch on Albertine, was paralysing and deadening in me all those imaginative impulses of the mind, all those inspirations of the will, which enable us to guess and to forestall what a person is going to do. It was all the more dangerous because by nature I have always been more open to the world of potentiality than to the world of contingent reality. This helps one to understand the human heart, but one is apt to be taken in by individuals. My jealousy was born of mental images, to produce a specific suffering, not based on probability. Now there may occur in the lives of men and of nations (and there was to occur in mine) a moment when we need to have within us a chief of police, a clear-sighted diplomat, a master-detective, who instead of pondering over the possible contingencies that extend to all the points of the compass, reasons soundly and says to himself: "If Germany announces this, it means that she intends to do something else, not just 'something' in the abstract but precisely this or that or the other, which she may perhaps have already begun to do," or "If so-and-so has fled, it is not in the direction *a* or *b* or *d*, but to the point *c*, and the place to which we must direct our search for him is *c*." Alas, I allowed this faculty, which was.

not highly developed in me, to grow numb, to lose strength, to disappear, by letting myself be lulled as soon as others were engaged in keeping watch on my behalf.

As for the reason for my desire to remain at home, I should have been very reluctant to explain it to Albertine. I told her that the doctor had ordered me to stay in bed. This was not true. And if it had been true, his instructions would have been powerless to prevent me from accompanying my mistress. I asked her to excuse me from going out with herself and Andrée. I shall mention only one of my reasons, which was dictated by prudence. Whenever I went out with Albertine, if she left my side for a moment I became anxious, began to imagine that she had spoken to or simply looked at somebody. If she was not in the best of tempers, I thought that I must be causing her to miss or to postpone some appointment. Reality is never more than a lead towards an unknown on the road to which one can never progress very far. It is better not to know, to think as little as possible, not to feed one's jealousy with the slightest concrete detail. Unfortunately, in the absence of an outer life, incidents are created by the inner life too; in the absence of expeditions with Albertine, the random course of my solitary reflexions furnished me at times with some of those tiny fragments of the truth which attract to themselves, like a magnet, an inkling of the unknown, which from that moment becomes painful. Even if one lives under the equivalent of a bell jar, associations of ideas, memories, continue to act upon us. But these internal shocks did not occur immediately; no sooner had Albertine set off on her drive than I was revivified, if only for a few moments, by the exhilarating virtues of solitude. I took my share in the pleasures of the new day; the arbitrary desire—the capricious and purely solipsistic impulse—to savour them would not have sufficed to place them within my reach, had not the particular state of the weather not merely evoked for me their past images but affirmed their present reality, immediately accessible to all men whom a contingent and consequently negligible circumstance did not compel to remain at home. On certain fine days, the weather was so cold, one was in such full communication with the street, that it seemed as though the outer walls of the house had been dismantled, and, whenever a tramcar passed, the sound of its bell reverberated like that of a silver knife striking a wall of glass. But it was above all in myself that I heard, with rapture, a new sound emitted by the violin within. Its strings are tautened or relaxed by mere differences in the temperature or the light outside. Within our being, an instrument which the uniformity of habit has rendered mute, song is born of these divergences, these variations, the source of all music: the change of weather on certain days makes us pass at once from one note to another. We recapture the forgotten tune the mathematical necessity of which we might have deduced, and which for the first few moments we sing without recognising it. These modifications alone, internal though they had come from without, gave me a fresh vision of the external world. Communicating doors, long barred, reopened in my brain. The life of certain towns, the gaiety of certain excursions, resumed their place in my consciousness. With my whole being quivering around the vibrating string, I would have sacrificed my former existence and my life to come, erasing them with the india-rubber of habit, for such a unique state of soul.

If I had not gone out with Albertine on her long expedition, my mind would stray all the further afield, and, because I had refused to savour with my senses this particular morning, I enjoyed in imagination all the similar mornings, past or possible, or more precisely a certain type of morning of which all those of the same kind were but the intermittent apparition which I had at once recognised; for the sharp air blew the book open of its own accord at the right page, and I found before me, already marked, so that I might follow it from my bed, the Gospel for the day. This ideal morning filled my mind full of a permanent reality identical with all similar mornings, and infected me with a joyousness which my physical debility did not diminish: for, a sense of well-being resulting far less from the soundness of our health than from the surplus of our energies, we can achieve it just as well by restricting the scope of our activity as by increasing our strength. The activity with which I was overflowing and which I kept constantly charged as I lay in bed, made me throb and leap internally, like a machine which, prevented from moving from its position, turns over on itself.

Françoise would come in to light the fire, and in order to make it draw, would throw upon it a handful of twigs, the scent of which, forgotten for a year past, traced round the fireplace a magic circle within which, glimpsing myself poring over a book, now at Combray, now at Doncières, I was as joyful, while remaining in my bedroom in Paris, as if I had been on the point of setting out for a walk along the Méséglise way, or of going to join Saint-Loup and his friends on manoeuvres. It often happens that the pleasure which everyone takes in turning over the keepsakes that his memory has collected is keenest in those whom the tyranny of physical illness and the daily hope of its cure prevent, on the one hand, from going out to seek in nature scenes that resemble those memories and, on the other hand, leave so convinced that they will shortly be able to do so that they can remain gazing at them in a state of desire and appetite and not regard them merely as memories or pictures. But, even if they could never have been more than this for me, even if, in recalling them, I could see them as pictures only, they none the less suddenly recreated out of my present self, the whole of that self, by virtue of an identical sensation, the child or the youth who had first seen them. There had been not merely a change in the weather outside, or, inside the room, a change of smells; there had been in myself an alteration in age, the substitution of another person. The scent, in the frosty air, of the twigs of brushwood was like a fragment of the past, an invisible ice-floe detached from some bygone winter advancing into my room, often, moreover, striated with this or that perfume or gleam of light, as though with different annular rings, in which I found myself once more submerged, overwhelmed, even before I had identified them, by the exhilaration of hopes long since abandoned. The sun's rays fell upon my bed and passed through the transparent shell of my attenuated body, warmed me, made me glow like crystal. Then, like a famished convalescent already battening upon all the dishes that are still forbidden him, I wondered whether marriage with Albertine might not spoil my life, not only by making me assume the too arduous task of devoting myself to another person, but by forcing me to live apart from myself because of her continual presence and depriving me forever of the joys of solitude.

And not of these alone. Even if one asks of the day nothing but desires, there are some—those that are excited not by things but by people—whose character it is to be personal and particular. So that if, on rising from my bed, I went to the window and drew the curtain aside for a moment, it was not merely, as a pianist for a moment turns back the lid of his instrument, to ascertain whether, on the balcony and in the street, the sunlight was tuned to exactly the same pitch as in my memory, but also to catch a glimpse of some laundress carrying her linen-basket, a baker-woman in a blue apron, a dairymaid with a tucker and white linen sleeves, carrying the yoke from which her milk-churns are suspended, some haughty fair-haired girl escorted by her governess—an image, in short, which differences of outline, perhaps quantitatively insignificant, were enough to make as different from any other as, in a phrase of music, the difference between two notes, an image but for the vision of which I should have dispossessed my day of the goals which it might have to offer to my desires of happiness. But if the access of joy brought me by the spectacle of women whom it was impossible to imagine *a priori* made the street, the town, the world, more desirable, more deserving of exploration, it set me longing, for that very reason, to recover my health, to go out of doors and, without Albertine, to be a free man. How often, at the moment when the unknown woman who was to haunt my dreams passed beneath the window, sometimes on foot, sometimes at full speed in a motor-car, did I not suffer from the fact that my body could not follow my gaze which kept pace with her, and falling upon her as though shot from the embrasure of my window by an arquebus, arrest the flight of the face that held out for me the offer of a happiness which, thus cloistered, I should never know!

Of Albertine, on the other hand, I had nothing more to learn. Every day she seemed to me less pretty. Only the desire that she aroused in others, when, on learning of it, I began to suffer again and wanted to challenge their possession of her, raised her in my eyes to a lofty pinnacle. She was capable of causing me pain, but no longer any joy. Pain alone kept my wearisome attachment alive. As soon as it subsided, and with it the need to appease it, requiring all my attention like some agonising distraction, I felt how utterly meaningless she was to me, as I must be to her. I was miserable at the thought that this state of affairs should persist, and, at certain moments, I longed to hear of something terrible that she had done, something that would keep us estranged until I was cured, giving us a chance to make it up and to reconstitute in a different and more flexible form the chain that bound us.

In the meantime, I relied on countless events, on countless pleasures, to procure for her in my company the illusion of that happiness which I did not feel capable of giving her. I should have liked, as soon as I was cured, to set off for Venice, but how was I to manage it, if I married Albertine, I who was so jealous of her that even in Paris whenever I decided to stir from my room it was to go out with her? Even when I stayed in the house all the afternoon, my thoughts accompanied her on her drive, traced a distant blue horizon, created round the centre that was myself a fluctuating zone of vague uncertainty. "How completely," I said to myself, "would Albertine spare me the anguish of separation if, in the course of one of these drives, seeing that I had ceased to talk of marriage, she decided not to come back, and went off to her aunt's without my having to say good-bye to her!" My heart, now that its scar had begun to heal, was beginning to detach itself from hers; I could, in my imagination, shift her, separate her from myself without pain. No doubt, failing myself, some other man would be her husband, and in her freedom she would indulge in those amorous adventures which filled me with horror. But the day was so fine, I was so certain that she would return in the evening, that even if the idea of possible misbehaviour did enter my mind, I could, by an exercise of free will, imprison it in a part of my brain in which it had no more importance than the vices of an imaginary person would have had in my real life; manipulating the supple hinges of my thought, with an energy which I felt, in my head, at once physical and mental, as it were a muscular movement and a spiritual impulse, I had broken away from the state of perpetual preoccupation in which I had hitherto been confined, and was beginning to move in a free atmosphere, in which the idea of sacrificing everything in order to prevent Albertine from marrying someone else and to put an obstacle in the way of her taste for women seemed as unreasonable in my own eyes as in those of a person who had never known her.

However, jealousy is one of those intermittent maladies the cause of which is capricious, arbitrary, always identical in the same patient, sometimes entirely different in another. There are asthma sufferers who can assuage their attacks only by opening the windows, inhaling the high winds, the pure air of mountains, others by taking refuge in the heart of the city, in a smoke-filled room. There are few jealous men whose jealousy does not allow certain derogations. One will consent to infidelity provided he is told of it, another provided it is concealed from him, wherein they are equally absurd, since if the latter is more literally deceived inasmuch as the truth is not disclosed to him, the other demands from that truth the aliment, the extension, the renewal of his sufferings.

What is more, these two inverse idiosyncrasies of jealousy often extend beyond words, whether they implore or reject confidences. We see jealous lovers who are jealous only of the men with whom their mistress has relations in their absence, but allow her to give herself to another man, if it is done with their permission, near at hand, and, if not actually before their eyes, at least under their roof. This case is not at all uncommon among elderly men who are in love with a young woman. They feel the difficulty of winning her favours, sometimes their inability to satisfy her, and, rather than be deceived, prefer to allow into the house, into an adjoining room, some man whom they consider incapable of giving her bad advice, but not incapable of giving her pleasure. With others it will be just the opposite; never allowing their mistress to go out by herself for a single minute in a town they know, keeping her in a state of veritable bondage, they allow her to go for a month to a place they do not know, where they cannot picture to themselves what she may be doing. With regard to Albertine, I had both sorts of soothing quirk. I should not have been jealous if she had enjoyed her pleasures in my vicinity, with my encouragement, completely under my surveillance, thereby relieving me of any fear of mendacity; nor should I have been jealous if she had moved to a place so unfamiliar and remote that I could not imagine, had no possibility of knowing, and no temptation to know, her manner of life. In either case, my uncertainty would have been eliminated by a knowledge or an ignorance equally complete.

The decline of day plunging me back by an act of memory into a cool atmosphere of long ago, I would inhale it with the same delight as Orpheus the subtle air, unknown upon this earth, of the Elysian Fields. But already the day was ending and I would be overcome by the desolation of evening. Looking mechanically at the clock to see how many hours must elapse before Albertine's return, I would see that I still had time to dress and go downstairs to ask my landlady, Mme de Guermantes, for particulars of various pretty articles of clothing which I wanted to give Albertine. Sometimes I would meet the Duchess in the courtyard, going out shopping, even if the weather was bad, in a close-fitting hat and furs. I knew quite well that to a number of intelligent people she was merely a lady like any other, the name Duchesse de Guermantes signifying nothing, now that there are no longer any duchies or principalities; but I had adopted a different point of view in my manner of enjoying people and places. This lady in furs braving the bad weather seemed to me to carry with her all the castles of the territories of which she was duchess, princess, viscountess, as the figures carved over a portal hold in their hands the cathedral they have built or the city they have defended. But my mind's eyes alone could discern these castles and these forests in the gloved hand of the lady in furs who was a cousin of the king. My bodily eyes distinguished in it only, on days when the sky was threatening, an umbrella with which the Duchess did not hesitate to arm herself. "It's much wiser—one can never be certain, I may find myself miles from home, with a cabman demanding a fare *beyond my means*." The words "too dear" and "beyond my means" kept recurring all the time in the Duchess's conversation, as did also: "I'm too poor"—

without its being possible to decide whether she spoke thus because she thought it amusing to say that she was poor, being so rich, or because she thought it smart, being so aristocratic (that is to say affecting to be a peasant), not to attach to riches the importance that people give them who are merely rich and nothing else and who look down on the poor. Perhaps it was, rather, a habit contracted at a time in her life when, already rich, but not rich enough to satisfy her needs considering the expense of keeping up all those properties, she felt a certain financial embarrassment which she did not wish to appear to be concealing. The things about which we most often jest are generally, on the contrary, the things that worry us but that we do not wish to appear to be worried by, with perhaps a secret hope of the further advantage that the person to whom we are talking, hearing us treat the matter as a joke, will conclude that it is not true.

But on most evenings at this hour I could count on finding the Duchess at home, and I was glad of this, for it was more convenient for the purpose of discussing at length the particulars that Albertine required. And I would go down almost without thinking how extraordinary it was that I should be calling upon that mysterious Mme de Guermantes of my boyhood simply in order to make use of her for a practical purpose as one makes use of the telephone, a supernatural instrument before whose miracles we used to stand amazed, and which we now employ without giving it a thought, to summon our tailor or to order an ice cream.

The accessories of costume gave Albertine enormous pleasure. I could not resist giving her some new trifle every day. And whenever she had spoken to me rapturously of a scarf, a stole, a sunshade which, from the window or as they passed one another in the courtyard, her eyes, that so quickly distinguished anything connected with elegance of dress, had seen round the throat, over the shoulders, or in the hand of Mme de Guermantes, knowing how the girl's naturally fastidious taste (refined still further by the lessons in elegance which Elstir's conversation had been to her) would by no means be satisfied by any mere substitute, even of a pretty thing, such as fills its place in the eyes of the common herd

but differs from it entirely, I would go in secret to ask the
Duchess to explain to me where, how, from what model the
article had been created that had taken Albertine's fancy, how I
should set about obtaining one exactly similar, in what lay
the maker's secret, the charm (what Albertine called the
"*chic*," the "style") of its manner and—the beauty of the
material having also its importance—the name and quality of
the fabrics that I was to insist upon their using.

When I had mentioned to Albertine, on our return from
Balbec, that the Duchesse de Guermantes lived opposite us,
in the same building, she had assumed, on hearing the proud
title and great name, that more than indifferent, that hostile,
contemptuous air which is the sign of an impotent desire in
proud and passionate natures. Splendid though Albertine's
might be, the qualities that lay buried in it could develop only
amid those trammels which are our personal tastes, or that
bereavement of those of our tastes that we have been obliged
to forgo, as in Albertine's case snobbery: in other words,
what are called aversions. Albertine's aversion for society
people occupied very little room in her nature, and appealed
to me as an aspect of the revolutionary spirit—that is to say
an embittered love for the nobility—engraved upon the obverse
side of the French character to that which displays the aristocratic style of Mme de Guermantes. Albertine would perhaps
not have given a thought to this aristocratic style, in view of the
impossibility of achieving it, but remembering that Elstir
had spoken to her of the Duchess as the best-dressed woman in
Paris, her republican contempt for a duchess gave way to a
keen interest in a fashionable woman. She was always asking
me to tell her about Mme de Guermantes, and was glad that I
should call on the Duchess to obtain advice about her own
clothes. No doubt I could have got this from Mme Swann,
and indeed I did once write to her with this intention. But
Mme de Guermantes seemed to me to carry the art of dressing
even further. If, on going down for a moment to see her, after
making sure that she had not gone out and leaving word that
I was to be warned as soon as Albertine returned, I found the
Duchess swathed in the mist of a grey crêpe de Chine gown, I
accepted this aspect of her which I felt to be due to complex

causes and to be quite unalterable, and steeped myself in the atmosphere which it exhaled, like that of certain late afternoons cushioned in pearly grey by a vaporous fog; if, on the other hand, her indoor gown was Chinese with red and yellow flames, I gazed at it as at a glowing sunset; these garments were not a casual decoration alterable at will, but a given, poetical reality like that of the weather, or the light peculiar to a certain hour of the day.

Of all the outdoor and indoor gowns that Mme de Guermantes wore, those which seemed most to respond to a specific intention, to be endowed with a special significance, were the garments made by Fortuny from old Venetian models. Is it their historical character, or is it rather the fact that each one of them is unique, that gives them so special a significance that the pose of the woman who is wearing one while she waits for you to appear or while she talks to you assumes an exceptional importance, as though the costume had been the fruit of a long deliberation and your conversation was somehow detached from everyday life like a scene in a novel? In the novels of Balzac, we see his heroines put on this or that dress on purpose when they are expecting some particular visitor. The dresses of to-day have less character, always excepting the creations of Fortuny. There is no room for vagueness in the novelist's description, since the dress does really exist, its smallest details are as naturally preordained as those of a work of art. Before putting on one or another of them, the woman has had to make a choice between two garments that are not more or less alike but each one profoundly individual, and identifiable by name.

But the dress did not prevent me from thinking of the woman. Indeed, Mme de Guermantes seemed to me at this time more attractive than in the days when I was still in love with her. Expecting less of her (I no longer went to visit her for her own sake), it was almost with the relaxed negligence one exhibits when alone, with my feet on the fender, that I listened to her as though I were reading a book written in the language of long ago. I was sufficiently detached to enjoy in what she said that pure charm of the French language which we no longer find either in the speech or in the writing of the present day. I listened to her conversation as to a folk song deliciously and purely French; I understood why I should have heard her deriding Maeterlinck (whom in fact she now admired, out of feminine weak-mindedness, influenced by those literary fashions whose rays spread slowly), as I understood why Mérimée had derided Baudelaire, Stendhal Balzac, Paul-Louis Courier Victor Hugo, Meilhac Mallarmé. I was well aware that the critic had a far more restricted outlook than his victim, but also a purer vocabulary. That of Mme de Guermantes, almost as much as that of Saint-Loup's mother, was enchantingly pure. It is not in the bloodless pastiches of the writers of to-day who say *au fait* (for "in reality"), *singulièrement* (for "in particular"), *étonné* (for "struck with amazement"), and the like, that we recapture the old speech and the true pronunciation of words, but in conversing with a Mme de Guermantes or a Françoise. I had learned from the latter, when I was five years old, that one did not say "the Tarn" but "the Tar"; not "Béarn" but "Béar." The effect of which was that at twenty, when I began to go into society, I had no need to be taught there that one ought not to say, like Mme Bontemps, "Madame de Béar*n*."

It would not be true to say that the Duchess was unaware of this earthy and quasi-peasant quality that survived in her, or was entirely innocent of affectation in displaying it. But, on her part, it was not so much the false simplicity of a great lady aping the countrywoman, or the pride of a duchess bent upon snubbing the rich ladies who express contempt for the peasants whom they do not know, as the quasi-artistic preference of a woman who knows the charm of what she possesses and is not going to spoil it with a coat of modern varnish. In the same way, everybody used to know a Norman innkeeper, landlord of the "William the Conqueror" at Dives, who had carefully refrained—a rare thing indeed—from giving his hostelry the modern comforts of an hotel, and, albeit a millionaire, retained the speech and the smock of a Norman peasant and allowed you to enter his kitchen and watch him prepare with his own hands, as in a farmhouse, a dinner which was nevertheless infinitely better, and even more expensive, than in the most luxurious hotel.

All the local sap that survives in the old noble families is not enough; it must be embodied in a person of sufficient intelligence not to despise it, not to obliterate it beneath a society veneer. Mme de Guermantes, unfortunately clever and Parisian and, when I knew her, retaining nothing of her native soil but its accent, had at least, when she wished to describe her life as a girl, contrived for her speech one of those compromises (between what would have seemed too spontaneously provincial on the one hand or artificially literary on the other) which form the attraction of George Sand's *La Petite Fadette* or of certain legends related by Chateaubriand in his *Mémoires d'Outre-Tombe*. My chief pleasure was in hearing her tell some anecdote which brought peasants into the picture with herself. The historic names, the old customs, gave to these blendings of the castle with the village a distinctly attractive savour.

If there was no affectation, no deliberate effort to fabricate a special language, then this style of pronunciation was a regular museum of French history displayed in conversation. "My great-uncle Fitt-jam" was not at all surprising, for we know that the Fitz-James family are proud to boast that they are French nobles and do not like to hear their name pronounced in the English fashion. One must, however, marvel at the touching docility of the people who had previously supposed themselves obliged to pronounce certain names phonetically, and who, all of a sudden, after hearing the Duchesse de Guermantes pronounce them otherwise, adopted a pronunciation which they could never have guessed. Thus the Duchess, who had had a great-grandfather in the suite of the Comte de Chambord, liked to tease her husband for having turned Orleanist by proclaiming: "We old Frochedorf people. . . ." The visitor, who had always imagined that he was correct in saying "Frohsdorf," at once turned his coat, and ever afterwards might be heard saying "Frochedorf."

On one occasion when I asked Mme de Guermantes who a young blood was whom she had introduced to me as her nephew but whose name I had failed to catch, I was none the wiser when from the back of her throat the Duchess uttered in a very loud but quite inarticulate voice: "*C'est l'* . . . *i Eon* . . . *l* . . . *b* . . . *frère à Roert*. He claims to have the same shape of skull as the ancient Welsh." Then I realised that she had said: "*C'est le petit Léon,*" and that this was the Prince de Léon, who was indeed Robert de Saint-Loup's brother-in-law. "I know nothing about his skull," she went on, "but the way he dresses, and I must say he does dress very well, is not at all in the style of those parts. Once when I was staying at Josselin, with the Rohans, we all went over to a place of pilgrimage to which peasants had come from pretty well every part of Brittany. A great hulking villager from Léon stood gaping at Robert's brother-in-law in his beige breeches. 'What are you staring at me like that for?' said Léon, 'I bet you don't know who I am.' The peasant admitted as much. 'Well,' said Léon, 'I'm your Prince.' 'Oh!' said the peasant, taking off his cap and apologising. 'I thought you were an *Englische.*'"

And if, seizing this point of departure, I led Mme de Guermantes on to talk about the Rohans (with whom her own family had frequently intermarried), her conversation would become impregnated with a hint of the wistful charm of the Breton "pardons" and (as that true poet Pampille would say) with "the pungent flavour of buck-wheat pancakes cooked over a gorse fire."

Of the Marquis du Lau (whose sad end is familiar—when, himself deaf, he used to be taken to call on Mme H... who was blind), she would recall the less tragic years when, after the day's sport, at Guermantes, he would change into slippers before having tea with the Prince of Wales, to whom he did not regard himself as inferior, and with whom, as we see, he did not stand on ceremony. She described all this so picturesquely that she seemed to invest him with the plumed musketeer hat of the somewhat vainglorious gentlemen of Périgord.

But even in the mere designation of people Mme de Guermantes, having remained herself a countrywoman—which was her great strength—would take care to distinguish between different provinces, and place people within them, as a Parisian-born woman could never have done, and those simple names, Anjou, Poitou, Périgord, re-created, in her conversation, a series of landscapes round Saint-Simonian portraits.

To revert to the pronunciation and vocabulary of Mme de Guermantes, it is in this aspect that the nobility shows itself

truly conservative, with everything that the word implies
in the sense of being at once slightly puerile, slightly dangerous,
stubborn in its resistance to change, but at the same time
diverting to an artist. I wanted to know the original spelling
of the name Jean. I learned it when I received a letter from a
nephew of Mme de Villeparisis who signs himself—as he was
christened, as he figures in the Almanach de Gotha—Jehan de
Villeparisis, with the same handsome, superfluous, heraldic H
that we admire, illuminated in vermilion or ultramarine, in a
Book of Hours or in a stained-glass window.

Unfortunately, I never had time to prolong these visits
indefinitely, for I was anxious, as far as possible, not to return
home after Albertine. But it was only in driblets that I was
able to obtain from Mme de Guermantes that information
as to her clothes which was of use in helping me to order
costumes similar in style, so far as it was possible for a young
girl to wear them, for Albertine.

"For instance, Madame, that evening when you dined with
Mme de Saint-Euverte, and then went on to the Princesse de
Guermantes, you had a dress that was all red, with red shoes,
you were marvellous, you reminded me of a sort of great
blood-red blossom, a glittering ruby—now, what was that
dress called? Is it the sort of thing that a young girl can wear?"

The Duchess, imparting to her tired features the radiant
expression that the Princesse des Laumes used to wear when
Swann paid her compliments years ago, glanced quizzically
and delightedly, with tears of merriment in her eyes, at M. de
Bréauté who was always there at that hour and who sat beaming behind his monocle with an indulgent smile for this intellectual's rigmarole because of the physical excitement of youth
which seemed to him to underlie it. The Duchess appeared to be
saying: "What's the matter with him? He must be mad." Then
turning to me with a winning expression: "I wasn't aware that
I looked like a glittering ruby or a blood-red blossom, but I
do indeed remember that I had on a red dress: it was red satin,
which was being worn that season. Yes, a young girl can wear
that sort of thing at a pinch, but you told me that your friend
never went out in the evening. It's a full evening dress, not a
thing that she can put on to pay calls."

What is extraordinary is that of the evening in question, which after all was not so very remote, Mme de Guermantes remembered nothing but what she had been wearing, and had forgotten a certain incident which nevertheless, as we shall see presently, ought to have mattered to her greatly. It seems that among men and women of action (and society people are men and women of action on a minute, a microscopic scale, but action none the less), the mind, overtaxed by the need to attend to what is going to happen in an hour's time, commits very little to memory. As often as not, for instance, it was not with the object of deliberately misleading and making himself appear innocent of an error of judgment that M. de Norpois, when you reminded him of the prophecies he had uttered with regard to an alliance with Germany of which nothing had ever come, would say: "You must be mistaken, I have no recollection of it whatever, it isn't like me, for in that sort of conversation I am always most laconic, and I would never have predicted the success of one of those *coups d'éclat* which are often nothing more than *coups de tête* and habitually degenerate into *coups de force*. It is beyond question that in the remote future a Franco-German *rapprochement* might come into being and would be highly profitable to both countries; nor would France have the worse of the bargain, I dare say; but I have never spoken of it because the time is not yet ripe, and if you wish to know my opinion, in asking our late enemies to join with us in solemn wedlock, I consider that we would be courting a grave setback and would receive some unpleasant shocks." In saying this M. de Norpois was not being untruthful; he had simply forgotten. We quickly forget what we have not deeply considered, what has been dictated to us by the spirit of imitation, by the passions of the day. These change, and with them our memory undergoes alteration. Even more than diplomats, politicians are unable to remember the point of view which they adopted at a certain moment, and some of their palinodes are due less to an excess of ambition than to a deficiency of memory. As for society people, they remember very little.

Mme de Guermantes assured me that, at the party to which she had gone in a red dress, she did not remember Mme de

Chaussepierre's being present, and that I must be mistaken. And yet, heaven knows, the Chaussepierres had been present enough in the minds of both the Duke and the Duchess since then. For the following reason. M. de Guermantes had been the senior vice-president of the Jockey Club when the president died. Certain members of the club who were not popular in society and whose sole pleasure was to blackball the men who did not invite them to their houses launched a campaign against the Duc de Guermantes who, certain of being elected, and relatively indifferent to the presidency which was a small matter for a man in his social position, paid no attention. It was urged against him that the Duchess was a Dreyfusard (the Dreyfus case was long since over, but twenty years later people would still talk about it, and so far only two years had elapsed) and entertained the Rothschilds, that too much consideration had been shown of late to certain great international potentates like the Duc de Guermantes, who was half German. The campaign found sympathetic ears, clubs being always jealous of men who are in the public eye, and detesting big fortunes. Chaussepierre's was by no means meagre, but nobody could be offended by it; he spent hardly a sou, the couple lived in a modest apartment, the wife went about dressed in black wool. A passionate music-lover, she did indeed give little afternoon parties to which many more singers were invited than to the Guermantes. But no one talked about these parties, which occurred without any refreshments, often in the absence of the husband, in the obscurity of the Rue de la Chaise. At the Opéra, Mme de Chaussepierre passed unnoticed, always among people whose names recalled the most "die-hard" element of the intimate circle of Charles X, but who were retiring and unsocial. On the day of the election, to the general surprise, obscurity triumphed over glitter: Chaussepierre, the second vice-president, was elected president of the Jockey, and the Duc de Guermantes was left sitting—that is to say, in the senior vice-president's chair. Of course, being president of the Jockey means little or nothing to princes of the highest rank such as the Guermantes. But not to be president when it is your turn, to be passed over in favour of a Chaussepierre, whose wife's greeting Oriane not only had refused to acknowledge two years earlier but had gone so far as to show offence at being greeted by such an obscure scarecrow, this the Duke did find hard to swallow. He pretended to be above such setbacks, asserting incidentally that it was his long-standing friendship with Swann that was at the root of it. Actually, his anger never cooled.

One curious thing was that nobody had ever before heard the Duc de Guermantes make use of the quite commonplace expression "well and truly"; but ever since the Jockey Club election, whenever anybody referred to the Dreyfus case, out would come "well and truly." "Dreyfus case, Dreyfus case, it's easy to say, and it's a misuse of the term. It's not a question of religion, it's well and truly political." Five years might go by without your hearing him say "well and truly" again, if during that time nobody mentioned the Dreyfus case, but if, at the end of five years, the name Dreyfus cropped up, "well and truly" would at once follow automatically. The Duke could not in any case bear to hear any mention of the case, "which has been responsible," he would say, "for so many misfortunes," although he was really conscious of one only: his failure to become president of the Jockey.

And so on the afternoon in question—the afternoon on which I reminded Mme de Guermantes of the red dress she had worn at her cousin's party—M. de Bréauté was none too well received when, for want of anything better to say, by an association of ideas which remained obscure and which he did not illumïnate, he began, twisting his tongue about between his pursed lips: "Talking of the Dreyfus case . . ." (why the Dreyfus case?—we were talking simply of a red dress, and certainly poor Bréauté, whose only desire was to make himself agreeable, can have had no malicious intention, but the mere name of Dreyfus made the Duc de Guermantes knit his Jupiterian brows) ". . . I was told of a rather nice remark, damned clever, 'pon my word, that was made by our friend Cartier" (the reader may care to know that this Cartier, Mme de Villefranche's brother, had not the slightest connexion with the jeweller of that name), "not that I'm in the least surprised, for he's got wit enough and to spare."

"Oh!" broke in Oriane, "he can spare me his wit. I can't

tell you how much your friend Cartier has always *bored* me, and I've never been able to understand the boundless charm that Charles de La Trémoïlle and his wife seem to find in the creature, for I meet him there every time I go to their house."

"My dear Dutt-yess," replied Bréauté, who had difficulty in pronouncing *ch*, "I think you're a bit hard on Cartier. It's true that he has perhaps made himself rather excessively at home at the La Trémoïlles', but after all he does provide Tyarles with a sort of—what shall I say?—a sort of *fidus Achates*, and that has become a very rare bird indeed in these days. Anyhow, what he's supposed to have said is that if M. Zola had gone out of his way to stand his trial and to be convicted, it was in order to enjoy the only sensation he had never yet tried, that of being in prison."

"And so he ran away before they could arrest him," Oriane broke in. "Your story doesn't hold water. Besides, even if it was plausible, I find the remark absolutely idiotic. If that's what you call witty!"

"Good grate-ious, my dear Oriane," replied Bréauté who, finding himself contradicted, was beginning to lose confidence, "it's not my remark, I'm telling you it as it was told to me, take it for what it's worth. Anyhow, it earned M. Cartier a proper dressing-down from that excellent fellow La Trémoïlle who, quite rightly, doesn't like people to discuss what one might call, so to speak, current events in his drawing-room, and was all the more annoyed because Mme Alphonse Rothschild was present. Cartier was given a positive roasting by La Trémoïlle."

"Of course," said the Duke, in the worst of tempers, "the Alphonse Rothschilds, even if they have the tact never to speak of that abominable affair, are Dreyfusards at heart, like all the Jews. Indeed that is an argument *ad hominem*" (the Duke was a trifle vague in his use of the expression *ad hominem*) "which is not sufficiently exploited to prove the dishonesty of the Jews. If a Frenchman robs or murders somebody, I don't consider myself bound, because he's a Frenchman like myself, to find him innocent. But the Jews will never admit that one of their co-citizens is a traitor, although they know it perfectly well, and never think of the terrible repercussions" (the Duke was thinking, naturally, of that accursed defeat by Chausse-pierre) "which the crime of one of their people can bring even to . . . Come, Oriane, you're not going to pretend that it isn't damning to the Jews that they all support a traitor. You're not going to tell me that it isn't because they're Jews."

"I'm afraid I am," retorted Oriane (feeling, together with a trace of irritation, a certain desire to hold her own against Jupiter Tonans and also to put "intelligence" above the Dreyfus case). "Perhaps it's just because they are Jews and know themselves that they realise that a person can be a Jew and not necessarily a traitor and anti-French, as M. Drumont seems to maintain. Certainly, if he'd been a Christian, the Jews wouldn't have taken any interest in him, but they did so because they knew quite well that if he hadn't been a Jew people wouldn't have been so ready to think him a traitor *a priori*, as my nephew Robert would say."

"Women never understand a thing about politics," exclaimed the Duke, fastening his gaze upon the Duchess. "That shocking crime is not simply a Jewish cause, but *well and truly* an affair of vast national importance which may bring the most appalling consequences for France, which ought to have driven out all the Jews, whereas I'm sorry to say that the sanctions taken up to the present have been directed (in an ignoble fashion, which should be overruled) not against them but against the most eminent of their adversaries, against men of the highest rank who have been flung into the gutter to the ruin of our unhappy country."

I felt that the conversation had taken a wrong turning and reverted hurriedly to the topic of clothes.

"Do you remember, Madame," I said, "the first time that you were friendly to me . . ."

"The first time that I was friendly to him," she repeated, turning with a smile to M. de Bréauté, the tip of whose nose grew more pointed, and his smile more tender out of politeness to Mme de Guermantes, while his voice, like a knife on the grindstone, emitted a few vague and rusty sounds.

'. . . You were wearing a yellow dress with big black flowers."

"But, my dear boy, that's the same thing, those are evening dresses."

"And your hat with the cornflowers that I liked so much! Still, those are all things of the past. I should like to order for the girl I mentioned to you a fur coat like the one you had on yesterday morning. Would it be possible for me to see it?"

"Of course; Hannibal has to be going in a moment. You shall come to my room and my maid will show you everything. Only, my dear boy, though I shall be delighted to lend you anything you like, I must warn you that if you have things from Callot's or Doucet's or Paquin's copied by some small dressmaker, the result is never the same."

"But I never dreamed of going to a small dressmaker. I know quite well it wouldn't be the same thing, but I should be interested to hear you explain why."

"You know quite well I can never explain anything, I'm a perfect fool, I talk like a peasant. It's a question of handiwork, of style; as far as furs go, I can at least give you a line to my furrier, so that he shan't rob you. But you realise that even then it will cost you eight or nine thousand francs."

"And that indoor gown that you were wearing the other evening, with such a curious smell, dark, fluffy, speckled, streaked with gold like a butterfly's wing?"

"Ah! that's one of Fortuny's. Your young lady can quite well wear that in the house. I have heaps of them; you shall see them presently, in fact I can give you one or two if you like. But I should like you to see one that my cousin Talleyrand has. I must write to her for the loan of it."

"But you had such charming shoes as well. Were they Fortuny too?"

"No, I know the ones you mean, they're made of some gold kid we came across in London, when I was shopping with Consuelo Manchester. It was amazing. I could never make out how they did it, it was just like a golden skin, simply that, with a tiny diamond in front. The poor Duchess of Manchester is dead, but if it's any help to you I can write and ask Lady Warwick or the Duchess of Marlborough to try and get me some more. I wonder, now, if I haven't a piece of the stuff left. You might be able to have a pair made here. I shall look for it this evening, and let you know."

Since I endeavoured as far as possible to leave the Duchess

before Albertine had returned, it often happened, because of
the hour, that I met in the courtyard as I came away from her
door M. de Charlus and Morel on their way to have tea at
Jupien's, a supreme treat for the Baron! I did not encounter
them every day but they went there every day. It may, incidentally, be observed that the regularity of a habit is usually in
direct proportion to its absurdity. Really striking things we
do as a rule only by fits and starts. But insensate lives, of a
kind in which a crackpot deprives himself of all pleasure and
inflicts the greatest discomforts upon himself, are those that
change least. Every ten years, if we had the curiosity to
inquire, we should find the poor wretch still asleep at the hours
when he might be living his life, going out at the hours when
there is nothing to do but get oneself murdered in the streets,
sipping iced drinks when he is hot, still trying desperately to
cure a cold. A slight burst of energy, for a single day, would be
sufficient to change these habits for good and all. But the fact
is that lives of this sort are on the whole peculiar to people who
are incapable of energy. Vices are another aspect of these
monotonous existences which the exercise of will power would
suffice to render less painful. Both aspects were to be observed
simultaneously when M. de Charlus came every day with
Morel to have tea at Jupien's. A single outburst had marred
this daily custom. The tailor's niece having said one day to
Morel: "That's all right then, come to-morrow and I'll stand
you tea," the Baron had quite justifiably considered this
expression very vulgar on the lips of a person whom he regarded as almost a prospective daughter-in-law, but as he enjoyed
being offensive and became intoxicated by his own indignation,
instead of his simply asking Morel to give her a lesson in
refinement, the whole of their homeward walk was a succession
of violent scenes. In the most rude and arrogant tone the
Baron said: "So your 'touch' which, I can see, is not necessarily
allied to 'tact,' has hindered the normal development of your
sense of smell, since you could allow that fetid expression
'stand you tea'—at fifteen centimes, I suppose—to waft its
stench of sewage to my regal nostrils? When you have come
to the end of a violin solo, have you ever in my house been
rewarded with a fart, instead of frenzied applause or a silence

more eloquent still since it is due to fear of being unable to restrain, not what your young woman lavishes upon you, but the sob that you have brought to my lips?"

When a public official has had similar reproaches heaped upon him by his chief, he is invariably sacked next day. Nothing, on the contrary, could have been more painful to M. de Charlus than to dismiss Morel, and, fearing indeed that he had gone a little too far, he began to sing the girl's praises in the minutest detail, tastefully expressed and unconsciously sprinkled with impertinent observations. "She is charming; as you are a musician, I suppose that she seduced you by her voice, which is very beautiful in the high notes, where she seems to await the accompaniment of your B sharp. Her lower register appeals to me less, and that must bear some relation to the triple rise of her strange and slender throat, which when it seems to have come to an end begins again; but these are trivial details, it is her silhouette that I admire. And as she is a dressmaker and must be handy with her scissors, you must get her to give me a pretty paper cut-out of herself."

Charlie had paid but little attention to this eulogy, the charms which it extolled in his betrothed having completely escaped his notice. But he said, in reply to M. de Charlus: "That's all right, my boy, I shall tell her off properly, and she won't talk like that again." If Morel addressed M. de Charlus thus as his "boy," it was not that the handsome violinist was unaware that his own years numbered barely a third of the Baron's. Nor did he use the expression as Jupien would have done, but with that simplicity which in certain relations postulates that a suppression of the difference in age has tacitly preceded tenderness (a feigned tenderness in Morel's case, in others a sincere tenderness). Thus, at about this time M. de Charlus received a letter worded as follows: "My dear Pala-mède, when am I going to see you again? I miss you terribly and think of you often . . . etc. etc. Ever yours, PIERRE." M. de Charlus racked his brains to discover which of his relatives it could be who took the liberty of addressing him so familiarly, and must consequently know him intimately, although he failed to recognise the handwriting. All the princes to whom the Almanach de Gotha accords a few lines passed in procession through his mind for a few days. And then, all of a sudden, an address written on the back of the letter enlightened him: the writer was the doorman at a gambling club to which M. de Charlus sometimes went. This doorman had not felt that he was being discourteous in writing in this tone to M. de Charlus, for whom on the contrary he felt the deepest respect. But he felt that it would be uncivil not to address by his Christian name a gentleman who had kissed one several times, and thereby—he naïvely imagined—bestowed his affection on one. M. de Charlus was secretly delighted by this familiarity. He even brought M. de Vaugoubert away from an afternoon party in order to show him the letter. And yet, heaven knows M. de Charlus did not care to go about with M. de Vaugoubert. For the latter, his monocle stuck in his eye, would keep looking round at every passing youth. What was worse, shedding all restraint when he was with M. de Charlus, he adopted a form of speech which the Baron detested. He referred to everything male in the feminine, and, being intensely stupid, imagined this pleasantry to be extremely witty, and was continually in fits of laughter. As at the same time he attached enormous importance to his position in the diplomatic service, these deplorable sniggering exhibitions in the street were constantly interrupted by sudden fits of terror at the simultaneous appearance of some society person or, worse still, of some civil servant. "That little telegraph messenger," he said, nudging the scowling Baron with his elbow, "I used to know her, but she's turned respectable, the wretch! Oh, that messenger from the Galeries Lafayette, what a dream! Good God, there's the head of the Commercial Department. I hope he didn't notice anything. He's quite capable of mentioning it to the Minister, who would put me on the retired list, all the more so because it appears he's one himself." M. de Charlus was speechless with rage. At length, to bring this infuriating walk to an end, he decided to produce the letter and give it to the Ambassador to read, but warned him to be discreet, for he liked to pretend that Charlie was jealous, in order to be able to persuade people that he was loving. "And," he added with a priceless expression of benevolence, "we ought always to try to cause as little pain as possible."

Before we come back to Jupien's shop, the author would like to say how grieved he would be if the reader were to be offended by his portrayal of such weird characters. On the one hand (and this is the less important aspect of the matter), it may be felt that the aristocracy is, in these pages, disproportionately accused of degeneracy in comparison with the other classes of society. Were this true, it would be in no way surprising. The oldest families end by displaying, in a red and bulbous nose, or a misshapen chin, characteristic signs in which everyone recognises "blood." But among these persistent and increasingly pronounced features, there are others that are not visible, to wit tendencies and tastes. It would be a more serious objection, were there any foundation for it, to say that all this is alien to us, and that we ought to extract truth from the poetry that is close at hand. Art extracted from the most familiar reality does indeed exist and its domain is perhaps the largest of any. But it is none the less true that considerable interest, not to say beauty, may be found in actions inspired by a cast of mind so remote from anything we feel, from anything we believe, that they remain incomprehensible to us, displaying themselves before our eyes like a spectacle without rhyme or reason. What could be more poetic than Xerxes, son of Darius, ordering the sea to be scourged with rods for having engulfed his fleet?

We may be certain that Morel, relying on the influence which his personal attractions gave him over the girl, communicated to her, as coming from himself, the Baron's criticism, for the expression "stand you tea" disappeared as completely from the tailor's shop as, from a salon, some intimate acquaintance who used to call daily but with whom, for one reason or another, the hostess has quarrelled or whom she wants to keep out of sight and meets only outside. M. de Charlus was pleased by the development. He saw in it a proof of his own ascendancy over Morel and the removal of the one little blemish from the girl's perfection. In short, like everyone of his kind, while genuinely fond of Morel and of the girl who was all but engaged to him, and an ardent advocate of their marriage, he thoroughly enjoyed his power to create, as and when he pleased, more or less inoffensive little scenes, outside and above which he himself remained as Olympian as his brother would have done. Morel had told M. de Charlus that he loved Jupien's niece and wished to marry her, and the Baron enjoyed accompanying his young friend on visits in which he played the part of father-in-law to be, indulgent and discreet. Nothing pleased him better.

My personal opinion is that "stand you tea" had originated with Morel himself, and that in the blindness of her love the young seamstress had adopted an expression from her beloved which jarred horribly with her own pretty way of speaking. This way of speaking, the charming manners that went with it, and the patronage of M. de Charlus brought it about that many customers for whom she had worked received her as a friend, invited her to dinner, and introduced her to their friends, though the girl accepted their invitations only with the Baron's permission and on the evenings that suited him. "A young seamstress received in society?" the reader will exclaim, "how improbable!" If one thinks about it, it was no less improbable that at one time Albertine should have come to see me at midnight, and that she should now be living with me. And yet this might perhaps have been improbable of anyone else, but not of Albertine, a fatherless and motherless orphan, leading so free a life that at first I had taken her, at Balbec, for the mistress of a racing cyclist, a girl whose next of kin was Mme Bontemps who in the old days, at Mme Swann's, had particularly admired her niece's bad manners and who now shut her eyes, especially if by doing so she might be able to get rid of her by securing for her a wealthy marriage from which a little of the wealth would trickle into the aunt's pocket (in the highest society, very well-born and very penurious mothers, having succeeded in finding rich brides for their sons, allow themselves to be kept by the young couples, and accept presents of furs, motor-cars and money from daughters-in-law whom they do not like but whom they introduce to their friends).

The day may come when dressmakers will move in society—nor should I find it at all shocking. Jupien's niece, being an exception, cannot yet be regarded as a portent, for one swallow does not make a summer. At all events, if the very modest advancement of Jupien's niece did scandalise some people,

Morel was not among them, for on certain points his stupidity was so intense that not only did he label "rather a fool" this girl who was a thousand times cleverer than himself, and foolish perhaps only in loving him, but he actually took to be adventuresses, dressmakers' assistants in disguise playing at being ladies, the highly reputable ladies who invited her to their houses and whose invitations she accepted without a trace of vanity. Naturally these were not Guermantes, or even people who knew the Guermantes, but rich and elegant middle-class women broad-minded enough to feel that it is no disgrace to invite a dressmaker to your house and at the same time snobbish enough to derive some satisfaction from patronising a girl whom His Highness the Baron de Charlus was in the habit, in all propriety of course, of visiting daily.

Nothing could have pleased the Baron more than the idea of this marriage, for he felt that in this way Morel would not be taken from him. It appears that Jupien's niece had been, when scarcely more than a child, "in trouble." And M. de Charlus, while he sang her praises to Morel, would not have been averse to confiding this secret to his friend—who would have been furious—and thus sowing the seeds of discord. For M. de Charlus, although terribly spiteful, resembled a great many kind people who sing the praises of some man or woman to prove their own kindness, but would avoid like poison the soothing words, so rarely uttered, that would be capable of putting an end to strife. Notwithstanding this, the Baron refrained from making any insinuation, for two reasons. "If I tell him," he said to himself, "that his lady-love is not spotless, his vanity will be hurt and he will be angry with me. Besides, how am I to know that he is not in love with her? If I say nothing, this flash in the pan will soon subside, I shall be able to control their relations as I choose, and he will love her only to the extent that I shall allow. If I tell him of his betrothed's past transgression, who knows whether my Charlie may not still be sufficiently enamoured of her to become jealous? Then I shall by my own doing be converting a harmless and easily controlled flirtation into a serious passion, which is a difficult thing to manage." For these reasons, M. de Charlus preserved a silence which had only the outward appearance of discretion, but was in another respect meritorious, since it is almost impossible for men of his sort to hold their tongues.

Moreover, the girl herself was delightful, and M. de Charlus, who found that she satisfied all the aesthetic interest that he was capable of taking in women, would have liked to have hundreds of photographs of her. Not such a fool as Morel, he was delighted to hear the names of the respectable ladies who invited her to their houses, and whom his social instinct was able to place, but he took good care (wishing to retain his hold over him) not to say so to Charlie, who, a complete oaf in this respect, continued to believe that, apart from the "violin class" and the Verdurins, there existed only the Guermantes and the few almost royal houses enumerated by the Baron, all the rest being but "dregs" or "scum." Charlie interpreted these expressions of M. de Charlus literally.

What, you will say, M. de Charlus, awaited in vain every day of the year by so many ambassadors and duchesses, not dining with the Prince de Croy because one has to give precedence to the latter, M. de Charlus spent all the time that he denied to these great lords and ladies with a tailor's niece! In the first place—the paramount reason—Morel was there. But even if he had not been there, I see nothing improbable in it, or else you are judging things as one of Aimé's minions would have done. Few except waiters believe that an excessively rich man always wears dazzling new clothes and a supremely smart gentleman gives dinner parties for sixty and travels everywhere by car. They deceive themselves. Very often an excessively rich man wears constantly the same jacket; while a supremely smart gentleman is one who in a restaurant hobnobs only with the staff and, on returning home, plays cards with his valet. This does not prevent him from refusing to give precedence to Prince Murat.

Among the reasons which made M. de Charlus look forward to the marriage of the young couple was this, that Jupien's niece would then be in some sense an extension of Morel's personality, and so of the Baron's power over him and knowledge of him. It would never even have occurred to him to feel the slightest scruple about "betraying," in the conjugal sense, the violinist's future wife. But to have a "young couple" to guide, to feel himself the redoubtable and all-powerful protector of Morel's wife, who, looking upon the Baron as a god, would thereby prove that Morel had inculcated this idea into her, and would thus contain in herself something of Morel— all this would add a new variety to the form of M. de Charlus's domination and bring to light in his "creature," Morel, a creature the more—the husband—that is to say would give the Baron something different, new, curious, to love in him. Perhaps indeed this domination would be stronger now than it had ever been. For whereas Morel by himself, naked so to speak, often resisted the Baron whom he felt certain of winning back, once he was married he would soon fear for his household, his bed and board, his future, would offer to M. de Charlus's wishes a wider target, an easier hold. All this, and even at a pinch, on evenings when he was bored, the prospect of stirring up trouble between husband and wife (the Baron had always been fond of battle-pictures) was pleasing to him. Less pleasing, however, than the thought of the state of dependence upon himself in which the young people would live. M. de Charlus's love for Morel acquired a delicious novelty when he said to himself: "His wife too will be mine just as much as he is; they will always behave in such a way as not to annoy me, they will obey my every whim, and thus she will be a sign (hitherto unknown to me) of what I had almost forgotten, what is so very dear to my heart—that to all the world, to everyone who sees that I protect and house them, to myself, Morel is mine." This testimony, in the eyes of the world and in his own, pleased M. de Charlus more than anything. For the possession of what we love is an even greater joy than love itself. Very often, those who conceal this possession from the world do so only from the fear that the beloved object may be taken from them. And their happiness is diminished by this prudent reticence.

The reader may remember that Morel had once told the Baron that his great ambition was to seduce some young girl, and this one in particular, and that to succeed in his enterprise he would promise to marry her, but, the rape accomplished, would "buzz off"; but what with the declarations of love for

Jupien's niece which Morel had poured out to him, M. de Charlus had forgotten this confession. What was more, Morel had quite possibly forgotten it himself. There was perhaps a real gap between Morel's nature—as he had cynically admitted, perhaps even artfully exaggerated it—and the moment at which it would regain control of him. As he became better acquainted with the girl, she had appealed to him, he grew fond of her; he knew himself so little that he even perhaps imagined that he was in love with her, forever. True, his initial desire, his criminal intention remained, but concealed beneath so many superimposed feelings that there is nothing to prove that the violinist would not have been sincere in saying that this vicious desire was not the true motive of his action. There was, moreover, a brief period during which, without his admitting it to himself precisely, this marriage appeared to him to be necessary. Morel was suffering at the time from violent cramp in the hand, and found himself obliged to contemplate the possibility of having to give up the violin. Since, in everything but his art, he was astonishingly lazy, he was faced with the necessity of finding someone to keep him; and he preferred that it should be Jupien's niece rather than M. de Charlus, this arrangement offering him greater freedom and also a wide choice of different kinds of women, ranging from the apprentices, perpetually changing, whom he would persuade Jupien's niece to procure for him, to the rich and beautiful ladies to whom he would prostitute her. That his future wife might refuse to lend herself to these ploys, that she could be to such a degree perverse, never entered Morel's calculations for a moment. However, his cramp having ceased, they receded into the background and were replaced by pure love. His violin would suffice, together with his allowance from M. de Charlus, whose demands upon him would certainly be reduced once he, Morel, was married to the girl. This marriage was the urgent thing, because of his love, and in the interest of his freedom. He asked Jupien for his niece's hand, and Jupien consulted her. This was wholly unnecessary. The girl's passion for the violinist streamed around her, like her hair when she let it down, as did the joy in her beaming eyes. In Morel, almost everything that was agreeable or advantageous to him awakened moral emotions and words to correspond, sometimes even melting him to tears. It was therefore sincerely—if such a word can be applied to him—that he addressed to Jupien's niece speeches as steeped in sentimentality (sentimental too are the speeches that so many young noblemen who look forward to a life of idleness address to some charming daughter of a bourgeois plutocrat) as the theories he had expounded to M. de Charlus about the seduction and deflowering of virgins had been steeped in unmitigated vileness. However, there was another side to this virtuous enthusiasm for a person who afforded him pleasure and to the solemn promises that he made to her. As soon as the person ceased to cause him pleasure, or indeed if, for example, the obligation to fulfil the promises that he had made caused him displeasure, she at once became the object of an antipathy which he sought to justify in his own eyes and which, after some neurasthenic disturbance, enabled him to prove to himself, as soon as the balance of his nervous system was restored, that, even looking at the matter from a purely virtuous point of view, he was released from any obligation.

Thus, towards the end of his stay at Balbec, he had managed somehow to lose all his money and, not daring to mention the matter to M. de Charlus, looked about for someone to whom he might appeal. He had learned from his father (who at the same time had forbidden him ever to become a "sponger") that in such circumstances the correct thing is to write to the person whom you intend to ask for a loan saying that you have a "business matter to discuss with him," that you would like to make a "business appointment." This magic formula had so enchanted Morel that he would, I believe, have been glad to lose his money, simply to have the pleasure of asking for a "business" appointment. In the course of his life he had found that the formula did not have quite the magic power that he supposed. He had discovered that certain people, to whom otherwise he would never have written at all, did not reply within five minutes of receiving his letter asking to "talk business" to them. If the afternoon went by without his receiving an answer, it never occurred to him that, even on

the most optimistic assumption, it was quite possible that the
gentleman addressed had not yet come home, or had had other
letters to write, if indeed he had not gone away, or fallen ill,
or something of that sort. If, by an extraordinary stroke of
luck, Morel was given an appointment for the following morning, he would accost his intended creditor with: "I was quite
surprised not to get an answer, and I wondered whether there
was anything wrong; but I'm glad to see you're quite well,"
and so forth. So, at Balbec, without telling me that he wished
to talk "business" to him, he had asked me to introduce him
to that very Bloch to whom he had been so unpleasant a week
earlier in the train. Bloch had not hesitated to lend him—or
rather to get M. Nissim Bernard to lend him—five thousand
francs. From that moment Morel had worshipped Bloch. He
asked himself with tears in his eyes how he could show his
gratitude to a person who had saved his life. Finally, I undertook to ask on his behalf for a thousand francs a month from
M. de Charlus, a sum which he would at once forward to
Bloch who would thus find himself repaid within quite a
short time. The first month, Morel, still under the impact of
Bloch's generosity, sent him the thousand francs immediately,
but after this he doubtless decided that the remaining four
thousand francs might be put to more satisfactory use, for he
began to speak extremely ill of Bloch. The mere sight of him
was enough to fill his mind with dark thoughts, and Bloch
himself having forgotten the exact amount that he had lent
Morel, and having asked him for 3,500 francs instead of 4,000,
which would have left the violinist 500 francs to the good, the
latter took the line that, in view of so preposterous a fraud, not
only would he not pay another centime but his creditor might
consider himself very fortunate if Morel did not bring an
action against him. As he said this his eyes blazed. Not content
with asserting that Bloch and M. Nissim Bernard had no
cause for resentment against him, he was soon saying that they
might count themselves lucky that he showed no resentment
towards them. Finally, M. Nissim Bernard having apparently
stated that Thibaud played as well as Morel, the latter felt that
he ought to take the matter to court, such a remark being
calculated to damage him professionally; then, since there

was no longer any justice in France, especially against the Jews (anti-semitism having been in Morel the natural effect of a loan of 5,000 francs from a Jew), took to never going out without a loaded revolver.

A similar splenetic reaction in the wake of keen affection was soon to occur in Morel with regard to the tailor's niece. It is true that M. de Charlus may have been to some extent unwittingly responsible for this change, for he was in the habit of declaring, without meaning a word of it, and merely to tease them, that once they were married he would never see them again and would leave them to fend for themselves. This idea was in itself quite insufficient to detach Morel from the girl; but, lurking in his mind, it was ready when the time came to combine with other related ideas capable, once the compound was formed, of becoming a powerful disruptive agent.

It was not very often, however, that I was fated to meet M. de Charlus and Morel. Often they had already gone into Jupien's shop when I came away from the Duchess, for the pleasure that I found in her company was such that I was led to forget not merely the anxious expectation that preceded Albertine's return, but even the hour of that return.

I shall set apart from the other days on which I lingered at Mme de Guermantes's one that was marked by a trivial incident the cruel significance of which entirely escaped me and was not brought home to me until long afterwards. On this particular evening, Mme de Guermantes had given me, knowing that I was fond of them, some branches of syringa which had been sent to her from the South. When I left her and went upstairs to our flat, Albertine had already returned, and on the staircase I ran into Andrée, who seemed to be distressed by the powerful smell of the flowers that I was bringing home.

"What, are you back already?" I said.

"Only a moment ago, but Albertine had some letters to write, so she sent me away."

"You don't think she's up to any mischief?"

"Not at all, she's writing to her aunt, I think. But you know how she dislikes strong scents, she won't be particularly thrilled by your syringa."

"How stupid of me! I shall tell Françoise to put them out on the service stairs."

"Do you imagine Albertine won't notice the scent of them on you? Next to tuberoses they've the strongest scent of any flower, I always think. Anyhow, I believe Françoise has gone out shopping."

"But in that case, as I haven't got my latchkey, how am I to get in?"

"Oh, you've only got to ring the bell. Albertine will let you in. Besides, Françoise may have come back by this time."

I said good-bye to Andrée. I had no sooner pressed the bell than Albertine came to open the door, which she had some difficulty in doing since, in the absence of Françoise, she did not know where to turn on the light. At last she managed to let me in, but the scent of the syringa put her to flight. I took them to the kitchen, so that meanwhile my mistress, leaving her letter unfinished (I had no idea why), had time to go to my room, from which she called to me, and to lie down on my bed. Once again, at the actual moment I saw nothing in all this that was not perfectly natural, at the most a little confused, but in any case unimportant.*

In general, apart from this isolated incident, everything would be quite normal when I returned from my visits to the Duchess. Since Albertine never knew whether I might not wish to go out with her before dinner, I usually found in the hall her hat, coat and umbrella, which she had left lying there in case they should be needed. As soon as I caught sight of them on opening the door, the atmosphere of the house became breathable once more. I felt that, instead of a rarefied air, it was happiness that filled it. I was rescued from my melancholy, the sight of these trifles gave me possession of Albertine, and I would rush to greet her.

On the days when I did not go down to Mme de Guermantes, so that time should not hang too heavy for me during the

---

*She had nearly been caught with Andrée and had snatched a brief respite for herself by turning out all the lights, going to my room so that I should not see the disordered state of her bed, and pretending to be busy writing a letter. But we shall see all this later on, a situation the truth of which I never ascertained.

hour that preceded Albertine's return, I would take up an
album of Elstir's work, one of Bergotte's books, or Vinteuil's
sonata. Then, just as those works of art which seem to address
themselves to the eye or ear alone require that, if we are to
appreciate them, our awakened intelligence shall collaborate
closely with those organs, I would unconsciously summon up
from within me the dreams that Albertine had inspired in me
long ago before I knew her and that had been quenched by
the routine of everyday life. I would cast them into the composer's phrase or the painter's image as into a crucible, or use
them to enrich the book that I was reading. And no doubt the
latter appeared all the more vivid in consequence. But Albertine
herself gained just as much by being thus transported from
one into the other of the two worlds to which we have access
and in which we can place alternately the same object, by escaping thus from the crushing weight of matter to play freely in
the fluid spaces of the mind. I found myself suddenly and for
an instant capable of passionate feelings for this wearisome girl.
She had at that moment the appearance of a work by Elstir
or Bergotte, I felt a momentary ardour for her, seeing her in
the perspective of imagination and art.

Presently I would be told that she had returned; though
there was a standing order that her name was not to be mentioned if I was not alone, and if, for instance, I had Bloch
in the room with me, I would compel him to stay a little longer
so that there should be no risk of his meeting my mistress in
the hall. For I concealed the fact that she was staying in the
house, and even that I ever saw her there, so afraid was I that
one of my friends might become infatuated with her, and wait
for her outside, or that in a momentary encounter in the
passage or the hall she might make a signal and fix a rendezvous. Then I would hear the rustle of Albertine's skirt on her
way to her own room, for, out of tact and also no doubt in
the spirit in which, when we used to go to dinner at la
Raspelière, she went out of her way to ensure that I should
have no cause for jealousy, she did not come to my room when
she knew that I was not alone. But it was not only for this
reason, as I suddenly realised. I remembered; I had known a
different Albertine then all at once she had changed into

another, the Albertine of to-day. And for this change I could hold no one responsible but myself. Everything that she would have admitted to me readily and willingly when we were simply good friends had ceased to flow from her as soon as she had suspected that I was in love with her, or, without perhaps thinking of the word Love, had divined the existence in me of an inquisitorial sentiment that desires to know, suffers from knowing, and seeks to learn yet more. Ever since that day, she had concealed everything from me. She kept away from my room whether she thought my visitor was male or (as was not often the case) female, she whose eyes used at one time to sparkle so brightly whenever I mentioned a girl: "You must try and get her to come here. I'd be amused to meet her." "But she's what you call a bad type." "Precisely, that'll make it all the more fun." At that moment, I might perhaps have learned all that there was to know. And even when, in the little Casino, she had withdrawn her breasts from Andrée's, I believe that this was due not to my presence but to that of Cottard, who was capable, she doubtless thought, of giving her a bad reputation. And yet, even then, she had already begun to "freeze," confiding words no longer issued from her lips, her gestures became guarded. Then she had rid herself of everything that might have disturbed me. To those parts of her life of which I knew nothing she ascribed a character the inoffensiveness of which my ignorance conspired to accentuate. And now the transformation was completed; she went straight to her room if I was not alone, not merely from fear of disturbing me, but in order to show me that she was not interested in other people. There was one thing alone that she would never again do for me, that she would have done only in the days when it would have left me indifferent, that she would then have done without hesitation for that very reason, namely, confess. I should be forever reduced, like a judge, to drawing uncertain conclusions from verbal indiscretions that were perhaps explicable without postulating guilt. And always she would feel that I was jealous, and judging her.

Our engagement was assuming the aspect of a criminal trial, and gave her the timorousness of a guilty party. Now she changed the conversation whenever it turned on people, men or women, who were not of mature years. It was when she had not yet suspected that I was jealous of her that I should have asked her to tell me what I wanted to know. One ought always to take advantage of that period. It is then that one's mistress tells one about her pleasures and even the means by which she conceals them from other people. She would no longer have admitted to me now as she had admitted at Balbec, partly because it was true, partly by way of apology for not making her affection for me more evident, for I had already begun to weary her even then, and she had gathered from my kindness to her that she need not show as much affection to me as to others in order to obtain more from me than from them—she would no longer have admitted to me now as she had admitted then: "I think it stupid to let people see who one loves. I'm just the opposite: as soon as a person attracts me, I pretend not to take any notice. In that way, nobody knows anything about it."

What, it was the same Albertine of to-day, with her pretensions to frankness and indifference to everyone, who had told me that! She would never have expressed such a rule of conduct to me now! She contented herself, when she was chatting to me, with applying it by saying of some girl or other who might cause me anxiety: "Oh, I don't know, I didn't even look at her, she's too insignificant." And from time to time, to anticipate discoveries which I might make, she would proffer the sort of confessions whose very tone, before one knows the reality which they are intended to distort, to exculpate, already betrays them as lies.

As I listened to Albertine's footsteps with the consoling pleasure of thinking that she would not be going out again that evening, I marvelled at the thought that, for this girl whom at one time I had supposed that I could never possibly succeed in knowing, returning home every day actually meant returning to my home. The fugitive and fragmentary pleasure, compounded of mystery and sensuality, which I had felt at Balbec, on the night when she had come to sleep at the hotel, had been completed and stabilised, filling my hitherto empty dwelling with a permanent store of domestic, almost conjugal, bliss that radiated even into the passages and upon which all my senses, either actively or, when I was alone, in imagination as I awaited her return, peacefully fed. When I had heard the door of Albertine's room shut behind her, if I had a friend with me I made haste to get rid of him, not leaving him until I was quite sure that he was on the staircase, down which I might even escort him for a few steps.

Coming towards me in the passage, Albertine would greet me with: "I say, while I'm taking off my things, I shall send you Andrée. She's looked in for a minute to say hello." And still swathed in the big grey veil, falling from her chinchilla toque, which I had given her at Balbec, she would turn from me and go back to her room, as though she had guessed that Andrée, whom I had entrusted with the duty of watching over her, would presently, by relating their day's adventures in full detail, mentioning their meeting with some person of their acquaintance, impart a certain clarity of outline to the vague regions in which the day-long excursion had run its course and which I had been incapable of imagining.

Andrée's defects had become more marked; she was no longer as pleasant a companion as when I first knew her. One noticed now, on the surface, a sort of sour uneasiness, ready to gather like a swell on the sea, merely if I happened to mention something that gave pleasure to Albertine and myself. This did not prevent Andrée from being nicer to me and liking me better—and I had frequent proof of this—than other more amiable people. But the slightest look of happiness on a person's face, if it was not caused by herself, gave a shock to her nerves, as unpleasant as that given by a banging door. She could accept sufferings in which she had no part, but not pleasures; if she saw that I was unwell, she was distressed, was sorry for me, would have stayed to nurse me. But if I displayed a satisfaction as trifling as that of stretching myself with a blissful expression as I shut a book, saying: "Ah! I've just spent two delightful hours reading. What an enjoyable book!", these words, which would have given pleasure to my mother, to Albertine, to Saint-Loup, provoked in Andrée a sort of disapprobation, perhaps simply a sort of nervous uneasiness. My satisfactions caused her an irritation which she was unable to conceal. These defects were supplemented by others of a more serious nature; one day when I mentioned the young man so learned in matters of racing, gambling and golf, so uneducated in everything else, whom I had met with the little band at Balbec, Andrée said with a sneer: "You know that his father is a swindler, he only just missed being prosecuted. They're swaggering now more than ever, but I tell everybody about it. I should love them to bring an action for slander against me. I'd have something to say in the witness-box!" Her eyes sparkled. In fact I discovered that the father had done nothing wrong, and that Andrée knew this as well as anybody. But she had felt spurned by the son, had looked around for something that would embarrass him, put him to shame, and had concocted a whole string of evidence which she imagined herself called upon to give in court, and, by dint of repeating the details to herself, was perhaps herself unsure whether they were true or not. And so, in her present state (and even without her brief, mad hatreds), I should not have wished to see her, if only because of the malevolent touchiness that surrounded with a sour and frigid carapace her warmer and better nature. But the information which she alone could give me about my mistress interested me too much for me to be able to neglect so rare an opportunity of acquiring it.

Andrée would come into my room, shutting the door behind her. They had met a girl they knew, whom Albertine had never mentioned to me.

"What did they talk about?"

"I can't tell you; I took advantage of the fact that Albertine wasn't alone to go and buy some wool."

"Buy some wool?"

"Yes, it was Albertine who asked me to get it."

"All the more reason not to have gone. It was perhaps a pretext to get you out of the way."

"But she asked me to go for it before we met her friend."

"Ah!" I would reply, breathing again. At once my suspicions were revived: she might, for all I knew, have made an appointment beforehand with her friend and have provided herself with an excuse to be left alone when the time came. Besides, could I be certain that it was not my former hypothesis (according to which Andrée did not always tell me the truth) that was correct? Andrée was perhaps in league with Albertine.

Love, I used to say to myself at Balbec, is what we feel for a person; our jealousy seems rather to be directed towards that person's actions; we feel that if she were to tell us everything, we might perhaps easily be cured of our love. However skilfully jealousy is concealed by him who suffers from it, it is very soon detected by her who has inspired it, and who applies equal skill in her turn. She seeks to put us off the scent of what might make us unhappy, and easily succeeds, for, to the man who is not forewarned, how should a casual remark reveal the falsehoods that lie beneath it? We do not distinguish this remark from the rest; spoken apprehensively, it is received unheedingly. Later on, when we are alone, we shall return to this remark, which will seem to us not altogether consistent with the facts of the case. But do we remember it correctly? There seems to arise spontaneously in us, with regard to it and to the accuracy of our memory, a doubt of the sort which, in certain nervous conditions, prevents us from remembering whether we have bolted the door, no less after the fiftieth time than after the first; it would seem that we can repeat the action indefinitely without its ever being accompanied by a precise and liberating memory. But at least we can shut the door again for the fifty-first time. Whereas the disturbing remark exists in the past, in an imperfect hearing of it which it is not within our power to re-enact. Then we concentrate our attention upon other remarks which conceal nothing, and the sole remedy, which we do not want, is to be ignorant of everything in order not to have any desire for further knowledge.

As soon as jealousy is discovered, it is regarded by the person who is its object as a challenge which justifies deception. Moreover, in our endeavour to learn something, it is we who have taken the initiative in lying and deceit. Andrée or Aimé may promise us that they will say nothing, but will they keep their promise? Then Bloch could promise nothing because he knew nothing. And Albertine has only to talk to any of the three in order to learn, with the help of what Saint-Loup would have called "cross-checking," that we are lying to her when we claim to be indifferent to her actions and morally incapable of having her watched. Following thus upon my habitual boundless uncertainty as to what Albertine might be doing, an uncertainty too indeterminate not to remain painless, which was to jealousy what that incipient forgetfulness in which assuagement is born of vagueness is to grief, the little fragment of an answer which Andrée had just brought me at once began to raise fresh questions; in exploring one sector of the vast zone that extended round me, I had succeeded only in pushing back still further that unknowable thing which, when we seek to form a definite idea of it, another person's life invariably is to us. I would continue to interrogate Andrée while Albertine, from tact and in order to leave me free (was she conscious of this?) to question her friend, prolonged her toilet in her own room.

"I think Albertine's uncle and aunt both like me," I would thoughtlessly remark to Andrée, forgetting her peculiar nature.

At once I would see her glutinous features change, like a mixture that has turned; her face would seem permanently clouded. Her mouth would become bitter. Nothing remained in Andrée of that juvenile gaiety which, like all the little band and notwithstanding her delicate health, she had displayed in the year of my first visit to Balbec and which now (it is true that Andrée was several years older) became so rapidly eclipsed in her. But I would make it reappear involuntarily before Andrée left me that evening to go home to dinner. "Somebody was singing your praises to me to-day in the most glowing terms," I would say to her. Immediately a ray of joy would beam from her eyes; she looked as though she really loved me. She avoided my gaze but smiled at the empty air with a pair of eyes that had suddenly become quite round. "Who was it?" she would ask with an artless, avid interest. I would tell her, and, whoever it was, she was delighted. Then the time would come for her to leave me.

After Andrée's departure Albertine would come back to my room; she had undressed, and would be wearing one of the crêpe-de-Chine dressing-gowns or Japanese kimonos which I had asked Mme de Guermantes to describe to me, and for some of which supplementary details had been furnished me by Mme Swann, in a letter that began: "After your long eclipse,

I felt as I read your letter about my *tea-gowns* that I was hearing from a ghost."

Albertine had on her feet a pair of black shoes studded with brilliants which Françoise indignantly called clogs and which were modelled upon those which, from the drawing-room window, she had seen Mme de Guermantes wearing in the evening, just as a little later Albertine took to wearing slippers, some of gold kid, others of chinchilla, the sight of which gave me great pleasure because they were all of them signs (which other shoes would not have been) that she was living under my roof. She had also certain things which had not come to her from me, including a fine gold ring. I admired upon it the outspread wings of an eagle. "It was my aunt who gave me it," she explained. "She can be quite nice sometimes after all. It makes me feel terribly old, because she gave it to me on my twentieth birthday."

Albertine took a far keener interest in all these pretty things than the Duchess, because, like every obstacle in the way of a possession (in my own case the ill health which made travel so difficult and so desirable), poverty, more generous than opulence, gives to women far more than the clothes that they cannot afford to buy: the desire for those clothes which goes hand in hand with a genuine, detailed, thorough knowledge of them. She, because she had never been able to afford these things, and I, because in ordering them for her I was seeking to give her pleasure, were both of us like students who already know all about the pictures which they are longing to go to Dresden or Vienna to see. Whereas rich women, amid the vast quantities of their hats and gowns, are like those tourists to whom a visit to a gallery, being preceded by no desire, gives merely a sensation of bewilderment, boredom and exhaustion. A particular toque, a particular sable coat, a particular Doucet dressing-gown with pink-lined sleeves, assumed for Albertine, who had observed them, coveted them and, thanks to the exclusiveness and meticulousness that characterize desire, had at once isolated them from the rest against an empty background in which the lining or the sash stood out to perfection, and studied them down to the smallest detail—and for myself who had gone to Mme de Guermantes in quest of an explanation of what constituted the peculiar merit, the superiority, the stylishness of each garment and the inimitable cut of the great designer—an importance, a charm which they certainly did not possess for the Duchess, surfeited before she had even acquired an appetite, and would not, indeed, have possessed for me had I seen them a few years earlier while accompanying some lady of fashion on one of her wearisome tours of the dressmakers' shops.

To be sure, a woman of fashion was what Albertine too was gradually becoming. For, while each of the things that I ordered for her was the prettiest of its kind, with all the refinements that might have been added to it by Mme de Guermantes or Mme Swann, she was beginning to possess these things in abundance. But it mattered little, since she had admired them beforehand and in isolation. When we have been smitten by one painter, then by another, we may end by feeling for the whole gallery an admiration that is not frigid, for it is made up of successive enthusiasms, each one exclusive in its day, which finally have joined forces and become reconciled in one whole.

She was not, moreover, frivolous, read a great deal when she was alone, and read aloud to me when we were together. She had become extremely intelligent. She would say, quite falsely in fact: "I'm appalled when I think that but for you I should still be quite ignorant. Don't contradict. You have opened up a world of ideas to me which I never suspected, and whatever I may have become I owe entirely to you."

It will be remembered that she had spoken in similar terms of my influence over Andrée. Had either of them a real feeling for me? And, in themselves, what were Albertine and Andrée? To know the answer, I should have to immobilise you, to cease to live in that perpetual state of expectancy ending always in a different presentment of you, I should have to cease to love you in order to fix your image, cease to be conscious of your interminable and always disconcerting arrival, O girls, O successive rays in the swirling vortex wherein we throb with emotion on seeing you reappear while barely recognising you, in the dizzy velocity of light. We might perhaps remain unaware of that velocity, and everything would seem to us motionless, did not a sexual attraction set us in pursuit of

you, O drops of gold, always dissimilar and always surpassing
our expectation! Each time, a girl so little resembles what she
was the time before (shattering, as soon as we catch sight of
her, the memory that we had retained of her and the desire
that we had proposed to gratify), that the stability of nature
which we ascribe to her is purely fictitious and a convention of
speech. We have been told that some pretty girl is tender,
loving, full of the most delicate feelings. Our imagination
accepts this assurance, and when we behold for the first time,
beneath the woven girdle of her golden hair, the rosy disc of
her face, we are almost afraid that this too virtuous sister,
cooling our ardour by her very virtue, can never be to us the
lover for whom we have been longing. What secrets, however,
we confide to her from the first moment, on the strength of that
nobility of heart, what plans we make together! But a few
days later, we regret that we were so confiding, for the rosy-
cheeked girl, at our second meeting, addresses us in the
language of a lascivious Fury. As for the successive facets
which after pulsating for some days the roseate light, now
eclipsed, presents to us, it is not even certain that a momentum
external to these girls has not modified their aspect, and this
might well have happened with my band of girls at Balbec.
People extol to us the gentleness, the purity of a virgin. But
afterwards they feel that something more spicy would please
us better, and recommend her to show more boldness. In
herself was she one more than the other? Perhaps not, but
capable of yielding to any number of different possibilities in the
headlong current of life. With another, whose whole attraction
lay in a certain ruthlessness (which we counted upon subduing
to our own will), as, for instance, with the fearsome jumping
girl at Balbec who grazed in her leaps the bald pates of startled
old gentlemen, what a disappointment when, a new facet of
her personality being presented to us, just as we are making
tender declarations fired by the memory of her cruelty to
others, we hear her telling us, by way of an opening gambit,
that she is shy, that she can never say anything intelligent to
anyone at a first introduction, so frightened is she, and that it is
only after a fortnight or so that she will be able to talk to us at
her ease. The steel has turned to cotton wool, and there is

nothing left for us to attempt to break down, since of her own accord she has shed her hard integument. Of her own accord, but through our fault perhaps, for the tender words which we addressed to Harshness had perhaps, even without any deliberate calculation on her part, suggested to her that she ought to be gentle. (Distressing as the change may have been to us, it was not altogether maladroit, for our gratitude for all her gentleness may exact more from us than our delight at overcoming her cruelty.)

I do not say that a day will not come when, even to these luminous girls, we shall assign sharply defined characters, but that will be because they will have ceased to interest us, because their entry upon the scene will no longer be, for our heart, the apparition which it expected to be different and which, each time, leaves it overwhelmed by fresh incarnations. Their immobility will come from our indifference to them, which will deliver them up to the judgment of our intelligence. The latter's conclusions will not in fact be very much more categorical, for after deciding that some defect, predominant in the one, was happily absent from the other, it will see that this defect was offset by some precious quality. So that, from the false judgment of our intelligence, which comes into play only when we have lost interest, there will emerge well-defined, stable characters of girls, which will enlighten us no more than did the surprising faces that used to appear every day when, in the bewildering speed of our expectation, they presented themselves daily, weekly, too different to allow us, since their course was never arrested, to classify them, to award degrees of merit. As for our sentiments, we have said so too often to repeat it here, as often as not love is no more than the association of the image of a girl (whom otherwise we should soon have found intolerable) with the heartbeats inseparable from an endless wait in vain and her failure to turn up at the end of it. All this is true not only of impressionable young men in the face of changeable girls. At the stage that our narrative has now reached, it appears, as I later learned, that Jupien's niece had altered her opinion of Morel and M. de Charlus. My chauffeur, to reinforce her love for Morel, had extolled to her, as existing in the violinist, boundless refinements of delicacy in which she was all too ready to believe. And at the same time Morel never ceased to complain to her of the despotic treatment that he received from M. de Charlus, which she ascribed to malevolence, never imagining that it could be due to love. She was moreover forced to acknowledge that M. de Charlus was a tyrannical presence at all their meetings. And in corroboration of this, she had heard society women speak of the Baron's atrocious spitefulness. Lately, however, her judgment had been completely reversed. She had discovered in Morel (without ceasing for that reason to love him) depths of malevolence and perfidy, compensated it was true by frequent gentleness and genuine sensitivity, and in M. de Charlus an immense and unsuspected kindness mixed with incomprehensible asperities. And so she had been unable to arrive at a more definite judgment of what, each in himself, the violinist and his protector really were, than I was able to form of Andrée, whom nevertheless I saw every day, or of Albertine who was living with me.

On the evenings when the latter did not read aloud to me, she would play me some music or begin a game of draughts, or a conversation, which I would interrupt with kisses. Our relations had a simplicity that made them soothing. The very emptiness of her life gave Albertine a sort of eagerness to comply with the few demands I made on her. Behind this girl, as behind the purple light that used to filter beneath the curtains of my room at Balbec, while outside the concert blared, there shone the blue-green undulations of the sea. Was she not, after all (she in whose being there now existed an idea of me so habitual and familiar that, next to her aunt, I was perhaps the person whom she distinguished least from herself), the girl whom I had seen the first time at Balbec, beneath her flat cap, with her insistent laughing eyes, a stranger still, slender as a silhouette projected against the waves? These effigies preserved intact in our memory astonish us, when we recall them, by their dissimilarity from the person we know, and we realise what a task of remodelling is performed every day by habit. In the charm that Albertine had in Paris, by my fireside, there still survived the desire that had been aroused in me by that insolent and blossoming cortège along the beach, and just as Rachel retained in Saint-Loup's eyes, even after he had made her abandon it, the glamour of her stage life, so in this Albertine cloistered in my house, far from Balbec whence I had hurried her away, there persisted the excitement, the social confusion, the hollow restlessness, the roving desires of seaside life. She was so effectively caged that on certain evenings I did not even ask her to leave her room for mine, she whom at one time all the world pursued, whom I had found it so hard to overtake as she sped past on her bicycle, whom the liftboy himself was unable to bring back to me, leaving me with little hope of her coming, although I sat up waiting for her all night. Had not Albertine been—out there in front of the hotel —like a great actress of the blazing beach, arousing jealousy when she advanced upon that natural stage, speaking to no one, jostling the habitués, dominating her friends? And was not this so greatly coveted actress the same who, withdrawn by me from the stage, shut up in my house, was now here, shielded from the desires of all those who might henceforth seek for her in vain, sitting now in my room, now in her own, engaged in some work of design or engraving?

No doubt, in the first days at Balbec, Albertine seemed to exist on a parallel plane to that on which I was living, but one that had converged on it (after my visit to Elstir) and had finally joined it, as my relations with her, at Balbec, in Paris, then at Balbec again, grew more intimate. Moreover, what a difference there was between the two pictures of Balbec, on my first visit and on my second, pictures composed of the same villas from which the same girls emerged by the same sea! In Albertine's friends at the time of my second visit, whom I knew so well, whose good and bad qualities were so clearly engraved on their features, how could I recapture those fresh, mysterious strangers who once could not thrust open the doors of their chalets with a screech over the sand or brush past the quivering tamarisks without making my heart throb? Their huge eyes had sunk into their faces since then, doubtless because they had ceased to be children, but also because those ravishing strangers, those ravishing actresses of that first romantic year, about whom I had gone ceaselessly in quest of information, no longer held any mystery for me. They had become for me, obedient to my whims, a mere grove of budding girls, from among whom I was not a little proud of having plucked, and hidden away from the rest of the world, the fairest rose.

Between the two Balbec settings, so different one from the other, there was the interval of several years in Paris, the long expanse of which was dotted with all the visits that Albertine had paid me. I saw her in the different years of my life occupying, in relation to myself, different positions which made me feel the beauty of the intervening spaces, that long lapse of time during which I had remained without seeing her and in the diaphanous depths of which the roseate figure that I saw before me was carved with mysterious shadows and in bold relief. This was due also to the superimposition not merely of the successive images which Albertine had been for me, but also of the great qualities of intelligence and heart, and of the defects of character, all alike unsuspected by me, which Albertine, in a germination, a multiplication of herself, a fleshy efflorescence in sombre colours, had added to a nature that formerly could scarcely have been said to exist, but was now difficult to plumb. For other people, even those of whom we have dreamed so much that they have come to seem no more than pictures, figures by Benozzo Gozzoli against a greenish background, of whom we were inclined to believe that they varied only according to the point of vantage from which we looked at them, their distance from us, the effect of light and shade, such people, while they change in relation to ourselves, change also in themselves, and there had been an enrichment, a solidification and an increase of volume in the figure once simply outlined against the sea.

Moreover, it was not only the sea at the close of day that existed for me in Albertine, but at times the drowsy murmur of the sea upon the shore on moonlit nights. For sometimes, when I got up to fetch a book from my father's study, my mistress, having asked my permission to lie down while I was out of the room, was so tired after her long outing in the morning and afternoon in the open air that, even if I had been away for a moment only, when I returned I found her asleep and did not wake her. Stretched out at full length on my bed, in an attitude so natural that no art could have devised it, she reminded me of a long blossoming stem that had been laid there; and so in a sense she was: the faculty of dreaming, which I possessed only in her absence, I recovered at such moments in her presence, as though by falling asleep she had become a plant. In this way, her sleep realised to a certain extent the possibility of love: alone, I could think of her, but I missed her, I did not possess her; when she was present, I spoke to her, but was too absent from myself to be able to think of her; when she was asleep, I no longer had to talk, I knew that I was no longer observed by her, I no longer needed to live on the surface of myself.

By shutting her eyes, by losing consciousness, Albertine had stripped off, one after another, the different human personalities with which she had deceived me ever since the day when I had first made her acquaintance. She was animated now only by the unconscious life of plants, of trees, a life more different from my own, more alien, and yet one that belonged more to me. Her personality was not constantly escaping, as when we talked, by the outlets of her unacknowledged thoughts and of her eyes. She had called back into herself everything of her that lay outside, had withdrawn, enclosed, reabsorbed herself into her body. In keeping it in front of my eyes, in my hands, I had an impression of possessing her entirely which I never had when she was awake. Her life was submitted to me, exhaled towards me its gentle breath.

I listened to this murmuring, mysterious emanation, soft as a sea breeze, magical as a gleam of moonlight, that was her sleep. So long as it lasted, I was free to dream about her and yet at the same time to look at her, and, when that sleep grew deeper, to touch, to kiss her. What I felt then was a love as pure, as immaterial, as mysterious, as if I had been in the presence of those inanimate creatures which are the beauties of nature. And indeed, as soon as her sleep became at all deep, she ceased to be merely the plant that she had been; her sleep, on the margin of which I remained musing, with a fresh delight of which I never tired, which I could have gone on enjoying indefinitely, was to me a whole landscape. Her sleep brought within my reach something as serene, as sensually delicious as those nights of full moon on the bay of Balbec, calm as a lake over which the branches barely stir, where, stretched out upon the sand, one could listen for hours on end to the surf breaking and receding.

On entering the room, I would remain standing in the doorway, not venturing to make a sound, and hearing none but that of her breath rising to expire upon her lips at regular intervals, like the reflux of the sea, but drowsier and softer. And at the moment when my ear absorbed that divine sound, I felt that there was condensed in it the whole person, the whole life of the charming captive outstretched there before my eyes. Carriages went rattling past in the street, but her brow remained as smooth and untroubled, her breath as light, reduced to the simple expulsion of the necessary quantity of air. Then, seeing that her sleep would not be disturbed, I would advance cautiously, sit down on the chair that stood by the bedside, then on the bed itself.

I spent many a charming evening talking and playing with Albertine, but none so delicious as when I was watching her sleep. Granted that she had, as she chatted with me, or played cards, a naturalness that no actress could have imitated; it was a more profound naturalness, as it were at one remove, that was offered me by her sleep. Her hair, falling along her pink cheek, was spread out beside her on the bed, and here and there an isolated straight tress gave the same effect of perspective as those moonlit trees, lank and pale, which one sees standing erect and stiff in the backgrounds of Elstir's Raphaelesque pictures. If Albertine's lips were closed, her eyelids, on the other hand, seen from where I was placed, seemed so loosely joined that I might almost have questioned whether she really was asleep. At the same time those lowered lids gave her face that perfect continuity which is unbroken by the obtrusion of eyes. There are people whose faces assume an unaccustomed beauty and majesty the moment they cease to look out of their eyes.

I would gaze at Albertine stretched out below me. From time to time a slight, unaccountable tremor ran through her, as the leaves of a tree are shaken for a few moments by a sudden breath of wind. She would touch her hair and then, not having arranged it to her liking, would raise her hand to it again with

motions so consecutive, so deliberate, that I was convinced
that she was about to wake. Not at all; she grew calm again in
the sleep from which she had not emerged. Thereafter she lay
motionless. She had laid her hand on her breast with a droop
of the arm so artlessly childlike that I was obliged, as I gazed
at her, to suppress the smile that is provoked in us by the
solemnity, the innocence and the grace of little children.

I, who was acquainted with many Albertines in one person,
seemed now to see many more again reposing by my side. Her
eyebrows, arched as I had never noticed them, encircled the
globes of her eyelids like a halcyon's downy nest. Races,
atavisms, vices reposed upon her face. Whenever she moved
her head, she created a different woman, often one whose
existence I had never suspected. I seemed to possess not one
but countless girls. Her breathing, as it became gradually deeper, made her breast rise and fall in a regular rhythm, and above
it her folded hands and her pearls, displaced in a different way
by the same movement, like boats and anchor chains set
swaying by the movement of the tide. Then, feeling that the
tide of her sleep was full, that I should not run aground on
reefs of consciousness covered now by the high water of
profound slumber, I would climb deliberately and noiselessly
on to the bed, lie down by her side, clasp her waist in one arm,
and place my lips upon her cheek and my free hand on her
heart and then on every part of her body in turn, so that it too
was raised, like the pearls, by the breathing of the sleeping
girl; I myself was gently rocked by its regular motion: I had
embarked upon the tide of Albertine's sleep.

Sometimes it afforded me a pleasure that was less pure. For
this I had no need to make any movement, but allowed my
leg to dangle against hers, like an oar which one trails in the
water, imparting to it now and again a gentle oscillation like
the intermittent wing-beat of a bird asleep in the air. I chose,
in gazing at her, the aspect of her face which one never saw
and which was so beautiful. It is I suppose comprehensible
that the letters which we receive from a person should be
more or less similar to one another and combine to trace an
image of the writer sufficiently different from the person we
know to constitute a second personality. But how much

stranger is it that a woman should be conjoined, like Rosita with Doodica,[2] with another woman whose different beauty makes us infer another character, and that in order to see them we must look at one of them in profile and the other in full face. The sound of her breathing, which had grown louder, might have given the illusion of the panting of sexual pleasure, and when mine was at its climax, I could kiss her without having interrupted her sleep. I felt at such moments that I had possessed her more completely, like an unconscious and unresisting object of dumb nature. I was not troubled by the words that she murmured from time to time in her sleep; their meaning was closed to me, and besides, whoever the unknown person to whom they referred, it was upon my hand, upon my cheek that her hand, stirred by an occasional faint tremor, stiffened for an instant. I savoured her sleep with a disinterested, soothing love, just as I would remain for hours listening to the unfurling of the waves.

Perhaps people must be capable of making us suffer intensely before they can procure for us, in the hours of remission, the same soothing calm as nature does. I did not have to answer her as when we were engaged in conversation, and even if I could have remained silent, as for that matter I did when it was she who was talking, still while listening to her I did not penetrate so far into the depths of her being. As I continued to hear, to capture from moment to moment, the murmur, soothing as a barely perceptible breeze, of her pure breath, it was a whole physiological existence that was spread out before me, at my disposal; just as I used to remain for hours lying on the beach, in the moonlight, so long could I have remained there gazing at her, listening to her. Sometimes it was as though the sea was beginning to swell, as though the storm was making itself felt even inside the bay, and I would press myself against her and listen to the gathering roar of her breath.

Sometimes, when she was too warm, she would take off her kimono while she was already almost asleep and fling it over an armchair. As she slept I would tell myself that all her letters were in the inner pocket of this kimono, into which she always thrust them. A signature, an assignation, would have sufficed to prove a lie or to dispel a suspicion. When I

could see that Albertine was sound asleep, leaving the foot of
the bed where I had been standing motionless in contemplation
of her, I would take a step forward, seized by a burning curiosity, feeling that the secret of this other life lay offering itself
to me, flaccid and defenceless, in that armchair. Perhaps I took
this step forward also because to stand perfectly still and watch
her sleeping became tiring after a while. And so, on tiptoe,
constantly turning round to make sure that Albertine was not
waking, I would advance towards the armchair. There I
would stop short, and stand for a long time gazing at the kimono, as I had stood for a long time gazing at Albertine. But
(and here perhaps I was wrong) never once did I touch the
kimono, put my hand in the pocket, examine the letters. In
the end, realising that I would never make up my mind, I
would creep back to the bedside and begin again to watch
the sleeping Albertine, who would tell me nothing, whereas I
could see lying across an arm of the chair that kimono which
would perhaps have told me much.

And just as people pay a hundred francs a day for a room at
the Grand Hotel at Balbec in order to breathe the sea air, I
felt it to be quite natural that I should spend more than that
on her, since I had her breath upon my cheek, between my
lips which I laid half-open upon hers, through which her life
flowed against my tongue.

But this pleasure of seeing her sleep, which was as sweet to
me as that of feeling her live, was cut short by another pleasure,
that of seeing her wake. It was, carried to a more profound
and more mysterious degree, the same pleasure as I felt in
having her under my roof. It was gratifying to me, of course,
that when she alighted from the car in the afternoon, it should
be to my house that she was returning. It was even more so to
me that when, from the underworld of sleep, she climbed the
last steps of the staircase of dreams, it was in my room that she
was reborn to consciousness and life, that she wondered for
an instant: "Where am I?" and, seeing the objects by which
she was surrounded, and the lamp whose light scarcely made
her blink her eyes, was able to assure herself that she was at
home on realising that she was waking in *my* home. In that
first delicious moment of uncertainty, it seemed to me that

once again I was taking possession of her more completely, since, instead of her returning to her own room after an outing, it was my room that, as soon as Albertine should have recognised it, was about to enclose, to contain her, without there being any sign of misgiving in her eyes, which remained as calm as if she had never slept at all. The uncertainty of awakening, revealed by her silence, was not at all revealed in her eyes.

Then she would find her tongue and say: "My ——" or "My darling ——" followed by my Christian name, which, if we give the narrator the same name as the author of this book, would be "My Marcel," or "My darling Marcel." After this I would never allow a member of my family, by calling me "darling," to rob of their precious uniqueness the delicious words that Albertine uttered to me. As she uttered them, she pursed her lips in a little pout which she spontaneously transformed into a kiss. As quickly as she had earlier fallen asleep, she had awoken.

No more than my own progression in time, no more than the fact of looking at a girl sitting near me beneath a lamp that shed upon her a very different light from that of the sun when I used to see her striding along the seashore, was this material enrichment, this autonomous progress of Albertine, the determining cause of the difference between my present view of her and my original impression of her at Balbec. A longer term of years might have separated the two images without effecting so complete a change; it had come about, this sudden and fundamental change, when I had learned that Albertine had been virtually brought up by Mlle Vinteuil's friend. If at one time I had been overcome with excitement when I thought I detected mystery in Albertine's eyes, now I was happy only at times when from those eyes, from those cheeks even, as revealing as the eyes, at one moment so gentle but quickly turning sullen, I succeeded in expelling every trace of mystery. The image which I sought, upon which I relied, for which I would have been prepared to die, was no longer that of Albertine leading an unknown life, it was that of an Albertine as known to me as it was possible for her to be (and it was for this reason that my love could not be lasting unless it remained unhappy, for by definition it did not satisfy the need for mystery), an Albertine who did not reflect a distant world, but desired nothing else—there were moments when this did indeed appear to be the case—than to be with me, to be exactly like me, an Albertine who was the image precisely of what was mine and not of the unknown.

When it is thus from an hour of anguish in relation to another person that love is born, when it is from uncertainty whether we shall keep or lose that person, such a love bears the mark of the revolution that has created it, it recalls very little of what we had previously seen when we thought of the person in question. And although my first impressions of Albertine, silhouetted against the sea, might to some small extent persist in my love for her, in reality, these earlier impressions occupy but a tiny place in a love of this sort, in its strength, in its agony, in its need of comfort and its resort to a calm and soothing memory with which we would prefer to abide and to learn nothing more of the beloved, even if there were something horrible to be known. Even if the previous impressions are retained, such a love is made of very different stuff!

Sometimes I would put out the light before she came in. It was in the darkness, barely guided by the glow of a smouldering log, that she would lie down by my side. My hands and my cheeks alone identified her without my eyes seeing her, my eyes that were often afraid of finding her changed; so that, by virtue of these blind caresses, she may perhaps have felt bathed in a warmer tenderness than usual.

On other evenings, I undressed and went to bed, and, with Albertine perched on the side of the bed, we would resume our game or our conversation interrupted by kisses; and in the physical desire that alone makes us take an interest in the existence and character of another person, we remain so true to our own nature (even if, on the other hand, we abandon successively the different persons whom we have loved in turn) that on one occasion, catching sight of myself in the mirror at the moment when I was kissing Albertine and calling her "my little girl," the sorrowful, passionate expression on my own

face, similar to the expression it would have worn long ago
with Gilberte whom I no longer remembered, and would
perhaps assume one day with another if I were ever to forget
Albertine, made me think that, over and above any personal
considerations (instinct requiring that we consider the person
of the moment as the only real one), I was performing the
duties of an ardent and painful devotion dedicated as an obla-
tion to the youth and beauty of Woman. And yet with this
desire by which I was honouring youth with a votive offering,
with my memories too of Balbec, there was blended, in my
need to keep Albertine thus every evening by my side, something that had hitherto been foreign to my amorous existence
at least, if it was not entirely new in my life. It was a soothing
power the like of which I had not experienced since the evenings at Combray long ago when my mother, stooping over my
bed, brought me repose in a kiss. To be sure, I should have
been greatly astonished at that time had anyone told me that
I was not extremely kind and especially that I would ever seek
to deprive someone else of a pleasure. I must have known myself very imperfectly then, for my pleasure in having Albertine
to live with me was much less a positive pleasure than the
pleasure of having withdrawn from the world, where everyone
was free to enjoy her in turn, the blossoming girl who, if she
did not bring me any great joy, was at least withholding joy
from others. Ambition and fame would have left me unmoved.
Even more was I incapable of feeling hatred. And yet to love
carnally was none the less, for me, to enjoy a triumph over
countless rivals. I can never repeat it often enough: it was more
than anything else an appeasement.

For all that I might, before Albertine returned, have doubted
her, have imagined her in the room at Montjouvain, once she
was in her dressing-gown and seated facing my chair or (if,
as was more frequent, I had remained in bed) at the foot of my
bed, I would deposit my doubts in her, hand them over for
her to relieve me of them, with the abnegation of a worshipper
uttering a prayer. All through the evening she might have been
there, curled up in a mischievous ball on my bed, playing with
me like a cat; her little pink nose, the tip of which she made
even tinier with a coquettish glance which gave it a daintiness

characteristic of certain women who are inclined to be plump, might have given her an inflamed and provocative air; she might have allowed a tress of her long, dark hair to fall over her pale-pink waxen cheek and, half shutting her eyes, unfolding her arms, have seemed to be saying to me: "Do what you like with me"—but when the time came for her to leave me, and she drew close to me to say good-night, it was a softness that had become almost familial that I kissed on either side of her sturdy neck which then never seemed to me brown or freckled enough, as though these solid qualities were associated with a certain frank good nature in Albertine.

When it was Albertine's turn to bid me good-night, kissing me on either side of my neck, her hair caressed me like a wing of softly bristling feathers. Incomparable as were those two kisses of peace, Albertine slipped into my mouth, in making me the gift of her tongue, as it were a gift of the Holy Ghost, conveyed to me a viaticum, left me with a provision of tranquillity almost as precious as when my mother in the evening at Combray used to lay her lips upon my forehead.

"Are you coming with us to-morrow, old crosspatch?" she would ask before leaving me.

"Where are you going?"

"That will depend on the weather and on you. But have you written anything to-day, my little darling? No? Then it was hardly worth your while not coming with us. Tell me, by the way, when I came in this evening, you knew my step, you guessed at once who it was?"

"Of course. Could I possibly be mistaken? Couldn't I tell my little sparrow's hop among a thousand? She must let me take her shoes off before she goes to bed, it will give me such pleasure. You're so nice and pink in all that white lace."

Such was my answer; amid the sensual expressions, others will be recognised that were peculiar to my grandmother and my mother. For, little by little, I was beginning to resemble all my relations: my father who—in a very different fashion from myself, no doubt, for if things repeat themselves, it is with great variations—took so keen an interest in the weather; and not my father only, but, more and more, my aunt Léonie. Otherwise Albertine could not but have been a reason for my going out, so as not to leave her on her own, beyond my control. Although every day I found an excuse in some particular indisposition, what made me so often remain in bed was a person—not Albertine, not a person I loved but a person with more power over me than any beloved—who had transmigrated into me, a person despotic to the point of silencing at times my jealous suspicions or at least of preventing me from going to verify whether they had any foundation, and that person was my aunt Léonie—my aunt Léonie, who was entirely steeped in piety and with whom I could have sworn that I had not a single point in common, I who was so passionately fond of pleasure, apparently worlds apart from that religious maniac who had never known any pleasure in her life and lay mumbling her rosary all day long, I who suffered from my inability to embark upon a literary career whereas she had been the one person in the family who could never understand that reading was anything other than a means of whiling away the time, which made it, even at Eastertide, permissible on Sundays, when every serious occupation is forbidden in order that the day may be hallowed by prayer alone. And as if it were not enough that I should bear an exaggerated resemblance to my father, to the extent of not being satisfied like him with consulting the barometer, but becoming an animated barometer myself, as if it were not enough that I should allow myself to be ordered by my aunt Léonie to stay at home and watch the weather, from my bedroom window or even from my bed, here I was talking now to Albertine, at one moment as the child that I had been at Combray used to talk to my mother, at another as my grandmother used to talk to me. When we have passed a certain age, the soul of the child that we were and the souls of the dead from whom we sprang come and shower upon us their riches and their spells, asking to be allowed to contribute to the new emotions which we feel and in which, erasing their former image, we recast them in an original creation. Thus my whole past from my earliest years, and, beyond these, the past of my parents and relations, blended with my impure love for Albertine the tender charm of an affection at once filial and maternal. We have to give hospitality, at a certain stage in our lives, to all our relatives who have journeyed so far and gathered round us.

Before Albertine obeyed and took off her shoes, I would open her chemise. Her two little uplifted breasts were so round that they seemed not so much to be an integral part of her body as to have ripened there like fruit; and her belly (concealing the place where a man's is disfigured as though by an iron clamp left sticking in a statue that has been taken down from its niche) was closed, at the junction of her thighs, by two valves with a curve as languid, as reposeful, as cloistral as that of the horizon after the sun has set. She would take off her shoes, and lie down by my side.

O mighty attitudes of Man and Woman, in which there seeks to be united, in the innocence of the world's first days and with the humility of clay, what the Creation made separate, in which Eve is astonished and submissive before Man by whose side she awakens, as he himself, alone still, before God who has fashioned him! Albertine would fold her arms behind her dark hair, her hip swelling, her leg drooping with the inflexion of a swan's neck that stretches upwards and then curves back on itself. When she was lying completely on her side, there was a certain aspect of her face (so sweet and so beautiful from in front) which I could not endure, hook-nosed as in one of Leonardo's caricatures, seeming to betray the malice, the greed for gain, the deceitfulness of a spy whose presence in my house would have filled me with horror and whom that profile seemed to unmask. At once I took Albertine's face in my hands and altered its position.

"Be a good boy and promise me that if you don't come out to-morrow you'll work," she would say as she slipped her chemise on again.

"Yes, but don't put on your dressing-gown yet."

Sometimes I ended by falling asleep by her side. The room would grow cold, more wood would be wanted. I would try to find the bell above my head, but fail to do so, after fingering all the copper rods in turn save those between which it hung, and would say to Albertine who had sprung from the bed so that Françoise should not find us lying side by side: "No, come back for a moment, I can't find the bell."

Sweet, gay, innocent moments to all appearance, and yet moments in which there gathers the unsuspected possibility of disaster, which makes the amorous life the most precarious of all, that in which the unpredictable rain of sulphur and brimstone falls after the most radiant moments, whereupon, without having the heart or the will to draw a lesson from our misfortune, we set to work at once to rebuild upon the slopes of the crater from which nothing but catastrophe can emerge. I was as carefree as everyone who imagines that his happiness will last. It is precisely because this tenderness has been necessary to give birth to pain—and will return moreover at intervals to calm it—that men can be sincere with each other, and even with themselves, when they pride themselves on a woman's lovingness, although, taking things all in all, at the heart of their intimacy there lurks continuously and secretly, unavowed to the rest of the world, or revealed unintentionally by questions and inquiries, a painful disquiet. But this could not have come to birth without the preliminary tenderness, which even afterwards is intermittently necessary to make the pain bearable and to avoid ruptures; and concealment of the secret hell that a life shared with the woman in question really is, to the point of parading an allegedly tender intimacy, expresses a genuine point of view, a universal process of cause and effect, one of the modes whereby the production of grief and pain is rendered possible.

It no longer surprised me that Albertine should be in the house, and would not be going out to-morrow save with myself or in the custody of Andrée. These habits of shared life, these broad lines by which my existence was demarcated and within which nobody might penetrate but Albertine, and also (in the future plan, of which I was still unaware, of my life to come, like the plan drawn up by an architect for monuments which will not be erected until long afterwards) the remoter lines, parallel to these and broader still, by which, like an isolated hermitage, the somewhat rigid and monotonous prescription of my future loves was adumbrated, had in reality been traced that night at Balbec when, in the little train, after Albertine had revealed to me who it was that had brought her up, I had decided at all costs to remove her from certain influences and to prevent her from straying out of my sight for some days. Day after day had gone by, and these habits had become mechanical, but, like those primitive rites the meaning of which historians seek to discover, I could have said (though I would not have wished to say) to anybody who asked me to explain the meaning of this life of seclusion which I carried so far as no longer to go to the theatre, that its origin lay in the anxiety of a certain evening and my need to prove to myself, during the days that followed, that the girl of whose unfortunate childhood I had learned should have no possibility, whether she wished to or not, of exposing herself to similar temptations. I no longer thought, save very rarely, of these possibilities, but they were nevertheless to remain vaguely present in my consciousness. The fact that I was destroying them—or trying to do so—day by day was doubtless the reason why I took such pleasure in kissing those cheeks which were no more beautiful than many others; beneath any carnal attraction that goes at all deep, there is the permanent possibility of danger.

I had promised Albertine that, if I did not go out with her, I would settle down to work. But in the morning, just as if, taking advantage of our being asleep, the house had miraculously flown, I awoke in different weather beneath another clime. We do not begin to work as soon as we disembark in a strange country to the conditions of which we have to adapt ourselves. And each day was for me a different country. How could I even recognise my indolence itself, under the novel forms which it assumed? Sometimes, on days when the weather was generally agreed to be past praying for, mere residence in the house, situated in the midst of a steady and continuous rain, had all the gliding ease, the soothing silence, the interest of a sea voyage; another time, on a bright day, to lie still in bed was to let the lights and shadows play around me as round a tree-trunk. Or yet again, at the first strokes of the bell of a neighbouring convent, rare as the early morning worshippers, barely whitening the dark sky with their hesitant hail-showers, melted and scattered by the warm breeze, I would discern one of those tempestuous, disordered, delightful days, when the roofs, soaked by an intermittent downpour and dried by a gust of wind or a ray of sunshine, let fall a gurgling raindrop and, as they wait for the wind to turn again, preen their iridescent pigeon's-breast slates in the momentary sunshine; one of those days filled with so many changes of weather, atmospheric incidents, storms, that the idle man does not feel that he has wasted them because he has been taking an interest in the activity which, in default of himself, the atmosphere, acting as it were in his stead, has displayed; days similar to those times of revolution or war which do not seem empty to the schoolboy playing truant, because by loitering outside the Law Courts or by reading the newspapers he has the illusion of deriving from the events that have occurred, failing the work which he has neglected, an intellectual profit and an excuse for his idleness; days, finally, to which one may compare those on which some exceptional crisis has occurred in one's life from which the man who has never done anything imagines that he will acquire industrious habits if it is happily resolved: for instance, the morning on which he sets out for a duel which is to be fought under particularly dangerous conditions, and he is suddenly made aware, at the moment when it is perhaps about to be taken from him, of the value of a life of which he might have made use to begin some important work, or merely to enjoy a few pleasures, and of which he has failed to make any use at all. "If only I'm not killed," he says to himself, "how I shall settle down to work this very minute, and how I shall enjoy myself too!" Life has in fact suddenly acquired a higher value in his eyes, because he puts into life everything that it seems to him capable of giving, instead of the little that he normally demands of it. He sees it in the light of his desire, not as his experience has taught him that he was apt to make it, that is to say so tawdry. It has, at that moment, become filled with work, travel, mountain-climbing, all the splendid things which, he tells himself, the fatal outcome of the duel may render impossible, whereas they were already impossible before there was any question of a duel, owing to the bad habits which, even had there been no duel, would have persisted. He returns home without even a scratch, but he continues to find the same obstacles to pleasures, excursions, travel, to everything which for a moment he had feared that death would deprive him of; life is sufficient for that. As for work—exceptional circumstances having the effect of intensifying what previously existed in a man, work in the industrious, idleness in the lazy—he takes a holiday from it.

I followed his example, and did as I had always done since my first resolution to become a writer, which I had made long ago, but which seemed to me to date from yesterday, because I had regarded each intervening day as non-existent. I treated this day in a similar fashion, allowing its showers of rain and bursts of sunshine to pass without doing anything, and vowing that I would begin to work next day. But then I was no longer the same man beneath a cloudless sky; the golden note of the bells contained, like honey, not only light but the sensation of light (and also the sickly savour of preserved fruits, because at Combray it had often loitered like a wasp over our cleared dinner-table). On this day of dazzling sunshine, to remain until nightfall with my eyes shut was a thing permitted, customary, health-giving, pleasant, seasonable, like keeping the outside shutters closed against the heat. It was in such weather as this that at the beginning of my second visit to Balbec I used to hear the violins of the orchestra amid the blue-green surge of the rising tide. How much more fully did I possess Albertine today! There were days when the sound of a bell striking the hour bore upon the sphere of its sonority a plaque so spread with moisture or with light that it was like a transcription for the blind or, if you like, a musical interpretation of the charm of rain or the charm of sunlight. So much so that, at the moment, as I lay in bed with my eyes shut, I said to myself that everything is capable of transposition and that a universe that was exclusively audible might be as full of variety as the other. Travelling lazily upstream from day to day as in a boat, and seeing an endlessly changing succession of enchanted scenes appear before my eyes, scenes which I did not choose, which a moment earlier had been invisible to me, and which my

memory presented to me one after another without my being
free to choose them, I idly pursued over that smooth expanse
my stroll in the sunshine.

Those morning concerts at Balbec were not long past. And
yet, at that comparatively recent time, I had given but little
thought to Albertine. Indeed, on the very first days after my
arrival, I had not known that she was at Balbec. From whom
then had I learned it? Oh, yes, from Aimé. It was a fine sunny
day like this. He was glad to see me again. But he does not
like Albertine. Not everybody can like her. Yes, it was he
who told me that she was at Balbec. But how did he know?
Ah! he had met her, had thought that she was badly-behaved.
At that moment, as I approached Aimé's story by a different
facet from the one it had presented when he had told it to me,
my thoughts, which hitherto had been sailing blissfully over
these untroubled waters, exploded suddenly, as though they
had struck an invisible and perilous mine, treacherously moored
at this point in my memory. He had told me that he had met
her, that he had thought her badly-behaved. What had he
meant by bad behaviour? I had understood him to mean vulgar
behaviour, because, to contradict him in advance, I had declared that she was most refined. But no, perhaps he had meant
Gomorrhan behaviour. She was with another girl, perhaps
their arms were round one another's waists, perhaps they
were staring at other women, were indeed behaving in a
manner which I had never seen Albertine adopt in my presence.
Who was the other girl? Where had Aimé met her, this odious
Albertine?

I tried to recall exactly what Aimé had said to me, in order
to see whether it could be related to what I imagined, or
whether he had meant nothing more than common manners.
But in vain might I ask the question, the person who put it
and the person who could supply the recollection were, alas, one
and the same person, myself, who was momentarily duplicated
but without any additional insight. Question as I might, it
was myself who answered, I learned nothing more. I no
longer gave a thought to Mlle Vinteuil. Born of a new suspicion, the fit of jealousy from which I was suffering was new
too, or rather it was only the prolongation, the extension of that

suspicion; it had the same theatre, which was no longer Montjouvain but the road upon which Aimé had met Albertine,
and for its object one or other of the various friends who might
have been with Albertine that day. It was perhaps a certain
Elisabeth, or else perhaps those two girls whom Albertine
had watched in the mirror at the Casino, while appearing not to
see them. She had doubtless been having relations with them,
and also with Esther, Bloch's cousin. Such relations, had they
been revealed to me by a third person, would have been
enough almost to kill me, but since it was I who imagined
them, I took care to add sufficient uncertainty to deaden the
pain. We succeed in absorbing daily in enormous doses,
under the guise of suspicions, this same idea that we are being
betrayed, a quite small quantity of which might prove fatal
if injected by the needle of a shattering word. And it is no doubt
for that reason, and as a by-product of the instinct of self-
preservation, that the same jealous man does not hesitate to
form the most terrible suspicions upon a basis of innocuous
facts, provided that, whenever any proof is brought to him,
he refuses to accept the irrefutable evidence. Besides, love is an
incurable malady, like those diathetic states in which rheumatism affords the sufferer a brief respite only to be replaced by
epileptiform headaches. If my jealous suspicion was calmed,
I then felt a grudge against Albertine for not having been
tender enough, perhaps for having made fun of me with
Andrée. I thought with alarm of the idea that she must have
formed if Andrée had repeated all our conversations; the future
loomed black and menacing. This mood of depression left
me only if a new jealous suspicion drove me to further inquiries or if, on the other hand, Albertine's displays of affection
made my happiness seem to me insignificant. Who could this
girl be? I must write to Aimé, try to see him, and then check his
statement by talking to Albertine, making her confess. In the
meantime, convinced that it must be Bloch's cousin, I asked
Bloch himself, who had not the remotest idea of my purpose,
simply to let me see her photograph, or, better still, to arrange
for me to meet her.

How many persons, cities, roads jealousy makes us eager thus
to know! It is a thirst for knowledge thanks to which, with

regard to various isolated points, we end by acquiring every
possible notion in turn except the one that we require. One
can never tell whether a suspicion will not arise, for, all of a
sudden, one recalls a remark that was not clear, an alibi that
cannot have been given without a purpose. One has not seen
the person again, but there is such a thing as a retrospective
jealousy, that is born only after we have left the person, a
delayed-action jealousy. Perhaps the habit that I had acquired
of nursing within me certain desires, the desire for a young
girl of good family such as those I used to see pass beneath my
window escorted by their governesses, and especially for the
girl whom Saint-Loup had mentioned to me, the one who frequented houses of ill fame, the desire for handsome lady's-
maids, and especially for Mme Putbus's, the desire to go to the
country in early spring to see once again hawthorns, apple
trees in blossom, storms, the desire for Venice, the desire to
settle down to work, the desire to live like other people—
perhaps the habit of storing up all these desires, without assuag-
ing any of them, contenting myself with a promise to myself
not to forget to satisfy them one day—perhaps this habit, so
many years old already, of perpetual postponement, of what
M. de Charlus used to castigate under the name of procrastination, had become so prevalent in me that it took hold of my
jealous suspicions also and, while encouraging me to make a
mental note that I would not fail, some day, to have things out
with Albertine as regards the girl, or possibly girls (this part
of the story was confused and blurred in my memory and to
all intents and purposes indecipherable) with whom Aimé
had met her, made me also postpone this inquest. In any
case, I would not mention the subject to my mistress this
evening, for fear of making her think me jealous and so offending her.

And yet when, on the following day, Bloch sent me the
photograph of his cousin Esther, I made haste to forward it
to Aimé. And at the same moment I remembered that Albertine
had that morning refused me a pleasure which might indeed
have tired her. Was that in order to reserve it for someone
else, this afternoon, perhaps? For whom? Jealousy is thus
endless, for even if the beloved, by dying for instance, can

no longer provoke it by her actions, it may happen that memories subsequent to any event suddenly materialise and behave in our minds as though they too were events, memories which hitherto we had never explored, which had seemed to us unimportant, and to which our own reflexion upon them is sufficient, without any external factors, to give a new and terrible meaning. There is no need for there to be two of you, it is enough to be alone in your room, thinking, for fresh betrayals by your mistress to come to light, even though she is dead. And so we ought not to fear in love, as in everyday life, the future alone, but even the past, which often comes to life for us only when the future has come and gone—and not only the past which we discover after the event but the past which we have long kept stored within ourselves and suddenly learn how to interpret.

No matter, I was only too happy, as afternoon turned to evening, that the hour was not far off when I should be able to look to Albertine's presence for the appeasement which I needed. Unfortunately, the evening that followed was one of those when this appeasement was not forthcoming, when the kiss that Albertine would give me when she left me for the night, very different from her usual kiss, would no more soothe me than my mother's kiss had soothed me long ago, on days when she was vexed with me and I dared not call her back although I knew that I should be unable to sleep. Such evenings were now those on which Albertine had formed for the next day some plan about which she did not wish me to know. Had she confided it to me, I would have shown an eagerness to ensure its realisation that no one but Albertine could have inspired in me. But she told me nothing, and she had no need to tell me anything; as soon as she came in, before she had even crossed the threshold of my room, while she was still wearing her hat or toque, I had already detected the unknown, restive, desperate, uncontrollable desire. These were often the evenings when I had awaited her return with the most loving thoughts, and looked forward to throwing my arms round her neck with the warmest affection. Alas, misunderstandings such as I had often had with my parents, whom I would find cold or irritable when I ran to embrace them, overflowing with love, are as nothing in comparison with those that occur between lovers. The anguish then is far less superficial, far harder to endure; it has its seat in a deeper layer of the heart.

On this particular evening, however, Albertine was obliged to mention the plan that she had in mind; I gathered at once that she wished to go next day to pay a visit to Mme Verdurin, a visit to which in itself I would have seen no objection. But evidently her object was to meet someone there, to prepare some future pleasure. Otherwise she would not have attached so much importance to this visit. That is to say, she would not have kept on assuring me that it was of no importance. I had in the course of my life followed a progression which was the opposite of that adopted by peoples who make use of phonetic writing only after having considered the characters as a set of symbols; having, for so many years, looked for the real life and thought of other people only in the direct statements about them which they supplied me with of their own free will, in the absence of these I had come to attach importance, on the contrary, only to disclosures that are not a rational and analytical expression of the truth; the words themselves did not enlighten me unless they were interpreted in the same way as a rush of blood to the cheeks of a person who is embarrassed, or as a sudden silence. Such and such an adverb (for instance that used by M. de Cambremer when he understood that I was "literary" and, not having yet spoken to me, as he was describing a visit he had paid to the Verdurins, turned to me with: "*Incidentally*, Borelli was there!") bursting into flames through the involuntary, sometimes perilous contact of two ideas which the speaker has not expressed but which, by applying the appropriate methods of analysis or electrolysis, I was able to extract from it, told me more than a long speech. Albertine sometimes let fall in her conversation one or other of these precious amalgams which I made haste to "treat" so as to transform them into lucid ideas.

It is in fact one of the most terrible things for the lover that whereas particular details—which only experiment or espionage, among so many possible realisations, would ever make known to him—are so difficult to discover, the truth on the

other hand is so easy to detect or merely to sense. Often, at
Balbec, I had seen her fasten on girls who came past us a
sudden lingering stare, like a physical contact, after which, if
I knew the girls, she would say to me: "Suppose we asked
them to join us? I should so enjoy insulting them." And now,
for some time past, doubtless since she had succeeded in
reading my mind, no request to me to invite anyone, not a
word, not even a sidelong glance from her eyes, which had
become objectless and mute, and, with the abstracted, vacant
expression that accompanied them, as revealing as had been
their magnetic swerve before. Yet it was impossible for me to
reproach her, or to ply her with questions about things which
she would have declared to be so petty, so trivial, stored up
by me simply for the pleasure of "nit-picking." It is hard
enough to say: "Why did you stare at that girl who went past?"
but a great deal harder to say: "Why did you not stare at her?"
And yet I knew quite well—or at least I should have known if I
had not chosen instead to believe those affirmations of hers—
what Albertine's demeanour comprehended and proved, like
such and such a contradiction in the course of conversation
which often I did not perceive until long after I had left her,
which kept me in anguish all night long, which I never dared
mention to her again, but which nevertheless continued to
honour my memory from time to time with its periodical
visits. Even in the case of these furtive or sidelong glances
on the beach at Balbec or in the streets of Paris, I might sometimes wonder whether the person who provoked them was
not only an object of desire at the moment when she passed, but
an old acquaintance, or else some girl who had simply been
mentioned to her and whom, when I heard about it, I was
astonished that anybody could have mentioned to her, so
remote was she from what one would have guessed Albertine's
range of acquaintance to be. But the Gomorrah of to-day is a
jigsaw puzzle made up of pieces that come from places where
one least expected to find them. Thus I once saw at Rivebelle
a big dinner-party of ten women, all of whom I happened to
know, at least by name, and who, though as dissimilar as could
be, were none the less perfectly united, so much so that I never
saw a party so homogeneous, albeit so composite.

To return to the girls whom we passed in the street, never would Albertine stare at an old person, man or woman, with such fixity, or on the other hand with such reserve and as though she saw nothing. Cuckolded husbands who know nothing in fact know perfectly well. But it requires more accurate and abundant evidence to create a scene of jealousy. Besides, if jealousy helps us to discover a certain tendency to falsehood in the woman we love, it multiplies this tendency a hundredfold when the woman has discovered that we are jealous. She lies (to an extent to which she has never lied to us before), whether from pity, or from fear, or because she instinctively shies away in a flight that is symmetrical with our investigations. True, there are love affairs in which from the start a woman of easy virtue has posed as virtue incarnate in the eyes of the man who is in love with her. But how many others consist of two diametrically opposite periods! In the first, the woman speaks almost freely, with slight modifications, of her zest for pleasure and of the amorous life which it has made her lead, all of which she will deny later on with the utmost vigour to the same man when she senses that he is jealous of her and spying on her. He comes to regret the days of those first confidences, the memory of which torments him nevertheless. If the woman continued to make them, she would furnish him almost unaided with the secret of her conduct which he has been vainly pursuing day after day. And besides, what abandon those early confidences proved, what trust, what friendship! If she cannot live without being unfaithful to him, at least she would be doing so as a friend, telling him of her pleasures, associating him with them. And he thinks with regret of the sort of life which the early stages of their love seemed to promise, which the sequel has rendered impossible, turning that love into something agonisingly painful, which will make a final parting, according to circumstances, either inevitable or impossible.

Sometimes the script from which I deciphered Albertine's lies, without being ideographic, needed simply to be read backwards; thus this evening she had tossed at me casually the message, intended to pass almost unnoticed: "I may go and see the Verdurins tomorrow. I don't really know whether I will go, I don't particularly want to." A childish anagram of the admission: "It's absolutely certain that I'll go to see the Verdurins tomorrow. It's of the greatest possible importance." This apparent hesitation indicated a firm resolution and was intended to diminish the importance of the visit while informing me of it. Albertine always adopted a dubitative tone for irrevocable decisions. Mine was no less irrevocable: I would see that this visit to Mme Verdurin did not take place. Jealousy is often only an anxious need to be tyrannical applied to matters of love. I had doubtless inherited from my father this abrupt, arbitrary desire to threaten the people I loved best in the hopes with which they were lulling themselves with a sense of security which I wanted to expose to them as false; when I saw that Albertine had planned without my knowledge, behind my back, an expedition which I would have done everything in the world to make easier and more pleasant for her had she taken me into her confidence, I said casually, in order to make her tremble, that I intended to go out the next day myself.

I began to suggest to Albertine other expeditions in directions which would have made the visit to the Verdurins impossible, in words stamped with a feigned indifference beneath which I strove to conceal my agitation. But she had detected it. It encountered in her the electric power of a contrary will which violently repulsed it; I could see the sparks flash from Albertine's pupils. What use was it, though, to pay attention to what her eyes were saying at that moment? How had I failed to observe long ago that Albertine's eyes belonged to the category which even in a quite ordinary person seem to be composed of a number of fragments because of all the places in which the person wishes to be—and to conceal the desire to be—on that particular day. Eyes mendaciously kept always immobile and passive, but none the less dynamic, measurable in the yards or miles to be traversed before they reach the desired, the implacably desired meeting-place, eyes that are not so much smiling at the pleasure which tempts them as shadowed with melancholy and discouragement because there may be a difficulty in their getting to the meeting-place. Even when you hold them in your hands, such persons are fugitives. To understand the emotions which they arouse, and which others, even better-looking, do not, we must recognise that they are not immobile but in motion, and add to their person a sign corresponding to that which in physics denotes speed.

If you upset their plans for the day, they confess to you the pleasure they had concealed from you: "I did so want to go and have tea with so and so who I'm fond of." And then, six months later, if you come to know the person in question, you will learn that the girl whose plans you had upset, who, trapped, in order that you might set her free had confessed to you that she was thus in the habit of taking tea with a dear friend every day at the hour at which you did not see her, has never once been inside this person's house, that they have never had tea together, since the girl used to explain that her whole time was taken up by none other than yourself. And so the person with whom she confessed that she was going to tea, with whom she begged you to allow her to go to tea, that person was merely the excuse that necessity made her plead; there was still something else, someone else! What else? Who else?

Alas, the kaleidoscopic eyes, far-ranging and melancholy, might enable us perhaps to measure distance, but do not indicate direction. The boundless field of possibilities extends before us, and if by any chance the reality presented itself to our eyes, it would be so far outside the limits of the possible that, knocking suddenly against this looming wall, we should fall over backwards in a daze. It is not even essential that we should have proof of her movement and flight, it is enough that we should guess them. She had promised us a letter; we were calm, we were no longer in love. The letter has not come; each mail fails to bring it; what can have happened? Anxiety is born afresh, and love. It is such people more than any others who inspire love in us, to our distress. For every new anxiety that we feel on their account strips them in our eyes of some of their personality. We were resigned to suffering, thinking that we loved outside ourselves, and we perceive that our love is a function of our sorrow, that our love perhaps is our sorrow, and that its object is only to a very small extent the girl with the raven hair. But, when all is said, it is such people more than any others who inspire love.

More often than not, a body becomes the object of love only when an emotion, fear of losing it, uncertainty of getting it back, is merged into it. Now this sort of anxiety has a great affinity for bodies. It adds to them a quality which surpasses beauty itself, which is one of the reasons why we see men who are indifferent to the most beautiful women fall passionately in love with others who appear to us ugly. To such beings, such fugitive beings, their own nature and our anxiety fasten wings. And even when they are with us the look in their eyes seems to warn us that they are about to take flight. The proof of this beauty, surpassing beauty itself, that wings add is that often, for us, the same person is alternately winged and wingless. Afraid of losing her, we forget all the others. Sure of keeping her, we compare her with those others whom at once we prefer to her. And as these fears and these certainties may vary from week to week, a person may one week see everything that gave us pleasure sacrificed to her, in the following week be sacrificed herself, and so on for weeks and months on end. All of which would be incomprehensible did we not know (from the experience, which every man shares, of having at least once in a lifetime ceased to love a woman, forgotten her) how very insignificant in herself a woman is when she is no longer—or is not yet—permeable to our emotions. And, of course, if we speak of fugitive beings it is equally true of imprisoned ones, of captive women whom we think we shall never be able to possess. Hence men detest procuresses, because they facilitate flight and dangle temptations, but if on the other hand we are in love with a cloistered woman, we willingly have recourse to a procuress to snatch her from her prison and bring her to us. In so far as relations with women whom we abduct are less permanent than others, the reason is that the fear of not succeeding in procuring them or the dread of seeing them escape is the whole of our love for them and that once they have been carried off from their husbands, torn from their footlights, cured of the temptation to leave us, dissociated in short from our emotion whatever it may be, they are only themselves, that is to say next to nothing, and, so long desired, are soon forsaken by the very man who was so afraid of their forsaking him.

I have said: "How could I have failed to guess?" But had I
not guessed it from the first day at Balbec? Had I not detected
in Albertine one of those girls beneath whose envelope of
flesh more hidden persons stir, I will not say than in a pack of
cards still in its box, a closed cathedral or a theatre before we
enter it, but the whole vast ever-changing crowd? Not only
all these persons, but the desire, the voluptuous memory, the
restless search for all these persons. At Balbec I had not been
troubled because I had never even supposed that one day I
should be following a trail, even a false trail. Nevertheless, it
had given Albertine, in my eyes, the plenitude of someone
filled to the brim by the superimposition of so many persons,
of so many desires and voluptuous memories of persons.
And now that she had one day let fall the name "Mlle
Vinteuil," I should have liked, not to tear off her dress to
see her body, but through her body to see and read the
whole diary of her memories and her future passionate assignations.

Strange how the things that are probably most insignificant
suddenly assume an extraordinary value when a person
whom we love (or who has lacked only this duplicity to make
us love her) conceals them from us! In itself, suffering does
not of necessity inspire in us sentiments of love or hatred
towards the person who causes it: a surgeon can hurt us
without arousing any personal emotion in us. But with a
woman who has continued for some time to assure us that
we are everything in the world to her, without being herself
everything in the world to us, a woman whom we enjoy
seeing, kissing, taking on our knee, we are astonished if we
merely sense from a sudden resistance that she is not at our
entire disposal. Disappointment may then revive in us the
forgotten memory of an old anguish, which we nevertheless
know to have been provoked not by this woman but by others
whose betrayals stretch back like milestones through our past.
And indeed, how have we the heart to go on living, how can
we move a finger to preserve ourselves from death, in a world
in which love is provoked only by lies and consists solely in
our need to see our sufferings appeased by the person who has
made us suffer? To escape from the depths of despondency

that follow the discovery of this lying and this resistance, there is the sad remedy of endeavouring to act, against her will, with the help of people whom we feel to be more closely involved than we are in her life, upon her who is resisting us and lying to us, to play the cheat in turn, to make ourselves loathed. But the suffering caused by such a love is of the kind which must inevitably lead the sufferer to seek an illusory comfort in a change of position. These means of action are not wanting, alas! And the horror of the kind of love which anxiety alone has engendered lies in the fact that we turn over and over incessantly in our cage the most trivial utterances; not to mention that rarely do the people for whom we feel this love appeal to us physically to any great extent, since it is not our deliberate preference, but the accident of a moment's anguish (a moment indefinitely prolonged by our weakness of character, which repeats its experiments every evening until it yields to sedatives) that has chosen for us.

No doubt my love for Albertine was not the most barren of those to which, through lack of will-power, a man may descend, for it was not entirely platonic; she did give me some carnal satisfaction, and moreover she was intelligent. But all this was supererogatory. What occupied my mind was not something intelligent that she might have said, but a chance remark that had aroused in me a doubt as to her actions; I tried to remember whether she had said this or that, in what tone, at what moment, in response to what words, to reconstruct the whole scene of her dialogue with me, to recall at what moment she had expressed a desire to visit the Verdurins, what word of mine had brought that look of vexation to her face. The most important event might have been at issue without my going to so much trouble to establish the truth of it, to reconstitute its precise atmosphere and colour. No doubt, after these anxieties have intensified to a degree which we find unbearable, we sometimes manage to calm them altogether for an evening. We too are invited to the party which the woman we love was to attend and the true nature of which has been obsessing us for days; she has neither looks nor words for anyone but us; we take her home and then, all our anxieties dispelled, we enjoy a repose as complete and

as healing as the deep sleep that comes after a long walk. And
no doubt such repose is worth a high price. But would it not
have been simpler not to buy ourselves, deliberately, the
preceding anxiety, and at an even higher price? Besides, we
know all too well that however profound these temporary
respites may be, anxiety will still prevail. Often, indeed, it is
revived by a remark that was intended to set our mind at rest.
The demands of our jealousy and the blindness of our credulity
are greater than the woman we love could ever suppose.
When, spontaneously, she swears to us that such and such a
man is no more to her than a friend, she shatters us by informing us—something we never suspected—that he has been her
friend. While she is telling us, in proof of her sincerity, how
they had tea together that very afternoon, at each word that
she utters the invisible, the unsuspected, takes shape before
our eyes. She admits that he has asked her to be his mistress,
and we suffer agonies at the thought that she can have listened
to his overtures. She refused them, she says. But presently,
when we recall her story, we wonder whether that refusal is
really genuine, for there is wanting, between the different
things that she said to us, that logical and necessary connexion
which, more than the facts related, is the sign of truth. Besides, there was that frightening note of scorn in her voice:
"I said to him no, categorically," which is to be found in every
class of society when a woman is lying. We must nevertheless
thank her for having refused, encourage her by our kindness
to repeat these painful confidences in the future. At the most,
we may remark: "But if he had already made advances to you,
why did you accept his invitation to tea?" "So that he should
not hold it against me and say that I hadn't been nice to him."
And we dare not reply that by refusing she would perhaps
have been nicer to us.

Albertine alarmed me further when she said that I was
quite right to say, out of regard for her reputation, that I was
not her lover, since "for that matter," she went on, "it's
perfectly true that you aren't." I was not perhaps her lover in
the full sense of the word, but then, was I to suppose that all
the things that we did together she did also with all the other
men whose mistress she swore to me that she had never been?

The desire to know at all costs what Albertine was thinking, whom she saw, whom she loved—how strange that I should sacrifice everything to this need, since I had felt the same need to know in the case of Gilberte, names and facts which now meant nothing to me! I was perfectly well aware that in themselves Albertine's actions were of no greater interest. It is curious that a first love, if by the fragile state in which it leaves one's heart it paves the way for subsequent loves, does not at least provide one, in view of the identity of symptoms and sufferings, with the means of curing them. Besides, is there any need to know a fact? Are we not aware beforehand, in a general way, of the mendacity and even the discretion of those women who have something to conceal? Is there any possibility of error? They make a virtue of their silence, when we would give anything to make them speak. And we feel certain that they have assured their accomplice: "I never say anything. It won't be through me that anybody will hear about it, I never say anything."

A man may give his fortune and even his life for a woman, and yet know quite well that in ten years' time, more or less, he would refuse her the fortune, prefer to keep his life. For then that woman would be detached from him, alone, that is to say non-existent. What attaches us to people are the countless roots, the innumerable threads which are our memories of last night, our hopes for to-morrow morning, the continuous weft of habit from which we can never free ourselves. Just as there are misers who hoard from generosity, so we are spend-thrifts who spend from avarice, and it is not so much to a person that we sacrifice our life as to everything of ours that may have become attached to that person, all those hours and days, all those things compared with which the life we have not yet lived, our life in the relative future, seems to us more remote, more detached, less intimate, less our own. What we need is to extricate ourselves from these bonds which are so much more important than the person, but they have the effect of creating in us temporary obligations which mean that we dare not leave the person for fear of being badly thought of, whereas later on we would so dare, for, detached from us, that person would no longer be part of us, and because in reality we create obligations (even if, by an apparent contradiction, they should lead to suicide) towards ourselves alone.

If I was not in love with Albertine (and of this I could not be sure) then there was nothing extraordinary in the place that she occupied in my life: we live only with what we do not love, with what we have brought to live with us only in order to kill the intolerable love, whether it be for a woman, for a place, or again for a woman embodying a place. Indeed we should be terrified of beginning to love again if a new separation were to occur. I had not yet reached this stage with Albertine. Her lies, her admissions, left me to complete the task of elucidating the truth: her innumerable lies, because she was not content with merely lying, like everyone who imagines that he or she is loved, but was by nature, quite apart from this, a liar (and so inconsistent moreover that, even if she told me the truth every time about, for instance, what she thought of other people, she would say something different every time); her admissions, because, being so rare, so quickly cut short, they left between them, in so far as they concerned the past, huge blanks over the whole expanse of which I was obliged to retrace—and for that first of all to discover—her life.

As for the present, so far as I could interpret the sibylline utterances of Françoise, it was not only on particular points but over a whole area that Albertine lied to me, and "one fine day" I would see what Françoise pretended to know, what she refused to tell me, what I dared not ask her. It was no doubt with the same jealousy that she had shown in the past with regard to Eulalie that Françoise would speak of the most unlikely things, but so vaguely that at most one could deduce therefrom the highly improbable insinuation that the poor captive (who was a lover of women) preferred marriage with somebody who did not appear to be me. If this had been so, how, in spite of her telepathic powers, could Françoise have come to hear of it? Certainly, Albertine's statements could give me no definite enlightenment, for they were as different day by day as the colours of a spinning-top that has almost come to a standstill. However, it seemed that it was hatred more than anything else that impelled Françoise to speak.

Not a day went by without her addressing to me, and I in my mother's absence enduring, such speeches as:

"To be sure, you're very nice, and I shall never forget the debt of gratitude that I owe you" (this probably so that I might establish fresh claims upon her gratitude) "but the house has become infected ever since niceness brought in deceitfulness, ever since cleverness has been protecting the stupidest person that ever was seen, ever since refinement, good manners, wit, dignity in all things, the appearance and the reality of a prince, allow themselves to be dictated to and plotted against and me to be humiliated—me who've been forty years in the family—by vice, by everything that's most vulgar and base."

What Françoise resented most about Albertine was having to take orders from somebody who was not one of ourselves, and also the strain of the additional housework which, affecting the health of our old servant (who would not, for all that, accept any help in the house, not being a "good for nothing"), in itself would have accounted for her irritability and her furious hatred. Certainly, she would have liked to see Albertine-Esther banished from the house. This was Françoise's dearest wish. And, by consoling her, its fulfilment would in itself have given our old servant some rest. But to my mind there was more to it than this. So violent a hatred could have originated only in an over-strained body. And, more even than of consideration, Françoise was in need of sleep.

Albertine went to take off her things and, to lose no time in finding out what I wanted to know, I seized the telephone receiver and invoked the implacable deities, but succeeded only in arousing their fury which expressed itself in the single word "Engaged." Andrée was in fact engaged in talking to someone else. As I waited for her to finish her conversation, I wondered why it was—now that so many of our painters are seeking to revive the feminine portraits of the eighteenth century, in which the cleverly devised setting is a pretext for portraying expressions of expectation, sulkiness, interest, reverie—why it was that none of our modern Bouchers or Fragonards had yet painted, instead of "The Letter" or "The Harpsichord," this scene which might be entitled "At the telephone," in which there would come spontaneously to the lips of the listener a smile that is all the more genuine because it is conscious of being unobserved.

Finally I got through to Andrée: "Are you coming to call for Albertine to-morrow?" I asked, and as I uttered Albertine's name, I thought of the envy Swann had aroused in me when he had said to me, on the day of the Princesse de Guermantes's party: "Come and see Odette," and I had thought how potent, when all was said, was a Christian name which, in the eyes of the whole world including Odette herself, had on Swann's lips alone this entirely possessive sense. Such a monopoly—summed up in a single word—over the whole existence of another person had appeared to me, whenever I was in love, to be sweet indeed! But in fact, when we are in a position to say it, either we no longer care, or else habit, while not blunting its tenderness, has changed its sweetness to bitterness.* I knew that I alone was in a position to say "Albertine" in that tone to Andrée. And yet, to Albertine, to Andrée, and to myself, I felt that I was nothing. And I realised the impossibility which love comes up against. We imagine that it has as its object a being that can be laid down in front of us, enclosed within a body. Alas, it is the extension of that being to all the points in space and time that it has occupied and will occupy. If we do not possess its contact with this or that place, this or that hour, we do not possess that being. But we cannot touch all these points. If only they were indicated to us, we might perhaps contrive to reach out to them. But we grope for them without finding them. Hence mistrust, jealousy, persecutions. We waste precious time on absurd clues and pass by the truth without suspecting it.

But already one of the irascible deities with the breathtakingly agile handmaidens was becoming irritated, not because I was speaking but because I was saying nothing.

"Come along, I've been holding the line for you all this time; I shall cut you off."

However, she did nothing of the sort but, evoking Andrée's presence, enveloped it, like the great poet that a damsel of the telephone always is, in the atmosphere peculiar to the home, the district, the very life itself of Albertine's friend.

"Is that you?" asked Andrée, whose voice was projected towards me with an instantaneous speed by the goddess whose privilege it is to make sound more swift than light.

"Listen," I replied; "go wherever you like, anywhere, except to Mme Verdurin's. You must at all cost keep Albertine away from there to-morrow."

"But that's just where she's supposed to be going."

"Ah!"

But I was obliged to break off the conversation for a moment and to make menacing gestures, for if Françoise continued—as though it were something as unpleasant as vaccination or as dangerous as the aeroplane—to refuse to learn to use the telephone, whereby she would have spared us the trouble of conversations which she might intercept without any harm, on the other hand she would at once come into the room whenever I was engaged in a conversation so private that I was particularly anxious to keep it from her ears. When she had left the room at last, not without lingering to take away various objects that had been lying there since the previous day and might perfectly well have been left there for an hour longer, and to put on to the fire a log made quite superfluous by the burning heat generated in me by the intruder's presence and my fear of finding myself "cut off" by the operator, "I'm sorry," I said to Andrée, "I was interrupted. Is it absolutely certain that she has to go to the Verdurins' tomorrow?"

"Absolutely, but I can tell her that you don't want her to."

"No, not at all, but I might possibly come with you."

"Ah!" said Andrée, in a voice that sounded annoyed and somehow alarmed by my audacity, which was incidentally fortified as a result.

"Well then, good-night, and please forgive me for disturbing you for nothing."

"Not at all," said Andrée, and (since, now that the telephone has come into general use, a decorative ritual of polite phrases has grown up round it, as round the tea-tables of the past) she added: "It's been a great pleasure to hear your voice."

I might have said the same, and with greater truth than Andrée, for I had been deeply affected by the sound of her voice, having never noticed before that it was so different from the voices of other people. Then I recalled other voices still, women's voices especially, some of them slowed down by the precision of a question and by mental concentration, others made breathless, even interrupted at moments, by the lyrical flow of what they were relating; I recalled one by one the voices of all the girls I had known at Balbec, then Gilberte's, then my grandmother's, then Mme de Guermantes's; I found them all dissimilar, moulded by a speech peculiar to each of them, each playing on a different instrument, and I thought to myself how thin must be the concert performed in paradise by the three or four angel musicians of the old painters, when I saw, mounting to the throne of God by tens, by hundreds, by thousands, the harmonious and multiphonic salutation of all the Voices. I did not leave the telephone without thanking, in a few propitiatory words, the goddess who reigns over the speed of sound for having kindly exercised on behalf of my humble words a power which made them a hundred times more rapid than thunder. But my thanksgiving received no other response than that of being cut off.

When Albertine came back to my room, she was wearing a black satin dress which had the effect of making her seem paler, of turning her into the pallid, intense Parisian woman, etiolated by lack of fresh air, by the atmosphere of crowds and perhaps by the practice of vice, whose eyes seemed the more uneasy because they were not brightened by any colour in her cheeks.

"Guess," I said to her, "who I've just been talking to on the telephone. Andrée!"

"Andrée?" exclaimed Albertine in a loud, astonished, excited voice that so simple a piece of intelligence hardly seemed to call for. "I hope she remembered to tell you that we met Mme Verdurin the other day."

"Mme Verdurin? I don't remember," I replied as though I were thinking of something else, in order to appear indifferent to this meeting and not to betray Andrée who had told me where Albertine was going next day. But how could I tell whether Andrée was not herself betraying me, whether she would not tell Albertine to-morrow that I had asked her to prevent her at all costs from going to the Verdurins', and

whether she had not already revealèd to her that I had on
several occasions made similar recommendations. She had
assured me that she had never repeated anything, but the
value of this assertion was counterbalanced in my mind by the
impression that for some time past Albertine's face had ceased
to show the trust that she had placed in me for so long.*

Suffering, when we are in love, ceases from time to time,
but only to resume in a different form. We weep to see the
beloved no longer respond to us with those bursts of affection,
those amorous advances of earlier days; we suffer even more
when, having relinquished them with us, she resumes them
with others; then, from this suffering, we are distracted by a
new and still more agonising pang, the suspicion that she
has lied to us about how she spent the previous evening, when
she was no doubt unfaithful to us; this suspicion in turn is
dispelled, and we are soothed by our mistress's affectionate
kindness; but then a forgotten word comes back to us; we
had been told that she was ardent in moments of pleasure,
whereas we have always found her calm; we try to picture to
ourselves these passionate frenzies with others, we feel how
very little we are to her, we observe an air of boredom, longing,
melancholy while we are talking, we observe like a black sky
the slovenly clothes she puts on when she is with us, keeping
for other people the dresses with which she used to flatter us.
If, on the contrary, she is affectionate, what joy for a moment!
But when we see that little tongue stuck out as though in
invitation, we think of those to whom that invitation was so
often addressed that even perhaps with me, without her thinking of those others, it had remained for Albertine, by force of
long habit, an automatic signal. Then the feeling that she is
bored by us returns. But suddenly this pain is reduced to
nothing when we think of the unknown evil element in her
life, of the places, impossible to identify, where she has been,
where she still goes perhaps during the hours when we are not
with her, if indeed she is not planning to live there altogether,
those places in which she is separated from us, does not belong
to us, is happier than when she is with us. Such are the revolving searchlights of jealousy.

Jealousy is moreover a demon that cannot be exorcised,

but constantly reappears in new incarnations. Even if we could succeed in exterminating them all, in keeping the beloved for ever, the Spirit of Evil would then adopt another form, more pathetic still, despair at having obtained fidelity only by force, despair at not being loved.

Tender and sweet though Albertine was on certain evenings, she no longer had any of those spontaneous impulses which I remembered from Balbec when she used to say "How very nice you are!" and her whole heart seemed to go out to me unrestrained by any of those grievances which she now felt and which she kept to herself because she doubtless considered them irremediable, impossible to forget, unavowable, but which nevertheless created between us a significant verbal prudence on her part or an impassable barrier of silence.

"And may one be allowed to know why you telephoned to Andrée?"

"To ask whether she had any objection to my joining you to-morrow and paying the Verdurins the visit I've been promising them since la Raspelière."

"Just as you like. But I warn you, there's an appalling fog this evening, and it's sure to last over to-morrow. I mention it because I shouldn't like you to make yourself ill. Personally, I need hardly say that I'd love you to come with us. However," she added with a thoughtful air, "I'm not at all sure that I'll go to the Verdurins. They've been so kind to me that I ought, really. . . . Next to you, they've been nicer to me than anybody, but there are some things about them that I don't quite like. I simply must go to the Bon Marché or the Trois-Quartiers and get a white bodice to wear with this dress which is really too black."

To allow Albertine to go by herself into a big shop crowded with people perpetually brushing against one, provided with so many exits that a woman can always say that when she came out she could not find her carriage which was waiting farther along the street, was something that I was quite determined never to consent to, but the thought of it made me extremely unhappy. And yet it did not occur to me that I ought long ago to have ceased to see Albertine, for she had entered, for me, upon that lamentable period in which a person, scattered in

space and time, is no longer a woman but a series of events on
which we can throw no light, a series of insoluble problems, a
sea which, like Xerxes, we scourge with rods in an absurd
attempt to punish it for what it has engulfed. Once this period
has begun, we are perforce vanquished. Happy are they who
understand this in time not to prolong unduly a futile, exhausting struggle, hemmed in on every side by the limits of the
imagination, a struggle in which jealousy plays so sorry a part
that the same man who, once upon a time, if the eyes of the
woman who was always by his side rested for an instant
upon another man, imagined an intrigue and suffered endless
torments, now resigns himself to allowing her to go out by
herself, sometimes with the man whom he knows to be her
lover, preferring to the unknowable this torture which at
least he knows! It is a question of the rhythm to be adopted,
which afterwards one follows from force of habit. Neurotics
who could never stay away from a dinner-party will eventually
take rest cures which never seem to them to last long enough;
women who recently were still of easy virtue live in penitence.
Jealous lovers who, to keep an eye on the woman they loved,
cut short their hours of sleep, deprived themselves of rest,
now feeling that her desires, the world so vast and secret, and
time are too much for them, allow her to go out without
them, then to travel, and finally separate from her. Jealousy
thus perishes for want of nourishment and has survived so
long only by clamouring incessantly for fresh food. I was still
a long way from this state.

I was now at liberty to go out with Albertine as often as I
wished. As there had recently sprung up round Paris a number
of aerodromes, which are to aeroplanes what harbours are to
ships, and as, ever since the day when, on the way to la Raspelière, that almost mythological encounter with an airman, at
whose passage overhead my horse had reared, had been to me
like a symbol of liberty, I often chose to end our day's excursion—with the ready approval of Albertine, a passionate lover of
every form of sport—at one of these aerodromes. We went
there, she and I, attracted by that incessant stir of departure and
arrival which gives so much charm to a stroll along a jetty,
or merely along a beach, to those who love the sea, and to

loitering about an "aviation centre" to those who love the sky. From time to time, amid the repose of the machines that lay inert and as though at anchor, we would see one being laboriously pulled by a number of mechanics, as a boat is dragged across the sand at the bidding of a tourist who wishes to go for an outing on the sea. Then the engine was started, the machine ran along the ground, gathered speed, until finally, all of a sudden, at right angles, it rose slowly, in the braced and as it were static ecstasy of a horizontal speed suddenly transformed into a majestic, vertical ascent. Albertine could not contain her joy, and would demand explanations of the mechanics who, now that the machine was in the air, were strolling back to the sheds. The passenger, meanwhile, was covering mile after mile; the huge skiff, upon which our eyes remained fixed, was now no more than a barely visible dot in the sky, a dot which, however, would gradually recover its solidity, its size, its volume, when, as the time allowed for the excursion drew to an end, the moment came for landing. And we watched with envy, Albertine and I, as he sprang to earth, the passenger who had gone up like that to enjoy in the solitary expanses of the open sky the calm and limpidity of evening. Then, whether from the aerodrome or from some museum or church that we had been visiting, we would return home together for dinner. And yet I did not return home calmed, as I used to be at Balbec by less frequent excursions which I rejoiced to see extend over a whole afternoon and used afterwards to contemplate standing out like clustering flowers against the rest of Albertine's life as against an empty sky beneath which one muses pleasantly, without thinking. Albertine's time did not belong to me then in such ample quantities as to-day. Yet it had seemed to me then to belong to me much more, because I then took into account—my love rejoicing in them as in the bestowal of a favour—only the hours that she spent with me, whereas now—my jealousy searching anxiously among them for the possibility of a betrayal—it was only those hours that she spent apart from me.

Tomorrow, evidently, she was looking forward to a few such hours. I must choose to cease from suffering or to cease from loving. For, just as in the beginning it is formed by desire, so afterwards love is kept in existence only by painful anxiety. I felt that part of Albertine's life eluded me. Love, in the pain of anxiety as in the bliss of desire, is a demand for a whole. It is born, and it survives, only if some part remains for it to conquer. We love only what we do not wholly possess. Albertine was lying when she told me that she probably would not go to see the Verdurins, as I was lying when I said that I wished to go. She was seeking merely to dissuade me from going out with her, and I, by my abrupt announcement of this plan which I had no intention of putting into practice, to touch what I felt to be her most sensitive spot, to track down the desire that she was concealing and to force her to admit that my company next day would prevent her from gratifying it. She had virtually made this admission by ceasing suddenly to wish to go to see the Verdurins.

"If you don't want to go to the Verdurins'," I told her, "there is a splendid charity show at the Trocadéro." She listened to my exhortations to attend it with a doleful air. I began to be harsh with her as at Balbec, at the time of my first fit of jealousy. Her face reflected her disappointment, and in reproaching her I used the same arguments that had been so often advanced against me by my parents when I was small, and that had appeared so unintelligent and cruel to my misunderstood childhood. "No, in spite of your gloomy look," I said to Albertine, "I can't feel sorry for you; I should feel sorry for you if you were ill, if you were in trouble, if you had suffered some bereavement; not that you would mind in the least, I dare say, considering your expenditure of false sensibility over nothing. Besides, I'm not very impressed by the sensibility of people who pretend to be so fond of us and are quite incapable of doing us the smallest favour, and whose minds wander so that they forget to deliver the letter we have entrusted to them on which our whole future depends."

A great part of what we say being no more than a recitation from memory, I had often heard these words uttered by my mother, who (always ready to explain to me that one ought not to confuse genuine sensibility with sentimentality, what the Germans, whose language she greatly admired despite my grandfather's loathing for that nation, called *Empfindung* and *Empfindelei*) once, when I was in tears, had gone so far as to tell me that Nero was probably highly-strung and was none the better for that. Indeed, like those plants which bifurcate as they grow, side by side with the sensitive boy which was all that I had been, there was now a man of the opposite sort, full of common sense, of severity towards the morbid sensibility of others, a man resembling what my parents had been to me. No doubt, as each of us is obliged to continue in himself the life of his forebears, the level-headed, caustic individual who did not exist in me at the start had joined forces with the sensitive one, and it was natural that I should become in my turn what my parents had been to me. What is more, at the moment when this new personality took shape in me, he found his language ready made in the memory of the sarcastic, scolding things that had been said to me, that I must now say to others, and that came so naturally to my lips, either because I evoked them through mimicry and association of memories, or because the delicate and mysterious incrustations of genetic energy had traced in me unawares, as upon the leaf of a plant, the same intonations, the same gestures, the same attitudes as had been characteristic of those from whom I sprang. Indeed it often happened to my mother (so many obscure unconscious currents caused everything in me even down to the tiniest movements of my fingers to be drawn into the same cycles as my parents) to imagine that it was my father at the door, so similar was my knock to his.

Moreover the coupling of contrary elements is the law of life, the principle of fertilisation, and, as we shall see, the cause of many misfortunes. As a rule we detest what resembles ourselves, and our own faults when observed in another person exasperate us. How much the more does a man who has passed the age at which one instinctively displays them, a man who, for instance, has maintained an expression of icy calm through the most aggravating moments, execrate those same faults if it is another man, younger or simpler or stupider, who displays them! There are sensitive people for whom merely to see in other people's eyes the tears which they themselves have held back is infuriating. It is excessive similarity that, in spite of affection, and sometimes all the more the greater the affection, causes division to reign in families.

Possibly in myself, as in many other people, the second man that I had become was simply another aspect of the first, excitable and sensitive where he himself was concerned, a sage mentor to others. Perhaps it was so also with my parents according to whether they were considered in relation to me or in themselves. In the case of my grandmother and mother it was only too clear that their severity towards me was deliberate on their part and indeed cost them dear, but perhaps even my father's coldness too was only an external aspect of his sensibility. For it was perhaps the human truth of this twofold aspect—the one concerned with the inner life, the other with social relations—that was expressed in a remark which seemed to me at the time as false in substance as it was commonplace in form, when someone said of my father: "Beneath his icy exterior, he conceals an extraordinary sensibility; the real truth is that he's ashamed of his own feelings." Did it not in fact conceal incessant secret storms, that calm of his, interspersed at times with sententious reflections and ironical comments on the awkward manifestations of sensibility, which now I too affected in my relations with everyone and above all never swerved from, in certain circumstances, with Albertine?

I really believe that I came near that day to making up my mind to break with her and to set out for Venice. What bound me anew in my chains had to do with Normandy, not that she showed any inclination to go to that region where I had been jealous of her (for it was my good fortune that her plans never impinged upon the painful zones in my memory), but because when I happened to say to her: "It's as though I were speaking to you about your aunt's friend who lived at Infreville," she replied angrily, delighted—like everyone in an argument who is anxious to muster as many points as possible on his side— to show me that I was in the wrong and herself in the right: "But my aunt never knew anybody at Infreville, and I've never been near the place." She had forgotten the lie that she had told me one afternoon about the touchy lady with whom she simply must go and have tea, even if by visiting this lady she were to forfeit my friendship and shorten her own life.

I did not remind her of her lie. But it shattered me. And once
again I postponed our rupture to another day. A person has
no need of sincerity, nor even of skill in lying, in order to be
loved. Here I mean by love reciprocal torture.

I saw nothing reprehensible that evening in speaking to her
as my grandmother—that mirror of perfection—used to speak
to me, nor, when I told her that I would escort her to the
Verdurins', in having adopted the brusque manner of my
father, who would never inform us of any decision except in a
manner calculated to cause us the maximum of agitation, out
of all proportion to the decision itself. So that it was easy for
him to call us absurd for appearing so distressed by so small a
matter, our distress corresponding in reality to the perturbation
that he had aroused in us. And if—like the inflexible wisdom
of my grandmother—these arbitrary whims of my father's
had been passed on to me to complement the sensitive nature
to which they had so long remained alien and, throughout my
whole childhood, had caused so much suffering, that sensitive
nature informed them very exactly as to the points at which
they could most effectively be aimed: there is no better in-
former than a reformed thief, or a subject of the nation one is
fighting. In certain untruthful families, a brother who has
come to call without any apparent reason and makes some
casual inquiry on the doorstep as he leaves, appearing scarcely
to listen to the answer, indicates thereby to his brother that this
inquiry was the sole object of his visit, for the brother is
quite familiar with that air of detachment, those words uttered
as though in parentheses and at the last moment, having
frequently had recourse to them himself. Similarly, there are
pathological families, kindred sensibilities, fraternal tempera-
ments, initiated into that mute language which enables the
members of a family to understand each other without speaking.
Thus who can be more nerve-racking than a neurotic? And then
there may have been a deeper and more general cause for my
behaviour in these cases. In those brief but inevitable moments
when we hate someone we love—moments which last sometimes for a whole lifetime in the case of people we do not love
—we do not wish to appear kind in order not to be pitied, but
at once as unpleasant and as happy as possible so that our

happiness may be truly hateful and wound to the very soul the occasional or permanent enemy. To how many people have I not untruthfully maligned myself, simply in order that my "successes" might seem to them the more immoral and infuriate them the more! The proper thing to do would be to take the opposite course, to show without arrogance that we have generous feelings, instead of taking such pains to hide them. And this would be easy if we were capable of never hating, of always loving. For then we should be so happy to say only the things that can make other people happy, melt their hearts, make them love us.

True, I felt some remorse at being so insufferable to Albertine, and said to myself: "If I didn't love her, she would be more grateful to me, for I wouldn't be nasty to her; but no, it would be the same in the end, for I should also be less nice." And I might, in order to justify myself, have told her that I loved her. But the avowal of that love, apart from the fact that it would have told Albertine nothing new, would perhaps have made her colder towards me than the harshness and deceit for which love was the sole excuse. To be harsh and deceitful to the person whom we love is so natural! If the interest that we show towards other people does not prevent us from being gentle towards them and complying with their wishes, it is because our interest is not sincere. Other people leave us indifferent, and indifference does not prompt us to unkindness.

The evening was drawing to a close. Before Albertine went to bed, there was no time to lose if we wished to make peace, to renew our embraces. Neither of us had yet taken the initiative.

Meanwhile, feeling that in any case she was angry with me, I took the opportunity of mentioning Esther Lévy.

"Bloch tells me," I said untruthfully, "that you're a great friend of his cousin Esther."

"I shouldn't know her if I saw her," said Albertine with a vague look.

"I've seen her photograph," I continued angrily.

I did not look at Albertine as I said this, so that I did not see her expression, which would have been her sole reply, for she said nothing.

It was no longer the peace of my mother's kiss at Combray that I felt when I was with Albertine on these evenings, but, on the contrary, the anguish of those on which my mother scarcely bade me good-night, or even did not come up to my room at all, either because she was cross with me or was kept downstairs by guests. This anguish—not merely its trans-position into love but this anguish itself—which for a time had specialised in love and which, when the separation, the division of the passions occurred, had been assigned to love alone, now seemed once more to be extending to them all, to have be-come indivisible again as in my childhood, as though all my feelings, which trembled at the thought of my not being able to keep Albertine by my bedside, at once as a mistress, a sister, a daughter, and as a mother too, of whose regular good-night kiss I was beginning once more to feel the childish need, had begun to coalesce, to become unified in the premature evening of my life which seemed fated to be as short as a winter day. But if I felt the same anguish as in my childhood, the different person who caused me to feel it, the difference in the feeling she inspired in me, the very transformation in my character, made it impossible for me to demand its appeasement from Albertine as in the old days from my mother. I could no longer say: "I'm unhappy." I confined myself, with a heavy heart, to speaking of inconsequential matters that took me no further towards a happy solution. I waded knee-deep in painful platitudes. And with that intellectual egoism which, if some insignificant fact happens to have a bearing on our love, makes us pay great respect to the person who has discovered it, as fortuitously perhaps as the fortune-teller who has foretold some trivial event which has afterwards come to pass, I came near to regarding Françoise as more inspired than Bergotte and Elstir because she had said to me at Balbec: "That girl will bring you nothing but trouble."

Every minute brought me nearer to Albertine's good-night, which at length she said. But that evening her kiss, from which she herself was absent and which made no impression on me, left me so anxious that, with a throbbing heart, I watched her make her way to the door, thinking: "If I'm to find a pretext for calling her back, keeping her here, making peace with her,

I must be quick; only a few steps and she will be out of the
room, only two, now one, she's turning the handle; she's
opening the door, it's too late, she has shut it behind her!"
But perhaps it was not too late after all. As in the old days at
Combray when my mother had left me without soothing me
with her kiss, I wanted to rush after Albertine, I felt that there
would be no peace for me until I had seen her again, that this
renewed encounter would turn into something tremendous
which it had not been before and that—if I did not succeed
by my own efforts in ridding myself of this misery—I might
perhaps acquire the shameful habit of going to beg from
Albertine. I sprang out of bed when she was already in her
room, I paced up and down the corridor, hoping that she
would come out of her room and call me; I stood stock still
outside her door for fear of failing to hear some faint summons, I returned for a moment to my own room to see whether
she might not by some lucky chance have forgotten her handkerchief, her bag, something which I might have appeared to
be afraid of her needing during the night, and which would
have given me an excuse for going to her room. No, there was
nothing. I returned to my station outside her door, but the
crack beneath it no longer showed any light. Albertine had
put out the light, she was in bed; I remained there motionless,
hoping for some lucky accident which did not occur; and long
afterwards, frozen, I returned to bestow myself between my
own sheets and cried for the rest of the night.

But on certain such evenings I had recourse to a ruse which
won me Albertine's kiss. Knowing how quickly sleep came
to her as soon as she lay down (she knew it also, for, instinctively, before lying down, she would take off the slippers which
I had given her, and her ring which she placed by the bedside,
as she did in her own room when she went to bed), knowing
how heavy her sleep was, how affectionate her awakening,
I would find an excuse for going to look for something and
make her lie down on my bed. When I returned she would be
asleep and I saw before me the other woman that she became
whenever one saw her full face. But her personality quickly
changed when I lay down beside her and saw her again in
profile. I could take her head, lift it up, press her face to my

lips, put her arms round my neck, and she would continue to sleep, like a watch that never stops, like a climbing plant, a convolvulus which continues to thrust out its tendrils whatever support you give it. Only her breathing was altered by each touch of my fingers, as though she were an instrument on which I was playing and from which I extracted modulations by drawing different notes from one after another of its strings. My jealousy subsided, for I felt that Albertine had become a creature that breathes and is nothing else besides, as was indicated by that regular suspiration in which is expressed that pure physiological function which, wholly fluid, has the solidity neither of speech nor of silence; and, in its ignorance of all evil, drawn seemingly rather from a hollowed reed than from a human being, that breath, truly paradisiacal to me who at such moments felt Albertine to be withdrawn from everything, not only physically but morally, was the pure song of the angels. And yet, in that breathing, I thought to myself of a sudden that perhaps many names of people, borne on the stream of memory, must be revolving.

Sometimes indeed the human voice was added to that music. Albertine would murmur a few words. How I longed to catch their meaning! It would happen that the name of a person of whom we had been speaking and who had aroused my jealousy would come to her lips, but without making me unhappy, for the memory that it brought with it seemed to be only that of the conversations that she had had with me on the subject. One evening, however, when with her eyes still shut she half awoke, she said tenderly, addressing me: "Andrée." I concealed my emotion. "You're dreaming, I'm not Andrée," I said to her, smiling. She smiled also: "Of course not, I wanted to ask you what Andrée said to you this evening." "I assumed that you must be used to lying beside her like that." "Oh no, never," she said. But, before making this reply, she had hidden her face for a moment in her hands. So her silences were merely screens, her surface affection merely kept beneath the surface a thousand memories which would have rent my heart, her life was full of those incidents the good-natured, bantering account of which forms one's daily gossip at the expense of other people, people who do not matter, but which, so long as a

woman remains buried in the depths of one's heart, seem to
us so precious a revelation of her life that, for the privilege of
exploring that underlying world, we would gladly sacrifice
our own. Then her sleep would seem to me a marvellous and
magic world in which at.certain moments there rises from the
depths of the barely translucent element the avowal of a secret
which we shall not understand. But as a rule, when Albertine
was asleep, she seemed to have recaptured her innocence. In
the attitude which I had imposed upon her, but which in her
sleep she had speedily made her own, she seemed to trust
herself to me. Her face had lost any expression of cunning or
vulgarity, and between herself and me, towards whom she
raised her arm, on whom she rested her hand, there seemed to
be an absolute surrender, an indissoluble attachment. Her sleep
moreover did not separate her from me and allowed her to
retain the consciousness of our affection; its effect was rather to
abolish everything else; I would kiss her, tell her that I was
going to take a turn outside, and she would half-open her eyes
and say to me with a look of surprise—for the hour was indeed
late—"But where are you off to, my darling——" (calling me
by my Christian name), and at once fall asleep again. Her sleep
was no more than a sort of blotting out of the rest of her life,
an even silence over which from time to time familiar words of
tenderness would pass in their flight. By putting these words
together, one might have arrived at the unalloyed conversation,
the secret intimacy of a pure love. This calm slumber delighted
me, as a mother, reckoning it a virtue, is delighted by her
child's sound sleep. And her sleep was indeed that of a child.
Her awakening also, so natural and so loving, before she even
knew where she was, that I sometimes asked myself with
dread whether she had been in the habit, before coming to live
with me, of not sleeping alone but of finding, when she opened
her eyes, someone lying by her side. But her childlike grace
was more striking. Like a mother again, I marvelled that she
should always awake in such a good humour. After a few
moments she would recover consciousness, would utter
charming words, unconnected with one another, mere twitter-
ings. By a sort of reversal of roles, her throat, which as a rule
one seldom remarked, now almost startlingly beautiful, had

acquired the immense importance which her eyes, by being closed in sleep, had lost, her eyes, my regular interlocutors to which I could no longer address myself after the lids had closed over them. Just as the closed lids impart an innocent, grave beauty to the face by suppressing all that the eyes express only too plainly, there was in the words, not devoid of meaning but interrupted by moments of silence, which Albertine uttered as she awoke, a pure beauty of a kind that is not constantly tarnished, as is conversation, by habits of speech, stale repetitions, traces of familiar defects. Moreover, when I had decided to wake Albertine, I would have been able to do so without fear, knowing that her awakening would bear no relation to the evening that we had passed together, but would emerge from her sleep as morning emerges from night. As soon as she had begun to open her eyes with a smile, she would have offered me her lips, and before she had even said a word, I would have savoured their freshness, as soothing as that of a garden still silent before the break of day.

The day after the evening when Albertine had told me that she might perhaps, then that she might not, be going to see the Verdurins, I awoke early, and, while I was still half asleep, my joy informed me that it was a spring day interpolated in the middle of the winter. Outside, popular themes skilfully transposed for various instruments, from the horn of the china repairer, or the trumpet of the chair mender, to the flute of the goatherd who seemed, on a fine morning, to be a Sicilian drover, were lightly orchestrating the matutinal air with an "Overture for a Public Holiday." Our hearing, that delightful sense, brings us the company of the street, of which it traces every line for us, sketches all the figures that pass along it, showing us their colours. The iron shutters of the baker's shop and of the dairy, which had been lowered last night over every possibility of feminine bliss, were now being raised, like the canvas of a ship that is getting under way and about to set sail across the transparent sea, on to a vision of young shopgirls. This sound of the iron shutters being raised would perhaps have been my sole pleasure in a different part of the town. In this quarter a hundred other sounds contributed to my joy, of which I would not have missed a single one by

remaining too long asleep. It is one of the enchantments of the
old aristocratic quarters that they are at the same time plebeian.
Just as, sometimes, cathedrals used to have them within a
stone's throw of their portals (which have even preserved the
name, like the door of Rouen cathedral styled the Booksellers',
because these latter used to expose their merchandise in the
open air beside it), so various minor trades, but in this case
itinerant, passed in front of the noble Hôtel de Guermantes,
and made one think at times of the ecclesiastical France of long
ago. For the beguiling calls which they launched at the little
houses on either side had, with rare exceptions, little connection with song. They differed from song as much as the declamation—scarcely tinged by even the most imperceptible
modulation—of *Boris Godunov* and *Pelléas*; but on the other
hand recalled the drone of a priest intoning his office, of
which these street scenes are but the good-humoured, secular,
and yet half-liturgical counterpart. Never had I so delighted in
them as since Albertine had come to live with me; they seemed
to me a joyous signal of her awakening, and by interesting me
in the life of the world outside made me all the more conscious
of the soothing virtue of a beloved presence, as constant as I
could wish. Several of the foodstuffs peddled in the street,
which personally I detested, were greatly to Albertine's liking,
so much so that Françoise used to send her young footman
out to buy them, slightly humiliated perhaps at finding himself
mixing with the plebeian crowd. Very distinct in this peaceful
quarter (where the noises were no longer a cause of lamentation
to Françoise and had become a source of pleasure to myself),
there reached my ears, each with its different modulation,
recitatives declaimed by these humble folk as they would be in
the music—so entirely popular—of *Boris*, where an initial
tonality is barely altered by the inflexion of one note leaning
upon another, music of the crowd, which is more speech than
music. It was "Winkles, winkles, a ha'porth of winkles!" that
brought people running to buy the cornets in which were sold
those horrid little shellfish, which, if Albertine had not been
there, would have repelled me, as did the snails which I heard
being peddled at the same hour. Here again it was of the barely
musical declamation of Moussorgsky that the vendor reminded

me, but not of it alone. For after having almost "spoken" the refrain: "Who'll buy my snails, fine, fresh snails?" it was with the vague sadness of Maeterlinck, transposed into music by Debussy, that the snail vendor, in one of those mournful cadences in which the composer of *Pelléas* shows his kinship with Rameau: "If vanquished I must be, is it for thee to be my vanquisher?"[3] added with a singsong melancholy: "Only tuppence a dozen. . . ."

I have always found it difficult to understand why these perfectly simple words were sighed in a tone so far from appropriate, as mysterious as the secret which makes everyone look sad in the old palace to which Mélisande has not succeeded in bringing joy, and as profound as one of the thoughts of the aged Arkel who seeks to utter in the simplest words the whole lore of wisdom and destiny. The very notes upon which the voice of the old King of Allemonde or that of Golaud rises with ever-increasing sweetness to say: "We do not know what is happening here. It may seem strange. Perhaps nothing that happens is in vain," or else: "You mustn't be frightened . . . she was a poor little mysterious creature, like everyone," were those which served the snail vendor to repeat in an endless cantilena: "Only tuppence a dozen . . ." But this metaphysical lamentation scarcely had time to expire upon the shore of the infinite before it was interrupted by a shrill trumpet. This time it was not a question of victuals; the words of the libretto were: "Dogs clipped, cats trimmed, tails and ears docked."

It was true that the fantasy or wit of each vendor or vendress frequently introduced variations into the words of all these chants that I used to hear from my bed. And yet a ritual suspension interposing a silence in the middle of a word, especially when it was repeated a second time, constantly evoked the memory of old churches. In his little cart drawn by a she-ass which he stopped in front of each house before entering the courtyard, the old-clothes man, brandishing a whip, intoned: "Old clothes, any old clothes, old . . . clothes" with the same pause between the final syllables as if he had been intoning in plainchant: "*Per omnia saecula saeculo . . . rum*" or "*requiescat in pa . . . ce*" although he had no reason to believe in the immortality of his clothes, nor did he offer them as cerements for the eternal rest in peace. And similarly, as the motifs, even at this early hour, were beginning to interweave with one another, a costermonger pushing her little hand-cart employed in her litany the Gregorian division:

> Tender green artichokes,
> Tender and young,
> Ar . . . tichokes

although she had probably never heard of the antiphonary, or of the seven tones that symbolise, four the arts of the quadrivium and three those of the trivium.

Drawing from a penny whistle, or from a bagpipe, airs of his own southern country whose sunlight harmonised well with these fine days, a man in a smock, carrying a bull's pizzle in his hand and wearing a beret on his head, stopped before each house in turn. It was the goatherd with two dogs driving before him his string of goats. As he came from a distance, he arrived fairly late in our quarter; and the women came running out with bowls to receive the milk that was to give strength to their little ones. But with the Pyrenean airs of this benign shepherd was now blended the bell of the grinder, who cried: "Knives, scissors, razors." With him the saw-setter was unable to compete, for, lacking an instrument, he had to be content with calling: "Here comes the saw-setter. Any saws to set?" while in a gayer mood the tinker, after enumerating the pots, pans and everything else that he repaired, struck up the refrain:

> Tan, ran, tan, tan, ran, tan,
> For pots or cans, oh! I'm your man.
> I'll mend them all with a tink, tink, tink,
> And never leave a chink, chink, chink,

and little Italians carrying big iron boxes painted red, upon which the numbers—winning and losing—were marked, and springing their rattles, issued the invitation: "Enjoy yourselves, ladies, here's a treat."

Françoise brought in the *Figaro*. A glance was sufficient to show me that my article had still not appeared. She told me that Albertine had asked whether she might come to my room and sent word that she had after all given up the idea of calling upon the Verdurins and had decided to go, as I had advised her, to the "special" matinée at the Trocadéro—what nowadays would be called, though with considerably less significance, a "gala" matinée—after a short ride which she had promised to take with Andrée. Now that I knew that she had abandoned her possibly nefarious intention of going to see Mme Verdurin, I said with a laugh: "Tell her to come in," and told myself that she might go wherever she chose and that it was all the same to me. I knew that by the end of the afternoon, when dusk began to fall, I should probably be a different man, moping, attaching to every one of Albertine's movements an importance that they did not possess at this morning hour when the weather was so fine. For my insouciance was accompanied by a clear notion of its cause, but was in no way modified thereby.

"Françoise assured me that you were awake and that I wouldn't be disturbing you," said Albertine as she entered the room. And since, next to making me catch cold by opening the window at the wrong moment, what Albertine most dreaded was to come into my room when I was asleep: "I hope I haven't done wrong," she went on. "I was afraid you'd say to me:

> What insolent mortal comes to meet his doom?"

And she laughed that laugh which I always found so disturbing.
I replied in the same jesting vein:

> Was it for you this stern decree was made?

And, lest she should ever venture to infringe it, added: "Although I'd be furious if you did wake me."
"I know, I know, don't be frightened," said Albertine.
To show that I was mollified, I added, still enacting the scene from *Esther* with her, while in the street below the cries continued, drowned by our conversation:

> I find in you alone a certain grace
> That charms me and of which I never tire

(and to myself I thought: "Yes, she does tire me very often"). And remembering what she had said to me the night before, as

I thanked her extravagantly for having given up the Verdurins, so that another time she would obey me similarly with regard to something else, I said: "Albertine, you distrust me although I love you and you place your trust in people who don't love you" (as though it were not natural to distrust the people who love you and who alone have an interest in lying to you in order to find out things, to thwart you), and added these lying words: "It's funny, you don't really believe that I love you. As a matter of fact, I don't *adore* you." She lied in her turn when she told me that she trusted nobody but myself and then became sincere when she assured me that she knew quite well that I loved her. But this affirmation did not seem to imply that she did not believe me to be a liar who spied on her. And she seemed to forgive me as though she saw these defects as the agonising consequence of a great love or as though she herself did not feel entirely guiltless.

"I beg of you, my darling girl, no more of that trick riding you were practising the other day. Just think, Albertine, if you were to have an accident!"*

Of course I did not wish her any harm. But how delighted I should have been if, with her horses, she had taken it into her head to ride off somewhere, wherever she chose, and never come back to my house again! How it would have simplified everything, that she should go and live happily somewhere else, I did not even wish to know where!

"Oh! I know you wouldn't survive me for forty-eight hours. You'd kill yourself."*

Thus did we exchange lying speeches. But a truth more profound than that which we would utter were we sincere may sometimes be expressed and announced by another channel than that of sincerity.

"You don't mind all that noise outside?" she asked me. "Personally I love it. But you're such a light sleeper."

I was on the contrary often an extremely heavy sleeper (as I have already said, but am compelled to repeat in view of what follows), especially when I only fell asleep in the morning. As this kind of sleep is—on an average—four times as refreshing, it seems to the awakened sleeper to have lasted four times as long, when it has really been four times as short. A splendid, sixteenfold error in multiplication which gives so much beauty to our awakening and gives life a veritable new dimension, like those drastic changes of rhythm which, in music, mean that in an andante a quaver has the same duration as a minim in a prestissimo, and which are unknown in our waking state. There, life is almost always the same, whence the disappointments of travel. Yet it would seem that our dreams are sometimes made of the coarsest stuff of life, but that stuff is as it were treated, kneaded so thoroughly—with a protraction due to the fact that none of the temporal limitations of the waking state is there to prevent it from tapering off into unbelievable heights—that we fail to recognise it. On the mornings after this good fortune had befallen me, after the sponge of sleep had wiped from my brain the signs of everyday occupations that are traced upon it as on a blackboard, I was obliged to bring my memory back to life; by an exercise of will we can recapture what the amnesia of sleep or of a stroke has made us forget, what gradually returns to us as our eyes open or our paralysis disappears. I had lived through so many hours in a few minutes that, wishing to address Françoise, for whom I had rung, in words that corresponded to the facts of real life and were regulated by the clock, I was obliged to exert all my inner power of compression in order not to say: "Well, Françoise, here we are at five o'clock in the evening and I haven't set eyes on you since yesterday afternoon." And seeking to dispel my dreams, giving them the lie and lying to myself as well, I said brazenly, compelling myself with all my might to silence, the direct opposite: "Françoise, it must be at least ten o'clock!" I did not even say ten o'clock in the morning, but simply ten o'clock, so that this incredible hour might appear to be uttered in a more natural tone. And yet to say these words, instead of those that continued to run in the mind of the half-awakened sleeper that I still was, demanded the same effort of equilibrium that a man requires when, jumping out of a moving train and running for some yards along the platform, he manages to avoid falling. He runs for a moment because the environment that he has just left was one animated by great velocity, and utterly unlike the inert soil to which his feet find it difficult to accustom themselves.

Because the dream world is not the waking world, it does not follow that the waking world is less real; far from it. In the world of sleep, our perceptions are so overloaded, each of them blanketed by a superimposed counterpart which doubles its bulk and blinds it to no purpose, that we are unable even to distinguish what is happening in the bewilderment of awakening: was it Françoise who had come to me, or I who, tired of calling her, went to her? Silence at that moment was the only way of revealing nothing, as when we are brought before a magistrate cognisant of all the charges against us when we ourselves have not been informed of them. Was it Françoise who had come, or was it I who had summoned her? Was it not, indeed, Françoise who had been asleep and I who had just awoken her? To go further still, was not Françoise contained within me, for the distinction between persons and their interaction barely exists in that murky obscurity in which reality is no more translucent than in the body of a porcupine, and our all but non-existent perception may perhaps give us an idea of the perception of certain animals? Besides, in the state of limpid unreason that precedes these heavy slumbers, if fragments of wisdom float there luminously, if the names of Taine and George Eliot are not unknown, the waking state remains none the less superior to the extent that it is possible to continue it every morning, but not to continue the dream life every night. But perhaps there are other worlds more real than the waking world. Even it we have seen transformed by each new revolution in the arts, and still more, at the same time, by the degree of proficiency or culture that distinguishes an artist from an ignorant fool.

And often an extra hour of sleep is an attack of paralysis after which we must recover the use of our limbs and learn to speak. Our will would not be adequate for this task. We have slept too long, we no longer exist. Our waking is barely felt, mechanically and without consciousness, as a water pipe might feel the turning off of a tap. A life more inanimate than that of the jellyfish follows, in which we could equally well believe that we had been drawn up from the depths of the sea or released from gaol, were we but capable of thinking anything at all. But then from the highest heaven the goddess

Mnemotechnia bends down and holds out to us in the formula "the habit of ringing for coffee" the hope of resurrection. Even then, the instantaneous gift of memory is not always so simple. Often we have at our disposal, in those first minutes in which we allow ourselves to glide into the waking state, a variety of different realities among which we imagine that we can choose as from a pack of cards. It is Friday morning and we have just returned from a walk, or else it is teatime by the sea. The idea of sleep and that we are lying in bed in our nightshirt is often the last thing that occurs to us. The resurrection is not effected at once; we think we have rung the bell, but we have not done so, and we utter senseless remarks. Movement alone restores thought, and when we have actually pressed the electric button we are able to say slowly but distinctly: "It must be at least ten o'clock, Françoise. Bring me my coffee."

Françoise, *mirabile dictu*, could have had no suspicion of the sea of unreality in which I was still wholly immersed and through which I had had the energy to make my strange question penetrate. Her answer would be: "It's ten past ten," which made me appear quite rational and enabled me not to betray the fantastic conversations by which I had been interminably lulled (on days when a mountain of non-existence had not crushed all life out of me). By force of will, I had reintegrated myself with reality. I was still enjoying the last shreds of sleep, that is to say of the only source of invention, the only novelty that exists in story-telling, since none of our narrations in the waking state, even when embellished with literary graces, admit those mysterious differences from which beauty derives. It is easy to speak of the beauty created by opium. But to a man who is accustomed to sleeping only with the aid of drugs, an unexpected hour of natural sleep will reveal the vast, matutinal expanse of a landscape as mysterious and more refreshing. By varying the hour and the place in which we go to sleep, by wooing sleep in an artificial manner, or on the contrary by returning for a day to natural sleep—the strangest kind of all to whomsoever is in the habit of putting himself to sleep with soporifics—we succeed in producing a thousand times as many varieties of sleep as a gardener could produce of carnations or roses. Gardeners produce

flowers that are delicious dreams, and others too that are like
nightmares. When I fell asleep in a certain way I used to wake
up shivering, thinking that I had caught the measles, or,
what was far more painful, that my grandmother (of whom I
no longer ever thought) was hurt because I had mocked her
that day at Balbec when, in the belief that she was about to die,
she had wished me to have a photograph of her. At once,
although I was awake, I felt that I must go and explain to her
that she had misunderstood me. But already my bodily warmth
was returning. The diagnosis of measles was set aside, and my
grandmother was so far away that she no longer made my
heart ache. Sometimes over these different kinds of sleep a
sudden darkness fell. I was afraid to continue my walk along an
entirely unlighted avenue, where I could hear prowling footsteps. Suddenly an argument broke out between a policeman
and one of those women whom one often saw driving hackney
carriages, and mistook at a distance for young coachmen.
Upon her box among the shadows I could not see her, but she
was speaking, and in her voice I could read the perfections of
her face and the youthfulness of her body. I strode towards
her, in the darkness, to get into her carriage before she drove
off. It was a long way. Fortunately, her argument with the
policeman was prolonged. I overtook the carriage which was
still stationary. This part of the avenue was lighted by street
lamps. The driver became visible. It was indeed a woman, but
large and old and corpulent, with white hair tumbling beneath
her cap, and a strawberry mark on her face. I walked past her,
thinking: "Is this what happens to the youth of women? If we
have a sudden desire to see those we have met in the past, have
they grown old? Is the young woman we desire like a character
on the stage when, through the defection of the actress who
created the part, the management is obliged to entrust it to a
new star? But then it is no longer the same."

Then I would be overcome with a feeling of sadness. We
have thus in our sleep countless images of pity, like Renaissance Pietà's, not, like them, wrought in marble, but on the
contrary unsubstantial. They have their purpose, however,
which is to remind us of a more compassionate, more humane
view of things, which we are too apt to forget in the icy com-

mon sense, sometimes full of hostility, of the waking state. Thus I was reminded of the vow that I had made at Balbec that I would always treat Françoise with compassion. And for the whole of that morning at least I would manage to compel myself not to be irritated by Françoise's quarrels with the butler, to be gentle with Françoise to whom everyone else showed so little kindness. For that morning only, and I would have to try to frame a code that was a little more permanent; for, just as nations are not governed for any length of time by a policy of pure sentiment, so men are not governed for long by the memory of their dreams. Already this dream was beginning to fade away. In attempting to recall it in order to portray it I made it fade all the faster. My eyelids were no longer so firmly sealed over my eyes. If I tried to reconstruct my dream, they would open completely. We must constantly choose between health and sanity on the one hand, and spiritual pleasures on the other. I have always been cowardly enough to choose the former. Moreover, the perilous power that I was renouncing was even more perilous than one might suppose. Those dreams, those images of pity, do not fly away alone. When we alter thus the conditions in which we go to sleep, it is not our dreams alone that fade, but, for days on end, sometimes for years, the faculty not merely of dreaming but of going to sleep. Sleep is divine but by no means stable; the slightest shock makes it volatile. A friend to habit, it is kept night after night in its appointed place by habit, more steadfast than itself, protected from any possible disturbance; but if it is displaced, if it is no longer subjugated, it melts away like a vapour. It is like youth and love, never to be recaptured.

In these various forms of sleep, as likewise in music, it was the lengthening or shortening of the interval that created beauty. I enjoyed this beauty, but on the other hand I had missed in my sleep, however brief, a good number of the street cries which render perceptible to us the peripatetic life of the tradesmen, the victuallers of Paris. And so, habitually (without, alas, foreseeing the drama in which these late awakenings and the draconian, Medo-Persian laws of a Racinian Assuerus were presently to involve me) I made an effort to wake early so as to miss none of these cries. In addition to the pleasure of knowing how fond Albertine was of them and of being out of doors myself without leaving my bed, I heard in them as it were the symbol of the atmosphere of the world outside, of the dangerous stirring life through the midst of which I did not allow her to move save under my tutelage, in an external prolongation of her seclusion, and from which I withdrew her at the hour of my choosing to make her return home to my side.

Hence it was with the utmost sincerity that I was able to say in answer to Albertine: "On the contrary, they give me pleasure because I know that you like them."

"Seafood, oysters, seafood."

"Oh, oysters! I've been simply longing for some!"

Fortunately Albertine, partly from fickleness, partly from docility, quickly forgot the things for which she had been longing, and before I had time to tell her that she would find better oysters at Prunier's, she wanted in succession all the things that she heard cried by the fish woman: "Prawns, lovely prawns, alive, alive-o." "Skate, nice fresh skate." "Whiting to fry, to fry." "Here comes the mackerel, freshly caught mackerel. Here's mackerel, ladies, beautiful mackerel." "Who'll buy my mussels, fine fat mussels!"

In spite of myself, the warning: "Here comes the mackerel" made me shudder. But as this warning could not, I felt, apply to our chauffeur, I thought only of the fish of that name, which I detested, and my uneasiness did not last.[4]

"Ah! mussels," said Albertine, "I should so like some mussels."

"My darling! They were all very well at Balbec, but here they're not worth eating; besides, I implore you, remember what Cottard told you about mussels."

But my remark was all the more ill-chosen in that the next costermonger announced a thing that Cottard had forbidden even more strictly:

> Lettuce, cos lettuce, not to hawk,
> Lovely cos lettuce out for a walk.

Albertine consented, however, to forgo the cos lettuces, on the condition that I would promise to buy for her in a few days' time from the woman who cried: "Argenteuil asparagus, lovely green asparagus." A mysterious voice, from which one would have expected some stranger utterance, insinuated: "Barrels, barrels ..." One was obliged to remain under the disappointing impression that nothing more was being offered than barrels, for the word was almost entirely drowned by the cry: "Glazier, gla-zier, any broken panes, here comes the gla-zier," a Gregorian division which reminded me less, however, of the liturgy than did the call of the rag-and-bone man, unwittingly reproducing one of those abrupt changes of tone in the middle of a prayer which are common enough in the ritual of the church: "*Praeceptis salutaribus moniti et divina institutione formati, audemus dicere,*" says the priest, ending briskly upon "*dicere.*" Without irreverence, as the populace of the Middle Ages used to perform farces and satires on the very threshold of the church, it was of that "*dicere*" that the rag-and-bone man reminded one when, after drawling the other words, he uttered the final syllable with a brusqueness befitting the accentuation laid down by the great seventh-century Pope: "Any old rags, any old iron, any ..." (all this chanted slowly, as were the two syllables that followed, whereas the last concluded more briskly than "*dicere*") "rabbit ... skins." The oranges ("Valencia oranges, lovely ripe oranges"), the humble leeks even ("Here's fine leeks"), the onions ("Threepence a rope") sounded for me as 'it were an echo of the rolling waves in which, left to herself, Albertine might have perished, and thus assumed the sweetness of a *suave mari magno.*

> Here's carrots for lunch
> At tuppence a bunch.

"Oh!" exclaimed Albertine, "cabbages, carrots, oranges. All the things I want to eat. Do make Françoise go out and buy some. She shall cook us a dish of creamed carrots. Besides, it will be so nice to eat all these things together. It will be all the shouts we're hearing transformed into a good dinner..." ("Skate, alive, alive-o!") "Oh, please, ask Françoise to give us instead a *raie au beurre noir*. It's so good!"

"Very well, my little darling. But don't stay any longer,

otherwise you'll be asking for every single thing on the bar-
rows."

"All right, I'm off, but I never want anything again for our
dinners, except what we've heard cried in the street. It's
such fun. And to think that we shall have to wait two whole
months before we hear: 'Green and tender beans, fresh green
beans!' How true that is: tender beans; you know I like them
as soft as soft, dripping with oil and vinegar, you wouldn't
think you were eating them, they melt in the mouth like drops
of dew. Oh dear, it's the same with the cream cheese, such a
long time to wait: 'Good cream cheese, fresh cheese!' And the
water-grapes from Fontainebleau: 'Best chasselas for sale.'"
(And I thought with dismay of all the time that I should have
to spend with her before the water-grapes were in season.)
"Wait, though. I said I wanted only the things that we had
heard cried, but of course I make exceptions. And so it's by
no means impossible that I may look in at Rebattet's and order
an ice for the two of us. You'll tell me that it's not the season
for them, but I do so want one!"

I was disturbed by this plan of going to Rebattet's, rendered
more certain and more suspect in my eyes by the words "it's
by no means impossible." It was the day on which the Verdurins
were "at home," and, ever since Swann had informed them that
Rebattet's was the best place, it was there that they ordered
their ices and pastries.

"I have no objection to an ice, my darling Albertine, but
let me order it for you, I don't know myself whether it will
be from Poiré-Blanche's, or Rebattet's, or the Ritz, anyhow I
shall see."

"Then you're going out?" she said with a look of mistrust.

She always maintained that she would be delighted if I
went out more often, but if anything I said gave her to suppose
that I would not be staying indoors, her uneasy air made me
think that the joy she would evince on seeing me go out more
often was perhaps not altogether sincere.

"I may perhaps go out, perhaps not. You know quite well
that I never make plans beforehand. In any case ices are not a
thing that's hawked in the streets, so why do you want one?"

And then she answered me in words which showed me what

a fund of intelligence and latent taste had suddenly developed in her since Balbec, in words akin to those which, she maintained, were due entirely to my influence, to living continually in my company, words which, however, I should never have uttered, as though I had been somehow forbidden by an unknown authority ever to decorate my conversation with literary forms. Perhaps the future was not destined to be the same for Albertine as for myself. I had almost a presentiment of this when I saw her eagerness to employ in speech images so "bookish," which seemed to me to be reserved for another, more sacred use, of which I was still in ignorance. She said to me (and I was, in spite of everything, deeply touched, for I thought to myself: True, I myself wouldn't speak like that, and yet, all the same, but for me *she* wouldn't be speaking like that. She has been profoundly influenced by me, and cannot therefore help but love me, since she is my creation): "What I like about these foodstuffs that the peddlers cry is that a thing heard like a rhapsody changes its nature when it comes to the table and addresses itself to my palate. As for ices (for I hope that you won't order me one that isn't cast in one of those old-fashioned moulds which have every architectural shape imaginable), whenever I eat them, temples, churches, obelisks, rocks, a sort of picturesque geography is what I see at first before converting its raspberry or vanilla monuments into coolness in my gullet."

I thought that this was a little too well expressed, but she felt that I thought that it was well expressed and went on, pausing for a moment when she had brought off a simile to laugh that beautiful laugh of hers which was so painful to me because it was so voluptuous.

"Oh dear, at the Ritz I'm afraid you'll find Vendôme Columns of ice, chocolate ice or raspberry, and then you'll need a lot of them so that they may look like votive pillars or pylons erected along an avenue to the glory of Coolness. They make raspberry obelisks too, which will rise up here and there in the burning desert of my thirst, and I shall make their pink granite crumble and melt deep down in my throat which they will refresh better than any oasis" (and here the deep laugh broke out, whether from satisfaction at talking so well, or in self-mockery for using such carefully contrived images, or, alas, from physical pleasure at feeling inside herself something so good, so cool, which was tantamount to a sexual pleasure). "Those mountains of ice at the Ritz sometimes suggest Monte Rosa, and indeed, if it's a lemon ice, I don't object to its not having a monumental shape, its being irregular, abrupt, like one of Elstir's mountains. It mustn't be too white then, but slightly yellowish, with that look of dull, dirty snow that Elstir's mountains have. The ice needn't be at all big, only half an ice if you like, those lemon ices are still mountains, reduced to a tiny scale, but our imagination restores their dimensions, like those Japanese dwarf trees which one feels are still cedars, oaks, manchineels; so much so that if I arranged a few of them beside a little trickle of water in my room I should have a vast forest, stretching down to a river, in which children would lose their way. In the same way, at the foot of my yellowish lemon ice, I can see quite clearly postillions, travellers, post-chaises over which my tongue sets to work to roll down freezing avalanches that will swallow them up" (the cruel delight with which she said this excited my jealousy); "just as," she went on, "I set my lips to work to destroy, pillar by pillar, those Venetian churches of a porphyry that is made with strawberries, and send what's left over crashing down upon the worshippers. Yes, all those monuments will pass from their stony state into my inside which throbs already with their melting coolness. But, you know, even without ices, nothing is so exciting or makes one so thirsty as the advertisements for thermal springs. At Montjouvain, at Mlle Vinteuil's, there was no good confectioner who made ices in the neighbourhood, but we used to make our own tour of France in the garden by drinking a different mineral water every day, like Vichy water which, as soon as you pour it out, sends up from the bottom of the glass a white cloud which fades and dissolves if you don't drink it at once."

But to hear her speak of Montjouvain was too painful, and I cut her short.

"I'm boring you, good-bye my darling," she said.

What a change from Balbec, where I would defy Elstir himself to have been able to divine in Albertine this wealth of poetry, though a poetry less strange, less personal than that of Céleste Albaret, I need hardly say! Albertine would never have thought of the things that Céleste used to say to me, but love, even when it seems to be nearing its end, is partial. I preferred the picturesque geography of her ices, the somewhat facile charm of which seemed to me a reason for loving Albertine and a proof that I had some power over her, that she loved me.

As soon as Albertine had gone out, I felt how exhausting was her perpetual presence, insatiable in its restless animation, which disturbed my sleep with its movements, made me live in a perpetual chill by her habit of leaving doors open, and forced me—in order to find excuses that would justify my not accompanying her, without, however, appearing too unwell, and at the same time seeing that she was not unaccompanied—to display every day greater ingenuity than Sheherazade. Unfortunately, if by a similar ingenuity the Persian story-teller postponed her own death, I was hastening mine. There are thus in life certain situations that are not all created, as was this, by amorous jealousy and a precarious state of health which does not permit us to share the life of a young and active person, situations in which nevertheless the problem of whether to continue a shared life or to return to the separate existence of the past poses itself almost in medical terms: to which of the two sorts of repose ought we to sacrifice ourselves (by continuing the daily strain, or by returning to the agonies of separation)—to that of the head or that of the heart?

In any event, I was very glad that Andrée was to accompany Albertine to the Trocadéro, for certain recent and on the whole fairly trivial incidents had persuaded me that—though I still had, of course, the same confidence in the chauffeur's honesty—his vigilance, or at least the perspicacity of his vigilance, was not quite what it had once been. It happened that, only a short while before, I had sent Albertine alone in his charge to Versailles, and she told me that she had had lunch at the Réservoirs; as the chauffeur had mentioned Vatel's restaurant, on discovering this contradiction I found an excuse to go downstairs and speak to him (it was still the same man, whose acquaintance we made at Balbec) while Albertine was dressing.

"You told me that you had lunch at Vatel's, but Mlle Albertine mentioned the Réservoirs. What's the explanation?"

The chauffeur replied: "Oh, I said I had my lunch at Vatel's, but I've no idea where Mademoiselle had hers. She left me as soon as we reached Versailles to take a horse cab, which she prefers when it isn't a long drive."

Already I was furious at the thought that she had been alone; still, it was only during the time that it took her to have lunch.

"You might surely," I suggested mildly (for I did not wish to appear to be keeping Albertine actually under surveillance, which would have been humiliating to myself, and doubly so, for it would have shown that she concealed her activities from me), "have had your lunch, I don't say at her table, but in the same restaurant?"

"But she told me not to bother to meet her before six o'clock in the Place d'Armes. I wasn't to call for her after lunch."

"Ah!" I said, making an effort to conceal my dismay. And I returned upstairs. So it was for more than seven hours on end that Albertine had been alone, left to her own devices. I could reassure myself, it is true, that the cab had not been merely an expedient whereby to escape from the chauffeur's supervision. In town, Albertine preferred dawdling in a cab, saying that one had a better view, that the air was milder. Nevertheless, she had spent seven hours about which I should never know anything. And I dared not think of the manner in which she must have spent them. I felt that the driver had been extremely maladroit, but my confidence in him was henceforth absolute. For if he had been to the slightest extent in league with Albertine, he would never have admitted that he had left her unguarded from eleven o'clock in the morning until six in the evening. There could be but one other explanation (and it was absurd) of the chauffeur's admission. This was that some quarrel between Albertine and himself had prompted him, by making a minor disclosure to me, to show her that he was not the sort of man who could be silenced, and that if, after this first gentle warning, she did not toe the line with him, he would simply spill the beans. But this explanation was absurd;

it first of all presupposed a non-existent quarrel between him and Albertine, and then meant attributing the character of a blackmailer to this handsome chauffeur who had always shown himself so affable and obliging. In fact, two days later I saw that he was more capable than in my suspicious frenzy I had for a moment supposed of exercising over Albertine a discreet and perspicacious vigilance. Having managed to take him aside and talk to him of what he had told me about Versailles, I said to him in a casual, friendly tone: "That drive to Versailles you told me about the other day was everything that it should have been, you behaved perfectly as you always do. But if I may give you just a little hint, nothing of any great consequence, I feel such a responsibility now that Mme Bontemps has placed her in my charge, I'm so afraid of accidents, I feel so guilty about not accompanying her, that I'd be happier if it were you alone, you who are so safe, so wonderfully skilful, to whom no accident can possibly happen, who drove Mlle Albertine everywhere. Then I need fear nothing."

The charming apostolic motorist smiled a subtle smile, his hand resting upon the consecration-cross of his wheel.[5] Then he answered me in the following words which (banishing all the anxiety from my heart and filling it instead with joy) made me want to fling my arms round his neck.

"Never fear," he said to me. "Nothing can happen to her, for when my wheel isn't guiding her, my eye follows her everywhere. At Versailles, I went quietly along and visited the town with her, as you might say. From the Réservoirs she went to the Château, from the Château to the two Trianons, with me following her all the time without appearing to see her, and the amazing thing is that she never saw me. Oh, even if she had it wouldn't have been such a calamity. It was only natural, since I had the whole day before me with nothing to do, that I should visit the Château too. All the more so because Mademoiselle certainly can't have failed to notice that I've read a bit myself and take an interest in all those old curiosities." (This was true; indeed I should have been surprised if I had learned that he was a friend of Morel's, so far did he surpass the violinist in taste and sensitivity.) "Anyhow, she didn't see me."

"She must have met some of her friends, of course, for she has several at Versailles."

"No, she was alone all the time."

"Then people must have stared at her, such a dazzling young lady all by herself."

"Why, of course they stared at her, but she knew practically nothing about it; she went round all the time with her eyes glued to her guide-book, or gazing up at the pictures."

The chauffeur's story seemed to me all the more accurate in that it was indeed a postcard representing the Château, and another representing the two Trianons, that Albertine had sent me on the day of her visit. The care with which the obliging chauffeur had followed every step of her itinerary touched me deeply. How could I have supposed that this rectification—in the form of a generous amplification—of the account he had given two days earlier was due to the fact that in those two days Albertine, alarmed that the chauffeur should have spoken to me, had submitted and made her peace with him? This suspicion never even occurred to me. What is certain is that this version of the chauffeur's story, by ridding me of any fear that Albertine might have deceived me, quite naturally cooled my ardour towards my mistress and made me take less interest in the day that she had spent at Versailles. I think, however, that the chauffeur's explanations, which, by absolving Albertine, made her seem even more boring to me than before, would not perhaps have been sufficient to calm me so quickly. Two little pimples which she had on her forehead for a few days were perhaps even more effective in modifying the feelings of my heart. Finally, these feelings were diverted further still from her (so far that I was conscious of her existence only when I set eyes on her) by the strange confidence volunteered me by Gilberte's maid, whom I met by chance. I learned that, when I used to go to see Gilberte every day, she was in love with a young man of whom she saw a great deal more than of myself. I had had a momentary inkling of this at the time, and indeed I had questioned this very maid. But, as she knew that I was in love with Gilberte, she had denied the story, had sworn that Mlle Swann had never set eyes on the young man. Now, however, knowing that my love had long since

died, that for years past I had left all her letters unanswered—
and also perhaps because she was no longer in Gilberte's
service—of her own accord she gave me a full account of the
amorous episode of which I had known nothing. This seemed
to her quite natural. I assumed, remembering the oaths she had
sworn at the time, that she had not been aware of what was going
on. Not at all; it was she herself who used to go, on the orders
of Mme Swann, to inform the young man whenever the one I
loved was alone. The one I loved then . . . But I asked myself
whether my love of those days was as dead as I thought, for
this story pained me. Since I do not believe that jealousy can
revive a dead love, I supposed that my painful impression was
due, in part at least, to the injury to my self-esteem, for a number of people whom I did not like and who at that time and even
a little later—their attitude has since altered—affected a
contemptuous attitude towards me, knew perfectly well,
while I was in love with Gilberte, that I was being duped.
And this made me wonder retrospectively whether in my love
for Gilberte there had not been an element of self-love, since
it so pained me now to discover that all the hours of tenderness
which had made me so happy were recognised, by people I
did not like, as downright deception on Gilberte's part at my
expense. In any case, love or self-love, Gilberte was almost
dead in me, but not entirely, and the result of this chagrin
was to prevent me from worrying unduly about Albertine,
who occupied so small a place in my heart. Nevertheless, to
return to her (after so long a digression) and to her expedition
to Versailles, the postcards of Versailles (is it possible, then,
to have one's heart thus obliquely assailed by two simultaneous
and interwoven jealousies, each inspired by a different person?)
gave me a slightly disagreeable impression whenever my eye
fell upon them as I tidied my papers. And I thought that if the
chauffeur had not been such a worthy fellow, the accordance
of his second narrative with Albertine's cards would not have
amounted to much, for what are the first things that people
send you from Versailles but the Château and the Trianons,
unless the cards have been chosen by some sophisticated person
who adores a certain statue, or by some idiot who selects as a
"view" of Versailles the horse tramway station or the goods

depot. But perhaps I am wrong in saying an idiot, such post-cards not having always been bought by a person of that sort at random, for their interest as coming from Versailles. For two whole years men of intelligence, artists, used to find Siena, Venice, Granada a "bore," and would say of the humblest omnibus, of every railway carriage: "There you have true beauty." Then this fancy passed like the rest. Indeed, I am not sure that people did not revert to the "sacrilege of destroying the noble relics of the past." At any rate, a first-class railway carriage ceased to be regarded as *a priori* more beautiful than St Mark's in Venice. People continued to say: "Here you have real life, the return to the past is artificial," but without drawing any definite conclusion. At all events, while retaining full confidence in the chauffeur, to ensure that Albertine would be unable to desert him without his daring to stop her for fear of being taken for a spy, I no longer allowed her to go out after this without the reinforcement of Andrée, whereas for a time I had found the chauffeur sufficient. I had even allowed her then (a thing I would never dare do now) to stay away for three whole days by herself with the chauffeur and to go almost as far as Balbec, such a craving did she have for travelling at high speed in an open car. Three days during which my mind had been quite at rest, although the rain of postcards that she had showered upon me did not reach me, owing to the appalling state of the Breton postal system (good in summer, but dis-organised, no doubt, in winter), until a week after the return of Albertine and the chauffeur, in such health and vigour that on the very morning of their return they resumed their daily outings as though nothing had happened. I was delighted that Albertine should be going this afternoon to the Trocadéro, to this "special" matinée, but above all reassured by the fact that she would have a companion there in the shape of Andrée.

Dismissing these reflexions, now that Albertine had gone out, I went and stood for a moment at the window. There was at first a silence, amid which the whistle of the tripe vendor and the hooting of the trams reverberated through the air in different octaves, like a blind piano-tuner. Then gradually the interwoven motifs became distinct, and others were combined with them. There was also a new whistle, the call of a vendor

the nature of whose wares I never discovered, a whistle that
exactly resembled the whistle of the trams, and since it was
not carried out of earshot by its own velocity, it gave the
impression of a single tram-car, not endowed with motion, or
broken down, immobilised, screeching at brief intervals like
a dying animal. And I felt that, should I ever have to leave
this aristocratic quarter—unless it were to move to one that
was entirely plebeian—the streets and boulevards of central
Paris (where the greengrocery, fishmongering and other
trades, stabilised in big stores, rendered superfluous the cries
of the street hawkers, who in any case would have been unable
to make themselves heard) would seem to me very dreary,
quite uninhabitable, stripped, drained of all these litanies of the
small trades and itinerant victuals, deprived of the orchestra
that came every morning to charm me. On the pavement a
woman with no pretence to fashion (or else obedient to an
ugly fashion) came past, too brightly dressed in a sack overcoat of goatskin; but no, it was not a woman, it was a chauffeur
who, enveloped in his ponyskin, was proceeding on foot
to his garage. Winged messengers of variegated hue, escaped
from the big hotels, were speeding towards the stations bent
over their handlebars, to meet the arrivals by the morning
trains. The throbbing of a violin was due at one time to the
passing of a motor-car, at another to my not having put enough
water in my electric hot-water bottle. In the middle of the
symphony an old-fashioned tune rang out; replacing the sweet-
seller, who generally accompanied her song with a rattle, the
toy-seller, to whose kazoo was attached a jumping-jack which
he sent bobbing in all directions, paraded other puppets for
sale, and, indifferent to the ritual declamation of Gregory the
Great, the reformed declamation of Palestrina or the lyrical
declamation of the moderns, warbled at the top of his voice, a
belated adherent of pure melody:

> Come along all you mammies and dads,
> Here's toys for your lasses and lads!
> I make them myself,
> And I pocket the pelf.
> Tralala, tralala, tralalee.
> Come along youngsters . . .

Making no attempt to compete with this lively aria, little Italians in berets offered their statuettes for sale in silence. Soon, however, a young fifer compelled the toy merchant to move on and to chant more inaudibly, though in brisk time: "Come along all you mammies and dads!" Was this young fifer one of the dragoons whom I used to hear in the mornings at Doncières? No, for what followed was: "Here comes the china restorer. I repair glass, marble, crystal, bone, ivory and antiques. Here comes the restorer." In a butcher's shop, between an aureole of sunshine on the left and a whole ox suspended from a hook on the right, a young assistant, very tall and slender, with fair hair and a long neck emerging from a sky-blue collar, was displaying a lightning speed and a religious conscientiousness in putting on one side the most exquisite fillets of beef, on the other the coarsest parts of the rump, and placing them on glittering scales surmounted by a cross from which there dangled a set of beautiful chains, and—although he did nothing afterwards but arrange in the window a display of kidneys, steaks and ribs—was really far more reminiscent of a handsome angel who, on the Day of Judgment, will organise for God, according to their quality, the separation of the good and the wicked and the weighing of souls. And once again the thin, shrill music of the fife rose into the air, herald no longer of the destruction that Françoise used to dread whenever a regiment of cavalry filed past, but of "repairs" promised by an "antiquary," simpleton or rogue, who, in either case highly eclectic and very far from specialising, applied his art to the most diverse materials. The little bakers' girls hastened to stuff into their baskets the long loaves ordered for some luncheon party, while the dairymaids deftly attached the milk-churns to their yokes. Could it, I wondered, be altogether warranted, the nostalgic view I had of these young creatures? Would it not have been different if I had been able to detain for a few moments at close quarters one of those whom from the height of my window I saw only inside their shops or in motion? To estimate the loss that I suffered by my seclusion, that is to say the riches that the day had to offer me, I should have had to intercept in the long unwinding of the animated frieze some damsel carrying her laundry or her milk, transfer her for a moment, like the silhouette of a mobile piece of décor between the uprights of a stage flat, into the proscenium arch of my bedroom door, and keep her there before my eyes for long enough to elicit some information about her which would enable me to find her again some day, like the identification discs which ornithologists or ichthyologists attach before setting them free to the legs or bellies of the birds or fishes whose migrations they are anxious to trace.

And so I told Françoise that I wanted some shopping done, and asked her to send up to me, should any of them call, one or other of the girls who were constantly coming to the house with laundry or bread or jugs of milk, and whom she herself used often to send on errands. In doing so I was like Elstir, who, obliged to remain closeted in his studio, on certain days in spring when the knowledge that the woods were full of violets gave him a hunger to see some, used to send his concièrge out to buy him a bunch; and then it was not the table upon which he had posed the little floral model, but the whole carpet of undergrowth where in other years he had seen, in their thousands, the serpentine stems bowed beneath the weight of their tiny blue heads, that Elstir would fancy that he had before his eyes, like an imaginary zone defined in his studio by the limpid odour of the sweet, evocative flower.

Of a laundry girl, on a Sunday, there was not the slightest prospect. As for the baker's girl, as ill luck would have it she had rung the bell when Françoise was not about, had left her loaves in their basket on the landing, and had made off. The greengrocer's girl would not call until much later. Once, I had gone to order a cheese at the dairy, and among the various young female employees had noticed a startling towhead, tall in stature though little more than a child, who seemed to be day-dreaming, amid the other errand-girls, in a distinctly haughty attitude. I had seen her from a distance only, and for so brief an instant that I could not have described her appearance, except to say that she must have grown too fast and that her head supported a mane that gave the impression far less of capillary characteristics than of a sculptor's stylised rendering of the separate meanderings of parallel snowtracks on a mountainside. This was all that I had been able to make out, apart from a sharply defined nose (a rare thing in a child) in a thin face, which recalled the beaks of baby vultures. It was not only the clustering of her comrades round her that prevented me from seeing her distinctly, but also my uncertainty whether the sentiments which I might, at first sight and subsequently, inspire in her would be those of fierce pride, or of irony, or of a scorn which she would express later on to her friends. These alternative suppositions which I had formed about her in a flash had thickened the blurred atmosphere around her in which she was veiled like a goddess in a cloud shaken by thunder. For moral uncertainty is a greater obstacle to an exact visual perception than any defect of vision would be. In this too skinny young person, who also struck one's attention too forcibly, the excess of what another person would perhaps have called her charms was precisely what was calculated to repel me, but had nevertheless had the effect of preventing me from even noticing, let alone remembering, anything about the other dairymaids, whom the hooked nose of this one and her uninviting look, pensive, private, seeming to be passing judgment, had totally eclipsed, as a white streak of lightning plunges the surrounding countryside into darkness. And thus, of my call to order a cheese at the dairy, I had remembered (if one can say "remember" in speaking of someone so carelessly observed that one adapts to the nullity of the face ten different noses in succession), I had remembered only the girl I had found unpleasing. This can be enough to set a love affair in motion. And yet I might have forgotten the startling towhead and might never have wished to see her again, had not Françoise told me that, though still quite a nipper, she had all her wits about her and would shortly be leaving her employer, since she had been going too fast and owed money in the neighbourhood. It has been said that beauty is a promise of happiness. Conversely, the possibility of pleasure may be a beginning of beauty.

I began to read Mamma's letter. Behind her quotations from Mme de Sévigné ("If my thoughts are not entirely black at Combray, they are at least dark grey; I think of you constantly; I long for you; your health, your affairs, your absence: think how they must seem to me when the dusk descends") I sensed

that my mother was vexed to find Albertine's stay in the house
prolonged, and my intention of marriage, although not yet
announced to the betrothed, confirmed. She did not express
her annoyance more directly because she was afraid that I
might leave her letters lying about. Even then, veiled as they
were, she reproached me for not informing her immediately,
after each of them, that I had received it: "You remember how
Mme de Sévigné used to say: 'When one is far away, one no
longer laughs at letters which begin: *I have received yours.*'"
Without referring to what distressed her most, she expressed
displeasure at my lavish expenditure: "Where on earth does
all your money go? It is distressing enough that, like Charles
de Sévigné, you do not know what you want and are 'two or
three people at once,' but do try at least not to be like him in
spending money so that I may never have to say of you: 'He
has discovered how to spend and have nothing to show, how
to lose without staking and how to pay without clearing himself of debt.'"

I had just finished Mamma's letter when Françoise returned
to tell me that she had in the house that very same slightly
forward young dairymaid of whom she had spoken to me.
"She can quite well take Monsieur's letter and do his shopping
for him if it's not too far. You'll see, she's just like a Little Red
Ridinghood." Françoise went to fetch the girl, and I could
hear her showing the way and saying: "Come along now,
frightened because there's a passage! Stuff and nonsense, I
never thought you'd be such a goose. Have I got to lead you
by the hand?" And Françoise, like a good and faithful servant
who means to see that her master is respected as she respects
him herself, had draped herself in the majesty that ennobles
the procuress in the paintings of the old masters, wherein the
mistress and the lover fade into insignificance by comparison.

Elstir, when he gazed at the violets, had no need to bother
about what they were doing. The entry of the young dairymaid at once robbed me of my contemplative calm; I could
no longer think of anything except how to give plausibility
to the fable of the letter that she was to deliver and I began
to write quickly without venturing to cast more than a furtive
glance at her, so that I might not seem to have brought her into

my room to be scrutinised. She was invested for me with that charm of the unknown which would not have existed for me in a pretty girl whom I had found in one of those houses where they attend on one. She was neither naked nor in disguise, but a genuine dairymaid, one of those whom we picture to ourselves as being so pretty when we do not have the time to approach them; she was a particle of what constitutes the eternal desire, the eternal regret of life, the twofold current of which is at length diverted, directed towards us. Twofold, for if it is a question of the unknown, of a person who, from her stature, her proportions, her indifferent glance, her haughty calm, we suspect must be divine, at the same time we want this woman to be thoroughly specialised in her profession, enabling us to escape from ourselves into that world which a special costume makes us romantically believe to be different. Indeed, if we wanted to embody in a formula the law of our amorous curiosities, we should have to seek it in the maximum divergence between a woman glimpsed and a woman approached and caressed. If the women of what used at one time to be called the closed houses, if prostitutes themselves (provided that we know them to be prostitutes) attract us so little, it is not because they are less beautiful than other women, but because they are ready and waiting; because they already offer us precisely what we seek to attain; it is because they are not conquests. The divergence, there, is at its minimum. A whore smiles at us in the street as she will smile when she is by our side. We are sculptors. We want to obtain of a woman a statue entirely different from the one she has presented to us. We have seen a girl strolling, indifferent and insolent, along the seashore, we have seen a shop-assistant, serious and active behind her counter, who will answer us curtly if only to avoid being subjected to the jibes of her comrades, or a fruit-vendor who barely answers us at all. Whereupon we will not rest until we can discover by experiment whether the proud girl on the seashore, the shop-assistant obsessed with what other people will say, the aloof fruit-vendor, cannot be made, by skilful handling on our part, to relax their uncompromising attitude, to throw about our necks those arms that were laden with fruit, to bend towards our lips, with a smile of consent, eyes hitherto cold or absent—oh, the beauty of the eyes of a working-girl, eyes which were stern in working hours when she was afraid of the scandalmongering of her companions, eyes which shunned our obsessive gaze and which, now that we have seen her alone and face to face, allow their pupils to light up with sunny laughter when we speak of making love. Between the shopgirl, or the laundress busy with her iron, or the fruit seller, or the dairymaid, and that self-same wench when she is about to become one's mistress, the maximum divergence is attained, stretched indeed to its extreme limits, and varied by those habitual gestures of her profession which make a pair of arms describe, during the hours of toil, an arabesque as different as it is possible to imagine from those supple bonds that already every evening are fastened about one's neck while the mouth shapes itself for a kiss. And so one spends one's life in anxious approaches, constantly renewed, to serious working girls whose calling seems to distance them from one. Once they are in one's arms, they are no longer what they were, the distance that one dreamed of bridging is abolished. But one begins anew with other women, one devotes all one's time, all one's money, all one's energy to these enterprises, one is enraged by the too cautious driver who may make us miss the first rendezvous, one works oneself up into a fever. And yet one knows that this first rendezvous will bring the end of an illusion. No matter: as long as the illusion lasts one wants to see whether one can convert it into reality, and then one thinks of the laundress whose coldness one remarked. Amorous curiosity is like the curiosity aroused in us by the names of places; perpetually disappointed, it revives and remains for ever insatiable.

Alas, as soon as she stood before me, the fair dairymaid with the streaky locks, stripped of all the desires and imaginings that had been aroused in me, was reduced to her mere self. The quivering cloud of my suppositions no longer enveloped her in a dizzying haze. She acquired an almost apologetic air from having (in place of the ten, the twenty that I recalled in turn without being able to fix them in my memory) but a single nose, rounder than I had thought, which gave her a hint of stupidity and had in any case lost the faculty of multiplying itself. This flyaway caught on the wing, inert, crushed, incapable of adding anything to its own paltry appearance, no longer had my imagination to collaborate with it. Fallen into the inertia of reality, I sought to spring back again; her cheeks, which I had not noticed in the shop, appeared to me so pretty that I was abashed, and to recover my composure said to the young dairymaid: "Would you be so kind as to hand me the *Figaro* which is lying there. I must make sure of the address to which I am going to send you." Thereupon, as she picked up the newspaper, she disclosed as far as her elbow the red sleeve of her jersey and handed me the conservative sheet with a neat and courteous gesture which pleased me by its swift familiarity, its fluffy appearance and its scarlet hue. While I was opening the *Figaro*, for the sake of something to say, and without raising my eyes, I asked the girl: "What do you call that red knitted thing you're wearing? It's very pretty." She replied: "It's my sweater." For, by a slight downward tendency common to all fashions, the garments and words which a few years earlier seemed to belong to the relatively smart world of Albertine's friends, were now the currency of working-girls. "Are you quite sure it won't be giving you too much trouble," I said, while I pretended to be searching the columns of the *Figaro*, "if I send you rather a long way?" As soon as I myself thus appeared to consider the job I wanted her to do for me somewhat arduous, she began to feel that it would be a nuisance to her: "The only thing is, I'm supposed to be going for a ride on my bike this afternoon. You see, Sunday's the only day we've got." "But won't you catch cold, going bare-headed like that?" "Oh, I shan't be bare-headed, I'll have my cap, and I could get on without it with all the hair I have." I raised my eyes to those flavescent, frizzy locks and felt myself caught in their swirl and swept away, with a throbbing heart, amid the lightning and the blasts of a hurricane of beauty. I continued to study the newspaper, but although it was only to keep myself in countenance and to gain time, while only pretending to read I nevertheless took in the meaning of the words that were before my eyes, and my attention was caught by the following: "To the programme already announced for this afternoon in the great hall of the Trocadéro must be added the name of Mlle Léa who has consented to appear in *Les Fourberies de Nérine*. She will of course sustain the part of Nérine, which she plays with dazzling verve and bewitching gaiety." It was as though an invisible hand had brutally torn from my heart the bandage beneath which its wound had begun to heal since my return from Balbec. The flood of my anguish came pouring out in torrents. Léa was the actress friend of the two girls at Balbec whom Albertine, without appearing to see them, had watched in the mirror, one afternoon at the Casino. It was true that at Balbec Albertine, at the name of Léa, had adopted a special tone of hushed solemnity in order to say to me, almost shocked that anyone could suspect such a pattern of virtue: "Oh no, she isn't in the least that sort of woman. She's a very nice person." Unfortunately for me, when Albertine made an assertion of this kind, it was invariably a first stage in a series of different assertions. Shortly after the first would come this second one: "I don't know her." In the third phase, after Albertine had spoken to me of somebody who was "above suspicion" and whom (in the second place) she did not know, she would gradually forget first of all that she had said that she did not know the person and then, unwittingly contradicting herself, would inform me that she did. This first lapse of memory having occurred, and the new assertion been made, a second lapse of memory would begin, concerning the person's being above suspicion. "Isn't so and so," I would ask, "one of those women?" "Why, of course, everybody knows that!" Immediately the note of solemnity was sounded afresh in an assertion which was a vague echo, greatly reduced, of the first assertion of all. "I'm bound to say that she has always behaved perfectly properly with me. Of course, she knows that I'd soon send her about her business if she tried it on. But that's neither here nor there. I'm obliged to give her credit for the genuine respect she has always shown me. It's easy to see she knew the sort of person she had to deal with." We remember the truth because it has a name, is rooted in the past, but a makeshift lie is quickly forgotten. Albertine would forget this latest lie, her fourth, and, one day when she was anxious to gain my confidence by confiding in me, would open up to me with regard to the same person who at the outset had been so respectable and whom she did not know: "She took quite a fancy to me at one time. Three or four times she asked me to walk home with her and to come up and see her. I saw no harm in walking home with her, in front of lots of people, in broad daylight, in the open air. But when we reached her front door I always made some excuse and I never went upstairs." Shortly after this, Albertine would make some remark about the beautiful things that this lady had in her house. By proceeding from one approximation to another one would doubtless have succeeded in getting her to tell the truth, a truth which was perhaps less serious than I was inclined to believe, for, though susceptible to women, she perhaps preferred a male lover, and, now that she had me, might not have given a thought to Léa.

Already, in the case of quite a number of women at any rate, it would have been enough for me to gather together and present to my mistress a synthesis of her contradictory statements, in order to convict her of her misdeeds (misdeeds which, like astronomical laws, it is a great deal easier to deduce by a process of reasoning than to detect and observe in reality). But then she would have preferred to say that one of her statements had been a lie, the withdrawal of which would thus bring about the collapse of my whole system of deduction, rather than acknowledge that everything she had told me from the start was simply a tissue of mendacious tales. There are similar tales in the *Arabian Nights* which we find charming. They pain us coming from a person whom we love, and thereby enable us to penetrate a little deeper in our knowledge of human nature instead of being content to play around on its surface. Grief enters into us and forces us, out of painful curiosity, to probe. Whence emerge truths which we feel that we have no right to keep hidden, so much so that a dying atheist who has discovered them, certain of his own extinction, indifferent to fame, will nevertheless devote his last hours on earth to an attempt to make them known.

However, I was still at the first stage of enlightenment with regard to Léa. I was not even aware whether Albertine knew her. No matter, it came to the same thing. I must at all costs prevent her from renewing this acquaintance or making the acquaintance of this stranger at the Trocadéro. I say that I did not know whether she knew Léa or not; yet I must in fact have learned this at Balbec, from Albertine herself. For amnesia obliterated from my mind as well as from Albertine's a great many of the statements that she had made to me. Memory, instead of being a duplicate, always present before one's eyes, of the various events of one's life, is rather a void from which at odd moments a chance resemblance enables one to resuscitate dead recollections; but even then there are innumerable little details which have not fallen into that potential reservoir of memory, and which will remain forever unverifiable. One pays no attention to anything that one does not connect with the real life of the woman one loves; one forgets immediately what she has said to one about such and such an incident or such and such people one does not know, and her expression while she was saying it. And so when, in due course, one's jealousy is aroused by these same people, and seeks to ascertain whether or not it is mistaken, whether it is indeed they who are responsible for one's mistress's impatience to go out, and her annoyance when one has prevented her from doing so by returning earlier than usual, one's jealousy, ransacking the past in search of a clue, can find nothing; always retrospective, it is like a historian who has to write the history of a period for which he has no documents; always belated, it dashes like an enraged bull to the spot where it will not find the dazzling, arrogant creature who is tormenting it and whom the crowd admire for his splendour and cunning. Jealousy thrashes around in the void, uncertain as we are in those dreams in which we are distressed because we cannot find in his empty house a person whom we have known well in life, but who here perhaps is another person and has merely borrowed the features of our friend, uncertain as we are even more after we awake when we seek to identify this or that detail of our dream. What was one's mistress's expression when she told one that? Did she not look happy, was she not actually whistling, a thing that she never does unless she has some amorous thought in her mind and finds one's presence importunate and irritating? Did she not tell one something that is contradicted by what she now affirms, that she knows or does not know such and such a person? One does not know, and one will never know; one searches desperately among the unsubstantial fragments of a dream, and all the time one's life with one's mistress goes on, a life that is oblivious of what may well be of importance to one, and attentive to what is perhaps of none, a life hagridden by people who have no real connexion with one, full of lapses of memory, gaps, vain anxieties, a life as illusory as a dream.

I suddenly realised that the young dairymaid was still in the room. I told her that the place was undoubtedly a long way off, and that I did not need her. Whereupon she also decided that it would be too much trouble: "There's a fine match this afternoon, and I don't want to miss it." I felt that she must already be in the habit of saying "Sport's the thing," and that in a few years' time she would be talking about "living her own life." I told her that I certainly did not need her any longer, and gave her five francs. Immediately, having little expected this largesse, and telling herself that if she got five francs for doing nothing she would get a great deal more for doing my errand, she began to find that her match was of no importance. "I could easily have taken your message. I can always find time." But I pushed her towards the door, for I needed to be alone: I must at all costs prevent Albertine from meeting Léa's girl friends at the Trocadéro. It was essential that I should succeed in doing so, but I did not yet know how, and during these first few moments I opened my hands, gazed at them, cracked my knuckles, whether because the mind, when it cannot find what it is seeking, in a fit of laziness decides to halt for an instant during which it is vividly aware of the most insignificant things, like the blades of grass on a railway embankment which we see from the carriage window trembling in the wind, when the train stops in the open country—an immobility that is not always more fruitful than that of a captured animal which, paralysed by fear or mesmerised, gazes without moving a muscle—or because I was holding my body in readiness— with my mind at work inside it and, in my mind, the means of action against this or that person—as though it were simply a weapon from which would be fired the shot that would separate Albertine from Léa and her two friends. It is true that, earlier that morning, when Françoise had come in to tell me that Albertine was going to the Trocadéro, I had said to myself:

"Albertine is at liberty to do as she pleases," and had supposed that in this radiant weather her actions would remain without any perceptible importance to me until the evening. But it was not only the morning sun, as I had thought, that had made me so carefree; it was because, having obliged Albertine to abandon the plans that she might perhaps have initiated or even realised at the Verdurins', and having reduced her to attending a matinée which I myself had chosen and with a view to which she could not have planned anything, I knew that whatever she did would of necessity be innocent. Similarly, if Albertine had said a few moments later: "I don't really care if I kill myself," it was because she was certain that she would not kill herself. Surrounding both myself and Albertine there had been this morning (far more than the sunny day) that environment which itself is invisible but through the translucent and changing medium of which we saw, I her actions, she the importance of her own life—that is to say those beliefs which we do not perceive but which are no more assimilable to a pure vacuum than is the air that surrounds us; composing round about us a variable atmosphere, sometimes excellent, often unbreathable, they deserve to be studied and recorded as carefully as the temperature, the barometric pressure, the season, for our days have their own singularity, physical and moral. The belief, which I had failed to notice this morning but in which nevertheless I had been joyously enveloped until the moment when I had looked a second time at the *Figaro*, that Albertine would do nothing that was not blameless—that belief had vanished. I was no longer living in the fine sunny day, but in another day carved out of it by my anxiety lest Albertine might renew her acquaintance with Léa, and more easily still with the two girls if, as seemed to me probable, they went to applaud the actress at the Trocadéro where it would not be difficult for them to meet Albertine during one of the intervals. I no longer gave a thought to Mlle Vinteuil; the name of Léa had brought back to my mind, to make me jealous, the image of Albertine in the Casino watching the two girls. For I possessed in my memory only a series of Albertines, separate from one another, incomplete, a collection of profiles or snapshots, and so my jealousy was restricted to a discontinuous expression, at once fugitive and fixed, and to the people who had caused that expression to appear upon Albertine's face. I remembered her when, at Balbec, she was eyed with undue intensity by the two girls or by women of that sort; I remembered the distress that I felt when I saw her face subjected to an active scrutiny, like that of a painter preparing to make a sketch, entirely enveloped in it, and, doubtless on account of my presence, submitting to this contact without appearing to notice it, with a passivity that was perhaps clandestinely voluptuous. And before she pulled herself together and spoke to me, there was an instant during which Albertine did not move, smiled into the empty air, with the same air of feigned spontaneity and secret pleasure as if she were posing for somebody to take her photograph, or even seeking to assume before the camera a more dashing pose—the one she had adopted at Doncières when we were walking with Saint-Loup, and, laughing and passing her tongue over her lips, she pretended to be playing with a dog. Certainly at such moments she was not at all the same as when it was she who was interested in little girls who passed by. Then, on the contrary, her intense and silky gaze fastened itself, glued itself to the passer-by, so prehensile, so corrosive, that you felt that, in withdrawing, it must tear away the skin. But that look, which did at least give her a certain gravity, almost as though she were ill, seemed to me a pleasant relief after the vacant, blissful look she had worn in the presence of the two girls, and I should have preferred the sombre expression of the desire that she may perhaps have felt at times to the beaming expression caused by the desire which she aroused. However much she tried to conceal her awareness of it, it bathed her, enveloped her, vaporous, voluptuous, made her whole face glow. But who knows whether, once my back was turned, Albertine would continue to suppress everything that at such moments she held in suspension within herself, that radiated around her and gave me such anguish, whether, now that I was no longer there, she would not respond boldly to the advances of the two girls? Certainly these memories caused me great pain; they were like a complete admission of Albertine's proclivities, a general confession of infidelity, against which the specific pledges that she gave me and that I wanted to believe, the negative results of my incomplete inquiries, the assurances of Andrée, given perhaps with Albertine's connivance, were powerless to prevail. Albertine might deny specific betrayals; but by words that she let fall, more potent than her declarations to the contrary, by those looks alone, she had confessed to what she would have wished to hide far more than any specific facts, to what she would have let herself be killed sooner than admit: her natural tendency. For there is no one who will willingly deliver up his soul.

In spite of the pain that these memories caused me, could I have denied that it was the programme of the matinée at the Trocadéro that had revived my need of Albertine? She was one of those women whose very failings can sometimes take the place of absent charms, and, no less than their failings, the tenderness that follows upon them and brings us that assuagement which, like an invalid who is never well for two days in succession, we are incessantly obliged to recapture in their company. Besides, even more than their faults while we are in love with them, there are their faults before we knew them, and first and foremost their nature. For what makes this sort of love painful is the fact that there pre-exists it a sort of original sin of Woman, a sin which makes us love them, so that, when we forget it, we feel less need of them, and to begin to love again we must begin to suffer again. At this moment, the thought that she must not meet the two girls again and the question whether or not she knew Léa were what was chiefly occupying my mind, in spite of the rule that one ought not to take an interest in particular facts except in relation to their general significance, and notwithstanding the childishness, as great as that of longing to travel or to make friends with women, of frittering one's curiosity against such elements of the invisible torrent of painful realities which will always remain unknown to one as have fortuitously crystallised in one's mind. Moreover, even if one succeeded in destroying those elements, they would at once be replaced by others. Yesterday I was afraid lest Albertine should go to see Mme Verdurin. Now my only thought was of Léa. Jealousy, which is blindfold, is not merely powerless to discover anything in the darkness that enshrouds it; it is also one of those tortures where the task must be incessantly repeated, like that of the Danaides, or of Ixion. Even if the two girls were not there, what impression might not Léa make on her, beautified by her stage attire, haloed with success, what thoughts might she not leave in Albertine's mind, what desires, which, even if she repressed them in my company, would give her an aversion for a life in which she was unable to gratify them!

Besides, how could I be certain that she did not already know Léa, and would not pay her a visit in her dressing-room? And even if Léa did not know her, who could assure me that, having certainly seen her at Balbec, she would not recognise her and make a signal to her from the stage that would enable Albertine to gain admission back-stage? A danger seems perfectly avoidable when it has been averted. This one was not yet averted, and because I was afraid that it might never be, it seemed to me all the more terrible. And yet this love for Albertine, which I felt almost vanish when I attempted to realise it, seemed somehow at this moment to acquire a proof of its existence from the intensity of my anguish. I no longer cared about anything else, I thought only of how to prevent her from remaining at the Trocadéro, I would have offered any sum in the world to Léa to persuade her not to go there. If then we prove our predilection by the action that we perform rather than by the idea that we form, I must have been in love with Albertine. But this renewal of my suffering gave no greater consistency to the image of Albertine that I retained within me. She caused my ills like a deity who remains invisible. Making endless conjectures, I sought to ward off my suffering without thereby realising my love.

First of all, I must make certain that Léa was really going to perform at the Trocadéro. After dismissing the dairymaid, I telephoned to Bloch, whom I knew to be on friendly terms with Léa, in order to ask him. He knew nothing about it and seemed surprised that it could be of any interest to me. I decided that I must act quickly, remembered that Françoise was dressed and ready to go out and that I was not, and while I got up and dressed I told her to take a motor-car and go to the Trocadéro, buy a seat, search the auditorium for Albertine and give her a note from me. In this note I told Albertine that I was greatly upset by a letter which I had just received from that same lady on whose account she would remember that I had been so wretched one night at Balbec. I reminded her that, on the following day, she had reproached me for not having sent for her. And so I was taking the liberty, I told her, of asking her to sacrifice her matinée and to join me at home so that we might take the air together, which might help me to recover from the shock. But since it would be some time before I was dressed and ready, she would oblige me, seeing that she had Françoise as an escort, by calling at the Trois-Quartiers (this shop, being smaller, seemed to me less dangerous than the Bon Marché) to buy the white tulle bodice that she required.

My note was probably not superfluous. To tell the truth, I knew nothing that Albertine had done since I had come to know her, or even before. But in her conversation (she might, had I mentioned it to her, have replied that I had misunderstood her) there were certain contradictions, certain embellishments which seemed to me as decisive as catching her red-handed, but less usable against Albertine who, often caught out like a child, had invariably, by dint of sudden, strategic changes of front, stultified my cruel attacks and retrieved the situation. Cruel, most of all, to myself. She employed, not by way of stylistic refinement, but in order to correct her imprudences, abrupt breaches of syntax not unlike that figure which the grammarians call anacoluthon or some such name. Having allowed herself, while discussing women, to say: "I remember, the other day, I . . .," she would suddenly, after a "semiquaver rest," change the "I" to "she": it was something that she had witnessed as an innocent spectator, not a thing that she herself had done. It was not she who was the subject of the action. I should have liked to recall exactly how the sentence had begun, in order to decide for myself, since she had broken off in the middle, what the conclusion would have been. But since I had been awaiting that conclusion, I found it hard to remember the beginning, from which perhaps my air of interest had made her deviate, and was left still anxious to know her real thoughts, the actual truth of her recollection. The beginnings of a lie on the part of one's mistress are like the beginnings of one's own love, or of a vocation. They take shape, accumulate, pass unnoticed by oneself. When one wants to remember in what manner one began to love a woman, one is already in love with her; day-dreaming about her beforehand, one did not say to oneself: "This is the prelude to love; be careful!"—and one's day-dreams advanced unobtrusively, scarcely noticed by oneself. In the same way, save in a few comparatively rare cases, it is only for narrative convenience that I have frequently in these pages confronted one of Albertine's false statements with her previous assertion on the same subject. This previous assertion, as often as not, since I could not read the future and did not at the time guess what contradictory affirmation was to form a pendant to it, had slipped past unperceived, heard it is true by my ears, but without my isolating it from the continuous flow of Albertine's speech. Later on, faced with the self-evident lie, or seized by an anxious doubt, I would endeavour to recall it; but in vain; my memory had not been warned in time; it had thought it unnecessary to keep a copy.

I instructed Françoise to let me know by telephone when she had got Albertine out of the theatre, and to bring her home whether she was willing or not.

"It really would be the last straw if she wasn't willing to come and see Monsieur," replied Françoise.

"But I don't know that she's as fond of seeing me as all that."

"Then she must be an ungrateful wretch," went on Françoise, in whom Albertine was renewing after all these years the same torment of envy that Eulalie used at one time to cause her in my aunt's sickroom. Unaware that Albertine's position in my household was not of her own seeking but had been willed by me (a fact which, from motives of self-esteem and to infuriate Françoise, I preferred to conceal from her), she was amazed and incensed by the girl's cunning, called her when she spoke of her to the other servants a "play-actress," a "wily customer" who could twist me round her little finger. She dared not yet declare open war on her, showed her a smiling face and sought to acquire merit in my eyes by the services she did her in her relations with me, deciding that it was useless to say anything to me and that she would gain nothing by doing so, but always on the look-out for an opportunity, so that if ever she discovered a crack in Albertine's armour, she was determined to enlarge it, and to separate us for good and all.

"Ungrateful? No, Françoise, I think it's I who am ungrateful. You don't know how good she is to me." (It was so comforting to me to appear to be loved!) "Off you go."

"All right, I'll hop it, double quick."

Her daughter's influence was beginning to contaminate Françoise's vocabulary. So it is that all languages lose their purity by the addition of new words. For this decadence of Françoise's speech, which I had known in its golden period, I was in fact myself indirectly responsible. Françoise's daughter would not have made her mother's classic language degenerate into the vilest slang if she had stuck to conversing with her in dialect. She had never hesitated to do so, and if they had anything private to say to each other when they were both with me, instead of shutting themselves up in the kitchen they provided themselves, right in the middle of my room, with a protective screen more impenetrable than the most carefully closed door, by conversing in dialect. I supposed merely that the mother and daughter were not always on the best of terms, if I was to judge by the frequency with which they employed the only word that I could make out: *m'esasperate* (unless it was myself who was the object of their exasperation). Unfortunately the most unfamiliar tongue becomes intelligible in time when we are always hearing it spoken. I was sorry that it was dialect, for I succeeded in picking it up, and should have been no less successful had Françoise been in the habit of expressing herself in Persian. In vain did Françoise, when she became aware of my progress, accelerate the speed of her delivery, and her daughter likewise; there was nothing to be done. The mother was greatly put out that I understood their dialect, then delighted to hear me speak it. I am bound to admit that her delight was a mocking delight, for although I came in time to pronounce the words more or less as she herself did, she found a gulf between our two pronunciations which gave her infinite joy, and she began to regret that she no longer saw people to whom she had not given a thought for years but who, it appeared, would have rocked with laughter which it would have done her good to hear if they could have heard me speaking their dialect so badly. The mere idea of it filled her with gaiety and nostalgia, and she enumerated various peasants who would have laughed until they cried. However, no amount of joy could mitigate her sorrow at the fact that, however badly I might pronounce it, I understood it perfectly well. Keys become useless when the person whom we seek to prevent from entering can avail himself of a skeleton key or a jemmy. Dialect having become useless as a means of defence, she took to conversing with her daughter in a French which rapidly became that of the most debased epochs.

I was now ready, but Françoise had not yet telephoned. Should I set out without waiting for a message? But how could I be sure that she would find Albertine, that the latter hadn't gone back-stage, that even if Françoise did find her, she would allow herself to be brought home? Half an hour later the telephone bell began to tinkle and my heart throbbed tumultuously with hope and fear. There came, at the bidding of an operator, a flying squadron of sounds which with an instantaneous speed brought me the voice of the telephonist, not that of Françoise whom an ancestral timidity and melancholy, when she was brought face to face with any object unknown to her fathers, prevented from approaching a telephone receiver, although she would readily visit a person suffering from a contagious disease. She had found Albertine in the lobby by herself, and Albertine, after going off to tell Andrée that she was not going to stay, had come straight back to Françoise.

"She wasn't angry? Oh, I beg your pardon; will you please ask the lady whether the young lady was angry?"

"The lady asks me to say that she wasn't at all angry, quite the contrary, in fact; anyhow, if she wasn't pleased, she didn't show it. They're now going to go to the Trois-Quartiers, and will be home by two o'clock."

I gathered that two o'clock meant three, for it was already past two. But Françoise suffered from one of those peculiar, permanent, incurable defects which we call diseases: she was never able either to read or to express the time correctly.

When, after consulting her watch at two o'clock, she said "It's one o'clock" or "It's three o'clock," I was never able to understand whether the phenomenon that occurred was situated in her vision or in her mind or in her speech; the one thing certain is that the phenomenon never failed to occur. Humanity is a very old institution. Heredity and cross-breeding have given insuperable strength to bad habits, faulty reflexes. One person sneezes and gasps because he is passing a rose-bush, another breaks out in a rash at the smell of wet paint; others get violent stomach-aches if they have to set out on a journey, and grandchildren of thieves who are themselves rich and generous cannot resist the temptation to rob you of fifty francs. As for discovering the cause of Françoise's incapacity to tell the time correctly, she herself never threw any light upon the problem. For, notwithstanding the fury that her inaccurate replies regularly provoked in me, Françoise never attempted either to apologise for her mistake or to explain it. She remained silent, seeming not to hear, and thereby making me lose my temper altogether. I should have liked to hear a few words of justification, if only to be able to demolish them; but not a word, an indifferent silence. However, as far as today was concerned there could be no doubt; Albertine was coming home with Françoise at three o'clock, Albertine would not be meeting Léa or her friends. Whereupon, the danger of her renewing relations with them having been averted, it at once began to lose its importance in my eyes and I was amazed, seeing with what ease it had been averted, that I should have supposed that I would not succeed in averting it. I felt a keen impulse of gratitude towards Albertine, who, I could see, had not gone to the Trocadéro to meet Léa's friends, and who showed me, by leaving the matinée and coming home at a word from me, that she belonged to me, even for the future, more than I had imagined. My gratitude was even greater when a cyclist brought me a note from her bidding me be patient, and full of the charming expressions that she was in the habit of using. "My darling dear Marcel, I return less quickly than this cyclist, whose bike I should like to borrow in order to be with you sooner. How could you imagine that I might be angry or that I could enjoy anything better than to

be with you? It will be nice to go out, just the two of us together; it would be nicer still if we never went out except
together. The ideas you get into your head! What a Marcel!
What a Marcel! Always and ever your Albertine."

The dresses that I bought for her, the yacht of which I
had spoken to her, the Fortuny gowns—all these things, having
in this obedience on Albertine's part not their recompense
but their complement, appeared to me now as so many privileges
that I exercised; for the duties and expenses of a master are
part of his dominion, and define it, prove it, fully as much as
his rights. And these rights which she acknowledged were
precisely what gave my expenditure its true character: I had a
woman of my own, who, at the first word that I sent her out
of the blue, informed me deferentially by telephone that she
was coming, that she was allowing herself to be brought home,
at once. I was more of a master than I had supposed. More of a
master, in other words more of a slave. I no longer felt the
slightest impatience to see Albertine. The certainty that she
was at this moment engaged in shopping with Françoise,
that she would return with her at an approaching moment
which I would willingly have postponed, lit up like a calm
and radiant star a period of time which I would now have been
far better pleased to spend alone. My love for Albertine had
made me get up and prepare to go out, but it would prevent
me from enjoying my outing. I reflected that on a Sunday
afternoon like this little shopgirls, midinettes, prostitutes
must be strolling in the Bois. And with the words *midinettes*,
little shopgirls (as had often happened to me with a proper
name, the name of a girl read in the account of a ball), with the
image of a white bodice, a short skirt, since beneath them I
placed an unknown person who might perhaps come to love
me, I created out of nothing desirable women, and said to
myself: "How delightful they must be!" But of what use
would it be to me that they were delightful, seeing that I
was not going out alone? Taking advantage of the fact that
I still was alone, and drawing the curtains together so that the
sun should not prevent me from reading the notes, I sat down
at the piano, opened at random Vinteuil's sonata which happened to be lying there, and began to play; seeing that Alber-

tine's arrival was still a matter of some time but was on the other hand certain, I had at once time to spare and peace of mind. Lulled by the confident expectation of her return escorted by Françoise and by the assurance of her docility as by the blessedness of an inner light as warming as the light of the sun, I could dispose of my thoughts, detach them for a moment from Albertine, apply them to the sonata. I did not even go out of my way to notice how, in the latter, the combination of the sensual and the anxious motifs corresponded more closely now to my love for Albertine, from which jealousy had been for so long absent that I had been able to confess to Swann my ignorance of that sentiment. No, approaching the sonata from another point of view, regarding it in itself as the work of a great artist, I was carried back upon the tide of sound to the days at Combray—I do not mean Montjouvain and the Méséglise way, but to my walks along the Guermantes way—when I myself had longed to become an artist. In abandoning that ambition *de facto*, had I forfeited something real? Could life console me for the loss of art? Was there in art a more profound reality, in which our true personality finds an expression that is not afforded it by the activities of life? For every great artist seems so different from all the rest, and gives us so strongly that sensation of individuality for which we seek in vain in our everyday existence! Just as I was thinking thus, I was struck by a passage in the sonata. It was a passage with which I was quite familiar, but sometimes our attention throws a different light upon things which we have known for a long time and we remark in them what we have never seen before. As I played the passage, and although Vinteuil had been trying to express in it a fancy which would have been wholly foreign to Wagner, I could not help murmuring "*Tristan*," with the smile of an old family friend discovering a trace of the grandfather in an intonation, a gesture of the grandson who has never set eyes on him. And as the friend then examines a photograph which enables him to specify the likeness, so, on top of Vinteuil's sonata, I set up on the music-rest the score of *Tristan*, a selection from which was being given that afternoon, as it happened, at a Lamoureux concert. In admiring the Bayreuth master, I had none of the scruples of those who, like Nietzsche, are bidden by a sense of duty to shun in art as in life the beauty that tempts them, and who, tearing themselves from *Tristan* as they renounce *Parsifal*, and, in their spiritual asceticism, progressing from one mortification to another, succeed, by following the most painful of *viae Crucis*, in exalting themselves to the pure cognition and perfect adoration of *Le Postillon de Longjumeau*.[6] I was struck by how much reality there is in the work of Wagner as I contemplated once more those insistent, fleeting themes which visit an act, recede only to return again and again, and, sometimes distant, drowsy, almost detached, are at other moments, while remaining vague, so pressing and so close, so internal, so organic, so visceral, that they seem like the reprise not so much of a musical motif as of an attack of neuralgia.

Music, very different in this respect from Albertine's society, helped me to descend into myself, to discover new things: the variety that I had sought in vain in life, in travel, but a longing for which was none the less renewed in me by this sonorous tide whose sunlit waves now came to expire at my feet. A twofold diversity. As the spectrum makes visible to us the composition of light, so the harmony of a Wagner, the colour of an Elstir, enable us to know that essential quality of another person's sensations into which love for another person does not allow us to penetrate. Then a diversity inside the work itself, by the sole means that exist of being effectively diverse: to wit, combining diverse individualities. Where a minor composer would claim to be portraying a squire, or a knight, while making them both sing the same music, Wagner on the contrary allots to each separate appellation a different reality, and whenever a squire appears, it is an individual figure, at once complicated and simplified, that, with a joyous, feudal clash of warring sounds, inscribes itself in the vast tonal mass. Whence the plenitude of a music that is indeed filled with so many different strains, each of which is a person. A person or the impression that is given us by a momentary aspect of nature. Even that which, in this music, is most independent of the emotion that it arouses in us preserves its outward and absolutely precise reality; the song of a bird, the ring of a hunter's horn, the air that a shepherd plays upon his pipe, each carves its silhouette of sound against the horizon. True, Wagner would bring them forward, appropriate them, introduce them into an orchestral whole, make them subservient to the highest musical concepts, but always respecting their original nature, as a carpenter respects the grain, the peculiar essence of the wood that he is carving.

But notwithstanding the richness of these works in which the contemplation of nature has its place alongside the action, alongside the individuals who are not merely the names of characters, I thought how markedly, all the same, these works partake of that quality of being—albeit marvellously—always incomplete, which is the characteristic of all the great works of the nineteenth century, that century whose greatest writers somehow botched their books, but, watching themselves work as though they were at once workman and judge, derived from this self-contemplation a new form of beauty, exterior and superior to the work itself, imposing on it a retroactive unity, a grandeur which it does not possess. Without pausing to consider the man who belatedly saw in his novels a *Human Comedy*, or those who entitled heterogeneous poems or essays *The Legend of the Centuries* or *The Bible of Humanity*, can we not say none the less of the last of these that he so admirably personifies the nineteenth century that the greatest beauties in Michelet are to be sought not so much in his work itself as in the attitudes that he adopts towards his work, not in his *History of France* nor in his *History of the Revolution*, but in his prefaces to those books? Prefaces, that is to say pages written after the books themselves, in which he considers the books, and with which we must include here and there certain sentences beginning as a rule with a: "Dare I say?" which is not a scholar's precaution but a musician's cadence. The other musician, he who was delighting me at this moment, Wagner, retrieving some exquisite fragment from a drawer of his writing-table to introduce it, as a retrospectively necessary theme, into a work he had not even thought of at the time he composed it, then having composed a first mythological opera, and a second, and afterwards others still, and perceiving all of a sudden that he had written a tetralogy, must have felt

something of the same exhilaration as Balzac when the latter,
casting over his books the eye at once of a stranger and of a
father, finding in one the purity of Raphael, in another the
simplicity of the Gospel, suddenly decided, shedding a
retrospective illumination upon them, that they would be
better brought together in a cycle in which the same characters
would reappear, and touched up his work with a swift brush-
stroke, the last and the most sublime. An ulterior unity, but
not a factitious one, otherwise it would have crumbled into
dust like all the other systematisations of mediocre writers
who with copious titles and sub-titles give themselves the
appearance of having pursued a single and transcendent design.
Not factitious, perhaps indeed all the more real for being
ulterior, for being born of a moment of enthusiasm when it is
discovered to exist among fragments which need only to be
joined together; a unity that was unaware of itself, hence vital
and not logical, that did not prohibit variety, dampen invention. It emerges (but applied this time to the work as a
whole) like such and such a fragment composed separately,
born of an inspiration, not required by the artificial development
of a thesis, which comes to be integrated with the rest. Before
the great orchestral movement that precedes the return of
Isolde, it is the work itself that has attracted towards itself
the half-forgotten air of a shepherd's pipe. And, no doubt,
just as the orchestra swells and surges at the approach of the
ship, when it takes hold of these notes of the pipe, transforms
them, imbues them with its own intoxication, breaks their
rhythm, clarifies their tonality, accelerates their movement,
expands their instrumentation, so no doubt Wagner himself
was filled with joy when he discovered in his memory the
shepherd's tune, incorporated it in his work, gave it its full
wealth of meaning. This joy moreover never forsakes him. In
him, however great the melancholy of the poet, it is consoled,
transcended—that is to say, alas, to some extent destroyed—
by the exhilaration of the fabricator. But then, no less than by
the similarity I had remarked just now between Vinteuil's
phrase and Wagner's, I was troubled by the thought of this
Vulcan-like skill. Could it be this that gave to great artists the
illusory aspect of a fundamental, irreducible originality, ap-

parently the reflexion of a more than human reality, actually
the result of industrious toil? If art is no more than that, it is
no more real than life and I had less cause for regret. I went on
playing *Tristan*. Separated from Wagner by the wall of sound,
I could hear him exult, invite me to share his joy, I could hear
the immortally youthful laughter and the hammer-blows of
Siegfried ring out with redoubled vigour; but the more
marvellously those phrases were struck, the technical skill of
the craftsman served merely to make it easier for them to leave
the earth, birds akin not to Lohengrin's swan but to that
aeroplane which I had seen at Balbec convert its energy into
vertical motion, glide over the sea and vanish in the sky.
Perhaps, as the birds that soar highest and fly most swiftly
have more powerful wings, one of these frankly material
vehicles was needed to explore the infinite, one of these
120 horse-power machines—brand-name Mystère—in which
nevertheless, however high one flies, one is prevented to some
extent from enjoying the silence of space by the overpowering
roar of the engine!

Somehow or other the course of my musings, which hitherto
had wandered among musical memories, turned now to those
men who have been the best performers of music in our day,
among whom, slightly exaggerating his merit, I included Morel.
At once my thoughts took a sharp turn, and it was Morel's
character, certain peculiarities of that character, that I began
to consider. As it happened—and this might be connected
though not confused with the neurasthenia to which he was
a prey—Morel was in the habit of talking about his life, but
always presented so shadowy a picture of it that it was difficult
to make anything out. For instance, he placed himself entirely
at M. de Charlus's disposal on the understanding that he must
keep his evenings free, as he wished to be able after dinner to
attend an algebra course. M. de Charlus conceded this, but
insisted on seeing him after the lessons.

"Impossible, it's an old Italian painting" (this witticism
means nothing when written down like this; but M. de Charlus
having made Morel read *l'Education sentimentale*, in the penultimate chapter of which Frédéric Moreau uses this expression,
it was Morel's idea of a joke never to say the word "impossible"

without following it up with "it's an old Italian painting"),
"the lessons go on very late, and they're already enough of an
inconvenience to the teacher, who naturally would be annoyed
if I came away in the middle."

"But there's no need to have lessons. Algebra isn't a thing
like swimming, or even English, you can learn it equally well
from a book," replied M. de Charlus, who had guessed from
the first that these algebra lessons were one of those images of
which it was impossible to decipher anything at all. It was
perhaps some affair with a woman, or, if Morel was seeking
to earn money in shady ways and had attached himself to the
secret police, a nocturnal expedition with detectives, or
possibly, what was even worse, an engagement as a gigolo
whose services may be required in a brothel.

"A great deal more easily from a book," Morel assured M. de
Charlus, "for it's impossible to make head or tail of the lessons."

"Then why don't you study it in my house, where you would
be far more comfortable?" M. de Charlus might have answered,
but took care not to do so, knowing that at once, preserving
only the same essential element that the evening hours must
be set apart, the imaginary algebra course would change to
obligatory lessons in dancing or drawing. In this M. de Charlus
could see that he was mistaken, partially at least, for Morel
often spent his time at the Baron's in solving equations.
M. de Charlus did raise the objection that algebra could be of
little use to a violinist. Morel replied that it was a distraction
which helped him to pass the time and to conquer his neurasthenia. No doubt M. de Charlus might have made inquiries,
have tried to find out what actually were these mysterious and
inescapable algebra lessons that were given only at night. But
M. de Charlus was too caught up in the toils of his own social
life to be able to unravel the tangled skein of Morel's occupations. The visits he received or paid, the time he spent at his
club, the dinner-parties, the evenings at the theatre, prevented
him from thinking about the problem, or for that matter about
the malevolence, at once violent and deceitful, to which (it
was reported) Morel had been wont to give vent and which he
had at the same time sought to conceal in the successive
circles, the different towns through which he had passed, and

where people still spoke of him with a shudder, with bated breath, never daring to say anything about him.

It was unfortunately one of the outbursts of this neurotic venom that I was destined to hear that day when, rising from the piano, I went down to the courtyard to meet Albertine, who had still not arrived. As I passed by Jupien's shop, in which Morel and the girl who, I supposed, was shortly to become his wife were alone together, Morel was screaming at the top of his voice, thereby revealing an accent that I hardly recognised as his, a coarse peasant accent, suppressed as a rule, and very strange indeed. His words were no less strange, and faulty from the point of view of the French language, but his knowledge of everything was imperfect.[7] "Will you get out of here, *grand pied de grue*, *grand pied de grue*, *grand pied de grue*," he repeated to the poor girl who at first had clearly not understood what he meant, and now, trembling and indignant, stood motionless before him. "Didn't I tell you to get out of here, *grand pied de grue*, *grand pied de grue*. Go and fetch your uncle till I tell him what you are, you whore." Just at that moment the voice of Jupien, who was returning home with one of his friends, was heard in the courtyard, and as I knew that Morel was an utter coward, I decided that it was unnecessary to add my forces to those of Jupien and his friend, who in another moment would have entered the shop, and retired upstairs again to avoid Morel, who, for all his having pretended (probably in order to frighten and subjugate the girl by a piece of blackmail based perhaps on nothing at all) to be so anxious that Jupien should be fetched, made haste to depart as soon as he heard him in the courtyard. The words I have set down here are nothing, and would not explain why my heart was beating so violently as I went upstairs. These scenes which we witness from time to time in our lives acquire an incalculable element of potency from what soldiers call, in speaking of a military offensive, the advantage of surprise, and however agreeably I might be soothed by the knowledge that Albertine, instead of remaining at the Trocadéro, was coming home to me, I still heard ringing in my ears those words ten times repeated: "*Grand pied de grue, grand pied de grue,*" which had so shattered me.

Gradually my agitation subsided. Albertine was on her way home. I would hear her ring the bell in a moment. I felt that my life was no longer even what it could have been, and that to have a woman in the house like this with whom quite naturally, when she returned home, I would go out, to the adornment of whose person the energy and activity of my being were to be more and more diverted, made of me as it were a bough that has blossomed, but is weighed down by the abundant fruit into which all its reserves of strength have passed. In contrast to the anxiety that I had been feeling only an hour earlier, the calm induced in me by the prospect of Albertine's return was even vaster than that which I had felt in the morning before she left the house. Anticipating the future, of which my mistress's docility made me to all intents and purposes master, more resistant, as though it were filled and stabilised by the imminent, importunate, inevitable, gentle presence, it was the calm (dispensing us from the obligation to seek our happiness in ourselves) that is born of family feeling and domestic bliss. Familial and domestic: such was again, no less than the feeling which had brought me such peace while I was waiting for Albertine, that which I experienced later when I drove out with her. She took off her glove for a moment, either to touch my hand, or to dazzle me by letting me see on her little finger, next to the ring that Mme Bontemps had given her, another upon which was displayed the large and liquid surface of a bright sheet of ruby.

"What, another new ring, Albertine! Your aunt *is* generous!"

"No, I didn't get this from my aunt," she said with a laugh. "I bought it myself, since thanks to you I can save up ever so much money. I don't even know whose it was before. A visitor who was short of money left it with the proprietor of a hotel where I stayed at Le Mans. He didn't know what to do with it, and would have sold it for much less than it was worth. But it was still far too dear for me. Now that, thanks to you, I'm becoming a smart lady, I wrote to ask him if he still had it. And here it is."

"That makes a great many rings, Albertine. Where will you put the one that I am going to give you? Anyhow, this one's very pretty. I can't quite make out what that is carved round the ruby, it looks like a man's grinning face. But my eyesight isn't good enough."

"Even if it was better than it is it wouldn't get you very far. I can't make it out either."

In the past it had often happened to me, on reading a book of memoirs or a novel in which a man is always going out with a woman, or having tea with her, to long to be able to do likewise. I had thought sometimes that I had succeeded in doing so, as for instance when I took Saint-Loup's mistress out with me, or went to dinner with her. But however much I summoned to my assistance the idea that I was at that moment actually impersonating the character I had envied in the novel, this idea assured me that I ought to find pleasure in Rachel's company and yet afforded me none. For, whenever we attempt to imitate something that has really existed, we forget that this something was brought about not by the desire to imitate but by an unconscious force which itself is also real; but this unique impression, which all my longing to taste a delicate pleasure by going out with Rachel had failed to give me, I was now experiencing, without having looked for it in the slightest, but for quite other reasons, reasons that were sincere and profound; to take a single instance, for the reason that my jealousy prevented me from losing sight of Albertine, and, the moment I was able to leave the house, from letting her go anywhere without me. I was experiencing it only now because our knowledge is not of the external objects which we want to observe, but of involuntary sensations, because in the past, though a woman might indeed be sitting in the same carriage as myself, she was not *really* by my side as long as she was not continually re-created there by a need for her such as I felt for Albertine, as long as the constant caress of my gaze did not incessantly restore to her those tints that need to be perpetually refreshed, as long as my senses, appeased perhaps but still freshly remembering, were not aware of the savour and substance beneath those colours, as long as, combined with the senses and with the imagination that exalts them, jealousy was not maintaining that woman in a state of equilibrium at my side by a compensated attraction as powerful as the law of gravity. Our motor-car sped along the boulevards and the avenues, whose rows of houses, a pink congelation of sunshine and cold, reminded me of my visits to Mme Swann in the soft light of her chrysanthemums, before it was time to ring for the lamps.

I had barely time to make out, being separated from them by the glass of the motor-car as effectively as I should have been by that of my bedroom window, a young fruit-seller, or a dairymaid, standing in the doorway of her shop, illuminated by the sunshine like a heroine whom my desire was sufficient to launch upon exquisite adventures, on the threshold of a romance which I should never know. For I could not ask Albertine to let me stop, and already the young women whose features my eyes had barely distinguished, and whose fresh complexions they had barely caressed, were no longer visible in the golden haze in which they were bathed. The emotion that gripped me when I caught sight of a wine-merchant's girl at her cash-desk or a laundress chatting in the street was the emotion that we feel on recognising a goddess. Now that Olympus no longer exists, its inhabitants dwell upon the earth. And when, in composing a mythological scene, painters have engaged to pose as Venus or Ceres young women of the people following the humblest callings, so far from committing sacrilege they have merely added or restored to them the quality, the divine attributes of which they had been stripped.

"What did you think of the Trocadéro, you little gadabout?"

"I'm jolly glad I came away from it to go out with you. Architecturally it's pretty measly, isn't it? It's by Davioud, I believe."

"But how learned my little Albertine is becoming! It is indeed by Davioud, but I'd forgotten."

"While you're asleep I read your books, you old lazybones."

"I say, little one, you're changing so fast and becoming so intelligent" (this was true, but even had it not been true I was not sorry that she should have the satisfaction, failing others, of saying to herself that at least the time she spent in my house was not being entirely wasted) "that I don't mind telling you things which would generally be regarded as false but which correspond to a truth that I'm searching for. You know what is meant by impressionism?"

"Of course!"

"Very well then, this is what I mean: you remember the church at Marcouville l'Orgueilleuse which Elstir disliked because it was new? Isn't it rather a denial of his own impressionism when he abstracts such buildings from the global impression in which they're included, brings them out of the light in which they're somehow dissolved and scrutinises their intrinsic merit like an archaeologist? When he paints, haven't a hospital, a school, a poster on a hoarding the same value as a matchless cathedral which stands by their side in a single indivisible image? Remember how the façade was baked by the sun, how that carved frieze of saints floated on the sea of light. What does it matter that a building is new, if it appears old, or even if it doesn't? All the poetry that the old quarters contain has been squeezed out to the last drop, but if you look at some of the houses that have been built lately for well-to-do tradesmen in the new districts, where the stone is all freshly cut and still too white, don't they seem to rend the torrid mid-day air of July, at the hour when the shopkeepers go home to lunch in the suburbs, with a cry as sharp and acidulous as the smell of the cherries waiting for the meal to begin in the darkened dining-room, where the prismatic glass knife-rests throw off a multicoloured light as beautiful as the windows of Chartres?"

"How wonderful you are! If I ever do become clever, it will be entirely owing to you."

"Why, on a fine day, tear your eyes away from the Trocadéro, whose giraffe-neck towers remind one of the Charterhouse of Pavia?"

"It reminded me also, standing up like that on its knoll, of a Mantegna that you have, I think it's of St Sebastian, where in the background there's a terraced city where you'd swear you'd find the Trocadéro."

"There, you see! But how did you come across the Mantegna reproduction? You're absolutely staggering."

We had now reached a more plebeian neighbourhood, and the installation of an ancillary Venus behind each counter made it as it were a suburban altar at the foot of which I would gladly have spent the rest of my life.

As one does on the eve of a premature death, I drew up a

mental list of the pleasures of which I was deprived by the fact that Albertine had put a full stop to my freedom. At Passy it was in the middle of the street itself, so crowded were the footways, that a pair of girls, their arms encircling one another's waists, enthralled me with their smiles. I had not time to distinguish them clearly, but it is unlikely that I was over-rating their charms; in any crowd, after all, in any crowd of young people, it is not unusual to come upon the effigy of a noble profile. So that these assembled masses on public holidays are as precious to the voluptuary as is to the archaeologist the disordered jumble of a site whose excavation will bring ancient medals to light. We arrived at the Bois. I reflected that, if Albertine had not come out with me, I might at this moment, in the enclosure of the Champs-Elysées, have been hearing the Wagnerian storm set all the rigging of the orchestra ascream, draw into its frenzy, like a light spindrift, the tune of the shepherd's pipe which I had just been playing to myself, set it flying, mould it, distort it, divide it, sweep it away in an ever-increasing whirlwind. I was determined, at any rate, that our drive should be short and that we should return home early, for, without having mentioned it to Albertine, I had decided to go that evening to the Verdurins'. They had recently sent me an invitation which I had flung into the waste paper basket with all the rest. But I had changed my mind as far as this evening was concerned, for I meant to try to find out who Albertine might have been hoping to meet there in the afternoon. To tell the truth, I had reached that stage in my relations with Albertine when, if everything remains the same, if things go on normally, a woman no longer serves any purpose for one except as a transitional stage before another woman. She still retains a corner in one's heart, but a very small corner; one is impatient to go out every evening in search of unknown women, especially unknown women who are known to her and can tell one about her life. Herself, after all, we have possessed, and exhausted everything that she has consented to yield to us of herself. Her life is still herself, but precisely that part of her which we do not know, the things about which we have questioned her in vain and which we shall be able to gather from fresh lips.

If my life with Albertine was to prevent me from going to Venice, from travelling, at least I might this afternoon, had I been alone, have been making the acquaintance of the young midinettes scattered about in the sunlight of this fine Sunday, in the sum total of whose beauty I gave a considerable place to the unknown life that animated them. Are they not, those eyes one sees, shot through with a look behind which we do not know what images, memories, expectations, disdains lie concealed, and from which we cannot separate them? Will not that life, which is that of the woman passing by, impart a different value, according to what it is, to the frown on that forehead, the dilating of those nostrils? Albertine's presence debarred me from approaching them, and perhaps thus ceasing to desire them. The man who would maintain in himself the desire to go on living and a belief in something more delicious than the things of daily life, must go out driving; for the streets, the avenues, are full of goddesses. But the goddesses do not allow us to approach them. Here and there, among the trees, at the entrance to some café, a waitress was watching like a nymph on the edge of a sacred grove, while beyond her three girls were seated by the sweeping arc of their bicycles that were stacked beside them, like three immortals leaning against the clouds or the fabulous coursers upon which they perform their mythological journeys. I noticed that, whenever Albertine looked for a moment at these girls with deep attentiveness, she at once turned round towards me. But I was not unduly troubled, either by the intensity of this contemplation, or by its brevity which was compensated by that intensity; indeed, as to the latter, it often happened that Albertine, whether from exhaustion, or because it was an attentive person's way of looking at other people, would gaze thus in a sort of brown study either at my father or at Françoise; and as for the rapidity with which she turned to look at me, it might be due to the fact that Albertine, knowing my suspicions, might wish, even if they were unjustified, to avoid laying herself open to them. This attention, moreover, which would have seemed to me criminal on Albertine's part (and quite as much so if it had been directed at young men), I myself fastened upon all the midinettes without thinking it reprehensible for a moment, almost deciding indeed that it was reprehensible of Albertine to prevent me, by her presence, from stopping the car and going to join them. We consider it innocent to desire, and heinous that the other person should do so. And this contrast between what concerns oneself on the one hand, and on the other the person one loves, is not confined only to desire, but extends also to lying. What is more usual than a lie, whether it is a question of masking the daily weaknesses of a constitution which we wish to be thought strong, of concealing a vice, or of going off, without offending other people, to the thing that we prefer? It is the most necessary means of self-preservation, and the one that is most widely used. Yet this is the thing that we actually propose to banish from the life of the person we love; we watch for it, scent it, detest it everywhere. It distresses us, it is sufficient to bring about a rupture, it seems to us to conceal the gravest misdemeanours, except when it conceals them so effectively that we do not suspect their existence. A strange state, this, in which we are so inordinately sensitive to a pathogenic agent whose universal proliferation makes it inoffensive to other people and so baneful to the wretch who finds that he is no longer immune to it!

The life of these pretty girls (since, because of my long periods of reclusion, I so rarely met any) appeared to me, as to everyone in whom ease of fulfilment has not deadened the power of imagining, a thing as different from anything that I knew, and as desirable, as the most marvellous cities that travel holds in store for us.

The disappointment I had felt with the women I had known, or in the cities I had visited, did not prevent me from falling for the attraction of others or from believing in their reality. Hence, just as seeing Venice—Venice, for which this spring weather filled me also with longing, and which marriage with Albertine would prevent me from knowing—seeing Venice in a diorama which Ski would perhaps have declared to be more beautiful in tone than the place itself, would to me have been no substitute for the journey to Venice the length of which, determined without my having any hand in it, seemed to me an indispensable preliminary, so in the same way, however pretty she might be, the midinette whom a procuress had

artificially provided for me could not possibly be a substitute
for the gangling girl who was slouching at this moment under
the trees, laughing with a friend. Even if the girl I found in the
house of assignation were prettier than this one, it could not be
the same thing, because we do not look at the eyes of a girl we
do not know as we would look at little chunks of opal or
agate. We know that the little ray that colours them or the
diamond dust that makes them sparkle is all that we can see of
a mind, a will, a memory in which is contained the family
home that we do not know, the intimate friends whom we
envy. The enterprise of gaining possession of all this, of
something so difficult, so recalcitrant, is what gives its attraction
to that gaze far more than its merely physical beauty (which
may serve to explain why the same young man can awaken
a whole romance in the imagination of a woman who has
heard somebody say that he is the Prince of Wales but pays
no further attention to him after learning that she is mistaken).
To find the midinette in the house of assignation is to find
her emptied of that unknown life which permeates her and
which we aspire to possess with her; it is to approach a pair
of eyes that have indeed become mere precious stones, a
nose whose wrinkling is as devoid of meaning as that of a
flower. No, what my life with Albertine was depriving me of
was precisely that unknown midinette who was passing at that
moment, and it seemed to me as essential, if I wished to continue to believe in her reality, to face up to her resistance by
adapting my methods of approach, challenging a rebuff,
returning to the charge, obtaining an assignation, waiting for
her outside her place of work, getting to know, episode by
episode, everything that constituted the girl's life, experiencing
whatever was represented for her by the pleasure I was
seeking, and traversing the distance which her different
habits, her special mode of life, set between me and the attention, the favour which I wished to obtain from her—all this
seemed to me as essential as making a long journey by train if I
wished to believe in the reality of Pisa and would see it not
simply as a panoramic show in a World Fair. But these
very similarities between desire and travel made me vow to
myself that one day I would grasp a little more closely the

nature of this force, invisible but as powerful as any belief or, in the world of physics, as atmospheric pressure, which exalted cities and women to such a height so long as I did not know them, and, slipping away from beneath them as soon as I had approached them, made them at once collapse and fall flat on to the dead level of the most commonplace reality.

Further on, another little girl was kneeling beside her bicycle, which she was putting to rights. The repair finished, the young racer mounted her machine, but without straddling it as a man would have done. For a moment the bicycle swerved, and the young body seemed to have added to itself a sail, a huge wing; and presently we saw the young creature speed away, half-human, half-winged, angel or peri, pursuing her course.

This was what the presence of Albertine, this was what my life with Albertine, deprived me of. Deprived me, did I say? Should I not have thought rather: what it presented to me? If Albertine had not been living with me, if she had been free, I should have imagined, and with reason, every one of these women as a possible or indeed a probable object of her desire, of her pleasure. They would have appeared to me like dancers in a diabolical ballet, representing the Temptations to one person, and shooting their darts into the heart of another. Midinettes, schoolgirls, actresses, how I should have hated them all! Objects of horror, for me they would have been excluded from the beauty of the universe. Albertine's servitude, by releasing me from suffering on their account, restored them to the beauty of the world. Now that they were harmless, having lost the sting that stabs the heart with jealousy, I was free to admire them, to caress them with my eyes, another day more intimately perhaps. By shutting Albertine away, I had at the same time restored to the universe all those glittering wings that flutter in public gardens, ballrooms, theatres, and which became tempting once more to me because she could no longer succumb to their temptation. They composed the beauty of the world. They had at one time composed that of Albertine. It was because I had seen her first as a mysterious bird, then as a great actress of the beach, desired, perhaps won, that I had thought her wonderful. As soon as she was a captive in my house, the bird that I had seen one afternoon advancing with measured tread along the front, surrounded by a congregation of other girls like seagulls alighted from who knew where, Albertine had lost all her colours, together with all the opportunities that other people had of securing her for themselves. Gradually she had lost her beauty. It required excursions like this, in which I imagined her, but for my presence, accosted by some woman or by some young man, to make me see her again amid the splendour of the beach, although my jealousy was on a different plane from the decline of the pleasures of my imagination. But in spite of these abrupt reversions in which, desired by other people, she once more became beautiful in my eyes, I might very well have divided her stay with me into two periods, in the first of which she was still, although less so every day, the glittering actress of the beach, and in the second of which, become the grey captive, reduced to her drab self, she needed these flashes in which I remembered the past to restore her colour to her.

Sometimes, in the hours in which I felt most indifferent towards her, there came back to me the memory of a far-off moment on the beach, before I yet knew her, when, not far from a lady with whom I was on bad terms and with whom I was almost certain now that she had had relations, she burst out laughing, staring me in the face in an insolent fashion. All round her hissed the blue and polished sea. In the sunshine of the beach, Albertine, in the midst of her friends, was the most beautiful of them all. It was this magnificent girl, who, in her familiar setting of boundless waters—she, a precious object in the eyes of the admiring lady—had inflicted this insult on me. It was definitive, for the lady had returned perhaps to Balbec, had registered perhaps, on the luminous and echoing beach, the absence of Albertine; but she was unaware that the girl was living with me, was wholly mine. The vast expanse of blue water, her obliviousness of the predilection she had had for this particular girl and had now diverted to others, had closed over the insult that Albertine had offered me, enshrining it in a glittering and unbreakable casket. Then hatred of that woman gnawed my heart; of Albertine too, but a hatred mingled with admiration of the beautiful, adulated girl, with her marvellous hair, whose laughter upon the beach

had been an affront. Shame, jealousy, the memory of my first
desires and of the brilliant setting, had restored to Albertine
her former beauty and worth. And thus there alternated with
the somewhat oppressive boredom that I felt in her company
a throbbing desire, full of resplendent images and of regrets,
according to whether she was by my side in my room or I
set her free again in my memory, on the sea-front, in her gay
beach clothes, to the sound of the musical instruments of the
sea,—Albertine, now abstracted from that environment,
possessed and of no great value, now plunged back into it,
escaping from me into a past which I should never get to
know, humiliating me before the lady who was her friend as
much as the splashing of the waves or the dizzying heat of the
sun,—Albertine restored to the beach or brought back again
to my room, in a sort of amphibious love.

Elsewhere, a numerous band were playing ball. All these
girls had come out to make the most of the sunshine, for these
February days, even when they are as dazzling as this one,
do not last long, and the splendour of their light does not
postpone the hour of its decline. Before that hour drew near,
we had a spell of chiaroscuro, because after we had driven
as far as the Seine, where Albertine admired, and by her presence
prevented me from admiring, the reflexions of red sails upon
the wintry blue of the water, and a tiled house nestling in the
distance like a single red poppy against the clear horizon of
which Saint-Cloud seemed, further off still, to be the fragmentary, friable, ribbed petrifaction, we left our motor-car and
walked a long way together. For some moments I even gave
her my arm, and it seemed to me that the ring which her arm
formed round mine united our two persons in a single self
and linked our separate destinies together.

Our shadows, now parallel, now close together and linked,
traced an exquisite pattern at our feet. It seemed to me already
wonderful enough, at home, that Albertine should be living
with me, that it should be she who came and lay down on my
bed. But it was as it were the transportation of that marvel
to the outside world, into the heart of nature, that by the shore
of that lake in the Bois which I loved so much, beneath the
trees, it should be her shadow and none other, the pure and

simplified shadow of her leg, of her bust, that the sun delineated in monochrome by the side of mine upon the gravel of the
path. And the fusion of our shadows had a charm for me that
was doubtless more insubstantial, but no less intimate, than the
contiguity, the fusion of our bodies. Then we returned to the
car. And it chose, for our homeward journey, a succession of
little winding lanes along which the wintry trees, clothed, like
ruins, in ivy and brambles, seemed to be pointing the way to the
dwelling of some magician. No sooner had we emerged from
their shady cover than we found, leaving the Bois, the daylight
still so bright that I thought I should still have time to do
everything I wanted to do before dinner, when, only a few
moments later, as the car approached the Arc de Triomphe, it
was with a sudden start of surprise and dismay that I perceived,
over Paris, the moon prematurely full, like the face of a clock
that has stopped and makes us think that we are late for an
engagement. We had told the driver to take us home. For
Albertine, this also meant returning to my home. The presence
of women, however dear to us, who are obliged to leave us to
return home does not bestow that peace which I found in the
presence of Albertine seated in the car by my side, a presence
that was conveying us not to the emptiness of the hours when
lovers are apart, but to an even more stable and more sheltered
reunion in my home, which was also hers, the material symbol
of my possession of her. True, in order to possess, one must
first have desired. We do not possess a line, a surface, a mass
unless it is occupied by our love. But Albertine had not been
for me during our drive, as Rachel had once been, a meaningless dust of flesh and clothing. At Balbec, the imagination of my
eyes, my lips, my hands had so solidly constructed, so tenderly
polished her body that now, in this car, in order to touch that
body, to contain it, I had no need to press my own body against
Albertine, nor even to see her; it was enough for me to hear
her, and, if she was silent, to know that she was by my side;
my interwoven senses enveloped her completely and when,
on our arrival at the house, she quite naturally alighted, I
stopped for a moment to tell the chauffeur to call for me later,
but my eyes enveloped her still as she passed ahead of me under
the arch, and it was still the same inert, domestic calm that I

felt as I saw her thus, solid, flushed, opulent and captive, returning home quite naturally with me, like a woman who belonged to me, and, protected by its walls, disappearing into our house. Unfortunately she seemed to feel herself in prison there, and—judging by her mournful, weary look that evening as we dined together in her room—to share the opinion of that Mme de La Rochefoucauld who, when asked whether she was not glad to live in so beautiful a home as Liancourt, replied: "There is no such thing as a beautiful prison." I did not notice it at first; and it was I who bemoaned the thought that, had it not been for Albertine (for with her I should have suffered too acutely from jealousy in an hotel where all day long she would have been exposed to contact with so many people), I might at that moment be dining in Venice in one of those little low-ceilinged restaurants like a ship's saloon, from which one looks out on the Grand Canal through little curved windows encircled with Moorish mouldings.

I ought to add that Albertine greatly admired a big bronze I had by Barbedienne which with ample justification Bloch considered extremely ugly. He had perhaps less reason to be surprised at my having kept it. I had never sought, like him, to furnish for aesthetic effect, to arrange rooms artistically. I was too lazy for that, too indifferent to the things that I was in the habit of seeing every day. Since my taste was not involved, I had a right not to modulate my interiors. I might perhaps, in spite of this, have discarded the bronze. But ugly and expensive things are extremely useful, for they possess, in the eyes of people who do not understand us, who do not share our taste and with whom we may be in love, a glamour which a fine object that does not reveal its beauty may lack. Now the people who do not understand us are precisely the people with regard to whom it may be useful to us to take advantage of a prestige which our intellect is enough to ensure for us among superior people. Although Albertine was beginning to show some taste, she still had a certain respect for the bronze, and this was reflected back upon me in an esteem which, coming from Albertine, mattered infinitely more to me than the question of keeping a bronze which was a trifle degrading, since I loved Albertine.

But the thought of my bondage ceased of a sudden to weigh upon me and I looked forward to prolonging it still further, because I seemed to perceive that Albertine was sorely conscious of her own. True, whenever I had asked her whether she was unhappy in my house, she had always replied that she did not know where it would be possible for her to be happier. But often these words were contradicted by an air of nostalgia and edginess.

Certainly if she had the tastes with which I had credited her, this prevention from ever satisfying them must have been as frustrating to her as it was calming to myself, calming to such an extent that I should have decided that the hypothesis of my having accused her unjustly was the most probable, had it not been so difficult to fit into this hypothesis the extraordinary pains that Albertine took never to be alone, never to be free to go out with anyone, never to stop for a moment outside the front door when she came in, always to insist on being ostentatiously accompanied, whenever she went to the telephone, by someone who would be able to repeat to me what she had said—by Françoise or Andrée—always to leave me alone with the latter (without appearing to be doing so on purpose) after they had been out together, so that I might obtain a detailed report of their outing. Contrasted with this marvellous docility were occasional gestures of impatience, quickly repressed, which made me wonder whether Albertine might not be planning to shake off her chains. Certain incidental circumstances seemed to corroborate my supposition. Thus, one day when I had gone out by myself, I ran into Gisèle in the neighbourhood of Passy, and we chatted about this and that. Presently, not without pride at being able to do so, I informed her that I saw Albertine constantly. Gisèle asked me where she could find her, since she *happened* to have something to tell her. "Why, what is it?" "Something to do with some young friends of hers." "What friends? I may perhaps be able to tell you, though that needn't prevent you from seeing her." "Oh, girls she knew years ago, I don't remember their names," Gisèle replied vaguely, beating a retreat. She left me, supposing herself to have spoken with such prudence that I could not conceivably have suspected anything. But falsehood is so unexacting, needs so little help to make itself manifest! If it had been a question of friends of long ago, whose very names she no longer remembered, why did she "happen" to need to speak to Albertine about them? This "happen," akin to an expression dear to Mme Cottard: "It couldn't be better timed," could be applicable only to something particular, opportune, perhaps urgent, relating to specific persons. Besides, simply the way she opened her mouth, as though about to yawn, with a vague expression, when she said to me (almost retreating bodily, as she went into reverse at this point in our conversation): "Oh, I don't know, I don't remember their names," made her face, and in harmony with it her voice, as clear a picture of falsehood as the wholly different air, keen, animated, forthcoming, of her "I happen to have" was of truth. I did not cross-examine Gisèle. Of what use would it have been to me? Of course she did not lie in the same way as Albertine. And of course Albertine's lies pained me more. But they had obviously a point in common: the fact of the lie itself, which in certain cases is self-evident. Not evidence of the reality that the lie conceals. We know that each murderer, individually, imagines that he has arranged everything so cleverly that he will not be caught, but in general, murderers are almost always caught. Liars, on the contrary, are rarely caught, and, among liars, more particularly the woman with whom we are in love. We do not know where she has been, what she has been doing. But as soon as she opens her mouth to speak, to speak of something else beneath which lies hidden the thing that she does not mention, the lie is immediately perceived, and our jealousy increased, since we are conscious of the lie, and cannot succeed in discovering the truth. With Albertine, the impression that she was lying was conveyed by a number of characteristics which we have already observed in the course of this narrative, but especially by the fact that, when she was lying, her story erred either from inadequacy, omission, implausibility, or on the contrary from a surfeit of petty details intended to make it seem plausible. Plausibility, notwithstanding the idea that the liar holds of it, is by no means the same as truth. Whenever, while listening to something that is true, we hear something that is only plausible, that is perhaps more plausible than the truth, that is perhaps too plausible, an ear that is at all musical senses that it is not correct, as with a line that does not scan or a word read aloud in mistake for another. The ear senses it, and if we are in love, the heart takes alarm. Why do we not reflect at the time, when we change the whole course of our life because we do not know whether a woman went along the Rue de Berri or the Rue Washington, why do we not reflect that these few yards of difference, and the woman herself, will be reduced to the hundred millionth part of themselves (that is to say to dimensions far beneath our perception), if we only have the wisdom to remain for a few years without seeing the woman, and that she who has out-Gullivered Gulliver in our eyes will shrink to a Lilliputian whom no microscope—of the heart, at least, for that of the disinterested memory is more powerful and less fragile—can ever again discern! However that may be, if there was a point in common—mendacity itself—between Albertine's lies and Gisèle's, still Gisèle did not lie in the same way as Albertine, nor indeed in the same way as Andrée, but their respective lies dovetailed so neatly into one another, while presenting a great variety, that the little band had the impenetrable solidity of certain commercial houses, booksellers for example or newspaper publishers, where the wretched author will never succeed, notwithstanding the diversity of the persons employed in them, in discovering whether or not he is being swindled. The director of the newspaper or review lies with an attitude of sincerity all the more solemn in that he is frequently obliged to conceal the fact that he himself does exactly the same things and indulges in the same commercial practices as he denounced in other newspaper or theatre directors, in other publishers, when he chose as his banner, when he raised against them the standard of Honesty. The fact of a man's having proclaimed (as leader of a political party, or in any other capacity) that it is wicked to lie obliges him as a rule to lie more than other people, without on that account abandoning the solemn mask, doffing the august tiara of sincerity. The "honest" gentleman's partner lies in a different and more ingenuous fashion. He deceives his author as he deceives his wife, with tricks from the vaudeville stage. The sub-editor, a crude, straightforward man, lies quite simply, like an architect who promises that your house will be ready at a date when it will not have been begun. The editor, an angelic soul, flutters from one to another of the three, and without knowing what the matter is, gives them, out of brotherly scruple and affectionate solidarity, the precious support of an unimpeachable word. These four persons live in a state of perpetual dissension to which the arrival of the author puts a stop. Over and above their private quarrels, each of them remembers the paramount military duty of rallying to the support of the threatened "corps." Without realising it, I had long been playing the part of this author in relation to the little band. If Gisèle had been thinking, when she used the word "happen," of one of Albertine's friends who was prepared to go away with her as soon as my mistress should have found some pretext or other for leaving me, and had meant to warn Albertine that the hour had now come or would shortly strike, she, Gisèle, would have let herself be torn to pieces rather than tell me so; it was quite useless therefore to ply her with questions.

Meetings such as this one with Gisèle were not alone in reinforcing my doubts. For instance, I admired Albertine's paintings. The touching pastimes of a captive, they moved me so that I congratulated her upon them. "No, they're dreadfully bad, but I've never had a drawing lesson in my life." "But one evening at Balbec you sent word to me that you had stayed at home to have a drawing lesson." I reminded her of the day and told her that I had realised at the time that people did not have drawing lessons at that hour in the evening. Albertine blushed. "It's true," she said, "I wasn't having drawing lessons. I told you a great many lies at the beginning, that I admit. But I never lie to you now." How I should have loved to know what were the many lies that she had told me at the beginning! But I knew beforehand that her answers would be fresh lies. And so I contented myself with kissing her. I asked her to tell me one only of those lies. She replied: "Oh, well; for instance when I said that the sea air was bad for me." I ceased to insist in the face of this unwillingness to oblige.

To make her chains appear lighter, the clever thing seemed to me to be to make her believe that I myself was about to break them. But I could not confide this mendacious plan to her at that moment, since she had returned so sweetly from the Trocadéro that afternoon; the most I could do, far from distressing her with the threat of a rupture, was to keep to myself those dreams of a perpetual life together which my grateful heart had formed. As I looked at her, I found it hard to restrain myself from pouring them out to her, and she may perhaps have noticed this. Unfortunately the expression of such feelings is not contagious. The case of an affected old woman like M. de Charlus who, by dint of never seeing in his imagination anything but a proud young man, thinks that he has himself become a proud young man, all the more so the more affected and ridiculous he becomes—this case is more general, and it is the misfortune of an impassioned lover not to realise that while he sees in front of him a beautiful face, his mistress is seeing his face, which is not made any more beautiful, far from it, when it is distorted by the pleasure that is aroused in it by the sight of beauty. Nor indeed does love exhaust the generality of this case; we do not see our own bodies, which other people see, and we "follow" our own train of thought, the object, invisible to other people, which is before our eyes. At times the artist reveals this object in his work. Whence it arises that the admirers of that work are disappointed in its author, on whose face that inner beauty is imperfectly reflected.

Every person we love, indeed to a certain extent every person, is to us like Janus, presenting to us a face that pleases us if the person leaves us, a dreary face if we know him or her to be at our perpetual disposal. In the case of Albertine, the prospect of her continued society was painful to me in another way which I cannot explain in this narrative. It is terrible to have the life of another person attached to one's own like a bomb which one holds in one's hands, unable to get rid of it without committing a crime. But one has only to compare this with the ups and downs, the dangers, the anxieties, the fear that false but probable things will come to be believed when we will no longer be able to explain them—

feelings that one experiences if one lives on intimate terms with a madman. For instance, I pitied M. de Charlus for living with Morel (immediately the memory of the scene that afternoon made me feel that the left side of my chest was heavier than the other); leaving aside the relations that may or may not have existed between them, M. de Charlus must have been unaware at the outset that Morel was mad. Morel's beauty, his stupidity, his pride must have deterred the Baron from exploring so deeply, until the days of melancholia when Morel accused M. de Charlus of responsibility for his sorrows, without being able to furnish any explanation, abused him for his want of trust with the help of false but extremely subtle arguments, threatened him with desperate resolutions in the midst of which there persisted the most cunning regard for his own most immediate interests. But all this is only a comparison. Albertine was not mad.

I learned that a death had occurred that day which distressed me greatly—that of Bergotte. It was known that he had been ill for a long time past. Not, of course, with the illness from which he had suffered originally and which was natural. Nature scarcely seems capable of giving us any but quite short illnesses. But medicine has developed the art of prolonging them. Remedies, the respite that they procure, the relapses that a temporary cessation of them provokes, produce a simulacrum of illness to which the patient grows so accustomed that he ends by making it permanent, just as children have regular fits of coughing long after they have been cured of the whooping cough. Then the remedies begin to have less effect, the doses are increased, they cease to do any good, but they have begun to do harm thanks to this lasting indisposition. Nature would not have offered them so long a tenure. It is a great wonder that medicine can almost rival nature in forcing a man to remain in bed, to continue taking some drug on pain of death. From then on, the artificially grafted illness has taken root, has become a secondary but a genuine illness, with this difference only, that natural illnesses are cured, but never those which medicine creates, for it does not know the secret of their cure.

For years past Bergotte had ceased to go out of doors. In any case he had never cared for society, or had cared for it for a day only, to despise it as he despised everything else, and in the same fashion, which was his own, namely to despise a thing not because it was beyond his reach but as soon as he had attained it. He lived so simply that nobody suspected how rich he was, and anyone who had known would still have been mistaken, having thought him a miser whereas no one was ever more generous. He was generous above all towards women—girls, one ought rather to say—who were ashamed to receive so much in return for so little. He excused himself in his own eyes because he knew that he could never produce such good work as in an atmosphere of amorous feelings. Love is too strong a word, but pleasure that is at all deeply rooted in the flesh is helpful to literary work because it cancels all other pleasures, for instance the pleasures of society, those which are the same for everyone. And even if this love leads to disillusionment, it does at least stir, even by so doing, the surface of the soul which otherwise would be in danger of becoming stagnant. Desire is therefore not without its value to the writer in detaching him first of all from his fellow men and from conforming to their standards, and afterwards in restoring some degree of movement to a spiritual machine which, after a certain age, tends to come to a standstill. We do not achieve happiness but we gain some insights into the reasons which prevent us from being happy and which would have remained invisible to us but for these sudden revelations of disappointment. Dreams, we know, are not realisable; we might not form any, perhaps, were it not for desire, and it is useful to us to form them in order to see them fail and to learn from their failure. And so Bergotte said to himself: "I spend more than a multimillionaire on girls, but the pleasures or disappointments that they give me make me write a book which brings me in money." Economically, this argument was absurd, but no doubt he found some charm in thus transmuting gold into caresses and caresses into gold. We saw, at the time of my grandmother's death, how a weary

old age loves repose. Now in society there is nothing but
conversation. Vapid though it is, it has the capacity to eliminate
women, who become nothing more than questions and
answers. Removed from society, women become once more
what is so reposeful to a weary old man, an object of contemplation. In any case, now there was no longer any question
of all this. I have said that Bergotte never went out of doors,
and when he got out of bed for an hour in his room, he would
be smothered in shawls, rugs, all the things with which a
person covers himself before exposing himself to intense cold
or going on a railway journey. He would apologise for them
to the few friends whom he allowed to penetrate to his sanctuary; pointing to his tartan plaids, his travelling-rugs, he
would say merrily: "After all, my dear fellow, life, as Anaxa-
goras has said, is a journey." Thus he went on growing
steadily colder, a tiny planet offering a prophetic image of the
greater, when gradually heat will withdraw from the earth,
then life itself. Then the resurrection will have come to an end,
for, however far forward into future generations the works
of men may shine, there must none the less be men. If certain
species hold out longer against the invading cold, when there
are no longer any men, and if we suppose Bergotte's fame to
have lasted until then, suddenly it will be extinguished for all
time. It will not be the last animals that will read him, for it is
scarcely probably that, like the Apostles at Pentecost, they will
be able to understand the speech of the various races of mankind without having learned it.

In the months that preceded his death, Bergotte suffered
from insomnia, and what was worse, whenever he did fall
asleep, from nightmares which, if he awoke, made him reluctant to go to sleep again. He had long been a lover of
dreams, even bad dreams, because thanks to them, thanks to
the contradiction they present to the reality which we have
before us in our waking state, they give us, at the moment of
waking if not before, the profound sensation of having slept.
But Bergotte's nightmares were not like that. When he spoke
of nightmares, he used in the past to mean unpleasant things
that happened in his brain. Latterly, it was as though from
somewhere outside himself that he would see a hand armed

with a damp cloth which, rubbed over his face by an evil woman, kept trying to wake him; or an intolerable itching in his thighs; or the rage—because Bergotte had murmured in his sleep that he was driving badly—of a raving lunatic of a cabman who flung himself upon the writer, biting and gnawing his fingers. Finally, as soon as it had grown sufficiently dark in his sleep, nature would arrange a sort of undress rehearsal of the apoplectic stroke that was to carry him off. Bergotte would arrive in a carriage beneath the porch of Swann's new house, and would try to get out. A shattering attack of dizziness would pin him to his seat; the concierge would try to help him out; he would remain seated, unable to lift himself up or straighten his legs. He would cling to the stone pillar in front of him, but could not find sufficient support to enable him to stand.

He consulted doctors who, flattered to be summoned by him, saw in his virtues as an incessant worker (he had done nothing for twenty years), in overwork, the cause of his ailments. They advised him not to read frightening stories (he never read anything), to take more advantage of the sunshine, which was "indispensable to life" (he had owed a few years of comparative health only to his rigorous confinement at home), to take more nourishment (which made him thinner, and nourished nothing but his nightmares). One of his doctors was blessed with an argumentative and contrary spirit, and whenever Bergotte saw him in the absence of the others and, in order not to offend him, suggested to him as his own ideas what the others had advised, this doctor, thinking that Bergotte was trying to get him to prescribe something that he liked, would at once forbid it, often for reasons invented so hurriedly to meet the case that, in face of the material objections which Bergotte raised, the doctor, contradicting him, was obliged in the same sentence to contradict himself, but, for fresh reasons, repeated the original prohibition. Bergotte would return to one of the previous doctors, a man who prided himself on his wit, especially in the presence of one of the masters of the pen, and who, if Bergotte insinuated: "I seem to remember, though, that Dr X—— told me—long ago, of course—that that might affect my kidneys and my brain . . ."

would smile mischievously, raise his finger and enounce: "I said use, I did not say abuse. Naturally every drug, if one takes it in excess, becomes a double-edged weapon." There is in the human body a certain instinct for what is beneficial to us, as there is in the heart for what is our moral duty, an instinct which no authorisation by a doctor of medicine or divinity can replace. We know that cold baths are bad for us, but we like them: we can always find a doctor to recommend them, not to prevent them from doing us harm. From each of these doctors Bergotte took something which, in his own wisdom, he had forbidden himself for years past. After a few weeks, his old troubles had reappeared and the new ones had become worse. Maddened by uninterrupted pain, to which was added insomnia broken only by brief spells of nightmare, Bergotte called in no more doctors and tried with success, but to excess, different narcotics, trustingly reading the prospectus that accompanied each of them, a prospectus which proclaimed the necessity of sleep but hinted that all the preparations which induce it (except the one contained in the bottle round which the prospectus was wrapped, which never produced any toxic effect) were toxic, and therefore made the remedy worse than the disease. Bergotte tried them all. Some of these drugs may be of a different family from those to which one is accustomed, by-products, for instance, of amyl and ethyl. When one absorbs a new drug, entirely different in composition, it is always with a delicious expectancy of the unknown. One's heart beats as at a first assignation. To what unknown forms of sleep, of dreams, is the newcomer going to lead one? It is inside one now, it is in control of one's thoughts. In what way is one going to fall asleep? And, once asleep, by what strange paths, up to what peaks, into what unfathomed gulfs will this all-powerful master lead one? What new group of sensations will one meet with on this journey? Will it lead to illness? To blissful happiness? To death? Bergotte's death came to him the day after he had thus entrusted himself to one of these friends (a friend? or an enemy, rather?) who proved too strong for him. The circumstances of his death were as follows. A fairly mild attack of uraemia had led to his being ordered to rest. But, an art critic having written somewhere that in

Vermeer's *View of Delft* (lent by the Gallery at The Hague for an exhibition of Dutch painting), a picture which he adored and imagined that he knew by heart, a little patch of yellow wall (which he could not remember) was so well painted that it was, if one looked at it by itself, like some priceless specimen of Chinese art, of a beauty that was sufficient in itself, Bergotte ate a few potatoes, left the house, and went to the exhibition. At the first few steps he had to climb, he was overcome by an attack of dizziness. He walked past several pictures and was struck by the aridity and pointlessness of such an artificial kind of art, which was greatly inferior to the sunshine of a windswept Venetian palazzo, or of an ordinary house by the sea. At last he came to the Vermeer which he remembered as more striking, more different from anything else he knew, but in which, thanks to the critic's article, he noticed for the first time some small figures in blue, that the sand was pink, and, finally, the precious substance of the tiny patch of yellow wall. His dizziness increased; he fixed his gaze, like a child upon a yellow butterfly that it wants to catch, on the precious little patch of wall. "That's how I ought to have written," he said. "My last books are too dry, I ought to have gone over them with a few layers of colour, made my language precious in itself, like this little patch of yellow wall." Meanwhile he was not unconscious of the gravity of his condition. In a celestial pair of scales there appeared to him, weighing down one of the pans, his own life, while the other contained the little patch of wall so beautifully painted in yellow. He felt that he had rashly sacrificed the former for the latter. "All the same," he said to himself, "I shouldn't like to be the headline news of this exhibition for the evening papers."

He repeated to himself: "Little patch of yellow wall, with a sloping roof, little patch of yellow wall." Meanwhile he sank down on to a circular settee; whereupon he suddenly ceased to think that his life was in jeopardy and, reverting to his natural optimism, told himself: "It's nothing, merely a touch of indigestion from those potatoes, which were under-cooked." A fresh attack struck him down; he rolled from the settee to the floor, as visitors and attendants came hurrying to his assistance. He was dead. Dead forever? Who can say? Certainly, experiments in spiritualism offer us no more proof than the dogmas of religion that the soul survives death. All that we can say is that everything is arranged in this life as though we entered it carrying a burden of obligations contracted in a former life; there is no reason inherent in the conditions of life on this earth that can make us consider ourselves obliged to do good, to be kind and thoughtful, even to be polite, nor for an atheist artist to consider himself obliged to begin over again a score of times a piece of work the admiration aroused by which will matter little to his worm-eaten body, like the patch of yellow wall painted with so much skill and refinement by an artist destined to be forever unknown and barely identified under the name Vermeer. All these obligations, which have no sanction in our present life, seem to belong to a different world, a world based on kindness, scrupulousness, self-sacrifice, a world entirely different from this one and which we leave in order to be born on this earth, before perhaps returning there to live once again beneath the sway of those unknown laws which we obeyed because we bore their precepts in our hearts, not knowing whose hand had traced them there—those laws to which every profound work of the intellect brings us nearer and which are invisible only—if then!—to fools. So that the idea that Bergotte was not dead forever is by no means improbable.

They buried him, but all through that night of mourning, in the lighted shop-windows, his books, arranged three by three, kept vigil like angels with outspread wings and seemed, for him who was no more, the symbol of his resurrection.

I learned, as I have said, that Bergotte had died that day. And I was amazed at the inaccuracy of the newspapers which— each of them reproducing the same paragraph—stated that he had died the day before. For Albertine had met him the day before, as she informed me that very evening, and indeed she had been a little late in coming home, for he had chatted to her for some time. She was probably the last person to whom he had spoken. She knew him through me, for although I had long ceased to see him, as she had been anxious to be introduced to him I had written a year earlier to ask the old master whether I might bring her to see him. He had granted my request, though he was a trifle hurt, I fancy, that I should be visiting him only to give pleasure to another person, which was a confirmation of my indifference to him. These cases are frequent: sometimes the man or woman whom we approach not for the pleasure of conversing with them again, but on behalf of a third person, refuses so obstinately that our protégé concludes that we have boasted of an influence which we do not possess; more often the man of genius or the famous beauty consent, but, humiliated in their glory, wounded in their affection, they feel for us afterwards only a diminished, sorrowful, slightly contemptuous regard. It was not until long afterwards that I discovered that I had wrongly accused the newspapers of inaccuracy, since on the day in question Albertine had not in fact met Bergotte. At the time I had never suspected this for a single instant, so artlessly had she described the meeting to me, and it was not until much later that I discovered her charming skill in lying naturally. What she said, what she admitted, had to such a degree the same characteristics as the formal evidence of the case—what we see with our own eyes or learn from irrefutable sources—that she sowed thus in the gaps of her life episodes of another life the falsity of which I did not then suspect and began to perceive only at a much later date. I have used the word "admitted" for the following reason. Sometimes odd coincidences would give me jealous suspicions about her in which another person figured by her side in the past, or alas in the future. In order to appear certain of my facts, I would mention the person's name, and Albertine would say: "Yes, I met her a week ago, just outside the house. I acknowledged her greeting out of politeness. I walked a little way with her. But there's never been anything between us. There never will be." Now Albertine had not even met this person, for the simple reason that the person had not been in Paris for the last ten months. But my mistress felt that a complete denial would not sound very probable. Whence this imaginary brief encounter, related so simply that I could see the lady stop, greet her, and walk a little way with her. The evidence of my senses, if I had been in the street at that moment, would perhaps have informed me that the lady had not been with Albertine. But if I had known this to be the case, it was by one of those chains of reasoning in which the words of people in whom we have confidence insert strong links, and not by the evidence of my senses. To invoke this evidence by the senses I should have had to be in the street at that particular moment, and I had not been. One can imagine, however, that such a hypothesis is not improbable: I might have gone out, and have been passing along the street at the time at which Albertine was to tell me in the evening (not having seen me there) that she had walked a few steps with the lady, and I should then have known that Albertine was lying. But is this absolutely certain even then? A strange darkness would have clouded my mind, I should have begun to doubt whether I had seen her alone, I should hardly even have sought to understand by what optical illusion I had failed to perceive the lady, and I should not have been greatly surprised to find myself mistaken, for the stellar universe is not so difficult of comprehension as the real actions of other people, especially of the people we love, fortified as they are against our doubts by fables devised for their protection. For how many years on end can they not allow our apathetic love to believe that they have in some foreign country a sister, a brother, a sister-in-law who have never existed!

The evidence of the senses is also an operation of the mind in which conviction creates the facts. We have often seen her sense of hearing convey to Françoise not the word that was uttered but what she thought to be its correct form, which was enough to prevent her from hearing the implicit correction in a superior pronunciation. Our butler was cast in a similar mould. M. de Charlus was in the habit of wearing at this time—for he was constantly changing—very light trousers which were recognisable a mile off. Now our butler, who thought that the word *pissotière* (the word denoting what M. de Rambuteau[8] had been so annoyed to hear the Duc de Guermantes call a Rambuteau convenience) was really *pistière*, never once in the whole of his life heard a single person say *pissotière*, albeit the word was frequently pronounced thus in his hearing. But error is more obstinate than faith and does not examine the grounds of its belief. Constantly the butler would say: "I'm sure M. le Baron de Charlus must have caught a disease to stand about as long as he does in a *pistière*. That's what comes of running after the girls at his age. You can tell what he is by his trousers. This morning, Madame sent me with a message to Neuilly. As I passed the *pistière* in the Rue de Bourgogne I saw M. le Baron de Charlus go in. When I came back from Neuilly, a good hour later, I saw his yellow trousers in the same *pistière*, in the same place, in the middle stall where he always stands so that people shan't see him." I can think of no one more beautiful, more noble or more youthful than a certain niece of Mme de Guermantes. But I once heard the commissionaire of a restaurant where I used sometimes to dine say as she went by: "Just look at that old trollop, what a fright! And she must be eighty if she's a day." As far as age went, I find it difficult to believe that he meant what he said. But the pages clustered round him, who sniggered whenever she went past the hotel on her way to visit her charming great-aunts, Mmes de Fezensac and de Balleroy, who lived not far from there, saw upon the face of the young beauty the four-score years with which, seriously or in jest, the porter had endowed the "old trollop." You would have made them shriek with laughter had you told them that she was more distinguished than one of the two cashiers of the hotel, who, devoured by eczema, ridiculously fat, seemed to them a fine-looking woman. Perhaps sexual desire alone, if it had been let loose in the wake of the alleged old trollop, and if the pages had suddenly begun to covet the young goddess, would have been capable of preventing their error from taking shape. But for reasons unknown, which were most probably of a social nature, this desire had not come into play. The point is however highly debatable. The universe is real for us all and dissimilar to each one of us. If we were not obliged, in the interests of narrative tidiness, to confine ourselves to frivolous reasons, how many more serious reasons would enable us to demonstrate the mendacious flimsiness of the opening pages of this volume in which, from my bed, I hear the world awake, now to one sort of weather, now to another! Yes, I have been forced to whittle down the facts, and to be a liar, but it is not one universe, but millions, almost as many as the number of human eyes and brains in existence, that awake every morning.

To return to Albertine, I have never known any woman more amply endowed than herself with the happy aptitude for a lie that is animated, coloured with the very hues of life, unless it be one of her friends—one of my blossoming girls also, rose-pink as Albertine, but one whose irregular profile, concave in one place, then convex again, was exactly like certain clusters of pink flowers the name of which I have forgotten, but which have long and sinuous concavities. This girl was, from the point of view of story-telling, superior to Albertine, for her narrative was never interspersed with those painful moments, those furious innuendoes, which were frequent with my mistress. The latter was however charming, as I have said, when she invented a story which left no room for doubt, for one saw then in front of one the thing—albeit imaginary—which she was describing, through the eyes, as it were, of her words. Verisimilitude alone inspired Albertine, never the desire to make me jealous. For Albertine, not perhaps from motives of self-interest, liked people to be nice to her. And if in the course of this work I have had and shall have many occasions to show how jealousy intensifies love, it is from the lover's point of view that I write. But if that lover has a little pride, and even though he would die of a separation, he will not respond to a supposed betrayal with kind words or favours, but will turn away or, without withdrawing, will force himself to assume a mask of coldness. And so it is entirely to her own disadvantage that his mistress makes him suffer so acutely. If, on the contrary, she dispels with a tactful word, with loving caresses, the suspicions that have been torturing him for all his show of indifference, no doubt the lover does not feel that despairing increase of love to which jealousy drives him, but ceasing there and then to suffer, happy, mollified, relaxed as one is after a storm when the rain has stopped and one hears only at long intervals under the tall chestnut-trees the splash of the suspended raindrops which already the reappearing sun has dyed with colour, he does not know how to express his gratitude to her who has cured him. Albertine knew that I liked to reward her for being nice to me, and this perhaps explained why she used to invent, in order to exculpate herself, confessions as natural as these stories which I never doubted and one of which was her meeting with Bergotte when he was already dead. Previously I had never known any of Albertine's lies save those, for instance, which Françoise used to report to me at Balbec and which I have omitted from these pages although they caused me so much pain: "As she didn't want to come, she said to me: 'Couldn't you say to Monsieur that you couldn't find me, that I had gone out?' " But "inferiors" who love us as Françoise loved me take pleasure in wounding us in our self-esteem.

After dinner, I told Albertine that I wanted to take advantage of the fact that I was up to go and see some of my friends, Mme de Villeparisis, Mme de Guermantes, the Cambremers, anyone, in short, whom I might find at home. I omitted to mention only the people whom I did intend to visit, the Verdurins. I asked her if she would like to come with me. She pleaded that she had no suitable clothes. "Besides, my hair is so awful. Do you really want me to go on doing it like this?" And by way of farewell she held out her hand to me in that brusque fashion, the arm outstretched, the shoulders thrust back, which she used to adopt on the beach at Balbec and had since entirely abandoned. This forgotten gesture transformed the body which it animated into that of the Albertine who as yet scarcely knew me. It restored to Albertine, ceremonious beneath an air of brusqueness, her initial novelty, her mystery, even her setting. I saw the sea behind this girl whom I had never seen shake hands with me in this way since I was at the seaside. "My aunt thinks it ages me," she added glumly. "Would that her aunt were right!" thought I. "That Albertine by looking like a child should make Mme Bontemps appear younger than she is, is all that her aunt would ask, and also that Albertine should cost her nothing between now and the day when, by marrying me, she will bring her in money." But that Albertine should appear less young, less pretty, should turn fewer heads in the street, that is what I, on the contrary, hoped. For the agedness of a duenna is less reassuring to a jealous lover than that of the face of the woman he loves. I regretted only that the style in which I had asked her to do her hair should appear to Albertine an additional bolt on the door of her prison. And it was again this new domestic feeling that never ceased, even when I was away from Albertine, to bind me to her.

I said to Albertine, who was disinclined, as she had told me, to accompany me to the Guermantes' or the Cambremers', that I was not quite sure where I might go, and set off for the Verdurins'. At the moment when, on leaving the house, the thought of the concert that I was going to hear brought back to my mind the scene that afternoon: *"grand pied de grue, grand pied de grue,"*—a scene of disappointed love, of jealous love perhaps, but if so as bestial as the scene to which (minus the words) a woman might be subjected by an orang-outang that was, if one may so say, enamoured of her—at the moment when, having reached the street, I was about to hail a cab, I heard the sound of sobs which a man who was sitting upon a curbstone was endeavouring to stifle. I came nearer; the man, whose face was buried in his hands, appeared to be quite young, and I was surprised to see, from the gleam of white in the opening of his cloak, that he was wearing evening clothes and a white tie. On hearing me he uncovered a face bathed in tears, but at once, having recognised me, turned away. It was Morel. He saw that I had recognised him and, checking his tears with an effort, told me that he had stopped for a moment because he was in such anguish.

"I have grossly insulted, this very day," he said, "a person for whom I had the strongest feelings. It was a vile thing to do, for she loves me."

"She will forget perhaps, in time," I replied, without realising that by speaking thus I made it apparent that I had over-heard the scene that afternoon. But he was so absorbed in his grief that it never even occurred to him that I might know something about the affair.

"She may forget, perhaps," he said. "But I myself can never forget. I feel such a sense of shame, I'm so disgusted with myself! However, what I have said I have said, and nothing can unsay it. When people make me lose my temper, I don't know what I'm doing. And it's so bad for me, my nerves are all tied up in knots"—for, like all neurotics, he was keenly interested in his own health. If, during the afternoon, I had witnessed the amorous rage of an infuriated animal, this evening, within a few hours, centuries had elapsed and a new sentiment, a sentiment of shame, regret, grief, showed that an important stage had been reached in the evolution of the beast destined to be transformed into a human being. Nevertheless, I still heard ringing in my ears his "*grand pied de grue*" and feared an imminent return to the savage state. I had only a very vague idea, however, of what had happened, and this was all the more natural in that M. de Charlus himself was totally unaware that for some days past, and especially that day, even before the shameful episode which had no direct connexion with the violinist's condition, Morel had been suffering from a recurrence of his neurasthenia. He had, in the previous month, proceeded as rapidly as he had been able, which was a great deal less rapidly than he would have liked, towards the seduction of Jupien's niece, with whom he was at liberty, now that they were engaged, to go out whenever he chose. But as soon as he had gone a little too far in his attempts at rape, and especially when he suggested to his betrothed that she might make friends with other girls whom she would then procure for him, he had met with a resistance that had enraged him. All at once (either because she had proved too chaste, or on the contrary had finally given herself) his desire had subsided. He had decided to break with her, but feeling that the Baron, depraved though he might be, was far more moral than himself, he was afraid lest, in the event of a rupture, M. de Charlus might throw him out. And so he had decided, a fortnight ago, that he would not see the girl again, would leave M. de Charlus and Jupien to clean up the mess (he employed a more realistic term) by themselves, and, before announcing the rupture, to "bugger off" to an unknown destination.

This outcome had left him a little sad, and it is therefore probable that although his conduct towards Jupien's niece coincided exactly, down to the minutest details, with the plan of conduct which he had outlined to the Baron as they were dining together at Saint-Mars-le-Vêtu, in reality it had been somewhat different, and that sentiments of a less heinous nature, which he had not foreseen in his theoretical conduct, had embellished and softened it in practice. The sole point in which the reality was worse than the theory was this, that in the original plan it had not appeared to him possible that he could remain in Paris after such an act of betrayal. Now, on the contrary, actually to "bugger off" for so small a matter seemed to him excessive. It meant leaving the Baron, who would probably be furious, and forfeiting his position. He would lose all the money that the Baron was now giving him. The thought that this was inevitable made him hysterical; he whimpered for hours on end, and to take his mind off the subject dosed himself cautiously with morphine. Then suddenly he hit upon an idea which no doubt had gradually been taking shape in his mind and gaining strength there for some time, and this was that a rupture with the girl would not inevitably mean a complete break with M. de Charlus. To lose all the Baron's money was a serious thing. Morel in his uncertainty remained for some days a prey to black thoughts, such as came to him at the sight of Bloch. Then he decided that Jupien and his niece had been trying to set a trap for him, that they might consider themselves lucky to be rid of him so cheaply. He found in short that the girl had been in the wrong in having been so maladroit in failing to keep him attached to her through the senses. Not only did the sacrifice of his position with M. de Charlus seem to him absurd, but he even regretted the expensive dinners he had given the girl since they had become engaged, the exact cost of which he knew by heart, being a true son of the valet who used to bring his "book" every month for my uncle's inspection. For the word book, in the singular, which means a printed volume to humanity in general, loses that meaning among royalty and servants. To the latter it means their account-book, to the former the register in which we inscribe our names. (At Balbec one day when the Princesse de Luxembourg told me that she had not brought a book with her, I was about to offer her *Le Pêcheur d'Islande* and *Tartarin de Tarascon*, when I realised that she had meant not that she would pass the time less agreeably, but that it would be more difficult for me to get on to her list.)

Notwithstanding the change in Morel's point of view with regard to the consequences of his behaviour, although that behaviour would have seemed to him abominable two months earlier when he was passionately in love with Jupien's niece, whereas during the last fortnight he had never ceased to assure himself that the same behaviour was natural and praiseworthy, it could not fail to intensify the state of nervous tension in which, finally, he had served notice of the rupture that afternoon. And he was quite prepared to vent his rage, if not (save in a momentary outburst) upon the girl, for whom he still felt that lingering fear which is the last trace of love, at any rate upon the Baron. He took care, however, not to say anything to him before dinner, for, valuing his own professional virtuosity above everything, whenever he had any difficult music to play (as this evening at the Verdurins') he avoided (as far as possible, and the scene that afternoon was already more than ample) anything that might make his movements at all jerky. Similarly, a surgeon who is an enthusiastic motorist does not drive when he has an operation to perform. This explained to me why, as he was speaking to me, he kept bending his fingers gently one after another to see whether they had regained their suppleness. A slight frown seemed to indicate that there was still a trace of nervous stiffness. But in order not to aggravate it, he relaxed his features, as we try to prevent ourselves from getting agitated about not being able to sleep or to persuade a woman to give herself, for fear lest our phobia itself may retard the moment of sleep or of pleasure. And so, anxious to regain his serenity in order to be able to concentrate, as usual, on what he was going to play at the Verdurins', and anxious, so long as I was watching him, to let me see how unhappy he was, he decided that the simplest course was to entreat me to leave him immediately. The entreaty was superfluous, for it was a relief to me to get away from him. I had trembled lest, as we were due at the same house within a few minutes of one another, he might ask me to take him with me, my memory of the scene that afternoon being too vivid not to give me a certain distaste for the idea of having Morel by my side during the drive. It is quite possible that the love, and afterwards the indifference or hatred, felt by Morel for Jupien's niece had been sincere. Unfortunately, it was not the first time (nor would it be the last) that he had behaved thus, that he had suddenly "ditched" a girl to whom he had sworn undying love, going so far as to produce a loaded revolver and telling her that he would blow out his brains if ever he was vile enough to desert her. He would nevertheless desert her in time, and feel, instead of remorse, a sort of rancour against her. It was not the first time that he had behaved thus, and it was not to be the last, with the result that many young girls—girls less forgetful of him than he was of them—suffered—as Jupien's niece, continuing to love Morel while despising him, was to suffer for a long time—their heads ready to burst with the stabbing of an inner pain, because in each of them, like a fragment of a Greek sculpture, an aspect of Morel's face, hard as marble and beautiful as the art of antiquity, was embedded in the brain, with his blossoming hair, his fine eyes, his straight nose—forming a protuberance in a cranium not shaped to receive it, upon which no operation was possible. But in the fullness of time these stony fragments end by slipping into a place where they cause no undue laceration, from which they never stir again; their presence is no longer felt: the pain has been forgotten, or is remembered with indifference.

Meanwhile I had gained two things in the course of the day. On the one hand, thanks to the calm induced by Albertine's docility, there was the possibility, and in consequence the resolve, to break with her; on the other—the fruit of my reflexions during the interval that I had spent waiting for her, seated at the piano—the idea that Art, to which I would try to devote my reconquered liberty, was not something that was worth a sacrifice, something above and beyond life, that did not share in its fatuity and futility; the appearance of genuine individuality achieved in works of art being due merely to the illusion created by the artist's technical skill. If my afternoon had left behind it other deposits, possibly more profound, they were not to impinge upon my consciousness until much later. As for the two which I was able thus to ponder, they were not to be long-lived; for, from that very evening, my ideas about art were to recover from the diminution that they had suffered in the afternoon, while on the other hand my calm, and consequently the freedom that would enable me to devote myself to it, was once again to be withdrawn from me.

As my cab, driving along the riverside, was approaching the Verdurins' house, I made the driver pull up. I had just seen Brichot alighting from a tram at the corner of the Rue Bonaparte, after which he dusted his shoes with an old newspaper and put on a pair of pearl grey gloves. I went up to him on foot. For some time past, his sight having grown steadily worse, he had been equipped—as richly as an observatory—with new spectacles of a powerful and complicated kind, which, like astronomical instruments, seemed to be screwed into his eyes; he focused their exaggerated beams upon myself and recognised me. They—the spectacles—were in marvellous condition. But behind them I could see, minute, pallid, convulsive, expiring, a remote gaze placed under this powerful apparatus, as, in a laboratory too richly endowed for the work that is done in it, you may watch the last throes of some insignificant animalcule under the latest and most advanced type of microscope. I offered him my arm to guide him on his way. "This time it is not by great Cherbourg that we meet," he said to me, "but by little Dunkirk," a remark which I found extremely tiresome, as I did not understand what it meant; and yet I dared not ask Brichot, dreading not so much his scorn as his explanations. I replied that I was longing to see the drawing-room in which Swann used to meet Odette every evening. "What, so you know that old story, do you?" he said. "And yet from those days until Swann's death there's what the poet rightly calls '*grande spatium mortalis aevi.*' "

Swann's death had deeply distressed me at the time. Swann's death! Swann's, in this phrase, is something more than a mere genitive. I mean thereby his own particular death, the death assigned by destiny to the service of Swann. For we talk of "Death" for convenience, but there are almost as many different deaths as there are people. We do not possess a sense that would enable us to see, moving at full speed in every direction, these deaths, the active deaths aimed by destiny at this person or that. Often they are deaths that will not be entirely relieved of their duties until two or even three years later. They come in haste to plant a tumour in the side of a Swann, then depart to attend to other tasks, returning only when, the surgeons having performed their operations, it is necessary to plant the tumour there afresh. Then comes the moment when we read in the *Gaulois* that Swann's health has been causing anxiety but that he is now making an excellent recovery. Then, a few minutes before the last gasp, death, like a sister of charity who has come to nurse rather than to destroy us, enters to preside over our last moments, and crowns with a final aureole the cold and stiffening creature whose heart has ceased to beat. And it is this diversity of deaths, the mystery of their circuits, the colour of their fatal badge, that makes so moving a paragraph in the newspapers such as this:

"We learn with deep regret that M. Charles Swann passed away yesterday at his residence in Paris after a long and painful illness. A Parisian whose wit was widely appreciated, a discriminating but steadfastly loyal friend, he will be universally mourned, not only in those literary and artistic circles where the rare discernment of his taste made him a willing and a welcome guest, but also at the Jockey Club of which he was one of the oldest and most respected members. He belonged also to the Union and the Agricole. He had recently resigned his membership of the Rue Royale. His witty and striking personality never failed to arouse the interest of the public at all the great events of the musical and artistic seasons, notably at private views, where he was a regular attendant until the last few years, when he rarely left his house. The funeral will take place, etc."

From this standpoint, if one is not "somebody," the absence of a well-known title makes the process of decomposition even more rapid. No doubt it is more or less anonymously, without any individual identity, that a dead man remains the Duc d'Uzès. But the ducal coronet does for some time hold the elements of him together, as their moulds held together those artistically designed ices which Albertine admired, whereas the names of ultra-fashionable commoners, as soon as they are dead, melt and disintegrate, as it were taken out of their moulds. We have seen Mme de Guermantes speak of Cartier as the most intimate friend of the Duc de La Trémoïlle, as a man highly sought after in aristocratic circles. To a later generation, Cartier has become something so amorphous that it would almost be aggrandising him to ascribe to him a kinship with the jeweller Cartier, with whom he would have smiled to think that anybody could be so ignorant as to confuse him! Swann on the contrary was a remarkable intellectual and artistic personality, and although he had "produced" nothing, still he was lucky enough to survive a little longer. And yet, my dear Charles ——, whom I used to know when I was still so young and you were nearing your grave, it is because he whom you must have regarded as a young idiot has made you the hero of one of his novels that people are beginning to speak of you again and that your name will perhaps live. If, in Tissot's picture representing the balcony of the Rue Royale club, where you figure with Galliffet, Edmond de Polignac and Saint-Maurice, people are always drawing attention to you, it is because they know that there are some traces of you in the character of Swann.

To return to more general realities, it was of this death of his, foretold and yet unforeseen, that I had heard Swann speak himself to the Duchesse de Guermantes, on the evening of her cousin's party. It was the same death whose striking and specific strangeness had recurred to me one evening when, as I ran my eye over the newspaper, my attention was suddenly arrested by the announcement of it, as though traced in mysterious lines inopportunely interpolated there. They had sufficed to make of a living man someone who could never again respond to what one said to him, to reduce him to a mere name, a written name, that had suddenly passed from the real world to the realm of silence. It was they that even now gave me a desire to get to know the house in which the Verdurins had formerly lived, and where Swann, who at that time was not merely a row of letters printed in a newspaper, had dined so often with Odette. I must also add (and this is what for a long time made Swann's death more painful than any other, although these reasons bore no relation to the individual strangeness of *his* death) that I had never gone to see Gilberte as I promised him at the Princesse de Guermantes's; that he had never told me what the "other reason" was, to which he had alluded that evening, for his choosing me as the recipient of his conversation with the Prince; that countless questions occurred to me (as bubbles rise from the bottom of a pond) which I longed to ask him about the most disparate subjects: Vermeer, M. de Mouchy, Swann himself, a Boucher tapestry, Combray—questions which were doubtless not very urgent since I had put off asking them from day to day, but which seemed to me of cardinal importance now that, his lips being sealed, no answer would ever come.

"No," Brichot went on, "it wasn't here that Swann used to meet his future wife, or rather it was here only in the very latest period, after the fire that partially destroyed Mme Verdurin's former home."

Unfortunately, in my fear of displaying before the eyes of Brichot a luxury which seemed to me out of place, since the professor had no share in it, I had alighted too hastily from the carriage and the driver had not understood the words I had flung at him over my shoulder in order that I might be well clear of the carriage before Brichot caught sight of me. The consequence was that the driver drew alongside us and asked me whether he was to call for me later. I answered hurriedly in the affirmative and intensified all the more my respectful attentions to the professor who had come by omnibus.

"Ah! so you were in a carriage," he said gravely.

"Only by the purest accident. I never take one as a rule. I always travel by omnibus or on foot. However, it may perhaps earn me the great honour of taking you home to-night if you will oblige me by consenting to travel in that rattle-trap. We shall be packed rather tight. But you are always so kind to me."

Alas, in making him this offer, I am depriving myself of nothing, I reflected, since in any case I shall be obliged to go home because of Albertine. Her presence in my house, at an hour when nobody could possibly call to see her, allowed me to dispose as freely of my time as I had that afternoon, when I knew that she was on her way back from the Trocadéro and I was in no hurry to see her again. But at the same time, as also that afternoon, I felt that I had a woman in the house and that on returning home I would not taste the fortifying thrill of solitude.

"I heartily accept," replied Brichot. "At the period to which you allude, our friends occupied a magnificent ground floor apartment in the Rue Montalivet with an entresol and a garden behind, less sumptuous of course, and yet to my mind preferable to the old Venetian Embassy."

Brichot informed me that this evening there was to be at the "Quai Conti" (thus it was that the faithful spoke of the Verdurin salon since it had been transferred to that address) a great musical "jamboree" organized by M. de Charlus. He went on to say that in the old days to which I had referred, the little nucleus had been different and its tone not at all the same, not only because the faithful had then been younger. He told me of elaborate practical jokes played by Elstir (what he called "pure buffooneries"), as for instance one day when the painter, having pretended to "defect" at the last moment, had come disguised as an extra waiter and, as he handed round the dishes, murmured ribald remarks in the ear of the extremely prudish Baroness Putbus, who was crimson with anger and alarm; then, disappearing before the end of dinner, he had had a hip-bath carried into the drawing-room, out of which, when the party left the dinner-table, he had emerged stark naked uttering fearful oaths; and also of supper parties to which the guests came in paper costumes designed, cut out and painted by Elstir, which were veritable masterpieces, Brichot having worn on one occasion that of a nobleman of the court of Charles VII, with long pointed shoes, and another time that of Napoleon I, for which Elstir had fashioned a Grand Cordon of the Legion of Honour out of sealing-wax. In short Brichot, seeing again with the eyes of memory the salon of those days, the drawing-room with its high windows, its low settees bleached by the midday sun which had had to be replaced, declared that he preferred it to the drawing-room of to-day. Of course, I quite understood that by "salon" Brichot meant—as the word church implies not merely the religious edifice but the congregation of worshippers—not merely the apartment, but the people who frequented it, and the special pleasures that they came to enjoy there, and that were symbolised in his memory by those settees upon which, when you called to see Mme Verdurin in the afternoon, you waited until she was ready, while the blossom on the chestnut-trees outside, and the carnations in vases on the mantelpiece, seemed to offer a graceful and kindly thought for the visitor, expressed in the smiling welcome of their rosy hues, as they watched unblinkingly for the tardy appearance of the lady of the house. But if that salon seemed to him superior to the present one, it was perhaps because one's mind is an old Proteus who cannot remain the slave of any one shape and, even in the social world, suddenly transfers its allegiance from a salon which has slowly and arduously climbed to a pitch of perfection to another that is less brilliant, just as the "touched-up" photographs which Odette had had taken at Otto's, in which she queened it in a "princess" gown, her hair waved by Lenthéric, appealed less to Swann than a little snapshot taken at Nice, in which, in a plain cloth cape, her loosely dressed hair protruding beneath a straw hat trimmed with pansies and a black velvet bow, she looked, though a woman of fashion twenty years younger (for the earlier a photograph the older a woman looks in it), like a little maidservant twenty years older. Perhaps too he derived some pleasure from praising to me what I myself had never known, from showing me that he had enjoyed pleasures that I could never have. He succeeded, moreover, merely by citing the names of two or three people who were no longer alive and whom he invested with a kind of mysterious charm by the way he spoke of them. I felt that everything that had been told me about the Verdurins was far too crude; and indeed in the case of Swann, whom I had known, I reproached myself for not having paid sufficient attention to him, for not having paid attention to him in a sufficiently disinterested spirit, for not having listened to him properly when he used to entertain me while we waited for his wife to come home for lunch and he showed me his treasures, now that I knew that he was to be classed with the most brilliant talkers of the past.

Just as we were coming to Mme Verdurin's doorstep, I caught sight of M. de Charlus, steering towards us the bulk

of his huge body, drawing unwillingly in his wake one of those
ruffians or beggars who nowadays when he passed sprang out
without fail from even the most apparently deserted corners,
and by whom this powerful monster was, willy-nilly, invariably
escorted, although at a certain distance, as a shark is by its
pilot—in short, contrasting so markedly with the haughty
stranger of my first visit to Balbec, with his stern aspect,
his affectation of virility, that I seemed to be discovering,
accompanied by its satellite, a planet at a wholly different
period of its revolution, when one begins to see it full, or a
sick man devoured by the malady that a few years ago was but a
tiny spot which was easily concealed and the gravity of which
was never suspected. Although an operation that Brichot had
undergone had restored to some small extent the sight which
he had thought to be lost forever, I do not know whether he
had observed the ruffian following in the Baron's footsteps.
Not that this mattered much, for since la Raspelière, and notwithstanding the professor's friendly regard for M. de Charlus,
the sight of the latter always made him feel somehow uneasy.
No doubt to every man the life of every other extends along
shadowy paths of which he has no inkling. Lying, though it is
so often deceptive and is the basis of all conversation, conceals
less thoroughly a feeling of hostility, or of self-interest, or a visit
which one wants to appear not to have paid, or a short-lived
escapade with a mistress which one is anxious to keep from
one's wife, than a good reputation covers up—to the extent of
not letting its existence be guessed—sexual depravity. It may
remain unsuspected for a lifetime; an accidental encounter on a
pier, at night, discloses it; even then this accidental discovery
is frequently misunderstood and a third person who is in the
know must supply the elusive clue of which everyone is unaware. But, once known, it scares one by making one feel
that that way madness lies, far more than by its immorality.
Mme de Surgis le Duc could not be said to have a highly
developed moral sense, and would have tolerated in her sons
anything, however base, that could be explained by material
interest, which is comprehensible to all mankind. But she
forbade them to go on visiting M. de Charlus when she learned
that, by a sort of internal clockwork, he was inevitably drawn

upon each of their visits to pinch their chins and to make each of them pinch his brother's. She felt that uneasy sense of a physical mystery which makes us wonder whether the neighbour with whom we have been on friendly terms is not tainted with cannibalism, and to the Baron's repeated inquiry: "When am I going to see the young men?" she would reply, conscious of the wrath she was bringing down on herself, that they were very busy working for examinations, preparing to go abroad, and so forth. Irresponsibility aggravates faults, and even crimes, whatever may be said. Landru (assuming that he really did kill his women) may be pardoned if he did so from financial motives, which it is possible to resist, but not if it was from irresistible sadism.

The coarse pleasantries in which Brichot had indulged in the early days of his friendship with the Baron had given place, as soon as it was a question not of uttering commonplaces but of trying to understand, to an awkward feeling which was cloaked by gaiety. He reassured himself by recalling pages of Plato, lines of Virgil, because, being mentally as well as physically blind, he did not understand that in their day to love a young man was the equivalent (Socrates's jokes reveal this more clearly than Plato's theories) of keeping a dancing girl before getting engaged to be married in ours. M. de Charlus himself would not have understood, he who confused his ruling passion with friendship, which does not resemble it in the least, and the athletes of Praxiteles with obliging boxers. He refused to see that for nineteen hundred years ("a pious courtier under a pious prince would have been an atheist under an atheist prince," as La Bruyère reminds us) all conventional homosexuality—that of Plato's young friends as well as that of Virgil's shepherds—has disappeared, that what survives and increases is only the involuntary, the neurotic kind, which one conceals from other people and misrepresents to oneself. And M. de Charlus would have been wrong in not disowning frankly the pagan genealogy. In exchange for a little plastic beauty, how vast the moral superiority! The shepherd in Theocritus who sighs for love of a boy will have no reason later on to be less hard of heart, less dull of wit than the other shepherd whose flute sounds for Amaryllis. For the former is not suffering from a disease; he is conforming to the customs of his time. It is the homosexuality that survives in spite of obstacles, shameful, execrated, that is the only true form, the only form that corresponds in one and the same person to an intensification of the intellectual qualities. One is dismayed at the relationship that can exist between these and a person's bodily attributes when one thinks of the tiny dislocation of a purely physical taste, the slight blemish in one of the senses, that explains why the world of poets and musicians, so firmly barred against the Duc de Guermantes, opens its portals to M. de Charlus. That the latter should show taste in the furnishing of his home, which is that of a housewife with a taste for curios, need not surprise us; but the narrow loophole that opens upon Beethoven and Veronese! But this does not exempt the sane from a feeling of alarm when a madman who has composed a sublime poem, after explaining to them in the most logical fashion that he has been shut up by mistake through his wife's machinations, imploring them to intercede for him with the governor of the asylum, complaining of the promiscuous company that is forced upon him, concludes as follows: "You see that man in the courtyard, who I'm obliged to put up with; he thinks he's Jesus Christ. That should give you an idea of the sort of lunatics I've been shut up with; he *can't* be Jesus Christ, because *I'm* Jesus Christ!" A moment earlier, you were on the point of going to assure the psychiatrist that a mistake had been made. On hearing these words, even if you bear in mind the admirable poem at which this same man is working every day, you shrink from him, as Mme de Surgis's sons shrank from M. de Charlus, not because he had done them any harm, but because of the ceaseless invitations which ended up with his pinching their chins. The poet is to be pitied who must, with no Virgil to guide him, pass through the circles of an inferno of sulphur and brimstone, who must cast himself into the fire that falls from heaven in order to rescue a few of the inhabitants of Sodom! No charm in his work; the same severity in his life as in those of the unfrocked priests who follow the strictest rule of celibacy so that no one may be able to ascribe to anything but loss of faith their discarding of the cassock. Even then, it is not always so with these writers.

What asylum doctor has not had his own attack of madness by dint of continual association with madmen? He is lucky if he is able to affirm that it is not a previous latent madness that had predestined him to look after them. The subject of a psychiatrist's study often rebounds on him. But before that, what obscure inclination, what dreadful fascination had made him choose that subject?

Pretending not to see the shady individual who was gliding in his wake (whenever the Baron ventured on to the Boulevards or crossed the main hall of the Gare Saint-Lazare, these hangers-on who dogged his heels in the hope of touching him for a few francs could be counted by the dozen), and fearful lest the man might be bold enough to accost him, the Baron had devoutly lowered his mascara'ed eyelids which, contrasting with his powdered cheeks, gave him the appearance of a Grand Inquisitor painted by El Greco. But this priest was frightening and looked like an excommunicate, the various compromises to which he had been driven by the need to indulge his taste and to keep it secret having had the effect of bringing to the surface of his face precisely what the Baron sought to conceal, a debauched life betrayed by moral degeneration. This last, indeed, whatever be its cause, is easily detected, for it is never slow to materialise and proliferates upon a face, especially on the cheeks and round the eyes, as physically as the ochreous yellows of jaundice or the repulsive reds of a skin disease. Nor was it merely in the cheeks, or rather the chaps, of this painted face, in the mammiferous chest, the fleshy rump of this body abandoned to self-indulgence and invaded by obesity, that there now lingered, spreading like a film of oil, the vice at one time so jealously confined by M. de Charlus in the most secret recesses of his being. Now it overflowed into his speech.

"So this is how you prowl the streets at night, Brichot, with a good-looking young man," he said on joining us, while the disappointed ruffian made off. "A fine example. We must tell your young pupils at the Sorbonne that this is how you behave. But I must say the society of youth seems to agree with you, Monsieur le Professeur, you're as fresh as a rosebud. I've interrupted you though: you looked as though you were enjoying yourselves like a pair of giddy girls, and had no need

of an old Granny Killjoy like me. But I shan't go to confession
for it, since you were almost at your destination." The
Baron's mood was all the more blithe since he was totally
ignorant of the scene that afternoon, Jupien having decided
that he would be better advised to protect his niece against a
renewed onslaught than to go and inform M. de Charlus.
And so the Baron still looked forward to the marriage and was
delighted at the thought of it. One may suppose that it is a
consolation to these great solitaries to alleviate their tragic
celibacy with a fictitious fatherhood.

"But, upon my word, Brichot," he went on, turning towards
us with a laugh, "I feel quite embarrassed to see you in such
gallant company. You looked like a pair of lovers, going
along arm in arm. I say, Brichot, you do go the pace!" Ought
these remarks to have been ascribed to the senility of a mind
less capable than in the past of controlling its reflexes, which
in moments of automatism lets out a secret that has been so
carefully hidden for forty years? Or rather to that contempt for
the opinion of commoners which all the Guermantes felt in
their hearts, and which M. de Charlus's brother, the Duke,
displayed in a different form when, heedless of the fact that
my mother could see him, he used to shave by his bedroom
window in his unbuttoned nightshirt? Had M. de Charlus
contracted, during those stimulating journeys between Doncières and Douville, the dangerous habit of putting himself at
his ease and, just as he would push back his straw hat in order
to cool his huge forehead, of loosening—for a few moments
only at first—the mask that for too long had been rigorously
imposed upon his true face? His conjugal attitude towards
Morel might well have astonished anyone who was aware
that he no longer loved him. But M. de Charlus had reached
the stage when the monotony of the pleasures that his vice
nas to offer had become wearying. He had instinctively sought
after new exploits, and tiring of the strangers whom he picked
up, had gone to the opposite extreme, to what he used to
imagine that he would always loathe, the imitation of conjugal
life or of fatherhood. Sometimes even this did not suffice him;
he required novelty, and would go and spend the night with a
woman, just as a normal man may once in his life have wished

to go to bed with a boy, from a similar though inverse curiosity, in either case equally unhealthy. The Baron's existence as one of the "faithful," living, for Charlie's sake, exclusively among the little clan, by undermining the efforts he had made for years to keep up lying appearances, had had the same influence as a voyage of exploration or residence in the colonies has upon certain Europeans who discard the ruling principles by which they were guided at home. And yet, the internal revolution of a mind ignorant at first of the anomaly it carried within it, then appalled by this anomaly having recognised it, and finally becoming so accustomed to it as to fail to perceive that one cannot with impunity confess to other people what one has come round to confessing without shame to oneself, had been even more effective in liberating M. de Charlus from the last vestiges of social constraint than the time that he spent at the Verdurins'. No banishment, indeed, to the South Pole, or to the summit of Mont Blanc, can separate us so entirely from our fellow creatures as a prolonged sojourn in the seclusion of an inner vice, that is to say of a way of thinking that is different from theirs. A vice (so M. de Charlus used at one time to style it) to which the Baron now gave the genial aspect of a mere failing, extremely common, attractive on the whole and almost amusing, like laziness, absent-mindedness or greed. Conscious of the curiosity that his peculiar characteristics aroused, M. de Charlus derived a certain pleasure from satisfying, whetting, sustaining it. Just as a Jewish journalist will come forward day after day as the champion of Catholicism, not, probably, with any hope of being taken seriously, but simply in order not to disappoint the good-natured amusement of his readers, M. de Charlus would genially denounce sexual depravity in the company of the little clan, as he might have mimicked an English accent or imitated Mounet-Sully,[9] without waiting to be asked, simply to do his bit with good grace, by displaying an amateur talent in society; so that when he now threatened Brichot that he would report to the Sorbonne that he was in the habit of walking about with young men, it was in exactly the same way as the circumcised scribe keeps referring in and out of season to the "Eldest Daughter of the Church" and the "Sacred Heart of Jesus," that is to say without the least trace of hypocrisy, but with more than a hint of play-acting. It was not only the change in the words themselves, so different from those that he allowed himself to use in the past, that seemed to require some explanation, there was also the change that had occurred in his intonation and his gestures, which now singularly resembled what M. de Charlus used most fiercely to castigate; he would now utter involuntarily almost the same little squeaks (involuntary in his case and all the more deep-rooted) as are uttered voluntarily by those inverts who hail one another as "my dear!"—as though this deliberate "camping," against which M. de Charlus had for so long set his face, were after all merely a brilliant and faithful imitation of the manner that men of the Charlus type, whatever they may say, are compelled to adopt when they have reached a certain stage in their malady, just as sufferers from general paralysis or locomotor ataxia inevitably end by displaying certain symptoms. As a matter of fact—and this is what this purely unconscious "camping" revealed—the difference between the stern, black-clad Charlus with his hair *en brosse* whom I had known, and the painted and bejewelled young men, was no more than the purely apparent difference that exists between an excited person who talks fast and keeps fidgeting all the time, and a neurotic who talks slowly, preserves a perpetual phlegm, but is tainted with the same neurasthenia in the eyes of the physician who knows that each of the two is devoured by the same anxieties and marred by the same defects. At the same time one could tell that M. de Charlus had aged from wholly different signs, such as the extraordinary frequency in his conversation of certain expressions that had taken root in it and used now to crop up at every moment (for instance: "the concatenation of circumstances") and upon which the Baron's speech leaned in sentence after sentence as upon a necessary prop.

"Is Charlie already here?" Brichot asked M. de Charlus as we were about to ring the door-bell.

"Ah! I really don't know," said the Baron, raising his arms and half-shutting his eyes with the air of a person who does not wish to be accused of indiscretion, all the more so as he had probably been reproached by Morel for things which he had said and which the other, as cowardly as he was vain, and as ready to disown M. de Charlus as he was to boast of his friendship, had considered serious although they were quite trivial. "You know, I've no idea what he does."

If the conversations of two people bound by a tie of intimacy are full of lies, these crop up no less spontaneously in the conversations that a third person holds with a lover about the person with whom the latter is in love, whatever the sex of that person.

"Have you seen him lately?" I asked M. de Charlus, in order to appear at the same time not to be afraid of mentioning Morel to him and not to believe that they were actually living together.

"He came in, as it happened, for five minutes this morning while I was still half asleep, and sat down on the side of my bed, as though he wanted to ravish me."

I guessed at once that M. de Charlus had seen Charlie within the last hour, for if one asks a woman when she last saw the man whom one knows to be—and whom she may perhaps suppose that one suspects of being—her lover, if she has just had tea with him she replies: "I saw him for a minute before lunch." Between these two facts the only difference is that one is false and the other true. But both are equally innocent, or, if you prefer it, equally guilty. Hence one would be unable to understand why the mistress (and in this case, M. de Charlus) always chooses the false version, were one not aware that such replies are determined, unbeknownst to the person who makes them, by a number of factors which appear so out of proportion to the triviality of the incident that one does not bother to raise them. But to a physicist the space occupied by the tiniest ball of pith is explained by the clash or the equilibrium of laws of attraction or repulsion which govern far bigger worlds. Here we need merely record, as a matter of interest, the desire to appear natural and fearless, the instinctive impulse to conceal a secret assignation, a blend of decorum and ostentation, the need to confess what one finds so delightful and to show that one is loved, a divination of what one's interlocutor knows or guesses—but does not say—a divination which, exceeding or falling short of his, makes one now exaggerate, now under-estimate it, the unwitting desire to play with fire and the determination to rescue something from the

blaze. Just as many different laws acting in opposite directions
dictate the more general responses with regard to the innocence, the "platonic" nature, or on the contrary the carnal
reality, of one's relations with the person whom one says one
saw in the morning when one has seen him or her in the
evening. However, on the whole it must be said that M. de
Charlus, notwithstanding the aggravation of his malady which
perpetually urged him to reveal, to insinuate, sometimes quite
simply to invent compromising details, sought, during this
period in his life, to maintain that Charlie was not a man of the
same kind as himself and that they were friends and nothing
more. This (though it may quite possibly have been true) did
not prevent him from contradicting himself at times (as with
regard to the hour at which they had last met), either because
he forgot himself at such moments and told the truth, or
proffered a lie out of boastfulness or a sentimental affectation or
because he thought it amusing to mislead his interlocutor.

"You know that he is to me," the Baron went on, "a nice
little friend, for whom I have the greatest affection, as I am
sure" (did he doubt it, then, if he felt the need to say that he
was sure?) "he has for me, but there's nothing else between
us, nothing of that sort, you understand, nothing of that sort,"
said the Baron, as naturally as though he had been speaking of a
woman. "Yes, he came in this morning to pull me out of bed.
Though he knows that I hate being seen first thing in the
morning, don't you? Oh, it's horrible, it flusters one so, one
looks so perfectly hideous. Of course I'm no longer five-and-
twenty, they won't choose me to be Queen of the May, but
still one does like to feel that one's looking one's best."

It is possible that the Baron was sincere when he spoke of
Morel as a nice little friend, and that he was being even more
truthful than he supposed when he said: "I've no idea what
he does; I know nothing about his life."

Indeed we may mention (to anticipate by a few weeks
before resuming our narrative at the point where M. de Charlus,
Brichot and myself are arriving at Mme Verdurin's front door),
we may mention that shortly after this evening the Baron was
plunged into a state of grief and stupefaction by a letter
addressed to Morel which he had opened by mistake. This

letter, which was also indirectly to cause me acute distress, was written by the actress Léa, notorious for her exclusive taste for women. And yet her letter to Morel (whom M. de Charlus had never even suspected of knowing her) was written in the most passionate terms. Its indelicacy prevents us from reproducing it here, but we may mention that Léa addressed him throughout in the feminine gender, with such expressions as "Go on with you, naughty girl!" or "Of course you're one of us, you pretty sweetheart." And in this letter reference was made to various other women who seemed to be no less Morel's friends than Léa's. At the same time, Morel's sarcasm at the Baron's expense and Léa's at that of an officer who was keeping her, and of whom she said: "He keeps writing me letters begging me to be good! You bet! eh, my little white puss," revealed to M. de Charlus a state of things no less unsuspected by him than were Morel's peculiar and intimate relations with Léa. What most disturbed the Baron was the phrase "one of us." Ignorant at first of its application, he had eventually, now many moons ago, learned that he himself was "one of them." And now this notion that he had acquired was thrown back into question. When he had discovered that he was "one of them," he had supposed this to mean that his tastes, as Saint-Simon says, did not lie in the direction of women. And here was this expression taking on, for Morel, an extension of meaning of which M. de Charlus was unaware, so much so that Morel gave proof, according to this letter, of being "one of them" by having the same taste as certain women for other women. From then on the Baron's jealousy could no longer confine itself to the men of Morel's acquaintance, but would have to extend to the women also. So, to be "one of them" meant not simply what he had hitherto assumed, but to belong to a whole vast section of the inhabitants of the planet, consisting of women as well as of men, of men loving not merely men but women also, and the Baron, in the face of this novel meaning of a phrase that was so familiar to him, felt himself tormented by an anxiety of the mind as well as of the heart, born of this twofold mystery which combined an extension of the field of his jealousy with the sudden inadequacy of a definition.

M. de Charlus had never in his life been anything but an

amateur. That is to say that incidents of this sort could never be of any use to him. He worked off the painful impression that they might make upon him in violent scenes in which he was a past-master of eloquence, or in crafty intrigues. But to a person endowed with the qualities of a Bergotte, for instance, they might have been of inestimable value. This may indeed explain to a certain extent (since we act blindly, but choose, like the lower animals, the plant that is good for us) why men like Bergotte generally surround themselves with women who are inferior, false and ill-natured. Their beauty is sufficient for the writer's imagination, and excites his generosity, but does not in any way alter the nature of his mistresses, whose lives, situated thousands of feet below the level of his own, whose improbable connections, whose lies, carried further and moreover in a different direction from what might have been expected, appear in occasional flashes. The lie, the perfect lie, about people we know, about the relations we have had with them, about our motive for some action, formulated in totally different terms, the lie as to what we are, whom we love, what we feel with regard to people who love us and believe that they have fashioned us in their own image because they keep on kissing us morning, noon and night—that lie is one of the few things in the world that can open windows for us on to what is new and unknown, that can awaken in us sleeping senses for the contemplation of universes that otherwise we should never have known. As far as M. de Charlus is concerned, it must be said that if he was stupefied to learn with regard to Morel a certain number of things which the latter had carefully concealed from him, he was not justified in concluding from this that it is a mistake to make friends with the lower orders. Indeed, in the concluding section of this work, we shall see M. de Charlus himself engaged in doing things which would have stupefied the members of his family and his friends far more than he could possibly have been stupefied by Léa's revelations. (The revelation that he had found most painful had been that of a trip which Morel had made with Léa at a time when he had assured M. de Charlus that he was studying music in Germany. To build up his alibi he had made use of some obliging people to whom he had sent his letters in Germany, whence they were forwarded to M. de Charlus who, as it happened, was so positive that Morel was there that he had not even looked at the postmark.)

But it is time to rejoin the Baron as he advances with Brichot and myself towards the Verdurins' door.

"And what," he went on, turning to me, "has become of your young Hebrew friend whom we met at Doville? It occurred to me that, if you liked, one might perhaps invite him to the house one evening." For M. de Charlus, who did not shrink from employing a private detective agency to spy on Morel's every movement, for all the world like a husband or a lover, had not ceased to pay attention to other young men. The surveillance which he instructed one of his old servants to arrange for the agency to maintain over Morel was so indiscreet that his footmen thought they were being shadowed, and one of the housemaids lived in terror, no longer daring to go out into the street for fear of finding a detective at her heels. "She can do whatever she likes! Who'd waste time and money tailing her? As if her doings were of the slightest interest to us!" the old servant ironically exclaimed, for he was so passionately devoted to his master that although he in no way shared the Baron's tastes, he had come in time, with such ardour did he employ himself in their service, to speak of them as though they were his own. "He is the very best of good fellows," M. de Charlus would say of this old servant, for there is no one we appreciate more than a person who combines with other great virtues that of placing those virtues wholeheartedly at the service of our vices. It was of men alone that M. de Charlus was capable of feeling any jealousy so far as Morel was concerned. Women inspired in him none whatever. This is indeed an almost universal rule with the Charluses of this world. The love of the man they love for a woman is something else, which occurs in another animal species (a lion leaves tigers in peace), does not bother them, and if anything reassures them. Sometimes, it is true, in the case of those who exalt their inversion to the level of a priesthood, this love arouses disgust. These men resent their friends' having succumbed to it, not as a betrayal but as a degradation. A Charlus of a different variety from the Baron would have been as indignant to find Morel having relations with a woman as to read in a newspaper that he, the interpreter of Bach and Handel, was going to play Puccini. This is in fact why the young men who acquiesce in the love of Charluses for mercenary reasons assure them that women inspire them only with disgust, just as they would tell a doctor that they never touch alcohol and care only for spring water. But M. de Charlus, in this respect, departed to some extent from the general rule. Since he admired everything about Morel, the latter's successes with women, causing him no offence, gave him the same joy as his successes on the concert platform or at cards. "But do you know, my dear fellow, he has women," he would say, with an air of revelation, of scandal, possibly of envy, above all of admiration. "He's extraordinary," he would continue. "Wherever he goes, the most prominent whores have eyes for him alone. One notices it everywhere, whether it's on the underground or in the theatre. It's becoming such a bore! I can't go out with him to a restaurant without the waiter bringing him notes from at least three women. And always pretty women too. Not that it's anything to be wondered at. I was looking at him only yesterday, and I can quite understand them. He's become so beautiful, he looks like a sort of Bronzino; he's really marvellous." But M. de Charlus liked to show that he loved Morel, and to persuade other people, possibly to persuade himself, that Morel loved him. He took a sort of pride in having Morel always with him, in spite of the damage the young man might do to his social position. For (and this is often the case with men of some social standing and snobbish to boot, who, in their vanity, sever all their social ties in order to be seen everywhere with a mistress, a demi-mondaine or a lady of tarnished reputation who is no longer received in society but with whom nevertheless it seems to them flattering to be associated) he had arrived at the stage at which self-esteem devotes all its energy to destroying the goals to which it has attained, whether because, under the influence of love, a man sees a sort of glamour, which he is alone in perceiving, in ostentatious relations with the beloved object, or because, by the waning of social ambitions that have been gratified, and the rising tide of ancillary curiosities that are all the more absorbing for being platonic, the latter have not only reached but have passed the level at which the former found it difficult to sustain themselves.

As for other young men, M. de Charlus found that the existence of Morel was no obstacle to his taste for them, and that indeed his brilliant reputation as a violinist or his growing fame as a composer and journalist might in certain instances provide a bait. If a young composer of pleasing appearance was introduced to the Baron, it was in Morel's talents that he sought an opportunity of doing the newcomer a favour. "You must," he would tell him, "bring me some of your work so that Morel can play it at a concert or on tour. There's so little decent music written for the violin. It's a godsend to find something new. And abroad they appreciate that sort of thing enormously. Even in the provinces there are little musical societies where they love music with a fervour and intelligence that are quite admirable." Without any greater sincerity (for all this served only as bait and it was seldom that Morel condescended to fulfil these promises), Bloch having confessed that he was something of a poet ("in my idle moments," he had added with the sarcastic laugh with which he would accompany a trite remark when he could think of nothing original), M. de Charlus said to me: "You must tell your young Hebrew, since he writes verse, that he really must bring me some for Morel. For a composer that's always the stumbling block, finding something decent to set to music. One might even consider a libretto. It mightn't be uninteresting, and would acquire a certain value from the distinction of the poet, from my patronage, from a whole concatenation of auxiliary circumstances, among which Morel's talent would take the chief place. For he's composing a lot just now, and writing too, and very nicely—I must talk to you about it. As for his talent as an executant (there, as you know, he's already a real master), you shall see this evening how well the lad plays Vinteuil's music. He staggers me; at his age, to have such understanding while remaining such a schoolboy, such an urchin! Oh, this evening is only to be a little rehearsal. The big affair is to come off in two or three days. But it will be much more distinguished this evening. And so we're delighted that you've come," he went on, using the royal plural. "The programme is so magnificent that I've advised Mme Verdurin to give two parties: one in a few days' time, at which she will have all her own acquaintances, the other to-night at which the hostess is, as they say in legal parlance, 'disseized.' It is I who have issued the invitations, and I have collected a few people from another sphere, who may be useful to Charlie and whom it will be nice for the Verdurins to meet. It's all very well, don't you agree, to have the finest music played by the greatest artists, but the effect of the performance remains muffled, as though in cotton-wool, if the audience is composed of the milliner from across the way and the grocer from round the corner. You know what I think of the intellectual level of society people, but there are certain quite important roles which they can perform, among others the role which in public events devolves upon the press, and which is that of being an organ of dissemination. You understand what I mean: I have for instance invited my sister-in-law Oriane; it is not certain that she will come, but it is on the other hand certain that, if she does come, she will understand absolutely nothing. But one doesn't ask her to understand, which is beyond her capacity, but to talk, a task for which she is admirably suited, and which she never fails to perform. The result? To-morrow as ever is, instead of the silence of the milliner and the grocer, an animated conversation at the Mortemarts' with Oriane telling everyone that she has heard the most marvellous music, that a certain Morel, and so forth, and indescribable rage among the people not invited, who will say: 'Palamède obviously thought we were not worth asking; but in any case, who are these people in whose house it happened?'—a counterblast quite as useful as Oriane's praises, because Morel's name keeps cropping up all the time and is finally engraved in the memory like a lesson one has read over a dozen times. All this forms a concatenation of circumstances which may be of value to the artist, and to the hostess, may serve as a sort of megaphone for an event which will thus be made audible to a wide public. It really is worth the trouble; you shall see what progress Charlie has made. And what is more, we've discovered a new talent in him, my dear fellow: he writes like an angel. Like an angel, I tell you."

M. de Charlus omitted to say that for some time past he had been employing Morel, like those great noblemen of the seventeenth century who scorned to sign and even to write their own lampoons, to compose certain vilely calumnious little paragraphs at the expense of Comtesse Molé. Their effrontery being apparent even to those who merely glanced at them, how much more cruel were they to the young woman herself, who found in them, so slyly introduced that nobody but herself saw the point, certain passages from her own letters, quoted verbatim but twisted in a way that made them as deadly as the cruellest revenge. They killed the young woman. But there is published every day in Paris, Balzac would tell us, a sort of spoken newspaper, more terrible than its printed rivals. We shall see later on that this oral press reduced to nothing the power of a Charlus who had fallen out of fashion, and exalted far above him a Morel who was not worth the millionth part of his former patron. But at least this intellectual fashion is naïve and genuinely believes in the nullity of a gifted Charlus and in the incontestable authority of a crass Morel. The Baron was not so innocent in his implacable vindictiveness. Whence, no doubt, that bitter venom on his tongue the irruption of which seemed to dye his cheeks with jaundice when he was in a rage.

"Since you know Bergotte,"[10] M. de Charlus went on, "I thought that you might perhaps, by refreshing his memory with regard to the stripling's writings, as it were collaborate with me, help me to create a concatenation of circumstances capable of fostering a two-fold talent, that of a musician and a writer, which might one day acquire the prestige of that of Berlioz. As you know, the illustrious have often other things to think about, they are smothered in flattery, they take little interest except in themselves. But Bergotte, who is genuinely unpretentious and obliging, promised me that he would arrange for the *Gaulois*, or some such paper, to publish these little articles, a blend of the humorist and the musician, which are really very nicely done, and I should be so pleased if Charlie could combine with his violin this extra little hobby. I know I'm prone to exaggeration where he is concerned, like all the old fairy godmothers of the Conservatoire. What, my dear fellow, didn't you know that? You've clearly never noticed my hero-worshipping side. I pace up and down for hours on end outside the examination hall. I'm as happy as a queen. As for Charlie's prose, Bergotte assured me that it was really very good indeed."

M. de Charlus, who had long been acquainted with Bergotte through Swann, had indeed gone to see him to ask him to find an opening on some newspaper for a sort of half-humorous column by Morel about music. In doing so, M. de Charlus had felt some remorse, for, a great admirer of Bergotte, he was conscious that he never went to see him for his own sake, but in order—thanks to the respect, partly intellectual, partly social, that Bergotte had for him—to be able to do Morel or Mme Molé or others of his friends a good turn. That he no longer made use of the social world except for such purposes did not shock him, but to treat Bergotte thus seemed to him more reprehensible, because he felt that Bergotte was not at all calculating like society people, and deserved better. But his life was fully occupied and he could never find the time to spare unless he wanted something very badly, for instance when it affected Morel. Moreover, though he was himself extremely intelligent, the conversation of an intelligent man left him comparatively cold, especially that of Bergotte who was too much the man of letters for his liking, belonged to another clan and did not see things from his point of view. Bergotte for his part was well aware of the utilitarian motive for M. de Charlus's visits, but bore him no grudge; for though he was incapable of sustained kindness, he was anxious to give pleasure, tolerant, and impervious to the pleasure of administering a snub. As for M. de Charlus's vice, he had never to the smallest degree shared it, but found in it rather an element of colour in the person affected, *fas et nefas*, for an artist, consisting not in moral examples but in memories of Plato or of Sodoma.

"I should have very much liked him to come this evening, for he would have heard Charlie in the things he plays best. But I gather he doesn't go out, that he doesn't want to be bothered, and he's quite right. But you, fair youth, we never see you at the Quai Conti. You don't abuse their hospitality!"

I explained that I went out as a rule with my cousin.

"Do you hear that! He goes out with his cousin! What a most particularly pure young man!" said M. de Charlus to Brichot. Then, turning again to me: "But we are not asking you to give an account of your life, my boy. You are free to do anything that amuses you. We merely regret that we have no share in it. You have very good taste, by the way: your cousin is charming. Ask Brichot, she quite turned his head at Doville. Shall we be seeing her this evening? She really is extremely pretty. And she would be even prettier if she cultivated a little more the rare art, which she possesses naturally, of dressing well."

Here I must remark that M. de Charlus "possessed"—and this made him the exact opposite, the antithesis of me—the gift of observing minutely and distinguishing the details of a woman's clothes as much as of a painting. As regards dresses and hats, certain scandalmongers or certain over-dogmatic theorists will aver that, in a man, a fondness for male attractions is complemented by an innate taste, a knowledge and feeling for female dress. And this is indeed sometimes the case, as though, men having monopolised all the physical desire, all the deep tenderness of a Charlus, the other sex were to be favoured with what comes under the heading of "platonic" (a highly inappropriate adjective) taste, or quite simply everything that comes under the heading of taste, with the most subtle and assured discrimination. In this respect M. de Charlus merited the nickname which was given to him later on, "the dressmaker." But his taste and his gift for observation extended to many other things. The reader will have seen how, on the evening I went to see him after a dinner-party at the Duchesse de Guermantes', I had not noticed the masterpieces he had in his house until he pointed them out to me one by one. He recognised immediately things to which no one would ever have paid any attention, and this not only in works of art but in the dishes at a dinner-party (and everything else between painting and cooking). I always regretted that M. de Charlus, instead of restricting his artistic talents to the painting of a fan as a present for his sister-in-law (we have seen the Duchesse de Guermantes holding it in her hand and spreading it out not so much to fan

herself with it as to show it off and parade Palamède's friendship for her) and to the improvement of his pianistic technique
in order to accompany Morel's virtuoso flourishes without
playing wrong notes—I always regretted, as I say, and I still
regret, that M. de Charlus never wrote anything. Of course
one cannot draw from the eloquence of his conversation or
even of his correspondence the conclusion that he would have
been a talented writer. Those merits are not on the same plane.
One has come across purveyors of conversational banality
who have written masterpieces, and supreme talkers who have
proved inferior to the most mediocre hack as soon as they
turned to writing. Nevertheless I believe that if M. de Charlus
had tried his hand at prose, to begin with on those artistic
subjects about which he knew so much, the fire would have
blazed, the lightning would have flashed, and the society dilettante would have become a master of the pen. I often told him
so, but he never wished to try his hand, perhaps simply from
laziness, or because his time was taken up with dazzling entertainments and sordid diversions, or from a Guermantes need
to go on gossiping indefinitely. I regret it all the more because
in his most brilliant conversation the wit was never divorced
from the character, the inspired invention of the one from the
arrogance of the other. If he had written books, instead of
being admired and hated as he was in drawing-rooms where,
in his most remarkable moments of inventive intelligence, he
at the same time trampled down the weak, took revenge on
people who had not insulted him, basely sought to sow discord
between friends—if he had written books, one would have
had his wit and intellect in isolation, purged of evil, the admiration would have been unalloyed, and friendship would
have been kindled by many a delightful trait.

In any case, even if I am mistaken about what he might have
achieved with the merest page of prose, he would have performed a rare service by writing, for, while he observed and
distinguished everything, he also knew the name of everything
he distinguished. Certain it is that by talking to him, if I did
not learn to see (the natural tendency of my mind and sensibility
lying elsewhere), at least I glimpsed things that without him
would have remained invisible to me, though their names,

which would have helped me to recall their design or their colour, I always forgot fairly quickly. If he had written books, even bad ones (though I do not believe they would have been bad), what a delightful dictionary, what an inexhaustible inventory they would have been! But after all, who knows? Instead of bringing to the task his knowledge and his taste, perhaps, through that daemon that so often thwarts our destinies, he would have written insipid novels or pointless travel books.

"Yes, she knows how to dress, or more precisely how to wear clothes," M. de Charlus went on apropos of Albertine. "My only doubt is whether she dresses in conformity with her particular style of beauty, and I am in fact to some extent responsible for this, as a result of some rather ill-considered advice I gave her. What I often used to tell her on the way to la Raspelière, which was perhaps dictated—I regret to say—by the nature of the countryside, the proximity of the beaches, rather than by your cousin's distinctive type of looks, has made her err slightly on the side of flimsiness. I have seen her, I admit, in some very pretty muslins, some charming gauze scarves, and a certain pink toque by no means disfigured by a little pink feather. But I feel that her beauty, which is real and solid, demands more than dainty chiffons. Does a toque really suit that enormous head of hair which a kakochnyk would set off to full advantage? Very few women are suited by old-fashioned dresses which give an impression of theatre or fancy dress. But the beauty of this young girl who is already a woman is an exception, worthy of some old dress in Genoese velvet" (I thought at once of Elstir and of Fortuny's dresses) "which I would not be afraid of weighing down even more with incrustations or pendants of stones, marvellous and outmoded—I can think of no higher praise—such as the peridot, the marcasite and the incomparable labrador. Moreover she herself seems to have an instinct for the counter-balance that a somewhat heavy beauty calls for. Remember, on the way to dinner at la Raspelière, all that accompaniment of pretty cases and weighty bags, into which, when she is married, she will be able to put more than the whiteness of face-powder or the crimson of lipstick but—in a casket of lapis lazuli not too tinged

with indigo—those of pearls and rubies, not imitation ones, I
suspect, for she may well marry into money."

"Well, well, Baron," interrupted Brichot, fearing that I
might be distressed by these last words, for he had some doubts
as to the purity of my relations and the authenticity of my
cousinage with Albertine, "you *do* take an interest in young
ladies!"

"Will you please hold your tongue in front of this child,
you nasty thing," M. de Charlus replied with a giggle, raising
and lowering, in the gesture of imposing silence on Brichot,
a hand which he did not fail to let fall on my shoulder. "We
shall regret your cousin's absence this evening. But you did
just as well, perhaps, not to bring her with you. Vinteuil's
music is admirable. But I've heard that we are to meet the
composer's daughter and her friend, who have a terrible
reputation. That sort of thing is always awkward for a young
girl. They should be there, unless they've been detained in the
country, for they were to have been present without fail all
afternoon at a rehearsal which Mme Verdurin was giving
earlier and to which she had invited only the bores, the family,
the people who were not to be invited this evening. But just
before dinner, Charlie told me that the Misses Vinteuil, as we
call them, though positively expected, had failed to turn up."

In spite of the intense pain I felt at this sudden association
(as of the effect, of which alone I had been aware, with its cause,
at last discovered) of Albertine's desire to be there that afternoon with the expected presence (unknown to me) of Mlle
Vinteuil and her friend, I still had the presence of mind to
notice that M. de Charlus, who had told us a few minutes
earlier that he had not seen Charlie since the morning, was now
brazenly admitting that he had seen him before dinner. But my
anguish was becoming visible.

"Why, what's the matter with you?" said the Baron, "you've
turned quite green. Come, let's go in; you'll catch cold, you
don't look at all well."

It was not my first doubt as to Albertine's virtue that M. de
Charlus's words had awakened in me. Many others had penetrated my mind already. Each new doubt makes us feel that
the limit has been reached, that we cannot cope with it; then

we manage to find room for it all the same, and once it is introduced into the fabric of our lives it enters into competition there with so many longings to believe, so many reasons to forget, that we speedily become accustomed to it, and end by ceasing to pay attention to it. It lies there dormant like a half-healed pain, a mere threat of suffering which, the reverse side of desire, a feeling of the same order that has become, like it, the focus of our thoughts, irradiates them from infinite distances with wisps of sadness, as desire irradiates them with unidentifiable pleasures, wherever anything can be associated with the person we love. But the pain revives as soon as a new doubt enters our mind intact; even if we assure ourselves almost at once: "I shall deal with this, there'll be some way of avoiding suffering, it can't be true," nevertheless there has been a first moment in which we suffered as though we believed it. If we had merely limbs, such as legs and arms, life would be endurable. Unfortunately we carry inside us that little organ which we call the heart, which is subject to certain maladies in the course of which it is infinitely impressionable as regards everything that concerns the life of a certain person, so that a lie—that most harmless of things, in the midst of which we live so unconcernedly, whether the lie be told by ourselves or by others—coming from that person, causes that little heart, which we ought to be able to have surgically removed, intolerable spasms. Let us not speak of the brain, for our mind may go on reasoning interminably in the course of these spasms, but it does no more to mitigate them than by taking thought we can soothe an aching tooth. It is true that this person is blameworthy for having lied to us, for she had sworn to us that she would always tell us the truth. But we know, from our own shortcomings towards other people, how little such vows are worth. And we wanted to give credence to them when they came from her, the very person in whose interest it has always been to lie to us, and whom, moreover, we did not choose for her virtues. It is true that, later on, she would almost cease to have any need to lie to us—precisely when our heart will have grown indifferent to her lying—because then we shall no longer take an interest in her life. We know this, and, notwithstanding, we deliberately sacrifice our own life, either by killing ourselves for her sake, or by getting ourselves sentenced to death for having murdered her, or simply by spending our whole fortune on her in a few years and then being obliged to commit suicide because we have nothing left in the world. Moreover, however easy in one's mind one may imagine oneself to be when one loves, one always has love in one's heart in a state of precarious balance. The smallest thing is enough to place it in the position of happiness; one glows with it, one smothers with affection not her whom we love but those who have raised one in her esteem, who have protected her from every evil temptation; one feels easy in one's mind, and a single word is enough—"Gilberte is not coming," "Mademoiselle Vinteuil is expected"—for all the preconceived happiness towards which we were reaching out to collapse, for the sun to hide its face, for the compass card to revolve and let loose the inner tempest which one day we shall be incapable of resisting. On that day, the day on which the heart has become so fragile, friends who admire us will grieve that such trifles, that certain persons, can so affect us, can bring us to death's door. But what can they do? If a poet is dying of septic pneumonia, can one imagine his friends explaining to the pneumococcus that the poet is a man of talent and that it ought to let him recover? My doubt, in so far as it referred to Mlle Vinteuil, was not entirely new. But even to that extent, my jealousy of the afternoon, inspired by Léa and her friends, had abolished it. The danger of the Trocadéro once removed, I had felt, I had believed that I had recaptured for ever, complete peace of mind. But what was entirely new to me was a certain excursion as to which Andrée had told me: "We went to this place and that, and we didn't meet anyone," but during which, on the contrary, Mlle Vinteuil had evidently arranged to meet Albertine at Mme Verdurin's. At this moment I would gladly have allowed Albertine to go out by herself, to go wherever she might choose, provided that I might lock up Mlle Vinteuil and her friend somewhere and be certain that Albertine would not meet them. The fact is that jealousy is as a rule partial, inter- mittent and localised, whether because it is the painful exten- sion of an anxiety which is provoked now by one person, now by another of whom one's mistress may be enamoured, or because of the exiguity of one's thought which is able to realise only what it can represent to itself and leaves everything else in a vague penumbra from which one can suffer relatively little.

Just as we were about to enter the courtyard we were overtaken by Saniette, who had not at first recognised us. "And yet I contemplated you for some time," he told us breathlessly. "Is not it curious that I should have hesitated?"

To say "Is it not curious" would have seemed to him wrong, and he had acquired a familiarity with obsolete forms of speech that was becoming exasperating. "Albeit you are people whom one may acknowledge as friends." His grey complexion seemed to be illuminated by the livid glow of a storm. His breathlessness, which had been noticeable, as recently as last summer, only when M. Verdurin "jumped down his throat," was now continuous.

"I understand that an unknown work of Vinteuil is to be performed by excellent artists, and singularly by Morel."

"Why singularly?" inquired the Baron, who detected a criticism in the adverb.

"Our friend Saniette," Brichot made haste to explain, playing the part of interpreter, "is prone to speak, like the excellent scholar that he is, the language of an age in which 'singularly' was equivalent to our 'in particular.'"

As we entered the Verdurins' hall, M. de Charlus asked me whether I was engaged upon any work, and as I told him that I was not, but that I was greatly interested at the moment in old dinner-services of silver and porcelain, he assured me that I could not see any finer than those that the Verdurins had; that indeed I might have seen them at la Raspelière, since, on the pretext that one's possessions are also one's friends, they were foolish enough to take everything down there with them; that it would be less convenient to bring everything out for my benefit on the evening of a party, but that he would nevertheless ask them to show me anything I wished to see. I begged him not to do anything of the sort. M. de Charlus unbuttoned his overcoat and took off his hat, and I saw that the top of his head had now turned silver in patches. But like a precious shrub which is not only coloured with autumn tints but certain leaves of which are protected with cotton-wool or incrustations of plaster, M. de Charlus received from these few white hairs at his crest only a further variegation added to those of his face. And yet, even beneath the layers of different expressions, of paint and of hypocrisy which formed such a bad "make-up," his face continued to hide from almost everyone the secret that it seemed to me to be crying aloud. I was almost embarrassed by his eyes, for I was afraid of his surprising me in the act of reading it therein as in an open book, and by his voice which seemed to me to repeat it in every conceivable key, with unrelenting indecency. But secrets are well kept by such people, for everyone who comes in contact with them is deaf and blind. The people who learned the truth from someone else, from the Verdurins for instance, believed it, but only for so long as they had not met M. de Charlus. His face, so far from disseminating, dispelled every scandalous rumour. For we have so extravagant a notion of certain entities that we cannot identify it with the familar features of a person of our acquaintance. And we find it difficult to believe in such a person's vices, just as we can never believe in the genius of a person with whom we went to the Opera last night.

M. de Charlus was engaged in handing over his overcoat with the instructions of a familiar guest. But the footman to whom he was handing it was a newcomer, and quite young. Now M. de Charlus was inclined these days sometimes to "forget himself," as they say, and did not always remember what was or what was not "done." The praiseworthy desire that he had had at Balbec to show that certain topics did not alarm him, that he was not afraid to say of someone or other: "He's a nice-looking boy," to say, in a word, the same things as might have been said by somebody who was not like himself, this desire he had now begun to express by saying on the contrary things which nobody who was not like him could ever have said, things upon which his mind was so constantly fixed that he forgot that they do not form part of the habitual preoccupation of people in general. And so, looking at the new footman, he raised his forefinger in the air in a menacing fashion and, thinking that he was making an excellent joke, said: "You are not to make eyes at me like that, do you hear?" and, turning to Brichot: "He has a quaint little face, that boy, his nose is rather fun"; then, rounding off his pleasantry, or yielding to a desire, he lowered his forefinger horizontally, hesitated for an instant, and, unable to control himself any longer, thrust it irresistibly towards the footman and touched the tip of his nose, saying "Pif!", then walked into the drawing-room followed by Brichot, myself and Saniette, who told us that Princess Sherbatoff had died at six o'clock. "That's a rum card," the footman said to himself, and inquired of his companions whether the Baron was a joker or a madman. "It's just a way he has," said the butler (who regarded the Baron as slightly "touched," "a bit barmy"), "but he's one of Madame's friends for whom I've always had the greatest respect, he has a good heart."

"Will you be returning to Incarville this year?" Brichot asked me. "I believe that our hostess has taken la Raspelière again, although she had some trouble with her landlords. But that's nothing, a mere passing cloud," he added in the optimistic tone of the newspapers that say: "Mistakes have been made, it is true, but who does not make mistakes at times?" But I remembered the state of anguish in which I had left Balbec, and felt no desire to return there. I kept putting off to the morrow my plans for Albertine.

"Why, of course he's coming back, we need him, he's indispensable to us," declared M. de Charlus with the dictatorial and uncomprehending egoism of benevolence.

M. Verdurin, to whom we expressed our sympathy over Princess Sherbatoff, said: "Yes, I believe she is rather ill."

"No, no, she died at six o'clock," exclaimed Saniette.

"Oh you, you exaggerate everything," was M. Verdurin's brutal retort, for, the evening not having been cancelled, he preferred the hypothesis of illness, thereby unconsciously imitating the Duc de Guermantes.

Saniette, fearful of catching cold, for the outer door was continually being opened, stood waiting resignedly for someone to take his hat and coat.

"What are you hanging about there for like a whipped dog?" M. Verdurin asked him.

"I am waiting until one of the persons who are charged with the cloakroom can take my coat and give me a number."

"What's that you say?" demanded M. Verdurin with a stern expression. " 'Charged with the cloakroom'? Are you going gaga? 'In charge of the cloakroom,' is what we say. Have we got to teach you to speak your own language, like someone who's had a stroke?"

"Charged with a thing is the correct form," murmured Saniette in a wheezy tone; "the abbé Le Batteux . . ."

"You madden me, you do," cried M. Verdurin in a voice of thunder. "How you do wheeze! Have you just walked up six flights of stairs?"

The effect of M. Verdurin's rudeness was that the servants in the cloakroom allowed other guests to take precedence over Saniette and, when he tried to hand over his things, said to him: "Wait for your turn, Sir, don't be in such a hurry."

"There's system for you, there's competence. That's right, my lads," said M. Verdurin with an approving smile, in order to encourage them in their inclination to keep Saniette waiting till last. "Come along," he said to us, "the creature wants us all to catch our death hanging about in his beloved draught. Come and warm up in the drawing-room. 'Charged with the cloakroom,' indeed. What an idiot!"

"He *is* inclined to be a little precious, but he's not a bad fellow," said Brichot.

"I never said he was a bad fellow, I said he was an idiot," M. Verdurin retorted sourly.

Meanwhile Mme Verdurin was in deep conclave with Cottard and Ski. Morel had just declined (because M. de Charlus could not be present) an invitation from some friends of hers to whom she had promised the services of the violinist. The reason for Morel's refusal, which we shall presently see reinforced by others of a far more serious kind, might have found its justification in a habit peculiar to the leisured classes in general but more particularly to the little nucleus. To be sure, if Mme Verdurin intercepted between a newcomer and one of the faithful a whispered remark which might let it be supposed that they knew each other or wished to become better acquainted ("On Friday, then, at So-and-so's," or "Come to the studio any day you like. I'm always there until five o'clock, I shall look forward to seeing you"), she would become restless and excited, assuming that the newcomer occupied a "position" which would make him a brilliant recruit to the little clan, and while pretending not to have heard anything, and preserving in her fine eyes, ringed with dark shadows by the habit of listening to Debussy more than they would have been by that of sniffing cocaine, the exhausted look induced by musical intoxication alone, would revolve nevertheless behind her splendid brow, bulging with all those quartets and the resultant headaches, thoughts which were not exclusively polyphonic; and unable to contain herself any longer, unable to postpone the injection for another instant, would fling herself upon the speakers, draw them apart, and say to the newcomer, pointing to the "faithful" one: "You wouldn't care to come and dine with *him*, next Saturday, shall we say, or any day you like, with some really nice people? Don't speak too loud, as I don't want to invite all this mob" (a term used to designate for five minutes the little nucleus, disdained for the moment in favour of the newcomer in whom so many hopes were placed).

But this need for new enthusiasms, and also for bringing people together, had its reverse side. Assiduous attendance at their Wednesdays aroused in the Verdurins an opposite tendency. This was the desire to set people at odds, to estrange them from one another. It had been strengthened, had almost been carried to a frenzy during the months spent at la Raspelière, where they were all together morning, noon and night. M. Verdurin would go out of his way to catch someone out, to spin webs in which he might hand over to his spider mate some innocent fly. Failing a grievance, he would try ridicule. As soon as one of the faithful had been out of the house for half an hour, the Verdurins would make fun of him in front of the others, would feign surprise that their guests had not noticed how his teeth were never clean, or how on the contrary he had a mania for brushing them twenty times a day. If anyone took the liberty of opening a window, this want of breeding would cause host and hostess to exchange a glance of disgust. A moment later Mme Verdurin would ask for a shawl, which gave M. Verdurin an excuse for saying in a tone of fury: "No, I shall close the window. I wonder who had the impertinence to open it," in the hearing of the guilty wretch who blushed to the roots of his hair. You were rebuked indirectly for the quantity of wine you had drunk. "Doesn't it make you ill? It's all right for navvies!" If two of the faithful went for walks together without first obtaining permission from the Mistress, these walks were the subject of endless comment, however innocent they might be. Those of M. de Charlus with Morel were not innocent. It was only the fact that M. de Charlus was not staying at la Raspelière (because of Morel's garrison life) that retarded the hour of satiety, disgust, nausea. That hour was, however, about to strike.

Mme Verdurin was furious and determined to "enlighten" Morel as to the ridiculous and detestable role that M. de Charlus was making him play. "I must add," she went on (for when she felt that she owed someone a debt of gratitude which would weigh upon her, and was unable to rid herself of it by killing him, she would discover a serious defect in him which would honourably dispense her from showing her gratitude), "I must add that he gives himself airs in my house which I do not at all like." The truth was that Mme Verdurin had another reason more serious than Morel's refusal to play at her friends' party for resentment against M. de Charlus. The latter, highly conscious of the honour he was doing the Mistress by bringing to the Quai Conti people who after all would never have come there for her sake, had, on hearing the first few names put forward by Mme Verdurin of people who ought to be invited, pronounced the most categorical veto on them in a peremptory tone which blended the rancorous arrogance of a crotchety nobleman with the dogmatism of the artist who is an expert in questions of entertainment and who would withdraw his piece and withhold his collaboration sooner than agree to concessions which in his opinion would ruin the overall effect. M. de Charlus had given his approval, hedging it round with reservations, to Saintine alone, with whom, in order not to be lumbered with his wife, Mme de Guermantes had passed from a daily intimacy to a complete severance of relations, but whom M. de Charlus, finding him intelligent, continued to see. True, it was in a middle-class circle cross-bred with minor nobility, where people are merely very rich and connected by marriage with an aristocracy which the higher aristocracy does not know, that Saintine, at one time the flower of the Guermantes set, had gone to seek his fortune and, he imagined, a social foothold. But Mme Verdurin, knowing the blue-blooded pretensions of the wife's circle, and unaware of the husband's position (for it is what is immediately above our head that gives us the impression of altitude and not what is almost invisible to us, so far is it lost in the clouds), thought to justify an invitation for Saintine by pointing out that he knew a great many people, "having married Mlle ———." The ignorance which this assertion, the direct opposite of the truth, revealed in Mme Verdurin caused the Baron's painted lips to part in a smile of indulgent scorn and generous understanding. He did not deign to reply directly, but as he was always ready, in social matters, to elaborate theories in which his fertile intelligence and lordly pride were combined with the hereditary frivolity of his preoccupations, "Saintine ought to have consulted me before marrying," he said. "There's such a thing as social as well as physiological eugenics, in which I am perhaps the only specialist in existence. There could be no argument about Saintine's case: it was clear that, in marrying as he did, he was tying a stone round his neck, and hiding his light under a bushel. His social career was at an end. I should have explained this to him, and he would have understood me, for he is intelligent. Conversely, there was a certain person who had everything that he required to make his position exalted, predominant, world-wide, only a terrible cable bound him to the earth. I helped him, partly by pressure, partly by force, to break his moorings and now he has won, with a triumphant joy, the freedom, the omnipotence that he owes to me. It required, perhaps, a little determination on his part, but what a reward! Thus a man can himself, when he has the sense to listen to me, become the artificer of his destiny." (It was only too clear that M. de Charlus had not been able to influence his own; action is a different thing from words, however eloquent, and from thought, however ingenious.) "But, so far as I am concerned, I live the life of a philosopher who looks on with interest at the social reactions which he has foretold, but does not assist them. And so I have continued to see Saintine, who has always shown me the cordial deference which is my due. I have even dined with him in his new abode, where one is as heavily bored, in the midst of the most sumptuous splendour, as one used to be amused in the old days when, living from hand to mouth, he used to assemble the best society in a little attic. Him, therefore, you may invite; I authorise it. But I must impose a veto on all the other names that you have proposed. And you will thank me for it, for if I am an expert in the matter of marriages, I am no less an expert in the matter of festivities. I know the rising personalities who can lift a gathering, give it tone and distinction; and I know also the names that will bring it down to the ground, make it fall flat."

These exclusions of the Baron's were not always based on the resentments of a crackpot or the subtleties of an artist, but on the wiles of an actor. When he brought off, at the expense of somebody or something, an entirely successful tirade, he was anxious to let it be heard by the largest possible audience, but took care not to admit to the second performance the audience of the first who could have borne witness that the piece had not changed. He reconstituted his audience precisely because he did not alter his programme, and, when he had scored a success in conversation, would willingly have organised a tour and given performances in the provinces. Whatever the various motives for these exclusions, they did not merely annoy Mme Verdurin, who felt her authority as a hostess impaired; they also did her great damage socially, and for two reasons. The first was that M. de Charlus, even more touchy than Jupien, used to quarrel for no apparent reason with the people who were most suited to be his friends. Naturally, one of the first punishments that he could inflict upon them was that of not allowing them to be invited to a reception which he was organizing at the Verdurins'. Now these pariahs were often people who ruled the roost, as the saying is, but who in M. de Charlus's eyes had ceased to rule it from the day on which he had quarrelled with them. For his imagination, in addition to manufacturing faults in people in order to quarrel with them, was no less ingenious in stripping them of all importance as soon as they ceased to be his friends. If, for instance, the guilty person came of an extremely old family whose dukedom, however, dates only from the nineteenth century—the Montesquious for instance—from that moment all that counted for M. de Charlus was the seniority of the dukedom, the family becoming nothing. "They're not even dukes," he would exclaim. "It's the title of the Abbé de Montesquiou which passed most irregularly to a collateral, less than eighty years ago. The present duke, if duke he can be called, is the third. You may talk to me if you like of people like the Uzès, the la Trémoïlles, the Luynes, who are tenth or fourteenth dukes, or my brother who is twelfth Duc de Guermantes and seventeenth Prince de Condom. Even if the Montesquious are descended from an old family, what would that prove, supposing that it *were* proved? They have descended so far that they've reached the fourteenth storey below stairs." Had he on the contrary quarrelled with a gentleman who possessed an ancient dukedom, who boasted the most magnificent connexions, was related to ruling princes, but to whose line this distinction had come quite suddenly without any great length of pedigree, a Luynes for instance, the case was altered, pedigree alone counted. "I ask you—Monsieur Alberti, who does not emerge from the mire until Louis XIII! Why should we be impressed because court favour allowed them to pick up dukedoms to which they had no right?" What was more, with M. de Charlus the fall followed close upon the high favour because of that tendency peculiar to the Guermantes family to expect from conversation, from friendship, something that these are incapable of giving, as well as the symptomatic fear of becoming the object of slander. And the fall was all the greater the higher the favour had been. Now nobody had ever found such favour with the Baron as he had ostentatiously shown to Comtesse Molé. By what sign of indifference did she prove one fine day that she had been unworthy of it? The Countess herself always declared that she had never been able to discover. The fact remains that the mere sound of her name aroused in the Baron the most violent rage, provoked the most eloquent but the most terrible philippics. Mme Verdurin, to whom Mme Molé had been extremely amiable and who, as we shall see, was founding great hopes upon her, had rejoiced in anticipation at the thought that the Countess would meet in her house all the noblest names, as the Mistress said, "of France and of Navarre": she at once proposed inviting "Madame de Molé." "Goodness gracious me! I suppose it takes all sorts to make a world," M. de Charlus had replied, "and if you, Madame, feel a desire to converse with Mme Pipelet, Mme Gibout and Mme Joseph Prudhomme,[11] I'm only too delighted, but let it be on an evening when I am not present. I could see as soon as you opened your mouth that we don't speak the same language, since I was talking of aristocratic names and you come up with the most obscure names of parvenu commoners, sly, scandal-mongering and evil-minded, little women who imagine themselves patronesses of the arts because they echo an octave lower the manners of my Guermantes sister-in-law, like a jay trying to imitate a peacock. I must add that it would be positively indecent to admit to a celebration which I am pleased to give at Mme Verdurin's a person whom I have with good reason excluded from my society, a goose of a woman devoid of birth, loyalty or wit who is foolish enough to suppose that she is capable of playing the Duchesse de Guermantes and the Princesse de Guermantes, a combination which is in itself idiotic, since the Duchesse de Guermantes and the Princesse de Guermantes are poles apart. It is as though a person should pretend to be at once Reichenberg and Sarah Bernhardt. In any case, even if it were not wholly incompatible, it would be extremely ridiculous. Even though I myself may smile at times at the exaggerations of the one and regret the limitations of the other, that is my right. But that upstart little toad trying to inflate herself to the magnitude of two great ladies who at least always exhibit the incomparable distinction of blood, it's enough, as the saying is, to make a cat laugh. The Molé! That is a name which must not be uttered in my hearing, or else I must simply withdraw," he concluded with a smile, in the tone of a doctor who, having the good of his patient at heart in spite of the patient himself, lets it be understood that he will not tolerate the collaboration of a homoeopath.

In addition to this, certain persons whom M. de Charlus regarded as negligible might indeed be so for him but not for Mme Verdurin. M. de Charlus, from the height of his exalted birth, could afford to dispense with the most elegant people, the assemblage of whom would have made Mme Verdurin's drawing-room one of the first in Paris. But Mme Verdurin was beginning to feel that she had already on more than one occasion missed the bus, not to mention the enormous setback that the social error of the Dreyfus case had inflicted upon her—though it had not been an unmixed bane. "I forget whether I've told you," I might ask the reader, as one might ask a friend with regard to whom one has forgotten, after so many conversations, whether one has remembered or had a chance to tell him something, "how disapproving the Duchesse de Guermantes had been of certain persons of her world who, subordinating everything else to the Affair, excluded fashionable women from their drawing-rooms and admitted others who were not fashionable, because they were revisionist or anti-revisionist, and had then been criticised in her turn by those same ladies as being lukewarm, unsound in her views, and guilty of placing social distinctions above the national interest?" Whether I have done so or not, the attitude of the Duchesse de Guermantes at that time can easily be imagined, and indeed if we look at it in the light of subsequent history may appear, from the social point of view, perfectly correct. M. de Cambremer regarded the Dreyfus case as a foreign machination intended to destroy the Intelligence Service, to undermine discipline, to weaken the army, to divide the French people, to pave the way for invasion. Literature being, apart from a few of La Fontaine's fables, a closed book to the Marquis, he left it to his wife to show that the cruelly probing literature of the day had, by creating a spirit of disrespect, brought about a parallel upheaval. "M. Reinach and M. Hervieu are in league," she would say. Nobody will accuse the Dreyfus case of having premeditated such dark designs upon Society. But there it certainly broke down barriers. Society people who refuse to allow politics into their world are as far-sighted as soldiers who refuse to allow politics to permeate the army. Society is like sexual behaviour, in that no one knows what perversions it may develop once aesthetic considerations are allowed to dictate its choices.

The reason that they were Nationalists gave the Faubourg Saint-Germain the habit of entertaining ladies from another class of society; the reason vanished with Nationalism, but the habit remained. Mme Verdurin, thanks to Dreyfusism, had attracted to her house certain writers of distinction who for the moment were of no use to her socially, because they were Dreyfusards. But political passions are like all the rest, they do not last. New generations arise which no longer understand them; even the generation that experienced them changes, experiences new political passions which, not being modelled exactly upon their predecessors, rehabilitate some of the excluded, the reason for exclusion having altered. Monarchists no longer cared, at the time of the Dreyfus case, whether a man had been republican, or even radical, or even indeed anti-clerical, provided he was anti-semitic and nationalist. Should a war ever come, patriotism would assume another form and if a writer was chauvinistic enough nobody would stop to think whether he had or had not been a Dreyfusard.

It was thus that, from each political crisis, from each artistic revival, Mme Verdurin had picked up one by one, like a bird building its nest, the several scraps, temporarily unusable, of what would one day be her salon. The Dreyfus case had passed, Anatole France remained. Mme Verdurin's strength lay in her genuine love of art, the trouble she took for her faithful, the marvellous dinners that she gave for them alone, without inviting anyone from fashionable society. Each of the faithful was treated at her table as Bergotte had been treated at Mme Swann's. When a familiar guest of this sort becomes one fine day a famous man whom everyone wants to come and see, his presence in the house of a Mme Verdurin has none of the artificial, adulterated quality of an official or farewell banquet with a menu by Potel and Chabot,[12] but is like a delicious everyday meal which you would have found there in the same perfection on a day when there was no party at all. At Mme Verdurin's, the cast was trained to perfection, the repertory most select; all that was lacking was an audience. And now that the public taste had begun to turn from the rational Gallic art of Bergotte and was developing a taste for exotic forms of music, Mme Verdurin, a sort of accredited representative in Paris of all foreign artists, would soon be making her appearance, by the side of the exquisite Princess Yourbeletieff, as an aged Fairy Godmother, grim but all-powerful, to the Russian dancers. This charming invasion, against whose seductions only the stupidest of critics protested, infected Paris, as we know, with a fever of curiosity less agonising, more purely aesthetic, but quite as intense perhaps as that aroused by the Dreyfus case. There too Mme Verdurin, but with a very different result socially, was to be in the vanguard. Just as she had been seen by the side of Mme Zola, immediately below the judges' bench, during the trial in the Assize Court, so when the new generation, in their enthusiasm for the Russian ballet, thronged to the Opéra, crowned with the latest novelty in aigrettes, they invariably saw in a stage box Mme Verdurin by the side of Princess Yourbeletieff. And just as, after the excitements of the law courts, people used to go in the evening to Mme Verdurin's to meet Picquart or Labori in the flesh, and above all to hear the latest news, to learn what hopes might be placed in Zurlinden, Loubet, Colonel Jouaust, so years later, little inclined for sleep after the enthusiasm aroused by *Sheherazade* or the dances from *Prince Igor*, they would again repair to Mme Verdurin's, where, under the auspices of Princess Yourbeletieff and their hostess, an exquisite supper brought together every night the dancers themselves, who had abstained from dinner in order to remain more elastic, their director, their designers, the great composers Igor Stravinsky and Richard Strauss, a permanent little nucleus around which, as round the supper-table of M. and Mme Helvétius, the greatest ladies in Paris and foreign royalty were not too proud to gather. Even those society people who professed to be endowed with taste and drew otiose distinctions between the various Russian ballets, regarding the production of *Les Sylphides* as somehow more "delicate" than that of *Sheherazade*, which they were almost prepared to attribute to the inspiration of Negro art, were enchanted to meet face to face these great theatrical innovators who, in an art that is perhaps a little more artificial than painting, had created a revolution as profound as Impressionism itself.

To revert to M. de Charlus, Mme Verdurin would not have

minded so much if he had placed on his Index only Mme
Bontemps, whom she had picked out at Odette's on the strength
of her love of the arts, and who during the Dreyfus case had
come to dinner occasionally with her husband, whom Mme
Verdurin called "lukewarm" because he was not making any
move for a fresh trial but who, being extremely intelligent,
and glad to form relations in every camp, was delighted to
show his independence by dining at the same table as Labori,
to whom he listened without uttering a word that might compromise himself, but slipping in at the right moment a tribute
to the honesty, recognised by all parties, of Jaurès. But the
Baron had similarly proscribed several ladies of the aristocracy
with whom Mme Verdurin, on the occasion of some musical
festivity or fashion show, had recently formed an acquain-
tanceship and who, whatever M. de Charlus might think of
them, would have been, far more than himself, essential
ingredients in the formation of a fresh nucleus, this time aristocratic. Mme Verdurin had indeed been counting on this party
to mingle her new friends with ladies of the same set whom
M. de Charlus would be bringing, and had been relishing in
advance the surprise of the former on meeting at the Quai
Conti their own friends or relations invited there by the Baron.
She was disappointed and furious at his veto. It remained to
be seen whether, in these circumstances, the evening would
result in profit or loss to herself. The loss would not be too
serious if, at least, M. de Charlus's guests proved so well-
disposed towards her that they would become her friends in the
future. In this case no great harm would be done, and sooner or
later these two sections of the fashionable world, which the
Baron had insisted upon keeping apart, could be brought
together even if it meant excluding him on the evening in
question. And so Mme Verdurin was awaiting the Baron's
guests with a certain trepidation. It would not be long before
she discovered the frame of mind in which they were coming
and could judge what sort of relationship she could hope to
have with them. In the meantime she was taking counsel with
the faithful, but, on seeing M. de Charlus enter the room with
Brichot and myself, stopped short.

Greatly to our astonishment, when Brichot told her now

sorry he was to learn that her dear friend was so seriously ill,
Mme Verdurin replied: "You know, I'm bound to confess
that I feel no regret at all. It's no use feigning emotions one
doesn't feel. . . ." No doubt she spoke thus from want of energy,
because she shrank from the idea of wearing a long face
throughout her reception; from pride, in order not to appear
to be seeking excuses for not having cancelled it; yet also from
fear of what people might think of her and from social shrewd-
ness, because the absence of grief which she displayed was
more honourable if it could be attributed to a particular
antipathy, suddenly revealed, for the Princess, rather than to a
general insensitivity, and because her hearers could not fail
to be disarmed by a sincerity as to which there could be no
doubt: for if Mme Verdurin had not been genuinely indifferent
to the death of the Princess, would she, in order to explain
why she was entertaining, have gone so far as to accuse herself
of a far more serious fault? This was to forget that Mme
Verdurin would have had to admit, at the same time as confessing her grief, that she had not had the strength of mind to
forgo a pleasure; whereas the indifference of the friend was
something more shocking, more immoral, but less humiliating
and consequently easier to confess than the frivolity of the
hostess. In matters of crime, where there is danger for the
culprit, it is self-interest that dictates confessions; where the
offence incurs no penalty, it is self-esteem. Whether it was that,
doubtless finding rather hackneyed the excuse of people who,
in order not to allow a bereavement to interrupt their life of
pleasure, go about saying that it seems to them futile to wear
on their sleeves a grief which they feel in their hearts, she
preferred to imitate those intelligent culprits who are repelled
by the clichés of innocence and whose defence—a partial
admission, though they do not know it—consists in saying
that they would see no harm in doing what they are accused
of doing, although, as it happens, they have had no occasion
to do it, or whether, having adopted the theory of indifference
in order to explain her conduct, she found, once she had started
on the downward slope of her unnatural feeling, that there
was some originality in having felt it, a rare perspicacity in
having managed to diagnose it, and a certain "nerve" in

proclaiming it, Mme Verdurin kept dwelling upon her want of grief, not without something of the complacent pride of a paradoxical psychologist and daring dramatist.

"Yes, it's very odd," she said, "it made scarcely any impression on me. Of course, I don't mean to say that I wouldn't rather she were still alive, she wasn't a bad person."

"Yes she was," put in M. Verdurin.

"Ah! he doesn't approve of her because he thought I was doing myself harm by having her here, but he's rather pigheaded about that."

"Do me the justice to admit," said M. Verdurin, "that I never approved of the association. I always told you that she had a bad reputation."

"But I've never heard a thing against her," protested Saniette.

"What!" exclaimed Mme. Verdurin, "everybody knew; bad isn't the word, it was shameful, degrading. No, but it has nothing to do with that. I couldn't myself explain what I feel. I didn't dislike her, but she meant so little to me that when we heard that she was seriously ill my husband himself was quite surprised and said: 'Anyone would think you didn't mind.' Why, earlier this evening he offered to put off the rehearsal, and I insisted upon having it because I should have thought it a farce to show a grief which I don't feel."

She said this because she felt that it had an intriguing smack of the "independent theatre," and was at the same time singularly convenient; for avowed insensitivity or immorality simplifies life as much as does easy virtue; it converts reprehensible actions, for which one no longer need seek excuses, into a duty imposed by sincerity. And the faithful listened to Mme Verdurin's words with the mixture of admiration and uneasiness which certain cruelly realistic and painfully observant plays used at one time to cause; and while they marvelled to see their beloved Mistress display her rectitude and independence in a new form, more than one of them, although he assured himself that after all it would not be the same thing, thought of his own death, and wondered whether, on the day it occurred, they would draw the blinds or give a party at the Quai Conti.

"I'm very glad for my guests' sake that the evening hasn't

been cancelled," said M. de Charlus, not realising that in expressing himself thus he was offending Mme Verdurin.

Meanwhile I was struck, as was everybody who approached Mme Verdurin that evening, by a far from pleasant odour of rhino-gomenol. The reason was as follows. We know that Mme Verdurin never expressed her artistic emotions in an intellectual but always in a physical way, so that they might appear more inescapable and more profound. Now, if one spoke to her of Vinteuil's music, her favourite, she would remain unmoved, as though she expected to derive no emotion from it. But after looking at you for a few moments with a fixed, almost abstracted gaze, she would answer you in a sharp, matter of fact, scarcely civil tone (as though she had said to you: "I don't in the least mind your smoking, but it's because of the carpet; it's a very fine one—not that that matters either—but it's highly inflammable, I'm dreadfully afraid of fire, and I shouldn't like to see you all roasted because someone had carelessly dropped a cigarette end on it"), coldly expressing her regret that some of his music was being played that evening: "I have nothing against Vinteuil; to my mind, he's the greatest composer of the age. Only, I can never listen to that sort of stuff without weeping all the time" (there was not the slightest suggestion of pathos in the way she said "weeping"; she would have used precisely the same tone for "sleeping"; certain slandermongers used indeed to insist that the latter verb would have been more applicable, though no one could ever be certain, for she listened to the music with her face buried in her hands, and certain snoring sounds might after all have been sobs). "I don't mind weeping, not in the least; only I get the most appalling sniffles afterwards. It stuffs up my mucous membrane, and forty-eight hours later I look like nothing on earth. I have to inhale for days on end to get my vocal cords functioning. However, one of Cottard's pupils . . ." "Oh, by the way, I never offered you my condolences: he was carried off very quickly, poor fellow!" "Ah, yes, there we are, he died, as everyone has to. He'd killed enough people for it to be his turn to have a bit of his own medicine.[13] Anyhow, as I was saying, one of his pupils has been treating me for it. He goes by quite an original rule: 'Prevention is better than cure.' And he greases my nose before the music begins. The effect is radical. I can weep like all the mothers who ever lost a child, and not a trace of a cold. Sometimes a little conjunctivitis, that's all. It's completely efficacious. Otherwise I could never have gone on listening to Vinteuil. I was just going from one bronchial attack to another."

I could not refrain from mentioning Mlle Vinteuil. "Isn't the composer's daughter to be here," I asked Mme Verdurin, "with one of her friends?"

"No, I've just had a telegram," Mme Verdurin said evasively, "they were obliged to remain in the country."

I had a momentary hope that there might never have been any question of their coming and that Mme Verdurin had announced the presence of these representatives of the composer only in order to make a favourable impression on the performers and their audience.

"What, so they didn't even come to the rehearsal this afternoon?" said the Baron with feigned curiosity, anxious to appear not to have seen Charlie.

The latter came up to greet me. I whispered a question in his ear about Mlle Vinteuil's non-appearance; he seemed to me to know little or nothing about the matter. I signed to him to keep his voice down and told him we would talk again later. He bowed, and assured me that he would be entirely at my disposal. I observed that he was far more polite, far more respectful, than he had been in the past. I spoke warmly of him—since he might perhaps be able to help me to clear up my suspicions—to M. de Charlus who replied: "He only does what he should: there would be no point in his living among respectable people if he didn't learn good manners." These, according to M. de Charlus, were the old manners of France, without a hint of British stiffness. Thus when Charlie, returning from a tour in the provinces or abroad, arrived in his travelling suit at the Baron's, the latter, if there were not too many people present, would kiss him without ceremony on both cheeks, perhaps a little in order to banish by so ostentatious a display of his affection any idea of its being criminal, perhaps because he could not deny himself a pleasure, but still more, no doubt,

from historical piety, as upholding and illustrating the traditional manners of France, and, just as he would have protested
against the Munich or modern style of furniture by keeping
old armchairs that had come to him from a great-grandmother,
countering British phlegm with the affection of a warm-
hearted eighteenth-century father who does not conceal his
joy at seeing his son again. Was there indeed a trace of incest
in this paternal affection? It is more probable that the way in
which M. de Charlus habitually appeased his vice—as to which
we shall learn something in due course—did not meet his
emotional needs, which had remained unsatisfied since the
death of his wife; certain it is that after having thought more
than once of remarrying, he was now devoured by a maniacal
desire to adopt an heir, and certain persons close to him feared
that it might be fulfilled in favour of Morel. And there is
nothing extraordinary in this. The invert who has been unable
to feed his passion save on a literature written for women-
loving men, who used to think of men when he read Musset's
Nuits, feels the need to enter in the same way into all the social
activities of the man who is not an invert, to keep a lover, as
the old frequenter of the Opéra keeps ballet-girls, to settle
down, to marry or form a permanent tie, to become a father.

M. de Charlus took Morel aside, on the pretext of getting
him to explain what was going to be played, but above all
taking a sweet delight, while Charlie showed him his music,
in displaying thus publicly their secret intimacy. In the meantime I was surrounded by enchantment. For although the little
clan included few girls, a fair number were invited on big
occasions. There were several now present, and very pretty
ones, whom I knew. They wafted smiles of greeting to me
across the room. The air was thus continually spiced with
charming girlish smiles. They are the multifarious scattered
adornment of evenings as of days. One remembers an atmosphere because girls were smiling in it.

Many people might have been greatly surprised had they
overheard the furtive remarks which M. de Charlus exchanged
with a number of important men at this party. These were two
dukes, a distinguished general, a celebrated author, an eminent
physician and a great lawyer. And the remarks in question were:

"By the way, did you notice that footman, no, I mean the little fellow they take on the carriage ... And at your cousin Guermantes', you don't know of anyone?" "At the moment, no." "I say, though, outside the door, where the carriages stop, there was a little blonde person in short breeches, who seemed to me most attractive. She called my carriage most charmingly. I'd gladly have prolonged the conversation." "Yes, but I believe she's altogether hostile, and besides, she makes such a fuss! Since you like to get down to business at once, you'd be fed up. Anyhow, I know there's nothing doing, a friend of mine tried." "That's a pity, I thought the profile very fine, and the hair superb." "Really, you found her as nice as that? I think if you'd seen a little more of her you would have been disillusioned. No, in the supper-room only two months ago you would have seen a real marvel, a big strapping fellow over six feet tall, with a perfect skin, and loves it, too. But he's gone off to Poland." "Ah, that's a bit far." "You never know, he may come back. One always meets again somewhere." There is no great social function that does not, if one takes a cross-section of it and cuts sufficiently deep, resemble those parties to which doctors invite their patients, who utter the most intelligent remarks, have perfect manners, and would never show that they were mad if they did not whisper in your ear, pointing to some old gentleman going past: "That's Joan of Arc."

"I feel it's our duty to enlighten him," Mme Verdurin said to Brichot. "I don't mean any harm to Charlus, far from it. He's an agreeable man, and as for his reputation, I may say that it isn't of the kind that can do me any harm! You know how much, in the interests of our little clan and our table talk, I detest flirting, men talking nonsense to a woman in a corner instead of discussing interesting topics, but with Charlus I've never been afraid of what happened to me with Swann, and Elstir, and lots of others. With him I felt no need to worry; he would come to my dinners, all the women in the world might be there, yet you could be certain that the general conversation wouldn't be disturbed by flirting and whispering. Charlus is a special case, one doesn't have to worry, it's like having a priest. But he simply can't be allowed to take charge of the young men he meets here and cause trouble in our little nucleus, otherwise it will be even worse than having a womaniser." And Mme Verdurin was sincere in thus proclaiming her tolerance of Charlusism. Like every ecclesiastical power, she regarded human frailties as less dangerous than anything that might undermine the principle of authority, impair the orthodoxy, modify the ancient creed of her little Church. "Otherwise," she went on, "I shall bare my teeth. What do you say to a gentleman who prevents Charlie from coming to a recital because he himself hasn't been invited? So he's going to be taught a lesson, and I hope he'll profit by it, otherwise he can simply take his hat and go. Upon my word, he absolutely monopolises the boy!" And, using exactly the same expressions that almost anyone else might have used, for there are certain phrases not in common currency which some particular subject, some given circumstance, will recall almost infallibly to the mind of the talker who imagines he is speaking his mind freely when he is merely repeating mechanically the universal refrain, she continued: "It's impossible to see Morel nowadays without that great spindle-shanks hanging round him like a bodyguard."

M. Verdurin offered to take Charlie out of the room for a minute to talk to him, on the pretext of asking him something. Mme Verdurin was afraid that this might upset him, and that he would play badly in consequence. "It would be better to postpone this performance until after the other. Perhaps even until a later occasion." For however much Mme Verdurin might look forward to the delicious emotion that she would feel when she knew that her husband was engaged in enlightening Charlie in the next room, she was afraid, if the plan misfired, that he would lose his temper and fail to appear on the 16th.

What caused M. de Charlus's downfall that evening was the ill-breeding—so common in those circles—of the people whom he had invited and who were now beginning to arrive. Having come there partly out of friendship for M. de Charlus and also out of curiosity to explore these novel surroundings, each duchess made straight for the Baron as though it were he who was giving the party, and then said to me, within a yard of the Verdurins, who could hear every word: "Show me which is Mother Verdurin. Do you think I really need to get myself introduced to her? I do hope, at least, that she won't put my name in the paper to-morrow; nobody in my family would ever speak to me again. What, that woman with the white hair? But she looks quite presentable." Hearing some mention of Mlle Vinteuil, who, however, was not in the room, several of them said: "Ah! the sonata-man's daughter? Show me her." And, each of them finding a number of her friends, they formed a group by themselves, watched, bubbling over with ironical curiosity, the arrival of the faithful, but were able at the most to point a finger at the somewhat peculiar hair-style of a person who, a few years later, was to make this the fashion in the highest society, and, in short, regretted that they did not find this salon as different from the salons they knew as they had hoped to find it, feeling the same disappointment that they might have felt if, having gone to Bruant's night-club in the hope that the *chansonnier* would make a butt of them, they found themselves greeted on their arrival with a polite bow instead of the expected refrain: "Ah! look at that mug, look at that phizog. There's a sight for sore eyes."

M. de Charlus had, at Balbec, given me a perspicacious criticism of Mme de Vaugoubert who, in spite of her considerable intelligence, had brought about the irremediable disgrace after the unexpected prosperity of her husband. The rulers to whose court M. de Vaugoubert was accredited, King Theodosius and Queen Eudoxia, having returned to Paris, but this time for a prolonged visit, daily festivities had been held in their honour in the course of which the Queen, on friendly terms with Mme de Vaugoubert whom she had seen for the last ten years in her own capital, and knowing neither the wife of the President of the Republic nor the wives of his Ministers, had neglected these ladies and kept entirely aloof with the Ambassadress. The latter, believing her own position to be unassailable—M. de Vaugoubert having been responsible for the alliance between King Theodosius and France—had derived from the preference that the Queen showed for her society a self-satisfied pride but no anxiety at the danger which threatened her and which took shape a few months later in M. de Vaugoubert's abrupt retirement from the service, an event wrongly considered impossible by the over-confident couple. M. de Charlus, remarking in the "twister" upon the downfall of his childhood friend, expressed his astonishment that an intelligent woman had not in such circumstances used all her influence with the King and Queen to persuade them to behave as though she had none, and to transfer their civility to the wives of the President and his Ministers who would have been all the more flattered by it, that is to say all the more inclined in their self-contentedness to be grateful to the Vaugouberts, inasmuch as they would have supposed that civility to be spontaneous and not dictated by them. But the man who can see other people's errors often succumbs to them himself if sufficiently intoxicated by circumstances. And M. de Charlus, while his guests elbowed their way towards him to congratulate him and thank him as though he were the master of the house, never thought of asking them to say a few words to Mme Verdurin. Only the Queen of Naples, in whom survived the same noble blood that had flowed in the veins of her sisters the Empress Elisabeth and the Duchesse d'Alençon, made a point of talking to Mme Verdurin as though she had come for the pleasure of meeting her rather than for the music and for M. de Charlus, made endless gracious speeches to her hostess, never stopped telling her how much she had always wanted to make her acquaintance, complimented her on her house and spoke to her on all manner of subjects as though she were paying a call. She would so much have liked to bring her niece Elisabeth, she said (the niece who shortly afterwards was to marry Prince Albert of Belgium), who would be so disappointed! She stopped talking when she saw the musicians mount the platform, and asked which of them was Morel. She could scarcely have been under any illusion as to the motives that led M. de Charlus to desire that the young virtuoso should be surrounded with so much glory. But the venerable wisdom of a sovereign in whose veins flowed the blood of one of the noblest families in history, one of the richest in experience, scepticism and pride, made her merely regard the inevitable blemishes of the people whom she loved best, such as her cousin Charlus (whose mother had been a Duchess of Bavaria like herself), as misfortunes that rendered more precious to them the support that they might find in her and consequently gave her all the more pleasure in providing it. She knew that M. de Charlus would be doubly touched by her having taken the trouble to come in these circumstances. Only, being as kind as she had long ago shown herself brave, this heroic woman who, a soldier-queen, had herself fired her musket from the ramparts of Gaeta, always ready to place herself chivalrously on the side of the weak, seeing Mme Verdurin alone and abandoned, and moreover unaware that she ought not to leave the Queen, had sought to pretend that for her, the Queen of Naples, the centre of the evening, the focal point of attraction that had brought her there, was Mme Verdurin. She apologised endlessly for not being able to stay until the end, since, although she never went anywhere, she had to go on to another reception, and begged that on no account, when she had to go, should any fuss be made on her account, thus discharging Mme Verdurin from the honours which the latter did not even know that she ought to render her.

It must however be said in fairness to M. de Charlus that if he entirely forgot Mme Verdurin and allowed her to be ignored to a scandalous degree by the people "of his own world" whom he had invited, he did, on the other hand, realise that he must not allow them to display, during the "musical presentation" itself, the bad manners they were exhibiting towards the Mistress. Morel had already mounted the platform, and the musicians were assembling, but one could still hear conversations, not to say laughter, and remarks such as "Apparently you have to be initiated in order to understand it." Immediately M. de Charlus, drawing himself erect as though he had entered a different body from the one I had seen, a short while before, dragging itself towards Mme Verdurin's door, assumed a prophetic expression and glared at the assembly with a severity which signified that this was no time for laughter, thus bringing a sudden blush to the cheeks of more than one lady caught out like a schoolgirl by her teacher in front of the whole class. To my mind, M. de Charlus's attitude, so noble in other respects, was somehow slightly comic; for at one moment he withered the guests with his blazing eyes, and at the next, in order to indicate to them with a sort of vade-mecum the religious silence it was proper to observe, the detachment from any worldly preoccupation, he himself presented, raising his white-gloved hands to his handsome forehead, a model (to which they were expected to conform) of gravity, already almost of ecstasy, ignoring the greetings of late-comers so indelicate as not to realise that it was now the time for High Art. They were all hypnotised; no one dared to utter another sound, to move a chair; respect for music—by virtue of Palamède's prestige—had been instantaneously inculcated in a crowd as ill-bred as it was elegant.

When I saw not only Morel and a pianist but other instrumentalists too line up on the little platform, I supposed that the programme was to begin with works of composers other than Vinteuil. For I imagined that the only work of his in existence was his sonata for piano and violin.

Mme Verdurin sat alone, the twin hemispheres of her pale, slightly roseate brow magnificently bulging, her hair drawn back, partly in imitation of an eighteenth-century portrait, partly from the need for coolness of a feverish person reluctant to reveal her condition, aloof, a deity presiding over the musical rites, goddess of Wagnerism and sick-headaches, a sort of almost tragic Norn, conjured up by the spell of genius in the midst of all these "bores," in whose presence she would scorn even more than usual to express her feelings upon hearing a piece of music which she knew better than they. The concert began; I did not know what was being played; I found myself in a strange land. Where was I to place it? Who was the composer? I longed to know, and, seeing nobody near me whom I could ask, I should have liked to be a character in those *Arabian Nights* which I never tired of reading and in which, in moments of uncertainty, there appears a genie, or a maiden of ravishing beauty, invisible to everyone else but not to the perplexed hero to whom she reveals exactly what he wishes to learn. And indeed at that very moment I was favoured with just such a magical apparition. As when, in a stretch of country which one thinks one does not know and which in fact one has approached from a new direction, after turning a corner one finds oneself suddenly emerging on to a road every inch of which is familiar, but one had simply not been in the habit of approaching it that way, one suddenly says to oneself: "Why, this is the lane that leads to the garden gate of my friends the X—s; I'm only two minutes from their house," and there, indeed, is their daughter who has come out to greet one as one goes by; so, all of a sudden, I found myself, in the midst of this music that was new to me, right in the heart of Vinteuil's sonata; and, more marvellous than any girl, the little phrase, sheathed, harnessed in silver, glittering with brilliant sonorities, as light and soft as silken scarves, came to me, recognisable in this new guise. My joy at having rediscovered it was enhanced by the tone, so friendly and familiar, which it adopted in addressing me, so persuasive, so simple, and yet without subduing the shimmering beauty with which it glowed. Its intention, however, this time was merely to show me the way, which was not the way of the sonata, for this was an un-published work of Vinteuil in which he had merely amused himself, by an allusion that was explained at this point by a sentence in the programme which one ought to have been reading simultaneously, by reintroducing the little phrase for a moment. No sooner was it thus recalled than it vanished, and I found myself once more in an unknown world, but I knew now, and everything that followed only confirmed my knowledge, that this world was one of those which I had never even been capable of imagining that Vinteuil could have created, for when, weary of the sonata which was to me a universe thoroughly explored, I tried to imagine others equally beautiful but different, I was merely doing what those poets do who fill their artificial paradise with meadows, flowers and streams which duplicate those existing already upon earth. What was now before me made me feel as keen a joy as the sonata would have given me if I had not already known it, and consequently, while no less beautiful, was different. Whereas the sonata opened upon a lily-white pastoral dawn, dividing its fragile purity only to hover in the delicate yet compact entanglement of a rustic bower of honeysuckle against white geraniums, it was upon flat, unbroken surfaces like those of the sea on a morning that threatens storm, in the midst of an eerie silence, in an infinite void, that this new work began, and it was into a rose-red daybreak that this unknown universe was drawn from the silence and the night to build up gradually before me. This redness, so new, so absent from the tender, pastoral, unadorned sonata, tinged all the sky, as dawn does, with a mysterious hope. And a song already pierced the air, a song on seven notes, but the strangest, the most remote from anything I had ever imagined, at once ineffable and strident, no longer the cooing of a dove as in the sonata, but rending the air, as vivid as the scarlet tint in which the opening bars had been bathed, something like a mystical cock-crow, the ineffable but ear-piercing call of eternal morning. The atmosphere, cold, rain-washed, electric—of a quality so different, subject to quite other pressures, in a world so remote from the virginal, plant-strewn world of the sonata—changed continually, eclipsing the crimson promise of the dawn. At noon, however, in a burst of scorching but transitory sunlight, it seemed to reach fulfilment in a heavy, rustic, almost cloddish gaiety in which the lurching, riotous clangour of bells (like those which set the church square of Combray aglow and which Vinteuil, who must often have heard them, had perhaps discovered at that moment in his memory like a colour which a painter has at hand on his palette) seemed the material representation of the coarsest joy. Truth to tell, this joyous motif did not appeal to me aesthetically; I found it almost ugly, its rhythm was so laboriously earthbound that one could have imitated almost all its essentials simply with the noises made by rapping on a table with drumsticks in a particular way. It seemed to me that Vinteuil had been lacking, here, in inspiration, and consequently I was a little lacking also in the power of attention.

I looked at the Mistress, whose fierce immobility seemed to be a protest against the rhythmic noddings of the ignorant heads of the ladies of the Faubourg. She did not say: "You realise, of course, that I know a thing or two about this music! If I were to express all that I feel, you'd never hear the end of it!" She did not say this. But her upright, motionless body, her expressionless eyes, her straying locks said it for her. They spoke also of her courage, said that the musicians could carry on, that they need not spare her nerves, that she would not flinch at the andante, would not cry out at the allegro. I looked at the musicians. The cellist was hunched over the instrument which he clutched between his knees, his head bowed forward, his coarse features assuming an involuntary expression of disgust at the more mannerist moments; another leaned over his double bass, fingering it with the same domestic patience with which he might have peeled a cabbage, while by his side the harpist, a mere girl in a short skirt, framed behind the diagonal rays of her golden quadrilateral, recalling those which, in the magic chamber of a Sibyl, arbitrarily denote the ether according to the traditional forms, seemed to be picking out exquisite sounds here and there at designated points, just as though, a tiny allegorical goddess poised before the golden trellis of the heavenly vault, she were gathering, one by one, its stars. As for Morel, a lock, hitherto invisible and submerged in the rest of his hair, had fallen loose and formed a curl on his forehead.

I turned my head slightly towards the audience to discover what M. de Charlus might be feeling at the sight of this curl. But my eyes encountered only the face, or rather the hands, of Mme Verdurin, for the former was entirely buried in the latter. Did the Mistress wish to indicate by this meditative attitude that she considered herself as though in church, and regarded this music as no different from the most sublime of prayers? Did she wish, as some people do in church, to hide from prying eyes, out of modesty or shame, their presumed fervour or their culpable inattention or an irresistible urge to sleep? A regular noise which was not musical gave me momentarily to think that this last hypothesis was the correct one, but I realised later that it was produced by the snores, not of Mme Verdurin, but of her dog.

But very soon, the triumphant motif of the bells having been banished, dispersed by others, I succumbed once again to the music; and I began to realise that if, in the body of this septet, different elements presented themselves one after another to combine at the close, so also Vinteuil's sonata and, as I later discovered, his other works as well, had been no more than timid essays, exquisite but very slight, beside the triumphal and consummate masterpiece now being revealed to me.

And I could not help recalling by comparison that, in the same way too, I had thought of the other worlds that Vinteuil had created as being self-enclosed as each of my loves had been; whereas in reality I was obliged to admit that just as, within the context of the last of these—my love for Albertine— my first faint stirrings of love for her (at Balbec at the very beginning, then after the game of ferret, then on the night when she slept at the hotel, then in Paris on the foggy afternoon, then on the night of the Guermantes party, then at Balbec again, and finally in Paris where my life was now closely linked to hers) had been, so, if I now considered not my love for Albertine but my whole life, my other loves too had been no more than slight and timid essays that were paving the way, appeals that were unconsciously clamouring, for this vaster love: my love for Albertine. And I ceased to follow the music, in order to ask myself once again whether Albertine had or had not seen Mlle Vinteuil during the last few days, as one interrogates anew an inner pain from which one has been distracted for a moment. For it was in myself that Albertine's possible actions were performed. Of every person we know we possess a double; but, being habitually situated on the horizon of our imagination, of our memory, it remains more or less extraneous to us, and what it has done or may have done has no greater capacity to cause us pain than an object situated at a certain distance which provides us with only the painless sensations of vision. The things that affect these people we perceive in a contemplative fashion; we are able to deplore them in appropriate language which gives other people a sense of our kindness of heart, but we do not feel them. But ever since the wound I had received at Balbec, it was deep in my heart, and very difficult to extricate, that Albertine's double was lodged. What I saw of her hurt me, as a sick man would be hurt whose senses were so seriously deranged that the sight of a colour would be felt by him internally like an incision in his living flesh. It was fortunate that I had not already yielded to the temptation to break with Albertine; the tedium of having to rejoin her presently, when I went home, was a trifling matter compared with the anxiety that I should have felt if the separation had occurred when I

still had a doubt about her and before I had had time to grow
indifferent to her. And at the moment when I thus pictured her
waiting for me at home like a beloved wife, finding the time
of waiting long, perhaps having fallen asleep for a while in
her room, my ears were caressed by a passing phrase, tender,
homely and domestic, of the septet. Perhaps—everything
being so interwoven and superimposed in our inner life—it
had been inspired in Vinteuil by his daughter's sleep (that
daughter who was to-day the cause of all my distress) when it
enveloped the composer's work on peaceful evenings with its
quiet sweetness, this phrase which had so much power to
calm me by virtue of the same soft background of silence that
gives a hushed serenity to certain of Schumann's reveries,
during which, even when "the Poet speaks," one can tell that
"the child sleeps." Asleep or awake, I should find her again
this evening, Albertine, my little child, when I chose to return
home. And yet, I said to myself, something more mysterious
than Albertine's love seemed to be promised at the outset of this
work, in those first cries of dawn. I tried to banish the thought
of my mistress and to think only of the musician. Indeed, he
seemed to be present. It was as though, reincarnate, the composer lived for all time in his music; one could feel the joy with
which he chose the colour of some timbre, harmonising it
with the others. For with other and more profound gifts
Vinteuil combined that which few composers, and indeed
few painters, have possessed, of using colours not merely so
lasting but so personal that, just as time has been powerless to
spoil their freshness, so the disciples who imitate their dis-
coverer, and even the masters who surpass him, do not dim
their originality. The revolution that their apparition has
effected does not see its results merge unacknowledged in the
work of subsequent generations; it is unleashed, it explodes
anew, when, and only when, the works of the once-for-all-time
innovator are performed again. Each tone was identified by
a colour which all the rules in the world could not have taught
the most learned composers to imitate, with the result that
Vinteuil, although he had appeared at his appointed hour and
had his appointed place in the evolution of music, would always
leave that place to stand in the forefront whenever any of his

compositions was performed, compositions which would owe their appearance of having originated after the works of more recent composers to this apparently paradoxical and indeed deceptive quality of permanent novelty. A page of symphonic music by Vinteuil, familiar already on the piano, revealed, when one heard it played by an orchestra—like a ray of summer sunlight which the prism of the window decomposes before it enters a dark dining-room—all the jewels of the *Arabian Nights* in unsuspected, multicoloured splendour. But how could one compare to that motionless dazzle of light what was life, perpetual and blissful motion? This Vinteuil, whom I had known so timid and sad, had been capable—when he had to choose a timbre and to blend another with it—of an audacity, and in the full sense of the word a felicity, as to which the hearing of any of his works left one in no doubt. The joy that certain sonorities had caused him, the increase of strength they had given him wherewith to discover others, led the listener on too from one discovery to another, or rather it was the creator himself who guided him, deriving, from the colours he had just hit upon, a wild joy which gave him the strength to discover, to fling himself upon others which they seemed to call for, enraptured, quivering as though from the shock of an electric spark when the sublime came spontaneously to life at the clang of the brass, panting, intoxicated, unbridled, vertiginous, while he painted his great musical fresco, like Michelangelo strapped to his scaffold and from his upside-down position hurling tumultuous brush-strokes on to the ceiling of the Sistine Chapel. Vinteuil had been dead for many years; but in the sound of these instruments which he had loved, it had been given him to go on living, for an unlimited time, a part at least of his life. Of his life as a man solely? If art was indeed but a prolongation of life, was it worth while to sacrifice anything to it? Was it not as unreal as life itself? The more I listened to this septet, the less I could believe this to be so. No doubt the glowing septet differed singularly from the lily-white sonata; the timid question to which the little phrase replied, from the breathless supplication to find the fulfilment of the strange promise that had resounded, so harsh, so supernatural, so brief, setting the still inert crimson of the morning sky above the sea athrob. And yet these very different phrases were composed of the same elements; for, just as there was a certain world, perceptible to us in those fragments scattered here and there, in private houses, in public galleries, which was Elstir's world, the world he saw, the world in which he lived, so too the music of Vinteuil extended, note by note, stroke by stroke, the unknown, incalculable colourings of an unsuspected world, fragmented by the gaps between the different occasions of hearing his work performed; those two very dissimilar questions that governed the very different movement of the sonata and the septet, the former interrupting a pure, continuous line with brief calls, the latter welding together into an indivisible structure a medley of scattered fragments—one so calm and shy, almost detached and somehow philosophical, the other so restless, urgent, imploring—were nevertheless the same prayer, bursting forth like different inner sunrises, and merely refracted through the different mediums of other thoughts, of artistic researches carried on through the years in which he had sought to create something new. A prayer, a hope which was at heart the same, distinguishable beneath these disguises in the various works of Vinteuil, and at the same time not to be found elsewhere than in his works. For those phrases, historians of music could no doubt find affinities and pedigrees in the works of other great composers, but only for secondary reasons, external resemblances, analogies ingeniously discovered by reasoning rather than felt as the result of a direct impression. The impression conveyed by these Vinteuil phrases was different from any other, as though, in spite of the conclusions to which science seems to point, the individual did exist. And it was precisely when he was striving with all his might to create something new that one recognised, beneath the apparent differences, the profound similarities and the deliberate resemblances that existed in the body of a work; when Vinteuil took up the same phrase again and again, diversified it, amused himself by altering its rhythm, by making it reappear in its original form, those deliberate resemblances, the work of his intellect, necessarily superficial, never succeeded in being as striking as the disguised, involuntary resemblances, which broke out in different colours, between the two separate masterpieces; for then Vinteuil, striving to do something new, interrogated himself, with all the power of his creative energy, reached down to his essential self at those depths where, whatever be the question asked, it is in the same accent, that is to say its own, that it replies. Such an accent, the accent of Vinteuil, is separated from the accents of other composers by a difference far greater than that which we perceive between the voices of two people, even between the bellowings and the squeals of two animal species; by the real difference that exists between the thought of this or that other composer and the eternal investigations of Vinteuil, the question that he put to himself in so many forms, his habitual speculation, but as free from analytical forms of reasoning as if it were being carried out in the world of the angels, so that we can gauge its depth, but no more translate it into human speech than can disembodied spirits when, evoked by a medium, they are questioned by him about the secrets of death. And even when I bore in mind that acquired originality which had struck me that afternoon, that kinship, too, which musicologists might discover between composers, it is indeed a unique accent, an unmistakable voice, to which in spite of themselves those great singers that original composers are rise and return, and which is a proof of the irreducibly individual existence of the soul. Though Vinteuil might try to make more solemn, more grandiose, or to make more sprightly and gay, to re-create what he saw reflected in the mind of the public, in spite of himself he submerged it all beneath a ground-swell which makes his song eternal and at once recognisable. Where had he learned this song, different from those of other singers, similar to all his own, where had he heard it? Each artist seems thus to be the native of an unknown country, which he himself has forgotten, and which is different from that whence another great artist, setting sail for the earth, will eventually emerge. Certain it was that Vinteuil, in his latest works, seemed to have drawn nearer to that unknown country. The atmosphere was no longer the same as in the sonata, the questioning phrases had become more pressing, more unquiet, the answers more mysterious; the washed-out air of morning and evening seemed to affect the very strings of the instruments. Marvellously though Morel played, the sounds that came from his violin seemed to me singularly piercing, almost shrill. This harshness was pleasing, and, as in certain voices, one felt in it a sort of moral quality and intellectual superiority. But it could be found repellent. When his vision of the universe is modified, purified, becomes more adapted to his memory of his inner homeland, it is only natural that this should be expressed by a musician in a general alteration of sonorities, as of colours by a painter. In any case, the more intelligent section of the public is not misled, since Vinteuil's last compositions were ultimately declared to be his most profound. And yet no programme, no subject matter, supplied any intellectual basis for judgment. One simply sensed that it was a question of the transposition of creative profundity into terms of sound.

Composers do not actually remember this lost fatherland, but each of them remains all his life unconsciously attuned to it; he is delirious with joy when he sings in harmony with his native land, betrays it at times in his thirst for fame, but then, in seeking fame, turns his back on it, and it is only by scorning fame that he finds it when he breaks out into that distinctive strain the sameness of which—for whatever its subject it remains identical with itself—proves the permanence of the elements that compose his soul. But in that case is it not true that those elements—all the residuum of reality which we are obliged to keep to ourselves, which cannot be transmitted in talk, even from friend to friend, from master to disciple, from lover to mistress, that ineffable something which differentiates qualitatively what each of us has felt and what he is obliged to leave behind at the threshold of the phrases in which he can communicate with others only by limiting himself to externals, common to all and of no interest—are brought out by art, the art of a Vinteuil like that of an Elstir, which exteriorises in the colours of the spectrum the intimate composition of those worlds which we call individuals and which, without the aid of art, we should never know? A pair of wings, a different respiratory system, which enabled us to travel through space, would in no way help us, for if we visited Mars or Venus while keeping the same senses, they would clothe everything that we saw in the same aspect as the things of Earth. The only true voyage of discovery, the only really rejuvenating experience, would be not to visit strange lands but to possess other eyes, to see the universe through the eyes of another, of a hundred others, to see the hundred universes that each of them sees, that each of them is; and this we can do with an Elstir, with a Vinteuil; with men like these we do really fly from star to star.

The andante had just ended on a phrase filled with a tenderness to which I had entirely surrendered. There followed, before the next movement, a short interval during which the performers laid down their instruments and the audience exchanged impressions. A duke, in order to show that he knew what he was talking about, declared: "It's a difficult thing to play well." Other more agreeable people chatted for a moment with me. But what were their words, which like every human and external word left me so indifferent, compared with the heavenly phrase of music with which I had just been communing? I was truly like an angel who, fallen from the inebriating bliss of paradise, subsides into the most humdrum reality. And, just as certain creatures are the last surviving testimony to a form of life which nature has discarded, I wondered whether music might not be the unique example of what might have been—if the invention of language, the formation of words, the analysis of ideas had not intervened—the means of communication between souls. It is like a possibility that has come to nothing; humanity has developed along other lines, those of spoken and written language. But this return to the unanalysed was so intoxicating that, on emerging from that paradise, contact with more or less intelligent people seemed to me of an extraordinary insignificance. I had been able, while the music was playing, to remember people, to associate them with it; or rather I had associated with the music scarcely more than the memory of one person only, which was Albertine. And the phrase that ended the andante seemed to me so sublime that I told myself that it was a pity that Albertine did not know, and if she had known had not understood, what an honour it was to be associated with something as great as this phrase which reunited us, and the heartbreaking voice of which she seemed to have assumed. But

once the music was interrupted, the people who were there
seemed too insipid. Refreshments were handed round. M.
de Charlus hailed a footman now and then with: "How are
you? Did you get my note? Can you come?" No doubt there
was in these salutations the freedom of the great nobleman
who thinks he is flattering his interlocutor and is more one of
the people than the bourgeois, but there was also the cunning
of the delinquent who imagines that anything one flaunts is on
that account considered innocent. And he added, in the Guermantes tone of Mme de Villeparisis: "He's a good boy, a
friendly soul, I often employ him at home." But his adroitness
turned against the Baron, for people thought his intimate
courtesies and correspondence with footmen extraordinary.
The footmen themselves were not so much flattered as embarrassed in the presence of their comrades.

Meanwhile the septet, which had begun again, was moving
towards its close; again and again one phrase or another from
the sonata recurred, but altered each time, its rhythm and
harmony different, the same and yet something else, as things
recur in life; and they were phrases of the sort which, without
our being able to understand what affinity assigns to them as
their sole and necessary abode the past of a certain composer,
are to be found only in his work, and appear constantly in his
work, of which they are the spirits, the dryads, the familiar
deities; I had at first distinguished in the septet two or three
which reminded me of the sonata. Presently—bathed in the
violet mist which was wont to rise particularly in Vinteuil's
later work, so much so that, even when he introduced a dance
measure, it remained captive in the heart of an opal—I caught
a hint of another phrase from the sonata, still so distant that I
scarcely recognised it; hesitantly it approached, vanished as
though in alarm, then returned, intertwined with others that
had come, as I later learned, from other works, summoned
yet others which became in their turn seductive and persuasive
as soon as they were tamed, and took their places in the round,
the divine round that yet remained invisible to the bulk of the
audience, who, having before their eyes only a dim veil through
which they saw nothing, punctuated arbitrarily with admiring
exclamations a continuous boredom of which they thought

they would die. Then the phrases withdrew, save one which I saw reappear five times or six without being able to distinguish its features, but so caressing, so different—as no doubt the little phrase from the sonata had been for Swann—from anything that any woman had ever made me desire, that this phrase—this invisible creature whose language I did not know but whom I understood so well—which offered me in so sweet a voice a happiness that it would really have been worth the struggle to obtain, is perhaps the only Unknown Woman that it has ever been my good fortune to meet. Then this phrase broke up, was transformed, like the little phrase in the sonata, and became the mysterious call of the start. A phrase of a plaintive kind rose in answer to it, but so profound, so vague, so internal, almost so organic and visceral, that one could not tell at each of its re-entries whether it was a theme or an attack of neuralgia. Presently these two motifs were wrestling together in a close embrace in which at times one of them would disappear entirely, and then only a fragment of the other could be glimpsed. A wrestling match of disembodied energies only, to tell the truth; for if these creatures confronted one another, they did so stripped of their physical bodies, of their appearance, of their names, finding in me an inward spectator—himself indifferent, too, to names and particulars—to appreciate their immaterial and dynamic combat and follow passionately its sonorous vicissitudes. In the end the joyous motif was left triumphant; it was no longer an almost anxious appeal addressed to an empty sky, it was an ineffable joy which seemed to come from paradise, a joy as different from that of the sonata as some scarlet-clad Mantegna archangel sounding a trumpet from a grave and gentle Bellini seraph strumming a theorbo. I knew that this new tone of joy, this summons to a supra-terrestrial joy, was a thing that I would never forget. But would it ever be attainable to me? This question seemed to me all the more important inasmuch as this phrase was what might have seemed most eloquently to characterise—as contrasting so sharply with all the rest of my life, with the visible world—those impressions which at remote intervals I experienced in my life as starting-points, foundation-stones for the construction of a true life: the impression I had felt at the sight of the steeples of Martinville, or of a line of trees near Balbec. In any case, to return to the particular accent of this phrase, how strange it was that the presentiment most different from what life assigns to us on earth, the boldest approximation to the bliss of the Beyond, should have materialised precisely in the melancholy, respectable little bourgeois whom we used to meet in the Month of Mary at Combray! But above all, how was it possible that this revelation, the strangest that I had yet received, of an unknown type of joy, should have come to me from him, since, it was said, when he died he had left nothing but his sonata, everything else existing only as indecipherable scribblings. Indecipherable they may have been, but they had nevertheless been in the end deciphered, by dint of patience, intelligence and respect, by the only person who had been sufficiently close to Vinteuil to understand his method of working, to interpret his orchestral indications: Mlle Vinteuil's friend. Even in the lifetime of the great composer, she had acquired from his daughter the veneration that the latter felt for her father. It was because of this veneration that, in those moments in which people run counter to their true inclinations, the two girls had been able to take an insane pleasure in the profanations which have already been narrated. (Her adoration of her father was the very condition of his daughter's sacrilege. And no doubt they ought to have forgone the voluptuous pleasure of that sacrilege, but it did not express the whole of their natures.) And, moreover, the profanations had become rarer until they disappeared altogether, as those morbidly carnal relations, that troubled, smouldering conflagration, had gradually given way to the flame of a pure and lofty friendship. Mlle Vinteuil's friend was sometimes tormented by the nagging thought that she might have hastened Vinteuil's death. At any rate, by spending years unravelling the cryptic scroll left by him, by establishing the correct reading of those illegible hieroglyphs, she had the consolation of ensuring an immortal and compensatory glory for the composer over whose last years she had cast such a shadow. Relations which are not sanctioned by the law establish bonds of kinship as manifold, as complex, and even more solid, than those which spring from marriage. Indeed, without pausing to consider relations of so special a nature, do we not find every day that adultery, when it is based on genuine love, does not weaken family feelings and the duties of kinship, but rather revivifies them? Adultery then brings the spirit into what marriage would often have left a dead letter. A good daughter who will wear mourning for her mother's second husband for reasons of propriety has not tears enough to shed for the man whom her mother singled out as her lover. In any case Mlle Vinteuil had acted only out of sadism, which did not excuse her, though it gave me a certain consolation to think so later on. No doubt she must have realised, I told myself, at the moment when she and her friend had profaned her father's photograph, that what they were doing was merely morbidity, silliness, and not the true and joyous wickedness which she would have liked to feel. This idea that it was merely a pretence of wickedness spoiled her pleasure. But if this idea recurred to her later on, since it had spoiled her pleasure so it must have diminished her grief. "It wasn't me," she must have told herself, "I was out of my mind. *I* can still pray for my father's soul, and not despair of his forgiveness." Only it is possible that this idea, which had certainly occurred to her in her pleasure, may not have occurred to her in her grief. I would have liked to be able to put it into her mind. I am sure that I would have done her good and that I could have re-established between her and the memory of her father a more comforting relationship.

As in the illegible note-books in which a chemist of genius, who does not know that death is at hand, jots down discoveries which will perhaps remain forever unknown, Mlle Vinteuil's friend had disentangled, from papers more illegible than strips of papyrus dotted with a cuneiform script, the formula, eternally true and forever fertile, of this unknown joy, the mystic hope of the crimson Angel of the Dawn. And I for whom, albeit not so much, perhaps, as for Vinteuil, she had also been, had just been once more this very evening by reawakening my jealousy of Albertine, was to be above all in the future, the cause of so many sufferings, it was thanks to her, in compensation, that I had been able to apprehend the strange summons which I should henceforth never cease to hear, as the promise and proof that there existed something other, realisable no doubt through art, than the nullity that I had found in all my pleasures and in love itself, and that if my life seemed to me so futile, at least it had not yet accomplished everything.

What she had enabled us, thanks to her labour, to know of Vinteuil was to all intents and purposes the whole of Vinteuil's work. Compared with this septet, certain phrases from the sonata which were all that the public knew appeared so commonplace that it was difficult to understand how they could have aroused so much admiration. Similarly we are surprised that, for years past, pieces as trivial as the *Song to the Evening Star* or *Elisabeth's Prayer* can have aroused in the concert-hall fanatical worshippers who wore themselves out applauding and shouting *encore* at the end of what after all seems poor and trite to us who know *Tristan*, the *Rhinegold* and the *Mastersingers*. One must assume that those featureless melodies nevertheless already contained, in infinitesimal and for that reason perhaps more easily assimilable quantities, something of the originality of the masterpieces which alone matter to us in retrospect, but whose very perfection might perhaps have prevented them from being understood; those earlier melodies may have prepared the way for them in people's hearts. But the fact remains that, if they gave a vague presentiment of the beauties to come, they left these in complete obscurity. The same was true of Vinteuil; if at his death he had left behind him— excepting certain parts of the sonata—only what he had been able to complete, what we should have known of him would have been, in relation to his true greatness, as inconsiderable as in the case of, say, Victor Hugo if he had died after the *Pas d'Armes du Roi Jean*, the *Fiancée du Timbalier* and *Sarah la Baigneuse*, without having written a line of the *Légende des Siècles* or the *Contemplations*: what is to us his real achievement would have remained purely potential, as unknown as those universes to which our perception does not reach, of which we shall never have any idea.

Moreover this apparent contrast and profound union between genius (talent too and even virtue) and the sheath of vices in which, as had happened in the case of Vinteuil, it is so frequently contained and preserved, was detectable, as in a popular allegory, in the very assembly of the guests among whom I found myself once again when the music had come to an end. This assembly, albeit limited this time to Mme Verdurin's salon, resembled many others, the ingredients of which are unknown to the general public, and which journalist-philosophers, if they are at all well-informed, call Parisian, or Panamist, or Dreyfusard, never suspecting that they may equally well be found in Petersburg, Berlin, Madrid, and in every epoch; if as a matter of fact the Under Secretary of State for Fine Arts, an artist to his fingertips, well-born and snobby, several duchesses and three ambassadors with their wives were present this evening at Mme Verdurin's, the proximate, immediate cause of their presence lay in the relations that existed between M. de Charlus and Morel, relations which made the Baron anxious to give as wide a celebrity as possible to the artistic triumphs of his young idol, and to obtain for him the cross of the Legion of Honour; the remoter cause which had made this assembly possible was that a girl who enjoyed a relationship with Mlle Vinteuil analogous to that of Charlie and the Baron had brought to light a whole series of works of genius which had been such a revelation that before long a subscription was to be opened under the patronage of the Minister of Education, with the object of erecting a statue to Vinteuil. Moreover, these works had been assisted, no less than by Mlle Vinteuil's relations with her friend, by the Baron's relations with Charlie, a sort of short cut, as it were, thanks to which the world was enabled to catch up with these works without the detour, if not of an incomprehension which would long persist, at least of a complete ignorance which might have lasted for years. Whenever an event occurs which is within the range of the vulgar mind of the journalist-philosopher, a political event as a rule, the journalist-philosophers are convinced that there has been some great change in France, that we shall never see such evenings again, that no one will ever again admire Ibsen, Renan, Dostoievsky, D'Annunzio, Tolstoy, Wagner, Strauss. For the journalist-philosophers take their cue from the equivocal undercurrents of these official manifestations, in order to find something decadent in the art which is there celebrated and which as often as not is more austere than any other. There is not a name, among those most revered by these journalist-philosophers, which has not quite naturally given rise to some such strange gathering, although its strangeness may have been less flagrant and better concealed. In the case of this gathering, the impure elements that came together therein struck me from another aspect; true, I was as well able as anyone to dissociate them, having learned to know them separately; but those which concerned Mlle Vinteuil and her friend, speaking to me of Combray, spoke to me also of Albertine, that is to say of Balbec, since it was because I had long ago seen Mlle Vinteuil at Montjouvain and had learned of her friend's intimacy with Albertine that I was presently, when I returned home, to find, instead of solitude, Albertine awaiting me; and those which concerned Morel and M. de Charlus, speaking to me of Balbec, where I had seen, on the platform at Doncières, their intimacy begin, spoke to me of Combray and of its two "ways," for M. de Charlus was one of those Guermantes, Counts of Combray, inhabiting Combray without having any dwelling there, suspended in mid-air, like Gilbert the Bad in his window, while Morel was the son of that old valet who had introduced me to the lady in pink and enabled me, years after, to identify her as Mme Swann.*

At the moment when, the music having come to an end, his guests came to take leave of him, M. de Charlus committed the same error as on their arrival. He did not ask them to shake hands with their hostess, to include her and her husband in the gratitude that was being showered on himself. There was a long procession, a procession which led to the Baron alone, and of which he was clearly aware, for as he said to me a little later: "The form of the artistic celebration ended in a 'few-words-in-the-vestry' touch that was quite amusing." The guests even prolonged their expressions of gratitude with various remarks which enabled them to remain for a moment longer in the Baron's presence, while those who had not yet congratulated him on the success of his party hung around impatiently in the rear. (Several husbands wanted to go; but their wives, snobs even though duchesses, protested:

"No, no, even if we have to wait for an hour, we can't go away without thanking Palamède, who has gone to so much trouble. There's nobody else these days who can give entertainments like this." Nobody would have thought of asking to be introduced to Mme Verdurin any more than to the attendant in a theatre to which some great lady has for one evening brought the entire aristocracy.)

"Were you at Eliane de Montmorency's yesterday, cousin?" asked Mme de Mortemart, seeking an excuse to prolong their conversation.

"As a matter of fact, no; I'm fond of Eliane, but I never can understand her invitations. I must be very dense, I'm afraid," he went on with a beaming smile, while Mme de Mortemart realised that she was to be made the first recipient of "one of Palamède's" as she had often been of "one of Oriane's." "I did indeed receive a card a fortnight ago from the charming Eliane. Above the questionably authentic name of 'Montmorency' was the following kind invitation: 'My dear cousin, will you do me the honour of thinking of me next Friday at half-past nine.' Underneath were written the two less gracious words: 'Czech Quartet.' These seemed to me to be unintelligible, and in any case to have no more connexion with the sentence above than in those letters on the back of which one sees that the writer had begun another with the words 'My dear—' and nothing else, and failed to take a fresh sheet, either from absentmindedness or in order to save paper. I'm fond of Eliane, and so I bore her no ill-will; I merely ignored the strange and inappropriate allusion to a Czech Quartet, and, as I am a methodical man, I placed on my chimneypiece the invitation to think of Madame de Montmorency on Friday at half-past nine. Although renowned for my obedient, punctual and meek nature, as Buffon says of the camel"—at this, laughter seemed to radiate from M. de Charlus, who knew that on the contrary he was regarded as the most impossibly difficult man—"I was a few minutes late (the time that it took me to change my clothes), though without feeling undue remorse, thinking that half-past nine meant ten. At the stroke of ten, in a comfortable dressing-gown, with warm slippers on my feet, I sat down in my chimney corner to think of Eliane as she had requested me, and with an intensity which did not begin to falter until half-past ten. Do tell her, if you will, that I complied strictly with her audacious request. I am sure she will be gratified."

Mme de Mortemart swooned with laughter, in which M. de Charlus joined. "And to-morrow," she went on, oblivious of the fact that she had already long exceeded the time that could reasonably be allotted to her, "are you going to our La Rochefoucauld cousins?"

"Oh, that, now, is quite impossible. They have invited me, and you too, I see, to a thing it is utterly impossible to imagine, which is called, if I am to believe the invitation card, a '*thé dansant*.' I used to be considered pretty nimble when I was young, but I doubt whether I could ever decently have drunk a cup of tea while dancing. And I have never cared to eat or drink in an unseemly fashion. You will remind me that my dancing days are done. But even sitting down comfortably drinking my tea—of the quality of which I am in any case suspicious since it is called 'dancing'—I should be afraid lest other guests younger than myself, and less nimble possibly than I was at their age, might spill their cups over my tails and thus interfere with my pleasure in draining my own."

Nor was M. de Charlus content with leaving Mme Verdurin out of the conversation while he spoke of all manner of subjects (which he seemed to take a delight in developing and varying, for the cruel pleasure which he had always enjoyed of keeping indefinitely "queuing up" on their feet the friends who were waiting with excruciating patience for their turn to come); he even criticised all that part of the entertainment for which Mme Verdurin was responsible. "But, talking of cups, what in the world are those strange little bowls which remind me of the vessels in which, when I was a young man, people used to get sorbets from Poiré Blanche? Somebody said to me just now that they were for 'iced coffee.' But I have seen neither coffee nor ice. What curious little objects, with so ill-defined a purpose!"

While saying this M. de Charlus had placed his white-gloved hands vertically over his lips and cautiously swivelled his eyes with a meaning look as though he were afraid of being heard and even seen by his host and hostess. But this was only a pretence, for in a few minutes he would be offering the same criticisms to the Mistress herself, and a little later would be insolently enjoining her: "No more iced-coffee cups, remember! Give them to one of your friends whose house you wish to disfigure. But warn her not to have them in the drawing-room, or people might think that they had come into the wrong room, the things are so exactly like chamberpots."

"But, cousin," said the guest, lowering her voice too and casting a questioning glance at M. de Charlus, for fear of offending not Mme Verdurin but the Baron himself, "perhaps she doesn't yet quite know these things . . ."

"She shall be taught."

"Oh!" laughed the guest, "she couldn't have a better teacher! She *is* lucky! If you're in charge one can be sure there won't be a false note."

"There wasn't one, if it comes to that, in the music."

"Oh! it was sublime. One of those pleasures which can never be forgotten. Talking of that marvellous violinist," she went on, imagining in her innocence that M. de Charlus was interested in the violin for its own sake, "do you happen to know one whom I heard the other day playing a Fauré sonata wonderfully well. He's called Frank. . . ."

"Oh, he's ghastly," replied M. de Charlus, oblivious of the rudeness of a contradiction which implied that his cousin was lacking in taste. "As far as violinists are concerned, I advise you to confine yourself to mine."

This led to a fresh exchange of glances, at once furtive and watchful, between M. de Charlus and his cousin, for, blushing and seeking by her zeal to repair her blunder, Mme de Morte-mart was about to suggest to M. de Charlus that she might organise an evening to hear Morel play. Now, for her the object of the evening was not to bring an unknown talent into prominence, though this was the object which she would pretend to have in mind and which was indeed that of M. de Charlus. She regarded it simply as an opportunity for giving a particularly elegant reception and was calculating already whom she would invite and whom she would leave out. This process of selection, the chief preoccupation of people who give parties (the people whom "society" journalists have the nerve or the stupidity to call "the élite"), alters at once the expression—and the handwriting—of a hostess more profoundly than any hypnotic suggestion. Before she had even thought of what Morel was to play (which she rightly regarded as a secondary consideration, for even if everybody observed a polite silence during the music, from fear of M. de Charlus, nobody would even think of listening to it), Mme de Mortemart, having decided that Mme de Valcourt was not to be one of the "chosen," had automatically assumed that secretive, conspiratorial air which so degrades even those society women who can most easily afford to ignore what "people will say."

"Might it be possible for me to give a party for people to hear your friend play?" murmured Mme de Mortemart, who, while addressing herself exclusively to M. de Charlus, could not refrain, as though mesmerised, from casting a glance at Mme de Valcourt (the excluded one) in order to make certain that she was sufficiently far away not to hear her. "No, she can't possibly hear what I'm saying," Mme de Mortemart concluded inwardly, reassured by her own glance which in fact had had a totally different effect upon Mme de Valcourt from that intended: "Why," Mme de Valcourt had said to herself when she caught this glance, "Marie-Thérèse is arranging something with Palamède to which I'm not to be invited."

"You mean my protégé," M. de Charlus corrected, as merciless to his cousin's choice of words as he was to her musical endowments. Then, without paying the slightest attention to her mute entreaties, for which she herself apologised with a smile, "Why, yes ..." he said in a voice loud enough to be heard throughout the room, "although there is always a risk in that sort of exportation of a fascinating personality into surroundings that must inevitably diminish his transcendent gifts and would in any case have to be adapted to them."

Mme de Mortemart told herself that the mezza voce, the pianissimo of her question had been a waste of effort, after the megaphone through which the answer had issued. She was mistaken: Mme de Valcourt heard nothing, for the simple reason that she did not understand a single word. Her anxiety subsided, and would quickly have evaporated entirely, had not

Mme de Mortemart, afraid that she might have been given away and might have to invite Mme de Valcourt, with whom she was on too intimate terms to be able to leave her out if the other knew about her party beforehand, raised her eyelids once again in Edith's direction, as though not to lose sight of a threatening peril, lowering them again briskly so as not to commit herself too far. She intended, on the morning after the party, to write her one of those letters, the complement of the revealing glance, letters which are meant to be subtle but are tantamount to a full and signed confession. For instance: "Dear Edith, I've been missing you. I did not really expect you last night" ("How could she have expected me," Edith would say to herself, "since she never invited me?") "as I know that you're not very fond of gatherings of that sort which rather bore you. We should have been greatly honoured, all the same, by your company" (Mme de Mortemart never used the word "honoured," except in letters in which she attempted to cloak a lie in the semblance of truth). "You know that you are always welcome in our house. In any case you were quite right, as it was a complete failure, like everything that is got up at a moment's notice." But already the second furtive glance darted at her had enabled Edith to grasp everything that was concealed by the complicated language of M. de Charlus. This glance was indeed so potent that, after it had struck Mme de Valcourt, the obvious secrecy and intention to conceal that it betrayed rebounded upon a young Peruvian whom Mme de Mortemart intended, on the contrary, to invite. But being of a suspicious nature, seeing all too plainly the mystery that was being made without realising that it was not intended to mystify him, he at once conceived a violent hatred for Mme de Mortemart and vowed to play all sorts of disagreeable hoaxes on her, such as ordering fifty iced coffees to be sent to her house on a day when she was not entertaining, or, on a day when she was, inserting a notice in the papers to the effect that the party was postponed, and publishing mendacious accounts of subsequent parties in which would appear the notorious names of all the people whom for various reasons a hostess does not invite or even allow to be introduced to her.

Mme de Mortemart need not have bothered herself about

Mme de Valcourt. M. de Charlus was about to take it upon himself to denature the projected entertainment far more than that lady's presence would have done. "But, my dear cousin," she said in response to the remark about "adapting the surroundings," the meaning of which her momentary state of hyperaesthesia had enabled her to discern, "we shall spare you the least trouble. I undertake to ask Gilbert to arrange everything."

"Not on any account, and moreover he will not be invited. Nothing will be done except through me. The first thing is to exclude all those who have ears and hear not."

M. de Charlus's cousin, who had been reckoning on Morel as an attraction in order to give a party at which she could say that, unlike so many of her kinswomen, she had "had Palamède," abruptly switched her thoughts from this prestige of M. de Charlus's to all the people with whom he would get her into trouble if he took it upon himself to do the inviting and excluding. The thought that the Prince de Guermantes (on whose account, partly, she was anxious to exclude Mme de Valcourt, whom he declined to meet) was not to be invited alarmed her. Her eyes assumed an uneasy expression.

"Is this rather bright light bothering you?" inquired M. de Charlus with an apparent seriousness the underlying irony of which she failed to perceive.

"No, not at all. I was thinking of the difficulty, not because of me of course, but because of my family, if Gilbert were to hear that I had given a party without inviting him, when he never has half a dozen people in without. . . ."

"But precisely, we must begin by eliminating the half-dozen people, who would only jabber. I'm afraid that the din of talk has prevented you from realising that it was a question not of doing the honours as a hostess but of conducting the rites appropriate to every true celebration."

Then, having decided, not that the next person had been kept waiting too long, but that it did not do to exaggerate the favours shown to one who had in mind not so much Morel as her own visiting-list, M. de Charlus, like a doctor cutting short a consultation when he considers that it has lasted long enough, served notice on his cousin to withdraw, not by bidding her good-night but by turning to the person immediately behind her.

"Good evening, Madame de Montesquiou. It was marvellous, wasn't it? I didn't see Hélène. Tell her that any policy of general abstention, even the most noble, that is to say hers, must allow exceptions, if they are dazzling enough, as has been the case to-night. To show that one is rare is good, but to subordinate one's rarity, which is only negative, to what is precious is better still. In your sister's case—and I value more than anyone her systematic *absence* from places where what is in store for her is not worthy of her—here to-night, on the contrary, her presence at so memorable an occasion as this would have been a precedence, and would have given your sister, already so prestigious, an additional prestige."

Then he turned to a third lady.

I was greatly astonished to see there, as friendly and flattering towards M. de Charlus as he had been curt with him in the past, insisting on being introduced to Charlie and telling him that he hoped he would come and see him, M. d'Argencourt, that terrible scourge of the species of men to which M. de Charlus belonged. At the moment he was living in the thick of them. It was certainly not because he had become one of them himself. But for some time past he had more or less deserted his wife for a young society woman whom he adored. Being intelligent herself, she made him share her taste for intelligent people, and was most anxious to have M. de Charlus to her house. But above all M. d'Argencourt, extremely jealous and somewhat impotent, feeling that he was failing to satisfy his conquest and anxious to keep her amused, could do so without risk to himself only by surrounding her with innocuous men, whom he thus cast in the role of guardians of his seraglio. The latter found that he had become quite pleasant and declared that he was a great deal more intelligent than they had supposed, a discovery that delighted him and his mistress.

The remainder of M. de Charlus's guests drifted away fairly rapidly. Several of them said: "I don't want to go to the sacristy" (the little room in which the Baron, with Charlie by his side, was receiving congratulations, and to which he himself had given the name), "but I must let Palamède see me so that he knows that I stayed to the end." Nobody paid the slightest attention to Mme Verdurin. Some pretended not to recognise her and deliberately said good-night to Mme Cottard, appealing to me for confirmation with a "That *is* Mme Verdurin, isn't it?" Mme d'Arpajon asked me in our hostess's hearing: "Tell me, has there ever been a Monsieur Verdurin?" The duchesses who still lingered, finding none of the oddities they had expected in this place which they had hoped to find more different from what they were used to, made the best of a bad job by going into fits of laughter in front of Elstir's paintings; for everything else, which they found more in keeping than they had expected with what they were already familiar with, they gave the credit to M. de Charlus, saying: "How clever Palamède is at arranging things! If he were to stage a ballet in a shed or a bathroom, it would still be perfectly ravishing." The most noble ladies were those who showed most fervour in congratulating M. de Charlus upon the success of a party of the secret motive for which some of them were not unaware, without however being embarrassed by the knowledge, this class of society—remembering perhaps certain epochs in history when their own families had shown a similarly brazen effrontery--carrying their contempt for scruples almost as far as their respect for etiquette. Several of them engaged Charlie on the spot for different evenings on which he was to come and play them Vinteuil's septet, but it never occurred to any of them to invite Mme Verdurin.

The latter was already blind with fury when M. de Charlus who, his head in the clouds, was incapable of noticing her state, decided that it was only seemly to invite the Mistress to share his joy. And it was perhaps to indulge his taste for literature rather than from an overflow of pride that this specialist in artistic entertainments said to Mme Verdurin: "Well, are you satisfied? I think you have reason to be. You see that when I take it upon myself to organise a festivity there are no half-measures. I don't know whether your heraldic notions enable you to gauge the precise importance of the event, the weight that I have lifted, the volume of air that I have displaced for you. You have had the Queen of Naples, the brother of the King of Bavaria, the three premier peers. If Vinteuil is

Mohammed, we may say that we have brought to him some of the least movable of mountains. Bear in mind that to attend your party the Queen of Naples came up from Neuilly, which is a great deal more difficult for her than it was to leave the Two Sicilies," he added with malicious intent, notwithstanding his admiration for the Queen. "It's an historic event. Just think that it's perhaps the first time she has gone anywhere since the fall of Gaeta. It may well be that the history-books will record as climactic dates the day of the fall of Gaeta and that of the Verdurin reception. The fan that she laid down the better to applaud Vinteuil deserves to become more famous than the fan that Mme de Metternich broke because the audience hissed Wagner."

"In fact she left it here," said Mme Verdurin, momentarily appeased by the memory of the Queen's kindness to her, and she showed M. de Charlus the fan which was lying on a chair.

"Oh, how moving!" exclaimed M. de Charlus, approaching the relic with veneration. "It is all the more touching for being so hideous; the little violet is incredible!" And spasms of emotion and irony ran through him by turns. "Oh dear, I don't know whether you feel these things as I do. Swann would positively have died of convulsions if he had seen it. I know that whatever price it fetches, I shall buy that fan at the sale of the Queen's belongings, for she's bound to be sold up, she hasn't a penny," he went on, for he never ceased to intersperse the cruellest gossip with the most sincere veneration, although they sprang from two opposing natures, which, however, were combined in him. (They might even be brought to bear alternately on the same fact. For the M. de Charlus who from his comfortable position as a rich man jeered at the poverty of the Queen was the same who was often to be heard extolling that poverty and who, when anyone spoke of Princess Murat, Queen of the Two Sicilies, would reply: "I don't know who you mean. There is only one Queen of Naples, a sublime person who does not keep a carriage. But from her omnibus she annihilates every carriage in the street and one could kneel down in the dust on seeing her drive past.") "I shall bequeath it to a museum. In the meantime, it must be sent back to her, so that she need not hire a cab to come and fetch it. The wisest thing, in view of the historical interest of such an object, would be to steal the fan. But that would be awkward for her—since it is probable that she does not possess another!" he added with a shout of laughter. "Anyhow, you see that for my sake she came. And that is not the only miracle I have performed. I don't believe that anyone at the present day has the power to shift the people whom I persuaded to come. However, everyone must be given his due. Charlie and the rest of the musicians played divinely. And, my dear hostess," he added condescendingly, "you yourself have played your part on this occasion. Your name will not go unrecorded. History has preserved that of the page who armed Joan of Arc when she set out for battle. In sum, you served as a connecting link, you made possible the fusion between Vinteuil's music and its inspired interpreter, you had the intelligence to appreciate the cardinal importance of the whole concatenation of circumstances which would enable the interpreter to benefit from the whole weight of a considerable—if I were not referring to myself I might almost say providential—personage, whom you had the good sense to ask to ensure the success of the gathering, to bring before Morel's violin the ears directly attached to the tongues that have the widest hearing; no, no, it's by no means negligible. Nothing is negligible in so complete a realisation. Everything has its part. The Duras was marvellous. In fact, everything; that is why," he concluded, for he could not resist admonishing people, "I set my face against your inviting those human divisors who, among the superior people whom I brought you, would have played the part of the decimal points in a sum, reducing the others to a merely fractional value. I have a very exact appreciation of that sort of thing. You realise that we must avoid social blunders when we are giving a party which is to be worthy of Vinteuil, of his inspired interpreter, of yourself, and, I venture to say, of me. If you had invited the Molé woman, everything would have been spoiled. It would have been the tiny counteracting, neutralising drop which deprives a potion of its virtue. The electric lights would have fused, the pastries would not have arrived in time, the orangeade would have given everybody a stomach-ache.

She was the one person not to have here. At the mere sound
of her name, as in a fairy-tale, not a note would have issued
from the brass; the flute and the oboe would have suddenly
lost their voices. Morel himself, even if he had succeeded in
playing a few bars, would not have been in tune, and instead
of Vinteuil's septet you would have had a parody of it by
Beckmesser, ending amid catcalls. I who believe strongly in
the influence of personalities could feel quite plainly in the
blossoming of a certain *largo*, which opened out like a flower,
and in the supreme fulfilment of the finale, which was not
merely *allegro* but incomparably lively,[14] that the absence of
the Molé was inspiring the musicians and causing the very
instruments to swell with joy. In any case, when one is at home
to queens one does not invite one's concierge."

In calling her "the Molé" (as for that matter he said quite
affectionately "the Duras") M. de Charlus was doing the lady
justice. For all these women were the actresses of society,
and it is true that, even regarding her from this point of view,
the Comtesse Molé did not live up to the extraordinary reputation for intelligence that she had acquired, which reminded one
of those mediocre actors or novelists who at certain periods
are hailed as men of genius, either because of the mediocrity
of their competitors, among whom there is no supreme artist
capable of showing what is meant by true talent, or because of
the mediocrity of the public, which, if any extraordinary
individuality existed, would be incapable of understanding it.
In Mme Molé's case it is preferable, if not entirely accurate,
to settle for the former explanation. The social world being
the realm of nullity, there exist between the merits of different
society women only the most insignificant degrees, which
can however be crazily exaggerated by the rancours or the
imagination of a M. de Charlus. And certainly, if he spoke
as he had just been speaking in this language which was an
affected mixture of artistic and social elements, it was because
his old-womanly rages and his culture as a man of society
provided the genuine eloquence that he possessed with only the
most trivial themes. Since the world of differentials does not
exist on the surface of the earth among all the countries which our
perception renders uniform, all the more reason why it should

not exist in the social "world." But does it exist anywhere? Vinteuil's septet had seemed to tell me that it did. But where?

Since M. de Charlus also enjoyed repeating what one person had said of another, seeking to stir up trouble, to divide and rule, he added: "You have, by not inviting her, deprived Mme Molé of the opportunity of saying: 'I can't think why this Mme Verdurin should have invited me. I can't imagine who these people are, I don't know them.' She was already saying a year ago that you were wearying her with your advances. She's a fool; never invite her again. After all, she's nothing so very wonderful. She can perfectly well come to your house without making a fuss about it, seeing that I come here. In short," he concluded, "it seems to me that you have every reason to thank me, for, as far as it went, the whole thing was perfect. The Duchesse de Guermantes didn't come, but one never knows, perhaps it was better that she didn't. We shan't hold it against her, we'll think of her all the same another time, not that one can help remembering her, her very eyes say to us 'Forget me not!', for they remind one of those flowers" (here I thought to myself how strong the Guermantes spirit—the decision to go to one house and not to another—must be, to have outweighed in the Duchess's mind her fear of Palamède). "Faced with so complete a success, one is tempted like Bernardin de Saint-Pierre to see everywhere the hand of Providence. The Duchesse de Duras was enchanted. She even asked me to tell you so," added M. de Charlus, dwelling upon the words as though Mme Verdurin must regard this as a sufficient honour. Sufficient and indeed scarcely credible, for he thought it necessary, in order to be believed, to add "Yes, indeed," completely carried away by the madness of those whom Jupiter has decided to destroy. "She has engaged Morel to come to her house, where the same programme will be repeated, and I'm even thinking of asking her for an invitation for M. Verdurin." This civility to the husband alone was, although no such idea even occurred to M. de Charlus, the most cruel insult to the wife, who, believing herself to possess with regard to the violinist, by virtue of a sort of ukase which prevailed in the little clan, the right to forbid him to perform elsewhere without her express authorisation, was absolutely determined to forbid his appearance at Mme de Duras's party.

The Baron's volubility was in itself an irritation to Mme Verdurin, who did not like people to form separate conversational groups within the little clan. How often, even at la Raspelière, hearing M. de Charlus talking incessantly to Charlie instead of being content with taking his part in the concerted ensemble of the clan, had she not pointed to him and exclaimed: "What a windbag he is! What a windbag! He really is the most colossal windbag!"?[15] But this time it was far worse. Intoxicated by the sound of his own voice, M. de Charlus failed to realise that by acknowledging Mme Verdurin's role and confining it within narrow limits, he was unleashing that feeling of hatred which was in her only a special, social form of jealousy. Mme Verdurin was genuinely fond of her regular visitors, the faithful of the little clan, but wished them to be entirely devoted to their Mistress. Prepared to make some concessions, like those jealous lovers who will tolerate unfaithfulness, but only under their own roof and even in front of their eyes, that is to say when it scarcely counts as unfaithfulness, she would allow the men to have mistresses or even male lovers, on condition that the affair had no social consequence outside her own house, that the tie was formed and perpetuated in the shelter of her Wednesdays. In the old days, every furtive giggle that came from Odette when she was with Swann had gnawed at Mme Verdurin, and so of late had every aside exchanged by Morel and the Baron; she found one consolation alone for her vexations, which was to destroy the happiness of others. She would have been unable to endure the Baron's for long. And here was that rash individual precipitating the catastrophe by appearing to restrict the Mistress's position in her little clan. Already she could see Morel going into society, without her, under the Baron's aegis. There was only one remedy, to make Morel choose between the Baron and herself, and, taking advantage of the ascendancy that she had acquired over Morel by giving him proof of her extraordinary perspicacity thanks to reports which she commissioned and lies which she herself concocted, all of which served to corroborate what he himself was inclined to believe, and what would in time be made plain to him thanks to the booby-traps which she was preparing and into which her unsuspecting victims would fall—taking advantage of this ascendancy, to make him choose herself in preference to the Baron. As for the society ladies who had been present and had not even asked to be introduced to her, as soon as she grasped their hesitations or indifference, she had said: "Ah! I see what they are, the sort of old frumps that don't fit in with us. It's the last time they'll set foot in this house." For she would have died rather than admit that anyone had been less civil to her than she had hoped.

"Ah! my dear General," M. de Charlus suddenly exclaimed, abandoning Mme Verdurin on catching sight of General Deltour, Secretary to the Presidency of the Republic, who might be of great value in securing Charlie his medal, and who, after asking Cottard for a piece of advice, was slipping away. "Good evening, my dear, delightful friend. Trying to get away without saying good-bye to me, eh?" said the Baron with a genial, self-satisfied smile, for he knew quite well that people were always glad to stay a little longer to talk to him. And as, in his present state of exhilaration, he would answer his own questions in a shrill tone: "Well, did you enjoy it? Wasn't it really beautiful? The andante, what? It's the most touching thing that was ever written. I defy anyone to listen to the end without tears in his eyes. Charming of you to have come. By the way, I had the most excellent telegram this morning from Froberville, who tells me that as far as the Chancellery of the Legion goes the difficulties have been smoothed over, as they say." M. de Charlus's voice continued to rise, as piercing, as different from his normal voice, as that of a barrister grandiloquently addressing the court: a phenomenon of vocal amplification through over-excitement and nervous euphoria analogous to that which, at her own dinner-parties, raised to so high a pitch the voice and gaze alike of Mme de Guermantes.

"I intended to send you a note to-morrow by messenger to tell you of my enthusiasm, until I could find an opportunity to speak to you, but you were so popular! Froberville's support is not to be despised, but for my own part, I have the Minister's promise," said the General.

"Ah! excellent. Anyhow you've seen for yourself that it's no more than what such talent deserves. Hoyos was delighted. I didn't manage to see the Ambassadress. Was she pleased? Who would not have been, except those that have ears and hear not, which doesn't matter so long as they have tongues and can speak."

Taking advantage of the Baron's having moved away to speak to the General, Mme Verdurin beckoned to Brichot. The latter, who did not know what she was about to say, sought to amuse her, and without suspecting the anguish that he was causing me, said to the Mistress: "The Baron is delighted that Mlle Vinteuil and her friend didn't come. They shock him terribly. He declares that their morals are appalling. You can't imagine how prudish and severe the Baron is on moral questions." Contrary to Brichot's expectation, Mme Verdurin was not amused: "He's unspeakable," was her answer. "Suggest to him that he should come and smoke a cigarette with you, so that my husband can get hold of his Dulcinea without his noticing and warn him of the abyss that is yawning at his feet."

Brichot seemed to hesitate.

"I don't mind telling you," Mme Verdurin went on, to remove his final scruples, "that I don't feel at all safe with a man like that in the house. I know he's been involved in some nasty business and the police have their eye on him." And, as she had a certain talent for improvisation when inspired by malice, Mme Verdurin did not stop at this: "Apparently he's been in prison. Yes, yes, I've been told by people who knew all about it. In any case I know from a person who lives in his street that you can't imagine the ruffians he brings to his house." And as Brichot, who often went to the Baron's, began to protest, Mme Verdurin, growing more and more animated, exclaimed: "But I assure you! You can take my word for it," an expression with which she habitually sought to give weight to an assertion flung out more or less at random. "He'll be found murdered in his bed one of these days, as those people always are. It may not quite come to that, perhaps, because he's in the clutches of that Jupien whom he had the impudence to send to me and who's an ex-convict—yes, really,

I know it for a positive fact. He has a hold on him because of some letters which are perfectly dreadful, it seems. I got it from somebody who has seen them and who told me: 'You'd be sick on the spot if you saw them.' That's how Jupien gets him to toe the line and makes him cough up all the money he wants. I'd sooner die than live in the state of terror Charlus lives in. In any case, if Morel's family decides to bring an action against him, I've no desire to be dragged in as an accessory. If he goes on, it will be at his own risk, but I shall have done my duty. What is one to do? It's no joke, I can tell you."

And, already agreeably excited at the thought of her husband's impending conversation with the violinist, Mme Verdurin said to me: "Ask Brichot whether I'm not a courageous friend, and whether I'm not capable of sacrificing myself to save my comrades." (She was alluding to the circumstances in which she had forced him in the nick of time to break first of all with his laundress and then with Mme de Cambremer, as a result of which Brichot had gone almost completely blind and, people said, had taken to morphine.)

"An incomparable friend, farsighted and valiant," replied the Professor with ingenuous fervour.

"Mme Verdurin prevented me from doing something extremely foolish," Brichot told me when she had left us. "She doesn't hesitate to strike at the roots. She's an interventionist, as our friend Cottard would say. I admit, however, that the thought that the poor Baron is still unconscious of the blow that is about to fall upon him distresses me deeply. He's completely mad about that boy. If Mme Verdurin succeeds, there's a man who is going to be very miserable. However, I'm not at all sure she won't fail. I fear that she may only succeed in sowing discord between them, which in the end, without separating them, will only make them break with her."

It was often thus with Mme Verdurin and her faithful. But it was evident that the need she felt to preserve their friendship was more and more dominated by the requirement that this friendship should never be thwarted by the friendship they might feel for one another. She had no objection to homosexuality so long as it did not tamper with the orthodoxy of the little clan, but, like the Church, she preferred any sacrifice rather than a concession on orthodoxy. I was beginning to be afraid that her irritation with myself might be due to her having heard that I had prevented Albertine from going to her that day, and that she might presently set to work, if she had not already begun, upon the same task of separating her from me which her husband, in the case of Charlus, was now going to attempt with the violinist.

"Come along, get hold of Charlus, find some excuse, there's no time to lose," said Mme Verdurin, "and whatever you do, don't let him come back here until I send for you. Ah! what an evening," she added, revealing the true cause of her rage. "Performing a masterpiece in front of those nitwits. I don't include the Queen of Naples, she's intelligent, she's a nice woman" (which meant: "She was nice to me"). "But the others. Ah! it's enough to drive you mad. After all, I'm no longer a schoolgirl. When I was young, people used to tell me that one had to put up with a bit of boredom, so I made an effort; but now, ah! no, I just can't help it, I'm old enough to do as I please, life's too short. Allow myself to be bored stiff, listen to idiots, smile, pretend to think them intelligent—no, I simply can't do it. Come along, Brichot, there's no time to lose."

"I'm going, Madame, I'm going," said Brichot, as General Deltour moved away. But first of all the Professor took me aside for a moment: "Moral Duty," he said, "is less clearly imperative than our Ethics teach us. Whatever the theosophical coffee-houses and the Kantian beer-cellars may say, we are deplorably ignorant of the nature of the Good. I myself who, without wishing to boast, have lectured to my pupils, in all innocence, on the philosophy of the aforesaid Immanuel Kant, can see no precise directive for the case of social casuistry with which I am now confronted in that *Critique of Practical Reason* in which the great unfrocked priest of Protestantism platonised in the Teutonic manner for a prehistorically sentimental and aulic Germany, in the obscure interests of a Pomeranian mysticism. It's the *Symposium* once again, but held this time at Königsberg, in the local style, indigestible and chaste, and reeking of sauerkraut and without any good-looking boys. It is obvious on the one hand that I cannot refuse our excellent hostess the small service that she asks of me, in fully orthodox conformity with traditional Morality. One must avoid above all else—for there are few things that engender more inanities than that one—letting oneself be duped by words. But after all, one cannot but admit that if mothers were entitled to vote, the Baron would run the risk of being lamentably blackballed for the Chair of Virtue. It is unfortunately with the temperament of a rake that he pursues the vocation of a pedagogue. Mind you, I don't wish to speak ill of the Baron. He can be as amusing as a superior clown, whereas with the average colleague of mine, Academician though he be, I am bored, as Xenophon would say, at a hundred drachmas to the hour. Moreover this gentle man, who can carve a joint like nobody else, combines with a genius for anathema a wealth of kindness. But I fear that he is expending upon Morel rather more than a wholesome morality would enjoin, and without knowing to what extent the young penitent shows himself docile or recalcitrant to the special exercises which his catechist imposes upon him by way of mortification, one does not have to be a genius to be aware that we should be erring, as they say, on the side of indulgence with regard to this Rosicrucian who seems to have come down to us from Petronius by way of Saint-Simon, if we granted him with our eyes shut, duly signed and sealed, a licence to satanise. And yet, in keeping this man occupied while Mme Verdurin, for the sinner's good and indeed justly tempted by such a cure of souls, proceeds—by speaking unequivocally to the young harum-scarum—to remove from him all that he loves, to deal him perhaps a fatal blow, it seems to me that I am leading him into what might be termed an ambush, and I recoil from it as though from an act of treachery."

This said, he did not hesitate to commit it, but, taking me by the arm, approached M. de Charlus: "Shall we go and smoke a cigarette, Baron. This young man hasn't yet seen all the marvels of the house." I made the excuse that I was obliged to go home. "Wait just another minute," said Brichot. "You know you're supposed to be giving me a lift, and I haven't forgotten your promise." "Are you sure you wouldn't like me to get them to show you the silver plate? Nothing could be simpler," said M. de Charlus. "You promised me, remember, not a word about Morel's decoration. I mean to give him a surprise by announcing it presently when people have begun to leave, although he says that it is of no importance to an artist, but that his uncle would like him to have it" (I blushed, for the Verdurins knew through my grandfather who Morel's uncle was). "Then you wouldn't like me to get them to bring out the best pieces?" said M. de Charlus. "But you know them already, you've seen them a dozen times at la Raspelière."

I did not tell him that what might have interested me was not the mediocre glitter of even the most opulent bourgeois silver, but some specimen, were it only reproduced in a fine engraving, of Mme du Barry's. I was far too preoccupied and—even without this revelation as to Mlle Vinteuil's expected presence—always, in society, far too distracted and agitated to fasten my attention on objects, however beautiful. It could have been arrested only by the appeal of some reality that addressed itself to my imagination, as might have done, this evening, a picture of that Venice of which I had thought so much during the afternoon, or some general element, common to several aspects and truer than they, which, of its own accord, never failed to awake in me an inner spirit, habitually dormant, the ascent of which to the surface of my consciousness filled me with joy. Now, as I emerged from the room known as the concert-room and crossed the other drawing-rooms with Brichot and M. de Charlus, on discovering, transposed among others, certain pieces of furniture which I had seen at la Raspelière and to which I had paid no attention, I perceived, between the arrangement of the town house and that of the country house, a certain family resemblance, a permanent identity, and I understood what Brichot meant when he said to me with a smile: "There, look at this room, it may perhaps give you an idea of what things were like in the Rue Montalivet, twenty-five years ago, *grande mortalis aevi spatium.*" From his smile, a tribute to the defunct salon which he saw with his mind's eye, I understood that what Brichot, perhaps without realising it, preferred in the old drawing-room, more than the large windows, more than the gay youth of his hosts and their faithful, was that unreal aspect (which I myself could discern

from certain similarities between la Raspelière and the Quai
Conti) of which, in a drawing-room as in everything else, the
actual, external aspect, verifiable by everyone, is but the prolongation, the aspect which has detached itself from the outer
world to take refuge in our soul, to which it gives as it were a
surplus-value, in which it is absorbed into its habitual substance, transforming itself—houses that have been pulled down,
people long dead, bowls of fruit at suppers which we recall
—into that translucent alabaster of our memories of which
we are incapable of conveying the colour which we alone can
see, so that we can truthfully say to other people, when speaking of these things of the past, that they can have no conception
of them, that they are unlike anything they have seen, and that
we ourselves cannot inwardly contemplate without a certain
emotion, reflecting that it is on the existence of our thoughts
that their survival for a little longer depends, the gleam of
lamps that have been extinguished and the fragrance of arbours
that will never bloom again. And doubtless for this reason, the
drawing-room in the Rue Montalivet diminished, for Brichot,
the Verdurins' present home. But on the other hand it added
to this home, in the Professor's eyes, a beauty which it could
not have in those of a newcomer. Those pieces of the original
furniture that had been transplanted here, and sometimes arranged in the same groups, and which I myself remembered
from la Raspelière, introduced into the new drawing-room
fragments of the old which recalled it at moments to the point
of hallucination and then seemed themselves scarcely real
from having evoked in the midst of the surrounding reality
fragments of a vanished world which one seemed to see
elsewhere. A sofa that had risen up from dreamland between a
pair of new and thoroughly substantial armchairs, little chairs
upholstered in pink silk, the brocaded covering of a card-
table raised to the dignity of a person since, like a person, it
had a past, a memory, retaining in the chill and gloom of the
Quai Conti the tan of its sun-warming through the windows of
the Rue Montalivet (where it could tell the time of day as
accurately as Mme Verdurin herself) and through the glass
doors at la Raspelière, where they had taken it and where it
used to gaze out all day long over the flower-beds of the garden

at the valley below, until it was time for Cottard and the
violinist to sit down to their game; a bouquet of violets and
pansies in pastel, the gift of a painter friend, now dead, the
sole surviving fragment of a life that had vanished without
leaving any trace, epitomising a great talent and a long friendship, recalling his gentle, searching eyes, his shapely, plump
and melancholy hand as he painted it; the attractively disordered clutter of the presents from the faithful which had
followed the lady of the house from place to place and had
come in time to assume the fixity of a trait of character, of a
line of destiny; the profusion of cut flowers, of chocolate-
boxes, which here as in the country systematised their efflorescence in accordance with an identical mode of blossoming;
the curious interpolation of those singular and superfluous
objects which still appear to have just been taken from the
box in which they were offered and remain for ever what they
were at first, New Year presents; all those things, in short,
which one could not have isolated from the rest but which for
Brichot, an old habitué of Verdurin festivities, had that patina,
that velvety bloom of things to which, giving them a sort
of depth, a spiritual *Doppelgänger* has come to be attached—
all this sent echoing round him so many scattered chords,
as it were, awakening in his heart cherished resemblances,
confused reminiscences which, here in this actual drawing-
room that was speckled with them, cut out, defined, delimited
—as on a fine day a shaft of sunlight cuts a section in the atmosphere—the furniture and carpets, pursued, from a cushion to a
flower-stand, from a footstool to a lingering scent, from a
lighting arrangement to a colour scheme, sculpted, evoked,
spiritualised, called to life, a form which was as it were the
idealisation, immanent in each of their successive homes, of the
Verdurin drawing-room.

"We must try," Brichot whispered in my ear, "to get the
Baron on to his favourite topic. He's prodigious." Now on the
one hand I was glad of an opportunity to try to obtain from
M. de Charlus information as to the movements of Mlle
Vinteuil and her friend, information for which I had decided
to leave Albertine that evening. On the other hand, I did not
wish to leave the latter too long alone, not that she could (being

uncertain of the moment of my return, not to mention that, at so late an hour, she could not have received a visitor or left the house herself without being noticed) make any nefarious use of my absence, but simply so that she might not find it too prolonged. And so I told Brichot and M. de Charlus that I must shortly leave them.

"Come with us all the same," said the Baron, whose social excitement was beginning to flag, but feeling that need to prolong, to spin out a conversation, which I had already observed in the Duchesse de Guermantes as well as in himself, and which, while peculiarly characteristic of their family, extends in a more general fashion to all those who, offering their minds no other fulfilment than talk, that is to say an imperfect fulfilment, remain unsatisfied even after hours in company and attach themselves more and more hungrily to their exhausted interlocutor, from whom they mistakenly expect a satiety which social pleasures are incapable of giving. "Come, won't you," he repeated. "This is the pleasant moment at a party, the moment when all the guests have gone, the hour of Doña Sol; let us hope that it will end less tragically.[16] Unfortunately you're in a hurry, in a hurry, no doubt, to go and do things which you would much better leave undone. People are always in a hurry, and leave at the moment when they ought to be arriving. We're like Couture's philosophers,[17] this is the time to go over the events of the evening, to carry out what is called in military parlance a review of operations. We might ask Mme Verdurin to send us in a little supper to which we should take care not to invite her, and we might request Charlie—still *Hernani*—to play for us alone the sublime *adagio*. Isn't it simply beautiful, that *adagio*? But where *is* the young violinist, I should like to congratulate him; this is the moment for tender words and embraces. Do admit, Brichot, that they played like gods, Morel especially. Did you notice the moment when that lock of hair came loose? Ah, my dear fellow, then you saw nothing at all. There was an F sharp which was enough to make Enesco, Capet and Thibaud die of jealousy. Calm though I am, I don't mind telling you that at the sound of it I had such a lump in the throat I could scarcely control my tears. The whole room sat breathless. Brichot, my dear fellow," cried the Baron, gripping the other's arm and shaking it violently, "it was sublime. Only young Charlie preserved a stony immobility, you couldn't even see him breathe, he looked like one of those objects of the inanimate world of which Théodore Rousseau speaks, which make us think but do not think themselves. And then all of a sudden," cried M. de Charlus with a grandiloquent gesture as though miming a *coup de théâtre*, "then, the Forelock! And meanwhile, the graceful little quadrille of the *allegro vivace*. You know, that lock was a revelatory sign even for the most obtuse. The Princess of Taormina, deaf until then, for there are none so deaf as those that have ears and hear not, the Princess of Taormina, confronted by the message of the miraculous fore-lock, suddenly realised that it was music they were playing and not poker. Oh, that was indeed a solemn moment."

"Forgive me for interrupting you, Monsieur," I said to M. de Charlus, hoping to bring him to the subject in which I was interested, "you told me that the composer's daughter was to be present. I should have been most interested to meet her. Are you certain she was expected?"

"Oh, that I couldn't say."

M. de Charlus thus complied, perhaps involuntarily, with that universal rule by which one withholds information from a jealous lover, whether with the absurd intention of proving oneself a "good pal"—as a point of honour, and even if one hates her—to the woman who has excited his jealousy, or out of malice towards her because one guesses that jealousy would only intensify his love, or from that need to be disagreeable to other people which consists in telling the truth to the rest of the world but concealing it from the jealous, ignorance increasing their torment, or so at least they suppose—and in order to cause people pain one is guided by what they themselves believe, wrongly perhaps, to be most painful.

"You know," he went on, "in this house they're a trifle prone to exaggerate. They're charming people, but still they do like to entice celebrities of one sort or another. But you're not looking well, and you'll catch cold in this damp room," he said, pushing a chair towards me. "Since you haven't been well, you must take care of yourself. Let me go and fetch your coat. No, don't go for it yourself, you'll lose your way and catch cold. How careless people are; you might be an infant in arms, you want an old nanny like me to look after you." "Don't worry, Baron, I'll go," said Brichot, and went off at once: not being precisely aware perhaps of the very warm affection that M. de Charlus had for me and of the charming lapses into simplicity and devotedness that alternated with his frenzied outbursts of arrogance and persecution mania, he was afraid lest the Baron, whom Mme Verdurin had entrusted like a prisoner to his vigilance, might simply be seeking, under the pretext of asking for my overcoat, to return to Morel, and might thus upset the Mistress's plan.

Meanwhile Ski had sat down, uninvited, at the piano, and assuming—with a playful knitting of his brows, a distant gaze and a slight twist of his lips—what he imagined to be an artistic air, was insisting that Morel should play something by Bizet. "What, you don't like it, that boyish side to Bizet's music? Why, my dearr fellow," he said, with that rolling of the *r* which was one of his peculiarities, "it's rravishing." Morel, who did not like Bizet, said so in exaggerated terms and (as he had the reputation in the little clan of being, though it seems incredible, a wit) Ski, pretending to take the violinist's diatribes as paradoxes, burst out laughing. His laugh was not, like M. Verdurin's, the choking fit of a smoker. Ski first of all assumed a subtle air, then let out, as though in spite of himself, a single note of laughter, like the first clang from a belfry, followed by a silence in which the subtle look seemed to be judiciously examining the comic quality of what was said; then a second peal of laughter shook the air, followed presently by a merry angelus.

I expressed to M. de Charlus my regret that M. Brichot should have put himself out on my behalf. "Not at all, he's delighted. He's very fond of you, everyone's fond of you. Somebody was saying only the other day: 'But we never see him now, he's cut himself off.' Besides, he's such a good fellow, Brichot," M. de Charlus went on, doubtless never suspecting, in view of the frank and affectionate manner in which the Professor of Moral Philosophy conversed with

him, that he had no hesitation in pulling him to pieces behind
his back. "He is a man of great merit, immensely learned, and
his learning hasn't shrivelled him up, hasn't turned him into a
pedantic bookworm like so many of them. He has retained a
breadth of outlook, a tolerance, rare in his kind. Sometimes,
when one sees how well he understands life, with what a
natural grace he renders everyone his due, one wonders where
a humble little Sorbonne professor, an ex-schoolmaster, can
have picked it all up. I'm astonished at it myself."

I was even more astonished to see the conversation of this
Brichot, which the least discriminating of Mme de Guermantes's guests would have found so dull and heavy, impressing the most critical of them all, M. de Charlus. Among
the influences that had contributed towards this result were
those, in other respects different, by virtue of which Swann
had on the one hand so long enjoyed the company of the little
clan, when he was in love with Odette, and on the other hand,
after he married, seen an attraction in Mme Bontemps who,
pretending to adore the Swanns, came constantly to call on the
wife, revelled in the husband's stories, and spoke of them with
scorn. Like a writer who gives the palm for intelligence, not
to the most intelligent man, but to the worldling who utters a
bold and tolerant comment on the passion of a man for a
woman, a comment which makes the writer's blue-stocking
mistress agree with him in deciding that of all the people
who come to her house the least stupid is after all this old
beau who is experienced in matters of love, so M. de Charlus
found more intelligent than the rest of his friends Brichot,
who was not merely kind to Morel, but would cull from the
Greek philosophers, the Latin poets, the oriental storytellers,
appropriate texts which decorated the Baron's propensity
with a strange and charming florilegium. M. de Charlus had
reached the age at which a Victor Hugo chooses to surround
himself mainly with Vacqueries and Meurices.[18] He preferred
to all others those men who tolerated his outlook upon life.
"I see a great deal of him," he went on in a measured squeak,
allowing no movement save of his lips to disturb the grave,
powdered mask of his face, over which his ecclesiastical eyelids were deliberately lowered. "I attend his lectures: that

Latin Quarter atmosphere refreshes me: there's a studious, thoughtful breed of young bourgeois, more intelligent, better read than were, in a different milieu, my own contemporaries. It's another world, which you know probably better than I do: they're young *bourgeois*," he said, detaching the last word to which he prefixed a string of *b*s, and emphasising it from a sort of elocutionary habit, itself corresponding to a taste for fine shades of meaning that was peculiar to him, but perhaps also from inability to resist the pleasure of giving me a flick of his insolence. This did not in any way diminish the great and affectionate pity that M. de Charlus inspired in me (after Mme Verdurin had revealed her plan in my hearing); it merely amused me, and, even in circumstances when I did not feel so kindly disposed towards him, would not have offended me. I derived from my grandmother such a want of self-importance as could easily make me seem lacking in dignity. Doubtless I was little aware of this, and by dint of having seen and heard, from my schooldays onwards, my most highly regarded companions refuse to tolerate an affront, refuse to overlook disloyal behaviour, I had come in time to exhibit in my speech and actions a second nature which was tolerably proud. It was indeed considered to be extremely proud, because, being not in the least timorous, I was easily provoked into duels, the moral prestige of which, however, I diminished by making little of them, which easily persuaded other people that they were absurd. But the true nature which we repress continues nevertheless to abide within us. Thus it is that at times, if we read the latest masterpiece of a man of genius, we are delighted to find in it all those of our own reflexions which we have despised, joys and sorrows which we have repressed, a whole world of feelings we have scorned, and whose value the book in which we discover them afresh suddenly teaches us. I had come to learn from my experience of life that it was a mistake to smile a friendly smile when somebody made fun of me, instead of getting angry. But this absence of self-importance and resentment, if I had so far ceased to express it as to have become almost entirely unaware that it existed in me, was nevertheless the primordial vital element in which I was steeped. Anger and spite came to me only in a wholly different manner, in fits of rage. What was more, the notion of justice, to the extent of a complete absence of moral sense, was unknown to me. I was in my heart of hearts entirely on the side of the weaker party, and of anyone who was in trouble. I had no opinion as to the proportion in which good and evil might be blended in the relations between Morel and M. de Charlus, but the thought of the sufferings that were in store for M. de Charlus was intolerable to me. I would have liked to warn him, but did not know how to do so.

"The spectacle of that industrious little world is very pleasing to an old stick like myself. I do not know them," he went on, raising his hand with a deprecatory air, in order not to appear to be boasting, to testify to his own purity and not to allow any suspicion to hover over that of the students—"but they are most polite, they often go so far as to keep a place for me, since I'm a very old gentleman. Yes indeed, my dear boy, do not protest, I'm past forty," said the Baron, who was past sixty. "It's a trifle stuffy in the hall in which Brichot lectures, but it's always an interesting experience."

Although the Baron preferred to mingle with the scholarly young and indeed to be jostled by them, sometimes, to save him a long wait in the lecture-room, Brichot took him in by his own door. For all that Brichot was at home in the Sorbonne, at the moment when the beadle, loaded with his chains of office, stepped out before him, and the master so admired by his young students followed, he could not overcome a certain shyness, and much as he desired to profit by that moment in which he felt himself so important to display his affability towards Charlus, he was nevertheless slightly embarrassed; so that the beadle should allow him in, he said to him in an artificial tone and with a busy air: "Follow me, Baron, they'll find a place for you," then, without paying any further attention to him, to make his own entry he advanced briskly and alone down the aisle. On either side, a double hedge of young lecturers bowed to him; Brichot, anxious not to appear to be posing in front of these young men, in whose eyes he knew that he was a great pundit, bestowed on them countless winks, countless little nods of complicity, to which his desire to remain martial and thoroughly French gave the

effect of a sort of cordial encouragement, the *sursum corda* of
an old soldier saying: "We'll fight them, God damn it!" Then
the applause of the students broke out. Brichot sometimes
extracted from this attendance by M. de Charlus at his lectures
an opportunity for giving pleasure, almost for returning
hospitality. He would say to some parent, or to one of his
bourgeois friends: "If it would interest your wife or daughter,
I may tell you that the Baron de Charlus, Prince d'Agrigente,
a scion of the House of Condé, will be attending my lecture.
For a young person, to have seen one of the last descendants
of our aristocracy who preserves the type will be a memory to
cherish. If they care to come, they will recognise him from the
fact that he'll be seated next to my rostrum. Besides, he'll be
the only one, a stout man, with white hair and black moustaches, wearing the military medal." "Oh, thank you," the
father would say; and although his wife had other things to do,
in order not to offend Brichot he would force her to attend the
lecture, while the daughter, troubled by the heat and the
crowd, nevertheless gazed intently at the descendant of Condé,
surprised that he was not wearing a ruff and that he looked just
like a man of the present day. He, meanwhile, had no eyes for
her, but more than one student, who did not know who he
was, would be astonished at his friendly glances and become
self-conscious and stiff, and the Baron would depart full of
dreams and melancholy.

"Forgive me if I return to the subject," I said quickly to
M. de Charlus, for I could hear Brichot returning, "but could
you let me know by wire if you should hear that Mlle Vinteuil
or her friend is expected in Paris, letting me know exactly
how long they will be staying and without telling anybody
that I asked you."

I had almost ceased to believe that she had been expected,
but I wanted thus to be forewarned for the future.

"Yes, I will do that for you. First of all because I owe you
a great debt of gratitude. By not accepting what I proposed to
you long ago, you rendered me, to your own loss, an immense
service: you left me my liberty. It is true that I have abdicated
it in another fashion," he added in a melancholy tone which
betrayed a desire to confide in me. "But it's something that I

continue to regard as a major factor, a whole combination of
circumstances which you failed to turn to your own account,
possibly because fate warned you at that precise minute not
to obstruct my path. For always man proposes and God dis-
poses. If, that day when we came away together from Mme
de Villeparisis's, you had accepted, perhaps—who knows?
—many things that have since happened would never have
occurred."

In some embarrassment, I turned the conversation by
seizing on the name of Mme de Villeparisis, and saying how
sad I had been to hear of her death.[19] "Ah, yes," M. de Charlus
muttered drily and insolently, taking note of my condolences
without appearing to believe in their sincerity for a moment.
Seeing that in any case the subject of Mme de Villeparisis was
not painful to him, I sought to find out from him, since he was
so well qualified in every respect, for what reasons she had
been held at arm's length by the aristocratic world. Not only
did he not give me the solution to this little social problem,
he did not even appear to be aware of it. I then realised that the
position of Mme de Villeparisis, which was in later years to
appear great to posterity, and even in the Marquise's lifetime
to the ignorant commonalty, had appeared no less great—at the
opposite extremity of society, that which touched Mme de
Villeparisis—to the Guermantes family. She was their aunt;
they saw first and foremost birth, connexions by marriage, the
opportunity of impressing this or that sister-in-law with the
importance of their family. They saw it all less from the
social than from the family point of view. Now this was more
lustrous in the case of Mme de Villeparisis than I had supposed. I had been struck when I heard that the title Villeparisis
was falsely assumed. But there are other examples of great
ladies who have married beneath them and preserved a leading
position in society. M. de Charlus began by informing me that
Mme de Villeparisis was a niece of the famous Duchesse
de ——, the most celebrated member of the higher aristocracy
during the July Monarchy, who had nevertheless refused to
associate with the Citizen King and his family. I had so longed
to hear stories about this duchess! And Mme de Villeparisis,
the kind Mme de Villeparisis, with those cheeks that for me

had represented the cheeks of a middle-class lady, Mme de Villeparisis who sent me so many presents and whom I could so easily have seen every day, Mme de Villeparisis was her niece, brought up by her, in her very home, in the Hôtel de ——.

"She asked the Duc de Doudeauville," M. de Charlus told me, "speaking of the three sisters, 'Which of the sisters do you prefer?' And when Doudeauville said: 'Mme de Villeparisis,' the Duchesse de —— replied 'Pig!' For the Duchess was extremely *witty*," said M. de Charlus, giving the word the importance and the special emphasis that was customary among the Guermantes. That he should find the expression so "witty" did not moreover surprise me, for I had on many other occasions remarked the centrifugal, objective tendency which leads men to abjure, when they are relishing the wit of others, the severity with which they would judge their own, and to observe and treasure what they would have scorned to create.

"But what on earth is he doing. That's my overcoat he's bringing," he said, on seeing that Brichot had made so long a search to no better effect. "I would have done better to go myself. However, you can put it over your shoulders. Are you aware that it's highly compromising, my dear boy, it's like drinking out of the same glass: I shall be able to read your thoughts. No, not like that, come, let me do it," and arranging his overcoat round me, he smoothed it over my shoulders, fastened it round my throat, and brushed my chin with his hand apologetically. "At his age, he doesn't know how to put on a coat, one has to cosset him. I've missed my vocation, Brichot, I was born to be a nanny."

I wanted to leave, but M. de Charlus having expressed his intention of going in search of Morel, Brichot detained us both. Moreover, the certainty that when I went home I should find Albertine there, a certainty as absolute as that which I had felt in the afternoon that she would return home from the Trocadéro, made me at this moment as little impatient to see her as I had been then, while sitting at the piano after Françoise had telephoned me. And it was this sense of security that enabled me, whenever, in the course of this conversation, I attempted to rise, to obey the injunctions of Brichot who was afraid that my departure might prevent Charlus from remaining until Mme Verdurin came to fetch us.

"Come," he said to the Baron, "stay with us a little longer, you shall give him the accolade presently." Brichot focused upon me as he spoke his almost sightless eyes, to which the many operations that he had undergone had restored some degree of life, but which no longer had the mobility necessary to the sidelong expression of malice.

"The accolade, how absurd!" cried the Baron, in a shrill and rapturous tone. "I tell you, dear boy, he always imagines he's at a prize-giving, he day-dreams about his young pupils. I often wonder whether he doesn't sleep with them."

"You wish to meet Mlle Vinteuil," said Brichot, who had overheard the last words of our conversation. "I promise to let you know if she comes. I shall hear of it from Mme Verdurin." For he doubtless foresaw that the Baron was in grave danger of imminent expulsion from the little clan.

"I see, so you think that I have less claim than yourself upon Mme Verdurin," said M. de Charlus, "to be informed of the arrival of these terribly disreputable persons. They're quite notorious, you know. Mme Verdurin is wrong to allow them to come here, they're only fit for low company. They're friends with a terrible gang, and they must meet in the most appalling places."

At each of these words, my anguish was augmented by a new anguish, and its aspect constantly changed. And, suddenly remembering certain gestures of impatience which Albertine instantly repressed, I was terrified that she had already conceived a plan to leave me. This suspicion made it all the more necessary for me to prolong our life together until such time as I should have recovered my serenity. And in order to rid Albertine of the idea, if she entertained it, of forestalling my plan to break with her, in order to make her chains seem lighter until I could put my intention into practice without too much pain, the shrewd thing to do (perhaps I was infected by the presence of M. de Charlus, by the unconscious memory of the play-acting he liked to indulge in), the shrewd thing to do seemed to be to give Albertine to understand that I myself intended to leave her. As soon as I returned home, I would simulate farewells, a final rupture.

"Of course I don't think I have more influence with Mme Verdurin than you do," Brichot emphatically declared, afraid that he might have aroused the Baron's suspicions. And seeing that I was anxious to leave, he sought to detain me with the bait of the promised entertainment: "There is one thing which the Baron seems to me not to have taken into account when he speaks of the reputation of these two ladies, namely that a person's reputation may be at the same time appalling and undeserved. Thus for instance, in the more notorious of these groups which I may venture to call unofficial, it is certain that miscarriages of justice are many and that history has recorded convictions for sodomy against illustrious men who were wholly innocent of the charge. The recent discovery of Michelangelo's passionate love for a woman is a fresh fact which should entitle the friend of Leo X to the benefit of a posthumous acquittal. The Michelangelo case seems to me to be eminently calculated to excite the snobs and mobilise the hoi polloi when another case, in which anarchy was all the rage and became the fashionable sin of our worthy dilettantes, but which must not even be mentioned now for fear of stirring up quarrels, shall have run its course."

From the moment Brichot had begun to speak of masculine reputations, M. de Charlus had betrayed all over his features that special sort of impatience which one sees on the face of a medical or military expert when society people who know nothing about the subject begin to talk nonsense about points of therapeutics or strategy.

"You don't know the first thing about these matters," he finally said to Brichot. "Give me a single example of an undeserved reputation. Mention a few names . . . Yes, I know it all," he retorted vehemently to a timid interruption by Brichot, "the people who tried it once long ago out of curiosity, or out of affection for a dead friend, and the person who's afraid he has gone too far, and if you speak to him of the beauty of a man, replies that it's all Greek to him, that he can no more distinguish between a beautiful man and an ugly one than between the engines of two motor-cars, mechanics not being in his line. That's all stuff and nonsense. Mind you, I don't mean to say that a bad (or what is conventionally so called) and yet undeserved reputation is absolutely impossible. But it's so exceptional, so rare, that for practical purposes it doesn't exist. At the same time, I who am by nature inquisitive and enjoy ferreting things out, have known cases which were not mythical. Yes, in the course of my life I have verified (I mean scientifically verified—I'm not talking hot air) two unjustified reputations. They generally arise from a similarity of names, or from certain outward signs, a profusion of rings, for instance, which persons who are not qualified to judge imagine to be characteristic of what you were mentioning, just as they think that a peasant never utters a sentence without adding 'jarniguié,' or an Englishman 'Goddam.' It's the conventionalism of the boulevard theatre. What will surprise you is that the unjustified reputations are those most firmly established in the eyes of the public. You yourself, Brichot, who would stake your life on the virtue of some man or other who comes to this house and whom the initiated would recognise a mile away, you feel obliged to believe like everyone else in what is said about someone in the public eye who is the incarnation of those propensities to the common herd, when as a matter of fact he doesn't care a sou for that sort of thing. I say a sou, because if we were to offer five-and-twenty louis, we should see the number of plaster saints dwindle down to nothing. As things are, the average rate of sanctity, if you see any sanctity in that sort of thing, is somewhere between three and four out of ten."

If Brichot had transferred to the male sex the question of bad reputations, in my case, conversely, it was to the female sex that, thinking of Albertine, I applied the Baron's words. I was appalled at his statistic, even when I bore in mind that he probably inflated his figures in accordance with what he himself would have wished, and based them moreover on the reports of persons who were scandalmongers and possibly liars, and had in any case been led astray by their own desire, which, added to that of M. de Charlus himself, doubtless falsified his calculations.

"Three out of ten!" exclaimed Brichot. "Why, even if the

proportions were reversed I should still have to multiply the guilty a hundredfold. If it is as you say, Baron, and you are not mistaken, then we must confess that you are one of those rare visionaries who discern a truth which nobody round them has ever suspected. Just as Barrès made discoveries as to parliamentary corruption the truth of which was afterwards established, like the existence of Leverrier's planet. Mme Verdurin would cite for preference men whom I would rather not name who detected in the Intelligence Bureau, in the General Staff, activities inspired, I'm sure, by patriotic zeal but which I had never imagined. On freemasonry, German espionage, drug addiction, Léon Daudet concocts day by day a fantastic fairy-tale which turns out to be the barest truth. Three out of ten!" Brichot repeated in stupefaction. And it is true to say that M. de Charlus taxed the great majority of his contemporaries with inversion, excepting, however, the men with whom he himself had had relations, their case, provided there had been some element of romance in those relations, appearing to him more complex. So it is that we see Lotharios who refuse to believe in women's honour making an exception in the case of one who has been their mistress and of whom they protest sincerely and with an air of mystery: "No, no, you're mistaken, she isn't a whore." This unlooked-for tribute is dictated partly by their own vanity for which it is more flattering that such favours should have been reserved for them alone, partly by their gullibility which all too easily swallows everything that their mistress has led them to believe, partly from that sense of the complexity of life whereby, as soon as one gets close to other people, other lives, ready-made labels and classifications appear unduly crude. "Three out of ten! But have a care, Baron: less fortunate than the historians whose conclusions the future will justify, if you were to present to posterity the statistics that you offer us, it might find them erroneous. Posterity judges only on documentary evidence, and will insist on being shown your files. But as no document would be forthcoming to authenticate this sort of collective phenomenon which the initiated are only too concerned to leave in obscurity, the tender-hearted would be moved to indignation, and you would be regarded as nothing more than a slanderer or a lunatic. After having won top marks and unquestioned supremacy in the social examinations on this earth, you would taste the sorrows of being blackballed beyond the grave. The game is not worth the candle, to quote—may God forgive me —our friend Bossuet."

"I'm not interested in history," replied M. de Charlus, "this life is sufficient for me, it's quite interesting enough, as poor Swann used to say."

"What, you knew Swann, Baron? I didn't know that. Tell me, was he that way inclined?" Brichot inquired with an air of misgiving.

"What a mind the man has! So you think I only know men of that sort? No, I don't think so," said Charlus, looking at the ground and trying to weigh the pros and cons. And deciding that, since he was dealing with Swann whose contrary tendencies had always been so notorious, a half-admission could only be harmless to him who was its object and flattering to him who let it out in an insinuation: "I don't deny that long ago in our schooldays, once in a while," said the Baron, as though in spite of himself and thinking aloud; then pulling himself up: "But that was centuries ago. How do you expect me to remember? You're embarrassing me," he concluded with a laugh.

"In any case he was never what you'd call a beauty!" said Brichot who, himself hideous, thought himself good-looking and was always ready to pronounce other men ugly.

"Hold your tongue," said the Baron, "you don't know what you're talking about. In those days he had a peaches-and-cream complexion, and," he added, finding a fresh note for each syllable, "he was as pretty as a cherub. Besides he was always charming. The women were madly in love with him."

"But did you ever know his wife?"

"Why, it was through me that he came to know her. I had thought her charming in her boyish get-up one evening when she played Miss Sacripant; I was with some club-mates, and each of us took a woman home with him, and although all I wanted was to go to sleep, slanderous tongues alleged—it's terrible how malicious people are—that I went to bed with Odette. In any case she took advantage of the slanders to come and bother me, and I thought I might get rid of her by introducing her to Swann. From that moment on she never let me go. She couldn't spell the simplest word, it was I who wrote all her letters for her. And it was I who, later on, was responsible for taking her out. That, my boy, is what comes of having a good reputation, you see. Though I only half deserved it. She used to force me to get up the most dreadful orgies for her, with five or six men."

And the lovers whom Odette had had in succession (she had been with this, that and the other man, not one of whose names had ever been guessed by poor Swann, blinded by jealousy and by love, by turns weighing up the chances and believing in oaths more affirmative than a contradiction which the guilty woman lets slip, a contradiction far more elusive and yet far more significant, of which the jealous lover might take advantage more logically than of the information which he falsely pretends to have received, in the hope of alarming his mistress), these lovers M. de Charlus began to enumerate with as absolute a certainty as if he had been reciting the list of the Kings of France. And indeed the jealous lover, like the contemporaries of an historical event, is too close, he knows nothing, and it is for strangers that the chronicle of adultery assumes the precision of history, and prolongs itself in lists which are a matter of indifference to them and become painful only to another jealous lover, such as I was, who cannot help comparing his own case with that which he hears spoken of and wonders whether the woman he suspects cannot boast an equally illustrious list. But he can never find out; it is a sort of universal conspiracy, a "blind man's buff" in which everyone cruelly participates, and which consists, while his mistress flits from one to another, in holding over his eyes a bandage which he is perpetually trying to tear off without success, for everyone keeps him blindfold, poor wretch, the kind out of kindness, the cruel out of cruelty, the coarse-minded out of their love of coarse jokes, the well-bred out of politeness and good-breeding, and all alike respecting one of those conventions which are called principles.

"But did Swann ever know that you had enjoyed her favours?"

"What an idea! Confess such a thing to Charles! It's enough to make one's hair stand on end. Why, my dear fellow, he would have killed me on the spot, he was as jealous as a tiger. Any more than I ever confessed to Odette, not that she would have minded in the least, that . . . But you mustn't make my tongue run away with me. And the joke of it is that it was she who fired a revolver at him, and nearly hit me. Oh! I used to have a fine time with that couple; and naturally it was I who was obliged to act as his second against d'Osmond, who never forgave me. D'Osmond had carried off Odette, and Swann, to console himself, had taken as his mistress, or make-believe mistress, Odette's sister. But really you mustn't start making me tell you Swann's story, or we should be here all night—nobody knows more about it than I do. It was I who used to take Odette out when she didn't want to see Charles. It was all the more awkward for me as I have a very close kinsman who bears the name Crécy, without of course having any sort of right to it, but still he was none too well pleased. For she went by the name of Odette de Crécy, as she perfectly well could, being merely separated from a Crécy whose wife she still was—an extremely authentic one, he, a most estimable gentleman out of whom she had drained his last farthing. But why should I have to tell you about this Crécy? I've seen you with him on the twister, you used to have him to dinner at Balbec. He must have needed it, poor fellow, for he lived on a tiny allowance that Swann made him, and I'm very much afraid that, since my friend's death, that income must have stopped altogether. What I do not understand," M. de Charlus said to me, "is that, since you used often to go to Charles's, you didn't ask me this evening to present you to the Queen of Naples. In fact I can see that you're not interested in *people* as curiosities, and that always surprises me in someone who knew Swann, in whom that sort of interest was so highly developed that it's impossible to say whether it was I who initiated him in these matters or he me. It surprises me as much as if I met a person who had known Whistler and remained ignorant of what is meant by taste. However, it was chiefly important for Morel to meet her. He was passionately keen to as well, for he's nothing if not intelligent. It's a nuisance that she's gone.

However, I shall effect the conjunction one of these days. It's inevitable that he'll get to know her. The only possible obstacle would be if she were to die in the night. Well, it's to be hoped that that won't happen."

All of a sudden Brichot, who was still suffering from the shock of the proportion "three out of ten" which M. de Charlus had revealed to him, and had continued to pursue the idea all this time, burst out with an abruptness which was reminiscent of an examining magistrate seeking to make a prisoner confess but which was in reality the result of the Professor's desire to appear perspicacious and of the misgivings that he felt about launching so grave an accusation: "Isn't Ski like that?" he inquired of M. de Charlus with a sombre air. He had chosen Ski in order to show off his alleged intuitive powers, telling himself that since there were only three innocents in every ten, he ran little risk of being mistaken if he named Ski, who seemed to him a trifle odd, suffered from insomnia, used scent, in short was not entirely normal.

"But not in the *least*!" exclaimed the Baron with bitter, dogmatic, exasperated irony. "What you say is so wrong, so absurd, so wide of the mark! Ski is like that precisely to the people who know nothing about it. If he was, he wouldn't look so like it, be it said without any intention to criticise, for he has a certain charm, indeed I find there's something very engaging about him."

"But give us a few names, then," Brichot persisted. M. de Charlus drew himself up with a haughty air.

"Ah! my dear Sir, I, as you know, live in the world of the abstract; all this interests me only from a transcendental point of view," he replied with the querulous touchiness peculiar to men of his kind, and the affectation of grandiloquence that characterised his conversation. "To me, you understand, it's only general principles that are of any interest. I speak to you of this as I might of the law of gravity." But these moments of irritable retraction in which the Baron sought to conceal his true life lasted but a short time compared with the hours of continual progression in which he allowed it to betray itself, flaunted it with an irritating complacency, the need to confide being stronger in him than the fear of disclosure. "What I meant to say," he went on, "is that for one bad reputation that is unjustified there are hundreds of good ones which are no less so. Obviously, the number of those who don't deserve their reputations varies according to whether you rely on what is said by their own kind or by others. And it is true that if the malevolence of the latter is limited by the extreme difficulty they would find in believing that a vice as horrible to them as robbery or murder can be practised by people whom they know to be sensitive and kind, the malevolence of the former is stimulated to excess by the desire to regard as—how shall I put it?—accessible, men who attract them, on the strength of information given them by people who have been led astray by a similar desire, in fact by the very aloofness with which they are generally regarded. I've heard a man who was somewhat ill thought of on account of these tastes say that he supposed that a certain society figure shared them. And his sole reason for believing it was that this society figure had been polite to him! All the more reason for *optimism*," said the Baron artlessly, "in the computation of the number. But the true reason for the enormous disparity between the number calculated by the layman and the number calculated by the initiated arises from the mystery with which the latter surround their actions, in order to conceal them from the rest, who, lacking any means of knowing, would be literally stupefied if they were to learn merely a quarter of the truth."

"So in our day things are as they were among the Greeks," said Brichot.

"What do you mean, among the Greeks? Do you suppose that it hasn't been going on ever since? Take the reign of Louis XIV. You have Monsieur, young Vermandois, Molière, Prince Louis of Baden, Brunswick, Charolais, Boufflers, the Great Condé, the Duc de Brissac."

"Stop a moment. I knew about Monsieur, I knew about Brissac from Saint-Simon, Vendôme of course, and many others as well. But that old pest Saint-Simon often refers to the Great Condé and Prince Louis of Baden and never mentions it."

"It seems rather deplorable, I must say, that I should have to teach a Professor of the Sorbonne his history But, my dear fellow, you're as ignorant as a carp."

"You are harsh, Baron, but just. But wait a moment, now this will please you: I've just remembered a song of the period composed in macaronic verse about a storm in which the Great Condé was caught as he was going down the Rhône in the company of his friend the Marquis de La Moussaye. Condé says:

> *Carus Amicus Mussaeus,*
> *Ah! Quod tempus, bonus Deus!*
>   *Landerirette,*
> *Imbre sumus perituri.*

And La Moussaye reassures him with:

> *Securae sunt nostrae vitae.*
> *Sumus enim Sodomitae,*
> *Igne tantum perituri,*
>   *Landeriri.*"[20]

"I take back what I said," said Charlus in a shrill and mannered tone, "you are a well of learning. You'll write it down for me, won't you? I must preserve it in my family archives, since my great-great-great-grandmother was a sister of M. le Prince."

"Yes, but, Baron, with regard to Prince Louis of Baden I can think of nothing. However, I suppose that generally speaking the art of war. . . ."

"What nonsense! In that period alone you have Vendôme, Villars, Prince Eugène, the Prince de Conti, and if I were to tell you of all our heroes of Tonkin, Morocco, etc.—and I'm thinking of the ones who are truly sublime, and pious, and 'new generation'—you'd be amazed. Ah! I could teach them a thing or two, the people who conduct inquiries into the new generation, which has rejected the futile complications of its elders, M. Bourget tells us! I have a young friend out there, who's highly spoken of, who has done great things. . . . However, I'm not going to tell tales out of school; let's get back to the seventeenth century. You know that Saint-Simon says of the Maréchal d'Huxelles—one among many: 'Voluptuous in Grecian debaucheries which he made no attempt to conceal, he would accost young officers whom he trained to his purpose, not to mention stalwart young valets, and this openly, in the army and at Strasbourg.' You've probably read Madame's *Letters*: all his men called him 'Putana.' She's fairly explicit about it."

"And she was in a good position to judge, with her husband."

"Such an interesting character, Madame," said M. de Charlus. "One might take her as model for the definitive portrait, the lyrical synthesis of the 'Wife of an Auntie.' First of all, the masculine type; generally the wife of an Auntie is a man—that's what makes it so easy for him to give her children. Then Madame doesn't talk about Monsieur's vices, but she does talk incessantly about the same vice in other men, writing as someone in the know and from that habit which makes us enjoy finding in other people's families the same defects as afflict us in our own, in order to prove to ourselves that there's nothing exceptional or degrading in them. I was saying that things have been much the same in every age. Nevertheless, our own is especially remarkable in that respect. And notwithstanding the instances I've borrowed from the seventeenth century, if my great ancestor François de La Rochefoucauld were alive in our day, he might say of it with even more justification than of his own—come, Brichot, help me out: 'Vices are common to every age; but if certain persons whom everyone knows had appeared in the first centuries of our era, would anyone speak to-day of the prostitutions of Heliogabalus?' '*Whom everyone knows*' appeals to me immensely. I see that my sagacious kinsman understood the tricks of his most illustrious contemporaries as I understand those of my own. But men of that sort are not only far more numerous today. There's also something special about them."

I could see that M. de Charlus was about to tell us in what fashion these habits had evolved. And not for a moment while he was speaking, or while Brichot was speaking, was the semi-conscious image of my home, where Albertine awaited me—an image associated with the intimate and caressing motif of Vinteuil—absent from my mind. I kept coming back to Albertine, just as I would be obliged in fact to go back to her presently as to a sort of ball and chain to which I was somehow attached, which prevented me from leaving Paris and which at this moment, while from the Verdurin salon I pictured my home, made me think of it not as an empty space, exalting to the personality if a little melancholy, but as being filled—alike in this to the hotel in Balbec on a certain evening—with that immutable presence, which lingered there for me and which I was sure to find there whenever I chose. The insistence with which M. de Charlus kept reverting to this topic—into which his mind, constantly exercised in the same direction, had indeed acquired a certain penetration—was in a rather complex way distinctly trying. He was as boring as a specialist who can see nothing outside his own subject, as irritating as an initiate who prides himself on the secrets which he possesses and is burning to divulge, as repellent as those people who, whenever their own weaknesses are in question, blossom and expatiate without noticing that they are giving offence, as obsessed as a maniac and as uncontrollably imprudent as a criminal. These characteristics, which at certain moments became as striking as those that stamp a madman or a felon, brought me, as it happened, a certain consolation. For, subjecting them to the necessary transposition in order to be able to draw from them deductions with regard to Albertine, and remembering her attitude towards Saint-Loup and towards me, I said to myself, painful as one of these memories and melancholy as the other was to me, I said to myself that they seemed to preclude the kind of deformation, so distinctive and pronounced, the kind of specialisation, inevitably exclusive it seemed, that emanated so powerfully from the conversation as from the person of M. de Charlus. But the latter, unfortunately, made haste to destroy these grounds for hope in the same way as he had furnished me with them, that is to say unwittingly.

"Yes," he said, "I'm no longer a stripling, and I've already seen many things change round about me. I no longer recognise either society, in which all the barriers have been broken down, in which a mob devoid of elegance or decency dance the tango even in my own family, or fashion, or politics, or the arts, or religion, or anything. But I must admit that the thing that has changed most of all is what the Germans call homosexuality. Good heavens, in my day, leaving aside the

men who loathed women, and those who, caring only for
women, did the other thing merely with an eye to profit,
homosexuals were sound family men and never kept mistresses
except as a cover. Had I had a daughter to give away, it's
among them that I should have looked for my son-in-law if
I'd wanted to be certain that she wouldn't be unhappy. Alas!
things have changed. Nowadays they're also recruited from
among the most rabid womanisers. I thought I had a certain
flair, and that when I said to myself: 'Certainly not,' I couldn't
have been mistaken. Well, now I give up. One of my friends
who is well-known for it had a coachman whom my sister-in-
law Oriane found for him, a lad from Combray who had
dabbled in all sorts of trades but particularly that of chasing
skirts, and who, I would have sworn, was as hostile as possible
to that sort of thing. He broke his mistress's heart by deceiving
her with two women whom he adored, not to mention the
others, an actress and a barmaid. My cousin the Prince de
Guermantes, who has the irritating mind of people who are
too ready to believe anything, said to me one day: 'But why
in the world doesn't X—— sleep with his coachman? It might
give pleasure to Théodore' (which is the coachman's name)
'and he may even be rather hurt that his master doesn't make
advances to him.' I couldn't help telling Gilbert to hold his
tongue; I was irritated by that would-be perspicacity which,
when exercised indiscriminately, is a want of perspicacity,
and also by the blatant guile of my cousin who would have
liked X—— to test the ground so that he himself could follow
if the going was good."

"Then the Prince de Guermantes has those tastes too?"
asked Brichot with a mixture of astonishment and dismay.

"Good lord," replied M. de Charlus, highly delighted,
"it's so notorious that I don't think I'm being guilty of an
indiscretion if I tell you that he is. Well, the following year I
went to Balbec, where I heard from a sailor who used to
take me out fishing occasionally that my Théodore, whose
sister, I may mention, is the maid of a friend of Mme Verdurin,
Baroness Putbus, used to come down to the harbour to pick
up this or that sailor, with the most infernal cheek, to go for
a boat-trip 'with extras.' "

It was now my turn to inquire whether the employer, whom I had identified as the gentleman who at Balbec used to play cards all day long with his mistress, and who was the leader of the little group of four boon companions, was like the Prince de Guermantes.

"Why, of course, everyone knows. He doesn't even make any attempt to conceal it."

"But he had his mistress there with him."

"Well, and what difference does that make? How innocent these children are," he said to me in a fatherly tone, little suspecting the grief that I extracted from his words when I thought of Albertine. "She's charming, his mistress."

"So then his three friends are like himself?"

"Not at all," he cried, stopping his ears as though, in playing some instrument, I had struck a wrong note.

"Now he's gone to the other extreme. So a man no longer has the right to have friends? Ah! youth, youth; it gets everything wrong. We shall have to begin your education over again, my boy. Now," he went on, "I admit that this case—and I know of many others—however open a mind I may try to keep for every form of effrontery, does embarrass me. I may be very old-fashioned, but I fail to understand," he said in the tone of an old Gallican speaking of certain forms of Ultramontanism, of a liberal royalist speaking of the *Action Française* or of a disciple of Claude Monet speaking of the Cubists. "I don't condemn these innovators. I envy them if anything. I try to understand them, but I simply can't. If they're so passionately fond of women, why, and especially in this working-class world where it's frowned upon, where they conceal it from a sense of shame, have they any need of what they call 'a bit of brown'? It's because it represents something else to them. What?"

"What else can a woman represent to Albertine," I thought, and there indeed lay the cause of my anguish.

"Decidedly, Baron," said Brichot, "should the Board of Studies ever think of founding a Chair of Homosexuality, I shall see that your name is the first to be submitted. Or rather, no; an Institute of Specialized Psycho-physiology would suit you better. And I can see you, best of all, provided with a

Chair in the Collège de France, which would enable you to
devote yourself to personal researches the results of which
you would deliver, like the Professor of Tamil or Sanskrit, to
the handful of people who are interested in them. You would
have an audience of two, with your attendant, not that I
mean to cast the slightest aspersion upon our corps of beadles,
whom I believe to be above suspicion."

"You know nothing about it," the Baron retorted in a
harsh and cutting tone. "Besides you're wrong in thinking
that so few people are interested in the subject. It's just the
opposite." And without stopping to consider the incompatibility between the invariable trend of his own conversation
and the reproaches he was about to level at others, "It is,
on the contrary, most alarming," said the Baron with a
shocked and contrite air, "people talk about nothing else.
It's a disgrace, but I'm not exaggerating, my dear fellow!
It appears that the day before yesterday, at the Duchesse
d'Ayen's, they talked about nothing else for two hours on end.
Just imagine, if women have taken to discussing that sort of
thing, it's a positive scandal! The most revolting thing about
it," he went on with extraordinary fire and vigour, "is that
they get their information from pests, real scoundrels like
young Châtellerault, about whom there's more to be told than
anyone, who tell them stories about other men. I gather he's
been casting aspersions on me, but I don't care; I'm convinced
that the mud and filth flung by an individual who barely escaped being turned out of the Jockey for cheating at cards
can only rebound on him. I know that if I were Jane d'Ayen,
I should have sufficient respect for my salon not to allow such
subjects to be discussed there, nor to allow my own flesh and
blood to be dragged through the mire in my house. But
society's finished, there are no longer any rules, any proprie-
ties, in conversation any more than in dress. Ah, my dear fellow,
it's the end of the world. Everyone has become so malicious.
People vie with one another in speaking ill of their fellows.
It's appalling!"

As cowardly still as I had been long ago in my boyhood at
Combray when I used to run away in order not to see my
grandfather tempted with brandy and the vain efforts of my

grandmother imploring him not to drink it, I had but one
thought, which was to leave the Verdurins' house before the
execution of M. de Charlus occurred.

"I simply must go," I said to Brichot.

"I'm coming with you," he replied, "but we can't take
French leave. Come and say good-bye to Mme Verdurin,"
the Professor concluded, as he made his way to the drawing-
room with the air of a man who, in a parlour game, goes to
find out whether he may "come back."

While we had been talking, M. Verdurin, at a signal from
his wife, had taken Morel aside. Even if Mme Verdurin had
decided on reflexion that it was wiser to postpone Morel's
enlightenment, she was powerless now to prevent it. There are
certain desires, sometimes confined only to the lips, which,
as soon as we have allowed them to grow, insist upon being
gratified, whatever the consequences may be; one can no longer
resist the temptation to kiss a bare shoulder at which one has
been gazing for too long and on which one's lips pounce like
a snake upon a bird, or to bury one's sweet tooth in a cake
that has been titillating it; nor can one deny oneself the satisfaction of seeing the amazement, anxiety, grief or mirth to
which one can move another person by some unexpected
communication. So, drunk with melodrama, Mme Verdurin
had ordered her husband to take Morel out of the room and
at all costs to explain matters to him. The violinist had begun
by deploring the departure of the Queen of Naples before
he had had a chance of being presented to her. M. de Charlus
had told him so often that she was the sister of the Empress
Elizabeth and of the Duchesse d'Alençon that the sovereign
had assumed an extraordinary importance in his eyes. But the
Master explained to him that they were not there to talk about
the Queen of Naples, and then went straight to the point.
"Listen," he had concluded after a long explanation, "if
you like, we can go and ask my wife what she thinks. I give
you my word of honour, I've said nothing to her about it.
We'll see what she thinks of it all. My advice may not be right,
but you know how sound her judgment is, and besides, she
has an immense affection for you; let's go and submit the case
to her." And as Mme Verdurin, impatiently looking forward to

the excitement that she would presently be relishing when she talked to the musician, and then, after he had gone, when she made her husband give her a full report of their conversation, went on repeating to herself: "But what in the world can they be doing? I do hope that Gustave, in keeping him all this time, has managed to give him his cue," M. Verdurin reappeared with Morel, who seemed extremely agitated.

"He'd like to ask your advice," M. Verdurin said to his wife, in the tone of a man who does not know whether his request will be granted. Instead of replying to M. Verdurin, it was to Morel that, in the heat of her passion, Mme Verdurin addressed herself.

"I agree entirely with my husband. I consider that you cannot put up with it any longer," she exclaimed vehemently, discarding as a useless fiction her agreement with her husband that she was supposed to know nothing of what he had been saying to the violinist.

"How do you mean? Put up with what?" stammered M. Verdurin, endeavouring to feign astonishment and seeking, with an awkwardness that was explained by his dismay, to defend his falsehood.

"I guessed what you'd been saying to him," replied Mme Verdurin, undisturbed by the improbability of this explanation, and caring little what the violinist might think of her veracity when he recalled this scene. "No," Mme Verdurin continued, "I feel that you cannot possibly persist in this degrading promiscuity with a tainted person whom nobody will have in their house," she went on, regardless of the fact that this was untrue and forgetting that she herself entertained him almost daily. "You're the talk of the Conservatoire," she added, feeling that this was the argument that would carry most weight. "Another month of this life and your artistic future will be shattered, whereas without Charlus you ought to be making at least a hundred thousand francs a year."

"But I'd never heard a thing, I'm astounded, I'm very grateful to you," Morel murmured, the tears starting to his eyes. But, being obliged at once to feign astonishment and to conceal his shame, he had turned redder and was sweating more abundantly than if he had played all Beethoven's sonatas in succession, and tears welled from his eyes which the Bonn Master would certainly not have drawn from him.

"If you've never heard anything, you're unique in that respect. He is a gentleman with a vile reputation and has been mixed up in some very nasty doings. I know that the police have their eye on him and that is perhaps the best thing for him if he's not to end up like all such men, murdered by ruffians," she went on, for as she thought of Charlus the memory of Mme de Duras recurred to her, and in the intoxication of her rage she sought to aggravate still further the wounds that she was inflicting on the unfortunate Charlie, and to avenge herself for those that she herself had received in the course of the evening. "Anyhow, even financially he can be of no use to you; he's completely ruined since he has become the prey of people who are blackmailing him, and who can't even extract from him the price of the tune they call, any more than you can extract the price for yours, because everything's mortgaged up to the hilt, town house, country house, everything."

Morel was all the more inclined to believe this lie since M. de Charlus liked to confide in him his relations with ruffians, a race for which the son of a valet, however villainous himself, professes a feeling of horror as strong as his attachment to Bonapartist principles.

Already, in his cunning mind, a scheme had begun to take shape analogous to what was called in the eighteenth century a reversal of alliances. Resolving never to speak to M. de Charlus again, he would return on the following evening to Jupien's niece, and see that everything was put right with her. Unfortunately for him this plan was doomed to failure, M. de Charlus having made an appointment for that same evening with Jupien, which the ex-tailor dared not fail to keep in spite of recent events. Other events, as we shall see, having occurred as regards Morel, when Jupien in tears told his tale of woe to the Baron, the latter, no less woeful, assured him that he would adopt the forsaken girl, that she could take one of the titles that were at his disposal, probably that of Mlle d'Oloron, that he would see that she received a thorough finishing and married a rich husband. Promises which filled Jupien with joy but left his niece unmoved, for she still loved Morel, who, from stupidity or cynicism, would come into the shop and tease her in Jupien's absence. "What's the matter with you," he would say with a laugh, "with those big circles under your eyes? A broken heart? Dammit, time passes and things change. After all, a man has a right to try on a shoe, and all the more so a woman, and if she doesn't fit him. . . ." He lost his temper once only, because she cried, which he considered cowardly, unworthy of her. People are not always very tolerant of the tears which they themselves have provoked.

But we have looked too far ahead, for all this did not happen until after the Verdurin reception which we interrupted, and which we must take up again at the point where we left off.

"I'd never have suspected," Morel groaned, in answer to Mme Verdurin.

"Naturally people don't say it to your face, but that doesn't prevent your being the talk of the Conservatoire," Mme Verdurin went on wickedly, seeking to make it plain to Morel that it was not only M. de Charlus who was being criticised, but himself too. "I'm quite prepared to believe that you know nothing about it; all the same, people are talking freely. Ask Ski what they were saying the other day at Chevillard's concert within a few feet of us when you came into my box. In other words, people are pointing a finger at you. Personally I don't take a blind bit of notice, but what I do feel is that it makes a man supremely ridiculous and that he becomes a public laughing-stock for the rest of his life."

"I don't know how to thank you," said Charlie in the tone in which one speaks to a dentist who has just caused one the most excruciating pain without one's daring to show it, or to a too bloodthirsty second who has forced one into a duel on account of some casual remark of which he has said: "You can't swallow that."

"I believe that you have plenty of character, that you're a man," replied Mme Verdurin, "and that you will be capable of speaking out boldly, although he tells everybody that you'd never dare, that he's got you under his thumb."

Charlie, seeking a borrowed dignity in which to cloak the tatters of his own, found in his memory something that he had read or, more probably, heard quoted, and at once proclaimed: "I wasn't brought up to pocket that sort of affront. This very evening I shall break with M. de Charlus. The Queen of Naples has gone, hasn't she? Otherwise, before breaking with him, I'd have asked him. . . ."

"It isn't necessary to break with him altogether," said Mme Verdurin, anxious to avoid a disruption of the little nucleus. "There's no harm in your seeing him here, among our little group, where you are appreciated, where no one speaks ill of you. But you must insist upon your freedom, and not let him drag you about among all those stuck-up women who are friendly to your face; I wish you could have heard what they were saying behind your back. Anyhow, you need feel no regret. Not only are you getting rid of a stain which would have marked you for the rest of your life, but from the artistic point of view, even without this scandalous presentation by Charlus, I don't mind telling you that debasing yourself like this in these sham society circles would give people the impression that you aren't serious, would earn you the reputation of being an amateur, a mere salon performer, which is a terrible thing at your age. I can understand that to all those fine ladies it's highly convenient to be able to return their friends' hospitality by making you come and play for nothing, but it's your future as an artist that would foot the bill. I don't say that there aren't one or two. You mentioned the Queen of Naples—who has left, for she had to go on to another party—now she's a nice woman, and I may tell you that I think she has a poor opinion of Charlus. I'm sure she came here chiefly to please me. Yes, yes, I know she was longing to meet M. Verdurin and myself. That is a house in which you might play. And then of course if I take you—because the artists all know me, you understand, they've always been very sweet to me, and regard me almost as one of themselves, as their Mistress—that's quite a different matter. But whatever you do, you must never go near Mme de Duras! Don't go and make a bloomer like that! I know several artists who have come here and told me all about her. They know they can trust me," she said, in the sweet and simple tone which she knew how to adopt instantaneously, imparting an appropriate air of modesty to her features, an appropriate charm to

her eyes, "they come here, just like that, to tell me all their
little troubles; the ones who are said to be most taciturn go on
chatting to me sometimes for hours on end, and I can't tell
you how interesting they are. Poor Chabrier always used to
say: 'There's nobody like Mme Verdurin for getting them to
talk.' Well, do you know, I've seen them all, every one of them
without exception, literally in tears after having gone to play
for Mme de Duras. It's not only the way she enjoys making
her servants humiliate them, but they could never get an
engagement anywhere else, again. The agents would say:
'Oh yes, the fellow who plays at Mme de Duras's.' That settled
it. There's nothing like that for ruining a man's future. You
see, with society people it doesn't seem serious; you may have
all the talent in the world, it's a sad thing to have to say, but
one Mme de Duras is enough to give you the reputation of an
amateur. And artists, you realise—and after all I know them,
I've been moving among them for forty years, launching them,
taking an interest in them—well, when they say that somebody's an amateur, that's the end of it. And people were beginning to say it of you. Indeed, the number of times I've
been obliged to take up the cudgels on your behalf, to assure
them that you wouldn't play in some absurd drawing-room!
Do you know what the answer was: 'But he'll be forced to.
Charlus won't even consult him, he never asks him for his
opinion.' Somebody wanted to pay him a compliment by
saying: 'We greatly admire your friend Morel.' Do you know
the answer he gave, with that insolent air which you know
so well? 'But what do you mean by calling him my friend.
We're not of the same class. Say rather that he is my creature,
my protégé.' "

At this moment there stirred beneath the domed forehead
of the musical goddess the one thing that certain people cannot
keep to themselves, a word which it is not merely abject but
imprudent to repeat. But the need to repeat it is stronger than
honour or prudence. It was to this need that, after a few
convulsive twitches of her spherical and sorrowful brow,
the Mistress succumbed: "Someone actually told my husband
that he had said 'my servant,' but for that I cannot vouch,"
she added. It was a similar need that had impelled M. de

Charlus, shortly after he had sworn to Morel that nobody should ever know the story of his birth, to say to Mme Verdurin: "His father was a valet." A similar need again, now that the word had been said, would make it circulate from one person to another, each of whom would confide it under the seal of a secrecy which would be promised and not kept by the hearer, as by the informant himself. These words would end, as in the game called hunt-the-thimble, by being traced back to Mme Verdurin, bringing down upon her the wrath of the person concerned, who would finally have heard them. She knew this, but could not repress the word that was burning her tongue. "Servant" could not but offend Morel. She said "servant" nevertheless, and if she added that she could not vouch for the word, this was so as to appear certain of the rest, thanks to this hint of uncertainty, and to show her impartiality. She herself found this impartiality so touching that she began to speak tenderly to Charlie: "Because, don't you see, I don't blame him. He's dragging you down into his abyss, it is true, but it's not his fault since he wallows in it himself, since he wallows in it," she repeated in a louder tone, having been struck by the aptness of the image which had taken shape so quickly that her attention only now caught up with it and sought to make the most of it. "No, what I do reproach him for," she went on in a melting tone—like a woman drunk with her own success—"is a want of delicacy towards you. There are certain things that one doesn't say in public. For instance this evening, he was betting that he would make you blush with joy by telling you (stuff and nonsense, of course, for his recommendation would be enough to prevent your getting it) that you were to have the Cross of the Legion of Honour. Even that I could overlook, although I've never much liked," she went on with a delicate and dignified air, "seeing someone make a fool of his friends, but, don't you know, there are certain little things that do stick in one's gullet. Such as when he told us, with screams of laughter, that if you want the Cross it's to please your uncle and that your uncle was a flunkey."

"He told you that!" cried Charlie, believing, on the strength of this adroitly interpolated remark, in the truth of everything that Mme Verdurin had said. Mme Verdurin was overwhelmed with the joy of an old mistress who, just as her young lover is on the point of deserting her, succeeds in breaking up his marriage. And perhaps the lie had not been a calculated one, perhaps she had not even consciously lied. A sort of sentimental logic, or perhaps, more elementary still, a sort of nervous reflex, that impelled her, in order to brighten up her life and preserve her happiness, to sow discord in the little clan, may have brought impulsively to her lips, without giving her time to check their veracity, these assertions that were so diabolically effective if not strictly accurate.

"If he had only said it to us it wouldn't matter," the Mistress went on, "we know better than to pay any attention to what he says, and besides, what does a man's origin matter, you have your worth, you're what you make yourself, but that he should use it to make Mme de Portefin laugh" (Mme Verdurin named this lady on purpose because she knew that Charlie admired her) "that's what makes us sick. My husband said to me when he heard him: 'I'd sooner he had struck me in the face.' For he's as fond of you as I am, you know, is Gustave" (it was thus that one learned that M. Verdurin's name was Gustave). "He's really very sensitive."

"But I never told you I was fond of him," muttered M. Verdurin, acting the kind-hearted curmudgeon. "It's Charlus who's fond of him."

"Oh, no! Now I realise the difference. I was betrayed by a wretch and you, you're good," Charlie fervently exclaimed.

"No, no," murmured Mme Verdurin, seeking to safeguard her victory (for she felt that her Wednesdays were safe) but not to abuse it, "wretch is too strong; he does harm, a great deal of harm, unwittingly; you know that tale about the Legion of Honour was only a momentary squib. And it would be painful to me to repeat all that he said about your family," she added, although she would have been greatly embarrassed had she been asked to do so.

"Oh, even if it *was* only momentary, it proves that he's a traitor," cried Morel.

It was at this moment that we returned to the drawing-room. "Ah!" exclaimed M. de Charlus when he saw that Morel was in the room, and, advancing upon the musician with the

alacrity of a man who has skilfully organised a whole evening's
entertainment with a view to an assignation with a woman,
and in his excitement never imagines that he has with his
own hands set the snare in which he will presently be caught
and publicly thrashed by bravoes stationed in readiness by
her husband, "so here you are at last. Well, are you pleased,
young hero, and presently young knight of the Legion of
Honour? For very soon you will be able to sport your Cross,"
he said to Morel with a tender and triumphant air, but by the
very mention of the decoration endorsed Mme Verdurin's
lies, which appeared to Morel to be indisputable truth.

"Leave me alone. I forbid you to come near me," Morel
shouted at the Baron. "You know what I mean all right.
I'm not the first person you've tried to pervert!"

My sole consolation lay in the thought that I was about to
see Morel and the Verdurins pulverised by M. de Charlus.
For a thousand times less than that I had been visited with his
furious rage; no one was safe from it; a king would not have
intimidated him. Instead of which, an extraordinary thing
happened. M. de Charlus stood speechless, dumbfounded,
measuring the depths of his misery without understanding its
cause, unable to think of a word to say, raising his eyes to
gaze at each of the company in turn, with a questioning, outraged, suppliant air, which seemed to be asking them not so
much what had happened as what answer he ought to make.
And yet M. de Charlus possessed all the resources, not merely
of eloquence but of audacity, when, seized by a rage which
had been simmering for a long time, he reduced someone to
despair with the most cruel words in front of a shocked society
group which had never imagined that anyone could go so far.
M. de Charlus, on these occasions, almost foamed at the
mouth, working himself up into a veritable frenzy which left
everyone trembling. But in these instances he had the initiative,
he was on the attack, he said whatever came into his head (just
as Bloch was able to make fun of the Jews yet blushed if the
word Jew was uttered in his hearing). These people whom he
hated, he hated because he thought they looked down on him.
Had they been civil to him, instead of flying into a furious
rage with them he would have taken them to his bosom.

Perhaps what now struck him speechless was—when he saw
that M. and Mme Verdurin turned their eyes away from him
and that no one was coming to his rescue—his present anguish
and, still more, his dread of greater anguish to come; or else
the fact that, not having worked himself up and concocted
an imaginary rage in advance, having no ready-made thunderbolt at hand, he had been seized and struck down suddenly at a
moment when he was unarmed (for, sensitive, neurotic,
hysterical, he was genuinely impulsive but pseudo-brave—
indeed, as I had always thought, and it was something that
had rather endeared him to me, pseudo-cruel—and did not
have the normal reactions of an outraged man of honour);
or else that, in a milieu that was not his own, he felt less at
ease and less courageous than he would in the Faubourg.
The fact remains that, in this salon which he despised, this
great nobleman (in whom superiority over commoners was no
more essentially inherent than it had been in this or that
ancestor of his trembling before the revolutionary tribunal)
could do nothing, in the paralysis of his every limb as well as
his tongue, but cast around him terror-stricken, suppliant,
bewildered glances, outraged by the violence that was being
done to him. In a situation so cruelly unforeseen, this great
talker could do no more than stammer: "What does it all
mean? What's wrong?" His question was not even heard.
And the eternal pantomime of panic terror has so little changed
that this elderly gentleman to whom a disagreeable incident
had occurred in a Parisian drawing-room unconsciously re-
enacted the basic formal attitudes in which the Greek sculptors
of the earliest times symbolised the terror of nymphs pursued
by the god Pan.

The disgraced ambassador, the under-secretary placed
suddenly on the retired list, the man about town who finds
himself cold-shouldered, the lover who has been shown the
door, examine, sometimes for months on end, the event that
has shattered their hopes; they turn it over and over like a
projectile fired at them they know not from whence or by
whom, almost as though it were a meteorite. They long to
know the constituent elements of this strange missile which
has burst upon them, to learn what animosities may be de-

tected therein. Chemists have at least the means of analysis; sick men suffering from a disease the origin of which they do not know can send for the doctor; criminal mysteries are more or less unravelled by the examining magistrate. But for the disconcerting actions of our fellow-men we rarely discover the motives. Thus M. de Charlus—to anticipate the days that followed this evening to which we shall presently return—could see in Charlie's attitude one thing alone that was self-evident. Charlie, who had often threatened the Baron that he would tell people of the passion that he inspired in him, must have seized the opportunity to do so when he considered that he had now sufficiently "arrived" to be able to stand on his own feet. And he must, out of sheer ingratitude, have told Mme Verdurin everything. But how had she allowed herself to be taken in (for the Baron, having made up his mind to deny the story, had already persuaded himself that the sentiments of which he would be accused were imaginary)? Friends of Mme Verdurin's, themselves perhaps with a passion for Charlie, must have prepared the ground. Accordingly, during the next few days M. de Charlus wrote ferocious letters to a number of the faithful, who were entirely innocent and concluded that he must be mad; then he went to Mme Verdurin with a long and affecting tale, which had not at all the effect that he had hoped. For in the first place Mme Verdurin simply said to him: "All you need do is pay no more attention to him, treat him with scorn, he's a mere boy." Now the Baron longed only for a reconciliation, and to bring this about by depriving Charlie of everything he had felt assured of, he asked Mme Verdurin not to invite him again; a request which she met with a refusal that brought her angry and sarcastic letters from M. de Charlus. Flitting from one supposition to another, the Baron never hit upon the truth, which was that the blow had not come from Morel. It is true that he could have learned this by asking him if they could have a few minutes' talk. But he felt that this would be prejudicial to his dignity and to the interests of his love. He had been insulted; he awaited an explanation. In any case, almost invariably, attached to the idea of a talk which might clear up a misunderstanding, there is another idea which, for whatever reason, prevents us from agreeing to that talk. The man who has abased himself and shown his weakness on a score of occasions will make a show of pride on the twenty-first, the only occasion on which it would be advisable not to persist in an arrogant attitude but to dispel an error which is taking root in his adversary failing a denial. As for the social side of the incident, the rumour spread abroad that M. de Charlus had been turned out of the Verdurins' house when he had attempted to rape a young musician. The effect of this rumour was that nobody was surprised when M. de Charlus did not appear again at the Verdurins', and whenever he chanced to meet somewhere else one of the faithful whom he had suspected and insulted, as this person bore a grudge against the Baron who himself abstained from greeting him, people were not surprised, realising that no member of the little clan would ever wish to speak to the Baron again.

While M. de Charlus, momentarily stunned by Morel's words and by the attitude of the Mistress, stood there in the pose of a nymph seized with Panic terror, M. and Mme Verdurin had retired to the outer drawing-room, as a sign of diplomatic rupture, leaving M. de Charlus by himself, while on the platform Morel was putting his violin in its case: "Now you must tell us exactly what happened," Mme Verdurin exclaimed eagerly to her husband.

"I don't know what you can have said to him," said Ski. "He looked quite upset; there were tears in his eyes."

Pretending not to have understood, "I'm sure nothing that I said could have affected him," said Mme Verdurin, employing one of those stratagems which deceive no one, so as to force the sculptor to repeat that Charlie was in tears, tears which filled the Mistress with too much pride for her to be willing to run the risk that one or other of the faithful, who might have misheard, remained in ignorance of them.

"Oh, but it must have: I saw big tears glistening in his eyes," said the sculptor in a low voice with a smile of malicious connivance and a sidelong glance to make sure that Morel was still on the platform and could not overhear the conversation. But there was somebody who did overhear and whose presence, as soon as it was observed, would restore to Morel one of the hopes that he had forfeited. This was the Queen of Naples, who, having left her fan behind, had thought it more polite, on coming away from another party to which she had gone on, to call back for it in person. She had entered the room quietly, as though she were a little embarrassed, prepared to make apologies for her presence, and not to outstay her welcome now that the other guests had gone. But no one had heard her enter in the heat of the incident, the meaning of which she had at once gathered and which set her ablaze with indignation.

"Ski says he had tears in his eyes, Did you notice that?" said Mme Verdurin. "I didn't see any tears. Ah, yes, I remember now," she corrected herself, afraid that her denial might be believed. "As for old Charlus, he's almost done in, he ought to take a chair, he's tottering on his feet, he'll be on the floor in another minute," she said with a pitiless laugh.

At that moment Morel hastened towards her: "Isn't that lady the Queen of Naples?" he asked (although he knew quite well that she was), pointing to the sovereign who was making her way towards Charlus. "After what has just happened, I can no longer, I'm afraid, ask the Baron to introduce me."

"Wait, I shall take you to her myself," said Mme Verdurin, and, followed by a few of the faithful, but not by myself and Brichot who made haste to go and collect our hats and coats, she advanced upon the Queen who was chatting to M. de Charlus. The latter had imagined that the fulfilment of his great desire that Morel should be presented to the Queen of Naples could be prevented only by the improbable demise of that lady. But we picture the future as a reflexion of the present projected into an empty space, whereas it is the result, often almost immediate, of causes which for the most part escape our notice. Not an hour had passed, and now M. de Charlus would have given anything to prevent Morel from being presented to the Queen. Mme Verdurin made the Queen a curtsey. Seeing that the other appeared not to recognise her, "I am Mme Verdurin," she said. "Your Majesty doesn't remember me."

"Quite well," said the Queen, continuing to talk to M. de Charlus so naturally and with such a casual air that Mme Verdurin doubted whether it was to herself that this "Quite well" was addressed, uttered as it was in a marvellously off-hand tone, which wrung from M. de Charlus, despite his lover's anguish, the grateful and delighted smile of an expert in the art of rudeness. Morel, who had watched from the distance the preparations for his presentation, now approached. The Queen offered her arm to M. de Charlus. With him, too, she was vexed, but only because he did not make a more energetic stand against vile detractors. She was crimson with shame on his behalf that the Verdurins should dare to treat him in this fashion. The unaffected civility which she had shown them a few hours earlier, and the arrogant pride with which she now confronted them, had their source in the same region of her heart. The Queen was a woman of great kindness, but she conceived of kindness first and foremost in the form of an unshakable attachment to the people she loved, to her own family, to all the princes of her race, among whom was M. de Charlus, and, after them, to all the people of the middle classes or of the humblest populace who knew how to respect those whom she loved and were well-disposed towards them. It was as to a woman endowed with these sound instincts that she had shown kindness to Mme Verdurin. And no doubt this is a narrow conception of kindness, somewhat Tory and increasingly obsolete. But this does not mean that her kindness was any less genuine or ardent. The ancients were no less strongly attached to the human group to which they devoted themselves because it did not go beyond the limits of their city, nor are the men of to-day to their country, than those who in the future will love the United States of the World. In my own immediate surroundings, I had the example of my mother, whom Mme de Cambremer and Mme de Guermantes could never persuade to take part in any philanthropic undertaking, to join any patriotic workroom, to be a ticket-seller or a patroness for charity shows. I do not say that she was right in acting only when her heart had first spoken, and in reserving for her own family, for her servants, for the unfortunate whom chance brought in her way, the riches of her love and generosity, but I do know that these, like those of my grandmother, were inexhaustible and exceeded by far anything that Mme de Guermantes or Mme de Cambremer ever could have done or did. The case of the Queen of Naples was altogether different, but it must be admitted that lovable people were conceived of by her not at all as in those novels of Dostoievsky which Albertine had taken from my shelves and devoured, that is to say in the guise of wheedling parasites, thieves, drunkards, obsequious one minute, insolent the next, debauchees, even murderers. Extremes, however, meet, since the noble man, the brother, the outraged kinsman whom the Queen sought to defend was M. de Charlus, that is to say, notwithstanding his birth and all the family ties that bound him to the Queen, a man whose virtue was hedged round by many vices. "You don't look at all well, my dear cousin," she said to M. de Charlus. "Lean on my arm. You may be sure that it will always support you. It is strong enough for that." Then, raising her eyes proudly in front of her (where, Ski later told me, Mme Verdurin and Morel were standing): "You know how in the past, at Gaeta, it held the mob at bay. It will be a shield to you." And it was thus, taking the Baron on her arm and without having allowed Morel to be presented to her, that the glorious sister of the Empress Elizabeth left the house.

It might have been assumed, in view of M. de Charlus's ferocious temper and the persecutions with which he terrorised even his own family, that after the events of this evening he would have unleashed his fury and taken reprisals upon the Verdurins. We have seen why nothing of this sort occurred at first. Then the Baron, having caught cold a few days later, and contracted the septic pneumonia which was very rife that winter, was for long regarded by his doctors, and regarded himself, as being at the point of death, and lay for many months suspended between it and life. Was there simply a physical metastasis, and the substitution of a different malady for the neurosis that had previously made him lose all control of himself in veritable orgies of rage? For it is too simple to suppose that, never having taken the Verdurins seriously from the social point of view, he was unable to feel the same resentment against them as he would have felt against his equals; too simple also to recall that neurotics, irritated at the slightest provocation by imaginary and inoffensive enemies, become on the contrary inoffensive as soon as anyone takes the offensive against them, and that they are more easily calmed by flinging cold water in their faces than by attempting to prove to them the inanity of their grievances. But it is probably not in a metastasis that we ought to seek the explanation of this absence of rancour, but far more in the disease itself. It exhausted the Baron so completely that he had little leisure left in which to think about the Verdurins. He was almost moribund. We mentioned offensives; even those that will have only a posthumous effect require, if they are to be properly "staged," the sacrifice of a part of one's strength. M. de Charlus had too little strength left for the activity of preparation required. We hear often of mortal enemies who open their eyes to gaze on one another in the hour of death and close them again, satisfied. This must be a rare occurrence, except when death surprises us in the midst of life. It is, on the contrary, when we have nothing left to lose that we are not bothered by the risks which, when full of life, we would have undertaken lightly. The spirit of vengeance forms part of life; it deserts us as a rule—in spite of exceptions which, in one and the same character, as we shall see, are human contradictions—on the threshold of death. After having thought for a moment about the Verdurins, M. de Charlus felt that he was too weak, turned his face to the wall, and ceased to think about anything. It was not that he had lost his eloquence, which demanded little effort. It still flowed freely, but it had changed. Detached from the violence which it had so often adorned, it was now a quasi-mystical eloquence, embellished with words of meekness, parables from the Gospel, an apparent resignation to death. He talked especially on the days when he thought that he would live. A relapse made him silent. This Christian meekness into which his splendid violence had been transposed (as into *Esther* the so different genius of *Andromaque*) provoked the admiration of those who came to his bedside. It would have provoked that of the Verdurins themselves, who could not have helped adoring a man whose weaknesses had made them hate him. It is true that thoughts which were Christian only in appearance rose to the surface. He would implore the Archangel Gabriel to appear and announce to him, as to the Prophet, precisely when the Messiah would come. And, breaking off with a sweet and sorrowful smile, he would add: "But the Archangel mustn't ask me, as he asked Daniel, to have patience for 'seven weeks, and threescore and two weeks,' for I should be dead before then." The person whom he awaited thus was Morel. And so he asked the Archangel Raphael to bring him to him, as he had brought the young Tobias. And, introducing more human measures (like sick Popes who, while ordering masses to be said, do not neglect to send for their doctors), he insinuated to his visitors that if Brichot were to bring him without delay his young Tobias, perhaps the Archangel Raphael would consent to restore Brichot's sight, as he had done to the father of Tobias, or as had happened in the sheep-pool of Bethesda. But, notwithstanding these human lapses, the moral purity of M. de Charlus's conversation had none the less become charming. Vanity, slander, the madness of malevolence and pride, had alike disappeared. Morally M. de Charlus had risen far above the level at which he had lived in the past. But this moral improvement, as to the reality of which, it must be said, his oratorical skill was capable of deceiving somewhat his impressionable audience, vanished with the malady which had laboured on its behalf. M. de Charlus redescended the downward slope with a speed which, as we shall see, continued steadily to increase. But the Verdurins' attitude towards him was by that time no more than a somewhat distant memory which more immediate outbursts prevented from reviving.

To turn back to the Verdurin reception, when the host and hostess were alone, M. Verdurin said to his wife: "You know where Cottard has gone? He's with Saniette, whose attempt to recover his losses on the Stock Exchange has failed. When he got home just now after leaving us, and learned that he hadn't a penny in the world and nearly a million francs of debts, Saniette had a stroke."

"But then why did he gamble? It's idiotic, he was the last person in the world to succeed at that game. Cleverer men than he get plucked at it, and he was born to let himself be swindled by every Tom, Dick and Harry."

"But of course, we've always known he was an idiot," said M. Verdurin. "Anyhow, this is the result. Here you have a man who will be turned out of house and home to-morrow by his landlord, and who's going to find himself in utter penury; his relations don't like him, Forcheville is the last man in the world who would do anything for him. And so it occurred to me—I don't wish to do anything that doesn't meet with your approval, but we might perhaps be able to scrape up a small income for him so that he shan't be too conscious of his ruin, so that he can keep a roof over his head."

"I entirely agree with you, it's very good of you to have thought of it. But you say 'a roof'; the fool has kept on an apartment beyond his means, he can't remain in it, we shall have to find him a couple of rooms somewhere. I understand that at present he's still paying six or seven thousand francs."

"Six thousand five hundred. But he's greatly attached to his home. And after all, he's had a first stroke, he can scarcely live more than two or three years. Suppose we were to spend ten thousand francs on his behalf for three years. It seems to me that we should be able to afford that. We might for instance this year, instead of renting la Raspelière again, take somewhere more modest. With our income, it seems to me that to write off ten thousand francs a year for three years isn't out of the question."

"So be it. The only trouble is that people will get to know about it, and we'll be expected to do it for others."

"You can imagine that I thought of that. I shall do it only on the express condition that nobody knows about it. I've no wish for us to become the benefactors of the human race, thank you very much. No philanthropy! What we might do is to tell him that the money has been left to him by Princess Sherbatoff."

"But will he believe it? She consulted Cottard about her will."

"If the worst comes to the worst, we might take Cottard into our confidence. He's used to professional secrecy, he makes an enormous amount of money, he won't be like one of those busybodies for whom one's obliged to cough up. He may even perhaps be willing to say that the Princess appointed him as her executor. In that way we wouldn't even appear. That would avoid all the nuisance of scenes of gratitude, effusions and speeches."

M. Verdurin added an expression which made quite plain the kind of touching scenes and speeches which they were anxious to avoid. But it could not be reported to me precisely, for it was not a French expression, but one of those terms that are employed in certain families to denote certain things, annoying things especially, probably because people wish to be able to refer to them in the hearing of the persons concerned without being understood. An expression of this sort is generally a survival from an earlier condition of the family. In a Jewish family, for instance, it will be a ritual term diverted from its true meaning, and perhaps the only Hebrew word with which the family, now thoroughly Gallicised, is still acquainted. In a family that is strongly provincial, it will be a term of local dialect, albeit the family no longer speaks or even understands that dialect. In a family that has come from South America and no longer speaks anything but French, it will be a Spanish word. And, in the next generation, the word will no longer exist save as a childhood memory. It will be remembered perfectly well that the parents used to allude to the servants who were waiting at table by employing some such word, but the children have no idea what the word meant, whether it was Spanish, Hebrew, German, dialect, if indeed it ever belonged to any language and was not a proper name or a word entirely made up. The uncertainty can be cleared up only if they have a great-uncle or an old cousin still alive who must have used the same expression. As I never knew any relations of the Verdurins, I was never able to reconstruct the word. All I know is that it certainly drew a smile from Mme Verdurin, for the use of such a vocabulary, less general, more personal, more secret, than everyday speech, inspires in those who use it among themselves an egocentric feeling which is always accompanied by a certain self-satisfaction. After this moment of mirth, "But if Cottard talks," Mme Verdurin objected. "He won't talk." He did talk, to myself at least, for it was from him that I learned the story a few years later, actually at Saniette's funeral. I was sorry that I had not known of it earlier. For one thing the knowledge would have brought me more rapidly to the idea that we ought never to bear a grudge against people, ought never to judge them by some memory of an unkind action, for we do not know all the good that, at other moments, their hearts may have sincerely desired and realised. And thus, even simply from the point of view of prediction, one is mistaken. For doubtless the evil aspect which we have noted once and for all will recur; but the heart is richer than that, has many other aspects which will recur also in the same person and which we refuse to acknowledge because of his earlier bad behaviour. But from a more personal point of view, this revelation of Cottard's, if it had been made to me earlier, would have dispelled the suspicions I had formed as to the part that the Verdurins might be playing between Albertine and myself—would have dispelled them wrongly perhaps as it happened, for if M. Verdurin had virtues, he nevertheless teased and bullied to the point of the most savage persecution, and was so jealous of his position of dominance in the little clan as not to shrink from the basest falsehoods, from the fomentation of the most unjustified hatreds, in order to sever any ties among the faithful which had not as their sole object the strengthening of the little group. He was a man capable of disinterestedness, of unostentatious generosity, but that does not necessarily mean a man of feeling, or a likeable man, or a scrupulous or a truthful or always a kind man. A partial kindness—in which there subsisted, perhaps, a trace of the family whom my great-aunt had known—probably existed in him before I discovered it through this fact, as America or the North Pole existed before Columbus or Peary. Nevertheless, at the moment of my discovery, M. Verdurin's nature offered me a new and unsuspected facet; and I concluded that it is as difficult to present a fixed image of a character as of societies and passions. For a character alters no less than they do, and if one tries to take a snapshot of what is relatively immutable in it, one finds it presenting a succession of different aspects (implying that it is incapable of keeping still but keeps moving) to the disconcerted lens.

Seeing how late it was, and fearing that Albertine might be growing impatient, I asked Brichot, as we left the Ver-

durins' party, to be so kind as to drop me home first, and my
carriage would then take him on. He commended me for going
straight home like this (unaware that a girl was waiting for me
in the house) and for ending the evening so early and so wisely,
when in fact all I had done was postpone its real beginning.
Then he spoke to me about M. de Charlus. The latter would
doubtless have been amazed had he heard the Professor, who
was so amiable to him, the Professor who always assured him:
"I never repeat anything," speaking of him and of his life
without the slightest reticence. And Brichot's indignant amazement would perhaps have been no less sincere if M. de Charlus
had said to him: "I'm told you've been speaking ill of me."
Brichot did indeed have an affection for M. de Charlus, and
if he had had to call to mind some conversation that had turned
upon him, would have been far more likely to remember the
friendly feelings he had had for the Baron, while saying the
same things about him as everyone else, than those things themselves. He would not have thought that he was lying if he had
said: "I who speak of you with such friendliness," since he
did feel friendly when he was speaking about M. de Charlus.
The Baron had for Brichot the charm which he demanded
above all else from the world of society—that of offering
him real specimens of what he had long supposed to be an
invention of the poets. Brichot, who had often expounded the
second Eclogue of Virgil without really knowing whether
its fiction had any basis in reality, belatedly found, in conversing
with Charlus, some of the pleasure which he knew that his
masters, M. Mérimée and M. Renan, and his colleague M.
Maspéro, had felt when travelling in Spain, Palestine and
Egypt on recognising in the landscapes and the present inhabitants of Spain, Palestine and Egypt the settings and the
selfsame actors of the ancient scenes which they themselves
had expounded in their books.

"Be it said without offence to that knight of noble lineage,"
Brichot declared to me in the carriage that was taking us home,
"he is simply prodigious when he illustrates his satanic
catechism with a distinctly Bedlamite vigour and the obsessive-
ness, I was going to say the naïve candour, of a *blanc d'Espagne*[21]
or an *émigré*. I can assure you, if I dare express myself like

Mgr d'Hulst, I am by no means bored on the days when I
receive a visit from that feudal lord who, seeking to defend
Adonis against our age of miscreants, has followed the instincts
of his race, and, in all sodomist innocence, has gone crusading."

I listened to Brichot, and I was not alone with him. As,
for that matter, I had never ceased to feel since I left home that
evening, I felt myself, in however obscure a fashion, tied fast
to the girl who was at that moment in her bedroom. Even
when I was talking to someone or other at the Verdurins', I
had somehow felt that she was by my side, I had that vague
impression of her that we have of our own limbs, and if I
happened to think of her it was as we think, with annoyance
at being bound to it in complete subjection, of our own body.

"And what a fund of scandal," Brichot went on, "enough to
supply all the appendixes of the *Causeries du Lundi*, is the conversation of that apostle! Just imagine, I learned from him
that the treatise on ethics which I had always admired as the
most splendid moral edifice of our age was inspired in our
venerable colleague X by a young telegraph messenger. Needless to say, my eminent friend omitted to give us the name of this
ephebe in the course of his demonstrations. In this he showed
more circumspection, or, if you prefer, less gratitude, than
Phidias, who inscribed the name of the athlete whom he loved
upon the ring of his Olympian Zeus. The Baron had not heard
this last story. Needless to say, it appealed to his orthodoxy.
You can readily imagine that whenever I have to discuss with
my colleague a candidate's thesis, I find in his dialectic, which
for that matter is extremely subtle, the additional savour which
spicy revelations added, for Sainte-Beuve, to the insufficiently
confidential writings of Chateaubriand. From our colleague,
whose wisdom is golden but who had little money, the
telegraph-boy passed into the hands of the Baron, 'with the
most honourable intentions' (you should have heard his voice
when he said it). And as this Satan is the most obliging of
men, he found his protégé a post in the Colonies, from which
the young man, who has a sense of gratitude, sends him from
time to time the most excellent fruit. The Baron offers these
to his distinguished friends; some of the young man's pineapples appeared quite recently on the table at the Quai Conti,

causing Mme Verdurin to remark, with no malicious intent: 'You must have an uncle or a nephew in America, M. de Charlus, to get pineapples like these!' I admit that I ate them with a certain gaiety, reciting to myself the opening lines of an Horatian ode which Diderot loved to recall. In fact, like my colleague Boissier, strolling from the Palatine to Tibur, I derive from the Baron's conversation a singularly more vivid and more savoury idea of the writers of the Augustan age, without mentioning those of the Decadence, or harking back to the Greeks, although I once said to the excellent Baron that in his company I felt like Plato in the house of Aspasia. To tell the truth, I had considerably enlarged the scale of the two characters and, as La Fontaine says, my example was taken 'from smaller animals.' However that may be, you do not, I imagine, suppose that the Baron took offence. Never have I seen him so ingenuously delighted. A childish excitement caused him to depart from his aristocratic phlegm. 'What flatterers all these Sorbonnards are!' he exclaimed with rapture. 'To think that I should have had to wait until my age before being compared to Aspasia! An old fright like me! Oh, my youth!' I should have loved you to see him as he said this, outrageously powdered as he always is, and, at his age, scented like a young fop. All the same, beneath his genealogical obsessions, the best fellow in the world. For all these reasons, I should be distressed were this evening's rupture to prove final. What did surprise me was the way in which the young man turned on him. His manner towards the Baron has been, for some time past, that of a henchman, of a feudal vassal, which scarcely betokened such an insurrection. I hope that, in any event, even if (*Dii omen avertant*) the Baron were never to return to the Quai Conti, this schism will not extend to me. Each of us derives too much benefit from the exchange that we make of my feeble stock of learning with his experience." (We shall see that if M. de Charlus showed no violent rancour towards Brichot, at any rate his affection for the Professor vanished so completely as to allow him to judge him without indulgence.) "And I swear to you that the exchange is so much in my favour that when the Baron yields up to me what his life has taught him, I am unable to endorse the opinion of Sylvestre Bonnard that a library is still the best place in which to ponder the dream of life."

We had now reached my door. I got out of the carriage to give the driver Brichot's address. From the pavement, I could see the window of Albertine's room, that window, formerly quite black at night when she had not been staying in the house, which the electric light from inside, segmented by the slats of the shutters, striped from top to bottom with parallel bars of gold. This magic scroll, clear as it was to myself, tracing before my tranquil mind precise images, near at hand, of which I should presently be taking possession, was invisible to Brichot who had remained in the carriage and was almost blind, and would in any case have been incomprehensible to him since, like the friends who called on me before dinner, when Albertine had returned from her drive, the Professor was unaware that a girl who was all my own was waiting for me in a bedroom adjoining mine. The carriage drove off. I remained for a moment alone on the pavement. It was true that I endowed those luminous streaks which I could see from below, and which to anyone else would have seemed quite superficial, with the utmost plenitude, solidity and volume, because of all the significance that I placed behind them, in a treasure unsuspected by the rest of the world which I had hidden there and from which those horizontal rays emanated, but a treasure in exchange for which I had forfeited my freedom, my solitude, my thought. If Albertine had not been up there, and indeed if I had merely been in search of pleasure, I would have gone to demand it of unknown women, into whose life I should have attempted to penetrate, in Venice perhaps, or at least in some corner of nocturnal Paris. But now what I had to do when the time came for love-making was not to set out on a journey, was not even to leave my own house, but to return there. And to return there not to find myself alone and, after taking leave of the friends who provide one from the outside with food for one's thoughts, to find myself at any rate compelled to seek it in myself, but to be on the contrary less alone than when I was at the Verdurins', welcomed as I was about to be by the person to whom I had abdicated, to whom I had handed over most completely my own person, without having for an instant the leisure to think of myself nor even requiring the effort, since she would be by my side, to think of her. So that, as I raised my eyes for one last look from the outside at the window of the room in which I should presently find myself, I seemed to behold the luminous gates which were about to close behind me and of which I myself had forged, for an eternal slavery, the inflexible bars of gold.

Albertine had never told me that she suspected me of being jealous of her, preoccupied with everything that she did. The only words we had exchanged—fairly long ago, it must be said—on the subject of jealousy seemed to prove the opposite. I remembered that, on a fine moonlight evening towards the beginning of our relationship, on one of the first occasions when I had accompanied her home and would have been just as glad not to do so and to leave her in order to run after other girls, I had said to her: "You know, if I'm offering to take you home, it's not from jealousy; if you have anything else to do, I shall slip discreetly away." And she had replied: "Oh, I know quite well that you aren't jealous and that you don't care a fig, but I've nothing else to do except to stay with you." Another occasion was at la Raspelière, when M. de Charlus, not without casting a covert glance at Morel, had made a display of friendly gallantry towards Albertine; I had said to her: "Well, he gave you a good hug, I hope." And as I had added half ironically: "I suffered all the torments of jealousy," Albertine, employing the language proper either to the vulgar background from which she sprang or to that other, more vulgar still, which she frequented, replied: "What a kidder you are! I know quite well you're not jealous. For one thing, you told me so, and besides, it's perfectly obvious, get along with you!" She had never told me since then that she had changed her mind; but she must have formed a number of fresh ideas on the subject, which she concealed from me but which an accident might betray willy-nilly, for that evening when, on reaching home, after going to fetch her from her own room and taking her to mine, I said to her (with a certain awkwardness which I did not myself understand, for I had indeed told Albertine that I was going to pay a call and had said that I did not know where, perhaps on Mme de Villeparisis, perhaps on Mme de Guermantes, perhaps on Mme de Cambremer; it is true that I had not actually mentioned the Verdurins): "Guess where I've been—at the Verdurins'," I had barely had time to utter the words before Albertine, a look of utter consternation on her face, had answered me in words which seemed to explode of their own accord with a force which she was unable to contain: "I thought as much."

"I didn't know that you'd be annoyed by my going to see the Verdurins." (It is true that she had not told me that she was annoyed, but it was obvious. It is true also that I had not said to myself that she would be annoyed. And yet, faced with the explosion of her wrath, as with one of those events which a sort of retrospective second sight makes us imagine that we have already experienced in the past, it seemed to me that I could never have expected anything else.)

"Annoyed? What difference does it make to me? I couldn't care less. Wasn't Mlle Vinteuil to be there?"

Beside myself at these words, "You never told me you'd met her the other day," I said to her, to show her that I was better informed than she knew.

Believing that the person whom I reproached her for having met without telling me was Mme Verdurin and not, as I meant to imply, Mlle Vinteuil, "Did I meet her?" she inquired with a pensive air, addressing both herself, as though she were seeking to collect her fugitive memories, and me, as though it was I who could have enlightened her; and no doubt in order that I might indeed say what I knew, and perhaps also in order to gain time before making a difficult reply. But I was far less preoccupied with the thought of Mlle Vinteuil than with a fear which had already crossed my mind but which now gripped me more forcibly. Indeed I imagined that Mme Verdurin had purely and simply invented the story of having expected Mlle Vinteuil and her friend, in order to enhance her own prestige, so that I was quite calm on arriving home. Only Albertine, by saying: "Wasn't Mlle Vinteuil to be there?" had shown me that I had not been mistaken in my original suspicion; but anyhow my mind was at rest in that quarter as far as the future was concerned, since by giving up her plan of visiting the

Verdurins' Albertine had sacrified Mlle Vinteuil for my sake.

"Besides," I said to her angrily, "there are plenty of other things which you hide from me, even the most trivial things, such as for instance when you went for three days to Balbec—I mention it by the way." I had added the words "I mention it by the way" as a complement to "even the most trivial things" so that if Albertine said to me "What was there wrong about my trip to Balbec?" I might be able to answer: "Why, I've quite forgotten. The things people tell me get muddled up in my mind, I attach so little importance to them." And indeed if I referred to that three-day excursion she had made with the chauffeur to Balbec, from where her postcards had reached me after so long a delay, I did so purely at random, and regretted that I had chosen so bad an example, for in fact, as they had barely had time to go there and return, it was certainly the one excursion in which there had not even been time for the interpolation of a meeting that was at all protracted with anybody. But Albertine supposed, from what I had just said, that I knew the real truth and had merely concealed my knowledge from her. She had in any case been convinced, for some time past, that in one way or another, by having her followed, or in some such fashion, I was, as she had said the week before to Andrée, better informed about her life than she was herself. And so she interrupted me with a wholly unnecessary admission, for certainly I suspected nothing of what she now told me, and I was on the other hand shattered by it, so vast can the disparity be between the truth which a liar has travestied and the idea which, from her lies, the man who is in love with the said liar has formed of that truth. Scarcely had I uttered the words: "When you went for three days to Balbec, I mention it by the way," than Albertine, cutting me short, declared to me as something quite natural: "You mean I never went to Balbec at all? Of course I didn't! And I've always wondered why you pretended to believe that I did. All the same, there was no harm in it. The driver had some business of his own for three days. He didn't dare to mention it to you. And so out of kindness to him (it's typical of me, and I'm the one who always gets the blame), I invented a trip to Balbec. He simply put me down at Auteuil, at the house of a girl friend of mine

in the Rue de l'Assomption, where I spent the three days bored
to tears. You see it's not very serious, no great harm done. I
did begin to think that you perhaps knew all about it, when I
saw how you laughed when the postcards began to arrive, a
week late. I quite see that it was absurd, and that it would have
been better not to send any cards at all. But that wasn't my
fault. I'd bought them in advance and given them to the driver
before he dropped me at Auteuil, and then the fathead put them
in his pocket and forgot about them instead of sending them
on in an envelope to a friend of his near Balbec who was to
forward them to you. I kept on imagining they were about
to arrive. He only remembered them after five days, and instead of telling me, the idiot sent them on at once to Balbec.
When he did tell me, I really let him have it, I can tell you!
To go and worry you unnecessarily, the great fool, as a reward
for my shutting myself up for three whole days, so that he
could go and look after his family affairs! I didn't even venture
out into Auteuil for fear of being seen. The only time I did go
out, I was dressed as a man, just for a joke, really. And it
was just my luck that the first person I came across was your Yid
friend Bloch. But I don't believe it was from him that you
learned that my trip to Balbec never existed except in my
imagination, for he seemed not to recognise me."

I did not know what to say, not wishing to appear surprised,
and shattered by all these lies. A feeling of horror, which gave
me no desire to turn Albertine out of the house, far from it,
was combined with a strong inclination to burst into tears.
This last was caused not by the lie itself and by the annihilation
of everything that I had so firmly believed to be true that I
felt as though I were in a town that had been razed to the
ground, where not a house remained standing, where the
bare soil was merely heaped with rubble—but by the melancholy thought that, during those three days when she had been
bored to tears in her friend's house at Auteuil, Albertine had
never once felt the desire, that the idea had perhaps not even
occurred to her, to come and pay me a visit one day on the
quiet, or to send a message asking me to go and see her at
Auteuil. But I had no time to give myself up to these reflexions.
Whatever happened, I did not wish to appear surprised. I

smiled with the air of man who knows far more than he is prepared to say: "But that's only one thing out of hundreds.
For instance, only this evening, at the Verdurins', I learned
that what you had told me about Mlle Vinteuil. . . ."

Albertine gazed at me fixedly with a tormented air, seeking
to read in my eyes how much I knew. Now, what I knew and
what I was about to tell her was the truth about Mlle Vinteuil.
It is true that it was not at the Verdurins' that I had learned
it, but at Montjouvain long ago. But since I had always refrained, deliberately, from mentioning it to Albertine, I
could now appear to have learned it only this evening. And I
had a feeling almost of joy—after having felt such anguish in
the little train—at possessing this memory of Montjouvain,
which I would postdate, but which would nevertheless be the
unanswerable proof, a crushing blow to Albertine. This time
at least, I had no need to "seem to know" and to "make
Albertine talk": I *knew*, I had *seen* through the lighted window
at Montjouvain. It had been all very well for Albertine to
tell me that her relations with Mlle Vinteuil and her friend
had been perfectly pure, but how could she, when I swore to
her (and swore without lying) that I knew the habits of these
two women, how could she maintain any longer that, having
lived in daily intimacy with them, calling them "my big sisters,"
she had not been the object of approaches on their part which
would have made her break with them, if on the contrary she
had not acquiesced in them? But I had no time to tell her what
I knew. Albertine, imagining, as in the case of the pretended
excursion to Balbec, that I had learned the truth either from
Mlle Vinteuil, if she had been at the Verdurins', or simply from
Mme Verdurin herself, who might have mentioned her to
Mlle Vinteuil, did not allow me the chance to speak but made
a confession, precisely contrary to what I should have imagined,
which nevertheless, by showing me that she had never ceased
to lie to me, caused me perhaps just as much pain (especially
since I was no longer, as I said a moment ago, jealous of
Mlle Vinteuil). Taking the initiative, she spoke as follows:
"You mean that you found out this evening that I lied to you
when I pretended that I had been more or less brought up by
Mlle Vinteuil's friend. It's true that I did lie to you a little. But

I felt so looked down on by you, and I saw that you were so keen on that man Vinteuil's music, that as one of my school friends—this is true, I swear to you—had been a friend of Mlle Vinteuil's friend, I stupidly thought that I might make myself seem interesting to you by inventing the story that I had known the girls quite well. I felt that I bored you, that you thought me a goose; I thought that if I told you that those people used to see a lot of me, that I could easily tell you all sorts of things about Vinteuil's work, you'd think more highly of me, that it would bring us closer together. When I lie to you, it's always out of affection for you. And it needed this fatal Verdurin party to open your eyes to the truth, which perhaps they exaggerated a bit, incidentally. I bet Mlle Vinteuil's friend told you that she didn't know me. She met me at least twice at my friend's house. But of course, I'm not smart enough for people who've become so famous. They prefer to say that they've never met me."

Poor Albertine, when she had thought that to tell me that she had been on such intimate terms with Mlle Vinteuil's friend would postpone our separation, would bring her closer to me, she had, as so often happens, reached the truth by a different road from that which she had intended to take. Her showing herself better informed about music than I had supposed would never have prevented me from breaking with her that evening in the little train; and yet it was indeed that speech, which she had made with that object, that had immediately brought about far more than the impossibility of a rupture. Only she made an error of interpretation, not about the effect which that speech was to have, but about the cause by virtue of which it was to produce that effect—that cause being my discovery not of her musical culture but of her disreputable associations. What had abruptly drawn me closer to her—far more, fused indissolubly with her—was not the expectation of a pleasure—and pleasure is too strong a word, a mildly agreeable interest—but the grip of an agonising pain.

Once again I had to be careful not to keep too long a silence which might have led her to suppose that I was surprised. And so, touched by the discovery that she was so modest and had thought herself despised in the Verdurin circle, I said to her tenderly: "But, my darling, I'd gladly give you several hundred francs to let you go and play the fashionable lady wherever you please and invite M. and Mme Verdurin to a grand dinner."

Alas! Albertine was several persons in one. The most mysterious, most simple, most loathsome of these revealed herself in the answer which she made me with an air of disgust, and the exact words of which, to tell the truth, I could not quite make out (even the opening words, for she did not finish her sentence). I did not succeed in reconstituting them until some time later when I had guessed what was in her mind. We hear things retrospectively when we have understood them.

"Thank you for nothing! Spend money on them! I'd a great deal rather you left me free for once in a way to go and get myself b . . . (*me faire casser*) . . ."

At once her face flushed crimson, she looked appalled, and she put her hand over her mouth as though she could have thrust back the words which she had just uttered and which I had quite failed to catch.

"What did you say, Albertine?"

"Nothing, I was half asleep and talking to myself."

"Not a bit of it, you were wide awake."

"I was thinking about asking the Verdurins to dinner, it's very good of you."

"No, I mean what you said just now."

She gave me endless versions, none of which tallied in the least, not simply with her words which, having been interrupted, remained obscure to me, but with the interruption itself and the sudden flush that had accompanied it.

"Come, my darling, that's not what you were going to say, otherwise why did you stop short?"

"Because I felt that my request was presumptuous."

"What request?"

"To be allowed to give a dinner-party."

"No, no, that's not it, there's no need for ceremony between you and me."

"Indeed there is, we ought never to take advantage of the people we love. In any case, I swear to you that that was all."

On the one hand it was still impossible for me to doubt her sworn word; on the other hand her explanations did not satisfy my reason. I continued to press her. ' iyhow, you might at least have the courage to finish what you were saying, you stopped short at *casser*."

"No, leave me alone!"

"But why?"

"Because it's dreadfully vulgar, I'd be ashamed to say such a thing in front of you. I don't know what I was thinking of. The words—I don't even know what they mean, I heard them used in the street one day by some very low people—just came into my head without rhyme or reason. It had nothing to do with me or anybody else, I was simply dreaming aloud."

I felt that I would extract nothing more from Albertine. She had lied to me when she had sworn a moment ago that what had cut her short had been a social fear of being over-presumptuous, since it had now become the shame of using a vulgar expression in front of me. Now this was certainly another lie. For when we were alone together there was no expression too perverse, no word too coarse for us to utter amidst our embraces. However, it was useless to insist at that moment. But my memory remained obsessed by the word *casser*. Albertine often used expressions such as "casser du bois" or "casser du sucre," or would say "Ah! ce que je lui en ai cassé!" meaning "I fairly gave it to him!" But she would say this quite freely in my presence, and if it was this that she had meant to say, why had she suddenly stopped short, why had she blushed so deeply, placed her hands over her mouth, tried to refashion her sentence, and, when she saw that I had heard the word *casser*, offered a false explanation? Meanwhile, abandoning the pursuit of an interrogation from which I would get no response, the best thing to do was to appear to have lost interest in the matter, and, retracing my thoughts to Albertine's reproaches to me for having gone to the Mistress's, I said to her, somewhat clumsily, making indeed a sort of stupid excuse for my conduct: "Actually I'd been meaning to ask you to come to the Verdurins' party this evening," a remark that was doubly maladroit, for if I meant it, since I saw her all the time, why should I not have made the sugges-tion? Furious at my lie and emboldened by my timidity: "You could have gone on asking me for a thousand years," she said, "and I'd never have consented. Those people have always been against me, they've done everything they could to mortify me. There was nothing I didn't do for Mme Verdurin at Balbec, and look at the thanks I get. If she summoned me to her deathbed, I wouldn't go. There are some things it's impossible to forgive. As for you, it's the first time you've behaved badly to me. When Françoise told me you'd gone out (and she enjoyed telling me all right), I'd sooner have been bashed over the head. I tried not to show any sign, but never in my life have I felt so grossly insulted."

But while she was speaking there continued within me, in that curiously alive and creative sleep of the unconscious (a sleep in which the things that have barely touched us succeed in carving an impression, in which our sleeping hands take hold of the key that turns the lock, the key for which we have sought in vain), the quest for what it was that she had meant by that interrupted sentence, the missing end of which I was so anxious to know. And all of a sudden an appalling word, of which I had never dreamed, burst upon me: *le pot*.[22] I cannot say that it came to me in a single flash, as when, in a long passive submission to an incomplete recollection, while one tries gently and cautiously to unfold it, one remains ravelled in it, glued to it. No, in contrast to my habitual method of recall, there were, I think, two parallel lines of search: the first took into account not merely Albertine's words, but her look of exasperation when I had offered her a sum of money with which to give a grand dinner, a look which seemed to say: "Thank you, the idea of spending money upon things that bore me, when without money I could do things that I enjoy doing!" And it was perhaps the memory of the look she had given me that made me alter my method in order to discover the end of her unfinished sentence. Until then I had been hypnotised by the last word, *casser*. Break what? Break, break, break. And all at once her look, and her shrug, when I had suggested that she should give a dinner-party sent me back to the words that had preceded. And immediately I saw that she had not simply said *casser* but *me faire casser*. Horror! It was this that she would have preferred. Twofold horror! For even the vilest of prostitutes, who consents to such a thing, or even desires it, does not use that hideous expression to the man who indulges in it. She would feel it too degrading. To a woman alone, if she loves women, she might say it, to excuse herself for giving herself presently to a man. Albertine had not been lying when she told me that she was half dreaming. Her mind elsewhere, forgetting that she was with me, impulsively she had shrugged her shoulders and begun to speak as she would have spoken to one of those women, perhaps to one of my budding girls. And abruptly recalled to reality, crimson with shame, pushing back into her mouth what she was about to say, desperately ashamed, she had refused to utter another word. I had not a moment to lose if I was not to let her see the despair I was in. But already, after my first impulse of rage, the tears were coming to my eyes. As at Balbec, on the night that followed her revelation of her friendship with the Vinteuil pair, I must immediately invent a plausible reason for my grief, and one that was at the same time capable of having so profound an effect on Albertine as to give me a few days' respite before coming to a decision. And so, just as she was telling me that she had never felt so affronted as when she had heard that I had gone out alone, that she would sooner have died than be told this by Françoise, and just as, irritated by her absurd susceptibility, I was on the point of telling her that what I had done was trivial, that there was nothing wounding to her in my having gone out, my unconscious parallel search for what she had meant to say had come to fruition, and the despair into which my discovery plunged me could not be completely hidden, so that instead of defending, I accused myself. "My little Albertine," I said to her in a gentle voice which was drowned in my first tears, "I could tell you that you're mistaken, that what I did this evening was nothing, but I should be lying; it's you who are right, you have realised the truth, my poor sweet, which is that six months ago, three months ago, when I was still so fond of you, I should never have done such a thing. It's a mere nothing, and yet it's enormous, because of the immense change in my heart of which it is the sign. And since you have detected this change which I hoped to conceal from you, I feel impelled to say this to you: My little Albertine" (I went on in a tone of profound gentleness and melancholy), "don't you see that the life you're leading here is boring for you. It is better that we should part, and as the best partings are those that are effected most swiftly, I ask you, to cut short the great sorrow that I am bound to feel, to say good-bye to me to-night and to leave in the morning without my seeing you again, while I'm asleep."

She appeared stunned, incredulous and desolate: "To-morrow? You really mean it?"

And in spite of the anguish that I felt in speaking of our parting as though it were already in the past—partly perhaps because of that very anguish—I began to give Albertine the most precise instructions as to certain things which she would have to do after she left the house. And passing from one request to another, I soon found myself entering into the minutest details.

"Be so kind," I said with infinite sadness, "as to send me back that book of Bergotte's which is at your aunt's. There's no hurry about it, in three days, in a week, whenever you like, but remember that I don't want to have to write and ask you for it: that would be too painful. We have been happy together, but now we feel that we should be unhappy."

"Don't say that we feel that we'd be unhappy," Albertine interrupted me, "don't say 'we,' it's only you who feel that."

"Yes, very well, you or I, as you like, for one reason or another. But it's absurdly late, you must go to bed—we've decided to part to-night."

"Excuse me, *you*'ve decided, and I obey you because I don't want to upset you."

"Very well, it's I who have decided, but that doesn't make it any less painful for me. I don't say that it will be painful for long, you know that I'm not capable of remembering things for long, but for the first few days I shall be so miserable without you. And so I feel that it's no use stirring up the memory with letters, we must end everything at once."

"Yes, you're right," she said to me with a crushed air, which was enhanced by the signs of fatigue on her features due to the lateness of the hour, "rather than have one finger chopped off and then another, I prefer to lay my head on the block at once."

"Heavens, I'm appalled when I think how late I'm keeping you out of bed, it's madness. However, it's the last night! You'll have plenty of time to sleep for the rest of your life."

And thus while telling her that it was time to say good-night I sought to postpone the moment when she would have said it: "Would you like me, in order to take your mind off things during the first few days, to ask Bloch to send his cousin Esther to the place where you'll be staying. He'll do that for me."

"I don't know why you say that" (I had said it in an attempt to wrest a confession from Albertine), "there's only one person I care about, and that's you," Albertine said to me, and her words were infinitely sweet to me. But, the next moment, what a blow she dealt me! "I remember, of course, that I did give this Esther my photograph because she kept on asking me for it and I saw that it would give her pleasure, but as for having any great liking for her or wanting to see her again, never!" And yet Albertine was of so frivolous a nature that she went on: "If she wants to see me, it's all the same to me. She's very nice, but I don't care in the least either way."

Thus, when I had spoken to her of the photograph of Esther which Bloch had sent me (and which I had not even received when I mentioned it to her) Albertine had gathered that Bloch had shown me a photograph of herself which she had given to Esther. In my worst suppositions, I had never imagined that any such intimacy could have existed between Albertine and Esther. Albertine had been at a loss for words when I mentioned the photograph. And now, wrongly, supposing me to be in the know, she thought it advisable to confess. I was shattered.

"And, Albertine, let me ask you to do me one more favour: never attempt to see me again. If at any time, as may happen in a year, in two years, in three years, we should find ourselves in the same town, avoid me." And seeing that she did not answer my request in the affirmative, I went on: "My Albertine, don't do it, don't ever see me again in this life. It would hurt me too much. For I was really fond of you, you know. Of course, when I told you the other day that I wanted to see the friend I mentioned to you at Balbec again, you thought it was all settled. Not at all, I assure you, it was quite immaterial to me. You're convinced that I had long made up my mind to leave you, that my affection was all make-believe."

"Not at all, you're crazy, I never thought so," she said sadly.

"You're right, you must never think so, I did genuinely feel for you, not love perhaps, but a great, a very great affection, more than you can imagine."

"Of course I can imagine. And do you suppose that I don't love you!"

"It hurts me terribly to have to leave you."

"It hurts me a thousand times more," replied Albertine.

Already for some little time I had felt that I could no longer hold back the tears that came welling up in my eyes. And these tears did not spring from at all the same sort of misery which I had felt long ago when I said to Gilberte: "It is better that we should not see one another again; life is dividing us." No doubt when I wrote this to Gilberte, I said to myself that when I was in love not with her but with another, the excess of my love would diminish that which I might perhaps have been able to inspire, as though two people must inevitably have only a certain quantity of love at their disposal, of which the surplus taken by one is subtracted from the other, and that from her too, as from Gilberte, I should be doomed to part. But the situation was entirely different for several reasons, the first of which (and it had, in its turn, given rise to the others) was that the lack of will-power which my grandmother and my mother had observed in me with alarm, at Combray, and before which each of them, so great is the energy with which an invalid imposes his weakness upon others, had capitulated in turn, this lack of will-power had gone on increasing at an ever accelerated pace. When I felt that my presence bored Gilberte, I had still enough strength left to give her up; I had no longer the same strength when I had made a similar discovery with regard to Albertine, and could think only of keeping her by force. With the result that, whereas I wrote to Gilberte saying that I would not see her again and really meant it, I said this to Albertine quite untruthfully and in the hope of bringing about a reconciliation. Thus we presented each to the other an appearance which was very different from the

reality. And no doubt it is always so when two people are face
to face, since each of them is ignorant of a part of what exists
in the other (even what he knows, he can understand only in
part) and both of them reveal what is least personal to them,
either because they have themselves not properly untangled
and regard as negligible what is most personal or because
insignificant advantages which do not belong to them particularly seem more important and more flattering to themselves,
and at the same time they pretend not to care about certain
things they admire, in order not to be despised for not having
them, and these are precisely the things that they appear to
scorn above all else and even to abhor. But in love this misunderstanding is carried to its supreme pitch because, except
perhaps in childhood, we try to see to it that the appearance
we assume, instead of reflecting exactly what is in our thoughts,
is what is best calculated to enable us to obtain what we desire,
and this, in my case, since I had come in, was to be able to keep
Albertine as docile as she had been in the past, and to ensure
that she did not in her irritation ask me for greater freedom,
which I wanted to grant her some day but which at this
moment, when I was afraid of her hankerings after independence, would have made me too jealous. After a certain age,
from self-esteem and from sagacity, it is to the things we most
desire that we pretend to attach no importance. But in love,
mere sagacity—which in any case is probably not true wisdom
—drives us all too quickly to this kind of duplicity. What I had
dreamed of, as a child, as being the sweetest thing in love, what
had seemed to me to be the very essence of love, was to pour
out freely, to the one I loved, my tenderness, my gratitude for
her kindness, my longing for an everlasting life together. But
I had become only too well aware, from my own experience
and from that of my friends, that the expression of such sentiments is far from being contagious. The case of an affected
old woman like M. de Charlus who, as a result of seeing in
his mind's eye only a handsome young man, thinks he himself
has become a handsome young man, and betrays more and
more effeminacy in his risible affectations of virility—such a
case falls under a law which applies far more widely than to the
Charluses alone, a law so generalised that not even love itself

exhausts it entirely; we do not see our bodies, though others do, and we "follow" our thoughts, the object that is in front of us, invisible to others (made visible at times in a work of art, whence the frequent disillusionment of its admirers when they are admitted into the presence of the artist, whose inner beauty is so imperfectly reflected in his face). Once one has noticed this, one no longer "lets oneself go"; I had taken good care that afternoon not to tell Albertine how grateful I was to her that she had not remained at the Trocadéro. And to-night, having been afraid that she might leave me, I had feigned a desire to leave her, a pretence which moreover, as we shall see presently, had not been dictated solely by the experience I believed myself to have gained from my former loves and was seeking to turn to the profit of this one.

There was only one moment when I felt a kind of hatred for her, which merely sharpened my need to hold on to her. Since, being exclusively jealous of Mlle Vinteuil that night, I thought of the Trocadéro with the greatest indifference (not only because I had sent her there to avoid the Verdurins, but even when I thought of Léa's presence there, on account of which I had brought her back so that she should not meet her), I mentioned Léa's name without thinking, and Albertine, at once on her guard, supposing that I had perhaps heard something more, took the initiative and exclaimed volubly, but without looking me straight in the face: "I know her very well. Some of my friends and I went to see her act last year, and after the performance we went behind to her dressing-room. She changed in front of us. It was most interesting." Then my mind was compelled to relinquish Mlle Vinteuil and, in a despairing effort, in that fruitless hunt through the abysses of possible reconstructions, attached itself to the actress, to that evening when Albertine had gone to see her in her dressing-room. On the one hand, after all the oaths she had sworn me, and in so truthful a tone, after her complete sacrifice of her freedom, how could I possibly believe that there was anything wrong in it? And yet, on the other hand, were not my suspicions feelers pointing in the direction of the truth, since if she had given up the Verdurins for my sake in order to go to the Trocadéro, nevertheless at the Verdurins' Mlle Vinteuil had been expected, and at the Trocadéro, which she had moreover given up in order to go for a drive with me, there had been this Léa, who seemed to me to be disturbing me without cause and yet whom, in a remark which I had not extracted from her, she admitted having known on a larger scale than my fears had ever envisaged, in circumstances that were indeed dubious: for what could have induced her to go behind like that to her dressing-room? If I ceased to suffer on account of Mlle Vinteuil when I suffered because of Léa, those two tormentors of my day, it was either because of the inability of my mind to picture too many scenes at one time, or because of the intrusion of my nervous emotions of which my jealousy was but the echo. I could deduce from them only that she had no more belonged to Léa than to Mlle Vinteuil and that I believed in the Léa hypothesis only because she was now uppermost in my mind. But the fact that my jealousies subsided—to revive from time to time one after another—did not mean, either, that they did not correspond each to some truth of which I had had a foreboding, that of these various women I must not say to myself none, but all. I say a foreboding, for I could not project myself to all the points of time and space which I should have had to occupy; and besides, what instinct would have given me the sequence and the co-ordinates to enable me to surprise Albertine at such and such a time with Léa, or with the Balbec girls, or with that friend of Mme Bontemps whom she had brushed against, or with the girl on the tennis-court who had nudged her with her elbow, or with Mlle Vinteuil?

The fear that Albertine was perhaps going to say to me: "I want to be allowed to go out by myself at certain hours, I want to be able to stay away for twenty-four hours," or some such request for freedom which I did not attempt to define, but which alarmed me, this fear had crossed my mind for a moment during the Verdurin reception. But it had been dispelled, contradicted moreover by the memory of Albertine's constant assurances of how happy she was with me. The intention to leave me, if it existed in Albertine, manifested itself only in an obscure fashion, in certain mournful glances, certain gestures of impatience, remarks which meant nothing

of the sort but which, if one analysed them (and there was not
even any need for analysis, for one understands at once this
language of passion, even the most uneducated understand
these remarks which can be explained only by vanity, rancour,
jealousy, unexpressed as it happens, but detectable at once by
the interlocutor through an intuitive faculty which, like the
"good sense" of which Descartes speaks, is "the most evenly
distributed thing in the world"), could only be explained by
the presence in her of a sentiment which she concealed and
which might lead her to form plans for another life without
me. Just as this intention did not express itself in her speech
in a logical fashion, so the presentiment of this intention, which
I had felt to-night, remained just as vague in me. I continued
to live by the hypothesis which accepted as true everything that
Albertine told me. But it may be that during this time a wholly
contrary hypothesis, of which I refused to think, never left me;
this is all the more probable since otherwise I should not have
felt uncomfortable about telling Albertine that I had been to
the Verdurins', and my lack of astonishment at her anger
would not have been comprehensible. So that what probably
existed in me was an idea of Albertine entirely contrary to that
which my reason formed of her, and also to that which her own
words suggested, an Albertine who was none the less not
wholly invented, since she was like a prophetic mirror of
certain impulses that occurred in her, such as her ill-humour
at my having gone to the Verdurins'. Besides, for a long time
past, my constant anxieties, my fear of telling Albertine that I
loved her, all this corresponded to another hypothesis which
explained far more things and had also this to be said for it,
that if one adopted the first hypothesis the second became
more probable, for by allowing myself to give way to effusions
of tenderness for Albertine, I obtained from her nothing but
irritation (to which moreover she assigned a different cause).

I may say that what had seemed to me most serious and
had struck me most forcibly as a symptom of the fact
that she anticipated my accusation was that she had said
to me: "I believe Mlle Vinteuil was to be there," to which
I had replied in the cruellest possible way: "You didn't
tell me you'd met her." As soon as I found Albertine

less than nice, instead of telling her I was sad, I became nasty.

Analysing my feelings on the basis of this, on the basis of the unvarying system of ripostes expressing the opposite of what I felt, I can be quite certain that if, that night, I told her that I was going to leave her, it was because—even before I had realised it—I was afraid that she might desire some freedom (I should have been hard put to it to say what this freedom was that made me tremble, but anyhow a freedom which might have given her an opportunity of being unfaithful to me, or at least which was such that I should no longer have been able to be certain that she was not) and because I wanted to show her, from pride and from cunning, that I was very far from fearing anything of the sort, as I had already shown at Balbec, when I was anxious that she should have a good opinion of me, and later on, when I was anxious that she should not have time to feel bored with me.

Finally, the objection that might be offered to this second, unformulated hypothesis, that everything that Albertine said to me indicated on the contrary that the life which she preferred was the life she led in my house, rest, quiet, reading, solitude, a loathing for Sapphic loves, and so forth, need not be considered seriously. For if on her part Albertine had wanted to gauge what I felt from what I said to her, she would have learned the exact opposite of the truth, since I never expressed a desire to part from her except when I was unable to do without her, and at Balbec I had twice confessed to her that I was in love with another woman, first Andrée, then a mysterious stranger, on the two occasions when jealousy had revived my love for her. My words, therefore, did not in the least reflect my feelings. If the reader has no more than a faint impression of these, that is because, as narrator, I expose my feelings to him at the same time as I repeat my words. But if I concealed the former and he were acquainted only with the latter, my actions, so little in keeping with them, would so often give him the impression of strange reversals that he would think me more or less mad. A procedure which would not, for that matter, be much more false than the one I adopted, for the images which prompted me to action, so opposed to those which were portrayed in my words, were at that moment extremely obscure; I was but imperfectly aware of the nature which guided my actions; to-day, I have a clear conception of its subjective truth. As for its objective truth, that is to say whether the intuitions of that nature grasped more exactly than my reason Albertine's true intentions, whether I was right to trust to that nature or whether on the contrary it did not alter Albertine's intentions instead of making them plain— that I find difficult to say.

That vague fear which I had felt at the Verdurins' that Albertine might leave me had at first subsided. When I returned home, it had been with the feeling that I myself was a captive, not with that of finding a captive in the house. But the fear that had subsided had gripped me even more violently when, as soon as I informed Albertine that I had been to the Verdurins', I saw her face veiled with a look of enigmatic irritation which moreover was not making itself visible for the first time. I knew perfectly well that it was only the crystallisation in the flesh of reasoned grievances, of ideas clear to the person who forms but does not express them, a synthesis rendered visible but not therefore rational, which he who gathers its precious residue from the face of the beloved endeavours in his turn, so that he may understand what is occurring in her, to reduce by analysis to its intellectual elements. The approximate equation of that unknown quantity which Albertine's thoughts were to me had given me, more or less, the following: "I knew his suspicions, I was sure that he would attempt to verify them, and so that I might not hinder him, he has worked out his little plan in secret." But if this was the state of mind (which she had never expressed to me) in which Albertine was living, must she not regard with horror, no longer have the strength to lead, might she not at any moment decide to terminate, a life in which, if she was, in desire at any rate, guilty, she must feel herself suspected, hunted, prevented from ever yielding to her desires, without thereby disarming my jealousy, and in which, if she was innocent in intention and fact, she had had every right, for some time past, to feel discouraged, seeing that, ever since Balbec, where she had shown so much perseverance in avoiding the risk of ever being alone with Andrée, until this

very day when she had agreed not to go to the Verdurins'
and not to stay at the Trocadéro, she had not succeeded in
regaining my trust? All the more so because I could not say
that her behaviour was not exemplary. If at Balbec, when
anyone mentioned girls who behaved scandalously, she used
often to copy their laughter, their wrigglings, their general
manner, which was a torture to me because of what I supposed
it must mean to her girl friends, now that she knew my
opinion on the subject she ceased, as soon as anyone made
an allusion to things of that sort, to take part in the conversation, not only orally but with her facial expression. Whether
it was in order not to contribute her share to the slanders that
were being uttered about some woman or other, or for a quite
different reason, the only thing that was noticeable then, upon
those so mobile features, was that as soon as the topic was
broached they had made their inattention evident, while
preserving exactly the same expression as they had worn a
moment earlier. And this immobility of even a light expression
was as heavy as a silence. It would have been impossible to
say whether she blamed, whether she approved, whether she
knew or did not know about these things. Her features no
longer bore any relation to anything save one another. Her
nose, her mouth, her eyes formed a perfect harmony, isolated
from everything else; she looked like a pastel, and seemed
to have no more heard what had just been said than if it had
been uttered in front of a portrait by La Tour.

My servitude, which had again been brought home to me
when, as I gave the driver Brichot's address, I had seen her
lighted window, had ceased to weigh upon me shortly afterwards, when I saw that Albertine appeared so cruelly conscious
of her own. And in order that it might seem to her less burdensome, that she might not decide to break her bonds of her own
accord, I had felt that the most effective plan was to give her
the impression that it would not be permanent and that I
myself was looking forward to its termination. Seeing that my
feint had proved successful, I might well have felt happy,
in the first place because what I had so dreaded, Albertine's
supposed wish to leave me, seemed to be ruled out, and
secondly because, quite apart from the object that I had had

in mind, the very success of my feint, by proving that I was something more to Albertine than a scorned lover, whose jealousy is flouted, all of his ruses detected in advance, restored to our love a sort of virginity, revived for it the days in which she could still, at Balbec, so readily believe that I was in love with another woman. Doubtless she would no longer have believed that, but she gave credence to my feigned determination to part from her now and for ever.

She appeared to suspect that the cause of it might be something that had happened at the Verdurins'. I told her that I had seen a dramatist (Bloch), who was a great friend of Léa's and to whom Léa had said some strange things (I hoped by telling her this to make her think that I knew a great deal more than I cared to say about Bloch's cousins). But feeling a need to calm the agitation induced in me by my pretence of a rupture, I said to her: "Albertine, can you swear that you have never lied to me?"

She gazed fixedly into space before replying: "Yes . . . that is to say no. I was wrong to tell you that Andrée was greatly taken with Bloch. We never met him."

"Then why did you say so?"

"Because I was afraid that you believed other stories about her, that's all."

She stared once again into space and then said: "I ought not to have kept from you a three weeks' trip I went on with Léa. But I knew you so slightly in those days!"

"It was before Balbec?"

"Before the second time, yes."

And that very morning, she had told me that she did not know Léa! I watched a tongue of flame seize and devour in an instant a novel which I had spent millions of minutes in writing. To what end? To what end? Of course I realised that Albertine had revealed these two facts to me because she thought that I had learned them indirectly from Léa; and that there was no reason why a hundred similar facts should not exist. I realised too that Albertine's words, when one interrogated her, never contained an atom of truth, that the truth was something she let slip only in spite of herself, as a result of a sudden mixing together in her mind of the facts which she had previously been determined to conceal with the belief that one had got wind of them.

"But two things are nothing," I said to Albertine, "let's have as many as four, so that you may leave me with some memories. What other revelations have you got for me?"

Once again she stared into space. To what belief in a future life was she adapting her falsehood, with what gods less accommodating than she had supposed was she seeking to make a deal? It cannot have been an easy matter, for her silence and the fixity of her gaze continued for some time.

"No, nothing else," she said at length. And, notwithstanding my persistence, she adhered, easily now, to "nothing else." And what a lie! For, from the moment she had acquired those tastes until the day when she had been shut up in my house, how many times, in how many places, on how many excursions must she have gratified them! The daughters of Gomorrah are at once rare enough and numerous enough for one not to pass unnoticed by another in any given crowd. Thenceforward, a rendezvous is an easy matter.

I remembered with horror an evening which at the time had struck me as merely absurd. One of my friends had invited me to dine at a restaurant with his mistress and another of his friends who had also brought his. The two women were not long in coming to an understanding, but were so impatient to enjoy one another that already at the soup stage their feet were searching for one another, often finding mine. Presently their legs were intertwined. My two friends noticed nothing; I was in agonies. One of the women, who could contain herself no longer, stooped under the table, saying that she had dropped something. Then one of them complained of a headache and asked to go upstairs to the lavatory. The other remembered that it was time for her to go and meet a woman friend at the theatre. Finally I was left alone with my two friends, who suspected nothing. The lady with the headache reappeared, but begged to be allowed to go home by herself to wait for her lover at his house, so that she might take a sedative. The two women became great friends and used to go about together, one of them, dressed as a man, picking up little girls and taking them home to the other to be initiated.

One of them had a little boy with whom she would pretend to be displeased and would hand him over for correction to her friend, who went to it with a will. One may say that there was no place, however public, in which they did not do what is most secret.

"But Léa behaved perfectly properly with me all the time," Albertine told me. "In fact she was a great deal more reserved than plenty of society women."

"Are there any society women who have shown a lack of reserve with you, Albertine?"

"Never."

"Then what do you mean?"

"Oh, well, she was less free in her speech."

"For instance?"

"She would never, like many of the women you meet, have used the expression 'rotten,' or say: 'I don't care a damn for anybody.'"

It seemed to me that a part of the novel which the flames had so far spared had finally crumbled into ashes.

My discouragement might have persisted. Albertine's words, when I thought of them, made it give way to a furious rage. This subsided into a sort of tenderness. I too, since I had come home and declared that I wished to break with her, had been lying. Besides, even when I thought in fits and starts, in twinges, as we say of other bodily pains, of that orgiastic life which Albertine had led before she met me, I wondered all the more at the docility of my captive and ceased to feel any resentment.

However, the simulated rupture gradually affected me with something of the sadness which a genuine intention would have had and which I was obliged to visualise in order to feign it. Never, in the course of our life together, had I ceased to make it clear to Albertine that that life would in all probability be merely temporary, so that she might continue to find some charm in it. But to-night I had gone further, having feared that vague threats of separation were no longer suffi-cient, contradicted as they would doubtless be, in Albertine's mind, by her idea of a great and jealous love of her, which must have made me, she seemed to imply, go and investigate at the Verdurins'. That night I thought that, among the other reasons which might have made me suddenly decide to put on this act of rupture, without even realising what I was doing except as I went on, there was above all the fact that when, in one of those impulses to which my father was prone, I threatened another person's safety, since unlike him I did not have the courage to put a threat into practice, in order not to give the impression that it had been nothing but empty words, I would go to considerable lengths in pretending to carry out my threat and would recoil only when my adversary, genuinely convinced of my sincerity, had begun seriously to tremble.

Besides, we feel that in these lies there is indeed a grain of truth, that, if life does not bring about any changes in our loves, it is we ourselves who will seek to bring about or to feign them, so strongly do we feel that all love, and everything else in life, evolves rapidly towards a farewell. We want to shed the tears that it will bring long before it comes. No doubt there was, on this occasion, a practical reason for the scene that I had enacted. I had suddenly wanted to keep Albertine because I felt that she was scattered about among other people with whom I could not prevent her from mixing. But even if she had renounced them all for ever for my sake, I might perhaps have been still more firmly resolved never to leave her, for separation is made painful by jealousy but impossible by gratitude. I felt that in any case I was fighting the decisive battle in which I must conquer or fall. I would have offered Albertine in an hour all that I possessed, because I said to myself: "Everything depends upon this battle." But such battles are less like those of old, which lasted for a few hours, than like those of today which do not end the next day, or the day after, or the following week. We give all our strength, because we steadfastly believe that we shall never need it again. And more than a year goes by without producing a "decision."

Perhaps an unconscious reminiscence of lying scenes enacted by M. de Charlus, in whose company I had been when the fear of Albertine's leaving me had seized hold of me, had contributed thereto. But later on I heard my mother tell a story, of which I then knew nothing, which leads me to believe that I had found all the elements of this scene in myself, in those obscure reserves of heredity which certain emotions, acting in this as drugs such as alcohol or coffee act upon the residue of our stored-up strength, place at our disposal. When my aunt Léonie learned from Eulalie that Françoise, convinced that her mistress would never again leave the house, had secretly planned an outing of which my aunt was to know nothing, she pretended, the day before, to have suddenly decided to go for a drive next day. The incredulous Françoise was ordered not only to prepare my aunt's clothes beforehand, and to air those that had been put away for too long, but to order the carriage and to arrange all the details of the excursion down to the last quarter of an hour. It was only when Françoise, convinced or at any rate shaken, had been forced to confess to my aunt the plan that she herself had made, that my aunt publicly abandoned her own, so as not, she said, to interfere with Françoise's arrangements. Similarly, in order that Albertine should not think that I was exaggerating and in order to make her proceed as far as possible in the idea that we were to part, myself drawing the obvious inferences from the proposal I had advanced, I had begun to anticipate the time which was to begin next day and was to last for ever, the time when we should be separated, addressing to Albertine the same requests as if we were not presently to be reconciled. Like a general who considers that if a feint is to succeed in deceiving the enemy it must be pushed to the limit, I had used up almost as much of my store of sensibility as if it had been genuine. This fictitious parting scene ended by causing me almost as much grief as if it had been real, possibly because one of the actors, Albertine, by believing it to be real, had heightened the illusion for the other. We lived a day-to-day life which, however tedious, was still endurable, held down to earth by the ballast of habit and by that certainty that the next day, even if it should prove painful, would contain the presence of the other. And here was I foolishly destroying all that familiar, humdrum life. I was destroying it, it is true, only in a fictitious fashion, but this was enough to make me wretched; perhaps because the sad words which we utter, even mendaciously, carry in themselves their sorrow and inject it deeply into us; perhaps because we realise that, by feigning farewells, we anticipate an hour which must inevitably come sooner or later; then we cannot be certain that we have not triggered off the mechanism which will make it strike. In every bluff there is an element of uncertainty, however small, as to what the person whom we are deceiving is going to do. What if this make-believe parting should lead to a real parting! One cannot consider the possibility, however unlikely it may seem, without a pang of anguish. One is doubly anxious, because the parting would then occur at the moment when it would be most intolerable, when one has been made to suffer by the woman who would be leaving us before having healéd, or at least soothed, one's pain. Finally, one no longer has the solid ground of habit upon which to rest, even in one's sorrow. One has deliberately deprived oneself of it, one has given the present day an exceptional importance, detached it from the days before and after it; it floats without roots like a day of departure; one's imagination, ceasing to be paralysed by habit, has awakened, one has suddenly added to one's everyday love sentimental dreams which enormously enhance it, making indispensable to one a presence upon which in fact one is no longer certain that one can rely. No doubt it is precisely in order to assure oneself of that presence for the future that one has indulged in the make-believe of being able to dispense with it. But one has oneself been taken in by the game, one has begun to suffer anew because one has created something new and unfamiliar which thus resembles those cures that are destined in time to heal the malady from which one is suffering, but the first effects of which are to aggravate it.

I had tears in my eyes, like those people who, alone in their bedrooms, imagining, in the wayward course of their medita-tions, the death of someone they love, conjure up so precise a picture of the grief that they would feel that they end by feeling it. And so as I continued to advise Albertine as to the way in which she should behave towards me after we had parted, I seemed to feel almost as much distress as though we had not been on the verge of a reconciliation. Besides, was I so certain that I could bring about this reconciliation, bring Albertine back to the idea of a shared life, and, if I succeeded for the time being, that, in her, the state of mind which this scene had dispelled would not revive? I felt that I was in control of the future but I did not quite believe it because I realised that this feeling was due merely to the fact that the future did not yet exist, and that thus I was not crushed by its inevitability. And while I lied, I was perhaps putting into my words more truth than I supposed. I had just had an example of this, when I told Albertine that I would quickly forget her; this was what had indeed happened to me in the case of Gilberte, whom I now refrained from going to see in order to avoid, not suffering, but an irksome duty. And certainly I had suffered when I wrote to Gilberte to tell her that I would not see her any more. Yet I saw Gilberte only from time to time. Whereas the whole of Albertine's time belonged to me. And in love, it is easier to relinquish a feeling than to give up a habit. But all these painful words about our parting, if the strength to utter them had been given me because I knew them to be untrue, were on the other hand sincere on Albertine's lips when I heard her exclaim: "Ah! I promise I shall never see you again. Anything sooner than see you cry like that, my darling. I don't want to cause you pain. Since it must be, we'll never meet again." They were sincere, as they could not have been coming from me, because, since Albertine felt nothing stronger for me than friendship, on the one hand the renunciation that they promised cost her less, and on the other hand because my tears, which would have been so small a matter in a great love, seemed to her almost extraordinary and distressed her, transposed into the domain of that state of friendship in which she dwelt, a friendship greater than mine for her, to judge by what she had just said—what she had just said, because when two people part it is the one who is not in love who makes the tender speeches, since love does not express itself directly—what she had just said and what was perhaps not altogether untrue, for the countless kindnesses of love may end by arousing, in the person who inspires without feeling it, an affection and a gratitude less selfish than the sentiment that provoked them, which, perhaps, after years of separation, when nothing of that sentiment remains in the former lover, will still persist in the beloved.

"My little Albertine," I replied, "it is very good of you to make me this promise. Anyhow, for the first few years at least, I shall avoid the places where I might meet you. You don't know whether you'll be going to Balbec this year? Because in that case I should arrange not to go there myself." Now, if I went on in this way, anticipating the future in my lying inventions, it was less with the object of frightening Albertine than that of distressing myself. As a man who at first has had no serious reason for losing his temper becomes completely intoxicated by the sound of his own voice and lets himself be carried away by a fury engendered not by his grievance but by his anger itself as it steadily grows, so I was sliding faster and faster down the slope of my wretchedness, towards an ever more profound despair, with the inertia of a man who feels the cold grip him, makes no effort to struggle against it, and even finds a sort of pleasure in shivering. And if, presently, I had the strength at last to pull myself together, to react, to go into reverse, as I had every intention of doing, it was not so much for the pain that Albertine had caused me by greeting me with such hostility on my return, as for the pain I had felt in imagining, in order to pretend to be settling them, the formalities of an imaginary separation, in foreseeing its consequences, that Albertine's kiss, when the time came for her to bid me good-night, would have to console me now. In any case, it was important that this leave-taking should not come of its own accord from her, for that would have made more difficult the reversal whereby I would propose to her to abandon the idea of our parting. I therefore continued to remind her that the time to say good-night had long since come and gone, and this, by leaving the initiative to me, enabled me to put it off for a moment longer. And thus I interspersed the questions which I continued to put to Albertine with allusions to our exhaustion and the lateness of the hour.

"I don't know where I shall be going," she replied to the last of these questions with a preoccupied air. "Perhaps I shall go to Touraine, to my aunt's." And this first plan that she suggested froze me as though it were beginning actually to put our final separation into effect. She looked round the room, at the pianola, the blue satin armchairs. "I still can't get used to the idea that I shan't see all this again, to-morrow, or the next day, or ever. Poor little room. It seems to me quite impossible; I can't get it into my head."

"It had to be; you were unhappy here."

"No, I wasn't at all unhappy, it's now that I shall be unhappy."

"No, I assure you, it's better for you."

"For you, perhaps!"

I began to stare into space as though, tormented by a great uncertainty, I was struggling with an idea that had just occurred to me. Then, all of a sudden: "Listen, Albertine, you say that you're happier here, that you're now going to be unhappy."

"Why, of course."

"That appals me. Would you like us to try to carry on for a few weeks? Who knows, week by week, we may perhaps go on for a long time. You know that there are temporary arrangements which end by becoming permanent."

"Oh, it would be sweet of you!"

"Only in that case it's ridiculous of us to have made ourselves wretched like this over nothing for hours on end. It's like making all the preparations for a long journey and then staying at home. I'm absolutely dead beat."

I sat her on my knee, took Bergotte's manuscript which she so longed to have, and wrote on the cover: "To my little Albertine, in memory of a new lease of life."

"Now," I said to her, "go and sleep until to-morrow, my darling, for you must be worn out."

"Most of all I'm very happy."

"Do you love me a bit?"

"A hundred times more than ever."

I should have been wrong to be pleased with this little piece of play-acting. Even if it had stopped short of the sort of full-scale production I had given it, even if we had done no more than simply discuss a separation, it would have been serious enough. In conversations of this sort, we imagine that we are speaking not just insincerely, which is true, but freely. Whereas they are generally the first faint murmur of an unsuspected storm, whispered to us without our knowing it. In reality, what we express at such times is the opposite of our desire (which is to live for ever with the one we love), but also the impossibility of living together which is the cause of our daily suffering, a suffering preferred by us to that of a separation, which will, however, end by separating us in spite of ourselves. But not, as a rule, at once. More often than not it happens—this was not, as we shall see, my case with Albertine—that, some time after the words in which we did not believe, we put into action a vague attempt at a deliberate separation, not painful, temporary. We ask the woman, so that afterwards she may be happier in our company, so that we at the same time may momentarily escape from continual bouts of gloom and exhaustion, to go away without us, or to let us go away without her, for a few days—the first that we have spent away from her for a long time past, and something that we should have thought inconceivable. Very soon she returns to take her place by our fireside. Only this separation, short but effectuated, is not so arbitrarily decided upon, not so certainly the only one that we have in mind. The same bouts of gloom begin again, the same difficulty in living together makes itself felt, only a parting is no longer so difficult as before; we have begun by talking about it, and have then put it into practice amicably. But these are only premonitory symptoms which we have failed to recognise. Presently, the temporary and benign separation will be succeeded by the terrible and final separation for which, without knowing it, we have paved the way.

"Come to my room in five minutes and let me see something of you, my darling one. It would so nice if you would. But afterwards I shall fall asleep at once, for I'm almost dead."

It was indeed a dead woman that I saw when, presently, I entered her room. She had fallen asleep as soon as she lay down; her sheets, wrapped round her body like a shroud, had assumed, with their elegant folds, the rigidity of stone. It was as though, reminiscent of certain mediaeval Last Judgments, the head alone was emerging from the tomb, awaiting in its sleep the Archangel's trumpet. This head had been surprised by sleep almost upside down, the hair dishevelled. Seeing that expressionless body lying there, I asked myself what logarithmic table it constituted, that all the actions in which it might have been involved, from the nudge of an elbow to the brushing of a skirt, should be capable of causing me, stretched out to the infinity of all the points that it had occupied in space and time, and from time to time sharply reawakened in my memory, so intense an anguish, even though I knew that it was determined by impulses and desires of hers which in another person, in herself five years earlier or five years later, would have left me quite indifferent. It was all a lie, but a lie for which I had not the courage to seek any solution other than my own death. And so I remained, in the fur-lined coat which I had not taken off since my return from the Verdurins', beside that twisted body, that allegorical figure. Allegorising what? My death? My love? Presently I began to hear her regular breathing. I went and sat down on the edge of her bed to take that soothing cure of breath and contemplation. Then I withdrew very quietly so as not to wake her.

It was so late that, in the morning, I warned Françoise to tread very softly when she had to pass by the door of Albertine's room. And so Françoise, convinced that we had spent the night in what she used to call orgies, sarcastically warned the other servants not to "wake the Princess." And this was one of the things that I dreaded, that Françoise might one day be unable to contain herself any longer, might treat Albertine with insolence, and that this might introduce complications into our life. Françoise was now no longer, as at the time when it distressed her to see Eulalie treated generously by my aunt, of an age to endure her jealousy with fortitude. It distorted, paralysed our old servant's face to such an extent that at times I wondered, after some outburst of rage, whether she had not had a slight stroke. Having thus asked that Albertine's sleep should be respected, I was unable to sleep myself. I tried to understand Albertine's true state of mind. Was it a real peril that I had averted by that wretched farce which I had played, and notwithstanding her assurance that she was so happy living with me, had she really felt at certain moments a longing for freedom, or on the contrary was I to believe what she said? Which of these two hypotheses was the truth? If it often happened to me, especially later on, to extend an incident in my past life to the dimensions of history when I wished to understand some political event, conversely, that morning, in trying to understand the significance of our overnight scene, I could not help identifying it, in spite of all the differences, with a diplomatic incident that had just occurred. I had perhaps the right to reason thus. For it was highly probable that the example of M. de Charlus had guided me unwittingly in the sort of lying scene which I had so often seen him enact with such authority; and what else was this on his part than an unconscious importation into the domain of his private life of the innate tendency of his German blood, guilefully provocative and arrogantly bellicose at need?

Various persons, among them the Prince of Monaco, having suggested the idea to the French Government that, if it did not dispense with M. Delcassé, a menacing Germany would definitely declare war, the Minister for Foreign Affairs had been asked to resign. Thus the French Government had admitted the hypothesis of an intention to make war upon us if we did not yield. But others thought that it was all a mere "bluff" and that if France had stood firm Germany would not have drawn the sword. No doubt in this case the scenario was not merely different but almost the reverse, since the threat of a rupture had never been put forward by Albertine; but a series of impressions had led me to believe that she was thinking of it, as France had been led to believe it of Germany. On the other hand, if Germany desired peace, to have provoked in the French Government the idea that she was anxious for war was a questionable and dangerous trick. True, my conduct had been adroit enough, if it was the thought that I would never make up my mind to break with her that provoked in Albertine sudden longings for independence. And was it not difficult to believe that she did not have such longings, to shut one's eyes to a whole secret existence, directed towards the satisfaction of her vice, simply on the strength of the anger with which, on learning that I had gone to see the Verdurins, she had exclaimed: "I thought as much," and then gone on to reveal everything by saying: "Wasn't Mlle Vinteuil to be there?" All this was corroborated by Albertine's meeting with Mme Verdurin of which Andrée had informed me. And yet, perhaps, I told myself, when I tried to go against my own instinct, these sudden longings for independence were caused— supposing them to exist—or would eventually be caused by the opposite theory, to wit, that I had never had any intention of marrying her, that it was when I made, as though involuntarily, an illusion to our approaching separation that I was telling the truth, that I would leave her sooner or later whatever happened—a belief which the scene I had fabricated that night could then only have reinforced and which might end by engendering in her the resolution: "If it's bound to happen sooner or later, we might as well get it over with at once." Preparations for war, which are recommended by the most misleading of adages as the best way of ensuring peace, on the contrary create first of all the belief in each of the adversaries that the other desires a rupture, a belief which brings the rupture about, and then, when it has occurred, the further belief in each of the two that it is the other that has sought it. Even if the threat was not sincere, its success encourages a repetition. But the exact point up to which a bluff may succeed is difficult to determine; if one party goes too far, the other, which has yielded hitherto, advances in its turn; the first party, no longer capable of changing its methods, accustomed to the idea that to seem not to fear a rupture is the best way of avoiding one (which is what I had done that night with Albertine), and moreover driven by pride to prefer death to surrender, perseveres in its threat until the moment when neither can draw back. The bluff may also be blended with sincerity, may alternate with it, and what was yesterday a game may become a reality to-morrow. Finally it may also happen that one of the adversaries is really determined upon war—that Albertine, for instance, had the intention of sooner or later not continuing this life any longer, or on the contrary that the idea had never even entered her head and that my imagination had invented the whole thing from start to finish.

Such were the different hypotheses which I considered while she lay asleep that morning. And yet as to the last I can say that never, in the period that followed, did I threaten to leave Albertine unless in response to a hankering for a baleful freedom on her part, a hankering which she did not express to me, but which seemed to me to be implied by certain mysterious dissatisfactions, certain words, certain gestures, for which it could be the only possible explanation and for which she refused to give me any other. Even then, quite often, I noted them without making any allusion to a possible separation, hoping that they were the result of a bad mood which would end that same day. But sometimes that mood would continue without remission for weeks on end, during which Albertine seemed anxious to provoke a conflict, as though she knew of pleasures which were available at that moment in some more or less remote place and which would continue to influence her until they came to an end, like those atmospheric changes which, even by our own fireside, affect our nerves even when they are occurring as far away as the Balearic islands.

That morning, while Albertine lay asleep and I was trying to guess what was concealed in her, I received a letter from my mother in which she expressed her anxiety at having heard nothing of what I had decided in these words from Mme de Sévigné: "As for me, I am convinced that he will not marry; but then, why trouble this girl whom he will never marry? Why risk making her refuse suitors whom she will henceforth regard only with scorn? Why disturb the mind of a person whom it would be so easy to avoid?" This letter from my mother brought me back to earth. "Why do I go on seeking after a mysterious soul, interpreting a face, and feeling myself surrounded by presentiments which I dare not explore?" I asked myself. "I've been dreaming, the matter is quite simple. I am an indecisive young man, and it is a case of one of those marriages as to which it takes time to find out whether they will happen or not. There is nothing in this peculiar to Albertine." This thought brought me immense but short-lived relief. Very soon I said to myself: "One can of course reduce everything, if one regards it in its social aspect, to the most commonplace item of newspaper gossip. From outside, it is perhaps thus that I myself would look at it. But I know very well that what is true, what at least is also true, is everything that I have thought, what I have read in Albertine's eyes, the fears that torment me, the problem that I continually put to myself with regard to Albertine. The story of the hesitant suitor and the broken engagement may correspond to this, as the report of a theatrical performance made by an intelligent reporter may give us the subject of one of Ibsen's plays. But there is something beyond those facts that are reported. It is true that this other thing exists perhaps, were we capable of seeing it, in all hesitant suitors and in all engagements that drag on, because there is perhaps an element of mystery in everyday life." It was possible for me to neglect it in the lives of other people, but Albertine's life and my own I was living from within.

Albertine did not say to me after this midnight scene, any more than she had said before it: "I know you don't trust me, and I'm going to try to dispel your suspicions." But this idea, which she never expressed in words, might have served as an explanation of even her most trivial actions. Not only did she take care never to be alone for a moment, so that I could not help but know what she had been doing if I did not believe her own statements, but even when she had to telephone to Andrée, or to the garage, or to the livery stable or elsewhere, she pretended that it was too boring to stand about by herself waiting to telephone, what with the time the girls took to give you your number, and was careful that I should be with her at such times, or, failing me, Françoise, as though she were afraid that I might imagine reprehensible telephone conversations in which she would make mysterious assignations.

Alas, all this did not set my mind at rest. Aimé had sent me back Esther's photograph, saying that she was not the person. So there were yet others? Who? I sent this photograph back to Bloch. The one I should have liked to see was the one Albertine had given to Esther. How was she dressed in it? Perhaps in a low-cut dress. Who knew whether they had not been photographed together? But I dared not mention it to Albertine (for it would then have appeared that I had not seen the photograph), or to Bloch, since I did not wish him to think that I was interested in Albertine.

And this life, which anyone who knew of my suspicions and her bondage would have seen to be agonising both to myself and to Albertine, was regarded from without, by Françoise, as a life of unmerited pleasures of which full advantage was cunningly taken by that "temptress" and (as Françoise said, using the feminine form far more often than the masculine, for she was more envious of women) "charlatante." Indeed, as

Françoise, by contact with myself, had enriched her vocabulary with new expressions, but adapted them to her own style, she said of Albertine that she had never known a person of such "perfidity," who was so skilful at "drawing my money" by play-acting (which Françoise, who was as prone to mistake the particular for the general as the general for the particular and who had but a very vague idea of the various forms of dramatic art, called "acting a pantomime"). Perhaps I was myself to some extent responsible for this misconception as to the true nature of the life led by Albertine and myself, owing to the vague confirmations of it which, when I was talking to Françoise, I cunningly let fall, from a desire either to tease her or to appear, if not loved, at any rate happy. And yet it did not take her long to detect my jealousy and the watch I kept over Albertine (which I would have given anything for Françoise not to be aware of), guided, like a thought-reader who finds a hidden object while blindfolded, by that intuition which she possessed for anything that might be painful to me, which would not allow itself to be turned aside by any lies that I might tell in the hope of putting her off the scent, and also by that clairvoyant hatred which drove her—even more than it drove her to believe her enemies more prosperous, more cunning play-actresses than they really were—to uncover what might prove their undoing and precipitate their downfall. Françoise certainly never made any scenes with Albertine. But I knew her skill in the art of insinuation, the way she knew how to make the most of the implications of a particular situation, and I cannot believe that she resisted the temptation to let Albertine know, day after day, what a humiliating role she was playing in the household, to madden her by a slyly exaggerated portrayal of the confinement to which she was subjected. On one occasion I found Françoise, armed with a huge pair of spectacles, rummaging through my papers and replacing among them a sheet on which I had jotted down a story about Swann and his utter inability to do without Odette. Had she maliciously left it lying in Albertine's room? Besides, above all Françoise's innuendoes, which had merely been the muttering and perfidious accompaniment of it in the bass, it is probable that there must have risen, louder, clearer, more insistent, the accusing and calumnious voice of the Verdurins, irritated to see that Albertine was involuntarily keeping me and that I was voluntarily keeping her away from the little clan.

As for the money that I spent on Albertine, it was almost impossible for me to conceal it from Françoise, since I was unable to conceal any of my expenditure from her. Françoise had few faults, but those faults had created in her, for their own purposes, positive talents which she often lacked apart from the exercise of those faults. The principal one was her curiosity as to all money spent by us upon people other than herself. If I had a bill to pay or a tip to give, it was useless my going into a corner, she would find a plate to be put in the right place, a napkin to be picked up, which would give her an excuse for approaching. And however short a time I allowed her before dismissing her with fury, this woman who had almost lost her sight, who could scarcely count, guided by the same expert sense whereby a tailor, on catching sight of you, instinctively calculates the price of the stuff of which your coat is made, and indeed cannot resist fingering it, or a painter is immediately responsive to a colour effect, Françoise furtively glimpsed and instantaneously calculated the amount that I was giving. If, in order that she should not tell Albertine that I was corrupting her chauffeur, I tried to forestall her and, apologising for the tip, said: "I wanted to be generous to the chauffeur, so I gave him ten francs," Françoise, for whom the merciless glance of an old and almost blind eagle had sufficed, would reply: "No no, Monsieur gave him a tip of 43 francs. He told Monsieur that the charge was 45 francs, Monsieur gave him 100 francs, and he handed back only 12 francs." She had had time to see and to reckon the amount of the gratuity which I myself did not know.

I wondered whether Albertine, feeling herself watched, would not herself put into effect the separation with which I had threatened her, for life in its changing course makes realities of our fables. Whenever I heard a door open, I gave a start, as my grandmother used to start in her last moments whenever I rang the bell. I did not believe that she would have left the house without telling me, but my unconscious thought so, as my grandmother's unconscious quivered at the sound of the bell when she was no longer conscious. One morning, indeed, I had a sudden anxious fear that she had not only left the house but gone for good: I had just heard the sound of a door which seemed to me to be that of her room. I tiptoed towards the room, opened the door, and stood on the threshold. In the dim light the bedclothes bulged in a semicircle. It must be Albertine, lying in a curve, sleeping with her head and her feet nearest the wall. The hair on that head, abundant and dark, which alone showed above the bedclothes, made me realise that it was she, that she had not opened her door, had not stirred, and I sensed this motionless and living semicircle, in which a whole human life was contained and which was the only thing to which I attached any value; I sensed that it was there, in my despotic possession.

If Albertine's object was to restore my peace of mind, she was partly successful; my reason moreover asked nothing better than to prove to me that I had been mistaken as to her evil plans, as I had perhaps been mistaken as to her vicious instincts. No doubt I took into account, in assessing the value of the arguments with which my reason furnished me, my desire to find them sound. But in order to be really impartial and to have a chance of perceiving the truth, short of acknowledging that it can never be known save by presentiment, by a telepathic emanation, ought I not to tell myself that if my reason, in seeking to bring about my cure, let itself be guided by my desire, on the other hand, as regards Mlle Vinteuil, Albertine's vices, her intention to lead a different life, her plan of separation, which were the corollaries of her vices, my instinct, in trying to make me ill, might have allowed itself to be led astray by my jealousy? Besides, her seclusion, which Albertine herself contrived so ingeniously to render absolute, in eradicating my suffering gradually eradicated my suspicion and I could begin again, when evening revived my anxieties, to find in Albertine's presence the consolation of earlier days. Seated beside my bed, she would talk to me about one of those dresses or one of those objects which I was constantly giving her in order to make her life more agreeable and her prison more beautiful.

If I had questioned M. de Charlus about old French silver, this was because, when we had been planning to have a yacht—a plan which Albertine decided was impracticable, as I did also whenever I had begun to believe in her virtue, with the result that my diminishing jealousy no longer held in check other desires in which she had no place and which also needed money for their satisfaction—we had asked Elstir's advice on the off chance, even though Albertine did not believe that we would ever have one. Now, no less than in matters of women's dress, the painter was a refined and sensitive critic of the furnishing of yachts. He would allow only English furniture and old silver. This had led Albertine, who had at first thought only of clothes and furniture, to become interested in silver, and since our return from Balbec she had read books on the silversmith's art and on the hallmarks of the old craftsmen. But old French silver—having been melted down twice, at the time of the Treaty of Utrecht when the King himself, setting the example to his great nobles, sacrificed his silver plate, and again in 1789—is now extremely rare. At the same time, although modern silversmiths have managed to copy all this old plate from the Pont-aux-Choux designs, Elstir considered this reproduction work unworthy to enter the dwelling of a woman of taste, even a floating one. I knew that Albertine had read the description of the marvels that Roettiers had made for Mme du Barry. If any of these pieces remained, she longed to see them, and I to give them to her. She had even begun to form a neat collection which she installed with charming taste in a glass case and which I could not contemplate without affectionate dismay, for the skill with which she arranged them was that, born of patience, ingenuity, homesickness, the need to forget, in which prisoners excel.

In the matter of dress, what appealed to her most at this time was everything made by Fortuny. These Fortuny gowns, one of which I had seen Mme de Guermantes wearing, were those of which Elstir, when he told us about the magnificent garments of the women of Carpaccio's and Titian's day, had prophesied the imminent return, rising from their ashes, as magnificent as of old, for everything must return in time, as it is written beneath the vaults of St Mark's, and proclaimed, as they drink from the urns of marble and jasper of the Byzantine capitals, by the birds which symbolise at once death and resurrection. As soon as women had begun to wear them, Albertine had remembered Elstir's prophecy, had coveted them, and we were shortly to go and choose one. Now even if these gowns were not those genuine antiques in which women to-day seem a little too got up in fancy dress and which it is preferable to keep as collector's items (I was looking for some of these also, as it happens, for Albertine), neither did they have the coldness of the artificial, the sham antique. Like the theatrical designs of Sert, Bakst and Benois, who at that moment were recreating in the Russian ballet the most cherished periods of art with the aid of works of art impregnated with their spirit and yet original, these Fortuny gowns, faithfully antique but markedly original, brought before the eye like a stage decor, and with an even greater evocative power since the decor was left to the imagination, that Venice saturated with oriental splendour where they would have been worn and of which they constituted, even more than a relic in the shrine of St Mark, evocative as they were of the sunlight and the surrounding turbans, the fragmented, mysterious and complementary colour. Everything of those days had perished, but everything was being reborn, evoked and linked together by the splendour and the swarming life of the city, in the piecemeal reappearance of the still-surviving fabrics worn by the Doges' ladies. I had tried once or twice to obtain advice on this subject from Mme de Guermantes. But the Duchess did not care for clothes that gave the effect of fancy dress. She herself, though she possessed several, never looked so well as in black velvet with diamonds. And with regard to gowns like Fortuny's, she had little useful advice to give. Besides, I had scruples about asking her advice lest I might give the impression that I called on her only when I happened to need her help, whereas for a long time past I had been declining several invitations a week from her. It was not only from her, moreover, that I received them in such profusion. Certainly, she and many other women had always been extremely friendly to me. But my seclusion had undoubtedly multiplied their friendliness tenfold. It seems that in our social life, a minor echo of what occurs in love, the best way to get oneself sought after is to withhold oneself. A man may think up everything that he can possibly cite to his credit, in order to find favour with a woman; he may wear different clothes every day, look after his appearance; yet she will not offer him a single one of the attentions and favours which he receives from another woman to whom, by being unfaithful to her, and in spite of his appearing before her ill-dressed and without any artifice to attract, he has endeared himself for ever. Similarly, if a man were to regret that he was not sufficiently courted in society, I should not advise him to pay more calls, to keep an even finer carriage; I should tell him not to accept any invitation, to live shut up in his room, to admit nobody, and that then there would be a queue outside his door. Or rather I should not tell him so. For it is a sure way to become sought-after which succeeds only like the way to be loved, that is to say if you have not adopted it with that object in view, if, for instance, you confine yourself to your room because you are seriously ill, or think you are, or are keeping a mistress shut up with you whom you prefer to society (or for all these reasons at once), in the eyes of which, even if it is unaware of the woman's existence, and simply because you resist its overtures, it will simply be a reason to prefer you to all those who offer themselves, and to attach itself to you.

"We shall have to begin to think soon about your Fortuny dressing-gown," I said to Albertine one evening. Surely, for her, who had long desired them, who would choose them with me after long deliberation, who had a place reserved for them in advance, not only in her wardrobe but in her imagination, the possession of these gowns, every detail of which, before deciding among so many others, she would carefully examine, was something more than it would have been to a woman with too much money who has more dresses than she knows what to do with and never even looks at them. And yet, notwithstanding the smile with which Albertine thanked me, saying: "It's so sweet of you," I noticed how weary and even sad she was looking.

From time to time, while we were waiting for these gowns to be finished, I used to borrow others of the kind, sometimes merely the stuffs, and would dress Albertine in them, drape them over her; she walked about my room with the majesty of a Doge's wife and the grace of a mannequin. But alas, my captivity in Paris was made more burdensome to me by the sight of these garments which reminded me of Venice. True, Albertine was far more of a prisoner than I. And it was curious to remark how fate, which transforms persons, had contrived to penetrate the walls of her prison, to change her in her very essence, and turn the girl I had known at Balbec into a dreary, docile captive. Yes, the walls of her prison had not prevented that influence from reaching her; perhaps indeed it was they that had produced it. It was no longer the same Albertine, because she was not, as at Balbec, incessantly in flight upon her bicycle, impossible to find owing to the number of little watering-places where she would go to spend the night with friends and where moreover her lies made it more difficult to lay hands on her; because, shut up in my house, docile and alone, she was no longer what at Balbec, even when I had succeeded in finding her, she used to be upon the beach, that fugitive, cautious, deceitful creature, whose presence was expanded by the thought of all those assignations which she was skilled in concealing, which made one love her because they made one suffer and because, beneath her coldness to other people and her casual answers, I could sense yesterday's assignation and to-morrow's, and for myself a sly, disdainful thought; because the sea breeze no longer puffed out her skirts; because, above all, I had clipped her wings, and she had ceased to be a winged Victory and become a burdensome slave of whom I would have liked to rid myself.

Then, to change the course of my thoughts, rather than begin a game of cards or draughts with Albertine, I would ask her to give me a little music. I remained in bed, and she would go and sit down at the end of the room before the pianola, between the two bookcases. She chose pieces which were either quite new or which she had played to me only once or twice, for, beginning to know me better, she was aware that I liked to fix my thoughts only upon what was still obscure to me, and to be able, in the course of these successive renderings, thanks to the increasing but, alas, distorting and alien light of

my intellect, to link to one another the fragmentary and interrupted lines of the structure which at first had been almost
hidden in mist. She knew and, I think, understood the joy
that my mind derived, at these first hearings, from this task
of modelling a still shapeless nebula. And as she played, of all
Albertine's multiple tresses I could see but a single heart-
shaped loop of black hair clinging to the side of her ear like the
bow of a Velasquez Infanta. Just as the volume of that angel
musician was constituted by the multiple journeys between
the different points in the past which the memory of her occupied within me and the different signs, from the purely visual
to the innermost sensations of my being, which helped me to
descend into the intimacy of hers, so the music that she played
had also a volume, produced by the unequal visibility of the
different phrases, according as I had more or less succeeded
in throwing light on them and joining up the lines of the seemingly nebulous structure. She guessed that at the third or fourth
repetition my intellect, having grasped, having consequently
placed at the same distance, all the parts, and no longer having
to exert any effort on them, had conversely projected and
immobilised them on a uniform plane. She did not, however,
yet move on to another piece, for, without perhaps having any
clear idea of the process that was going on inside me, she knew
that at the moment when the exertions of my intelligence had
succeeded in dispelling the mystery of a work, it was very
rarely that, in compensation, it had not, in the course of its
baleful task, picked up some profitable reflexion. And when
in time Albertine said: "We might give this roll to Françoise
and get her to change it for something else," often there was
for me a piece of music the less in the world, perhaps, but a
truth the more.

I was so convinced that it would be absurd to be jealous of
Mlle Vinteuil and her friend, inasmuch as Albertine gave not
the least sign of wanting to see them again, and among all the
plans for a holiday in the country which we had formed had
herself rejected Combray, so near to Montjouvain, that often
I would ask her to play to me some of Vinteuil's music, without its causing me pain. Once only this music had been an
indirect cause of jealousy. This was when Albertine, who knew

that I had heard it performed at Mme Verdurin's by Morel, spoke to me one evening about him, expressing a keen desire to go and hear him play and to make his acquaintance. This, as it happened, was shortly after I had learned of the letter, unintentionally intercepted by M. de Charlus, from Léa to Morel. I wondered whether Léa might not have mentioned him to Albertine. The words "you naughty girl," "you vicious thing," came to my horrified mind. But precisely because Vinteuil's music was in this way painfully associated with Léa—and no longer with Mlle Vinteuil and her friend—when the anguish caused by Léa had subsided, I could listen to this music without pain; one malady had cured me of the possibility of the others. In the music I had heard at Mme Verdurin's, phrases I had not noticed, obscure phantoms that were then indistinct, turned into dazzling architectural structures; and some of them became friends, that I had scarcely distinguished, that at best had appeared to me to be ugly, so that I could never have supposed that they were like those people, antipathetic at first sight, whom we discover to be what they really are only after we have come to know them well. Between the two states there was a real transmutation. At the same time, phrases which had been quite distinct the first time but which I had not then recognised, I identified now with phrases from other works, such as that phrase from the Sacred Variation for Organ which, at Mme Verdurin's, had passed unperceived by me in the septet, where nevertheless, like a saint that had stepped down from the sanctuary, it found itself consorting with the composer's familiar sprites. Moreover, the phrase evoking the joyful clanging of the bells at noon, which had seemed to me too unmelodious, too mechanical in its rhythm, had now become my favourite, either because I had grown accustomed to its ugliness or because I had discovered its beauty. This reaction from the disappointment which great works of art cause at first may in fact be attributed to a weakening of the initial impression or to the effort necessary to lay bare the truth—two hypotheses which recur in all important questions, questions about the truth of Art, of Reality, of the Immortality of the Soul; we must choose between them; and, in the case of Vinteuil's music, this choice was constantly presenting itself under a variety of forms. For instance, this music seemed to me something truer than all known books. At moments I thought that this was due to the fact that, what we feel about life not being felt in the form of ideas, its literary, that is to say intellectual expression describes it, explains it, analyses it, but does not recompose it as does music, in which the sounds seem to follow the very movement of our being, to reproduce that extreme inner point of our sensations which is the part that gives us that peculiar exhilaration which we experience from time to time and which, when we say "What a fine day! What glorious sunshine!" we do not in the least communicate to others, in whom the same sun and the same weather evoke quite different vibrations. In Vinteuil's music, there were thus some of those visions which it is impossible to express and almost forbidden to contemplate, since, when at the moment of falling asleep we receive the caress of their unreal enchantment, at that very moment in which reason has already deserted us, our eyes seal up and before we have had time to know not only the ineffable but the invisible, we are asleep. It seemed to me, when I abandoned myself to this hypothesis that art might be real, that it was something even more than the merely nerve-tingling joy of a fine day or an opiate night that music can give; a more real, more fruitful exhilaration, to judge at least by what I felt. It is inconceivable that a piece of sculpture or a piece of music which gives us an emotion that we feel to be more exalted, more pure, more true, does not correspond to some definite spiritual reality, or life would be meaningless. Thus nothing resembled more closely than some such phrase of Vinteuil the peculiar pleasure which I had felt at certain moments in my life, when gazing, for instance, at the steeples of Martinville, or at certain trees along a road near Balbec, or, more simply, at the beginning of this book, when I tasted a certain cup of tea. Like that cup of tea, all those sensations of light, the bright clamour, the boisterous colours that Vinteuil sent to us from the world in which he composed, paraded before my imagination, insistently but too rapidly for me to be able to apprehend it, something that I might compare to the perfumed silkiness of a geranium. But whereas in memory this vagueness may be, if not fathomed, at any rate identified, thanks to a pinpointing of circumstances which explain why a certain taste has been able to recall to us luminous sensations, the vague sensations given by Vinteuil coming not from a memory but from an impression (like that of the steeples of Martinville), one would have had to find, for the geranium scent of his music, not a material explanation, but the profound equivalent, the unknown, colourful festival (of which his works seemed to be the disconnected fragments, the scarlet-flashing splinters), the mode by which he "heard" the universe and projected it far beyond himself. Perhaps it was in this, I said to Albertine, this unknown quality of a unique world which no other composer had ever yet revealed, that the most authentic proof of genius lies, even more than in the content of the work itself. "Even in literature?" Albertine inquired. "Even in literature." And thinking again of the sameness of Vinteuil's works, I explained to Albertine that the great men of letters have never created more than a single work, or rather have never done more than refract through various media an identical beauty which they bring into the world. "If it were not so late, my sweet," I said to her, "I would show you this quality in all the writers whose works you read while I'm asleep, I would show you the same identity as in Vinteuil. These key-phrases, which you are beginning to recognise as I do, my little Albertine, the same in the sonata, in the septet, in the other works, would be, say for instance in Barbey d'Aurevilly, a hidden reality revealed by a physical sign, the physiological blush of the Bewitched, of Aimée de Spens, of old Clotte, the hand in the *Rideau cramoisi*, the old manners and customs, the old words, the ancient and peculiar trades behind which there is the Past, the oral history compiled by the peasants of the region, the noble Norman cities redolent of England and charming as a Scottish village, the cause of curses against which one can do nothing, la Vellini, the Shepherd, a similar sensation of anxiety in a passage, whether it be the wife seeking her husband in *Une vieille maîtresse*, or the husband in *l'Ensorcelée* scouring the plain and the Bewitched herself coming out from Mass. Another example of Vinteuil's key-phrases is that stonemason's geometry in the novels of Thomas Hardy."

Vinteuil's phrases made me think of the "little phrase" and I told Albertine that it had been as it were the national anthem of the love of Swann and Odette, "the parents of Gilberte, whom I believe you know. You told me she was a bad girl. Didn't she try to have relations with you? She spoke to me about you."

"Yes, you see, her parents used to send a carriage to fetch her from school when the weather was bad, and I seem to remember she took me home once and kissed me," she said, after a momentary pause, laughing as though it were an amusing revelation. "She asked me all of a sudden whether I was fond of women." (But if she only "seemed to remember" that Gilberte had taken her home, how could she say with such precision that Gilberte had asked her this odd question?) "In fact, I don't know what weird idea came into my head to fool her, but I told her that I was." (It was as though Albertine was afraid that Gilberte had told me this and did not want me to see that she was lying to me.) "But we did nothing at all." (It was strange, if they had exchanged these confidences, that they should have done nothing, especially as, before this, they had kissed, according to Albertine.) "She took me home like that four or five times, perhaps more, and that's all."

It cost me a great effort not to ply her with questions, but, mastering myself so as to appear not to be attaching any importance to all this, I returned to Thomas Hardy. "Do you remember the stonemasons in *Jude the Obscure*, and in *The Well-Beloved* the blocks of stone which the father hews out of the island coming in boats to be piled up in the son's work-shop where they are turned into statues; and in *A Pair of Blue Eyes* the parallelism of the tombs, and also the parallel line of the boat and the nearby railway coaches containing the lovers and the dead woman; and the parallel between *The Well-Beloved*, where the man loves three women, and *A Pair of Blue Eyes*, where the woman loves three men, and in short all those novels which can be superimposed on one another like the houses piled up vertically on the rocky soil of the island. I can't sum up the greatest writers like this in a few moments, but you'll see in Stendhal a certain sense of altitude symbolising the life of the spirit: the lofty place in which Julien Sorel is imprisoned, the tower at the top of which Fabrice is incarcerated, the belfry in which the Abbé Blanès pores over his astrology and from which Fabrice has such a magnificent bird's-eye view. You told me you had seen some of Vermeer's pictures: you must have realised that they're fragments of an identical world, that it's always, however great the genius with which they have been recreated, the same table, the same carpet, the same woman, the same novel and unique beauty, an enigma at that period in which nothing resembles or explains it, if one doesn't try to relate it all through subject matter but to isolate the distinctive impression produced by the colour. Well, this novel beauty remains identical in all Dostoievsky's works. Isn't the Dostoievsky woman (as distinctive as a Rembrandt woman) with her mysterious face, whose engaging beauty changes abruptly, as though her apparent good nature was only play-acting, into coarse ferocity (although at heart it seems that she is more good than bad), isn't she always the same, whether it's Nastasia Philipovna writing love letters to Aglaya and telling her that she hates her, or in a visit that's absolutely identical with this—as also the one where Nastasia Philipovna insults Gania's family—Grushenka, as charming in Katerina Ivanovna's house as the latter had supposed her to be terrible, then suddenly revealing her malevolence by insulting Katerina Ivanovna (although Grushenka is good at heart)? Grushenka, Nastasia—figures as original, as mysterious, not merely as Carpaccio's courtesans but as Rembrandt's Bathsheba. Mind you, he certainly didn't only know how to depict that striking dual face, with its sudden explosions of furious pride, which makes the woman seem other than she is ("You are not like that," says Myshkin to Nastasia during the visit to Gania's family, and Alyosha might have said the same to Grushenka during the visit to Katerina Ivanovna). But on the other hand when he wants to try out 'pictorial ideas' they're always stupid and produce at best the pictures where Myshkin wants to see the representation of a condemned man at the moment when . . . etc., or the Virgin Mary at the moment when . . . etc. But to return to the new kind of beauty that Dostoievsky brought to the world, just as, in Vermeer, there's the creation of a certain soul, of a certain colour of fabrics and places, so in Dostoievsky there's the creation not only of people but of their homes, and the house of the Murder in *The Brothers Karamazov*, with its dvornik, isn't it as marvellous as the masterpiece of the house of Murder in *The Idiot*, that sombre house of Rogozhin's, so long, and so high, and so vast, in which he kills Nastasia Philipovna. That new and terrible beauty of a house, that new and two-sided beauty of a woman's face, that is the unique thing that Dostoievsky has given to the world, and the comparisons that literary critics may make, between him and Gogol, or between him and Paul de Kock, are of no interest, being external to this secret beauty. Besides, if I've said to you that from one novel to another it's the same scene, it's in the compass of a single novel that the same scenes, the same characters reappear if the novel is at all long. I could illustrate this to you easily in *War and Peace*, and a certain scene in a carriage. . . ."

"I didn't want to interrupt you, but now that I see that you're leaving Dostoievsky, I'm afraid I might forget. My sweet, what was it you meant the other day when you said: 'It's like the Dostoievsky side of Mme de Sévigné.' I must confess that I didn't understand. It seems to me so different."

"Come, little girl, let me give you a kiss to thank you for remembering so well what I say. You shall go back to the pianola afterwards. And I must admit that what I said was rather stupid. But I said it for two reasons. The first is a special reason. What I meant was that Mme de Sévigné, like Elstir, like Dostoievsky, instead of presenting things in their logical sequence, that is to say beginning with the cause, shows us first of all the effect, the illusion that strikes us. That is how Dostoievsky presents his characters. Their actions seem to us as deceptive as those effects in Elstir's pictures where the sea appears to be in the sky. We're quite surprised to find later on that some sly-looking individual is really the best of men, or vice versa."

"Yes, but give me an example in Mme de Sévigné."

"I admit," I answered her with a laugh, "that it's very far-fetched, but still I could find examples. For instance . . ."[23]

"But did he ever murder anyone, Dostoievsky? The novels of his that I know might all be called *The Story of a Crime*. It's an obsession with him, it isn't natural that he should always be talking about it."

"I don't think so, dear Albertine. I know little about his life. It's certain that, like everyone else, he was acquainted with sin, in one form or another, and probably in a form which the laws condemn. In that sense he must have been a bit criminal, like his heroes—who in any case are not entirely criminal, who are found guilty with extenuating circumstances. And perhaps it wasn't necessary for him to be criminal himself. I'm not a novelist; it's possible that creative writers are tempted by certain forms of life of which they have no personal experience. If I come with you to Versailles as we arranged, I shall show you the portrait of an ultra-respectable man, the best of husbands, Choderlos de Laclos, who wrote the most appallingly perverse book, and just opposite it the portrait of Mme de Genlis who wrote moral tales and, not content with betraying the Duchesse d'Orléans, tortured her by turning her children against her. I admit all the same that in Dostoievsky this preoccupation with murder is something extraordinary which makes him very alien to me. I'm amazed enough when I hear Baudelaire say:

> Si le viol, le poison, le poignard, l'incendie . . .
> C'est que notre âme, hélas! n'est pas assez hardie.

But I can at least assume that Baudelaire is not sincere. Whereas Dostoievsky. . . . All that sort of thing seems to me as remote from myself as possible, unless there are parts of myself of which I know nothing, for we realise our own nature only in the course of time. In Dostoievsky I find the deepest wells of insight but only into certain isolated regions of the human soul. But he is a great creator. For one thing, the world which he describes does really appear to have been created by him. All those buffoons who keep on reappearing, like Lebedev, Karamazov, Ivolgin, Segrev, that incredible procession, are human types even more fantastic than those that people Rembrandt's *Night Watch*. And yet perhaps they're fantastic only in the same way, by the effect of lighting and costume, and are quite normal really. In any case the whole thing is full of profound and unique truths, which belong only to Dostoievsky. They almost suggest, those buffoons, some trade or calling that no longer exists, like certain characters in the old drama, and yet how they reveal true aspects of the human soul! What I find so boring is the solemn manner in which people talk and write about Dostoievsky. Have you ever noticed the part that self-esteem and pride play in his characters? It's as though, for him, love and the most passionate hatred, goodness and treachery, timidity and insolence, are merely two aspects of a single nature, their self-esteem, their pride preventing Aglaya, Nastasia, the Captain whose beard Mitya pulls, Krassotkin, Alyosha's enemy-friend, from showing themselves in their true colours. But there are many other great qualities as well. I know very few of his books. But what a simple, sculptural notion it is, worthy of the most classical art, a frieze interrupted and resumed in which the theme of vengeance and expiation is unfolded in the crime of old Karamazov getting the poor simpleton with child, the mysterious, animal, unexplained impulse whereby the mother, herself unconsciously the instrument of an avenging destiny, obeying also obscurely her maternal instinct, feeling perhaps a combination of resentment and physical gratitude towards her violator, comes to give birth to her child in old Karamazov's garden. This is the first episode, mysterious, grandiose, august, like the Creation of Woman in one of the sculptures at Orvieto. And as counterpart, the second episode more than twenty years later, the murder of old Karamazov, the infamy committed against the Karamazov family by the madwoman's son, Smerdiakov, followed shortly afterwards by another act as mysteriously sculpturesque and unexplained, of a beauty as obscure and natural as the childbirth in old Karamazov's garden, Smerdiakov hanging himself, his crime accomplished. Actually I wasn't straying as far from Dostoievsky as you thought when I mentioned Tolstoy, who imitated him a great deal. In Dostoievsky there's concentrated, still tense and peevish, a great deal of what was to blossom later on in Tolstoy. There's that proleptic gloom of the primitives which their disciples will brighten and dispel."

"What a bore it is that you're so lazy, my sweet. Just look at your view of literature, so much more interesting than the way we were made to study it; the essays that they used to make us write about *Esther*: 'Monsieur,'—you remember," she said with a laugh, less from a desire to make fun of her masters and herself than from the pleasure of finding in her memory, in our common memory, a recollection that was already quite venerable.

But while she was speaking, and I thought once more of Vinteuil, it was the other, the materialist hypothesis, that of there being nothing, that in turn presented itself to my mind. I began to doubt again; I told myself that after all it might be the case that, if Vinteuil's phrases seemed to be the expression of certain states of soul analogous to that which I had experienced when I tasted the madeleine soaked in tea, there was nothing to assure me that the vagueness of such states was a sign of their profundity rather than of our not having yet learned to analyse them, so that there might be nothing more real in them than in other states. And yet that happiness, that sense of certainty in happiness while I was drinking the cup of tea, or when I smelt in the Champs-Elysées a smell of mouldering wood, was not an illusion. In any case, whispered the spirit of doubt, even if these states are more profound than others that occur in life, and defy analysis for that very reason, because they bring into play too many forces of which we have hitherto been unaware, the charm of certain phrases of Vinteuil's music makes us think of them because it too defies analysis, but this does not prove that it has the same profundity; the beauty of a phrase of pure music can easily appear to be the image of or at least akin to a non-intellectual impression which we have received, but simply because it is unintellectual. And why then do we suppose to be specially profound those mysterious phrases which haunt certain quartets and this septet by Vinteuil?

It was not, however, his music alone that Albertine played me; the pianola was to us at times like a scientific magic lantern (historical and geographical), and on the walls of this room in Paris, supplied with inventions more modern than my room at Combray, I would see extending before me, according to whether Albertine played me Rameau or Borodin, now an eighteenth-century tapestry sprinkled with cupids and roses, now the Eastern steppe in which sounds are muffled by the boundless distances and the soft carpet of snow. And these

fleeting decorations were as it happened the only ones in my
room, for although, at the time of inheriting my aunt Léonie's
fortune, I had resolved to become a collector like Swann, to buy
pictures and statues, all my money went on horses, a motor-car,
dresses for Albertine. But did not my room contain a work of
art more precious than all these—Albertine herself? I looked
at her. It was strange to me to think that it was she, she whom
I had for so long thought it impossible even to know, who
now, a wild beast tamed, a rosebush to which I had acted as
the prop, the framework, the trellis of its life, was seated thus,
day by day, at home, by my side, before the pianola, with her
back to my bookcase. Her shoulders, which I had seen
drooping sullenly when she was carrying her golf-clubs, now
leaned against my books. Her shapely legs, which on the
first day I had with good reason imagined as having manipulated throughout her girlhood the pedals of a bicycle, now rose
and fell alternately upon those of the pianola, upon which
Albertine, who had acquired an elegance which made me feel
her more my own, because it was from myself that it came,
pressed her shoes of cloth of gold. Her fingers, at one time
accustomed to handle-bars, now rested upon the keys like those
of a St Cecilia. Her throat, the curve of which, seen from my
bed, was strong and full, at that distance and in the lamplight
appeared pinker, less pink however than her face, bent forward in profile, which my gaze, issuing from the innermost
depths of myself, charged with memories and burning with
desire, invested with such a brilliancy, such an intensity of life
that its relief seemed to stand out and turn with the same almost
magic power as on the day, in the hotel at Balbec, when my
vision was clouded by my overpowering desire to kiss her;
and I prolonged each of its surfaces beyond what I was able to
see and beneath what concealed it from me and made me feel
all the more strongly—eyelids which half hid her eyes, hair
that covered the upper part of her cheeks—the relief of those
superimposed planes; her eyes (like two facets that alone have
yet been polished in the matrix in which an opal is still embedded), become more resistant than metal while remaining
more brilliant than light, disclosed, in the midst of the blind
matter overhanging them, as it were the mauve, silken wings

of a butterfly placed under glass; and her dark, curling hair, presenting different conformations whenever she turned to ask me what she was to play next, now a splendid wing, sharp at the tip, broad at the base, black, feathered and triangular, now massing the contours of its curls in a powerful and varied chain, full of crests, of watersheds, of precipices, with its soft, creamy texture, so rich and so multiple, seeming to exceed the variety that nature habitually achieves and to correspond rather to the desire of a sculptor who accumulates difficulties in order to emphasise the suppleness, the vibrancy, the fullness, the vitality of his creation, brought out more strongly, by interrupting in order to cover it, the animated curve and, as it were, the rotation of the smooth, roseate face, with its glazed matt texture as of painted wood. And, by contrast with all this relief, by the harmony also which united them with her, who had adapted her attitude to their form and purpose, the pianola which half concealed her like an organ-case, the bookcase, the whole of that corner of the room, seemed to be reduced to the dimensions of a lighted sanctuary, the shrine of this angel musician, a work of art which, presently, by a charming magic, was to detach itself from its niche and offer to my kisses its precious, rose-pink substance. But no, Albertine was for me not at all a work of art. I knew what it meant to admire a woman in an artistic fashion, having known Swann. For my own part, however, no matter who the woman might be, I was incapable of doing so, having no sort of power of detached observation, never knowing what it was that I saw, and I had been amazed when Swann added retrospectively an artistic dignity—by comparing her to me, as he liked to do gallantly to her face, to some portrait by Luini, by recalling in her attire the gown or the jewels of a picture by Giorgione— to a woman who had seemed to me to be devoid of interest. Nothing of that sort with me. The pleasure and the pain that I derived from Albertine never took the line of taste and intellect in order to reach me; indeed, to tell the truth, when I began to regard Albertine as an angel musician glazed with a marvellous patina whom I congratulated myself upon possessing, it was not long before I found her uninteresting; I soon became bored in her company; but these moments were of brief duration: one only loves that in which one pursues the inaccessible, one only loves what one does not possess, and very soon I began to realise once more that I did not possess Albertine. I saw flitting across her eyes, now the hope, now the memory, perhaps the regret, of joys which I could not guess at, which in that case she preferred to renounce rather than reveal to me, and which, glimpsing no more of them than that gleam in her pupils, I no more perceived than does the spectator who has been refused admission to the theatre, and who, his face glued to the glass panes of the door, can take in nothing of what is happening on the stage. (I do not know whether this was the case with her, but it is a strange thing—like evidence of a belief in God in the most incredulous—this perseverance in falsehood shown by all those who deceive us. It would be no good our telling them that their lies hurt us more than a confession, it would be no good their realising it for themselves, they would start lying again a moment later, to remain consistent with what they had always told us that they were, or with what they had told us that we were to them. Similarly, an atheist who values his life will let himself be burned alive rather than give the lie to the view that is generally held of his bravery.) During these hours, I used sometimes to see hover over her face, in her expression, in her pout, in her smile, the reflexion of those inner visions the contemplation of which made her on these evenings unlike her usual self, remote from me to whom they were denied. "What are you thinking about, my darling?" "Why, nothing." Sometimes, in answer to the reproaches I made to her that she told me nothing, she would at one moment tell me things which she was not unaware that I knew as well as anyone (like those statesmen who will never give you the least bit of news, but speak to you instead of what you could have read for yourself in the papers the day before), at another would describe without any precise details, in a sort of false confidence, bicycle rides that she had had at Balbec, the year before our first meeting. And as though I had guessed aright long ago, when I inferred therefrom that she must be a girl who was allowed a great deal of freedom, who went on long jaunts, the mention of those rides insinuated between

Albertine's lips the same mysterious smile that had captivated me in those first days on the front at Balbec. She spoke to me also of the excursions she had made with some girl friends through the Dutch countryside, of returning to Amsterdam in the evening, at a late hour, when a dense and happy crowd of people, almost all of whom she knew, thronged the streets and the towpaths of the canals, of which I felt that I could see reflected in Albertine's brilliant eyes, as in the glancing windows of a fast-moving carriage, the innumerable, flickering lights. How much more deserving of the name indifference is so-called aesthetic curiosity compared with the painful, unwearying curiosity I felt as to the places in which Albertine had stayed, as to what she might have been doing on a particular evening, her smiles, the expressions in her eyes, the words that she had uttered, the kisses that she had received! No, never would the jealousy that I had felt one day of Saint-Loup, if it had persisted, have caused me this immense uneasiness. This love between women was something too unfamiliar; there was nothing to enable me to form a precise and accurate idea of its pleasures, its quality. How many people, how many places (even places which did not concern her directly, vague haunts of pleasure where she might have enjoyed some pleasure, places where there are a great many people, where people brush against one) had Albertine—like a person who, shepherding all her escort, a whole crowd, past the barrier in front of her, secures their admission to the theatre—from the threshold of my imagination or of my memory, where I paid no attention to them, introduced into my heart! Now, the knowledge that I had of them was internal, immediate, spasmodic, painful. Love is space and time made perceptible to the heart.

And yet perhaps, had I myself been entirely faithful, I might not have suffered because of infidelities which I would have been incapable of conceiving; whereas what it tortured me to imagine in Albertine was my own perpetual desire to find favour with new women, to start up new romances, was to suppose her guilty of the glance which I had been unable to resist casting, the other day, even while I was by her side, at the young bicyclists seated at tables in the Bois de Boulogne. As there is no knowledge, one might almost say that there is no jealousy, save of oneself. Observation counts for little. It is only from the pleasure that we ourselves have felt that we can derive knowledge and pain.

At moments, in Albertine's eyes, in the sudden inflammation of her cheeks, I felt as it were a gust of warmth pass furtively through regions more inaccessible to me than the sky, in which Albertine's memories, unknown to me, lived and moved. Then this beauty which, when I thought of the various years in which I had known Albertine, whether on the beach at Balbec or in Paris, I found that I had but recently discovered in her, and which consisted in the fact that she existed on so many planes and embodied so many days that had passed, this beauty became almost heartrending. Then beneath that rose-pink face I felt that there yawned like a gulf the inexhaustible expanse of the evenings when I had not known Albertine. I could, if I chose, take Albertine on my knee, hold her head in my hands, I could caress her, run my hands slowly over her, but, just as if I had been handling a stone which encloses the salt of immemorial oceans or the light of a star, I felt that I was touching no more than the sealed envelope of a person who inwardly reached to infinity. How I suffered from that position to which we are reduced by the obliviousness of nature which, when instituting the division of bodies, never thought of making possible the interpenetration of souls! And I realised that Albertine was not even for me (for if her body was in the power of mine, her thoughts eluded the grasp of my thoughts) the marvellous captive with whom I had thought to enrich my home, while concealing her presence there as completely, even from the friends who came to see me and never suspected that she was at the end of the corridor, in the room next to my own, as did that man of whom nobody knew that he kept the Princess of China sealed in a bottle; urging me with cruel and fruitless insistence in quest of the past, she resembled, if anything, a mighty goddess of Time. And if I had to waste years of my life and much of my fortune for her sake—and provided that I can tell myself, which is by no means certain, alas, that she herself lost nothing—I have nothing to regret. No doubt solitude would have been better, more fruitful, less painful. But if I had led the collector's life which Swann counselled, and the joys of which M. de Charlus reproached me with not knowing, when, with a blend of wit, insolence and good taste, he complained to me how ugly my rooms were, what statues, what pictures long pursued, at length possessed, or even, to put it in the best light, contemplated with detachment, would—like the little wound which healed quickly enough, but which the unconscious tactlessness of Albertine, or of people generally, or of my own thoughts, was never long in reopening—have given me access to that way out of oneself, that connecting road which, though private, opens on to the highway along which passes what we learn to know only from the day when it has made us suffer: the life of other people?

Sometimes there was such a beautiful moonlight that, an hour after Albertine had gone to bed, I would go to her bedside to tell her to look out of the window. I am certain that it was for this reason that I went to her room, and not to assure myself that she was really there. What likelihood was there of her being able to escape, even if she had wished? It would have required an improbable collusion with Françoise. In the dim room, I could see nothing except, against the whiteness of the pillow, a slender diadem of dark hair. But I could hear Albertine's breathing. Her sleep was so deep that I hesitated at first to go as far as the bed. Then I sat down on the edge of it. Her sleep continued to flow with the same murmur. What I find it impossible to express is how gay her awakenings were. I would kiss her and shake her. At once she would cease to sleep, without even a moment's interval, would break out in a laugh, saying as she twined her arms round my neck: "I was just beginning to wonder whether you were coming," and then laugh even more blithely and tenderly. It was as though her charming head, when she slept, was filled with nothing but gaiety, affection and laughter. And in waking her I had merely, as when we cut open a fruit, released the gushing juice which quenches thirst.

Meanwhile winter was at an end; the fine weather returned, and often when Albertine had just bidden me good-night, my curtains and the wall above the curtains being still quite dark, in the nuns' garden next door I could hear, rich and mellow in the silence like a harmonium in church, the modulation of an unknown bird which, in the Lydian mode, was already chanting matins, and into the midst of my darkness flung the rich dazzling note of the sun that it could see.

Presently the nights grew shorter still, and before what had been the hour of daybreak, I could see already stealing above my window-curtains the daily increasing whiteness of the dawn. If I resigned myself to allowing Albertine to continue to lead this life in which, notwithstanding her denials, I felt that she had the impression of being a prisoner, it was only because I was sure that on the following day I should be able not only to set to work but to get up, to go out, to prepare our departure for some country place which we should buy and where Albertine would be able to lead, more freely and without anxiety on my account, the open-air life of the country or the seaside, of boating or hunting, which appealed to her. Only, the next day, from that past which I loved and detested by turns in Albertine (since, when it is the present, everyone, from calculation, or politeness, or pity, sets to work to weave, between himself and us, a curtain of falsehood which we mistake for the truth) it would happen that, retrospectively, one of the hours which composed it, even of those which I thought I knew, presented to me all of a sudden an aspect which she no longer made any attempt to conceal from me and which was then quite different from the aspect in which it had previously appeared to me. Behind some look in her eyes, in place of the benign thought which I had formerly supposed that I could read in it, a hitherto unsuspected desire would reveal itself, alienating from me a fresh region of Albertine's heart which I had believed to be assimilated to my own. For instance, when Andrée had left Balbec in the month of July, Albertine had never told me that she was to see her again shortly, and I imagined that she had seen her even sooner than she expected since, because of the great unhappiness that I had suffered at Balbec, on that night of the fourteenth of September, she had made me the sacrifice of not remaining there and of returning at once to Paris. When she had arrived there on the fifteenth, I had asked her to go and see Andrée and had said to her: "Was she pleased to see you again?" Now one day Mme Bontemps called round to bring something for Albertine. I saw her for a moment and told her that Albertine had gone out with Andrée: "They've gone for a drive in the country."

"Yes," replied Mme Bontemps, "Albertine is always ready to go to the country. Three years ago, for instance, she simply had to go every day to the Buttes-Chaumont." At the name Buttes-Chaumont, a place where Albertine had told me that she had never been, my breath stopped for a moment. The truth is the most cunning of enemies. It delivers its attacks at the point in one's heart where one was least expecting them and where one has prepared no defence. Had Albertine been lying, to her aunt then, when she said that she went every day to the Buttes-Chaumont, or to myself since, when she told me that she did not know the place? "Fortunately," Mme Bontemps went on, "that poor Andrée will soon be leaving for a more bracing countryside, for the real countryside. She needs it badly, she's not looking at all well. It's true that she didn't get all the fresh air she needs last summer. You see, she left Balbec at the end of July, expecting to go back there in September, and then her brother put his knee out, and she was unable to go back."

So Albertine was expecting her at Balbec and had concealed this from me! It is true that it was all the more kind of her to have offered to return to Paris with me. Unless. . . .

"Yes, I remember Albertine's mentioning it to me" (this was untrue). "When did the accident occur, again? I'm a bit muddled about it all."

"Actually, in a way it happened just at the right moment, because a day later the lease of the villa would have begun, and Andrée's grandmother would have had to pay a month's rent for nothing. He damaged his leg on the fourteenth of September, and she had time to cable Albertine on the morning of the fifteenth that she wasn't coming and Albertine was in time to warn the agency. A day later, and the lease would have run on to the middle of October."

And so, no doubt, when Albertine, changing her mind, had said to me: "Let's go this evening," what she saw with her mind's eye was an apartment unknown to me, that of Andrée's grandmother, where, as soon as we returned, she would be able to see the friend whom, without my suspecting it, she had hoped to see again shortly at Balbec. The kind words with which she had expressed her willingness to return to Paris with me, in contrast to her stubborn refusal a little earlier, I had sought to attribute to a genuine change of heart. In fact they were simply the reflection of one of those changes in a situation of which we do not know, and which are the whole secret of the variations in the conduct of women who do not love us. They obstinately refuse to meet us the following evening, because they are tired, because their grandfather insists on their dining with him: "But come later," we insist. "He keeps me very late. He may want to see me home." The simple truth is that they have a rendezvous with some man whom they like. Suddenly he is no longer free. And they come to tell us how sorry they are to have hurt us, that the grandfather can go to hell, and that there is nothing in the world that could keep them from remaining with us. I ought to have recognised these phrases in what Albertine had said to me on the day of my departure from Balbec. But to interpret her words I should have needed not only to recognise those phrases but to remember two traits peculiar to Albertine's character which now recurred to my mind, one to console me, the other to make me wretched, for we find a little of everything in our memory; it is a sort of pharmacy, a sort of chemical laboratory, in which our groping hand may come to rest now on a sedative drug, now on a dangerous poison. The first trait, the consoling one, was that habit of making a single action serve the pleasure of several persons, that multiple utilisation of whatever she did, which was characteristic of Albertine. It was quite in keeping with her character that, returning to Paris (the fact that Andrée was not coming back might have made it inconvenient for her to remain at Balbec without this meaning that she could not do without Andrée), she should use that single journey as an opportunity for pleasing two people of whom she was genuinely fond: myself by making me believe that it was in order not to leave me on my own, in order that I should not be unhappy, out of devotion to me, and Andrée by persuading her that, since she was not coming to Balbec, she herself did not wish to remain there a moment longer, that she had prolonged her stay there only in the hope of seeing Andrée and was now hurrying back to join her. Now, Albertine's departure with me was such an immediate sequel, on the one hand to my access of grief and my desire to return to Paris, and on the other hand to Andrée's telegram, that it was quite natural that Andrée and I, respectively unaware, she of my grief, I of her telegram, should both have supposed that Albertine's departure from Balbec was the effect of the one cause that each of us knew, which indeed it followed at so short an interval and so unexpectedly. And in this case, it was still possible for me to believe that the thought of keeping me company had been Albertine's real object, though she had not wanted to neglect an opportunity of thereby establishing a claim to Andrée's gratitude.

But unfortunately I remembered almost at once another of Albertine's characteristics, which was the swiftness with which she was seized by the irresistible temptation of a pleasure. And I recalled how, when she had decided to leave, she had been so impatient to get to the train, how she had pushed past the hotel manager who in trying to detain us might have made us miss the omnibus, the shrug of complicity which she had given me and by which I had been so touched when, on the twister, M. de Cambremer had asked us whether we could not "postpone it by a sennight." Yes, what she saw in front of her eyes at that moment, what made her so feverishly anxious to leave, what she was so impatient to get to, was an uninhabited apartment I had once visited, belonging to Andrée's grandmother, a luxurious apartment looked after by an old butler, facing south, but so empty, so silent, that the sun appeared to spread dust-sheets over the sofa and the armchairs of the room in which Albertine and Andrée would ask the respectful caretaker, perhaps unsuspecting, perhaps conniving, to allow them to rest for a while. I saw it constantly now, empty, with a bed or a sofa, and a servant who was either a dupe or an accomplice, that apartment to which, whenever Albertine seemed serious and in a hurry, she set off to meet her friend, who had doubtless arrived there before her since her time was more her own. Until then I had never given a thought to that apartment, which now possessed for me a horrible beauty. The unknown element in the lives of other people is like that of nature, which each fresh scientific discovery merely reduces but does not abolish. A jealous lover exasperates the woman he loves by depriving her of a thousand unimportant pleasures, but those pleasures which are the keystone of her life she conceals in a place where, even at moments when he thinks that he is showing the most intelligent perspicacity and third parties are keeping him most closely informed, he never dreams of looking. However, at least Andrée was going to leave Paris. But I did not want Albertine to be in a position to despise me as having been the dupe of herself and Andrée. One of these days I would tell her. And thus I would force her perhaps to speak to me more frankly, by showing her that I was after all informed of the things that she concealed from me. But I did not wish to mention it to her for the moment, first of all because, so soon after her aunt's visit, she would guess where my information came from, would block that source and would not be worried about other, unknown ones; and then because I did not want to run the risk, so long as I was not absolutely certain of keeping Albertine for as long as I chose, of provoking her irritation to the extent of making her decide to leave me. It is true that if I reasoned, sought the truth, prognosticated the future on the basis of her words, which always approved of all my plans, assuring me how much she loved this life, how little her seclusion deprived her of, I had no doubt that she would remain with me always. I was in fact dismayed by the thought; I felt that life and the world, whose fruits I had never really tasted, were passing me by, bartered for a woman in whom I could no longer find anything new. I could not even go to Venice, where, while I lay in bed, I should be too tormented by the fear of the advances that might be made to her by the gondolier, the people in the hotel, the Venetian women. But if on the contrary I reasoned on the basis of the other hypothesis, that which rested not upon Albertine's words but upon silences, looks, blushes, sulks, and even fits of anger, which I could quite easily have shown her to be unfounded and which I preferred to appear not to notice, then I told myself that she was finding this life unbearable, that she felt constantly deprived of what she loved, and that inevitably she would leave me one day. All that I wished, if she did so, was that I might choose the moment, a moment when it would not be too painful

to me, and also at a time of the year when she could not go to
any of the places in which I imagined her debaucheries,
neither to Amsterdam nor to Andrée's, nor to Mlle Vinteuil's,
though she would see them again, it was true, a few months
later. But in the meantime I should have become calmer and
it would no longer matter to me. In any case, before even
thinking of it I must wait until I was cured of the slight relapse
that had been caused by my discovery of the reasons on account
of which Albertine, at a few hours' interval, had been determined not to leave, and then to leave Balbec immediately;
I must allow time for the symptoms to disappear, since they
could only go on diminishing if I learned nothing new, but
were still too acute not to render more painful, more difficult, a
process of separation now recognised as inevitable, but in no
sense urgent, and one that would be better performed in
"cold blood." I could control the choice of moment, for if
she decided to leave me before I had made up my mind, as
soon as she informed me that she had had enough of this life,
there would always be time enough for me to think up some
way of countering her arguments, to offer her a larger freedom,
to promise her some great pleasure in the near future which
she herself would be anxious not to miss, and at worst, if I
could find no other recourse but to appeal to her heart, to
confess my anguish to her. My mind was therefore at rest from
this point of view though I was not being very logical with
myself. For, though the basis of this hypothesis was that I
precisely disregarded what she said or intimated, I was assuming that, when the question of her leaving me arose, she would
give me her reasons beforehand, would allow me to resist and
overcome them.

I felt that my life with Albertine was on the one hand, when I
was not jealous, nothing but boredom, and on the other hand,
when I was jealous, nothing but pain. If there had been any
happiness in it, it could not last. In the same spirit of wisdom
which had inspired me at Balbec, on the evening when we
had been happy together after Mme de Cambremer's visit, I
wanted to leave her, because I knew that by carrying on I
should gain nothing. Only, even now, I imagined that the
memory that I retained of her would be like a sort of vibration,

prolonged by a pedal, of the last moment of our parting. Hence I was anxious to choose a moment of sweetness, so that it might be it that continued to vibrate in me. I must not be too particular, and wait too long, I must be sensible. And yet, having waited so long, it would be madness not to wait a few days longer, until an acceptable moment should offer itself, rather than risk seeing her depart with that same sense of revolt which I had felt in the past when Mamma left my bedside without bidding me good-night, or when she said good-bye to me at the station. To be on the safe side, I heaped more and more presents on her. As regards the Fortuny gowns, we had at length decided upon one in blue and gold lined with pink which was just ready. And I had ordered all the same the other five which she had relinquished with regret in favour of this one. Yet with the coming of spring, two months after her aunt's conversation with me, I lost my temper with her one evening. It was the very evening on which Albertine had put on for the first time the indoor gown in gold and blue by Fortuny which, by reminding me of Venice, made me feel all the more strongly what I was sacrificing for her, who showed no corresponding gratitude towards me. If I had never seen Venice, I had dreamed of it incessantly since those Easter holidays which, when still a boy, I had been going to spend there, and earlier still, since the Titian prints and Giotto photographs which Swann had given me long ago at Combray. The Fortuny gown which Albertine was wearing that evening seemed to me the tempting phantom of that invisible Venice. It was covered with Arab ornamentation, like the Venetian palaces hidden like sultan's wives behind a screen of pierced stone, like the bindings in the Ambrosian Library, like the columns from which the oriental birds that symbolised alternatively life and death were repeated in the shimmering fabric, of an intense blue which, as my eyes drew nearer, turned into a malleable gold by those same transmutations which, before an advancing gondola, change into gleaming metal the azure of the Grand Canal. And the sleeves were lined with a cherry pink which is so peculiarly Venetian that it is called Tiepolo pink.

In the course of the day, Françoise had let fall in my hearing that Albertine was satisfied with nothing, that when I sent word to her that I would be going out with her, or that I would not be going out, that the motor-car would or would not come to fetch her, she almost shrugged her shoulders and would barely give a polite answer. That evening when I felt that she was in a bad mood, and when the first heat of summer had wrought upon my nerves, I could not restrain my anger and reproached her for her ingratitude. "Yes, you can ask anybody," I shouted at the top of my voice, quite beside myself, "you can ask Françoise, it's common knowledge." But immediately I remembered how Albertine had once told me how terrifying she found me when I was angry, and had applied to me the lines from *Esther*:

> Jugez combien ce front irrité contre moi
> Dans mon âme troublée a dû jeter d'émoi.
> Hélas! sans frissonner quel cœur audacieux
> Soutiendrait les éclairs qui partent de vos yeux?

I felt ashamed of my violence. And, to make amends for what I had done, without however acknowledging defeat, so that my peace might be an armed and formidable peace, while at the same time I thought it as well to show her once again that I was not afraid of a rupture so that she might not feel tempted to provoke it: "Forgive me, my little Albertine, I'm ashamed of my violence, I don't know how to apologise. If we can't get on together, if we're to be obliged to part, it mustn't be like this, it wouldn't be worthy of us. We will part, if part we must, but first of all I wish to beg your pardon most humbly and from the bottom of my heart." I decided that, to atone for my outburst and also to make certain of her intention to remain with me for some time to come, at any rate until Andrée should have left Paris, which would be in three weeks' time, it would be as well, next day, to think of some pleasure greater than any that she had yet had, but fairly far ahead; and since I was going to wipe out the offence that I had given her, perhaps it would be as well to take advantage of this moment to show her that I knew more about her life than she supposed. The resentment that she would feel would be removed next day by my generosity, but the warning would remain in her mind. "Yes, my little Albertine, forgive me if I was violent. But I'm not quite as much to blame as you think. There are wicked people in the world who are trying to make us quarrel; I've always refrained from mentioning it, as I didn't want to torment you. But sometimes I'm driven out of my mind by these accusations." And wishing to make the most of the fact that I was going to be able to show her that I was in the know as regards the departure from Balbec, I went on: "For instance, you knew that Mlle Vinteuil was expected at Mme Verdurin's that afternoon when you went to the Trocadéro."

She blushed: "Yes, I knew that."

"Can you swear to me that it was not in order to renew your relations with her that you wanted to go to the Verdurins'."

"Why, of course I can swear it. Why do you say *renew*, I never had any relations with her, I swear it."

I was distressed to hear Albertine lie to me like this, deny the facts which her blush had made all too evident. Her mendacity appalled me. And yet, as it contained a protestation of innocence which, almost unconsciously, I was prepared to accept, it hurt me less than her sincerity when, after I had asked her: "Can you at least swear to me that the pleasure of seeing Mlle Vinteuil again had nothing to do with your anxiety to go to the Verdurins' that afternoon?" she replied: "No, that I cannot swear. It would have been a great pleasure to see Mlle Vinteuil again."

A moment earlier, I had been angry with her because she concealed her relations with Mlle Vinteuil, and now her admission of the pleasure she would have felt at seeing her again turned my bones to water. True, when Albertine had said to me, on my return from the Verdurins': "Wasn't Mlle Vinteuil to be there," she had revived all my anguish by proving that she knew of her coming. But doubtless in the meantime I had reasoned thus: "She knew of her coming, which gave her no pleasure in the least, but since she must have realised, after the event, that it was the revelation that she knew someone with such a bad reputation as Mlle Vinteuil that had so distressed me at Balbec, she didn't want to mention it." And now here she was being obliged to admit that the prospect of seeing Mlle Vinteuil gave her pleasure. Besides, the mystery in which she had cloaked her intention of going to see the Verdurins

ought to have been a sufficient proof. But I had not given the
matter enough thought. And so, while saying to myself now:
"Why does she only half confess? It's even more stupid than
wicked and sad," I was so crushed that I did not have the
heart to pursue the question, as to which I was not in a
strong position, having no damning evidence to produce, and
to recover my ascendancy I hurriedly turned to the subject of
Andrée which would enable me to put Albertine to rout:
"Anyhow," I said to her, "now I'm being tormented and persecuted again with reports of your relations, this time with
Andrée."

"With Andrée?" she cried. Her face was ablaze with fury.
And astonishment or the desire to appear astonished made
her open her eyes wide. "How charming! And may one know
who has been telling you these pretty tales? May I be allowed to
speak to these persons, to learn from them what basis they
have for their slanders?"

"My little Albertine, I don't know, the letters are anonymous, but from people whom you would perhaps have no
difficulty in finding" (this to show her that I did not believe
that she would try) "for they must know you quite well. The
last one, I must admit (and I mention it because it deals with a
trivial thing and there's nothing at all unpleasant in it), made me
furious all the same. It informed me that if, on the day when
we left Balbec, you first of all wished to remain there and then
decided to go, that was because in the meantime you had received
a letter from Andrée telling you that she wasn't coming."

"I know quite well that Andrée wrote to tell me that she
wasn't coming, in fact she telegraphed; I can't show you the
telegram because I didn't keep it, but it wasn't that day.
Besides, even if it had been that day, what difference do you
suppose it could make to me whether Andrée came or not?"

The words "what difference do you suppose it could make
to me" were a proof of anger and that it did make some difference, but were not necessarily a proof that Albertine had
returned to Paris solely from a desire to see Andrée. Whenever
Albertine saw one of the real or alleged motives of one of her
actions discovered by a person to whom she had pleaded a
different motive, she became angry, even if the person was

someone for whose sake she had really performed the action. That Albertine believed that this information about what she had been doing did not come to me from anonymous letters which I had received willy-nilly but was eagerly solicited by me could never have been deduced from the words which she next uttered, in which she appeared to accept my story of the anonymous letters, but rather from her look of fury with me, a fury which appeared to be merely the explosion of her previous ill humour, just as the espionage in which, on this hypothesis, she must suppose that I had been indulging would have been only the culmination of a surveillance of all her actions which she had suspected for a long time past. Her anger extended even to Andrée herself, and deciding no doubt that from now on I should no longer be unworried even when she went out with Andrée, she went on: "Besides, Andrée exasperates me. She's a deadly bore. I never want to go anywhere with her again. You can tell that to the people who informed you that I came back to Paris for her sake. Suppose I were to tell you that after all the years I've known Andrée I couldn't even describe her face to you, so little have I ever looked at it!"

But at Balbec, that first year, she had said to me: "Andrée is lovely." It is true that this did not mean that she had had amorous relations with her, and indeed I had never heard her speak at that time save with indignation of any relations of that sort. But was it not possible that she had changed, even without being aware that she had changed, not thinking that her amusements with a girl friend were the same thing as the immoral relations, not very clearly defined in her own mind, which she condemned in other women? Was this not possible, since this same change, and this same unawareness of change, had occurred in her relations with myself, whose kisses she had repulsed at Balbec with such indignation, kisses which afterwards she was to give me of her own accord every day, which, I hoped, she would give me for a long time to come, which she was going to give me in a moment?

"But, my darling, how do you expect me to tell them when I don't know who they are?"

This answer was so forceful that it ought to have dissolved

the objections and doubts which I saw crystallised in Albertine's pupils. But it left them intact. I was now silent, and yet she continued to gaze at me with that persistent attention which we give to someone who has not finished speaking. I asked her forgiveness once more. She replied that she had nothing to forgive me. She had become very gentle again. But, beneath her sad and troubled features, it seemed to me that a secret plan had taken shape. I knew quite well that she could not leave me without warning me; in fact she could neither want to leave me (it was in a week's time that she was to try on the new Fortuny gowns), nor decently do so, as my mother was returning to Paris at the end of the week and her aunt also. Why, since it was impossible for her to leave, did I repeat to her several times that we should be going out together next day to look at some Venetian glass which I wished to give her, and why was I comforted when I heard her say that that was agreed? When it was time for her to say good-night and I kissed her, she did not behave as usual, but turned her face away—it was barely a minute or two since I had been thinking how pleasing it was that she now gave me every evening what she had refused me at Balbec—and did not return my kiss. It was as though, having quarrelled with me, she was not prepared to give me a token of affection which might later on have appeared to me an act of duplicity that belied the quarrel. It was as though she was attuning her actions to that quarrel, and yet with moderation, whether so as not to announce it, or because, while breaking off carnal relations with me, she wished nevertheless to remain my friend. I kissed her then a second time, pressing to my heart the shimmering golden azure of the Grand Canal and the mating birds, symbols of death and resurrection. But for the second time, instead of returning my kiss, she drew away with the sort of instinctive and baleful obstinacy of animals that feel the hand of death. This presentiment which she seemed to be expressing overcame me too, and filled me with such anxious dread that when she had reached the door I could not bear to let her go, and called her back.

"Albertine," I said to her, "I'm not at all sleepy. If you don't want to go to sleep yourself, you might stay here a little longer, if you like, but I don't really mind, and I don't on any account want to tire you." I felt that if I had been able to make her undress, and to have her there in her white nightdress, in which she seemed pinker and warmer, in which she excited my senses more keenly, the reconciliation would have been more complete. But I hesitated for an instant, for the sky-blue border of her dress added to her face a beauty, a luminosity, without which she would have seemed to me harder.

She came back slowly and said to me very sweetly, and still with the same downcast, sorrowful expression: "I can stay as long as you like, I'm not sleepy." Her reply calmed me, for, so long as she was in the room, I felt that I could prepare for the future, and it also reflected friendliness and obedience, but of a certain sort, which seemed to me to be limited by that secret which I sensed behind her sorrowful gaze, her altered manner, altered partly in spite of herself, partly no doubt to attune it in advance to something which I did not know. I felt that, all the same, I needed only to have her all in white, with her throat bare, in front of me, as I had seen her at Balbec in bed, to find the courage which would oblige her to yield.

"Since you're being kind enough to stay here a moment to console me, you ought to take off your gown, it's too hot, too stiff, I dare not approach you for fear of crumpling that fine stuff, and there are those fateful birds between us. Undress, my darling."

"No, I couldn't possibly take off this dress here. I shall undress in my own room presently."

"Then you won't even come and sit down on my bed?"

"Why, of course."

She remained, however, some way away from me, by my feet. We talked. Suddenly we heard the regular rhythm of a plaintive call. It was the pigeons beginning to coo. "That proves that day has come already," said Albertine; and, her brows almost knitted, as though she missed, by living with me, the joys of the fine weather, "Spring has begun, if the pigeons have returned." The resemblance between their cooing and the crow of the cock was as profound and as obscure as, in Vinteuil's septet, the resemblance between the theme of the adagio and that of the opening and closing passages, it being built on the same key-theme but so transformed by differences of tonality, tempo, etc. that the lay listener who opens a book on Vinteuil is astonished to find that they are all three based on the same four notes, four notes which for that matter he may pick out with one finger upon the piano without recognising any of the three passages. Likewise, this melancholy refrain performed by the pigeons was a sort of cockcrow in the minor key, which did not soar up into the sky, did not rise vertically, but, regular as the braying of a donkey, enveloped in sweetness, went from one pigeon to another along a single horizontal line, and never raised itself, never changed its lateral plaint into that joyous appeal which had been uttered so often in the allegro of the introduction and the finale. I know that I then uttered the word "death," as though Albertine were about to die. It seems that events are larger than the moment in which they occur and cannot be entirely contained in it. Certainly they overflow into the future through the memory that we retain of them, but they demand a place also in the time that precedes them. One may say that we do not then see them as they are to be, but in memory are they not modified too?

When I saw that she deliberately refrained from kissing me, realising that I was merely wasting my time, that it was only after a kiss that the really soothing moments would begin, I said to her: "Good-night, it's too late," because that would make her kiss me and we would go on kissing afterwards. But after saying to me, "Good-night, try and sleep well," she contented herself with letting me kiss her on the cheek, exactly as she had done twice before. This time I dared not call her back. But my heart beat so violently that I could not lie down again. Like a bird flying from one end of its cage to the other I alternated between anxiety lest Albertine should leave me and a state of comparative calm. This calm was produced by the argument which I kept repeating several times a minute: "She cannot go without warning me, and she never said anything about going," and I was more or less calmed. But at once I said to myself: "But what if to-morrow I find her gone! My very anxiety must be founded on something. Why didn't she kiss me?" At this my heart ached horribly. Then it was slightly soothed by the argument which I advanced once more, but I ended with a headache, so incessant and monotonous was this fluctuation of my thoughts. There are thus certain mental states, and especially anxiety, which, offering us only two alternatives, are somehow as atrociously circumscribed as a simple physical pain. I perpetually repeated both the argument which justified my anxiety and the one which proved it false and reassured me, within as narrow a space as the sick man who explores without ceasing, on an internal impulse, the organ that is causing his suffering and withdraws for an instant from the painful spot only to return to it a moment later. Suddenly, in the silence of the night, I was startled by a noise which, though apparently insignificant, filled me with terror, the noise of Albertine's window being violently opened. When I heard nothing more, I wondered why this noise had caused me such alarm. In itself there was nothing so extraordinary about it, but I probably gave it two interpretations which alarmed me equally. In the first place it was one of the conventions of our life together that, since I was afraid of draughts, nobody must ever open a window at night. This had been explained to Albertine when she came to stay in the house, and although she was convinced that this was a fad on my part and thoroughly unhealthy, she had promised me that she would never infringe the rule. And she was so timorous about everything that she knew to be my wish, even if she disapproved of it, that she would have gone to sleep amid the fumes of a smouldering fire rather than open her window, just as, however important the circumstances, she would not have had me woken up in the morning. It was only one of the minor conventions of our life, but if she was prepared to violate this one without consulting me, might it not mean that she no longer needed to behave with circumspection, that she would violate them all just as easily? Besides, the noise had been violent, almost rude, as though she had flung the window open, crimson with rage, saying to herself: "This life is stifling me. I don't care, I must have air!" I did not exactly say all this to myself, but I continued to think, as of an omen more mysterious and more funereal than the hoot of an owl, of that sound of the window which Albertine had opened. Filled with an agitation such as I had not perhaps felt since the evening at Combray when Swann had been dining downstairs, I paced the corridor all night long, hoping, by the noise that I made, to attract Albertine's attention, hoping that she would take pity on me and would call me to her, but I heard no sound from her room. At Combray, I had asked my mother to come. But with my mother I feared only her anger; I knew that I would not diminish her affection by displaying mine. This made me hesitate to call out to Albertine. Gradually I began to feel that it was too late. She must long have been asleep. I went back to bed. In the morning, as soon as I awoke, since no one ever came to my room, whatever happened, without a summons, I rang for Françoise. And at the same time I thought: "I must speak to Albertine about a yacht which I mean to have built for her." As I took my letters I said to Françoise without looking at her: "I shall have something to say to Mlle Albertine presently. Is she up yet?" "Yes, she got up early." I felt untold anxieties which I could scarcely contain rise up in me as in a gust of wind. The tumult in my chest was so great that I was quite out of breath, as though buffeted by a storm. "Ah! but where is she just now?" "I expect she's in her room." "Ah! good! Well, I shall see her presently." I breathed again; my agitation subsided; Albertine was here; it was almost a matter of indifference to me whether she was or not. Besides, had it not been absurd of me to suppose that she could possibly not be there? I fell asleep, but, in spite of my certainty that she would not leave me, it was a light sleep and its lightness related to her alone. For the sounds that were obviously connected with work in the courtyard, while I heard them vaguely in my sleep, left me untroubled, whereas the slightest rustle that came from her room, when she left it, or noiselessly returned, pressing the bell so gently, made me start, ran through my whole body, left me with a palpitating heart, although I had heard it in a deep drowse, just as my grandmother in the last days before her death, when she was plunged in a motionless torpor which nothing could disturb and which the doctors called coma, would begin, I was told, to tremble for a moment like a leaf when she heard the three rings with which I was in the habit of summoning Françoise, and which, even when

I made them softer, during that week, so as not to disturb the
silence of the death-chamber, nobody, Françoise assured me,
could mistake for anyone else's ring because of a way that I
had, and was quite unconscious of having, of pressing the
bell. Had I then myself entered into my last agony? Was this
the approach of death?

That day and the next we went out together, since Albertine
refused to go out again with Andrée. I did not even mention
the yacht to her. These outings had completely restored my
peace of mind. But in the evening she had continued to embrace me in the same new way, which left me furious. I could
interpret it now in no other way than as a means of showing
me that she was sulking, which seemed to me perfectly absurd
after the kindnesses I continued to heap upon her. And so,
no longer receiving from her even those carnal satisfactions
on which I depended, finding her positively ugly in her ill
humour, I felt all the more keenly my deprivation of all the
women and of the travels for which these first warm days
reawakened my desire. Thanks no doubt to scattered memories
of forgotten assignations that I had had, while still a schoolboy, with women, beneath trees already in full leaf, this springtime region in which the journey of our dwelling-place through
the seasons had halted three days since beneath a clement sky,
and in which all the roads sped away towards picnics in the
country, boating parties, pleasure trips, seemed to me to be
the land of women just as much as it was the land of trees, and
the land in which the pleasure that was everywhere on offer
became permissible to my convalescent strength. Resigning
myself to idleness, resigning myself to chastity, to tasting
pleasure only with a woman whom I did not love, resigning
myself to remaining shut up in my room, to not travelling,
all this was possible in the old world in which we had been
only yesterday, in the empty world of winter, but was no
longer possible in this new universe bursting with green
leaves, in which I had awoken like a young Adam faced for
the first time with the problem of existence, of happiness,
and not bowed down beneath the accumulation of previous
negative solutions. Albertine's presence weighed upon me. I
looked at her, grim-faced and sullen, and felt it was a pity we

had not broken with each other. I wanted to go to Venice, I wanted in the meantime to go to the Louvre to look at Venetian pictures and to the Luxembourg to see the two Elstirs which, as I had just heard, the Duchesse de Guermantes had recently sold to that gallery, those that I had so greatly admired, the *Pleasures of the Dance* and the *Portrait of the X Family*. But I was afraid that, in the former, certain lascivious poses might give Albertine a desire, a nostalgic longing for popular rejoicings, might make her think that perhaps a certain life which she had never led, a life of fireworks and country taverns, had something to recommend it. Already, in anticipation, I was afraid lest, on the Fourteenth of July, she would ask me to take her to a popular ball and I longed for some impossible event which would do away with the national holiday. And besides, there were also in those Elstirs certain nude female figures in exotic southern landscapes which might make Albertine think of certain pleasures, albeit Elstir himself (but would she not degrade his work?) had seen in them no more than sculptural beauty, or rather the beauty of white monuments, which women's bodies seated amidst verdure assume. And so I resigned myself to abandoning that pleasure and decided instead to go to Versailles. Albertine had remained in her room, reading, in her Fortuny dressing-gown. I asked her if she would like to go with me to Versailles. She had the charming quality of being always ready for anything, perhaps because she had been accustomed in the past to spend half her time as the guest of other people, and, just as she had made up her mind to come to Paris in two minutes, she said to me: "I can come as I am if we don't get out of the car." She hesitated for a moment between two Fortuny coats beneath which to conceal her dressing-gown—as she might have hesitated between two friends in choosing an escort—chose a beautiful dark-blue one, and stuck a pin into a hat. In a minute, she was ready, before I had put on my overcoat, and we went to Versailles. This very promptitude, this absolute docility left me more reassured, as though, without having any precise reason for anxiety, I had indeed been in need of reassurance. "After all I have nothing to fear. She does everything that I ask, in spite of the noise of her window the other night. The

moment I spoke of going out, she flung that blue coat over
her gown and out she came. That's not what a rebel would have
done, a person who was no longer on friendly terms with me,"
I said to myself as we went to Versailles. We stayed there a long
time. The sky consisted entirely of that radiant and slightly
pale blue which the wayfarer lying in a field sees at times above
his head, but so uniform and so deep that one feels that the
pigment of which it is composed has been applied without the
least alloy and with such an inexhaustible richness that one
might delve more and more deeply into its substance without
encountering an atom of anything but the same blue. I thought
of my grandmother who—in human art as in nature—loved
grandeur, and who used to enjoy gazing at the steeple of Saint-
Hilaire soaring into that same blue. Suddenly I felt once again a
longing for my lost freedom on hearing a noise which I did
not at first recognise and which my grandmother would also
have loved. It was like the buzz of a wasp. "Look," said
Albertine, "there's an aeroplane, high up there, very very high."
I looked all over the sky but could see only, unmarred by any
black spot, the unbroken pallor of the unalloyed blue. I
continued nevertheless to hear the humming of the wings,
which suddenly entered my field of vision. Up there, a pair of
tiny wings, dark and flashing, punctured the continuous blue
of the unalterable sky. I had at last been able to attach the
buzzing to its cause, to that little insect throbbing up there in
the sky, probably six thousand feet above me; I could see it
hum. Perhaps at a time when distances by land had not yet
been habitually shortened by speed as they are to-day, the
whistle of a passing train two thousand yards away was endowed with that beauty which now and for some time to come
will stir our emotions in the drone of an aeroplane six thousand feet up, at the thought that the distances traversed in this
vertical journey are the same as those on the ground, and that
in this other direction, where measurements appear different to
us because the reach seemed impossible, an aeroplane at six
thousand feet is no further away than a train at two thousand
yards, is nearer even, the identical trajectory occurring in a purer
medium, with no obstacle between the traveller and his starting
point, just as on the sea or across the plains, in calm weather,

the wake of a ship that is already far away or the breath of a single zephyr will furrow the ocean of water or of corn.

We returned home very late, in a half-light through which here and there, by the roadside, a pair of red breeches pressed against a skirt revealed an amorous couple. Our carriage passed in through the Porte Maillot. For the monuments of Paris had been substituted, pure, linear, two-dimensional, a drawing of the monuments of Paris, as though in an attempt to recapture the appearance of a city that had been destroyed. But, at the edges of this picture, there rose so delicately the pale-blue mounting in which it was framed that one's thirsty eyes sought everywhere for a little more of that delicious hue which was too sparingly meted out to them: the moon was shining. Albertine admired the moonlight. I dared not tell her that I would have admired it more if I had been alone, or in quest of an unknown woman. I recited to her some lines of verse or passages of prose about moonlight, pointing out to her how from "silvery" which it had been at one time, it had turned "blue" in Chateaubriand, and in the Victor Hugo of *Eviradnus* and *La Fête chez Thérèse*, to become in turn yellow and metallic in Baudelaire and Leconte de Lisle. Then, reminding her of the image that is used for the crescent moon at the end of *Booz endormi*, I recited the whole of that poem to her.

"By the way, since neither of us is really hungry, we might look in at the Verdurins'," Albertine said to me. "This is their day and their hour."

"But I thought you were cross with them?"

"Oh! there are all sorts of stories about them, but really they're not so bad as all that. Madame Verdurin has always been very nice to me. Besides, one can't keep on quarrelling all the time with everybody. They have their faults, but who hasn't?"

"You're not properly dressed, you would have to go home and dress, and that would make us very late."

"Yes, you're right, let's just go home," replied Albertine with that marvellous docility which never ceased to amaze me.

Looking back, I find it difficult to describe how densely her life was covered in a network of alternating, fugitive, often contradictory desires. No doubt falsehood complicated this still further, for, as she retained no accurate memory of our conversations, if, for example, she had said to me: "Ah! that was a pretty girl, if you like, and a good golfer," and, when I had asked the girl's name, had answered with that detached, universal, superior air of which no doubt there is always enough and to spare, for all liars of this category borrow it for a moment when they do not wish to answer a question, and it never fails them: "Ah, I'm afraid I don't know" (with regret at her inability to enlighten me), "I never knew her name, I used to see her on the golf course, but I didn't know what she was called"— if, a month later, I said to her: "Albertine, you remember that pretty girl you mentioned to me, who used to play golf so well," "Ah, yes," she would answer without thinking, "Emilie Daltier, I don't know what's become of her." And the lie, like a line of earthworks, was carried back from the defence of the name, now captured, to the possibilities of meeting her again. "Oh, I couldn't say, I never knew her address. I can't think of anyone who could give it to you. Oh, no! Andrée never knew her. She wasn't one of our little band, now so scattered."

At other times the lie took the form of a base admission: "Ah! if I had three hundred thousand francs a year. . . ." She bit her lip. "Well? what would you do then?" "I should ask your permission," she said, kissing me, "to stay with you always. Where else could I be so happy?"

But, even allowing for her lies, it was incredible how spasmodic her life was, how fugitive her strongest desires. She would be mad about a person whom, three days later, she would refuse to see. She could not wait for an hour while I sent out for canvas and colours, for she wished to start painting again. For two whole days she would be impatient, almost shed the tears, quickly dried, of an infant that has just been weaned from its nurse. And this instability of her feelings with regard to people, things, occupations, arts, places, was in fact so universal that, if she did love money, which I do not believe, she cannot have loved it for longer than anything else. When she said: "Ah! if I had three hundred thousand francs a year!" or even if she expressed a nefarious but very short-lived thought, she could not have held on to it any longer than to the idea of going to Les Rochers, of which she had seen an engraving in my grandmother's edition of Mme de Sévigné, of meeting an old friend from the golf course, of going up in an aeroplane, of going to spend Christmas with her aunt, or of taking up painting again.

One evening we stopped at a big pastry-cook's, situated almost outside the town, which at the time enjoyed a certain vogue. A lady was leaving the place, and asked the proprietress for her things. And after the lady had gone, Albertine cast repeated glances at the proprietress as though she wished to attract her attention while she was putting away cups, plates, cakes, for it was getting late. She approached us only if I asked for something. And it happened then that, as the woman, who incidentally was extremely tall, was standing up while she waited on us and Albertine was seated beside me, Albertine, each time, in an attempt to attract her attention, raised vertically towards her a sunny gaze which compelled her to elevate her pupils to an inordinate height since, the woman being close up against us, Albertine had no possibility of tempering the angle with a sidelong glance. She was obliged, without raising her head unduly, to make her eyes ascend to that disproportionate height at which the woman's eyes were situated. Out of consideration for me, Albertine would quickly lower her eyes and then, the woman having paid no attention to her, would begin again. This led to a series of vain imploring elevations before an inaccessible deity. Then the proprietress moved away to clear a large table next to ours. Now Albertine's look could be natural. But never once did the woman's eyes come to rest upon my mistress. This did not surprise me, for I knew that this woman, with whom I was slightly acquainted, had lovers, although she was married, but managed skilfully to conceal her intrigues, which astonished me vastly in view of her prodigious stupidity. I studied the woman while we finished our meal. Engrossed in her task, she carried her disregard for Albertine's glances (which incidentally were in no way improper) almost to the point of rudeness. She went on clearing away and arranging things without letting anything distract her. The counting and putting away of the coffee-spoons, the fruit-knives, might have been entrusted not to this large and handsome woman, but, by a "labour-saving" device, to a mere machine, and you would not have seen so complete an isolation from Albertine's attention; and yet she did not lower her eyes, did not appear self-absorbed, allowed her eyes, her charms to shine in an undivided attention to her work. It is true that if this woman had not been a particularly stupid person (not only was this her reputation, but I knew it from experience), this detachment might have been a supreme proof of guile. And I know very well that the stupidest person, if his desire or his pocket is involved, can, in that sole instance, emerging from the nullity of his stupid life, adapt himself immediately to the workings of the most complicated mach-chinery; all the same, this would have been too subtle a supposition in the case of a woman as brainless as this. Her stupidity even took her to improbable lengths of impoliteness. Not once did she look at Albertine whom, after all, she could not help seeing. It was not very flattering for my mistress, but, when all was said, I was delighted that Albertine should receive this little lesson and should see that frequently women paid no attention to her. We left the pastry-cook's, got into our carriage and were already on our way home when I was seized by a sudden regret that I had not taken the proprietress aside and begged her on no account to tell the lady who had come out of the shop as we were going in my name and address, which she must know perfectly well because of the orders I had constantly left with her. It was undesirable that the lady should be enabled thus to learn, indirectly, Albertine's address. But I felt that it was not worth while turning back for so small a matter, and that I should appear to be attaching too great an importance to it in the eyes of the idiotic and deceitful proprietress. I decided, however, that I should have to return there, in a week's time, to make this request, and that it is a great bore, since one always forgets half the things one has to say, to have to do even the simplest things in instalments.

The fine weather, that night, made a leap forward as the mercury in a thermometer darts upwards in the heat. On those early-risen spring mornings I could hear from my bed the tram-cars rumbling through a cloud of perfumes, in an atmosphere which became more and more saturated by the prevailing warmth until it reached the solidification and density of noon. In my bedroom where it was cooler, when the unctuous air had succeeded in glazing and isolating the smell of the wash-stand, the smell of the wardrobe, the smell of the sofa, simply by the sharpness with which they stood out, vertical and erect, in adjacent but distinct slices, in a pearly chiaroscuro which added a softer glaze to the shimmer of the curtains and the blue satin armchairs, I saw myself, not by a mere caprice of my imagination but because it was physically possible, following, in some new suburban quarter like that in which Bloch's house at Balbec was situated, the streets blinded by the sun, and finding in them not the dull butchers' shops and the white freestone facings, but the country dining-room which I could reach in no time, and the smells that I would find there on my arrival, the smell of the bowl of cherries and apricots, the smell of cider, the smell of gruyère cheese, held in suspense in the luminous coagulation of shadow which they delicately vein like the heart of an agate, while the knife-rests of prismatic glass scatter rainbows athwart the room or paint the oilcloth here and there with peacock-eyes.

Like a wind that swells in a steady roar, I heard with joy a motor-car beneath the window. I sniffed its smell of petrol. The latter may seem regrettable to the oversensitive (who are always materialists and for whom it spoils the country), and to certain thinkers (materialists after their own fashion also) who, believing in the importance of facts, imagine that man would be happier, capable of higher flights of poetry, if his eyes were able to perceive more colours and his nostrils to distinguish more scents, a philosophical misrepresentation of the naïve idea of those who believe that life was finer when men wore sumptuous costumes instead of the black coats of to-day. But to me (just as an aroma, unpleasing perhaps in itself, of naphthaline and vetiver would have thrilled me by bringing back to me the blue purity of the sea on the day of my arrival at Balbec), this smell of petrol which, together with the smoke from the exhaust of the car, had so often melted into the pale azure on those scorching days when I used to drive from Saint-Jean de la Haise to Gourville, since it had accompanied me on my excursions during those summer afternoons when I

left Albertine painting, called into blossom now on either side
of me, for all that I was lying in my darkened bedroom, cornflowers, poppies and red clover, intoxicated me like a country
scent, not circumscribed and fixed like that of the hawthorns
which, held in by its dense, oleaginous elements, hangs with a
certain stability about the hedge, but like a scent before which
the roads sped away, the landscape changed, stately houses
came hurrying to meet me, the sky turned pale, my strength
was increased tenfold, a scent which was like a symbol of
elastic motion and power and which revived the desire that I
had felt at Balbec to climb into the cage of steel and crystal,
but this time no longer to pay visits to familiar houses with a
woman I knew too well, but to make love in new places with a
woman unknown. A scent that was accompanied incessantly
by the horns of passing motors, which I set to words like a
military summons: "Parisian, get up, get up, come out and
picnic in the country, and take a boat on the river, under the
trees, with a pretty girl; get up, get up!" And all these day-
dreams were so agreeable that I congratulated myself upon the
"stern decree" which prescribed that until I had rung my bell
no "timid mortal," whether Françoise or Albertine, should
dare come in and disturb me "within this palace" where "a
dread majesty contrives to render me invisible to my subjects."[24]
But all of a sudden the scene changed; it was the memory,
no longer of old impressions but of an old desire, only recently
reawakened by the Fortuny gown in blue and gold, that spread
before me another spring, a spring not leafy at all but on the
contrary suddenly stripped of its trees and flowers by the name
that I had just murmured to myself: "Venice"; a decanted
springtime, which is reduced to its own essence and expresses
the lengthening, the warming, the gradual unfolding of its
days in the progressive fermentation, no longer, now, of
an impure soil, but of a blue and virginal water, springlike
without bud or blossom, which could answer the call of May
only by gleaming facets fashioned and polished by May,
harmonising exactly with it in the radiant, unalterable nakedness
of its dusky sapphire. Likewise, too, no more than the seasons
to its flowerless creeks, do modern times bring any change to
the Gothic city; I knew it, even if I could not imagine it, or

rather, imagining it, this was what I longed for with the same desire which long ago, when I was a boy, in the very ardour of departure, had broken and robbed me of the strength to make the journey: to find myself face to face with my Venetian imaginings, to observe how that divided sea enclosed in its meanderings, like the sinuosities of the ocean stream, an urbane and refined civilisation, but one that, isolated by their azure girdle, had evolved independently, had had its own schools of painting and architecture, to admire that fabulous garden of fruits and birds in coloured stone, flowering in the midst of the sea which kept it refreshed, lapped the base of the columns with its tide, and, like a sombre azure gaze watching in the shadows, kept patches of light perpetually flickering on the bold relief of the capitals.

Yes, I must go, the time had come. Now that Albertine no longer appeared to be angry with me, the possession of her no longer seemed to me a treasure in exchange for which one is prepared to sacrifice every other. For perhaps one would have done so only to rid oneself of a grief, an anxiety, which are now appeased. One has succeeded in jumping through the calico hoop through which one thought for a moment that one would never be able to pass. One has weathered and banished the storm, returned to a smiling serenity. The agonising mystery of a hatred with no known cause, and perhaps no end, is dispelled. Henceforward one finds oneself once more face to face with the problem, momentarily thrust aside, of a happiness which one knows to be impossible.

It might well occur to us, were we better able to analyse our loves, to see that women often attract us only because of the counterpoise of all the men with whom we have to compete for them, although we suffer agonies from having thus to compete; this counterpoise removed, the charm of the woman declines. We have a painful and cautionary example of this in the predilection men have for women who have strayed before they came to know them, for those women whom they feel to be sinking in perilous quicksands and whom they must spend the whole period of their love in rescuing; a posthumous example, on the other hand, and one that is not in the least tragic, in the man who, conscious of a decline in his affection for the woman he loves, spontaneously applies the rules that he has deduced, and, to make sure that he does not cease to love the woman, places her in a dangerous environment where he is obliged to protect her daily. (The opposite of the men who insist on a woman's retiring from the stage even though it was because she was on the stage that they fell in love with her.)

Now that life with Albertine had become possible once again, I felt that I could derive nothing from it but misery, since she did not love me; better to part from her in the gentle solace of her acquiescence, which I would prolong in memory. Yes, this was the moment; I must make quite certain of the date on which Andrée was leaving Paris, use all my influence with Mme Bontemps to make sure that at that moment Albertine should not be able to go either to Holland or to Montjouvain; and when in this way there were no immediate drawbacks to Albertine's departure, choose a fine day like this—and there would be plenty of them before long—when she had ceased to matter to me, when I was tempted by countless desires. I should have to let her leave the house without my seeing her, then, getting up and preparing myself in haste, leave a note for her, taking advantage of the fact that as she could not for the time being go anywhere that would upset me, I might be spared, during my travels, from imagining the wicked things which she might do—and which in any case for the moment seemed quite unimportant—and, without seeing her again, set off for Venice.

I rang for Françoise to ask her to buy me a guide-book and a time-table, as I had done as a boy when already I wanted to prepare in advance a journey to Venice, the fulfilment of a desire as violent as that which I felt at this moment. I forgot that, in the meantime, there was a desire which I had attained without any satisfaction—the desire for Balbec—and that Venice, being also a visible phenomenon, was probably no more able than Balbec to fulfil an ineffable dream, that of the Gothic age made actual by a springtime sea, that now teased my mind from moment to moment with an enchanted, caressing, elusive, mysterious, confused image. Françoise, having heard my ring, came into the room: "I was very worried," she said to me, "that Monsieur should be so late in ringing this morning. I didn't know what I ought to do. This morning at eight o'clock Mademoiselle Albertine asked me for her boxes. I dared not refuse her, and I was afraid that Monsieur might scold me if I came and waked him. It was no use lecturing her, telling her to wait an hour because I expected all the time that Monsieur would ring; she wouldn't have it, she left this letter with me for Monsieur, and at nine o'clock off she went." Then—so ignorant can we be of what is inside us, since I was convinced of my indifference to Albertine—my breath was cut short, I gripped my heart in my hands, which were suddenly moistened by a perspiration I had not experienced since the revelation she had made to me on the little train with regard to Mlle Vinteuil's friend, and I was incapable of saying anything else but: "Ah! very good, Françoise, you were of course quite right not to wake me. Leave me now for a moment, I shall ring for you presently."

THE FUGITIVE

THE FUGITIVE

"MADEMOISELLE Albertine has gone!" How much further does anguish penetrate in psychology than psychology itself! A moment before, in the process of analysing myself, I had believed that this separation without having seen each other again was precisely what I wished, and, comparing the mediocrity of the pleasures that Albertine afforded me with the richness of the desires which she prevented me from realising (and which the certainty of her presence in my home, as it were the pressure of my mental atmosphere, allowed to occupy the foreground of my feelings, but which at the news of Albertine's departure could no longer even begin to compete with her, for they had vanished instantaneously), I had felt that I was being subtle, had concluded that I no longer wished to see her, that I no longer loved her. But now these words: "Mademoiselle Albertine has gone," had produced in my heart an anguish such that I felt I could not endure it much longer; I must put an end to it at once; tender towards myself as my mother had been towards my dying grandmother, I said to myself with that genuine wish that one has to relieve the suffering of a person one loves: "Be patient for a moment, we shall find something to take the pain away, don't fret, we're not going to allow you to suffer like this." And, vaguely surmising that if just now, before I had yet rung the bell, Albertine's departure had appeared to me to be a matter of indifference, even something desirable, it was because I had thought it impossible, it was in this category of ideas that my instinct of self-preservation sought for the first sedatives to lay upon my open wound: "None of this is of the slightest importance, because I'm going to bring her back at once. I shall have to think how, but in any case she will be here this evening. Therefore it's useless to torment myself." "None of this is of the slightest importance"—I had not been content merely with giving myself this assurance, but had tried to convey the same impression to Françoise by not allowing her to see my suffering, because, even at the moment when I was feeling it so acutely, my love did not forget how important it was that it should appear a happy love, a mutual love, especially in the eyes of Françoise, who disliked Albertine and had always doubted her sincerity.

Yes, a moment ago, before Françoise came into the room, I had believed that I no longer loved Albertine, I had believed that I was leaving nothing out of account, like a rigorous analyst; I had believed that I knew the state of my own heart. But our intelligence, however lucid, cannot perceive the elements that compose it and remain unsuspected so long as, from the volatile state in which they generally exist, a phenomenon capable of isolating them has not subjected them to the first stages of solidification. I had been mistaken in thinking that I could see clearly into my own heart. But this knowledge, which the shrewdest perceptions of the mind would not have given me, had now been brought to me, hard, glittering, strange, like a crystallised salt, by the abrupt reaction of pain. I was so much in the habit of having Albertine with me, and now I suddenly saw a new aspect of Habit. Hitherto I had regarded it chiefly as an annihilating force which suppresses the originality and even the awareness of one's perceptions; now I saw it as a dread deity, so riveted to one's being, its insignificant face so incrusted in one's heart, that if it detaches itself, if it turns away from one, this deity that one had barely distinguished inflicts on one sufferings more terrible than any other and is then as cruel as death itself.

The first thing to be done was to read Albertine's letter, since I was anxious to think of some way of bringing her back. I felt that this lay in my power, because, as the future is what exists as yet only in the mind, it seems to us to be still alterable by the intervention, at the eleventh hour, of the will. But at the same time, I remembered that I had seen forces other than my own act upon it, forces against which, even if I had had more time, I could never have prevailed. Of what use is it that the hour has not yet struck if we can do nothing to influence what will happen when it does? When Albertine was living in the house I had been quite determined to retain the initiative in our parting. And then she had gone. I opened her letter. It ran as follows:

"MY DEAR FRIEND,

Forgive me for not having dared to say to you in person what I am now writing, but I am such a coward, and have always been so afraid in your presence, that however much I tried to force myself I could not find the courage to do so. This is what I should have said to you. Our life together has become impossible; indeed you must have realised, from your outburst the other evening, that there had been a change in our relations. What we were able to patch up that night would become irreparable in a few days' time. It is better for us, therefore, since we have had the good fortune to be reconciled, to part as friends. That is why, my darling, I am sending you this line, and I beg you to be kind enough to forgive me if I am causing you a little grief when you think of the immensity of mine. Dearest one, I do not want to become your enemy; it will be bad enough to become by degrees, and all too soon, a stranger to you; and so, as I have absolutely made up my mind, before sending you this letter by Françoise I shall have asked her to let me have my boxes. Good-bye: I leave you the best of myself.

ALBERTINE"

"All this means nothing," I told myself, "it's even better than I thought, for as she doesn't mean a word of what she says, she obviously wrote it only in order to give me a shock, to frighten me. I must think of something at once: Albertine must be brought back this evening. It's sad to think that the Bontemps are unscrupulous people who make use of their niece to extort money from me. But what does that matter? Even if, to bring Albertine back here this evening, I have to give half my fortune to Mme Bontemps, we shall still have enough left, Albertine and I, to live in comfort." And at the same time I calculated whether I had time to go out that morning and order the yacht and the Rolls-Royce which she coveted, quite forgetting, all my doubts having vanished, that I had decided that it would be unwise to give them to her. "Even if

Mme Bontemps' agreement isn't enough, if Albertine refuses to obey her aunt and makes it a condition of her return that she shall enjoy complete independence, well, however much it may distress me, I shall let her have it; she shall go out by herself, as and when she likes. One must be prepared to make sacrifices, however painful they may be, for the thing to which one attaches most importance, which is, in spite of everything I decided this morning on the strength of my precise and absurd arguments, that Albertine shall continue to live here." Can I say moreover that to grant her that freedom would have been altogether painful to me? I should be lying if I did. Already I had often felt that the anguish of leaving her free to misbehave far away from me was perhaps less acute even than the sort of misery which I used to feel when I sensed that she was bored in my company, under my roof. No doubt at the actual moment of her asking me to let her go somewhere, allowing her to do so, with my mind obsessed by the idea of organised orgies, would have been agonising for me. But to say to her: "Take our yacht, or the train, and go away for a month, to some place which I have never seen, where I shall know nothing of what you're doing,"—this had often appealed to me, because of the thought that, by force of contrast, when she was far away from me, she would hanker after my society, and would be happy when she returned. "Besides, it's certainly what she herself wants; she doesn't in the least demand that freedom on which more-over, by offering her every day some new pleasure, I could easily succeed in imposing day by day some further restriction. No, what Albertine wanted was for me not to go on behaving insufferably to her, and above all—like Odette with Swann—for me to make up my mind to marry her. Once she is married, her independence will cease to matter to her; we shall stay here, together, in perfect happiness." No doubt this meant giving up any thought of Venice. But the cities for which we have most longed (and *a fortiori* the most agreeable hostesses, the most pleasurable diversions—even more than Venice, the Duchesse de Guermantes or the theatre), how pale, insignifi-cant, dead they become when we are tied to another's heart by a bond so painful that it prevents us from tearing ourselves away! "Besides, Albertine is perfectly right about our marriage.

Mamma herself was saying that all this procrastination was ridiculous. Marry her, that's what I ought to have done long ago, that's what I must do now, that's what made her write her letter without meaning a word of it; it's only to bring about our marriage that she has postponed for a few hours what she must desire as keenly as I do: her return to this house. Yes, that's what she wanted, that was the purpose of her action," my compassionate reason assured me; but I felt that, in doing so, my reason was still basing itself on the same hypothesis which it had adopted from the start. Whereas I was well aware that it was the other hypothesis which had invariably proved correct. No doubt this second hypothesis would never have been so bold as to formulate in so many words the notion that Albertine could have been on intimate terms with Mlle Vinteuil and her friend. And yet, when I had been overwhelmed by the impact of that terrible revelation, as the train slowed down before stopping at Incarville station, it was the second hypothesis that had been confirmed. This hypothesis had subsequently never conceived the idea that Albertine might leave me of her own accord, in this fashion, without warning me and giving me time to prevent her departure. But all the same, if, after the immense new jolt which life had just given me, the reality that confronted me was as novel as that which is presented to us by the discovery of a scientist, by the inquiries of an examining magistrate or the researches of a historian into the hidden aspects of a crime or a revolution, this reality, while exceeding the puny predictions of my second hypothesis, nevertheless fulfilled them. This second hypothesis was not an intellectual one, and the panic fear that had gripped me on the evening when Albertine had refused to kiss me, or the night when I had heard the sound of her window being opened, was not based upon reason. But—and what follows will show it even more clearly, as many episodes must have indicated it already—the fact that our intelligence is not the subtlest, most powerful, most appropriate instrument for grasping the truth is only one reason the more for beginning with the intelligence, and not with an unconscious intuition, a ready-made faith in presentiments. It is life that, little by little, case by case, enables us to observe that what is most important to our hearts or to our minds is taught us not by reasoning but by other powers. And then it is the intelligence itself which, acknowledging their superiority, abdicates to them through reasoning and consents to become their collaborator and their servant. Experimental faith. It seemed to me that the unforeseen calamity with which I found myself grappling was also something that I had already known (as I had known of Albertine's friendship with a pair of Lesbians), from having read it in so many signs in which (notwithstanding the contrary affirmations of my reason, based upon Albertine's own statements) I had discerned the weariness, the loathing that she felt at having to live in that state of slavery, signs that had so often seemed to me to be written as though in invisible ink behind her sad, submissive eyes, upon her cheeks suddenly inflamed with an unaccountable blush, in the sound of the window that had suddenly been flung open. Doubtless I had not dared to explore them fully or to form explicitly the idea of her sudden departure. I had thought, with a mind kept in equilibrium by Albertine's presence, only of a departure arranged by myself at an undetermined date, that is to say a date situated in a non-existent time; consequently I had had merely the illusion of thinking of a departure, just as people imagine that they are not afraid of death when they think of it while they are in good health and are actually doing no more than introduce a purely negative idea into a healthy state which the approach of death would of course precisely alter. Besides, the idea of Albertine's departure on her own initiative might have occurred to my mind a thousand times over, in the clearest, the most sharply defined form, without my suspecting any the more what, in relation to myself, that is to say in reality, that departure would be, what an unprecedented, appalling, unknown thing, how entirely novel a calamity. I might have gone on thinking of that departure (had I foreseen it) unceasingly for years on end, without all those thoughts, placed end to end, having the faintest connection, not merely in intensity but in kind, with the unimaginable hell the curtain of which Françoise had raised for me when she said: "Mademoiselle Albertine has gone." In order to picture to itself an unknown situation the imagination borrows elements that are already familiar and, for that reason, cannot picture it. But the sensibility, even in its most physical form, receives, like the wake of a thunderbolt, the original and for long indelible imprint of the novel event. And I hardly dared say to myself that, if I had foreseen this departure, I would perhaps have been incapable of picturing it to myself in all its horror, or indeed, with Albertine informing me of it, and myself threatening, imploring her, of preventing it. How far removed from me now was the desire to go to Venice! Just as, long ago at Combray, had been the desire to know Mme de Guermantes when the moment came at which I longed for one thing only, to have Mamma in my room. And it was indeed all the anxieties I had felt ever since my childhood which, at the bidding of this new anguish, had come hastening to reinforce it, to amalgamate themselves with it in a homogeneous mass that suffocated me.

To be sure, the physical blow which such a parting administers to the heart, and which, because of that terrible capacity for registering things with which the body is endowed, makes the pain somehow contemporaneous with all the epochs in our life in which we have suffered,—to be sure, this blow to the heart which—so little compunction do we feel for the sufferings of others—she who wishes to give the maximum intensity to the regret she causes, whether because, her departure being only a sham, she merely wants to demand better terms, or because, leaving us for ever—for ever!—she desires to wound us, or in order to avenge herself, or to continue to be loved, or (with an eye to the quality of the memory that she will leave behind her) to destroy the web of lassitude and indifference which she has felt being woven about her—to be sure, this blow to the heart is something we had vowed that we would avoid, assuring ourselves that we would part on good terms. But it is seldom indeed that one does part on good terms, because if one were on good terms one would not part. And then the woman to whom we show the utmost indifference nevertheless obscurely feels that in growing tired of her, by virtue of an identical force of habit, we have grown more and more attached to her, and she reflects that one of the essential elements in parting on good terms is to warn the other person before one goes. But she is afraid, by warning, of preventing.

Every woman feels that, the greater her power over a man, the more impossible it is to leave him except by sudden flight: a fugitive precisely because a queen. True, there is an extraordinary discrepancy between the boredom which she inspired a moment ago and, because she has gone, this furious desire to have her back again. But for this—over and above those which have been given in the course of this work and others which will be given later on—there are reasons. For one thing, her departure occurs as often as not at the moment when her companion's indifference—real or imagined—is greatest, at the extreme point of the swing of the pendulum. The woman says to herself: "No, this can't go on any longer," precisely because the man speaks of nothing but leaving her, or thinks of nothing else; and it is she who leaves him. Then, the pendulum swinging back to the other extreme, the distance is all the greater. In an instant it returns to this point; once more, apart from all the reasons that have been given, it is so natural! The heart still beats; and besides, the woman who has gone is no longer the same as the woman who was with us. Her life under our roof, all too well known, is suddenly enlarged by the addition of the lives with which she is inevitably to be associated, and it is perhaps to associate herself with them that she has left us. So that this new richness of the life of the woman who has gone retroacts upon the woman who was with us and was perhaps premeditating her departure. To the sequence of psychological facts which we are able to deduce and which form part of her life with us, our too evident boredom in her company, our jealousy too (and the effect of which is that men who have been left by a number of women have been left almost always in the same way because of their character and of certain always identical reactions which can be calculated: everyone has his own way of being betrayed, as he has his own way of catching cold), to this sequence that is not too mysterious for us there doubtless corresponded a sequence of facts of which we were unaware. She must for some time past have been keeping up relations, written, or verbal, or through messengers, with some man, or some woman, have been awaiting some signal which we may perhaps have given her unwittingly ourselves when we said: "X called yesterday to see me," if she had arranged with X that on the eve of the day when she was to join him he was to call on me. How many possible hypotheses! Possible only. I constructed the truth so well, but in the realm of possibility only, that, having one day opened by mistake a letter addressed to one of my mistresses, a letter written in a pre-arranged code which said: "Still awaiting signal to go to the Marquis de Saint-Loup's; please inform tomorrow by telephone," I reconstructed a sort of projected flight; the name of the Marquis de Saint-Loup was there only as a substitute for some other name, for my mistress did not know Saint-Loup, but had heard me speak of him, and moreover the signature was some sort of nickname, without any intelligible form. As it happened, the letter was addressed not to my mistress but to another person in the building who bore a different name which had been misread. The letter was written not in a code but in bad French because it was from an American woman, who was indeed a friend of Saint-Loup, as he himself told me. And the odd way in which this American woman formed certain letters had given the appearance of a nickname to a name which was quite genuine, only foreign. And so I had on that occasion been utterly mistaken in my suspicions. But the intellectual structure which had linked these facts, all of them false, together in my mind was itself so strict and accurate a model of the truth that when, three months later, my mistress (who had at that time been meaning to spend the rest of her life with me) left me, it was in a fashion absolutely identical with that which I had imagined on the former occasion. A letter arrived, containing the same peculiarities which I had wrongly attributed to the former letter, but this time it was indeed meant as a signal.

The present calamity was the worst that I had experienced in my life. And yet the suffering that it caused me was perhaps even exceeded by my curiosity to learn the causes of this calamity: who Albertine had desired and gone to join. But the sources of great events are like those of rivers; in vain do we explore the earth's surface, we can never find them. Had Albertine been planning her flight for a long time past? I have not mentioned the fact (because at the time it had seemed to me simply affectation and ill-humour, what in the case of Françoise we called "a fit of the sulks") that, from the day when she had ceased to kiss me, she had gone about as though tormented by a devil, stiffly erect, unbending, saying the simplest things in a mournful voice, slow in her movements, never smiling. I cannot say that there was any concrete proof of conspiracy with the outer world. True, Françoise told me later that, having gone into Albertine's room two days before her departure, she had found it empty, with the curtains drawn, but had sensed from the atmosphere of the room and from the noise that the window was open. And indeed she had found Albertine on the balcony. But it is difficult to see with whom she could have been communicating from there, and moreover the drawn curtains screening the open window could doubtless be explained by the fact that she knew I was afraid of draughts, and that even if the curtains afforded me little protection they would prevent Françoise from seeing from the passage that the shutters had been opened so early. No, I can see nothing save one trifling fact which proves merely that on the day before her departure she knew that she was going. For during that day she took from my room without my noticing it a large quantity of wrapping paper and packing cloth which was kept there, and in which she spent the whole night packing her innumerable negligées and dressing-gowns so that she might leave the house in the morning. This is the only fact; that was all. I cannot attach any importance to her having almost forced upon me that evening a thousand francs which she owed me; there is nothing extraordinary in that, for she was extremely scrupulous about money.

Yes, she took the wrapping paper the night before, but it was not only then that she knew that she was going to leave me! For it was not resentment that made her leave but the decision, already taken, to leave me, to abandon the life of which she had dreamed, that gave her that air of resentment. A resentful air, almost solemnly cold towards myself, except on the last evening when, after staying in my room longer than she had intended, she said—a remark which surprised me, coming from her who had always sought to postpone the moment of parting—she said to me from the door: "Good-bye, little one, good-bye." But I did not take any notice of this at the time. Françoise told me that next morning when Albertine informed her that she was going (but this may be explained also by exhaustion, for she had not undressed and had spent the whole night packing everything except the things she had to ask Françoise for, as they were not in her bedroom or her dressing-room), she was still so sad, so much more erect, so much stiffer than during the previous days that Françoise thought, when Albertine said to her: "Good-bye, Françoise," that she was about to fall. When one is told a thing like that one realises that the woman who appealed to us so much less than any of the women whom one meets so easily in the course of the briefest outing, the woman who makes us resent having to sacrifice them to her, is on the contrary the one we would a thousand times prefer. For the choice lies no longer between a certain pleasure—which has become by force of habit, and perhaps by the mediocrity of its object, almost null and void— and other pleasures which tempt and thrill us, but between these latter pleasures and something that is far stronger than they, compassion for suffering.

When I vowed to myself that Albertine would be back in the house before night, I had proceeded as quickly as possible to cover with a fresh belief the open wound from which I had torn the belief that had been my mainstay until then. But, swiftly though my instinct of self-preservation had acted, I had, when Françoise spoke to me, been left helpless for an instant, and for all that I now knew that Albertine would be back that same evening, the pain I had felt during the instant in which I had not yet assured myself of her return (the instant that had followed the words: "Mademoiselle Albertine has asked for her boxes; Mademoiselle Albertine has gone"), this pain reawoke in me of its own accord, as sharp as it had been before, that is to say as if I had still been unaware of Albertine's imminent return. However, it was essential that she should return of her own accord. On any assumption, to appear to be taking the first step, to be begging her to return, would be to defeat my own object. True, I lacked the strength to give her up as I had given up Gilberte. Even more than to see Albertine again, what I wanted was to put an end to the physical anguish which my heart, less robust than of old, could endure no longer.

Then, by dint of accustoming myself not to use my will-power, whether it was a question of work or of anything else, I had become more cowardly. But above all, this anguish was incomparably more intense for a number of reasons of which the most important was perhaps not that I had never tasted any sensual pleasure with Mme de Guermantes or with Gilberte, but that, not seeing them every day, and at every hour of the day, having no opportunity and consequently no need to see them, there had been lacking, in my love for them, the immense force of Habit. Perhaps, now that my heart, incapable of willing and of voluntarily enduring suffering, could think of only one possible solution, that Albertine should return at all costs, perhaps the opposite solution (a deliberate renunciation, a gradual resignation) would have seemed to me a novelist's solution, improbable in real life, had I not myself opted for it in the case of Gilberte. I knew therefore that this other solution might be accepted also, and by one and the same man, for I had remained more or less the same. But time had played its part, time which had aged me, time which moreover had kept Albertine perpetually in my company while we were living together. But at least, without giving her up, what survived in me of all that I had felt for Gilberte was the pride which made me refuse to be to Albertine a despicable plaything by begging her to return; I wanted her to come back without my appearing to care whether she did or not. I got up, in order to lose no more time, but my anguish made me pause; this was the first time that I had got out of bed since Albertine had left me. Yet I must dress at once in order to go and make inquiries of Albertine's concierge.

Suffering, the prolongation of a spiritual shock that has come from without, keeps aspiring to change its form; one hopes to be able to dispel it by making plans, by seeking information; one wants it to pass through its countless metamorphoses, for this requires less courage than keeping our suffering intact; the bed on which we lie down with our grief appears so narrow, hard and cold. I therefore put my feet to the ground, and I stepped across the room with infinite care, placing myself in such a way as not to see Albertine's chair, the pianola on the pedals of which she used to press her golden slippers, or a single one of the things which she had used and all of which, in the secret language that my memories had taught them, seemed to be seeking to give me a translation, a different version, to break the news to me for a second time, of her departure. But even without looking at them I could see them: my strength left me; I sank down on one of those blue satin armchairs, the glossy surface of which an hour earlier, in the dimness of my bedroom anaesthetised by a ray of morning light, had made me dream dreams which then I had passionately caressed but which were infinitely remote from me now. Alas, I had never sat in one of them until this minute except when Albertine was still with me. And so I could not remain sitting there, and stood up again; and thus, at every moment, there was one more of those innumerable and humble "selves" that compose our personality which was still unaware of Albertine's departure and must be informed of it; I was obliged—and this was more cruel than if they had been strangers and did not share my susceptibility to suffering —to announce to all these beings, to all these "selves" who did not yet know of it, the calamity that had just occurred; each of them in turn must hear for the first time the words:"Albertine has asked for her boxes"—those coffin-shaped boxes which I had seen loaded on to the train at Balbec with my mother's— "Albertine has gone." Each of them had to be told of my grief, the grief which is in no way a pessimistic conclusion freely drawn from an accumulation of baneful circumstances, but is the intermittent and involuntary reviviscence of a specific impression that has come to us from without and was not chosen by us. There were some of these "selves" which I had not encountered for a long time past. For instance (I had not remembered that it was the day on which the barber called) the "self" that I was when I was having my hair cut. I had forgotten this "self," and his arrival made me burst into tears, as, at a funeral, does the appearance of an old retired servant who has not forgotten the deceased. Then all of a sudden I remembered that, during the past week, I had from time to time been seized by panic fears which I had not confessed to myself. At those moments, however, I had debated the question, saying to myself: "No need, of course, to consider the hypothesis of her suddenly leaving me. It's absurd. If I were to confide it to a sensible, intelligent man" (and I would have done so to set my mind at rest, had not jealousy prevented me from confiding in anyone) "he would be sure to say to me: 'Why, you're mad. It's impossible.' (And, as a matter of fact, during these last days we had not quarrelled once.) People leave you for a reason. They tell you the reason. They give you a chance to reply. They don't run away like that. No, it's perfectly childish. It's the only really absurd hypothesis." And yet, every day, on finding her still there in the morning when I rang my bell, I had heaved an immense sigh of relief. And when Françoise handed me Albertine's letter, I had at once been certain that it referred to the one thing that could not happen, to this departure which I had somehow perceived several days in advance, in spite of the logical reasons for feeling reassured. I had told myself this, almost with self-satisfaction at my perspicacity in my despair, like a murderer who knows that he cannot be found out but is nevertheless afraid and all of a sudden sees his victim's name written at the top of a document on the table of the examining magistrate who has sent for him.

My only hope was that Albertine had gone to Touraine, to her aunt's house, where after all she would be under some sort of surveillance and could not do anything very serious before I brought her back. My worst fear was that she might have stayed in Paris, or have gone to Amsterdam or to Montjouvain, in other words that she had escaped in order to pursue some intrigue the preliminaries of which I had failed to observe. But in reality, when I said to myself Paris, Amsterdam, Montjouvain, that is to say several places, I was thinking of places that were merely potential. And so, when Albertine's hall porter informed me that she had gone to Touraine, that place of residence which I had thought desirable seemed to me the most dreadful of all, because it was real, and because for the first time, tortured by the certainty of the present and the uncertainty of the future, I pictured Albertine starting on a life which she had deliberately chosen to lead apart from me, perhaps for a long time, perhaps for ever, a life in which she would realise that unknown element which in the past had so often troubled me, even though I enjoyed the good fortune of possessing, of caressing what was its outer shell, that charming face, impenetrable and captive. It was this unknown element that formed the core of my love. As for Albertine herself, she scarcely existed in me save under the form of her name, which, but for certain rare moments of respite when I awoke, came and engraved itself upon my brain and continued incessantly to do so. If I had thought aloud, I should have kept on repeating it, and my speech would have been as monotonous, as limited, as if I had been transformed into a bird, a bird like the one in the fable whose song repeated incessantly the name of her whom it had loved when a man. One says the name to oneself, and since one remains silent it is as though one were inscribing it inside oneself, as though it were leaving its trace on one's brain, which must end up, like a wall on which somebody has amused himself scribbling, by being entirely covered with the name, written a thousand times over, of the woman one loves. One rewrites it all the time in one's mind when one is happy, and even more when one is unhappy. And one feels a constantly recurring need to repeat this name which brings one nothing more than what one already knows, until, in course of time, it wearies us. I did not even give a thought to carnal pleasure at this moment; I did not even see in my mind's eye the image of that Albertine who had been the cause of such an upheaval of my being, I did not perceive her body, and if I had tried to isolate the idea—for there is always one—that was bound up with my suffering, it would have been, alternately, on the one hand my doubt as to the intention with which she had left me, with or without any thought of returning, and on the other hand the means of bringing her back. Perhaps there is something symbolical and true in the infinitesimal place occupied in our anxiety by the one who is its cause. The fact is that her person itself counts for little or nothing; what is almost everything is the series of emotions and anxieties which chance occurrences have made us feel in the past in connexion with her and which habit has associated with her. What proves this clearly is (even more than the boredom which we feel in moments of happiness) the extent to which seeing or not seeing the person in question, being or not being admired by her, having or not having her at our disposal, will

seem to us utterly irrelevant when we no longer have to pose
ourselves the problem (so otiose that we shall no longer take
the trouble to consider it) save in relation to the person herself
—the series of emotions and anxieties being forgotten, at least
so far as she is concerned, for it may have developed anew, but
transferred to another. Before this, when it was still attached to
her, we supposed that our happiness was dependent upon her
person; it depended merely upon the cessation of our anxiety.
Our unconscious was therefore more clairvoyant than ourselves at that moment, when it made the figure of the beloved
so minute, a figure which we had even perhaps forgotten, which
we might have been comparatively unfamiliar with and thought
mediocre, in the terrible drama in which seeing her again in
order to cease waiting for her could be a matter of life and
death for us. Minuscule proportions of the woman's form;
logical and necessary effect of the manner in which love
develops; clear allegory of the subjective nature of that love.

Outside the door of Albertine's house I found a little poor
girl who gazed at me with huge eyes and who looked so sweet-
natured that I asked her whether she would care to come
home with me, as I might have taken home a dog with faithful
eyes. She seemed pleased at the suggestion. When I got home,
I held her for some time on my knee, but very soon her presence,
by making me feel too keenly Albertine's absence, became
intolerable. And I asked her to go away, after giving her a
five-hundred franc note. And yet, soon afterwards, the thought
of having some other little girl in the house with me, of never
being alone without the comfort of an innocent presence,
was the only thing that enabled me to endure the idea that
Albertine might perhaps remain away for some time. The
spirit in which Albertine had left me was similar no doubt to
that of nations who pave the way by a demonstration of their
armed force for the exercise of their diplomacy. She must have
left me only in order to obtain from me better terms, greater
freedom, more luxury. In that case, of the two of us, the one
who prevailed would have been myself, had I had the strength
to await the moment when, seeing that she could gain nothing,
she would return of her own accord. But if at cards, or in
war, where victory alone matters, we can hold out against

bluff, the conditions are not the same as those created by love and jealousy, not to mention suffering. If, in order to wait, to "hold out," I allowed Albertine to remain away from me for several days, for several weeks perhaps, I was ruining what had been my sole purpose for more than a year: never to leave her by herself for a single hour. All my precautions would be rendered fruitless if I allowed her the time and the opportunity to be unfaithful to me to her heart's content; and if in the end she capitulated, I should never be able to forget the time when she had been alone, and even though victorious in the end, nevertheless in the past, that is to say irreparably, I should be the vanquished one.

As for the means of bringing Albertine back, they had all the more chance of success the more plausible the hypothesis appeared that she had left me only in the hope of being summoned back on more favourable terms. And of course to the people who did not believe in Albertine's sincerity, certainly to Françoise for instance, it was indeed plausible. But my reason, to which, before I knew anything, the only explanation of certain bouts of ill-humour, of certain attitudes, had appeared to be that she had planned to leave for good, found it difficult to believe that, now that her departure had occurred, it was a mere feint. I say my reason, not myself. The hypothesis of a feint became all the more necessary to me the more improbable it was, and gained in strength what it lost in probability. When we find ourselves on the verge of despair and it seems as though God has forsaken us, we no longer hesitate to expect a miracle of him.

I realise that in all this I was the most apathetic, albeit the most anxious of detectives. But Albertine's flight had not restored to me the faculties of which the habit of having her watched by other people had deprived me. I could think of one thing only: employing another person to search for her. This other person was Saint-Loup, who agreed. The transference of the anxiety of so many days to another person filled me with joy and I jigged about, certain of success, my hands becoming suddenly dry again as in the past, and no longer moist with the sweat in which Françoise had soaked me when she said: "Mademoiselle Albertine has gone."

It will be remembered that when I decided to live with Albertine, and even to marry her, it was in order to guard her, to know what she was doing, to prevent her from returning to her old habits with Mlle Vinteuil. It had been in the appalling anguish caused by her revelation at Balbec, when she had told me, as a thing which was quite natural, and which I succeeded, although it was the greatest sorrow I had ever experienced in my life, in appearing to find quite natural, the thing which in my worst suppositions I should never have been bold enough to imagine. (It is astonishing what a want of imagination jealousy, which spends its time making petty suppositions that are false, shows when it comes to discovering what is true.) Now this love, born first and foremost of a need to prevent Albertine from doing wrong, this love had thereafter preserved the traces of its origin. Being with her mattered little to me so long as I could prevent the fugitive creature from going to this place or to that. In order to prevent her, I had had recourse to the vigilance, to the company, of the people who escorted her, and they had only to give me at the end of the day a report that was fairly reassuring for my anxieties to dissolve into good humour.

Having given myself the assurance that, whatever steps I might have to take, Albertine would be back in the house that same evening, I had granted a respite to the pain which Françoise had caused me when she told me that Albertine had gone (because at that moment my mind, caught unawares, had believed for an instant that her departure was final). But after an interruption, when under the momentum of its own independent life the initial pain revived spontaneously in me, it was just as agonising as before, because it pre-existed the consoling promise that I had given myself to bring Albertine back that evening. My suffering was oblivious of this promise which would have calmed it. To set in motion the means of bringing about her return, once again I was condemned—not that such an attitude had ever proved very successful, but because I had always adopted it since I had been in love with Albertine—to behave as though I did not love her, as though I was not hurt by her departure; I was condemned to continue to lie to her. I could be all the more energetic in my efforts to bring her back in that personally I should appear to have given her up for good. I proposed to write Albertine a farewell letter in which I would regard her departure as final, while at the same time I would send Saint-Loup down, as though without my knowledge, to put the most brutal pressure on Mme Bontemps to make Albertine return as soon as possible. No doubt I had had experience with Gilberte of the danger of letters expressing an indifference which, feigned at first, ends by becoming genuine. And this experience ought to have restrained me from writing to Albertine letters of the same sort as those I had written to Gilberte. But what we call experience is merely the revelation to our own eyes of a trait in our character which naturally reappears, and reappears all the more markedly because we have already once brought it to light, so that the spontaneous impulse which guided us on the first occasion finds itself reinforced by all the suggestions of memory. The human plagiarism which is most difficult to avoid, for individuals (and even for nations which persevere in their faults and indeed intensify them), is self-plagiarism.

Knowing that Saint-Loup was in Paris, I summoned him there and then; he hastened round at once, swift and efficient as he had been long ago at Doncières, and agreed to set off at once for Touraine. I suggested to him the following arrangement. He was to take the train to Châtellerault, find out where Mme Bontemps lived, and wait until Albertine had left the house, since there was a risk of her recognising him. "But does the girl in question know me, then?" he asked. I told him that I did not think so. This plan of action filled me with indescribable joy. It was nevertheless diametrically opposed to my original intention: to arrange things so that I should not appear to be seeking Albertine's return; whereas by so acting I must inevitably appear to be seeking it. But this plan had the inestimable advantage over "the proper thing to do" that it enabled me to say to myself that someone sent by me was going to see Albertine, and would doubtless bring her back with him. And if I had been able to see clearly into my own heart at the outset, I might have foreseen that it was this solution, which was hidden in the shadows and which I thought deplorable, that would ultimately prevail over the alternative course of patience which I had decided to adopt, from lack of will-power. As Saint-Loup already appeared slightly surprised to learn that a girl had been living with me through the whole winter without my having said a word to him about her, as moreover he had often spoken to me of the girl he had seen at Balbec and I had never said in reply: "But she's living here," he might have been offended by my lack of trust. It was true that Mme Bontemps might talk to him about Balbec. But I was too impatient for his departure, and for his arrival at the other end, to be willing or able to think of the possible consequences of his journey. As for the risk of his recognising Albertine (whom in any case he had resolutely refrained from looking at when he had met her at Doncières), she had, everyone said, so changed and put on weight that it was hardly likely. He asked me whether I had a picture of Albertine. I replied at first that I had not, so that he might not have a chance of recognising Albertine, from her photograph, taken at about the time of our stay at Balbec, though he had had no more than a glimpse of her in the railway carriage. But then I realised that in the photograph she would be already as different from the Albertine of Balbec as the living Albertine now was, and that he would recognise her no better from her photograph than in the flesh. While I was looking for it, he laid his hand gently on my forehead, by way of consoling me. I was touched by the distress which the grief that he guessed me to be feeling was causing him. In the first place, however final his breach with Rachel, what he had felt at that time was not yet so remote for him not to have a special sympathy, a special pity for sufferings of that kind, as one feels closer to a person who is afflicted with the same illness as oneself. Besides, he had so strong an affection for me that the thought of my suffering was intolerable to him. Hence he conceived a mixture of rancour and admiration for the girl who was the cause of it. He regarded me as so superior a being that he felt that for me to be in thrall to another creature she must be quite out of the ordinary. I quite expected that he would think Albertine pretty in her photograph, but since at the same time I did not imagine that it would produce upon him the impression that Helen made upon the Trojan elders, as I continued to look for it I said modestly: "Oh, you know, you mustn't get ideas into your head. For one thing it's a bad photograph, and besides there's nothing startling about her, she's not a beauty, she's merely very nice."

"Oh, but she must be wonderful," he said with a naïve, sincere enthusiasm as he sought to form a mental picture of the person who was capable of plunging me into such despair and agitation. "I'm angry with her for hurting you, but at the same time one can't help seeing that someone who's an artist to his finger-tips as you are, someone who loves beauty in all its forms and with so passionate a love, that you were predestined to suffer more than an ordinary person when you found it in a woman."

At last I had found the photograph. "She's bound to be wonderful," Robert was still saying, not yet having seen that I was holding out the photograph to him. All at once he caught sight of it, and held it for a moment between his hands. His face expressed a stupefaction which amounted to stupidity. "Is this the girl you love?" he said at length in a tone in which astonishment was curbed by his fear of offending me. He made no comment, but he had assumed the reasonable, prudent, unavoidably somewhat disdainful air which one assumes in front of a sick person—even if he is a man of outstanding gifts, and your friend—who is now nothing of the sort, for, raving mad, he speaks to you of a celestial being who has appeared to him, and continues to behold this being where you, being sane, can see nothing but a quilt on the bed. I at once understood Robert's astonishment, realising that it was the same as that which the sight of his mistress had provoked in me, the only difference being that I had recognised in her a woman whom I already knew, where he imagined that he had never seen Albertine. But no doubt the difference between our respective impressions of the same person was equally great. The time was long past when I had all too tentatively begun at Balbec by adding to my visual sensations when I gazed at Albertine sensations of taste, of smell, of touch. Since then, other more profound, more tender, more indefinable sensations had been added to them, and afterwards painful sensations. In short, Albertine was merely, like a stone round which snow has gathered, the generating centre of an immense structure which rose above the plane of my heart. Robert, to whom all this stratification of sensations was invisible, grasped only a residue which it prevented me, on the contrary, from perceiving. What had struck Robert when his eyes fell upon Albertine's photograph was not the thrill of wonderment that overcame the Trojan elders seeing Helen go by and saying:

One glance from her eclipses all our ills[25]

but precisely the opposite impression which may be expressed by: "What, it's for this that he has worked himself into such a state, has grieved himself so, has done so many idiotic things!" It must indeed be admitted that this sort of reaction at the sight of the person who has caused the suffering, upset the life, sometimes brought about the death of someone we love, is infinitely more frequent than that of the Trojan elders, indeed to all intents and purposes the habitual one. This is not merely because love is individual, nor because, when we ourselves do not feel it, finding it avoidable and philosophising about the folly of others comes naturally to us. No, it is because, when it has reached the stage at which it causes such misery, the edifice of the sensations interposed between the face of the woman and the eyes of her lover—the huge egg of pain which encases it and conceals it as a mantle of snow conceals a fountain—is already raised so high that the point at which the lover's gaze comes to rest, the point at which he finds his pleasure and his sufferings, is as far from the point which other people see as is the real sun from the place in which its refracted light enables us to see it in the sky. And what is more, during this time, beneath the chrysalis of grief and tenderness which renders the worst metamorphoses of the beloved object invisible to the lover, her face has had time to grow old and to change. With the result that, if the face which the lover saw for the first time is very far removed from that which he has seen since he has loved and suffered, it is, in the opposite sense, equally far from the face which may now be seen by the indifferent onlooker. (What would have happened if, instead of the photograph of one who was still a girl, Robert had seen the photograph of an elderly mistress?) And indeed, in order to feel this astonishment, we have no need to see for the first time the woman who has caused such ravages. Often we know her already, as my great-uncle knew Odette. So the difference in optics extends not only to people's physical appearance but to their character, and to their individual importance. It is more likely than not that the woman who is causing the man who loves her to suffer has always behaved good-naturedly towards someone who was indifferent to her, as Odette, who was so cruel to Swann, had been the kind, attentive "lady in pink" to my great-uncle, or indeed that the person whose every decision is computed in advance by the man who loves her, with as much dread as that of a deity, appears as a person of no consequence, only too glad to do anything he asks, in the eyes of the man who does not love her, as Saint-Loup's mistress had appeared to me who saw in her merely that "Rachel when from the Lord" who had so repeatedly been offered to me. I recalled my own amazement, the first time I met her with Saint-Loup, at the thought that anybody could be tormented by not knowing what such a woman had been doing one evening, what she might have whispered to someone, why she had desired a rupture. And I felt that all this past existence—but, in this case, Albertine's—towards which every fibre of my heart, of my life, was directed with a throbbing and importunate pain, must appear just as insignificant to Saint-Loup, and would one day, perhaps, appear so to me; I felt that I might gradually pass, so far as the insignificance or gravity of Albertine's past was concerned, from the state of mind in which I was at the moment to that of Saint-Loup, for I was under no illusion as to what Saint-Loup might be thinking, as to what anyone else than the lover himself may think. And I was not unduly distressed. Let us leave pretty women to men with no imagination. I recalled that tragic explanation of so many lives which is furnished by an inspired but not lifelike portrait such as Elstir's portrait of Odette, which is a portrait not so much of a mistress as of the distortions of love. All that it lacked was—what so many portraits have—the fact of coming at once from a great painter and from a lover (and even then it was said that Elstir had been Odette's). The whole life of a lover, of a lover whose folly nobody understands—the whole life of a Swann—goes to prove this disparity. But let the lover be embodied in a painter like Elstir and then we have the clue to the enigma, we have at last before our eyes those lips which the common herd have never perceived, that nose which nobody has ever seen, that unsuspected carriage. The portrait says: "What I have loved, what has made me suffer, what I have never ceased to behold, is this." By an inverse gymnastic, I who had made a mental effort to add to Rachel all that Saint-Loup had added to her of himself, I now attempted to subtract the contribution of my heart and mind from the composition of Albertine and to picture her to myself as she must appear to Saint-Loup, as Rachel had appeared to me. But how much importance does all this have? Would we give credence to these differences, even if we could see them ourselves? When, in the summer at Balbec, Albertine used to wait for me beneath the arcades of Incarville and jump into my carriage, not only had she not yet "thickened," but, as a result of too much exercise, she had lost weight; thin, made plainer by an ugly hat which left visible only the tip of an ugly nose and, at a side-view, pale cheeks like white slugs, there was very little of her that I recognised, enough, however, to know, when she sprang into the carriage, that it was she, that she had been punctual in keeping our appointment and had not gone somewhere else; and this was enough; what we love is too much in the past, consists too much in the time that we have wasted together for us to require the whole woman; we wish only to be sure that it is she, not to be mistaken as to her identity, a thing far more important than beauty to those who love; her cheeks may grow hollow, her body thin, even to those who were originally proudest, in the eyes of the world, of their domination over a beauty, and yet that little tip of nose, that sign which epitomises the permanent personality of a woman, that algebraical formula, that constant factor, is sufficient to prevent a man who is courted in the highest society, and was once fond of it, from having a single evening free because he spends his time combing and uncombing, until it is time to go to sleep, the hair of the woman he loves, or simply sitting by her side, in order to be with her, or in order that she may be with him, or merely in order that she may not be with other men.

"Are you sure," Robert asked me, "that I can offer this

woman thirty thousand francs just like that for her husband's election committee? She's as dishonest as all that? If you're right, three thousand francs would be enough."

"No, I beg of you, don't be cheeseparing about a thing that matters so much to me. This is what you're to say to her (and it's to some extent true): 'My friend had borrowed these thirty thousand francs from a relative for the election expenses of the uncle of the girl he was engaged to marry. It was because of this engagement that the money was given him. And he had asked me to bring it to you so that Albertine should know nothing about it. And now Albertine has gone and left him. He doesn't know what to do. He's obliged to pay back the thirty thousand francs if he doesn't marry Albertine. And if he *is* going to marry her, then if only to keep up appearances she ought to return immediately, because it will make a very bad impression if she stays away for long.' You think I've made all this up?"

"Not at all," Saint-Loup assured me out of kindness, out of tact, and also because he knew that circumstances are often stranger than one supposes.

After all, it was by no means impossible that in this tale of the thirty thousand francs there might be, as I assured him, a large element of truth. It was possible, but it was not true, and this element of truth was in fact a lie. But we lied to each other, Robert and I, as in every conversation when one friend is genuinely anxious to help another who is unhappy in love. The friend who is being counsellor, prop, comforter, may pity the other's distress but cannot share it, and the kinder he is to him the more he lies. And the other confesses to him as much as is necessary in order to secure his help, but, precisely in order to secure that help, perhaps, conceals many things from him. And the happy one of the two is, when all is said, he who takes trouble, goes on a journey, carries out a mission, but has no inner anguish. I was at this moment the person Robert had been at Doncières when he thought that Rachel had left him.

"Very well, just as you like; if I get a snub, I accept it in advance for your sake. And even if it does seem a bit queer to make such an undisguised bargain, I know that in our world there are plenty of duchesses, even the stuffiest of them, who if you offered them thirty thousand francs would do things far more difficult than telling their nieces not to stay in Touraine. Anyhow, I'm doubly glad to be doing you a service, since it's the only thing that will make you agree to see me. If I marry," he went on, "don't you think we might see more of one another, won't you regard my house as your own? . . ."

He suddenly stopped short, the thought having occurred to him (as I supposed at the time) that, if I too were to marry, Albertine might not be a suitable friend for his wife. And I remembered what the Cambremers had said to me about the probability of his marrying a niece of the Prince de Guermantes.

He consulted the time-table, and found that he could not leave Paris until the evening. Françoise inquired: "Am I to take Mlle Albertine's bed out of the study?" "On the contrary," I said, "you must make it for her." I hoped that she would return any day and did not wish Françoise to suppose that there could be any doubt of this. Albertine's departure must appear to have been agreed between ourselves, and not in any way to imply that she loved me less than before. But Françoise looked at me with an air, if not of incredulity, at any rate of doubt. She too had her alternative hypotheses. Her nostrils flared, she scented a quarrel, she must have felt it in the air for a long time past. And if she was not absolutely sure of it, this was perhaps only because, like myself, she hesitated to believe unconditionally what would have given her too much pleasure.

Saint-Loup could scarcely have been in the train when I ran into Bloch in my hall. I had not heard his ring, and was obliged to let him stay with me for a while. He had met me recently with Albertine (whom he had known at Balbec) on a day when she was in a bad mood. "I met M. Bontemps at dinner," he told me, "and as I have a certain influence over him, I told him that I was grieved that his niece was not nicer to you, and that he ought to have a word with her about it." I choked with rage; these remonstrations and complaints would destroy the whole effect of Saint-Loup's intervention and involve me directly in the eyes of Albertine, whom I now seemed to be imploring to return. To make matters worse, Françoise, who was lingering in the hall, could hear every word. I heaped every imaginable reproach upon Bloch, telling him that I had never authorised him to do anything of the sort and that, besides, the whole thing was nonsense. From then on, Bloch never left off smiling, less, I think, from joy than from embarrassment at having annoyed me. He laughingly expressed his surprise at having provoked such anger. Perhaps he said this in the hope of minimising in my eyes the importance of his indiscreet intervention, perhaps because he was of a cowardly nature and lived gaily and idly in an atmosphere of falsehood, as jelly-fish float upon the surface of the sea, perhaps because, even if he had been a man of a different kind, other people can never see things from our point of view and therefore do not realise the magnitude of the injury that words uttered at random can do us. I had barely shown him out, unable to think of any remedy for the mischief he had done, when the bell rang again and Françoise brought me a summons from the head of the Sûreté. The parents of the little girl whom I had brought into the house for an hour had decided to bring a charge against me for abduction of a minor. There are moments in life when a sort of beauty is born of the multiplicity of the troubles that assail us, intertwined like Wagnerian leitmotifs, and also from the notion, which then emerges, that events are not situated in the sum of the reflections portrayed in the wretched little mirror which the mind holds in front of it and which it calls the future, that they are somewhere outside and spring up as suddenly as a person who comes to accuse us of a crime. Even when left to itself, an event becomes modified, whether frustration amplifies it for us or satisfaction reduces it. But it is rarely unaccompanied. The feelings aroused by each one of them contradict one another, and fear, to a certain extent, as I felt on my way to see the head of the Sûreté, is an at least temporary and fairly efficacious revulsant against sentimental miseries.

At the Sûreté, I found the girl's parents, who insulted me and with the words "We'd rather starve" handed me back the five hundred francs which I did not want to take, and the head of the Sûreté who, setting himself the inimitable example of the judicial facility in repartee, seized upon a word in each sentence that I uttered for the purpose of concocting a witty and crushing retort. My innocence of the alleged crime was never taken into consideration, for that was the sole hypothesis which nobody was willing to accept for an instant. Nevertheless the difficulty of proving the charge enabled me to escape with this castigation, which was extremely violent for as long as the parents were in the room. But as soon as they had gone, the head of the Sûreté, who had a weakness for little girls, changed his tone and admonished me as man to man: "Next time, you must be more careful. Gad, you can't pick them up as easily as that, or you'll get into trouble. Anyhow, you'll find dozens of little girls who are better-looking than that one, and far cheaper. It was a perfectly ridiculous amount to pay." I was so certain that he would fail to understand me if I attempted to tell him the truth that without saying a word I took advantage of his permission to withdraw. Every passer-by, until I was safely at home, seemed to me an inspector appointed to spy on my every movement. But this leitmotif, like that of my anger with Bloch, died away, leaving the field clear for that of Albertine's departure.

The latter resumed on an almost joyous note now that Saint-Loup had set out. Since he had undertaken to go and see Mme Bontemps, the burden of the affair no longer rested on my overwrought mind, but on him. I had even become quite elated at the moment of his departure, because I had taken a decision: "I reacted in a flash." And my sufferings had been dispelled. I believed that this was because I had acted, and I believed it sincerely, for we never know what is concealed in our hearts of hearts. But what really made me happy was not, as I supposed, that I had unburdened my indecisions on to Saint-Loup. I was not in fact entirely mistaken; the specific for curing an unfortunate event (and three events out of four are unfortunate) is a decision; for it has the effect, by a sudden reversal of our thoughts, of interrupting the flow of those that come from the past event and prolong its vibration, and breaking it with a counter-flow of thoughts from the outside, from the future. But these new thoughts are most of all beneficial to us (and this was the case with the thoughts that assailed me at this moment) when from the depths of that future it is a hope that they bring us. What really made me so happy was the secret certainty that Saint-Loup's mission could not fail and that Albertine was bound to return. I realised this; for not having received any word from Saint-Loup on the following day, I began to suffer anew. My decision, my transference to him of plenipotentiary powers, was not, therefore, the cause of my joy, which in that case would have persisted; its cause was rather the "Success is certain" which had been in my mind when I said "Come what may." And the thought, aroused by his delay, that after all his mission might not prove successful, was so hateful to me that all my gaiety evaporated. It is in reality our anticipation, our hope of happy events that fills us with a joy which we ascribe to other causes and which ceases, plunging us once more into misery, if we are no longer so certain that what we desire will come to pass. It is always an invisible belief that sustains the edifice of our sensory world and deprived of which it totters. We have seen that it created for us the merit or the nullity of other people, our excitement or boredom at seeing them. It similarly creates the possibility of enduring a grief which seems to us trivial simply because we are convinced that it will presently be brought to an end, or its sudden intensification to the point where a person's presence matters to us as much as, sometimes even more than, life itself.

One thing finally succeeded in making my heartache as acute as it had been in the first instant and (I am bound to admit) no longer was. This was when I re-read a sentence in Albertine's letter. However much we love people, the pain of losing them—when in our isolation we are confronted with it alone, to which our mind to a certain extent gives whatever form it chooses—is endurable and different from that other pain, less human, less our own—as unforeseen and unusual as an accident in the moral world and in the region of the heart—which is caused not so much by the people themselves as by the manner in which we have learned that we will never see them again. I could think of Albertine while weeping gently and accepting the fact that I should not be seeing her to-night any more than I had yesterday; but to re-read "my decision is irrevocable" was another matter; it was like taking a dangerous drug which had given me a heart attack from which I might never recover. There is in inanimate objects, in events, in fare-well letters, a special danger which amplifies and alters the very nature of the grief that people are capable of causing us. But this pain did not last long. I was, when all was said, so sure of Saint-Loup's skill, of his eventual success, Albertine's return seemed to me so certain, that I wondered whether I had been right to wish for it. Nevertheless, I rejoiced at the thought. Unfortunately, although I had assumed that the business with the Sûreté was over and done with, Françoise came in to tell me that an inspector had called to inquire whether I was in the habit of having girls in the house, that the concierge, supposing him to be referring to Albertine, had replied in the affirmative, and that since then it seemed as though the house was being watched. Henceforth it would be impossible for me ever to bring a little girl into the house to console me in my grief, without risking the shame of an inspector suddenly appearing and of her taking me for a criminal. And in the same instant I realised how much more important certain longings are to us than we suppose, for this impossibility of my ever taking a little girl on my knee again seemed to me to strip life of all its value forever, but what was more, I realised how understandable it is that people will readily refuse wealth and risk death, whereas we imagine that pecuniary interest and the fear of dying rule the world. For, rather than think that even an unknown little girl might be given a bad impression of me by the arrival of a policeman, I should have preferred to kill myself! Indeed there was no possible comparison between the two degrees of suf-fering. Yet in everyday life people never bear in mind that those to whom they offer money, or whom they threaten to kill, may have mistresses, or merely friends, whose respect they value even if they do not value their own. But all of a sudden, by a confusion of which I was not aware (for it did not occur to me that Albertine, being of age, was free to live under my roof and even to be my mistress), it seemed to me that the charge of corrupting minors might apply to Albertine also. Thereupon my life appeared to me to be hedged in on every side. And reflecting that I had not lived chastely with her, I saw, in the punishment that had been inflicted upon me for having dandled an unknown little girl on my knee, that relation which almost always exists in human sanctions, whereby there is hardly ever either a just sentence or a judicial error, but a sort of compromise between the false idea that the judge forms of an innocent act and the culpable deeds of which he is unaware. But then when I thought that Albertine's return might involve me in an ignominious charge which would degrade me in her eyes and might perhaps even do her some damage for which she would not forgive me, I ceased to look forward to her return, it terrified me. I wanted to cable her to tell her not to come back. And immediately, a passionate desire for her return overwhelmed me, drowning everything else. The fact was that, having envisaged for a moment the possibility of telling her not to return and of living without her, all of a sudden I felt on the contrary ready to abandon all travel, all pleasure, all work, if only Albertine would return!

Ah, how my love for Albertine, the course of which I had imagined that I could foretell on the basis of my love for Gilberte, had developed differently from the latter, indeed in perfect contrast with it! How impossible it was for me to live without seeing her! And with each of my actions, even the most trivial, since they had all been steeped beforehand in the blissful atmosphere which was Albertine's presence, I was obliged time after time, at renewed cost, with the same pain, to relive the first experience of separation. Then the competition of other forms of life thrust this new pain into the background, and during those days which were the first days of spring, as I waited until Saint-Loup had managed to see Mme Bontemps, I even enjoyed a few moments of agreeable calm in imagining Venice and beautiful, unknown women. As soon as I was conscious of this, I felt within me a panic terror. This calm which I had just enjoyed was the first apparition of that great intermittent force which was to wage war in me against grief, against love, and would ultimately get the better of them. This state of which I had just had a foretaste and had received the warning was for a moment only what would in time to come be my permanent state, a life in which I should no longer be able to suffer on account of Albertine, in which I should no longer love her. And my love, which had just seen and recognised the one enemy by whom it could be conquered, forgetfulness, began to tremble, like a lion which in the cage in which it has been confined has suddenly caught sight of the python that will devour it.

I thought of Albertine all the time, and Françoise, when she came into my room, never said to me "There are no letters" quickly enough to curtail my anguish. From time to time I succeeded, by letting some current or other of ideas flow through my grief, in freshening, in airing to some slight extent the vitiated atmosphere of my heart; but at night, if I succeeded in going to sleep, then it was as though the memory of Albertine had been the drug that had procured my sleep and the cessation of whose influence would awaken me. I thought all the time of Albertine while I was asleep. It was a special sleep of her own that she gave me, and one in which, moreover, I was no longer at liberty, as when awake, to think of other things. Sleep and the memory of her were like two substances which one must mix together and take at one draught in order to sleep. When I was awake, meanwhile, my suffering went on increasing day by day instead of diminishing. Not that oblivion was not performing its task, but by that very fact it encouraged the idealisation of the lamented image and thereby the assimilation of my initial suffering to other analogous sufferings which intensified it. At least that image was endurable. But if all of a sudden I thought of her room, of her room in which the bed stood empty, of her piano, of her motor-car, all my strength left me, I shut my eyes and let my head droop on my shoulder like someone who is about to faint. The sound of doors being opened hurt me almost as much because it was not she that was opening them. When it was possible that a telegram might have come from Saint-Loup, I dared not ask: "Is there a telegram?" At length one did come, but brought with it only a postponement, with the message: "The ladies have gone away for three days."

No doubt, if I had endured the four days that had already elapsed since her departure, it was because I said to myself: "It's only a matter of time. By the end of the week she will be here." But this consideration did not alter the fact that for my heart, for my body, the action to be performed was the

same: living without her, returning home and not finding
her in the house, passing the door of her room (as for opening
it, I did not yet have the courage to do that) knowing that she
was not inside, going to bed without having said good-night
to her—such were the tasks that my heart had been obliged to
perform in their terrible entirety, and for all the world as
though I was not going to see Albertine again. But the fact
that my heart had already performed this daily task four times
proved that it was now capable of continuing to perform it.
And soon, perhaps, the consideration that was helping me
thus to go on living—the prospect of Albertine's return—
would cease to be necessary to me; I should be able to say to
myself: "She will never come back," and go on living all the
same as I had already done for the last four days, like a cripple
who has recovered the use of his legs and can dispense with his
crutches. No doubt when I came home at night I still found,
taking my breath away, suffocating me in the vacuum of
solitude, the memories, placed end to end in an interminable
series, of all the evenings on which Albertine had been waiting
for me; but already I also found the memory of last night, of
the night before and of the two previous nights, that is to
say the memory of the four nights that had passed since
Albertine's departure, during which I had remained without
her, alone, through which none the less I had lived, four nights
already forming a strip of memories which was very slender
compared with the other, but which would be filled out,
perhaps, by every day that went by.

I shall say nothing of the letter conveying a declaration of
affection which I received at this time from a niece of Mme de
Guermantes who was considered to be the prettiest girl in
Paris, or of the overtures made to me by the Duc de Guermantes on behalf of her parents, resigned, in their anxiety to
secure their daughter's happiness, to the inequality of the
match, to an apparent misalliance. Such incidents which might
prove gratifying to one's self-esteem are too painful when one
is in love. One might have the desire but not the indelicacy to
communicate them to her who has a less flattering opinion of
one, an opinion which moreover would not be modified by
the knowledge that one is capable of inspiring a quite different

one. What the Duke's niece wrote to me could only have irritated Albertine.

From the moment of waking, when I picked up my grief again at the point where I had left it before going to sleep, like a book which had been shut for a while but which I would keep before my eyes until night, it was invariably to some thought concerning Albertine that I related every sensation, whether it came to me from without or from within. The bell would ring: it must be a letter from her, or she herself perhaps! If I felt well and not too miserable, I was no longer jealous, I no longer had any grievance against her, I wanted to see her at once, to kiss her, to live happily with her ever after. The act of telegraphing to her "Come at once" seemed to me to have become a perfectly simple thing, as though my new mood had changed not merely my attitude, but things external to myself, had made them easier. If I was in a sombre mood, all my anger with her revived, I no longer felt any desire to kiss her, I felt how impossible it was that she could ever make me happy, I sought only to harm her and to prevent her from belonging to other people. But the outcome of these two opposite moods was identical: it was essential that she should return as soon as possible. And yet, whatever joy I might feel at the moment of her return, I sensed that very soon the same difficulties would recur and that to seek happiness in the satisfaction of a desire of the mind was as naïve as to attempt to reach the horizon by walking straight ahead. The further the desire advances, the further does real possession recede. So that if happiness, or at least the absence of suffering, can be found, it is not the satisfaction, but the gradual reduction and the eventual extinction of desire that one should seek. One seeks to see the beloved object, but one ought to seek not to: forgetfulness alone brings about the ultimate extinction of desire. And I imagine that if an author were to publish truths of this sort he would dedicate the book that contained them to a woman with whom he would thus take pleasure in striking up a relationship, saying to her: "This book is yours." And thus, while telling the truth in his book, he would be lying in his dedication, for he will attach to the book's being hers only the importance that he attaches to the stone which came to him from her and which will remain precious to him only so long as he is in love with her. The bonds between ourselves and another person exist only in our minds. Memory as it grows fainter loosens them, and notwithstanding the illusion by which we want to be duped and with which, out of love, friendship, politeness, deference, duty, we dupe other people, we exist alone. Man is the creature who cannot escape from himself, who knows other people only in himself, and when he asserts the contrary, he is lying. And I should have been so afraid of being robbed (had anyone been capable of so robbing me) of this need of her, this love for her, that I convinced myself that it was a precious necessity in my life. To be able to hear, without being charmed and pained by them, the names of the stations through which the train passed on its way to Touraine would have seemed to me a diminution of myself (for no other reason really than that it would have proved that I was becoming indifferent to Albertine). It was right, I told myself, that by incessantly asking myself what she could be doing, thinking, wishing, at every moment, whether she intended, whether she was going to return, I should keep open that communicating door which love had opened up in me, and feel another person's life flooding through open sluices to fill the reservoir which must not again become stagnant.

Presently, as Saint-Loup's silence persisted, a subordinate anxiety—my expectation of a further telegram or a telephone call from him—masked the first, my uncertainty as to the result, whether Albertine was going to return. Listening for every sound in expectation of the telegram became so intolerable that I felt that, whatever its contents might be, the arrival of the telegram, which was the only thing I could think of at the moment, would put an end to my sufferings. But when at last I received a telegram from Robert in which he informed me that he had seen Mme Bontemps but that in spite of all his precautions Albertine had seen him, and that this had upset everything, I burst out in a torrent of fury and despair, for this was what I had wanted at all costs to avoid. Once it came to Albertine's knowledge, Saint-Loup's mission gave me an appearance of needing her which could only dissuade her from returning and my horror of which was moreover all that I had retained of the pride that my love had boasted in Gilberte's day and had since lost. I cursed Robert, then told myself that, if this scheme had failed, I would try another. Since man is capable of influencing the external world, how could I fail, by bringing into play cunning, intelligence, money, affection, to alter this terrible fact: Albertine's absence? We believe that we can change the things around us in accordance with our desires—we believe it because otherwise we can see no favourable outcome. We do not think of the outcome which generally comes to pass and is also favourable: we do not succeed in changing things in accordance with our desires, but gradually our desires change. The situation that we hoped to change because it was intolerable becomes unimportant to us. We have failed to surmount the obstacle, as we were absolutely determined to do, but life has taken us round it, led us past it, and then if we turn round to gaze into the distance of the past, we can barely see it, so imperceptible has it become.

From the floor above I could hear one of the neighbours playing some tunes from *Manon*. I applied their words, which I knew, to Albertine and myself, and was stirred so deeply that I began to cry. The words were:

> Hélas, l'oiseau qui fuit ce qu'il croit l'esclavage,
> Le plus souvent la nuit
> D'un vol désespéré revient battre au vitrage,

and the death of Manon:

> Manon, réponds-moi donc, seul amour de mon âme,
> Je n'ai su qu'aujourd'hui la bonté de ton coeur.

Since Manon returned to Des Grieux, it seemed to me that I was to Albertine the one and only love of her life. Alas, it is probable that, if she had been listening at that moment to the same tune, it would not have been me that she cherished under the name of Des Grieux, and, even if the idea had occurred to her at all, the memory of me would have prevented her from wallowing in this music which, though subtler and better-written, was very much of the kind that she admired. As for me, I had not the heart to abandon myself to the consoling thought of Albertine calling me her "heart's only love" and realising that she had been mistaken over what she "had thought to be bondage." I knew that one can never read a novel without giving its heroine the form and features of the woman one loves. But however happy the book's ending may be, our love has not advanced an inch and, when we have shut it, she whom we love and who has come to us at last in its pages, loves us no better in real life.

In a fit of fury, I telegraphed to Saint-Loup to return as quickly as possible to Paris, in order to avoid at least the appearance of an aggravating persistence in a mission which I had been so anxious to keep secret. But even before he had returned in obedience to my instructions, it was from Albertine herself that I received the following message:

"My dear, you have sent your friend Saint-Loup to my aunt, which was foolish. My dearest, if you needed me, why did you not write to me direct? I should have been only too delighted to come back. Do not let us have any more of these absurd approaches."

"I should have been only too delighted to come back"! If she said this, it must mean that she regretted her departure, and was only waiting for an excuse to return. I had only to do what she said, to write to her that I needed her, and she would return. So I was going to see her again, her, the Albertine of Balbec (for since her departure this was what she had once more become for me; like a sea-shell to which one ceases to pay any attention when it is always there on one's chest of drawers, and once one has parted with it, either by giving it away or by losing it, one begins to think about again, she recalled to me all the joyous beauty of the blue mountains of the sea). And it was not only she that had become a creature of the imagination, that is to say desirable, but life with her had become an imaginary life, that is to say a life freed from all difficulties, so that I said to myself: "How happy we are going to be!" But, now that I was assured of her return, I must not appear to be seeking to hasten it, but must on the contrary efface the bad impression left by Saint-Loup's intervention, which I could always disavow later on by saying that he had acted on his own initiative, because he had always been in favour of our marriage.

Meanwhile, I read her letter again, and was after all disappointed to be reminded of how little there is of a person in a letter. Doubtless the characters traced on the paper express our thoughts, as do also our features; it is still a thought of some kind that we are confronted with. But even so, in the person, the thought is not apparent to us until it has been diffused through the corolla of the face opened up like a waterlily. This modifies it considerably, after all. And it is perhaps one of the causes of our perpetual disappointments in love, this perpetual displacement whereby, in response to our expectation of the ideal person whom we love, each meeting provides us with a person in flesh and blood who yet contains so little trace of our dream. And then, when we demand something of this person, we receive from her a letter in which even of the person very little remains, as in the letters of an algebraical formula there no longer remains the precise value of the arithmetical figures, which themselves do not contain the qualities of the fruit or flowers that they enumerate. And yet "love," the "beloved," her letters, are perhaps nevertheless translations (unsatisfying though it may be to pass from one to the other) of the same reality, since the letter seems to us inadequate only while we are reading it, but we sweat blood until its arrival, and it is sufficient to calm our anguish, if not to appease, with its tiny black symbols, our desire which knows that it contains after all only the equivalent of a word, a smile, a kiss, not those things themselves.

I wrote to Albertine:

"Dear friend, I was just about to write to you. Thank you for saying that if I had been in need of you you would have come at once; it is good of you to have so exalted a sense of loyalty to an old friend, and my regard for you can only be increased thereby. But no, I did not ask and I shall not ask you to return; our seeing each other again—for a long time to come—might not perhaps be painful to you, a heartless girl. To me, whom at times you have thought so cold, it would be most painful. Life has driven us apart. You have made a decision which I consider very wise, and which you made at the right moment, with wonderful prescience, for you left me on the day when I had just received my mother's consent to my asking for your hand. I would have told you this when I awoke, when I received her letter (at the same time as yours). Perhaps you would have been afraid of hurting me by leaving there and then. And we might perhaps have linked our lives together in what (who knows?) could have been unhappiness. If that was what was in store for us, then I bless you for your wisdom. We should lose all the fruit of it were we to meet again. This is not to say that I should not find it a temptation. But I claim no great credit for resisting it. You know what an inconstant person I am and how quickly I forget. Therefore I am not greatly to be pitied. As you have told me often, I am first and foremost a man of habit. The habits which I am beginning to form in your absence are not as yet very strong. Naturally, for the moment, the habits which I shared with you and which your departure has disturbed are still the stronger. They will not remain so for very long. For that reason, indeed, I had thought of taking advantage of these last few days in which our meeting would not yet be for me what it will be in a fortnight's time, perhaps even sooner, a ... (forgive my frankness) an inconvenience—I had thought of taking advantage of them, before oblivion finally comes, in order to settle certain little material questions with you, in which you might, as a kind and charming friend, have rendered a service to him who for five minutes imagined himself your future husband. Since I never doubted my mother's approval, and since moreover I desired that we should each of us enjoy all that liberty of which you had too generously and abundantly made a sacrifice which was acceptable for a few weeks' living together but would have become as hateful to you as to myself now that we were to spend the rest of our lives together (it almost pains me as I write to you to think that this nearly happened, that we came within a few seconds of it), I had thought of organising our existence in the most independent manner possible, and to begin with I wished you to have that yacht in which you could go cruising while I, not being well enough to accompany you, would wait for you in port (I had written to Elstir to ask for his advice, since you admire his taste); and on land I wished you to have a motor-car to yourself, for your very own, in which you could go out, could travel wherever you chose. The yacht was almost ready; it is named, after a wish that you expressed at Balbec, the *Swan*. And remembering that you preferred Rolls-Royces to any other cars, I had ordered one. But now that we are never to meet again, as I have no hope of persuading you to accept either the boat or the car (to me they would be quite useless), I had thought—as I had ordered them through a middleman, in your name—that you might perhaps by countermanding them yourself save me the expense of the yacht and the car which are no longer required. But this, and many other matters, would have needed to be discussed. And I find that so long as I am capable of falling in love with you again, which will not be for long, it would be madness, for the sake of a sailing boat and a Rolls-Royce, to meet again and to jeopardise your life's happiness since you have decided that it lies in your living apart from me. No, I prefer to keep the Rolls and even the yacht. And as I shall make no use of them and they are likely to remain for ever, one in its dock, dismantled, the other in its garage, I shall have engraved on the ... of the yacht (Heavens, I'm afraid of calling it the wrong thing and committing a heresy which would shock you) those lines of Mallarmé which you used to like ... You remember—it is the poem that begins:

> Le vierge, le vivace et le bel aujourd'hui. ...

Alas, to-day is no longer either virginal or fair. But those who, like me, know that they will very soon make of it an endurable "to-morrow" are seldom *endurable* themselves. As for the Rolls, it would deserve rather those other lines of the same poet which you said you could not understand:

> Tonnerre et rubis aux moyeux
> Dis si je ne suis pas joyeux
> De voir dans l'air que ce feu troue
>
> Flamber les royaumes épars
> Comme mourir pourpre la roue
> Du seul vespéral de mes chars.[26]

Farewell for ever, my little Albertine, and thank you once again for the enjoyable drive which we went for together on the eve of our separation. I retain a very pleasant memory of it.

P.S. I make no reference to what you tell me of the alleged suggestions which Saint-Loup (whom I do not for a moment believe to be in Touraine) may have made to your aunt. It's pure Sherlock Holmes. What do you take me for?"

No doubt, just as I had said in the past to Albertine: "I don't love you," in order that she should love me, "I forget people when I don't see them," in order that she might see me often, "I have decided to leave you," in order to forestall any idea of separation, now it was because I was absolutely determined that she must return within a week that I said to her: "Farewell for ever"; it was because I wished to see her again that I said to her: "I think it would be dangerous to see you"; it was because living apart from her seemed to me worse than death that I wrote to her: "You were right, we would be unhappy together." Alas, in writing this sham letter in order to appear not to need her (the only vestige of pride that survived from my former love for Gilberte in my love for Albertine), and also to enjoy the pleasure of saying certain things which were only capable of moving me and not her, I ought to have foreseen from the start that it was possible that it would invite a negative response, that is to say, one which confirmed what I had said; that this was indeed probable, for even had Albertine been less intelligent than she was, she would never have doubted for an instant that what I said to her was untrue. Indeed, without pausing to consider the intentions that I expressed in this letter, the mere fact of my writing it, even if it had not been preceded by Saint-Loup's intervention, was enough to prove to her that I desired her return and to prompt her to let me become more and more inextricably ensnared. Then, having foreseen the possibility of a negative reply, I ought also to have foreseen that this reply would at once revive in its fullest intensity my love for Albertine. And I ought, still before posting my letter, to have asked myself whether, in the event of Albertine's replying in the same tone and refusing to return, I should have sufficient control over my grief to force myself to remain silent, not to telegraph to her "Come back," not to send her some other emissary—all of which, after I had written to her to say that we would never meet again, would make it perfectly obvious that I could not do without her, and would lead to her refusing more emphatically than ever, whereupon, unable to endure my anguish for another moment, I would go down to her myself and might, for all I knew, be refused admission. And doubtless this would have been, after three enormous blunders, the worst of all, after which there would be nothing left but to kill myself in front of her house. But the disastrous way in which the psychopathological universe is constructed has decreed that the clumsy act, the act which we ought most sedulously to avoid, is precisely the act that will calm us, the act that, opening before us, until we discover its outcome, fresh avenues of hope, momentarily relieves us of the intolerable pain which a refusal has aroused in us. So that, when the pain is too acute, we dash headlong into the blunder that consists in writing to, in sending somebody to intercede with, in going in person to see, in proving that we cannot do without, the woman we love.

But I foresaw none of all this. The probable outcome of my letter seemed to me on the contrary to be to make Albertine return to me at once. And so, with this outcome in mind, I had felt a sweet pleasure in writing the letter. But at the same time I had not ceased to shed tears while writing it; partly, first of all, in the same way as on the day when I had acted a pretence of separation, because, as the words represented for me the idea which they expressed to me although they were addressed to a different end (uttered mendaciously because my pride forbade me to admit that I loved), they carried their own load of sorrow, but also because I felt that the idea contained a grain of truth.

As this letter seemed to me to be certain of its effect, I began to regret that I had sent it. For when I pictured to myself Albertine's return and what an easy matter it was after all, suddenly all the reasons which made our marriage a thing disastrous to myself returned in their fullest force. I hoped that she would refuse to come back. I was in the process of calculating that my liberty, my whole future depended upon her refusal, that I had been mad to write to her, that I ought to have retrieved my letter which, alas, had gone, when Françoise brought it back to me (at the same time handing me the newspaper which she had just brought upstairs). She was

not certain how many stamps it required. But immediately I
changed my mind; I hoped that Albertine would not return, but
I wanted the decision to come from her, so as to put an end to
my anxiety, and I handed the letter back to Françoise. I
opened the newspaper. It announced a performance by Berma.
Then I remembered the two different ways in which I had
listened to *Phèdre*, and it was now in a third way that I thought
of the declaration scene. It seemed to me that what I had so
often recited to myself, and had seen and heard in the theatre,
was the statement of the laws which I was to experience in my
life. There are things in our hearts to which we do not realise
how strongly we are attached. Or else, if we live without them,
it is because day after day, from fear of failure, or of being
made to suffer, we put off entering into possession of them.
This was what had happened to me in the case of Gilberte,
when I thought that I was giving her up. If before the time
comes when we are entirely detached from these things—a time
long subsequent to that in which we believe ourselves to be
detached from them—the girl we love becomes, for instance,
engaged to someone else, we are driven mad, we can no longer
endure the life which appeared to us to be so mournfully
calm. Or else, if the thing is already in our possession, we feel
that it is a burden, that we should be only too glad to be rid of
it; and this was what had happened to me in the case of Albertine. But let a sudden departure remove the unwanted person from us, and we can no longer bear to live. Now, did not
the "argument" of *Phèdre* combine these two cases? Hippolyte
is about to leave. Phèdre, who until then has gone out of her
way to court his enmity, from qualms of conscience, she says
(or rather the poet makes her say), but really because she does
not see that it can lead anywhere and feels that she is not loved,
Phèdre can endure the situation no longer. She comes to him
to confess her love, and this was the scene which I had so often
recited to myself:

On dit qu'un prompt départ vous éloigne de nous. . . .

Doubtless Hippolyte's departure is a secondary reason, one
may feel, compared to the death of Thésée. And similarly when,

a few lines further on, Phèdre pretends for a moment that she has been misunderstood:

Aurais-je perdu tout le soin de ma gloire?

we may suppose that it is because Hippolyte has repulsed her declaration:

Madame, oubliez-vous
Que Thésée est mon père, et qu'il est votre époux?

But if he had evinced no indignation, Phèdre, her happiness achieved, might have had the same feeling that it did not amount to much. Whereas, as soon as she sees that it still eludes her grasp, that Hippolyte thinks he has misunderstood her and makes apologies, then, like myself when I decided to give my letter back to Françoise, she decides that the refusal must come from him, decides to stake everything on one last throw of the dice:

Ah! cruel, tu m'as trop entendue.

And even the very harshness with which, I had been told, Swann had treated Odette, or with which I myself had treated Albertine, a harshness which substituted for the original love a new love composed of pity, tenderness, the need for an out-pouring of emotion which was merely a variant of the first, is to be found also in this scene:

Tu me haïssais plus, je ne t'aimais pas moins.
Tes malheurs te prêtaient encor de nouveaux charmes.

What proves that it is not to the "thought of her own reputation" that Phèdre attaches most importance is that she would have forgiven Hippolyte and turned a deaf ear to Oenone's advice had she not learned that Hippolyte was in love with Aricie. For jealousy, which in love is equivalent to the loss of all happiness, outweighs mere loss of reputation. It is then that she allows Oenone (who is merely a name for the baser side of herself) to slander Hippolyte without taking upon herself the "burden of his defence" and thus sends the man who will have none of her to a fate the calamities of which are moreover no consolation to herself, since her own suicide follows immediately upon the death of Hippolyte. Thus at least it was that,

reducing the part played by all the "Jansenist scruples," as Bergotte would have put it, which Racine ascribed to Phèdre to make her appear less guilty, I saw this scene, as a sort of prophecy of the amorous episodes in my own life. These reflections had, however, in no way altered my resolve, and I handed my letter to Françoise so that she might post it after all, in order to carry into effect that approach to Albertine which seemed to me to be essential now that I had learned that my former attempt had failed. And no doubt we are wrong when we suppose that the fulfilment of our desire is a small matter, since as soon as we believe that it cannot be realised we become intent upon it once again, and decide that it was not worth our while to pursue it only when we are quite certain that our attempt will not fail. And yet we are right also. For if that fulfilment, if the achievement of happiness, appears of small account only in the light of certainty, nevertheless it is an unstable element from which only sorrows can arise. And those sorrows will be all the greater the more completely our desire will have been fulfilled, all the more impossible to endure when our happiness has been, in defiance of the law of nature, prolonged for a certain time, when it has received the consecration of habit. In another sense, too, these two tendencies, in this particular case that which made me anxious that my letter should be posted, and, when I thought that it had gone, that which made me regret the fact, have each of them a certain element of truth. As regards the first tendency, it is only too understandable that we should go in pursuit of our happiness—or misery—and that at the same time we should hope to keep before us, by this latest action which is about to involve us in its consequences, a state of expectancy which does not leave us in absolute despair, in a word that we should seek to convert into other forms which, we imagine, must be less painful to us, the malady from which we are suffering. But the other tendency is no less important, for, born of our belief in the success of our enterprise, it is simply an anticipation of the disillusionment which we should very soon feel in the presence of a satisfied desire, our regret at having fixed for ourselves, at the expense of others which are necessarily excluded, this particular form of happiness.

I gave the letter back to Françoise and asked her to go out at once and post it. As soon as it had gone, I began once more to think of Albertine's return as imminent. The thought did not fail to introduce into my mind certain pleasing images which neutralised to some extent the dangers I foresaw in her return. The pleasure, so long lost, of having her with me was intoxicating.

Time passes, and little by little everything that we have spoken in falsehood becomes true; I had learned this only too well with Gilberte; the indifference I had feigned while never ceasing to weep had eventually become a fact; gradually life, as I told Gilberte in a lying formula which retrospectively had come true, life had driven us apart. I remembered this, saying to myself: "If Albertine allows a few months to go by, my lies will become the truth. And now that the worst moments are over, ought I not to hope that she will allow these months to elapse without returning? If she returns, I shall have to renounce the true life which certainly I am not in a fit state to enjoy as yet, but which as time goes on may begin to offer me attractions while my memory of Albertine grows fainter."

I do not say that the process of forgetting was not beginning to operate. But one of the effects of forgetting was precisely—since it meant that many of Albertine's less pleasing aspects, of the boring hours that I had spent with her, no longer figured in my memory, ceased therefore to be reasons for my wanting her not to be there as I used to when she was—that it gave me a more concise impression of her enhanced by all the love that I had ever felt for other women. In this particular form, forgetfulness, although it was working towards inuring me to separation from her, nevertheless, by showing me a sweeter and more beautiful Albertine, made me long all the more for her return.

Often, since her departure, when I was confident that I showed no trace of tears, I had rung for Françoise and said to her: "We must make sure that Mademoiselle Albertine hasn't forgotten anything. See that you do her room so that it's nice and tidy for her when she comes." Or simply: "Only the other day Mademoiselle Albertine was saying to me, let me think now, it was the day before she left. ...." I wanted to diminish Françoise's detestable pleasure at Albertine's departure by giving her the impression that it was not to be prolonged. I wanted, too, to show Françoise that I was not afraid to speak of this departure, to proclaim it—like certain generals who describe a forced retreat as a strategic withdrawal in conformity with a prearranged plan—as deliberate, as constituting an episode the true meaning of which I was concealing for the moment, but in no way implying the end of my friendship with Albertine. I wanted, finally, by repeating her name incessantly, to introduce, like a breath of air, something of her into that room in which her departure had left a vacuum, in which I could no longer breathe. Besides, one seeks to reduce the dimensions of one's grief by fitting it into one's everyday talk between ordering a suit of clothes and ordering dinner.

While she was doing Albertine's room, Françoise, out of curiosity, opened the drawer of a little rosewood table in which my mistress used to put away the ornaments which she discarded when she went to bed. "Oh! Monsieur, Mademoiselle Albertine has forgotten to take her rings, they're still in the drawer."

My first impulse was to say: "We must send them after her." But this would make me appear uncertain of her return. "Oh well," I replied after a moment's silence, "it's hardly worth while sending them to her as she's coming back so soon. Give them to me, I shall see about them."

Françoise handed me the rings with some misgiving. She loathed Albertine, but, judging me by her own standards, she reckoned that one could not give me a letter in my mistress's handwriting without the risk of my opening it. I took the rings.

"Monsieur must take care not to lose them," said Françoise. "They're real beauties, they are! I don't know who gave them to her, whether it was Monsieur or someone else, but I can tell it was someone rich, who had good taste!"

"It wasn't me," I assured her, "and besides, they don't both come from the same person. One was given her by her aunt and the other she bought for herself."

"Not from the same person!" Françoise exclaimed. "Monsieur must be joking, they're exactly the same, except for the ruby that's been added to one of them, there's the same eagle on both, the same initials inside. . . ."

I do not know whether Françoise was conscious of the pain she was causing me, but a smile began to flicker across her lips and thereafter never left them.

"What do you mean, the same eagle? You're talking nonsense. It's true that the one without the ruby has an eagle on it, but the other has a sort of man's head carved on it."

"A man's head? Where did Monsieur see that? I had only to put on my specs to see at once that it was one of the eagle's wings. If Monsieur takes his magnifying glass, he'll see the other wing on the other side, and the head and the beak in the middle. You can count every feather. Oh, it's a fine piece of work."

My intense anxiety to know whether Albertine had lied to me made me forget that I ought to maintain a certain dignity in Françoise's presence and deny her the wicked pleasure that she felt, if not in torturing me, at least in harming Albertine. I almost gasped for breath as Françoise went to fetch my magnifying glass. I took it from her, and asked her to show me the eagle on the ring with the ruby. She had no difficulty in making me pick out the wings, stylised in the same way as on the other ring, the relief of the feathers, the head. She also pointed out to me the similar inscriptions, to which, it is true, others were added on the ring with the ruby. And on the inside of both was Albertine's monogram.

"But I'm surprised that it should need all this to make Monsieur see that the rings are the same," said Françoise. "Even without examining them, you can see that it's the same style, the same way of turning the gold, the same shape. As soon as I looked at them I could have sworn they came from the same place. You can tell straight away, just as you can tell the dishes of a good cook."

And indeed, to the curiosity of a servant fanned by hatred and trained to observe details with terrifying precision, there had been added, to assist her in this expert criticism, her natural taste, that same taste, in fact, which she showed in her cookery

and which was sharpened perhaps, as I had noticed on the way
to Balbec in the way she dressed, by the coquetry of a woman
who has once been pretty and has studied the jewelry and dresses
of other women. I might have picked up the wrong bottle of
pills and, instead of swallowing a few veronal tablets on a day
when I felt that I had drunk too many cups of tea, might have
swallowed as many caffeine tablets, and my heart would not
have throbbed more violently. I asked Françoise to leave the
room. I would have liked to see Albertine immediately. My
horror at her lie, my jealousy of the unknown donor, was
combined with pain at the thought that she should have allowed
herself to accept presents. I gave her even more, it is true, but a
woman whom we are keeping does not seem to us to be a
kept woman as long as we are unaware that she is being kept
by other men. And yet, since I had never ceased to spend a
great deal of money on her, I had taken her in spite of this
moral baseness; I had encouraged this baseness of hers, I had
perhaps increased, perhaps even created it. Then, just as we
have the faculty of making up stories to soothe our anguish, just
as we manage, when we are dying of hunger, to persuade ourselves that a stranger is going to leave us a fortune of a hundred
millions, I imagined Albertine in my arms, explaining to me
without the slightest hesitation that it was because of the
similarity of its workmanship that she had bought the second
ring, that it was she who had had her initials engraved on it.
But this explanation was still fragile, it had not yet had time
to thrust into my mind its beneficent roots, and my pain could
not be so quickly assuaged. And I reflected that many men
who tell their friends that their mistress is very sweet to them
must suffer similar torments. Thus it is that they lie to others
and to themselves. They do not altogether lie; they do spend in
her company hours that are genuinely delightful; but the
sweetness which she shows her lover in front of his friends and
which enables him to preen himself, and the sweetness which
she shows him when they are alone together and which enables
him to bless her, conceal all too many unrecorded hours in
which the lover has suffered, doubted, sought everywhere in
vain to discover the truth! Such sufferings are inseparable
from the pleasure of loving, of delighting in a woman's most

trivial remarks, remarks which we know to be trivial but which we perfume with her fragrance. At that moment, I was no longer capable of delighting, through memory, in the fragrance of Albertine. Shattered, holding the two rings in my hand, I stared at that pitiless eagle whose beak was rending my heart, whose wings, chiselled in high relief, had borne away the trust that I still retained in my mistress, in whose claws my tortured mind was unable to escape for an instant from the incessantly recurring questions concerning the stranger whose name the eagle doubtless symbolised though without allowing me to decipher it, whom she had doubtless loved in the past, and whom she had doubtless seen again not so long ago, since it was on the day, so peaceful, so loving and so intimate, of our drive together through the Bois that I had seen, for the first time, the second ring, the one in which the eagle appeared to be dipping its beak in the bright blood of the ruby.

If, however, from morning till night, I never ceased to grieve over Albertine's departure, this did not mean that I thought only of her. For one thing, her charm having for a long time past spread gradually over things which had since become quite remote from her, but were none the less electrified by the same emotion as she gave me, if something made me think of Incarville, or of the Verdurins, or of some new part that Léa was playing, a sudden flux of pain would overwhelm me. For another thing, what I myself called thinking of Albertine meant thinking of how I might get her back, how I might join her, how I might discover what she was doing. With the result that if, during those hours of incessant torment, a pictogram could have represented the images that accompanied my sufferings, it would have shown pictures of the Gare d'Orsay, of the bank-notes offered to Mme Bontemps, of Saint-Loup stooping over the sloping desk of a telegraph office filling in a telegram form to me, never the picture of Albertine. Just as, throughout the whole course of one's life, one's egoism sees before it all the time the objects that are of concern to the self, but never takes in that "I" itself which is incessantly observing them, so the desire which directs our actions descends towards them, but does not reach back to itself, whether because, being unduly utilitarian, it plunges into the action and disdains all knowledge of it, or because it looks to the future to compensate for the disappointments of the present, or because the inertia of the mind urges it to slide down the easy slope of imagination, rather than to climb the steep slope of introspection. In reality, during those hours of crisis in which we would stake our whole life, in proportion as the woman upon whom it depends reveals more and more clearly the immensity of the place that she occupies for us, leaving nothing in the world that is not disrupted by her, so the image of that woman diminishes until it is no longer perceptible. We find in everything the effect of her presence in the emotion that we feel; herself, the cause, we find nowhere. I was so incapable during those days of forming any picture of Albertine that I could almost have believed that I did not love her, just as my mother, in the moments of despair when she was incapable of ever picturing my grandmother (save once in the chance encounter of a dream, the importance of which she felt so strongly, although asleep, that she strove with all the strength that remained to her in her sleep to make it last), might have accused and did in fact accuse herself of not missing her mother, whose death had been a mortal blow to her but whose features eluded her memory.*

Why should I have supposed that Albertine did not care for women? Because she had said, especially of late, that she did not care for them: but did not our life rest upon a perpetual lie? Never once had she said to me: "Why can't I go out as and when I choose? Why do you always ask other people what I have been doing?" And yet, after all, the conditions of her life were so unusual that she must have asked me this had she not herself guessed the reason. And was it not understandable that my silence as to the causes of her confinement should be matched by a similar and constant silence on her part as to her perpetual desires, her innumerable memories, her countless hopes and longings? Françoise looked as though she knew that I was lying when I alluded to the imminence of Albertine's return. And her belief seemed to be founded upon something more than that truth which generally guided our old housekeeper, to the effect that masters do not like to be humiliated in front of their servants, and allow them to know only so much of the truth as does not depart too far from a flattering fiction calculated to maintain respect for themselves. This time, Françoise's belief seemed to be founded upon something else, as though she had herself aroused and fostered distrust in Albertine's mind, stimulated her anger, driven her, in short, to the point at which she could predict her departure as inevitable. If this was true, my version of a temporary absence, of which I had known and approved, could be received with nothing but incredulity by Françoise. But the idea that she had formed of Albertine's venal nature, the exasperation with which, in her hatred, she magnified the "profit" that Albertine was supposed to be making out of me, might to some extent belie that certainty. And so when in her hearing I made an allusion, as if to something perfectly natural, to Albertine's imminent return, Françoise would look at my face to see whether I was making it up, in the same way as, when the butler teased her by pretending to read out some political news which she hesitated to believe, as for instance the closing of churches and the expulsion of the clergy, even from the other end of the kitchen, and without being able to read it, she would stare instinctively and greedily at the paper, as though she were capable of seeing whether the report was really written there.

But when Françoise saw that after writing a long letter I looked up the exact address of Mme Bontemps, her alarm that Albertine might return, hitherto quite vague, began to increase. It grew to the point of consternation when one morning she had to bring me with the rest of my mail a letter on the envelope of which she had recognised Albertine's handwriting. She wondered whether Albertine's departure had not been a mere sham, a supposition which distressed her twice over as finally ensuring Albertine's future presence in the house, and as constituting for me, and thereby, as I was her employer, for herself, the humiliation of having been tricked by Albertine. Impatient though I was to read the letter, I could not refrain from studying for a moment Françoise's eyes from which all hope had fled, inferring from this omen the imminence of Albertine's return, as a lover of winter sports concludes with joy that the cold weather is at hand when he sees the swallows fly south. At length Françoise left me, and when I had made sure that she had shut the door behind her, I opened, noiselessly so as not to appear anxious, the letter which ran as follows:

"Dear friend, thank you for all the nice things you wrote to me. I am at your disposal for the countermanding of the Rolls, if you think that I can help in any way, as I am sure I can. You have only to let me know the name of the agents. You would let yourself be taken for a ride by these people who are only interested in selling, and what would you do with a motor-car, you who never stir out of the house? I am deeply touched that you have kept a happy memory of our last outing. You may be sure that for my part I shall never forget that doubly crepuscular drive (since night was falling and we were about to part) and that it will be effaced from my memory only when the darkness is complete."

I felt that this last sentence was merely phrase-making and that Albertine could not possibly retain until death any such sweet memory of this drive from which she had certainly derived no pleasure since she had been impatient to leave me. But I was impressed also, when I thought of the cyclist, the golfer of Balbec, who had read nothing but *Esther* before she came to know me, to see how gifted she was and how right I had been in thinking that she had enriched herself in my house with new qualities which made her different and more complete. And thus, the words that I had said to her at Balbec: "I feel that my friendship would be of value to you, that I am just the person who could give you what you lack" (I had written by way of dedication on a photograph I gave her: "with the certainty of being providential"), words which I uttered without believing them and simply that she might derive some benefit from my society which would outweigh any possible boredom, these words turned out to have been true as well; as, for that matter, had been my remark to her that I did not wish to see her for fear of falling in love with her. I had said this because on the contrary I knew that in constant proximity my love became deadened and that separation kindled it, but in reality constant proximity had given rise to a need of her that was infinitely stronger than my love in the first weeks at Balbec, so that that remark too had proved true.

But Albertine's letter in no way advanced matters. She spoke to me only of writing to the agents. It was essential to break out of this situation, to hasten things on, and I had the following idea. I sent a letter at once to Andrée in which I told her that Albertine was at her aunt's, that I felt very lonely, that she would give me immense pleasure if she came and stayed with me for a few days and that, as I did not wish to make any mystery of it, I begged her to inform Albertine. And at the same time I wrote to Albertine as though I had not yet received her letter:

"Dear friend, forgive me for doing something which I am sure you will understand. I have such a hatred of secrecy that I wanted you to be informed both by her and by myself. I have acquired, from having you staying so charmingly in the house with me, the bad habit of not being able to be alone. Since we have decided that you will not come back, it occurred to me that the person who would best fill your place, because she would make least change in my life, would remind me most of you, is Andrée, and I have asked her to come. So that all this should not appear too sudden, I have spoken to her only of a short visit, but between ourselves I am pretty certain that this time it will be a permanent thing. Don't you agree that I'm right? You know that your little group of girls at Balbec has always been the social unit that exerted the greatest influence upon me, in which I was most happy to be eventually included. No doubt this influence is still making itself felt. Since the fatal incompatibility of our characters and the mischances of life have decreed that my little Albertine can never be my wife, I believe that I shall nevertheless find a wife—less charming than herself but one whom greater natural affinities will enable perhaps to be happier with me—in Andrée."

But after I had sent off this letter, the suspicion occurred to me suddenly that, when Albertine had written to me to say: "I should have been only too delighted to come back if you had written to me direct," she had said this only because I had not written to her, and that had I done so she would still not have come back, that she would be glad to know that Andrée was with me, and was to be my wife, provided that she herself remained free, because she could now, as already for a week past, stultifying the hourly precautions which I had taken during more than six months in Paris, abandon herself to her vices and do what, minute by minute, I had prevented her from doing. I told myself that she was probably making an improper use of her freedom down there, and no doubt this idea which I formed seemed to me sad but remained general, showing me no specific details, and, by the indefinite number of possible mistresses which it allowed me to imagine, prevented me from stopping to consider any one of them, drew my mind on in a sort of perpetual motion not untinged with pain, but with a pain which the absence of any concrete image rendered endurable. It ceased, however, to be endurable and became atrocious when Saint-Loup arrived.

Before I explain why the information that he gave me made me so unhappy, I must relate an incident which occurred immediately before his visit and the memory of which so disturbed me afterwards that it weakened, if not the painful impression made on me by my conversation with Saint-Loup, at any rate the practical effect of that conversation. This incident was as follows. Burning with impatience to see Saint-Loup, I was waiting for him on the staircase (a thing which I could not have done had my mother been at home, for it was what she most abominated, next to "talking out of the window") when I heard the following words: "What! you mean to say you don't know how to get a fellow you don't like sacked? It's not difficult. For instance, you need only hide the things he has to take in. Then, when they're in a hurry and ring for him, he can't find anything, he loses his head. My aunt will be furious with him, and will say to you: 'But what's the man doing?' When he does show his face, everybody will be raging, and he won't have what's wanted. After this has happened four or five times you may be sure that he'll be sacked, especially if you take care to dirty the things that he's supposed to bring in clean, and a dozen other tricks of that kind."

I remained speechless with astonishment, for these cruel, Machiavellian words were uttered by the voice of Saint-Loup. Now I had always regarded him as so kind, so tender-hearted a person that these words had the same effect on me as if he had been rehearsing the role of Satan for a play: it could not be in his own name that he was speaking.

"But, after all, a man has to earn his living," said the other person, of whom I then caught sight and who was one of the Duchesse de Guermantes's footmen.

"What the hell does that matter to you so long as you're all right?" Saint-Loup replied callously. "It will be all the more fun for you, having a whipping-boy. You can easily spill ink over his livery just when he has to go and wait at a big dinner-party, and never leave him in peace for a moment until he's only too glad to give notice. Anyhow, I can put a spoke in his wheel. I shall tell my aunt that I admire your patience in working with a great lout like that, and so dirty too."

I showed myself, and Saint-Loup came to greet me, but my confidence in him was shaken since I had heard him speak in a manner so different from anything that I knew. And I wondered whether a person who was capable of acting so cruelly towards a poor and defenceless man might not have played the part of a traitor towards me on his mission to Mme Bontemps. This reflection served mainly, after he had left, to help me not to regard his failure as a proof that I myself might not succeed. But while he was with me, it was still of the Saint-Loup of old, and especially of the friend who had just come from Mme Bontemps, that I thought. He began by saying: "You feel that I ought to have telephoned to you more often, but I was always told that you were engaged." But the point at which my pain became unendurable was when he said: "To begin where my last telegram left you, after going through a sort of shed, I went into the house and at the end of a long passage was shown into a drawing-room."

At these words, shed, passage, drawing-room, and before he had even finished uttering them, my heart was shattered more instantaneously than by an electric current, for the force that circles the earth most times in a second is not electricity but pain. How I repeated to myself these words, shed, passage, drawing-room, renewing the shock at will, after Saint-Loup had left me! In a shed one girl can hide with another. And in that drawing-room, who knew what Albertine did when her aunt was not there? Had I then imagined the house in which she was living as incapable of possessing either a shed or a drawing-room? No, I had not imagined it at all, except as a vague dwelling. I had suffered first of all when the place where Albertine was had acquired a geographical identity, when I had learned that, instead of being in two or three possible places, she was in Touraine; those words uttered by her concierge had marked in my heart as upon a map the place where I must suffer. But once I had grown accustomed to the idea that she was in a house in Touraine, I had still not seen the house; never had there occurred to my imagination this appalling idea of a drawing-room, a shed, a passage, which struck me now, facing me in the retina of Saint-Loup's eyes which had seen them, as the rooms in which Albertine came and went, lived her life, as those rooms in particular and not an infinity of possible rooms which had cancelled one another out. With the words shed, passage, drawing-room, I became aware of my folly in having left Albertine for a week in that accursed place whose *existence* (instead of its mere possibility) had just been revealed to me. Alas! when Saint-Loup told me also that in this drawing-room he had heard someone singing at the top of her voice in an adjoining room and that it was Albertine who was singing, I realised with despair that, rid of me at last, she was happy! She had regained her freedom. And I had been thinking that she would come to take the place of Andrée! My grief turned to anger with Saint-Loup.

"That's the one thing in the world I asked you to avoid, that she should know of your coming."

"Do you think it was easy! They assured me that she wasn't in the house. Oh, I know very well that you're not pleased with me, I could tell that from your telegrams. But you're not being fair; I did what I could."

Set free once more, released from the cage in which, here at home, I used to leave her for days on end without letting her come to my room, Albertine had regained all her attraction in my eyes; she had become once more the girl whom everyone pursued, the marvellous bird of the earliest days.

"Anyhow, to sum up—as regards the money, I don't know what to say to you. I found myself addressing a woman who seemed to me to be so scrupulous that I was afraid of offending her. However, she didn't say a word when I mentioned the money. In fact, a little later she told me that she was touched to

find that we understood one another so well. And yet everything that she said afterwards was so delicate, so refined, that it
seemed to me impossible that she could have been referring to
my offer of money when she said: 'We understand one another
so well,' for after all I was behaving like a cad."

"But perhaps she didn't understand what you meant,
perhaps she didn't hear. You ought to have repeated the offer,
because then it would certainly have worked."

"But how could she possibly not have heard? I spoke to
her as I'm speaking to you, and she's neither deaf nor mad."

"And she made no comment?"

"None."

"You ought to have repeated the offer."

"How do you mean, repeat it? As soon as we met I saw what
sort of person she was. I said to myself that you'd been
mistaken, that you were making me commit the most awful
gaffe, and that it would be terribly difficult to offer her the
money like that. I did it, however, to oblige you, convinced
that she'd turn me out of the house."

"But she didn't. Therefore, either she hadn't heard you and
you should have started afresh, or you could have pursued the
subject."

"You say: 'She hadn't heard,' because you were here in Paris,
but, I repeat, if you'd been present at our conversation, there
wasn't a sound to interrupt us, I said it quite plainly, it's not
possible that she failed to understand."

"But anyhow she's quite convinced that I've always wished
to marry her niece?"

"No, as to that, if you want my opinion, she didn't believe
that you had any intention of marrying the girl. She told me
that you yourself had informed her niece that you wished to
leave her. I'm not really sure that she's convinced even now
that you want to marry."

This reassured me slightly by showing me that I was in a
less humiliating position, and therefore more capable of being
still loved, more free to take some decisive action. Nevertheless
I was tormented.

"I'm sorry, because I can see you're not pleased," Saint-
Loup went on.

"Well, I'm touched by your kindness, and I'm grateful to you, but it seems to me that you might have . . ."

"I did my best. No one else could have done more or even as much. Try sending someone else."

"No, no, as a matter of fact, if I had known I wouldn't have sent you, but the failure of your attempt prevents me from making another."

I heaped reproaches on him: he had tried to do me a service and had not succeeded.

On leaving the Bontemps' house he had met some girls arriving. I had already conjectured often enough that Albertine knew other girls in the neighbourhood; but this was the first time that I felt the pain of that conjecture. It would seem that nature has endowed the mind with the means of secreting a natural antidote which destroys the suppositions that we form unremittingly but without danger to ourselves; but nothing could immunise me against these girls whom Saint-Loup had met. But were not all these details precisely what I had sought to learn from everyone with regard to Albertine? Was it not I who, in order to learn them more fully, had begged Saint-Loup, summoned back to Paris by his colonel, to come and see me at all costs? Was it not I, therefore, who had desired them, or rather my famished grief, longing to feed and to wax fat upon them? Finally Saint-Loup told me that he had had the pleasant surprise of meeting down there—the only familiar face that had reminded him of the past—a former friend of Rachel, a pretty actress who was taking a holiday in the neighbourhood. And the name of this actress was enough to make me say to myself: "Perhaps she's the one"; was enough to make me see, in the very arms of a woman whom I did not know, Albertine smiling and flushed with pleasure. And, after all, why should this not have been so? Had I myself refrained from thinking of other women since I had known Albertine? On the evening of my first visit to the Princesse de Guermantes, when I returned home, had I not been thinking far less of her than of the society girl of whom Saint-Loup had told me, who frequented houses of assignation, and of Mme Putbus's maid? Was it not in the hope of meeting the latter that I had returned to Balbec? More recently, had I not longed

to go to Venice? Why then might Albertine not have longed
to go to Touraine? Only, when it came to the point, as I now
realised, I would not have left her, I would not have gone to
Venice. Indeed, in my heart of hearts, when I said to myself:
"I shall leave her soon," I knew that I would never leave her,
just as I knew that I would never settle down to work, or live
a healthy life, or do any of the things which, day after day, I
vowed that I would do to-morrow. Only, whatever I might
feel in my heart, I had thought it more adroit to let her live
under the perpetual threat of a separation. And no doubt,
thanks to my detestable adroitness, I had convinced her only
too well. In any case, things could not now go on like this; I
could not leave her in Touraine with those girls, with that
actress; I could not endure the thought of that life which eluded
me. I would await her reply to my letter: if she was doing wrong,
alas! a day more or less made no difference (and perhaps I said
this to myself because, being no longer in the habit of taking
note of every minute of her life, a single one of which wherein
she was unobserved would formerly have thrown me into a
panic, my jealousy no longer observed the same time scale).
But as soon as I received her answer, if she was not coming back
I would go and fetch her; willy-nilly, I would tear her away from
her women friends. Besides, was it not better for me to go down
in person, now that I had discovered Saint-Loup's hitherto
unsuspected duplicity? Might he not, for all I knew, have
organised a plot to separate me from Albertine?

Was it because I had changed, or because I had been incapable of imagining then that natural causes would bring
me one day to this unprecedented pass? At all events, how I
should have lied now had I written to her, as I had said to her
in Paris, that I hoped that no accident might befall her! Ah! if
some accident had happened to her, my life, instead of being
poisoned for ever by this incessant jealousy, would at once
regain, if not happiness, at least a state of calm through the
suppression of suffering.

The suppression of suffering? Can I really have believed it,
have believed that death merely strikes out what exists, and
leaves everything else in its place, that it removes the pain from
the heart of him for whom the other's existence has ceased to

be anything but a source of pain, that it removes the pain and substitutes nothing in its place? The suppression of pain! As I glanced at the news items in the papers, I regretted that I had not had the courage to form the same wish as Swann. If Albertine could have been the victim of an accident, were she alive I should have had a pretext for hastening to her bedside, were she dead I should have recovered, as Swann said, my freedom to live. Did I believe this? He had believed it, that subtlest of men who thought that he knew himself well. How little do we know of what we have in our hearts! How clearly, a little later, had he been still alive, I could have proved to him that his wish was not only criminal but absurd, that the death of the woman he loved would have delivered him from nothing!

I forsook all pride with regard to Albertine, and sent her a despairing telegram begging her to return on any terms, telling her that she could do whatever she liked, that I asked only to be allowed to take her in my arms for a minute three times a week, before she went to bed. And if she had said once a week only, I would have accepted the restriction.

She never came back. My telegram had just gone off to her when I myself received one. It was from Mme Bontemps. The world is not created once and for all for each of us individually. There are added to it in the course of our lives things of which we have never had any suspicion. Alas! it was not a suppression of suffering that the first two lines of the telegram produced in me: "My poor friend, our little Albertine is no more. Forgive me for breaking this terrible news to you who were so fond of her. She was thrown by her horse against a tree while she was out riding. All our efforts to restore her to life were unavailing. If only I had died in her stead!" No, not the suppression of suffering, but a suffering until then unimagined, that of realising that she would not come back. But had I not told myself many times that she might not come back? I had indeed done so, but now I saw that I had never believed it for a moment. As I needed her presence, her kisses, to enable me to endure the pain that my suspicions caused me, I had formed, since Balbec, the habit of being always with her. Even when she had gone out, when I was alone, I was kissing her still. I had continued to do so since her departure for Touraine. I had less need of her fidelity than of her return. And if my reason might with impunity cast doubt upon it now and again, my imagination never ceased for an instant to picture it for me. Instinctively I drew my hand over my throat, over my lips, which felt themselves kissed by her lips still after she had gone away, and would never be kissed by them again; I drew my hand over them, as Mamma had caressed me at the time of my grandmother's death, saying to me: "My poor boy, your grandmother who was so fond of you will never kiss you again." All my life to come seemed to have been wrenched from my heart. My life to come? Had I not, then, thought at times of living it without Albertine? Of course not! Had I then for a long time past pledged her every minute of my life until my death? I had indeed! This future indissolubly blended with hers was something I had never had the vision to perceive, but now that it had just been shattered, I could feel the place that it occupied in my gaping heart. Françoise, who still knew nothing, came into my room. In a sudden fury I shouted at her: "What do you want?" Then (sometimes there are words that set a different reality in the same place as that which confronts us; they bewilder us in the same way as a fit of dizziness) she said to me: "Monsieur has no need to look cross. On the contrary he's going to be pleased. Here are two letters from Mademoiselle Albertine."

I felt, afterwards, that I must have stared at her with the eyes of a man whose mind has become unbalanced. I was not even glad, nor was I incredulous. I was like a person who sees the same place in his room occupied by a sofa and by a grotto: nothing seeming real to him any more, he collapses on the floor. Albertine's two letters must have been written shortly before the fatal ride. The first said:

"My dear, I must thank you for the proof of your confidence which you give me when you tell me of your intention to bring Andrée to live with you. I am sure that she will be delighted to accept, and I think that it will be a very good thing for her. Gifted as she is, she will know how to make the most of the companionship of a man like yourself, and of the admirable influence which you manage to exert over other people.

I feel that you have had an idea from which as much good may spring for her as for yourself. And so, if she should make the slightest difficulty (which I do not believe she will), telegraph to me and I will undertake to bring pressure to bear upon her."

The second was dated the following day. (In fact she must have written them both within a few minutes of one another, perhaps at the same time, and must have predated the first. For, all the time, I had been forming absurd ideas of her intentions, which had simply been to return to me, and which anyone not directly interested in the matter, a man without imagination, the negotiator of a peace treaty, the merchant who has to examine a transaction, would have judged more accurately than myself.) It contained only these words:

"Is it too late for me to return to you? If you have not yet written to Andrée, would you be prepared to take me back? I shall abide by your decision, but I beg you not to be long in making it known to me; you can imagine how impatiently I shall be waiting. If it is to tell me to return, I shall take the train at once. Yours with all my heart, Albertine."

For the death of Albertine to have been able to eliminate my suffering, the shock of the fall would have had to kill her not only in Touraine but in myself. There, she had never been more alive. In order to enter into us, another person must first have assumed the form, have adapted himself to the framework of time; appearing to us only in a succession of momentary flashes, he has never been able to reveal to us more than one aspect of himself at a time, to present us with more than a single photograph of himself. A great weakness no doubt for a person, to consist merely of a collection of moments; a great strength also: he is a product of memory, and our memory of a moment is not informed of everything that has happened since; this moment which it has recorded endures still, lives still, and with it the person whose form is outlined in it. And moreover, this disintegration does not only make the dead one live, it multiplies him or her. In order to be consoled I would have to forget, not one, but innumerable Albertines. When I had succeeded in bearing the grief of losing this Albertine, I must begin again with another, with a hundred others.

So then my life was entirely altered. What had constituted its sweetness—not because of Albertine, but concurrently with her, when I was alone—was precisely the perpetual resurgence, at the bidding of identical moments, of moments from the past. From the sound of pattering raindrops I recaptured the scent of the lilacs at Combray; from the shifting of the sun's rays on the balcony the pigeons in the Champs-Elysées; from the muffling of sounds in the heat of the morning hours, the cool taste of cherries; the longing for Brittany or Venice from the noise of the wind and the return of Easter. Summer was at hand, the days were long, the weather was warm. It was the season when, early in the morning, pupils and teachers repair to the public gardens to prepare for the final examinations under the trees, seeking to extract the sole drop of coolness vouchsafed by a sky less ardent than in the midday heat but already as sterilely pure. From my darkened room, with a power of evocation equal to that of former days but capable now of evoking only pain, I felt that outside, in the heaviness of the atmosphere, the setting sun was plastering the vertical fronts of houses and churches with a tawny distemper. And if Françoise, when she came in, accidentally disturbed the folds of the big curtains, I stifled a cry of pain at the rent that had just been made in my heart by that ray of long-ago sunlight which had made beautiful in my eyes the modern façade of Marcouville l'Orgueilleuse when Albertine had said to me: "It's restored." Not knowing how to account to Françoise for my groan, I said to her: "Oh, I'm so thirsty." She left the room, then returned, but I turned sharply away under the impact of the painful discharge of one of the thousand invisible memories which incessantly exploded around me in the darkness: I had noticed that she had brought me cider and cherries, things which a farm-lad had brought out to us in the carriage, at Balbec, "kinds" in which I should have made the most perfect communion, in those days, with the prismatic gleam in shuttered dining-rooms on days of scorching heat. Then I thought for the first time of the farm called Les Ecorres, and said to myself that on certain days when Albertine had told me, at Balbec, that she would not be free, that she was obliged to go somewhere with her aunt, she had perhaps been with one or another of her girl friends at some farm to which she knew that I was not in the habit of going, and, while I waited desperately for her at Marie-Antoinette where they told me: "No, we haven't seen her to-day," had been saying to her friend the same words as she used to say to me when we went out together: "He'll never think of looking for us here, so there's no fear of our being disturbed." I told Françoise to draw the curtains together, so that I would no longer see that ray of sunlight. But it continued to filter through, just as corrosively, into my memory. "It doesn't appeal to me, it's been restored, but to-morrow we'll go to Saint-Mars-le-Vêtu, and the day after to. . . ." To-morrow, the day after, it was a prospect of life together, perhaps for ever, that was opening up; my heart leapt towards it, but it was no longer there, Albertine was dead.

I asked Françoise the time. Six o'clock. At last, thank God, that oppressive heat, of which in the past I used to complain to Albertine and which we so enjoyed, was about to die down. The day was drawing to its close. But what did that profit me? The cool evening air was rising; it was sunset; in my memory, at the end of a road which we had taken, she and I, on our way home, I saw it now, beyond the furthest village, like some distant place, inaccessible that evening, which we would spend at Balbec, still together. Together then; now I must stop short on the brink of that same abyss; she was dead. It was not enough now to draw the curtains; I tried to stop the eyes and ears of my memory in order not to see that band of orange in the western sky, in order not to hear those invisible birds responding from one tree to the next on either side of me who was then so tenderly embraced by her who was now dead. I tried to avoid those sensations that are produced by the dampness of leaves in the evening air, the rise and fall of humpback roads. But already those sensations had gripped me once more, carrying me far enough back from the present moment to give the necessary recoil, the necessary momentum to strike me anew, to the idea that Albertine was dead. Ah! never again would I enter a forest, never again would I stroll beneath the trees. But would the broad plains be less painful to me? How often had I crossed, on the way to fetch Albertine, how often had I retrodden, on the way back with her, the great plain of Cricqueville, sometimes in foggy weather when the swirling mists gave us the illusion of being surrounded by a vast lake, sometimes on limpid evenings when the moonlight, dematerialising the earth, making it appear from a few feet away as celestial as it is, in the daytime, in the distance only, enclosed the fields and the woods with the firmament to which it had assimilated them in the moss-agate of a universal blue!

Françoise must have been pleased by Albertine's death, and in fairness to her it should be said that by a sort of tact and decorum she made no pretence of sorrow. But the unwritten laws of her immemorial code and the tradition of the mediæval peasant woman who weeps as in the romances of chivalry were older than her hatred of Albertine and even of Eulalie. Thus, on one of these late afternoons, as I was not quick enough in concealing my distress, she caught sight of my tears, prompted by her instinct as a former peasant girl which at one time had led her to catch and maltreat animals, to feel nothing but merriment in wringing the necks of chickens and in boiling lobsters alive, and, when I was ill, in observing, as it might be the wounds that she had inflicted on an owl, my suffering expression which she afterwards proclaimed in a sepulchral tone as a presage of coming disaster. But her Combray "customary" did not permit her to treat tears and sorrow lightly —things which in her judgment were as fatal as shedding one's flannel vest or toying with one's food. "Oh, no, Monsieur, it doesn't do to cry like that, it isn't good for you." And in trying to stem my tears she looked as anxious as if they had been torrents of blood. Unfortunately I adopted a chilly air that cut short the effusions in which she was hoping to indulge and which might well have been sincere. Her attitude towards Albertine was perhaps akin to her attitude towards Eulalie, and, now that my mistress could no longer derive any profit from me, Françoise had ceased to hate her. She felt bound, however, to let me see that she was perfectly well aware that I was crying, and that, following the deplorable example set by my family, I did not wish to "show it." "You mustn't cry, Monsieur," she adjured me, in a calmer tone this time, and with the intention of proving her perspicacity rather than displaying her pity. And she added: "It was bound to happen; she was too happy, poor creature, she never knew how happy she was."

How slow the day is in dying on these interminable summer evenings! A pale ghost of the house opposite continued indefinitely to tinge the sky with its persistent whiteness. At last it was dark in the apartment; I stumbled against the furniture in the hall, but in the door that opened on to the staircase, in the midst of the darkness I had thought to be complete, the glazed panel was translucent and blue, with the blueness of a flower, the blueness of an insect's wing, a blueness that would have seemed to me beautiful had I not felt it to be a last glint, sharp as a steel blade, a final blow that was being dealt me, in its indefatigable cruelty, by the day. Finally, however, complete darkness came, but then a glimpse of a star behind the tree in the courtyard was enough to remind me of the times when we used to set out in a carriage, after dinner, for the woods of Chantepie, carpeted with moonlight. And even in the streets I might chance to isolate upon the back of a bench, to glean the natural purity of a moonbeam in the midst of the artificial lights of Paris—of Paris over which, by restoring the city for a moment, in my imagination, to a state of nature, with the infinite silence of the fields thus evoked, it enthroned the heart-rending memory of the walks that I had taken there with Albertine. Ah! when would the night end? But at the first coolness of dawn I shivered, for it had brought back to me the sweetness of that summer when, from Balbec to Incarville, from Incarville to Balbec, we had so many times escorted each other home until daybreak. I had now only one hope left for the future—a hope far more poignant than any fear— and that was that I might forget Albertine. I knew that I should forget her one day; I had forgotten Gilberte and Mme de Guermantes; I had forgotten my grandmother. And it is our most just and cruel punishment for that forgetfulness, as total and as tranquil as the oblivion of the graveyard, through which we have detached ourselves from those we no longer love, that we should recognise it to be inevitable in the case of those we love still. In reality, we know that it is not a painful state but a state of indifference. But not being able to think at one and the same time of what I was and of what I would be, I thought with despair of all that integument of caresses, of kisses, of friendly slumber, of which I must presently let myself be stripped forever. The influx of these tender memories, breaking against the idea that Albertine was dead, oppressed me with such a clash of warring currents that I could not remain still; I rose, but all of a sudden I stopped, overwhelmed with anguish; the same faint daybreak that I used to see when I had just left Albertine, still radiant and warm from her kisses, had just drawn above the curtains its now sinister blade whose whiteness, cold, implacable and compact, glinted like a dagger thrust into my heart.

Presently the sounds from the street would begin, enabling me to tell from the qualitative scale of their sonorities the degree of the steadily increasing heat in which they resounded. But in this heat which a few hours later would become saturated with the fragrance of cherries, what I found (as in a medicine which the substitution of one ingredient for another is sufficient to transform from the stimulant and tonic that it was into a depressant) was no longer the desire for women but the anguish of Albertine's departure. Besides, the memory of all my desires was as much impregnated with her, and with suffering, as the memory of my pleasures. Venice, where I had thought that her company would be irksome (doubtless because I had felt in a confused way that it would be necessary to me), no longer attracted me now that Albertine was no more. Albertine had seemed to me to be an obstacle interposed between me and all other things, because she was for me their container, and it was from her alone, as from a vase, that I could receive them. Now that this vase was shattered, I no longer felt that I had the courage to grasp things, and there was not one of them from which I did not now turn away, despondent, preferring not to taste it. So that my separation from her did not in the least throw open to me the field of possible pleasures which I had imagined to be closed to me by her presence. Besides, the obstacle which her presence had perhaps indeed been in the way of my travelling and enjoying life had merely (as always happens) concealed from me other obstacles which reappeared intact now that this one had been removed. Likewise, in the past, when some friendly call had prevented me from working, if on the following day I was left undisturbed I did not work any better. Let an illness, a duel, a runaway horse make us see death face to face, and how richly we should have enjoyed the life of pleasure, the travels in unknown lands, which are about to be snatched from us! And no sooner is the danger past than we resume once more the same dull life in which none of those delights existed for us.

No doubt these short summer nights last only for a brief season. Winter would at length return, when I should no longer have to dread the memory of drives with her until the too early dawn. But would not the first frosts bring back to me, preserved in their ice, the germ of my first desires, when at midnight I used to send for her, when the time seemed so long until I heard her ring at the door, a sound for which I might now wait everlastingly in vain? Would they not bring back to me the germ of my first anxieties, when twice I thought she would not come? At that time I saw her only rarely, but even those intervals between her visits which made her suddenly appear, after many weeks, from the heart of an unknown life which I made no attempt to possess, ensured my peace of mind by preventing the first inklings, constantly interrupted, of my jealousy from coagulating, from forming a solid mass in my heart. Soothing though they may have been at the time, in retrospect those intervals were stamped with pain since the unknown things she might have done in the course of them had ceased to be a matter of indifference to me, and especially now that no visit from her would ever occur again; so that those January evenings on which she used to come, and which for that reason had been so dear to me, would inject into me now with their biting winds an anxiety which was unknown to me then, and would bring back to me (but now grown pernicious) the first germ of my love. And when I thought of the recurrence of that cold season which, since the time of Gilberte and our games in the Champs-Elysées, had always seemed to me so melancholy, when I thought of evenings like that evening of snow when I had waited in vain for Albertine far into the night, then, like an invalid—in his case physically, fearing for his chest, in my case mentally—what at such moments I still dreaded most, for my grief, for my heart, was the return of the intense cold, and I said to myself that what it would be hardest to live through was perhaps the winter.

Linked as it was to each of the seasons, in order for me to discard the memory of Albertine I should have had to forget them all, even if it meant having to get to know them all over again, like an old man learning to read again after a stroke; I should have had to renounce the entire universe. Nothing, I told myself, but a veritable extinction of myself would be capable (but that is impossible) of consoling me for hers. It did not occur to me that the death of oneself is neither impossible nor extraordinary; it is effected without our knowledge, sometimes against our will, every day of our lives. And I should have to suffer from the recurrence of all sorts of days which not only nature, but adventitious circumstances, a purely conventional order, introduce into a season. Presently would return the day when I had gone to Balbec that last summer and when my love, which was not yet inseparable from jealousy and did not concern itself with what Albertine was doing all day, was to undergo so many vicissitudes, before becoming that very different love of recent months, that this final year, in which Albertine's destiny had begun to change and had received its quietus, appeared to me as full, as multiform and as vast as a whole century. Then it would be the memory of days more dilatory but dating from still earlier years, the rainy Sundays on which nevertheless everyone else had gone out, in the emptiness of the afternoon, when the sound of wind and rain would in the past have bidden me stay at home, to "philosophise in my garret"; with what anxiety would I see the hour approach at which Albertine, so little expected, had come to visit me, had caressed me for the first time, breaking off when Françoise had brought in the lamp, in that time now doubly dead when it had been Albertine who was curious about me, when my tenderness for her could legitimately cherish so many hopes! And even, later in the season, those glorious evenings when the doors and windows of pantries and shops and girls' schools, standing open to the view like wayside shrines, adorn the street with a diadem of those demi-goddesses who, conversing not far from us with others of their kind, fill us with a feverish longing to penetrate into their mythological existence, now reminded me only of the tenderness of Albertine, whose presence by my side had been an obstacle to my approaching them.

Moreover, to the memory even of hours that were purely natural would inevitably be added the psychological background that makes each of them a thing apart. When, later on, I should hear the goatherd's horn, on a first fine almost Italian morning, that same day would blend alternately with its sunshine the anxiety of knowing that Albertine was at the Trocadéro, possibly with Léa and the two girls, then the homely, familial sweetness, almost that of a wife who seemed to me then an embarrassment and whom Françoise was bringing home to me. That telephone message from Françoise which had conveyed to me the dutiful homage of an Albertine returning with her had seemed to me then to be a matter for pride. I was mistaken. If it had exhilarated me, it was because it had made me feel that she whom I loved was really mine, lived only for me, and even at a distance, without my needing to occupy my mind with her, regarded me as her lord and master, returning home at a sign from me. And thus that telephone message had been a fragment of sweetness, coming to me from afar, sent out from that Trocadéro district where there happened to be, for me, sources of happiness directing towards me molecules of comfort, healing balms, restoring to me at length so precious an equanimity of mind that I need do no more—surrendering myself without the slightest qualm or reservation to Wagner's music—than await the certain arrival of Albertine, without anxiety, with an entire absence of impatience in which I had not had the perspicacity to recognise happiness. And the cause of this happiness at the knowledge of her returning home, of her obeying me and belonging to me, lay in love and not in pride. It would have been quite immaterial to me now to have at my behest fifty women returning, at a sign from me, not from the Trocadéro but from the Indies. But that day, thinking of Albertine coming dutifully home to me as I sat alone in my room making music, I had breathed in one of those substances, scattered like motes in a sunbeam, which, just as others are salutary to the body, do good to the soul. Then there had been, half an hour later, the arrival of Albertine, then the drive with Albertine, both of which had seemed to me boring because they were accompanied for me by certainty, but which, because of that very certainty, had, from the moment of Françoise's telephoning to me that she was bringing Albertine home, poured a golden balm over the hours that followed, had made of them as it were a second day, wholly unlike the first, because it had a very different emotional basis, an emotional basis which made it a uniquely original day, one to be added to the variety of the days that I had previously known, a day which I should never have been able to imagine—any more than we could imagine the delicious idleness of a summer day if such days did not exist in the calendar of those through which we have lived—a day of which I could not say absolutely that I recalled it, for to this calm I added now an anguish which I had not felt at the time. But much later, when I went back gradually, in reverse order, over the times through which I had passed before I had come to love Albertine so much, when my healed heart could detach itself without suffering from Albertine dead, then I was able to recall at length without suffering that day on which Albertine had gone shopping with Françoise instead of remaining at the Trocadéro; I recalled it with pleasure as belonging to an emotional season which I had not known until then; I recalled it at last exactly, no longer injecting it with suffering, but rather, on the contrary, as we recall certain days in summer which we found too hot while they lasted, and from which only after they have passed do we extract their unalloyed essence of pure gold and indestructible azure.

So that these few years imposed upon my memory of Albertine, which made them so painful, successive colourings, the different modulations, the embers, not only of their seasons or of their hours, from late afternoons in June to winter evenings, from moonlight on the sea to daybreak on the way home, from snow in Paris to fallen leaves at Saint-Cloud, but also of each of the particular ideas of Albertine that I successively formed, of the physical aspect in which I pictured her at each of those moments, the degree of frequency with which I had seen her during that season, which itself appeared con-

sequently more or less dispersed or compact, the anxieties
which she might have caused me by keeping me waiting, the
charm which I may have had for her at such and such a
moment, the hopes formed and then shattered—all this modified the character of my retrospective sadness fully as much as
the impressions of light or of perfume which were associated
with it, and complemented each of the solar years through
which I had lived and which, simply with their springs, their
autumns, their winters, were already so sad because of the
inseparable memory of her, endowed it with a sort of sentimental counterpart in which the hours were defined not by the
sun's position, but by the time spent waiting for a rendezvous,
in which the length of the days or the changes in the temperature were measured by the soaring of my hopes, the progress of our intimacy, the gradual transformation of her face,
the journeys she had made, the frequency and style of the
letters she had written me during her absence, her more or less
eager anxiety to see me on her return. And lastly, if these
changes of weather, these variegated days, each brought me
back a different Albertine, it was not only through the evocation of similar moments. It will be remembered that always,
even before I began to love, each season had made me a
different person, swayed by other desires because he had other
perceptions, a person who, having dreamed only of cliffs and
storms overnight, if the indiscreet spring daybreak had insinuated a scent of roses through the gaps in the ill-fitting
enclosure of his sleep, would wake up on the way to Italy.
Even in the course of my love, had not the volatile state of my
emotional climate, the varying pressure of my beliefs, had they
not one day reduced the visibility of the love that I was feeling,
and the next day indefinitely extended it, one day embellished
it to a smile, another day condensed it to a storm? We exist
only by virtue of what we possess, we possess only what is
really present to us, and many of our memories, our moods,
our ideas sail away on a voyage of their own until they are lost
to sight. Then we can no longer take them into account in the
total which is our personality. But they know of secret paths by
which to return to us. And on certain nights, having gone to
sleep almost without missing Albertine any more—we can

only miss what we remember—on awakening I found a whole fleet of memories which had come to cruise upon the surface of my clearest consciousness and which I could distinguish perfectly. Then I wept over what I could see so plainly, though the night before it had been non-existent to me. In an instant, Albertine's name, her death, had changed their meaning; her betrayals had suddenly resumed their old importance.

How could she have seemed dead to me when now, in order to think of her, I had at my disposal only those same images one or other of which I used to recall when she was alive? By turns either swift-moving and bent over her handle-bars, as she was on rainy days, speeding through Balbec on her mythological wheels beneath the warrior's tunic of her waterproof, or else, on the evenings when we had taken champagne with us to the woods of Chantepie, her voice provocative, husky, altered, her face suffused with that warm pallor, tinged with red only on the cheekbones, which, unable to distinguish it in the darkness of the carriage, I drew into the moonlight, and which I tried now in vain to recapture, to see again in a darkness that would never end. A little statuette on the drive to the island in the Bois; plump, with slightly coarse-grained skin, at the pianola—by turns rain-soaked and swift, provoking and diaphanous, motionless and smiling, an angel of music. So that what I should have to annihilate in myself was not one, but innumerable Albertines. Each was attached to a moment, to the date of which I found myself carried back when I saw again that particular Albertine. And these moments of the past do not remain still; they retain in our memory the motion which drew them towards the future—towards a future which has itself become the past—drawing us along in their train. Never had I caressed the waterproofed Albertine of the rainy days; I wanted to ask her to take off that armour, in order to experience with her the love of the tented field, the fraternity of travel. But this was no longer possible, for she was dead. Never, either, for fear of corrupting her, had I shown any sign of comprehension on the evenings when she seemed to be offering me pleasures which, but for my self-restraint, she might not perhaps have sought from others, and which aroused in me now a frantic desire. I should not have found them the same in any other woman, but I might scour the whole world now without encountering the woman who was prepared to give them to me, for Albertine was dead. It seemed that I had to choose between two facts, to decide which of them was true, to such an extent was the fact of Albertine's death—arising for me from a reality which I had not known, her life in Touraine—in contradiction with all my thoughts of her, my desires, my regrets, my tenderness, my rage, my jealousy. So great a wealth of memories borrowed from the treasury of her life, such a profusion of feelings evoking, implicating her life, seemed to make it incredible that Albertine should be dead. Such a profusion of feelings, for my memory, in preserving my affection, left it all its variety. It was not Albertine alone who was a succession of moments, it was also myself. My love for her was not simple: to a curiosity about the unknown had been added a sensual desire, and to a feeling of almost conjugal sweetness, at one moment indifference, at another a furious jealousy. I was not one man only, but as it were the march-past of a composite army in which there were passionate men, indifferent men, jealous men—jealous men not one of whom was jealous of the same woman. And no doubt it would be from this that one day would come the cure for which I had no wish. In a composite mass, the elements may one by one, without our noticing it, be replaced by others, which others again eliminate, until in the end a change has been brought about which it would be impossible to conceive if we were a single person. The complexity of my love, of my person, multiplied and diversified my sufferings. And yet they could still be ranged in the two categories whose alternation had made up the whole life of my love for Albertine, swayed alternately by trust and by jealous suspicion.

If I found it difficult to imagine that Albertine, so alive in me (wearing as I did the double harness of the present and the past), was dead, perhaps it was equally paradoxical in me that this suspicion of the misdeeds which Albertine, stripped now of the flesh that had enjoyed them, of the mind that had conceived the desire for them, was no longer either capable of or responsible for, should excite in me such suffering, which I should only have blessed could I have seen it as the token of the spiritual reality of a person materially non-existent, instead of the reflection, destined itself to fade, of impressions that she had made on me in the past. A woman who could no longer experience pleasures with others ought no longer to have excited my jealousy, if only my tenderness had been able to come to the surface. But it was precisely this that was impossible, since it could not find its object, Albertine, save among memories in which she was still alive. Since, merely by thinking of her, I brought her back to life, her infidelities could never be those of a dead woman, the moment at which she had committed them becoming the present moment, not only for Albertine, but for that one of my various selves thus suddenly evoked who happened to be thinking of her. So that no anachronism could ever separate the indissoluble couple, in which each new culprit was immediately mated with a jealous lover, pitiable and always contemporaneous. I had, during the last months, kept her shut up in my own house. But in my imagination now, Albertine was free; she was abusing her freedom, was prostituting herself to this person or that. Formerly, I used constantly to think of the uncertainty of the future that stretched before us, and endeavour to read its message. And now, what lay ahead of me, like a counterpart of the future—as worrying as the future because it was equally uncertain, equally difficult to decipher, equally mysterious, and crueller still because I did not have, as with the future, the possibility, or the illusion, of influencing it, and also because it would go on unfolding throughout the whole length of my life without my companion's being present to soothe the anguish that it caused me—was no longer Albertine's future, it was her past. Her past? That is the wrong word, since for jealousy there can be neither past nor future, and what it imagines is invariably the present.

Atmospheric changes, provoking other changes in the inner man, awaken forgotten selves, counteract the torpor of habit, restore their old force to certain memories, to certain sufferings. How much more so with me if this change of weather recalled to me the weather in which Albertine, at Balbec, in the lashing rain, had set out, heaven knows why, on long rides, in the clinging tunic of her waterproof! If she had lived, no doubt to-day, in this so similar weather, she would be setting out on a comparable expedition in Touraine. Since she could do so no longer, I ought not to have suffered from the thought; but, as with people who have lost a limb, the slightest change in the weather revived the pain I felt in the limb that no longer existed.

Then a recollection that had not come back to me for a long time—for it had remained dissolved in the fluid and invisible expanse of my memory—suddenly crystallised. Many years ago, when somebody mentioned her bath-wrap, Albertine had blushed. At that time I was not jealous of her. But since then I had intended to ask her if she could remember that conversation, and why she had blushed. It had preoccupied me all the more because I had been told that the two girls who were friends of Léa's frequented the bathing establishment of the hotel, and, it was said, not merely for the purpose of taking showers. But, for fear of annoying Albertine, or else pending some more opportune moment, I had always put off mentioning it to her and in time had ceased to think about it. And all of a sudden, some time after Albertine's death, I recalled this memory, stamped with the character, at once tormenting and solemn, of puzzles left for ever insoluble by the death of the one person who could have explained them. Might I not at least try to find out whether Albertine had ever done anything wrong or even behaved suspiciously in that bathing establishment? By sending someone to Balbec, I might perhaps succeed in doing so. Had she been alive, I should doubtless have been unable to learn anything. But tongues become strangely loosened and will readily talk about a misdeed when the culprit's resentment need no longer be feared. As the constitution of our imagination, which has remained rudimentary and over-simplified (not having undergone the countless transformations which improve upon the primitive models of human inventions, whether it be the barometer, the balloon, the telephone, or anything else, which become barely recognisable in their ultimate perfection), allows us to see only a very few things at one time, the memory of the bathing establishment occupied the whole field of my inner vision. It was as though nothing else had ever happened in the whole of Albertine's life.

Sometimes I came into collision in the dark lanes of sleep with one of those bad dreams which are not very serious because for one thing the sadness they engender lasts for barely an hour after we awake, like the faintness caused by an artificial soporific, and for another we encounter them only very rarely, no more than once in two or three years. And, moreover, it remains uncertain whether we have encountered them before, whether they have not rather that aspect of not being seen for the first time which is projected on to them by an illusion, a subdivision (for duplication would not be a strong enough term). Of course, since I entertained doubts as to the life and the death of Albertine, I ought long since to have begun to make inquiries, but the same lassitude, the same cowardice which had made me give way to Albertine when she was with me prevented me from undertaking anything since I had ceased to see her. And yet, from a weakness that has dragged on for years, a flash of energy sometimes emerges. I decided to make this investigation at least, partial though it was.

I wondered who I could best send down to make inquiries on the spot, at Balbec. Aimé seemed to me to be a suitable person. Apart from his thorough knowledge of the place, he belonged to that category of working-class people who have a keen eye to their own advantage, are loyal to those they serve and indifferent to any form of morality, and of whom—because, if we pay them well, they prove themselves, in their obedience to our will, as incapable of indiscretion, lethargy or dishonesty as they are devoid of scruples—we say: "They are excellent people." In such we can have absolute confidence. When Aimé had gone, I thought how much more to the point it would have been if I could now interrogate Albertine herself about what he was going to try to find out down there. And at once the thought of this question which I would have liked to put, which it seemed to me that I was about to put to her, having brought Albertine to my side, not by dint of a conscious effort of resuscitation but as though by one of those chance encounters which, as is the case with photographs that are not posed, with snapshots, always make the person appear more alive, at the same time as I imagined our conversation I became aware of its impossibility; I had just approached from a new angle the idea that Albertine was dead, Albertine who inspired in me that tenderness we feel for absent ones the sight of whom does not come to correct the embellished image, inspiring also sorrow at the thought that this absence was eternal and that the poor child had been deprived for ever of the joys of life. And immediately, by an abrupt transposition, from the torments of jealousy I passed to the despair of separation.

What filled my heart now, instead of odious suspicions, was the affectionate memory of hours of confiding tenderness spent with the sister that her death had really deprived me of, since my grief was related not to what Albertine had been to me, but to what my heart, anxious to participate in the most general emotions of love, had gradually persuaded me that she was; then I became aware that the life that had bored me so (or so I thought) had been on the contrary delicious; the briefest moments spent in talking to her about even the most trivial things were now augmented, blended with a pleasure which at the time—it is true—had not been perceived by me, but which was already the cause of my having sought those moments so persistently to the exclusion of any others; the most trivial incidents which I recalled, a movement she had made in the carriage by my side, or when sitting down to dinner in her room, sent through my heart a surge of sweet sadness which gradually overwhelmed it altogether.

That room in which we used to dine had never seemed to me attractive; I had told Albertine that it was, merely in order that she should be content to live in it. Now, the sight of the curtains, the chairs, the books, had ceased to be a matter of indifference to me. Art is not alone in imparting charm and mystery to the most insignificant things; pain is endowed with the same power to bring them into intimate relation with ourselves. At the time I had paid no attention to the dinner which we had eaten together after our return from the Bois, before I went to the Verdurins', and towards the beauty, the solemn sweetness of which I now turned with my eyes full of tears. An impression of love is out of proportion to the other impressions of life, but when it is lost in their midst we are incapable of appreciating it. It is not from immediately below, in the tumult of the street and amid the thronging houses, but

when we have moved away, that, from the slope of a neighbouring hill, at a distance from which the whole town seems to
have vanished or forms only a confused heap at ground level,
we can appreciate, in the calm detachment of solitude and dusk,
the towering splendour of a cathedral, unique, enduring and
pure. I tried to embrace the image of Albertine through my
tears as I thought of all the serious and sensible things that she
had said that evening.

One morning, I thought I saw the oblong shape of a hill
swathed in mist, and sniffed the warm odour of a cup of
chocolate, while my heart was horribly wrung by the memory
of the afternoon on which Albertine had come to see me and
I had kissed her for the first time: the fact was that I had
heard the hiccough of the hot-water system which had just
been turned on. And I flung angrily away an invitation which
Françoise brought me from Mme Verdurin. How much more
forcibly the impression I had felt when I went to dine for the
first time at la Raspelière, that death does not strike us all at the
same age, overcame me now that Albertine had died so young,
while Brichot continued to dine with Mme Verdurin who was
still entertaining and would perhaps continue to entertain for
many years to come! At once the name of Brichot recalled to
me the close of that same evening when he had accompanied
me home, when I had seen from the street the light of Albertine's lamp. I had already thought of it many times, but I had
not approached this memory from the same angle. For, if our
memories do indeed belong to us, they do so after the fashion
of those country properties which have little hidden gates of
which we ourselves are often unaware, and which someone in
the neighbourhood opens for us, so that from one direction at
least which is new to us, we find ourselves back in our own
house. Then, when I thought of the void which I should now
find on returning home, when I realised that never again would
I see Albertine's window from the street, that its light was
extinguished forever, I remembered how that evening, on
leaving Brichot, I had felt irritated and regretful at my inability
to roam the streets and make love elsewhere, and I saw how
greatly I had been mistaken, that it was only because the
treasure whose reflections came down to me from above had

seemed to be entirely in my possession that I had failed to appreciate its value, so that it appeared necessarily inferior to pleasures, however slight, whose value I enhanced in seeking to imagine them. I realised all the plenitude, the life, the sweetness that that light which seemed to me to issue from a prison had contained for me; I realised that that life which I had led in Paris in a home which was also her home was precisely the realisation of that profound peace which I had dreamed of and believed forever impossible on the night when Albertine had slept under the same roof as myself in the Grand Hotel at Balbec.

Remembering the conversation I had had with Albertine after our return from the Bois before that party at the Verdurins', I would have been inconsolable had I felt that it had never occurred, that conversation which had to some extent involved Albertine in my intellectual life and in certain respects had made us one. For no doubt, if I returned with tender emotion to her intelligence and her sweetness to me, it was not because they had been any greater than those of other persons whom I had known; had not Mme de Cambremer said to me at Balbec: "What! you could be spending your days with Elstir, who is a genius, and you spend them with your cousin!" Albertine's intelligence pleased me because, by association, it reminded me of what I called her sweetness, as we call the sweetness of a fruit a certain sensation which exists only in our palate. And in fact, when I thought of Albertine's intelligence, my lips instinctively protruded and savoured a memory of which I preferred that the reality should remain external to me and should consist in the objective superiority of a person. There could be no denying that I had known people whose intelligence was greater. But the infinitude of love, or its egoism, brings it about that the people whom we love are those whose intellectual and moral physiognomy is least objectively defined in our eyes; we alter them incessantly to suit our desires and fears, we do not separate them from ourselves, they are simply a vast, vague arena in which to exteriorise our emotions. We do not have as clear an outline of our own body, into which so many sensations of pain and pleasure perpetually flow, as we have of a tree or a house or a passer-by. And where I had been wrong was perhaps in not making a greater effort to know Albertine in herself. Just as, from the point of view of her charm, I had long considered only the different positions that she occupied in my memory on the plane of the years, and had been surprised to see that she had become spontaneously enriched with modifications which were not due merely to the difference of perspective, so I ought to have sought to understand her character as that of an ordinary person, and thus perhaps, grasping the reason for her persistence in keeping her secret from me, might have avoided prolonging between us, what with that strange obstinacy of hers and my perpetual forebodings, the conflict which had led to her death. And I then felt, together with an intense pity for her, a sort of shame at having survived her. It seemed to me indeed, in the hours when I suffered least, that I had somehow benefited from her death, for a woman is of greater utility to our life if, instead of being an element of happiness in it, she is an instrument of suffering, and there is not a woman in the world the possession of whom is as precious as that of the truths which she reveals to us by causing us to suffer. In these moments, juxtaposing the deaths of my grandmother and of Albertine, I felt that my life was defiled by a double murder from which only the cowardice of the world could absolve me. I had dreamed of being understood by Albertine, of not being misjudged by her, thinking that it was for the great happiness of being understood, of not being misjudged, when so many other people could have done it better. One wants to be understood because one wants to be loved, and one wants to be loved because one loves. The understanding of others is a matter of indifference to us and their love importunate. My joy at having possessed a little of Albertine's intelligence and of her heart arose not from their intrinsic worth, but from the fact that this possession was a stage further towards the complete possession of Albertine, a possession which had been my goal and my dream ever since the day when I had first set eyes on her. When we speak of the "niceness" of a woman, we are doing no more perhaps than project outside ourselves the pleasure that we feel in seeing her, like children when they say: "My dear little bed, my dear little pillow, my dear little hawthorns." Which explains, incidentally, why men never say of a woman who is not unfaithful to them: "She is so nice," and say it so often of a woman by whom they are betrayed.

Mme de Cambremer was right in thinking that Elstir's intellectual charm was greater. But one cannot judge in the same way the charm of a person who is external to oneself like every other person, painted upon the horizon of one's mind, and that of a person who, as a result of an error in localisation consequent upon certain accidents but nevertheless tenacious, has lodged herself in one's own body to the point where wondering retrospectively whether or not she looked at a woman on a particular day in the corridor of a little seaside railway-train causes one the same pain as would a surgeon probing for a bullet in one's heart. A simple slice of bread, but one that we eat, gives us more pleasure than all the ortolans, leverets and francolins that were set before Louis XV, and the blade of grass quivering a few inches in front of our eyes as we lie on the hillside may conceal from us the vertiginous summit of a mountain if the latter is several miles away.

Moreover, our error does not lie in prizing the intelligence and amiability of a woman whom we love, however slight they may be. Our error is to remain indifferent to the amiability and intelligence of others. Falsehood begins to cause us the indignation, and kindness the gratitude, which they ought always to arouse in us, only if they come from a woman whom we love, and physical desire has the marvellous faculty of giving intelligence its true value and providing solid foundations for the moral life. Never should I find again that divine thing, a person with whom I could talk freely of everything, in whom I could confide. Confide? But did not others offer me greater confidence than Albertine? With others, did I not have more extensive conversations? The fact is that confidence and conversation are trivial things in themselves, and what does it matter if they are less than perfect if only there enters into them love, which alone is divine. I could see Albertine now, seated at her pianola, pink-faced beneath her dark hair; I could feel against my lips, which she would try to part, her tongue, her maternal, incomestible, nutritious, hallowed tongue, whose strange moist warmth, even when she merely ran it over the surface of my neck or my stomach, gave to those caresses of hers, superficial but somehow administered by the inside of her flesh, externalised like a piece of material reversed to show its lining, as it were the mysterious sweetness of a penetration.

I cannot even say that what I felt at the loss of all those moments of sweetness which nothing could ever restore to me was despair. To feel despair, we must still be attached to that life which can no longer be anything but unhappy. I had been in despair at Balbec when I saw the day break and realised that none of the days to come could ever be a happy one for me. I had remained just as selfish since then, but the self to which I was now attached, the self which constituted those vital reserves that bring the instinct of self-preservation into play, this self was no longer alive; when I thought of my inner strength, of my vital force, of what was best in me, I thought of a certain treasure which I had possessed (which I had been alone in possessing since others could not know exactly the feeling, hidden within myself, that it had inspired in me) and which no one could ever again take from me since I possessed it no longer. And in fact I had only ever possessed it because I had wanted to imagine myself as possessing it. I had not merely committed the imprudence, in looking at Albertine with my lips and lodging the treasure in my heart, of making it live within me, and that other imprudence of combining a quasi-domestic love with the pleasure of the senses. I had sought also to persuade myself that our relations were love, that we were mutually practising the relations that are called love, because she obediently returned the kisses that I gave her. And through having acquired the habit of believing this, I had lost not merely a woman whom I loved but a woman who loved me, my sister, my child, my tender mistress. And on the whole I had had a happiness and a misfortune which Swann had not experienced, for, after all, during the whole of the time in which he had loved Odette and had been so jealous of her, he had barely seen her, having found it so difficult, on certain days when she put him off at the last moment, to gain admission to her. But afterwards he had had her to himself, as his wife, and until the day of his death. I, on the contrary, while I was so jealous of Albertine, more fortunate than Swann, had

had her with me in my own house. I had experienced in
actuality what Swann had so often dreamed of and had experienced only when he had become indifferent to it. But, after
all, I had not managed to keep Albertine as he had kept Odette.
She had fled from me, she was dead. For nothing ever repeats
itself exactly, and the most analogous lives which, thanks to
kinship of character and similarity of circumstances, we may
select in order to represent them as symmetrical, remain in
many respects contrasting. And moreover the principal contrast (art) had not yet manifested itself.

By losing my life I should not have lost very much; I should
have lost only an empty form, the empty frame of a work of
art. Indifferent as to what I might henceforth put into it, but
happy and proud to think of what it had contained, I dwelt
upon the memory of those hours of sweetness, and this moral
support gave me a feeling of comfort which the approach of
death itself would not have disturbed. How she used to hasten
to see me at Balbec when I sent for her, lingering only to
sprinkle scent on her hair to please me! These images of Balbec
and Paris which I loved thus to see again were the pages, still
so recent, and so quickly turned, of her short life. All this,
which for me was only memory, had been for her action, action
speeding headlong, as in a tragedy, towards a swift death. For
people develop in one way inside us, but in another way outside us (I had felt this strongly on those evenings when I
remarked in Albertine an enrichment of qualities which was due
not only to my memory), and these two ways inevitably react
upon each other. Although, in seeking to know Albertine, then
to possess her entirely, I had merely obeyed the need to reduce
by experiment to elements meanly akin to those of our own ego
the mystery of every person, every place, which our imagination has made to seem different, and to impel each of our
profound joys towards its own destruction, I had been unable
to do so without in my turn exercising an influence over
Albertine's life. Perhaps my wealth, the prospect of a brilliant
marriage, had attracted her; my jealousy had kept her; her
kindness, or her intelligence, or her sense of guilt, or her shrewd
cunning, had made her accept, and had led me on to make
harsher and harsher, a captivity in chains forged simply by the

internal development of my mental toil, which had none the less
had repercussions on Albertine's life, themselves destined, by a
natural backlash, to pose new and ever more painful problems
to my psychology, since from my prison she had escaped to go
and kill herself on a horse which but for me she would not have
owned, leaving me, even after she was dead, with suspicions
the verification of which, if it was to come, would perhaps be
more painful to me than the discovery at Balbec that Albertine
had known Mlle Vinteuil, since Albertine would no longer be
there to soothe me. So that the long plaint of the soul which
thinks that it is living shut up within itself is a monologue in
appearance only, since the echoes of reality alter its course, and
a given life is like an essay in subjective psychology spontaneously pursued, but providing from a distance the "plot"
for the purely realistic novel of another existence, the vicissitudes of which come in their turn to inflect the curve and
change the direction of the psychological essay. How highly
geared had been the mechanism, how rapid had been the
evolution of our love, and, notwithstanding a few delays,
interruptions and hesitations at the start, as in certain of
Balzac's tales or Schumann's ballads, how sudden the dénouement! It was in the course of this last year, as long as a century
to me—so often had Albertine changed position in relation to
my thoughts between Balbec and her departure from Paris, and
also, independently of me and often without my knowing it,
changed in herself—that I must place the whole of that happy
life of tenderness which had lasted so short a while and which
yet appeared to me with an amplitude, almost an immensity,
which now was for ever impossible and yet was indispensable
to me. Indispensable without perhaps having been in itself and
at the outset something necessary, since I should not have
known Albertine had I not read in an archæological treatise a
description of the church at Balbec, had not Swann, by telling
me that this church was almost Persian, directed my taste to the
Byzantine Norman, had not a financial syndicate, by erecting at
Balbec a hygienic and comfortable hotel, made my parents
decide to grant my wish and send me to Balbec. To be sure, in
that Balbec so long desired, I had not found the Persian church
of my dreams, nor the eternal mists. Even the famous 1.22 train

had not corresponded to my mental picture of it. But in exchange for what our imagination leads us to expect and we give ourselves so much futile trouble trying to find, life gives us something which we were very far from imagining. Who would have told me at Combray, when I lay waiting for my mother's good-night with so heavy a heart, that those anxieties would be healed, and would then break out again one day, not for my mother, but for a girl who would at first be no more, against the horizon of the sea, than a flower upon which my eyes would daily be invited to gaze, but a thinking flower in whose mind I was so childishly anxious to occupy a prominent place that I was distressed by her not being aware that I knew Mme de Villeparisis? Yes, it was for the good-night kiss of such an unknown girl that, in years to come, I was to suffer as intensely as I had suffered as a child when my mother did not come up to my room. And yet if Swann had not spoken to me of Balbec, I should never have known this Albertine who had become so necessary, of love for whom my soul was now almost exclusively composed. Her life would perhaps have been longer, mine would have been devoid of what was now making it a martyrdom. And thus it seemed to me that, by my entirely selfish love, I had allowed Albertine to die just as I had murdered my grandmother. Even later, even after I had already got to know her at Balbec, it is possible that I might not have loved her as I eventually did. For, when I gave up Gilberte and knew that I might love another woman some day, I hardly dared entertain a doubt as to whether, at any rate as regards the past, I could have loved anyone else but Gilberte. Whereas in the case of Albertine I no longer even had any doubt, I was sure that it might well not have been her that I loved, that it might have been someone else. It would have been enough that Mme de Stermaria, on the evening when I was to dine with her on the island in the Bois, should not have cancelled the appointment. There was still time then, and it would have been upon Mme de Stermaria that I would have directed that activity of the imagination which makes us extract from a woman so special a notion of individuality that she appears to us unique in herself and predestined and necessary for us. At the most, adopting an almost physiological point of view, I could say that I might have been able to feel that same exclusive love for another woman but not for *any* other woman. For Albertine, plump and dark, did not resemble Gilberte, slim and fair, and yet they were fashioned of the same healthy stuff, and above the same sensual cheeks there was a look in the eyes of both whose meaning was difficult to grasp. They were women of a sort that would not attract the attention of men who for their part would go mad about other women who "meant nothing" to me. A man has almost always the same way of catching cold, of falling ill; that is to say, he requires for it to happen a particular combination of circumstances; it is natural that when he falls in love he should love a certain type of woman, a type which for that matter is very widespread. The first glances from Albertine which had set me dreaming were not absolutely different from Gilberte's first glances. I could almost believe that the obscure personality, the sensuality, the wilful, cunning nature of Gilberte had returned to tempt me, incarnate this time in Albertine's body, a body quite different and yet not without analogies. In Albertine's case, thanks to a wholly different life shared with me where no fissure of distraction or obliviousness had been able to penetrate a block of thoughts in which a painful preoccupation maintained a permanent cohesion, her living body had not, like Gilberte's, ceased one day to be the vessel in which I found what I subsequently recognised as being to me (what they would not have been to other men) the attributes of feminine charm. But she was dead. In time I would forget her. Who could say whether the same qualities of rich blood, of uneasy brooding would then return one day to create turmoil in me? But in what feminine form they would be embodied I could not foretell. The example of Gilberte would as little have enabled me to form an idea of Albertine and guess that I should fall in love with her, as the memory of Vinteuil's sonata would have enabled me to imagine his septet. Indeed, what was more, the first few times I had seen Albertine, I had even managed to believe that it was others I would love. Moreover, she might even have appeared to me, had I met her a year earlier, as dull as a grey sky in which dawn has not yet broken. If I had changed in relation to her, she herself had changed too, and the girl who had come

and sat on my bed on the day of my letter to Mme de Stermaria
was no longer the same girl I had known at Balbec, whether by
virtue of the explosion of womanhood which occurs at the age
of puberty, or as a result of circumstances which I was never
able to discover. In any case, even if the woman I was one day
to love must to a certain extent resemble her, that is to say if
my choice of a woman was not entirely free, this nevertheless
meant that, directed in a manner that was perhaps predetermined, it was directed towards something more considerable
than an individual, towards a type of woman, and this removed
all necessitude from my love for Albertine. We are well aware
that the woman whose face we have before our eyes more
constantly than light itself, since even with our eyes shut we
never cease for an instant to adore her beautiful eyes, her
beautiful nose, to arrange opportunities of seeing them again—
that this woman who to us is unique might well have been
another if we had been in a different town from the one in
which we met her, if we had explored other quarters of the
town, if we had frequented a different salon. Unique, we
suppose? She is legion. And yet she is compact and indestructible in our loving eyes, irreplaceable for a long time to come
by any other. The truth is that this woman has merely raised to
life by a sort of magic countless elements of tenderness existing
in us already in a fragmentary state, which she has assembled,
joined together, bridging every gap between them, and it is we
ourselves who by giving her her features have supplied all the
solid matter of the beloved object. Whence it arises that even
if we are only one among a thousand to her and perhaps the
last of them all, to us she is the only one, the one towards whom
our whole life gravitates. It was, indeed, true that I had been
quite well aware that this love was not inevitable, not only
because it might have crystallised round Mme de Stermaria,
but even apart from that, through knowing the feeling itself,
finding it to be only too like what it had been for others, and
also sensing it to be vaster than Albertine, enveloping her, unconscious of her, like a tide swirling round a tiny rock. But
gradually, by dint of living with Albertine, I was no longer able
to fling off the chains which I myself had forged; the habit of
associating Albertine's person with the sentiment which she

had not inspired made me none the less believe that it was peculiar to her, as habit gives to the mere association of ideas between two phenomena, according to a certain school of philosophy, the illusory force and necessity of a law of causation. I had thought that my connexions, my wealth, would dispense me from suffering, and only too effectively perhaps, since it seemed to dispense me from feeling, loving, imagining; I envied a poor country girl whom the absence of connexions, even by telegraph, allows to day-dream for months on end about a sorrow which she cannot artificially put to sleep. And now I began to realise that if, in the case of Mme de Guermantes, endowed with everything that must make the gulf between her and myself infinite, I had seen that gulf suddenly bridged by abstract opinion, for which social advantages are no more than inert and transmutable matter, so, in a similar albeit converse fashion, my social relations, my wealth, all the material means by which not only my own position but the civilisation of my age enabled me to profit, had done no more than postpone the conclusion of my struggle against the contrary, inflexible will of Albertine, upon which no pressure had had any effect—as in those modern wars where artillery preparations, the formidable range of weapons, merely delay the moment when men fling themselves on one another and it is the bravest heart that prevails. True, I had been able to exchange telegrams and telephone messages with Saint-Loup, to remain in constant communication with the post office at Tours, but had not the delay in waiting for them proved useless, the result nil? And country girls without social advantages or connexions, or human beings in general before these improvements of civilisation—do they not suffer less, because one desires less, because one regrets less what one has always known to be inaccessible, what for that reason has continued to seem unreal? One desires more the woman who has yet to give herself to us; hope anticipates possession; regret is an amplifier of desire. Mme de Stermaria's refusal to come and dine with me on the island in the Bois was what had prevented her from becoming the object of my love. It might also have sufficed to make me love her if afterwards I had seen her again in time. As soon as I knew that she would not come, entertaining the improbable hypothesis—which had been proved correct—that perhaps she had a jealous lover who kept her away from other men and that therefore I should never see her again, I had suffered so intensely that I would have given anything in the world to see her, and it was one of the most desolating agonies that I had ever felt that Saint-Loup's arrival had assuaged. But after we have reached a certain age our loves, our mistresses, are begotten of our anguish; our past, and the physical lesions in which it is recorded, determine our future. In the case of Albertine in particular, the fact that it was not necessarily she that I was predestined to love was inscribed, even without those circumambient loves, in the history of my love for her, that is to say for herself and her friends. For it was not even a love like my love for Gilberte, but was created by division among a number of girls. Conceivably it was because of her and because they appeared to me more or less similar to her that I had been attracted to her friends. The fact remains that for a long time it was possible for me to waver between them all, for my choice to stray from one to another, and when I thought that I preferred one, it was enough that another should keep me waiting, should refuse to see me, to make me feel the first premonitions of love for her. Often it might happen that, when Andrée was coming to see me at Balbec, if I had been preparing to say to her mendaciously, in order not to appear to care for her: "Alas! if only you'd come a few days earlier! Now I love someone else, but it doesn't matter, you can console me," Albertine would let me down shortly before Andrée's visit, my heart would throb without ceasing, I felt that I would never see her again and that it was she whom I loved. And when Andrée came it was quite truthfully that I said to her (as I said to her in Paris after I had learned that Albertine had known Mlle Vinteuil) what she might suppose me to be saying with an ulterior motive, insincerely, what I would indeed have said and in the same words had I been happy with Albertine the day before: "Alas! if you had only come sooner, now I love someone else." Even then, in this case of Andrée being replaced by Albertine after I learned that the latter had known Mlle Vinteuil, my love had alternated between them, so that after all there had been only one love at a time. But there had been previous cases where I had fallen out with two of the girls. The one who took the first step towards a reconciliation would restore my peace of mind, but it was the other that I would love if she remained hostile, which does not mean that it was not with the former that I would form a definitive tie, for she would console me—however ineffectually —for the harshness of the other, whom I would end by forgetting if she did not return to me. Now, it sometimes happened that, convinced though I was that one or the other at least would come back to me, for some time neither of them did so. My anguish was therefore twofold, and twofold my love; pending the likelihood of my ceasing to love the one who came back, in the meantime I continued to suffer on account of them both. It is our fate at a certain stage in life, which may come to us quite early, to be made less lovesick by a person than by a desertion, in which event we end by knowing one thing and one thing only about the person, her face being dim, her soul non-existent, our preference quite recent and unexplained: namely that what we need to make our suffering cease is a message from her: "May I come and see you?" My separation from Albertine on the day when Françoise had said to me: "Mademoiselle Albertine has gone" was like a very faint allegory of countless other separations. For very often, in order that we may discover that we are in love, perhaps indeed in order that we may fall in love, the day of separation must first have come.

In these cases, when it is an unkept appointment, a letter of refusal, that dictates one's choice, one's imagination, goaded by suffering, sets about its work so swiftly, fashions with so frenzied a rapidity a love that had scarcely begun and remained inchoate, destined, for months past, to remain in embryo, that there are times when one's intelligence, which has been unable to keep pace with one's heart, cries out in astonishment: "But you must be mad. What are these strange thoughts that are making you so miserable? None of this has anything to do with real life." And indeed at that moment, had one not been roused to action by the unfaithful one, a few healthy distractions that would calm one's heart physically would be sufficient to nip one's infatuation in the bud. In any case, if this life with

Albertine was not in its essence necessary, it had become indispensable to me. I had trembled when I was in love with Mme de Guermantes because I said to myself that, with her too abundant means of seduction, not only beauty but position and wealth, she would be too much at liberty to give herself to too many people, that I should have too little hold over her. Albertine, being penniless and obscure, must have been anxious to marry me. And yet I had not been able to possess her exclusively. Whatever our social position, however wise our precautions, when the truth is confessed we have no hold over the life of another person.

Why had she not said to me: "I have those tastes"? I would have yielded, would have allowed her to gratify them. In a novel I had read there was a woman whom no objurgation from the man who was in love with her could induce to speak. When I read the book, I had thought this situation absurd; had I been the hero, I assured myself, I would first of all have forced the woman to speak, then we could have come to an understanding. What was the good of all those futile miseries? But I saw now that we are not free to refrain from forging the chains of our own misery, and that however well we may know our own will, other people do not obey it.

And yet how often we had expressed them, those painful, those ineluctable truths which dominated us and to which we were blind, the truth of our feelings, the truth of our destiny, how often we had expressed them without knowing it, without meaning it, in words which doubtless we ourselves thought mendacious but the prophetic force of which had been established by subsequent events. I remembered many words that each of us had uttered without knowing at the time the truth that they contained, which indeed we had said thinking that we were play-acting and yet the falseness of which was very slight, very uninteresting, wholly confined within our pitiable insincerity, compared with what they contained unbeknownst to us—lies and errors falling short of the profound reality which neither of us perceived, truth extending beyond it, the truth of our natures, the essential laws of which escape us and require time before they reveal themselves, the truth of our destinies also. I had believed myself to be lying when I said to her at

Balbec: "The more I see you, the more I shall love you" (and yet it was that constant intimacy which, through the medium of jealousy, had attached me so strongly to her), "I feel that I could be of use to you intellectually"; and in Paris: "Do be careful. Remember that if you met with an accident, it would break my heart" (and she: "But I may meet with an accident"); in Paris too, on the evening when I had pretended that I wished to leave her: "Let me look at you once again since presently I shall not be seeing you again, and it will be for ever!" and she, when that same evening she had looked round the room: "To think that I shall never see this room again, those books, that pianola, the whole house, I cannot believe it and yet it's true." In her last letters again, when she had written (probably saying to herself that it was eye-wash): "I leave you the best of myself" (and was it not now indeed to the fidelity, to the strength—also too frail, alas—of my memory that her intelligence, her kindness, her beauty were entrusted?) and: "That doubly crepuscular moment, since night was falling and we were about to part, will be effaced from my thoughts only when the darkness is complete" (that sentence written on the eve of the day when her mind had indeed been plunged into complete darkness, and when, in those last brief glimmers which the anguish of the moment subdivides ad infinitum, she had indeed perhaps recalled our last drive together and in that instant when everything forsakes us and we create a faith for ourselves, as atheists turn Christian on the battlefield, she had perhaps summoned to her aid the friend whom she had so often cursed but had so deeply respected, who himself—for all religions are alike—was cruel enough to hope that she had also had time to see herself as she was, to give her last thought to him, to confess her sins at length to him, to die in him).

But to what purpose, since even if, at that moment, she had had time to see herself as she was, we had both of us understood where our happiness lay, what we ought to do, only when, only because, that happiness was no longer possible, when and because we could no longer do it—whether it be that, so long as things are possible, we postpone them, or that they cannot assume that force of attraction, that apparent ease of realisation save when, projected on to the ideal void of the imagination, they are removed from their deadening and degrading submersion in physical being. The idea that one will die is more painful than dying, but less painful than the idea that another person is dead, that, becoming once more a still, plane surface after having engulfed a person, a reality extends, without even a ripple at the point of disappearance, from which that person is excluded, in which there no longer exists any will, any knowledge, and from which it is as difficult to reascend to the idea that that person has lived as, from the still recent memory of his life, it is to think that he is comparable with the insubstantial images, the memories, left us by the characters in a novel we have been reading.

At any rate I was glad that before she died she had written me that letter, and above all had sent me that final message which proved to me that she would have returned had she lived. It seemed to me that it was not merely more soothing, but more beautiful also, that the event would have been incomplete without that telegram, would not have had so markedly the form of art and destiny. In reality it would have been just as markedly so had it been different; for every event is like a mould of a particular shape, and, whatever it may be, it imposes, upon the series of incidents which it has interrupted and seems to conclude, a pattern which we believe to be the only possible one, because we do not know the other which might have been substituted for it.

Why, I repeated to myself, had she not said to me: "I have those tastes"? I would have yielded, would have allowed her to gratify them; at this moment I would be kissing her still. How sad it was to have to remind myself that she had lied to me thus when she swore to me, three days before she left me, that she had never had with Mlle Vinteuil's friend those relations which at the moment when she swore it her blush had confessed! Poor child, she had at least had the honesty to be reluctant to swear that the pleasure of seeing Mlle Vinteuil again had no part in her desire to go that day to the Verdurins'. Why had she not made her admission complete? Perhaps, however, it was partly my fault that she had never, despite all my entreaties which were powerless against her denial, been willing to say to me: "I have those tastes." It was perhaps partly my fault because at Balbec, on the day when, after Mme de Cambremer's visit, I had had things out with Albertine for the first time, and when I was so far from imagining that she could possibly have had anything more than a rather too passionate friendship with Andrée, I had expressed with undue violence my disgust at those proclivities, had condemned them too categorically. I could not recall whether Albertine had blushed when I had naïvely expressed my horror of that sort of thing, for it is often only long afterwards that we long to know what attitude a person adopted at a moment when we were paying no attention to it, an attitude which, later on, when we think again of our conversation, would elucidate an agonising problem. But in our memory there is a blank, there is no trace of it. And very often we have not paid sufficient attention, at the actual moment, to the things which might even then have seemed to us important, we have not properly heard a sentence, have not noticed a gesture, or else we have forgotten them. And when later on, eager to discover a truth, we work back from deduction to deduction, leafing through our memory like a sheaf of written evidence, when we arrive at that sentence, at that gesture, we find it impossible to remember, and we repeat the process a score of times, in vain: the road goes no further. Had she blushed? I do not know whether she had blushed, but she could not have failed to hear, and the memory of my words had pulled her up later on when perhaps she had been on the point of confessing to me. And now she no longer existed anywhere; I could have scoured the earth from pole to pole without finding Albertine; the reality which had closed over her was once more unbroken, had obliterated every trace of the being who had sunk without trace. She was now no more than a name, like that Mme de Charlus of whom people who had known her said with indifference: "She was charming." But I could not conceive for more than an instant the existence of this reality of which Albertine had no knowledge, for in me she existed only too vividly, in me whose every feeling, every thought, related to her life. Perhaps, if she had known, she would have been touched to see that her lover had not forgotten her, now that her own life was finished, and would have been sensitive to things which in the past had left her indifferent. But as we would choose to abstain from infidelities, however secret, so fearful are we that she whom we love is not abstaining from them, I was terrified by the thought that if the dead do exist somewhere, my grandmother was as well aware of my forgetfulness as Albertine of my remembrance. And when all is said, even in the case of a single dead person, can we be sure that the joy we should feel in learning that she knows certain things would compensate for our alarm at the thought that she knows them *all*; and, however agonising the sacrifice, would we not sometimes forbear to keep those we have loved as friends after their death, for fear of having them also as judges?

My jealous curiosity as to what Albertine might have done was unbounded. I suborned any number of women from whom I learned nothing. If this curiosity was so tenacious, it was because people do not die for us immediately, but remain bathed in a sort of *aura* of life which bears no relation to true immortality but through which they continue to occupy our thoughts in the same way as when they were alive. It is as though they were travelling abroad. This is a thoroughly pagan survival. Conversely, when we have ceased to love, the curiosity which people arouse dies before they themselves are dead. Thus I would no longer have taken a single step to find out with whom Gilberte had been strolling on a certain evening in the Champs-Elysées. Now, I was well aware that these two forms of curiosity were absolutely identical, had no value in themselves, were incapable of lasting. But I continued to sacrifice everything to the cruel satisfaction of this transient curiosity, although I knew in advance that my enforced separation from Albertine, by the fact of her death, would lead me to the same indifference as had resulted from my voluntary separation from Gilberte.

If she could have known what was going to happen, she would have stayed with me. But this simply amounted to saying that, once she saw herself dead, she would have preferred to remain alive with me. Because of the very contradiction that it implied, such a supposition was absurd. But it was not innocuous, for in imagining how glad Albertine would be, if she could know, if she could retrospectively understand, to come back to me, I saw her before me, I wanted to kiss her, and alas, it was impossible, she would never come back, she was dead.

My imagination sought for her in the sky, at nightfall when we had been wont to gaze at it while still together; beyond that moonlight which she loved, I tried to raise up to her my tenderness so that it might be a consolation to her for being no longer alive, and this love for a being who was now so remote was like a religion; my thoughts rose towards her like prayers. Desire is powerful indeed: it engenders belief; I had believed that Albertine would not leave me because I desired that she should not do so. Because I desired it, I began to believe that she was not dead; I took to reading books about table-turning; I began to believe in the possibility of the immortality of the soul. But that did not suffice me. I required that, after my own death, I should find her again in her body, as though eternity were like life. Life, did I say? I was more exacting still. I should have liked not to be forever deprived by death of the pleasures of which in any case it is not alone in robbing us. For without it they would eventually have lost their edge; indeed they had already begun to do so through the effect of long-established habit, of fresh curiosities. Besides, had she been alive, Albertine, even physically, would gradually have changed; day by day I would have adapted myself to that change. But my memory, calling up only detached moments of her life, demanded to see her again as she would already have ceased to be had she lived; what it wanted was a miracle that would satisfy the natural and arbitrary limitations of memory, which cannot escape from the past. And yet, with the naïvety of the old theologians, I imagined this living creature vouchsafing me not simply the explanations which she might possibly have given me but, by a final contradiction, those that she had always refused me during her life. And thus, her death being a sort of dream, my love would seem to her an unlooked-for happiness; all I retained of death was the comfort and the optimism of a dénouement which simplifies, which settles everything.

Sometimes it was not so far off, it was not in another world, that I imagined our reunion. Just as, in the past, when I knew Gilberte only from playing with her in the Champs-Elysées, at home in the evening I used to imagine that I was about to receive a letter from her in which she would confess her love for me, that she was about to come into the room, so a similar force of desire, no more troubled by the laws of nature which inhibited it than on the former occasion, in the case of Gilberte (when after all it had not been mistaken since it had had the last word), made me think now that I was about to receive a message from Albertine, informing me that she had indeed had a riding accident but that for romantic reasons (and as, after all, has sometimes happened with people whom we have long believed to be dead) she had not wished me to hear of her recovery and now, repentant, asked to be allowed to come and live with me for ever. And—giving me an insight into the nature of certain mild lunacies in people who otherwise appear sane—I felt co-existing in me the certainty that she was dead and the incessant hope that I might see her come into the room.

I had not yet received news from Aimé, although he must by now have reached Balbec. No doubt my inquiry turned upon a secondary point, and one quite arbitrarily chosen. If Albertine's life had been really culpable, it must have contained many other things of far greater importance, which chance had not allowed me to consider as it had in the case of the conversation about the bathing-wrap and Albertine's blushes. But those things precisely did not exist for me since I had not seen them. But it was quite arbitrarily that I had hit upon that particular day and, several years later, was trying to reconstruct it. If Albertine had been a lover of women, there were thousands of other days in her life which I did not know how she had spent and about which it might be just as interesting for me to learn; I might have sent Aimé to many other places in Balbec, to many other towns besides Balbec. But these other days, precisely because I did not know how she had spent them, did not present themselves to my imagination, had no existence for it. Things and people did not begin to exist for me until they assumed in my imagination an individual existence. If there were thousands of others like them, they became for me representative of all the rest. If I had long felt a desire to know, in the matter of my suspicions with regard to Albertine, what exactly had happened in the baths, it was in the same manner in which, in the matter of my desires for women, and although

I knew that there were any number of young girls and lady's-maids who could satisfy them and whom chance might just as easily have brought to my notice, I wished to know—since it was of them that Saint-Loup had spoken to me—the girl who frequented houses of ill fame and Mme Putbus's maid. The difficulties which my health, my indecision, my "procrastination," as M. de Charlus called it, placed in the way of my carrying anything through, had made me put off from day to day, from month to month, from year to year, the elucidation of certain suspicions as well as the accomplishment of certain desires. But I retained them in my memory, promising myself that I would not forget to learn the truth of them, because they alone obsessed me (since the others had no form in my eyes, did not exist), and also because the very accident that had chosen them out of the surrounding reality gave me a guarantee that it was indeed in them that I should come in contact with a trace of the reality, of the true and coveted life. Besides, is not a single small fact, if it is well chosen, sufficient to enable the experimenter to deduce a general law which will reveal the truth about thousands of analogous facts? Although Albertine might exist in my memory, as she had successively appeared to me in the course of her life, only as a series of fractions of time, my mind, re-establishing unity in her, made her a single person, and it was on this person that I wished to arrive at a general judgment, to know whether she had lied to me, whether she loved women, whether it was in order to associate with them freely that she had left me. What the woman in the baths would have to say might perhaps put an end forever to my doubts as to Albertine's proclivities.

My doubts! Alas, I had supposed that it would be immaterial to me, even agreeable, not to see Albertine again, until her departure had revealed to me my error. Similarly her death had shown me how greatly I had been mistaken in believing that I sometimes wished for her death and supposed that it would be my deliverance. So it was that, when I received Aimé's letter, I realised that if I had not until then suffered too painfully from my doubts as to Albertine's virtue it was because in reality they were not doubts at all. My happiness, my life required that Albertine should be virtuous; they had laid it down once and for all that she was. Armed with this self-protective belief, I could with impunity allow my mind to play sadly with suppositions to which it gave a form but lent no credence. I said to myself, "She is perhaps a woman-lover," as we say "I may die to-night"; we say it, but we do not believe it, we make plans for the following day. This explains why, believing mistakenly that I was uncertain whether Albertine did or did not love women, and believing in consequence that a proof of Albertine's guilt would not tell me anything that I had not already envisaged, I experienced, in the face of the images, insignificant to anyone else, which Aimé's letter evoked for me, an unexpected anguish, the most painful that I had ever yet felt, and one that formed with those images, with the image, alas! of Albertine herself, a sort of precipitate, as they say in chemistry, in which the whole was indivisible and of which the text of Aimé's letter, which I isolate in a purely conventional fashion, can give no idea whatsoever, since each of the words that compose it was immediately transformed, coloured forever by the suffering it had just aroused.

"MONSIEUR,
"Monsieur will kindly forgive me for not having written sooner to Monsieur. The person whom Monsieur instructed me to see had gone away for a few days, and, anxious to justify the confidence which Monsieur had placed in me, I did not wish to return empty-handed. I have just spoken at last to this person who remembers (Mlle A.) very well." (Aimé, who possessed certain rudiments of culture, meant to put "Mlle A." in italics or between inverted commas. But when he meant to put inverted commas he put brackets, and when he meant to put something in brackets he put it between inverted commas. In the same way Françoise would say that someone *stayed* in my street meaning that he *dwelt* there, and that one could *dwell* for a few minutes, meaning *stay*, the mistakes of popular speech consisting merely, as often as not, in interchanging—as for that matter the French language has done—terms which in the course of centuries have replaced one another.) "According to her the thing that Monsieur supposed is absolutely certain. For one thing, it was she who looked after Mlle Albertine whenever

she came to the baths. (Mlle A.) came very often to take her
shower with a tall woman older than herself, always dressed in
grey, whom the shower-attendant without knowing her name
recognised from having often seen her going after girls. But
she took no notice of any of them after she met (Mlle A.). She
and (Mlle A.) always shut themselves up in the cabin, remained
there a very long time, and the lady in grey used to give at least
10 francs as a tip to the person I spoke to. As this person said
to me, you can imagine that if they were just stringing beads
they wouldn't have given a ten-franc tip. (Mlle A.) also used to
come sometimes with a woman with a very dark skin and a
lorgnette. But (Mlle A.) came most often with girls younger
than herself, especially one with very red hair. Apart from the
lady in grey, the people (Mlle A.) was in the habit of bringing
were not from Balbec and must even quite often have come
from quite a distance. They never went in together, but (Mlle
A.) would come in, and ask for the door of her cabin to be left
unlocked—as she was expecting a friend, and the person I spoke
to knew what that meant. This person could not give me any
other details as she did not remember very well, 'which is easy
to understand after such a long time.' Besides, this person did
not try to find out, because she is very discreet and it was to her
advantage because (Mlle A.) brought her in a lot of money.
She was quite sincerely touched to hear that she was dead. It is
true that so young it is a great calamity for her and for her
family. I await Monsieur's orders to know whether I may leave
Balbec where I do not think that I can learn anything more. I
thank Monsieur again for the little holiday that he has procured
me, and which has been very pleasant especially as the weather
is as fine as could be. The season promises well for this year.
Everyone hopes that Monsieur will come and put in a little
apparition.

"I can think of nothing else to say that will interest Monsieur," etc.

To understand how deeply these words penetrated my being,
it must be remembered that the questions which I had been
asking myself with regard to Albertine were not secondary,
insignificant questions, questions of detail, the only questions

in fact that one asks about anyone who is not oneself, whereby one is enabled to carry on, wrapped in the imperviousness of one's thoughts, through the midst of suffering, falsehood, vice and death. No, in Albertine's case they were essential questions: In her heart of hearts what was she? What were her thoughts? What were her loves? Did she lie to me? Had my life with her been as lamentable as Swann's life with Odette? Hence Aimé's reply, although it was not a general but a particular reply—indeed precisely because of that—struck home, in Albertine and in myself, to the quintessential depths.

At last I saw before my eyes, in that arrival of Albertine at the baths along the narrow lane with the lady in grey, a fragment of that past which seemed to me no less mysterious, no less horrifying than I had feared when I imagined it enclosed in the memory, in the look in the eyes of Albertine. No doubt anyone but myself might have dismissed as insignificant these details on which, now that Albertine was dead, my inability to secure a denial of them from her conferred the equivalent of a sort of probability. It is indeed probable that for Albertine, even if they had been true, even if she had admitted them, her own misdeeds (whether her conscience had thought them innocent or reprehensible, whether her sensuality had found them exquisite or somewhat insipid) would not have been accompanied by that inexpressible sense of horror from which I was unable to detach them. I myself, with the help of my own love of women, and although they could not have meant the same thing to Albertine, could more or less imagine what she felt. And indeed there was already an initial pain in my picturing her to myself desiring as I had so often desired, lying to me as I had so often lied to her, preoccupied with this or that girl, putting herself out for her, as I had done for Mlle de Stermaria and so many others, for the peasant girls I met on country roads. Yes, all my own desires helped me to a certain extent to understand hers; it was by this time an immense anguish in which all desires were transformed into torments that were all the more cruel the more intense they had been; as though in this algebra of sensibility they reappeared with the same coefficient but with a minus instead of a plus sign. To Albertine, so far as I was capable of judging her by my own standard, her misdeeds—

however anxious she might have been to conceal them from me (which made me suppose that she considered herself guilty or was afraid of hurting me)—because she had planned them to suit her own taste in the clear light of the imagination in which desire operates, must after all have appeared as things of the same kind as the rest of life, pleasures for herself which she had not had the strength to deny herself, griefs for me which she had sought to avoid causing me by concealing them from me, but pleasures and griefs which might be numbered among the other pleasures and griefs of life. But for me, it was from the outside, without my having been forewarned, without my having been able myself to elaborate them, it was from Aimé's letter that there had come to me the visions of Albertine arriving at the baths and preparing her tip. (Nevertheless I loved her more now; she was far away from me; presence, by distracting us from the only reality, the reality one thinks, allays suffering, and absence revives it, together with love.)

No doubt it was because in that silent and deliberate arrival of Albertine with the woman in grey I read the assignation they had made, that convention of going to make love in a shower-cabin, which implied an experience of corruption, the well-concealed organisation of a double life, it was because these images brought me the terrible tidings of Albertine's guilt, that they had immediately caused me a physical grief from which they would never be detached. But at once my grief had reacted upon them: an objective fact, an image, differs according to the internal state in which we approach it. And grief is as powerful a modifier of reality as intoxication. Combined with these images, my suffering had at once made of them something absolutely different from what might be for anyone else a lady in grey, a tip, a shower, the street which had witnessed the purposeful arrival of Albertine with the lady in grey: a vista of a life of lies and iniquities such as I had never conceived; my suffering had immediately altered them in their very essence; I did not see them in the light that illuminates earthly spectacles, they were a fragment of another world, of an unknown and accursed planet, a glimpse of Hell. My Hell was the whole region of Balbec, all those neighbouring villages from which, according to Aimé's letter, she frequently collected girls younger than herself whom she took to the baths. That mystery which I had long ago imagined in the country around Balbec and which had been dispelled after I had lived there, which I had then hoped to grasp again when I knew Albertine because, when I saw her pass by on the beach, when I was mad enough to hope that she was not virtuous, I thought that she must be its incarnation—how fearfully now everything that related to Balbec was impregnated with it! The names of those watering-places, Toutainville, Epreville, Parville, Apollonville, that had become so familiar, so soothing, when I heard them shouted at night as I returned from the Verdurins, now that I thought how Albertine had been staying at one, had gone from there to another, must often have ridden on her bicycle to a third, aroused in me an anxiety more cruel than on the first occasion, when I had observed them with such misgivings from the little local train with my grandmother before arriving at a Balbec which I did not yet know.

It is one of the faculties of jealousy to reveal to us the extent to which the reality of external facts and the sentiments of the heart are an unknown element which lends itself to endless suppositions. We imagine that we know exactly what things are and what people think, for the simple reason that we do not care about them. But as soon as we have a desire to know, as the jealous man has, then it becomes a dizzy kaleidoscope in which we can no longer distinguish anything. Had Albertine been unfaithful to me? With whom? In what house? On what day? On the day when she had said this or that to me, when I remembered that I had in the course of it said this or that? I could not tell. Nor did I know what her feelings were for me, whether they were inspired by self-interest or by affection. And all of a sudden I remembered some trivial incident, for instance that Albertine had wished to go to Saint-Martin-le-Vêtu, saying that the name interested her, and perhaps simply because she had made the acquaintance of some peasant girl who lived there. But it was useless that Aimé should have informed me of what he had learned from the woman at the baths, since Albertine must remain eternally unaware that he had informed me, the need to know having always been exceeded, in my love for Albertine, by the need to show her that I knew; for this broke down the partition of different illusions that stood between us, without having ever had the result of making her love me more, far from it. And now, since she was dead, the second of these needs had been amalgamated with the effect of the first: the need to picture to myself the conversation in which I would have informed her of what I had learned, as vividly as the conversation in which I would have asked her to tell me what I did not know; that is to say, to see her by my side, to hear her answering me kindly, to see her cheeks become plump again, her eyes shed their malice and assume an air of melancholy; that is to say, to love her still and to forget the fury of my jealousy in the despair of my loneliness. The painful mystery of this impossibility of ever making known to her what I had learned and of establishing our relations upon the truth of what I had only just discovered (and would not have been able, perhaps, to discover but for her death) substituted its sadness for the more painful mystery of her conduct. What? To have so desperately desired that Albertine—who no longer existed—should know that I had heard the story of the baths! This again was one of the consequences of our inability, when we have to consider the fact of death, to picture to ourselves anything but life. Albertine no longer existed; but to me she was the person who had concealed from me that she had assignations with women at Balbec, who imagined that she had succeeded in keeping me in ignorance of them. When we try to consider what will happen to us after our own death, is it not still our living self which we mistakenly project at that moment? And is it much more absurd, when all is said, to regret that a woman who no longer exists is unaware that we have learned what she was doing six years ago than to desire that of ourselves, who will be dead, the public shall still speak with approval a century hence? If there is more real foundation in the latter than in the former case, the regrets of my retrospective jealousy proceeded none the less from the same optical error as in other men the desire for posthumous fame. And yet, if this impression of the solemn finality of my separation from Albertine had momentarily supplanted my idea of her misdeeds, it only succeeded in aggravating them by bestowing upon them an irremediable character. I saw myself astray in life as on an endless beach where I was alone and where, in whatever direction I might turn, I would never meet her.

Fortunately, I found most opportunely in my memory—as there are always all sorts of things, some noxious, others salutary, in that jumble from which recollections come to light only one by one—I discovered, as a craftsman discovers the object that will serve for what he wishes to make, a remark of my grandmother's. She had said to me, with reference to an improbable story which the bath-attendant had told Mme de Villeparisis: "She is a woman who must suffer from a disease of mendacity." This memory was a great comfort to me. What significance could there be in the story she had told Aimé? Especially as, after all, she had seen nothing. A girl can come and take a shower with her friends without necessarily meaning any harm. Perhaps the woman had exaggerated the size of the tip in order to boast. I had indeed heard Françoise maintain once that my aunt Léonie had said in her hearing that she had "a million a month to spend," which was utter nonsense; another time that she had seen my aunt Léonie give Eulalie four thousand-franc notes, whereas a fifty-franc note folded in four seemed to me scarcely probable. And thus I sought to rid myself—and gradually succeeded in ridding myself—of the painful certainty which I had taken such trouble to acquire, tossed to and fro as I still was between the desire to know and the fear of suffering. Then my tenderness could revive anew, but, simultaneously with it, a sorrow at being parted from Albertine which made me perhaps even more wretched than I had been during the recent hours when it had been jealousy that tormented me. But the latter suddenly revived at the thought of Balbec, because of the vision which all at once reappeared (and which until then had never made me suffer and indeed appeared one of the most innocuous in my memory) of the dining-room at Balbec in the evening, with all that populace crowded together in the dark on the other side of the window, as in front of the luminous wall of an aquarium, watching the strange creatures moving around in the light but (and this I had never thought of) in its conglomeration causing the fisher-girls and other daughters of the people to brush

against girls of the bourgeoisie envious of that luxury, new to
Balbec, from which, if not their means, at any rate parsimony
and tradition excluded their parents, girls among whom there
had certainly been almost every evening Albertine whom I did
not know and who doubtless used to pick up some little girl
whom she would meet a few minutes later in the dark, upon
the sands, or else in a deserted bathing hut at the foot of the
cliff. Then my sadness would return as I heard like a sentence
of banishment the sound of the lift, which instead of stopping
at my floor went on higher. And yet the only person from
whom I could have hoped for a visit would never come again,
for she was dead. And in spite of this, when the lift did stop at
my floor, my heart leapt, and for an instant I said to myself:
"What if it was only a dream after all! Perhaps it's her—she's
going to ring the bell, she has come back, Françoise will come
in and say with more alarm than anger—for she's even more
superstitious than vindictive, and would be less afraid of the
living girl than of what she will perhaps take for a ghost—
'Monsieur will never guess who's here.' " I tried not to think
of anything, to take up a newspaper. But I found it impossible
to read all those articles written by men who felt no real grief.
Of a trivial song, one of them said: "It moves one to *tears*,"
whereas I myself would have listened to it with joy had
Albertine been alive. Another, albeit a great writer, having
been greeted with applause when he alighted from a train, said
that he had received "an *unforgettable* welcome," whereas I, if it
had been I who received that welcome, would not have given
it even a moment's thought. And a third assured his readers
that but for tiresome politics life in Paris would be "altogether
delightful," whereas I knew well that even without politics
that life could not but be odious to me, and would have seemed
to me delightful, even with politics, if I had found Albertine
again. The field sports correspondent said (we were in the
month of May): "This season of the year is truly distressing,
nay, catastrophic, to the true sportsman, for there is nothing,
absolutely nothing in the way of game," and the art critic said
of the Salon: "Faced with this method of arranging an exhibition one is overcome by an immense discouragement, by an
infinite gloom. . . ." If the strength of my feelings made me

regard as untruthful and colourless the expressions of men who had no true happiness or sorrow in their lives, on the other hand the most insignificant lines which could, however, remotely, be related either to Normandy, or to Touraine, or to hydrotherapeutic establishments, or to Léa, or to the Princesse de Guermantes, or to love, or to absence, or to infidelity, at once brought back before my eyes the image of Albertine, without my having the time to turn away from it, and my tears started afresh. In any case, usually I could not even read these newspapers, for the mere act of opening one of them reminded me at once that I used to open them when Albertine was alive, and that she was alive no longer; and I let it drop without having the strength to unfold its pages. Each impression called up an impression that was identical but marred, because Albertine's existence had been excised from it, so that I never had the heart to live to the end these mutilated minutes which suffered in my heart. Even when she gradually ceased to be present in my thoughts and all-powerful over my heart, I felt a sudden pang if I had occasion, as in the time when she was there, to go into her room, to grope for the light, to sit down by the pianola. Divided into a number of little household gods, she dwelt for a long time in the flame of the candle, the door-knob, the back of a chair, and other domains more immaterial such as a night of insomnia or the emotion that was caused me by the first visit of a woman who had attracted me. In spite of this the few sentences which I read in the course of a day, or which my mind recalled that I had read, often aroused in me a cruel jealousy. To do this, they required not so much to supply me with a valid proof of the immorality of women as to revive an old impression connected with the life of Albertine. Transported then to a forgotten moment the force of which had not been blunted by the habit of thinking of it, and in which Albertine still lived, her misdeeds became more immediate, more painful, more agonising. Then I asked myself whether I could be certain that the bath-attendant's revelations were false. A good way of finding out the truth would be to send Aimé to Touraine, to spend a few days in the neighbourhood of Mme Bontemps's villa. If Albertine enjoyed the pleasures which one woman takes with others, if it was in order not to be deprived of them any longer that she had left me, she must, as soon as she was free, have sought to indulge in them and have succeeded, in a neighbourhood which she knew and to which she would not have chosen to withdraw had she not expected to find greater facilities there than with me. No doubt there was nothing extraordinary in the fact that Albertine's death had so little altered my preoccupations. When one's mistress is alive, a large proportion of the thoughts which form what one calls one's love comes to one during the hours when she is not by one's side. Thus one acquires the habit of having as the object of one's musings an absent person, and one who, even if she remains absent for a few hours only, during those hours is no more than a memory. Hence death does not make any great difference. When Aimé returned, I asked him to go down to Châtellerault, and thus by virtue not only of my thoughts, my sorrows, the emotion caused me by a name connected, however remotely, with a certain person, but also of all my actions, the inquiries that I undertook, the use that I made of my money, all of which was devoted to the discovery of Albertine's actions, I may say that throughout the whole of that year my life remained fully occupied with a love affair, a veritable liaison. And she who was its object was dead. It is often said that something may survive of a person after his death, if that person was an artist and put a little of himself into his work. It is perhaps in the same way that a sort of cutting taken from one person and grafted on to the heart of another continues to carry on its existence even when the person from whom it had been detached has perished.

Aimé took lodgings close to Mme Bontemps's villa; he made the acquaintance of a maidservant, and of a jobmaster from whom Albertine had often hired a carriage by the day. These people had noticed nothing. In a second letter, Aimé informed me that he had learned from a young laundry-girl in the town that Albertine had a peculiar way of gripping her arm when she brought back the washing. "But," she said, "the young lady never did anything more." I sent Aimé the money to pay for his journey, to pay for the pain he had caused me by his letter, and meanwhile I was doing my best to heal it by telling myself that what he had described was a familiarity which gave no proof of any vicious desire, when I received a telegram from him: "Have learned most interesting things. Have heaps of news for Monsieur. Letter follows." On the following day came a letter the envelope of which was enough to make me tremble; I had recognised that it was from Aimé, for every person, even the humblest, has under his control those little familiar creatures, at once alive and reclining in a sort of torpor upon the paper: the characters of his handwriting which he alone possesses.

"At first the young laundry-girl refused to tell me anything, she assured me that Mlle Albertine had never done anything more than pinch her arm. But to get her to talk, I took her out to dinner and gave her plenty to drink. Then she told me that Mlle Albertine often used to meet her on the bank of the Loire, when she went to bathe, that Mlle Albertine, who was in the habit of getting up very early to go and bathe, was in the habit of meeting her by the water's edge, at a spot where the trees are so thick that nobody can see you, and besides there is nobody who can see you at that hour in the morning. Then the laundry-girl brought her girl friends and they bathed and afterwards, as it is already very hot down there and the sun beats down on you even through the trees, they used to lie about on the grass drying themselves and playing and stroking and tickling one another. The young laundry-girl confessed to me that she enjoyed playing around with her girl friends and that seeing that Mlle Albertine was always rubbing up against her in her bathing-wrap she made her take it off and used to caress her with her tongue along the throat and arms, even on the soles of her feet which Mlle Albertine held out to her. The laundry-girl undressed too, and they played at pushing each other into the water. After that she told me nothing more, but being always at your service and ready to do anything to oblige you, I took the young laundry-girl to bed with me. She asked me if I would like her to do to me what she used to do to Mlle Albertine when she took off her bathing-dress. And she said to me: (If you could have seen how she used to wriggle, that young lady, she said to me (oh, it's too heavenly) and she got so excited that she could not keep from biting me.) I could still see the marks on the laundry-girl's arms. And I can understand

Mlle Albertine's pleasure, for that young wench is really a very good performer."

I had suffered indeed at Balbec when Albertine told me of her friendship with Mlle Vinteuil. But Albertine was there to console me. Then, when by my excessive curiosity as to her actions I had succeeded in making Albertine leave me, when Françoise informed me that she was no longer in the house and I found myself alone, I had suffered even more. But at least the Albertine whom I had loved remained in my heart. Now, in her place—to punish me for having pushed even further a curiosity to which, contrary to what I had supposed, death had not put an end—what I found was a different girl, heaping up lies and deceit in an area where the other had so sweetly reassured me by swearing that she had never tasted the pleasures which, in the intoxication of her recaptured liberty, she had set out to enjoy to the point of swooning ecstasy, to the point of biting that young laundress whom she used to meet at sunrise, on the bank of the Loire, and to whom she used to say "Oh, it's too heavenly." A different Albertine, not only in the sense in which we understand the word different when we apply it to other people. If people are different from what we have supposed, as this difference does not affect us deeply, and the pendulum of intuition cannot swing outward with a greater oscillation than that of its inward swing, it is only in superficial areas of their being that we situate these differences. Formerly, when I learned that a woman loved other women, she did not seem to me on that account to be a quintessentially different woman. But in the case of a woman one loves, in order to rid oneself of the pain one feels at the thought that such a thing is possible, one wants to know not only what she has done, but what she felt while she was doing it, what she thought of what she was doing; then, probing ever more deeply, through the intensity of one's pain one arrives at the mystery, the quintessence. I suffered to the very depths of my being, in my body and in my heart, far more than the pain of losing my life would have made me suffer, from this curiosity to which all the force of my intelligence and my unconscious contributed; and thus it was into the core of Albertine's own being that I now projected everything that I learned about her.

And the pain that the revelation of her vice had thus driven into me to such a depth was to render me, much later, a final service. Like the harm that I had done my grandmother, the harm that Albertine had done me was a last bond between her and myself which outlived memory even, for with the conservation of energy which belongs to everything that is physical, suffering has no need of the lessons of memory. Thus a man who has forgotten the glorious nights spent by moonlight in the woods, suffers still from the rheumatism which he then contracted.

Those tastes which she had denied but which were hers, those tastes the discovery of which had come to me not by a cold process of reasoning but in the burning anguish I had felt on reading the words "Oh, it's too heavenly," an anguish that gave them a qualitative distinction, those tastes were not merely added to the image of Albertine as the new shell which it drags after it is affixed to the hermit crab, but rather as a salt which, coming in contact with another salt, alters not only its colour but, by a sort of chemical precipitate, its very nature. When the laundry-girl must have said to her friends, "Just fancy, I'd never have believed it, but the young lady is one too," to me it was not merely a vice hitherto unsuspected by them that they added to Albertine's person, but the discovery that she was another person, a person like themselves, speaking the same language, and this, by making her the compatriot of other women, made her even more alien to myself, proved that what I had possessed of her, what I carried in my heart, was only quite a small part of her, and that the rest, which was made so extensive by not being merely that thing which is already mysteriously important enough, an individual desire, but being shared with others, she had always concealed from me, had kept me away from, as a woman might conceal from me that she was a native of an enemy country and a spy, and far more treacherously even than a spy, for the latter deceives us only as to her nationality, whereas Albertine had deceived me as to her profoundest humanity, the fact that she did not belong to ordinary humankind, but to an alien race which moves among it, hides itself among it and never merges with it. I had as it happened seen two paintings by Elstir showing naked women in a thickly wooded landscape. In one of them, a girl is raising her foot as Albertine must have raised hers when she offered it to the laundress. With her other foot she is pushing into the water another girl who gaily resists, her thigh raised, her foot barely dipping into the blue water. I remembered now that the raised thigh made the same swan's-neck curve with the angle of the knee as was made by the droop of Albertine's thigh when she was lying by my side on the bed, and I had often meant to tell her that she reminded me of those paintings. But I had refrained from doing so, for fear of awakening in her mind the image of naked female bodies. Now I saw her, side by side with the laundry-girl and her friends, recomposing the group which I had so loved when I was sitting among Albertine's friends at Balbec. And if I had been an art-lover responsive to beauty alone, I should have recognised that Albertine re-composed it a thousand times more ravishingly, now that its elements were the nude statues of goddesses like those which the great sculptors scattered among the groves of Versailles or arrayed round the fountains to be washed and polished by the caresses of their waters. Now, beside the laundry-girl, I saw her as a water-maiden far more than she had been for me at Balbec: in their twofold nudity of marble statues in the midst of a grove of vegetation and dipping into the water like bas-reliefs of Naiads. Remembering Albertine as she lay on my bed, I seemed to see the curve of her thigh, I saw it as a swan's neck, seeking the other girl's mouth. Then I no longer even saw a thigh, but simply the bold neck of a swan, like the one that can be seen in a voluptuous sketch seeking the mouth of a Leda who is rapt in the palpitating specificity of feminine pleasure, because there is no one else with her but a swan, and she seems more alone, just as one discovers on the telephone the in-flexions of a voice which one fails to perceive so long as it is not dissociated from a face in which one objectivises its ex-pression. In this sketch, the pleasure, instead of reaching out to the woman who inspires it and who is absent, replaced by an expressionless swan, is concentrated in her who feels it. At moments the contact between my heart and my memory was interrupted. What Albertine had done with the laundry-girl was indicated to me now only by quasi-algebraic abbreviations which no longer meant anything to me; but a hundred times an hour the interrupted current was restored, and my heart was pitilessly scorched by a fire from hell, while I saw Albertine, resurrected by my jealousy, really alive, stiffen beneath the caresses of the young laundry-girl to whom she was saying: "Oh, it's too heavenly."

As she was alive at the moment when she committed her misdeed, that is to say at the moment at which I myself found myself placed, it was not enough for me to know of the misdeed, I wanted her to know that I knew. Hence, if at those moments I thought with regret that I should never see her again, this regret bore the stamp of my jealousy, and, very different from the lacerating regret of the moments when I loved her, was only regret at not being able to say to her: "You thought I'd never know what you did after you left me. Well, I know everything—the laundry-girl on the bank of the Loire, and your saying to her 'Oh, it's too heavenly,' and I've seen the bite." Of course I said to myself: "Why torment yourself? She who took her pleasure with the laundry-girl no longer exists, and consequently was not a person whose actions retain any importance. She isn't telling herself that you know. But neither is she telling herself that you don't know, since she isn't telling herself anything." But this line of reasoning convinced me less than the visual image of her pleasure which brought me back to the moment in which she had experienced it. What we feel is the only thing that exists for us, and we project it into the past, or into the future, without letting ourselves be stopped by the fictitious barriers of death. If my regret that she was dead was subjected at such moments to the influence of my jealousy and assumed such a peculiar form, that influence naturally extended to my thoughts about occultism and immortality, which were no more than an effort to realise what I desired. Hence, at those moments, if I could have succeeded in evoking her by table-turning as Bergotte had at one time thought possible, or in meeting her in the other life as the abbé X thought, I would have wished to do so only in order to say to her: "I know about the laundry-girl. You said to her: 'Oh, it's too heavenly,' and I've seen the bite."

What came to my rescue against this image of the laundry-girl—certainly when it had lasted for some time—was that image itself, because we only truly know what is new, what suddenly introduces into our sensibility a change of tone which strikes us, what habit has not yet replaced with its colourless facsimiles. But it was above all that fragmentation of Albertine into many parts, into many Albertines, that was her sole mode of existence in me. Moments recurred in which she had simply been kind, or intelligent, or serious, or even primarily addicted to sport. And was it not right, after all, that this fragmentation should soothe me? For if it was not in itself something real, if it arose from the continuously changing shape of the hours in which she had appeared to me, a shape which remained that of my memory as the curve of the projections of my magic lantern depended on the curve of the coloured slides, did it not in its own way represent a truth, a thoroughly objective truth too, to wit, that none of us is single, that each of us contains many persons who do not all have the same moral value, and that if a vicious Albertine had existed, it did not mean that there had not been others, the Albertine who enjoyed talking to me about Saint-Simon in her room, the Albertine who on the night when I had told her that we must part had said so sadly: "This pianola, this room, to think that I shall never see any of these things again" and, when she saw the distress which I had finally communicated to myself by my lie, had exclaimed with sincere pity: "Oh, no, anything rather than make you unhappy, I promise that I shall never try to see you again." Then I was no longer alone; I felt the barrier that separated us vanish. As soon as this good Albertine had returned, I had found once more the only person who could provide me with the antidote to the sufferings which Albertine was causing me. True, I still wanted to speak to her about the story of the laundry-girl, but no longer in order to score a cruel triumph and to show her maliciously how much I knew. I asked her tenderly, as I should have asked her had she been alive, whether the story about the laundry-girl was true. She swore to me that it was not, that Aimé was not very truthful and that, wishing to appear to have earned the money I had given him, he had not liked to return empty-handed, and had made the girl tell him what he wished to hear. No doubt Albertine had never ceased to lie to me. And yet, in the ebb and flow of her contradictions, I felt that there had been a certain progression due to myself. That she had not, indeed, confided some of her secrets to me at the beginning (perhaps, it is true, involuntarily, in a remark that escaped her lips) I would not have absolutely sworn. I no longer remembered. And besides, she had such odd ways of naming certain things that they could be interpreted one way or the other. But the impression she had received of my jealousy had led her afterwards to retract with horror what at first she had complacently admitted. In any case, Albertine had no need to tell me this. To be convinced of her innocence it was enough for me to embrace her, and I could do so now that the barrier that separated us was down, that impalpable but hermetic barrier which rises between two lovers after a quarrel and against which kisses would be shattered. No, she had no need to tell me anything. Whatever she might have done, whatever she might have wished to do, the poor child, there were sentiments in which, over the barrier that divided us, we could be united. If the story was true, and if Albertine had concealed her tastes from me, it was in order not to make me unhappy. I had the comfort of hearing this Albertine say so. Besides, had I ever known any other? The two chief causes of error in one's relations with another person are, having oneself a kind heart, or else being in love with that other person. We fall in love for a smile, a look, a shoulder. That is enough; then, in the long hours of hope or sorrow, we fabricate a person, we compose a character. And when later on we see much of the beloved being, we can no more, whatever the cruel reality that confronts us, divest the woman with that look, that shoulder, of the sweet nature and loving character with which we have endowed her than we can, when she has grown old, eliminate her youthful face from a person whom we have known since her girlhood. I recalled the kind and compassionate look in the eyes of that Albertine, her plump cheeks, the somewhat grainy texture of her neck. It was the image of a dead woman, but, as this dead woman was alive, it was easy for me to do immediately what I should inevitably have done if she had been by my side in her living body (what I should do were I ever to meet her again in another life), I forgave her.

The hours which I had lived through with this Albertine were so precious to me that I did not want to let any of them escape me. And occasionally, as one recovers the remnants of a squandered fortune, I recaptured some of them which I had thought to be lost: for instance, tying a scarf behind my neck instead of in front, I remembered a drive which I had never thought of since, during which, in order that the cold air might not reach my throat, Albertine had arranged my scarf for me in this way after first kissing me. That simple drive, restored to my memory by so humble a gesture, gave me the same pleasure as the intimate objects belonging to a dead woman who was dear to us which are brought to us by her old servant and which we find so precious; my grief was enriched by it, all the more so as I had never given another thought to the scarf in question. As with the future, it is not all at once but grain by grain that one savours the past.

Moreover my grief assumed so many forms that at times I no longer recognised it; I wanted to experience a great love; I wanted to find a woman who would live with me; this seemed to me to be the sign that I no longer loved Albertine, whereas it meant that I loved her still; for this need to experience a great love was, quite as much as the desire to kiss Albertine's plump cheeks, merely a part of my regret. And at heart I was happy not to fall in love with another woman; I realised that this continuing love for Albertine was like the ghost of the feeling I had had for her, reproducing its various stages and obeying the same laws as the sentimental reality which it reflected on the further side of death. For I was well aware that if I could extend the intervals between my thoughts of Albertine, I should have ceased to love her if the gap had been too wide; I should have become indifferent to her as I was now indifferent to my grandmother. Too much time spent without thinking of her would have broken, in my memory, the continuity which is the very principle of life, though it may recover and resume after a certain lapse of time. Had not this been the case with my love for Albertine when she was alive, a love which had been able to revive after a quite long interval

during which I had not given her a thought? My memory must
have been obedient to the same laws, must have been unable to
endure longer intervals, for it simply went on reflecting, like an
aurora borealis, after Albertine's death the feeling I had had for
her; it was like the phantom of my love. It was when I had
forgotten her that I might think it wiser and happier to live
without love. Thus my regret for Albertine, because it was it
that aroused in me the need of a sister, made that need un-
assuageable. And as my regret for Albertine grew fainter, the
need of a sister, which was only an unconscious form of that
regret, would become less imperious. And yet these two
residues of my love did not follow the same rate of progress in
their gradual decline. There were hours when I was determined to marry, so completely had the former been eclipsed,
while the latter on the contrary remained very strong. And on
the other hand, later on, my jealous memories having died
away, suddenly at times a feeling of tenderness for Albertine
would well up in my heart, and then, thinking of my own love
affairs with other women, I told myself that she would have
understood, would have shared them—and her vice became
almost a reason for loving her. At times my jealousy revived in
moments when I no longer remembered Albertine, although it
was of her that I was jealous. I thought that I was jealous of
Andrée, apropos of whom I heard at that time of an amorous
adventure she was having. But Andrée was to me merely a
substitute, a by-road, a connecting link which brought me
indirectly to Albertine. So it is that in dreams we give a
different face, a different name to a person as to whose underlying identity we are not mistaken. When all was said, notwithstanding the continuing ebb and flow which upset in these
particular instances the general law, the sentiments that Albertine had bequeathed to me were more difficult to extinguish
than the memory of their original cause. Not only the sentiments, but the sensations. Different in this respect from Swann
who, when he had begun to cease to love Odette, had not even
been able to recreate in himself the sensation of his love, I felt
myself still reliving a past which was now no more than the
story of another person; my personality was now somehow
split in two, and while the upper part was already hard and

chilled, it still burned at its base whenever a spark made the old current pass through it, even after my mind had long ceased to conceive of Albertine. And as no image of her accompanied the painful palpitations that were substituted for it, and the tears that were brought to my eyes by a cold breeze blowing as at Balbec through apple-trees already pink with blossom, I came to wonder whether the renewal of my grief was not due to entirely pathological causes and whether what I took to be the revival of a memory and the final period of a lingering love was not rather the first stage of heart-disease.

There are in certain affections secondary symptoms which the sufferer is too apt to confuse with the malady itself. When they cease, he is surprised to find himself nearer to recovery than he had supposed. Of this sort had been the suffering caused me—the "complication" brought about—by Aimé's letters with regard to the bathing establishment and the laundry-girls. But a spiritual healer, had such a person visited me, would have found that, in other respects, my grief itself was on the way to recovery. Doubtless, since I was a man, one of those amphibious creatures who are plunged simultaneously in the past and in the reality of the present, there still existed in me a contradiction between the living memory of Albertine and my consciousness of her death. But this contradiction was in a sense the converse of what it had been before. The idea that Albertine was dead, which at first used to contest so furiously with the idea that she was alive that I was obliged to run away from it as children run away from an oncoming wave, by the very force of its incessant onslaughts had ended by capturing the place in my mind that a short while before was still occupied by the idea of her life. Without my being precisely aware of it, it was now this idea of Albertine's death—no longer the present memory of her life—that for the most part formed the basis of my unconscious musings, with the result that if I interrupted them suddenly to reflect upon myself, what surprised me was not, as during the first days, that Albertine, so alive in me, could be no longer existent upon the earth, could be dead, but that Albertine, who no longer existed upon the earth, who was dead, should have remained so alive in me. Built up and held together by the contiguity of the memories that followed one another, the black tunnel in which my thoughts had lain dreaming so long that they had even ceased to be aware of it was suddenly broken by an interval of sunlight, bathing in the distance a blue and smiling universe where Albertine was no more than a memory, insignificant and full of charm. Was it she, I wondered, who was the true Albertine, or was it the person who, in the darkness through which I had so long been travelling, seemed to me the sole reality? The person I had been so short a time ago, who lived only in the perpetual expectation of the moment when Albertine would come in to say good-night and kiss him, was now made to appear to me, by a sort of multiplication of myself, as no more than a faint fragment of me, already half stripped away, and, like a flower unfolding its petals, I felt the rejuvenating refreshment of an exfoliation. However, these brief illuminations succeeded perhaps only in making me more conscious of my love for Albertine, as happens with every idea that is too constant, needing opposition to make it affirm itself. People who were alive during the war of 1870, for instance, say that the idea of war ended by seeming to them natural, not because they did not think enough about the war, but because they thought of it all the time. And in order to understand how strange and momentous a fact war is, it was necessary that, something else wrenching them out of their permanent obsession, they should forget for a moment that a state of war prevailed and should find themselves once again as they had been in peace-time, until all of a sudden, against that momentary blank, there stood out clearly at last the monstrous reality which they had long ceased to see, since there had been nothing else visible.

If only this withdrawal of my different impressions of Albertine had at least been carried out not in echelon but simultaneously, evenly, frontally, along the whole line of my memory, the recollections of her infidelities receding at the same time as those of her sweetness, forgetting would have brought me solace. It was not so. As upon a beach where the tide recedes unevenly, I would be assailed by the onrush of one of my suspicions when the image of her tender presence had already withdrawn too far from me to be able to bring me its remedial balm.

The betrayals had made me suffer because, however remote the year in which they had occurred, to me they were not remote; but I suffered from them less when they became remote, that is to say when I pictured them to myself less vividly, for the remoteness of a thing is in proportion rather to the visual power of the memory that is looking at it than to the real duration of the intervening days, as the memory of last night's dream may seem to us more distant in its imprecision and dimness than an event which is many years old. But, although the idea of Albertine's death made some headway in me, the reflux of the sensation that she was alive, if it did not arrest that progress, obstructed it nevertheless and prevented its being regular. And I realise now that during this period (doubtless because of my having forgotten the hours in which she had been cloistered in my house, hours which, by dispelling my anguish at misdeeds which seemed to me almost unimportant because I knew that she was not committing them, had become tantamount to so many proofs of her innocence), I underwent the martyrdom of living in the constant company of an idea quite as novel as the idea that Albertine was dead (until then I had always started from the idea that she was alive), with an idea which I should have supposed it to be equally impossible to endure and which, without my noticing it, was gradually forming the basis of my consciousness, substituting itself for the idea that Albertine was innocent: the idea that she was guilty. When I thought I was doubting her, I was on the contrary believing in her; similarly I took as the starting point of my other ideas the certainty—often proved false as the contrary idea had been—of her guilt, while continuing to imagine that I still felt doubts. I must have suffered a great deal during this period, but I realise that it had to be so. One is cured of suffering only by experiencing it to the full. By protecting Albertine from any contact with the outside world, by creating for myself the illusion that she was innocent, and also, later on, by adopting as the basis of my reasoning the thought that she was alive, I was merely postponing the hour of recovery, because I was postponing the long hours of necessary suffering that must precede it. Now with regard to these ideas of Albertine's guilt, habit, were it to come into play, would do so in accordance with the same laws as I had already experienced in the course of my life. Just as the name Guermantes had lost the significance and the charm of a road bordered with red and purple flowers and of the window of Gilbert the Bad, Albertine's presence that of the blue undulations of the sea, the names of Swann, of the lift-boy, of the Princesse de Guermantes and so many others, all that they had meant to me—that charm and that significance leaving me with a mere word which they considered big enough to stand on its own feet, as a man who comes to set a subordinate to work gives him his instructions and after a few weeks withdraws—similarly the painful knowledge of Albertine's guilt would be expelled from me by habit. Moreover between now and then, like an attack launched from both flanks at once, in this action undertaken by habit two allies would mutually lend a hand. It was because this idea of Albertine's guilt would become for me more probable, more habitual, that it would become less painful. But at the same time, because it would be less painful, the objections against my certainty of her guilt, which were inspired in my mind only by my desire not to suffer too acutely, would collapse one by one; and, one action precipitating another, I should pass quickly enough from the certainty of Albertine's innocence to the certainty of her guilt. I had to live with the idea of Albertine's death, with the idea of her misdeeds, in order for these ideas to become habitual, that is to say in order to be able to forget these ideas and in the end forget Albertine herself.

I had not yet reached this stage. At one time it was my memory, made clearer by some intellectual excitement—such as reading a book—which revived my grief; at other times it was on the contrary my grief—when it was aroused, for instance, by the anguish of a spell of stormy weather—which raised higher, brought nearer to the light, some memory of our love.

Moreover these revivals of my love for Albertine might occur after an interval of indifference interspersed with other curiosities, as, after the long interval which had begun with her refusal to let me kiss her at Balbec and during which I had thought far more about Mme de Guermantes, about Andrée, about Mlle de Stermaria, it had revived when I had started

seeing her regularly again. But even now various preoccupations could bring about a separation—from a dead woman, this
time—in which she left me more indifferent. All this for the
same reason, that she was a living person for me. And even
later on, when I loved her less, it remained nevertheless for me
one of those desires of which we quickly tire, but which revive
when we have allowed them to lie dormant for a while. I pursued one living woman, then another, then I returned to my
dead one. Often it was in the most obscure recesses of myself,
when I could no longer form any clear idea of Albertine, that
a name would come by chance to stimulate painful reactions
which I supposed to be no longer possible, like those dying
people whose brain is no longer capable of thought and who
are made to contract their muscles by the prick of a needle.
And, during long periods, these stimulations occurred to me
so rarely that I was driven to seek for myself occasions for
grief, for a pang of jealousy, in an attempt to re-establish contact with the past, to remember her better. For, since regret for
a woman is only a recrudescence of love and remains subject to
the same laws, the keenness of my regret was intensified by the
same causes which in Albertine's lifetime had increased my love
for her and in the front rank of which had always appeared
jealousy and grief. But as a rule these occasions—for an illness
or a war can always last far longer than the most prophetic
wisdom has calculated—took me unawares and caused me such
violent shocks that I thought far more of protecting myself
against suffering than of appealing to them for a memory.

Moreover a word did not even need to be connected, like
"Chaumont," with some suspicion (even a syllable common to
two different names was sufficient for my memory—as for an
electrician who is happy with any substance that is a good
conductor—to restore the contact between Albertine and my
heart) in order to reawaken that suspicion, to be the password,
the "Open Sesame" unlocking the door of a past which one
had ceased to take into account because, having seen more than
enough of it, literally one no longer possessed it; one had been
shorn of it, had supposed that by this subtraction one's own
personality had changed its form, like a geometrical figure
which by the removal of an angle would lose one of its sides;

certain phrases, for instance, in which there occurred the name of a street or a road where Albertine might have been, were sufficient to incarnate a potential, non-existent jealousy, in the quest of a body, a dwelling, some physical location, some particular realisation.

Often it was simply during my sleep that these "reprises," these "da capos" of one's dreams, which turn back several pages of one's memory, several leaves of the calendar at once, brought me back, made me regress to a painful but remote impression which had long since given place to others but which now became present once more. As a rule, it was accompanied by a whole stage-setting, clumsy but striking, which, giving me the illusion of reality, brought before my eyes, voiced in my ears, what thenceforward dated from that night. Besides, in the history of a love-affair and of its struggles against forgetfulness, do not our dreams occupy an even larger place than our waking state, since they take no account of the infinitesimal divisions of time, suppress transitions, oppose sharp contrasts, undo in an instant the web of consolation so slowly woven during the day, and contrive for us, by night, a meeting with her whom we would eventually have forgotten, provided always that we did not see her again? For whatever people may say, we can perfectly well have in a dream the impression that what is happening in it is real. It would be impossible only for reasons drawn from our waking experience, an experience which at that moment is hidden from us. With the result that this supposititious life seems to us real. Sometimes, by a defect in the internal lighting which spoiled the success of the play, my well-staged memories giving me the illusion of life, I really believed that I had arranged to meet Albertine, that I was seeing her again, but then I found myself incapable of advancing to meet her, of uttering the words which I meant to say to her, of relighting in order to see her the torch that had gone out—impossibilities which were simply in my dream the immobility, the dumbness, the blindness of the sleeper—as suddenly one sees a huge shadow which ought not to be visible obliterate the figures on the screen of a magic lantern, a shadow which is that of the lantern itself, or that of the operator. At other times Albertine was present in my dream, and proposed to leave me once again, without my being moved by her resolve. This was because a warning ray of light had managed to filter into the darkness of my sleep, and what deprived Albertine's future actions, her threatened departure, of any importance for me was the knowledge that she was dead. But often, even more clearly, this memory that Albertine was dead was combined, without destroying it, with the sensation that she was alive. I chatted to her, and while I was speaking my grandmother moved to and fro at the back of the room. Part of her chin had crumbled away like a corroded statue, but I found nothing unusual in that. I told Albertine that I had various questions to ask her with regard to the bathing establishment at Balbec, and to a certain laundress in Touraine, but I would put them off till later since we had plenty of time and there was no longer any urgency. She assured me that she was not doing anything wrong and that she had merely, the day before, kissed Mlle Vinteuil on the lips. "What? Is she here?" "Yes, in fact it's time for me to leave you, as I have to go and see her presently." And since, now that Albertine was dead, I no longer kept her a prisoner in my house as in the last months of her life, her visit to Mlle Vinteuil perturbed me. I did not want to show it; Albertine told me that she had done no more than kiss her, but she was evidently beginning to lie again as in the days when she used to deny everything. Presently, no doubt, she would not be content merely with kissing Mlle Vinteuil. Doubtless from a certain point of view I was wrong to let myself be disturbed like this, since, according to what we are told, the dead can feel nothing, can do nothing. People say so, but this did not alter the fact that my grandmother, who was dead, had continued nevertheless to live for many years, and at that moment was walking to and fro in my room. And no doubt, once I was awake, this idea of a dead woman who continued to live ought to have become as impossible for me to understand as it is to explain. But I had already formed it so many times in the course of those transient periods of madness which are our dreams, that I had become in time familiar with it; our memory of dreams may become lasting, if they repeat themselves often enough. And long after my dream had ended, I remained tormented by that kiss which Albertine had told me

she had given in words which I thought I could still hear. And
indeed they must have passed very close to my ear since it was
I myself who had uttered them. All day long, I continued to
talk to Albertine; I questioned her, I forgave her, I made up for
my forgetfulness of the things which I had always meant to say
to her during her life. And all of a sudden I was startled by the
thought that the creature invoked by memory to whom all
these remarks were addressed no longer bore any relation to
reality, that death had destroyed the various parts of the face to
which the continual thrust of the will to live, now abolished,
had alone given the unity of a person.

At other times, without my having dreamed, as soon as I
awoke I felt that the wind had changed in me; it was blowing
coldly and steadily from another direction, issuing from the
remotest past, bringing back to me the sound of a clock striking
far-off hours, of the whistle of departing trains which I did not
ordinarily hear. One day I tried to interest myself in a book. I
reopened a novel by Bergotte of which I had been especially
fond. Its congenial characters appealed to me greatly, and very
soon, reconquered by the charm of the book, I began to hope,
as for a personal pleasure, that the wicked woman might be
punished, while my eyes grew moist when the happiness of the
young lovers was assured. "But then," I exclaimed in despair,
"I cannot conclude, from the fact that I attach so much importance to what Albertine may have done, that her personality
is something real which cannot be destroyed, that I shall find
her one day in her own likeness in heaven, if I invoke with so
many entreaties, await with such impatience, welcome with
such floods of tears the success of a person who has never
existed save in Bergotte's imagination, whom I have never seen,
whose appearance I am at liberty to imagine as I please!"
Besides, in this novel, there were seductive girls, amorous
correspondences, deserted paths in which lovers meet, and all
this, reminding me that one may love clandestinely, revived my
jealousy, as though Albertine had still been able to stroll along
deserted paths. And the novel also pictured a man who after
fifty years meets a woman whom he loved in her youth, fails to
recognise her, is bored in her company. And this reminded me
that love does not last for ever and shattered me as though I

were destined to be parted from Albertine and to meet her
again with indifference in my old age. If I caught sight of a map
of France, my fearful eyes took care not to fall upon Touraine
so that I might not be jealous, nor, so that I might not be
miserable, upon Normandy, where would certainly be indicated at least Balbec and Doncières, between which I could
situate all those places we had traversed so many times together. In the midst of other names of towns or villages of
France, names which were merely visible or audible, the name
of Tours, for instance, seemed to be differently composed, to be
made up, not of intangible images, but of venomous substances
which acted instantaneously on my heart, making it beat faster
and more painfully. And if this force extended to certain names,
making them so different from the rest, how, when I stayed
closer to myself, when I confined myself to Albertine herself,
could I be astonished that this force which I found irresistible,
and to produce which any other woman might have served,
had been the result of an entanglement, of a bringing into contact of dreams, desires, habits, affections, with the requisite
conjunction of alternating pains and pleasures? And this continued her life in death, memory being sufficient to sustain the
reality of life, which is mental. I recalled Albertine alighting
from a railway carriage and telling me that she wanted to go to
Saint-Mars-le-Vêtu, and I saw her again before that, with her
"polo" pulled down over her cheeks; I thought of new possibilities of happiness, towards which I sprang, saying to myself:
"We might have gone on together to Quimperlé, to Pont-
Aven." There was no watering-place in the neighbourhood of
Balbec in which I did not see her, with the result that that
country, like a mythological land which had been preserved,
restored to me, living and cruel, the most ancient, the most
charming legends, those that had been most obliterated by the
sequel of my love. Ah, what anguish were I ever to have to
sleep again in that bed at Balbec around whose brass frame, as
around an immovable pivot, a fixed bar, my life had moved and
evolved, bringing successively into its compass gay conversations with my grandmother, the nightmare of her death,
Albertine's soothing caresses, the discovery of her vice, and
now a new life into which, looking at the glazed bookcases in

which the sea was reflected, I knew that Albertine would never come again! Was it not, that Balbec hotel, like the single set of a provincial theatre, in which for years past the most diverse plays have been performed, which has served for a comedy, for first one tragedy, then another, for a purely poetical drama, that hotel which already stretched quite far back into my past, with invariably, within its walls, new periods of my life? The fact that this part alone remained always the same, with its walls, its bookcases, its mirror, made me better aware that, all in all, it was everything else, it was myself that had changed, and gave me thus that impression which children do not have, believing in their pessimistic optimism that the mysteries of life, of love, of death are reserved, that they have no share in them, and which one perceives with sorrowful pride to have formed an integral part of one's own life through the course of the years.

I tried at times to take an interest in the newspapers. But I found the act of reading them repellent, and moreover by no means innocuous. The fact is that from each of our ideas, as from a crossroads in a forest, so many paths branch off in different directions that at the moment when I least expected it I found myself faced by a fresh memory. The title of Fauré's melody *le Secret* had led me to the Duc de Broglie's *Secret du Roi*, the name Broglie to that of Chaumont;[27] or else the words "Good Friday" had made me think of Golgotha, Golgotha of the etymology of the word which is, it seems, the equivalent of *Calvus Mons*, Chaumont. But, whatever the path by which I had arrived at Chaumont, at that moment I received so violent a shock that I was far more concerned to ward off pain than to probe for memories. Some moments after the shock, my intelligence, which like the sound of thunder travels less rapidly, produced the reason for it. Chaumont had made me think of the Buttes-Chaumont, where Mme Bontemps had told me that Andrée used often to go with Albertine, whereas Albertine had told me that she had never seen the Buttes-Chaumont. After a certain age our memories are so intertwined with one another that what we are thinking of, the book we are reading, scarcely matters any more. We have put something of ourselves everywhere, everything is fertile, everything is dangerous, and we can make discoveries no less precious than in Pascal's *Pensées* in an advertisement for soap.

No doubt a fact such as the one about the Buttes-Chaumont, which at the time had appeared to me trifling, was in itself far less serious, far less decisive evidence against Albertine than the story of the bath-attendant or the laundry-girl. But in the first place, a memory which comes to one fortuitously finds in one an intact capacity for imagining, that is to say in this case for suffering, which one has partly used up when one has deliberately applied one's mind to recreating a memory. And then to these latter memories (those that concerned the bath-attendant and the laundry-girl), ever present albeit obscured in my consciousness, like the furniture placed in the semi-darkness of a gallery which, without being able to see, one avoids knocking into, I had grown accustomed. Whereas it was a long time since I had given a thought to the Buttes-Chaumont, or, to take another instance, to Albertine's scrutiny of the mirror in the casino at Balbec, or to her unexplained delay on the evening when I had waited so long for her after the Guer-mantes party, or any of those parts of her life which remained outside my heart and which I would have liked to know in order that they might become assimilated, annexed to it, merged with the sweeter memories formed therein by an interior Albertine, an Albertine genuinely possessed. Lifting a corner of the heavy curtain of habit (stupefying habit, which during the whole course of our life conceals from us almost the whole universe, and in the dead of night, without changing the label, substitutes for the most dangerous or intoxicating poisons of life something anodyne that procures no delights), such memories would come back to me as at the time itself with that fresh and piercing novelty of a recurring season, of a change in the routine of our hours, which, in the realm of pleasures also, if we get into a carriage on the first fine day in spring, or leave the house at sunrise, makes us observe our own most trivial actions with a lucid exaltation which makes that intense minute worth more than the sum-total of the preceding days. Days in the past cover up little by little those that preceded them and are themselves buried beneath those that follow them. But each past day has remained deposited in us, as in a vast library where, even of the oldest books, there is a copy which doubtless nobody will ever ask to see. And yet should this day from the past, traversing the translucency of the intervening epochs, rise to the surface and spread itself inside us until it covers us entirely, then for a moment names resume their former meaning, people their former aspect, we ourselves our state of mind at the time, and we feel, with a vague suffering which however is endurable and will not last for long, the problems which have long ago become insoluble and which caused us such anguish at the time. Our ego is composed of the superimposition of our successive states. But this superimposition is not unalterable like the stratification of a mountain. Incessant upheavals raise to the surface ancient deposits. I found myself once more after the party at the Princesse de Guermantes's, awaiting Albertine's arrival. What had she been doing that evening? Had she been unfaithful to me? With whom? Aimé's revelations, even if I accepted them, in no way diminished for me the anxious, despairing interest of this unexpected question, as though each different Albertine, each new memory, set a special problem of jealousy, to which the solutions of the other problems could not apply.

But I would have liked to know not only with what woman she had spent that evening, but what special pleasure it represented to her, what was happening inside her at that moment. Sometimes, at Balbec, Françoise had gone to fetch her, and had told me that she had found her leaning out of her window with an anxious, questing air, as though she were expecting somebody. Supposing I learned that the girl she was awaiting was Andrée—what was the state of mind in which Albertine awaited her, that state of mind concealed behind the anxious, questing gaze? How important were those tastes to Albertine? How large a place did they occupy in her thoughts? Alas, remembering my own agitation whenever I had caught sight of a girl who attracted me, sometimes when I had merely heard her spoken of without having seen her, my anxiety to look my best, to show myself to advantage, my cold sweats, I had only, in order to torture myself, to imagine the same voluptuous excitement in Albertine, as though by means of the apparatus which, after the visit of a certain practitioner who had shown some scepticism about her malady, my aunt Léonie had wished to see invented, and which would enable the doctor to undergo all the sufferings of his patient in order to understand better. And already it was enough to torture me, to tell me that, compared with this other thing, serious conversations with me about Stendhal and Victor Hugo must have counted for very little with her, to feel her heart being drawn towards other people, detaching itself from mine, implanting itself elsewhere. But even the importance which this desire must have for her and the reserve with which she surrounded it could not reveal to me what it was qualitatively, still less how she referred to it when she spoke of it to herself. In physical suffering, at least we do not have to choose our pain ourselves. The malady determines it and imposes it on us. But in jealousy we have, so to speak, to try out sufferings of every shape and size, before we arrive at the one which seems to fit. And how much more difficult this is in the case of a suffering such as that of feeling that she whom we loved is finding pleasure with beings who are different from us, who give her sensations which we are not capable of giving her, or who at least by their configuration, their aspect, their ways, represent to her something quite different from us! Ah, if only Albertine had fallen in love with Saint-Loup, how much less, it seemed to me, I should have suffered!

It is true that we are unaware of the particular sensibility of each of our fellow-creatures, but as a rule we do not even know that we are unaware of it, for this sensibility of other people is a matter of indifference to us. So far as Albertine was concerned, my misery or happiness would have depended upon the nature of this sensibility; I was well aware that it was unknown to me, and the fact that it was unknown to me was painful in itself. Once, I had the illusion of seeing these unknown desires and pleasures of Albertine's, when, some time after her death, Andrée came to see me.

For the first time she seemed to me beautiful. I said to myself that her almost frizzy hair, her dark, shadowed eyes, were doubtless what Albertine had loved so much, the materialisation before my eyes of what she pictured in her amorous day-dreams, what she saw with the expectant eyes of desire on the day when she had so suddenly decided to leave Balbec. Like a strange, dark flower brought back to me from beyond the grave, from the innermost being of a person in whom I had been unable to discover it, I seemed to see before me, the unlooked-for exhumation of a priceless relic, the incarnate desire of Albertine which Andrée was to me, as Venus was the desire of Jove. Andrée regretted Albertine's death, but I sensed at once that she did not miss her. Forcibly removed from her friend by death, she seemed to have easily reconciled herself to a final separation which I would not have dared to ask of her while Albertine was alive, so afraid would I have been of failing to obtain her consent. She seemed on the contrary to accept this renunciation without difficulty, but precisely at the moment when it could no longer be of any advantage to me. Andrée abandoned Albertine to me, but dead, and having lost for me not only her life but retrospectively a little of her reality, now that I saw that she was not indispensable and unique to Andrée who had been able to replace her with others.

While Albertine was alive, I would not have dared to ask Andrée to confide in me about the nature of their friendship both mutually and with Mlle Vinteuil's friend, being uncertain, towards the end, whether Andrée did not repeat to Albertine everything I said to her. But now such an inquiry, even if it were to prove fruitless, would at least be unattended by danger. I spoke to Andrée, not in a questioning tone but as though I had known all the time, perhaps from Albertine, of the fondness that she herself, Andrée, had for women and of her own relations with Mlle Vinteuil. She admitted it all without the slightest reluctance, smiling as she spoke. I could not help drawing the most painful conclusions from this avowal; first of all because Andrée, so affectionate and coquettish with many of the young men at Balbec, would never have been suspected by anyone of practices which she made no attempt to deny, so that by analogy, when I discovered this new Andrée, I felt that Albertine would have confessed them with the same ease to anyone other than myself, whom she felt to be jealous. But at the same time, Andrée having been Albertine's best friend, and the friend for whose sake she had probably returned in haste from Balbec, and Andrée having admitted to these tastes, the conclusion that was forced upon my mind was that Albertine and Andrée had always indulged them together. Of course, just as, in the presence of a stranger, we do not always dare to examine the gift he has brought us, the wrapper of which we shall not unfasten until the donor has gone, so long as Andrée was with me I did not retire into myself to examine the pain she had brought me. Although I could feel that it was already causing my bodily servants, my nerves, my heart, the greatest turmoil, out of good manners I pretended not to notice, chatting away on the contrary with the utmost affability to the girl who was my guest without diverting my gaze to these internal incidents. It was especially painful to me to hear Andrée say of Albertine: "Oh, yes, she always loved going to the Chevreuse valley." To the vague and non-existent universe in which Albertine's excursions with Andrée occurred, it seemed to me that the latter, by a posthumous and diabolical act of creation, had just added to God's work an accursed valley. I felt that Andrée was going to tell me everything that she had been in the habit of doing with Albertine, and, as I went on trying, from politeness, from force of habit, from pride, perhaps from gratitude, to appear more and more affectionate, while the space that I had still been able to concede to Albertine's innocence became smaller and smaller, it seemed to me that, despite my efforts, I presented the paralysed aspect of an animal round which a bird of prey is wheeling in steadily narrowing circles, unhurriedly because it is confident of being able to swoop on its helpless victim whenever it chooses. I gazed at her nevertheless, and, with such liveliness, naturalness and assurance as a person can muster who is trying to make it appear that he is not afraid of being hypnotised by someone's stare, I said casually to Andrée: "I've never mentioned the subject to you for fear of offending you, but now that we both find pleasure in talking about her, I may as well tell you that I found out long ago all about the things of that sort that you used to do with Albertine. And I can tell you something that you will be glad to hear although you know it already: Albertine adored you."

I told Andrée that it would be of great interest to me if she would allow me to see her (even if she simply confined herself to caresses which would not embarrass her unduly in my presence) performing such actions with those of Albertine's friends who shared her tastes, and I mentioned Rosemonde, Berthe, each of Albertine's friends, in the hope of finding out something.

"Apart from the fact that not for anything in the world would I do the things you mention in your presence," Andrée replied, "I don't believe that any of the girls whom you've named have those tastes."

Drawing closer in spite of myself to the monster that was mesmerising me, I answered: "What! You don't expect me to believe that of all your group Albertine was the only one with whom you did that sort of thing!"

"But I never did anything of the sort with Albertine."

"Come now, my dear Andrée, why deny things which I've known for at least three years? I see nothing wrong in them, far from it. For instance, that evening when she was so anxious to go with you the next day to Mme Verdurin's, you may remember perhaps. . . ."

Before I had completed my sentence, I saw in Andrée's eyes, which it sharpened to a pin-point like those stones which for that reason jewellers find it difficult to use, a fleeting, worried look, like the look on the face of a person privileged to go behind the scenes who draws back the edge of the curtain before the play has begun and at once withdraws in order not to be seen. This anxious look vanished and everything was back in place, but I sensed that whatever I saw from now on would have been artificially arranged for my benefit. At that moment I caught sight of myself in the mirror, and was struck by a certain resemblance between myself and Andrée. If I had not long since ceased to shave my upper lip and had had only a faint shadow of a moustache, this resemblance would have been almost complete. It was perhaps on seeing my moustache at Balbec when it had scarcely begun to grow again that Albertine had suddenly felt that impatient, furious desire to return to Paris.

"But I still can't say things that aren't true simply because you see no harm in them. I swear to you that I never did anything with Albertine, and I'm convinced that she detested that sort of thing. The people who told you that were lying to you, probably with some ulterior motive," she said with a questioning, defiant air.

"Oh, very well then, since you won't tell me," I replied, pretending to appear to be unwilling to furnish a proof which in fact I did not possess. However, I mentioned vaguely and at random the Buttes-Chaumont.

"I may have gone to the Buttes-Chaumont with Albertine, but is it a place that has a particularly evil reputation?"

I asked her whether she could not raise the subject with Gisèle who had at one time been on intimate terms with Albertine. But Andrée told me that because of a vile thing that Gisèle had done to her recently, asking a favour of her was the one thing that she must absolutely decline to do for me. "If you see her," she went on, "don't tell her what I've said to you about her; there's no point in making an enemy of her. She knows what I think of her, but I've always preferred to avoid having violent quarrels with her which only have to be patched up afterwards. And besides, she's dangerous. But you must understand that when one has read the letter which I had in my hands a week ago, and in which she lied with such absolute treachery, nothing, not even the noblest actions in the world, can wipe out the memory of such a thing."

On the whole I felt that if, in spite of the fact that Andrée had those tastes to the extent of making no pretence of concealing them, and the fact that Albertine had felt for her the great affection which she undoubtedly had felt, Andrée had none the less never had any carnal relations with Albertine and had never been aware that Albertine had those tastes, this meant that Albertine did not have them, and had never enjoyed with anyone those relations which, rather than with anyone else, she would have enjoyed with Andrée. And so when Andrée had left me, I realised that her categorical assertion had brought me some peace of mind. But perhaps it had been dictated by a sense of the obligation, which Andrée felt that she owed to the dead girl whose memory still survived in her, not to let me believe what Albertine, while she was alive, had doubtless begged her to deny.

Having thought for a moment, contemplating Andrée, that

I could actually see these pleasures of Albertine's which I had so often tried to imagine, on another occasion I received an intimation of them otherwise than through the eyes: I thought I heard them. I had had two young laundry-girls, from a district where Albertine had often gone, brought to a house of assignation. One of them, beneath the caresses of the other, suddenly began to utter sounds which at first I found difficult to identify, for one never understands precisely the meaning of an original sound expressive of a sensation which one does not experience oneself. Hearing it from a neighbouring room without being able to see, one may mistake for a chuckle the noise which is forced by pain from a patient being operated on without an anaesthetic; and as for the noise emitted by a mother who has just been told that her child has died, it can seem to us, if we are unaware of its origin, as difficult to translate into human terms as the noise emitted by an animal or by a harp. It takes us a little time to realise that those two noises express what, by analogy with the (very different) sensations we ourselves may have felt, we call pain; and it took me some time, too, to understand that *this* noise expressed what, by analogy with the (very different) sensations I myself had felt, I called pleasure; and the pleasure must have been very great to overwhelm to this extent the person who was expressing it and to extract from her this strange utterance which seemed to describe and comment on the exquisite drama which the young woman was living through and which was concealed from my eyes by the curtain that is forever lowered for other people over what happens in the mysterious intimacy of every human creature. In any case these two girls could tell me nothing, as they had no idea who Albertine was.

Novelists sometimes pretend in an introduction that while travelling in a foreign country they have met somebody who has told them the story of another person's life. They then withdraw in favour of this chance acquaintance, and the story that he tells them is nothing more or less than their novel. Thus the life of Fabrice del Dongo was related to Stendhal by a canon of Padua. How gladly would we, when we are in love, that is to say when another person's existence seems to us mysterious, find some such well-informed narrator! And undoubtedly he exists. Do we not ourselves frequently relate the story of some woman or other quite dispassionately to one of our friends, or to a stranger, who has known nothing of her love-affairs and listens to us with keen interest? Such a person as I was when I spoke to Bloch about the Princesse de Guermantes or Mme Swann, such a person existed, who could have spoken to me of Albertine, such a person exists always . . . but we never come across him. It seemed to me that if I had been able to find women who had known her I should have learned everything I did not yet know. And yet to strangers it must have seemed that nobody could have known as much about her life as I did. Indeed, did I not know her dearest friend, Andrée? Thus one imagines that the friend of a Minister must know the truth about some political affair or cannot be implicated in a scandal. From his own experience the friend has found that whenever he discussed politics with the Minister the latter confined himself to generalisations and told him nothing more than what had already appeared in the newspapers, or that if he was in any trouble, his repeated attempts to secure the Minister's help have invariably been met with an "It's not in my power" against which the friend is himself powerless. I said to myself: "If I could have known such and such witnesses!"—from whom, if I had known them, I should probably have been unable to extract anything more than from Andrée, herself the custodian of a secret which she refused to surrender. Differing in this respect also from Swann who, when he was no longer jealous, ceased to feel any curiosity as to what Odette might have done with Forcheville, I found that, even after my jealousy had subsided, the thought of making the acquaintance of Albertine's laundry-girl, of people in her neighbourhood, of reconstructing her life in it, her intrigues, alone had any charm for me. And as desire always springs from an initial glamour, as had happened to me in the past with Gilberte and with the Duchesse de Guermantes, it was the women of Albertine's background, in the districts in which she had formerly lived, that I sought to know, and whose presence alone I could have desired. Whether or not I could learn anything from them, the only women towards whom I felt attracted were those whom Albertine had known or whom she might have known, women

of her own background or of the sort with whom she liked to
associate, in a word those women who had in my eyes the distinction of resembling her or of being of the type that might
have appealed to her. And among these last, especially girls
of the working class, because of that life, so different from the
life that I knew, which is theirs. No doubt it is only in one's
mind that one possesses things, and one does not possess
a picture because it hangs in one's dining-room if one is
incapable of understanding it, or a landscape because one lives
in it without even looking at it. But still, I had had in the past
the illusion of recapturing Balbec, when in Paris Albertine
came to see me and I held her in my arms, and similarly I
established some contact, restricted and furtive though it might
be, with Albertine's life, the atmosphere of workrooms, a conversation across a counter, the spirit of the slums, when I
embraced a seamstress. Andrée, and these other women, all of
them in relation to Albertine—like Albertine herself in relation
to Balbec—were to be numbered among those substitute pleasures, replacing one another in a gradual declension, which
enable us to dispense with the pleasure to which we can no
longer attain, a trip to Balbec or the love of Albertine, pleasures
which (just as going to the Louvre to look at a Titian consoles
us for not being able to go to Venice where it originally was),
separated one from another by indistinguishable gradations,
convert one's life into a series of concentric, contiguous, har-
monic and graduated zones, encircling an initial desire which
has set the tone, eliminated everything that does not combine
with it, applied the dominant colour (as had, for instance,
occurred to me also in the cases of the Duchesse de Guermantes and of Gilberte). Andrée and these women were to the
desire, which I knew I could no longer gratify, to have Albertine by my side, what had been, one evening, before I knew
Albertine except by sight and felt that she could never be mine,
the writhing, sun-drenched freshness of a cluster of grapes.
Recalling thus either Albertine herself or the type for which she
doubtless had a predilection, these women aroused in me a
painful feeling of jealousy or regret, which later, when my
grief subsided, changed into a curiosity that was not devoid
of charm.

Associated now with the memory of my love, Albertine's physical and social attributes, in spite of which I had loved her, oriented my desire on the contrary towards what at one time it would least readily have chosen: dark-haired girls of the lower middle class. Indeed what was beginning partially to revive in me was that immense desire which my love for Albertine had been unable to assuage, that immense desire to know life which I used to feel on the roads round Balbec, in the streets of Paris, that desire which had caused me so much suffering when, supposing it to exist in Albertine's heart also, I had sought to deprive her of the means of satisfying it with anyone but myself. Now that I was able to endure the idea of her desire, since that idea was at once aroused by my own desire, these two immense appetites coincided; I would have liked us to be able to indulge them together, saying to myself: "That girl would have appealed to her," and led by this sudden detour to think of her and of her death, I felt too unhappy to be able to pursue my own desire any further. As, long ago, the Méséglise and Guermantes ways had laid the foundations of my taste for the countryside and prevented me thereafter from finding any real charm in a place where there was no old church, where there were no cornflowers or buttercups, so it was by linking them in my mind to a past full of charm that my love for Albertine made me seek out exclusively a certain type of woman; I was beginning once more, as before I loved her, to feel the need for overtones from her which would be interchangeable with a memory that had become gradually less exclusive. I could not have found pleasure now in the company of a golden-haired and haughty duchess, because she would not have aroused in me any of the emotions that sprang from Albertine, from my desire for her, from my jealousy of her love-affairs, from my grief at her death. For our sensations, in order to be strong, need to release inside us something different from themselves, a sentiment which cannot find its satisfaction in pleasure, but which adds itself to desire, swells it, makes it cling desperately to pleasure. Gradually, as the love that Albertine may have felt for certain women ceased to cause me pain, it attached those women to my past, made them somehow more real, as the memory of Combray gave to buttercups and hawthorn-blossom a greater reality than to unfamiliar flowers. Even of Andrée, I no longer said to myself with rage in my heart: "Albertine loved her," but on the contrary, in order to explain my desire to myself, in a tone of affectionate tenderness: "Albertine was fond of her." I could now understand the widowers whom we suppose to have found consolation and who prove on the contrary that they are inconsolable because they marry their deceased wife's sister.

Thus my waning love seemed to make new loves possible for me, and Albertine, like those women long loved for themselves who later, feeling their lover's desire fade, preserve their power by contenting themselves with the role of procuresses, provided me, as the Pompadour provided Louis XV, with fresh damsels. In the past, my time had been divided into periods in which I desired this woman or that. When the violent pleasures afforded by one had subsided, I longed for the other who would give me an almost pure affection until the need of more sophisticated caresses brought back my desire for the first. Now these alternations had come to an end, or at least one of the periods was being indefinitely prolonged. What I would have liked was that the newcomer should take up her abode in my house, and should give me at night, before leaving me, a friendly, sisterly kiss. So that I might almost have believed— had I not had experience of the intolerable presence of another person—that I regretted a kiss more than a certain pair of lips, a pleasure more than a love, a habit more than a person. I would have liked also that the newcomers should be able to play Vinteuil's music to me like Albertine, to talk to me as she had talked about Elstir. All this was impossible. Their love would not match up to hers, I thought; either because a love which embraced all those episodes, visits to picture galleries, evenings at concerts, a whole complicated existence which allows correspondence, conversations, a flirtation preliminary to the more intimate relations, a serious friendship afterwards, possesses more resources than love for a woman who can only offer herself, as an orchestra possesses more resources than a piano; or because, more profoundly, my need of the same sort of tenderness as Albertine used to give me, the tenderness of a girl of a certain culture who would at the same time be a sister to me, was—like my need for women of the same background as Albertine—merely a recrudescence of my memory of Albertine, of my memory of my love for her. And once again I discovered, first of all that memory has no power of invention, that it is powerless to desire anything else, let alone anything better, than what we have already possessed; secondly that it is spiritual, in the sense that reality cannot provide it with the state which it seeks; and lastly that, stemming from a dead person, the resurrection that it incarnates is not so much that of the need to love, in which it makes us believe, as that of the need for the absent person. So that even the resemblance to Albertine of the woman I had chosen, the resemblance of her tenderness, if I succeeded in winning it, to Albertine's, only made me the more conscious of the absence of what I had been unconsciously seeking, of what was indispensable to the revival of my happiness, that is to say, Albertine herself, the time we had lived together, the past in the search for which I was unwittingly engaged.

Certainly, on fine days, Paris seemed to me innumerably aflower with all the girls, not whom I desired, but who thrust down their roots into the obscurity of the desire and the unknown nocturnal life of Albertine. It was of one such that she had said to me at the outset, when she had not yet begun to be wary of me: "She's ravishing, that girl. What pretty hair she has!" All that I had wanted to know about her life in the past when I knew her only by sight, and at the same time all my desires in life, merged into this one sole curiosity, to know in what manner Albertine experienced pleasure, to see her with other women, perhaps because thus, when they had left her, I should have remained alone with her, the last and the master. And seeing her hesitations as to whether it would be worth her while to spend the evening with this or that girl, her satiety when the other had gone, perhaps her disappointment, I should have elucidated, I should have restored to its true proportions, the jealousy that Albertine inspired in me, because seeing her thus experience them I should have taken the measure and discovered the limit of her pleasures. Of how many pleasures, of what an agreeable life she deprived us, I said to myself, by that stubborn obstinacy in denying her tastes! And as once again I sought to discover what could have been the reason for that obstinacy, all of a sudden the memory came back to me of a remark that I had made to her at Balbec on the day when she gave me a pencil. As I reproached her for not having allowed me to kiss her, I had told her that I thought a kiss just as natural as I thought it revolting that a woman should have relations with another woman. Alas, perhaps Albertine had never forgotten that imprudent speech.

I took home with me the girls who would have appealed to me least, I stroked sleek virginal tresses, I admired a small and well-shaped nose or a Spanish pallor. True, in the past, even with a woman I had merely glimpsed on a road near Balbec or in a street in Paris, I had felt the individuality of my desire and that it would be adulterating it to seek to assuage it with another person. But life, by disclosing to me little by little the permanence of our needs, had taught me that failing one person we must content ourselves with another, and I felt that what I had demanded of Albertine could have been given to me by another, by Mlle de Stermaria. But it had been Albertine; and between the satisfaction of my need for tenderness and the distinctive characteristics of her body, such an inextricable network of memories had been woven that I could no longer detach it from any new physical desire. She alone could give me that happiness. The idea of her uniqueness was no longer a metaphysical *a priori* based upon what was individual in Albertine, as in the case of the women I passed in the street long ago, but an *a posteriori* created by the contingent and indissoluble overlapping of my memories. I could no longer desire physically without feeling a need for her, without suffering from her absence. Hence the mere resemblance of the woman chosen, the caresses sought, to the happiness I had known only made me the more conscious of all that they lacked wherewith to revive it. The same vacuum that I had found in my room since Albertine had left, and had supposed that I could fill by taking women in my arms, I found in them. They had never spoken to me, these women, of Vinteuil's music, of Saint-Simon's memoirs, they had not sprayed themselves with an overpowering scent before coming to see me, they had not played at intertwining their eyelashes with mine, all of which things are important because they seem to enable one to weave dreams round the sexual act itself and to give oneself the illusion of love, but in reality because they formed part of my memory of Albertine and it was she whom I wanted there. What these women had in common with Albertine made me feel all the more strongly what was lacking of her in them, which was everything, and would never exist again since Albertine was dead. And so my love for Albertine, which had drawn me towards these women, made me indifferent to them, and my regret for Albertine and the persistence of my jealousy, which had already outlasted my most pessimistic calculations, would perhaps never have altered appreciably if their existence, isolated from the rest of my life, had been subjected merely to the play of my memories, to the actions and reactions of a psychology applicable to immobile states, and had not been drawn into a vaster system in which souls move in time as bodies move in space.

As there is a geometry in space, so there is a psychology in time, in which the calculations of a plane psychology would no longer be accurate because we should not be taking account of time and one of the forms that it assumes, forgetting—forgetting, the force of which I was beginning to feel and which is so powerful an instrument of adaptation to reality because it gradually destroys in us the surviving past which is in perpetual contradiction with it. And I really ought to have discovered sooner that one day I should no longer be in love with Albertine. When I had realised, from the difference that existed between what the importance of her person and of her actions was to me and what it was to other people, that my love was not so much a love for her as a love in myself, I might have drawn various conclusions from this subjective nature of my love and in particular deduced that, being a mental state, it might survive the person for some time, but also that, having no real connexion with that person, it must, like every mental state, even the most lasting, find itself one day obsolete, be "replaced," and that when that day came everything that seemed to attach me so sweetly, indissolubly, to the memory of Albertine would no longer exist for me. It is the tragedy of other people that they are merely showcases for the very perishable collections of one's own mind. For this very reason one bases upon them projects which have all the fervour of thought; but thought languishes and memory decays: the day would come when I would readily admit the first comer to Albertine's room, as I had without the slightest regret given Albertine the agate marble or other gifts that I had received from Gilberte. It was not that I did not still love Albertine, but I no longer loved her in the same fashion as in the final phase. No, it was in the fashion of the earlier days, when everything connected with her, places or people, made me feel a curiosity in which there was more charm than suffering. And indeed I was well aware now that before I forgot her altogether, before I got back to the initial stage of indifference, I should have to traverse in the opposite direction, like a traveller who returns by the same route to his starting-point, all the sentiments through which I had passed before arriving at my great love. But these stages, these moments of the past are not immobile; they have retained the tremendous force, the happy ignorance of the hope that was then soaring towards a time which has now become the past, but which a hallucination makes us for a moment mistake retrospectively for the future. I read a letter from Albertine in which she had announced her intention of coming to see me that evening, and I felt for an instant the joy of expectation. In these return journeys along the same line from a place to which one will never return, when one recognises the names and the appearance of all the places through which one passed on the outward journey, it happens that, while one's train is halted at one of the stations, for an instant one has the illusion of setting off again, but in the direction of the place from which one has come, as on the former journey. The illusion vanishes at once, but for an instant one had felt oneself being carried towards it once more: such is the cruelty of memory.

At times the reading of a novel that was at all sad carried me suddenly back, for certain novels are like great but temporary bereavements, abolishing habit, bringing us once more into contact with the reality of life, but for a few hours only, like a nightmare, since the force of habit, the oblivion it creates, the gaiety it restores to us because of the powerlessness of the brain to fight against it and to re-create the truth, infinitely outweigh the almost hypnotic suggestion of a good book which, like all such influences, has very transient effects.

And yet if, before returning to the state of indifference from which one started, one cannot avoid covering in the reverse direction the distances one had traversed in order to arrive at love, the itinerary one follows, the line one takes, are not necessarily the same. They have this in common, that they are not direct, because the process of forgetting is no more regular than that of love. But they do not necessarily take the same routes. And on the route which I followed on my return journey there were three stages, when I was already well on the way towards my destination, which I remember particularly, doubtless because I perceived in them things that had no part in my love for Albertine, or at most were linked to it only to the extent to which what existed already in one's heart before a great love becomes associated with it, whether by fostering it, or by combating it, or by offering contrasts with it or images of it for one's intelligence to analyse.

The first of these stages began early one winter, on a fine Sunday, which was also All Saints' Day, when I had ventured out of doors. As I approached the Bois, I remembered sadly how Albertine had come back to join me from the Trocadéro, for it was the same day, only without Albertine. Sadly and yet not without pleasure all the same, for the repetition in the minor, in a melancholy key, of the same motif that had filled that earlier day, the very absence of Françoise's telephone message, of Albertine's return, which was not something negative but the suppression in reality of what I remembered, gave the day a certain sadness, made of it something more beautiful than a simple, unbroken day, because what was no longer there, what had been torn from it, remained as it were etched upon it. I hummed a few phrases of Vinteuil's sonata. The thought that Albertine had so often played it to me no longer saddened me unduly, for almost all my memories of her had entered into that secondary chemical state in which they no longer cause an anxious oppression of the heart, but rather a certain sweetness. From time to time, in the passages which she used to play most often, when she was in the habit of making some observation which at the time I thought charming, of suggesting some reminiscence, I said to myself: "Poor child," but not sadly, merely investing the musical phrase with an additional value, as it were an historical, a curiosity value, like that which the portrait of Charles I by Van Dyck, already so beautiful in itself, acquires from the fact that it found its way into the national collection because of Mme du Barry's desire to impress the King. When the little phrase, before disappearing altogether, dissolved into its various elements in which it floated still for a moment in scattered fragments, it was not for me, as it had been for Swann, a messenger from a vanishing Albertine. It was not altogether the same associations of ideas that the little phrase had aroused in me as in Swann. I had been struck most of all by the elaboration, the trial runs, the repetitions, the gradual evolution of a phrase which developed through the course of the sonata as that love had developed through the course of my life. And now, aware that, day by day, one element after another of my love was vanishing, the jealous side of it, then some other, drifting gradually back in a vague remembrance to the first tentative beginnings, it was my love that, in the scattered notes of the little phrase, I seemed to see disintegrating before my eyes.

As I followed the paths through thickets whose gauzy screen of leaves grew thinner each day, the memory of a drive during which Albertine was by my side in the carriage on the way home with me, and during which I felt that my life was wrapped up in her, now floated round about me, in the vague mist of the darkening branches in the midst of which the setting sun lit up the tenuous horizontal strips of golden foliage so that they seemed suspended in the empty air. My heart kept fluttering from moment to moment, as happens to anyone who is haunted by an obsession which gives to every woman standing at the end of a path the resemblance or even the possible identity with the woman he is thinking of. "Perhaps it is she!" One looks round, the carriage continues on its way, and one does not go back. I did not simply contemplate this foliage with the eyes of memory; it interested me, touched me, like those purely descriptive pages into which an artist, to make them more complete, introduces a fiction, a whole romance;

and this work of nature thus assumed the sole charm of melancholy which was capable of reaching my heart. The reason for this charm seemed to me to be that I still loved Albertine as much as ever, whereas the true reason was on the contrary that oblivion was continuing to make such headway in me that the memory of Albertine was no longer painful to me, that is to say had changed; but however clearly we may discern our impressions, as I then thought that I could discern the reason for my melancholy, we are unable to trace them back to their more distant meaning. Like those symptoms which the doctor hears his patient describe to him and with the help of which he works back to a deeper cause of which the patient is unaware, similarly our impressions, our ideas, have only a symptomatic value. My jealousy being kept in abeyance by the impression of charm and sweet sadness which I was feeling, my senses reawakened. Once again, as when I had ceased to see Gilberte, the love of women arose in me, relieved of any exclusive association with a particular woman already loved, and floated like those essences that have been liberated by previous destructions and stray suspended in the springtime air, asking only to be reunited with a new creature. Nowhere do so many flowers, "forget-me-nots" though they be styled, germinate as in a cemetery. I looked at the girls with whom this fine day was so multitudinously aflower, as I would have looked at them long ago from Mme de Villeparisis's carriage or from the carriage in which, on a similar Sunday, I had come there with Albertine. At once, the glance which I now gave one or other of them was matched immediately by the curious, furtive, speculative glance, reflecting unimaginable thoughts, which Albertine would surreptitiously have cast at them and which, duplicating my own with a mysterious, swift, steel-blue wing, wafted along these paths, so natural until then, the tremor of an unknown life with which my own desire would not have sufficed to animate them had it remained alone, for it, to me, contained nothing that was unfamiliar.

At Balbec, when I had first longed to know Albertine, was it not because she had seemed to me representative of those girls the sight of whom had so often brought me to a standstill in the streets of towns or on country roads, and because she might epitomise their life for me? And was it not natural that now the waning star of my love in which they had been condensed should disperse once again in this scattered dust of nebulae? All of them seemed to me Albertines—the image that I carried inside me making me find copies of her everywhere—and indeed, at the bend of an avenue, a girl getting into a motor-car recalled her so strongly, was so exactly of the same build, that I wondered for an instant whether it was not her that I had just seen, whether people had not been deceiving me when they sent me the report of her death. I recalled her thus at the corner of an avenue, perhaps at Balbec, getting into a car in the same way, at a time when she was so full of confidence in life. And I did not merely record with my eyes, as one of those superficial phenomena which occur so often in the course of a walk, this other girl's action in climbing into the car: become a sort of sustained action, it seemed to me to extend also into the past by virtue of the memory which had been superimposed upon it and which pressed so deliciously, so sadly against my heart. But by this time the girl had vanished.

A little further on I saw a group of three girls, slightly older, young women perhaps, whose elegant and energetic appearance corresponded so closely with what had attracted me on the day when I first saw Albertine and her friends that I hastened in pursuit of them and, when they stopped a carriage, looked frantically in every direction for another. I found one, but it was too late. I failed to overtake them. A few days later, however, on coming home, I saw emerging from the portico of our house the three girls whom I had followed in the Bois. They were absolutely typical, the two dark ones especially, save that they were slightly older, of those well-born girls who so often, seen from my window or encountered in the street, had made me form countless plans, had given me a taste for life, but whom I had never succeeded in getting to know. The fair one had a rather more delicate, almost an invalid air, which appealed to me less. It was she, nevertheless, who was responsible for my not contenting myself with gazing at them for a moment, having stopped dead, with one of those looks which, by their fixed absorption, their application as to a problem, seem to be concerned with something far beyond what meets the eye.

I should doubtless have allowed them to disappear, as I had allowed so many others, if, as they walked past me, the fair-haired one—was it because I was scrutinising them so closely? —had not darted a furtive glance at me and then, turning round after having passed me, a second one that set me aflame. However, as she ceased to pay attention to me and resumed her conversation with her friends, my ardour would doubtless have subsided, had it not been increased a hundredfold by the following discovery. When I asked the concierge who they were, "They asked for Mme la Duchesse," he informed me. "I think only one of them knows her and the others were simply accompanying her as far as the door. Here's the name, I don't know whether I've taken it down properly." And I read: "Mlle Déporcheville," which it was easy to correct to "d'Eporcheville," that is to say the name, more or less, so far as I could remember, of the girl of excellent family, vaguely connected with the Guermantes, whom Robert had told me that he had met in a disorderly house and with whom he had had relations. I now understood the meaning of her glance, why she had turned round without letting her companions see. How often I had thought about her, trying to visualise her from the name that Robert had given me! And here I had just seen her, in no way different from her friends, save for that clandestine glance which established between herself and me a secret entry into the parts of her life which were evidently hidden from her friends and which made her appear more accessible—already almost half mine—and more soft-hearted than girls of the aristocracy usually are. In the mind of this girl, she and I now had in common the hours that we might have spent together if she was free to make an assignation with me. Was it not this that her glance had sought to express to me with an eloquence that was intelligible to me alone? My heart beat wildly. I could not have given an exact description of Mlle d'Eporcheville's appearance, I could only picture vaguely a fair-skinned face viewed from the side; but I was madly in love with her. All of a sudden I realised that I was reasoning as though, of the three girls, Mlle d'Eporcheville must be the fair one who had turned round and looked at me twice. But the concierge had not told me this.

I returned to his lodge and questioned him again. He told me that he could not enlighten me on the subject, because they had come today for the first time and while he was not there. But he would ask his wife who had seen them once before. She was busy at the moment scrubbing the service stairs. Which of us has not experienced in the course of his life exquisite uncertainties more or less similar to this? A charitable friend, to whom one describes a girl one has seen at a ball, concludes from the description that she must be one of his friends and invites one to meet her. But among so many others, and on the basis of a mere verbal portrait, is there not a possibility of error? The girl you are about to see may well turn out to be a different girl from the one you desire. On the other hand, you may be about to see, holding out her hand to you with a smile, precisely the girl whom you hoped that she would be. This latter case is not infrequent, and, without being justified always by a reasoning as convincing as mine with respect to Mlle d'Eporcheville, arises from a sort of intuition as well as from that wind of fortune which favours us at times. Then, on seeing her, one says to oneself: "She was the one." I remembered that, among the little band of girls who used to parade along the beach, I had guessed correctly which was named Albertine Simonet. This memory caused me a sharp but transient pang, and while the concierge went in search of his wife, my chief anxiety—as I thought of Mlle d'Eporcheville, and since in those minutes spent waiting during which a name or piece of information which we have for some reason or other fitted to a face finds itself free for an instant and floats between several, ready, if it belongs to a new one, to make the original face to which it had applied retrospectively strange, innocent, elusive—was that the concierge was perhaps going to inform me that Mlle d'Eporcheville was, on the contrary, one of the two dark girls. In that event, the being in whose existence I believed would vanish, the being whom I already loved, whom I now thought only of possessing, that sly, blonde Mlle d'Eporcheville whom the fateful answer must then separate into two distinct elements, which I had arbitrarily united after the fashion of a novelist who blends diverse elements borrowed from reality in order to create an imaginary character, elements which, taken separately—the name failing to corroborate the supposed intention of the glance—lost all their meaning. In that case my arguments would be nullified, but how greatly, on the contrary, they found themselves strengthened when the concierge returned to tell me that Mlle d'Eporcheville was indeed the fair girl.

From then on I could no longer believe that it was a case of homonymy. It would have been too great a coincidence that of these three girls one should be named Mlle d'Eporcheville, that she should be precisely (and this was an initial, highly relevant corroboration of my supposition) the one who had looked at me in that way, almost smiling at me, and that it should not be she who frequented houses of assignation.

Then began a day of wild excitement. Even before setting out to buy everything in which I thought it proper to array myself in order to create a favourable impression when I went to call upon Mme de Guermantes two days later, when (the concierge had informed me) the young lady would be coming back to see the Duchess, in whose house I should thus find a willing girl with whom I would arrange a rendezvous (for I could easily find an opportunity of speaking to her alone in a corner of the drawing-room), I decided, to make assurance doubly sure, to telegraph Robert to ask him for the girl's exact name and description, hoping to have his reply within forty-eight hours (I did not think for an instant of anything else, not even of Albertine), for I was determined, whatever might happen to me in the meantime, even if I had to be carried down in a chair because I was too ill to walk, to pay a call on the Duchess at the appropriate hour. If I telegraphed to Saint-Loup it was not that I had any lingering doubt as to the identity of the person, it was not that the girl whom I had seen and the girl of whom he had spoken were still distinct personalities in my mind. I had no doubt whatever that they were the same person. But in my impatience at the enforced interval of forty-eight hours, it was a pleasure to me, it gave me already a sort of secret power over her, to receive a telegram concerning her, filled with detailed information. At the telegraph office, as I drafted my message with the animation of a man who is fired by hope, I remarked how much less helpless I was now than in my boyhood, and in relation to Mlle d'Eporcheville than I had been in relation to Gilberte. I had merely had to take the trouble to write out my telegram, and thereafter the clerk had only to take it from me, and the swiftest channels of electric communication to transmit it, and the whole length and breadth of France and the Mediterranean, together with the whole of Robert's roistering life applied to the identification of the person I had just met, would be placed at the service of the romance which I had just sketched out and to which I need no longer give a thought, for they would undertake to bring it to a conclusion one way or the other before twenty-four hours had passed. Whereas in the old days, brought home by Françoise from the Champs-Elysées, brooding alone in the house over my impotent desires, unable to make use of the practical devices of civilisation, I loved like a savage, or indeed, for I was not even free to move about, like a flower. From this moment onwards I was in a continual fever; a request from my father to go away with him for a couple of days, which would have obliged me to forgo my visit to the Duchess, filled me with such rage and despair that my mother intervened and persuaded my father to allow me to remain in Paris. But for several hours my fury refused to be allayed, while my desire for Mlle d'Eporcheville was increased a hundredfold by the obstacle that had been placed between us, by the fear which I had felt for a moment that those hours of my visit to Mme de Guermantes, at the prospect of which I smiled in constant anticipation, as at an assured blessing of which nothing could deprive me, might not occur. Certain philosophers assert that the external world does not exist, and that it is within ourselves that we develop our lives. However that may be, love, even in its humblest beginnings, is a striking example of how little reality means to us. Had I been obliged to draw from memory a portrait of Mlle d'Eporcheville, to furnish a description of her, or even to recognise her in the street, I should have found it impossible. I had glimped her in profile, on the move, and she had struck me as being simple, pretty, tall and fair; I could not have said more. But all the reflexes of desire, of anxiety, of the mortal blow struck by the fear of not seeing her if my father took me away, all these things, associated

with an image of which on the whole I knew nothing, and
as to which it was enough that I knew it to be agreeable,
already constituted a state of love. At last, on the following
morning, after a night of happy sleeplessness I received Saint-
Loup's telegram: "De l'Orgeville, *de* particle, *orge* barley,
ville town, small, dark, plump, is at present in Switzerland."
It was not the girl.

A moment later my mother came into my room with the
mail, put it down carelessly on my bed as though she were
thinking of something else, and withdrew at once to leave me
on my own. And I, who was familiar with my dear Mamma's
little subterfuges and knew that one could always read the
truth in her face without fear of being mistaken, if one took
as a key to the cipher her desire to give pleasure to others, I
smiled and thought: "There must be something interesting
for me in the post, and Mamma assumed that indifferent,
absent-minded air so that my surprise might be complete and
so as not to be like the people who take away half your pleasure
by telling you of it beforehand. And she didn't stay with me
because she was afraid that out of pride I might conceal my
pleasure and so feel it less keenly." Meanwhile, on reaching the
door, my mother had run into Françoise who was coming into
the room, and forcing her to turn back, had dragged her out
with her, somewhat alarmed and surprised; for Françoise
considered that her duties conferred upon her the privilege
of entering my room at any hour of the day and of remaining
there if she chose. But already, upon her features, astonishment
and anger had vanished beneath a dark and sticky smile of
transcendent pity and philosophical irony, a viscous liquid
secreted, in order to heal her wound, by her outraged self-
esteem. So that she might not feel herself despised, she despised
us. Moreover she knew that we were masters, in other words
capricious creatures, who, not being conspicuously intelligent,
take pleasure in imposing by fear upon clever people, upon
servants, in order to prove that they are the masters, absurd
tasks such as boiling water in times of epidemic, washing down
a room with a damp cloth, and leaving it at the very moment
when you wanted to come into it. In her haste, Mamma had
taken away the candle. But I noticed that she had left the post

by my side, so that I might not overlook it. I could see however that it consisted only of newspapers. No doubt there
was some article by a writer whom I admired, which, as he
wrote seldom, would be a surprise for me. I went to the
window, and drew back the curtains. Above the pale and misty
daylight, the sky glowed pink, like the stoves that are being
lighted in kitchens at that hour, and the sight of it filled me
with hope and with a longing to spend the night in a train and
awake at the little country station where I had seen the milk-
girl with the rosy cheeks.

Meanwhile I could hear Françoise who, indignant at having
been banished from my room, into which she considered that
she had the right of entry, was grumbling: "It's a proper
shame, a kid I saw brought into the world. I didn't see him
when his mother bore him, to be sure. But when I first knew
him, to say the most, it wasn't five years since he was birthed!"

I opened the *Figaro*. What a bore! The main article had the
same title as the article which I had sent to the paper and which
had not appeared. But not merely the same title . . . why,
here were several words that were absolutely identical. This
was really too bad. I must write and complain. But it wasn't
merely a few words, it was the whole thing, and there was my
signature . . . It was my article that had appeared at last!
But my brain which, even at that period, had begun to show
signs of age and to tire easily, continued for a moment longer
to reason as though it had not understood that this was my
article, like an old man who is obliged to complete a movement
that he has begun even if it has become unnecessary, even if
an unforeseen obstacle, in the face of which he ought at once
to draw back, makes it dangerous. Then I considered the
spiritual bread of life that a newspaper is, still warm and damp
from the press in the murky air of the morning in which it is
distributed, at daybreak, to the housemaids who bring it to
their masters with their morning coffee, a miraculous, self-
multiplying bread which is at the same time one and ten thousand, which remains the same for each person while penetrating
innumerably into every house at once.

What I was holding in my hand was not a particular copy
of the newspaper, but one out of the ten thousand; it was

not merely what had been written by me, but what had been written by me and read by everyone; it was not only what I had written, but the symbol of its incarnation in countless minds. To appreciate exactly the phenomenon which was occurring at this moment in other houses, it was essential that I read this article not as its author but as one of the readers of the paper. But then came an initial anxiety. Would the reader who had not been forewarned see this article? I opened the paper carelessly as would such a reader, even assuming an air of not knowing what there was this morning in my paper, of being in a hurry to look at the social and political news. But my article was so long that my eye, which was avoiding it (in order to be absolutely fair and not load the dice in my favour, as a person who is waiting counts very slowly on purpose) picked up a fragment of it in passing. But many of those readers who notice the main article and even read it do not notice the signature; I myself would be quite incapable of saying who had written the main article of the day before. And I now made up my mind always to read them, and the author's name too; but, like a jealous lover who refrains from being unfaithful to his mistress in order to believe in her fidelity, I reflected sadly that my own future attention would not compel, had not compelled the reciprocal attention of other people. And besides, there were those who would have gone out shooting, and those who would have left the house too early. But still, a few people would read it. I did as they would do: I began. Although I was well aware that many people who read this article would find it detestable, at the moment of reading it the meaning that each word conveyed to me seemed to me to be printed on the paper, and I could not believe that every other reader on opening his eyes would not see directly the images that I saw, assuming—with the same naïvety as those who believe that it is the actual speech they have uttered that proceeds just as it is along the telephone wires—that the author's thought is directly perceived by the reader, whereas quite other thoughts form in the latter's mind; at the very moment in which I was trying to be an ordinary reader, my mind was redoing as author the work of those who would read my article. If M. de Guermantes did not understand some sentence which would appeal to Bloch, he might, on the other hand, be amused by some reflection which Bloch would scorn. Thus, a fresh admirer presenting himself for each section which the previous reader seemed to disregard, the article as a whole was lifted to the skies by a swarm of readers and prevailed over my own self-distrust, since I no longer needed to bolster it. The truth of the matter is that the value of an article, however remarkable it may be, is like that of those passages in parliamentary reports in which the words "We shall see," uttered by the Minister, are only a part, and perhaps the least important part, of a passage which must be read thus: THE PRIME MINISTER, MINISTER OF THE INTERIOR AND OF RELIGIOUS AFFAIRS: "We shall see!" (*Loud exclamations on the extreme Left.* "*Hear, hear,*" *from some Left and Centre benches*)—an ending better than the middle and worthy of the beginning. In both cases part of the beauty— and it is the original flaw in this type of literature, from which the famous *Lundis* are not exempt—lies in the impression made on the readers. It is a collective Venus, of which we have but one truncated limb if we confine ourselves to the thought of the author, for it is fully realised only in the minds of his readers. In them it finds completion. And since a crowd, even a select crowd, is not an artist, this final seal which it sets upon the article must always retain a trace of the commonplace. Thus Sainte-Beuve, on a Monday, could imagine Mme de Boigne in her four-poster bed reading his article in the *Constitutionnel,* and appreciating some pretty sentence which he had taken a long delight in composing and which might never, perhaps, have flowed from his pen had he not thought it opportune to stuff it into his article in order to make a more wide-reaching impression. Doubtless the Chancellor,[28] reading it too, would mention it during the visit he would pay to his old friend and mistress a little later. And when he dropped him home in his carriage that evening, the Duc de Noailles in his grey trousers would tell him what had been thought of it in society, if a note from Mme d'Arbouville had not already informed him.

And setting my own self-distrust against the ten-thousand-fold approbation which now sustained me, I drew as much strength and hope for my talent from reading the article at this moment as I drew misgivings when what I had written was addressed only to myself. I saw at that same hour my thought—or at least, failing my thought for those who were incapable of understanding it, the repetition of my name and as it were an embellished evocation of my person—shine on countless people, colour their own thoughts in an auroral light which filled me with more strength and triumphant joy than the multiple dawn which at that moment was blushing at every window. I saw Bloch, M. de Guermantes, Legrandin, Andrée, Monsieur X, extracting each in turn from every sentence the images that it enclosed at the very moment in which I was endeavouring to be an ordinary reader, while reading as author. In order that the impossible creature I was endeavouring to be should combine all the opposites that might be most favourable to me, if I read as an author I judged myself as a reader, without any of the qualms that may be felt about a written text by him who compares it with the ideal which he has sought to express in it. Those passages which, when I wrote them, were so colourless in comparison with my thought, so complicated and opaque in comparison with my harmonious and transparent vision, so full of gaps which I had not managed to fill, that the reading of them was a torture to me, had only accentuated in me the sense of my own impotence and of my incurable lack of talent. But now, in forcing myself to be a reader, I transferred to others the painful duty of judging me, and I succeeded at least in making a clean sweep of what I had attempted to do in reading what I had written. I read the article while forcing myself to imagine that it had been written by someone else. Then all my images, all my reflections, all my epithets taken in themselves, untarnished by the memory of the failure which they represented in relation to my aims, charmed me by their brilliance, their unexpectedness, their profundity. And when I became aware of too blatant a weakness, taking refuge in the spirit of the ordinary and astonished reader, I said to myself: "Bah! how could a reader possibly notice that? There may well be something lacking there, but good heavens, they ought to be pleased! There are enough good things in it to be getting on with, more than they usually get." And thus, no sooner had I finished this comfort-

ing perusal than I who had not had the courage to re-read my
manuscript wanted to start again immediately, for there is
nothing of which one can say more aptly than of an old article
by oneself that "it bears re-reading." I made up my mind to
send Françoise out to buy more copies—in order to give them
to my friends, I would tell her, but in reality to feel at first
hand the miracle of the multiplication of my thought and to
read, as though I were another person who had just opened
the *Figaro*, the same sentences in another copy. It was, as it
happened, a very long time since I had seen the Guermantes:
I would go and pay them a visit in order to find out what
people thought of my article.

I imagined some female reader into whose room I would
have loved to penetrate and to whom the newspaper would
convey, if not my thought, which she would be incapable of
understanding, at least my name, like a eulogy of me which
someone had delivered for her benefit. But eulogies of people
one does not love do not captivate the heart any more than the
thoughts of a mind one is unable to penetrate attract the mind.
With regard to other friends, however, I told myself that if
the state of my health continued to grow worse and I could
no longer see them, it would be pleasant to continue to write,
in order thus to have access to them still, to speak to them
between the lines, to make them share my thoughts, to please
them, to be received into their hearts. I told myself this
because, social relations having hitherto had a place in my
daily life, a future in which they would no longer figure
alarmed me, and because this expedient which would enable
me to remain in the thoughts of my friends, perhaps to arouse
their admiration, until the day when I should be well enough
to begin to see them again, was a solace to me; I told myself
this, but I was well aware that it was not true, that although I
chose to imagine their attention as the object of my pleasure,
that pleasure was an internal, spiritual, self-generated pleasure
which they could not give me and which I could find not in
conversing with them, but in writing far away from them, and
that if I began to write in the hope of seeing them indirectly,
in the hope they might have a better idea of me, in the hope of
preparing for myself a better position in society, perhaps

writing would relieve me of the wish to see them, and I should no longer have any desire to enjoy the position in society which literature might have given me, because my pleasure would be no longer in society but in literature.

After lunch, when I went down to Mme de Guermantes, it was less for the sake of Mlle d'Eporcheville, who had been stripped, by Saint-Loup's telegram, of the better part of her personality, than in the hope of finding in the Duchess herself one of those readers of my article who would enable me to form an idea of the impression that it had made upon those members of the public who were subscribers to or purchasers of the *Figaro*. It was not, incidentally, without pleasure that I went to see Mme de Guermantes. Although I told myself that what made her house different to me from all the rest was the fact that it had for so long haunted my imagination, by knowing the reason for this difference I did not abolish it. Moreover, the name Guermantes existed for me in many forms. If the form which my memory had merely noted down as in an address-book was not accompanied by any poetry, older forms, those which dated from the time when I did not know Mme de Guermantes, were liable to renew themselves in me, especially when I had not seen her for some time and the glaring light of the person with human features did not quench the mysterious radiance of the name. Then once again I began to think of Mme de Guermantes's dwelling as of something that was beyond the bounds of reality, in the same way as I began to think again of the misty Balbec of my early day-dreams as though I had not since then made that journey, or of the 1.22 train as though I had never taken it. I forgot for an instant my own knowledge that none of this existed, as we think at times of a beloved friend forgetting for an instant that he is dead. Then the idea of reality returned as I entered the Duchess's hall. But I consoled myself with the reflection that in spite of everything she was for me the real point of inter-section between reality and dream.

On entering the drawing-room, I saw the fair girl whom I had supposed for twenty-four hours to be the girl of whom Saint-Loup had spoken to me. It was she who asked the Duchess to "reintroduce" me to her. And indeed, the moment

I came into the room I had the impression that I knew her quite well, an impression which the Duchess however dispelled by saying: "Oh! so you've met Mlle de Forcheville before?" For, on the contrary, I was certain that I had never been introduced to any girl of that name, which would certainly have struck me, so familiar was it in my memory ever since I had been given a retrospective account of Odette's love-affairs and Swann's jealousy. In itself my twofold error as to the name, in having remembered "de l'Orgeville" as "d'Eporcheville" and in having reconstructed as "d'Eporcheville" what was in reality "Forcheville," was in no way extraordinary. Our mistake lies in supposing that things present themselves as they really are, names as they are written, people as photography and psychology give an unalterable notion of them. But in reality this is not at all what we ordinarily perceive. We see, we hear, we conceive the world in a lopsided fashion. We repeat a name as we have heard it spoken until experience has corrected our mistake—something that does not always happen. Everyone at Combray had spoken to Françoise for twenty-five years of Mme Sazerat and Françoise continued to say "Mme Sazerin," not from that deliberate and proud perseverance in error which was habitual with her, which was strengthened by our contradictions, and which was all that she had added of the egalitarian principles of 1789 to the France of Saint-André-des-Champs in her make-up (she claimed only one civic right, that of not pronouncing words as we did and of maintaining that "hôtel," "été" and "air" were of the feminine gender), but because she really did continue to hear "Sazerin." This perpetual error, which is precisely "life," does not bestow its countless forms merely upon the visible and the audible universe, but upon the social universe, the sentimental universe, the historical universe, and so forth. The Princesse de Luxembourg is no better than a prostitute in the eyes of the Judge's wife, which of course is of little consequence; what is of slightly more consequence is the fact that Odette is in Swann's eyes a difficult woman to conquer, whence he builds up a whole romance which becomes all the more painful when he discovers his error; what is of even more consequence still, the French are thinking only of revenge in the eyes of the Germans. We have of the universe only inchoate, fragmentary visions, which we complement by arbitrary associations of ideas, creative of dangerous illusions. I should therefore have had no reason to be surprised when I heard the name Forcheville (and I was already wondering whether she was related to the Forcheville of whom I had so often heard) had not the fair girl said to me at once, anxious no doubt to forestall, tactfully, questions which would have been disagreeable to her: "Don't you remember that you knew me well long ago . . . you used to come to our house . . . your friend Gilberte. I could see that you didn't recognise me. I recognised you at once." (She said this as if she had recognised me at once in the drawing-room, but the truth is that she had recognised me in the street and had greeted me, and later Mme de Guermantes informed me that she had told her, as something very comic and extraordinary, that I had followed her and brushed against her, mistaking her for a tart.) I did not discover until after her departure why she was called Mlle de Forcheville. After Swann's death, Odette, who astonished everyone by her profound, prolonged and sincere grief, found herself an extremely rich widow. Forcheville married her, after making a long round of country houses and ascertaining that his family would acknowledge his wife. (The family raised some difficulties at first, but yielded to the material advantage of no longer having to provide for the expenses of a needy relative who was about to pass from comparative penury to opulence.) Shortly after this, an uncle of Swann's, in whose hands the successive demise of innumerable relatives had accumulated an enormous inheritance, died, leaving the whole of his fortune to Gilberte who thus became one of the richest heiresses in France. But this was a time when in the aftermath of the Dreyfus case an anti-semitic trend had arisen parallel to a growing trend towards the penetration of society by Jews. The politicians had not been wrong in thinking that the discovery of the judicial error would be a severe blow to anti-semitism. But, temporarily at least, a form of social anti-semitism was on the contrary enhanced and exacerbated thereby. Forcheville, who, like every petty nobleman, had derived from conversations in the family circle the certainty that his name was more ancient than that of La Rochefoucauld, considered that, in marrying the widow of a Jew, he had performed a similar act of charity to that of a millionaire who picks up a prostitute in the street and rescues her from poverty and squalor. He was prepared to extend his bounty to Gilberte, whose prospects of marriage would be assisted by all her millions but hindered by that absurd name "Swann." He declared that he would adopt her. We know that Mme de Guermantes, to the astonishment of her friends—which she enjoyed and was in the habit of provoking—had refused, after Swann's marriage, to meet his daughter as well as his wife. This refusal had appeared all the more cruel inasmuch as what the possibility of marriage to Odette had long represented to Swann was the prospect of introducing his daughter to Mme de Guermantes. And doubtless he ought to have known, he who had already had so long an experience of life, that these scenes which we picture to ourselves are never realised for a diversity of reasons, among which there is one which meant that he seldom regretted his inability to effect that introduction. This reason is that, whatever the image may be—from the prospect of eating a trout at sunset, which makes a sedentary man decide to take the train, to the desire to be able to astonish the proud lady at a cash desk one evening by stopping outside her door in a magnificent carriage, which makes an unscrupulous man decide to commit murder or to long for the death of rich relatives, according to whether he is brave or lazy, whether he follows his ideas through or remains fondling the first link in the chain—the act which is destined to enable us to attain to it, whether the act be travel, marriage, crime or whatever, modifies us so profoundly that not merely do we cease to attach any importance to the reason which made us perform it, but the image conceived by the man who was not then a traveller, or a husband, or a criminal, or a recluse (who has set himself to work with the idea of fame and simultaneously lost all desire for fame), may perhaps never even once recur to his mind. Moreover, even if we are stubbornly determined to prove that our wish to act was not an idle one, it is probable that the sunset effect would fail to materialise, that feeling cold at that moment we would long for a bowl of soup by the fireside and not for a trout in the open air, that our carriage would fail to impress the cashier who perhaps for wholly different reasons had a great regard for us and in whom this sudden opulence would arouse suspicion. In short, we have seen Swann, once married, attach importance above all else to the relations of his wife and daughter with Mme Bontemps, etc.

To all the reasons, derived from the Guermantes way of looking at social life, which had made the Duchess decide never to allow Mme and Mlle Swann to be introduced to her, we may add also that happy complacency with which people who are not in love dissociate themselves from that which they condemn in lovers and which is explained by their love. "Oh! I don't get mixed up in all that. If it amuses poor Swann to behave idiotically, that's his affair, but I'm not going to be dragged into that sort of thing; it may end very badly; I leave them to get on with it." It is the *suave mari magno* which Swann himself recommended to me with regard to the Verdurins, when he had long ceased to be in love with Odette and no longer cared about the little clan. It is what makes so wise the judgments of third persons with regard to passions which they themselves do not feel and the complications of behaviour which those passions bring about.

Mme de Guermantes had in fact applied to the ostracism of Mme and Mlle Swann a perseverance that caused general surprise. When Mme Molé and Mme de Marsantes had begun to make friends with Mme Swann and to bring a quantity of society ladies to her house, Mme de Guermantes had not only remained intractable but had contrived to sabotage the lines of communication and to see that her cousin the Princesse de Guermantes followed her example. On one of the gravest days of the crisis during Rouvier's Ministry when it was thought that there was going to be war with Germany, I dined at Mme de Guermantes's with M. de Bréauté and found the Duchess looking worried. I supposed that, since she was always dabbling in politics, this was a manifestation of her fear of war, as when, appearing at the dinner-table one evening looking similarly pensive and barely replying in monosyllables, upon somebody's inquiring timidly what was the cause of her anxiety, she had answered solemnly: "I'm worried about

China." But a moment later Mme de Guermantes, herself volunteering an explanation of that preoccupied air which I had put down to fear of a declaration of war, said to M. de Bréauté: "I'm told that Marie-Aynard intends to launch the Swanns. I simply must go and see Marie-Gilbert to-morrow and get her to help me prevent it. Otherwise there'll be no society left. The Dreyfus case is all very well. But then the grocer's wife round the corner has only to call herself a Nationalist and expect us to invite her to our houses in return." And this remark was in such frivolous contrast to the one I expected to hear that I felt the same astonishment as a reader who, turning to the usual column of the *Figaro* for the latest news of the Russo-Japanese war, finds instead the list of people who have given wedding-presents to Mlle de Mortemart, the importance of an aristocratic marriage having relegated the battles on land and sea to the back of the paper. Moreover the Duchess had come to derive from this immoderate perseverance of hers a self-satisfied pride which she lost no opportunity of expressing. "Babal," she said, "maintains that we are the two most elegant people in Paris because he and I are the only two people who do not allow Mme and Mlle Swann to greet us. For he assures me that elegance consists in not knowing Mme Swann." And the Duchess laughed heartily.

However, when Swann was dead, it came to pass that her determination not to know his daughter had ceased to provide Mme de Guermantes with all the satisfactions of pride, independence, autocracy and cruelty which she was capable of deriving from it and which had come to an end with the passing of the man who had given her the exquisite sensation that she was resisting him, that he could not compel her to revoke her decrees. Then the Duchess had proceeded to the promulgation of other decrees which, being applied to people who were still alive, could make her feel that she was free to act as she thought fit. She did not think about the Swann girl, but, when anyone mentioned her, she would feel a certain curiosity, as about some place that she had never visited, which was no longer suppressed by the desire to stand out against Swann's pretensions. Besides, so many different sentiments may contribute to the formation of a single one that it could not be said that there was not a lingering trace of affection for Swann in this interest. No doubt—for at every level of society a worldly and frivolous life paralyses the sensibility and robs people of the power to resuscitate the dead—the Duchess was one of those people who require a personal presence—that presence which, like a true Guermantes, she excelled in protracting—in order to love truly, but also, and this is less common, in order to hate a little. So that often her friendly feeling for people, suspended during their lifetime by the irritation caused her by some action or other on their part, revived after their death. She then felt almost a longing to make reparation, because she pictured them now—though very vaguely—with only their good qualities, and stripped of the petty satisfactions, the petty pretensions, which had irritated her in them when they were alive. This imparted at times, notwithstanding the frivolity of Mme de Guermantes, something rather noble—mixed with much that was base—to her conduct. For, whereas three-quarters of the human race flatter the living and pay no attention to the dead, she often did after their deaths what those whom she had treated badly would have wished her to do while they were alive.

As for Gilberte, all the people who were fond of her and had a certain respect for her dignity could rejoice at the change in the Duchess's attitude towards her only by thinking that Gilberte, by scornfully rejecting advances coming after twenty-five years of insults, would be able to avenge them at last. Unfortunately, moral reflexes are not always identical with what common sense imagines. A man who, by an untimely insult, thinks that he has forfeited for ever all hope of winning the friendship of a person whom he cares about, finds that, on the contrary, he has thereby assured himself of it. Gilberte, who remained fairly indifferent to the people who were kind to her, never ceased to think with admiration of the insolent Mme de Guermantes, to ask herself the reasons for such insolence; once indeed (and this would have made all the people who were at all fond of her die of shame on her behalf) she had thought of writing to the Duchess to ask her what she had against a girl who had never done her any harm. The Guermantes had assumed in her eyes proportions which their birth would have been powerless to give them. She placed them not only above all the nobility, but even above all the royal houses.

Some of Swann's former women-friends took a great interest in Gilberte. When the aristocracy learned of her latest inheritance, they began to remark how well brought up she was and what a charming wife she would make. People said that a cousin of Mme de Guermantes, the Princesse de Nièvre, was thinking of Gilberte for her son. Mme de Guermantes hated Mme de Nièvre. She spread the word that such a marriage would be a scandal. Mme de Nièvre took fright and swore that she had never considered such a thing. One day, after lunch, as the sun was shining and M. de Guermantes was going to take his wife for a drive, Mme de Guermantes was arranging her hat in front of the mirror, her blue eyes gazing at their own reflection and at her still golden hair, her maid holding in her hand various sunshades among which her mistress might choose. The sun was flooding in through the window and they had decided to take advantage of the fine weather to pay a visit to Saint-Cloud, and M. de Guermantes, all ready to set off with his pearl-grey gloves and topper, said to himself: "Oriane is really astounding still; I find her delicious," and went on, aloud, seeing that his wife seemed to be in a good humour: "By the way, I have a message for you from Mme de Virelef. She wanted to ask you to the Opéra on Monday, but as she's having the Swann girl she didn't dare, and asked me to explore the ground. I don't express any opinion, I simply convey the message. But really, it seems to me that we might. . . ." he added evasively, for, their attitude towards people being a collective one, springing up identically in each of them, he knew from his own feelings that his wife's hostility to Mlle Swann had subsided and that she was curious to meet her. Mme de Guermantes settled her veil to her liking and chose a sunshade. "Just as you like. What difference do you suppose it makes to me? I see no objection to our meeting the child. You know quite well that I've never had anything *against* her. I simply didn't want us to appear to be countenancing the dubious establishments of our friends. That's all." "And you were perfectly right," replied the Duke. "You are wisdom incarnate, Madame, and you are more ravishing than ever in that hat." "You're very kind," said Mme de Guermantes with a smile at her husband as she made her way to the door. But, before entering the carriage, she insisted on giving him a further explanation: "Lots of people call on the mother now. Besides, she has the sense to be ill for nine months of the year. . . . Apparently the child is quite charming. Everybody knows that we were very fond of Swann. People will think it quite natural." And they set off together for Saint-Cloud.

A month later, the Swann girl, who had not yet taken the name of Forcheville, came to lunch with the Guermantes. They talked about a variety of things, and at the end of the meal, Gilberte said timidly: "I believe you knew my father quite well." "Why, of course we did," said Mme de Guermantes in a melancholy tone which proved that she understood the daughter's grief and with a spurious intensity as though to conceal the fact that she was not sure whether she did remember the father very clearly. "We knew him very well, I remember him *very well*." (As indeed she might, seeing that he had come to see her almost every day for twenty-five years.) "I know quite well who he was, let me tell you," she went on, as though she were seeking to explain to the daughter what sort of man her father had been and to provide her with some information about him, "he was a great friend of my mother-in-law and he was also very attached to my brother-in-law Palamède." "He used to come here too, in fact he used to come to luncheon here," added M. de Guermantes with ostentatious modesty and a scrupulous regard for accuracy. "You remember, Oriane. What a fine man your father was! One felt that he must come of a very decent family. As a matter of fact, I once saw his father and mother long ago. What excellent people they were, he and they!"

One felt that if Swann and his parents had still been alive, the Duc de Guermantes would not have hesitated to recommend them for jobs as gardeners. And this is how the Faubourg Saint-Germain speaks to any bourgeois about other bourgeois, either to flatter him with the exception being made in his favour (for as long as the conversation lasts) or rather, or at the same time, to humiliate him. Thus it is that an anti-semite, at the very moment when he is smothering a Jew with affability, will speak ill of Jews, in a general fashion which enables him to be wounding without being rude.

But, queen of the present moment, when she knew how to be infinitely amiable to you, and could not bring herself to let you go, Mme de Guermantes was also its slave. Swann might have managed at times to give the Duchess the illusion, in the excitement of conversation, that she was genuinely fond of him, but he could do so no longer. "He was charming," said the Duchess with a wistful smile, fastening upon Gilberte a soft and kindly gaze which would at least, if the girl should prove to be a sensitive soul, show her that she was understood and that Mme de Guermantes, had the two been alone to-gether and had circumstances permitted, would have loved to reveal to her all the depth of her sensibility. But M. de Guermantes, whether because he was indeed of the opinion that the circumstances forbade such effusions, or because he considered that any exaggeration of sentiment was a matter for women and that men had no more part in it than in the other feminine attributions, save food and wine which he had reserved to himself, knowing more about them than the Duch-ess, felt it incumbent upon him not to encourage, by taking part in it, this conversation to which he listened with visible impatience.

However, this burst of sensibility having subsided, Mme de Guermantes added with worldly frivolity, addressing Gilberte: "Why, he was not only a *gggreat* friend of my brother-in-law Charlus, he was also on very good terms with Voisenon" (the country house of the Prince de Guermantes), not only as though Swann's acquaintance with M. de Charlus and the Prince had been a mere accident, as though the Duchess's brother-in-law and cousin were two men with whom Swann had happened to become friendly through some fortuitous circumstance, whereas Swann had been on friendly terms with all the people in that set, but also as though Mme de Guer-mantes wanted to explain to Gilberte roughly who her father had been, to "place" him for her by means of one of those characteristic touches whereby, when one wants to explain how it is that one happens to know somebody whom one would not naturally know, or to point up one's story, one invokes the names of his particular social sponsors.

As for Gilberte, she was all the more glad to find the subject being dropped, in that she herself was only too anxious to drop it, having inherited from Swann his exquisite tact combined with a delightful intelligence that was recognised and appreciated by the Duke and Duchess, who begged her to come again soon. Moreover, with the passion for minutiae of people whose lives are purposeless, they would discern, one after another, in the people with whom they became acquainted, qualities of the simplest kind, exclaiming at them with the artless wonderment of a townsman who on going into the country discovers a blade of grass, or on the contrary magnifying as with a microscope, endlessly commenting upon and inveighing against the slightest defects, and often applying both processes alternately to the same person. In Gilberte's case it was first of all upon her agreeable qualities that the idle perspicacity of M. and Mme de Guermantes was brought to bear: "Did you notice the way she pronounces certain words?" the Duchess said to her husband after the girl had left them; "it was just like Swann, I seemed to hear him speaking." "I was just about to say the very same thing, Oriane." "She's witty, she has exactly the same cast of mind as her father." "I consider that she's even far superior to him. Think how well she told that story about the sea-bathing. She has a vivacity that Swann never had." "Oh! but he was, after all, quite witty." "I'm not saying that he wasn't witty, I'm saying that he lacked vivacity," said M. de Guermantes in a querulous tone, for his gout made him irritable, and when he had no one else upon whom to vent his irritation, it was to the Duchess that he displayed it. But being incapable of any clear understanding of its causes, he preferred to adopt an air of being misunderstood.

This friendly attitude on the part of the Duke and Duchess meant that from now on, if the occasion arose, they would have said to her "your poor father," but this would no longer do, since it was just about this time that Forcheville adopted the girl. She addressed him as "Father," charmed all the dowagers by her politeness and distinction, and it was generally acknowledged that, if Forcheville had behaved admirably towards her, the child was very good-hearted and more than recompensed him. True, since she was able at times and anxious to show a great deal of naturalness and ease, she had reintroduced herself to me and had spoken to me about her real father. But this was an exception and no one now dared utter the name Swann in her presence.

As it happened, on entering the drawing-room I had caught sight of two sketches by Elstir which formerly had been banished to a little room upstairs where I had seen them only by chance. Elstir was now in fashion. Mme de Guermantes could not forgive herself for having given so many of his pictures away to her cousin, not because they were in fashion, but because she now appreciated them. For fashion is composed of the collective enthusiasm of a number of people of whom the Guermantes are typical. But she could not think of buying other pictures by him, for they had now begun to fetch absurdly high prices. She was determined to have something at least by Elstir in her drawing-room and had brought down these two drawings which, she declared, she "preferred to his paintings."

Gilberte recognised the technique. "They look like Elstirs," she said. "Why, yes," replied the Duchess without thinking, "in fact it was your fa . . . some friends of ours who made us buy them. They're admirable. To my mind, they're superior to his paintings."

Not having heard this conversation, I went up to one of the drawings to examine it, and exclaimed: "Why, this is the Elstir that. . . ." I saw Mme de Guermantes's desperate signals. "Ah, yes, the Elstir that I admired upstairs. It looks much better here than in that passage. Talking of Elstir, I mentioned him yesterday in an article in the *Figaro*. Did you happen to read it?"

"You've written an article in the *Figaro*?" exclaimed M. de Guermantes with the same violence as if he had exclaimed: "Why, she's my cousin."

"Yes, yesterday."

"In the *Figaro*, are you sure? I can't believe it. Because we each of us get our *Figaro*, and if one of us had missed it, the other would certainly have noticed it. That's so, isn't it, Oriane, there was nothing."

The Duke sent for the *Figaro* and only yielded to the evidence of his own eyes, as though up till then the probability had been that I had made a mistake as to the newspaper for which I had written.

"What's that? I don't understand. So you've written an article in the *Figaro*?" said the Duchess, making an obvious effort in speaking of something that did not interest her. "Come, Basin, you can read it afterwards."

"No, the Duke looks so nice like that with his great beard dangling over the paper," said Gilberte. "I shall read it as soon as I get home."

"Yes, he wears a beard now that everybody else is clean-shaven," said the Duchess. "He never does anything that other people do. When we were first married, he shaved not only his beard but his moustache as well. The peasants who didn't know him by sight thought that he couldn't be French. At that time he was called the Prince des Laumes."

"Is there still a Prince des Laumes?" asked Gilberte, who was interested in everything that concerned the people who had refused to acknowledge her existence during all those years.

"Why, no," the Duchess replied with a melancholy, caressing gaze.

"Such a charming title! One of the finest titles in France!" said Gilberte, a certain sort of banality springing inevitably, as a clock strikes the hour, to the lips of certain quite intelligent persons.

"Ah, yes, I'm sorry too. Basin would like his sister's son to adopt it, but it isn't the same thing; though it would be possible, since it doesn't have to be the eldest son, it can be passed to a younger brother. I was telling you that in those days Basin was clean-shaven. One day, at a pilgrimage—you remember, my dear," she turned to her husband, "that pilgrimage at Paray-le-Monial—my brother-in-law Charlus, who always enjoys talking to peasants, was saying to one after another: 'Where do you come from?' and as he's extremely generous, he would give them something, take them off to have a drink. For nobody was ever at the same time simpler and more haughty than Mémé. You'll see him refuse to bow to a Duchess whom he doesn't think duchessy enough, and heap kindnesses on a kennelman. So then I said to Basin: 'Come, Basin, say something to them too.' My husband, who is not always very inventive . . ." ("Thank you, Oriane," said the Duke, without interrupting his reading of my article in which he was immersed) ". . . went up to one of the peasants and repeated his brother's question in so many words: 'Where do you come from?' 'I'm from Les Laumes.' 'You're from Les Laumes? Why, I'm your Prince.' Then the peasant looked at Basin's hairless face and replied: 'That ain't true. You're an English.' "29

In these little anecdotes of the Duchess's, such great and eminent titles as that of Prince des Laumes seemed to stand out in one's mind's eye in their true setting, in their original state and their local colour, as in certain Books of Hours one recognises amid the mediaeval crowd the soaring steeple of Bourges.

Some visiting-cards were brought to her which a footman had just left at the door. "I can't think what's got into her, I don't know her. It's to you that I'm indebted for this, Basin. Although that sort of acquaintance hasn't done you much good, my poor dear," and, turning to Gilberte: "I really don't know how to explain to you who she is, you've certainly never heard of her, she's called Lady Rufus Israel."

Gilberte flushed crimson: "No, I don't know her," she said (which was all the more untrue in that Lady Israel and Swann had been reconciled two years before the latter's death and she addressed Gilberte by her Christian name), "but I know quite well, from hearing about her, who it is that you mean."

Later I learned that one day, a young society girl having asked her out of tactlessness or malice what the name of her real, not her adoptive father was, in her confusion and as though to euphemise the name a little, instead of pronouncing it "Souann" she said "Svann," a change, as she soon realised, for the worse, since it made this name of English origin a German patronymic. And she had even gone on to say, abasing herself with the object of self-enhancement: "All sorts of different stories have been told about my birth, but I'm not supposed to know anything about it."

Ashamed though Gilberte must have felt at certain moments, when she thought of her parents (for even Mme Swann represented for her, and was, a good mother), of such a way of looking at life, it must alas be borne in mind that its elements were doubtless borrowed from her parents, for we do not create ourselves of our own accord out of nothing. But to a certain quantity of egoism which exists in the mother, a different egoism, inherent in the father's family, is admixed, which does not invariably mean that it is superadded, nor even precisely that it serves as a multiple, but rather that it creates a fresh egoism infinitely stronger and more redoubtable. And ever since the world began, ever since families in which some defect exists in one form have been intermarrying with families in which the same defect exists in another, thereby creating a peculiarly complete and detestable variety of that defect in the offspring, the accumulated egoisms (to confine ourselves, for the moment, to this defect) must have acquired such force that the whole human race would have been destroyed, did not the malady itself engender natural restrictions, capable of reducing it to reasonable proportions, analogous to those which prevent the infinite proliferation of the infusoria from destroying our planet, the unisexual fertilisation of plants from bringing about the extinction of the vegetable kingdom, and so forth. From time to time a virtue combines with this egoism to produce a new and disinterested force. The combinations by which, in the course of generations, moral chemistry thus stabilises and renders innocuous the elements that were becoming too powerful, are infinite, and would give an exciting variety to family history. Moreover, with these accumulated egoisms, such as must have existed in Gilberte, there may coexist some charming virtue of the parents; it appears for a moment to perform an interlude by itself, to play its touching part with an entire sincerity. No doubt Gilberte did not always go so far as when she insinuated that she was perhaps the natural daughter of some great personage; but as a rule she concealed her origins. Perhaps it was simply too painful for her to confess them and she preferred that people should learn of them from others. Perhaps she really believed that she was concealing them, with that dubious belief which at the same time is not doubt, which leaves room for the possibility of what we wish to be true, of which Musset furnishes an example when he speaks of Hope in God.

"I don't know her personally," Gilberte went on. Did she, in fact, when she called herself Mlle de Forcheville, expect that people would not know that she was Swann's daughter? Some people, perhaps, who, she hoped, would in time become everybody. She could not be under any illusion as to their number at the moment, and doubtless knew that many people must be whispering: "Isn't that Swann's daughter?" But she knew it only with that knowledge which tells us of people taking their lives in desperation while we are going to a ball, that is to say, a remote and vague knowledge for which we are at no pains to substitute a more precise knowledge based on direct observation. Gilberte belonged, during those years at least, to the most widespread variety of human ostriches, the kind that bury their heads not in the hope of not being seen, which they consider highly improbable, but in the hope of not seeing that they can be seen, which seems to them something to the good and enables them to leave the rest to chance. As distance makes things appear smaller, more indistinct, less dangerous, Gilberte preferred not to be near other people at the moment when they made the discovery that she was by birth a Swann. And as we are near the people whom we picture to ourselves, and we can picture people reading their news-paper, Gilberte preferred the newspapers to style her Mlle de Forcheville. It is true that with the writings for which she her-self was responsible, her letters, she prolonged the transition for some time by signing herself "G. S. Forcheville." The real hypocrisy in this signature was made manifest by the suppres-sion not so much of the other letters of the name "Swann" as of those of the name "Gilberte." For, by reducing the inno-cent Christian name to a simple "G," Mlle de Forcheville seemed to insinuate to her friends that the similar amputation applied to the name "Swann" was due equally to the necessity of abbreviation. Indeed she gave a special significance to the "S," extending it with a sort of long tail which ran across the

"G," but which one felt to be transitory and destined to disappear like the tail which, still long in the monkey, has ceased to exist in man.

In spite of all this, there was something of Swann's intelligent curiosity in her snobbishness. I remember that, in the course of that same afternoon, she asked Mme de Guermantes whether she could meet M. du Lau, and that when the Duchess replied that he was an invalid and never went out, Gilberte asked what he was like, for, she added with a faint blush, she had heard a great deal about him. (The Marquis du Lau had in fact been one of Swann's most intimate friends before the latter's marriage, and Gilberte may perhaps even have caught a glimpse of him, but at a time when she was not interested in such people.) "Would M. de Bréauté or the Prince d'Agrigente be at all like him?" she asked. "Oh! not in the least," exclaimed Mme de Guermantes, who had a keen sense of these provincial differences and drew portraits that were sober and restrained but coloured by her husky, golden voice, beneath the gentle efflorescence of her violet-blue eyes. "No, not in the least. Du Lau was very much the Périgord squire, full of charm, with all the good manners and informality of his province. At Guermantes, when we had the King of England with whom du Lau was on the friendliest terms, we used to have a little meal after the men came in from shooting. . . . It was the hour when du Lau was in the habit of going to his room to take off his boots and put on big woollen slippers. Well, the presence of King Edward and all the grand-dukes didn't disturb him in the last, he came down to the great hall at Guermantes in his woollen slippers. He felt that he was the Marquis du Lau d'Allemans who had no reason to stand on ceremony with the King of England. He and that charming Quasimodo de Breteuil, they were the two I liked best. Actually they were great friends of . . ." (she was about to say "your father" and stopped short). "No, there's no resemblance at all, either to Gri-gri or to Bréauté. He was the typical nobleman from Périgord. Incidentally, Mémé quotes a page from Saint-Simon about a Marquis d'Allemans, and it's just like him."

I recited the opening words of the portrait: "M. d'Allemans,

who was a man of great distinction among the nobility of
Périgord, through his own birth and through his merit, and
was regarded by every soul alive there as a general arbiter
to whom each had recourse because of his probity, his capacity
and the suavity of his manners, as it were the cock of his
province."

"Yes, that's it," said Mme de Guermantes, "all the more so
as du Lau was always as red as a turkey cock."

"Yes, I remember hearing that description quoted," said
Gilberte, without adding that it had been quoted by her father,
who was, as we know, a great admirer of Saint-Simon.

She liked also to speak of the Prince d'Agrigente and of M.
de Bréauté for another reason. The Prince d'Agrigente had
inherited his title from the House of Aragon, but the family
domains were in Poitou. As for his country house, the house,
that is to say, in which he lived, it was not the property of
his own family but had come to him from his mother's first
husband, and was situated approximately halfway between
Martinville and Guermantes. And so Gilberte spoke of him
and of M. de Bréauté as of country neighbours who reminded
her of her old home. Strictly speaking there was an element of
falsehood in this attitude, since it was only in Paris, through
the Comtesse Molé, that she had come to know M. de Bréauté,
albeit he had been an old friend of her father's. As for her
pleasure in speaking of the country round Tansonville, it
may have been sincere. Snobbery is with certain people
analogous to those beverages in which the agreeable is mixed
with the beneficial. Gilberte took an interest in some lady of
fashion because she possessed priceless books and portraits
by Nattier which my former friend would probably not have
taken the trouble to inspect in the Bibliothèque Nationale or
the Louvre, and I imagine that, in spite of their even greater
proximity, the magnetic influence of Tansonville would have
had less effect in drawing Gilberte towards Mme Sazerat or
Mme Goupil than towards M. d'Agrigente.

"Oh! poor Babal and poor Gri-gri," said Mme de Guermantes, "they're in a far worse state than du Lau. I'm afraid
they haven't long to live, either of them."

When M. de Guermantes had finished reading my article,

he complimented me in somewhat qualified terms. He regretted the slightly hackneyed and conventional style with its "turgid metaphors as in the antiquated prose of Chateaubriand"; on the other hand he congratulated me wholeheartedly for "keeping myself busy": "I like a man to do something with what God gave him. I don't like useless people who are always self-important or fidgety. A fatuous breed!"

Gilberte, who was acquiring the ways of society with extreme rapidity, declared how proud she would be to be able to say that she was the friend of an author. "You can imagine that I shall tell people that I have the pleasure, the *honour* of your acquaintance."

"You wouldn't care to come with us to-morrow to the Opéra-Comique?" the Duchess asked me; and it struck me that it would be doubtless in that same box in which I had first beheld her, and which had seemed to me then as inaccessible as the underwater realm of the Nereids. But I replied in a melancholy tone: "No, I'm not going to the theatre just now; I've lost a friend to whom I was greatly attached." I almost had tears in my eyes as I said this, and yet for the first time it gave me a sort of pleasure to speak about it. It was from that moment that I began to write to everyone saying that I had just experienced a great sorrow, and to cease to feel it.

When Gilberte had gone, Mme de Guermantes said to me: "You didn't understand my signals. I was trying to hint to you not to mention Swann." And, as I apologised: "But I absolutely sympathise: I was on the point of mentioning him myself, but I stopped short just in time, it was terrible. You know, it really is a great bore," she said to her husband, seeking to mitigate my own error by appearing to believe that I had yielded to a propensity common to everyone and difficult to resist.

"What am I supposed to do about it?" replied the Duke. "You'd better tell them to take those drawings upstairs again, since they make you think about Swann. If you don't think about Swann, you won't speak about him."

On the following day I received two congratulatory letters which surprised me greatly, one from Mme Goupil whom I had not seen for many years and to whom, even at Combray, I had scarcely ever spoken. A lending library had given her the

chance of seeing the *Figaro*. Thus, when anything occurs in
one's life which makes some stir, messages come to one from
people situated so far outside the zone of one's acquaintance,
and one's memory of whom is already so remote, that they
seem to be placed at a great distance, especially in the dimension of depth. A forgotten friendship of one's schooldays,
which has had a score of opportunities of recalling itself to
one's mind, gives us a sign of life, though sometimes in a negative sense. Thus for instance Bloch, whose opinion of my
article I should have loved to know, did not write to me.
It is true that he had read the article and was to admit it later,
but as it were backhandedly. For he himself contributed an
article to the *Figaro* some years later, and was anxious to inform
me immediately of the event. Since what he regarded as a
privilege had fallen to him as well, the envy that had made him
pretend to ignore my article ceased, as though by the lifting
of a compressor, and he spoke to me about it, though not at all
in the way in which he hoped to hear me talk about his: "I
knew that you too had written an article," he told me, "but I
didn't think I ought to mention it to you, for fear of hurting
your feelings, because one oughtn't to speak to one's friends
about the humiliating things that happen to them. And it's
obviously humiliating to write in the organ of the sabre and
the aspergillum, of afternoon tea, not to mention the holy-
water-stoup." His character remained unaltered, but his style
had become less precious, as happens to certain people who
shed their mannerisms, when, ceasing to compose symbolist
poetry, they take to writing serial novels.

To console myself for his silence, I re-read Mme Goupil's
letter; but it was lacking in warmth, for if the aristocracy
employ certain formulas which form a sort of palisade, between them, between the initial "*Monsieur*" and the "*sentiments
distingués*" of the close, cries of joy and admiration may spring
up like flowers, and their clusters waft over the palisade their
adoring fragrance. But bourgeois conventionality enwraps
even the content of letters in a tissue of "your well-deserved
success," at best "your great success." Sisters-in-law, faithful
to their upbringing and tight-laced in their respectable stays,
think that they have overflowed into the most distressing

enthusiasm if they have written "my kindest regards." "Mother joins me" is a superlative with which one is rarely indulged.

I received another letter as well as Mme Goupil's, but the name of the writer, Sanilon, was unknown to me. It was in an illiterate hand and a charming style. I was distressed not to be able to discover who had written to me.

Two days later I found myself rejoicing at the thought that Bergotte was a great admirer of my article, which he had been unable to read without envy. But a moment later my joy subsided. For Bergotte had written me not a word. I had simply wondered whether he would have liked the article, fearing that he would not. As I was asking myself the question, Mme de Forcheville had replied that he admired it enormously and considered it the work of a great writer. But she had told me this while I was asleep: it was a dream. Almost all our dreams respond thus to the questions which we put to ourselves with complicated statements, elaborate productions with several characters, which however lead to nothing.

As for Mlle de Forcheville, I could not help feeling saddened when I thought of her. She, Swann's daughter, whom he would have so loved to see at the Guermantes's, whom the latter had refused to give their great friend the pleasure of inviting—to think that she was now spontaneously sought after by them, time having passed, time that renews all things, that infuses a new personality, based upon what we have been told about them, into people whom we have not seen for a long time, during which we ourselves have grown a new skin and acquired new tastes. But when, to this daughter of his, he used from time to time to say, taking her in his arms and kissing her: "How comforting it is, my darling, to have a daughter like you; one day when I'm no longer here, if people still mention your poor papa, it will be only to you and because of you," Swann, in thus pinning a timorous and anxious hope of survival on his daughter after his death, was as mistaken as an old banker who, having made a will in favour of a little dancer whom he is keeping and who has very nice manners, tells himself that though to her he is no more than a great friend, she will remain faithful to his memory. She had very nice manners while her feet under the table sought the feet of those of the old banker's friends who attracted her, but all this very discreetly, beneath excellent appearances. She will wear mourning for the worthy man, will feel relieved to be rid of him, will enjoy not only the ready money, but the real estate, the motor-cars that he has bequeathed to her, taking care to remove the monogram of the former owner which makes her feel slightly ashamed, and will never associate her enjoyment of the gift with any regret for the giver. The illusions of paternal love are perhaps no less poignant than those of the other kind; many daughters regard their fathers merely as the old men who leave their fortunes to them. Gilberte's presence in a drawing-room, instead of being an occasion for people to speak of her father from time to time, was an obstacle in the way of their seizing the opportunities that might still have remained for them to do so, and that were becoming more and more rare. Even in connexion with the things he had said, the presents he had given, people acquired the habit of not mentioning him, and she who ought to have kept his memory young, if not perpetuated it, found herself hastening and completing the work of death and oblivion.

And it was not only with regard to Swann that Gilberte was gradually completing the process of forgetting; she had accelerated in me that process with regard to Albertine. Under the influence of desire, and consequently of the desire for happiness which Gilberte had aroused in me during the few hours in which I had supposed her to be someone else, a certain number of miseries, of painful preoccupations, which only a little while earlier had obsessed my mind, had slipped away from me, carrying with them a whole block of memories, probably long since crumbling and precarious, with regard to Albertine. For if many memories, which were connected with her, had at the outset helped to keep alive in me my grief for her death, in return that grief had itself fixed those memories. So that the modification of my sentimental state, prepared for no doubt obscurely day by day by the continuous erosions of forgetfulness, but realised abruptly as a whole, gave me the impression, which I remember having felt that day for the first time, of a void, of the suppression in myself of a whole segment of my associations of ideas, such as a man feels in whose brain a long-impaired artery has burst, so that a whole section of his memory is abolished or paralysed. I no longer loved Albertine. At most, on certain days, when the weather was of the sort which, by modifying, by awakening one's sensibility, brings one back into relationship with the real, I felt painfully sad in thinking of her. I was suffering from a love that no longer existed. Thus does an amputee, in certain kinds of weather, feel pain in the limb that he has lost.

The disappearance of my suffering, and of all that it carried away with it, left me diminished, as recovery from an illness which has occupied a big place in one's life often does. No doubt it is because memories are not always true that love is not eternal, and because life is made up of a perpetual renewal of cells. But this renewal, in the case of memories, is nevertheless retarded by one's attention, which temporarily arrests and freezes what is bound to change. And since it is the case with grief as with the desire for women that one magnifies it by thinking about it, having plenty of other things to do should make it easier not only to be chaste but to forget.

By another reaction, if (though it was a distraction—the desire for Mlle d'Eporcheville—that had suddenly brought home to me the tangible reality of forgetting) it remains true that it is time that gradually brings forgetfulness, forgetfulness in its turn does not fail to alter profoundly our notion of time. There are optical errors in time as there are in space. The persistence within me of an old impulse to work, to make up for lost time, to change my way of life, or rather to begin to live, gave me the illusion that I was still as young as in the past; and yet the memory of all the events that had succeeded one another in my life (and also of those that had succeeded one another in my heart, for when one has greatly changed, one is misled into supposing that one has lived longer) in the course of those last months of Albertine's existence, had made them seem to me much longer than a year, and now this forgetfulness of so many things, separating me by gulfs of empty space from quite recent events which they made me think remote, because I had had what is called "the time" to forget them, by its fragmentary, irregular interpolation in my memory—like a thick fog at sea which obliterates all the landmarks—distorted, dislocated my sense of distances in time, contracted in one place, distended in another, and made me suppose myself now further away from things, now much closer to them, than I really was. And as in the new spaces, as yet unexplored, which extended before me, there would be no more trace of my love for Albertine than there had been, in the time lost which I had just traversed, of my love for my grandmother, my life appeared to me—offering a succession of periods in which, after a certain interval, nothing of what had sustained the previous period survived in that which followed—as something utterly devoid of the support of an individual, identical and permanent self, something as useless in the future as it was protracted in the past, something that death might as well put an end to at this point or that, without in the least concluding it, as those courses of French history in the sixth form at school which stop short indiscriminately, according to the whim of the curriculum or the professor, at the Revolution of 1830, or that of 1848, or the end of the Second Empire.

Perhaps then the fatigue and sadness that I felt arose not so much from my having loved in vain what I was already forgetting as from my beginning to enjoy the company of new living people, purely social figures, mere friends of the Guermantes, offering no interest in themselves. It was easier perhaps to reconcile myself to the discovery that she whom I had loved was no more, after a certain interval of time, than a pale memory, than to the rediscovery in myself of that futile activity which makes us waste time decorating our lives with a human vegetation which is robust but parasitic, which likewise will become nothing when it is dead, which already is alien to all that we have ever known, but which nevertheless our garrulous, melancholy, conceited senility seeks to cultivate. The newcomer who would find it easy to endure the prospect of life without Albertine had made his appearance in me, since I had been able to speak of her at Mme de Guermantes's in the language of grief without any real suffering. The possible advent of these new selves, which ought each to bear a different name from the preceding one, was something I had always dreaded, because of their indifference to the object of my love —long ago in connexion with Gilberte when her father told

me that if I went to live in Oceania I would never wish to
return, quite recently when I had read with such a pang in my
heart the passage in Bergotte's novel where he treats of the
character who, separated by the vicissitudes of life from a
woman whom he had adored when he was young, meets her
as an old man without pleasure, without any desire to see her
again. Yet he was bringing me on the contrary, this newcomer, at the same time as oblivion an almost complete elimination of suffering, a possibility of comfort—this newcomer, so
dreaded yet so beneficent, who was none other than one of
those spare selves which destiny holds in reserve for us, and
which, paying no more heed to our entreaties than a clear-
sighted and thus all the more authoritative physician, it substitutes in spite of us, by a timely intervention, for the self that
has been too seriously wounded. This process, as it happens,
automatically occurs from time to time, like the decay and
renewal of our tissues, but we notice it only if the former self
contained a great grief, a painful foreign body, which we are
surprised to find no longer there, in our amazement at having
become another person to whom the sufferings of his predecessor are no more than the sufferings of a stranger, of
which we can speak with compassion because we do not feel
them. Indeed we are unconcerned about having undergone
all those sufferings, since we have only a vague remembrance of
having suffered them. It may well be that likewise our nightmares are horrifying. But on waking we are another person,
who cares little that the person whose place he takes has had
to flee from a gang of cut-throats during the night.

No doubt this self still maintained some contact with the
old, as a friend who is indifferent to a bereavement speaks of it
nevertheless to the persons present in a suitable tone of sorrow,
and returns from time to time to the room in which the widower who has asked him to receive the company for him may still
be heard weeping. I too still wept when I became once again
for a moment the former friend of Albertine. But it was into a
new personality that I was tending to change altogether. It
is not because other people are dead that our affection for them
fades; it is because we ourselves are dying. Albertine had no
cause to reproach her friend. The man who was usurping his

name was merely his heir. We can only be faithful to what we remember, and we remember only what we have known. My new self, while it grew up in the shadow of the old, had often heard the other speak of Albertine; through that other self, through the stories it gathered from it, it thought that it knew her, it found her lovable, it loved her; but it was only a love at second hand.

Another person in whom the process of forgetting, as far as Albertine was concerned, was probably more rapid at this time, and indirectly enabled me to register a little later a new advance which that process had made in myself (and this is my memory of my second stage before finally forgetting), was Andrée. I can scarcely indeed but cite this forgetting of Albertine as, if not the sole cause, if not even the principal cause, at any rate a conditioning and necessary cause of a conversation which occurred between Andrée and myself about six months after the conversation I have already reported, and in which her words were very different from those that she had used on the former occasion. I remember that it was in my room because at that moment I found pleasure in having semi-carnal relations with her, by reason of the collective aspect which my love for the girls of the little band had originally had and now assumed once more, a love that had long been undivided among them and only for a while associated exclusively with Albertine's person, during the months that had preceded and followed her death.

We were in my room for another reason as well which enables me to date this conversation quite accurately. This was that I had been banished from the rest of the apartment because it was Mamma's "at-home" day. After some hesitation she had gone to lunch with Mme Sazerat, thinking that, since the latter always contrived, even at Combray, to invite one to meet boring people, she would be able without sacrificing any pleasure to return home in good time. And she had indeed returned in time and without regrets, Mme Sazerat having had nobody but the most deadly people who were in any case chilled by the special voice that she adopted when she had company, what Mamma called her Wednesday voice. My mother was none the less fond of her, and sympathised with

her ill-fortune—the result of the indiscretions of her father
who had been ruined by the Duchesse de X—which compelled her to live all the year round at Combray, with a few
weeks at her cousin's house in Paris and a long "pleasure-
trip" every ten years.

I remember that the day before this, after months of entreaty
from me, and because the Princess was always begging her to
come, Mamma had gone to call on the Princesse de Parme,
who paid no calls herself and at whose house people as a rule
contented themselves with signing their names, but who had
insisted on my mother's coming to see her, since the rules of
etiquette forbade Her Highness to come to us. My mother had
come home thoroughly cross: "You sent me on a wild goose
chase," she told me. "The Princesse de Parme barely greeted
me. She turned back to the ladies she was talking to without
paying any attention to me, and after ten minutes, as she hadn't
addressed a word to me, I came away without her even offering
me her hand. I was extremely annoyed. However, on the doorstep, as I was leaving, I met the Duchesse de Guermantes who
was very kind and spoke to me a great deal about you. What a
strange idea of yours to talk to her about Albertine! She told
me that you'd said to her that her death had been a great blow
to you. I shall never go near the Princesse de Parme again.
You've made me make a fool of myself."

The next day, which was my mother's "at-home" day,
Andrée came to see me. She did not have much time, as she
had to go and call for Gisèle with whom she was very anxious
to dine. "I know her faults, but she's after all my best friend
and the person for whom I feel most affection," she told me.
And she even appeared to be slightly alarmed at the thought
that I might ask her to let me dine with them. She was hungry
for people, and a third person who knew her too well, such as
myself, by preventing her from letting herself go, would prevent her from enjoying herself to the full in their company.

It is true that I was not there when she came; she was waiting for me in my room, and I was about to go through my
small sitting-room to join her when I realised, on hearing a
voice, that I had another visitor. Impatient to see Andrée, and
not knowing who the other person was (who evidently did not

know her since he had been put in another room), I listened
for a moment at the door of the small sitting-room; for my
visitor was not alone, he was speaking to a woman. *"Oh! ma
chérie, c'est dans mon coeur!"* he warbled to her, quoting Armand
Silvestre. "Yes, you will always remain my darling in spite of
everything you've done to me:

> *Les morts dorment en paix dans le sein de la terre.*
> *Ainsi doivent dormir nos sentiments éteints.*
> *Ces reliques du coeur ont aussi leur poussière;*
> *Sur leurs restes sacrés ne portons pas les mains.*[30]

It's a bit outmoded, but how pretty it is! And also what I
might have said to you from the first:

> *Tu les feras pleurer, enfant belle et chérie . . .*

What, you don't know it?

> *. . . Tous ces bambins, hommes futurs,*
> *Qui suspendent déjà leur jeune rêverie*
> *Aux cils câlins de tes yeux purs.*

Ah! for a moment I thought I could say to myself:

> *Le premier soir qu'il vint ici*
> *De fierté je n'eus plus souci.*
> *Je lui disais: Tu m'aimeras*
> *Aussi longtemps que tu pourras.*
> *Je ne dormais bien qu'en ses bras."*

Curious to see the woman to whom this deluge of poems
was addressed, even though it meant postponing for a moment
my urgent meeting with Andrée, I opened the door. They
were being recited by M. de Charlus to a young soldier whom
I soon recognised as Morel, and who was about to set off for his
fortnight's auxiliary service. He was no longer on friendly
terms with M. de Charlus, but saw him from time to time to
ask some favour of him. M. de Charlus, who usually gave a
more masculine style to his love-making, also had his moments
of weakness. Moreover, during his childhood, in order to be
able to feel and understand the words of the poets, he had been
obliged to imagine them as being addressed not to faithless
beauties but to young men. I left them as soon as I could,
although I sensed that paying visits with Morel was an immense satisfaction to M. de Charlus, to whom it gave the

momentary illusion of having married again. And besides, he combined in his person the snobbery of queens with the snobbery of servants.

The memory of Albertine had become so fragmentary that it no longer caused me any sadness and was no more now than a transition to fresh desires, like a chord which announces a change of key. And indeed, any idea of a passing sensual whim being ruled out, in so far as I was still faithful to Albertine's memory, I was happier at having Andrée in my company than I would have been at having an Albertine miraculously restored to life. For Andrée could tell me more things about Albertine than Albertine herself had ever told me. Now the problems concerning Albertine still remained in my mind although my tenderness for her, both physically and mentally, had already vanished. And my desire to know about her life, because it had diminished less, was now relatively greater than my need of her presence. Moreover, the idea that a woman had perhaps had relations with Albertine no longer aroused in me anything save the desire to have relations with that woman myself. I told Andrée this, caressing her as I spoke. Then, without making the slightest effort to make her words consistent with those of a few months earlier, Andrée said to me with a lurking smile: "Ah! yes, but you're a man. And so we can't do quite the same things as I used to do with Albertine." And whether because she felt that it would increase my desire (in the hope of extracting confidences, I had told her that I would like to have relations with a woman who had had them with Albertine) or my grief, or perhaps destroy a sense of superiority to herself which she might suppose me to feel at being the only person who had had relations with Albertine, she went on: "Ah! we spent many happy hours together; she was so caressing, so passionate. But it wasn't only with me that she liked to enjoy herself. She had met a handsome young man at Mme Verdurin's called Morel. They came to an understanding at once. He undertook—having her permission to enjoy them himself, for he liked little novices, and as soon as he had set them on the path of evil would abandon them—he undertook to entice young fisher-girls in remote villages, or young laundry-girls, who would fall for a boy but might not

have responded to a girl's advances. As soon as a girl was well
under his control, he'd bring her to a safe place and hand her
over to Albertine. For fear of losing Morel, who took part in
it all too, the girl always obeyed, and yet she lost him all the
same, because, as he was afraid of what might happen and also
as once or twice was enough for him, he would run off leaving
a false address. Once he had the nerve to bring one of these
girls, with Albertine, to a brothel at Couliville, where four or
five of the women had her together, or in turn. That was his
passion, and Albertine's too. But Albertine suffered terrible
remorse afterwards. I believe that when she was with you she
had conquered her passion and put off indulging it from day to
day. Besides, her affection for you was so great that she had
scruples. But it was quite certain that if she ever left you
she'd begin again. Only I think that after having left you, if
she succumbed to that overpowering urge, her remorse must
have been even greater. She hoped that you would rescue her,
that you would marry her. She felt in her heart that her obsession was a sort of criminal lunacy, and I've often wondered
whether it wasn't after an incident of that sort, which had
led to a suicide in a family, that she killed herself on purpose.
I must confess that in the early days of her stay with you she
hadn't entirely given up her games with me. There were days
when she seemed to need it, so much so that once, when it
would have been so easy elsewhere, she couldn't bring herself
to say good-bye without taking me to bed with her, in your
house. We were out of luck, and were very nearly caught.
She'd taken advantage of the fact that Françoise had gone out
to do some shopping, and you weren't yet home. Then she'd
turned out all the lights so that when you let yourself in with
your key it would take you some time to find the switch;
and she'd left the door of her room open. We heard you come
upstairs, and I only just had time to tidy myself up and come
down. Which was quite unnecessary as it happened, for by an
incredible chance you'd left your key at home and had to ring
the bell. But we lost our heads all the same, so that to conceal
our embarrassment we both of us, without having a chance to
consult each other, had the same idea: to pretend to dread the
scent of syringa which as a matter of fact we adored. You were

bringing a big branch of it home with you, which enabled me to turn my head away and hide my confusion. This didn't prevent me from telling you in the most idiotic way that perhaps Françoise had come back and would let you in, when a moment earlier I had told you the lie that we'd only just come in from our drive and that when we arrived Françoise hadn't yet left the house (which was true). But the big mistake we made—assuming that you had your key—was to turn out the light, for we were afraid that as you came upstairs you'd see it being turned on again; or at least we hesitated too long. And for three nights on end Albertine couldn't get a wink of sleep because she was constantly afraid that you might be suspicious and ask Françoise why she hadn't turned on the light before leaving the house. For Albertine was terribly afraid of you, and at times she maintained that you were treacherous and nasty and that you hated her really. After three days she gathered from your calm that you hadn't said anything to Françoise, and she was able to sleep again. But she never resumed her relations with me after that, either from fear or from remorse, for she made out that she did really love you, or perhaps she was in love with someone else. At all events, nobody could ever mention syringa again in her hearing without her turning crimson and putting her hand over her face in the hope of hiding her blushes."

Like certain strokes of fortune, there are strokes of misfortune that come too late, and do not assume the magnitude they would have had in our eyes a little earlier. One such was the misfortune that Andrée's terrible revelation was to me. No doubt, even when a piece of bad news is bound to make us unhappy, it may happen that, in the absorption, the regular give and take of conversation, it will pass in front of us without stopping and, preoccupied as we are by all the things we have to say in reply, transformed into someone else by the desire to please our present interlocutors, protected for a few moments in this new environment against the affections and the sufferings that we discarded upon entering it and will return to when the brief spell is broken, we do not have the time to take them in. However, if these affections and these sufferings are too predominant, we enter only distractedly into

the zone of a new and momentary environment, in which, too
faithful to our sufferings, we are incapable of becoming other;
and then the words that we hear said enter at once into relation
with our heart, which has not been neutralised. But for some
time past words that concerned Albertine, like a poison that has
evaporated, had lost their toxic power. She was already too
remote from me. As an afternoon stroller, seeing a misty
crescent in the sky, thinks: "So that's the vast moon," I said
to myself: "What, so that truth which I've sought for so long,
which I've so dreaded, is nothing more than these few words
uttered in the course of conversation, words to which one
cannot even give one's whole attention because one isn't
alone!" Besides, it took me at a serious disadvantage, as I had
exhausted myself with Andrée. Really, I would have liked to
have more strength to devote to a truth of such magnitude;
it remained extraneous to me, but this was because I had not
yet found a place for it in my heart. We would like the truth
to be revealed to us by novel signs, not by a sentence similar
to those which we have constantly repeated to ourselves. The
habit of thinking prevents us at times from experiencing
reality, immunises us against it, makes it seem no more than
another thought. There is no idea that does not carry in itself
its possible refutation, no word that does not imply its opposite.

In any case, if it was true, it was by this time the sort of
useless truth about the life of a dead mistress that rises up from
the depths and reveals itself when we can no longer have any
use for it. Then, thinking doubtless of some other woman
whom we now love and with regard to whom the same thing
may occur (for to her whom we have forgotten we no longer
give a thought), we lament, and say to ourselves: "If she who
is alive could only understand all this and realise that when
she is dead I shall know everything that she is hiding from
me." But it is a vicious circle. If I could have caused Albertine
to be restored to life, I should at the same time have caused
Andrée to reveal nothing. It is to some extent the same thing
as the everlasting "You'll see when I no longer love you,"
which is so true and so absurd, since one would indeed elicit
much if one no longer loved, but one would no longer be
interested in eliciting it. In fact it is precisely the same thing.

For if the woman you see again when you no longer love her then tells you all, it is because it is no longer she, or because it is no longer you: the person who loved has ceased to exist. There too death has passed by, and has made everything simple and pointless. I pursued these reflections basing myself on the assumption that Andrée was truthful—which was possible—and had been prompted to sincerity with me precisely because she had now had relations with me, from that Saint-André-des-Champs side of her nature which Albertine too had shown me at the start. She was encouraged in this case by the fact that she was no longer afraid of Albertine, for the reality of other people survives their death for only a short time in our minds, and after a few years they are like those gods of obsolete religions whom one offends without fear because one has ceased to believe in their existence. But the fact that Andrée no longer believed in the reality of Albertine might mean that she no longer feared (any more than to betray a secret which she had promised not to reveal) to concoct a lie which retrospectively slandered her alleged accomplice. Had this absence of fear permitted her to reveal the truth at last in telling me all that, or else to concoct a lie, if, for some reason, she supposed me to be full of happiness and pride and wished to cause me pain? Perhaps she was irritated with me (an irritation that had been held in abeyance so long as she saw that I was miserable, disconsolate) because I had had relations with Albertine and she envied me, perhaps—supposing that I considered myself on that account more favoured than her—an advantage which she herself had never, perhaps, obtained, nor even sought. Thus it was that I had often heard her say how ill they were looking to people whose look of radiant health, and in particular their awareness of it, exasperated her, and add, in the hope of annoying them, that she herself was very well, a fact that she never ceased to proclaim when she was seriously ill until the day when, in the detachment of death, it no longer mattered to her that others should be well and should know that she herself was dying. But that day was still remote. Perhaps she was angry with me, for what reason I had no idea, as long ago she had been filled with rage against the young man so learned in sporting matters, so ignorant of everything else, whom we had met at Balbec, who since then had been living with Rachel, and on the subject of whom Andrée poured forth defamatory remarks, hoping to be sued for slander in order to be able to formulate discreditable accusations against his father the falseness of which he would be unable to prove. Quite possibly this rage against myself had simply revived, having doubtless ceased when she saw how miserable I was. For the very same people whom, her eyes flashing with rage, she had longed to disgrace, to kill, to send to prison, by false testimony if need be, had only to reveal themselves to be unhappy or humiliated, for her to cease to wish them any harm, and to be ready to overwhelm them with kindness. For she was not fundamentally wicked, and if her unapparent, slightly deeper nature was not the niceness which one assumed at first from her delicate attentions, but rather envy and pride, her third nature, deeper still, the true but not entirely realised nature, tended towards kindness and the love of her fellow-creatures. Only, like all those people who in a certain state desire a better one, but, knowing it only through desiring it, do not realise that the first condition is to break away from the former state—like neurasthenics or drug-addicts who are anxious to be cured, but at the same time not to be deprived of their neuroses or their drugs, or like those world-loving religious or artistic spirits who long for solitude but seek none the less to envisage it as not implying an absolute renunciation of their former existence—Andrée was prepared to love all her fellow-creatures, but on the condition that she should first of all have succeeded in not having to visualise them as triumphant, and to that end should have humiliated them in advance. She did not understand that one should love even the proud, and conquer their pride by love and not by an even more overweening pride. But the fact is that she was like those invalids who wish to be cured by the very means that prolong their disease, which they like and would cease at once to like if they renounced them. But people wish to learn to swim and at the same time to keep one foot on the ground.

As regards the young sportsman, the Verdurins' nephew, whom I had met during my two visits to Balbec, it may be recounted here, incidentally and prematurely, that, some time after Andrée's visit, the account of which will be resumed in a moment, certain events occurred which caused a great sensation. First of all, this young man (perhaps in memory of Albertine with whom I did not then know that he had been in love) became engaged to Andrée and married her, to the despair of Rachel, of which he took no notice. Andrée no longer said then (that is to say some months after the visit of which I have been speaking) that he was a wretch, and I realised later on that she had said so only because she was madly in love with him and felt that he did not want her. But another fact made an even greater impression. This young man produced certain sketches for the theatre, with settings and costumes designed by himself, which effected in contemporary art a revolution at least equal to that brought about by the Russian ballet. In fact, the best-qualified critics regarded his works as being of cardinal importance, almost works of genius, and indeed I agree with them, confirming thus, to my own astonishment, the opinion long held by Rachel. The people who had known him at Balbec, intent only on seeing whether the cut of the clothes of the men with whom he associated was elegant or not, spending all his time at baccarat, at the races, on the golf-course or on the polo-ground, who knew that at school he had always been a dunce and had even been expelled from the lycée (to annoy his parents, he had gone to live for two months in the smart brothel in which M. de Charlus had hoped to surprise Morel), thought that perhaps his productions were the work of Andrée, who was prepared out of love to allow him all the glory, or that more probably he was paying, out of his huge personal fortune at which his excesses had barely nibbled, some inspired but needy professional to create them (this kind of wealthy society, unpolished by contact with the aristocracy and having no idea of what constitutes an artist—who to them is either an actor whom they engage to recite monologues at their daughter's engagement party, handing him his fee discreetly there and then in another room, or a painter to whom they make her sit once she is married, before the children come and when she is still at her best—are apt to believe that all the society people who write, compose or paint have their work done for them and pay to obtain a reputation as a creative artist as other men pay to secure a seat in Parliament). But all this was untrue, and this young man was indeed the author of those admirable works. When I learned this, I found myself torn between a number of different suppositions. Either he had indeed been for long years the dullard that he appeared to be, and some physiological cataclysm had awakened the dormant genius in him, like a Sleeping Beauty; or else at the time of his turbulent schooldays, of his failures to matriculate, of his heavy gambling losses at Balbec, of his reluctance to get into the little "tram" with his aunt Verdurin's faithful because of their hideous clothes, he was already a man of genius, distracted perhaps from his genius, which he had left in abeyance in the effervescence of juvenile passions; or again, already a conscious man of genius, and at the bottom of his class only because, while the master was spouting platitudes about Cicero, he himself was reading Rimbaud or Goethe. True, there were no grounds for any such hypothesis when I met him at Balbec, where his interests seemed to me to be centred exclusively on turning out a smart carriage and pair and mixing cocktails. But even this is not an irrefutable objection. He may have been extremely vain—something that is not incompatible with genius—and have sought to shine in the manner which he knew was best calculated to dazzle in the world in which he lived, that is to say, not by showing a profound knowledge of *Elective Affinities*, but far rather a knowledge of how to drive four-in-hand. Moreover, I am not at all sure that later on, when he had become the creator of those fine and original works, he would have cared greatly, outside the theatres in which he was known, to greet anyone who was not in evening dress, like the "faithful" in their earlier manner, which would be a proof in him not of stupidity but of vanity, and indeed of a certain practical sense, a certain perceptiveness in adapting his vanity to the mentality of the imbeciles whose esteem he valued and in whose eyes a dinner-jacket might perhaps shine with greater brilliance than the gaze of a thinker. Who can say whether, seen from without, some man of talent, or even a man devoid of talent but a lover of the things of the mind, myself for instance, would not have appeared, to anyone who met him at Rivebelle, in the hotel at Balbec, or on the esplanade, the most perfect and pretentious fool? Not to mention that for Octave matters of art must have been something so intimate, inhabiting the most secret recesses of his being, that doubtless it would never have occurred to him to speak of them, as Saint-Loup, for instance, would have done, Saint-Loup for whom the arts had all the glamour that horses and carriages had for Octave. And then he may have had a passion for gambling, and it is said that he retained it. But all the same, if the piety which brought to light the unknown work of Vinteuil emerged from the murky environment of Montjouvain, I was no less struck by the thought that what were perhaps the most extraordinary masterpieces of our day had emerged not from the *concours général*, from a model, academic education *à la* Broglie, but from the frequentation of paddocks and fashionable bars. In any case, in those days at Balbec, the reasons which made me anxious to know him, and which made Albertine and her friends anxious that I should not know him, were equally extraneous to his merit, and could only have illustrated the eternal misunderstanding between an "intellectual" (represented in this instance by myself) and society (represented by the little band) with regard to a social personality (the young golfer). I had no inkling of his talent, and his prestige in my eyes—like that of Mme Blatin long ago—had been that of being, whatever they might say, the friend of my girl friends, and more one of their band than myself. On the other hand, Albertine and Andrée, symbolising in this respect the incapacity of society people to bring a sound judgment to bear upon the things of the mind and their propensity to attach themselves in that connexion to false appearances, not only thought me almost idiotic because I took an interest in such an imbecile, but were astonished above all that, golfer for golfer, my choice should have fallen upon the poorest player of them all. If, for instance, I had chosen to make friends with young Gilbert de Bellœuvre, apart from golf he was a boy who had a certain amount of conversation, who had secured a *proxime accessit* in the *concours général* and was an agreeable versifier (as a matter of fact he was the stupidest of them all). Or again, if my object had been to "make a study for a book," Guy Saumoy, who was completely insane, who had abducted two girls, was at least a singular type who might "interest" me.

These two might have been allowed me, but the other, what attraction could I find in him? He was the epitome of the "great lout," of the "thick numbskull."

To return to Andrée's visit, after the disclosure that she had just made to me of her relations with Albertine, she added that the main reason for which Albertine had left me was concern about what her friends of the little band, and other people as well, might think of her living like that with a young man to whom she was not married: "Of course I know it was in your mother's house. But that makes no difference. You can't imagine what that sort of girls' community is like, what they conceal from one another, how they dread one another's opinion of them. I've seen some of them being terribly severe with young men simply because they knew their friends and they were afraid that certain things might be repeated, and then I've happened by chance to see those very same girls in a totally different light, much to their chagrin."

A few months earlier, this knowledge which Andrée appeared to possess of the motives that swayed the girls of the little band would have seemed to me the most precious thing in the world. What she said was perhaps sufficient to explain why Albertine, who had given herself to me afterwards in Paris, had refused to do so at Balbec where I was constantly meeting her friends, a fact which I had absurdly supposed to be so great an advantage for the purpose of being on good terms with her. Perhaps indeed it was because she had seen signs of my confiding in Andrée, or because I had rashly told the latter that she was coming to spend the night at the Grand Hotel, that Albertine, who an hour earlier was perhaps ready to let me enjoy certain favours as though that were the simplest thing in the world, had abruptly changed her mind and threatened to ring the bell. But then, she must have been accommodating to lots of others. This thought rekindled my jealousy and I told Andrée that there was something that I wished to ask her.

"You did those things in your grandmother's empty apartment?"

"Oh, no, never, we'd have been disturbed."

"Why, I thought . . . it seemed to me. . . ."

"Besides, Albertine chiefly liked doing it in the country."

"Oh! where?"

"Originally, when she hadn't time to go very far, we used to go to the Buttes-Chaumont. She knew a house there. Or else we would lie under the trees, there's never anyone about. In the grotto of the Petit Trianon, too."

"There, you see; how am I to believe you? You swore to me, not a year ago, that you'd never done anything at the Buttes-Chaumont."

"I was afraid of hurting you."

As I have said, I thought (although not until much later) that on the contrary it was on this second occasion, the day of her confessions, that Andrée had sought to hurt me. And this thought would have occurred to me at once, because I should have felt the need of it, if I had still been as much in love with Albertine. But Andrée's words did not hurt me sufficiently to make it essential for me to dismiss them immediately as untrue. On the whole, if what Andrée said was true, and I did not doubt it at the time, the real Albertine whom I now discovered, after having known so many diverse forms of Albertine, differed very little from the young bacchante who had loomed up and at once been detected that first day, on the front at Balbec, and who had offered me so many different aspects in succession, as a town alters the disposition of its buildings one after the other as we approach it, to the point of crushing, obliterating the principal monument which alone we could see from a distance, until finally, when we know it well and can judge it exactly, its true proportions prove to be those which the perspective of the first glance had indicated, the rest, through which we passed, being no more than that succession of lines of defence which everything in creation raises against our vision, and which we must cross one after another, at the cost of how much suffering, before we arrive at the heart. If, however, I had no need to believe absolutely in Albertine's innocence because my suffering had diminished, I can say that conversely, if I did not suffer unduly at this revelation, it was because, some time since, the belief in Albertine's innocence that I had fabricated for myself had been gradually replaced, without my realising it, by the belief, ever present in my mind,

in her guilt. Now if I no longer believed in Albertine's innocence, it was because I had already ceased to feel the need, the
passionate desire to believe in it. It is desire that engenders
belief, and if we are not as a rule aware of this, it is because
most belief-creating desires—unlike the desire which had
persuaded me that Albertine was innocent—end only with our
own life. To all the evidence that corroborated my original
version, I had stupidly preferred mere assertions by Albertine.
Why had I believed them? Lying is essential to humanity.
It plays as large a part perhaps as the quest for pleasure, and
is moreover governed by that quest. One lies in order to protect one's pleasure, or one's honour if the disclosure of one's
pleasure runs counter to one's honour. One lies all one's life
long, even, especially, perhaps only, to those who love one.
For they alone make us fear for our pleasure and desire their
esteem. I had at first thought Albertine guilty, and it was only
my desire, by utilising the powers of my intelligence to construct an edifice of doubt, that had put me on the wrong track.
Perhaps we live surrounded by electric, seismic signs which we
must interpret in good faith in order to know the truth about
people's characters. If the truth be told, saddened as I was in
spite of everything by Andrée's words, I thought it fitter that
the reality should finally turn out to accord with what my
instinct had originally foreboded rather than with the wretched
optimism to which I had later so cravenly surrendered. I
preferred that life should remain on the same level as my
intuitions. Those, moreover, that I had had that first day on
the beach, when I had believed that these girls were the
incarnation of frenzied pleasure, of vice, and again on the
evening when I had seen Albertine's governess leading that
passionate girl home to the little villa, as one drives into its
cage a wild animal which nothing, later on, despite appearances, will ever succeed in taming—did not those intuitions
accord with what Bloch had told me when he had made the
world seem so fair to my eyes by showing me, making me
quiver with excitement on all my walks, at every encounter,
the universality of desire? Perhaps, when all was said, it was
better that I should not have found those first intuitions verified afresh until now. While the whole of my love for Albertine

endured, they would have made me suffer too acutely and it was better that there should have subsisted of them only a trace, my perpetual suspicion of things which I did not see and which nevertheless happened continually so close to me, and perhaps another trace as well, earlier, vaster, which was *my love itself*. For was it not, despite all the denials of my reason, tantamount to knowing Albertine in all her hideousness, actually to choose her, to love her? And even in the moments when mistrust is stilled, is not love the persistence of that mistrust and a transformation of it, is it not a proof of clairvoyance (a proof unintelligible to the lover himself), since desire, reaching out always towards what is most opposite to oneself, forces one to love what will make one suffer? There is no doubt that, inherent in a woman's charm, in her eyes, her lips, her figure, are the elements, unknown to us, most calculated to make us unhappy, so much so that to feel attracted to her, to begin to love her, is, however innocent we may pretend it to be, to read already, in a different version, all her betrayals and her misdeeds. And may not those charms which, to attract me, corporealised thus the noxious, dangerous, fatal elements of a person, have stood in a more direct relation of cause and effect to those secret poisons than do the seductive luxuriance and the toxic juice of certain venomous flowers? It was perhaps, I told myself, Albertine's vice itself, the cause of my future sufferings, that had produced in her that honest, frank manner, creating the illusion that one enjoyed with her the same loyal and unqualified comradeship as with a man, just as a parallel vice had produced in M. de Charlus a feminine delicacy of sensibility and mind. In the midst of the most complete blindness, perspicacity subsists in the form of predilection and tenderness; so that it is a mistake to speak of a bad choice in love, since as soon as there is a choice it can only be a bad one.

"Did those excursions to the Buttes-Chaumont take place when you used to call for her here?" I asked Andrée.

"Oh! no, from the day Albertine came back from Balbec with you, except the time I told you about, she never did anything again with me. She wouldn't even allow me to mention such things to her."

"But my dear Andrée, why go on lying to me? By the

merest chance, for I never try to find out anything, I've learned
in the minutest detail things of that sort which Albertine did,
I can tell you exactly, on the bank of a river with a laundry-
girl, only a few days before her death."

"Ah! perhaps after she'd left you, that I can't say. She felt
that she'd failed, that she'd never again be able to regain your
trust."

These last words shattered me. Then I thought again of the
evening of the syringa, and remembered that about a fortnight
later, as my jealousy kept changing its object, I had asked
Albertine whether she had ever had relations with Andrée,
and she had replied: "Oh! never! Of course, I adore Andrée;
I have a deep affection for her, but as I might have for a sister,
and even if I had the tastes which you seem to suppose, she's
the last person I should have thought of in that connexion.
I can swear to you by anything you like, the honour of my aunt,
the grave of my poor mother." I had believed her. And yet even
if my suspicions had not been aroused by the contradiction
between her former partial admissions with regard to certain
matters and the vehemence with which she had afterwards
denied them as soon as she saw that I was not indifferent to
them, I ought to have remembered Swann, convinced of the
platonic nature of M. de Charlus's friendships and assuring
me of it on the evening of the very day I had seen the tailor
and the Baron in the courtyard; I ought to have reflected that
there are two worlds one behind the other, one consisting of
the things that the best, the sincerest people say, and behind
it the world composed of the sequence of what those same
people do; so that when a married woman says to you of a
young man: "Oh! it's perfectly true that I have an immense
affection for him, but it's something quite innocent, quite
pure, I could swear it on the memory of my parents," one
ought oneself, instead of feeling any hesitation, to swear to
oneself that she has probably just come out of the bathroom
into which, after every assignation she has with the young
man in question, she rushes in order not to have a child. The
spray of syringa made me profoundly sad, as did also the
thought that Albertine could have believed, and said, that I
was treacherous and hostile; and most of all perhaps, certain

lies so unexpected that I had difficulty in grasping them. One day Albertine had told me that she had been to an aerodrome where one of the airmen was a friend of hers (this doubtless in order to divert my suspicions from women, thinking that I was less jealous of men), and that it had been amusing to see how dazzled Andrée was by the said airman, by all the compliments he paid Albertine, until finally Andrée had wanted to go up in his aeroplane with him. Now this was a complete fabrication; Andrée had never visited the aerodrome in question.

When Andrée left me, it was dinner-time. "You'll never guess who has been to see me and stayed at least three hours," said my mother. "I call it three hours, but it was perhaps longer. She arrived almost on the heels of my first visitor, who was Mme Cottard, sat still and watched everybody come and go— and I had more than thirty callers—and left me only a quarter of an hour ago. If you hadn't had your friend Andrée with you, I'd have sent for you."

"Well, who was it?"

"A person who never pays calls."

"The Princesse de Parme?"

"Why, I have a cleverer son than I thought. It's no fun making you guess a name; you hit on it at once."

"Did she apologise for her coldness yesterday?"

"No, that would have been stupid. The visit itself was her apology. Your poor grandmother would have thought it admirable. It seems that about two o'clock she sent a footman to ask whether I had an 'at-home' day. She was told that this was the very day and so up she came."

My first thought, which I did not dare mention to Mamma, was that the Princesse de Parme, surrounded the day before by people of rank and fashion with whom she was on intimate terms and enjoyed conversing, on seeing my mother come into the room had felt an annoyance which she had made no attempt to conceal. And it was quite in the style of the great ladies of Germany, which for that matter the Guermantes had largely adopted—that haughtiness for which they thought to atone by a scrupulous affability. But my mother believed, and I came in time to share her opinion, that the Princesse de Parme, having simply failed to recognise her, had not felt bound to pay any attention to her, and that she had learned after my mother's departure who she was, either from the Duchesse de Guermantes whom my mother had met below or from the list of her visitors, whose names were requested by the ushers before they entered her presence and inscribed in a register. She had felt that it would be ungracious to send word or to say to my mother: "I didn't recognise you," and instead— and this was no less in keeping with the code of manners of the German courts and with the ways of the Guermantes than my original version—had thought that a visit, an exceptional action on the part of a royal personage, and what was more a visit of several hours' duration, would convey the explanation to my mother in an indirect but no less convincing form, which is just what did happen.

But I did not stay to hear my mother's account of the Princess's visit, for I had just recalled a number of facts concerning Albertine as to which I had intended but had forgotten to question Andrée. How little, for that matter, did I know, would I ever know, of this story of Albertine, the only story that really interested me, or was at least beginning to interest me again at certain moments. For man is that ageless creature who has the faculty of becoming many years younger in a few seconds, and who, surrounded by the walls of the time through which he has lived, floats within them as in a pool the surface-level of which is constantly changing so as to bring him within range now of one epoch, now of another. I wrote to Andrée asking her to come again. She was unable to do so until a week later. Almost as soon as she entered the room I said to her: "Very well, then, since you maintain that Albertine never did that sort of thing while she was staying here, according to you it was to be able to do it more freely that she left me, but for which of her friends?"

"Certainly not, it wasn't that at all."

"Then because I was too disagreeable?"

"No, I don't think so. I think she was forced to leave you by her aunt who had designs for her future upon that guttersnipe, you know, the young man you used to call 'I'm a wash-out,' the young man who was in love with Albertine and had asked for her hand. Seeing that you weren't marrying her, they were afraid that the shocking length of her stay in your house might prevent the young man from doing so. And so Mme Bontemps, on whom the young man was constantly bringing pressure to bear, summoned Albertine home. Albertine after all needed her uncle and aunt, and when she realised that they were forcing her hand she left you."

I had never in my jealousy thought of this explanation, but only of Albertine's desire for women and of my own surveillance of her; I had forgotten that there was also Mme Bontemps who might eventually regard as strange what had shocked my mother from the first. At least Mme Bontemps was afraid that it might shock this possible husband whom she was keeping in reserve for Albertine in case I failed to marry her.

So that it was possible that a long debate had gone on in Albertine's mind between staying with me and leaving me, but that her decision to leave me had been made on account of her aunt, or of that young man, and not on account of women to whom perhaps she had never given a thought. The most disturbing thing to my mind was that Andrée, who after all no longer had anything to conceal from me as to Albertine's morals, swore to me that nothing of the sort had ever occurred between Albertine on the one hand and Mlle Vinteuil or her friend on the other (Albertine herself was unconscious of her own proclivities when she first met them, and they, from the fear of being mistaken in the object of one's desire which breeds as many errors as desire itself, regarded her as extremely hostile to that sort of thing. Perhaps later on they had learned that her tastes were similar to their own, but by that time they knew Albertine and Albertine knew them too well for there to be any question of their doing those things together).

"But, my dear Andrée, you're lying again. Remember—you admitted it to me yourself when I telephoned to you the evening before, don't you remember?—that Albertine had been so anxious, and kept it from me as though it was something that I mustn't know about, to go to the afternoon party at the Verdurins' at which Mlle Vinteuil was expected."

"Yes, but Albertine hadn't the slightest idea that Mlle Vinteuil was to be there."

"What? You yourself told me that she'd met Mme Verdurin a few days earlier. Besides, Andrée, there's no point in our trying to deceive one another. I found a note one morning in Albertine's room, a note from Mme Verdurin urging her to come that afternoon."

And I showed her this note which, as a matter of fact, Françoise had taken care to bring to my notice by placing it on top of Albertine's belongings a few days before her departure, and, I regret to say, leaving it there to make Albertine suppose that I had been rummaging among her things, to let her know in any case that I had seen it. And I had often wondered whether Françoise's ruse had not been largely responsible for the departure of Albertine, who saw that she could no longer conceal anything from me, and felt disheartened, defeated. I showed Andrée the note: *I feel no compunction, on the strength of this genuine family feeling.* . . . "You know very well, Andrée, that Albertine used always to say that Mlle Vinteuil's friend was indeed a mother, an elder sister to her."

"But you've misinterpreted this note. The person Mme Verdurin wished Albertine to meet that afternoon wasn't Mlle Vinteuil's friend at all, it was the young man you call 'I'm a wash-out,' and the family feeling is what Mme Verdurin felt for the brute, who is after all her nephew. However, I think Albertine did hear afterwards that Mlle Vinteuil was to be there—Mme Verdurin may have let her know incidentally. And of course the thought of seeing her friend again gave her pleasure, reminded her of happy times in the past, just as you'd be glad, if you were going somewhere, to know that Elstir would be there, but no more than that, not even as much. No, if Albertine was unwilling to say why she wanted to go to Mme Verdurin's, it was because it was a rehearsal to which Mme Verdurin had invited a very small party, including that nephew of hers whom you met at Balbec, to whom Mme Bontemps was hoping to marry Albertine off and to whom Albertine wanted to talk. He was a real blackguard . . ."

And so Albertine, contrary to what Andrée's mother used to think, had had after all the prospect of a wealthy marriage. And when she had wanted to visit Mme Verdurin, when she had spoken to her in secret, when she had been so annoyed that I should have gone there that evening without warning her, the intrigue between her and Mme Verdurin had had as its object her meeting not Mlle Vinteuil but the nephew who loved Albertine and for whom Mme Verdurin, with that satisfaction at the prospect of certain marriages which surprise one in some families into whose state of mind one does not enter completely, did not desire a rich bride. Now I had never given another thought to this nephew who had perhaps been the initiator thanks to whom I had received Albertine's first kiss. And for the whole structure of Albertine's motives and anxieties which I had built up, I must now substitute another, or rather superimpose it, for perhaps it did not exclude the other, a taste for women not being incompatible with marriage. Was this marriage really the reason for Albertine's departure, and had she, out of self-respect, so as not to appear to be dependent on her aunt, or to force me to marry her, preferred not to mention it? I was beginning to realise that the system of multiple motives for a single action, of which Albertine showed her mastery in her relations with her friends when she allowed each of them to suppose that it was for her sake that she had come, was only a sort of symbol, artificial and premeditated, of the different aspects that an action assumes according to the point of view from which we look at it. It was not the first time I had felt astonishment and a sort of shame at never once having told myself that Albertine was in a false position in my house, a position that might give offence to her aunt; it was not the first, nor was it the last. How often has it happened to me, after having sought to understand the relations between two people and the crises that they entail, to hear all of a sudden a third person speak to me of them from his own point of view, for he has even closer relations with one of the two, a point of view which has perhaps been the cause of the crisis! And if people's actions remain so unpredictable, how should not the people themselves be equally so? Listening to the people who maintained that Albertine was a schemer who had tried to get one man after another to marry her, it was not difficult to imagine how they would have defined her life with me. And yet to my mind she had been a victim, a victim

who perhaps was not altogether pure, but in that case guilty for
other reasons, on account of vices which people did not
mention.

But above all we must remember this: on the one hand,
lying is often a trait of character; on the other hand, in women
who would not otherwise be liars, it is a natural defence,
improvised at first, then more and more organised, against that
sudden danger which would be capable of destroying all life:
love. Furthermore, it is not by mere chance that sensitive,
intellectual men invariably give themselves to insensitive and
inferior women, and moreover remain attached to them, and
that the proof that they are not loved does not in the least
cure them of the urge to sacrifice everything to keep such
women with them. If I say that such men need to suffer, I am
saying something that is accurate while suppressing the preliminary truths which make that need—involuntary in a sense
—to suffer a perfectly understandable consequence of those
truths. Not to mention the fact that, complete natures being
rare, a man who is highly sensitive and highly intellectual
will generally have little will-power, will be the plaything of
habit and of that fear of suffering in the immediate present
which condemns to perpetual suffering—and that in these
conditions he will never be prepared to repudiate the woman
who does not love him. One may be surprised that he should be
content with so little love, but one ought rather to picture to
oneself the anguish that may be caused him by the love which
he himself feels. An anguish which one ought not to pity
unduly, for those terrible commotions that are caused by an
unrequited love, by the departure or the death of a mistress,
are like those attacks of paralysis which at first leave us helpless, but after which the muscles tend gradually to recover
their vital elasticity and energy. What is more, this anguish
does not lack compensation. These sensitive and intellectual
persons are as a rule little inclined to falsehood. It takes them
all the more unawares in that, however intelligent they may be,
they live in the world of the possible, live in the anguish which
a woman has just inflicted on them rather than in the clear
perception of what she wanted, what she did, what she loved,
a perception granted chiefly to self-willed natures which need

it in order to prepare against the future instead of lamenting the past. And so these persons feel that they are betrayed without quite knowing how. Wherefore the mediocre woman whom we are astonished to see them loving enriches the universe for them far more than an intelligent woman would have done. Behind each of her words, they feel that a lie is lurking, behind each house to which she says that she has gone, another house, behind each action, each person, another action, another person. Of course they do not know what or whom, they do not have the energy, would not perhaps find it possible, to discover. A lying woman, by an extremely simple trick, can beguile, without taking the trouble to change her method, any number of people, and, what is more, the very person who ought to have discovered the trick. All this confronts the sensitive intellectual with a universe full of depths which his jealousy longs to plumb and which are not without interest to his intelligence. Without being precisely a man of that category, I was going perhaps to learn, now that Albertine was dead, the secret of her life. Here again, do not these indiscretions which occur only after a person's life on earth is ended prove that nobody really believes in a future life? If these indiscretions are true, one ought to fear the resentment of a woman whose actions one reveals fully as much in anticipation of meeting her in heaven as one feared it while she was alive and one felt bound to keep her secret. And if these indiscretions are false, invented because she is no longer present to contradict them, one ought to be even more afraid of the dead woman's wrath if one believed in heaven. But no one does believe in it.

On the whole, I did not understand any better than before why Albertine had left me. If the face of a woman can with difficulty be grasped by the eyes, which cannot take in the whole of its mobile surface, or by the lips, or still less by the memory, if it is shrouded in obscurity according to her social position, according to the level at which we are situated, how much thicker is the veil drawn between those of her actions which we see and her motives! Motives are situated at a deeper level, which we do not perceive, and moreover engender actions other than those of which we are aware and often in absolute contradiction to them. When has there not been some man in public life, regarded as a saint by his friends, who is discovered to have forged documents, robbed the State, betrayed his country? How often is a great nobleman robbed by a steward whom he has brought up from childhood, ready to swear that he was an excellent man, as possibly he was! And how much more impenetrable does it become, this curtain that screens another's motives, if we are in love with that person, for it clouds our judgment and also obscures the actions of one who, feeling that she is loved, ceases suddenly to set any store by what otherwise would have seemed to her important, such as wealth for example. Perhaps also it induces her to feign to some extent this scorn for wealth in the hope of obtaining more by making us suffer. The bargaining instinct may also enter into everything else; and even actual incidents in her life, an intrigue which she has confided to no one for fear of its being revealed to us, which many people might for all that have discovered had they felt the same passionate desire to know it as we ourselves while preserving a greater equanimity of mind and arousing fewer suspicions in the guilty party, an intrigue of which certain people have in fact not been unaware—but people whom we do not know and would not know how to find. And among all these reasons for her adopting an inexplicable attitude towards us, we must include those idiosyncrasies of character which impel people, whether from indifference to their own interests, or from hatred, or from love of freedom, or under the impulse of anger, or from fear of what certain people will think, to do the opposite of what we expected. And then there are the differences of environment, of upbringing, in which we refuse to believe because, when we are talking together, they are effaced by our words, but which return when we are apart to direct the actions of each of us from so opposite a point of view that no true meeting of minds is possible.

"Anyhow there's no need to seek out all these explanations," Andrée went on. "Heaven knows I was fond of Albertine, and she was a really nice creature, but, especially after she had typhoid (a year before you first met us all), she was an absolute madcap. All of a sudden she would get sick of what she was doing, all her plans would have to be changed that very minute, and she herself probably couldn't say why. You remember the year when you first came to Balbec, the year when you met us all? One fine day she got somebody to send her a telegram calling her back to Paris; she barely had time to pack her trunks. But there was absolutely no reason for her to go. All the pretexts she gave were false. Paris would be a deadly bore at that moment. We were all of us still at Balbec. The golf club wasn't closed, indeed the heats for the cup which she was so keen on winning weren't finished. She'd certainly have won it. It only meant staying on for another week. Well, off she went. I often spoke to her about it later. She said herself that she didn't know why she had left, that she felt home-sick (the home being Paris, you can imagine how likely that was), that she didn't feel happy at Balbec, that she thought there were people there who sneered at her."

And there was this much truth in what Andrée said: that if differences between minds account for the different impressions produced upon one person and another by the same work, and differences of feeling for the impossibility of captivating a person who does not love you, there are also differences between characters, peculiarities in a single character, which are also motives for action. Then I ceased to think about this explanation and said to myself how difficult it is to know the truth in this world.

I had indeed noticed Albertine's desire to go to Mme Verdurin's and her concealment of it: I had not been mistaken on that point. But then even if we do thus manage to grasp one fact, all the others, which we perceive only in their outward appearance, pass us by, and we see only a succession of flat silhouettes of which we say to ourselves: it may be this, it may be that, it may be because of her, or it may be because of someone else. The revelation of the fact that Mlle Vinteuil was expected had seemed to me the true explanation, all the more so because Albertine, forestalling me, had spoken to me about it. And subsequently had she not refused to swear to me that Mlle Vinteuil's presence gave her no pleasure? And here, with regard to this young man, I remembered a point

which I had forgotten. A short time before, while Albertine
was living with me, I had met him, and he had been—in
contrast to his attitude at Balbec—extremely friendly, even
affectionate towards me, had begged me to allow him to
call on me, a request which I had refused for a number of
reasons. And now I realised that it was quite simply because,
knowing that Albertine was living in my house, he had
wanted to be on good terms with me so as to have every facility
for seeing her and for carrying her off from me, and I concluded that he was a scoundrel. Some time later, when I
attended the first performances of this young man's work,
although I continued to think that if he had been so anxious
to call on me, it was for Albertine's sake, and although I felt
this to be reprehensible, I remembered that in the past, if I
had gone down to Doncières to see Saint-Loup, it was really
because I was in love with Mme de Guermantes. It is true that
the two cases were not quite the same: Saint-Loup not being
in love with Mme de Guermantes, there was in my display of
affection for him a trace of duplicity perhaps, but no treason.
But I reflected afterwards that this affection which one feels
for the person who possesses the object of one's desire is
something that one feels equally even if he himself also loves
that object. No doubt, one ought in that case to resist a
friendship which will lead one straight to betrayal. And I think
that this is what I have always done. But in the case of those
who lack the strength to resist, we cannot say that the friendship they affect for their rival is a mere sham; they feel it
sincerely and for that reason display it with a fervour which,
once the betrayal has been accomplished, can cause the betrayed husband or lover to say with amazed indignation: "If
you had heard the protestations of affection that the wretch
showered on me! That a person should come to rob a man of
his treasure, that I can understand. But that he should feel the
diabolical need to assure him of his friendship first of all strikes
me as a degree of ignominy and perversity almost impossible
to imagine." No, in fact, there is no perverse pleasure in it,
nor even an absolutely conscious lie.

The affection of this sort which Albertine's pseudo-fiancé
had manifested for me that day had yet another excuse, being

more complex than a simple by-product of his love for
Albertine. It was only a short time since he had known himself
to be, confessed himself to be, been anxious to be proclaimed
an intellectual. For the first time, values other than sporting
or hedonistic existed for him. The fact that I enjoyed the
esteem of Elstir and Bergotte, that Albertine had perhaps
told him of the way I talked about writers, which had led
her to imagine that I might myself be able to write, meant
that all of a sudden I had become to him (to the new man
whom he at last realised himself to be) an interesting person
whose friendship he would have liked to cultivate, to whom
he would have liked to confide his plans, whom he might
perhaps have asked for an introduction to Bergotte. So that
he was in fact sincere when he asked if he might call on me,
expressing a regard for me to which intellectual reasons as
well as a reflection of Albertine imparted a certain veracity.
No doubt it was not *for that* that he was so anxious to come and
see me and would have dropped everything in order to do so.
But of this last reason, which did little more than raise to a
sort of impassioned paroxysm the two other reasons, he was
perhaps unaware himself, and the other two existed really, as
might really have existed in Albertine, when she had been
anxious to go to Mme Verdurin's on the afternoon of the
rehearsal, the perfectly respectable pleasure that she would
feel in meeting again friends of her childhood who in her eyes
were no more depraved than she was in theirs, in talking to
them, in showing them, by the mere fact of her presence at the
Verdurins', that the poor little girl whom they had known
was now invited to a noted salon, the pleasure also that she
might perhaps have felt in listening to Vinteuil's music. If all
this was true, the blush that had risen to Albertine's cheeks
when I had mentioned Mlle Vinteuil was due to the fact that
I had done so in the context of that afternoon party which she
had tried to keep secret from me because of the marriage
proposal of which I was not to know. Albertine's refusal to
swear to me that she would have felt no pleasure in meeting
Mlle Vinteuil again at that party had at the moment intensified
my torment, strengthened my suspicions, but proved to me in
retrospect that she had wanted to be sincere, even over an

innocent matter, perhaps simply because it was an innocent matter. There nevertheless remained what Andrée had told me about her relations with Albertine. Perhaps, however, even without going so far as to believe that Andrée had invented them solely in order that I might cease to be happy and cease to be able to feel superior to her, it was still possible for me to suppose that she had slightly exaggerated her account of what she used to do with Albertine, and that Albertine, by a mental reservation, also minimised slightly what she had done with Andrée, Jesuitically making use of certain definitions which I had stupidly formulated on the subject, judging that her relations with Andrée did not fall into the category of what she was obliged to confess to me and that she could deny them without lying. But why should I believe that it was she rather than Andrée who was lying? Truth and life are very difficult to fathom, and I retained of them, without really having got to know them, an impression in which sadness was perhaps actually eclipsed by exhaustion.

As for the third occasion on which I remember being conscious of nearing total indifference with regard to Albertine (and this time to the extent of feeling that I had finally arrived at it), it was some little while after Andrée's last visit, in Venice.

My mother had taken me to spend a few weeks there, and— as beauty may exist in the most precious as well as in the humblest things—I received there impressions analogous to those which I had felt so often in the past at Combray, but transposed into a wholly different and far richer key. When, at ten o'clock in the morning, my shutters were thrown open, I saw blazing there, instead of the gleaming black marble into which the slates of Saint-Hilaire used to turn, the golden angel on the campanile of St Mark's. Glittering in a sunlight which made it almost impossible to keep one's eyes upon it, this angel promised me, with its outstretched arms, for the moment when I appeared on the Piazzetta half an hour later, a joy more certain than any that it could ever in the past have been bidden to announce to men of good will. I could see nothing else so long as I remained in bed, but as the whole world is merely a vast sun-dial, a single sunlit segment of which enables us to tell what time it is, on the very first morning I was reminded of the shops in the Place de l'Eglise at Combray, which, on Sunday mornings, were always on the point of shutting when I arrived for mass, while the straw in the market place smelt strongly in the already hot sunlight. But on the second morning, what I saw on awakening, what made me get out of bed (because they had taken the place in my memory and in my desire of the recollections of Combray), were the impressions of my first morning stroll in Venice, in Venice where everyday life was no less real than in Combray, where as in Combray on Sunday mornings one had the pleasure of stepping down into a festive street, but where that street was entirely paved with sapphire-blue water, cooled by warm breezes and of a colour so durable that my tired eyes might rest their gaze upon it in search of relaxation without fear of its blenching. Like the good folk of the Rue de l'Oiseau at Combray, so also in this strange town, the inhabitants actually emerged from houses lined up side by side along the main street, but the role played there by houses of casting a patch of shade at their feet was entrusted in Venice to palaces of porphyry and jasper, above the arched doors of which the head of a bearded god (breaking the alignment, like the knocker on a door at Combray) had the effect of darkening with its shadow, not the brownness of the earth, but the splendid blueness of the water. On the Piazza, the shadow that would have been produced at Combray by the awning over the draper's shop and the barber's pole was a carpet of little blue flowers strewn at its feet upon the desert of sun-scorched flagstones by the relief of a Renaissance façade, which is not to say that, when the sun beat down, one was not obliged, in Venice as at Combray, to pull down the blinds, even beside the canal, but they hung between the quatrefoils and foliage of Gothic windows. Of this sort was the window in our hotel behind the balusters of which my mother sat waiting for me, gazing at the canal with a patience which she would not have displayed in the old days at Combray, at a time when, cherishing hopes for my future which had never been realised, she was unwilling to let me see how much she loved me. Nowadays she was well aware that an apparent coldness on her part would alter nothing, and the affection she lavished upon me was like those forbidden foods which are no longer withheld from invalids when it is certain that they are past recovery. True, the humble details which gave an individuality to the window of my aunt Léonie's bedroom seen from the Rue de l'Oiseau, the impression of asymmetry caused by its unequal distance from the windows on either side of it, the exceptional height of its wooden ledge, the angled bar which served to open the shutters, the two curtains of glossy blue satin tied back with loops—the equivalent of all these things existed in this hotel in Venice where I could hear also those words, so distinctive and so eloquent, which enable us to recognise from a distance the dwelling to which we are going home to lunch, and afterwards remain in our memory as testimony that, for a certain period of time, that dwelling was ours; but the task of uttering them had, in Venice, devolved not, as at Combray and most other places, upon the simplest, not to say the ugliest things, but upon the ogive, still half Arab, of a façade which is reproduced in all the architectural museums and all the illustrated art books as one of the supreme achievements of the domestic architecture of the Middle Ages; from a long way away and when I had barely passed San Giorgio Maggiore, I caught sight of this ogival window which had already seen me, and the thrust of its pointed arches added to its smile of welcome the distinction of a loftier, scarcely comprehensible gaze. And because, behind its multi-coloured marble balusters, Mamma was sitting reading while she waited for me to return, her face shrouded in a tulle veil as heart-rending in its whiteness as her hair to me who sensed that, hiding her tears, she had pinned it to her straw hat not so much with the idea of appearing "dressed" in the eyes of the hotel staff as in order to appear to me to be less in mourning, less sad, almost consoled for the death of my grandmother; because, not having recognised me at first, as soon as I called to her from the gondola, she sent out to me, from the bottom of her heart, a love which stopped only where there was no longer any corporeal matter to sustain it, on the surface of her impassioned gaze which she brought as close to me as possible, which she tried to thrust forward to the advanced post of her lips, in a smile which seemed to be kissing me, within the frame and beneath the canopy of the more discreet smile of the arched window lit up by the midday sun—because of this, that window has assumed in my memory the precious quality of things that have had, simultaneously with us, side by side with us, their share in a certain hour that struck, the same for us and for them; and however full of admirable tracery its mullions may be, that illustrious window retains in my eyes the intimate aspect of a man of genius with whom we have spent a month in some holiday resort, where he has acquired a friendly regard for us; and if, ever since then, whenever I see a cast of that window in a museum, I am obliged to hold back my tears, it is simply because it says to me the thing that touches me more than anything else in the world: "I remember your mother so well."

And as I went indoors to join my mother who by now had left the window, on leaving the heat of the open air I had the same sensation of coolness that I experienced long ago at Combray when I went upstairs to my room; but in Venice it was a breeze from the sea that kept the air cool, and no longer on a little wooden staircase with narrow steps, but on the noble surfaces of marble steps continually splashed by shafts of blue-green sunlight, which, to the valuable instruction in the art of Chardin acquired long ago, added a lesson in that of Veronese. And since, in Venice, it is works of art, things of priceless beauty, that are entrusted with the task of giving us our impressions of everyday life, it is to falsify the character of that city, on the grounds that the Venice of certain painters is coldly aesthetic in its most celebrated parts (let us make an exception of the superb studies of Maxime Dethomas), to represent only its poverty-stricken aspects, in the districts where nothing of its splendour is to be seen, and, in order to make Venice more intimate and more genuine, to give it a resemblance to Aubervilliers. It has been the mistake of some very great artists, from a quite natural reaction against the artificial Venice of bad painters, to concentrate exclusively on the Venice of the more humble *campi*, the little deserted *rii*, which they found more real.

It was this Venice that I used often to explore in the afternoon, when I did not go out with my mother. The fact was that it was easier to find there women of the people, match-sellers, pearl-stringers, glass or lace makers, young seamstresses in black shawls with long fringes, whom there was nothing to prevent me from loving, because I had to a large extent forgotten Albertine, and who seemed to me more desirable than others, because I still remembered her a little. Who, in any case, could have told me precisely, in this passionate quest of mine for Venetian women, how much there was of themselves, how much of Albertine, how much of my old, long-cherished desire to visit Venice? Our slightest desire, though unique as a chord, nevertheless includes the fundamental notes on which the whole of our life is built. And sometimes, if we were to eliminate one of them, even one that we do not hear, that we are not aware of, one that has no connexion with the object of our quest, we would nevertheless see our whole desire for that object disappear. There were many things that I made no attempt to identify in the excitement I felt as I went in search of Venetian women.

My gondola followed the course of the small canals; like the mysterious hand of a genie leading me through the maze of this oriental city, they seemed, as I advanced, to be cutting a path for me through the heart of a crowded quarter which they bisected, barely parting, with a slender furrow arbitrarily traced, the tall houses with their tiny Moorish windows; and as though the magic guide had been holding a candle in his hand and were lighting the way for me, they kept casting ahead of them a ray of sunlight for which they cleared a route. One felt that between the mean dwellings which the canal had just parted, and which otherwise would have formed a compact whole, no open space had been reserved; so that a campanile or a garden trellis vertically overhung the *rio*, as in a flooded city. But, for both churches and gardens, thanks to the same transposition as in the Grand Canal, the sea so readily served as means of communication, as substitute for street or alley, that on either side of the *canaletto* the belfries rose from the water in this poor and populous district like those of humble and much-frequented parish churches bearing

the stamp of their necessity, of their use by crowds of simple
folk, the gardens traversed by the canal cutting trailed their
startled leaves and fruit in the water, and on the ledges of the
houses whose crudely cut stone was still rough as though it
had only just been sawn, urchins surprised by the gondola sat
back trying to keep their balance and allowing their legs to
dangle vertically, like sailors seated upon a swing-bridge the
two halves of which have been swung apart, allowing the sea
to pass between them. Now and again would appear a hand-
somer building that happened to be there like a surprise in a
box which one has just opened, a little ivory temple with its
Corinthian columns and an allegorical statue on its pediment,
somewhat out of place among the ordinary surroundings in
the midst of which the peristyle with which the canal had
provided it retained the look of a landing-stage for market
gardeners.

I returned on foot through narrow lanes; I accosted plebeian
girls as Albertine perhaps had done, and I should have liked to
have her with me. Yet these could not be the same girls;
at the time when Albertine had been in Venice, they would
have been children still. But, after having been unfaithful in
the past, in a basic sense and out of cowardice, to each of the
desires that I had conceived as unique—since I had sought an
analogous object and not the same one, which I despaired of
finding again—now I systematically sought women whom
Albertine had not known, just as I no longer sought those that
I had desired in the past. True, it often happened to me to
recall, with an extraordinary violence of desire, some wench
of Méséglise or Paris, or the milk-girl I had seen early in the
morning at the foot of a hill during my first journey to Balbec.
But alas! I remembered them as they were then, that is to say
as they certainly would not be now. So that if in the past I had
been led to qualify my impression of the uniqueness of a desire
by seeking, in place of a convent-girl I had lost sight of, a
similar convent-girl, now, in order to recapture the girls who
had troubled my adolescence or that of Albertine, I had to
consent to a further departure from the principle of the
individuality of desire: what I must look for was not those who
were sixteen then, but those who were sixteen to-day, for now,

in the absence of that which was most distinctive in the person and which eluded me, what I loved was youth. I knew that the youth of those I had known existed no longer save in my impassioned recollection, and that it was not them, however anxious I might be to make contact with them when my memory recalled them to me, that I must cull if I really wished to harvest the youth and the blossom of the year.

The sun was still high in the sky when I went to meet my mother on the Piazzetta. We would call for a gondola. "How your poor grandmother would have loved this simple grandeur!" Mamma would say to me, pointing to the Doges' Palace which stood contemplating the sea with the thoughtful expression that had been bequeathed to it by its architect and that it faithfully retained in its mute attendance on its vanished lords. "She would even have loved those soft pink tints, because they are unmawkish. How she would have loved the whole of Venice, and what informality, worthy of nature itself, she would have found in all these beauties, this plethora of objects that seem to need no formal arrangement but present themselves just as they are—the Doges' Palace with its cubic shape, the columns which you say are those of Herod's palace, slap in the middle of the Piazzetta, and, even less deliberately placed, put there as though for want of anywhere better, the pillars from Acre, and those horses on the balcony of St Mark's! Your grandmother would have had as much pleasure seeing the sun setting over the Doges' Palace as over a mountain." And there was indeed an element of truth in what my mother said, for, as the gondola brought us back along the Grand Canal, we watched the double line of palaces between which we passed reflect the light and angle of the sun upon their pink flanks, and alter with them, seeming not so much private habitations and historic buildings as a chain of marble cliffs at the foot of which one goes out in the evening in a boat to watch the sunset. Seen thus, the buildings arranged along either bank of the canal made one think of objects of nature, but of a nature which seemed to have created its works with a human imagination. But at the same time (because of the always urban character of the impressions which Venice gives almost in the open sea, on those waters whose ebb and flow makes itself felt twice daily, and which alternately cover at high tide and uncover at low tide the splendid outside stairs of the palaces), as we should have done in Paris on the boulevards, in the Champs-Elysées, in the Bois, in any wide and fashionable avenue, we passed the most elegant women in the hazy evening light, almost all foreigners, who, languidly reclining against the cushions of their floating carriages, followed one another in procession, stopped in front of a palace where they had a friend to call on, sent to inquire whether she was at home, and while, as they waited for the answer, they prepared to leave a card just in case, as they would have done at the door of the Hôtel de Guermantes, turned to their guide-books to find out the period and the style of the palace, being shaken the while, as though upon the crest of a blue wave, by the wash of the glittering, swirling water, which took alarm on finding itself pent between the dancing gondola and the resounding marble. And thus any outing, even when it was only to pay calls or to leave visiting-cards, was threefold and unique in this Venice where the simplest social coming and going assumed at the same time the form and the charm of a visit to a museum and a trip on the sea.

Several of the palaces on the Grand Canal had been converted into hotels, and for the sake of a change or out of hospitality towards Mme Sazerat whom we had encountered— the unexpected and inopportune acquaintance whom one invariably meets when one travels abroad—and whom Mamma had invited to dine with us, we decided one evening to try an hotel which was not our own and in which we had been told that the food was better. While my mother was paying the gondolier and taking Mme Sazerat to the drawing-room which she had engaged, I slipped away to inspect the great hall of the restaurant with its fine marble pillars and walls and ceiling that were once entirely covered with frescoes, recently and badly restored. Two waiters were conversing in an Italian which I translate:

"Are the old people going to dine in their room? They never let us know. It's annoying; I never know whether I ought to keep their table for them (*non so se bisogna conservargli la loro tavola*). Serve them right if they come down and find it's been taken! I don't understand how they can take in *forestieri* like that in such a smart hotel. They're not the sort of people you expect here."

Notwithstanding his scorn, the waiter was anxious to know what action he was to take with regard to the table, and was about to send the lift-boy upstairs to inquire when, before he had had time to do so, he received his answer: he had just caught sight of the old lady who was entering the room. I had no difficulty, despite the air of melancholy and weariness that comes with the weight of years, and despite a sort of eczema, of red leprosy that covered her face, in recognising beneath her bonnet, in her black jacket made by W— but to the untutored eye exactly like that of an old charwoman, the Marquise de Villeparisis. The place where I was standing, engaged in studying the remains of a fresco between two of the beautiful marble panels, happened by chance to be immediately behind the table at which Mme de Villeparisis had just sat down.

"Then M. de Villeparisis won't be long. They've been here a month now, and they've only once not eaten together," said the waiter.

I was wondering who could be the relative with whom she was travelling and who was named M. de Villeparisis, when a few moments later I saw her old lover, M. de Norpois, advance towards the table and sit down beside her.

His great age had weakened the resonance of his voice, but had in compensation imparted to his speech, formerly so reserved, a positive intemperance. The cause of this was perhaps to be sought in ambitions for the realisation of which he felt that little time remained to him and which filled him with all the more vehemence and ardour; perhaps in the fact that, cut off from a world of politics to which he longed to return, he imagined, in the naïvety of his desire, that he could turn out of office, by the savage criticisms which he launched at them, the men he was determined to replace. Thus do we see politicians convinced that the Cabinet of which they are not members cannot hold out for three days. It would, however, be an exaggeration to suppose that M. de Norpois had entirely forgotten the traditions of diplomatic speech. Whenever "important matters" were at issue, he became once more, as we shall see, the man whom we remember in the past. but for the rest of the time he would inveigh against this man and that with the senile violence which makes certain octogenarians hurl themselves at women to whom they are no longer capable of doing any serious damage.

Mme de Villeparisis preserved, for some minutes, the silence of an old woman who in the exhaustion of age finds it difficult to rise from recollection of the past to consideration of the present. Then, turning to one of those eminently practical questions that indicate the survival of a mutual affection:

"Did you call at Salviati's?"

"Yes."

"Will they send it to-morrow?"

"I brought the bowl back myself. You shall see it after dinner. Let us look at the menu."

"Did you send instructions about my Suez shares?"

"No; at the present moment the Stock Exchange is entirely taken up with oil shares. But there's no hurry, in view of the propitious state of the market. Here is the menu. As a first course there is red mullet. Shall we try them?"

"I shall, but you are not allowed them. Ask for a risotto instead. But they don't know how to cook it."

"Never mind. Waiter, some mullet for Madame and a risotto for me."

A fresh and prolonged silence.

"Here, I've brought you the papers, the *Corriere della Sera*, the *Gazzetta del Popolo*, and all the rest of them. Did you know that there is a strong likelihood of a diplomatic reshuffle in which the first scapegoat will be Paléologue, who is notoriously inadequate in Serbia. He may perhaps be replaced by Lozé, and there will be a vacancy at Constantinople. But," M. de Norpois hastened to add in a biting tone, "for an Embassy of such scope, in a capital where it is obvious that Great Britain must always, whatever happens, occupy the chief place at the council-table, it would be prudent to turn to men of experience better equipped to counter the subterfuges of the enemies of our British ally than are diplomats of the modern school who would walk blindfold into the trap." The angry volubility with which M. de Norpois uttered these last words was due principally to the fact that the newspapers, instead of suggesting his name as he had recommended them to do, named as a "hot favourite" a young minister plenipotentiary. "Heaven knows that the men of years and experience are far from eager to put themselves forward, after all manner of tortuous manoeuvres, in the place of more or less incapable recruits. I have known many of these self-styled diplomats of the empirical school who centred all their hopes in a trial balloon which it did not take me long to deflate. There can be no question that if the Government is so lacking in wisdom as to entrust the reins of state to unruly hands, at the call of duty any conscript will always answer 'Present!' But who knows" (and here M. de Norpois appeared to know perfectly well to whom he was referring) "whether it would not be the same on the day when they came in search of some veteran full of wisdom and skill. To my mind, though everyone may have his own way of looking at things, the post at Constantinople should not be accepted until we have settled our existing difficulties with Germany. We owe no man anything, and it is intolerable that every six months they should come and demand from us, by fraudulent machinations and against our better judgment, some quietus or other which is invariably advocated by a venal press. This must cease, and naturally a man of high distinction who has proved his merit, a man who would have, if I may say so, the Emperor's ear, would enjoy greater authority than anyone else in bringing the conflict to an end."

A gentleman who was finishing his dinner bowed to M. de Norpois.

"Why, there's Prince Foggi," said the Marquis.

"Ah, I'm not sure that I know who you mean," muttered Mme de Villeparisis.

"But, of course you do—Prince Odo. He's the brother-in-law of your cousin Doudeauville. Surely you remember that I went shooting with him at Bonnétable?"

"Ah! Odo, is he the one who went in for painting?"

"Not at all, he's the one who married the Grand Duke N—'s sister."

M. de Norpois uttered these remarks in the cross tone of a

schoolmaster who is dissatisfied with his pupil, and stared fixedly at Mme de Villeparisis out of his blue eyes.

When the Prince had drunk his coffee and was leaving his table, M. de Norpois rose, hastened towards him and with a majestic sweep of his arm, stepping aside himself, presented him to Mme de Villeparisis. And during the few minutes that the Prince was standing beside their table, M. de Norpois never ceased for an instant to keep his azure pupils trained on Mme de Villeparisis, with the mixture of indulgence and severity of an old lover, but principally from fear of her committing one of those verbal solecisms which he had relished but which he dreaded. Whenever she said anything to the Prince that was not quite accurate he corrected her mistake and stared into the eyes of the abashed and docile Marquise with the steady intensity of a hypnotist.

A waiter came to tell me that my mother was waiting for me. I went to join her and made my apologies to Mme Sazerat, saying that I had been amused to see Mme de Villeparisis. At the sound of this name, Mme Sazerat turned pale and seemed about to faint. Controlling herself with an effort: "Mme de Villeparisis who was Mlle de Bouillon?" she inquired.

"Yes."

"Couldn't I just get a glimpse of her for a moment? It has been the dream of my life."

"Then there's no time to lose, Madame, for she will soon have finished her dinner. But how do you come to take such an interest in her?"

"Because Mme de Villeparisis was, before her second marriage, the Duchesse d'Havré, beautiful as an angel, wicked as a demon, who drove my father to distraction, ruined him and then abandoned him immediately. Well, she may have behaved to him like the lowest prostitute, she may have been the cause of our having had to live, my family and myself, in humble circumstances at Combray, but now that my father is dead, my consolation is to think that he loved the most beautiful woman of his generation, and as I've never set eyes on her, it will be a sort of solace in spite of everything . . ."

I escorted Mme Sazerat, trembling with emotion, to the restaurant and pointed out Mme de Villeparisis.

But, like a blind person who looks everywhere but in the right direction, Mme Sazerat did not bring her eyes to rest upon the table at which Mme de Villeparisis was dining, but, looking towards another part of the room, said:

"But she must have gone, I don't see her where you say she is."

And she continued to gaze round the room in quest of the loathed, adored vision that had haunted her imagination for so long.

"Yes, there she is, at the second table."

"Then we can't be counting from the same point. At what I count as the second table there's only an old gentleman and a little hunchbacked, red-faced, hideous woman."

"That's her!"

Meanwhile, Mme de Villeparisis having asked M. de Norpois to invite Prince Foggi to sit down, a friendly conversation ensued among the three of them. They discussed politics, and the Prince declared that he was indifferent to the fate of the Cabinet and would spend another week at least in Venice. He hoped that by that time all risk of a ministerial crisis would have been avoided. Prince Foggi thought for a few moments that these political topics did not interest M. de Norpois, for the latter, who until then had been expressing himself with such vehemence, had become suddenly absorbed in an almost angelic silence which seemed capable of blossoming, should his voice return, only into some innocent and tuneful melody by Mendelssohn or César Franck. The Prince supposed also that this silence was due to the reserve of a Frenchman who naturally would not wish to discuss Italian affairs in the presence of an Italian. Now in this the Prince was completely mistaken. Silence and an air of indifference had remained, in M. de Norpois, not a sign of reserve but the habitual prelude to an intervention in important affairs. The Marquis had his eye upon nothing less (as we have seen) than Constantinople, after the prior settlement of the German question, with a view to which he hoped to force the hand of the Rome Cabinet. He considered, in fact, that an action on his part of international significance might be the worthy consummation of his career, perhaps even a prelude to fresh honours, to difficult tasks to which he had not relinquished his pretensions. For old age makes us incapable of doing but not, at first, of desiring. It is only in a third period that those who live to a very great age relinquish desire, as they have already had to forgo action. They no longer even present themselves as candidates in futile elections where they have so often tried to win success, such as that for the Presidency of the Republic. They content themselves with taking the air, eating, reading the newspapers; they have outlived themselves.

The Prince, to put the Marquis at his ease and to show him that he regarded him as a compatriot, began to speak of the possible successors to the Prime Minister then in office. Successors who would have a difficult task before them. When Prince Foggi had mentioned more than twenty names of politicians who seemed to him suitable for office, names to which the ex-Ambassador listened with his eyelids drooping over his blue eyes and without moving a muscle, M. de Norpois broke his silence at length to utter the words which were to provide the chancelleries with food for conversation for many years to come, and afterwards, when they had been forgotten, would be exhumed by some personage signing himself "One Who Knows" or "Testis" or "Machiavelli" in a newspaper in which the very oblivion into which they had fallen enabled them to create a fresh sensation. So, Prince Foggi had mentioned more than twenty names to the diplomat who remained as motionless and silent as a deaf-mute, when M. de Norpois raised his head slightly, and, in the form in which his most pregnant and far-reaching diplomatic interventions had been couched, albeit this time with greater audacity and less brevity, shrewdly inquired: "And has no one mentioned the name of Signor Giolitti?" At these words the scales fell from Prince Foggi's eyes; he could hear a celestial murmur. Then at once M. de Norpois began to speak about one thing and another, no longer afraid to make a noise, as, when the last note of a sublime aria by Bach has died away, the audience are no longer afraid to talk aloud, to call for their hats and coats in the cloakroom. He made the break even more marked by begging the Prince to pay his most humble respects to Their Majesties the King and Queen when next he should see them, a farewell phrase corresponding to the shout for a coachman at the end of a concert: "Auguste, from the Rue de Belloy." We cannot say what exactly were Prince Foggi's impressions. He must certainly have been delighted to have heard the gem: "And has no one mentioned Signor Giolitti's name?" For M. de Norpois, in whom age had extinguished or deranged his most outstanding qualities, had on the other hand, as he grew older, perfected his bravura, as certain aged musicians, who in all other respects have declined, acquire and retain until the end, in the field of chamber-music, a perfect virtuosity which they did not formerly possess.

However that may be, Prince Foggi, who had intended to spend a fortnight in Venice, returned to Rome that very night and was received a few days later in audience by the King in connexion with certain properties which, as we may perhaps have mentioned already, the Prince owned in Sicily. The Cabinet hung on for longer than might have been expected. When it fell, the King consulted various statesmen as to the most suitable leader of a new Cabinet. Then he sent for Signor Giolitti, who accepted. Three months later a newspaper reported Prince Foggi's meeting with M. de Norpois. The conversation was reported as we have given it here, with the difference that, instead of: "M. de Norpois shrewdly inquired," one read: "M. de Norpois said with that shrewd and charming smile which is so characteristic of him." M. de Norpois considered that "shrewdly" had in itself sufficient explosive force for a diplomat and that this addition was, to say the least, excessive. He had even asked the Quai d'Orsay to issue an official denial, but the Quai d'Orsay did not know which way to turn. For, ever since the conversation had been made public, M. Barrère had been telegraphing several times hourly to Paris complaining of this unofficial ambassador to the Quirinal and describing the indignation with which the incident had been received throughout the whole of Europe. This indignation was nonexistent, but the other ambassadors were too polite to contradict M. Barrère's assertion that everyone was up in arms. M. Barrère, guided only by his own reaction, mistook this courteous silence for assent. Immediately he telegraphed to Paris: "I have just had an hour's conversation with the Marchese

Visconti-Venosta," and so forth. His secretaries were worn out.

M. de Norpois, however, had at his disposal a French news-paper of very long standing, which already in 1870, when he was French Minister in a German capital, had been of great service to him. This paper (especially its leading article, which was unsigned) was admirably written. But the paper became a thousand times more interesting whenever this leading article (styled "premier-Paris" in those far-off days and now, no one knows why, "editorial") was on the contrary badly expressed, with endless repetitions of words. Everyone sensed then, with great excitement, that the article had been "inspired." Perhaps by M. de Norpois, perhaps by some other man of the hour. To give an anticipatory idea of the Italian incident, let us show how M. de Norpois made use of this paper in 1870, to no purpose, it may be thought, since war broke out nevertheless, but most efficaciously, according to M. de Norpois, whose axiom was that one ought first and foremost to prepare public opinion. His articles, every word in which was weighed, resembled those optimistic bulletins which are at once followed by the death of the patient. For instance, on the eve of the declaration of war in 1870, when mobilisation was almost complete, M. de Norpois (remaining, of course, in the background) had felt it his duty to send to this famous newspaper the following "editorial":

"The opinion seems to prevail in authoritative circles that, since the afternoon hours of yesterday, the situation, without of course being of an alarming nature, might well be envisaged as serious and even, from certain angles, as susceptible of being regarded as critical. M. le Marquis de Norpois would appear to have had several conversations with the Prussian Minister, with a view to examining, in a firm and conciliatory spirit, and in a wholly concrete fashion, the various existing causes of friction, if one may so put it. Unfortunately, we have not yet heard, at the time of going to press, whether Their Excellencies have been able to agree upon a formula that may serve as the basis for a diplomatic instrument."

Stop press: "It has been learned with satisfaction in well-informed circles that a slight slackening of tension seems to have occurred in Franco-Prussian relations. Particular importance would appear to be attached to the fact that M. de Norpois is reported to have met the British Minister 'unter den Linden' and to have conversed with him for fully twenty minutes. This report is regarded as highly satisfactory." (There was added, in brackets, after the word "satisfactory" its German equivalent "*befriedigend.*") And on the following day one read in the editorial: "It would appear that, notwithstanding all the dexterity of M. de Norpois, to whom everyone must hasten to render homage for the skill and energy with which he has defended the inalienable rights of France, a rupture is now, one might say, virtually inevitable."

The newspaper could not refrain from following an editorial couched in this vein with a selection of comments, furnished of course by M. de Norpois. The reader may perhaps have observed in these last pages that the conditional was one of the Ambassador's favourite grammatical forms in the literature of diplomacy. ("Particular importance would appear to be attached" for "Particular importance is attached.") But the present indicative employed not in its usual sense but in that of the old "optative" was no less dear to M. de Norpois. The comments that followed the editorial were as follows:

"Never has the public shown itself so admirably calm" (M. de Norpois would have liked to believe that this was true but feared that it was precisely the opposite of the truth). "It is weary of fruitless agitation and has learned with satisfaction that the Government of His Majesty the Emperor would assume their responsibilities whatever the eventualities that might occur. The public asks" (optative) "nothing more. To its admirable composure, which is in itself a token of success, we shall add a piece of intelligence eminently calculated to reassure public opinion, were there any need of that. We are assured that M. de Norpois who, for reasons of health, was ordered long ago to return to Paris for medical treatment, would appear to have left Berlin where he considered that his presence no longer served any purpose."

Stop press: "His Majesty the Emperor left Compiègne this morning for Paris in order to confer with the Marquis de Norpois, the Minister for War and Marshal Bazaine in whom public opinion has especial confidence. H. M. the Emperor has cancelled the banquet which he was to give for his sister-in-law the Duchess of Alba. This action created everywhere, as soon as it became known, a particularly favourable impression. The Emperor has held a review of his troops, whose enthusiasm is indescribable. Several corps, by virtue of a mobilisation order issued immediately upon the Sovereign's arrival in Paris, are, in any contingency, ready to move in the direction of the Rhine."*

Sometimes at dusk as I returned to the hotel I felt that the Albertine of long ago, invisible to my eyes, was nevertheless enclosed within me as in the *Piombi* of an inner Venice, the tight lid of which some incident occasionally lifted to give me a glimpse of that past.

Thus for instance one evening a letter from my stockbroker reopened for me for an instant the gates of the prison in which Albertine dwelt within me, alive, but so remote, so profoundly buried that she remained inaccessible to me. Since her death I had ceased to indulge in the speculations that I had made in order to have more money for her. But time had passed; the wisest judgments of the previous generation had been belied by the next, as had occurred in the past to M. Thiers who had said that railways could never prove successful, and the stocks of which M. de Norpois had said to us: "The income from them may not be very great, but at least the capital will never depreciate," were, more often than not, those which had declined most in value. In the case of my English Consols and Raffineries Say shares alone, I had to pay out such considerable sums in brokers' commissions, as well as interest and contango fees, that in a rash moment I decided to sell out everything and found that I now possessed barely a fifth of the fortune that I had inherited from my great-aunt and still possessed when Albertine was alive. This became known at Combray among the surviving members of our family and their friends who, knowing that I went about with the Marquis de Saint-Loup and the Guermantes family, said to themselves: "Pride goes before a fall!" They would have been greatly astonished to learn that it was for a girl of Albertine's modest background, almost a protégée of my grandmother's former piano-teacher, Vinteuil, that I had made these speculations. Besides, in that Combray world in which everyone is classified forever, as in an Indian caste, according to the income he is known to enjoy, no one would have been capable of imagining the great freedom that prevailed in the world of the Guermantes, where no importance was attached to wealth and where poverty was regarded as being as disagreeable as, but no more degrading, having no more effect on a person's social position, than a stomach-ache. Doubtless people at Combray imagined, on the contrary, that Saint-Loup and M. de Guermantes must be ruined aristocrats with heavily mortgaged estates, to whom I had been lending money, whereas if I had been ruined they would have been the first to offer, unavailingly, to come to my assistance. As for my comparative penury, it was all the more awkward at the moment, inasmuch as my Venetian interests had been concentrated for some little time past on a young vendor of glassware whose blooming complexion offered to the delighted eye a whole range of orange tones and filled me with such a longing to see her daily that, realising that my mother and I would soon be leaving Venice, I had made up my mind to try to create some sort of position for her in Paris which would spare me the distress of parting from her. The beauty of her seventeen summers was so noble, so radiant, that it was like acquiring a genuine Titian before leaving the place. But would the scant remains of my fortune be enough to tempt her to leave her native land and come to live in Paris for my sole convenience?

But as I came to the end of the stockbroker's letter, a passage in which he said: "I shall look after your credits" reminded me of a scarcely less hypocritically professional expression which the bath-attendant at Balbec had used in speaking to Aimé of Albertine: "It was I who looked after her," she had said. And these words which had never recurred to my mind acted like an "Open sesame!" upon the hinges of the prison door. But a moment later the door closed once more upon the immured victim—whom I was not to blame for not wishing to join since I was no longer able to see her, to call her to mind, and since other people exist for us only through the idea that we have of them—but who for a moment had been rendered more touching by my desertion of her, albeit she was unaware of it, so that for the duration of a lightning-flash I had thought with longing of the time, already remote, when I used to suffer night and day from the companionship of her memory. Another time, in San Giorgio degli Schiavoni, an eagle accompanying one of the Apostles, and conventionalised in the same manner, revived the memory and almost the suffering caused by the two rings the similarity of which Françoise had revealed to me, and as to which I had never learned who had given them to Albertine.

One evening, however, an incident occurred of such a nature that it seemed as though my love must revive. No sooner had our gondola stopped at the hotel steps than the porter handed me a telegram which the messenger had already brought three times to the hotel, for owing to the inaccurate rendering of the addressee's name (which I recognised nevertheless, through the corruptions introduced by the Italian clerks, as my own) the post office required a signed receipt certifying that the telegram was indeed for me. I opened it as soon as I was in my room, and, glancing through the message which was filled with inaccurately transmitted words, managed nevertheless to make out: "My dear friend, you think me dead, forgive me, I am quite alive, I long to see you, talk about marriage, when do you return? Affectionately. Albertine." Then there occurred in me in reverse order a process parallel to that which had occurred in the case of my grandmother. When I had learned the fact of my grandmother's death, I had not at first felt any grief. And I had been really grieved by her death only when certain involuntary memories had brought her alive again for me. Now that Albertine no longer lived for me in my thoughts, the news that she was alive did not cause me the joy that I might have expected. Albertine had been no more to me than a bundle of thoughts, and she had survived her physical death so long as those thoughts were alive in me; on the other hand, now that those thoughts were dead, Albertine did not rise again for me with the resurrection of her body. And when I realised that I felt no joy at the thought of her being alive, that I no longer loved her, I ought to have been more shattered than a man who, looking at his reflection in a mirror, after months of travel or sickness, discovers that he has white hair and a different face, that of a middle-aged or an old man. This is shattering because its message is: "the man that I was, the fair-haired young man, no longer exists, I am another person." And yet, was not the impression that I now felt the proof of as profound a change, as total a death of my former self and of the no less complete substitution of a new self for that former self, as the sight of a wrinkled face topped with a white wig instead of the face of long ago? But one is no more distressed at having become another person, after a lapse of years and in the natural sequence of time, than one is at any given moment by the fact of being, one after another, the incompatible persons, malicious, sensitive, refined, caddish, disinterested, ambitious which one can be, in turn, every day of one's life. And the reason why one is not distressed is the same, namely that the self which has been eclipsed—momentarily in this latter case and when it is a question of character, permanently in the former case and when the passions are involved—is not there to deplore the other, the other which is for the moment, or from then onwards, one's whole self; the caddish self laughs at his caddishness because one is the cad, and the forgetful self does not grieve about his forgetfulness precisely because one has forgotten.

I should have been incapable of resuscitating Albertine because I was incapable of resuscitating myself, of resuscitating the self of those days. Life, in accordance with its habit which is, by incessant, infinitesimal labours, to change the face of the world, had not said to me on the morrow of Albertine's death: "Become another person," but, by changes too imperceptible for me to be conscious even that I was changing, had altered almost everything in me, with the result that my mind was already accustomed to its new master—my new self—when it became aware that it had changed; it was to this new master that it was attached. My feeling for Albertine, my jealousy, stemmed, as we have seen, from the irradiation, by the association of ideas, of certain pleasant or painful impressions, the memory of Mlle Vinteuil at Montjouvain, the precious goodnight kisses that Albertine used to give me. But as these impressions had grown gradually fainter, the vast field of impressions which they coloured with a hue that was agonising or soothing reverted to neutral tones. As soon as oblivion had taken hold of certain dominant points of suffering and pleasure, the resistance offered by my love was overcome, I no longer loved Albertine. I tried to recall her image to my mind. I had been right in my presentiment when, a couple of days after Albertine's flight, I was appalled by the discovery that I had been able to live for forty-eight hours without her. It had been the same as when I wrote to Gilberte long ago saying to myself: "If this goes on for a year or two, I shall no longer love her." And if, when Swann asked me to come and see Gilberte again, this had seemed to me as embarrassing as greeting a dead woman, in Albertine's case death—or what I had supposed to be death—had achieved the same result as a prolonged breach in Gilberte's. Death merely acts in the same way as absence. The monster at whose apparition my love had trembled, oblivion, had indeed, as I had feared, ended by devouring that love. Not only did the news that she was alive fail to revive my love, not only did it enable me to realise how far I had already proceeded along the road towards indifference, it at once and so abruptly accelerated that process that I wondered retrospectively whether the opposite report, that of Albertine's death, had not, conversely, by completing the effect of her departure, rekindled my love and delayed its decline. Yes, now that the knowledge that she was alive and the possibility of our reunion made her suddenly cease to be so precious to me, I wondered whether Françoise's insinuations, our rupture itself, and even her death (imaginary, but believed to be real) had not prolonged my love, to such an extent do the efforts of third persons, and even those of fate, to separate us from a woman succeed only in attaching us to her. Now it was the contrary process that had occurred. Anyhow, I tried to recall her image and perhaps because I had only to raise a finger for her to be mine once more, the memory that came to me was that of a somewhat stout and mannish-looking girl from whose faded features protruded already, like a sprouting seed, the profile of Mme Bontemps. What she might or might not have done with Andrée or with other girls no longer interested me. I no longer suffered from the malady which I had so long thought to be incurable, and really I might have foreseen this.

Certainly, regret for a lost mistress and retrospective jealousy are physical maladies fully as much as tuberculosis or leucaemia. And yet among physical maladies it is possible to distinguish those which are caused by a purely physical agency, and those which act upon the body only through the medium of the intelligence. If the part of the mind which serves as carrier is the memory—that is to say if the cause is obliterated or remote—however agonising the pain, however profound the disturbance to the organism may appear to be, it is very seldom (the mind having a capacity for renewal or rather an incapacity for conservation which the tissues lack) that the prognosis is not favourable. At the end of a given period after which a man who has been attacked by cancer will be dead, it is very seldom that the grief of an inconsolable widower or father is not healed. Mine was healed. Was it for this girl whom I saw in my mind's eye so bloated and who had certainly aged, as the girls whom she had loved had aged—was it for her that I must renounce the dazzling girl who was my memory of yesterday, my hope for to-morrow, to whom I could no longer give a sou, any more than to any other, if I married Albertine, that I must renounce this "new Albertine" whom I loved "not as hell had beheld her . . . but faithful, and proud, and even rather shy"?[31] It was she who was now what Albertine had been in the past: my love for Albertine had been but a transitory form of my devotion to youth. We think that we are in love with a girl, whereas we love in her, alas! only that dawn the glow of which is momentarily reflected on her face.

The night went by. In the morning I gave the telegram back to the hotel porter explaining that it had been brought to me by mistake and that it was not addressed to me. He told me that now it had been opened he might get into trouble, that it would be better if I kept it; I put it back in my pocket, but made up my mind to behave as though I had never received it. I had finally ceased to love Albertine. So that this love, after departing so greatly from what I had anticipated on the basis of my love for Gilberte, after obliging me to make so long and painful a detour, had ended too, after having proved an exception to it, by succumbing, like my love for Gilberte, to the general law of oblivion.

But then I thought to myself: I used to value Albertine more than myself; I no longer value her now because for a certain time past I have ceased to see her. My desire not to be parted from myself by death, to rise again after my death—that desire was not like the desire never to be parted from Albertine; it still persisted. Was this due to the fact that I valued myself more highly than her, that when I loved her I loved myself more? No, it was because, having ceased to see her, I had ceased to love her, whereas I had not ceased to love myself because my everyday links with myself had not been severed like those with Albertine. But if my links with my body, with myself, were severed also. . . ? Obviously, it would be the same. Our love of life is only an old liaison of which we do not know how to rid ourselves. Its strength lies in its permanence. But death which severs it will cure us of the desire for immortality.

After lunch, when I was not going to roam about Venice by myself, I went up to my room to get ready to go out with my mother and to collect the notebooks in which I would take notes for some work I was doing on Ruskin. In the abrupt angles of the walls I sensed the restrictions imposed by the sea, the parsimony of the soil. And when I went downstairs to join Mamma who was waiting for me, at that hour when at Combray it was so pleasant to feel the sun close at hand in the darkness preserved by the closed shutters, here, from top to bottom of the marble staircase where one could no more tell than in a Renaissance picture whether it was in a palace or on a galley, the same coolness and the same sense of the splendour of the scene outside were imparted thanks to the awnings which stirred outside the ever-open windows through which, upon an incessant stream of air, the warm shade and the greenish sunlight flowed as if over a liquid surface and suggested the weltering proximity, the glitter, the shimmering instability of the sea.

As often as not we would set off for St Mark's, with all the more pleasure because, since one had to take a gondola to go there, the church represented for me not simply a monument but the terminus of a voyage on these vernal, maritime waters, with which, I felt, St Mark's formed an indivisible and living whole. My mother and I would enter the baptistery, treading

underfoot the marble and glass mosaics of the paving, in front
of us the wide arcades whose curved pink surfaces have been
slightly warped by time, thus giving the church, wherever the
freshness of this colouring has been preserved, the appearance
of having been built of a soft and malleable substance like the
wax in a giant honeycomb, and, where time has shrivelled and
hardened the material and artists have embellished it with gold
tracery, of being the precious binding, in the finest Cordoba
leather, of the colossal Gospel of Venice. Seeing that I needed
to spend some time in front of the mosaics representing the
Baptism of Christ, and feeling the icy coolness that pervaded
the baptistery, my mother threw a shawl over my shoulders.
When I was with Albertine at Balbec, I felt that she was revealing one of those insubstantial illusions which clutter the minds
of so many people who do not think clearly, when she used to
speak of the pleasure—to my mind baseless—that she would
derive from seeing works of art with me. To-day I am sure that
the pleasure does exist, if not of seeing, at least of having seen,
a beautiful thing with a particular person. A time has now come
when, remembering the baptistery of St Mark's—contemplating the waters of the Jordan in which St John immerses Christ,
while the gondola awaited us at the landing-stage of the
Piazzetta—it is no longer a matter of indifference to me that,
beside me in that cool penumbra, there should have been a
woman draped in her mourning with the respectful and
enthusiastic fervour of the old woman in Carpaccio's *St Ursula*
in the Accademia, and that that woman, with her red cheeks
and sad eyes and in her black veils, whom nothing can ever
remove from that softly lit sanctuary of St Mark's where I am
always sure to find her because she has her place reserved there
as immutably as a mosaic, should be my mother.

Carpaccio, as it happens, who was the painter we visited most
readily when I was not working in St Mark's, almost succeeded
one day in reviving my love for Albertine. I was seeing for the
first time *The Patriarch of Grado exorcising a demoniac*. I looked at
the marvellous rose-pink and violet sky and the tall encrusted
chimneys silhouetted against it, their flared stacks, blossoming
like red tulips, reminiscent of so many Whistlers of Venice.
Then my eyes travelled from the old wooden Rialto to that

fifteenth-century Ponte Vecchio with its marble palaces decorated with gilded capitals, and returned to the canal on which the boats are manoeuvred by adolescents in pink jackets and plumed toques, the spitting image of those avowedly inspired by Carpaccio in that dazzling *Legend of Joseph* by Sert, Strauss and Kessler. Finally, before leaving the picture, my eyes came back to the shore, swarming with the everyday Venetian life of the period. I looked at the barber wiping his razor, at the negro humping his barrel, at the Muslims conversing, at the noblemen in wide-sleeved brocade and damask robes and hats of cerise velvet, and suddenly I felt a slight gnawing at my heart. On the back of one of the *Compagni della Calza* identifiable from the emblem, embroidered in gold and pearls on their sleeves or their collars, of the merry confraternity to which they were affiliated, I had just recognised the cloak which Albertine had put on to come with me to Versailles in an open carriage on the evening when I so little suspected that scarcely fifteen hours separated me from the moment of her departure from my house. Always ready for anything, when I had asked her to come out with me on that melancholy evening which she was to describe in her last letter as "doubly crepuscular in that dusk was falling and we were about to part," she had flung over her shoulders a Fortuny cloak which she had taken away with her next day and which I had never thought of since. It was from this Carpaccio picture that that inspired son of Venice had taken it, it was from the shoulders of this *Compagno della Calza* that he had removed it in order to drape it over the shoulders of so many Parisian women who were certainly unaware, as I had been until then, that the model for it existed in a group of noblemen in the foreground of the *Patriarch of Grado* in a room in the Accademia in Venice. I had recognised it down to the last detail, and, that cloak having restored to me as I looked at it the eyes and the heart of him who had set out that evening with Albertine for Versailles, I was overcome for a few moments by a vague feeling of desire and melancholy.

There were days when my mother and I were not content with visiting the museums and churches of Venice only, and once, when the weather was particularly fine, in order to see the "Virtues" and "Vices" of which M. Swann had given me reproductions that were probably still hanging on the wall of the schoolroom at Combray, we went as far afield as Padua. After walking across the garden of the Arena in the glare of the sun, I entered the Giotto chapel, the entire ceiling of which and the background of the frescoes are so blue that it seems as though the radiant daylight has crossed the threshold with the human visitor in order to give its pure sky a momentary breather in the coolness and shade, a sky merely of a slightly deeper blue now that it is rid of the glitter of the sunlight, as in those brief moments of respite when, though no cloud is to be seen, the sun has turned its gaze elsewhere and the azure, softer still, grows deeper. This sky transplanted on to the blue-washed stone was peopled with flying angels which I was seeing for the first time, for M. Swann had given me reproductions only of the Vices and Virtues and not of the frescoes depicting the life of the Virgin. Watching the flight of these angels, I had the same impression of actual movement, literally real activity, that the gestures of Charity and Envy had given me. For all the celestial fervour, or at least the childlike obedience and application, with which their minuscule hands are joined, they are represented in the Arena chapel as winged creatures of a particular species that had really existed, that must have figured in the natural history of biblical and apostolic times. Constantly flitting about above the saints whenever the latter walk abroad, these little beings, since they are real creatures with a genuine power of flight, can be seen soaring upwards, describing curves, "looping the loop," diving earthwards head first, with the aid of wings which enable them to support themselves in positions that defy the laws of gravity, and are far more reminiscent of an extinct species of bird, or of young pupils of Garros practising gliding,[32] than of the angels of the Renaissance and later periods whose wings have become no more than emblems and whose deportment is generally the same as that of heavenly beings who are not winged.

On returning to the hotel I would meet young women, mainly Austrians, who came to Venice to spend the first fine days of this flowerless spring. There was one in particular whose features did not resemble Albertine's but who attracted me by the same fresh complexion, the same gay, light-hearted look. Soon I became aware that I was beginning to say the same things to her as I had said to Albertine at the start, that I concealed the same misery when she told me she would not be seeing me the following day because she was going to Verona, and that I immediately wanted to go to Verona too. It did not last—she was soon to leave for Austria and I would never see her again—but already, vaguely jealous as one is when one begins to fall in love, looking at her charming and enigmatic face I wondered whether she too loved women, whether what she had in common with Albertine, that clear complexion, that bright-eyed look, that air of friendly candour which charmed everyone and which stemmed more from the fact that she was not in the least interested in knowing about other people's actions, which interested her not at all, than that she was confessing her own, which on the contrary she concealed beneath the most puerile lies—I wondered whether all this constituted the morphological characteristics of the woman who loves other women. Was it this about her that, without my being able rationally to grasp why, exercised its attraction upon me, caused my anxieties (perhaps a deeper cause of my attraction towards her by virtue of the fact that we are drawn towards that which will make us suffer), gave me when I saw her so much pleasure and sadness, like those magnetic elements in the air of certain places which we do not see but which cause us such physical discomfort? Alas, I should never know. I should have liked, when I tried to read her face, to say to her: "You really should tell me, it would interest me as an example of human natural history," but she would never tell me. She professed an especial loathing for anything that resembled that vice, and was extremely distant towards her women friends. Perhaps indeed this was proof that she had been mocked or reviled for it, and the air that she assumed in order that people should not think such things of her was like an animal's instinctive and revealing recoil from someone who has beaten it. As for my finding out about her life, it was impossible; even in the case of Albertine, how long it had taken me to get to know anything! It had taken her death to loosen people's tongues, such prudent circumspection had Albertine, like this young woman, observed in all her conduct. And in any case, could I be certain that I had discovered anything about Albertine? Moreover, just as the conditions of life that we most desire become a matter of indifference to us if we cease to love the person who, without our realising it, made us desire them because they enabled us to be close to her, to be in a position to please her, so it is with certain kinds of intellectual curiosity. The scientific importance which I attached to knowing the particular kind of desire that lay hidden beneath the delicate pink petals of those cheeks, in the brightness, a sunless brightness as at daybreak, of those pale eyes, in those days that were never accounted for, would doubtless subside when I had entirely ceased to love Albertine or when I had entirely ceased to love this young woman.

After dinner, I went out alone, into the heart of the enchanted city where I found myself in the middle of strange purlieus like a character in the *Arabian Nights*. It was very seldom that, in the course of my wanderings, I did not come across some strange and spacious *piazza* of which no guidebook, no tourist had ever told me. I had plunged into a network of little alleys, or *calli*, packed tightly together and dissecting in all directions with their furrows a chunk of Venice carved out between a canal and the lagoon, as if it had crystallised in accordance with these innumerable, tenuous and minute patterns. Suddenly, at the end of one of these alleys, it seemed as though a distension had occurred in the crystallised matter. A vast and splendid *campo* of which, in this network of little streets, I should never have guessed the scale, or even found room for it, spread out before me surrounded by charming palaces silvery in the moonlight. It was one of those architectural ensembles towards which, in any other town, the streets converge, lead you and point the way. Here it seemed to be deliberately concealed in a labyrinth of alleys, like those palaces in oriental tales whither mysterious agents convey by night a person who, brought back home before daybreak, can never find his way back to the magic dwelling which he ends by believing that he visited only in a dream.

The next day, I set out in quest of my beautiful nocturnal *piazza*, following *calle* after *calle* which were exactly like one another and refused to give me the smallest piece of information, except such as would lead me further astray. Sometimes a vague landmark which I seemed to recognise led me to suppose that I was about to see appear, in its seclusion, solitude and silence, the beautiful exiled *piazza*. At that moment, some evil genie which had assumed the form of a new *calle* made me unwittingly retrace my steps, and I found myself suddenly brought back to the Grand Canal. And as there is no great difference between the memory of a dream and the memory of a reality, I finally wondered whether it was not during my sleep that there had occurred, in a dark patch of Venetian crystallisation, that strange mirage which offered a vast *piazza* surrounded by romantic palaces to the meditative eye of the moon.

But, far more than certain places, it was the desire not to lose forever certain women that kept me while in Venice in a state of agitation which became febrile when, towards the end of the day on which my mother had decided that we should leave, and our luggage was already on the way to the station in a gondola, I read in the register of guests expected at the hotel: "Mme Putbus and attendants." At once, the thought of all the hours of casual pleasure of which our departure would deprive me raised this desire, which existed in me in a chronic state, to the level of a feeling, and drowned it in a vague melancholy. I asked my mother to put off our departure for a few days, and her air of not for a moment taking my request into consideration, of not even listening to it seriously, reawakened in my nerves, exacerbated by the Venetian springtime, that old desire to rebel against an imaginary plot woven against me by my parents, who imagined that I would be forced to obey them, that defiant spirit which drove me in the past to impose my will brutally upon the people I loved best in the world, though finally conforming to theirs after I had succeeded in making them yield. I told my mother that I would not leave Venice, but she, thinking it wiser not to appear to believe that I was saying this seriously, did not even answer. I went on to say that she would soon see whether I was serious or not. The porter brought us three letters, two for her, and one for me which I put in my wallet among several others without even looking at the envelope. And when the hour came at which, accompanied by all my belongings, she set off for the station, I ordered a drink to be brought out to me on the terrace overlooking the canal, and settled down there to watch the sunset, while from a boat that had stopped in front of the hotel a musician sang *O sole mio*.

The sun continued to sink. My mother must be nearing the station. Soon she would be gone, and I should be alone in Venice, alone with the misery of knowing that I had distressed her, and without her presence to comfort me. The hour of the train's departure was approaching. My irrevocable solitude was so near at hand that it seemed to me to have begun already and to be complete. For I felt myself to be alone; things had become alien to me; I no longer had calm enough to break out of my throbbing heart and introduce into them a measure of stability. The town that I saw before me had ceased to be Venice. Its personality, its name, seemed to me to be mendacious fictions which I no longer had the will to impress upon its stones. I saw the palaces reduced to their basic elements, lifeless heaps of marble with nothing to choose between them, and the water as a combination of hydrogen and oxygen, eternal, blind, anterior and exterior to Venice, oblivious of the Doges or of Turner. And yet this unremarkable place was as strange as a place at which one has just arrived, which does not yet know one, or a place which one has left and which has forgotten one already. I could no longer tell it anything about myself, I could leave nothing of myself imprinted upon it; it contracted me into myself until I was no more than a throbbing heart and an attention strained to follow the development of *O sole mio*. In vain might I fix my mind despairingly upon the beautiful and distinctive curve of the Rialto, it seemed to me, with the mediocrity of the obvious, a bridge not merely inferior to but as alien to the notion I had of it as an actor of whom, in spite of his blond wig and black garments, we know quite well that in his essence he is not Hamlet. So it was with the palaces, the canal, the Rialto, divested of the idea that constituted their reality and dissolved into their vulgar material elements. But at the same time this mediocre place seemed to me less distant. In the dock basin of the Arsenal, because of an element which itself also was scientific, namely latitude, there was that singularity in things whereby, even when similar in appearance to those of our own land, they reveal themselves to be alien, in exile beneath other skies; I felt that that horizon so close at hand, which I could have reached in an hour by boat, was a curvature of the earth quite different from that of France, a distant curvature which, by the artifice of travel, happened to be moored close to where I was; so that the dock basin of the Arsenal, at once insignificant and remote, filled me with that blend of distaste and alarm which I had felt as a child when I first accompanied my mother to the Deligny baths, where, in that weird setting of a pool of water reflecting neither sky nor sun, which nevertheless amid its fringe of cabins one felt to be in communication with invisible depths crowded with human bodies, I had asked myself whether those depths, concealed from mortal eyes by hutments which made their existence impossible to divine from the street, were not the entry to arctic seas which began at that point, in which the poles were comprised, and whether that narrow space was not indeed the open water that surrounds the pole; and in this lonely, unreal, icy, unfriendly setting in which I was going to be left alone, the strains of *O sole mio*, rising like a dirge for the Venice I had known, seemed to bear witness to my misery. No doubt I ought to have ceased to listen to it if I wished to be able to join my mother and take the train with her; I ought to have made up my mind to leave without losing another second. But this was precisely what I was powerless to do; I remained motionless, incapable not merely of rising, but even of deciding that I would rise from my chair. My mind, in order not to have to consider the decision I had to take, was entirely occupied in following the course of the successive phrases of *O sole mio*, singing them to myself with the singer, anticipating each surge of melody, soaring aloft with it, sinking down with it once more.

No doubt this trivial song which I had heard a hundred times did not interest me in the least. I could give no pleasure to myself or anyone else by listening to it religiously like this to the end as though I were fulfilling a duty. After all, none of the already familiar phrases of this sentimental ditty was capable of furnishing me with the resolution I needed; what was more, each of these phrases, when it came and went in its turn, became an obstacle in the way of my putting that resolution into effect, or rather it forced me towards the contrary resolution not to leave Venice, for it made me too late for the train. Wherefore this occupation, devoid of any pleasure in itself, of listening to O sole mio was charged with a profound, almost despairing melancholy. I was well aware that in reality it was the resolution not to go that I was making by remaining there without stirring, but to say to myself: "I'm not going," which in that direct form was impossible, became possible in this indirect form: "I'm going to listen to one more phrase of O sole mio"; possible but infinitely painful, for the practical significance of this figurative language did not escape me and, while I said to myself: "After all, I'm only listening to one more phrase," I knew that the words meant: "I shall remain by myself in Venice." And it was perhaps this melancholy, like a sort of numbing cold, that constituted the despairing but hypnotic charm of the song. Each note that the singer's voice uttered with a force and ostentation that were almost muscular stabbed me to the heart. When the phrase was completed down below and the song seemed to be at an end, the singer had still not had enough and resumed at the top as though he needed to proclaim once more my solitude and despair.

My mother must by now have reached the station. In a little while she would be gone. I was gripped by the anguish that was caused me by the sight of the Canal which had become diminutive now that the soul of Venice had fled from it, of that commonplace Rialto which was no longer the Rialto, and by the song of despair which O sole mio had become and which, bellowed thus beside the insubstantial palaces, finally reduced them to dust and ashes and completed the ruin of Venice; I looked on at the slow realisation of my distress, built up artistically, without haste, note by note, by the singer as he stood beneath the astonished gaze of the sun arrested in its course beyond San Giorgio Maggiore, with the result that the fading light was to combine for ever in my memory with the throb of my emotion and the bronze voice of the singer in an equivocal, unalterable and poignant alloy.

Thus I remained motionless, my will dissolved, no decision

in sight. Doubtless at such moments our decision has already been made: our friends can often predict it, but we ourselves are unable to do so, otherwise we should be spared a great deal of suffering.

But suddenly, from caverns darker than those from which flashes the comet which we can predict—thanks to the unsuspected defensive power of inveterate habit, thanks to the hidden reserves which by a sudden impulse it hurls at the last moment into the fray—my will to action arose at last; I set off in hot haste and arrived, when the carriage doors were already shut, but in time to find my mother flushed with emotion and with the effort to restrain her tears, for she thought that I was not coming. "You know," she said, "your poor grandmother used to say: It's curious, there's nobody who can be as unbearable or as nice as that child." Then the train started and we saw Padua and Verona come to meet us, to speed us on our way, almost on to the platforms of their stations, and, when we had drawn away from them, return—they who were not travelling and were about to resume their normal life—one to its plain, the other to its hill.

The hours went by. My mother was in no hurry to read her two letters, which she had merely opened, and tried to prevent me from pulling out my pocket-book at once to take from it the letter which the hotel porter had given me. She was always afraid of my finding journeys too long and too tiring, and put off as long as possible, so as to keep me occupied during the final hours, the moment at which she would seek fresh distractions for me, bring out the hard-boiled eggs, hand me the newspapers, untie the parcel of books which she had bought without telling me. We had long passed Milan when she decided to read the first of her two letters. At first I sat watching her, as she read it with an air of astonishment, then raised her head, her eyes seeming to come to rest upon a succession of distinct and incompatible memories which she could not succeed in bringing together. Meanwhile I had recognised Gilberte's handwriting on the envelope which I had just taken from my pocket-book. I opened it. Gilberte wrote to inform me that she was marrying Robert de Saint-Loup. She told me that she had sent me a telegram about it to Venice but had had no reply. I remembered that I had been told that the telegraphic service there was inefficient. I had never received her telegram. Perhaps she would refuse to believe this. All of a sudden I felt in my brain a fact, which was installed there in the guise of a memory, leave its place and surrender it to another fact. The telegram that I had received a few days earlier, and had supposed to be from Albertine, was from Gilberte. As the somewhat laboured originality of Gilberte's handwriting consisted chiefly, when she wrote a line, in introducing into the line above it the strokes of her *t*'s which appeared to be underlining the words, or the dots over her *i*'s which appeared to be punctuating the sentence above them, and on the other hand in interspersing the line below with the tails and flourishes of the words immediately above, it was quite natural that the clerk who dispatched the telegram should have read the loops of *s*'s or *y*'s in the line above as an "-ine" attached to the word "Gilberte." The dot over the *i* of Gilberte had climbed up to make a full stop. As for her capital *G*, it resembled a Gothic *A*. The fact that, in addition to this, two or three words had been misread, had dovetailed into one another (some of them indeed had seemed to me incomprehensible), was sufficient to explain the details of my error and was not even necessary. How many letters are actually read into a word by a careless person who knows what to expect, who sets out with the idea that the message is from a certain person? How many words into the sentence? We guess as we read, we create; everything starts from an initial error; those that follow (and this applies not only to the reading of letters and telegrams, not only to all reading), extraordinary as they may appear to a person who has not begun at the same starting-point, are all quite natural. A large part of what we believe to be true (and this applies even to our final conclusions) with an obstinacy equalled only by our good faith, springs from an original mistake in our premises.

"Oh, it's too incredible," said my mother. "You know at my age one has ceased to be astonished at anything, but I assure you that nothing could be more unexpected than the news I've just read in this letter."

"Well," I replied, "I don't know what it is, but however

astonishing it may be, it can't be quite so astonishing as what I've learnt from mine. It's a marriage. Robert de Saint-Loup is marrying Gilberte Swann."

"Ah!" said my mother, "then that must be what's in the other letter, which I haven't yet opened, for I recognised your friend's hand."

And my mother smiled at me with that faint trace of emotion which, ever since she had lost her own mother, she felt at every event, however insignificant, that concerned human creatures who were capable of grief and recollection and who themselves also mourned their dead. And so my mother smiled at me and spoke to me in a gentle voice, as though she were afraid, by treating this marriage lightly, of belittling the melancholy feelings that it might arouse in Swann's widow and daughter, in Robert's mother who had resigned herself to being parted from her son, all of whom Mamma, in her kindness of heart, in her gratitude for their kindness to me, endowed with her own faculty of filial, conjugal and maternal emotion.

"Was I right in saying that you wouldn't produce anything as astonishing?" I asked her.

"On the contrary," she replied in a gentle tone, "it's I who have the most extraordinary news, I shan't say the greatest or the smallest, for that quotation from Sévigné which everyone produces who knows nothing else that she ever wrote used to sicken your grandmother as much as 'What a pretty thing haymaking is.' We don't deign to collect such hackneyed Sévigné. This letter is to announce the marriage of the Cambremer boy."

"Oh!" I remarked with indifference, "to whom? But in any case the personality of the bridegroom robs this marriage of any sensational character."

"Unless the bride's personality supplies it."

"And who is the bride in question?"

"Ah, if I tell you straight away, that will spoil the fun. Come on, see if you can guess," said my mother who, seeing that we had not yet reached Turin, wished to keep something in reserve for me as meat and drink for the rest of the journey.

"But how do you expect me to know? Is it someone brilliant? If Legrandin and his sister are satisfied, we may be sure that it's a brilliant marriage."

"I can't answer for Legrandin, but the person who informs me of the marriage says that Mme de Cambremer is delighted. I don't know whether you will call it a brilliant marriage. To my mind, it suggests the days when kings used to marry shepherdesses, and in this case the shepherdess is even humbler than a shepherdess, charming as she is. It would have amazed your grandmother, but would not have displeased her."

"But who in the world is this bride?"

"It's Mlle d'Oloron."

"That sounds to me tremendous and not in the least shepherdessy, but I don't quite gather who she can be. It's a title that used to be in the Guermantes family."

"Precisely, and M. de Charlus conferred it, when he adopted her, upon Jupien's niece."

"Jupien's niece! It isn't possible!"

"It's the reward of virtue. It's a marriage from the last chapter of one of Mme Sand's novels," said my mother. ("It's the wages of vice, a marriage from the end of a Balzac novel," thought I.)

"After all," I said to my mother, "it's quite natural, when you think of it. Here are the Cambremers established in that Guermantes clan among which they never hoped to pitch their tent; what is more, the girl, adopted by M. de Charlus, will have plenty of money, which was indispensable since the Cambremers have lost theirs; and after all she's the adopted daughter, and in the Cambremers' eyes probably the real daughter—the natural daughter—of a person whom they regard as a Prince of the Blood. A bastard of a semi-royal house has always been regarded as a flattering alliance by the nobility of France and other countries. Indeed, without going so far back, to the Lucinges,[33] only the other day, not more than six months ago, you remember the marriage of Robert's friend and that girl whose only social qualification was that she was supposed, rightly or wrongly, to be the natural daughter of a sovereign prince."

My mother, without abandoning the caste ethos of Combray in the light of which my grandmother ought to have been scandalised by such a marriage, being anxious above all to show the validity of her mother's judgment, added: "Anyhow,

the girl is worth her weight in gold, and your dear grandmother wouldn't have had to draw upon her immense goodness, her infinite tolerance, to keep her from condemning
young Cambremer's choice. Do you remember how distinguished she thought the girl was, long ago, when she went
into the shop to have a stitch put in her skirt? She was only a
child then. And now, even if she has rather run to seed and
become an old maid, she's a different woman, a thousand times
more perfect. But your grandmother saw all that at a glance.
She found the little niece of a jobbing tailor more 'noble' than
the Duc de Guermantes."

But even more necessary than to extol my grandmother was
it for my mother to decide that it was "better" for her that she
had not lived to see the day. This was the culmination of her
daughterly love, as though she were sparing my grandmother
a final grief.

"And yet, can you imagine for a moment," my mother said
to me, "what old Swann—not that you ever knew him, of
course—would have felt if he could have known that he would
one day have a great-grandchild in whose veins the blood of
old mother Moser who used to say: 'Ponchour Mezieurs' would
mingle with the blood of the Duc de Guise!"

"But you know, Mamma, it's much more surprising than
that. Because the Swanns were very respectable people, and,
given the social position that their son acquired, his daughter,
if he himself had made a decent marriage, might have married
very well indeed. But everything had to start again from
scratch because he married a whore."

"Oh, a whore, you know, people were perhaps rather
malicious. I never quite believed it all."

"Yes, a whore; indeed I shall let you have some ... family
revelations one of these days."

Lost in reverie, my mother said: "To think of the daughter
of a woman whom your father would never allow me to greet
marrying the nephew of Mme de Villeparisis on whom your
father wouldn't allow me to call at first because he thought her
too grand for me!" Then: "And the son of Mme de Cambremer to whom Legrandin was so afraid of having to give us
a letter of introduction because he didn't think us smart

enough, marrying the niece of a man who would never dare to come to our flat except by the service stairs! . . . Your poor grandmother was absolutely right—you remember—when she said that the high aristocracy did things that would shock the middle classes and that Queen Marie-Amélie was spoiled for her by the overtures she made to the Prince de Condé's mistress to get her to persuade him to make his will in favour of the Duc d'Aumale. You remember too how it shocked her that for centuries past daughters of the house of Gramont who were veritable saints had borne the name Corisande in memory of Henri IV's liaison with one of their ancestresses. These things may perhaps also occur among the middle classes, but they conceal them better. Can't you imagine how it would have amused your poor grandmother!" Mamma added sadly, for the joys which it grieved us to think that my grandmother was deprived of were the simplest joys of life—an item of news, a play, or even something more trifling still, a piece of mimicry, which would have amused her. "Can't you imagine her astonishment! But still, I'm sure that your grandmother would have been shocked by these marriages, that they would have grieved her; I feel that it's better that she never knew about them," my mother went on, for, when confronted with any event, she liked to think that my grandmother would have received an utterly distinctive impression from it which would have stemmed from the marvellous singularity of her nature and have been uniquely significant. If anything sad or painful occurred which could not have been foreseen in the past—the disgrace or ruin of one of our old friends, some public calamity, an epidemic, a war, a revolution—my mother would say to herself that perhaps it was better that Grandmamma had known nothing about it, that it would have grieved her too much, that perhaps she would not have been able to endure it. And when it was a question of something shocking like these two marriages, my mother, by an impulse directly opposite to that of the malicious people who like to imagine that others whom they do not like have suffered more than is generally supposed, would not, in her tenderness for my grandmother, allow that anything sad or diminishing could ever have happened to her. She always imagined my grandmother as being above the assaults even of any evil which might not have been expected to occur, and told herself that my grandmother's death had perhaps been a blessing on the whole, inasmuch as it had shut off the too ugly spectacle of the present day from that noble nature which could never have become resigned to it. For optimism is the philosophy of the past. The events that have occurred being, among all those that were possible, the only ones which we have known, the harm that they have caused seems to us inevitable, and we give them the credit for the slight amount of good that they could not help bringing with them, for we imagine that without them it would not have occurred. My mother sought at the same time to form a more accurate idea of what my grandmother would have felt when she learned these tidings, and to believe that it was impossible for our minds, less exalted than hers, to form any such idea. "Can't you imagine," she said to me first of all, "how astonished your poor grandmother would have been!" And I felt that my mother was distressed by her inability to tell her the news, regretting that my grandmother would never know it, and feeling it to be somehow unjust that the course of life should bring to light facts which my grandmother would never have believed, thus rendering erroneous and incomplete, retrospectively, the knowledge of people and society which my grandmother had taken to the grave, the marriage of the Jupien girl and Legrandin's nephew being calculated to modify her general notions of life, no less than the news—had my mother been able to convey it to her—that people had succeeded in solving the problems, which my grandmother had regarded as insoluble, of aerial navigation and wireless telegraphy. But as we shall see, this desire that my grandmother should share in the blessings of our modern science was soon, in its turn, to appear too selfish to my mother.

What I was to learn later on—for I had been unable to keep in touch with it all from Venice—was that Mlle de Forcheville's hand had been sought both by the Duc de Châtellerault and by the Prince de Silistrie, while Saint-Loup was seeking to marry Mlle d'Entragues, the Duc de Luxembourg's daughter.

This is what had occurred. Mlle de Forcheville possessing a hundred million francs, Mme de Marsantes had decided that she would be an excellent match for her son. She made the mistake of saying that the girl was charming, that she herself had not the slightest idea whether she was rich or poor, that she did not wish to know, but that even without a dowry it would be a piece of good luck for the most exacting young man to find such a wife. This was going rather too far for a woman who was tempted only by the hundred millions, which made her shut her eyes to everything else. People realised at once that she was thinking of the girl for her own son. The Princesse de Silistrie went round protesting loudly, expatiating on Saint-Loup's social grandeur, and proclaiming that if he should marry the daughter of Odette and a Jew then it was the end of the Faubourg Saint-Germain. Mme de Marsantes, sure of herself as she was, dared not proceed further and retreated before the indignant protests of the Princesse de Silistrie, who immediately made a proposal on behalf of her own son. She had protested only in order to keep Gilberte for herself. Meanwhile Mme de Marsantes, refusing to own herself defeated, had turned at once to Mlle d'Entragues, the Duc de Luxembourg's daughter. Having no more than twenty millions, the latter suited her purpose less, but Mme de Marsantes told everyone that a Saint-Loup could not marry a Mlle Swann (there was no longer any mention of Forcheville). Some time later, somebody having thoughtlessly remarked that the Duc de Châtellerault was thinking of marrying Mlle d'Entragues, Mme de Marsantes, who was the most punctilious woman in the world, mounted her high horse, changed her tactics, returned to Gilberte, made a formal offer of marriage on Saint-Loup's behalf, and the engagement was immediately announced.

This engagement was to provoke keen comment in the most different social circles.

Several of my mother's friends, who had met Saint-Loup in our house, came to her "day," and inquired whether the bridegroom was indeed the same person as my friend. Certain people went so far as to maintain, with regard to the other marriage, that it had nothing to do with the Legrandin-Cambremers. They had this on good authority, for the

Marquise, *née* Legrandin, had denied it on the very eve of the day on which the engagement was announced. I, for my part, wondered why M. de Charlus on the one hand, Saint-Loup on the other, each of whom had had occasion to write to me shortly before and had spoken in such friendly terms of various travel plans the realisation of which must have precluded the wedding ceremonies, had said nothing whatever to me about them. I came to the conclusion, forgetting the secrecy which people maintain until the last moment in affairs of this sort, that I was less their friend than I had supposed, a conclusion which, so far as Saint-Loup was concerned, saddened me. Though why, when I had already remarked that the affability, the egalitarian, "man-to-man" attitude of the aristocracy was all a sham, should I be surprised to find myself its victim? In the establishment for women—where men were now to be procured in increasing numbers—in which M. de Charlus had spied on Morel, and in which the "assistant matron,"[34] a great reader of the *Gaulois*, used to discuss the social gossip with her clients, this lady, while conversing with a stout gentleman who used to come to her to drink bottle after bottle of champagne with young men, because, being already very stout, he wished to become obese enough to be certain of not being "called up" should there ever be a war, declared: "It seems young Saint-Loup is 'one of those,' and young Cambremer too. Poor wives! In any case, if you know these bridegrooms, you must send them to us. They'll find everything they want here, and there's plenty of money to be made out of them." Whereupon the stout gentleman, albeit he was himself "one of those," indignantly retorted, being something of a snob, that he often met Cambremer and Saint-Loup at his cousins' the Ardonvillers, and that they were great womanisers, and quite the opposite of "those." "Ah!" the assistant matron concluded in a sceptical tone, but possessing no proof of the assertion, and convinced that in our century the perversity of morals was rivalled only by the absurd exaggeration of slanderous tittle-tattle.

Certain people whom I no longer saw wrote to me and asked me "what I thought" of these two marriages, precisely as though they were conducting an inquiry into the height of women's hats in the theatre or the psychological novel. I had not the heart to answer these letters. Of these two marriages I thought nothing at all, but I felt an immense sadness, as when two parts of one's past existence, which have been anchored near to one, and upon which one has perhaps been basing idly from day to day an unacknowledged hope, remove themselves finally, with a joyous crackling of flames, for unknown destinations, like a pair of ships. As for the prospective bridegrooms themselves, their attitude towards their own marriages was perfectly natural, since it was a question not of other people but of themselves—though hitherto they had never tired of mocking at such "grand marriages" founded upon some secret taint. And even the Cambremer family, so ancient in its lineage and so modest in its pretensions, would have been the first to forget Jupien and to remember only the unimaginable grandeur of the House of Oloron, had not an exception appeared in the person who ought to have been most gratified by this marriage, the Marquise de Cambremer-Legrandin. Being spiteful by nature, she reckoned the pleasure of humiliating her family above that of glorifying herself. And so, not being enamoured of her son, and having rapidly taken a dislike to her future daughter-in-law, she declared that it was a calamity for a Cambremer to marry a person who had sprung from heaven knew where, and had such bad teeth. As for young Cambremer, who had already shown a propensity towards the society of men of letters such as Bergotte and even Bloch, it may be imagined that so brilliant a marriage did not have the effect of making him more of a snob than before, but that, feeling himself to have become the successor of the Ducs d'Oloron— "sovereign princes" as the newspapers said—he was sufficiently persuaded of his own grandeur to be able to mix with anyone he chose. And he deserted the minor nobility for the intelligent bourgeoisie on the days when he did not confine himself to royalty. The notices in the papers, especially when they referred to Saint-Loup, invested my friend, whose royal ancestors were endlessly enumerated, with a renewed grandeur which, however, could only sadden me, as though he had become someone else, the descendant of Robert the Strong rather than the friend who, only a little while since, had taken the folding seat in the carriage in order that I might be more comfortable in the back; the fact that I had had no previous suspicion of his marriage with Gilberte—the prospect of which had appeared to me suddenly, in my letter, so different from anything that I could have expected of either of them the day before, as unexpected as a chemical precipitate—pained me, whereas I ought to have reflected that he had had a great deal to do, and that moreover in the fashionable world marriages are often arranged thus all of a sudden, as a substitute for a different combination which has come to grief. And the gloom, as dismal as the depression of moving house, as bitter as jealousy, that these marriages caused me by the accident of their sudden impact was so profound that people used to remind me of it later, congratulating me absurdly on my perspicacity, as having been, quite contrary to what it was at the time, a two-fold, indeed a three-fold and four-fold presentiment.

The people in society who had taken no notice of Gilberte said to me with an air of solemn interest: "Ah! she's the one who's marrying the Marquis de Saint-Loup," and studied her with the attentive gaze of people who not only relish all the social gossip of Paris but are anxious to learn and believe in the profundity of their observation. Those who on the other hand had known only Gilberte gazed at Saint-Loup with the closest attention, asked me (these were often people who scarcely knew me) to introduce them, and returned from the presentation to the bridegroom radiant with the joys of the festivity saying to me: "He's a fine figure of a man." Gilberte was convinced that the name "Marquis de Saint-Loup" was a thousand times grander than "Duc d'Orléans," but since she was very much of her knowing generation, she did not want to appear less witty than others, and delighted in saying *mater semita*, to which she would add in order to show herself wittier still: "In my case, however, it's my *pater*."

"It appears that it was the Princesse de Parme who arranged young Cambremer's marriage," Mamma said to me. And this was true. The Princess had known for a long time, through her charitable activities, on the one hand Legrandin whom she regarded as a distinguished man, on the other hand Mme de

Cambremer who changed the subject whenever the Princess asked her whether it was true that she was Legrandin's sister. The Princess knew how deeply Mme de Cambremer regretted having remained on the threshold of aristocratic high society without ever being invited in. When the Princess, who had undertaken to find a husband for Mlle d'Oloron, asked M. de Charlus whether he knew anything about an amiable and cultivated man called Legrandin de Méséglise (it was thus that M. Legrandin now styled himself), the Baron first of all replied in the negative, then suddenly the memory recurred to him of a man whose acquaintance he had made in the train one night and who had given him his card. He smiled a vague smile. "It's perhaps the same man," he said to himself. When he learned that the prospective bridegroom was the son of Legrandin's sister, he said: "Why, that would be really extraordinary! If he took after his uncle, it wouldn't alarm me; after all, I've always said that they made the best husbands." "Who are *they*?" inquired the Princess. "Ah, madame, I could explain it all to you if we met more often. With you one can talk freely. Your Highness is so intelligent," said Charlus, seized by a desire to confide which, however, went no further. The name Cambremer pleased him, although he did not like the boy's parents; he knew that it was one of the four Baronies of Brittany and everything he could possibly have hoped for his adopted daughter; it was an old and respected name, with solid connexions in its native province. A prince would have been out of the question and, moreover, not altogether desirable. This was the very thing. The Princess then asked Legrandin to call. Physically he had changed considerably of late, on the whole for the better. Like those women who deliberately sacrifice their faces to the slimness of their figures and never stir from Marienbad, he had acquired the breezy air of a cavalry officer. He had taken up tennis at the age of fifty-five. In proportion as M. de Charlus had thickened and slowed down, Legrandin had become slimmer and brisker, the contrary effect of an identical cause. This velocity of movement had its psychological reasons as well. He was in the habit of frequenting certain low haunts where he did not wish to be seen going in or coming out: he would hurl himself into them.

When the Princesse de Parme spoke to him of the Guermantes family and of Saint-Loup, he declared that he had known them all his life, making a sort of compound of the fact that he had always known *by name* the proprietors of Guermantes and the fact that he had met *in person*, at my aunt's house, Swann, the father of the future Mme de Saint-Loup—although he had always refused to have anything to do with Swann's wife and daughter at Combray. "Indeed, I travelled quite recently with the brother of the Duc de Guermantes, M. de Charlus. It was he who spontaneously engaged me in conversation, which is always a good sign, for it proves that a man is neither a strait-laced fool nor a pretentious snob. Oh, I know all the things that people say about him. But I never pay any attention to gossip of that sort. Besides, the private life of other people is not my business. He gave me the impression of having a sensitive nature and a cultivated mind." Then the Princesse de Parme spoke of Mlle d'Oloron. In the Guermantes circle people waxed sentimental about the nobility of heart of M. de Charlus who, generous as always, was securing the future happiness of a penniless but charming girl. And the Duc de Guermantes, who suffered from his brother's reputation, let it be understood that, fine as this conduct was, it was wholly natural. "I don't know if I make myself clear, but everything in the affair is natural," he said, with calculated maladroitness. His object was to indicate that the girl was a daughter of his brother whom the latter acknowledged. This accounted at the same time for Jupien. The Princesse de Parme hinted at this version of the story to show Legrandin that after all young Cambremer would be marrying something in the nature of Mlle de Nantes, one of those bastards of Louis XIV who were scorned neither by the Duc d'Orléans nor by the Prince de Conti.

These two marriages which my mother and I discussed in the train that was taking us back to Paris had quite remarkable effects upon several of the characters who have figured in the course of this narrative. First of all upon Legrandin; needless to say, he swept like a hurricane into M. de Charlus's town house, for all the world as though he were entering a house of ill-fame where he must on no account be seen, and also, at the same time, to display his mettle and to conceal his age—for our habits accompany us even into places where they serve no useful purpose—and scarcely anybody observed that M. de Charlus greeted him with a smile which was hard to detect and harder still to interpret; this smile was similar in appearance— though in fact it was precisely the opposite—to the smile which two men who are in the habit of meeting in the best society exchange if they happen to meet in what they regard as disreputable surroundings (such as the Elysée where General de Froberville, whenever he met Swann there in the old days, would assume, on catching sight of him, an expression of ironical and mysterious complicity appropriate between two habitués of the salon of the Princesse des Laumes who were compromising themselves by visiting M. Grévy). But what was rather remarkable was the genuine improvement in Legrandin's character. For a long time past—ever since the days when I used to go as a child to spend my holidays at Combray—he had been surreptitiously cultivating relations with the aristocracy, productive at the most of an isolated invitation to a sterile house party. All of a sudden, his nephew's marriage having supervened to join up these scattered fragments, Legrandin stepped into a social position to which, retroactively, his former relations with people who had known him only in private but had known him well, gave a sort of solidity. Ladies to whom people offered to introduce him revealed that for the last twenty years he had stayed with them in the country for a fortnight annually, and that it was he who had given them the beautiful old barometer in the small drawing-room. It also transpired that he had been photographed in "groups" which included dukes who were now related to him. But as soon as he had acquired this social position, he ceased to take advantage of it. This was not merely because, now that people knew that he was received everywhere, he no longer derived any pleasure from being invited, but because, of the two vices that had long struggled for mastery in him, the less natural, snobbishness, was now giving way to another that was less artificial, since it did at least show a sort of return, however circuitous, towards nature. No doubt the two are not incompatible, and a nocturnal prowl may be undertaken immediately after leaving a duchess's party. But the dampening effect of age discouraged Legrandin from combining too many pleasures, from venturing out except with a definite purpose, and also made his enjoyment of the pleasures of nature fairly platonic, consisting chiefly in friendships, in time-consuming conversations, which, making him spend almost all his time among the people, left him very little for the life of society.

Mme de Cambremer herself became almost indifferent to the friendly overtures of the Duchesse de Guermantes. The latter, obliged to see something of the Marquise, had noticed, as happens whenever we come to see more of our fellow creatures, that is to say as combinations of good qualities which we eventually discover and defects to which we eventually grow accustomed, that Mme de Cambremer was a woman endowed with an intelligence and culture which were little to my taste but which appeared remarkable to the Duchess. And so she often went to see Mme de Cambremer in the late afternoon and paid her long visits. But the fabulous charm which her hostess imagined to exist in the Duchesse de Guermantes vanished as soon as she found herself sought after by her, and she received her out of politeness rather than pleasure.

A more striking change manifested itself in Gilberte, a change at once symmetrical with and different from that which occurred in Swann after his marriage. It is true that during the first few months Gilberte had been happy to open her doors to the most select society. It was doubtless only because of the inheritance that she invited the intimate friends to whom her mother was attached, but on certain days only when there was no one but themselves, segregated from the fashionable people, as though the contact of Mme Bontemps or Mme Cottard with the Princesse de Guermantes or the Princesse de Parme might, like that of two unstable powders, have produced irreparable catastrophes. Nevertheless the Bontemps, the Cottards and such, although disappointed to find themselves dining among themselves, were proud to be able to say: "We dined with the Marquise de Saint-Loup," all the more so because she sometimes went so far as to invite with them Mme de Marsantes, who showed herself emphatically the "great lady" with her tortoise-shell and ostrich-feather fan—also in the interests of the legacy. She merely made a point of paying tribute from time to time to the discreet people whom one never sees except when they are invited, a word to the wise subject to which she bestowed upon the Cottards, the Bontemps and their ilk her most gracious and lofty salutation. Perhaps because of my "Balbec girl friend," by whose aunt I liked to be seen in these surroundings, I should have preferred to be included in that group. But Gilberte, in whose eyes I was now principally a friend of her husband and of the Guermantes (and who—perhaps even from the Combray days, when my parents did not call upon her mother—at the age when we do not merely add this or that to the value of things but classify them according to their species, had endowed me with the sort of prestige which one never afterwards loses), regarded these evenings as unworthy of me, and would say to me as I left: "It's delightful to have seen you, but you must come the day after to-morrow; you'll find my aunt Guermantes, and Mme de Poix; to-day it was just a few of Mamma's friends, to please Mamma." But this state of things lasted for a few months only, and then everything was totally transformed. Was this because Gilberte's social life was fated to exhibit the same contrasts as Swann's? However that may be, Gilberte had been for only a short time the Marquise de Saint-Loup (in the process of becoming, as we shall see, Duchesse de Guermantes)[35] when, having attained to the most brilliant and most rarefied position, she decided that the name Guermantes was now embodied in her like a glowing enamel and that, whatever the society she frequented, from now onwards she would remain for all the world the Marquise de Saint-Loup—sharing, in short, the opinion of the character in the operetta who declares: "My name, I think, dispenses me from saying more."[36] Wherein she was mistaken, for the value of a title, like that of stocks and shares, rises with the demand and falls when it is offered in the market. Everything that seems to us imperishable tends towards decay; a position in society, like anything else, is not created once and for all, but, just as much as the power of an Empire, is continually rebuilding itself by a sort of perpetual process of creation, which explains the apparent anomalies in social or political history in the course of half a century. The creation of the world did not occur at the beginning of time, it occurs every day. The Marquise de Saint-Loup said to herself, "I am the Marquise de Saint-Loup," and she knew that, the day before, she had refused three invitations to dine with duchesses. But if to a certain extent her name aggrandised the very unaristocratic people whom she entertained, by an inverse process the people whom she entertained diminished the name that she bore. Nothing can hold out against such trends; the greatest names succumb to them in the end. Had not Swann known a princess of the House of France whose drawing-room, because anyone at all was welcomed there, had fallen to the lowest rank? One day when the Princesse des Laumes had gone to pay a brief duty call on this Highness, in whose drawing-room she had found only nonentities, arriving immediately afterwards at Mme Leroi's, she had said to Swann and the Marquis de Modène: "At last I find myself upon friendly soil. I have just come from Mme la Comtesse de X—, and there weren't three faces I knew in the room." At all events, Gilberte suddenly began to flaunt her contempt for what she had once so ardently desired, to declare that all the people in the Faubourg Saint-Germain were idiots, simply not worth meeting, and, suiting her actions to her words, ceased to meet them. People who did not make her acquaintance until after this period, and who, in the first stages of that acquaintance, heard her, by that time Duchesse de Guermantes, being very funny at the expense of the society in which she could so easily have moved, never inviting a single person from that society, and, if any of them, even the most brilliant, should venture into her drawing-room, yawning openly in their faces, blush now in retrospect at the thought that they themselves could ever have seen any glamour in the fashionable world, and would never dare to confess this humiliating secret of their past weaknesses to a woman whom they assume to have been, by an essential loftiness in her nature, incapable from the beginning of understanding such things. They hear her poking such delicious fun at dukes, and see her (which is more significant) matching her behaviour so entirely to her mockery! No doubt they do not think of inquiring into the causes of the accident which turned Mlle Swann into Mlle de Forcheville, Mlle de Forcheville into the

Marquise de Saint-Loup, and finally into the Duchesse de Guermantes. Possibly it does not occur to them either that the effects of this accident would serve no less than its causes to explain Gilberte's subsequent attitude, association with commoners not being regarded in quite the same light in which Mlle Swann would have regarded it by a lady who is addressed by all and sundry as "Madame la Duchesse" and, by other duchesses who bore her so much, as "cousin." One is always ready to despise a goal which one has not succeeded in attaining, or has finally attained. And this contempt seems to us to form part of the character of people whom one did not know before. Perhaps, if we were able to go back over the years, we should find them devoured, more savagely than anyone, by those same weaknesses which they have succeeded so completely in disguising or conquering that we reckon them incapable not only of ever having been infected by them themselves but even of ever excusing them in others, because of their inability to imagine them. At all events, very soon the drawing-room of the new Marquise de Saint-Loup assumed its permanent aspect (from the social point of view at least, for we shall see what troubles were brewing in it in other respects). Now this aspect was surprising for the following reason. People still remembered that the most grandiose and glittering receptions in Paris, as brilliant as those given by the Princesse de Guermantes, had been those of Mme de Marsantes, Saint-Loup's mother. At the same time, in recent years Odette's salon, infinitely lower in the social scale, had been no less dazzling in its elegance and splendour. Saint-Loup, however, happy to have, thanks to his wife's vast fortune, everything that he could desire in the way of comfort, wished only to rest quietly in his armchair after a good dinner with a musical entertainment by good performers. And this young man who had seemed at one time so proud and so ambitious invited to share his luxury old friends whom his mother would not have admitted to her house. Gilberte, for her part, put into practice Swann's maxim: "Quality doesn't matter, what I dread is quantity." And Saint-Loup, very much on his knees before his wife, both because he loved her and because it was to her that he owed this extreme luxury, took care not to interfere with tastes that were so similar to his own. With the result that the great receptions that had been given year after year by Mme de Marsantes and Mme de Forcheville, principally with an eye to the establishing of their children in ostentatious splendour, gave rise to no receptions by M. and Mme de Saint-Loup. They had the best of saddle-horses on which to go out riding together, the finest of yachts in which to cruise—but they never took more than a couple of guests with them. In Paris, every evening, they would invite three or four friends to dine, never more; with the result that, by an unforeseen but at the same time quite natural retrogression, the two vast maternal aviaries had been replaced by a silent nest.

The person who profited least by these two marriages was the young Mlle d'Oloron who, already stricken with typhoid on the day of the religious ceremony, was barely able to crawl to the church and died a few weeks later. In the letter of intimation that was sent out some time after her death, names such as Jupien's were juxtaposed with some of the greatest in Europe, such as those of the Vicomte and Vicomtesse de Montmorency, H.R.H. the Comtesse de Bourbon-Soissons, the Prince of Modena-Este, the Vicomtesse d'Edumea, Lady Essex, and so forth. No doubt, even to a person who knew that the deceased was Jupien's niece, this plethora of grand marriage connections could cause no surprise. The great thing, after all, is to have a grand marriage. Then, the *casus foederis* coming into play, the death of a simple little seamstress plunges all the princely families of Europe into mourning. But many young people of the rising generation, who were not familiar with the real situation, might, apart from the possibility of their mistaking Marie-Antoinette d'Oloron, Marquise de Cambremer, for a lady of the noblest birth, have been guilty of many other errors had they read this communication. Thus, supposing their excursions through France to have given them some slight familiarity with the country round Combray, when they saw that the Comte de Méséglise figured among the first of the signatories, close to the Duc de Guermantes, they might not have been at all surprised: the Méséglise way and the Guermantes way are cheek by jowl. "Old nobility of the same region, perhaps inter-related for generations," they might have said to themselves. "Who knows? It's perhaps a branch of the Guermantes family which bears the title of Comte de Méséglise." As it happened, the Comte de Méséglise had no connection with the Guermantes and was not even enrolled on the Guermantes side, but on the Cambremer side, since the Comte de Méséglise, who by a rapid advancement had remained Legrandin de Méséglise for only two years, was our old friend Legrandin. No doubt, if they had to choose between bogus titles, few could have been so disagreeable to the Guermantes as this one. They had been connected in the past with the authentic Comtes de Méséglise, of whom there survived only one female descendant, tne daughter of obscure parents who had come down in the world, herself married to one of my aunt's tenant farmers named Ménager, who had become rich and bought Mirougrain from her and now styled himself "Ménager de Mirougrain," with the result that when it was said that his wife was born "de Méséglise" people thought that she must simply have been born at Méséglise and that she was "from Méséglise" as her husband was "from Mirougrain."

Any other sham title would have caused less annoyance to the Guermantes family. But the aristocracy knows how to tolerate such irritations, and many others as well, the moment a marriage is at stake which is deemed advantageous, from whatever point of view. Shielded by the Duc de Guermantes, Legrandin was, to part of that generation, and would be to the whole of the generation that followed it, the real Comte de Méséglise.

Yet another mistake which any young reader not acquainted with the facts might have been led to make was that of supposing that the Baron and Baronne de Forcheville figured on the list in the capacity of parents-in-law of the Marquis de Saint-Loup, that is to say on the Guermantes side. But on this side they had no right to appear since it was Robert who was related to the Guermantes and not Gilberte. No, the Baron and Baronne de Forcheville, despite these deceptive appearances, did figure on the wife's side, it is true, and not on the Cambremer side, not because of the Guermantes, but because of Jupien, who, the better informed reader knows, was Odette's first cousin.

All M. de Charlus's favour had been transferred after the marriage of his adopted daughter on to the young Marquis de Cambremer; the young man's tastes, which were similar to those of the Baron, since they had not prevented the Baron from choosing him as a husband for Mlle d'Oloron, naturally made him appreciate him all the more when he was left a widower. This is not to say that the Marquis did not have other qualities which made him a charming companion for M. de Charlus. But even in the case of a man of real merit, it is a quality not to be despised by the person who admits him into his private life, and one that makes him particularly useful if he can also play whist. The intelligence of the young Marquis was remarkable, and, as they had already begun to say at Féterne when he was barely out of his cradle, he "took" entirely after his grandmother, had the same enthusiasms, the same love of music. He reproduced also some of her idiosyncrasies, but these more by imitation, like all the rest of the family, than from atavism. Thus it was that, some time after the death of his wife, having received a letter signed "Léonor," a name which I did not remember as being his, I realised who it was that had written to me only when I had read the closing formula: "*Croyez à ma sympathie vraie.*" The placing of that *vraie* infallibly added to the Christian name Léonor the surname Cambremer.

The train reached Paris before my mother and I had finished discussing these two pieces of news, which, so that the journey might not seem to me too long, she had deliberately reserved for the latter part of it, not allowing me to learn about them until after Milan. My mother had soon reverted to the point of view which for her was the only possible one, that of my grandmother. Mamma had first of all said that my grandmother would have been surprised, then that she would have been saddened, which was simply a way of saying that such a surprising event would have given her pleasure, and my mother, unable to accept that my grandmother should have been deprived of a pleasure, preferred to think that all was for the best, this news being of the kind that could only have caused her sorrow. But no sooner had we reached home than my mother felt that it was still too selfish of her to regret being unable to share with my grandmother all the surprises that life brings. She preferred to believe that this news would not have surprised my grandmother, since it merely confirmed her predictions. She wanted to see it as a confirmation of my grandmother's foresight, proof that she had been even more profound, more perceptive, more sagacious than we had thought. And so, in order to arrive at this attitude of pure admiration, it was not long before my mother was adding: "And yet, who knows whether your grandmother wouldn't have approved? She was so kind and tolerant. And then you know, for her, social status meant nothing; natural distinction was what mattered. And curiously enough, don't you remember, she liked both of them. Remember that first visit of hers to Mme de Villeparisis, when she came back and told us how common she thought M. de Guermantes was, and by comparison how full of praise she was for those Jupiens. Poor Mamma, do you remember her saying about the father: 'If I had another daughter, I'd give her to him as a wife, and his daughter is even nicer.' And the little Swann girl! She used to say of her: '*I* think she's charming; you'll see that she'll marry well.' Poor Mamma, if only she'd lived to see how right she was! Right up to the end she'll go on giving us lessons in goodness and foresight and judgment." And since the joys which we suffered to see my grandmother deprived of were all the humble little joys of life—the imitation of an actor's voice which would have amused her, a dish she would have enjoyed, a new novel by a favourite author—Mamma said: "How surprised she would have been! How it would have interested her! What a lovely letter she would have written in reply!" And my mother went on: "Just imagine, poor Swann who so longed for Gilberte to be received by the Guermantes, how happy he would be if he could see his daughter become a Guermantes!"

"Under another name than his, led to the altar as Mlle de Forcheville—do you think he would be so happy after all?"

"Ah, that's true, I hadn't thought of it."

"That's what makes it impossible for me to be happy for her sake, the thought that the little wretch could have had the heart to give up her father's name, when he was so good to her."

"Yes, you're right; all things considered, it's perhaps just as well that he never knew." So difficult is it for us to know, with the dead as with the living, whether a thing would cause them joy or sorrow! "It appears that the Saint-Loups are going to live at Tansonville," my mother went on. "Old Swann, who was so anxious to show your poor grandfather his pond, could never have dreamed that the Duc de Guermantes would see it constantly, especially if he had known of his son's shameful marriage. And then, you've talked so often to Saint-Loup about the hawthorns and lilacs and irises at Tansonville, he'll see what you meant now. They'll be his property."

Thus there proceeded in our dining-room, in the lamplight that is so congenial to them, one of those long chats in which the wisdom not of nations but of families, taking hold of some event, a death, a betrothal, an inheritance, a bankruptcy, and slipping it under the magnifying glass of memory, brings it into high relief, detaches, thrusts back, and places in perspective at different points in space and time things which to those who have not lived through it seem to be juxtaposed on a single plane, the names of the deceased, successive addresses, the origins of a fortune and its vicissitudes, transfers of property. It is the wisdom inspired by the Muse whom it is best to ignore for as long as possible if we wish to retain some freshness of impressions, some creative power, but whom even those who have ignored her meet in the evening of their lives in the nave of an old country church, at a point when suddenly they feel less susceptible to the eternal beauty expressed in the carvings on the altar than to the thought of the vicissitudes of fortune which those carvings have undergone, passing into a famous private collection or a chapel, from there to a museum, then returning at length to the church, or to the feeling that as they walk around it they may be treading upon a flagstone almost endowed with thought, which is made of the ashes of Arnauld or Pascal, or simply to deciphering (forming perhaps a mental picture of a fresh-faced country girl) on the brass plate of the wooden prie-dieu the names of the daughters of the squire or the notable—the Muse who has gathered up everything that the more exalted Muses of philosophy and art have rejected, everything that is not founded upon truth, everything that is merely contingent, but that reveals other laws as well: the Muse of History.

Some old friends of my mother, who belonged more or less to Combray, came to see her to discuss Gilberte's marriage, which did not dazzle them in the least. "You know who Mlle de Forcheville is, she's simply Mlle Swann. And her witness at the marriage, the 'Baron' de Charlus, as he calls himself, is the old man who used to keep her mother at one time, under Swann's very nose, and no doubt to his advantage." "But what do you mean?" my mother protested; "in the first place, Swann was extremely rich." "One must assume that he wasn't as rich as all that if he needed other people's money. But what is there about that woman, that she hangs on to her old lovers like that? She managed to persuade the first to marry her, then the third, and she drags out the second when he has one foot in the grave to get him to be a witness at the marriage of the daughter she had by the first or by someone else—for how is one to tell who the father was? She can't be certain herself! I said the third, but I should have said the three hundredth. Mind you, even if the girl's no more a Forcheville than you or I, that puts her on the same level as the bridegroom who of course isn't noble at all. You can imagine that only an adventurer would marry a girl like that. It appears he's just a plain Monsieur Dupont or Durand or something. If it weren't that we have a Radical mayor now at Combray, who doesn't even lift his hat to the priest, I should know all about it. Because, you understand, when they published the banns, they were obliged to give the real name. It's all very nice, for the newspapers or for the stationer who sends out the invitations, to describe yourself as the Marquis de Saint-Loup. That does no harm to anyone, and if it can give any pleasure to those worthy people, I should be the last person in the world to object! What harm can it do me? As I shall never dream of going to call on the daughter of a woman who has let herself be talked about, she can have a string of titles as long as my arm for the benefit of her servants. But in an official document it's not the same thing. Ah, if my cousin Sazerat was still deputy-mayor, I'd have written to him, and he would certainly have let *me* know what name the man was registered under."

I saw a good deal of Gilberte at this time, as it happened, having renewed my friendship with her: for our life, in the long run, is not calculated according to the duration of our friendships. Let a certain period of time elapse, and you will see (just as, in politics, former ministries reappear, or, in the theatre, forgotten plays are revived) friendships renewed between the same persons as before, after long years of interruption, and renewed with pleasure. After ten years, the reasons which made one party love too passionately, the other unable to endure a too exacting despotism, no longer exist. The affinity alone survives, and everything that Gilberte would have refused me in the past, that had seemed to her intolerable, impossible, she granted me quite readily—doubtless because I no longer desired it. Although neither of us had ever mentioned the reason for this change, if she was always ready to come to me, never in a hurry to leave me, it was because the obstacle had vanished: my love.

Some time later, I went to spend a few days at Tansonville. This excursion was something of an inconvenience, for I was keeping a girl in Paris who slept in a bachelor flat which I had rented. As other people need the aroma of forests or the ripple of a lake, so I needed her sleep by my side during the night and, by day, to have her always by my side in the carriage. For even if one love has passed into oblivion, it may determine the form of the love that is to follow it. Already, even in the midst of the previous love, daily habits existed, the origin of which we did not ourselves remember; perhaps it was a moment of anguish early on that had made us passionately desire, then permanently adopt, like customs the meaning of which has been forgotten, the habit of those homeward drives to the beloved's door, or her residence in our home, our presence or the presence of someone we trust during all her outings. All these habits, which are like great uniform high-roads along which our love passes daily and which were forged long ago in the volcanic fire of an ardent emotion, nevertheless survive the woman, survive even the memory of the woman. They become the pattern, if not of all our loves, at least of certain of our loves which alternate with the others. And thus my home had demanded, in memory of a forgotten Albertine, the presence of my mistress of the moment whom I concealed from visitors and who filled my life as Albertine had filled it in the past. And in order to go to Tansonville I had to obtain her consent to being looked after for a few days by one of my friends who did not care for women. But I had heard that Gilberte was unhappy, because Robert was unfaithful to her, though not in the fashion which everyone believed, which perhaps she herself still believed, which in any case she alleged. A belief that could be explained by pride, by the desire to hoodwink other people and to hoodwink oneself, not to mention the imperfect knowledge of infidelities which is all that betrayed spouses ever acquire, all the more so as Robert, a true nephew of M. de Charlus, went about openly with women whom he compromised, whom the world believed and whom Gilberte on the whole believed to be his mistresses. It was even thought in society that he was too barefaced, never stirring, at a party, from the side of some woman whom he afterwards accompanied home, leaving Mme de Saint-Loup to return as best she could. Anyone who had said that the other woman whom he compromised thus was not really his mistress would have been regarded as a fool, incapable of seeing what was staring him in the face; but I had been pointed, alas, in the direction of the truth, a truth which caused me infinite distress, by a few words let fall by Jupien. A few months before my visit to Tansonville I had gone to inquire after M. de Charlus, in whom certain cardiac symptoms had been causing his friends great anxiety, and having mentioned to Jupien, whom I found alone, some love-letters addressed to Robert and signed Bobette which Mme de Saint-Loup had discovered, I was stupefied to learn from the Baron's former factotum that the person who used the signature Bobette was none other than the violinist who had played so important a part in M. de Charlus's life.[37] Jupien could not speak of him without indignation: "The boy was free to do whatever he liked. But if there was one direction in which he ought never to have looked, that was in the direction of the Baron's nephew. All the more so as the Baron loved his nephew like his own son. He has tried to break up the marriage

—it's really shameful. And he must have gone about it with the most devilish cunning, for no one was ever more opposed to that sort of thing by nature than the Marquis de Saint-Loup. You've only to think of the follies he committed for the sake of his mistresses! No, however despicably—there's no other word for it—he deserted the Baron, that was his business. But to take up with the nephew! There are some things that just aren't done."

Jupien was sincere in his indignation; among so-called immoral people, moral indignation is quite as violent as among other people, only its object is slightly different. What is more, people whose own hearts are not directly involved always regard unfortunate entanglements, disastrous marriages, as though one were free to choose whom one loves, and do not take into account the exquisite mirage which love projects and which envelops so entirely and so uniquely the person with whom one is in love that the "folly" a man commits by marrying his cook or the mistress of his best friend is as a rule the only poetical action that he performs in the course of his existence.

I gathered that Robert and his wife had been on the brink of a separation (though Gilberte had not yet discovered the precise nature of the trouble) and that it was Mme de Marsantes, a loving, ambitious and philosophical mother, who had arranged and enforced their reconciliation. She belonged to a world in which perennial inbreeding and the impoverishment of patrimonies constantly bring out, in the realm of the passions as in that of pecuniary interest, inherited vices and compromises. It was with the same energy that in the past she had patronised Mme Swann, encouraged the marriage of Jupien's niece and arranged that of her own son to Gilberte, exercising thus on her own behalf, with a pained resignation, the same atavistic wisdom which she deployed for the benefit of the entire Faubourg. And perhaps what had made her at a certain moment expedite Robert's marriage to Gilberte—which had certainly caused her less trouble and fewer tears than making him break with Rachel—had been the fear of his forming with another harlot—or perhaps with the same one, for Robert took a long time to forget Rachel—a fresh attachment which might have been his salvation. Now I understood what Robert had meant when he said to me at the Princesse de Guermantes's: "It's a pity your Balbec girl friend hasn't the fortune that my mother insists upon. I believe she and I would have got on very well together." He had meant that she belonged to Gomorrah as he belonged to Sodom, or perhaps, if he did not yet belong, that he had ceased to enjoy women whom he could not love in a certain fashion and together with other women. Gilberte, too, might have been able to enlighten me as to Albertine. If therefore, apart from rare moments of recollection, I had not lost all my curiosity as to the life of my dead mistress, I could have questioned not only Gilberte but her husband about her. And on the whole it was the same thing that had given both Robert and myself a desire to marry Albertine—to wit, the knowledge that she was a lover of women. But the causes of our desire, as for that matter its objects, were the reverse of each other. In my case, it was the despair in which I had been plunged by the discovery, in Robert's the satisfaction; in my case to prevent her, by perpetual vigilance, from indulging her predilection; in Robert's to cultivate it, and by granting her her freedom to make her bring her girl friends to him.

If Jupien traced back to a quite recent origin the new orientation, so divergent from their original course, that Robert's carnal desires had assumed, a conversation which I had with Aimé and which made me extremely unhappy showed me that the head waiter at Balbec traced this divergence, this inversion, back to a far earlier date. The occasion of this conversation had been a brief visit I paid to Balbec, where Saint-Loup himself had also come with his wife, whom during this first phase he never allowed out of his sight. I had been struck by the extent to which Rachel's influence over Robert still made itself felt. Only a young husband who has long been keeping a mistress knows how to take off his wife's cloak as they enter a restaurant, how to treat her with due attentiveness. He has received, during the course of his liaison, the education which a good husband requires. Not far from him, at a table adjoining mine, Bloch, among a party of pretentious young academics, was assuming a spuriously relaxed air, and shouted at the top of his voice to one of his friends, as he ostentatiously passed him the menu with a gesture which upset two carafes of water: "No, no, my dear fellow, you order! Never in my life have I been able to make head or tail of these documents. I've never known how to order dinner!" he repeated with a pride that was obviously insincere and, blending literature with greed, decided at once upon a bottle of champagne which he liked to see "in a purely symbolic fashion" adorning a conversation. Saint-Loup, on the other hand, did know how to order. He was seated by the side of Gilberte—already pregnant (subsequently he did not fail to keep her continually supplied with offspring)[38]—as he slept by her side in their double bed in the hotel. He spoke to no one but his wife; the rest of the hotel appeared not to exist for him; but whenever a waiter came to take an order, and stood close beside him, he swiftly raised his blue eyes and darted a glance at him which did not last for more than two seconds, but in its limpid penetration seemed to indicate a kind of investigative curiosity entirely different from that which might have inspired any ordinary diner scrutinising, even at greater length, a page or waiter with a view to making humorous or other observations about him which he would communicate to his friends. This little glance, brief, disinterested, showing that the waiter interested him in himself, would have revealed to anyone who intercepted it that this excellent husband, this once so passionate lover of Rachel, had another plane in his life, and one that seemed to him infinitely more interesting than the one on which he moved from a sense of duty. But it was not otherwise visible. Already his eyes had returned to Gilberte who had noticed nothing; he introduced her to a passing friend and left the room to stroll with her outside. It was then that Aimé spoke to me of a far earlier time, the time when I had made Saint-Loup's acquaintance through Mme de Ville-parisis, in this same Balbec.

"Why, of course, Monsieur," he said to me, "it's common knowledge, I've known it for ever so long. The first year Monsieur came to Balbec, M. le Marquis shut himself up with my lift-boy, on the pretext of developing some photographs of Monsieur's grandmother. The boy made a complaint, and we had the greatest difficulty in hushing the matter up. And besides, Monsieur, Monsieur remembers the day, no doubt, when he came to lunch at the restaurant with M. le Marquis de Saint-Loup and his mistress, whom M. le Marquis was using as a screen. Monsieur doubtless remembers that M. le Marquis left the room, pretending that he had lost his temper. Of course I don't suggest for a moment that Madame was in the right. She was leading him a regular dance. But as to that day, no one will ever make me believe that M. le Marquis's anger wasn't put on, and that he hadn't a good reason to get away from Monsieur and Madame."

So far as that day was concerned, I am convinced that, if Aimé was not deliberately lying, he was entirely mistaken. I remembered too well the state Robert was in, the blow he had struck the journalist. And, for that matter, it was the same with the Balbec incident; either the lift-boy had lied, or it was Aimé who was lying. At least so I believed; I could not be absolutely certain, for we never see more than one aspect of things, and had it not been that the thought distressed me, I should have found a certain beauty in the fact that, whereas for me sending the lift-boy to Saint-Loup had been the most convenient way of conveying a letter to him and receiving his answer, for him it had meant making the acquaintance of a person who had taken his fancy. For everything is at least dual. On to the most insignificant action that we perform, another man will graft a series of entirely different actions. Certain it is that Saint-Loup's adventure with the lift-boy, if it occurred, no more seemed to me to be inherent in the commonplace dispatch of my letter than that a man who knew nothing of Wagner save the duet in *Lohengrin* would be able to foresee the prelude to *Tristan*. True, things offer men only a limited number of their innumerable attributes, because of the paucity of our senses. They are coloured because we have eyes; how many other epithets would they not merit if we had hundreds of senses? But this different aspect which they might present is made more comprehensible to us by the occurrence in life of even the most trivial event of which we know a part which we suppose to be the whole, and at which another person looks as through a window opened up on the other side of the house and offering a different view. Supposing that Aimé had not been mistaken,

Saint-Loup's blush when Bloch spoke to him of the lift-boy had not perhaps been due after all to my friend's pronouncing the word as "lighft." But I was convinced that Saint-Loup's physiological evolution had not begun at that period and that he had then been still exclusively a lover of women. More than by any other sign, I could tell this retrospectively by the friendship that Saint-Loup had shown me at Balbec. It was only while he still loved women that he was really capable of friendship. Afterwards, for some time at least, to the men who did not attract him physically he displayed an indifference which was to some extent, I believe, sincere—for he had become very curt—but which he exaggerated as well in order to make people think that he was interested only in women. But I remember all the same that one day at Doncières, when I was on my way to dine with the Verdurins and he had just been staring rather hard at Morel, he had said to me: "Curious, that fellow reminds me in some ways of Rachel. Doesn't it strike you? They seem to me identical in some ways. Not that it can be of the slightest interest to me." And yet his eyes had afterwards remained for a long time gazing abstractedly at the horizon, as when we think, before returning to the card-table or going out to dinner, of one of those long journeys which we think we shall never make, but for which we have felt a momentary longing. But if Robert found something of Rachel in Charlie, Gilberte, for her part, sought to give herself some resemblance to Rachel in order to appear more attractive to her husband, wearing, like her, bows of scarlet or pink or yellow ribbon in her hair, which she dressed in a similar style, for she believed that her husband was still in love with Rachel, and so was jealous of her. That Robert's love may have hovered at times on the boundary which divides the love of a man for a woman from the love of a man for a man was quite possible. In any case, the memory of Rachel now played only an aesthetic role in this context. It is indeed improbable that it could have played any other. One day Robert had gone to her to ask her to dress up as a man, to leave a lock of hair hanging down, and nevertheless had contented himself with gazing at her, unsatisfied. He remained none the less attached to her and paid her scrupulously, though without pleasure, the enormous income which he had promised her and which did not prevent her from treating him in the most abominable fashion later on. This generosity towards Rachel would not have distressed Gilberte if she had known that it was merely the resigned fulfilment of a promise which no longer bore any trace of love. But love was, on the contrary, precisely what he pretended to feel for Rachel. Homosexuals would be the best husbands in the world if they did not put on an act of loving other women. Not that Gilberte made any complaint. It was the belief that Robert had been loved, and loved for so long, by Rachel that had made her desire him, had made her reject more glittering matches; it seemed that he was making a sort of concession to her in marrying her. And indeed, at first, any comparison between the two women (incommensurable though they were in charm and beauty) did not favour the delicious Gilberte. But the latter subsequently grew in her husband's esteem while Rachel visibly diminished.

There was another person who changed her tune, namely Mme Swann. If, in Gilberte's eyes, Robert before their marriage was already crowned with the double halo conferred on him on the one hand by his life with Rachel, perpetually advertised by Mme de Marsantes's lamentations, and on the other hand by the prestige which the Guermantes family had always had in her father's eyes and which she had inherited from him, Mme de Forcheville for her part would have preferred a more brilliant, perhaps a princely marriage (there were impoverished royal families who would not have refused the money—which incidentally proved to be considerably less than the promised eighty million—disinfected as it was by the name Forcheville) and a son-in-law less depreciated in social value by a life spent in comparative seclusion. She had been unable to overcome Gilberte's determination, and had complained bitterly to all and sundry, denouncing her son-in-law. One fine day her attitude changed completely; her son-in-law had become an angel, and she no longer said anything against him except surreptitiously. The fact was that age had left Mme Swann (now Mme de Forcheville) with the taste she had always had for being kept, but, by the desertion of her admirers, had deprived her of the means. She longed every day for another

necklace, a new dress studded with brilliants, a more sumptuous motor-car, but she had only a small income, Forcheville
having squandered most of it, and—what Jewish strain influenced Gilberte in this?—she had an adorable but fearfully
avaricious daughter, who counted every sou that she gave her
husband, and naturally even more so her mother. Then suddenly she had sniffed out and found her natural protector in
Robert. That she was no longer in her first youth mattered
little to a son-in-law who was not a lover of women. All that
he asked of his mother-in-law was to smooth down any little
difficulty that might arise between Gilberte and himself, to
obtain his wife's consent to his going on a trip with Morel.
Odette, having applied herself thereto, was at once rewarded
with a magnificent ruby. To pay for this, it was necessary for
Gilberte to be more generous to her husband. Odette urged
her in this direction with all the more fervour in that it was she
herself who would benefit by her daughter's generosity. Thus,
thanks to Robert, she was enabled, on the threshold of her
fifties (some said her sixties), to dazzle every table at which she
dined, every party at which she appeared, with an unparalleled
splendour without needing to have, as in the past, a "friend"
who now would no longer have coughed up, or even fallen for
her. And so she had entered, permanently it seemed, into the
period of final chastity, and yet she had never been so elegant.

It was not merely the malice, the rancour of the once poor
boy against the master who has enriched him and has moreover
(this was in keeping with the character and still more with the
vocabulary of M. de Charlus) made him feel the difference of
their positions, that had made Charlie turn to Saint-Loup in
order to aggravate the Baron's sufferings. He may also have
had an eye to his own profit. I had the impression that Robert
must be giving him a great deal of money. After an evening
party at which I had met Robert before I went down to Combray—and where the manner in which he flaunted himself by
the side of a lady of fashion who was reputed to be his mistress,
glued to her, never leaving her for a moment, enveloped
publicly in the folds of her skirt, reminded me, but with something more hectic and jumpy about it, of a sort of involuntary
repetition of an ancestral gesture which I had had an oppor-

tunity of observing in M. de Charlus, when he appeared to be wrapped in the finery of Mme Molé, the banner of a gynophil cause which was not his own but which, without having any right to do so, he loved to flaunt thus, whether because he found it useful as a protection or aesthetically charming—I had been struck, as we came away, by the discovery that this young man, so generous when he was far less rich, had become so stingy. That a man clings only to what he possesses, and that he who used to scatter money when he so rarely had any now hoards that with which he is amply supplied, is no doubt a common enough phenomenon, and yet in this instance it seemed to me to have assumed a more particular form. Saint-Loup refused to take a cab, and I saw that he had kept a tramway transfer-ticket. No doubt in so doing Saint-Loup was exercising, for different ends, talents which he had acquired in the course of his liaison with Rachel. A young man who has lived for years with a woman is not as inexperienced as the novice for whom the woman he marries is the first. One had only to see, on the rare occasions when Robert took his wife out to a restaurant, the adroit and considerate way he looked after her, his skill and poise in ordering dinner and giving instructions to waiters, the care with which he smoothed Gilberte's sleeves before she put on her jacket, to realise that he had been a woman's lover for a long time before being this one's husband. Similarly, having had to enter into the minutest details of Rachel's domestic economy, partly because she herself was useless as a housekeeper, and later because his jealousy made him determined to keep a firm control over her domestic staff, he was able, in the administration of his wife's property and the management of their household, to go on playing this skilful and competent role which Gilberte, perhaps, might have been unable to fulfil and which she gladly relinquished to him. But no doubt he did so principally in order to be able to give Charlie the benefit of his candle-end economies, maintaining him in affluence without Gilberte's either noticing it or suffering from it—and perhaps even assuming the violinist to be a spendthrift "like all artists" (Charlie styled himself thus without conviction and without conceit, in order to excuse himself for not answering letters and for a mass of other defects which he

believed to form part of the undisputed psychology of the
artist). Personally, I found it absolutely immaterial from a moral
point of view whether one took one's pleasure with a man or
with a woman, and only too natural and human that one
should take it where one could find it. If, therefore, Robert had
not been married, his liaison with Charlie ought not to have
caused me pain. And yet I realised that the pain I felt would
have been as acute if Robert had been a bachelor. In anyone
else, his conduct would have left me indifferent. But I wept
when I reflected that I had once had so great an affection for a
different Saint-Loup, an affection which, I sensed all too clearly
from the cold and evasive manner which he now adopted, he
no longer felt for me, since men, now that they were capable of
arousing his desires, could no longer inspire his friendship.
How could these tastes have come to birth in a young man who
had loved women so passionately that I had seen him brought
to a state of almost suicidal despair because "Rachel when from
the Lord" had threatened to leave him? Had the resemblance
between Charlie and Rachel—invisible to me—been the plank
which had enabled Robert to pass from his father's tastes to
those of his uncle, in order to complete the physiological
evolution which even in the latter had occurred fairly late? At
times, however, Aimé's words came back to my mind to make
me uneasy; I remembered Robert that year at Balbec; he had
had a trick, when he spoke to the lift-boy, of not paying any
attention to him which strongly resembled M. de Charlus's
manner when he addressed certain men. But Robert might
easily have derived this from M. de Charlus, from a certain
hauteur and a certain physical posture peculiar to the Guermantes family, without for a moment sharing the Baron's
heterodox tastes. For instance, the Duc de Guermantes, who
was wholly innocent of such tastes, had the same nervous trick
as M. de Charlus of turning his wrist, as though he were
straightening a lace cuff round it, and also in his voice certain
shrill and affected intonations, mannerisms to all of which, in
the case of M. de Charlus, one might have been tempted to
ascribe another meaning, to which he had given another
meaning himself, the individual expressing his distinctive
characteristics by means of impersonal and atavistic traits

which are perhaps simply age-old characteristics ingrained in his gestures and voice. On this latter assumption, which borders upon natural history, it would not be M. de Charlus whom one described as a Guermantes affected with a blemish and expressing it to a certain extent by means of traits peculiar to the Guermantes stock, but the Duc de Guermantes who, in a perverted family, would be the exception whom the hereditary disease has so effectively spared that the external stigmata it has left upon him have lost all meaning. I remembered that on the day when I had seen Saint-Loup for the first time at Balbec, so fair-complexioned, fashioned of so rare and precious a substance, his monocle fluttering in front of him, I had found in him an effeminate air which was certainly not the effect of what I had now learned about him, but sprang rather from the grace peculiar to the Guermantes, from the fineness of that Dresden china in which the Duchess too was moulded. I recalled his affection for myself, his tender, sentimental way of expressing it, and told myself that this too, which might have deceived anyone else, meant at the time something quite different, indeed the direct opposite of what I had just learned about him. But when did the change date from? If from the year of my return to Balbec, how was it that he had never once come to see the lift-boy, had never once mentioned him to me? And as for the first year, how could he have paid any attention to the boy, passionately enamoured as he then was of Rachel? That first year, I had found Saint-Loup unusual, as was every true Guermantes. Now he was even odder than I had supposed. But things of which we have not had a direct intuition, which we have learned only through other people, are such that we no longer have the means, we have missed the chance, of conveying them to our inmost soul; its communications with the real are blocked and so we cannot profit by the discovery, it is too late. Besides, upon any consideration, this discovery distressed me too deeply for me to be able to appreciate it intellectually. Of course, after what M. de Charlus had told me in Mme Verdurin's house in Paris, I no longer doubted that Robert's case was that of any number of respectable people, to be found even among the best and most intelligent of men. To learn this of anyone else would not have affected me, of anyone in the world save Robert. The doubt that Aimé's words had left in my mind tarnished all our friendship at Balbec and Doncières, and although I did not believe in friendship, or that I had ever felt any real friendship for Robert, when I thought about those stories of the lift-boy and of the restaurant in which I had had lunch with Saint-Loup and Rachel, I was obliged to make an effort to restrain my tears.

TIME REGAINED

TIME REGAINED

I SHOULD have no occasion to dwell upon this visit which I paid to the neighbourhood of Combray at perhaps the moment in my life when I thought least about Combray, had it not, precisely for that reason, brought me what was at least a provisional confirmation of certain ideas which I had first conceived along the Guermantes way, and also of certain other ideas which I had conceived on the Méséglise way. I repeated every evening, in the opposite direction, the walks which we used to take at Combray, in the afternoon, when we went the Méséglise way. One dined now at Tansonville at an hour at which in the past one had long been asleep at Combray. And because of the seasonal heat, and also because Gilberte spent the afternoon painting in the chapel attached to the house, one did not go out for one's walk until about two hours before dinner. The pleasure of those earlier walks, which was that of seeing, on the way home, the crimson sky framing the Calvary or mirroring itself in the Vivonne, was now replaced by the pleasure of setting forth at nightfall, when one encountered nothing in the village save the blue-grey, irregular and shifting triangle of a flock of sheep being driven home. Over one half of the fields the sun had already set; above the other half the moon was already alight and would soon bathe them in their entirety. It sometimes happened that Gilberte let me go without her, and I set off, trailing my shadow behind me, like a boat gliding across enchanted waters. But as a rule Gilberte came with me. The walks that we took thus together were very often those that I used to take as a child: how then could I help but feel much more acutely even than in the past on the Guermantes way the conviction that I would never be able to write, reinforced by the conviction that my imagination and my sensibility had weakened, when I found how incurious I was about Combray? I was distressed to see how little I relived my early years. I found the Vivonne narrow and ugly alongside

the towpath. Not that I noticed any great physical discrepancies
from what I remembered. But, separated as I was by a whole
lifetime from places I now happened to be passing through
again, there was lacking between them and me that contiguity
from which is born, even before we have perceived it, the
immediate, delicious and total deflagration of memory. Having
doubtless no very clear conception of its nature, I was saddened by the thought that my faculty of feeling and imagining
things must have diminished since I no longer took any pleasure in these walks. Gilberte herself, who understood me even
less than I understood myself, increased my melancholy by
sharing my astonishment. "What," she would say, "you feel no
excitement when you turn into this little footpath which you
used to climb?" And she herself had changed so much that I no
longer thought her beautiful, that she was no longer beautiful
at all. As we walked, I saw the landscape change; we had to
climb hills, followed by downward slopes. We chatted—very
agreeably for me. Not without difficulty, however. In so many
people there are different strata which are not alike: the character of the father, then of the mother; one traverses first one,
then the other. But, next day, the order of their superimposition
is reversed. And finally one does not know who will decide
between the contestants, to whom one is to appeal for the
verdict. Gilberte was like one of those countries with which
one dare not form an alliance because of their too frequent
changes of government. But in reality this is a mistake. The
memory of the most multiple person establishes a sort of
identity in him and makes him reluctant to go back on promises which he remembers, even if he has not countersigned
them. As for intelligence, Gilberte's, in spite of certain absurdities inherited from her mother, was very acute. But, quite
unrelated to this, I remember that, in the course of our conversations during these walks, on several occasions she surprised me a great deal. The first time was when she said to me:
"If you were not too hungry and if it was not so late, by taking
that road to the left and then turning to the right, in less than
a quarter of an hour we should be at Guermantes." It was as
though she had said to me: "Turn to the left, then bear right,
and you will touch the intangible, you will reach the in-

accessibly remote tracts of which one never knows anything on this earth save the direction, save" (what I thought long ago to be all that I could ever know of Guermantes, and perhaps in a sense I had not been mistaken) "the 'way.'" One of my other surprises was that of seeing the "source of the Vivonne," which I imagined as something as extra-terrestrial as the Gates of Hell, and which was merely a sort of rectangular basin in which bubbles rose to the surface. And the third occasion was when Gilberte said to me: "If you like, we might after all go out one afternoon and then we can go to Guermantes, taking the road by Méséglise, which is the nicest way," a sentence which upset all the ideas of my childhood by informing me that the two "ways" were not as irreconcilable as I had supposed. But what struck me most forcibly was how little, during this stay, I re-lived my childhood years, how little I desired to see Combray, how narrow and ugly I thought the Vivonne. But where Gil-berte corroborated some of my childhood imaginings along the Méséglise way was during one of those walks which were more or less nocturnal even though they occurred before dinner—for she dined so late. Before descending into the mystery of a deep and flawless valley carpeted with moonlight, we stopped for a moment like two insects about to plunge into the blue calyx of a flower. Gilberte then uttered, perhaps simply out of the politeness of a hostess who is sorry you are going away so soon and would have liked to show you more of a countryside which you seem to appreciate, an avowal of the sort in which her practice as a woman of the world skilled in putting to the best advantage silence, simplicity, sobriety in the expression of her feelings, makes you believe that you occupy a place in her life which no one else could fill. Opening my heart to her suddenly with a tenderness born of the exquisite air, the fragrant evening breeze, I said to her: "You were speaking the other day of the little footpath. How I loved you then!" She replied: "Why didn't you tell me? I had no idea. I loved you too. In fact I flung myself twice at your head." "When?" "The first time at Tansonville. You were going for a walk with your family, and I was on my way home. I'd never seen such a pretty little boy. I was in the habit," she went on with a vaguely bashful air, "of going to play with little boys I knew in the ruins of the keep of Roussainville. And you will tell me that I was a very naughty girl, for there were girls and boys there of all sorts who took advantage of the darkness. The altar-boy from Combray church, Théodore, who, I must admit, was very nice indeed (goodness, how handsome he was!) and who has become quite ugly (he's the chemist now at Méséglise), used to amuse himself with all the peasant girls of the district. As I was allowed to go out by myself, whenever I was able to get away, I used to rush over there. I can't tell you how I longed for you to come there too; I remember quite well that, as I had only a moment in which to make you understand what I wanted, at the risk of being seen by your people and mine, I signalled to you so vulgarly that I'm ashamed of it to this day. But you stared at me so crossly that I saw that you didn't want to."

And suddenly I thought to myself that the true Gilberte, the true Albertine, were perhaps those who had at the first moment yielded themselves with their eyes, one through the hedge of pink hawthorn, the other on the beach. And it was I who, having been incapable of understanding this, having failed to recapture the impression until much later in my memory after an interval in which, as a result of my conversation, a dividing hedge of sentiment had made them afraid to be as frank as in the first moments, had ruined everything by my clumsiness. I had "botched it" more completely—although in fact the comparative failure with them was less absurd—and for the same reasons as Saint-Loup with Rachel.

"And the second time," Gilberte went on, "was years later when I passed you in the doorway of your house, the day before I met you again at my aunt Oriane's. I didn't recognise you at first, or rather I did unconsciously recognise you because I felt the same attraction as I had felt at Tansonville."

"But in the meantime there'd been, after all, the Champs-Elysées."

"Yes, but there you were too fond of me. I felt you were prying into everything I did."

I did not think to ask her who the young man was with whom she had been walking along the Avenue des Champs-Elysées on the day when I had set out to call on her again, when I might have been reconciled with her while there was still time, that day which would perhaps have changed the whole course of my life, if I had not caught sight of those two shadowy figures strolling side by side in the dusk. If I had asked her, she would perhaps have confessed the truth, as would Albertine had she been restored to life. And indeed when we meet again after many years women whom we no longer love, is there not the abyss of death between them and us, quite as much as if they were no longer of this world, since the fact that our love exists no longer makes the people that they were or the person that we were then as good as dead? Perhaps, too, she might not have remembered, or she might have lied. In any case I was no longer interested to know, since my heart had changed even more than Gilberte's face. This face gave me little pleasure, but above all I was no longer unhappy, and I should have been incapable of conceiving, had I thought about it again, that I could have been so unhappy at the sight of Gilberte tripping along by the side of a young man that I had said to myself: "It's all over, I shall never attempt to see her again." Of the state of mind which, in that far-off year, had been tantamount to a long-drawn-out torture for me, nothing survived. For in this world of ours where everything withers, everything perishes, there is a thing that decays, that crumbles into dust even more completely, leaving behind still fewer traces of itself, than Beauty: namely Grief.

And so I am not surprised that I did not ask her then with whom she had been walking in the Champs-Elysées, for I had already seen too many examples of the incuriosity that is brought about by Time, but I am a little surprised that I did not tell her that before I saw her that evening I had sold a Chinese porcelain bowl in order to buy her flowers. It had indeed, during the gloomy period that followed, been my sole consolation to think that one day I should be able with impunity to tell her of so tender an intention. More than a year later, if I saw another carriage about to crash into mine, my sole reason for wishing not to die was that I might be able to tell this to Gilberte. I consoled myself with the thought: "There's no hurry, I have a whole lifetime in which to tell her." And for this reason I was anxious not to lose my life. Now it would have seemed to me an unseemly, almost ridiculous thing to say, and a thing that would "involve consequences."

I did not ask then with whom she had been walking that evening. (I asked her later. It was Léa dressed as a man. Gilberte was aware that she knew Albertine, but could tell me nothing more. Thus it is that certain persons always reappear in one's life to herald one's pleasures or one's griefs.) What reality there had been beneath the appearance on that occasion had become quite immaterial to me. And yet for how many days and nights had I not tormented myself with wondering who it had been, had I not been obliged, even more perhaps than in the effort not to go downstairs to say good-night to Mamma in this very Combray, to control the beating of my heart! It is said, and this is what accounts for the gradual disappearance of certain nervous affections, that our nervous system grows old. This is true not merely of our permanent self, which continues throughout the whole duration of our life, but of all our successive selves which, after all, to a certain extent compose it.

"Moreover," Gilberte went on, "even on the day when I passed you in the doorway, you were still just the same as at Combray; if you only knew how little you'd changed!"

I pictured Gilberte again in my memory. I could have drawn the rectangle of light which the sun cast through the hawthorns, the spade which the little girl was holding in her hand, the slow gaze that she fastened on me. Only I had supposed, because of the coarse gesture that accompanied it, that it was a contemptuous gaze because what I longed for it to mean seemed to me to be a thing that little girls did not know about and did only in my imagination, during my hours of solitary desire. Still less could I have supposed that so casually, so rapidly, almost under the eyes of my grandfather, one of them would have had the audacity to suggest it.

And so I was obliged, after an interval of so many years, to touch up a picture which I recalled so well—an operation which made me quite happy by showing me that the impassable gulf which I had then supposed to exist between myself and a certain type of little girl with golden hair was as imaginary as Pascal's gulf, and which I thought poetic because of the long sequence of years at the end of which I was called upon to perform it. I felt a stab of desire and regret when I thought of the dungeons of Roussainville. And yet I was glad to be able to tell myself that the pleasure towards which I used to strain every nerve in those days, and which nothing could restore to me now, had indeed existed elsewhere than in my mind, in fact so close at hand, in that Roussainville of which I used to speak so often, and which I could see from the window of the orris-scented closet. And I had known nothing! In short, the image of Gilberte summed up everything that I had desired during my walks to the point of being unable to make up my mind to return home, seeming to see the tree-trunks part asunder and take human form. What I had so feverishly longed for then she had been ready, if only I had been able to understand and to meet her again, to let me taste in my boyhood. More completely even than I had supposed, Gilberte had been in those days truly part of the Méséglise way.

And even on the day when I had passed her in a doorway, although she was not Mlle de l'Orgeville, the girl whom Robert had met in houses of assignation (and what an absurd coincidence that it should have been to her future husband that I had applied for information about her), I had not been altogether mistaken as to the meaning of her glance, nor as to the sort of woman that she was and confessed to me now that she had been. "All that is a long time ago," she said to me, "I've never given a thought to anyone but Robert since the day of our engagement. And, let me tell you, it isn't those childish whims that I feel most guilty about . . ."[39]

All day long, in that slightly too countrified house which seemed no more than a place for a rest between walks or during a sudden downpour, one of those houses in which all the sitting-rooms look like arbours and, on the wall-paper in the bedrooms, here the roses from the garden, there the birds from the trees outside join you and keep you company, isolated from the world—for it was old wall-paper on which every rose was so distinct that, had it been alive, you could have picked it, every bird you could have put in a cage and tamed, quite different from those grandiose bedroom decorations of to-day where, on a silver background, all the apple trees of Normandy display their outlines in the Japanese style to hallucinate the hours you spend in bed—all day long I remained in my room which looked over the fine greenery of the park and the lilacs at the entrance, over the green leaves of the tall trees by the edge of the lake, sparkling in the sun, and the forest of Méséglise. Yet I looked at all this with pleasure only because I said to myself: "How nice to be able to see so much greenery from my bedroom window," until the moment when, in the vast verdant picture, I recognised, painted in a contrasting dark blue simply because it was further away, the steeple of Combray church. Not a representation of the steeple, but the steeple itself, which, putting in visible form a distance of miles and of years, had come, intruding its discordant tone into the midst of the luminous verdure—a tone so colourless that it seemed little more than a preliminary sketch—and engraved itself upon my window-pane. And if I left my room for a moment, I saw at the end of the corridor, in a little sitting-room which faced in another direction, what seemed to be a band of scarlet—for this room was hung with a plain silk, but a red one, ready to burst into flames if a ray of sun fell upon it.

The love of Albertine had disappeared from my memory. But it seems that there exists too an involuntary memory of the limbs, a pale and sterile imitation of the other but longer-lived, just as there are animals or vegetables without intelligence which are longer-lived than man. Our legs and our arms are full of torpid memories. And once, when I had said good-night to Gilberte rather early, I woke up in the middle of the night in my room at Tansonville and, still half-asleep, called out: "Albertine!" It was not that I had thought of her or dreamt of her, nor that I was confusing her with Gilberte, but a memory in my arm, opening like a flower, had made me fumble behind my back for the bell, as though I had been in my bedroom in Paris. And not finding it, I had called out: "Albertine!", thinking that my dead mistress was lying by my side, as she had often done in the evening, and that we were both dropping off to sleep, and reckoning, as I woke up, that, because of the time it would take Françoise to reach my room, Albertine might without imprudence pull the bell which I could not find.

During our walks Gilberte intimated to me that Robert was turning away from her, but only in order to run after other women. And it is true that many women encumbered his life, yet always these associations, like certain masculine friendships in the lives of men who love women, had that quality of ineffectual resistance, of purposelessly filling an empty space that often in a house may be seen in objects which are not there to be used.

He came several times to Tansonville while I was there and I found him very different from the man I had known. His life had not coarsened him or slowed him down, as had happened with M. de Charlus; on the contrary, working in him an inverse change, it had given him, in a degree in which he had never had it before—and this although he had resigned his commission on his marriage—the grace and ease of a cavalry officer. Gradually, just as M. de Charlus had grown heavier, Robert (it is true that he was very much younger, but one felt that with age he would only get nearer and nearer to this ideal), had, like those women who resolutely sacrifice their faces to their figures and after a certain moment never stir from Marienbad (they realise that they cannot preserve more than one kind of youth and think that a youthful figure will serve best to represent youth in general), become slimmer and taken to moving more rapidly, a contrary effect of an identical vice. This swiftness of movement had, moreover, various psychological causes, the fear of being seen, the wish to conceal that fear, the feverishness which is generated by self-dissatisfaction and boredom. He was in the habit of visiting certain low haunts into which, as he did not wish to be seen going in or coming out, he would hurl himself in such a way as to present the smallest possible target to the unfriendly glances of possible passers-by, like a soldier going into an attack.[40] And this manner of moving like a gust of wind had become a habit. Perhaps also it symbolised the superficial intrepidity of a man who wants to show that he is not afraid and does not want to give himself time to think. We must mention too, if our account is to be complete, a desire, the older he grew, to appear young, and also the impatience characteristic of those perpetually bored and perpetually cynical men that people inevitably turn into when they are too intelligent for the relatively idle lives they lead, in which their faculties do not have full play. No doubt idleness, in these men as in others, may express itself in inertia. But in these days especially, when physical exercise is so much in favour, there exists also, even outside the actual hours of sport, an athletic form of idleness which finds expression not in inertia but in a feverish vivacity that hopes to leave boredom neither time nor space to develop in.

Becoming—at any rate during this tiresome phase—much harder in his manner, towards his friends, towards for example myself, he now exhibited scarcely any trace of sensibility. Towards Gilberte on the other hand he behaved with an affectation of sentiment carried to the point of theatricality, which was most disagreeable. Not that he was in fact indifferent to her. No, he loved her. But he lied to her all the time and his untruthfulness, if not the actual purpose of his lies, was invariably detected; and then he thought that the only way to extricate himself was to exaggerate to a ridiculous degree the genuine distress which he felt at having hurt her. He would arrive at Tansonville, obliged, he said, to leave again the next morning because of some business with a certain neighbouring landowner who was supposed to be waiting for him in Paris; but the neighbour, when they happened to meet him near Combray the same evening, would unintentionally expose the lie, of which Robert had neglected to inform him, by saying that he had come to the country for a month's rest and would not be going back to Paris during his stay. Robert would blush, would observe Gilberte's melancholy and knowing smile, get rid of the blundering friend with a few sharp words, go home before his wife, send her a desperate note saying that he had told this lie in order not to hurt her, so that she should not think, when she saw him go off for a reason which he could not avow to her, that he did not love her (and all this, though Robert thought that he was lying when he wrote it, was in substance true), and then would ask permission to come to her room and there—part genuine distress, part the nervous strain of the life he led, part a pretence which became every day more

brazen—would sob, plunge his head into cold water, talk about
his imminent death, sometimes throw himself on the floor as
though he had been taken ill. Gilberte did not know how far
she should believe him, supposed that in each particular case
he was lying but that in a general way he loved her, and was
worried by this presentiment of an imminent death, thinking
that he perhaps had some illness she did not know of, so that
for that reason she did not dare to thwart him or ask him to
give up his travels. All this, however, did not help me to
understand why Robert insisted on Morel's being accepted as
the son of the house—as much a part of it as Bergotte[41]—
wherever he and his wife were, in Paris or at Tansonville.

Françoise, who had seen all that M. de Charlus had done for
Jupien and saw now all that Robert de Saint-Loup was doing
for Morel, did not conclude that this was a characteristic which
reappeared from generation to generation in the Guermantes
family. She, who was so moral and so full of prejudices, had
come rather to believe—as Legrandin too was so kind to
Théodore—that this was a custom rendered respectable by its
universality. She would say of a young man, whether it were
Morel or Théodore: "He has found a gentleman who takes an
interest in him and has done a great deal to help him." And as
in such cases it is the protectors who love and suffer and forgive, Françoise, faced with a choice between the "gentlemen"
and the youths whom they seduced, did not hesitate to award
her sympathy to the seducers, to decide that it was they who
"really had hearts." She blamed Théodore for all the tricks he
played on Legrandin—and yet it seemed scarcely possible that
she could have any doubt about the nature of their relations,
for she would add: "Then the boy realised that it was his turn
to make a move and said: 'Take me with you, I will love you,
I will do my best to please you,' and upon my word the gentleman has such a heart that I'm sure Théodore is sure to do well
with him. Perhaps much better than he deserves, for he's a
proper madcap, but the gentleman is so good that I've often
said to Jeannette (Théodore's fiancée): 'My girl, if ever you're
in trouble, go to the gentleman. He'd give you his bed rather
than let you sleep on the floor. He's been too fond of that lad
(Théodore) to turn him out. You can be sure he'll never desert

him.'" Out of politeness I inquired what was the surname of
Théodore, who was now living somewhere in the south of
France, and she told me that it was Sanilon. "Then that's who
it was," I exclaimed, "who wrote to me about my article in
Le Figaro."

In the same way Françoise had a higher esteem for Saint-
Loup than for Morel and gave it as her opinion that, in spite
of all the tricks the lad (Morel) had played, the Marquis would
always come to his rescue if he were in trouble, for he was a
man with a real heart—or if he didn't, it would only be because
he himself had suffered some great disaster.

Saint-Loup insisted that I should stay on at Tansonville and
once, although he never now visibly sought to give me pleasure, let slip the remark that my coming had been so great a
joy to his wife that it had caused her, as she had told him, a
transport of happiness which lasted a whole evening, an
evening when she had been feeling so miserable that my unexpected arrival had miraculously saved her from despair,
"Perhaps from something worse," he added. He asked me to
try to persuade her that he loved her and told me that, though
he loved another woman, he loved her less than his wife and
would soon break with her. "And yet," he continued, with
such self-satisfaction and such an evident need to confide that
there were moments when I thought the name of Charlie
would, for all Robert's efforts, "come up" like a number in a
lottery, "I had something to be proud of. This woman who
has given me so many proofs of her affection and whom I am
about to sacrifice to Gilberte, had never looked at a man before,
she even thought herself incapable of falling in love. I am the
first man in her life. I knew that she had refused offers right
and left, so that when I received the marvellous letter in which
she told me that there would be no happiness for her except
with me, I just could not get over it. Obviously, there would
be something here for me to lose my head about, were it not
that the thought of seeing poor Gilberte in tears is intolerable
to me. Don't you see something of Rachel in her?" he went on.
And indeed I had been struck by a vague resemblance which
one could, if one tried, now find between them. Perhaps it was
due to a real similarity of certain features (owing possibly to

the Jewish origin of both, though of this there was little evidence in Gilberte) which had caused Robert, when his family had insisted that he should marry, to feel himself more attracted to Gilberte than to any other girl who was equally rich. But it was due also to the fact that Gilberte, having come across some hidden photographs of Rachel, whose name even had been unknown to her, tried to please Robert by imitating certain habits dear to the actress, such as always wearing a red ribbon in her hair and a black velvet ribbon on her arm, and by dyeing her hair in order to look dark. Then, feeling that her unhappiness was spoiling her looks, she tried to do something about it. Sometimes she went a great deal too far. One day, when Robert was coming to Tansonville for a single night, I was astounded to see her take her place at table looking so strangely different, not merely from what she had been in the past, but from her present self of every day, that I sat dumbfounded as if I had before my eyes an actress, a sort of Empress Theodora. I felt that in spite of myself I was staring at her, so curious was I to know what it was that was changed. My curiosity was soon satisfied when she blew her nose—in spite of all the precautions with which she did this. For from the many colours which were left on her handkerchief, turning it into a sumptuous palette, I saw that she was heavily made up. This it was that gave her that blood-red mouth which she tried hard to control into laughter in the belief that it was becoming to her, while the thought that the time of her husband's train was approaching and still she did not know whether he would really come or whether he would send one of those telegrams of which M. de Guermantes had wittily fixed the formula: "Cannot come, lie follows," turned her cheeks pale beneath the violet sweat of her grease-paint and drew dark rings round her eyes.

"Ah! don't you see?" he would say to me—in an artificially affectionate manner which contrasted painfully with his spontaneous affection of the old days, with the voice of an alcoholic and an actor's intonations—"Gilberte happy, there is nothing I would not give to see that. She has done so much for me. You can't possibly know." And the most disagreeable part of all this was once again his vanity, for he was flattered at being loved by Gilberte and, without daring to say that it was

Charlie whom he loved, gave, nevertheless, of the love which
the violinist was supposed to feel for him, details which he, the
Saint-Loup from whom Charlie every day demanded more and
more money, knew to be wildly exaggerated if not invented
from start to finish. And so, entrusting Gilberte to my care, he
would go off to Paris again. In Paris (to anticipate a little, for I
am still at Tansonville) I once had an opportunity of observing
him at a party and from a distance and on this occasion, though
the way in which he spoke was still alive and charming and
enabled me to rediscover the past, I was struck by the great
changes taking place in him. More and more he resembled his
mother: the haughtily elegant manner which he had inherited
from her and which she, by means of the most elaborate training, had perfected in him was now freezing into exaggeration;
the penetrating glance proper to him as a Guermantes gave
him the air of inspecting every place in which he happened to
be, but of doing this in an almost unconscious fashion, as
though from habit, in obedience to a sort of animal characteristic. Even when he was at rest the colouring which he
possessed in a greater degree than any other Guermantes—that
air of being merely the solidified sunniness of a golden day—
gave him as it seemed a plumage so strange, made of him a
species so rare and so precious, that one would have liked to
acquire him for an ornithological collection; but when, in
addition, this ray of light metamorphosed into a bird started
into movement, into action, when for instance I saw Robert de
Saint-Loup enter this evening party at which I was present, the
way in which he tossed back his head, so silkily and proudly
crested with the golden tuft of his slightly moulting hair, and
moved his neck from side to side, was so much more supple, so
much more aloof and yet more delicate than anything to be
expected of a human being that, fired by the sight with curiosity
and wonder, half social and half zoological, one asked oneself
whether one was really in the Faubourg Saint-Germain and not
rather in the Zoological Gardens, whether one was watching
the passage of a great nobleman through a drawing-room or a
bird pacing its cage. And if one was prepared to exercise a little
imagination, the twittering lent itself just as well to this second
interpretation as the plumage. For he was beginning to use

phrases which he thought redolent of the age of Louis XIV, and though in this he was simply imitating the manners of the Guermantes, in him some indefinable nuance was turning them into the manners of M. de Charlus. "I must leave you for a moment," he said to me for instance, at this party, at which Mme de Marsantes was standing a little way away from us. "I have to present my humble respects to my mother."

To return to this "love," of which he could not stop talking to me, it was not only love for Charlie, although this was the only love that counted for him. Whatever be the nature of a man's loves, one always makes mistakes as to the number of people with whom he has affairs, partly from wrongly interpreting friendships as love affairs, an error which exaggerates the total, but also through believing that one proved love affair excludes another, which is an error of a contrary kind. Two people may say: "X's mistress, yes, I know her," they may pronounce two different names and neither of them may be mistaken. A woman whom we love seldom satisfies all our needs and we deceive her with a woman whom we do not love. As to the species of loves that Saint-Loup had inherited from M. de Charlus, a husband who is that way inclined usually makes his wife happy. This is a general rule to which the Guermantes contrived to be an exception, because those of them who had this taste wanted it to be believed that on the contrary they were fond of women. So they made themselves conspicuous with one woman or another and drove their own wives to despair. The Courvoisiers were more sensible. The young Vicomte de Courvoisier thought he was the only man alive, perhaps the only man since the beginning of the world, to be tempted by someone of his own sex. Supposing this inclination to come to him from the devil, he struggled against it, married an extremely pretty wife and had children by her. Then one of his cousins taught him that the tendency is fairly wide-spread and was even so kind as to take him to places where he could indulge it. M. de Courvoisier became fonder than ever of his wife and redoubled his philoprogenitive zeal, and he and she were quoted as the happiest couple in Paris. That could not possibly be said of the Saint-Loups, because Robert, instead of being content with inversion, made his wife ill with jealousy by keeping mistresses without pleasure to himself.

It is possible that Morel, being excessively dark, was necessary to Saint-Loup in the way that shadow is necessary to the sunbeam. Can one not imagine some golden-haired aristocrat sprung from an ancient family such as his, intelligent and endowed with every kind of prestige, concealing within him, unbeknown to all his friends, a secret taste for negroes?

Robert never allowed the conversation to touch upon his own species of loves. If I said a word about it, "Oh! I don't know," he would reply, with a detachment so profound that it caused him to drop his monocle, "I am utterly ignorant about those things. If you want information about them, my dear boy, I advise you to go elsewhere. I am a soldier, that's all I can say for myself. The things you speak of leave me cold. What I *am* interested in, passionately, is the course of the Balkan war. That sort of thing interested you too once, the 'etymology' of battles. I told you in those days that we should see again, even in greatly changed circumstances, battles conforming to certain types, for example the great exercise in lateral envelopment, the battle of Ulm. Well! However special these Balkan wars may be, Lüleburgaz is Ulm all over again: lateral envelopment. These are the subjects you can talk to me about. As for the sort of thing you allude to, it means about as much to me as Sanskrit."

While Robert thus expressed his disdain for the subject, Gilberte on the contrary, after he had left, was very willing to raise it in the conversations which I had with her. Not with reference to her husband certainly, for she knew, or pretended to know, nothing. But she liked to discuss it at length in so far as other men were concerned, whether because she saw in this a sort of indirect excuse for Robert or because he, divided like his uncle between an austere silence with regard to the subject and a need to let himself go and talk slander, had opened her eyes in many directions. M. de Charlus was one of those who were not spared, doubtless because Robert, without mentioning Charlie to Gilberte, could not help, when he was with her, repeating in one form or another what the violinist had told him; and the latter pursued his former benefactor with un-

relenting hate. These conversations, and Gilberte's evident
liking for them, gave me a chance to ask her whether, in a
parallel category, Albertine, whose name I had first heard from
Gilberte herself when they were attending the same classes, had
comparable tastes. Gilberte could not give me any information
on this point. And in any case it had long ceased to be of
interest to me. But I continued to make inquiries mechanically,
as an old man with a failing memory from time to time asks
for news of the son he has lost.

What is odd, though I cannot here enlarge upon the topic,
is the degree to which at the time I am writing about all the
people whom Albertine loved, all those who might have been
able to persuade her to do what they wanted, asked, entreated,
I will even say begged to be allowed to have, if not my friendship, at least some sort of acquaintance with me. No longer
should I have had to offer money to Mme Bontemps as an
inducement to send Albertine back to me. But this turn of
fortune's wheel, taking place when it was no longer of the
slightest use, merely saddened me profoundly, not because of
Albertine, whom I would have received without pleasure had
she been brought back not from Touraine but from the other
world, but because of a young woman with whom I was in
love and whom I could not contrive to meet. I told myself
that, if she died, or if I no longer loved her, all those who might
have brought us together would suddenly be at my feet.
Meanwhile, I tried in vain to work upon them, not having
been cured by experience, which ought to have taught me—if
ever it taught anybody anything—that loving is like an evil
spell in a fairy-story against which one is powerless until the
enchantment has passed.

"As a matter of fact the book I'm reading at the moment
talks about that sort of thing," Gilberte said to me. "It is an
old Balzac which I am swotting up so as to be as well-informed
as my uncles, *La Fille aux Yeux d'Or*. But it is absurd, improbable, nightmarish. For one thing, I suppose a woman
might be kept under surveillance in that way by another
woman, but surely not by a man." "You are wrong, I once
knew a woman who was loved by a man who in the end literally
imprisoned her; she was never allowed to see anybody, she

could only go out with trusted servants." "Well, you who are so kind must be horrified at the idea. By the way, we were saying, Robert and I, that you ought to get married. Your wife would improve your health and you would make her happy." "No, I have too bad a character." "How absurd!" "I mean it. Besides, I was engaged once. But I couldn't quite make up my mind to marry the girl—and anyhow she thought better of it herself, because of my undecided and cantankerous character." This was, in fact, the excessively simple light in which I regarded my adventure with Albertine, now that I saw it only from outside.

Back in my bedroom again, I thought sadly that I had not once been back to revisit Combray church, which seemed to be waiting for me amidst green foliage in a violet-tinted window. "Never mind," I said to myself, "that can wait for another year, if I don't die in the meanwhile," seeing no other possible obstacle but my own death and not envisaging that of the church which must, as I supposed, endure for centuries after my death as it had for centuries before my birth.

One day I spoke to Gilberte about Albertine, and asked her whether Albertine loved women. "Not in the least!" "But you used to say that you didn't approve of her." "I said that? No, I'm sure you're mistaken. In any case, if I said it—but you're wrong about that—what I was referring to was flirtations with young men. And anyhow, at her age, it probably didn't go very far." Did Gilberte say this in order to conceal from me that she herself—or so Albertine had told me—loved women and had made advances to Albertine? Or did she (for other people are often better informed about our life than we think) know that I had loved and been jealous of Albertine, and did she (since, though others may know more of the truth about us than we think, they may also stretch it too far and fall into the error of supposing too much, whereas we had hoped that they made the mistake of supposing nothing at all) imagine that this was still the case, was she, out of kindness, placing over my eyes that bandage with which we are always ready to blindfold the jealous? In any case, Gilberte's remarks, from the "disapproval" of the old days to the present certificate of respectability, were pursuing an opposite course to the statements of Albertine, who in the end had almost admitted some sort of relations with Gilberte. In this Albertine had astonished me, just as I had been astonished by what Andrée had told me, for with all the girls in the little band, if I had at first believed, before knowing them, in their perversity, I had come round to the view that my suspicions were false, as must often happen when one finds a virtuous girl, almost ignorant of the facts of love, in surroundings which one had wrongly supposed to be extremely depraved. Then later I had travelled the same road in the opposite direction, back to a belief in the truth of my original suspicions. But perhaps Albertine had told me this because she wanted to appear more experienced than she was and to dazzle me in Paris with the prestige of her depravity, as on the earlier occasion at Balbec with that of her virtue; or quite simply, when I had talked about women who loved women, had not wanted to appear not to know what I meant, just as, if Fourier or Tobolsk is mentioned in a conversation, one tries to look as if one understood even if one has no idea what they are. She had perhaps lived, though in proximity to Mlle Vinteuil's friend and to Andrée, yet separated from them by a watertight partition, so that they thought that she was "not one," and had perhaps only got to know about the subject later—in the spirit of a woman who marries a man of letters and tries to improve her mind—in order to please me by making herself capable of answering my questions, until the day when she realised that the questions were inspired by jealousy, when she had hastily gone into reverse. Unless it was Gilberte who was lying to me. It even occurred to me that it was because he had learnt from Gilberte, while flirting with her with an eye all the while on his real interests, that she did not altogether dislike women, that Robert had married her, hoping for pleasures which, since he now went elsewhere for them, he must have failed to obtain from her. None of these hypotheses was absurd, for with women like Odette's daughter or the girls of the little band there is such a diversity, such an accumulation of alternating if not actually simultaneous tastes, that they pass easily from an affair with a woman to a great love for a man, so that to define the real and dominating taste must always be difficult.

I did not want to borrow Gilberte's copy of *La Fille aux Yeux d'Or* as she was reading it herself. But she lent me to read in bed, on that last evening of my stay with her, a book which produced on me a strong but mixed impression, which did not, however, prove to be lasting. It was a volume of the unpublished Journal of the Goncourts. And when, before putting out my candle, I read the passage which I am about to transcribe, my lack of talent for literature, of which I had had a presentiment long ago on the Guermantes way and which had been confirmed during the stay of which this was the last evening—one of those evenings before a departure when we emerge from the torpor of habits about to be broken and attempt to judge ourselves—struck me as something less to be regretted, since literature, if I was to trust the evidence of this book, had no very profound truths to reveal: and at the same time it seemed to me sad that literature was not what I had thought it to be. At the same time, the state of ill-health which was soon to shut me up in a sanatorium seemed to me also less to be regretted, if the beautiful things of which books speak were not more beautiful than what I had seen myself. And yet, by an odd contradiction, now that they were being spoken of in this book I had a desire to see them. Here are the pages that I read before fatigue closed my eyes . . .

"The day before yesterday Verdurin drops in here to carry me off to dine with him—Verdurin, former critic of the *Revue*, author of that book on Whistler in which the workmanship, the painterly colouration of the American eccentric is interpreted sometimes with great delicacy by the lover of all the refinements, all the *prettinesses* of the painted canvas that Verdurin is. And while I am getting dressed to accompany him, he treats me to a long narrative, almost at moments a timidly stammered confession, about his renunciation of writing immediately after his marriage to Fromentin's 'Madeleine,' a renunciation brought about, he says, by his addiction to morphine and which had the result, according to Verdurin, that most of the frequenters of his wife's drawing-room did not even know that her husband had ever been a writer and spoke to him of Charles Blanc, of

Saint-Victor, of Sainte-Beuve, of Burty, as individuals to whom
they considered him, Verdurin, altogether inferior. 'Now, you
Goncourts, you know—and Gautier knew too—that my *Salons*
were on a different plane to those pitiful *Maîtres d'Autrefois*
which are deemed a masterpiece in my wife's family.' Then,
through a dusk in which, as we pass the towers of the Trocadéro, the last glimmer of a gleam of daylight makes them
positively resemble those towers of red-currant jelly that
pastry-cooks used to make, the conversation continues in the
carriage on its way to the Quai Conti, where is their mansion,
which its owner claims was once the mansion of the Venetian
Ambassadors and in which there is a room used as a smoking-
room which Verdurin tells me was transported lock, stock and
barrel, as in a tale of the *Thousand and One Nights*, from a
celebrated *palazzo* whose name I forget, a *palazzo* boasting a
well-head decorated with a Coronation of the Virgin which
Verdurin maintains is positively one of Sansovino's finest
things and which now, he says, their guests find useful as a
receptacle for cigar-ash. And upon my word, when we arrive,
in the watery shimmer of a moonlight really just like that in
which the painting of the great age enwraps Venice, against
which the silhouetted dome of the Institute makes one think of
the Salute in Guardi's pictures, I have almost the illusion of
looking out over the Grand Canal. And the illusion is preserved
by the way in which the house is built so that from the first
floor one cannot see the quay, and by the evocative remark of
its owner, who affirms that the name of the Rue du Bac—the
devil if ever I'd thought of it—comes from the ferry which once
upon a time used to take an order of nuns, the Miramiones,
across to attend services in Notre-Dame. A whole quarter
which my childhood used idly to explore when my aunt de
Courmont lived there, and which I am inspired to *re-love* by rediscovering, almost next door to the Verdurin mansion, the
sign of 'Little Dunkirk,' one of the rare shops surviving elsewhere than in the crayon and wash vignettes of Gabriel de
Saint-Aubin, to which the eighteenth-century connoisseur
would come to pass a few leisure moments in cheapening
trinkets French and foreign and 'all the newest products of the
arts,' as an invoice of this Little Dunkirk puts it, an invoice of

which we two, Verdurin and myself, are, I believe, alone in possessing copies, one of those flimsy masterpieces of engraved paper upon which the reign of Louis XV made out its accounts, with a headpiece representing a billowy sea laden with vessels, a sea of billows which might be an illustration, in the Fermiers Généraux La Fontaine, to 'The Oyster and the Litigants.' The mistress of the house, who has placed me next to her at dinner, graciously tells me before we go in that she has flowered her table with nothing but Japanese chrysanthemums—but chrysanthemums displayed in vases which are the rarest masterpieces, one in particular of bronze on which petals of red-gold copper seem to have been shed by the living flower. Cottard, the doctor, is there, his wife, the Polish sculptor Viradobetski, Swann the collector, and an aristocratic Russian lady, a princess with a name ending in -off which I fail to catch (Cottard whispers in my ear that she is the woman who is supposed to have fired point-blank at the Archduke Rudolf), according to whom in Galicia and the whole of the north of Poland my reputation stands extraordinarily high, no young girl ever giving her consent to an offer of marriage without first ascertaining whether her fiancé is an admirer of *La Faustin*. 'You cannot understand that, you western Europeans,'—this is thrown in as a sort of coda by the Princess, who, upon my word, strikes me as a person of a really superior intelligence—'that penetration by a writer of a woman's most intimate feelings.' A man with a close-shaven chin and lip and the side-whiskers of a butler, rolling out in a condescending tone the witticisms of a fifth-form schoolmaster unbending among his prize pupils on the feast of St Charlemagne—this is Brichot, of the university. I am introduced to him by Verdurin but he utters not a word of reference to our books, and I am filled with a mixture of discouragement and anger at this conspiracy organised against us by the Sorbonne, which brings even into this pleasant dwelling where I am received as an honoured guest the contradiction, the hostility, of deliberate silence. We go in to dinner, and there follows an extraordinary cavalcade of plates which are nothing less than masterpieces of the porcelainist's art, that artist whose chatter, during an exquisite meal, is heard with more pleasure than any fellow-guest's by the titillated attention of the connoisseur—Yung Cheng plates with nasturtium-coloured borders and purple-blue irises, leafless and tumid, and those supremely decorative flights of kingfishers and cranes trailing across a dawn sky, a dawn that has just the early-morning tones glimpsed daily from Boulevard Montmorency by my awakening eyes—Dresden plates daintier and of more graceful workmanship, with drowsy, bloodless roses fading into violet, with ragged-edged tulips the colour of wine-lees, with the rococo elegance of a pink or a forget-me-not—Sèvres plates meshed with the close guilloche of their white fluting, whorled in gold, or knotted with a golden ribbon that stands in gallant relief upon the creamy smoothness of the paste—finally a whole service of silver plate arabesqued with those myrtles of Luciennes that were not unknown to the Dubarry. And what is perhaps equally rare is the truly quite remarkable quality of the things served upon these plates, a meal most subtly concocted, a real spread such as Parisians, one cannot say it too emphatically, never have at their really grand dinner-parties and which reminds me of certain prize dishes of Jean d'Heurs. Even the foie gras bears no resemblance to the insipid mousse customarily served under that name; and I do not know many places in which a simple potato salad is made as it is here with potatoes firm as Japanese ivory buttons and patina'd like those little ivory spoons with which Chinese women sprinkle water over their new-caught fish. Into the Venetian glass which I have before me is poured, like a rich cascade of red jewels, an extraordinary Léoville bought at M. Montalivet's sale, and it is a delight to the imagination of the eye and also, I am not afraid to say it, of what used to be called the gullet, to see a brill placed before us which has nothing in common with those anything but fresh brills that are served at the most luxurious tables, which in the slow course of their journey from the sea have had the pattern of their bones imprinted upon their backs; a brill that is served not with the sticky paste prepared under the name of white sauce by so many chefs in great houses, but with a genuine white sauce, made with butter that costs five francs a pound; to see this brill brought in on a wonderful Ching Hon dish streaked with the purple rays of a sun setting above a sea upon which ludicrously sails a flotilla of large

lobsters, their spiky stippling rendered with such extraordinary
skill that they seem to have been moulded from living shells,
with a border too depicting a little Chinaman who plays with
rod and line a fish whose silver and azure belly makes it a marvel
of iridescent colour. When I remark to Verdurin what an
exquisite pleasure it must be for him to eat this rare and subtle
grub off a collection such as no prince to-day possesses in his
show cases: 'It is easy to see that you don't know him,' gloomily
interjects the mistress of the house. And she speaks to me of her
husband as of an original and a crank, indifferent to all these
dainties, 'a crank,' she repeats, 'yes, that is the only word for it,
a crank who would get more enjoyment from a bottle of cider
drunk in the somewhat plebeian coolness of a Normandy farm.'
And this charming woman, whose speech betrays her positive
adoration of local colouring, talks with overflowing enthusiasm of the Normandy in which they once lived, a Normandy,
so she says, like an immense English park, with the fragrance
of tall woodlands that Lawrence might have painted, with the
cryptomeria-coloured velvet of natural lawns bordered with
the porcelain of pink hydrangeas, with crumpled sulphur-roses
which, as they cascade over a cottage-door, above which the
incrustation of two entwined pear-trees has the effect of a purely
decorative sign over a shop, make one think of the free arabesque of a flowery branch of bronze in a candle-bracket by
Gouthière, a Normandy absolutely unsuspected by the Parisian
holiday-makers, protected by the iron gates of each of its little
properties, gates which the Verdurins confessed to me that they
did not scruple to open one and all. At the end of the day, in the
drowsy extinguishment of all colours, when the only light was
from an almost curdled sea, blue-white like whey ('No, not in
the least like the sea you know,' frantically protests my neighbour, when I start to tell her that Flaubert once took us, my
brother and me, to Trouville, 'not the slightest bit, you must
come with me, otherwise you will never find out'), they would
go home, through the forests—absolute forests abloom with
pink tulle—of the great rhododendrons, quite drunk with the
smell of the sardine fisheries which gave her husband terrible
attacks of asthma—'Yes,' she insists, 'I mean it, real attacks of
asthma.' Thereupon, the following summer, they returned,

lodging a whole colony of artists in an old cloister which they rented for next to nothing, and which made an admirable mediaeval abode. And upon my word, as I listen to this woman who, in passing through so many social circles of real distinction, has nevertheless preserved in her speech a little of the freshness and freedom of language of a woman of the people, a language which shows you things with the colour which your imagination sees in them, my mouth waters at the life which she avows to me they lived down there, each one working in his cell and the whole party assembling before luncheon, in a drawing-room so vast that it had two fireplaces, for really intelligent conversation interspersed with parlour games, a life which makes me think of the one we read of in that masterpiece of Diderot, the *Lettres à Mademoiselle Volland*. Then, after luncheon, they would all go out, even on the days when the weather was unsettled, in a brief burst of sunshine or the diffused radiance of a shower, a shower whose filtered light sharpened the knotted outlines of a magnificent avenue of century-old beeches which began just behind the house and brought almost up to the iron grill that vegetable embodiment of 'the beautiful' so dear to eighteenth-century taste, and of the ornamental trees which held suspended in their branches not buds about to flower but drops of rain. They would stop to listen to the delicate splish-splash of a bull-finch, enamoured of coolness, bathing itself in the tiny dainty Nymphenburg bath made for it by the corolla of a white rose. And when I mention to Mme Verdurin Elstir's delicate pastel sketches of the landscapes and the flowers of that coast: 'But it is through me that he discovered all those things,' she bursts out, with an angry toss of the head, 'all of them, yes, all, make no mistake about it, the interesting spots, every one of his subjects—I threw it in his teeth when he left us, didn't I, Auguste?—every one of the subjects he has painted. *Things* he has always known about, there one must be fair, one must admit that. But as for flowers, he had never seen any, he couldn't tell a mallow from a hollyhock. It was I who taught him—you won't believe this—to recognise jasmine.' And one must admit that it is a curious ïought that the artist who is cited by connoisseurs today as our leading flower-painter, superior even to Fantin-Latour, would perhaps never, without the help of the woman sitting beside me, have known how to paint jasmine. 'Yes, honestly, jasmine. And all the roses he has done have been painted in my house, or else it was I who took them to him. Among us he was always known simply as Monsieur Tiche; ask Cottard, ask Brichot, ask anybody here, whether we treated him as a great man. He would have laughed at the idea himself. I taught him to arrange his flowers; at first he couldn't manage it at all. He never learnt how to make a bouquet. He had no natural taste in selecting, I had to say to him: "No, don't paint that, that's no good, paint this." Ah! if he had listened to us about the arrangement of his life as he did about the arrangement of his flowers, and hadn't made that vile marriage!' And of a sudden, her eyes feverish from her absorption in thoughts of the past, plucking nervously at the silk sleeves of her bodice as she frenziedly tenses her fingers, she presents, in the distortion of her grief-stricken pose, an admirable picture which has, I think, never been painted, a picture in which one would see portrayed all the restrained revolt, all the passionate susceptibilities of a female friend outraged in the delicate feelings, the modesty of a woman. Thereupon she talks about the admirable portrait which Elstir did for her, the portrait of the Cottard family, which she gave to the Luxembourg at the time of her quarrel with the painter, confessing that it was she who gave him the idea of painting the man in dress clothes in order to get all that splendid ebullition of fine linen, and she who chose the woman's velvet gown which forms a solid mass amid all the glitter of the bright tones of the carpets, the flowers, the fruit, the little girls' muslin dresses that look like dancers' tutus. It was she too, she tells me, who gave him the idea of the woman brushing her hair, an idea for which the artist was subsequently much praised and which consisted simply in painting her not as if she were on show but surprised in the intimacy of her everyday life. ' "In a woman doing her hair," I used to say to him, "or wiping her face, or warming her feet, when she thinks she is not observed, there is a multitude of interesting movements, movements of a grace and charm that are positively Leonardesque!" ' But at a sign from Verdurin indicating that the revival of these old indignations is dangerous for the health of his wife, who is really a mass of nerves, Swann points out to me the wonderful necklace of black pearls which the mistress of the house is wearing, which she bought, as a necklace of white pearls, at the sale of a descendant of Mme de La Fayette, to whom they were given by Henrietta of England, and which became black as the result of a fire which destroyed part of a house which the Verdurins had in a street whose name I do not remember, after which fire the casket containing these pearls was found, with the pearls completely black inside it. 'And I know the portrait of these pearls, on the shoulders of Mme de La Fayette herself, yes, positively their portrait,' insists Swann, checking the exclamations of the somewhat dumbfounded guests, 'their authentic portrait, in the collection of the Duc de Guermantes.' A collection which has not its equal in the world, proclaims Swann, and which I ought to go and see, a collection inherited by the celebrated Duke, who was her favourite nephew, from his aunt Mme de Beausergent, who afterwards became Mme d'Hazfeld and was the sister of the Marquise de Villeparisis and of the Princess of Hanover, in whose house years ago my brother and I became so fond of him under the guise of the charming infant known as Basin, which is indeed the Duke's first name. Thereupon Doctor Cottard, with that keen intelligence which shows him to be a man of real distinction, harks back to the story of the pearls and informs us that catastrophes of this kind can produce changes in people's brains which are just like those that may be observed in inanimate matter, and, discoursing in a philosophical vein well beyond the powers of most doctors, quotes as an example Mme Verdurin's own valet, who from the terrible shock of this fire in which he very nearly lost his life became a changed man, with a handwriting so altered that when his master and mistress, then in Normandy, first received a letter from him with the news of the fire, they thought that someone was playing a practical joke upon them. And not only an altered handwriting, according to Cottard, who maintains that this man, hitherto always sober, became such an abominable sot that Mme Verdurin was obliged to get rid of him. And the Doctor's stimulating dissertation passes, upon a gracious sign from the mistress of the house, from the dining-room to the Venetian smoking-room, where he tells us that he has witnessed cases of what can only be called dual personality, citing as an instance one of his patients, whom he is so kind as to offer to bring to my house, whose temples he only has to touch, so he says, to awaken him to a second life, a life during which he remembers nothing of his first life and so different that, while he behaves most respectably in the first, he has more than once been arrested for thefts committed in the second, in which he is nothing more nor less than an abominable scoundrel. Whereupon Mme Verdurin acutely observes that medical science could provide the theatre with truer themes than those now in favour, themes in which the comicality of the plot would be based upon misunderstandings of a pathological kind, and this, by a natural transition, leads Mme Cottard to say that a very similar subject has been employed by a story-teller who is her children's favourite at bedtime, the Scotsman Stevenson, a name which brings from Swann the peremptory statement: 'But he is a really great writer, Stevenson, I assure you, M. de Goncourt, a very great writer, equal to the greatest.' Next, after I have admired the ceiling of the room where we are smoking, with its escutcheoned coffers from the old Barberini palace, when I intimate my regret at the progressive blackening of a certain stone basin by the ash of our 'Havanas' and Swann remarks that similar stains on books from the library of Napoleon which are now, despite his anti-Bonapartist opinions, in the possession of the Duc de Guermantes, bear witness to the fact that the Emperor chewed tobacco, Cottard, who evinces a truly penetrating curiosity in all things, declares that the stains do not come from that at all—'No, no, no, not at all,' he insists with authority—but from the habit the Emperor had of always, even on the field of battle, clutching in his hand the liquorice tablets which he took to relieve the pain in his liver. 'For he had a disease of the liver and that is what he died of,' concludes the Doctor."

There I stopped, for I was leaving the next morning; and besides it was the hour at which I was habitually summoned by that other master in whose service we spend, every day, a part of our time. The task which he assigns to us we accom-

plish with our eyes closed. Every morning he hands us back to
the master who shares us with him, knowing that, unless he
did so, we should be remiss in his own service. Curious, when
our intelligence reopens its eyes, to know what we can have
done under this master who first makes his slaves lie down and
then puts them to work at full speed, the most artful among us
try, the moment their task is finished, to take a covert glance.
But sleep is racing against them to obliterate the traces of what
they would like to see. And after all these centuries we still
know very little about the matter.

I closed the Journal of the Goncourts. Prestige of literature!
I wished I could have seen the Cottards again, asked them all
sorts of details about Elstir, gone to look at the shop called
Little Dunkirk, if it still existed, asked permission to visit the
Verdurin mansion where I had once dined. But I felt vaguely
depressed. Certainly, I had never concealed from myself that I
knew neither how to listen nor, once I was not alone, how to
look. My eyes were blind to the sort of necklace an old woman
might be wearing, and the things I might be told about her
pearls never entered my ears. All the same, I had known these
people in daily life, I had dined with them often, they were
simply the Verdurins and the Duc de Guermantes and the
Cottards, and each one of them I had found just as commonplace as my grandmother had found that Basin of whom she
had no suspicion that he was the darling nephew, the enchanting young hero, of Mme de Beausergent, each one of them had
seemed to me insipid; I could remember the vulgarities without
number of which each of them was composed. . . .

Et que tout cela fasse un astre dans la nuit![42]

But provisionally I decided to ignore the objections against
literature raised in my mind by the pages of Goncourt which
I had read on the evening before I left Tansonville. Even without taking into account the manifest naïvety of this particular
diarist, I could in any case reassure myself on various counts.
First, in so far as my own character was concerned, my incapacity for looking and listening, which the passage from the
Journal had so painfully illustrated to me, was nevertheless not
total. There was in me a personage who knew more or less how

to look, but it was an intermittent personage, coming to life only in the presence of some general essence common to a number of things, these essences being its nourishment and its joy. Then the personage looked and listened, but at a certain depth only, without my powers of superficial observation being enhanced. Just as a geometer, stripping things of their sensible qualities, sees only the linear substratum beneath them, so the stories that people told escaped me, for what interested me was not what they were trying to say but the manner in which they said it and the way in which this manner revealed their character or their foibles; or rather I was interested in what had always, because it gave me specific pleasure, been more particularly the goal of my investigations: the point that was common to one being and another. As soon as I perceived this my intelligence—until that moment slumbering, even if sometimes the apparent animation of my talk might disguise from others a profound intellectual torpor—at once set off joyously in pursuit, but its quarry then, for instance the identity of the Verdurin drawing-room in various places and at various times, was situated in the middle distance, behind actual appearances, in a zone that was rather more withdrawn. So the apparent, copiable charm of things and people escaped me, because I had not the ability to stop short there—I was like a surgeon who beneath the smooth surface of a woman's belly sees the internal disease which is devouring it. If I went to a dinner-party I did not see the guests: when I thought I was looking at them, I was in fact examining them with X-rays. And the result was that, when all the observations I had succeeded in making about the guests during the party were linked together, the pattern of the lines I had traced took the form of a collection of psychological laws in which the actual purport of the remarks of each guest occupied but a very small space. But did this take away all merit from my portraits, which in fact I did not intend as such? If, in the realm of painting, one portrait makes manifest certain truths concerning volume, light, movement, does that mean that it is necessarily inferior to another completely different portrait of the same person, in which a thousand details omitted in the first are minutely transcribed, from which second portrait one would conclude that the model was ravish-

ingly beautiful while from the first one would have thought
him or her ugly, a fact which may be of documentary, even of
historical importance, but is not necessarily an artistic truth?
Furthermore my frivolity, the moment I was not alone, made
me eager to please, more eager to amuse by chattering than to
acquire knowledge by listening, unless it happened that I had
gone out into society in search of information about some
particular artistic question or some jealous suspicion which my
mind had previously been revolving. Always I was incapable
of seeing anything for which a desire had not already been
roused in me by something I had read, anything of which I had
not myself traced in advance a sketch which I wanted now to
confront with reality. How often—and I was well aware of this
even without being apprised of it by these pages of Goncourt
—have I remained incapable of bestowing my attention upon
things or people that later, once their image has been presented
to me in solitude by an artist, I would have travelled many
miles, risked death to find again! Then and then only has my
imagination been set in motion, has it begun to paint. And of
something which a year before had made me yawn I have said
to myself with anguish, longingly contemplating it in advance:
"Shall I really be unable to see this thing? I would give anything
for a sight of it!" When one reads articles about people, perhaps
mere fashionable people, who are described as "the last representatives of a society of which no eye-witness now exists," one
may of course exclaim: "Fancy using such extravagant language
about so insignificant a creature! This is what I should have
lamented never having known if I had only read the newspapers and the monthly reviews and had not met the man!" But
I was tempted rather, when I read such pages in the newspapers,
to think: "How unfortunate that in those days when I was
solely preoccupied with meeting Gilberte or Albertine again I
did not pay more attention to this gentleman! I took him for a
society bore, a mere dummy. On the contrary he was a Distinguished Figure!" The pages of Goncourt which I had read
made me regret this tendency of mine. For though I might have
inferred from them that life teaches us to cheapen the value of a
book, and shows us that what a writer extols was in fact worth
very little, it was equally possible for me to come to the

contrary conclusion, that reading teaches us to take a more exalted view of the value of life, a value at the time we did not know how to appreciate and of whose magnitude we have only become aware through the book. We may, without too much difficulty, console ourselves for having taken little pleasure in the society of a Vinteuil, a Bergotte. But the prudish respectability of the one, the intolerable defects of the other, even the pretentious vulgarity of an Elstir in his early days—for I had discovered from the Goncourt Journal that he was none other than the "Monsieur Tiche" whose twaddle had once exasperated Swann in the Verdurins' drawing-room—prove nothing against them: their genius is manifested in their works. What man of genius has not in his conversation adopted the irritating mannerisms of the artists of his set, before attaining (as Elstir had eventually done, though this does not always happen) to a good taste that rises above them? Are not Balzac's letters, for instance, strewn with vulgar expressions which Swann would have suffered a thousand deaths rather than employ? Yet can one doubt that Swann, finely intelligent as he was, purged of all odious absurdities, would have been incapable of writing *La Cousine Bette* or *Le Curé de Tours*? As for the Vinteuils, the Bergottes, the Elstirs, the question whether it is we or the writers of memoirs who are at fault when they represent the society of these men as charming whereas we found it disagreeable, it is a question of slight importance, since even if our estimate were the correct one, this would be no argument against the value of a life that can produce such geniuses.

Right at the other pole of experience, when I saw that the most piquant anecdotes, which form the inexhaustible material of the Goncourt Journal and provide the reader with entertainment for many solitary evenings, had been related to the writer by these people whom he had met at dinner and who, though on the evidence of his pages we should certainly have wanted to meet them, had in my mind left no trace of any interesting recollection, that too was not altogether difficult to explain. In spite of the naïvety of Goncourt, who inferred from the interest of these anecdotes the probable distinction of the man who related them, it might well be that commonplace men had seen during their lives, or heard related, remarkable things which they in their turn had described. Goncourt knew how to listen, just as he knew how to see; I did not. Besides, all these facts needed to be considered and judged separately. Certainly M. de Guermantes had not given me the impression of that adorable model of the youthful graces which my grandmother so wished she had known and which she set before me, in the Memoirs of Mme de Beausergent, as an inimitable example. But one must remember that Basin was then seven years old, that the writer was his aunt, and that even a husband who within a few months will be suing for divorce will praise his wife to the skies. In one of his most delightful poems Sainte-Beuve describes an apparition beside a fountain—a little girl crowned with every gift and every grace, young Mlle de Champlâtreux, whose age at the time cannot have been ten. And in spite of all the affectionate respect which the poet of genius who is the Comtesse de Noailles bore for her husband's mother, the Duchesse de Noailles née Champlâtreux, one wonders whether, had she had occasion to portray her, the result might not have contrasted rather sharply with the portrait drawn by Sainte-Beuve fifty years earlier.

More puzzling perhaps were the people in between the two extremes, those in whom what the writer says of them implies more than a memory which has succeeded in retaining a piquant anecdote, with whom, nevertheless, one has not, as with the Vinteuils, the Bergottes, the resource of judging them on their work, for they have created none: they have only—to the great astonishment of us who found them so commonplace —inspired the work of others. I could, it is true, understand how the drawing-room which, seen on the walls of a museum, will give a greater impression of elegance than anything since the great paintings of the Renaissance, might be that of the ridiculous middle-class woman whom, had I not known her, I would have longed, as I stood before the picture, to be able to approach in reality, hoping to learn from her the most precious secrets of the painter's art which his canvas did not reveal to me, and how her lace and her stately train of velvet might have become a piece of painting as lovely as anything in Titian. For I had already realised long ago that it is not the man with the liveliest mind, the most well-informed, the best supplied with friends and acquaintances, but the one who knows how to become a mirror and in this way can reflect his life, commonplace though it may be, who becomes a Bergotte (even if his contemporaries once thought him less witty than Swann, less erudite than Bréauté), and could one not say as much, and with better reason, of a painter's models? The artist may paint anything in the world that he chooses, but when beauty is awakened within him, the model for that elegance in which he will find themes of beauty will be provided for him by people a little richer than he is himself, in whose house he will find what is not normally to be seen in the studio of an unrecognised man of genius selling his canvases for fifty francs: a drawing-room with chairs and sofas covered in old brocades, an abundance of lamps, beautiful flowers, beautiful fruit, beautiful dresses—people in a relatively modest position, or who would seem to be so to people of real social brilliance (who are not even aware of their existence), but who, for that reason, are more within reach of the obscure artist's acquaintance, more likely to appreciate him, to invite him, to buy his pictures, than men and women of the aristocracy who, like the Pope and Heads of State, get themselves painted by academicians. Will not posterity, when it looks at our time, find the poetry of an elegant home and beautifully dressed women in the drawing-room of the publisher Charpentier as painted by Renoir, rather than in the portraits of the Princesse de Sagan or the Comtesse de La Rochefoucauld by Cotte or Chaplin? The artists who have given us the most splendid visions of elegance have gathered the materials for them from among people who were rarely the leaders of fashion in their age, for the leaders of fashion rarely commission pictures from the unknown bearer of a new type of beauty which they are unable to distinguish in his canvases, concealed as it is by the interposition of that formula of hackneyed charm which floats in the eye of the public like the subjective visions which a sick man supposes really to exist before his eyes. This, I say, I could understand; but that these commonplace models whom I had known should in addition have inspired and advised certain arrangements which had enchanted me, that the presence of one or another of them in a painting should be not merely that of a model but of a friend whom an artist wants to put into his pictures, this made me ask myself whether all the people whom we regret not having known because Balzac depicted them in his novels or dedicated books to them in homage and admiration, the people about whom Sainte-Beuve or Baudelaire wrote their loveliest poems, still more whether all the Récamiers, all the Pompadours, would not have seemed to me insignificant creatures, either owing to an infirmity of my nature, which, if it were so, made me furious at being ill and therefore unable to go back and see again all the people whom I had misjudged, or because they owed their prestige only to an illusory magic of literature, in which case I had been barking up the wrong tree and need not repine at being obliged almost any day now by the steady deterioration of my health to break with society, renounce travel and museums, and go to a sanatorium for treatment.

These ideas, tending on the one hand to diminish, and on the other to increase, my regret that I had no gift for literature, were entirely absent from my mind during the long years—in which I had in any case completely renounced the project of writing—which I spent far from Paris receiving treatment in a sanatorium, until there came a time, at the beginning of 1916, when it could no longer get medical staff. I then returned to a Paris very different from the city to which, as we shall see presently, I had come back once before in August 1914 for a medical consultation, after which I had withdrawn again to my sanatorium.

On one of the first evenings of my second return, in 1916, wanting to hear people talk about the only thing that interested me at the time, the war, I went out after dinner to call on Mme Verdurin, who was, with Mme Bontemps, one of the queens of this war-time Paris which made one think of the Directory. As if by the germination of a tiny quantity of yeast, apparently of spontaneous generation, young women now went about all day with tall cylindrical turbans on their heads, as a contemporary of Mme Tallien's might have done, and from a sense of patriotic duty wore Egyptian tunics, straight and dark and very "war," over very short skirts; they wore thonged footwear recalling the buskin as worn by Talma, or else long gaiters recalling those of our dear boys at the front; it was, so they said, because they did not forget that it was their duty to rejoice the eyes of these "boys at the front," that they still decked themselves of an evening not only in flowing dresses, but in jewellery which suggested the army by its choice of decorative themes, when indeed the actual material from which it was made did not come from, had not been wrought in the army; for instead of Egyptian ornaments recalling the campaign in Egypt, the fashion now was for rings or bracelets made out of fragments of exploded shells or copper bands from 75 millimetre ammunition, and for cigarette-lighters constructed out of two English pennies to which a soldier, in his dug-out, had succeeded in giving a patina so beautiful that the profile of Queen Victoria looked as if it had been drawn by the hand of Pisanello; and it was also because they never stopped thinking of the dear boys, so they said, that when one of their own kin fell they scarcely wore mourning for him, on the pretext that "their grief was mingled with pride," which permitted them to wear a bonnet of white English crêpe (a bonnet with the most charming effect, "authorising every hope" and "inspired by an invincible confidence in final victory") and to replace the cashmere of former days by satin and chiffon, and even to keep their pearls, "while observing the tact and propriety of which there is no need to remind Frenchwomen."

The Louvre and all the other museums were closed, and when one saw at the head of an article in a newspaper the words: "A sensational exhibition," one could be sure that the exhibition in question was not one of paintings but of dresses, of dresses moreover which aimed at reviving "those refined joys of art of which the women of Paris have for too long been deprived." So it was that fashion and pleasure had returned, fashion, in the absence of the arts, apologising for its survival as the arts had done in 1793, in which year the artists exhibiting in the revolutionary Salon proclaimed that, though "stern Republicans might find it strange that we should occupy ourselves with the arts when Europe united in coalition is besieging the soil of liberty," they would be wrong. The same sort of thing was said in 1916 by the dressmakers, who, with the

self-conscious pride of artists, affirmed that "to create something new, to get away from banality, to assert an individual
character, to prepare for victory, to evolve for the post-war
generations a new formula of beauty, such was the ambition
that tormented them, the chimaera that they pursued, as would
be apparent to anyone who cared to visit their salons, delight-
fully installed in the Rue de la . . ., where to efface by a note of
luminous gaiety the heavy sadness of the hour seems to be the
watchword, with the discretion, naturally, that circumstances
impose. The sadness of the hour"—it was true—"might prove
too strong for feminine energies, were it not that we have so
many lofty examples of courage and endurance to contemplate.
So, as we think of our warriors dreaming in their trenches of
more comfort and more pretty things for the girl they have left
behind them, we shall not pause in our ever more strenuous
efforts to create dresses that answer to the needs of the moment.
The vogue"—and what could be more natural?—"is for the
fashion-houses of our English allies, and the rage this year is
the barrel-dress, which, with its charming informality, gives us
all an amusing little *cachet* of rare distinction. We may even say
that one of the happiest consequences of this sad war will be,"
added the delightful chronicler (and one expected: "the return
of our lost provinces" or "the reawakening of national sentiment")—"one of the happiest consequences of this sad war
will be that we have achieved some charming results in the
realm of fashion, without ill-considered and unseemly luxury,
with the simplest materials, that we have created prettiness out
of mere nothings. To the dresses of the great designers, reproduced in a number of copies, women prefer just now dresses
made at home, which affirm the intelligence, the taste and the
personal preferences of the individual."

As for charity, the thought of all the miseries that had sprung
from the invasion, of all the wounded and disabled, meant
naturally that it was obliged to develop forms "more ingenious
than ever before," and this meant that the ladies in tall turbans
were obliged to spend the latter part of the afternoon at "teas"
round a bridge table, discussing the news from the "front,"
while their cars waited at the door with a handsome soldier in
the driver's seat who chatted to the footman. It was, moreover,

not only the headdresses with their strange cylinders towering above the ladies' faces that were new. The faces were new themselves. These ladies in new-fangled hats were young women who had come one did not quite know from where and had been the flower of fashion, some for six months, others for two years, others for four. And these differences were of as much importance for them as had been, at the time when I took my first steps in society, for two families like the Guermantes and the La Rochefoucaulds a difference of three or four centuries of proven antiquity. The lady who had known the Guermantes since 1914 looked upon the lady who had been introduced to them in 1916 as an upstart, greeted her with the air of a dowager, quizzed her with her lorgnette, and admitted with a little grimace that no one even knew for certain whether or no she was married. "It is all rather nauseating," concluded the lady of 1914, who would have liked the cycle of new admissions to have come to a halt after herself. These new ladies, whom the young men found pretty ancient and whom, also, certain elderly men who had not moved exclusively in the best circles, thought that they recognised as being not so new as all that, did not merely recommend themselves to society by offering it its favourite amusements of political conversation and music in intimate surroundings; part of their appeal was that it was *they* who offered these amenities, for in order that things should appear new even if they are old—and indeed even if they are new—there must in art, as in medicine and in fashion, be new names. (New names indeed there were in certain spheres. For instance, Mme Verdurin had visited Venice during the war, but—like those people who cannot bear sad talk or display of personal feelings—when she said that "it" was "marvellous" she was referring not to Venice, or St Mark's, or the palaces, all that I had so loved and she thought so unimportant, but to the effect of the searchlights in the sky, of which searchlights she could give you a detailed account supported by statistics. So from age to age is reborn a certain realism which reacts against what the previous age has admired.)

The Saint-Euverte salon was a faded banner now, and the presence beneath it of the greatest artists, the most influential ministers, would have attracted nobody. But people would run

to listen to the secretary of one of these same artists or a subordinate official of one of the ministers holding forth in the
houses of the new turbaned ladies whose winged and chattering
invasion filled Paris. The ladies of the first Directory had a
queen who was young and beautiful and was called Mme
Tallien. Those of the second had two, who were old and ugly
and were called Mme Verdurin and Mme Bontemps. Who
could now hold it against Mme Bontemps that in the Dreyfus
affair her husband had played a role which the *Echo de Paris* had
sharply criticised? The whole Chamber having at a certain
moment become revisionist, it was inevitably from among
former revisionists—and also from among former socialists—
that the party of social order, of religious tolerance, of military
preparedness, had been obliged to enlist its recruits. Time was
when M. Bontemps would have been abominated, because then
the antipatriots bore the name of Dreyfusards. But presently
this name had been forgotten and replaced by that of "opponent of the law of three years' military service." M. Bontemps,
far from being its opponent, was one of the sponsors of this
law; consequently he was a patriot. In society (and this social
phenomenon is merely a particular case of a much more general
psychological law) novelties, whether blameworthy or not,
excite horror only so long as they have not been assimilated
and enveloped by reassuring elements. It was the same with
Dreyfusism as with that marriage between Saint-Loup and the
daughter of Odette which had at first produced such an outcry.
Now that "everybody one knew" was seen at the parties given
by the Saint-Loups, Gilberte might have had the morals of
Odette herself but people would have "gone there" just the
same and would have thought it quite right that she should
disapprove like a dowager of any moral novelties that had not
been assimilated. Dreyfusism was now integrated in a scheme
of respectable and familiar things. As for asking oneself whether
intrinsically it was good or bad, the idea no more entered
anybody's head, now when it was accepted, than in the past
when it was condemned. It was no longer "shocking" and that
was all that mattered. People hardly remembered that it had
once been thought so, just as, when a certain time has elapsed,
they no longer know whether a girl's father was a thief or not.

One can always say, if the subject crops up: "No, it's the brother-in-law, or someone else with the same name, that you're thinking of. There has never been a breath of scandal about her father." In the same way, there had undeniably been Dreyfusism and Dreyfusism, and a man who was received by the Duchesse de Montmorency and was helping to pass the three years law could not be bad. And then, as the saying goes, no sin but should find mercy. If Dreyfusism was accorded an amnesty, so, *a fortiori*, were Dreyfusards. In fact, there no longer were Dreyfusards in politics, since at one moment every politician had been one if he wanted to belong to the government, even those who represented the contrary of what at the time of its shocking novelty—the time when Saint-Loup had been getting into bad ways—Dreyfusism had incarnated: anti-patriotism, irreligion, anarchy, etc. So the Dreyfusism of M. Bontemps, invisible and constitutional like that of every other politician, was no more apparent than the bones beneath the skin. No one troubled to remember that he had been a Dreyfusard, for people in society are scatter-brained and forgetful and, besides, all *that* had been a very long time ago, a "time" which these people affected to think longer than it was, for one of the ideas most in vogue was that the pre-war days were separated from the war by something as profound, something of apparently as long a duration, as a geological period, and Brichot himself, that great nationalist, when he alluded to the Dreyfus case now talked of "those pre-historic days." (The truth is that this profound change wrought by the war was in inverse ratio to the quality of the minds which it affected, at least above a certain level. At the very bottom of the scale the really stupid people, who lived only for pleasure, did not bother about the fact that there was a war. But, at the other end of the scale too, people who have made for themselves a circum-ambient interior life usually pay small regard to the importance of events. What profoundly modifies their system of thought is much more likely to be something that in itself seems to have no importance, something that reverses the order of time for them by making them contemporaneous with another epoch in their lives. And that this is so we may see in practice from the beauty of the writing which is inspired in this particular way: the song of a bird in the park at Montboissier, or a breeze laden with the scent of mignonette, are obviously phenomena of less consequence than the great events of the Revolution and the Empire; but they inspired Chateaubriand to write pages of infinitely greater value in his *Mémoires d'Outre-tombe*.) The words Dreyfusard and anti-Dreyfusard no longer had any meaning then. But the very people who said this would have been dumbfounded and horrified if one had told them that probably in a few centuries, or perhaps even sooner, the word Boche would have only the curiosity value of such words as *sans-culotte, chouan* and *bleu*.

Things had altered so little that people still found it quite natural to use the old catchwords "right-minded" and "not right-minded." And yet change of a kind there was, for, just as former partisans of the Commune had at a later date been anti-revisionists, so now the most extreme Dreyfusards of the old days wanted to shoot people right and left, and the generals supported them in this policy just as they had supported Galliffet's opponents at the time of the Affair.

M. Bontemps did not want there to be any question of peace until Germany had been broken up into tiny states as it had been in the Middle Ages, the fall of the House of Hohenzollern pronounced, and the Kaiser stood up against a wall and shot. In a word he was what Brichot called a *jusquauboutiste*, and this was the highest certificate of patriotism that could be conferred upon him. Doubtless for the first three days Mme Bontemps had been a little bewildered in the midst of the people who had asked Mme Verdurin to introduce them to her, and it was in a tone of some slight asperity that Mme Verdurin had replied: "No, my dear, the Comte," when Mme Bontemps said to her "That was the Duc d'Haussonville you introduced to me just now, wasn't it?", either out of total ignorance and failure to associate the name Haussonville with any title whatsoever or, on the contrary, from excess of information and an association of ideas with the "Party of the Dukes," to which she had been told that in the Academy M. d'Haussonville belonged. But by the fourth day she had begun to be firmly installed in the Faubourg Saint-Germain. Sometimes there could still be seen around her the nameless fragments of a world that one did not know, which, in those who knew the egg from which Mme Bontemps had emerged, evoked no more surprise than the débris of shell around a chick. But after a fortnight she had shaken them off, and before the end of the first month, when she said: "I am going to the Lévis'," everybody understood, without her having to explain herself, that it was the Lévis-Mirepoix she meant, and not a duchess would have gone to bed without having inquired of Mme Bontemps or Mme Verdurin, at least by telephone, what there had been in the evening communiqué, what had been deliberately left out, how the Greek situation was developing, what offensive was being prepared, in a word all the news that the public would know only on the following day or later but of which the two ladies staged the equivalent of a dressmaker's private view. In conversation, when she was announcing news, Mme Verdurin would say "we" when she meant France. "Now listen: we demand of the King of Greece that he should withdraw from the Peloponnese, etc.; we send him, etc." And in all her stories there was constant mention of G.H.Q. ("I telephoned to G.H.Q."), an abbreviation which gave her, as it fell from her lips, the pleasure that in former days women who did not know the Prince d'Agrigente had got from asking with a smile, when his name was mentioned, so as to show that they were in the swim: "Grigri?", a pleasure which in untroubled times is confined to the fashionable world but in great crises comes within the reach of the lower classes. Our butler, for instance, if the King of Greece was mentioned, was able, thanks to the newspapers, to say like the Kaiser Wilhelm: "Tino?", whereas hitherto his familiarity with kings had been of his own invention and of a more plebeian kind, as when at one time he had been in the habit of referring to the King of Spain as "Fonfonse." Another noticeable change was that, as more and more smart people made advances to Mme Verdurin, inversely the number of those whom she dubbed "bores" diminished. By a sort of magical transformation, every bore who had come to call on her and asked to be invited to her parties immediately became a charming and intelligent person. In short, at the end of a year, the number of bores had dwindled to such an extent that "the fear and awfulness of being bored," which had filled so large a place in the conversation and played so great a role in the life of Mme Verdurin, had almost entirely disappeared. In her latter days, it seemed, this awfulness of being bored (which anyhow, as she had formerly assured people, she had not known in her early youth) afflicted her less, just as certain kinds of migraine, certain nervous asthmatic conditions lose their force as one grows older. And the terror of being bored would doubtless, for want of bores, have entirely abandoned Mme Verdurin had she not, in some slight degree, replaced the vanishing bores by others recruited from the ranks of the former faithful.

Be that as it may, to conclude the subject of the duchesses who now frequented Mme Verdurin's house, they came, though they did not realise this, in search of exactly the same thing as the Dreyfusards had sought there in the old days, that is to say a social pleasure so compounded that their enjoyment of it at the same time assuaged their political curiosities and satisfied their need to discuss with others like themselves the incidents about which they had read in the newspapers. Mme Verdurin said: "Come at 5 o'clock to talk about the war" as she would have said in the past: "Come and talk about the Affair," or at an intermediate period: "Come to hear Morel."

Morel, incidentally, ought not to have been there, for the reason that he had not, as was supposed, been invalided out of the army. He had simply failed to rejoin his regiment and was a deserter, but nobody knew this.

One of the stars of the salon was "I'm a wash-out," who in spite of his sportive tastes had got himself exempted and whom I now thought of mainly as the author of remarkable works of art which were constantly in my thoughts. To such an extent had he assumed for me this new character that it was only by chance, when from time to time I established a transverse current linking two series of memories, that it crossed my mind that he was also the person who had brought about the depar-ture of Albertine from my house. And even this transverse current ended, as far as these vestigial memories of Albertine were concerned, in a channel which petered out completely at a distance of several years from the present. For I never thought of her now. That was a channel of memories, a route, which I had quite ceased to take. Whereas the works of "I'm a wash-out" were recent and this route of memory was one perpetually visited and used by my mind.

I ought to say that the acquaintance of Andrée's husband was neither very easy nor very agreeable to make, and that any attempt to make friends with him was destined to numerous disappointments. He was, in fact, at this time already seriously ill and spared himself all fatigues except those which he thought likely to give him pleasure. Now in this category he included only meetings with people whom he did not yet know, whom his ardent imagination represented to him doubtless as being possibly different from others. When it came to people he was already acquainted with, he knew too well what they were like and what they would be like again and they no longer seemed to him worth the trouble of a fatigue that would be dangerous and might even be fatal to him. In short, he was a very poor friend. And perhaps in his taste for new people there was still something to be found of the frenzied daring which he had shown in the old days at Balbec, in sport, in gambling, in excesses of eating and drinking.

Whenever Andrée and I were there together Mme Verdurin tried to introduce me to her, being unable to accept the fact that we were already acquainted. Andrée did not often come with her husband, but she at least was an admirable and sincere friend to me. Faithful to the aesthetic ideas of her husband, who had reacted against the Russian Ballet, she was always saying of the Marquis de Polignac: "He's had his house decorated by Bakst. How can one sleep with all that round one? I would rather have Dubuffe." The Verdurins, too, swept along by the fatal progress of aestheticism which ends by eating its own tail, said now that they could not endure *art nouveau* (besides, it came from Munich) or white rooms; they cared only for old French furniture in a sombre colour-scheme.

I saw a lot of Andrée at this time. We did not know what to say to each other, and once there came into my mind that name, Juliette, which had risen from the depths of Albertine's memory like a mysterious flower. Mysterious then, but now it no longer stirred any feeling in me: many subjects that were indifferent to me I discussed but on this subject I was silent;

not that it meant less to me than others, but a sort of super-saturation takes place when one has thought about a thing too much. Perhaps the epoch in my life when I saw so many mysteries in that name was the true one. But as these epochs will not last for ever, it is a mistake for a man to sacrifice his health and his fortune to the elucidation of mysteries which one day will no longer interest him.

Now that Mme Verdurin could get anyone she wanted to come to her house, people were very surprised to see her make indirect advances to someone she had completely lost sight of, Odette, the general opinion being that Odette could add noth-ing to the brilliant set that the little group had become. But a prolonged separation, which has the effect of appeasing resent-ments, in some cases also reawakens feelings of friendship. And then too the phenomenon of the dying man who pronounces none but familiar names from the past, or the old man who finds pleasure in his childhood memories, has its social equi-valent. To succeed in the project of making Odette return to her, Mme Verdurin employed, naturally, not the "ultras" but the less faithful members of the group who had kept a foot in each of the two drawing-rooms. "I can't think why we no longer see her here," she said to them. "She may have fallen out with me, I haven't with her. After all, what harm have I done her? It was in my house that she met both her husbands. If she wants to come back, let her know that the door is open." These words, which would have involved a sacrifice of pride for the Mistress if they had not been dictated to her by her imagination, were passed on, but without success. Mme Verdurin waited in vain for Odette, until events which will come to our notice later brought about, for entirely different reasons, what the intercession of the "deserters," for all their zeal, had been unable to achieve. So rarely do we meet either with easy success or with irreversible defeat.

To these parties Mme Verdurin used to invite a few ladies of rather recent origin, known for their good works, who at first came magnificently dressed, with great pearl necklaces that Odette, who had a necklace just as beautiful the display of which she had herself formerly overdone, regarded, now that she was "dressed for war" in imitation of the ladies of the

Faubourg, with some severity. But women know how to adapt themselves. After three or four appearances they realised that the clothes which they had thought smart were precisely the ones proscribed by people who were smart; they laid aside their gold dresses and resigned themselves to simplicity.

"It is too bad," Mme Verdurin would say. "I must telephone to Bontemps to get things put right for to-morrow, they have *blue-pencilled* the whole of the end of Norpois's article and just because he hinted that Percin had been *bowler-hatted*." For the idiocy of the times caused people to pride themselves on using the expressions of the times; in this way they hoped to show that they were in the fashion, like the middle-class woman who says, when MM. de Bréauté or d'Agrigente or de Charlus is mentioned: "You mean Babal de Bréauté? Grigri? Mémé de Charlus?" As a matter of fact duchesses dò this too, and duchesses felt the same pleasure in saying "bowler-hatted," for it is in their names that these ladies—for the commoner with a poetical imagination—are exceptional; in their language and their ideas they conform to the intellectual category to which they belong and to which also belong a vast number of middle-class people. The classes of the intellect take no account of birth.

All this telephoning that Mme Verdurin did was not, however, without its disadvantages. Although we have forgotten to mention the fact, the Verdurin "salon," if it continued to exist in spirit and in all essentials, had been temporarily transferred to one of the largest hotels in Paris, the lack of coal and light making it too difficult for the Verdurins to entertain in the former mansion of the Venetian Ambassadors, which was extremely damp. But the new drawing-room was not altogether disagreeable. Just as, in Venice, the restrictions that water imposes upon a site dictate the shape of a palace, and in Paris a scrap of garden is more ravishing than a whole park in the country, so the narrow dining-room that Mme Verdurin had in the hotel made, with the dazzling white walls of its irregular quadrilateral, a sort of screen upon which figured every Wednesday, indeed almost every day of the week, all the most interesting men of every kind, all the smartest women in Paris, only too delighted to avail themselves of the luxury of the

Verdurins, which went on increasing, with their wealth, at a time when other very rich people were economising, because part of their income was frozen. In their altered form the receptions had not ceased to enchant Brichot, who, as the circle of the Verdurins' acquaintance grew wider and wider, found in their parties ever new pleasures, packed tight together in a tiny space like surprises in a Christmas stocking. On some days the guests were so numerous that the dining-room of the private suite was too small and the dinner was given in the huge dining-room downstairs, where the faithful, if they feigned a hypocritical regret for the intimacy of upstairs, were at heart delighted—while keeping themselves to themselves, as in the old days on the little train—to be a spectacle and an object of envy for neighbouring tables. Doubtless, under normal peace-time conditions, a "society" note surreptitiously sent to *Le Figaro* or *Le Gaulois* would have informed a larger public than could be contained in the dining-room of the Majestic that Brichot had dined with the Duchesse de Duras. But since the war, the social reporters having suppressed this type of news (they made up for it, however, in funerals, "mentions in despatches" and Franco-American banquets), publicity could only be attained through a more embryonic, a more restricted medium, worthy of primitive ages and anterior to the discovery of Gutenberg: one had actually to be seen at Mme Verdurin's table. After dinner the guests went upstairs to the Mistress's reception rooms, and then the telephoning began. But many large hotels were at this period peopled with spies, who duly noted the news announced over the telephone by Bontemps with an indiscretion which might have had serious consequences but for a fortunate lack of accuracy in his reports, which invariably were contradicted by events.

Before the hour at which the afternoon tea-parties came to an end, at the close of the day, in the still light sky one saw, far off, little brown dots which one might have taken, in the blue evening, for midges or birds. In the same way, when one sees a mountain at a great distance one can imagine it to be a cloud. But because one knows that this "cloud" is huge, solid

and resistant one's emotions are stirred. And I too was moved
by the thought that the brown dot in the summer sky was
neither midge nor bird but an aeroplane with a crew of men
keeping guard over Paris. (The memory of the aeroplanes
which I had seen with Albertine on our last drive, near Versailles, played no part in this emotion, for the memory of that
drive had become indifferent to me.)

When the time came for dinner, the restaurants were full;
and if, passing in the street, I saw a wretched soldier on leave,
escaped for six days from the constant danger of death and
about to return to the trenches, halt his gaze for a moment
upon the illuminated windows, I suffered as I had in the hotel
at Balbec when fishermen used to watch us at dinner, but I
suffered more now because I knew that the misery of the soldier
is greater than that of the poor, since it combines in itself all
miseries, and more touching still because more resigned, more
noble, and because it was with a philosophical shake of the
head, without hatred, that on the eve of setting out again for
the war the soldier would say to himself, as he saw the shirkers
jostling one another in their efforts to secure a table: "You'd
never know there was a war on here." Then at half past nine,
before anyone had had time to finish dinner, the lights were all
suddenly turned out because of the police regulations, so that
at nine thirty-five the second jostling of shirkers snatching their
overcoats from the page-boys of the restaurant where I had
dined with Saint-Loup one evening when he was on leave took
place in a mysterious half-darkness which might have been that
of a room in which slides are being shown on a magic lantern,
or of the auditorium, during the exhibition of a film, of one of
those cinemas towards which the men and women who had
been dining would presently rush.

But at any later hour for those who, like myself on the evening which I am going to describe, had had dinner at home and
were going out to see friends, Paris, at least in certain quarters,
was even blacker than had been the Combray of my childhood;
the visits that people paid one another were like the visits of
country neighbours. Ah! if Albertine had been alive, how
delightful it would have been, on the evenings when I had
dined out, to arrange to meet her out of doors, under the

arcades! At first I should have seen nothing, I should have had
the pang of thinking that she had failed to turn up, when
suddenly I should have seen one of her beloved grey dresses
emerge from the black wall, then her smiling eyes which had
already seen me, and we could have walked along with our
arms round each other without any fear of being recognised or
disturbed, and then at length gone home. But alas, I was alone
and I felt as if I was setting out to pay a neighbourly visit in the
country, like those that Swann used to pay us after dinner,
without meeting more people on his way through the darkness
of Tansonville, along the little tow-path and as far as the Rue
du Saint-Esprit, than I now met in the streets, transformed into
winding rustic lanes, between Sainte-Clotilde and the Rue
Bonaparte. Or again—since the effect of those fragments of
landscape which travel in obedience to the moods of the
weather was no longer nullified by surroundings which had
become invisible—on evenings when the wind was chasing an
icy shower of rain I had, now, much more strongly the impression of being on the shore of that raging sea of which I had
once so longingly dreamed than I had had when I was actually
at Balbec; and other natural features also, which had not existed
in Paris hitherto, helped to create the illusion that one had just
got out of the train and arrived to spend a holiday in the depth
of the country: for example the contrast of light and shadow
on the ground that one had all round one on evenings when
the moon was shining. There were effects of moonlight normally unknown in towns, sometimes in the middle of winter
even, when the rays of the moon lay outpoured upon the snow
on the Boulevard Haussmann, untouched now by the broom of
any sweeper, as they would have lain upon a glacier in the
Alps. Against this snow of bluish gold the silhouettes of the
trees were outlined clear and pure, with the delicacy that they
have in certain Japanese paintings or in certain backgrounds of
Raphael; and on the ground at the foot of the tree itself there
was stretched out its shadow as often one sees trees' shadows
in the country at sunset, when the light inundates and polishes
to the smoothness of a mirror some meadow in which they are
planted at regular intervals. But by a refinement of exquisite
delicacy the meadow upon which were displayed these shadows

of trees, light as souls, was a meadow of paradise, not green but
of a whiteness so dazzling because of the moonlight shining
upon the jade-like snow that it might have been a meadow
woven entirely from petals of flowering pear trees. And in the
squares the divinities of the public fountains, holding a jet of
ice in their hand, looked like statues wrought in two different
materials by a sculptor who had decided to marry pure bronze
to pure crystal. On these exceptional days all the houses were
black. But in the spring, on the contrary, here and there, defy-
ing the regulations of the police, a private house, or simply one
floor of a house, or even simply one room of one floor, had
failed to close its shutters and appeared, mysteriously supported
by dark impalpable shadows, to be no more than a projection
of light, an apparition without substance. And the woman
whom, if one raised one's eyes high above the street, one could
distinguish in this golden penumbra, assumed, in this night in
which one was oneself lost and in which she too seemed to be
hidden away, the mysterious and veiled charm of an oriental
vision. Then one passed on and nothing more interrupted the
rustic tramp, wholesome and monotonous, of one's feet
through the darkness.

I reflected that it was a long time since I had seen any of the
personages who have been mentioned in this work. In 1914, it
was true, during the two months that I had spent in Paris, I
had caught a glimpse of M. de Charlus and seen something
of Bloch and Saint-Loup, the latter only twice. The second
occasion was certainly that on which he had been most himself;
he had quite effaced that disagreeable impression of insincerity
which he had made on me during the stay at Tansonville that
I have described, and I had once more recognised in him all the
fine qualities of his earlier days. On the earlier occasion, which
was less than a week after the declaration of war, while Bloch
made a display of the most chauvinistic sentiments, Saint-Loup,
once Bloch had left us, was unashamedly cynical about the fact
that he himself had not joined his regiment, and I had been
almost shocked at the violence of his tone. (Saint-Loup had
just come back from Balbec. I learnt later, indirectly, that he
had made unsuccessful advances to the manager of the restaurant. The latter owed his position to the money he had

inherited from M. Nissim Bernard. He was, in fact, none other than the young waiter whom in the past Bloch's uncle had "protected." But wealth in his case had brought with it virtue and it was in vain that Saint-Loup had attempted to seduce him. Thus, by a process of compensation, while virtuous young men abandon themselves in their later years to the passions of which they have at length become conscious, promiscuous youths turn into men of principle from whom any Charlus who turns up too late on the strength of old stories will get an unpleasant rebuff. It is all a question of chronology.) "No," he exclaimed, gaily and with force, "if a man doesn't fight, whatever reason he may give, it is because he doesn't want to be killed, because he is *afraid*." And with the same affirming gesture, even more energetic than that which he had used to underline the fear of others, he added: "And that goes for me too. If I haven't rejoined my regiment, it is quite simply from *fear*—so there!" I had already observed in more than one person that the affectation of praiseworthy sentiments is not the only method of covering bad ones; another less obvious method is to make a display of these bad sentiments, so that at least one does not appear to be unaware of them. Moreover, in Saint-Loup this tendency was strengthened by his habit, when he had committed an indiscretion or made a blunder for which he expected to be blamed, of proclaiming it aloud and saying that it had been done on purpose. A habit which, I believe, must have come to him from some instructor at the Ecole de Guerre whom he had known well and greatly admired. I had, therefore, no hesitation in interpreting this outburst as the verbal confirmation of a sentiment which, since it had dictated the conduct of Saint-Loup and his non-participation in the war now beginning, he preferred to proclaim aloud. "Have you heard the rumour," he asked, as he left me, "that my aunt Oriane is going to get a divorce? Personally I know nothing about it whatsoever. There have been rumours of the kind from time to time, and I have so often heard that it's imminent that I shall wait until it happens before I believe it. I must admit, it would be very understandable. My uncle is a charming man, not only socially but as a friend and in the family. He even, in a way, has much more heart than my aunt, who is a saint but makes him terribly aware of it. Only he is a dreadful husband, who has never ceased to be unfaithful to his wife, to insult her, to bully her, to keep her short of money. It would be so natural for her to leave him that that is a reason for the story to be true, but also a reason why it may not be true—the idea occurs to people and inevitably they talk about it. And then she has put up with him for so long! Of course I know quite well that there are lots of things which are reported falsely, and then denied, but later do become true." This put it into my head to ask him whether there had ever been any question of his marrying Mlle de Guermantes. He seemed amazed and assured me that there had not, that it was merely one of those rumours of the fashionable world which arise from time to time one does not know why and vanish in the same way, without their falsity causing those who believed them to be any more cautious when a new rumour arises, of an engagement or a divorce, or a political rumour, in giving credence to it and spreading it.

Forty-eight hours had not elapsed before certain facts which I learnt proved to me that I had been absolutely wrong in my interpretation of Robert's words: "If a man is not at the front, it is because he is afraid." Saint-Loup had said this in order to shine in conversation, to appear in the role of an original psychologist, so long as he was not sure that his own enlistment would be accepted. But meanwhile he was moving heaven and earth to bring this about and showing himself in this less "original," in the meaning that he thought it necessary to give to the word, but more profoundly a Frenchman of Saint-André-des-Champs, more in conformity with all that at this moment was best in the Frenchmen of Saint-André-des-Champs, lords, citizens and serfs—feudally respectful serfs and serfs in revolt, those two divisions, both equally French, of the same family, the Françoise branch and the Morel branch, from which two arrows were now converging upon a common target, the frontier. Bloch had been enchanted to hear a confession of cowardice from a nationalist (who was, as a matter of fact, so little of a nationalist) and when Saint-Loup had asked him whether he himself would soon be off, had assumed a high-priestly air and replied: "Short-sighted." But Bloch had com-

pletely changed his mind about the war a few days later, when
he came to see me in a state of frenzy. Although short-sighted,
he had been passed fit for service. I was accompanying him
home when we met Saint-Loup, who was on his way to an
interview at the Ministry of War with a colonel to whom he
was to be introduced by a retired officer—"M. de Cambremer,"
he said to me, and added: "Oh! but of course, he is an old
acquaintance of yours. You know Cancan as well as I do." I
replied that I did indeed know him and his wife too, and that
I didn't have a particularly high opinion of them. But I was so
much in the habit, ever since I had first met them, of considering the wife as in her way a remarkable woman, who knew her
Schopenhauer and at least had access to an intellectual sphere
which was closed to her boorish husband, that I was at first
astonished to hear Saint-Loup reply: "His wife is idiotic, I
won't try to defend her. But *he* is an excellent man—he was
talented once and is still a very pleasant person." By the
"idiocy" of the wife, Saint-Loup meant no doubt her desperate
desire to move in grand society, which is the thing that grand
society judges most severely; by the good qualities of the
husband, he meant perhaps something of the qualities that
were recognised in him by his niece when she declared that he
was the best of the family. He, at least, did not worry about
duchesses, though this it must be admitted is a form of "intelligence" which differs as much from the intelligence that
characterises thinkers as the "intelligence" admired by the
public in this or that rich man who has "been clever enough to
make a fortune." However Saint-Loup's words did not displease me, because they reminded me that pretentiousness is
near akin to stupidity and that simplicity has a flavour which
though it lies beneath the surface is agreeable. I had, it is true,
had no opportunity to savour that of M. de Cambremer. But
this was merely an instance of the law that a person is many
different persons according to who is judging him, quite apart
from the different standards by which different people judge.
In the case of M. de Cambremer, I had known only the rind.
His flavour, therefore, though avouched to me by others, was
to me personally unknown.

Bloch left us outside his house, overflowing with bitterness against Saint-Loup and saying to his face that men of his sort, privileged dandies who strutted about at headquarters, ran no risks and that he, as a plain private soldier, had no wish to "get a hole in his skin just because of William." "It seems that the Emperor William is seriously ill," replied Saint-Loup. Bloch, like everybody connected with the Stock Exchange, was more than usually credulous of sensational reports. "Yes," he said, "there is even a strong rumour that he is dead." In Stock Exchange circles every monarch who is ill, whether it be Edward VII or William II, is dead, every town which is about to be besieged has already been captured. "It is only being kept secret," added Bloch, "in order not to damage the morale of the Boches. But he died the night before last. My father has it from an absolutely first-class source." Absolutely first-class sources were the only ones to which M. Bloch senior paid any attention, and it was always with such a source that thanks to his "important connexions" he was fortunate enough to be in touch, when he heard before anyone else that Foreign Bonds were going to go up or that De Beers were going to fall. However, if just at that moment De Beers had a rise or Foreign Bonds "came on offer," if the market in the former was "firm and active" and that in the latter "hesitant and weak, with a note of caution," the first-class source did not, for that reason, cease to be a first-class source. So Bloch informed us of the death of the Kaiser with an air of mystery and self-importance, but also of fury. He was exasperated beyond measure at hearing Robert say: "the Emperor William." I believe that under the blade of the guillotine Saint-Loup and M. de Guermantes could not have spoken otherwise. Two men of "society," surviving alone on a desert island where they would have nobody to impress by a display of good manners, would recognise each other by these little signs of breeding, just as two Latinists in the same circumstances would continue to quote Virgil correctly. Saint-Loup, even under torture at the hands of the Germans, could never have used any other expression than "the Emperor William." And this good breeding, whatever else one may think of it, is a symptom of formidable mental shackles. The man who cannot throw them off can never be more than a man of the world. However, his elegant mediocrity

—particularly when it is allied, as is often the case, with hidden generosity and unexpressed heroism— is a delightful quality in comparison with the vulgarity of Bloch, at once coward and braggart, who started now to scream at Saint-Loup: "Can't you simply say William? The trouble is you've got the wind up. Even in Paris you crawl on your belly before him! Pooh! we're going to have some fine soldiers at the frontier, they'll lick the boots of the Boches. You and your friends in fancy uniforms, you're fit to parade in a tournament and that's about all."

"Poor Bloch is absolutely determined that I am to do nothing but strut about on parade," said Saint-Loup to me with a smile, when we had left our friend. And I sensed that this was not at all what Robert wished to do, although at the time I did not realise what his intentions were as clearly as I did later when, as the cavalry remained inactive, he got leave to serve as an officer in the infantry and then in the light infantry, or when, later still, there came the sequel which the reader will learn in due course. But Robert's patriotism was something that Bloch was unaware of simply because Robert chose not to display it. If Bloch had treated us to a viciously anti-militarist profession of faith once he had been passed as "fit," he had previously made the most chauvinistic statements when he thought that he would be discharged on the grounds of short sight. But Saint-Loup would have been incapable of making these statements; in the first place from that sort of moral delicacy which prevents people from expressing sentiments that lie too deep within them and that seem to them quite natural. My mother, in the past, would not only not have hesitated for a second to die for my grandmother, but would have suffered horribly if anyone had prevented her from doing so. Nevertheless, I cannot retrospectively imagine on her lips any such phrase as "I would give my life for my mother." And the same reticence, in his love of France, was displayed by Robert, who at this moment seemed to me much more Saint-Loup (in so far as I could form a picture of his father) than Guermantes. And then Robert would also have been saved from expressing the chauvinistic sentiments of Bloch by the fact that his intelligence was in itself to some extent a moral quality. Among intelligent and genuinely serious workers there is a certain aversion for those who make literature out of the subject they are engaged on, those who use it for self-display. Robert and I had not been at the Lycée or at the Sorbonne together, but we had attended, independently, certain courses of lectures by the same teachers, and I remember the smile he had for the ones who—as happens sometimes when a man is giving a remarkable series of lectures —tried to pass themselves off as geniuses by giving their theories an ambitious name. We only had to mention them for Robert to burst out laughing. Our personal and instinctive preference was, naturally, not for the Cottards or the Brichots, but we had nevertheless a certain respect for any man with a really thorough knowledge of Greek or medicine who did not for that reason think himself entitled to behave as a charlatan. I have said that, if in the past all Mamma's actions had as their basis the sentiment that she would have given her life for her mother, she had yet never formulated this sentiment to herself, and that in any case it would have seemed to her not merely unnecessary and ridiculous but shocking and shameful to express it to others; in the same way it was impossible for me to imagine on the lips of Saint-Loup—talking to me about his equipment, the things he had to do in Paris, our chances of victory, the weakness of the Russian army, how England would act—it is impossible for me to imagine on his lips even the most eloquent phrase that even the most deservedly popular minister might have addressed to a wildly cheering Chamber of Deputies. I cannot, however, say that in this negativeness which checked him from expressing the noble sentiments that he felt he was not to some extent influenced by the "Guermantes spirit," of which we have seen so many similar instances in Swann. For, if I found him more Saint-Loup than anything else, he was, nevertheless, also Guermantes, and consequently, among the numerous motives which animated his courage, there were some which did not exist for his friends of Doncières, those young men enamoured of their profession with whom I had dined night after night and of whom so many went to their deaths at the battle of the Marne or elsewhere, leading their men into action.

As for the young socialists who were at Doncières when I was there but whom I did not get to know because they did not belong to the same set as Saint-Loup, they could see now for themselves that the officers of that set were by no means "nobs," with the implications of haughty pride and base self-indulgence which the "plebs," the ex-ranker officers, the freemasons attached to that word. And conversely, this same patriotism was found by the officers of aristocratic birth to exist in full measure among the socialists whom I had heard them accuse, while I was at Doncières at the height of the Dreyfus case, of being "men without a country." The patriotism of the military caste, as sincere and profound as any other, had assumed a fixed form which the members of that caste regarded as sacrosanct and which they were infuriated to see heaped with "opprobrium," but the radical-socialists, who were independent and to some extent unconscious patriots without any fixed patriotic religion, had failed to perceive the profound and living reality that lay behind what they thought were empty and malignant formulas.

No doubt, like his friends, Saint-Loup had formed the habit of inwardly cultivating, as the truest part of himself, the search for and the elaboration of the best possible manoeuvres which would lead to the greatest strategic and tactical successes, so that, for him as for them, the life of the body was something relatively unimportant which could easily be sacrificed to this inner part of the self, the real vital core within them, around which their personal existence was of value only as a protective outer skin. But in Saint-Loup's courage there were also more individual elements, and amongst these it would have been easy to recognise the generosity which in its early days had constituted the charm of our friendship, and also the hereditary vice which had later awoken from dormancy in him and which, at the particular intellectual level which he had not been able to transcend, caused him not only to admire courage but to exaggerate his horror of effeminacy into a sort of intoxication at any contact with virility. He derived, chastely no doubt, from spending days and nights in the open with Senegalese soldiers who might at any moment be called upon to sacrifice their lives, a cerebral gratification of desire into which there entered a vigorous contempt for "little scented gentlemen" and which, however contrary it might seem, was not so very different from that which he had obtained from the cocaine in

which he had indulged excessively at Tansonville and of which
heroism—one drug taking the place of another—was now
curing him. And another essential part of his courage was that
double habit of courtesy which, on the one hand, caused him
to bestow praise on others but where he himself was concerned
made him content to do what had to be done and say nothing
about it—the opposite of a Bloch, who had said to him just
now "You—of course you'd funk it," and yet was doing nothing
himself—and on the other hand impelled him to hold as of no
value the things that he himself possessed, his fortune, his rank,
and even his life, so that he was ready to give them away: in a
word, the true nobility of his nature.

"Are we in for a long war?" I said to Saint-Loup. "No, I
believe it will be very short," he replied. But here, as always,
his arguments were bookish. "Bearing in mind the prophecies
of Moltke, re-read," he said to me, as if I had already read it,
"the decree of the 28th October, 1913, about the command of
large formations; you will see that the replacement of peace-
time reserves has not been organised or even foreseen, a thing
which the authorities could not have failed to do if the war
were likely to be a long one." It seemed to me that the decree
in question could be interpreted not as a proof that the war
would be short, but as a failure on the part of its authors to
foresee that it would be long, and what kind of war it would be,
the truth being that they suspected neither the appalling wastage
of material of every kind that would take place in a war of stable
fronts nor the interdependence of different theatres of operations.

Outside the limits of homosexuality, among the men who
are most opposed by nature to homosexuality, there exists a
certain conventional idea of virility, which the homosexual
finding at his disposal proceeds, unless he is a man of unusual
intelligence, to distort. This ideal—to be seen in certain professional soldiers, certain diplomats—can be singularly exasperating. In its crudest form it is simply the gruffness of the
man with the heart of gold who is determined not to show his
emotions, the man who at the moment of parting from a friend
who may very possibly be killed has a secret desire to weep,
which no one suspects because he conceals it beneath a mounting anger which culminates, at the actual moment of farewell,

in a sort of explosion: "Well, now, damn it! Shake hands with me, you old ruffian, and take this purse, it's no use to me, don't be an idiot." The diplomat, the officer, the man who believes that nothing counts except a great task in the service of the nation but who was fond nevertheless of the "poor boy" in his legation or his battalion who has died from a fever or a bullet exhibits the same taste for virility in a form that is less clumsy, and more sophisticated, but at bottom just as odious. He does not want to mourn for the "poor boy," he knows that soon he and everybody else will forget him, just as a kind-hearted surgeon soon forgets though for a whole evening after some little girl has died in an epidemic he feels a grief which he does not express. Should the diplomat be a writer and describe this death, he will not say that he felt grief. No—first from "manly reticence," secondly from that skilled artistry which arouses emotion by dissembling it. With one of his colleagues he will watch by the side of the dying man. Not for one second will they say that they feel grief. They will talk of the affairs of the legation or the battalion and their remarks may be even more terse than usual: "B. said to me: 'Don't forget we have the general's inspection tomorrow. See to it that your men are well turned out.' Habitually so gentle, he spoke in a sharper tone than usual. I noticed that he avoided looking at me, I too felt myself to be overwrought." And the reader understands that this "sharp tone" is simply grief showing itself in men who do not want to appear to feel grief, an attitude which might be ridiculous and nothing more but is in fact also sinister and ugly, because it is the manner of feeling grief of those who think that grief does not matter, that there are more serious things in life than being parted from one's friends, etc., so that when someone dies they give the same impression of falsehood, of nothingness, as on New Year's Day the gentleman who hands you a present of *marrons glacés* and just manages to say with a titter: "With the compliments of the season!"

To conclude the narrative of the officer or the diplomat watching at the deathbed, his head covered because the wounded or sick man has been carried out of doors, the moment comes when all is over. "'I must go back and get my kit cleaned,' I thought. But I do not know why, at the moment when the doctor let go the pulse, simultaneously B. and I, without any sign passing between us—the sun was beating vertically down, perhaps we were hot standing beside the bed—removed our caps." And the reader knows that it was not because of the heat of the sun but from emotion in the presence of the majesty of death that the two virile men, on whose lips the words grief and affection were almost unknown, now bared their heads.

In homosexuals like Saint-Loup the ideal of virility is not the same, but it is just as conventional and just as false. The falsehood consists for them in the fact that they do not want to admit to themselves that physical desire lies at the root of the sentiments to which they ascribe another origin. M. de Charlus had detested effeminacy. Saint-Loup admired the courage of young men, the intoxication of cavalry charges, the intellectual and moral nobility of friendships between man and man, entirely pure friendships, in which each is prepared to sacrifice his life for the other. War, which turns capital cities, where only women remain, into an abomination for homosexuals, is at the same time a story of passionate adventure for homosexuals if they are intelligent enough to concoct dream figures, and not intelligent enough to see through them, to recognise their origin, to pass judgment on themselves. So that while some young men were enlisting simply in order to join in the latest sport—in the spirit in which one year everybody plays diabolo —for Saint-Loup, on the other hand, war was the very ideal which he imagined himself to be pursuing in his desires (which were in fact much more concrete but were clouded by ideology), an ideal which he could serve in common with those whom he preferred to all others, in a purely masculine order of chivalry, far from women, where he would be able to risk his life to save his orderly and die inspiring a fanatical love in his men. And thus, though there were many elements in his courage, the fact that he was a great nobleman was one of them, and another, in an unrecognisable and idealised form, was M. de Charlus's dogma that it was of the essence of a man to have nothing effeminate about him. But just as in philosophy and in art ideas acquire their value only from the manner in which they are developed, and two analogous ones may differ greatly according to whether they have been expounded by Xenophon or by Plato, so, while I recognise how much, in his behaviour, the one has in common with the other, I admire Saint-Loup, for asking to be sent to the point of greatest danger, infinitely more than I do M. de Charlus for refusing to wear brightly coloured cravats.

I spoke to Saint-Loup about my friend the manager of the Grand Hotel at Balbec, who, it seems, had alleged that at the beginning of the war there had been in certain French regiments defections, which he called "defectuosities," and had accused what he called the "Prussian militariat" of having provoked them; he had even, at one moment, believed in a simultaneous landing by the Japanese, the Germans and the Cossacks at Rivebelle as threatening Balbec, and had said that the only thing to do was to "decramp." He also thought that the departure of the government and the ministries for Bordeaux was a little precipitous and declared that they were wrong to "decramp" so soon. This German-hater would say with a laugh of his brother: "He is in the trenches, twenty-five yards away from the Boches," until the authorities, having discovered that he was a "Boche" himself, put him in a concentration camp. "Talking of Balbec, do you remember the lift-boy who used to be in the hotel?" said Saint-Loup as he left me, in a tone suggesting that he did not quite know who the lift-boy was and was counting on me for enlightenment. "He is joining up and has written to ask me to get him into the flying corps." No doubt the young man was tired of going up in the captive cage of the lift, and the heights of the staircase of the Grand Hotel no longer sufficed him. He was going to "get his stripes" otherwise than by becoming a hall-porter, for our destiny is not always what we had supposed. "I shall certainly support his application," said Saint-Loup. "I was saying to Gilberte only this morning, we shall never have enough aeroplanes. It is aeroplanes that will enable us to see what the enemy is preparing, and aeroplanes that will rob him of the greatest advantage of attack, which is surprise. The best army will be, perhaps, the army with the best eyes. And tell me about poor Françoise, has she succeeded in getting her nephew exempted?" But Françoise, who for a long time had been making every effort to achieve this, and who, when she had been offered through the Guermantes a recommendation to General de Saint-Joseph, had replied in a tone of despair: "Oh no, that would be quite useless, there's nothing to be got from that old fogy, he's as bad as could be, he's patriotic," Françoise, as soon as there had been any question of war, however much she suffered at the thought of it, was of the opinion that it would be wrong to abandon the "poor Russians" since we were "allianced" to them. The butler, who in any case was convinced that the war would only last ten days and would end in a brilliant victory for France, would not have dared, for fear of being contradicted by events —and would not even have had enough imagination—to predict a long and indecisive war. But from this complete and immediate victory he tried at least to extract in advance the maximum of suffering for Françoise. "Things may well take an ugly turn, because it seems there are lots who refuse to march, boys of sixteen in floods of tears." And this habit of telling her disagreeable things in order to "vex" her was what he called "putting the wind up her," "making her flesh creep," "giving her a bit of a jolt." "Sixteen, Holy Mother!" said Françoise, and then suspicious for a moment: "But they said they only took them at twenty, at sixteen they're still children." "Naturally the papers have been told to say nothing about it. Anyhow, the young men, one and all, will be off to the front and there won't be many to come back. In one way it'll do some good. A good blood-letting, you know, is useful now and again. And then it will help trade. And I promise you, if there are any lads who are a bit soft and think twice about it, they'll be for the firing-squad, bang, bang, bang! I suppose it has to be done. And then, the officers, what does it matter to them? They get paid their screw, that's all they ask." Françoise turned so pale whenever one of these conversations took place that we were afraid the butler might cause her death from a heart attack.

But this did not mean that she had lost her old faults. Whenever I had a visit from a girl, however much her old servant's legs might be hurting her, if I happened to leave my room for a moment there she was at the top of a step-ladder in the dressing-room, searching, so she said, for some overcoat of mine to see if the moths had got into it, but really in

order to eavesdrop. And she still, in spite of all my complaints, had her insidious manner of asking questions in an
indirect way, the phrase she now used for this purpose being
"because of course." Not daring to say to me: "Has this lady
her own house?" she would say, her eyes timidly raised like the
eyes of a good dog: "Because of course this lady has her own
house . . .," avoiding a blatant interrogative not so much in
order to be polite as in order not to seem too curious. Then
again, as the servants whom we love most—and this is particularly true when they have almost ceased to give us either the
service or the respect proper to their employment—remain,
unfortunately, servants and only make more clear the limitations of their caste, which we ourselves would like to do away
with, when they imagine that they are penetrating most successfully into ours, Françoise often addressed me ("to get under my
skin," as the butler would have said) with odd remarks which
someone of my own class could not have made: for instance,
with a joy carefully dissembled but as profound as if she had
detected a serious illness, she would say to me if I was hot and
there were beads of sweat which I had not noticed on my forehead: "But you're absolutely dripping," looking astonished as
though this were some strange phenomenon and at the same
time with that little smile of contempt with which we greet an
impropriety ("Are you going out? You know you've forgotten
to put your tie on") and also with the anxious voice which we
assume when we want to alarm someone about the state of his
health. One would have thought that no one in the world had
ever been "dripping" before. Finally, she no longer spoke good
French as she had in the past. For in her humility, in her
affectionate admiration for people infinitely inferior to herself,
she had come to adopt their ugly habits of speech. Her daughter
having complained to me about her and having used the words
(I do not know where she had heard them): "She's always
finding fault with me because I don't shut the doors properly
and *patatipatali* and *patatatipatala*," Françoise clearly thought
that only her imperfect education had deprived her until now
of this beautiful idiom. And from those lips which I had once
seen bloom with the purest French I heard several times a day:
"And *patatipatali* and *patatatipatala*." It is indeed curious how

little not only the expressions but also the ideas of an individual vary. The butler, having got into the habit of declaring that M. Poincaré was a wicked man, not because he was after money but because he had been absolutely determined to have a war, repeated this seven or eight times a day to an audience which was always the same and always just as interested. Not a word was altered, not a gesture or an intonation. The performance only lasted two minutes, but it was unvarying, like that of an actor. And his faulty French was quite as much to blame as that of her daughter for corrupting the language of Françoise. He thought that what M. de Rambuteau had been so annoyed one day to hear the Duc de Guermantes call "Rambuteau shelters" were called "rinals." No doubt in his childhood he had failed to hear the "u" and had never realised his mistake, so every time he used the word—and he used it frequently—he mispronounced it. Françoise, embarrassed at first, ended by using it too, and liked to complain that the same sort of thing did not exist for women as well as for men. But as a result of her humility and her admiration for the butler she never said "urinals" but—with a slight concession to customary usage— "arinals."

She no longer slept, no longer ate. Every day she insisted on the bulletins, of which she understood nothing, being read to her by the butler who understood hardly more of them than she did, and in whom the desire to torment Françoise was frequently dominated by a patriotic cheerfulness: he would say, with a sympathetic laugh, referring to the Germans: "Things are hotting up for them, it won't be long before old Joffre puts salt on the tail of the comet." Françoise had no idea what comet he was alluding to, but this strengthened her conviction that the phrase was one of those amiable and original extravagances to which a well-bred person is required by the laws of courtesy to respond good-humouredly, so gaily shrugging her shoulders as if to say: "He's always the same," she tempered her tears with a smile. At least she was happy that her new butcher's boy, who in spite of his trade was anything but courageous (his first job nevertheless had been in the slaughterhouses), was not old enough to be called up. Otherwise she would have been quite capable of going to see the Minister of War to get him exempted.

The butler had not enough imagination to realise that the bulletins were not excellent and that we were not advancing towards Berlin, since he kept reading: "We have repulsed with heavy enemy losses, etc.," actions which he celebrated as a succession of victories. I, however, was alarmed at the speed with which the scene of these victories was approaching Paris, and was astonished that even the butler, having seen in one bulletin that an engagement had taken place near Lens, was not disturbed to read in the newspaper next day that it had been followed by satisfactory operations in the neighbourhood of Jouy-le-Vicomte, of which the approaches were firmly in our hands. Now the butler knew Jouy-le-Vicomte well by name, for it was not so very far from Combray. But we read the newspapers as we love, blindfold. We do not try to understand the facts. We listen to the soothing words of the editor as we listen to the words of our mistress. We are "beaten and happy" because we believe that we are not beaten but victorious.

I had, in any case, not remained long in Paris but had returned very soon to my sanatorium. Although in principle the doctor's treatment consisted in isolation, I had been allowed to receive, at different times, a letter from Gilberte and a letter from Robert. Gilberte wrote (this was in about September 1914) that, however much she would have liked to stay in Paris in order to get news of Robert more easily, the constant Taube raids on the city had caused her such alarm, particularly for her little girl, that she had fled by the last train to leave for Combray, that the train had not even got as far as Combray, and that it was only thanks to a peasant's cart, on which she had had an appalling journey of ten hours, that she had succeeded in reaching Tansonville! "And there, imagine what awaited your old friend," she concluded her letter. "I had left Paris to escape from the German aeroplanes, supposing that at Tansonville I should be perfectly safe. Before I had been there two days you will never imagine what turned up: the Germans, who having defeated our troops near La Fère were overrunning the district. A German headquarters staff, with a regiment just behind it, presented itself at the gates of Tansonville and I was obliged to take them in, and not a hope of getting away, no more trains, nothing." Whether the German staff had really

behaved well, or whether it was right to detect in Gilberte's
letter the influence, by contagion, of the spirit of those Guermantes who were of Bavarian stock and related to the highest
aristocracy of Germany, she was lavish in her praise of the
perfect breeding of the staff-officers, and even of the soldiers
who had only asked her for "permission to pick a few of the
forget-me-nots growing near the pond," a good breeding
which she contrasted with the disorderly violence of the fleeing
French troops, who had pillaged everything as they crossed the
property before the arrival of the German generals. In any case,
if Gilberte's letter was in some ways impregnated with the
spirit of the Guermantes—others would say the spirit of Jewish
internationalism, which would probably have been unfair to
her, as we shall see—the letter which I received several months
later from Robert was, on the other hand, much more Saint-
Loup than Guermantes and reflected in addition all the liberal
culture which he had acquired. Altogether, it was a delightful
letter. Unfortunately, he did not talk about strategy as he had
in our conversations at Doncières, nor did he tell me to what
extent he considered that the war confirmed or invalidated the
principles which he had then expounded to me. All he said was
that since 1914 there had in reality been a series of wars, the
lessons of each one influencing the conduct of the one that
followed. For example, the theory of the "break-through" had
been supplemented by a new idea: that it was necessary, before
breaking through, for the ground held by the enemy to be
completely devastated by the artillery. But then it had been
found that on the contrary this devastation made it impossible
for the infantry and the artillery to advance over ground in
which thousands of shell-holes created as many obstacles.
"War," he wrote, "does not escape the laws of our old friend
Hegel. It is in a state of perpetual becoming." This was meagre
in comparison with what I should have liked to know. But
what was still more annoying was that he was forbidden to
mention the names of generals. And anyhow, according to the
little that the newspapers told me, the generals as to whom at
Doncières I had been so eager to know which among them
would prove most effective and courageous in a war, were not
the ones who were now in command. Geslin de Bourgogne,

Galliffet, Négrier were dead. Pau had retired from active service almost at the beginning of the war. Of Joffre, of Foch, of Castelnau, of Pétain, Robert and I had never spoken. "My dear boy," he wrote, "I recognise that expressions like *passeront pas* and *on les aura* are not agreeable; they have always set my teeth on edge as much as *poilu* and the rest, and of course it is tiresome to be composing an epic with words and phrases which are—worse than an error of grammar or of taste—an appalling contradiction in terms, a vulgar affectation and pretension of the kind that you and I abominate, as bad as when people think it clever to say 'coco' instead of 'cocaine.' But if you could see everybody here, particularly the men of the humbler classes, working men and small shopkeepers, who did not suspect what heroism they concealed within them and might have died in their beds without suspecting it—if you could see them running under fire to help a comrade or carry off a wounded officer and then, when they have been hit themselves, smiling a few moments before they die because the medical officer has told them that the trench has been recaptured from the Germans, I assure you, my dear boy, it gives you a magnificent idea of the French people, makes you begin to understand those great periods in history which seemed to us a little extraordinary when we learned about them as students. The epic is so magnificent that you would find, as I do, that words no longer matter. Cannot Rodin or Maillol create a masterpiece from some hideous raw material which he transforms out of all recognition? At the touch of such greatness, the word *poilu* has for me become something of which I no more feel that it may originally have contained an allusion or a joke than one does, for instance, when one reads about the *chouans*. But I do know that *poilu* is already waiting for great poets, like other words, 'deluge,' or 'Christ,' or 'barbarians,' which were already instinct with greatness before Hugo, Vigny and the rest made use of them. As I say, the people, the working men, are the best of all, but everybody is splendid. Poor young Vaugoubert, the ambassador's son, was wounded seven times before he was killed, and each time he came back from a raid without having 'copped it' he seemed to want to apologise and to say that it was not his fault. He was a charming creature. We had become close friends.

His parents were given permission to come to the funeral, on condition that they did not wear mourning and only stayed five minutes because of the shelling. The mother, a great horse of a woman whom I dare say you know, was no doubt deeply moved but showed no sign of it. But the poor father was in such a state that I assure you that I, who am now totally unfeeling because I have got used to seeing the head of the comrade who is talking to me suddenly ripped open by a landmine or even severed from its trunk, I could not contain myself when I saw the collapse of poor Vaugoubert, who was an utter wreck. The general tried to tell him that it was for France, that his son had behaved like a hero, but it was no use, this only redoubled the sobs of the poor man, who could not tear himself away from his son's body. The fact is, and that is why we must learn to put up with *passeront pas*, it is men like these, like my poor valet, like Vaugoubert, who have prevented the Germans from 'passing.' You may think we are not advancing much, but logic is beside the point, there is a secret inner feeling which tells an army that it is victorious—or a dying man that he is finished. We know that victory will be ours and we are determined that it shall be, so that we can dictate a just peace, I don't mean 'just' simply for ourselves, but truly just, just to the French and just to the Germans."

I do not wish to imply that the "calamity" had raised Saint-Loup's intelligence to a new level. But just as soldier heroes with commonplace and trivial minds, if they happened to write poems during their convalescence, placed themselves, in order to describe the war, at the level not of events, which in themselves are nothing, but of the commonplace aesthetic whose rules they had obeyed in the past, and talked, as they would have ten years earlier, of the "blood-stained dawn," "victory's tremulous wings," and so on, so Saint-Loup, by nature much more intelligent and much more of an artist, remained intelligent and an artist, and it was with the greatest good taste that he now recorded for my benefit the observations of landscape which he made if he had to halt at the edge of a marshy forest, very much as he would have done if he had been out duck-shooting. To help me to understand certain contrasts of light and shade which had been "the enchantment of his morning," he alluded in his letter to certain paintings which we both loved and was not afraid to cite a passage of Romain Rolland, or even of Nietzsche, with the independent spirit of the man at the front, who had not the civilian's terror of pronouncing a German name, and also—in thus quoting an enemy—with a touch of coquetry, like Colonel du Paty de Clam who, waiting among the witnesses at Zola's trial and chancing to pass Pierre Quillard, the violently Dreyfusard poet, whom he did not even know, recited some lines from his symbolist play, *La Fille aux Mains Coupées*. In the same way if Saint-Loup had occasion in a letter to mention a song by Schumann, he never gave any but the German title, nor did he use any periphrasis to tell me that, when at dawn on the edge of the forest he had heard the first twittering of a bird, his rapture had been as great as though he had been addressed by the bird in that "sublime *Siegfried*" which he so looked forward to hearing after the war.

And now, on my second return to Paris, I had received, the day after I arrived, another letter from Gilberte, who had doubtless forgotten, or at least forgotten what she had said in, the letter I have described, for in this new letter her departure from Paris at the end of 1914 was presented retrospectively in a very different light. "Perhaps you do not know, my dear friend," she wrote, "that I have now been at Tansonville for nearly two years. I arrived here at the same time as the Germans. Everybody had tried to prevent me from leaving. I was regarded as mad. 'What,' my friends said, 'here you are safe in Paris and you want to go off to enemy-occupied territory just when everybody is trying to escape from it.' I was quite aware of the strength of this argument. But I can't help it; if I have one good quality, it is that I am not a coward, or perhaps I should say, I am loyal, and when I knew that my beloved Tansonville was threatened, I simply could not leave our old bailiff to defend it alone. I felt that my place was by his side. And it was, in fact, thanks to this decision that I succeeded in more or less saving the house when all the other big houses in the neighbourhood, abandoned by their panic-stricken owners, were almost without exception reduced to ruins—and in saving not only the house but the valuable collections too, which dear Papa was so fond of." In a word, Gilberte was now persuaded that she had gone to Tansonville not, as she had written to me in 1914, in order to escape from the Germans and be in a safe place, but on the contrary in order to face them and defend her house against them. They had, as a matter of fact, not stayed long at Tansonville, but since then the house had witnessed a constant coming and going of soldiers, far more intensive than that marching up and down the streets of Combray which had once drawn tears to the eyes of Françoise, and Gilberte had not ceased, as she said, this time quite truly, to live the life of the front. So that the newspapers spoke with the highest praise of her wonderful conduct and there was some question of giving her a decoration. The end of the letter was absolutely truthful. "You have no idea what this war is like, my dear friend, or of the importance that a road, a bridge, a height can assume. How often have I thought of you, of those walks of ours together which you made so delightful, through all this now ravaged countryside, where vast battles are fought to gain possession of some path, some slope which you once loved and which we so often explored together! Probably, like me, you did not imagine that obscure Roussainville and boring Méséglise, where our letters used to be brought from and where the doctor was once fetched when you were ill, would ever be famous places. Well, my dear friend, they have become for ever a part of history, with the same claim to glory as Austerlitz or Valmy. The battle of Méséglise lasted for more than eight months; the Germans lost in it more than six hundred thousand men, they destroyed Méséglise, but they did not capture it. As for the short cut up the hill which you were so fond of and which we used to call the hawthorn path, where you claim that as a small child you fell in love with me (whereas I assure you in all truthfulness it was I who was in love with you), I cannot tell you how important it has become. The huge field of corn upon which it emerges is the famous Hill 307, which you must have seen mentioned again and again in the bulletins. The French blew up the little bridge over the Vivonne which you said did not remind you of your childhood as much as you would have wished, and the Germans have thrown other bridges across the river. For a year and a half they held one half of Combray and the French the other."

The day after I received this letter, that is to say two days before the evening on which, as I have described, I made my way through the dark streets with the sound of my footsteps in my ears and all these memories revolving in my mind, Saint-Loup, arrived from the front and very shortly to return to it, had come to see me for a few moments only, and the mere announcement of his visit had violently moved me. Françoise had been tempted to fling herself upon him, in the hope that he could obtain an exemption for the timid butcher's boy whose class was to be called up the following year. But she had been checked, without my saying anything to her, by the thought of the futility of this endeavour, for the timid slaughterer of animals had moved to another butcher's some time previously. And whether our butcher's wife was afraid of losing our custom, or whether she was telling the truth, she declared to Françoise that she did not know where the boy—who, in any case, would never make a good butcher—was working. Françoise had searched everywhere. But Paris is large and butcher's shops are numerous, and although she had visited a great many she had never succeeded in finding the timid and blood-stained young man.

When Saint-Loup came into my room I had gone up to him with that feeling of shyness, that impression of something supernatural which was in fact induced by all soldiers on leave and which one feels when one enters the presence of a man suffering from a fatal disease, who still, nevertheless, leaves his bed, gets dressed, goes for walks. It seemed (above all it had seemed at first, for upon those who had not lived, as I had, at a distance from Paris, there had descended Habit, which cuts off from things which we have witnessed a number of times the root of profound impression and of thought which gives them their real meaning), it seemed almost that there was something cruel in these leaves granted to the men at the front. When they first came on leave, one said to oneself: "They will refuse to go back, they will desert." And indeed they came not merely from places which seemed to us unreal, because we had only heard them spoken of in the newspapers and could not conceive how a man was able to take part in these titanic battles and emerge with nothing worse than a bruise on his shoulder; it was from the shores of death, whither they would soon return, that they came to spend a few moments in our midst, incomprehensible to us, filling us with tenderness and terror and a feeling of mystery, like phantoms whom we summon from the dead, who appear to us for a second, whom we dare not question, and who could, in any case, only reply: "You cannot possibly imagine." For it is extraordinary how, in the survivors of battle, which is what soldiers on leave are, or in living men hypnotised or dead men summoned by a medium, the only effect of contact with mystery is to increase, if that be possible, the insignificance of the things people say. Such were my feelings when I greeted Robert, who still had a scar on his forehead, more august and more mysterious in my eyes than the imprint left upon the earth by a giant's foot. And I had not dared to put a single question to him and he had made only the simplest remarks to me. Remarks that even differed very little from the ones he might have made before the war, as though people, in spite of the war, continued to be what they were; the tone of conversation was the same, only the subject-matter differed— and even that not so very much!

I guessed from what he told me that in the army he had found opportunities which had gradually made him forget that Morel had behaved as badly towards him as towards his uncle. However, he still felt a great affection for him and was seized by sudden cravings to see him again, though he always postponed doing this. I thought it kinder to Gilberte not to inform Robert that to find Morel he had only to pay a call on Mme Verdurin.

I remarked apologetically to Robert how little one felt the war in Paris. He replied that even in Paris it was sometimes "pretty extraordinary." This was an allusion to a Zeppelin raid which had taken place the previous night and he went on to ask me if I had had a good view, very much as in the old days he might have questioned me about some spectacle of great aesthetic beauty. At the front, I could see, there might be a sort of bravado in saying: "Isn't it marvellous? What a pink! And that pale green!" when at any moment you might be killed, but here in Paris there could be no question of any such pose in Saint-Loup's way of speaking about an insignificant raid, which had in fact looked marvellously beautiful from our balcony when the silence of the night was broken by a display which was more than a display because it was real, with fireworks that were purposeful and protective and bugle-calls that did more than summon on parade. I spoke of the beauty of the aeroplanes climbing up into the night. "And perhaps they are even more beautiful when they come down," he said. "I grant that it is a magnificent moment when they climb, when they fly off in *constellation*, in obedience to laws as precise as those that govern the constellations of the stars—for what seems to you a mere spectacle is the rallying of the squadrons, then the orders they receive, their departure in pursuit, etc. But don't you prefer the moment, when, just as you have got used to thinking of them as stars, they break away to pursue an enemy or to return to the ground after the all-clear, the moment of *apocalypse*, when even the stars are hurled from their courses? And then the sirens, could they have been more Wagnerian, and what could be more appropriate as a salute to the arrival of the Germans? —it might have been the national anthem, with the Crown Prince and the Princesses in the imperial box, the *Wacht am Rhein*; one had to ask oneself whether they were indeed pilots and not Valkyries who were sailing upwards." He seemed to be delighted with this comparison of the pilots to Valkyries, and went on to explain it on purely musical grounds: "That's it, the music of the sirens was a 'Ride of the Valkyries'! There's no doubt about it, the Germans have to arrive before you can hear Wagner in Paris." In some ways the simile was not misleading. The town from being a black shapeless mass seemed suddenly to rise out of the abyss and the night into the luminous sky, where one after another the pilots soared upwards in answer to the heart-rending appeal of the sirens, while with a movement slower but more insidious, more alarming—for their gaze made one think of the object, still invisible but perhaps already very near, which it sought—the searchlights strayed ceaselessly to and fro, scenting the enemy, encircling him with their beams until the moment when the aeroplanes should be unleashed to bound after him in pursuit and seize him. And squadron after squadron, each pilot, as he soared thus above the town, itself now transported into the sky, resembled indeed a Valkyrie. Meanwhile on ground-level, at the height of the houses, there were also scraps of illumination, and I told Saint-Loup that, if he had been at home the previous evening, he might, while contemplating the apocalypse in the sky, at the same time have watched on the ground (as in El Greco's *Burial of Count Orgaz*, in which the two planes are distinct and parallel) a first-rate farce acted by characters in night attire, whose famous names merited a report to some successor of that Ferrari whose society paragraphs had so often provided amusement to the two of us, Saint-Loup and myself, that we used also to amuse ourselves by inventing imaginary ones. And that is what we did once more on the day I am describing, just as though we were not in the middle of a war, although our theme, the fear of the Zeppelins, was very much a "war" one: "Seen about town: the Duchesse de Guermantes magnificent in a night-dress, the Duc de Guermantes indescribable in pink pyjamas and a bath-robe, etc."

"I am sure," he said, "that in all the large hotels you would have seen American Jewesses in their night-dresses, hugging to their ravaged bosoms the pearl necklaces which will enable them to marry a ruined duke. The Ritz, on these evenings when the Zeppelins are overhead, must look like Feydeau's *Hôtel du libre échange*."

"Do you remember," I said to him, "our conversations at Doncières?"

"Ah! those were the days! What a gulf separates us from them! Will those happy times ever re-emerge

> *du gouffre interdit à nos sondes,*
> *Comme montent au ciel les soleils rajeunis*
> *Après s'être lavés au fond des mers profondes?*"[43]

"But don't let's think about those conversations simply in order to remind ourselves how delightful they were," I said. "I was attempting in them to arrive at a certain kind of truth. What do you think, does the present war, which has thrown everything into confusion—and most of all, so you say, the idea of war—does it render null and void what you used to tell me then about the types of battle, the battles of Napoleon, for instance, which would be imitated in the wars of the future?"

"Not in the least," he said, "the Napoleonic battle still exists, particularly in this war, since Hindenburg is imbued with the Napoleonic spirit. His rapid movements of troops, his feints—the device, for instance, of leaving only a small covering force opposite one of his enemies, while he falls with his united strength upon the other (Napoleon in 1814) or the other stratagem of pressing home a diversion so strongly that the enemy is compelled to keep up his strength on a front which is not the really important one (for example, Hindenburg's feint before Warsaw, which tricked the Russians into concentrating their resistance there and brought about their defeat at the Masurian Lakes)—his tactical withdrawals, analogous to those with which Austerlitz, Arcola, Eckmühl began, everything in Hindenburg is Napoleonic, and we haven't seen the end of him. I must add that if, when we are no longer together, you try, as the war proceeds, to interpret its events, you should not rely too exclusively on this particular aspect of Hindenburg to reveal to you the meaning of what he is doing and the key to what he is about to do. A general is like a writer who sets out to write a certain play, a certain book, and then the book itself, with the unexpected potentialities which it reveals here, the impassable obstacles which it presents there, makes him deviate to an enormous degree from his preconceived plan. You know, for instance, that a diversion should only be made against a position which is itself of considerable importance; well, suppose the diversion succeeds beyond all expectation, while the principal operation results in a deadlock: the diversion may then become the principal operation. But there is one type of Napoleonic battle which I am waiting to see Hindenburg attempt, and that is the one which consists in driving a wedge between two allies, in this case the English and ourselves."

I have said that the war had not altered the stature of Saint-Loup's intelligence, but I ought to add that this intelligence, developing in accordance with laws in which heredity counted for much, had acquired a brilliancy which I had never seen in him before. What a difference between the fair-haired boy who had once been run after by smart women or women who were hoping to become smart, and the voluble talker, the theorist who never stopped juggling with words! In another generation, grafted upon another stock, like an actor re-interpreting a part played years ago by Bressant or Delaunay, he was like a successor—pink, fair and golden, whereas the other had been half and half very dark and quite white—of M. de Charlus. It was true that he did not agree with his uncle about the war, since he had ranged himself with that section of the aristocracy which put France above everything else in the world while M. de Charlus was at heart defeatist, but nevertheless he could demonstrate to anyone who had not seen the "creator of the part" what a success could be made in the role of verbal acrobat.

"It seems that Hindenburg is a revelation," I said to him.

"An old revelation," he retorted instantly, "or a future revolution. Instead of being soft with the enemy, we should have supported Mangin in his offensive, then we might have smashed Austria and Germany and europeanised Turkey instead of balkanising France."

"But soon we shall have the help of the United States," I said.

"Meanwhile, I see here only the spectacle of the disunited states. Why refuse to make more generous concessions to Italy for fear of dechristianising France?"

"How shocked your uncle Charlus would be to hear you!" I said. "The fact is that you would be only too pleased to give the Pope another slap in the face, while your uncle is in despair at the thought of the damage that may be done to the throne of Franz Josef. And in this he says that he is in the tradition of Talleyrand and the Congress of Vienna."

"The age of the Congress of Vienna is dead and gone," he replied; "the old secret diplomacy must be replaced by concrete diplomacy. My uncle is at heart an impenitent monarchist, who can be made to swallow carps like Mme Molé and scamps like Arthur Meyer provided that both carps and scamps are à la Chambord. He so hates the tricolour flag that I believe he would rather serve under the duster of the Red Bonnet, which he would take in good faith for the white flag of the Monarchists."

Admittedly, this was mere play on words and Saint-Loup was far from possessing the sometimes profound originality of his uncle. But he was as affable and agreeable in character as the other was jealous and suspicious. And he had remained charming and pink as he had been at Balbec beneath his shock of golden hair. And one family characteristic he possessed in at least as high a degree as his uncle, that attitude of mind of the Faubourg Saint-Germain which remains deeply implanted in the men of that world who fancy that they have most completely detached themselves from it, the attitude which combines respect for clever men who are not of good family (a respect which flourishes, truly, only among the aristocracy, and which makes revolutions so unjust) with a fatuous satisfaction with themselves. Through this mixture of humility and pride, of acquired intellectual curiosity and innate authority, M. de Charlus and Saint-Loup, by different paths, and with opposite opinions, had become, with the gap of a generation between them, intellectuals whom every new idea interested and talkers whom no interruption could silence. So that a not very intelligent person might, according to the humour in which he happened to be, have found both the one and the other either dazzling or insufferably tedious.

I had gone on walking as I turned over in my mind this recent meeting with Saint-Loup and had come a long way out of my way; I was almost at the Pont des Invalides. The lamps (there were very few of them, on account of the Gothas) had already been lit, a little too early because "the clocks had been put forward" a little too early, when the night still came rather quickly, the time having been "changed" once and for all for the whole of the summer just as a central heating system is turned on or off once and for all on a fixed date; and above the city with its nocturnal illumination, in one whole quarter of the sky—the sky that knew nothing of summer time and winter time and did not deign to recognise that half past eight had become half past nine—in one whole quarter of the sky from which the blue had not vanished there was still a little daylight. Over that whole portion of the city which is dominated by the towers of the Trocadéro the sky looked like a vast sea the colour of turquoise, from which gradually there emerged, as it ebbed, a whole line of little black rocks, which might even have been nothing more than a row of fishermen's nets and which were in fact small clouds—a sea at that moment the colour of turquoise, sweeping along with it, without their noticing, the whole human race in the wake of the vast revolution of the earth, that earth upon which they are mad enough to continue their own revolutions, their futile wars, like the war which at this very moment was staining France crimson with blood. But if one looked for long at the sky, this lazy, too beautiful sky which did not condescend to change its time-table and above the city, where the lamps had been lit, indolently prolonged its lingering day in these bluish tones, one was seized with giddiness: it was no longer a flat expanse of sea but a vertically stepped series of blue glaciers. And the towers of the Trocadéro which seemed so near to the turquoise steps must, one realised, be infinitely remote from them, like the twin towers of certain towns in Switzerland which at a distance one would suppose to be near neighbours of the upper mountain slopes.

I retraced my steps, but once I had left the Pont des Invalides there was no longer any trace of day in the sky and there was practically no light in the town, so that stumbling here and there against dust-bins and mistaking one direction for another, I found to my surprise that, by mechanically following a labyrinth of dark streets, I had arrived on the boulevards. There, the impression of an oriental vision which I had had earlier in the evening came to me again, and I thought too of the Paris of an earlier age, not now so much of the Paris of the Directory as of the Paris of 1815. As in 1815 there was a march past of allied troops in the most variegated uniforms; and among them, the Africans in their red divided skirts, the Indians in their white turbans were enough to transform for me this Paris through which I was walking into a whole imaginary exotic city, an oriental scene which was at once meticulously accurate with respect to the costumes and the colours of the faces and arbitrarily fanciful when it came to the background, just as out of the town in which he lived Carpaccio made a Jerusalem or a Constantinople by assembling in its streets a crowd whose marvellous motley was not more rich in colour than that of the crowd around me. Walking close behind two zouaves who seemed hardly to be aware of him, I noticed a tall,

stout man in a soft felt hat and a long heavy overcoat, to whose
purplish face I hesitated whether I should give the name of an
actor or a painter, both equally notorious for innumerable
sodomist scandals. I was certain in any case that I was not
acquainted with him; so I was not a little surprised, when his
glance met mine, to see that he appeared to be embarrassed and
deliberately stopped and came towards me like a man who
wants to prove that you have not surprised him in an occupation which he would prefer to remain secret. For a second I
asked myself who it was that was greeting me: it was M. de
Charlus. One may say that for him the evolution of his malady
or the revolution of his vice had reached the extreme point at
which the tiny original personality of the individual, the
specific qualities he has inherited from his ancestors, are entirely
eclipsed by the transit across them of some generic defect or
malady which is their satellite. M. de Charlus had travelled as
far as was possible from himself, or rather he was himself but
so perfectly masked by what he had become, by what belonged
not to him alone but to many other inverts, that for a moment
I had taken him for some other invert, as he walked behind
these zouaves down the wide pavement of the boulevard, for
some other invert who was not M. de Charlus, who was not a
great nobleman or a man of imagination and intelligence, and
whose only point of resemblance to the Baron was the look that
was common to them all, which in him now, at least until one
had taken the trouble to observe him carefully, concealed every
other quality from view.

Thus it was that, having intended to call on Mme Verdurin,
I had met M. de Charlus. And certainly I should not now as in
the past have found him in her drawing-room; their quarrel had
grown steadily more bitter and Mme Verdurin even took
advantage of present events to discredit him further. Having
said for years that she found him stale, finished, more out of
date in his professed audacities than the dullest philistine, she
now summed up this condemnation in such a way as to make
him an object of general aversion, by saying that he was
"pre-war." The war had set between him and the present, so
the little clan declared, an abyss which left him stranded in
the deadest of dead pasts. Besides—and this was addressed

particularly to the political world, which was less well informed —she made him out to be just as "bogus," just as much an "outsider" from the point of view of social position as from that of intellectual merit. "He sees nobody, nobody invites him," she said to M. Bontemps, whom she easily convinced. Anyhow, there was an element of truth in these words. The position of M. de Charlus had changed. Caring less and less about society, having quarrelled, because of his cantankerous character, and having disdained, because of his high opinion of his own social importance, to reconcile himself with most of the men and women who were the flower of society, he lived in a relative isolation which was not caused, like that in which Mme de Villeparisis had died, by the fact that the aristocracy had ostracised him, but which nevertheless in the eyes of the public for two reasons appeared to be worse. The bad reputation which M. de Charlus was now known to enjoy made ill-informed people think that it was for this reason that his company was not sought by people whom in fact he himself made a point of refusing to see. So that what was really the result of his own spleen seemed to be due to the contempt of the people upon whom he vented it. Secondly, Mme de Villeparisis had had one great bulwark: the family. But between his family and himself M. de Charlus had multiplied quarrels. His family in any case—particularly the "old Faubourg" side of it, the Courvoisier side—had always seemed to him uninteresting. And he was far from suspecting, he who, from a spirit of opposition to the Courvoisiers, had made such audacious advances in the direction of art, that the feature in him which would most have interested, for example, a Bergotte, was precisely his kinship with the whole of this old Faubourg which he despised, and the descriptions he could have given of the almost provincial life led by his female cousins, in that district bounded by the Rue de la Chaise and the Place du Palais-Bourbon in one direction and the Rue Garancière in the other.

And then, considering the question from another point of view, less transcendent and more practical, Mme Verdurin affected to believe that he was not French. "What is his nationality exactly, isn't he an Austrian?" M. Verdurin would ask innocently. "No, certainly not," Comtesse Molé would reply, her first reaction being one rather of common sense than of resentment. "No, he is Prussian," the Mistress would say. "Yes, I know what I am talking about, he has told us countless times that he is a hereditary member of the Prussian Chamber of Peers and a Durchlaucht." "Still, the Queen of Naples told me . . ." "You know she is a dreadful spy," screamed Mme Verdurin, who had not forgotten how the fallen sovereign had behaved in her house one evening. "I know—there is absolutely no question about it—that that is what she has been living on. If we had a more energetic government, she and her kind ought all to be in a concentration camp. I mean it! In any case, you will be wise not to receive visits from that charming set, because I know that the Minister of the Interior has his eye on them, your house would be watched. I have not the slightest doubt that for two years Charlus did nothing but spy on us all." And thinking probably that there might be some doubt as to the interest that the German government would show in even the most circumstantial reports on the organisation of the little clan, Mme Verdurin went on, with a mild and perspicacious air, like someone who knows that the value of what she is saying will only seem greater if she does not raise her voice: "Let me tell you, I said to my husband the very first day: 'I don't like the way that man wormed his way into my house. There's something shady here.' We had a property which stood on very high ground, looking down over a bay. Quite obviously he had been sent by the Germans to prepare a base for their submarines. There were many things which surprised me at the time, but which I understand now. For instance, at first, he would not come by the train with my other regular guests. I was so kind as to offer to put him up in the house. But no, he preferred to stay at Doncières, which was swarming with soldiers. All this stank to high heaven of espionage."

About the first of the charges brought against the Baron de Charlus, that of being out of date, fashionable people were only too ready to agree with Mme Verdurin. In this they were ungrateful, for M. de Charlus was to some extent their poet, the man who had been able to extract from the world of fashion a sort of essential poetry, which had in it elements of history, of beauty, of the picturesque, of the comic, of frivolous elegance. But people in society, incapable of understanding this poetry, did not see that it existed in their own lives; they sought for it rather elsewhere, and placed on an infinitely higher peak than M. de Charlus men who were much stupider than him but who professed to despise "society" and liked instead to hold forth about sociology and political economy. M. de Charlus, for instance, took a delight in repeating unconsciously characteristic remarks of the Duchesse de Montmorency and in describing the studied charm of her clothes, and spoke of her as if she were something sublime, but this merely gave him the reputation of an utter idiot in the eyes of the sort of society women who thought that the Duchesse de Montmorency was an uninteresting fool, and that dresses are made to be worn but without the wearer appearing to give them a moment's attention, and who meanwhile gave proof of their own superior intelligence by running to hear lectures at the Sorbonne or Deschanel speak in the Chamber.

In short, people in society had become disillusioned about M. de Charlus, not from having penetrated too far, but without having penetrated at all, his rare intellectual merit. The reason why he was found to be "pre-war," old-fashioned, was that the people who are least capable of judging the worth of individuals are also the most inclined to adopt fashion as a principle by which to classify them; they have not exhausted, or even grazed the surface of, the talented men of one generation, when suddenly they are obliged to condemn them all *en bloc*, for here is a new generation with a new label which will be no better understood than its predecessor.

As for the second accusation, that of being pro-German, fashionable people because of their dislike of extreme views tended to reject it, but the charge had an unwearying and particularly cruel advocate in Morel, who, having managed to retain in the newspapers and even in society the position which M. de Charlus had first achieved for him and then tried equally hard, but without success, to undermine, pursued the Baron with a hatred that was all the more infamous since, whatever the precise relations between them had been, Morel had seen and known the side of him that he concealed from so many people: his profound kindness. M. de Charlus had shown such generosity, such delicacy towards the violinist, had been so scrupulous about fulfilling his promises to him that, when Charlie left him, the image of the Baron that remained in his mind was not at all that of a vicious man (at most he regarded the Baron's vice as a disease) but of a man with loftier ideas than any other he had ever known, a man with extraordinary capacity for feeling, a kind of saint. So little disposed was he to deny this that even after the quarrel he would say in all sincerity to a young man's parents: "You can trust your son to him, he can only have the most excellent influence on him." And so when by his articles in the papers he tried to make him suffer, it was in his imagination not vice but virtue incarnate that he was scourging. Not long before the war there had begun to appear short "pieces," transparent to the so-called initiated, in which M. de Charlus was most monstrously libelled. Of one, entitled *The Misfortunes of a Dowager ending in -us or the Latter Days of the Baroness*, Mme Verdurin had bought fifty copies in order to be able to lend it to her acquaintances and M. Verdurin, declaring that Voltaire himself did not write better, took to reading it aloud. Since the war the tone of these pieces had changed. Not only was the Baron's inversion denounced, but also his alleged Germanic nationality: "Frau Bosch," "Frau von den Bosch" were the names habitually used to designate M. de Charlus. A little composition of a poetic nature appeared with the title—borrowed from some of Beethoven's dances—*Une Allemande*. Finally two short stories, *The Uncle from America and the Aunt from Frankfurt* and *The Jolly Sailor*, read in proof in the little clan, had delighted even Brichot himself, who exclaimed: "So long as the most high and puissant Lady Censorship does not blue-pencil us!" The articles themselves were cleverer than their ridiculous titles. Their style derived from Bergotte but in a way which, for the reason that follows, perhaps no one but myself perceived. Bergotte's *writings* had had not the slightest influence on Morel. The fertilisation had been effected in a most unusual way, which I record here only because of its rarity. I have described earlier the very special manner which Bergotte had, when he spoke, of choosing and pronouncing his words. Morel, who for a long time had been in the habit of meeting him at the Saint-Loups, had at that period done "imitations" of him, in which he exactly mimicked his voice, using just the words that Bergotte would have chosen. And now that he had taken to writing, Morel used to transcribe passages of "spoken Bergotte," but without first transposing them in the way which would have turned them into "written Bergotte." Not many people having known Bergotte as a talker, the tone of his voice was not recognised, since it differed from the style of his pen. This oral fertilisation is so rare that I have thought it worth mentioning here. The flowers that it produces are, however, always sterile.

Morel, who was in the Press Office, found after a while, his French blood boiling in his veins like the juice of the grapes of Combray, that there was not much to be said for being in an office during the war, and he ended by joining up, although Mme Verdurin did everything she could to persuade him to stay in Paris. Admittedly she was indignant that M. de Cambremer, at his age, should be on the general staff, and of every man who did not come to her parties she would say: "I can't think where the wretch has managed to hide himself all this time," and if someone assured her that the wretch had been in the front line since the first day, would reply, without any scruple about telling a lie or perhaps just because she was so used to getting things wrong: "Not at all, he has not budged from Paris, he's doing something about as dangerous as taking a Minister for walks, I know what I am talking about, you can take my word for it, I was told by someone who has seen him at it"; but where the faithful were concerned it was not the same thing, she did not want to let them go off to the war, and looked upon it as a great "bore" that caused them to defect. And so she pulled every possible string to keep them in Paris, which would give her the double pleasure of having them at her dinner-parties and at the same time, before they arrived or after they left, making scathing remarks about their inactivity. However, the faithful in each case had to be made to agree to the soft job she had found for them and she was bitterly distressed to find Morel recalcitrant; in vain had she said to him over and over again: "But don't you see, you are *serving* in your office, and serving more than you would be at the front. The important thing is to be useful, to be really part of the war, to be in it. There are those who are in it, and there are the shirkers. Now you, you're in it, you have nothing to worry about, everybody knows this, nobody's going to throw stones at you." In the same way, in different circumstances, although men were at that time not so scarce and she had not been, as she was now, obliged to have a preponderance of women, if a man had lost his mother she had not hesitated to try and convince him that there was no objection to his continuing to come to her parties. "Grief is worn in the heart. If you wanted to go to a dance" (she never gave one) "I should be the first to advise you not to do it, but here, at my little Wednesdays, or in a box, nobody will be in the least surprised. We all know you have had a great grief. . . ." Men were scarcer now and mourning more frequent though no longer needed to prevent men from going to parties, the war itself having put a stop to that. Mme Verdurin hung on to the survivors. She tried to persuade them that they were more useful to France if they stayed in Paris, just as in the past she would have assured them that the deceased would have been happy to see them enjoying themselves. In spite of all her efforts she did not have many men; perhaps sometimes she regretted that between herself and M. de Charlus she had brought about a rupture which left no hope of a return to their former relations.

But, if M. de Charlus and Mme Verdurin no longer saw one another, they continued nevertheless, Mme Verdurin to entertain, M. de Charlus to pursue his pleasures, very much as if nothing had changed. A few little differences there were, but of no great importance: Cottard, for instance, was now to be seen at Mme Verdurin's parties in a colonel's uniform which might have come out of Loti's *Ile du Rêve* (it bore a striking resemblance to that of a Haitian admiral and at the same time, with its broad sky-blue ribbon, recalled that of the "Children of Mary"); and M. de Charlus, finding himself in a town from which the mature men for whom he had hitherto had a taste had vanished, followed the example of those Frenchmen who, after being womanisers in France, go to live in the colonies: from necessity he had acquired first the habit of and then the taste for little boys.

But the first of these newly acquired characteristics was not in evidence for long: Cottard soon died "facing the enemy," so the newspapers said, though he had never left Paris—but it was true that he had exerted himself too much for his age—and he was soon followed by M. Verdurin, whose death caused grief to one person only and that, strangely enough, was Elstir. For whereas I had been able to study Elstir's work from a point of view which was to some extent objective, the painter himself, particularly as he grew older, linked it superstitiously to the society which had provided him with models and which had also, after thus transforming itself within him through the alchemy of impressions into a work of art, given him his public, his spectators. More and more he was inclined to believe materialistically that a not inconsiderable part of beauty is inherent in objects, and just as, at the beginning, he had adored in Mme Elstir the archetype of that rather heavy beauty which he had pursued and caressed in his paintings and in tapestries, so now in the death of M. Verdurin he saw the disappearance of one of the last relics of the social frame-work, the perishable frame-work—as swift to crumble away as the very fashions in clothes which form part of it—which supports an art and certifies its authenticity, and he was as saddened and distressed by this event as a painter of *fêtes galantes* might have been by the Revolution which destroyed the elegances of the eighteenth century, or Renoir by the disappearance of Montmartre and the Moulin de la Galette; but more than this, with M. Verdurin he saw disappear the eyes, the brain, which had had the truest vision of his painting, in which, in the form of a cherished memory, his painting was to some extent inherent. No doubt young men had come along who also loved painting, but painting of another kind; they had not, like Swann, like M. Verdurin, received lessons in taste from Whistler, lessons in truth from Monet, lessons which alone would have qualified them to judge Elstir with justice. So the death of M. Verdurin left Elstir feeling lonelier, although they had not been on speaking terms for a great many years: it was for him as though a little of the beauty of his own work had been eclipsed, since there had perished a little of the universe's sum total of awareness of its special beauty.

As for the change which had overtaken the pleasures of M. de Charlus, this was no more than intermittent: by maintaining a correspondence with numerous soldiers at the front, who sometimes came on leave, he did not altogether lack the company of mature men.

At the time when I believed what people said I should have been tempted, hearing Germany, or later Bulgaria or Greece, protest their pacific intentions, to give credence to these statements. But since life with Albertine and with Françoise had accustomed me to suspect in them thoughts and projects which they did not disclose, I now allowed no pronouncement, however specious, of William II or Ferdinand of Bulgaria or Constantine of Greece, to deceive my instinct and prevent it from divining what each one of them was plotting. Of course my quarrels with Françoise or with Albertine had been merely private quarrels, of interest only to the life of that little cell, endowed with mind, that a human being is. But just as there are animal bodies and human bodies, each one of which is an assemblage of cells as large in relation to a single cell as Mont Blanc, so there exist huge organised accumulations of individuals which are called nations: their life does no more than repeat on a larger scale the lives of their constituent cells, and anybody who is incapable of comprehending the mystery, the reactions, the laws of these smaller lives, will only make futile pronouncements when he talks about struggles between nations. But if he is master of the psychology of individuals, then these colossal masses of conglomerated individuals will assume in his eyes, as they confront one another, a beauty more potent than that of the struggle which arises from a mere conflict between two characters; and they will seem to him as huge as the body of a tall man would seem to the infusoria of which more than ten thousand would be required to fill the space of a cubic millimetre. So it had been now for some time past: the huge irregular geometric figure France, filled to its perimeter with millions of little polygons of various shapes, and another figure filled with an even greater number of polygons, Germany, had been engaged in one of these quarrels. And considered from this point of view, the body Germany and the body France, and the allied and enemy bodies, were behaving to some extent like individuals, and the blows which they were exchanging were governed by the innumerable rules of that art of boxing which Saint-Loup had expounded to me; but since, even if one chose to consider them as individuals, they were at the same time giant assemblages of individuals, the quarrel took on immense and magnificent forms, like the surge of a million-waved ocean which tries to shatter an age-old line of cliffs, or like gigantic glaciers which with their slow destructive oscillations attempt to break down the frame of mountains which surrounds them. But in spite of this, life continued almost unchanged for many of these who have played a part in this story, and not least for M. de Charlus and the Verdurins, just as if the Germans had not been as near them as they were, since the threat of a danger momentarily checked but permanently alive leaves us absolutely indifferent if we do not picture it to ourselves. People, as they go about their pleasures, do not normally stop to think that, if certain moderating and weakening influences should happen to be suspended, the proliferation of infusoria would attain its maximum theoretical rate and after a very few days the organisms that might have been contained in a cubic millimetre would take a leap of many millions of miles and become a mass a million times greater than the sun, having in the process destroyed all our oxygen and all the substances on which we live, so that there would exist neither humanity nor animals nor earth, nor do they reflect that an irremediable and by no means improbable catastrophe may one day be generated in the ether by the incessant and frenzied activity which lies behind the apparent immutability of the sun; they busy themselves with their own affairs without thinking about these two worlds, the one too small, the other too large for us to be aware of the cosmic menaces with which they envelop us.

So it was that the Verdurins gave dinner-parties (then, after a time, Mme Verdurin gave them alone, for M. Verdurin died) and M. de Charlus went about his pleasures and hardly ever stopped to reflect that the Germans—immobilised, it is true, by a bloody barrier perpetually renewed—were only an hour by car from Paris. The Verdurins, one would imagine, did think about this fact, since they had a political salon in which every evening they and their friends discussed the situation not only of the armies but of the fleets. They thought certainly of these hecatombs of regiments annihilated and passengers swallowed by the waves; but there is a law of inverse proportion which multiplies to such an extent anything that concerns our own welfare and divides by such a formidable figure anything that does not concern it, that the death of unknown millions is felt by us as the most insignificant of sensations, hardly even as disagreeable as a draught. Mme Verdurin, who suffered even more from her headaches now that she could no longer get croissants to dip in her breakfast coffee, had eventually obtained a prescription from Cottard permitting her to have them specially made in a certain restaurant of which we have spoken. This had been almost as difficult to wangle with the authorities as the appointment of a general. The first of these special croissants arrived on the morning on which the newspapers reported the sinking of the *Lusitania*. As she dipped it in her coffee and gave a series of little flicks to her newspaper with one hand so as to make it stay open without her having to remove her other hand from the cup, "How horrible!" she said. "This is something more horrible than the most terrible stage tragedy." But the death of all these drowned people must have been reduced a thousand million times before it impinged upon her, for even as, with her mouth full, she made these distressful observations, the expression which spread over her face, brought there (one must suppose) by the savour of that so precious remedy against headaches, the croissant, was in fact one of satisfaction and pleasure.

As for M. de Charlus, his case was a little different, but worse even, for he went beyond not passionately desiring the victory of France: he desired rather, without admitting it to himself, that Germany should, if not triumph, at least not be crushed as everybody hoped she would be. And for this attitude of his the reason was, again, that the great collections of individuals called nations themselves behave to some extent like individuals. The logic that governs them is an inner logic, wrought and perpetually re-wrought by passions, like that of men and women at grips with one another in an amorous or domestic quarrel, the quarrel of a son with his father, or of a cook with her mistress, or a wife with her husband. The party who is in the wrong believes nevertheless that he is in the right—this was so in the case of Germany—and the party who is in the right sometimes supports his excellent cause with arguments which appear to him to be irrefutable only because they answer to his own passionate feelings. In these quarrels of individuals, the surest way of being convinced of the excellence of the cause of one party or the other is actually to be that party: a spectator will never to the same extent give his unqualified approval. Now within a nation the individual, if he is truly part of the nation, is simply a cell of the nation-individual. It is ridiculous to talk about the power of propaganda. Had the French been told that they were going to be beaten, no single Frenchman would have given way to despair any more than he would if he had been told that he was going to be killed by the Berthas. The real propaganda is what—if we are genuinely a living member of a nation—we tell ourselves because we have hope, hope being a symbol of a nation's instinct of self-preservation. To remain blind to the unjustness of the cause of the individual "Germany," to recognise at every moment the justness of the cause of the individual "France," the surest way was not for a German to be without judgment, or for a Frenchman to possess it, it was, both for the one and for the other, to be possessed of patriotism. M. de Charlus, who had rare moral qualities, who was susceptible to pity, generous, capable of affection and devotion, on the other hand for various reasons—among which the fact that his mother had been a Duchess of Bavaria may have played a part—did not have patriotism. He belonged, in consequence, no more to the body France than to the body Germany. Even I myself, had I been devoid of patriotism, had I not felt myself to be one of the cells of the body France, could not, it seems to me, have judged the quarrel in the manner in which I might have judged it in the past. In my adolescence, when I believed word for word what I was told, I should no doubt, hearing the German government protest its good faith, have been tempted to believe that this good faith existed; but I had learned long ago that our thoughts do not always accord with our words; not only had I one day, from the window on the staircase, discovered a Charlus whose existence I did not suspect; more important, in Françoise, and then, alas, in Albertine, I had seen the formation of opinions and projects so contrary to their words that now, even in the role of mere spectator, I should not have allowed any of the pronouncements of the Kaiser or the King of Bulgaria to deceive my instinct. But after all I can only conjecture what I might have done if I had not been an actor in the drama, if I had not been a part of the actor France in the same way as, in my quarrels with Albertine, my sad gaze and the choking feeling in my throat had been parts of the individual "me" who was passionately interested in my cause; I could not arrive at detachment. That of M. de Charlus was complete. And given that he was nothing more than a spectator, and that, without being genuinely French, he was living in France, there was every reason why he was likely to be pro-German. In the first place, he was very intelligent and in every country fools form the bulk of the population; no doubt, had he lived in Germany, the German fools defending foolishly and with passion an unjust cause would have irritated him; but living as he did in France, the French fools defending foolishly and with passion a just cause irritated him quite as much. The logic of passion, even if it happens to be in the service of the best possible cause, is never irrefutable for the man who is not himself passionate. Inevitably M. de Charlus with his critical intelligence seized on every weak point in the reasoning of the patriots. And then the complacency that an imbecile derives from the excellence of his cause, and the certainty of victory, are particularly irritating phenomena. Inevitably M. de Charlus was irritated by the triumphant optimism of people who did not know Germany and Germany's strength as he did, who believed every month in a crushing victory for the following month, and at the end of the year were as confident in making fresh predictions as though they had never, with equal confidence, made false ones —which they had, however, forgotten, saying, if they were reminded of them, that it "was not the same thing." (Yet M. de Charlus, profound as his intelligence was in some directions, would perhaps have failed to see that this same reasoning applies also to new developments in art and that when a conservative critic of Manet replies to the argument "But people said the same thing about Delacroix" by saying "This is not the same thing," it is the critic who is wrong.)

Then again, M. de Charlus was merciful, the idea of a vanquished opponent caused him pain, he was always on the side of the underdog, he refrained from reading the law reports in the newspapers in order not to have to suffer in his own flesh from the anguish of the condemned man and from the impossibility of assassinating the judge, the executioner and the crowd that stood gloating to see "justice done." He was certain in any case that France could not be defeated now, and he knew on the other hand that the Germans were suffering from famine and would be obliged sooner or later to surrender unconditionally. And this idea too he more particularly disliked owing to the fact that he was living in France. His memories of Germany, after all, were distant, while the French who spoke of the crushing defeat of Germany with a joy which disgusted him, were people whose defects were known to him, their personalities unsympathetic. In such circumstances we pity more readily those whom we do not know, whom we merely imagine, than those who are near us in the vulgarity of daily life, unless—once again—we ourselves altogether are the latter and form but one flesh with them, since patriotism accomplishes the miracle that we are "for" our country as in a quarrel between lovers we are "for" ourself. So the war for M. de Charlus was an extraordinarily fertile breeding-ground of those hatreds he was prone to which sprang up in him in a moment and had only a very brief existence, during which, however, he would have abandoned himself to any violent impulse. When he read the newspapers, the air of triumph with which day after day the journalists portrayed Germany as beaten—"the Beast at bay, reduced to impotence"—while the contrary was only too true, their cheerful and savage stupidity, intoxicated him with rage. The newspapers at this moment were written partly by well-known men who found this a means of "serving their country again," men such as Brichot, Norpois, Morel even, and Legrandin. M. de Charlus longed to meet them, to heap the most bitter sarcasms on their heads. Always particularly well-informed about sexual irregularities, he knew of some in individuals who, believing their own to be unknown, complacently denounced such things in the sovereigns of the "Empires of Prey," in Wagner, etc. He had a furious desire to find himself face to face with these men, to rub their noses in their own vice before the eyes of the world and leave them, these insulters of a vanquished opponent, dishonoured and gasping for breath.

Finally, M. de Charlus had also more particular reasons for being the pro-German that he was. One was that, himself a man of the world, he had lived much among men of the world, honourable men and men of honour, men who will not shake hands with a scoundrel; he was acquainted with their scruples and also with their hardness, he knew them to be insensible to the tears of a man whom they expel from a club or with whom they refuse to fight a duel, even if this act of "moral hygiene" should bring about the death of the black sheep's mother. And so in spite of himself, whatever admiration he might feel for England and for the admirable fashion in which she entered the war, nevertheless this impeccable England—incapable of false-hood but forbidding the entry of wheat and milk into Germany —was in his eyes a little too much the man of honour among nations, the professional second in duels, the arbiter of affairs of honour, whereas his experience told him that men of a different type, men with a blot upon their reputation, scoun-drels like some of Dostoievsky's characters, may in fact be better—though I have never been able to understand why he identified the Germans with such men, since falsehood and deceit are in themselves no evidence of a kind heart, which is something the Germans do not seem to have displayed.

One last trait must be mentioned to complete this account of the pro-Germanism of M. de Charlus: he owed it, and through a most bizarre reaction, to his "Charlusism." He found the Germans very ugly, perhaps because they were rather too near to his own blood—it was the Moroccans he was mad about and even more the Anglo-Saxons, in whom he saw living statues by Phidias. Now in him pleasure was not unaccompanied by a certain idea of cruelty of which I had not at that time learned the full force: the man whom he loved appeared to him in the guise of a delightful torturer. In taking sides against the Germans he would have seemed to himself to be acting as he did only in his hours of physical pleasure, to be acting, that is, in a manner contrary to his merciful nature, fired with passion for seductive evil and helping to crush virtuous ugliness. This too was his reaction at the time of the murder of Rasputin, an event which, happening as it did at a supper-party *à la* Dostoievsky, caused a general surprise because people found in it so strong a Russian flavour (this impression would have been stronger still had the public not been unaware of aspects of the case that were perfectly well known to M. de Charlus), because life disappoints us so often that in the end we come to believe that literature bears no relation to it and we are therefore astounded when we see the precious ideas that literature has revealed to us display themselves, without fear of getting spoiled, gratuitously, naturally, in the midst of daily life, when we see, for instance, that a supper-party and a murder taking place in Russia actually have something Russian about them.

The war dragged on indefinitely and those who, already several years earlier, had reported on good authority that negotiations for peace had been begun, even specifying the clauses of the treaty, were at no pains now, when they talked to you, to make excuses for their previous false rumours. They had forgotten them and were ready in all sincerity to propagate others which they would forget just as quickly. It was the period when there were constant Gotha raids; the air was perpetually buzzing with the vibration, vigilant and sonorous, of French aeroplanes. But at intervals the siren rang out like the heart-rending scream of a Valkyrie—the only German music to have been heard since the war—until the moment when the fire-engines announced that the alert was over, while beside them, like an invisible street-urchin, the all-clear at regular intervals commented on the good news and hurled its cry of joy into the air.

M. de Charlus was astonished to see that even men like Brichot who before the war had been militarists and had never ceased to reproach France for her lack of military preparedness, were not content now with reproaching Germany for the excesses of her militarism, but criticised even her admiration of the army. No doubt they expressed quite different opinions the moment there was any danger of slowing down the war against Germany and continued, for the best reasons, to denounce the pacifists of their own country. But Brichot, for example, having consented, in spite of his bad eyesight, to discuss in some lectures certain works which had appeared in neutral countries, gave high praise to a novel by a Swiss author which has a satirical passage about two children—militarists in embryo— who are struck dumb with symbolic admiration at the sight of a dragoon. There were other reasons why this satire was likely to displease M. de Charlus, who deemed that a dragoon may be a very beautiful thing. But above all he did not understand Brichot's admiration, if not for the book, which the Baron had not read, at least for its spirit, so different from that which had animated Brichot himself before the war. At that time every-thing that a military man did was right, even the irregularities of General de Boisdeffre, the disguises and strategies of Colonel du Paty de Clam, the forgery of Colonel Henry. By what extraordinary *volte-face* (it was in reality merely another aspect of the same very noble passion, the passion of patriotism, which, from being militarist when it was struggling against Dreyfusism, a phenomenon of anti-militarist tendencies, had been obliged itself to become almost anti-militarist now that the struggle was against the hyper-militaristic Germany) had Brichot come to exclaim: "O marvellous and mighty spectacle, fit lure for the youth of an age that is all brutality and knows only the cult of force: a dragoon! Well may one judge what the base soldiery will be of a generation reared in the cult of these manifestations of brutal force." He approved too of another Swiss novelist Spitteler, who "wanting something to oppose to the hideous conception of the sword supreme, symbolically exiled to the depths of the forests the dreamy figure, mocked, calumniated and solitary, whom he calls the Mad Student, his delightful incarnation of the sweetness—unfashionable, alas, and perhaps soon to be forgotten if the grim rule of the ancient god of the militarists is not destroyed—the adorable sweetness of the times of peace."

"Now tell me," M. de Charlus said to me, "you know Cottard and you know Cambremer. Every time I see them, they talk to me about Germany's extraordinary lack of psychology. But between ourselves, do you think that hitherto they have cared much about psychology, or that even now they are

capable of giving proof of any skill in it? You may be sure that
I am not exaggerating. Even if he is talking about the very
greatest of Germans, about Nietzsche or Goethe himself, you
will hear Cottard say: 'with the habitual lack of psychology
which characterises the Teutonic race.' Naturally there are
things in the war which cause me greater distress, but you must
admit that this is exasperating. Norpois is more intelligent, I
grant you, although since the beginning of the war he has on
every occasion been wrong. But what can one say of these
articles of Brichot's which are arousing universal enthusiasm?
You know as well as I do, my dear sir, the merit of the man,
whom I like very much, even after the schism which has cut me
off from his little church, which causes me to see much less of
him than I used to. But still I have a certain regard for this
usher with the gift of the gab and a vast amount of learning,
and I confess that it is very touching that at his age—and with
his strength failing as it clearly has been failing for some years
past—he should, as he says, have taken it upon himself to
'serve again.' But after all, good intentions are one thing, talent
is another, and talent Brichot has never had. I admit that I share
his admiration for certain elements of greatness in the present
war. I do, however, find it strange that a blind partisan of
antiquity like Brichot, who could not be sarcastic enough about
Zola for discovering more poetry in a working-class home or a
coal-mine than in the famous palaces of history, or about
Goncourt for elevating Diderot above Homer and Watteau
above Raphael, should incessantly drum into our ears that
Thermopylae and even Austerlitz were nothing compared with
Vauquois. And this time, to make things worse, the public,
after resisting the modernists of literature and art, is falling into
line with the modernists of war, because it is an accepted
fashion to think like this and also because little minds are
crushed, not by the beauty, but by the hugeness of the action.
It is true that *kolossal* is now spelt only with a *k*, but fundamentally, what people are bowing the knee to is simply the
colossal. By the way, talking of Brichot, have you seen Morel?
I am told that he wants to see me again. He has only to take the
first step. I am the older man, it is not for me to make a move."

Unfortunately only the next day, to anticipate a little, M. de

Charlus found himself face to face with Morel in the street; Morel, to inflame his jealousy, took him by the arm and told him various tales which were more or less true and which agitated M. de Charlus and made him feel that he needed Morel's presence beside him that evening, that he must not be allowed to go anywhere else. But the young man, catching sight of a friend of his own age, quickly said good-bye to M. de Charlus, whereupon the Baron, hoping that this threat —which naturally he would never carry out—would make Morel stay, said to him: "Take care, I shall have my revenge." Morel, however, went off with a laugh, giving his astonished young friend a pat on the neck and putting his arm round his waist.

No doubt the remark which M. de Charlus had just made to me about Morel's wishing to see him was proof of the extent to which love—and that of the Baron must have been extremely persistent—while it makes a man more imaginative and quicker to take offence, at the same time makes him more credulous and less proud. But when M. de Charlus went on: "He is a boy who is mad about women and thinks of nothing else," his words were truer than he thought. He said this out of vanity and out of love, so that people might suppose that Morel's attachment for him had not been followed by others of the same nature. I certainly did not believe a word of it, I who had seen, what M. de Charlus still did not know, that for fifty francs Morel had once given himself to the Prince de Guermantes for a night. And if, when he saw M. de Charlus pass in the street, Morel (except on the days when, from a need to confess, he would bump into him so as to have the opportunity to say gloomily: "Oh! I am so sorry, I quite see that I have behaved disgustingly towards you"), seated at a café on the pavement with his friends, would join them in noisily pointing at the Baron and making those little clucking noises with which people make fun of an old invert, I was persuaded that this was in order to conceal his own activities; and that likewise, taken aside by the Baron, each one of these public accusers would have done everything that the latter asked of him. I was wrong. If a strange development had brought to inversion—and in every social class—men like Saint-Loup who were furthest removed from it, a movement in the contrary direction had detached from these practices those in whom they were most habitual. In some the change had been wrought by tardy religious scruples, by the emotion they had felt when certain scandals had blazed into publicity, or by the fear of non-existent diseases in which they had been made to believe either, in all sincerity, by a relative who was often a concierge or a valet, or, disingenuously, by a jealous lover who had thought that in this way he would keep for himself alone a young man whom he had, on the contrary, succeeded in detaching from himself as well as from others. Thus it was that the former lift-boy at Balbec would now not have accepted for silver or gold propositions which he had come to regard as no less criminal than treasonable proposals from the enemy. In the case of Morel, however, his refusal of all offers without exception, as to which M. de Charlus had unwittingly spoken a truth which at one and the same time justified his illusions and destroyed his hopes, came from the fact that, two years after having left M. de Charlus, he had fallen in love with a woman whom he now lived with and that she, having the stronger will of the two, had managed to impose upon him an absolute fidelity. So that Morel, who at the time when M. de Charlus was showering so much money upon him had given a night to the Prince de Guermantes for fifty francs, would not now have accepted from the latter or from any other man whatever an offer even of fifty thousand. In default of honour and disinterestedness, his mistress had inculcated in him some concern for people's opinion of him, which made him not averse even to demonstrating, with a show of bravado, that all the money in the world meant nothing to him when it was offered on certain conditions. Thus, in the flowering of the human species, the interplay of different psychological laws operates always in such a way as to compensate for any process that might otherwise, in one direction or the other, through plethora or through rarefaction, bring about the annihilation of the race. And thus, too, among flowers, a similar wisdom, which Darwin was the first to bring to light, governs their different modes of fertilisation, opposing them successively one to another.

"It is a strange thing," M. de Charlus went on, in the shrill little voice with which he sometimes spoke, "I hear people who appear to be perfectly happy all day long and enjoy their cocktails, declare that they will never last until the end of the war, that their hearts won't stand it, that they can think of nothing else, that they will quite suddenly die. And what is really extraordinary is that this does in fact happen! How curious it is! Is it a question of nourishment, because the food they eat is all so badly prepared now, or is it because, to prove their zeal, they harness themselves to tasks which are useless but destroy the mode of life which kept them alive? Anyhow, I have noted an astonishing number of these strange premature deaths, premature at least from the point of view of the deceased. I forget what I was saying to you just now, about Norpois and his admiration for the war. But what a singular manner he has of writing about it! First, have you noticed the pullulation in his articles of new expressions which, when they have eventually worn themselves out by dint of being employed day after day —for really Norpois is indefatigable, I think the death of my aunt Villeparisis must have given him a second youth—are immediately replaced by yet other commonplaces? In the old days I remember you used to amuse yourself by recording the fashionable phrases which appeared and had their vogue and then disappeared: 'he who sows the wind reaps the whirlwind'; 'the dogs bark, the caravan passes'; 'give me sound politics and I will give you sound finances, as Baron Louis said'; 'these are symptoms which it would be exaggerated to take tragically but wise to take seriously'; 'to work for the King of Prussia' (this last, inevitably, has come to life again). Well, since then, alas, how many of the species have I seen born and die! We have had 'the scrap of paper,' 'the Empires of Prey,' 'the famous *Kultur* which consists in massacring defenceless women and children,' 'victory belongs, as the Japanese say, to the side which can hold out for a quarter of an hour longer than the other,' 'the Germano-Turanians,' 'scientific barbarism,' 'if we want to win the war, as Mr Lloyd George has forcibly said' (but that's out of date now), and 'the fighting spirit of our troops' or 'the pluck of our troops.' Even the syntax of the excellent Norpois has undergone in consequence of the war as profound a change as the baking of bread or the speed of transport. Have you observed that the excellent man, wanting to proclaim his own desires as a truth on the verge of being realised, does not dare nevertheless to employ the future pure and simple, since this would run the risk of being contradicted by events, but has adopted as a sign of future tense the verb 'to know'?"

I confessed to M. de Charlus that I did not quite understand what he meant.

(I ought to mention here that the Duc de Guermantes by no means shared his brother's pessimism. Furthermore, he was as anglophile as M. de Charlus was anglophobe. And he regarded M. Caillaux as a traitor who deserved a thousand times over to be shot. When his brother asked him for proofs of the man's treason, M. de Guermantes replied that, if we were only to convict people who signed a statement saying "I am a traitor," the crime of treason would never be punished. But in case I should not have occasion to return to the subject, I will mention also that a few years later, when Caillaux was on trial, the Duc de Guermantes, animated as he was by the purest anti-Caillautism, met an English military attaché and his wife, an exceptionally cultivated couple with whom he made friends, as he had done at the time of the Dreyfus case with the three charming ladies; that on the first day of the acquaintance he was astounded, talking of Caillaux, whom he regarded as obviously guilty and certain to be convicted, to hear the cultivated and charming couple say: "But he will probably be acquitted, there is absolutely no evidence against him." M. de Guermantes tried to argue that M. de Norpois, in the witness box, had fixed the unhappy Caillaux with his gaze and said to him: "You are the Giolitti of France, yes, Monsieur Caillaux, you are the Giolitti of France." But the cultivated and charming couple had smiled, made fun of M. de Norpois, cited proofs of his senility and concluded that, though Le Figaro might have said that he had addressed these words to "the unhappy M. Caillaux," he had probably in fact addressed them to a highly amused M. Caillaux. The Duc de Guermantes lost no time in changing his opinions. That this change could be brought about by the influence of an Englishwoman is not so extraordinary as one might have supposed had it been foretold even as late as 1919, when the English still spoke of the Germans only as "the Huns" and demanded savage penalties for the guilty. For their opinions too had changed and now—less than a year later—they approved every decision which was likely to distress France and be of help to Germany.)

To return to M. de Charlus: "Yes," he said, in reply to my confession that I did not quite understand. "I mean exactly what I say: 'to know,' in the articles of Norpois, indicates the future, it indicates, that is to say, the desires of Norpois, and indeed the desires of us all," he added, perhaps without complete sincerity. "I am sure you will agree with me. If 'to know' had not become simply a sign of the future tense, one might just find it intelligible for the subject of this verb to be a country. For instance, every time Norpois says: 'America would not know how to remain indifferent to these repeated violations of international law,' 'the Dual Monarchy would not know how to fail to come to its senses,' it is clear that such phrases express the desires of Norpois (they are also mine, and yours)—but here nevertheless the verb can still just retain its original meaning, for a country can 'know,' America can 'know,' the Dual Monarchy itself can 'know' (in spite of its eternal 'lack of psychology'). But when Norpois writes: 'These systematic devastations would not know how to persuade the neutrals,' 'the region of the Lakes would not know how to fail to fall speedily into the hands of the Allies,' 'the results of these neutralist elections would not know how to reflect the opinion of the vast majority of the country,' there is no longer any possibility of doubt. For it is certain that these devastations, these regions, these electoral results are inanimate things which cannot 'know.' And in using this formula Norpois is simply addressing to the neutrals an injunction (which, I regret to say, they do not appear to be obeying) to abandon their neutrality, or to the region of the Lakes an injunction no longer to belong to the 'Boches'" (M. de Charlus gave the impression of having to pluck up courage to pronounce the word "Boche," very much as in the past, in the "tram" at Balbec, he had when he had talked about men whose taste is not for women). "And then, have you noticed the wily fashion in which, ever since 1914, Norpois has begun his articles to the neutrals? He starts by declaring that of course it is not for France to interfere in the

politics of Italy (or of Rumania or Bulgaria or whatever country
it may be). These powers alone must decide, in full independence and with only their own national interests in view,
whether or no it is their duty to abandon neutrality. But if these
opening statements of the article (what would once have been
called the exordium) are disinterested, the sequel is generally
much less so. 'Nevertheless,'—this is the gist of what Norpois
goes on to say—'it is quite clear that only those nations will
derive a material benefit from the struggle which have ranged
themselves on the side of Law and Justice. It cannot be expected that the Allies should reward, by bestowing upon them the
territories which for centuries have resounded with the groans
of their oppressed brethren, those peoples who, taking the line
of least resistance, have not drawn their sword in the service of
the Allies.' Once he has taken this first step towards a counsel
of intervention, there is no holding Norpois, it is not only the
principles but the moment of intervention as to which, with
less and less attempt at disguise, he delivers advice. 'Certainly,'
he says, sailing, as he himself would say, under false colours, 'it
is for Italy, for Rumania alone to decide when the hour has
come to strike and what form their intervention shall take.
They cannot, however, be unaware that, if they protract their
tergiversations, they run the risk of losing their opportunity.
Already the hoofs of the Russian cavalry are sending a shiver
of unspeakable panic through the trapped millions of Germany.
It must be evident that the peoples who have done nothing
more than fly to the help of that victory of which already we
see the resplendent dawn, will have no right or title to the
reward that they may still, if they hasten, etc.' It is like the
notices you see at the theatre: 'Book now. The last remaining
seats will soon be sold.' And what makes this reasoning all the
stupider is that Norpois has to revise it every six months, saying to Rumania at regular intervals: 'The hour has come for
Rumania to determine whether or no she wishes to realise her
national aspirations. Any further delay and it may be too late.'
But though he has been saying this for three years, not only has
the 'too late' not yet come, the offers that are made to Rumania
are constantly being improved. In the same way he invites
France, etc., to intervene in Greece by virtue of her status as a

protective power because the treaty that bound Greece to Serbia has not been observed. But, candidly, if France were not at war and did not desire the assistance or the benevolent neutrality of Greece, would she take it into her head to intervene as a protective power? Those moral sentiments which make France raise her voice in horror because Greece has not kept her engagements towards Serbia, are they not silent the moment it is a question of the equally flagrant violation of treaties by Rumania or Italy, which countries—rightly I think, and the same is true of Greece—have failed to carry out their obligations (though these are less imperative and less far-reaching than they are said to be) as Allies of Germany? The truth is that people see everything through the medium of their newspaper, and what else could they do, seeing that they are not personally acquainted with the men or the events under discussion? At the time of the Affair in which you took so passionate and so bizarre an interest, in that epoch from which it is now the convention to say that we are separated by centuries—for the philosophers of the war have spread the doctrine that all links with the past are broken—I was shocked to see men and women of my family express high esteem for anti-clericals with a Communard past whom their newspaper represented to them as anti-Dreyfusards, and at the same time severe disapproval of a Catholic general of good family who happened to be a revisionist. I am no less shocked now to see all Frenchmen execrate that same Emperor Franz Josef whom once they venerated—and rightly, I may say, I who have known him well and whom he is gracious enough to treat as his cousin. Ah! I haven't written to him since the war," he added, as if he were boldly confessing a fault for which he knew quite well he could not be blamed. "No, the first year I did write, but once only. But what would you have me do? My respect for him is unaltered, but I have many young relatives here fighting in our lines who would, I know, be most displeased were I to carry on a regular correspondence with the head of a nation that is at war with us. How could I? Criticise me who will," he continued, and again he seemed bravely to invite my reproaches, "but in these times I have not wanted a letter signed Charlus to arrive in Vienna. There is only one point in the conduct of the old monarch that I would wish to criticise at all severely, and that is that a nobleman of his rank, head of one of the most ancient and illustrious houses of Europe, should have allowed himself to be led astray by a petty land-owner—a very intelligent man, of course, but still a complete upstart—like William of Hohenzollern. It is one of the more shocking anomalies of this war."

And as, the moment he returned to considerations of genealogy and precedence, which for him fundamentally dominated all others, M. de Charlus became capable of extraordinary childishness, he said to me, in the tone that he might have used in speaking of the Marne or Verdun, that there were important and extremely curious things which ought not to be omitted by anyone who came to write the history of this war. "For instance," he said, "everybody is so ignorant that no one has bothered to point out this very striking fact: the Grand Master of the Order of Malta, who is a pure Boche, continues none the less to live in Rome where, as Grand Master of our order, he enjoys the privilege of extraterritoriality. Most interesting," he added significantly, as if to say: "You see that you have not wasted your evening by meeting me." I thanked him, and he assumed the modest air of one who asks no reward for services rendered.

M. de Charlus still retained all his respect and all his affection for certain great ladies who were accused of defeatism, just as he had in the past for others who had been accused of Dreyfusism. He regretted only that by stooping to meddle in politics they had given a handle to the "polemics of the journalists." In his own attitude to them nothing had changed. So systematic was his frivolity that for him birth, combined with beauty and with other sources of prestige, was the durable thing and the war, like the Dreyfus case, merely a vulgar and fugitive fashion. Had the Duchesse de Guermantes been shot for trying to make a separate peace with Austria, he would still have considered her no less noble than before, no more dishonoured by this mischance than is Marie-Antoinette in our eyes from having been condemned to the guillotine. He was speaking seriously now and for a brief instant, with the noble air of a Saint-Vallier or a Saint-Mégrin, erect and stiff and solemn, he was free of all those mannerisms by which men of his sort betray themselves. And yet, why is it that not one of these men can ever have a voice which hits absolutely the right note? Even at this moment, when M. de Charlus's voice was so very near to solemnity, its pitch was still false, it still needed the tuning-fork to correct it. "Now, what was I saying to you?" he went on. "Ah! yes, that people hate Franz Josef now, because they take their cue from their newspaper. As for King Constantine of Greece and the Tsar of Bulgaria, the public has oscillated more than once between aversion and sympathy, according as it has been said turn and turn about that they would join the side of the Entente or of what Brichot calls the Central Empires. Brichot, by the way, is telling us at every moment that 'the hour of Venizelos will strike.' Now I do not doubt that M. Venizelos is a statesman of great capabilities, but who says that the Greeks are so particularly eager to have him? We are told that he wanted Greece to keep her engagements towards Serbia. Even so, it would be as well to know what these engagements were and whether they were more far-reaching than those which Italy and Rumania did not scruple to violate. We display for the manner in which Greece implements her treaties and respects her constitution an anxiety which we certainly would not display were it not in our interest to do so. Had there been no war, do you think the 'guarantor' powers would even have noticed the dissolution of the Chambers? What I see is simply that one by one the supports of the King of Greece are being withdrawn from him, so that when the day arrives when he no longer has an army to defend him he can be thrown out of the country or put into prison. I was saying just now that the public judges the King of Greece and the King of the Bulgars only as it is told to judge them by the newspapers. But here again, what opinion of these monarchs could people have except that of their newspapers, seeing that they are not acquainted with them? I personally have seen a great deal of them both, I knew Constantine of Greece very well indeed when he was Diadoch, he is a really splendid man. I have always thought that the Emperor Nicholas had a great affection for him. Of course I mean to imply nothing dishonourable. Princess Christian used to talk openly about it, but she is a terrible scandalmonger. As for the Tsar of the Bulgars, he is an out-and-out nancy and a monstrous liar, but very intelligent, a remarkable man. He likes me very much."

M. de Charlus, who could be so delightful, became horrid when he touched on these subjects. He brought to them that same sort of complacency which we find so exasperating in the invalid who keeps drawing attention to his good health. I have often thought that in the "twister" of Balbec the faithful who so longed to hear the admission which he was too secretive to make, would in fact have been unable to endure any real display of his mania; ill at ease, breathing with difficulty as one does in a sick-room or in the presence of a morphine addict who takes out his syringe in public, they would themselves have put a stop to the confidences which they imagined they desired. It was, indeed, exasperating to hear the whole world accused, and often without any semblance of proof, by someone who omitted himself from the special category to which one knew perfectly well that he belonged and in which he so readily included others. In spite of all his intelligence, he had in this context fabricated for himself a narrow little philosophy (at the bottom of which there was perhaps just a spark of that interest in the curiousness of life which Swann had felt) which explained everything by reference to these special causes and in which, as always happens when a man stoops to the level of his own vice, he was not only unworthy of himself but exceptionally satisfied with himself. Thus it was that this dignified and noble man put on the most imbecile smile to complete the following little speech: "As there are strong presumptions of the same kind as for Ferdinand of Coburg in the case of the Emperor William, this may well be the reason why Tsar Ferdinand has joined the side of the 'Empires of Prey.' After all, it is very understandable, one is indulgent to a *sister*, one refuses her nothing. To my mind that would be a very pretty explanation of Bulgaria's alliance with Germany." And at this stupid explanation M. de Charlus pealed with laughter as though he really found it most ingenious—an explanation which, even had it been based upon true facts, was in the same puerile category as the observations which M. de Charlus made about the war when he judged it from the point of view of a feudal lord or a Knight of St John of Jerusalem. He ended with a more sensible remark: "What is astonishing," he said, "is that this public which judges the men and events of the war solely from the newspapers, is persuaded that it forms its own opinions."

In this M. de Charlus was right. I have been told that it was fascinating to see the moments of silence and hesitation, so exactly like those that are necessary not merely to the pronouncement but to the formation of a personal opinion, which Mme de Forcheville used to have before declaring, as though it were a heart-felt sentiment: "No, I do not think they will take Warsaw"; "I have the impression that it cannot last another winter"; "the worst thing that could happen is a patched-up peace"; "what alarms me, if you want to know, is the Chamber"; "yes, I believe all the same that we shall succeed in breaking through." And to make these statements Odette assumed a simpering air which became even more exaggerated when she said: "I don't say the German armies do not fight well, but they lack what is called pluck." In pronouncing the word "pluck" (and it was the same when she merely said "fighting spirit") she executed with her hand the sculptural gesture, and with her eyes the wink, of an art student employing a technical term of the studios. Her language now, however, even more than in the past bore witness to her admiration for the English, whom she was no longer obliged to call, as formerly, merely "our neighbours across the Channel," or at most "our friends the English": they were "our loyal allies." Needless to say she never failed, relevant or not, to quote the expression *fair play* (and to point out that in the eyes of the English the Germans were unfair players) and also: "the important thing is to win the war, as our brave allies say." She even had an unfortunate habit of associating the name of her son-in-law with the subject of English soldiers and of referring to the pleasure which he derived from living cheek by jowl with Australians and Scotsmen, New Zealanders and Canadians. "My son-in-law Saint-Loup has learned the slang of all the brave *tommies*, he can make himself understood by the ones from the most distant *dominions*—and I don't mean just the general in command of the base, he fraternises with the humblest *private*."

May this parenthesis on Mme de Forcheville serve as my excuse, while I am strolling along the boulevards side by side with M. de Charlus, for embarking upon another, of greater length but useful as an illustration of this era, on the relations of Mme Verdurin with Brichot. The truth is that if, as we have seen, poor Brichot was judged without indulgence by M. de Charlus (because the latter was both extremely intelligent and more or less unconsciously pro-German), he was treated still worse by the Verdurins. They no doubt were chauvinistic, and this ought to have made them appreciate Brichot's articles, which were in any case quite as good as many pieces of writing which delighted Mme Verdurin. But first, the reader may remember that already at la Raspelière Brichot had become for the Verdurins, instead of the great man that he had once been in their eyes, if not actually a scapegoat like Saniette at any rate a target for their scarcely disguised ridicule. Still, at that period he remained a faithful of the faithful and thus was entitled to a share in the advantages tacitly conferred by the statutes upon all the founding or associate members of the little group. But while, under cover of the war perhaps, or through the rapid crystallisation of a long-delayed social prestige, of which in fact all the necessary elements had for a long time existed in it, invisible and in a state of saturation, the drawing-room of the Verdurins had been opening itself to a new world and the faithful, at first the baits to attract this new world, had ended by being invited less and less themselves, at the same time a parallel phenomenon had been taking place in the life of Brichot. In spite of the Sorbonne, in spite of the Institut, before the war he had been a celebrity only inside the Verdurin drawing-room. But when he began to write, almost every day, articles adorned with that second-rate brilliance which we have so often seen him scatter open-handed in the presence of the faithful, yet enriched too with a perfectly genuine learning which, like a true man of the Sorbonne, he made no attempt to conceal however he might clothe it in agreeable forms, the "great world" was literally dazzled. And for once it had bestowed its favour upon someone who was far from being a nonentity, upon a man who could hold the attention of an audience by the fertility of his intelligence and the resources of his memory. So that now, while three duchesses spent the evening with Mme Verdurin, three other duchesses contested the honour of having the great man at their dinner table, and one of these invitations the great man usually accepted, feeling all the freer to do this since Mme Verdurin, exasperated by the success of his articles with the Faubourg Saint-Germain, was careful never to ask him to her house when some smart woman was to be there whom he did not yet know and who would lose no time in luring him away. Thus journalism (into which he was really doing no more than pour belatedly, with applause and in return for a magnificent financial reward, what all his life he had squandered incognito and for nothing in the Verdurin drawing-room—for his articles, since he had so much knowledge and wrote with such ease, cost him no more trouble than his conversation) might have led, indeed at one moment seemed to be leading Brichot to an indefeasible glory, had it not been for Mme Verdurin. Admittedly, these articles were far from being as remarkable as fashionable people supposed. The vulgarity of the man was apparent in every line beneath the pedantry of the scholar. And side by side with images which had absolutely no meaning ("the Germans will no longer be able to look Beethoven's statue in the face; Schiller must have shuddered in his tomb; the ink which had guaranteed the neutrality of Belgium was scarcely dry; Lenin speaks, but his words are scattered on the winds of the steppe") there were trivialities such as: "twenty thousand prisoners, that is indeed a figure; our command will know how to keep a weather eye open; we mean to win, that sums it up in a nutshell." Yet mixed with all this, how much knowledge, how much intelligence, what just reasoning! Mme Verdurin, however, never began an article by Brichot without first dwelling upon the enjoyable thought that she was going to find ridiculous things in it, and she read it with the most sustained attention in order to be certain of not letting them escape her. And unfortunately it could not be denied that ridiculous things there were. But the faithful did not even wait until they had found them. The most felicitous quotation from an author who was really very little known, at least in the work to which Brichot referred, was seized upon as proof of the most insufferable pedantry, and

Mme Verdurin could hardly wait for the hour of dinner when she would unloose the torrential laughter of her guests. "Well, what do you say to to-night's Brichot? I thought of you when I read the quotation from Cuvier. I honestly think the man is going mad." "I haven't read it yet," Cottard would say. "What, you haven't read it yet? But you don't know what delights you are missing. I promise you you will die of laughter." And pleased at heart that someone had not yet read the latest Brichot, since this meant that she herself could call attention to the ludicrous things in it, Mme Verdurin would tell the butler to bring *Le Temps* and would herself read the article aloud, lingering with emphasis on the most simple phrases. After dinner, for the whole of the evening, the anti-Brichot campaign would continue, but with hypocritical reservations. "I won't say it too loud because I am afraid that over there," she would say, indicating Comtesse Molé, "there is a good deal of admiration for this stuff. Fashionable people are more foolish than is generally supposed." In saying this she did her best, by speaking just loud enough, to let Mme Molé hear that she was being talked about, and at the same time to convey to her, by occasionally lowering her voice, that she did not want her to hear what she was saying. Mme Molé was cowardly enough to disown Brichot, whom in fact she thought the equal of Michelet. She said that of course Mme Verdurin was right, and so as to end by nevertheless saying something which seemed to her incontestably true, added: "What one must allow him, is that it is well written." "You call that well written?" said Mme Verdurin. "Personally, I consider that it might have been written by a pig"—an audacity which always made her fashionable guests laugh, particularly as Mme Verdurin, as though she herself were frightened by the word "pig," uttered it in a whisper, holding her hand to her lips. Her rage against Brichot was still further increased by the naïve fashion in which he displayed his pleasure at his success, in spite of the fits of ill humour provoked in him by the censorship every time that it —as he expressed it, for he liked to employ new words in order to show that he was not too donnish—"blue-pencilled" part of his article. In his presence, however, Mme Verdurin did not reveal too clearly, save by a certain grumpiness which might have been a warning to a more perspicacious man, the poor opinion which she had of the writings of "Chochotte." Only once did she criticise him, for using the word "I" too often. And it was true that he was in the habit of using it continually, firstly because, with his professorial habits, he was constantly employing phrases like "I grant that" and even (in the sense of "I am willing to admit that") "I am willing that," as for instance: "I am willing that the vast development of the fronts should necessitate, etc.," but principally because, as a militant anti-Dreyfusard of the old days who had had suspicions of German preparations long before the war, he had frequently had occasion to write: "Since 1897 I have been denouncing"; "I pointed out in 1901"; "In my little pamphlet, of the greatest rarity today (*habent sua fata libelli*) I drew attention," and the habit, once formed, had remained with him. He turned crimson at Mme Verdurin's remark, which had been made with acerbity. "You are right, Madame. A man who had no more love for the Jesuits than M. Combes—although he never had the honour of a preface from our sweet master of delicious scepticism, Anatole France, who was, if I am not mistaken, my adversary . . . before the Flood—observed that the first person singular is always odious."[44] From that moment Brichot replaced "I" by "one," but *one* did not prevent the reader from seeing that the author was speaking of himself, indeed it permitted him to speak of himself more frequently than ever, to comment on the most insignificant of his own phrases, to build a whole article round a single negative statement, always behind the protective screen of *one*. If for example Brichot had said, in another article perhaps, that the German armies had lost some of their strength, he would begin thus: "One does not camouflage the truth here. One has said that the German armies have lost some of their strength. One has not said that they do not still possess great strength. Still less will one write that the ground gained, if it is not, etc." In short, simply by enunciating all that he would not say and by recalling all that he had said some years ago and all that Clausewitz, Jomini, Ovid, Apollonius of Tyana and others had said in the more recent or more remote past, Brichot could easily have put together the material for a solid volume. It is to be regretted that he did not publish one, for these erudite articles are now difficult to come by. The Faubourg Saint-Germain, admonished by Mme Verdurin, began by laughing at Brichot in her drawing-room, but continued, after departing from the little clan, to admire him. Then after a while it became the fashion to scoff at him as it had previously been to admire him, and even those ladies who continued to find him interesting in secret while they were actually reading his articles, checked themselves and mocked as soon as they were no longer alone, so as not to appear less clever than their friends. Never was Brichot so much discussed in the little clan as at this period, but in a spirit of derision. The criterion for judging the intelligence of a newcomer was simply his opinion of Brichot's articles, and if the first time he gave the wrong reply no pains were spared to instruct him how it was that you were recognised to be foolish or clever.

"Well, my poor friend," M. de Charlus went on, "all this is very dreadful, and tedious articles are not the only things we have to deplore. We hear talk of vandalism, of the destruction of statues. But the destruction of so many marvellous young men, who while they lived were incomparable polychrome statues, is that not also vandalism? Will not a town which has lost all its beautiful men be like a town of which all the sculpture has been smashed to pieces? What pleasure can I get from dining in a restaurant where I am served by moth-eaten old buffoons who look like Father Didon, if not by hags in mobcaps who make me think I have strayed into one of Duval's soup-kitchens? Yes, it's as bad as that, my boy, and I think I have the right to say these things, because Beauty is still Beauty when it exists in a living material. How delightful to be served by rachitic creatures with spectacles on their noses and the reason for their exemption from military service written all over their faces! In these changed times, if you wish to rest your eyes on someone nice-looking in a restaurant, you must look not among the waiters who are serving you but among the customers who are eating and drinking. And then in the old days one could always see a waiter a second time, although they frequently changed, but with some English lieutenant who has perhaps never been to the restaurant before and may well be killed to-morrow, what hope is there of finding out who he is and when he will return? When Augustus of Poland, as we are told by the charming Morand, the delightful author of *Clarisse*, exchanged one of his regiments for a collection of Chinese porcelain, it is my opinion that he made a bad bargain. To think that all those huge footmen six foot tall and more, who used to adorn the monumental staircases of the lovely hostesses whose houses we visited, have one and all been killed, and that most of them joined up because it was dinned into them that the war would last two months! Ah! they did not know as I do the strength of Germany, the courage of the Prussian race," he said, forgetting himself. And then, realising that he had revealed too much of his point of view, he went on: "It is not so much Germany that I fear for France as the war itself. People away from the front imagine that the war is no more than a gigantic boxing match, of which, thanks to the newspapers, they are spectators at a comfortable distance. But it is nothing of the sort. It is an illness which, when it seems to have been defeated at one point, returns at another. To-day Noyon will be recovered from the enemy, to-morrow there will be no bread or chocolate, the next day the man who thought he was safe and was prepared, if necessary, to face death on the battlefield because he had not imagined it, will be panic-stricken to read in the newspapers that his class has been called up. As for monuments, it is not so much the quality as the quantity of the destruction that appals me, I am less horrified at the disappearance of a unique monument like Rheims than at that of all the living entities which once made the smallest village in France instructive and charming."

My mind turned immediately to Combray, but in the past I had thought that I would lower myself in the eyes of Mme de Guermantes by confessing to the humble position which my family occupied there. I wondered now whether the facts had not been revealed to the Guermantes and to M. de Charlus, either by Legrandin or by Swann or Saint-Loup or Morel, and I said nothing, even this silence being less painful to me than a retrospective explanation. I only hoped that M. de Charlus would not mention Combray.

"I do not wish to speak ill of the Americans, Monsieur," he

went on, "it seems that they are inexhaustibly generous, and as there has been nobody to conduct the orchestra in this war, as each performer has joined in a long time after the one before and the Americans only began when we had almost finished, they may possibly have an ardour which in us four years of war have succeeded in damping. Even before the war they were fond of our country and our art, they paid high prices for our masterpieces. They have taken many home with them. But this uprooted art, as M. Barrès would call it, is precisely the opposite of what once formed the delicious charm of France. The *château* explained the church, which itself, because it had been a place of pilgrimage, explained the *chanson de geste*. I need not dwell upon the illustriousness of my family and my connexions, which in any case is not the subject that concerns us. But recently I had occasion, to settle a matter of business, and in spite of a certain coolness that exists between the young couple and myself, to visit my niece Saint-Loup who lives at Combray. Combray was simply a small town like hundreds of others. But the ancestors of my family were portrayed as donors in some of the windows in the church, and in others our armorial bearings were depicted. We had our chapel there, and our tombs. And now this church has been destroyed by the French and the English because it served as an observation-post to the Germans. All that mixture of art and still-living history that was France is being destroyed, and we have not seen the end of the process yet. Of course I am not so absurd as to compare, for family reasons, the destruction of the church of Combray with that of the cathedral of Rheims, that miracle of a Gothic cathedral which seemed, somehow naturally, to have rediscovered the purity of antique sculpture, or of the cathedral of Amiens. I do not know whether the raised arm of St Firmin is still intact to-day or whether it has been broken. If so, the loftiest affirmation of faith and energy ever made has disappeared from this world."

"You mean its symbol, Monsieur," I interrupted. "And I adore certain symbols no less than you do. But it would be absurd to sacrifice to the symbol the reality that it symbolises. Cathedrals are to be adored until the day when, to preserve them, it would be necessary to deny the truths which they teach. The raised arm of St Firmin said, with an almost military gesture of command: 'Let us be broken, if honour requires.' Do not sacrifice men to stones whose beauty comes precisely from their having for a moment given fixed form to human truths.''

"I understand what you mean," M. de Charlus replied, "and M. Barrès, who has sent us, alas, on too many pilgrimages to the statue of Strasbourg and the tomb of M. Déroulède, was both moving and graceful when he wrote that the cathedral of Rheims itself was less dear to us than the lives of our infantrymen. An assertion which makes nonsense of the wrath of our newspapers against the German general in command there who said that the cathedral of Rheims was less precious to him than the life of one German soldier. Indeed, the exasperating and depressing thing is that each country says the same. The reasons for which the industrialists of Germany declare the possession of Belfort indispensable for safeguarding their nation against our ideas of revenge, are the very same reasons as those which Barrès gives for demanding Mainz as a protection against the recurrent urge to invade which possesses the Boches. Why is it that the recovery of Alsace-Lorraine seemed to France an insufficient motive for embarking on a war, yet a sufficient motive for continuing one, for redeclaring it afresh year after year? You appear to believe that nothing can rob France of victory now and with all my heart I hope that you are right, you may be quite sure of that. But is it not a fact that since, rightly or wrongly, the Allies have come to believe that they are sure to win (for my part naturally I should be enchanted by this outcome, but what I see is mostly a profusion of victories on paper, Pyrrhic victories whose cost is not revealed to us) and the Boches no longer believe that they are sure to win, we see Germany striving to make peace quickly and France to prolong the war, France which is a just nation and does right to pronounce words of justice but is also sweet, gentle France and ought to pronounce words of mercy, were it only in order to spare her own children and to allow the flowers which bloom with each new spring to shed their lustre on other things than tombs? Be honest, my friend, you yourself once propounded a theory to me about things existing only in virtue of a creation which is perpetually renewed. The creation of the world did not take place once and for all, you said, it is, of necessity, taking place every day. Well, if you are sincere, you cannot except war from this theory. Never mind if the excellent Norpois has written (trotting out one of those oratorical phrases which are as dear to him as 'the dawn of victory' and 'General Winter'): 'Now that Germany has determined on war, the die is cast,' the truth is that every morning war is declared afresh. And the men who wish to continue it are as guilty as the men who began it, more guilty perhaps, for the latter perhaps did not foresee all its horrors. Besides, can we be sure that a war thus prolonged, even if it must eventually end in victory, is without danger? It is difficult to speak of things which have no precedent and of the repercussions upon an organism of an operation which is being attempted for the first time. Generally, it is true, novelties which people find alarming pass off very well. The most prudent republicans thought that it was mad to separate the Church from the State. It was as easy as sending a letter through the post. Dreyfus was rehabilitated, Picquart was made Minister of War, and nobody uttered a murmur. Yet what may we not fear from the stress and strain of a war which has continued without pause for several years? What will men do when they return from it? Will fatigue have broken them or will it have driven them mad? All this could have grave results, if not for France, at least for the government, perhaps even for the present form of government. You once made me read Maurras's excellent novel *Aimée de Coigny*. The original Aimée, you remember, was waiting for the collapse of the Empire to ensue from the war that it was waging in 1812, and I should be surprised if she has not her counterpart today. If a present-day Aimée de Coigny exists, will her hopes with regard to the Republic be fulfilled? I should be sorry to see that happen. But to return to the war itself, can we say that the man who first began it was the Emperor William? I am very doubtful about that. And if it was, what has he done that Napoleon, for instance, did not do—something that I certainly find abominable, but that I am astonished to see also inspiring such horror in those who burn incense before Napoleon, those who on the day that war was declared exclaimed like General

Pau: 'I have been waiting forty years for this day. It is the most glorious day of my life.' Heaven knows whether anyone protested with greater energy than myself at the time when a deference out of all proportion was paid by society to the nationalists and the military men, when every friend of the arts was accused of occupying himself with things of baleful import to France and all civilisation of an unwarlike nature was thought to be pernicious! In those days an authentic member of the best society hardly counted compared with a general. Some madwoman came within an inch of presenting *me* to M. Syveton, as if *I* were *his* inferior. You will tell me that the rules I was striving to maintain were merely social ones. But for all their apparent frivolity they might have prevented many excesses. I have always honoured the defenders of grammar or logic. We realise fifty years later that they have averted serious dangers. To-day our nationalists are the most anti-German of men, the most determined to persevere to the bitter end. But in the last fifteen years their philosophy has completely changed. It is true that they are pressing for the continuation of the war. But they are doing this only in order to exterminate a warlike race, they are doing it from love of peace. The idea of a martial civilisation, which fifteen years ago they thought so beautiful, now fills them with horror; not only do they reproach the Prussians for having allowed the military element to predominate in their state, they claim that throughout the ages military civilisations have been destructive of all that they now hold precious, not only of the arts but also of chivalry towards women. And if any critic of their views is converted to nationalism he at the same moment becomes a friend of peace. He is persuaded that in all martial civilisations women have been humiliated and crushed. One dare not reply that the 'lady' of a knight in the Middle Ages or Dante's Beatrice was perhaps placed upon a throne as elevated as the heroines of M. Becque. Any day now I expect to see myself placed at table beneath a Russian revolutionary or simply beneath one of these generals of ours who wage war out of horror of war and in order to punish a people for cultivating an ideal which fifteen years ago they themselves regarded as the only one that could invigorate a nation. It is not many months since the unhappy Tsar was

honoured for his part in assembling the conference at The
Hague. But now that people hail the advent of a free Russia
they forget his claim to glory. So turns the wheel of the world.
Meanwhile Germany uses expressions so similar to those of
France that one can hardly believe she is not quoting her, she
never tires of saying that she is 'struggling for existence.' When
I read: 'We shall struggle against an implacable and cruel
enemy until we have obtained a peace which will give us
guarantees for the future against all aggression and ensure that
the blood of our brave soldiers shall not have flowed in vain,'
or: 'he who is not for us is against us,' I do not know whether
the words are the Emperor William's or M. Poincaré's, for they
have both of them, with a few trifling differences, pronounced
such phrases twenty times, although to be truthful I must
admit that in this instance it is the Emperor who has copied the
President of the Republic. France would perhaps have been less
eager to prolong the war if she had remained weak, and
Germany certainly would have been in less of a hurry to end it
if she had not ceased to be strong. I should say, to be as strong
as she was; for strong, as you will see, she still is."

He had got into the habit of talking at the top of his voice,
from excitability, from the need to find an outlet for impressions of which, never having cultivated any art, he needed to
unburden himself—as an airman unloads his bombs, if necessary in open country—even where his words could impinge
upon nobody, particularly in society, where they fell completely
at random and where people listened to him out of snobbishness, uncritically and (to such an extent did he tyrannise his
audience) one may say under compulsion and even from fear.
On the boulevards this loud harangue of his was also a mark of
contempt for the passers-by, for whom he no more lowered his
voice than he would have stepped aside to avoid them. But it
struck a discordant note there and caused astonishment and,
worse than that, rendered audible to the people who turned
round to look at us remarks which might well have made them
take us for defeatists. I pointed this out to M. de Charlus but
succeeded only in arousing his mirth. "You must admit that
that would be most amusing," he said. "After all, one never
knows, every evening each one of us runs the risk of being part

of the next day's news. Is there really any reason why I should not be shot in a ditch at Vincennes? That is what happened to my great-uncle the Duc d'Enghien. The thirst for noble blood maddens a certain rabble—and here they show a greater fastidiousness than lions, for those beasts, as you know, would throw themselves even upon Mme Verdurin if she had so much as a scratch upon her nose. Upon what in my youth we would have called her boko!" And he began to roar with laughter as if we had been alone in a room.

At moments, seeing suspicious-looking individuals drawn out of the shadows by the passage of M. de Charlus conglomerate at a little distance from him, I wondered whether it would be more agreeable to him if I left him alone or remained with him. In the same way, if you meet an old man who is subject to frequent epileptic fits and see from the incoherence of his gait that an attack is probably imminent, you may ask yourself whether your company is more desired by him as a support or dreaded as that of a witness from whom he would prefer to conceal the attack and whose mere presence may perhaps suffice to bring it on, whereas absolute calm might succeed in averting it. But in the case of the sick man the possibility of the event upon which you are uncertain whether or no you ought to turn your back is revealed by his walking in circles as if he were drunk; while in that of M. de Charlus the divagations—sign of a possible incident as to which I did not know whether he desired or feared that my presence should prevent its occurrence—were transferred, as in an ingenious stage production, from the Baron himself, who was walking straight ahead, to a whole circle of supernumerary actors. All the same, it is my belief that he preferred to avoid the encounter, for he dragged me down a side-street, darker than the boulevard but into which nevertheless the latter was incessantly discharging—or else like a tributary stream they were flowing towards it—soldiers of every arm and of every nation, a rising youthful tide, compensatory and consoling for M. de Charlus, the reverse of that ebb-tide of all men towards the frontier which in the first days of mobilisation had made a vacuum in the capital. At every moment M. de Charlus expressed his admiration for the brilliant uniforms which passed before us, which made of Paris a town as cosmopolitan as a port, as unreal as a stage setting designed by a painter who has simply put up a few scraps of architecture as an excuse for assembling the most variegated and glittering costumes. Literally he did not know which way to turn his head; often he raised it, regretting that he did not have a pair of field-glasses (which would in fact have been of very little use to him), since because of the Zeppelin raid of two days earlier, which had caused the authorities to redouble their precautions, there were soldiers in greater numbers than usual even in the sky. The aeroplanes which a few hours earlier I had seen, like insects, as brown dots upon the surface of the blue evening, now passed like blazing fire-ships through the darkness of the night, which was made darker still by the partial extinction of the street lamps. And perhaps the greatest impression of beauty that these human shooting stars made us feel came simply from their forcing us to look at the sky, towards which normally we so seldom raise our eyes. In this Paris, whose beauty in 1914 I had seen awaiting almost defenceless the threat of the approaching enemy, there was certainly, as there had been then, the ancient unalterable splendour of a moon cruelly and mysteriously serene, which poured down its useless beauty upon the still untouched buildings of the capital; but as in 1914, and more now than in 1914, there was also something else, there were lights from a different source, intermittent beams which, whether they came from the aeroplanes or from the searchlights of the Eiffel Tower, one knew to be directed by an intelligent will, by a friendly vigilance which gave one the same kind of emotion, inspired the same sort of gratitude and calm that I had felt in Saint-Loup's room at Doncières, in the cell of that military cloister where so many fervent and disciplined hearts were exercising themselves in readiness for the day when, without hesitation, in the midst of their youth, they would consummate their sacrifice.

After the raid of two days earlier, when it had been more full of movement than the earth, the sky had become calm again as the sea becomes calm after a storm. But like the sea after a storm, it had not yet recovered absolute tranquillity. Aeroplanes were still mounting like rockets to the level of the stars, and searchlights, as they quartered the sky, wafted slowly

across it what looked like a pale dust of stars, of errant milky
ways. Meanwhile the aeroplanes took their places among the
constellations and seeing these "new stars" one might well have
supposed oneself to be in another hemisphere. M. de Charlus
spoke to me of his admiration for these airmen of ours, and
went on, since he was no more capable of checking the flow of
his pro-German feelings than of his other inclinations, even
though at the same time he denied both the one and the other
tendency: "I must add of course that I have just as much
admiration for the Germans who go up in the Gothas. And
when it comes to the Zeppelins, think of the courage that is
needed! They are heroes, there is no other word for it. What
difference can it make that they are attacking civilians, if guns
are firing at them? Are you afraid of the Gothas and the bombardment?" I admitted that I was not, but perhaps I was wrong.
No doubt, my idleness having given me the habit, when it was
a question of my work, of putting it off from one day to
another, I imagined that death too might be postponed in the
same fashion. How should one be afraid of a bombardment
when one is convinced that one will not be hit to-day? Anyhow,
formed in isolation, the idea of bombs being dropped, the idea
of the possibility of death, had added nothing tragic to the
image which I had in my mind of the German flying machines,
until from one of them, storm-tossed and partly hidden from
my sight by the thick billowing mists of an agitated sky, from
an aeroplane which, though I knew it to be murderous, I
imagined only as stellar and celestial, I had one evening seen
the gesture of a bomb dropped upon us. For the novel reality
of a danger is perceived only through the medium of that new
thing, not assimilable to anything that we already know, to
which we give the name "an impression" and which is often,
as in the present case, epitomised in a line, a line which defines
an intention and possesses the latent potentiality of the action
which has given it its particular form, like the invisible line
described by this falling bomb or those other lines which I had
seen at the same time from the Pont de la Concorde, on all sides
of the threatening, hunted aeroplane, as though they had been
reflections in the clouds of the fountains of the Champs-
Elysées and the Place de la Concorde and the Tuileries: the

beams of the searchlights travelling through the sky like luminous jets of water, which also were lines full of intention, full of the provident and protective intentions of men of power and wisdom to whom, as on that night in the barracks at Doncières, I felt grateful for condescending to employ their strength, with this so beautiful precision, in watching over our safety.

The night was as beautiful as in 1914, and the threat to Paris was as great. The moonlight was like a soft and steady magnesium flare, by the light of which some camera might, for the last time, have been recording nocturnal images of those lovely groups of buildings like the Place Vendôme and the Place de la Concorde, to which my fear of the shells that were perhaps about to destroy them imparted by contrast, as they stood in their still intact beauty, a sort of plenitude, as if they were bending forward and freely offering their defenceless architecture to the blows that might fall. "You are not afraid?" M. de Charlus repeated. "The people of Paris don't realise the situation. I am told that Mme Verdurin gives parties every day. I know it only from hearsay, personally I know absolutely nothing about them, I have completely broken off relations," he added, lowering not only his eyes as if a telegraph boy had passed, but also his head and his shoulders and raising his arm with the gesture that signifies, if not "I wash my hands of them" at any rate "I can tell you nothing about them" (not that I had asked him anything). "I know that Morel still goes there a lot," he went on (it was the first time that he had mentioned him again). "It is rumoured that he much regrets the past and would like to make it up with me," he continued, exhibiting at one and the same time the credulity of a man of the Faubourg who says· "People say that there are more talks than ever going on between France and Germany, and even that negotiations have been started," and that of the lover whom the most cruel rebuffs are unable to convince. "In any case, if he wants it, he only has to say so. I am older than he, it is not for me to take the first step." And certainly there was no need to say this, so evident was it. But it was not even sincere, and this made one very embarrassed for M. de Charlus, for one felt that, by saying that it was not for him to take the first step, he was in fact making one and was waiting for me to offer to undertake a reconciliation.

Naturally I was familiar with the credulity, naïve or feigned, of people who love someone, or simply are not invited to someone's house, and attribute to that someone a desire of which, in fact, in spite of wearisome solicitations, he has given no hint. But from the sudden tremor of the voice with which M. de Charlus pronounced these words, from the anxious look which flickered in the depths of his eyes, I got the impression that there was something more here than an ordinary attempt at bluff. I was not mistaken, and I will relate straight away the two facts which proved subsequently that I was right. (I take a leap of many years for the second of these incidents, which was posterior to the death of M. de Charlus, who was not to die until a much later period and whom we shall have occasion to see again a number of times, greatly changed from what we have known him to be, particularly the last time of all, when he had come to forget Morel completely.) The first of these incidents took place only two or three years after the evening on which I walked down the boulevards with M. de Charlus. About two years after this evening, I met Morel. I thought immediately of M. de Charlus, of the pleasure it would give him to see the violinist again, and I urged Morel to go and see him, even if it were only once. "He has been good to you," I said, "he is an old man now, he may die, you should settle old scores and obliterate all trace of your quarrel." Morel appeared to be entirely of my opinion as to the desirability of making peace, but he none the less refused categorically to visit M. de Charlus even once. "You are wrong," I said. "Is it from obstinacy, from indolence, from spite, from misplaced vanity, from concern for your virtue (you may be sure that it will not be attacked), from coquettishness?" At this point the violinist, twisting his features as he forced himself to make an admission which no doubt was extremely painful, replied with a shudder: "No, it is from none of all those things. As for virtue, I don't give a damn for it. Spite? On the contrary, I am beginning to pity him. It is not from coquettishness, which could serve no purpose. It is not from having too much to do, for there are whole days when I stay at home and twiddle my thumbs. No, it is not for any of these reasons. It is—but never say this to anybody, I am mad to tell you—it is, it is . . . from fear!" He began to tremble in every limb. I confessed that I did not understand him. "No, don't ask me, don't let's talk about it, you do not know him as I do, I may say that you do not know him at all." "But what harm can he do you? In any case, he won't want to harm you if you put an end to the bitterness that exists between you. And then, you know that at heart he is very kind." "Good heavens, yes! I know he is kind. And wonderfully considerate, and honest. But let me alone, don't let's talk about it, I beseech you—it's a shameful admission, but I am afraid!"

The second incident dates from after the death of M. de Charlus. I was brought one or two things which he had left me as mementoes, and also a letter enclosed in three envelopes, which he had written at least ten years before his death. He had been seriously ill at the time and had put all his affairs in order, but then had recovered, only to fall later into the condition in which we shall see him on the day of an afternoon party given by the Princesse de Guermantes—and the letter, put aside in a strong-box with the objects which he was bequeathing to a few friends, had remained there for seven years, seven years during which he had completely forgotten Morel. It was written in a firm and delicate hand-writing and was couched in the following terms:

"My dear friend, the ways of Providence are inscrutable. Sometimes a fault in a very ordinary man is made to serve its purposes by helping one of the just not to slip from his lofty eminence. You know Morel, you know the humbleness of his origin and the height (my own level, no less) to which I wished to raise him. You are aware that he preferred to return not to the dust and ashes from which every man—for man surely is the true phoenix—may be born again, but to the slime in which the viper crawls. He fell, and in so doing he saved me from falling from where I belong. You know that my arms contain the device of Our Lord himself: *Inculcabis super leonem et aspidem*, with the crest of a man having beneath the soles of his feet, as heraldic supporters, a lion and a serpent. Well, if I have succeeded as I have in crushing the lion proper that I am, it is thanks to the serpent and his prudence, which just now I was thoughtless enough to call a fault, for the profound wisdom of the Gospel makes a virtue of it, a virtue at least for other people. Our serpent, of the once harmonious and well modulated hisses, was, when he had a charmer—a charmer charmed, moreover—not merely musical and reptilian, he had, to the point of cowardice, that virtue, Prudence, which I now hold to be divine. This divine prudence it was that made him resist the appeals to come back and see me which I conveyed to him, and I shall have no peace in this world or hope of forgiveness in the next if I do not confess the truth to you. He was, in resisting my appeals, the instrument of divine Wisdom, for I was resolved, had he come, that he should not leave my house alive. One of us two had to disappear. I had decided to kill him. God counselled him prudence to preserve me from crime. I do not doubt that the intercession of the Archangel Michael, my patron saint, played a great part in this and I beseech him to pardon me for having so neglected him over many years and for having so ill responded to the innumerable favours which he has conferred upon me, especially in my struggle against evil. I owe it to this Servant of God—I say the words in the plenitude of my faith and my understanding—that the heavenly Father inspired Morel not to come. And so it is I who am now about to die.

Your faithfully devoted, *Semper idem*,
P. G. Charlus."

Reading these words I understood Morel's fear. Certainly there was in the letter more than a small element of pride and of literature. But the confession was true. And Morel had known better than I that the "practically mad side" of her brother-in-law's character which Mme de Guermantes used to hint at was not confined, as until this revelation I had supposed, to his momentary exhibitions of superficial and ineffective rage.

But I must return to my narrative. I am walking down the boulevards by the side of M. de Charlus, who has just made a vague attempt to use me as an intermediary for overtures of peace between himself and Morel. Seeing that I made no reply, "Anyhow," he went on, "I do not know why it is that he no longer gives concerts. There is no music now on the pretext that there is a war on, but people dance and go out to dinner and women invent something called Ambrine for their skin. Social amusements fill what may prove, if the Germans continue to advance, to be the last days of our Pompeii. And if the city is indeed doomed, that in itself will save it from frivolity. The lava of some German Vesuvius—and their naval guns are no less terrible than a volcano—has only to surprise these good people at their toilet and to eternise their gestures by interrupting them, and in days to come it will be part of a child's education to look at pictures in his school-books of Mme Molé about to put on a last layer of powder before going out to dine with a sister-in-law, or Sosthène de Guermantes adding the final touches to his false eyebrows; these things will be the subject of lectures by the Brichots of the future, for the frivolity of an age, when ten centuries have passed over it, is matter for the gravest erudition, particularly if it has been embalmed by a volcanic eruption or by the substances akin to lava which a bombardment projects. What documents for the future historian if asphyxiating gases, like the fumes of Vesuvius, and the collapse of a whole city, like the catastrophe which buried Pompeii, should preserve intact all the imprudent dowagers who have not yet sent off their paintings and their statues to safety in Bayonne! And indeed, for the last year, have we not already seen fragments of Pompeii every evening: people burying themselves in their cellars, not in order to emerge with some old bottle of Mouton Rothschild or Saint-Emilion, but to conceal along with themselves their most treasured belongings, like the priests of Herculaneum whom death surprised in the act of carrying away the sacred vessels? Attachment to an object always brings death to its possessor. True, Paris was not, like Herculaneum, founded by Hercules. But how many points of resemblance leap to the eye! And this lucid vision that is given to us is not unique to ourselves, it has been granted to every age. If I reflect that to-morrow we may suffer the fate of the cities of Vesuvius, these in their turn sensed that they were threatened with the doom of the accursed cities of the Bible.

On the wall of a house in Pompeii has been found the revealing inscription: *Sodoma, Gomora.*"

Perhaps it was this name of Sodom and the ideas that it evoked in him, or possibly the idea of the bombardment, that made M. de Charlus for an instant raise his eyes to heaven, but soon he brought them back to earth. "I admire all the heroes of this war," he said. "Why, my dear boy, those English soldiers whom at the beginning I rather thoughtlessly dismissed as mere football players presumptuous enough to measure themselves against professionals—and what professionals!—well, purely from the aesthetic point of view they are quite simply Greek athletes, you understand me, my boy, Greek athletes, they are the young men of Plato, or rather they are Spartans. I have a friend who has been to Rouen where their base is, he has seen marvels, marvels almost unimaginable. It is not Rouen any longer, it is another town. Of course the old Rouen still exists, with the emaciated saints of the cathedral. And naturally, that is beautiful too, but it is something quite different. And our *poilus*! I cannot tell you how deliciously full of character I find our *poilus*, the young Parisian boys, like that one there, for instance, who is passing us, with his knowing expression, his alert and humorous face. I often stop them for one reason or another and we chat for a moment or two, and what subtlety, what good sense! And the boys from the provinces, how amusing and nice they are, with the way they roll their *r*'s and their regional dialects! I have always lived a lot in the country, I have slept in farms, I know how to talk to them. Still, our admiration for the French must not make us depreciate our enemies, that would only be to disparage ourselves. And you don't know what a soldier the German soldier is; you haven't seen him, as I have, march past on parade, doing the goose-step, *unter den Linden.*"

And returning to that ideal of virility which he had outlined to me at Balbec and which, with time, had assumed a more philosophical form in his mind, but using also absurd arguments which at moments, even just after he had said something out of the ordinary, gave his hearer a glimpse of the flimsiness of mental fabric of a mere society gentleman, albeit an intelligent one: "You see," he said to me, "that splendid sturdy fellow the Boche soldier is strong and healthy and thinks only of the greatness of his country, *Deutschland über Alles*, which is not so stupid as you might think, whereas we, while they were preparing themselves in a virile fashion, were hopelessly sunk in dilettantism." This word probably signified for M. de Charlus something analogous to literature, for immediately, remembering no doubt that I was fond of literature and had at one time intended to devote myself to it, he slapped me on the shoulder (taking the opportunity to lean so heavily upon me that the blow hurt as much as, in the days when I was doing my military service, the recoil of a "76" against my shoulder-blade) and said, as if to soften the reproach: "Yes, we were sunk in dilettantism, all of us, you too, you may remember. Like me you may say your *mea culpa*. We have been too dilettante." From astonishment at this reproach, from lack of readiness in repartee, from deference towards my interlocutor, and also because I was touched by his friendly kindness, I replied as though I too, as he suggested, had cause to beat my breast—an idiotic reaction, for I could not be accused of the slightest suggestion of dilettantism. "Well," he said to me, "I must leave you here" (the group which had escorted him at a distance had finally abandoned us), "I am going off to bed like a very old gentleman, particularly as, so it seems, the war has changed all our habits—isn't that one of the imbecile aphorisms which Norpois is so fond of?" I knew, as a matter of fact, that when he went home at night M. de Charlus did not cease to be surrounded by soldiers, for he had turned his house into a military hospital and had done this, I believe, in obedience to the dictates much less of his imagination than of his kind heart.

It was a transparent and breathless night; I imagined that the Seine, flowing between the twin semi-circles of the span and the reflection of its bridges, must look like the Bosporus. And —a symbol perhaps of the invasion foretold by the defeatism of M. de Charlus, or else of the co-operation of our Muslim brothers with the armies of France—the moon, narrow and curved like a sequin, seemed to have placed the sky of Paris beneath the oriental sign of the crescent.

M. de Charlus lingered a few moments more, while he said good-bye to me with a shake of my hand powerful enough to crush it to pieces—a Germanic peculiarity to be found in those who think like the Baron. For several seconds he continued, as Cottard would have said, to "knead" my hand, as if he had wished to restore to my joints a suppleness which they had never lost. In certain blind men the sense of touch makes good to a certain extent the lack of sight. I do not exactly know what sense it was taking the place of here. Perhaps he thought that he was merely shaking my hand, as no doubt he thought that he was merely seeing a Senegalese soldier who passed in the darkness without deigning to notice that he was being admired. But in each case the Baron was mistaken, the intensity of contact and of gaze was greater than propriety permitted. "Don't you see all the Orient of Decamps and Fromentin and Ingres and Delacroix in this scene?" he asked me, still immobilised by the passage of the Senegalese. "As you know, I for my part am interested in things and in people only as a painter, a philosopher. Besides, I am too old. But how unfortunate that to complete the picture one of us two is not an odalisque!"

It was not the Orient of Decamps or even of Delacroix that began to haunt my imagination when the Baron had left me, but the old Orient of those *Thousand and One Nights* which I had been so fond of; losing myself gradually in the network of these dark streets, I thought of the Caliph Harun al-Rashid going in search of adventures in the hidden quarters of Baghdad. The weather was warm and my walk had made me hot and thirsty, but the bars had all closed long ago and, because of the scarcity of petrol, the rare taxis which I met, driven by Levantines or negroes, did not even take the trouble to respond to my signs. The only place where I might have been able to get something to drink and rest until I felt strong enough to walk home would have been a hotel. But in the street, rather remote from the centre of the town, to which I had penetrated, every hotel, since the Gothas had begun to drop their bombs on Paris, had closed. The same was true of almost all the shops, the shopkeepers, either owing to lack of staff or because they had taken fright themselves, having fled to the country and left on their door a hand-written notice announcing in some conventional phrase that they would re-open at a distant date (though even that seemed problematical). The few establishments which had managed to survive announced in the same fashion that they were open only twice a week. One felt that poverty, dereliction, fear inhabited the whole quarter. I was all the more surprised, therefore, to see that among these abandoned houses there was one in which life seemed, on the contrary, to have been victorious and terror and bankruptcy to have yielded to activity and wealth. Behind the closed shutters of each window the lights, dimmed on account of police regulations, revealed nevertheless a complete disregard for economy. And at every moment the door opened to allow some fresh visitor to enter or leave. It was a hotel which, because of the money its proprietors must be making, could not fail to have aroused the envy of all the neighbouring tradespeople; and I too became curious when, at a distance of fifteen yards, that is to say too far off for me to be able to make him out clearly in the profound darkness, I saw an officer come out and walk rapidly away.

Something, however, struck me: not his face, which I did not see, nor his uniform, which was disguised by a heavy greatcoat, but the extraordinary disproportion between the number of different points which his body successively occupied and the very small number of seconds within which he made good this departure which had almost the air of a sortie from a besieged town. So that my mind turned, if I did not explicitly recognise him—I will not say even to the build, nor to the slimness or the carriage or the swift movements of Saint-Loup—but to the sort of ubiquity which was so special to him. This military man with the ability to occupy so many different positions in space in such a short time disappeared down a side-street without seeing me, and I was left wondering whether it would be wise to enter a hotel whose modest appearance made me think that it could hardly have been Saint-Loup who had emerged. And yet I recalled involuntarily that he had—unjustly—been involved in a case of espionage because his name had been found in some letters captured on a German officer. He had, of course, been completely exonerated by the military authorities. But in spite of myself I associated this recollection with what I now saw. Was this hotel being used as a meeting-place of spies?

The officer had only just disappeared when I saw some private soldiers of various arms go in, which further strengthened my suspicions. I was now, however, extremely thirsty. I should probably be able to get something to drink inside and at the same time I might attempt, although I felt nervous at the prospect, to assuage my curiosity. And so, but not, I think, primarily from curiosity about the officer I had seen, I hesitated no longer but climbed the little staircase at the top of which the door of a sort of hall stood open, no doubt on account of the heat. I thought at first that I might fail to discover very much, for from the staircase, where I remained in shadow, I saw several people come and ask for a room and receive the answer that there were absolutely none left. The objection to these people, I guessed, was simply that they did not belong to the nest of espionage, for a moment later a common sailor presented himself and was promptly given room No. 28. From where I stood in the darkness I could, without being seen, observe a few soldiers and two men of the working classes who were chatting tranquilly in a stiflingly hot little room, gaudily decorated with coloured pictures of women cut from illustrated magazines and reviews.

These men, as they chatted quietly together, were expounding patriotic ideas: "After all, you've got to do what the other blokes do," said one. "Well, you can be jolly sure *I* don't mean to get killed," was the reply of another, who evidently was going off the next day to a dangerous post, to some expression of good wishes which I had not heard. "I reckon, at twenty-two, after only doing six months, it would be a bit hard," he exclaimed in a voice in which could be heard, even more plainly than the desire to go on living, the assurance that his reasoning was correct, as though the fact that he was only twenty-two could not fail to give him a better chance of survival, as though it were out of the question that he should be killed. "It's terrific in Paris," said another; "you'd never know there's a war on. How about you, Julot, d'you still mean to join up?" "Of course I do, I can't wait to take a pot shot or two at these filthy Boches." "This Joffre, you know, he's just a man who sleeps with the politicians' wives, he's never done a thing himself." "That's a dreadful way to talk," said a slightly older man,

an airman, and then, turning to the workman who had just
made the statement: "I should advise you not to talk like that
in the front line, the *poilus* would soon do you in." The banality
of these scraps of conversation did not inspire me with any
great wish to hear more, and I was about to make my entrance
or go back down the stairs when I was jolted out of my
indifference by hearing a series of remarks which made me
shudder: "I'm amazed the boss isn't back yet, damn it, at this
hour of the night I don't know where he's going to find any
chains." "Anyhow, the chap's already tied up." "Tied up?
Well, he is and he isn't. Tie me up like that and I'd soon untie
myself." "But the padlock's closed." "Of course it's closed, but
it's not so impossible to open it. The trouble is the chains aren't
long enough. Don't you try and tell me, I was beating the
stuffing out of him all last night until my hands were covered
with blood." "Are you doing the beating to-night?" "No. It's
not me, it's Maurice. But it'll be me on Sunday, the boss
promised me." I understood now why the strong arm of the
sailor had been needed. If peaceable citizens had been turned
away, it was not because the hotel was a nest of spies. An
appalling crime was about to be committed, unless someone
arrived in time to discover it and have the criminals arrested.
And yet the whole scene, in the midst of this peaceful and
threatened night, was like a dream or a fairy-tale, so that it was
at once with the pride of an emissary of justice and the rapture
of a poet that I at length, my mind made up, entered the hotel.

I touched my hat lightly and the people in the room, without
rising to their feet, replied more or less civilly to the greeting.
"Can you tell me who is in charge here? I should like a room
and something to drink sent up to it." "Will you wait a minute,
the boss has gone out." "There's the director, he's upstairs,"
suggested one of the men who had taken part in the conversation. "But you know he can't be disturbed." "Do you think
they will give me a room?" "Expect so." "43 must be free,"
said the young man who was sure he would not be killed
because he was twenty-two years old. And he moved a little
way along the sofa to make room for me. "Suppose we open
the window a bit, you can cut the smoke with a knife in here!"
said the airman; and indeed they all had their pipe or their

cigarette. "Yes, but in that case close the shutters first, you know it's forbidden to show any light because of the Zeppelins." "We've finished with the Zeppelins. There's even been something in the papers about their having all been shot down." "We've finished with this, we've finished with that, what d'you know about it? When you've done fifteen months at the front, as I have, and shot down your fifth Boche aeroplane, you'll be able to talk. What d'you want to believe the papers for? They were over Compiègne yesterday, they killed a mother and two children." "A mother and two children!" said the young man who hoped not to be killed, with blazing eyes and a look of profound compassion upon his energetic and open countenance, which I found very likeable. "There's been no news of big Julot lately. His 'godmother' hasn't had a letter from him for eight days, and it's the first time he's been so long without writing." "Who is she, his 'godmother'?" "The woman who looks after the toilets just beyond the Olympia." "Do they sleep together?" "What an idea! She's a married woman, she couldn't be more respectable. She sends him money every week out of pure kindness of heart. She's a real good sort." "Do you know him then, big Julot?" "Do I know him!" retorted scornfully the young man of twenty-two. "He's a close friend of mine and one of the best. There's not many I think as highly of as I do of him: a real pal, always ready to do you a good turn. Yes, it would be a catastrophe all right if anything had happened to him." Someone proposed a game of dice and, from the feverish haste with which the young man of twenty-two shook them and cried out the results, with his eyes starting out of his head, it was easy to see that he had the gambler's temperament. I did not quite catch the next remark that someone made to him, but he exclaimed with a note of profound pity in his voice: "Julot a ponce! You mean he *says* he's a ponce. But he's no more a ponce than I am. I've seen him with my own eyes paying his woman, yes, paying her. That's to say, I don't say Jeanne l'Algérienne didn't give him a little something now and then, but it was never more than five francs, and what's that from a woman in a brothel earning more than fifty francs a day? A present of five francs! Some men are just too stupid to live. And now she's at the front, well, her life may be hard,

I grant you, but she can earn as much as she wants—and she sends him nothing. Bah, that chap a ponce? There's plenty who could call themselves a ponce at that rate. Not only is he not a ponce, in my opinion he's an imbecile." The oldest of the group, whom the boss had no doubt for that reason put in charge of the others, with instructions to make them behave with a certain restraint, had been to the lavatory for a moment and heard only the end of this conversation. But he could not help looking in my direction and seemed visibly upset at the impression such talk must have made on me. Without addressing himself specially to the young man of twenty-two, though it was he who had been expounding this theory of venal love, he said, in a general manner: "You're talking too much and too loud, the window is open, there are people asleep at this hour. You know quite well that if the boss came back and heard you talking like that, he wouldn't be at all pleased."

At that very moment the door was heard to open and everyone was silent, thinking it was the boss, but it was only a foreign chauffeur who was welcomed as an old friend by everybody in the room. But seeing a magnificent watchchain displayed upon the chauffeur's jacket, the young man of twenty-two threw him a questioning and amused glance, followed by a frown and a severe wink in my direction. I understood that the first look meant: "What's that, did you steal it? My congratulations." And the second: "Don't say anything, because of this fellow we don't know." Suddenly the boss came in, carrying several yards of heavy iron chains—sufficient to secure quite a number of convicts—and sweating. "What a weight!" he said. "If you weren't all so idle, I shouldn't be obliged to fetch them myself." I told him that I wanted a room. "Just for a few hours. I can't find a cab and I am rather unwell. But I should like something to drink sent up." "Pierrot, go and fetch some *cassis* from the cellar and tell them to get No. 43 ready. There's 7 ringing again. They say they're ill. Ill my foot, I wouldn't be surprised if they'd been doping themselves, they look half cracked, it's time they were shown the door. Has anybody put a pair of sheets in 22? Good! There goes 7 again, run and see what it is. Well, Maurice, what are you standing there for? You know someone's waiting for you, go up to 14b.

And get a move on." And Maurice hurried out after the boss, who seemed a little annoyed that I had seen his chains and disappeared carrying them with him. "How is it you're so late?" the young man of twenty-two asked the chauffeur. "What do you mean, late? I'm an hour early. But it's too hot in the streets. My appointment's not till midnight." "Who have you come for then?" "Pretty Pamela," said the dark-skinned chauffeur, whose laugh uncovered a set of fine white teeth. "Ah!" said the young man of twenty-two.

Presently I was taken up to Room 43, but it was so unpleasantly stuffy and my curiosity was so great that, having drunk my *cassis*, I started to go downstairs again, then, changing my mind, turned round and went up past the floor of Room 43 to the top of the building. Suddenly from a room situated by itself at the end of a corridor, I thought I heard stifled groans. I walked rapidly towards the sounds and put my ear to the door. "I beseech you, mercy, have pity, untie me, don't beat me so hard," said a voice. "I kiss your feet, I abase myself, I promise not to offend again. Have pity on me." "No, you filthy brute," replied another voice, "and if you yell and drag yourself about on your knees like that, you'll be tied to the bed, no mercy for you," and I heard the noise of the crack of a whip, which I guessed to be reinforced with nails, for it was followed by cries of pain. At this moment I noticed that there was a small oval window opening from the room on to the corridor and that the curtain had not been drawn across it; stealthily in the darkness I crept as far as this window and there in the room, chained to a bed like Prometheus to his rock, receiving the blows that Maurice rained upon him with a whip which was in fact studded with nails, I saw, with blood already flowing from him and covered with bruises which proved that the chastisement was not taking place for the first time—I saw before me M. de Charlus.

Suddenly the door opened and a man came in who fortunately did not see me. It was Jupien. He went up to the Baron with an air of respect and a smile of understanding: "Well, you don't need me, do you?" The Baron asked Jupien to send Maurice out of the room for a moment. Jupien did so with perfect unconcern. "We can't be heard, can we?" said the Baron to Jupien, who assured him that this was the case. The Baron knew that Jupien, with an intelligence worthy of a man of letters, was yet quite lacking in practical sense and constantly talked about people in their presence with innuendoes which deceived nobody and nicknames which everybody understood.

"Just a second," interrupted Jupien, who had heard a bell ring in Room No. 3. It was a deputy of the Liberal Action party, who was about to leave. Jupien did not need to look at the bell-board, for he recognised the man's ring. Indeed the deputy came every day after lunch, but to-day he had been obliged to re-arrange his time-table, for at twelve o'clock he had given away his daughter in marriage at the church of Saint Pierre de Chaillot. So he had come in the evening but was anxious to leave early on account of his wife, who very easily became nervous if he was late in getting home, particularly in these days of bombardment. Jupien always liked to accompany him downstairs in order to show his deference for the status of "honourable," and in this he was quite disinterested. For although this deputy (who repudiated the exaggerations of *L'Action Française* and would in any case have been incapable of understanding a line of Charles Maurras or Léon Daudet) stood well with the Ministers, whom he flattered by inviting them to his shooting-parties, Jupien would not have dared to ask him for the slightest support in his difficulties with the police. He knew that, had he ventured to mention that subject to the affluent and apprehensive legislator, he would not have saved himself even the most harmless "raid" but would immediately have lost the most generous of his clients. After having escorted the deputy as far as the door, from which he set off with his hat pulled down over his eyes and his collar turned up and with a rapid gliding movement not unlike the style of his electoral manifestoes, by which devices he hoped to render his face invisible, Jupien went upstairs again to M. de Charlus. "It was Monsieur Eugène," he said to him. In Jupien's establishment, as in a sanatorium, people were referred to only by their Christian names, though their real names, either to satisfy the curiosity of the visitor or to enhance the prestige of the house, were invariably added in a whisper. Sometimes, however, Jupien was unaware of the real identity of a client and imagined and said that he was some well-known financier or nobleman or artist—fleeting errors not without charm for the man to whom the wrong name was attached—and in the end had to resign himself to the idea that he still did not know who Monsieur Victor was. Sometimes too, to please the Baron, he was in the habit of inverting the procedure that is customary on certain social occasions ("Let me introduce you to M. Lebrun," then a whisper: "He wants to be called M. Lebrun but he is really Grand Duke X—of Russia"). Jupien on the other hand felt that it was not quite sufficient to introduce M. de Charlus to a young milkman. He would murmur to him with a wink: "He's a milkman but he's also one of the most dangerous thugs in Belleville" (and it was with a superbly salacious note in his voice that Jupien uttered the word "thug"). And as if this recommendation were not sufficient, he would try to add one or two further "citations." "He has had several convictions for theft and burglary, he was in Fresnes for assaulting" (the same salacious note in his voice) "and practically murdering people in the street, and he's been in a punishment battalion in Africa. He killed his sergeant."

The Baron was slightly cross with Jupien for his lack of prudence, for he knew that in this house which he had instructed his factotum to purchase for him and to manage through a subordinate, everybody, thanks to the blunders of Mlle d'Oloron's uncle, was more or less aware of his identity and his name (many, however, thought that it was not a title but a nickname, and mispronounced and distorted it, so that their own stupidity and not the discretion of Jupien had served to protect the Baron). But he found it simpler to let himself be reassured by Jupien's assurances, and now, relieved to know that they could not be heard, he said to him: "I did not want to speak in front of that boy, who is very nice and does his best. But I don't find him sufficiently brutal. He has a charming face, but when he calls me a filthy brute he might be just repeating a lesson." "I assure you, nobody has said a word to him," replied Jupien, without perceiving how improbable this statement was. "And besides, he was involved in the murder of a concierge in La Villette." "Ah! that is extremely interesting," said the Baron with a smile. "But I'll tell you who

I have here: the killer of oxen, the man of the slaughter-houses, who is so like this boy; he happened to be passing. Would you care to try him?" "Yes, certainly I should." I saw the man of the slaughter-houses enter the room; he was indeed a little like Maurice, but—and this was odder—they both had in them something of a type which I had never myself consciously observed in Morel's face but which I now clearly saw to exist there; they bore a resemblance, if not to Morel as I had seen him, at least to a certain countenance which eyes seeing Morel otherwise than I did might have constructed out of his features. No sooner had I, out of features borrowed from my recollections of Morel, privately made for myself this rough model of what he might represent to somebody else, than I realised that the two young men, one of whom was a jeweller's assistant while the other worked in a hotel, were in a vague way substitutes for Morel. Was I to conclude that M. de Charlus, at least in a certain aspect of his loves, was always faithful to a particular type and that the desire which had made him select these two young men one after the other was the identical desire which had made him accost Morel on the platform at Doncières station; that all three resembled a little the ephebe whose form, engraved in the sapphire-like eyes of M. de Charlus, gave to his glance that strange quality which had alarmed me the first day at Balbec? Or that, his love for Morel having modified the type which he pursued, to console himself for Morel's absence he sought men who resembled him? A third hypothesis which occurred to me was that perhaps, in spite of appearances, there had never existed between him and Morel anything more than relations of friendship, and that M. de Charlus caused young men who resembled Morel to come to Jupien's establishment so that he might have the illusion, while he was with them, of enjoying pleasure with Morel himself. It is true that, if one thought of everything that M. de Charlus had done for Morel, this hypothesis was bound to seem most unlikely, did one not know that love drives us not only to the greatest sacrifices on behalf of the person we love, but sometimes even to the sacrifice of our desire itself, a desire which in any case we find all the harder to gratify if the loved person is aware of the strength of our love. And something

else that made this hypothesis less improbable than at first sight
it appears to be (though I have little doubt that it was not in
fact the true one) was the influence of the nervous temperament, the profoundly passionate character of M. de Charlus—
in this not unlike Saint-Loup—which in the early days of his
relations with Morel might have had the same negative effect
of making him behave with greater propriety that a similar
cause had had on his nephew in the early days of his relations
with Rachel. A man's relations with a woman whom he loves
(and the same may be true of love for a young man) may remain
platonic for a reason which is neither the woman's virtue nor
a lack of sensuality in the love which she inspires. The reason
may be that the lover, too impatient from the very excess of his
love, does not know how to wait with a sufficient show of indifference for the moment when he will obtain what he desires.
Over and over again he returns to the charge, he writes incessantly to the woman, he tries constantly to see her, she
refuses, he is in despair. Henceforth she understands that if she
accords him her company, her friendship, this happiness in
itself will seem so considerable to the man who thought he had
lost it, that she may spare herself the trouble of giving him
anything more and may take advantage of a moment when he
can no longer endure not to see her, when he is determined at
any price to end the war, to impose upon him a peace of which
the first condition will be the platonic nature of their relations.
In any case, during the period which preceded this treaty, the
lover, always anxious, hoping all the time for a letter, a glance,
has given up thinking of physical possession, which at first had
been the object of the desire which had tormented him; that
desire has withered away with waiting and its place has been
taken by needs of another order, needs which can, however, if
they remain unsatisfied, cause him yet greater pain. So that the
pleasure which at the beginning he had hoped to obtain from
caresses, he receives later not in its natural form but instead
from friendly words, from mere promises of the loved woman's
presence, which after the effects of uncertainty—sometimes
after a single look, black with a heavy cloud of disdain, which
has withdrawn her to such a distance that he thinks he will
never see her again—bring with them a delicious relief from

tension. A woman divines these things and knows that she can afford the luxury of never giving herself to a man who, because he has been too agitated to conceal it during the first few days, has allowed her to become aware of his incurable desire for her. She is only too pleased to receive, without giving anything in return, much more than she is accustomed to be given when she gives herself. Men with a nervous temperament believe therefore in the virtue of their idol. And the halo which they place round her is a product, but as we have seen an indirect one, of their excessive love. The woman then finds herself very much in the position—though she of course is conscious, while they are not—of those unwittingly crafty drugs like sleeping-draughts and morphine. It is not to the people to whom they bring the pleasure of sleep or a genuine well-being that these drugs are an absolute necessity; it is not by such people as these that they would be bought at any price, bartered against all the sick man's possessions, but by that other class of sick men (who may perhaps be the same individuals but become different with the passage of a few years), those whom the medicine does not send to sleep, to whom it gives no thrill of pleasure, but who, so long as they are without it, are prey to an agitation which at any price, even the price of their own death, they need desperately to end.

In the case of M. de Charlus, which on the whole, with slight discrepancies due to the identity of sex, accords very well with the general laws of love, for all that he belonged to a family more ancient than the Capets, that he was rich and vainly sought after by fashionable society while Morel was nobody, he would have got nowhere by saying to Morel, as he had once said to me: "I am a prince, I want to help you,"—it was still Morel who had the upper hand so long as he refused to surrender. And for him to persist in this refusal, it was perhaps enough that he should feel himself to be loved. The horror that grand people have for the snobs who move heaven and earth to make their acquaintance is felt also by the virile man for the invert, by a woman for every man who is too much in love with her. M. de Charlus possessed, and would have offered Morel a share in, immense advantages. But it is possible that all this might have hurled itself in vain against a determined will. And in that case, M. de Charlus would have suffered the same fate as the Germans—in whose ranks in fact his ancestry placed him—who in the war at that moment taking its course were indeed, as the Baron was a little too fond of repeating, victorious on every front. But of what use were their victories, since after every one they found the Allies yet more firmly resolved to refuse them the one thing that they, the Germans, wanted: peace and reconciliation? Napoleon too, as he advanced into Russia, had again and again magnanimously invited the authorities to meet him. But nobody came.

I made my way downstairs and went back into the little ante-room where Maurice, uncertain whether he would be sent for again (he had been told by Jupien to wait just in case), was engaged in a game of cards with one of his friends. There was a lot of excitement about a *croix de guerre* which had been found lying on the ground—nobody knew who had lost it and to whom it ought to be returned so that the owner should not be punished. Then there was talk of the generosity of an officer who had been killed trying to save his batman. "All the same, there are some good blokes among the rich. I'd gladly get myself killed for a chap like that," said Maurice, who evidently performed his terrible fustigations of the Baron simply from mechanical habit, as a result of a neglected education, from need of money and from a certain preference for making it in a manner which was supposed to be less trouble, and was perhaps really more trouble, than ordinary work. But as M. de Charlus had feared, he was perhaps really very kind-hearted and certainly, so it seemed, a young man of exemplary courage. He almost had tears in his eyes as he spoke of the death of this officer, and the young man of twenty-two was no less moved. "Yes, indeed, they're fine blokes. For poor chaps like us there's not much to lose, but when it's a toff who has a whole troop of flunkeys and can go to posh bars every night of his life, it's really terrific! You can scoff as much as you like, but when you see blokes like that dying, it really does something to you. Rich people like that, God shouldn't let them die—for one thing they're too useful to the working man. A death like that makes you want to kill every Boche to the last man. And then look what they did at Louvain, and cutting off the hands of little

children! No, I don't know, I'm no better than the next man,
but I'd rather face the music and be shot to bits than give in to
barbarians like that; they're not men, they're real barbarians,
don't you try and tell me anything else." All these young men
were patriots at heart. One only, who had been slightly wounded
in the arm but was soon going to have to return to the front,
did not rise to the level of the others. "Darn it," he said, "it
wasn't the right sort of wound" (the kind that gets you
invalided out), very much as in the past Mme Swann would
have said: "Somehow or other I've caught this most tiresome
influenza."

The door opened to re-admit the chauffeur, who had been
taking the air for a moment. "What, finished already? You
weren't long," he said, catching sight of Maurice, whom he
supposed to be still engaged in beating the individual whom,
in allusion to a newspaper which was appearing at that time,
they had nicknamed "the Man in Chains." "It may not have
seemed long to you out in the fresh air," replied Maurice,
vexed that the others should see that he had failed to give
satisfaction upstairs. "But if you'd been obliged to wallop away
with all your might in this heat, like me! If it wasn't for the
fifty francs he gives . . ." "And then, he's a man who talks well;
you can see he's educated. Does he say it will soon be over?"
"He says we'll never beat them, it will end without either side
really winning." "Bloody hell, if he says that he must be a
Boche. . . ." "I've already told you you're talking too loud,"
said the oldest of the group to the others, seeing that I had
returned, and then to me: "Have you finished with your
room?" "Shut your trap, you're not the boss here." "Yes, I've
finished, and I've come to pay." "It would be better if you paid
the *patron*. Maurice, go and fetch him." "But I don't want to
bother you." "It's no trouble." Maurice went upstairs, and
came back saying: "The *patron* will be down in a second." I
gave him two francs for his pains. He blushed with pleasure.
"Oh! thank you very much. I'll send it to my brother who's a
prisoner. No, he doesn't have a bad time. It depends a lot on
the camp you're in."

Meanwhile, two very smart clients, in white tie and tails and
wearing overcoats—two Russians, as I guessed from the very

slight accent with which they spoke—were standing in the door-way and deliberating whether they should enter. It was visibly the first time that they had been to the place, to which no doubt they had come on somebody's recommendation, and they appeared torn between desire, temptation and extreme fright. One of the two—a good-looking young man—kept repeating every ten seconds to the other, with a smile that was half a question and half an attempt at persuasion: "Well! After all, what do we care?" But though no doubt he meant by this that after all they did not care about the consequences, it is probable that he cared rather more than he implied, for the remark was not followed by any movement to cross the threshold but by a further glance at his companion, followed by the same smile and the same "After all, what do we care?" And in this "After all, what do we care?" I saw a perfect example of that portentous language, so unlike the language we habitually speak, in which emotion deflects what we had intended to say and causes to emerge in its place an entirely different phrase, issued from an unknown lake wherein dwell these expressions alien to our thoughts which by virtue of that very fact reveal them. I remember an occasion when Françoise, whose approach we had not heard, was about to come into the room while Albertine was completely naked in my arms, and Albertine, wanting to warn me, blurted out: "Good heavens, here's the beautiful Françoise!" Françoise, whose sight was no longer very good and who was merely going to cross the room at some distance from us, would no doubt have noticed nothing. But the unprecedented phrase "the beautiful Françoise," which Albertine had never uttered before in her life, was in itself enough to betray its origin; Françoise sensed that the words had been plucked at random by emotion and had no need to look to understand what was happening; she went out muttering in her dialect the word *poutana*. On another occasion, many years later, after Bloch had become the father of a family and had married off one of his daughters to a Catholic, an ill-mannered gentleman said to the young woman that he thought he had heard that her father was a Jew and asked what his name was. Whereupon she, who had been Mlle Bloch with a *k* sound from the day she was born, replied "Bloch" with

the Teutonic *ch* which the Duc de Guermantes would have
used.

The *patron*, to return to the scene in the hotel (into which the
two Russians had decided to penetrate—"After all, what do we
care?"), had still not arrived when Jupien came in to say that
they were talking too loud and that the neighbours would
complain. But seeing me he was rooted to the spot in amazement. "Go out on to the landing all of you." They were all
rising to their feet when I said to him: "It would be simpler if
these young men stayed where they are and you and I went
outside for a moment." He followed me, very agitated. I
explained to him why I had come. Clients could be heard
inquiring of the *patron* whether he could introduce them to a
footman, a choir-boy, a negro chauffeur. Every profession interested these old lunatics, every branch of the armed forces,
every one of the allied nations. Some asked particularly for
Canadians, influenced perhaps unconsciously by the charm of
an accent so slight that one does not know whether it comes
from the France of the past or from England. The Scots too,
because of their kilts and because dreams of a landscape with
lakes are often associated with these desires, were at a premium.
And as every form of madness is, if not in every case aggravated
by circumstances, at least imprinted by them with particular
characteristics, an old man in whom curiosity of every kind had
no doubt been satisfied was asking insistently to be introduced
to a disabled soldier. Slow footsteps were heard on the stairs.
With the indiscretion that was natural to him, Jupien could not
refrain from telling me that it was the Baron who was coming
down, and at all costs he must not see me, but that if I liked to
go into the bedroom adjoining the ante-room where the young
men were, he would open the ventilator, a device which he had
fixed up so that the Baron could see and hear without being
seen, and which he said he would use in my favour against him.
"Only don't move." And pushing me into the dark, he left me.
In any case he had no other room to give me, his hotel, in spite
of the war, being full. The one which I had just left had been
taken by the Vicomte de Courvoisier who, having got away
from the Red Cross at X—for two days, had come to Paris for
an hour's entertainment before going on to the Château de

Courvoisier to be reunited with his wife, to whom he would explain that he had not been able to catch the fast train. He had no suspicion that M. de Charlus was a few yards away from him, and the latter would have been equally surprised to know that his cousin was there, never having met him in the establishment of Jupien, who was himself ignorant of the Vicomte's carefully concealed identity.

The Baron soon entered the ante-room, walking with difficulty on account of his injuries, though doubtless he must have been used to them. Although his pleasure was at an end and he had only come in to give Maurice the money which he owed him, he directed at the young men a tender and curious glance which travelled round the whole circle, promising himself with each of them the pleasure of a moment's chat, platonic but amorously prolonged. And in the sprightly frivolity which he exhibited before this harem which appeared almost to intimidate him, I recognised those jerky movements of the body and the head, those languishing glances which had struck me on the evening of his first visit to la Raspelière, graces inherited from some grandmother whom I had not known, which in ordinary life were disguised by more virile expressions on his face but which from time to time were made to blossom there coquettishly, when circumstances made him anxious to please an inferior audience, by the desire to appear a great lady.

Jupien had recommended the young men to the Baron's favour by swearing that they were all pimps from Belleville and would sell you their own sisters for a few francs. And in this he was at the same time lying and telling the truth. Better, more soft-hearted than he made them out to be, they did not belong to a race of savages. But the clients who believed them to be thugs spoke to them nevertheless with complete truthfulness, a truthfulness which they imagined these terrible beings to share. For a man given to sadistic pleasures may believe that he is talking to a murderer but this will not alter his own purity of heart, he will still be astounded by the mendacity of his companion, who is not a murderer at all but wants to earn a little easy money and whose father or mother or sister alternately die, come to life, and die again as he contradicts himself in his conversation with the client whom he is attempting to please.

The client, in his naïvety, is astounded, for with his arbitrary conception of the gigolo, while he gets a thrill of delight from the numerous murders of which he believes him to be guilty, he is horrified by any simple contradiction or lie which he detects in his words.

Everybody in the room seemed to know him, and M. de Charlus stopped for a long time before each one, talking to them in what he thought was their language, both from a pretentious affectation of local colour and because he got a sadistic pleasure from contact with a life of depravity. "You're disgusting, you are, I saw you outside the Olympia with two tarts. After a bit of brass, no doubt. Just shows how faithful you are to me." Luckily for the man to whom these remarks were addressed, he did not have time to declare that he would never have accepted "brass" from a woman, a claim which would have damped the Baron's ardour, but reserved his protest for the final phrase, which he answered by saying: "But of course I'm faithful to you." This remark gave M. de Charlus a lively pleasure, and as, in spite of himself, the kind of intelligence that was natural to him showed through the character which he affected, he turned to Jupien: "How nice of him to say that! And how well he says it! One would really think it was true. And after all, what does it matter whether it is true or not since he manages to make me believe it? What charming little eyes he has! There, I'm going to give you two big kisses for your trouble, my dear boy. You will think of me in the trenches. Things are not too bad there?" "Whew, there are some days, when a grenade just misses you. . . ." And the young man proceeded to imitate the noise of the grenade, the aeroplanes, etc. "But one's got to do what the others do, and you can be absolutely sure that we will go on to the end." "To the end! If one only knew to what end!" said the Baron in a melancholy manner, giving rein to his "pessimism." "You haven't seen what Sarah Bernhardt said in the papers: 'France will go on to the end. If necessary, the French will let themselves be killed to the last man.' " "I do not doubt for a single moment that the French would bravely let themselves be killed to the last man," said M. de Charlus, as if this were the simplest thing in the world and although he himself had no intention of doing anything whatsoever, hoping by this remark to correct the impression of pacifism which he gave when he forgot himself. "That I do not doubt, but I ask myself to what extent *Madame* Sarah Bernhardt is qualified to speak in the name of France. . . . But I don't think I have made the acquaintance of this charming, this delightful young man," he added, spying another whom he did not recognise or perhaps had not seen before. He greeted him as he would have greeted a prince at Versailles, and making the most of this opportunity to have a supplementary pleasure for nothing—just as, when I was little and my mother had finished giving an order at Boissier's or Gouache's, I would accept the offer of a sweet which one of the ladies behind the counter would invite me to select from those glass bowls over which she and her colleagues held sway—he took the hand of the charming young man and gave it a long squeeze, in the Prussian manner, smilingly fixing him with his eyes for the interminable time which photographers used to take to pose you when the light was bad. "Sir, I am charmed, I am enchanted to make your acquaintance. What pretty hair he has!" he said, turning to Jupien. Next he went up to Maurice to give him his fifty francs, but first, putting his arm round his waist: "You never told me that you had knifed an old hag of a concierge in Belleville." And M. de Charlus shrieked with ecstatic laughter and brought his face close to that of Maurice. "Oh! Monsieur le Baron," said the gigolo, who had not been warned, "how can you believe such a thing?" Whether the report was in fact false, or whether it was true and the perpetrator of the deed nevertheless thought it abominable and one of those things that it is better to deny, he went on: "Me touch a fellow-creature? A Boche, yes, because that's war, but a woman, and an old woman at that!" This declaration of virtuous principles had the effect of a douche of cold water upon the Baron, who brusquely moved away from Maurice, having first handed him his money, but with the disgusted air of someone who has been cheated, who pays because he does not want to make a fuss but is far from pleased. The bad impression made upon the Baron was accentuated by the manner in which the recipient thanked him, with the words: "I shall send this to the old folks and keep a bit for my brother at the front as well." By these touching sentiments M. de Charlus was almost as gravely disappointed as he was irritated by the rather conventional peasant's language in which they were expressed. Occasionally Jupien warned the young men that they ought to be more perverse. Then one of them, as if he were confessing to something diabolical, would hazard: "I say, Baron, you won't believe me, but when I was a kid I used to watch my parents making love through the key-hole. Pretty vicious, wasn't it? You look as if you think that's a cock and bull story, but I swear it's the truth." And M. de Charlus was driven at once to despair and to exasperation by this factitious attempt at perversity, the result of which was only to reveal such depths both of stupidity and of innocence. Yet even the most determined thief or murderer would not have satisfied him, for that sort of man does not talk about his crimes; and besides there exists in the sadist—however kind he may be, in fact all the more the kinder he is—a thirst for evil which wicked men, doing what they do not because it is wicked but from other motives, are unable to assuage.

The young man realised his mistake and tried to repair it by saying that he loathed the sight of a copper and by daringly inquiring of the Baron: "How about a date?"—but it was too late, the charm was dispelled. One had a distinct feeling of sham, as with the books of authors who force themselves to write slang. It was in vain that the young man described in detail all the "filthy things" that he did with his wife; M. de Charlus merely reflected that these "filthy things" amounted to very little. And in this he was not simply being insincere. Nothing is more limited than pleasure and vice. In that sense one may say truly, altering slightly the meaning of the phrase, that we revolve always in the same vicious circle.

If M. de Charlus was believed to be not a baron but a prince, there was, conversely, general regret in the establishment for the death of someone of whom the gigolos said: "I don't know his name, but it seems that he is a baron," and who was none other than the Prince de Foix (the father of Saint-Loup's friend). Supposed by his wife to spend a lot of time at his club, in reality he would sit for hours at Jupien's, retailing fashionable gossip to an audience from the underworld. Like his son he was tall and good-looking. M. de Charlus, no doubt because he had always known him in society, remained strangely ignorant that the Prince shared his own tastes, to such a degree that he was even said to have had designs at one time upon his own son, Saint-Loup's friend, then still at school. This was probably untrue: on the contrary, excellently informed about activities whose existence many do not suspect, he watched with care over the company kept by his son. One day a man—and a man not of exalted origin—followed the young Prince de Foix as far as his father's house, where he threw a note in at the window, which the father picked up. But the follower, though genealogically this was not the case, from another point of view belonged to the same world as M. de Foix the father. He therefore had no difficulty in finding among those who shared their common secrets an intermediary who silenced M. de Foix by proving to him that it was his son who had himself provoked this rash act of an elderly man. And this was quite possible. For the Prince de Foix had succeeded in preserving his son from the external influence of bad company but not from heredity. The young Prince de Foix, however, remained, like his father, in this respect unknown to his social equals, although in a different world his behaviour was wild in the extreme.

"How simple he is! You would never say he was a baron," said some of the frequenters of the establishment when M. de Charlus had left, after being escorted to the street door by Jupien, to whom he did not fail to complain of the young man's virtuousness. From the air of annoyance of Jupien, whose duty it was to have trained the young man in advance, it was clear that the fictitious murderer would presently get a terrific dressing down. "The truth is exactly the opposite of what you told me," added the Baron, so that Jupien might profit by the lesson for another time. "He seems most good-natured, he expresses sentiments of respect for his family." "Still, he's on bad terms with his father," Jupien objected. "It's true they live together, but they work in different bars." Obviously this was not much of a crime compared with murder, but Jupien had been caught unprepared with an answer. The Baron said no more, for, if he wanted others to prepare his pleasures for him, he wanted to give himself the illusion that they were unprepared. "He is a real crook, he said all that to mislead you, you are too gullible," Jupien went on, in an attempt to exculpate himself which succeeded only in wounding the vanity of M. de Charlus.

"It seems that he has a million francs a day to spend," said the young man of twenty-two, who saw no improbability in this statement. The car which had come to fetch M. de Charlus was now heard to drive away. At the same moment there entered the room with a slow step, by the side of a soldier who had evidently emerged with her from a neighbouring bedroom, what appeared to me to be an elderly lady in a black skirt. I soon realised my mistake: it was a priest—that thing so rare, and in France altogether exceptional, a bad priest. Evidently the soldier was teasing his companion about the discrepancy between his conduct and his habit, for the other with a serious air, raising a finger towards his hideous face with the gesture of a doctor of theology, said sententiously: "What do you expect? I am not" (I expected him to say "a saint") "a good girl." He was, however, ready to depart and he said good-bye to Jupien, who had just come upstairs again after seeing the Baron to the door. But absentmindedly the bad priest had forgotten to pay for his room. Jupien, who had always a ready wit, shook the collecting box in which he placed the contribution of each client and said, as he made it clink: "For the expenses of the church, Monsieur l'Abbé!" The horrid creature apologised, put in his coin and disappeared.

Jupien came to fetch me from the cave of darkness in which I had been standing without daring to move. "Come into the hall for a moment where my young men are sitting, while I go upstairs and lock up the bedroom; since you have taken a room, it's quite natural." The *patron* was there, so I paid him. At that moment a young man in a dinner-jacket came in and asked the *patron* with an air of authority: "Will I be able to have Léon at a quarter to eleven instead of eleven to-morrow morning, as I have a luncheon engagement?" "That will depend," replied the *patron*, "on how long the Abbé keeps him." This reply appeared not to satisfy the young man in a dinner-jacket, who seemed to be on the point of launching into abuse of the Abbé, but his

TIME REGAINED

fury was diverted when he caught sight of me. Going straight
up to the *patron*: "Who is this? What does this mean?" he
muttered in a quiet but angry voice. The *patron*, very put out,
explained that my presence was quite harmless, that I had taken
a room. The young man in a dinner-jacket appeared to be not
in the slightest degree pacified by this explanation. He kept
repeating: "This is extremely unpleasant, things of this sort
ought not to happen, you know I detest them, if you are not
careful I will never set foot here again." The execution of this
threat did not, however, appear to be imminent, for he went off
in a rage, but not without asking that Léon should try to be
free at a quarter to eleven, or better still half past ten. Jupien
came back to fetch me and we went downstairs together and
out into the street.

"I do not want you to misjudge me," he said to me. "This
house does not bring me in as much profit as you might think.
I am obliged to let rooms to respectable people, though of
course if they were my only customers I should simply be
throwing money down the drain. Here, contrary to the doctrine
of the Carmelites, it is thanks to vice that virtue is able to live.
No, if I took this house, or rather if I got the manager whom
you have seen to take it, it was purely and simply in order to
render a service to the Baron and amuse his old age." Jupien
was here referring not merely to scenes of sadism like those
which I had witnessed and to the actual vicious practices of the
Baron. The latter, even for conversation, for company, for a
game of cards, now only enjoyed the society of lower-class
people who exploited him. No doubt the snobbery of the
gutter may be understood as easily as snobbery of the other
kind. The two had in fact long been united, alternating one
with the other, in M. de Charlus, who thought no one was
smart enough to be numbered among his social acquaintances,
no one sufficiently a ruffian to be worth knowing in other ways.
"I detest the intermediate style," he would say. "Bourgeois
comedy is stiff and affected. Let me have either the princesses of
classical tragedy or broad farce. No half-way houses—either
Phèdre or *Les Saltimbanques*." But in the end the balance
between the two forms of snobbery had been broken. Perhaps
because he was an old man and tired, perhaps because sensuality

had come to enter into even his trivial relationships, the Baron now lived only among his "inferiors," thus unintentionally taking his place as the successor of more than one among his great ancestors, the Duc de La Rochefoucauld, the Prince d'Harcourt, the Duc de Berry, whom we see in the pages of Saint-Simon passing their lives in the midst of their lackeys, who extracted enormous sums from them, and sharing their amusements, to such an extent that people who had to visit them were embarrassed, for their sakes, to find these great noblemen familiarly engaged in a game of cards or a drinking-bout with their domestic servants. "And above all," Jupien went on, "it is to keep him out of trouble, because the Baron, you know, is a big baby. Even now that he has here everything that he can desire, he still wanders about in search of sordid adventures. And with his generosity, that sort of thing could have disagreeable consequences in these days. Only the other day there was a page-boy from a hotel who was absolutely terrified because of all the money the Baron offered him if he would go to his house! (To his house, what imprudence!) The boy, who in fact only cares about women, was reassured when he understood what was wanted of him. Hearing all these promises of money, he had taken the Baron for a spy. And he was greatly relieved when he realised that he was being asked to sell not his country but his body, which is possibly not a more moral thing to do, but less dangerous and in any case easier." And listening to Jupien, I said to myself: "How unfortunate it is that M. de Charlus is not a novelist or a poet! Not merely so that he could describe what he sees, but because the position in which a Charlus finds himself with regard to desire by causing scandals to spring up round him compels him to take life seriously, to load pleasure with a weight of emotion. He cannot get stuck in an ironical and superficial view of things because a current of pain is perpetually re-awakened within him. Almost every time he makes a declaration of love he is violently snubbed, if he does not run the risk of being sent to prison." A slap in the face or a box on the ear helps to educate not only children but poets. If M. de Charlus had been a novelist, the house which Jupien had set up for him, by reducing so greatly the risks—at least (for a raid by the police was always a possibility) the risk emanating from an individual casually encountered in the street, of whose inclinations the Baron could not have felt certain—would have been a misfortune for him. But in the sphere of art M. de Charlus was no more than a dilettante, who never thought of writing and had no gift for it.

"Besides, I may as well admit to you," Jupien continued, "that I have very few scruples about making money in this way. The actual thing that is done here is—I can no longer conceal the fact from you—something that I like, it is what I have a taste for myself. Well, is it forbidden to receive payment for things that one does not regard as wickedness? You are better educated than I am, and you will tell me no doubt that Socrates was of the opinion that he could not accept money for his lessons. But in our age professors of philosophy do not hold that view, nor do doctors or painters or playwrights or theatrical producers. Do not imagine that this trade of mine brings me into contact only with the dregs of society. No doubt the director of an establishment of this kind, like a great courtesan, receives only men, but he receives men who are conspicuous in every walk of life and who are generally, on their own level, among the most intelligent, the most sensitive, the most agreeable of their profession. In no time at all, I assure you, this house could be transformed into an information bureau or a school of wit." Nevertheless, I was still under the impression of the blows which I had seen inflicted upon M. de Charlus.

And the truth is that, when one knew M. de Charlus well—his pride, his satiety with social pleasures, his fancies which changed easily into passions for men of the lowest class and the worst character—one could very easily understand that the possession of a huge fortune, the charm of which, had he been an upstart, would have been that it enabled him to marry his daughter to a duke and invite Highnesses to his shooting-parties, pleased him simply because it allowed him to have at his disposal in this way one or perhaps several establishments with a permanent supply of young men whose company he enjoyed. And perhaps this might have come to pass even without his special vice, heir as he was to so many great noblemen, dukes or princes of the blood, of whom Saint-Simon tells us

that they never associated with anybody "who could boast a
name."

"Meanwhile," I said to Jupien, "this house is anything but
what you say it might become. It is worse than a madhouse,
since the mad fancies of the lunatics who inhabit it are played
out as actual, visible drama—it is a veritable pandemonium. I
thought that I had arrived, like the Caliph in the *Thousand and
One Nights*, in the nick of time to rescue a man who was being
beaten, and in fact it was a different tale from the *Thousand
and One Nights* which I saw enacted before me, the one in which
a woman who has been turned into a dog willingly submits to
being beaten in order to recover her former shape." Jupien
appeared to be very upset by my words, for he realised that I
had seen the Baron being beaten. He was silent for a moment,
while I stopped a cab which was passing; then suddenly, with
that pretty wit which had so often struck me in this self-
educated man when in the courtyard of our house he had
greeted me or Françoise with some graceful phrase: "You have
mentioned one or two of the tales in the *Thousand and One
Nights*," he said. "But there is another I know of, not unrelated to the title of a book which I think I have seen at the
Baron's" (he was alluding to a translation of Ruskin's *Sesame
and Lilies* which I had sent M. de Charlus). "If ever you are
curious, one evening, to see, I will not say forty but a dozen
thieves, you have only to come here; to know whether I am in
the house you have only to look up at that window; if I leave
my little window open with a light visible it means that I am
in the house and you may come in; it is my private Sesame. I
say only Sesame. As for Lilies, if they are what you seek I
advise you to go elsewhere." And with a somewhat offhand
gesture of farewell—for an aristocratic clientele and the habit
of ruling like a pirate chief over a gang of young men had
imparted a certain lordliness to his manners—he was about to
take his leave of me when the noise of an explosion—a bomb
which had fallen before the sirens could give warning—made
him advise me to stay with him for a moment. Soon the anti-
aircraft barrage began, and with such violence that one could
sense very near, just above our heads, the presence of the
German aeroplane.

In an instant the streets became totally black. At moments only, an enemy aeroplane flying very low lit up the spot upon which it wished to drop a bomb. I set off, but very soon I was lost. I thought of that day when, on my way to la Raspelière, I had met an aeroplane and my horse had reared as at the apparition of a god. Now, I thought, it would be a different meeting—with the god of evil, who would kill me. I started to walk faster in order to escape, like a traveller pursued by a tidal wave; I groped my way round dark squares from which I could find no way out. At last the flames of a blazing building showed me where I was and I got back on to the right road, while all the time the shells burst noisily above my head. But my thoughts had turned to another subject. I was thinking of Jupien's house, perhaps by now reduced to ashes, for a bomb had fallen very near me just after I had left it—that house upon which M. de Charlus might prophetically have written *Sodoma*, as the unknown inhabitant of Pompeii had done, with no less prescience or perhaps when the volcano had already started to erupt and the catastrophe had begun. But what mattered sirens and Gothas to the men who had come to seek their pleasure? The social setting or the natural scene which surrounds our love-making barely impinges upon our thoughts. The tempest may rage over the sea, the ship roll and plunge in every direction, the sky pour down avalanches convulsed by the wind, and at most we bestow the attention of a single second, forced from us by physical discomfort, upon this immense scenic background against which we ourselves are so insignificant, both we and the body which we long to approach. The siren with its warning of bombs troubled Jupien's visitors no more than an iceberg would have done. Indeed, the threat of physical danger delivered them from the fear which for long had morbidly harassed them. For it is wrong to suppose that the scale of our fears corresponds to that of the dangers by which they are inspired. A man may be afraid of not sleeping and not in the least afraid of a serious duel, afraid of a rat and not of a lion. For a few hours now the police would have their hands full looking after something as trivial as the lives of the city's inhabitants and their reputations were temporarily in no danger. But if some, their fears allayed, remained in Jupien's establishment, others were tempted not so much by the thought of recovering their moral liberty as by the darkness which had suddenly settled upon the streets. Some of these, like the Pompeians upon whom the fire from heaven was already raining, descended into the passages of the Métro, black as catacombs. They knew that they would not be alone there. And darkness, which envelops all things like a new element, has the effect, irresistibly tempting for certain people, of suppressing the first halt on the road to pleasure—it permits us to enter without impediment into a region of caresses to which normally we gain access only after a certain delay. Whether the coveted object be a woman or a man, supposing even that the first approach is easy and that there is no need of the gallant speeches which in a drawing-room might run on for ever (at any rate in daylight), on a normal evening, even in the most dimly lit street, there is at least a preamble in which the eyes alone feed on the repast which cannot yet be enjoyed and the fear of passers-by, the fear also of the man or woman before us, prevents us from doing more than look and speak. In the darkness this time-honoured ritual is instantly abolished— hands, lips, bodies may go into action at once. There is always the excuse of darkness, and of the mistakes that darkness engenders, if we are not well received. And if we are, this immediate response of a body which does not withdraw but approaches, gives us of the woman (or the man) whom we have selected the idea that she is without prejudices and full of vice, which adds an extra pleasure to the happiness of having bitten straight into the fruit without first coveting it with our eyes and without asking permission. Meanwhile the darkness persisted; plunged into the new element, imagining that they had travelled to a distant country and were witnessing a natural phenomenon like a tidal wave or an eclipse, that they were enjoying not an artificially prepared, sedentary pleasure but a chance encounter in the unknown, the men who had come away from Jupien's house celebrated, while the bombs mimicked the rumbling of a volcano, deep in the earth as in a Pompeian house of ill fame, their secret rites in the shadows of the catacombs.

The Pompeian paintings of Jupien's house were admirably

suited, recalling as they did the later days of the Revolution, to the age so similar to the Directory which was about to begin. Already, without waiting for peace, concealing themselves in the darkness so as not too openly to infringe the regulations of the police, everywhere new-fangled dances were being evolved and frenziedly danced by their devotees throughout the night. And at the same time certain artistic opinions less anti-German in tone than those of the first years of the war were coming into vogue, allowing suffocated minds to breathe once more—but still before you dared to present these ideas you needed to produce a certificate of your patriotism. A professor might write a remarkable book on Schiller and it would be reviewed in the newspapers. But before discussing the author of the book they would record, as a sort of *imprimatur*, that he had been at the Marne or Verdun, that he had been mentioned in despatches five times or had two sons killed. Then and then only did they praise the lucidity, the depth of his work on Schiller, whom it was permissible to describe as "great" provided that he was called not "that great German" but "that great Boche." This was the pass-word, and having passed this test the article was allowed to proceed.

The clients who had not wished to leave had collected together in one room in Jupien's house. They were not acquainted with one another, but one could see that they all belonged nevertheless roughly to the same world, rich and aristocratic. The appearance of each one had in it something repugnant, a reflection, I presumed, of their failure to resist degrading pleasures. One, an enormous man, had a face covered with red blotches like a drunkard. I was told that formerly he had not drunk much himself but had merely enjoyed making young men drunk. But, terrified at the idea of being called up (although he seemed to be in his fifties) and being very stout, he had started to drink without stopping in order to get his weight above a hundred kilos, as nobody over this limit was accepted for the army. And now, this calculation having transformed itself into a passion, the moment that he was left alone, wherever it might be, he would disappear and be found again in a wine-shop. But as soon as he spoke I saw that, though his intelligence was commonplace, he was a man with a good deal of knowledge, education and culture. Another man came in, very young and of great physical distinction. This one, who clearly belonged to the best society, had as yet it is true no external marks of vice, but—and this was more disturbing—the interior signs were there. Very tall, with a charming face, his speech revealed an intelligence of quite a different order from that of his alcoholic neighbour, an intelligence that might without exaggeration be called really outstanding. But to everything that he said there was added a facial expression which would have suited a different phrase. As though, while possessing the whole treasure-house of the expressions of the human countenance, he lived in some world of his own, he displayed these expressions in the wrong order, appearing to scatter smiles and glances at random without any connexion with the remarks that were being addressed to him. I hope for his sake—if, as he certainly is, he is still alive—that he was the victim not of a lasting malady but of a brief intoxication. Probably, had one asked all these men for their visiting cards, one would have been surprised to see that they belonged to an exalted social class. But some vice or other, and that greatest of all vices, the lack of will-power which prevents a man from resisting any vice in particular, brought them together in this place, in isolated rooms it is true, but evening after evening so I was told, so that, though their names might be known to fashionable hostesses, the latter had gradually lost sight of their faces and no longer ever received their visits. Invitations might still be sent to them, but habit brought them back to their composite haunt of depravity. They made, moreover, little attempt at concealment, unlike the page-boys, young workmen, etc., who ministered to their pleasures. And this fact, for which a number of reasons could be given, is best explained by this one: for a man with a job, whether in industry or in domestic service, to go to Jupien's was much the same as for a woman supposed respectable to go to a house of assignation; some, while ready to admit that they had gone there, denied having gone more than once, and Jupien himself, lying to protect their reputations or to discourage competition, would declare: "Oh, no, he doesn't come to my establishment, he wouldn't go *there*." For men with a social position it was not so serious, particularly as other men with a social position who do not go *there* know nothing about the place and do not concern themselves with your life. But in an aeroplane factory, for instance, if one or two fitters have gone *there*, their comrades, who have spied on them, would not dream of following their example for fear of being found out.

As I made my way home, I reflected upon the speed with which conscience ceases to be a partner in our habits, which she allows to develop freely without bothering herself about them, and upon the astonishing picture which may consequently present itself to us if we observe simply from without, and in the belief that they engage tne whole of the individual, the actions of men whose moral or intellectual virtues may at the same time be developing independently in an entirely different direction. Clearly it was a gross fault in their education, or a complete absence of education, combined with a propensity for making money in the way which, if not the least painful (for there were many forms of work which must in the long run be pleasanter—but then does not an invalid in the same way fabricate for himself, with fads, privations and remedies, an existence much more painful than the one imposed upon him by the often trivial disease against which he imagines himself to be fighting by these methods?), was at least less laborious than any other, which had led these ordinary young men to do, quite innocently one may almost say and for a very moderate reward, things which caused them no pleasure and which must in the beginning have inspired in them a lively disgust. On this evidence one might have supposed them to be fundamentally bad, but not only were they in the war splendid soldiers, men of incomparable courage, in civil life too they had often been kind-hearted and sometimes wholly admirable people. They had long ceased to speculate upon the morality or immorality of the life they led, because it was the life that was led by everybody round them. So it is that, when we study certain periods of ancient history, we are astonished to see men and women individually good participate without scruple in mass assassinations or human sacrifices which probably seemed to them natural things. And our own age no doubt, when its history is read two thousand years hence, will seem to an equal degree

to have bathed men of pure and tender conscience in a vital
element which will strike the future reader as monstrously
pernicious, but to which at the time these men adapted themselves without difficulty. Similarly, I knew few men, I may
even say I knew none, who in point of intelligence and sensibility were as gifted as Jupien; for the store of knowledge
which gave such a delightful quality of wit to his conversation
came to him not from that instruction at school or that liberal
education at a university which might have made him indeed
a remarkable man, but from which many fashionable youths
derive no profit. It was simply his innate good sense, his
natural taste, which had enabled him, from a few books read
at random, without a guide, at odd moments, to construct that
correct and elegant manner of speaking in which all the sym-
metries of language were revealed and their beauty displayed.
Yet the trade that he followed might with good reason be
regarded, though certainly as one of the most lucrative, as the
lowest of all. As for M. de Charlus, whatever disdain his
aristocratic pride may have given him for the thought of what
people would say, how was it that some feeling of personal
dignity and self-respect had not forced him to refuse his
sensuality certain satisfactions for which the only imaginable
excuse might seem to be complete insanity? But in him, as in
Jupien, the practice of separating morality from a whole order
of actions (and this is something that must also often happen
to men who have public duties to perform, those of a judge for
instance or a statesman and many others as well) must have
been so long established that Habit, no longer asking Moral
Sentiment for its opinion, had grown stronger from day to day
until at last this consenting Prometheus had had himself nailed
by Force to the rock of Pure Matter.

No doubt, as I saw clearly enough, a new stage had been
reached in the malady of M. de Charlus, which since I had first
observed it had, to judge from the diverse phases which had
presented themselves to my vision, pursued its development
with ever-increasing speed. The poor Baron could not now be
very far from the malady's final term, from death itself, though
this possibly would be preceded, in accordance with the predictions and prayers of Mme Verdurin, by an imprisonment which

at his age could only hasten its coming. Yet I have perhaps been inaccurate in speaking of the rock of Pure Matter. In this Pure Matter it is possible that a small quantum of Mind still survived. This madman knew, in spite of everything, that he was the victim of a form of madness and during his mad moments he nevertheless was playing a part, since he knew quite well that the young man who was beating him was not more wicked than the little boy who in a game of war is chosen by lot to be "the Prussians," upon whom all the others hurl themselves in a fury of genuine patriotism and pretended hate. The victim of a madness, yet a madness into which there entered nevertheless a little of the personality of M. de Charlus. Even in these aberrations (and this is true also of our loves or our travels), human nature still betrays its need for belief by its insistent demands for truth. Françoise, if I spoke to her about a church in Milan, a town which she would probably never visit, or about the cathedral of Rheims—or even merely that of Arras!—which she would not be able to see since they had been more or less destroyed, spoke enviously of the rich who can afford to visit such treasures or else exclaimed with nostalgic regret: "Ah! how lovely it must have been!" although, after all these years that she had lived in Paris, she had never had the curiosity to go and see Notre-Dame. For Notre-Dame is part of Paris and Paris was the town in which the daily life of Françoise took its course, the town, in consequence, in which it was difficult for our old servant—as it would have been for me had not the study of architecture corrected in me at certain points the instincts of Combray—to situate the objects of her dreams. In the people whom we love, there is, immanent, a certain dream which we cannot always clearly discern but which we pursue. It was my belief in Bergotte and in Swann which had made me love Gilberte, my belief in Gilbert the Bad which had made me love Mme de Guermantes. And what a vast expanse of sea had been hidden away in my love—the most full of suffering, the most jealous, seemingly the most individual of all my loves—for Albertine! In any case, just because we are furiously pursuing a dream in a succession of individuals, our loves for people cannot fail to be more or less of an aberration. (And are not even the maladies of the body, at least those that are at all closely connected with the nervous system, in the nature of special tastes or special fears acquired by our organs or our joints, which indicate in this manner that they have conceived for certain climates a horror as inexplicable and as obstinate as the fondness which certain men betray for, it might be, women with an eye-glass or women on horseback? Who can say to what long-lived and unconscious dream is linked the desire that never fails to re-awaken at the sight of a woman on horseback, an unconscious dream as mysterious as is, for example, for a man who has suffered all his life from asthma, the influence of a certain town, in appearance no different from any other town, in which for the first time he breathes freely?) And if there is something of aberration or perversion in all our loves, perversions in the narrower sense of the word are like loves in which the germ of disease has spread victoriously to every part. Even in the maddest of them love may still be recognised. If M. de Charlus insisted that his hands and feet should be bound with chains of proven strength, if he asked repeatedly for the "bar of justice" and, so Jupien told me, for other ferocious instruments which it was almost impossible to obtain even from sailors—for they served to inflict punishments which have been abolished even on board ship where discipline is more rigorous than anywhere else—at the bottom of all this there persisted in M. de Charlus his dream of virility, to be attested if need be by acts of brutality, and all that inner radiance, invisible to us but projecting in this manner a little reflected light, with which his mediaeval imagination adorned crosses of judgment and feudal tortures. It was the same sentiment that made him, every time he arrived, say to Jupien: "I hope there will be no alert this evening, for already I see myself consumed by this fire from heaven like an inhabitant of Sodom." And he affected to be nervous of the Gothas, not that they caused him the slightest shadow of fear, but so as to have a pretext, as soon as the sirens sounded, to rush into the shelters in the Métro, where he hoped for pleasure from brief contact with unseen figures, accompanied by vague dreams of mediaeval dungeons and oubliettes. In short his desire to be bound in chains and beaten, with all its ugliness, betrayed a dream as poetical as, in other men, the longing to go to Venice or to keep ballet-dancers. And M. de Charlus was so determined that this dream should give him the illusion of reality that Jupien was obliged to sell the wooden bed which was in Room 43 and replace it by an iron bed which went better with the chains.

The all-clear sounded at last as I was approaching my house. A little boy in the street told me what a noise the fire-engines had made. I met Françoise coming up from the cellar with the butler. She thought that I had been killed. She told me that Saint-Loup had looked in, with apologies, to see whether he had not, in the course of the visit he had paid me during the morning, dropped his *croix de guerre*. For he had just noticed that he had lost it, and as he had to rejoin his regiment the following morning he had wanted to see whether it was in our flat. He had searched everywhere with Françoise and had found nothing. Françoise thought that he must have lost it before coming to see me, for, she said, she was almost sure, in fact she could have sworn that he was not wearing it when she saw him. In this she was mistaken. So much for the value of evidence and memory! In any case it was of no great importance. Saint-Loup was as much esteemed by his officers as loved by his men, and the matter could easily be arranged. However, I sensed immediately, from the unenthusiastic manner in which they spoke of him, that Saint-Loup had made a poor impression on Françoise and on the butler. True, whereas the butler's son and Françoise's nephew had made every effort to get themselves into safe jobs, Saint-Loup had made efforts of the opposite kind, and with success, to be sent to as dangerous a post as possible. But this, because they judged from their own natures, was something that Françoise and the butler were incapable of believing. They were convinced that the rich are always put where there is no danger. In any case, had they known the truth concerning the heroic courage of Robert, it would have left them unmoved. He did not say "Boches," he had praised the valour of the Germans, he did not attribute to treachery the fact that we had not been victorious from the first day. That is what they would have liked to hear, that is what would have seemed to them a sign of courage. So although they continued to search for the *croix de guerre*, I found them chilly on the subject of Robert. Having my suspicions as to where the cross had been forgotten, I advised Françoise and the butler to go to bed. (However, if Saint-Loup had amused himself that evening in the fashion which I suspected, it was only to pass the time of waiting, for he had been seized once more by the desire to see Morel and had made use of all his military connexions to find out in what regiment he was serving, so that he could go and see him, but so far had only received hundreds of contradictory answers.) But the butler was never in a hurry to leave Françoise now that, thanks to the war, he had found a means of torturing her even more efficacious than the expulsion of the nuns or the Dreyfus case. That evening, and every time I went near them during the few more days that I spent in Paris before leaving to go to a new sanatorium, I heard the butler say to a terrified Françoise: "They're not in a hurry of course, they're biding their time, but when the time is ripe they will take Paris, and on that day we shall see no mercy!" "Heavens above, Mother of God," cried Françoise, "aren't they satisfied to have conquered poor Belgium? She suffered enough, when they invaded her." "Belgium, Françoise? What they did in Belgium will be nothing compared to this!" And as the war had flooded the conversation of working-class people with a quantity of terms with which they had become acquainted through their eyes alone, by reading the newspapers, and which they consequently did not know how to pronounce, the butler went on to say: "I cannot understand how everybody can be so stupid. You will see, Françoise, they are preparing a new attack with a wider *scoop* than all the others." At this I rebelled, if not in the name of pity for Françoise and strategic common sense, at least in that of grammar, and declared that the word should be pronounced "scope," but succeeded only in causing the terrible phrase to be repeated to Françoise every time I entered the kitchen, for to the butler the pleasure of alarming his companion was scarcely greater than that of showing his master that, though he had once been a gardener at Combray and was a mere butler, he was nevertheless a good Frenchman according to the rule of Saint-André-des-Champs and possessed, by virtue of the Declaration of the Rights of Man, the right to use the pronunciation "scoop" in full independence and not to let himself be dictated to on a point which formed no part of his service and upon which in consequence, since the Revolution had made us all equals, he need listen to nobody.

To my annoyance, therefore, I had to listen to him talking to Françoise about an operation of wide "scoop" with an emphasis which was intended to prove to me that this pronunciation was the result not of ignorance but of an act of will following upon ripe reflection. He confounded the government and the newspapers in a single "they" full of mistrust, saying: "They tell us about the losses of the Boches, they don't tell us about our own, it seems that they are ten times as big. They tell us that the enemy are at the end of their tether, that they have nothing to eat, personally I believe they are a hundred times better off than we are for food. It's no use stuffing us with lies. If the enemy had nothing to eat, they wouldn't fight as they did the other day when they killed a hundred thousand of our young men not twenty years old." Thus at every moment he exaggerated the triumphs of the Germans, as in the past he had those of the Radicals; and at the same time he recounted their atrocities in order that these triumphs might be yet more painful to Françoise, who never stopped saying: "Ah! Holy Mother of the Angels! Ah! Mary, Mother of God!", and sometimes, in order to be disagreeable to her in a different way, he said: "Anyhow, we are no better than they are, what we're doing in Greece is no prettier than what they have done in Belgium. You will see that we shall turn everybody against us, we shall find ourselves fighting every nation in the world," whereas the truth was exactly the opposite. On days when the news was good he destroyed its effect by assuring Françoise that the war would last thirty-five years, and if there was talk of the possibility of an armistice, he declared that peace would not last more than a few months and would be followed by battles which would make the present ones look like child's play, such battles that after them there would be nothing left of France.

The victory of the Allies seemed, if not near at hand, at least more or less certain, and it must unfortunately be admitted that the butler was greatly distressed at the prospect. For he had reduced the "world" war, like everything else, to the war which he was secretly waging against Françoise (of whom, nevertheless, he was fond, just as one may be fond of the person whom one enjoys infuriating every day by beating him at dominoes) and victory in his eyes took the shape of the first conversation in which he would have the pain of hearing Françoise say: "Well, it's over at last, and they'll have to give us more than we gave them in '70." He believed, nevertheless, that this fatal day of reckoning was perpetually about to arrive, for an unconscious patriotism made him suppose, like all Frenchmen, victims of the same mirage as myself since my illness, that victory—like my recovery—was just round the corner. This event he anticipated by announcing to Françoise that victory might perhaps come, but that his heart bled at the thought, for revolution would follow hard on its heels and then invasion. "Ah! this blooming war, the Boches will be the only ones to recover from it quickly, Françoise. They have already made hundreds of thousands of millions out of it. But as for their coughing up a *sou* to us, what nonsense! They will print that in the newspapers perhaps," he added out of prudence and so as to be ready for any eventuality, "in order to appease the people, just as for three years now they have been saying that the war will be over to-morrow." Françoise was only too easily disturbed by these words, because, having at first believed the optimists rather than the butler, she saw now that the war, which she had thought would end in a fortnight in spite of "the *innovation* of poor Belgium," was indeed still going on, that we were not advancing (the phenomenon of fixed front warfare was beyond her comprehension) and that, according to one of the innumerable "godsons" to whom she gave everything that she earned with us, "they" were concealing various awkward facts. "It's the working man who will have to pay," concluded the butler. "They will take your field away from you, Françoise." "Ah! God in Heaven!" But to these distant misfortunes he preferred nearer ones and devoured the newspapers in the hope of being able to announce a defeat to Françoise. He waited for pieces of bad news as eagerly as if they had been Easter eggs, hoping that things would go badly enough to terrify Françoise but not badly enough to cause him any material suffering. Thus the prospect of a Zeppelin raid enchanted him: he would have the spectacle of Françoise hiding in the cellars, and at the same time he was persuaded that in a town as large as Paris the bombs would never happen to fall just on our house.

Françoise meanwhile was beginning at moments to return to her Combray pacifism. She almost had doubts about the "German atrocities." "When the war started we were told that the Germans were murderers, brigands, real bandits, BBBoches. . . ." (If she gave several *b*'s to Boche, it was because the accusation that the Germans were murderers seemed to her quite plausible, but the idea that they were Boches, because of the enormity of the accusation, improbable in the extreme. Only it was not at all easy to understand what mysteriously terrifying sense Françoise gave to the word Boche, since the period she was talking about was the very beginning of the war, and also on account of the air of doubt with which she pronounced the word. For a doubt whether the Germans were criminals might be ill-founded in fact but did not contain in itself, from the point of view of logic, any contradiction. But how was it possible to doubt that they were Boches, since the word, in the popular language, means nothing more nor less than German? Perhaps she was simply repeating in an indirect fashion the violent remarks she had heard at the time, in which the word Boche was emphasised with particular energy.) "I believed all that," she went on, "but I am wondering now whether we are not every bit as scoundrelly as they are." This blasphemous thought had been slyly prepared in Françoise's mind by the butler, who, seeing that she had a certain fondness for King Constantine of Greece, had not ceased to represent him to her as literally starved by us until the day when he would yield. So the abdication of this monarch had aroused strong feelings in Françoise, who went so far as to declare: "We are no better than they are. If we were in Germany, we would do just the same."

I saw little of her, in any case, during these few days, for she spent much time at the house of those cousins of whom Mamma had said to me one day: "But you know that they are richer than you are." These cousins had given an example of that beautiful conduct which was very frequent at this period throughout the country and which would bear witness, if there were a historian to perpetuate its memory, to the greatness of France, her greatness of soul, her greatness after the fashion of Saint-André-des-Champs, a kind of conduct displayed as much by thousands of civilians living in safety far from the front as by the soldiers who fell at the Marne. There had been killed at Berry-au-Bac a nephew of Françoise who was also a nephew of the millionaire cousins, former proprietors of a large café who had retired long since after making their fortune. The young man who was killed had been the owner of a very small café and quite poor; he had gone off, twenty-five years old, when the army was mobilised, leaving his young wife alone to look after the little bar to which he hoped to return in a few months. He had been killed. And then this is what happened. The millionaire cousins of Françoise, who were not related by blood to the young woman who was their nephew's widow, had left the home in the country to which they had retired ten years earlier and had set to work again as café proprietors, without putting a *sou* into their own pockets; every morning at six the millionairess, a real lady, was up and dressed together with Mademoiselle her daughter, ready to help their niece and cousin by marriage. And for nearly three years now they had been washing glasses and serving drinks from early morning until half past nine at night, without a day's rest. In this book in which there is not a single incident which is not fictitious, not a single character who is a real person in disguise, in which everything has been invented by me in accordance with the requirements of my theme, I owe it to the credit of my country to say that only the millionaire cousins of Françoise who came out of retirement to help their niece when she was left without support, only they are real people who exist. And persuaded as I am that I shall not offend their modesty, for the reason that they will never read this book, it is both with childish pleasure and with a profound emotion that, being unable to record the names of so many others who undoubtedly acted in the same way, to all of whom France owes her survival, I transcribe here the real name of this family: they are called—and what name could be more French?

—Larivière. If there were a few vile shirkers like the arrogant young man in a dinner-jacket whom I had seen in Jupien's establishment, whose only concern was to know whether he could have Léon at half past ten "as he had a luncheon engagement," they are redeemed by the innumerable throng of all the Frenchmen of Saint-André-des-Champs, by all the sublime soldiers and by those whom I rank as their equals, the Larivières.

The butler, to sharpen the fears of Françoise, showed her an old copy of *Lectures pour tous* which he had found, with a picture on its cover (it dated from before the war) of the "imperial family of Germany." "There's our lord and master to be," said the butler to Françoise, showing her "William." She goggled, then pointed to the feminine personage who stood by his side and said: "And there's the Williamess!"

My departure from Paris was delayed by a piece of news which caused me such grief that I was for some time rendered incapable of travelling. This was the death of Robert de Saint-Loup, killed two days after his return to the front while covering the retreat of his men. Never had any man felt less hatred for a nation than he (and as for the Emperor, for particular reasons, very possibly incorrect, he thought that William II had tried rather to prevent the war than to bring it about). Nor had he hated Germanism; the last words which I had heard on his lips, six days before he died, were the opening words of a Schumann song which he had started to hum in German on my staircase, until I had made him desist because of the neighbours. Accustomed by supreme good breeding to eliminate from his conduct all trace of apology or invective, all rhetoric, he had avoided in face of the enemy, as he had at the time of mobilisation, the actions which would have ensured his survival, through that tendency to efface himself before others of which all his behaviour was symbolic, down to his manner of coming out into the street bare-headed to close the door of my cab, every time I visited him. For several days I remained shut up in my room, thinking of him. I recalled his arrival the first time at Balbec, when, in an almost white suit, with his eyes greenish and mobile like the waves, he had crossed the hall adjoining the great dining-room whose windows gave on to the sea. I recalled the very special being that he had then seemed to me to be, the

being for whose friendship I had so greatly wished. That wish
had been realised beyond the limits of what I should ever have
thought possible, without, however, at the time giving me
more than a very slight pleasure; and then later I had come to
understand the many great virtues and something else as well
which lay concealed behind his elegant appearance. All this, the
good as well as the bad, he had given without counting the
cost, every day, as much on the last day when he advanced to
attack a trench, out of generosity and because it was his habit
to place at the service of others all that he possessed, as on that
evening when he had run along the backs of the seats in the
restaurant in order not to disturb me. And the fact that I had
seen him really so little but against such varied backgrounds,
in circumstances so diverse and separated by so many intervals
—in that hall at Balbec, in the café at Rivebelle, in the cavalry
barracks and at the military dinners in Doncières, at the theatre
where he had slapped the face of the journalist, in the house of
the Princesse de Guermantes—only had the effect of giving me,
of his life, pictures more striking and more sharply defined and
for his death a grief more lucid than we are likely to have in the
case of people whom we have loved more, but with whom our
association has been so nearly continuous that the image we
retain of them is no more than a sort of vague average between
an infinity of imperceptibly different images and our affection,
satiated, has not, as with those whom we have seen only for
brief moments, during meetings prematurely ended against
their wish and ours, the illusion that there was possible between
us a still greater affection of which circumstances alone have
defrauded us. A few days after the day on which I had seen him
pursuing his monocle and supposed him to be so haughty, in
that hall at Balbec, there was another living form which I had
seen for the first time on the beach at Balbec and which now,
like his, no longer existed save in the state of memory: Albertine, making her progress along the sand that first evening,
indifferent to everybody around her, a marine creature, like a
seagull. For her my love had come so swiftly that, in order to be
free to go out with her every day, I had never during my stay
at Balbec gone over to Doncières to see Saint-Loup. And yet
the history of my relations with him bore witness also to the

fact that at one period I had ceased to love Albertine, since if later I had installed myself for a while near Robert at Doncières, the reason lay in my unhappiness at seeing that the feeling which I had for Mme de Guermantes was not returned. His life and Albertine's, so late made known to me, both at Balbec, and so swiftly concluded, had scarcely crossed, though it was he, I told myself, perceiving that the nimble shuttles of the years weave links between those of our memories which seem at first most independent of each other, it was he whom I had sent to see Mme Bontemps after Albertine had left me. And then it had turned out that their two lives had each of them a parallel secret, which I had not suspected. Saint-Loup's secret caused me now more sadness perhaps than that of Albertine, whose life had become so alien to me. But I felt an inconsolable regret that her life as well as his had been so short. They had often said to me, both of them: "You who are ill . . .," they had looked after me. And yet it was they who were dead, while I, both of the one and of the other, could set side by side, separated by an interval which after all was really not very long, the final image—before the trench, in the river-bed—and the first image, which even in the case of Albertine I valued now only because it was associated in my mind with that of the sun setting over the sea.

Saint-Loup's death was received by Françoise with more compassion than that of Albertine. Immediately she assumed her role of hired mourner and descanted upon the memory of the dead man with frenzied threnodies and lamentations. She paraded her grief and only put on an unfeeling expression, at the same time averting her head, when in spite of myself I betrayed mine, which she wished to appear not to have seen. For like many emotional people, she was exasperated by the emotions of others, which bore no doubt too great a resemblance to her own. She loved now to draw attention to her slightest rheumatic twinge, to a fit of giddiness, to a bump. But if I referred to one of my symptoms, in an instant she was stoical and grave again and pretended not to have heard. "Poor Marquis," she said, although she continued to believe that he would have done anything in the world in order not to go to the front and, once there, in order to run away from danger.

"Poor lady," she said, thinking of Mme de Marsantes, "how she must have cried when she heard about her boy's death! If at least she had been able to see him again! But perhaps it's better that she didn't, because his nose was cut in two, he was completely disfaced." And the eyes of Françoise filled with tears, behind which, however, there was perceptible the cruel curiosity of the peasant woman. No doubt Françoise pitied the sorrow of Mme de Marsantes with all her heart, but she regretted not knowing the form which this sorrow had taken and not being able to enjoy the afflicting spectacle of it. And as she would dearly have loved to cry and to be seen by me to cry, she said, in order to work herself up: "This has really done something to me!" In me too she sought to detect the traces of grief, with an avidity which caused me to feign a certain indifference when I spoke of Robert. And, largely no doubt out of a spirit of imitation and because she had heard the phrase used—for there are clichés in the servants' hall as well as in social coteries —she kept repeating, not however without a poor man's smugness in her voice: "All his riches did not save him from dying like anybody else, and what use are they to him now?" The butler took advantage of the occasion to say to Françoise that of course it was sad, but that it hardly counted beside the millions of men who fell every day in spite of all the efforts which the government made to conceal the fact. But this time the butler did not succeed in augmenting the sorrow of Françoise as he had hoped. For she replied: "It is true that they also die for France, but they are nobodies; it is always more interesting when it is somebody whom one knows." And Françoise, who enjoyed crying, went on to add: "You must be sure to let me know if they talk about the death of the Marquis in the newspaper."

Robert had often said to me sadly, long before the war: "Oh! my life, don't let's talk about it, I am a condemned man from the start." Was he alluding to the vice which he had succeeded hitherto in concealing from the world, but of which he was himself aware and whose seriousness he perhaps exaggerated, just as children who make love for the first time, or merely before that age seek solitary pleasure, imagine themselves to be like a plant which cannot scatter its pollen without dying immediately afterwards? Perhaps this exaggeration, for Saint-Loup as for the children, came partly from the still unfamiliar idea of sin, partly from the fact that an entirely novel sensation has an almost terrible force which later will gradually diminish; or had he really, justifying it if need be by the death of his father at an early age, a presentiment of his own premature end? Such a presentiment would seem, no doubt, to be impossible. Yet death appears to be obedient to certain laws. Often for instance, one gets the impression that children of parents who have died very old or very young are almost compelled to disappear at the same age, the former protracting until their hundredth year their incurable miseries and ailments, the latter, in spite of a happy and healthy existence, swept away at the premature but inevitable date by an illness so opportune and so accidental (whatever deep roots it may have in the victim's temperament) that it appears to be merely the formality necessary for the realisation of death. And may it not be possible that accidental death too—like that of Saint-Loup, which was perhaps in any case linked to his character in more ways than I have thought it necessary to describe—is somehow recorded in advance, known only to the gods, invisible to men, but revealed by a peculiar sadness, half unconscious, half conscious (and even, insofar as it is conscious, proclaimed to others with that complete sincerity with which we foretell misfortunes which in our heart of hearts we believe we shall escape but which will nevertheless take place) to the man who bears and forever sees within himself, as though it were some heraldic device, a fatal date?

He must have been truly magnificent in those last hours. This man who throughout his life, even when sitting down, even when walking across a drawing-room, had seemed to be restraining an impulse to charge, while with a smile he dissembled the indomitable will which dwelt within his triangular head, at last had charged. Freed from the books which encumbered it, the feudal turret had become military once more. And this Guermantes had died more himself than ever before, or rather more a member of his race, into which slowly he dissolved until he became nothing more than a Guermantes, as was symbolically visible at his burial in the church of Saint-Hilaire at Combray, completely hung for the occasion with black draperies upon which stood out in red, beneath the closed circle of the coronet, without initials or Christian names or titles, the G of the Guermantes that he had again in death become.

Even before going to this burial, which did not take place immediately, I wrote to Gilberte. I ought perhaps to have written to the Duchesse de Guermantes, but I told myself that she would receive the death of Robert with the same indifference which I had seen her display towards the deaths of so many others who had seemed to be closely linked to her life, and that she would perhaps even, with her Guermantes wit, try to show that she did not share the superstition about ties of blood. And I was too unwell to write to everybody. In the past I had believed that she and Robert were fond of each other in the sense in which that phrase is used in society, that is to say that, when they were together, they said to each other tender things which at the moment they truly felt. But away from her, he did not hesitate to declare that she was an idiot, and if she sometimes derived an egotistical pleasure from seeing him, I had observed her on the other hand to be incapable of taking the slightest trouble, of making even the smallest use of her credit in order to render him a service or even to spare him an unpleasantness. Her unkindness in refusing to give Robert a recommendation to General de Saint-Joseph, at the time when he wanted to avoid returning to Morocco, proved surely that the devoted help which she had given him on the occasion of his marriage was no more than a sort of atonement which cost her almost nothing. So I was very astonished to hear—she was unwell at the moment when Robert was killed—that in order to spare her the shock which the news would cause her her family had thought it necessary to conceal from her for several days, under the most fallacious pretexts, the newspapers which would have informed her of his death. And my surprise increased when I heard that, after they had at last been obliged to tell her the truth, the Duchess wept for a whole day, fell sick and for a long time—more than a week, which was a long time for her—was inconsolable. When I heard of her grief, I was touched. It enabled society to say, and it enables me to vouch for the truth of the statement, that a great friendship existed between them. But then when I recall all the little malicious utterances, all the ill-natured refusals to help each other which this friendship had not excluded, I cannot help reflecting that in society a great friendship does not amount to much.

However, a little later, in circumstances which, if they touched my heart less, were historically more important, Mme de Guermantes showed herself, to my mind, in a yet more favourable light. This woman who as a girl, as the reader may remember, had behaved with such audacious impertinence towards the imperial family of Russia, and who after her marriage had addressed them always with a freedom which sometimes caused her to be charged with lack of tact, was perhaps alone, after the Russian Revolution, in giving proofs of a limitless devotion to the Grand Duchesses and the Grand Dukes. Only the year before the war she had not a little annoyed the Grand Duchess Vladimir by persistently referring to Countess Hohenfelsen, the morganatic wife of the Grand Duke Paul, as "the Grand Duchess Paul." Nevertheless, no sooner had the Russian Revolution broken out than our ambassador in St Petersburg, M. Paléologue ("Paléo" in diplomatic society, which like society at large has its supposedly witty abbreviations), was plagued with telegrams from the Duchesse de Guermantes asking for news of the Grand Duchess Maria Pavlovna. And for a long time the only marks of sympathy and respect which this Princess received came to her regularly and exclusively from Mme de Guermantes.

To various individuals Saint-Loup caused not so much by his death as by what he had done in the preceding weeks a distress greater than that which afflicted the Duchess. What happened was that, only the day after the evening on which I had seen him, and two days after the Baron had said to Morel "I will have my revenge," the inquiries which Saint-Loup had made about the whereabouts of Morel were successful; they succeeded, that is to say, in bringing to the notice of the general under whose command Morel should have been the fact that he was a deserter, whereupon the general had him searched for and arrested and, to apologise to Saint-Loup for the punishment which he was obliged to inflict upon someone in whom he took an interest, wrote to inform him how the matter stood.

Morel did not doubt that his arrest had been brought about by
the rancour of M. de Charlus. He remembered the words "I
will have my revenge," thought that this was the threatened
revenge, and asked to be allowed to make some disclosures.
"It is quite true," he declared, "that I am a deserter. But if I
have been led astray, is it altogether my fault?" He then told
apropos of M. de Charlus and M. d'Argencourt, with whom
also he had quarrelled, stories in which he had not in fact himself been directly involved, but which they, with the double
expansiveness of lovers and of inverts, had related to him, and
the result was the immediate arrest of both these gentlemen.
But each of them suffered less perhaps at being arrested than at
learning—what neither of them had known—that the other
was his rival, and the judicial examination revealed that they
had an enormous number of other obscure, quotidian rivals,
picked up in the street. M. de Charlus and M. d'Argencourt
were soon released. So was Morel, because the general's letter
to Saint-Loup was returned to him with the information:
"Deceased, killed in action." Out of respect for the dead man
the general so arranged things that Morel was merely sent to
the front. He conducted himself bravely there, survived every
danger and returned, when the war was over, with the cross
which M. de Charlus had in the past vainly solicited for him
and which in this indirect fashion was procured for him by the
death of Saint-Loup.

I have often thought since then, remembering the *croix de
guerre* which went astray in Jupien's establishment, that if
Saint-Loup had lived, he could easily have got himself elected
a deputy in the elections which followed the armistice, thanks
to the scum of universal fatuousness which the war left in its
wake and the halo which still adhered to military glory. For at
that time, if the loss of a finger could abolish centuries of pre-
judice and allow a man of humble birth to make a brilliant
marriage into an aristocratic family, the *croix de guerre*, even one
won by sitting in an office, sufficed for a triumphal election to
the Chamber of Deputies, if not to the Académie Française.
The election of Saint-Loup would have caused M. Arthur
Meyer to pour out floods of tears and ink about the new
deputy's "holy family." But perhaps he was too sincerely fond

of the people to be good at winning their votes, although on account of his quarterings of nobility they would probably have forgiven him his democratic ideas. These he would no doubt have expounded with success before a Chamber composed of aviators. Certainly these heroes would have understood him, and a few other exceptionally intelligent and highminded men. But thanks to the platitudinous mentality of the National Bloc, the old lags of politics who are invariably reelected had also turned up again, and such of them as failed to enter a Chamber of aviators solicited, so that they might at least get into the Académie Française, the suffrages of the Marshals, of the President of the Republic, the President of the Chamber, etc. These men would have looked with less favour upon Saint-Loup than they did upon another of Jupien's habitués, the deputy of Liberal Action, who was once more returned unopposed and who continued to wear the uniform of a territorial officer long after the war had been over. His election was hailed with joy by all the newspapers which had agreed to put his name forward, as well as by the noble and wealthy ladies who now dressed only in rags from feelings of propriety and from fear of taxes, while the gentlemen of the Bourse never stopped buying diamonds, not for their wives but because, having lost all confidence in the credit of any nation, they were seeking refuge in this tangible wealth and as a result sending up the price of De Beers by a thousand francs. All this tomfoolery was not exactly popular, but there was less disposition to blame the National Bloc when suddenly there appeared on the scene the victims of bolshevism, those Grand Duchesses in tatters whose husbands had been assassinated in carts, while their sons after being left to starve and then forced to work in the midst of abuse, had finally been thrown into wells and buried beneath stones because it was believed that they had the plague and might pass it on. Those of them who succeeded in escaping suddenly turned up in Paris.

The new sanatorium to which I withdrew was no more successful in curing me than the first one, and many years passed before I came away. During the train-journey which eventually took me back to Paris, the thought of my lack of talent for literature—a defect which I had first discovered, so I supposed, long ago on the Guermantes way, which I had again recognised, and been still more saddened by, in the course of the daily walks that I had taken with Gilberte before returning to dine very late at night at Tansonville, and which on the eve of my departure from that house I had come very near to identifying, after reading some pages of the Goncourt Journal, with the vanity, the falsehood of literature—this thought, less painful perhaps but more melancholy still if I referred it not to a private infirmity of my own but to the non-existence of the ideal in which I had believed, this thought, which for a very long time had not entered my mind, struck me afresh and with a force more painful than ever before. The train had stopped, I remember, in open country. The sun was shining on a row of trees that followed the railway line, flooding the upper halves of their trunks with light. "Trees," I thought, "you no longer have anything to say to me. My heart has grown cold and no longer hears you. I am in the midst of nature. Well, it is with indifference, with boredom that my eyes register the line which separates your radiant foreheads from your shadowy trunks. If ever I thought of myself as a poet, I know now that I am not one. Perhaps in the new, the so desiccated part of my life which is about to begin, human beings may yet inspire in me what nature can no longer say. But the years in which I might have been able to sing *her* praise will never return." But in thus consoling myself with the thought that the observation of humanity might possibly come to take the place of an unattainable inspiration, I knew that I was merely seeking to console myself, I knew that I knew myself to be worthless. If I really had the soul of an artist, surely I would be feeling pleasure at the sight of this curtain of trees lit by the setting sun, these little flowers on the bank which lifted themselves almost to the level of the steps of my compartment, flowers whose petals I was able to count but whose colour I would not, like many a worthy man of letters, attempt to describe, for can one hope to transmit to the reader a pleasure that one has not felt? A little later I had noticed with the same absence of emotion the glitter of gold and orange

which the sun splashed upon the windows of a house; and
finally, as the evening advanced, I had seen another house
which appeared to be built out of a strange pink substance. But
I had made these various observations with the same absolute
indifference as if, walking in a garden with a lady, I had seen a
pane of glass, and a little further on an object of an alabaster-
like material, the unusual colour of which had failed to draw
me out of the most languorous boredom, but as if, nevertheless, out of politeness towards the lady, in order to say something and also in order to show that I had noticed these colours,
I had pointed in passing to the tinted glass and the fragment of
stucco. In the same way, to satisfy my conscience, I indicated
to myself now as to someone who was travelling with me and
might be able to extract from them more pleasure than I, the
flame-like reflections in the windows and the pink transparency
of the house. But the companion whose attention I had drawn
to these curious effects was evidently of a less enthusiastic
nature than many more sympathetically disposed persons who
are enraptured by such sights, for he had taken cognisance of
the colours without any kind of joy.

My long absence from Paris had not prevented old friends
from continuing, as my name remained on their lists, faithfully
to send me invitations, and when on my return I found—
together with one to a tea-party given by Berma for her
daughter and her son-in-law—another to an afternoon party
with music which was to take place the following day at the
house of the Prince de Guermantes, the gloomy reflections
which had passed through my mind in the train were not the
least of the motives which urged me to accept. Really, I said
to myself, what point is there in forgoing the pleasures of
social life if, as seems to be the case, the famous "work" which
for so long I have been hoping every day to start the next day,
is something I am not, or am no longer, made for and perhaps
does not even correspond to any reality. This reasoning was, it
is true, completely negative and merely deprived of their force
those other reasons which might have dissuaded me from going
to this fashionable concert. The positive reason that made me
decide to go was the name of Guermantes, absent long enough
from my mind to be able, when I read it upon the invitation

card, to re-awaken a ray of my attention, to draw up from the depths of my memory a sort of section of the past of the Guermantes, attended by all the images of seigniorial forest and tall flowers which at that earlier time of my life had accompanied it, and to reassume for me the charm and the significance which I had found in it at Combray when, passing along the Rue de l'Oiseau on my way home, I used to see from outside, like some dark lacquer, the window of Gilbert the Bad, Lord of Guermantes. For a moment the Guermantes had once more seemed to me to be totally different from people in society, comparable neither with them nor with any living being, even a reigning prince, creatures begotten of the union of the sharp and windy air of the dark town of Combray in which my childhood had been spent with the past which could be sensed there, in the little street, at the height of the stained-glass window. I had had a longing to go to the Guermantes party as if in going there I must have been brought nearer to my childhood and to the depths of my memory where my childhood dwelt. And I had continued to read and re-read the invitation until in the end, rising in revolt, the letters which composed this name at once so familiar and so mysterious, like that of Combray itself, resumed their independence and outlined before my tired eyes a name that I seemed never to have seen before. (Mamma happened to be going to a little tea-party of Mme Sazerat's which she knew beforehand she would find extremely boring, so I had no scruples about going to the Princesse de Guermantes's.)

I took a cab to go to the Prince de Guermantes's house, which was no longer his former home but a magnificent mansion that he had recently built in the Avenue du Bois. One of the mistakes of society people is not to realise that, if they want us to believe in them, it is first necessary that they should believe in themselves, or at least should respect the essential elements of our belief. At the time when I believed, even if I knew the contrary to be true, that the Guermantes lived in this or that grand house in virtue of a hereditary right, to penetrate into the palace of the sorcerer or the fairy, to compel to open before me the doors which yield only when one has pronounced the magic formula, seemed to me as difficult as to obtain an interview with the sorcerer or the fairy themselves. To persuade myself that the old manservant engaged twenty-four hours earlier or supplied by Potel and Chabot was the son, the grandson, the scion of a whole line of menials who had been in the family's service since long before the Revolution was the easiest thing in the world, and I was only too happy to take for an ancestral portrait some painting which had been bought the previous month from Bernheim Jeune. But enchantment cannot be decanted from one vessel to another, memories are indivisible, and of the Prince de Guermantes, now that he had himself shattered the illusions of my belief by going to live in the Avenue du Bois, nothing much was left. The ceilings which I had once feared to see collapse upon the announcement of my name, those ceilings under which, for me, there would still have floated something of the enchantment and the fears of those early days, now looked down upon the parties of an American hostess in whom I took not the slightest interest. Intrinsically, material objects have in themselves no power, but, since it is our practice to bestow power upon them, doubtless at this moment some middle-class schoolboy was feeling, in front of the house in the Avenue du Bois, the same sentiments that I had once felt as I stood before the house where the Prince de Guermantes had lived in my youth. He, this schoolboy, was still at the age of beliefs, but I had passed beyond it, I had lost that privilege, just as after one's first years one loses the ability that a baby has to break up the milk which he ingests into digestible fragments, so that the prudent adult will drink milk only in small quantities whereas babies can continue to suck it in indefinitely without pausing for breath. But at least the Prince de Guermantes's change of residence had this advantage for me, that the cab which had come to fetch me and in which, as it took me to the party, I was making these reflections, was obliged to traverse the streets which lead to the Champs-Elysées. They were very badly paved at this time, but the moment I found myself in them I was, none the less, detached from my thoughts by that sensation of extraordinary physical comfort which one has when suddenly a car in which one is travelling rolls more easily, more softly, without noise, because the gates of a park have been opened and one is gliding over alleys covered with fine sand or dead leaves; materially nothing of the sort had happened, but I felt suddenly that all external obstacles had been eliminated, simply because I no longer had to make that effort of adaptation or attention which we make, sometimes without being conscious of it, in the presence of new things: the streets through which I was passing at this moment were those, so long forgotten, which I used once upon a time to take with Françoise when we went to the Champs-Elysées. The solid earth knew of its own accord where it had to go; its resistance was vanquished. And like an airman who hitherto has progressed laboriously along the ground, abruptly "taking off" I soared slowly towards the silent heights of memory. Among all the streets of Paris these streets will always stand out for me, as though they were made of a different substance from the others. When we reached the corner of the Rue Royale where once had stood the open-air vendor of the photographs beloved by Françoise, it seemed to me that the cab, feeling the pull of hundreds of former turns, could not do otherwise than turn of its own accord. I was not traversing the same streets as the people who were walking about the town that day, I was traversing a past, gliding, sad and sweet; a past which was moreover compounded of so many different pasts that it was difficult for me to recognise the cause of my melancholy, to know whether it was due to those walks in which the hope of meeting Gilberte had co-existed with the fear that she would not come, to the proximity of a certain house to which I had been told that Albertine had gone with Andrée, or to that vanity of all things which seems to be the significance of a route which one has followed a thousand times in a state of passion which has disappeared and which has borne no fruit, like the route which I used to take on those expeditions of feverish haste after luncheon to see, with the paste still damp upon them, the posters of *Phèdre* and *Le Domino noir*.

The cab turned into the Champs-Elysées and, as I did not particularly want to hear the whole of the concert which was being given at the Guermantes party, I stopped it and was preparing to get out in order to walk a few yards when I was struck by the spectacle presented by another cab which was also stopping. A man with staring eyes and hunched figure was placed rather than seated in the back, and was making, to keep himself upright, the efforts that might have been made by a child who has been told to be good. But his straw hat failed to conceal an unruly forest of hair which was entirely white, and a white beard, like those which snow forms on the statues of river-gods in public gardens, flowed from his chin. It was—side by side with Jupien, who was unremitting in his attentions to him—M. de Charlus, now convalescent after an attack of apoplexy of which I had had no knowledge (I had only been told that he had lost his sight, but in fact this trouble had been purely temporary and he could now see quite well again) and which, unless the truth was that hitherto he had dyed his hair and that he had now been forbidden to continue so fatiguing a practice, had had the effect, as in a sort of chemical precipitation, of rendering visible and brilliant all that saturation of metal which the locks of his hair and his beard, pure silver now, shot forth like so many geysers, so that upon the old fallen prince this latest illness had conferred the Shakespearian majesty of a King Lear. His eyes had not remained unaffected by this total convulsion, this metallurgical transformation of his head, but had, by an inverse phenomenon, lost all their brightness. But what was most moving was that one felt that this lost brightness was identical with his moral pride, and that somehow the physical and even the intellectual life of M. de Charlus had survived the eclipse of that aristocratic haughtiness which had in the past seemed indissolubly linked to them. To confirm this, at the moment which I am describing, there passed in a victoria, no doubt also on her way to the reception of the Prince de Guermantes, Mme de Saint-Euverte, whom formerly the Baron had not considered elegant enough for him. Jupien, who tended him like a child, whispered in his ear that it was someone with whom he was acquainted, Mme de Saint-Euverte. And immediately, with infinite laboriousness but with all the concentration of a sick man determined to show that he is capable of all the movements which are still difficult for him, M. de Charlus lifted his hat, bowed, and greeted Mme de Saint-Euverte as respectfully as if she had been the Queen of France or as if he had been a small child coming timidly in

obedience to his mother's command to say "How do you do?"
to a grown-up person. For a child, but without a child's pride,
was what he had once more become. Perhaps the very difficulty
that M. de Charlus had in making these gestures was in itself a
reason for him to make them, in the knowledge that he would
create a greater effect by an action which, painful for an invalid,
became thereby doubly meritorious on the part of the man who
performed it and doubly flattering to the individual to whom
it was addressed, invalids, like kings, practising exaggerated
civility. Perhaps also there was in the movements of the Baron
that lack of co-ordination which follows upon maladies of the
spinal column and the brain, so that his gestures went beyond
anything that he intended. What I myself saw in them was
above all a sort of gentleness, an almost physical gentleness,
and of detachment from the realities of life, phenomena so
strikingly apparent in those whom death has already drawn
within its shadow. And the exposure of the veins of silver in
his hair was less indicative of profound convulsions than this
unconscious humility which turned all social relations upside
down and abased before Mme de Saint-Euverte—as it would
have abased before the most vulgar of American hostesses
(who at last would have been able to congratulate herself on
the hitherto unattainable politeness of the Baron)—what had
seemed to be the proudest snobbishness of all. For the Baron
still lived, still thought; his intellect was not impaired. And
more than any chorus of Sophocles on the humbled pride of
Oedipus, more than death itself or any funeral oration on the
subject of death, the humble greeting, full of effort to please,
which the Baron addressed to Mme de Saint-Euverte proclaimed the fragile and perishable nature of the love of earthly
greatness and all human pride. M. de Charlus, who until this
moment would never have consented to dine with Mme de
Saint-Euverte, now bowed to the ground in her honour. To
receive the homage of M. de Charlus had been, for her, the
highest ambition of snobbery, just as, for the Baron, the central
principle of snobbery had been to be rude to her. And now this
inaccessible and precious essence which he had succeeded in
making Mme de Saint-Euverte believe to be part of his nature,
had at a single stroke been annihilated by M. de Charlus, by the

earnest timidity, the apprehensive zeal with which he raised a hat from beneath which, all the while that his head remained deferentially uncovered, there streamed with the eloquence of a Bossuet the torrents of his silvery hair. Jupien helped the Baron to descend and I greeted him. He spoke to me very rapidly, in a voice so inaudible that I could not distinguish what he was saying, which wrung from him, when for the third time I made him repeat his remarks, a gesture of impatience that astonished me by its contrast with the impassivity which his face had at first displayed, which was no doubt an after-effect of his stroke. But when after a while I had grown accustomed to this pianissimo of whispered words, I perceived that the sick man retained the use of his intelligence absolutely intact. There were, however, two M. de Charluses, not to mention any others. Of the two, one, the intellectual one, passed his time in complaining that he suffered from progressive aphasia, that he constantly pronounced one word, one letter by mistake for another. But as soon as he actually made such a mistake, the other M. de Charlus, the subconscious one, who was as desirous of admiration as the first was of pity and out of vanity did things that the first would have despised, immediately, like a conductor whose orchestra has blundered, checked the phrase which he had started and with infinite ingenuity made the end of his sentence follow coherently from the word which he had in fact uttered by mistake for another but which he thus appeared to have chosen. Even his memory was intact, and from it his vanity impelled him, not without the fatigue of the most laborious concentration, to drag forth this or that ancient recollection, of no importance, which concerned myself and which would demonstrate to me that he had preserved or recovered all his lucidity of mind. Without moving his head or his eyes, and without varying in the slightest degree the modulation of his voice, he said to me, for instance: "Look, there's a poster on that telegraph-pole like the one which I was standing near when I saw you for the first time at Avranches—no, I am mistaken, at Balbec." And it was in fact an advertisement for the same product.

I had found it difficult at first to understand what he was saying, just as one begins by seeing absolutely nothing in a room of which all the curtains are closed. But like one's eyes in half-darkness, my ears soon accustomed themselves to his pianissimo. The sound had in any case, I think, gradually grown in volume while the Baron was speaking, perhaps because the weakness of his voice was due in part to a nervous apprehension which was dispelled when he was distracted by the presence of another person and ceased to think about it, though possibly, on the other hand, the feeble voice corresponded to the real state of his health and the momentary strength with which he spoke in conversation was the result of an artificial, transient and even dangerous excitement, which might make strangers say: "He is much better, he must stop thinking about his illness," but in fact only aggravated the illness, which lost no time in resuming its sway. Whatever the explanation may be, the Baron at this moment (even making allowances for the improvement in my own hearing) was flinging down his words with greater force, as the tide, on days of bad weather, flings down its little contorted waves. And the traces of his recent attack caused one to hear at the back of his words a noise like that of pebbles dragged by the sea. Continuing to speak to me about the past, no doubt to prove to me that he had not lost his memory, he evoked it now—in a funereal fashion but without sadness—by reciting an endless list of all the people belonging to his family or his world who were no longer alive, less, it seemed, with any emotion of grief that they were dead than with satisfaction at having survived them. He appeared indeed, as he recalled their extinction, to enjoy a clearer perception of his own return towards health and it was with an almost triumphal sternness that he repeated, in a monotonous tone, stammering slightly and with a dull sepulchral resonance: "Hannibal de Bréauté, dead! Antoine de Mouchy, dead! Charles Swann, dead! Adalbert de Montmorency, dead! Boson de Talleyrand, dead! Sosthène de Doudeauville, dead!" And every time he uttered it, the word "dead" seemed to fall upon his departed friends like a spadeful of earth each heavier than the last, thrown by a grave-digger grimly determined to immure them yet more closely within the tomb.

The Duchesse de Létourville, who was not going to the

Princesse de Guermantes's reception because she had just recovered from a long illness, passed near us at that moment on foot, and seeing the Baron, of whose recent attack she knew nothing, stopped to say good-day to him. But the effect of her own illness was to make her not more understanding but more impatient—with a nervous ill-humour that was nevertheless perhaps not without a large element of compassion—of the illnesses of others. Hearing the Baron pronounce certain words with difficulty and incorrectly and seeing the painful effort he had to make to move his arm, she cast her eyes first upon Jupien and then upon myself as though to demand an explanation of so shocking a phenomenon. As we said nothing, it was to M. de Charlus himself that she addressed a long look full of sadness but also of reproach. She seemed to think it very wrong of him to be out of doors and in her company in a condition as unusual as if he had come out without a tie or without shoes. And when yet another error in pronunciation was perpetrated by the Baron, augmenting both the distress and the indignation of the Duchess, she cried out to him: "Palamède!" in the interrogative and exasperated tone of those nervous people who cannot bear to be kept waiting for a single moment and will say to you sharply, if you let them come into your room before you are ready (with a word of apology for being still engaged upon your toilet), not so as to excuse themselves but in order to accuse you: "Oh, I'm disturbing you, am I?" as if it was your fault that you were being disturbed. Finally she left us, looking crosser and crosser and saying to the Baron: "Really, you ought to go home."

M. de Charlus said he would like to sit down on a chair to rest while Jupien and I went for a little walk, and with some difficulty pulled out of his pocket a book which looked to me like a prayer-book. I was not displeased to have an opportunity to learn from Jupien various details of the Baron's state of health. "I am very glad to talk to you, sir," said Jupien, "but we won't go further than the Rond-Point. Thank heaven, the Baron is better now, but I dare not leave him alone for long, he is always the same, he is too kind-hearted, he would give away everything he possesses: and then that's not the only thing, he still tries to pick people up as if he was a young man, and I have to keep my eyes open." "Particularly as he has recovered the use of his own eyes," I replied; "I was very distressed when I was told that he had lost his sight." "Yes, it's true that his eyes were affected by his stroke. For a time he could see nothing at all. Just imagine, during the cure, which as a matter of fact did him a great deal of good, he was for several months unable to see more than a man born blind." "At least that must have made your surveillance largely unnecessary?" "Not at all, no sooner had he arrived in a hotel than he would ask me what this or that individual on the staff was like. I used to assure him that they were all horrors. But he realised that that couldn't be universally true, that I must sometimes be lying. Little rascal that he is! And then he was extraordinarily good at guessing, from the voice perhaps, I don't know. He used to contrive to send me on urgent errands. One day—you will excuse my telling you this, but you came once by chance to the Temple of Shamelessness and I have nothing to hide from you" (in fact, it was a disagreeable feature of his character that he seemed always to enjoy revealing secrets in his possession)—"I was returning from one of these supposedly urgent errands, all the faster because I guessed it to have been arranged on purpose, when as I approached the Baron's room I heard a voice saying: 'What?' and the Baron reply: 'You don't mean that this has never happened to you before?' I went into the room without knocking, and imagine my terror! The Baron, misled by a voice which was in fact deeper than is usual at that age (remember that at this period he was completely blind and in the old days, as you know, he had always been partial to men who were not quite young), was with a little boy who could not have been ten years old."

I have been told since that at that time he suffered almost every day from severe fits of mental depression, during which, though his mind was not actually wandering, he used to proclaim aloud before people whose presence or whose strict views he forgot opinions which normally he concealed, his pro-Germanism for instance. The war had long since ended, but still he groaned over the defeat of the Germans, amongst whose number he counted himself, and would say proudly: "And yet, inevitably, we shall have our revenge. For we have proved that we are the nation with the greatest capacity for resistance, and the best organisation too." Or else his confidences would take another direction, and he would cry out angrily: "Lord X— (or the Prince de XX—) had better not dare repeat what he said yesterday, it was all I could do not to reply: 'You know you're just as much one as I am.'" Needless to say, when, at the moments when he was "not quite all there," M. de Charlus made these avowals of his pro-German or other tendencies, anybody from his immediate circle who might be with him, whether it were Jupien or the Duchesse de Guermantes, would interrupt the imprudent remarks and interpret them for the benefit of others less intimately acquainted with the Baron and less discreet in a far-fetched but honourable sense.

"But, good heavens!" cried Jupien, "I was right not to want us to go too far. Look! He's already managed to get into conversation with a gardener's boy. I had better say good-bye to you, sir, I must not leave my invalid alone for a second, he is really just a big baby now."

I got out of my cab a second time just before it reached the house of the Princesse de Guermantes and I began once more to reflect upon the mood of lassitude and boredom in which I had attempted, the previous day, to note the characteristics of that line which, in a countryside reputed one of the loveliest of France, had separated upon the trunks of the trees the shadow from the light. Certainly the reasoned conclusions which I had drawn at the time did not cause me so much pain to-day. They were unchanged; but at this moment, as on every occasion when I found myself torn from my habits—in a new place, or going out at an unaccustomed hour—I was feeling a lively pleasure. The pleasure seemed to me to-day a purely frivolous one, that of going to an afternoon party given by Mme de Guermantes. But since I knew now that I could hope for nothing of greater value than frivolous pleasures, what point was there in depriving myself of them? I told myself again that I had felt, in attempting the description, not a spark of that enthusiasm which, if it is not the sole, is one of the first criteria of talent. I tried next to draw from my memory other "snapshots," those in particular which it had taken in Venice, but the mere word "snapshot" made Venice seem to me as boring as an exhibition of photographs, and I felt that I had no more taste, no more talent for describing now what I had seen in the past, than I had had yesterday for describing what at that very moment I was, with a meticulous and melancholy eye, actually observing. In a few minutes a host of friends whom I had not seen for years would probably ask me to give up being a recluse and devote my days to them. And what reason had I to refuse their request, now that I possessed the proof that I was useless and that literature could no longer give me any joy whatever, whether this was my fault, through my not having enough talent, or the fault of literature itself, if it were true that literature was less charged with reality than I had once supposed?

When I thought of what Bergotte had said to me: "You are ill, but one cannot pity you for you have the joys of the mind," how mistaken he had been about me! How little joy there was in this sterile lucidity! Even if sometimes perhaps I had pleasures (not of the mind), I sacrificed them always to one woman after another; so that, had fate granted me another hundred years of life and sound health as well, it would merely have added a series of extensions to an already tedious existence, which there seemed to be no point in prolonging at all, still less for any great length of time. As for the "joys of the intelligence," could I call by that name those cold observations which my clairvoyant eye or my power of accurate ratiocination made without any pleasure and which remained always unfertile?

But it is sometimes just at the moment when we think that everything is lost that the intimation arrives which may save us; one has knocked at all the doors which lead nowhere, and then one stumbles without knowing it on the only door through which one can enter—which one might have sought in vain for a hundred years—and it opens of its own accord. Revolving the gloomy thoughts which I have just recorded, I had entered the courtyard of the Guermantes mansion and in my absent-minded state I had failed to see a car which was coming towards me; the chauffeur gave a shout and I just had time to step out of the way, but as I moved sharply backwards I tripped against the uneven paving-stones in front of the coach-house. And at the moment when, recovering my balance, I put my foot on a stone which was slightly lower than its neighbour, all my discouragement vanished and in its place was that same happiness which at various epochs of my life had been given to me by the sight of trees which I had thought that I recognised in the course of a drive near Balbec, by the sight of the twin steeples of Martinville, by the flavour of a madeleine dipped in tea, and by all those other sensations of which I have spoken and of which the last works of Vinteuil had seemed to me to combine the quintessential character. Just as, at the moment when I tasted the madeleine, all anxiety about the future, all intellectual doubts had disappeared, so now those that a few seconds ago had assailed me on the subject of the reality of my literary gifts, the reality even of literature, were removed as if by magic. I had followed no new train of reasoning, discovered no decisive argument, but the difficulties which had seemed insoluble a moment ago had lost all importance. The happiness which I had just felt was unquestionably the same as that which I had felt when I tasted the madeleine soaked in tea. But if on that occasion I had put off the task of searching for the profounder causes of my emotion, this time I was determined not to resign myself to a failure to understand them. The emotion was the same; the difference, purely material, lay in the images evoked: a profound azure intoxicated my eyes, impressions of coolness, of dazzling light, swirled round me and in my desire to seize them—as afraid to move as I had been on the earlier occasion when I had continued to savour the taste of the madeleine while I tried to draw into my consciousness whatever it was that it recalled to me—I continued, ignoring the evident amusement of the great crowd of chauffeurs, to stagger as I had staggered a few seconds ago, with one foot on the higher paving-stone and the other on the lower. Every time that I merely repeated this physical movement, I achieved nothing; but if I succeeded, forgetting the Guermantes party, in recapturing what I had felt when I first placed my feet on the ground in this way, again the dazzling and indistinct vision fluttered near me, as if to say: "Seize me as I pass if you can, and try to solve the riddle of happiness which I set you." And almost at once I recognised the vision: it was Venice, of which my efforts to describe it and the supposed snapshots taken by my memory had never told me anything, but which the sensation which I had once experienced as I stood upon two uneven stones in the baptistery of St Mark's had, recurring a moment ago, restored to me complete with all the other sensations linked on that day to that particular sensation, all of which had been waiting in their place—from which with imperious suddenness a chance happening had caused them to emerge—in the series of forgotten days. In the same way the taste of the little madeleine had recalled Combray to me. But why had the images of Combray and of Venice, at these two different moments, given me a joy which was like a certainty and which sufficed, without any other proof, to make death a matter of indifference to me?

Still asking myself this question, and determined to-day to find the answer to it, I entered the Guermantes mansion, because always we give precedence over the inner task that we have to perform to the outward role which we are playing, which was, for me at this moment, that of guest. But when I had gone upstairs, a butler requested me to wait for a few minutes in a little sitting-room used as a library, next to the room where the refreshments were being served, until the end of the piece of music which was being played, the Princess having given orders for the doors to be kept shut during its performance. And at that very moment a second intimation came to reinforce the one which had been given to me by the two uneven paving-stones and to exhort me to persevere in my task. A servant, trying unsuccessfully not to make a noise, chanced to knock a spoon against a plate and again that same species of happiness which had come to me from the uneven paving-stones poured into me; the sensation was again of great heat, but entirely different: heat combined with a whiff of smoke and relieved by the cool smell of a forest background; and I recognised that what seemed to me now so delightful was that same row of trees which I had found tedious both to observe and to describe but which I had just now for a moment, in a sort of daze—I seemed to be in the railway carriage again, opening a bottle of beer—supposed to be before my eyes, so forcibly had the identical noise of the spoon knocking against the plate given me, until I had had time to remember where I was, the illusion of the noise of the hammer with which a rail-wayman had remedied some defect on a wheel of the train while we stopped near the little wood. And then it seemed as though the signs which were to bring me, on this day of all days, out of my disheartened state and restore to me my faith in literature, were thronging eagerly about me, for, a butler who had long been in the service of the Prince de Guermantes having recognised me and brought to me in the library where I was waiting, so that I might not have to go to the buffet, a selection of *petits fours* and a glass of orangeade, I wiped my mouth with the napkin which he had given me; and instantly, as though I had been the character in the *Thousand and One Nights* who unwittingly accomplishes the very rite which can cause to appear, visible to him alone, a docile genie ready to convey him to a great distance, a new vision of azure passed before my eyes, but an azure that this time was pure and saline and swelled into blue and bosomy undulations, and so strong was this impression that the moment to which I was trans-ported seemed to me to be the present moment: more bemused than on the day when I had wondered whether I was really going to be received by the Princesse de Guermantes or whether everything round me would not collapse, I thought that the servant had just opened the window on to the beach and that all things invited me to go down and stroll along the promenade while the tide was high, for the napkin which I had used to wipe my mouth had precisely the same degree of stiff-ness and starchedness as the towel with which I had found it so awkward to dry my face as I stood in front of the window on the first day of my arrival at Balbec, and this napkin now, in the library of the Prince de Guermantes's house, unfolded for me —concealed within its smooth surfaces and its folds—the plumage of an ocean green and blue like the tail of a peacock. And what I found myself enjoying was not merely these colours but a whole instant of my life on whose summit they rested, an instant which had been no doubt an aspiration to-wards them and which some feeling of fatigue or sadness had perhaps prevented me from enjoying at Balbec but which now, freed from what is necessarily imperfect in external perception, pure and disembodied, caused me to swell with happiness.

The piece of music which was being played might end at any moment, and I might be obliged to enter the drawing-room. So I forced myself to try as quickly as possible to discern the essence of the identical pleasures which I had just experienced three times within the space of a few minutes, and having done so to extract the lesson which they might be made to yield. The thought that there is a vast difference between the real impression which we have had of a thing and the artificial impression of it which we form for ourselves when we attempt by an act of will to imagine it did not long detain me. Remembering with what relative indifference Swann years ago had been able to speak of the days when he had been loved, because what he saw beneath the words was not in fact those days but something else, and on the other hand the sudden pain which he had been caused by the little phrase of Vinteuil when it gave him back the days themselves, just as they were when he had felt them in the past, I understood clearly that what the sensation of the uneven paving-stones, the stiffness of the napkin, the taste of the madeleine had reawakened in me had no connexion with what I frequently tried to recall to myself of Venice, Balbec, Combray, with the help of an undifferentiated memory; and I understood that the reason why life may be judged to be trivial although at certain moments it seems to us so beautiful is that we form our judgment, ordinarily, on the evidence not of life itself but of those quite different images which preserve nothing of life—and therefore we judge it disparagingly. At most I noticed cursorily that the differences which exist between every one of our real impressions—differences which explain why a uniform depiction of life cannot bear much resemblance to the reality—derive probably from the following cause: the slightest word that we have said, the most insignificant action that we have performed at any one epoch of our life was surrounded by, and coloured by the reflection of, things which logically had no connexion with it and which later have been separated from it by our intellect which could make nothing of them for its own rational purposes, things, however, in the midst of which—here the pink reflection of the evening upon the flower-covered wall of a country restaurant, a feeling of hunger, the desire for women, the pleasure of luxury;

there the blue volutes of the morning sea and, enveloped in them, phrases of music half emerging like the shoulders of water-nymphs—the simplest act or gesture remains immured as within a thousand sealed vessels, each one of them filled with things of a colour, a scent, a temperature that are absolutely different one from another, vessels, moreover, which being disposed over the whole range of our years, during which we have never ceased to change if only in our dreams and our thoughts, are situated at the most various moral altitudes and give us the sensation of extraordinarily diverse atmospheres. It is true that we have accomplished these changes imperceptibly; but between the memory which brusquely returns to us and our present state, and no less between two memories of different years, places, hours, the distance is such that it alone, even without any specific originality, would make it impossible to compare one with the other. Yes: if, owing to the work of oblivion, the returning memory can throw no bridge, form no connecting link between itself and the present minute, if it remains in the context of its own place and date, if it keeps its distance, its isolation in the hollow of a valley or upon the highest peak of a mountain summit, for this very reason it causes us suddenly to breathe a new air, an air which is new precisely because we have breathed it in the past, that purer air which the poets have vainly tried to situate in paradise and which could induce so profound a sensation of renewal only if it had been breathed before, since the true paradises are the paradises that we have lost.

And I observed in passing that for the work of art which I now, though I had not yet reached a conscious resolution, felt myself ready to undertake, this distinctness of different events would entail very considerable difficulties. For I should have to execute the successive parts of my work in a succession of different materials; what would be suitable for mornings beside the sea or afternoons in Venice would be quite wrong if I wanted to depict those evenings at Rivebelle when, in the dining-room that opened on to the garden, the heat began to resolve into fragments and sink back into the ground, while a sunset glimmer still illumined the roses on the walls of the restaurant and the last water-colours of the day were still visible in the sky—this would be a new and distinct material, of a transparency and a sonority that were special, compact, cool after warmth, rose-pink.

Over all these thoughts I skimmed rapidly, for another inquiry demanded my attention more imperiously, the inquiry, which on previous occasions I had postponed, into the cause of this felicity which I had just experienced, into the character of the certitude with which it imposed itself. And this cause I began to divine as I compared these diverse happy impressions, diverse yet with this in common, that I experienced them at the present moment and at the same time in the context of a distant moment, so that the past was made to encroach upon the present and I was made to doubt whether I was in the one or the other. The truth surely was that the being within me which had enjoyed these impressions had enjoyed them because they had in them something that was common to a day long past and to the present, because in some way they were extra-temporal, and this being made its appearance only when, through one of these identifications of the present with the past, it was likely to find itself in the one and only medium in which it could exist and enjoy the essence of things, that is to say: outside time. This explained why it was that my anxiety on the subject of my death had ceased at the moment when I had unconsciously recognised the taste of the little madeleine, since the being which at that moment I had been was an extra-temporal being and therefore unalarmed by the vicissitudes of the future. This being had only come to me, only manifested itself outside of activity and immediate enjoyment, on those rare occasions when the miracle of an analogy had made me escape from the present. And only this being had the power to perform that task which had always defeated the efforts of my memory and my intellect, the power to make me rediscover days that were long past, the Time that was Lost.

And perhaps, if just now I had been disposed to think Bergotte wrong when he spoke of the life of the mind and its joys, it was because what I thought of at that moment as "the life of the mind" was a species of logical reasoning which had no connexion with it or with what existed in me at this moment—an error like the one which had made me find society and life

itself tedious because I judged them on the evidence of untrue
recollections, whereas now, now that three times in succession
there had been reborn within me a veritable moment of the
past, my appetite for life was immense.

A moment of the past, did I say? Was it not perhaps very
much more: something that, common both to the past and to
the present, is much more essential than either of them? So
often, in the course of my life, reality had disappointed me
because at the instant when my senses perceived it my imagination, which was the only organ that I possessed for the enjoyment of beauty, could not apply itself to it, in virtue of that
ineluctable law which ordains that we can only imagine what
is absent. And now, suddenly, the effect of this harsh law had
been neutralised, temporarily annulled, by a marvellous expedient of nature which had caused a sensation—the noise made
both by the spoon and by the hammer, for instance—to be
mirrored at one and the same time in the past, so that my
imagination was permitted to savour it, and in the present,
where the actual shock to my senses of the noise, the touch of
the linen napkin, or whatever it might be, had added to the
dreams of the imagination the concept of "existence" which
they usually lack, and through this subterfuge had made it
possible for my being to secure, to isolate, to immobilise—for
a moment brief as a flash of lightning—what normally it never
apprehends: a fragment of time in the pure state. The being
which had been reborn in me when with a sudden shudder of
happiness I had heard the noise that was common to the spoon
touching the plate and the hammer striking the wheel, or had
felt, beneath my feet, the unevenness that was common to the
paving-stones of the Guermantes courtyard and to those of the
baptistery of St Mark's, this being is nourished only by the
essences of things, in these alone does it find its sustenance and
delight. In the observation of the present, where the senses
cannot feed it with this food, it languishes, as it does in the
consideration of a past made arid by the intellect or in the
anticipation of a future which the will constructs with fragments of the present and the past, fragments whose reality it
still further reduces by preserving of them only what is suitable
for the utilitarian, narrowly human purpose for which it intends

them. But let a noise or a scent, once heard or once smelt, be heard or smelt again in the present and at the same time in the past, real without being actual, ideal without being abstract, and immediately the permanent and habitually concealed essence of things is liberated and our true self which seemed— had perhaps for long years seemed—to be dead but was not altogether dead, is awakened and reanimated as it receives the celestial nourishment that is brought to it. A minute freed from the order of time has re-created in us, to feel it, the man freed from the order of time. And one can understand that this man should have confidence in his joy, even if the simple taste of a madeleine does not seem logically to contain within it the reasons for this joy, one can understand that the word "death" should have no meaning for him; situated outside time, why should he fear the future?

But this species of optical illusion, which placed beside me a moment of the past that was incompatible with the present, could not last for long. The images presented to us by the voluntary memory can, it is true, be prolonged at will, for the voluntary memory requires no more exertion on our part than turning over the pages of a picture-book. On the day, for instance, long ago, when I was to visit the Princesse de Guermantes for the first time, I had from the sun-drenched court-yard of our house in Paris idly regarded, according to my whim, now the Place de l'Eglise at Combray, now the beach at Balbec, as if I had been choosing illustrations for that particular day from an album of water-colours depicting the various places where I had been; and with the egotistical pleasure of a collec-tor, I had said to myself as I catalogued these illustrations stored in my memory: "At least I have seen some lovely things in my life." And of course my memory had affirmed that each one of these sensations was quite unlike the others, though in fact all it was doing was to make varied patterns out of elements that were homogeneous. But my recent experience of the three memories was something utterly different. These, on the con-trary, instead of giving me a more flattering idea of myself, had almost caused me to doubt the reality, the existence of that self. And just as on the day when I had dipped the madeleine in the hot tea, in the setting of the place where I happened at the time to be—on that first day my room in Paris, today at this moment the library of the Prince de Guermantes, a few minutes earlier the courtyard of his house—there had been, inside me and irradiating a little area outside me, a sensation (the taste of the madeleine dipped in the tea, a metallic sound, a step of a certain kind) which was common both to my actual surroundings and also to another place (my aunt Léonie's bedroom, the railway carriage, the baptistery of St Mark's). And now again, at the very moment when I was making these reflections, the shrill noise of water running through a pipe, a noise exactly like those long-drawn-out whistles which sometimes on summer evenings one heard the pleasure-steamers emit as they approached Balbec from the sea, made me feel—what I had once before been made to feel in Paris, in a big restaurant, by the sight of a luxurious dining-room, half-empty, summery and hot—something that was not merely a sensation analogous to the one I used to have at the end of the afternoon in Balbec when, the tables already laid and glittering with linen and silver, the vast window-bays still open from one end to the other on to the esplanade without a single interruption, a single solid surface of glass or stone, while the sun slowly descended upon the sea and the steamers in the bay began to emit their cries, I had, if I had wished to join Albertine and her friends who were walking on the front, merely to step over the low wooden frame not much higher than my ankle, into a groove in which the whole continuous range of windows had been wound down so that the air could come into the hotel. (The painful recollection of having loved Albertine was, however, absent from my present sensation. Painful recollections are always of the dead. And the dead decompose rapidly, and there remains even in the proximity of their tombs nothing but the beauty of nature, silence, the purity of the air.) It was no mere analogous sensation nor even a mere echo or replica of a past sensation that I was made to feel by the noise of the water in the pipe, it was that past sensation itself. And in this case as in all the others, the sensation common to past and present had sought to re-create the former scene around itself, while the actual scene which had taken the former one's place opposed with all the resistance of material inertia this incursion into a house in Paris of a Normandy beach or a railway embankment. The marine dining-room of Balbec, with its damask linen prepared like so many altar-cloths to receive the setting sun, had sought to shatter the solidity of the Guermantes mansion, to force open its doors, and for an instant had made the sofas around me sway and tremble as on another occasion it had done to the tables of the restaurant in Paris. Always, when these resurrections took place, the distant scene engendered around the common sensation had for a moment grappled, like a wrestler, with the present scene. Always the present scene had come off victorious, and always the vanquished one had appeared to me the more beautiful of the two, so beautiful that I had remained in a state of ecstasy on the uneven paving-stones or before the cup of tea, endeavouring to prolong or to reproduce the momentary appearances of the Combray or the Balbec or the Venice which invaded only to be driven back, which rose up only at once to abandon me in the midst of the new scene which somehow, nevertheless, the past had been able to permeate. And if the present scene had not very quickly been victorious, I believe that I should have lost consciousness; for so complete are these resurrections of the past during the second that they last, that they not only oblige our eyes to cease to see the room which is near them in order to look instead at the railway bordered with trees or the rising tide, they even force our nostrils to breathe the air of places which are in fact a great distance away, and our will to choose between the various projects which those distant places suggest to us, they force our whole self to believe that it is surrounded by these places or at least to waver doubtfully between them and the places where we now are, in a dazed uncertainty such as we feel sometimes when an indescribably beautiful vision presents itself to us at the moment of our falling asleep.

Fragments of existence withdrawn from Time: these then were perhaps what the being three times, four times brought back to life within me had just now tasted, but the contemplation, though it was of eternity, had been fugitive. And yet I was vaguely aware that the pleasure which this contemplation had, at rare intervals, given me in my life, was the only genuine and fruitful pleasure that I had known. The unreality of the others is indicated clearly enough—is it not?—either by their inability to satisfy us, as is the case with social pleasures, the only consequence of which is likely to be the discomfort provoked by the ingestion of unwholesome food, or with friendship, which is a simulacrum, since, for whatever moral reasons he may do it, the artist who gives up an hour of work for an hour of conversation with a friend knows that he is sacrificing a reality for something that does not exist (our friends being friends only in the light of an agreeable folly which travels with us through life and to which we readily accommodate ourselves, but which at the bottom of our hearts we know to be no more reasonable than the delusion of the man who talks to the furniture because he believes that it is alive), or else by the sadness which follows their satisfaction, a sadness which I had felt, for instance, on the day when I had been introduced to Albertine, at having taken pains (not even in fact very great pains) in order to achieve something—getting to know this girl—which seemed to me trivial simply because I had achieved it. And even a more profound pleasure, like the pleasure which I might have hoped to feel when I was in love with Albertine, was in fact only experienced inversely, through the anguish which I felt when she was not there, for when I was sure that she would soon be with me, as on the day when she had returned from the Trocadéro, I had seemed to experience no more than a vague dissatisfaction, whereas my exaltation and my joy grew steadily greater as I probed more and more deeply into the noise of the spoon on the plate or the taste of the tea which had brought into my bedroom in Paris the bedroom of my aunt Léonie and in its train all Combray and the two ways of our walks.

To this contemplation of the essence of things I had decided therefore that in future I must attach myself, so as somehow to immobilise it. But how, by what means, was I to do this? Naturally, at the moment when the stiffness of the napkin had restored Balbec to me and for an instant caressed my imagination not only with the sight of the sea as it had been that morning but with the smell of my room, the speed of the wind, the sensation of looking forward to lunch, of wondering which of the different walks I should take (all this being attached to the feel of the linen like those thousand wings of the angels which revolve a thousand times in a minute), or at the moment when the unevenness of the two paving-stones had extended in every direction and dimension the desiccated and insubstantial images which I normally had of Venice and St Mark's and of all the sensations which I had felt there, reuniting the piazza to the cathedral, the landing-stage to the piazza, the canal to the landing-stage, and to all that the eyes see the world of desires which is seen only by the mind—naturally at those moments I had been tempted, if not, because of the time of the year, to go and walk once more through the watery streets of Venice which for me were above all associated with the spring, at least to return to Balbec. But this thought did not for an instant detain me. I knew for one thing that countries were not such as their names painted them to my imagination, so that now it was scarcely ever except in my dreams, while I was asleep, that a place could lie spread before me wrought in that pure matter which is entirely distinct from the matter of the common things that we see and touch but of which, when I had imagined these common things without ever having seen them, they too had seemed to me to be composed: and I knew also that the same was true of that other species of image which is formed by the memory, so that not only had I failed to discover the beauty of Balbec as I had imagined it when I had gone there for the first time, I had failed also when I went back the second time to rediscover the remembered beauty which that first visit had left me. Experience had taught me only too well the impossibility of attaining in the real world to what lay deep within myself; I knew that Lost Time was not to be found again on the piazza of St Mark's any more than I had found it again on my second visit to Balbec or on my return to Tansonville to see Gilberte, and that travel, which merely dangled once more before me the illusion that these vanished impressions existed outside myself, could not be the means which I sought. And I did not want to let myself be side-tracked once more, for the task before me was to discover at long last whether or no it was possible to attain to what—disappointed as I had always been by the actuality of places and people—I had, although once the septet of Vinteuil had seemed to point to the contrary conclusion, come to think of as unrealisable. I did not intend, then, to make yet another experiment in a direction which I had long known could lead nowhere. Impressions such as those to which I wished to give permanence could not but vanish at the touch of a direct enjoyment which had been powerless to engender them. The only way to savour them more fully was to try to get to know them more completely in the medium in which they existed, that is to say within myself, to try to make them translucid even to their very depths. I had not known pleasure at Balbec any more than I had known pleasure when I lived with Albertine, for the pleasure of living with her had been perceptible to me only in retrospect. When I recapitulated the disappointments of my life as a lived life, disappointments which made me believe that its reality must reside elsewhere than in action, what I was doing was not merely to link different disappointments together in a purely fortuitous manner and in following the circumstances of my personal existence. I saw clearly that the disappointment of travel and the disappointment of love were not different disappointments at all but the varied aspects which are assumed, according to the particular circumstances which bring it into play, by our inherent powerlessness to realise ourselves in material enjoyment or in effective action. And thinking again of the extra-temporal joy which I had been made to feel by the sound of the spoon or the taste of the madeleine, I said to myself: "Was this perhaps that happiness which the little phrase of the sonata promised to Swann and which he, because he was unable to find it in artistic creation, mistakenly assimilated to the pleasures of love, was this the happiness of which long ago I was given a presentiment —as something more supraterrestrial even than the mood evoked by the little phrase of the sonata—by the call, the mysterious, rubescent call of that septet which Swann was never privileged to hear, having died like so many others before the truth that was made for him had been revealed? A truth that in any case he could not have used, for though the phrase perhaps symbolised a call, it was incapable of creating new powers and making Swann the writer that he was not."

And then, after I had dwelt for some little time upon these resurrections of the memory, the thought came to me that in another fashion certain obscure impressions, already even at Combray on the Guermantes way, had solicited my attention in a fashion somewhat similar to these reminiscences, except that they concealed within them not a sensation dating from an earlier time, but a new truth, a precious image which I had sought to uncover by efforts of the same kind as those that we make to recall something that we have forgotten, as if our finest ideas were like tunes which, as it were, come back to us although we have never heard them before and which we have to make an effort to hear and to transcribe. I remembered—with pleasure because it showed me that already in those days I had been the same and that this type of experience sprang from a fundamental trait in my character, but with sadness also when I thought that since that time I had never progressed—that already at Combray I used to fix before my mind for its attention some image which had compelled me to look at it, a cloud, a triangle, a church spire, a flower, a stone, because I had the feeling that perhaps beneath these signs there lay something of a quite different kind which I must try to discover, some thought which they translated after the fashion of those hieroglyphic characters which at first one might suppose to represent only material objects. No doubt the process of decipherment was difficult, but only by accomplishing it could one arrive at whatever truth there was to read. For the truths which the intellect apprehends directly in the world of full and unimpeded light have something less profound, less necessary than those which life communicates to us against our will in an impression which is material because it enters us through the senses but yet has a spiritual meaning which it is possible for us to extract. In fact, both in the one case and in the other, whether I was concerned with impressions like the one which I had received from the sight of the steeples of Martinville or with reminiscences like that of the unevenness of the two steps or the taste of the madeleine, the task was to interpret the given sensations as signs of so many laws and ideas, by trying to think—that is to say, to draw forth from the shadow—what I had merely felt, by trying to convert it into its spiritual equivalent. And this method, which seemed to me the sole method, what was it but the creation of a work of art? Already the consequences came flooding into my mind: first, whether I considered reminiscences of the kind evoked by the noise of the spoon or the taste of the madeleine, or those truths written with the aid of shapes for whose meaning I searched in my brain, where—church steeples or wild grass growing in a wall —they composed a magical scrawl, complex and elaborate, their essential character was that I was not free to choose them, that such as they were they were given to me. And I realised that this must be the mark of their authenticity. I had not gone in search of the two uneven paving-stones of the courtyard upon which I had stumbled. But it was precisely the fortuitous and inevitable fashion in which this and the other sensations had been encountered that proved the trueness of the past which they brought back to life, of the images which they released, since we feel, with these sensations, the effort that they make to climb back towards the light, feel in ourselves the joy of rediscovering what is real. And here too was the proof of the trueness of the whole picture formed out of those contemporaneous impressions which the first sensation brings back in its train, with those unerring proportions of light and shade, emphasis and omission, memory and forgetfulness to which conscious recollection and conscious observation will never know how to attain.

As for the inner book of unknown symbols (symbols carved in relief they might have been, which my attention, as it explored my unconscious, groped for and stumbled against and followed the contours of, like a diver exploring the ocean-bed), if I tried to read them no one could help me with any rules, for to read them was an act of creation in which no one can do our work for us or even collaborate with us. How many for this reason turn aside from writing! What tasks do men not take upon themselves in order to evade this task! Every public event, be it the Dreyfus case, be it the war, furnishes the writer with a fresh excuse for not attempting to decipher this book: he wants to ensure the triumph of justice, he wants to restore the moral unity of the nation, he has no time to think of literature. But these are mere excuses, the truth being that he has not or no longer has genius, that is to say instinct. For instinct dictates our duty and the intellect supplies us with

pretexts for evading it. But excuses have no place in art and
intentions count for nothing: at every moment the artist has to
listen to his instinct, and it is this that makes art the most real
of all things, the most austere school of life, the true last judgment. This book, more laborious to decipher than any other,
is also the only one which has been dictated to us by reality,
the only one of which the "impression" has been printed in us
by reality itself. When an idea—an idea of any kind—is left in
us by life, its material pattern, the outline of the impression
that it made upon us, remains behind as the token of its necessary truth. The ideas formed by the pure intelligence have no
more than a logical, a possible truth, they are arbitrarily chosen.
The book whose hieroglyphs are patterns not traced by us is
the only book that really belongs to us. Not that the ideas
which we form for ourselves cannot be correct in logic; that
they may well be, but we cannot know whether they are true.
Only the impression, however trivial its material may seem to
be, however faint its traces, is a criterion of truth and deserves
for that reason to be apprehended by the mind, for the mind,
if it succeeds in extracting this truth, can by the impression and
by nothing else be brought to a state of greater perfection and
given a pure joy. The impression is for the writer what experiment is for the scientist, with the difference that in the scientist
the work of the intelligence precedes the experiment and in the
writer it comes after the impression. What we have not had to
decipher, to elucidate by our own efforts, what was clear before
we looked at it, is not ours. From ourselves comes only that
which we drag forth from the obscurity which lies within us,
that which to others is unknown.

(A level ray of the setting sun recalls to me instantaneously
an episode in my early childhood to which I had never since
that time given a thought: my aunt Léonie had a fever which
Doctor Percepied feared might be typhoid and for a week I
was made to sleep in Eulalie's little room looking out on the
Place de l'Eglise, which had nothing but rush mats on the
floor and over the window a muslin curtain that was always
buzzing with a sunshine to which I was not accustomed. And
seeing how the recollection of this little old-fashioned servant's
bedroom suddenly added to my past life a long stretch of time

so different from the rest and so delicious, I thought by contrast of the nullity of the impressions which had been contributed to it by the most sumptuous entertainments in the most princely mansions. The only thing at all sad about this room of Eulalie's was that at night, because the viaduct was so near, one heard the hooting of the trains. But as I knew that these were bellowings produced by machines under human control, they did not terrify me as, in a prehistoric age, I might have been terrified by the ululations of a neighbouring mammoth taking a free and unco-ordinated stroll.)

I had arrived then at the conclusion that in fashioning a work of art we are by no means free, that we do not choose how we shall make it but that it pre-exists us and therefore we are obliged, since it is both necessary and hidden, to do what we should have to do if it were a law of nature, that is to say to discover it. But this discovery which art obliges us to make, is it not, I thought, really the discovery of what, though it ought to be more precious to us than anything in the world, yet remains ordinarily for ever unknown to us, the discovery of our true life, of reality as we have felt it to be, which differs so greatly from what we think it is that when a chance happening brings us an authentic memory of it we are filled with an immense happiness? In this conclusion I was confirmed by the thought of the falseness of so-called realist art, which would not be so untruthful if we had not in life acquired the habit of giving to what we feel a form of expression which differs so much from, and which we nevertheless after a little time take to be, reality itself. I began to perceive that I should not have to trouble myself with the various literary theories which had at moments perplexed me—notably those which practitioners of criticism had developed at the time of the Dreyfus case and had taken up again during the war, according to which "the artist must be made to leave his ivory tower" and the themes chosen by the writer ought to be not frivolous or sentimental but rather such things as great working-class movements or—in default of crowds—at least no longer as in the past unimportant men of leisure ("I must confess that the depiction of these useless characters rather bores me," Bloch had been fond of saying), but noble intellectuals or men of heroic stature. In any case, quite apart from what I might think of the logical propositions which they contained, these theories seemed to me to indicate very clearly the inferiority of those who upheld them—my reaction was that of the truly well-brought-up child who, lunching in a strange house and hearing his hosts say: "We are frank, we don't hide our light under a bushel here," feels that the remark indicates a moral quality inferior to right conduct pure and simple, which says nothing. Authentic art has no use for proclamations of this kind, it accomplishes its work in silence. Moreover, those who theorised in this way used hackneyed phrases which had a curious resemblance to those of the idiots whom they denounced. And it is perhaps as much by the quality of his language as by the species of aesthetic theory which he advances that one may judge of the level to which a writer has attained in the moral and intellectual part of his work. Quality of language, however, is something the critical theorists think that they can do without, and those who admire them are easily persuaded that it is no proof of intellectual merit, for this is a thing which they cannot infer from the beauty of an image but can recognise only when they see it directly expressed. Hence the temptation for the writer to write intellectual works—a gross impropriety. A work in which there are theories is like an object which still has its price-tag on it. (And as to the choice of theme, a frivolous theme will serve as well as a serious one for a study of the laws of character, in the same way that a prosector can study the laws of anatomy as well in the body of an imbecile as in that of a man of talent, since the great moral laws, like the laws of the circulation of the blood or of renal elimination, vary scarcely at all with the intellectual merit of individuals.) A writer reasons, that is to say he goes astray, only when he has not the strength to force himself to make an impression pass through all the successive states which will culminate in its fixation, its expression. The reality that he has to express resides, as I now began to understand, not in the superficial appearance of his subject but at a depth at which that appearance matters little; this truth had been symbolised for me by that clink of a spoon against a plate, that starched stiffness of a napkin, which had been of more value to me for my spiritual renewal than innumerable conversations of a humanitarian or patriotic or internationalist or metaphysical kind. "Enough of style," had been the cry, "enough of literature, let us have life!" And one may well imagine how since the beginning of the war even the simple theories of M. de Norpois, his denunciations of the "flute-players," had enjoyed a second vogue. For plenty of people who lack the artistic sense, who lack, that is to say, the faculty of submitting to the reality within themselves, may yet possess the ability to expatiate upon the theory of art until the crack of doom. And if they happen to be diplomats or financiers to boot, involved in the "realities" of the present age, they are likely to believe that literature is an intellectual game destined in the future to be progressively eliminated. (Some critics now liked to regard the novel as a sort of procession of things upon the screen of a cinematograph. This comparison was absurd. Nothing is further from what we have really perceived than the vision that the cinematograph presents.)

The idea of a popular art, like that of a patriotic art, if not actually dangerous seemed to me ridiculous. If the intention was to make art accessible to the people by sacrificing refinements of form, on the ground that they are "all right for the idle rich" but not for anybody else, I had seen enough of fashionable society to know that it is there that one finds real illiteracy and not, let us say, among electricians. In fact, an art that was "popular" so far as form was concerned would have been better suited to the members of the Jockey Club than to those of the General Confederation of Labour—and as for subject, the working classes are as bored by novels of popular life as children are by the books which are written specially for them. When one reads, one likes to be transported into a new world, and working men have as much curiosity about princes as princes about working men. At the beginning of the war M. Barrès had said that the artist (he happened to be talking about Titian) must first and foremost serve the glory of his country. But this he can do only by being an artist, which means only on condition that, while in his own sphere he is studying laws, conducting experiments, making discoveries which are as delicate as those of science, he shall think of nothing—not even his country—but the truth which is before him.

Let us not imitate the revolutionaries who out of "civic sense" despised, if they did not destroy, the works of Watteau and La Tour, painters who have brought more honour upon France than all those of the Revolution. Anatomy is not perhaps the occupation that a kind-hearted man would choose, if he or any artist had the possibility of choice, and certainly it was not the kindness of a virtuous heart (though he was a truly kind man) that made Choderlos de Laclos write *Les Liaisons dangereuses,* nor was it any affection for the lower or upper bourgeoisie that made Flaubert choose the themes of *Madame Bovary* and *L'Education sentimentale*—but this is no valid criticism of the work of these writers.

Some people were also saying that the art of an age of haste would be brief, just as many people before the war had predicted that it would be short. The railway, according to this mode of thinking, was destined to kill contemplation and there was no sense in regretting the age of the diligence. But in fact the car has taken over its function and once more deposits tourists outside forgotten churches.

As I entered the library where I had been pursuing this train of thought I had remembered what the Goncourts say about the magnificent first editions which it contains and I had promised myself that I would look at them while I was waiting. And all this while, without paying very much attention to what I was doing, I had been taking first one and then another of the precious volumes from the shelves, when suddenly, at the moment when I carelessly opened one of them—it was George Sand's *François le Champi*—I felt myself unpleasantly struck by an impression which seemed at first to be utterly out of harmony with the thoughts that were passing through my mind, until a moment later, with an emotion so strong that tears came to my eyes, I recognised how very much in harmony with them it was. Imagine a room in which a man has died, a man who has rendered great services to his country; the undertaker's men are getting ready to take the coffin downstairs and the dead man's son is holding out his hand to the last friends who are filing past it; suddenly the silence is broken by a flourish of trumpets beneath the windows and he feels outraged, thinking that this must be some plot to mock and insult his grief; but presently this man who until this moment has mastered his emotions dissolves into tears, for he realises that what he hears is the band of a regiment which has come to share in his mourning and to pay honour to his father's corpse. Like this dead man's son, I had just recognised how completely in harmony with the thoughts in my mind was the painful impression which I had experienced when I had seen this title on the cover of a book in the library of the Prince de Guermantes, for it was a title which after a moment's hesitation had given me the idea that literature did really offer us that world of mystery which I had ceased to find in it. And yet the book was not a very extraordinary one, it was *François le Champi*. But that name, like the name Guermantes, was for me unlike the names which I had heard for the first time only in later life. The memory of what had seemed to me too deep for understanding in the subject of *François le Champi* when my mother long ago had read the book aloud to me, had been reawakened by the title, and just as the name of Guermantes, after a long period during which I had not seen the Guermantes, contained for me the essence of the feudal age, so *François le Champi* contained the essence of the novel, and for a second this memory substituted itself for the quite commonplace idea of "one of George Sand's novels about Berry." At a dinner-party, where thought always remains superficial, I might no doubt have been able to talk about *François le Champi* and the Guermantes without either the novel or the family being what they had been to me at Combray. But alone, as I was at this moment, I was plunged by these names to a greater depth. At such moments the idea that some woman whom I had met at parties was a cousin of Mme de Guermantes, a cousin that is to say of a personage of the magic lantern, seemed to me incomprehensible, and equally incomprehensible was the idea that the best books I had ever read might be—I will not say superior to, though that is in fact of course what they were—but even equal to this extraordinary *François le Champi*. This was a very deeply buried impression that I had just encountered, one in which memories of childhood and family were tenderly intermingled and which I had not immediately recognised. My first r ction had been to ask myself, angrily, who this stranger was who was coming to trouble me. The stranger was none other than myself, the child I had been at that time, brought to life within me by the book, which knowing nothing of me except this child had instantly summoned him to its presence, wanting to be seen only by his eyes, to be loved only by his heart, to speak only to him. And this book which my mother had read aloud to me at Combray until the early hours of the morning had kept for me all the charm of that night. Admittedly the "pen" of George Sand, to borrow a phrase from Brichot, who was so fond of saying that a book was written with a "lively pen," no longer seemed to me, as for so long it had seemed to my mother before she had gradually come to model her literary tastes upon mine, in the least a magic pen. But it was a pen which, unintentionally, like a schoolboy amusing himself with a real pen, I had charged with electricity, and now a thousand trifling details of Combray which for years had not entered my mind came lightly and spontaneously leaping, in follow-my-leader fashion, to suspend themselves from the magnetised nib in an interminable and trembling chain of memories.

Certain people, whose minds are prone to mystery, like to believe that objects retain something of the eyes which have looked at them, that old buildings and pictures appear to us not as they originally were but beneath a perceptible veil woven for them over the centuries by the love and contemplation of millions of admirers. This fantasy, if you transpose it into the domain of what is for each one of us the sole reality, the domain of his own sensibility, becomes the truth. In that sense and in that sense alone (but it is a far more important one than the other), a thing which we have looked at in the past brings back to us, if we see it again, not only the eyes with which we looked at it but all the images with which at the time those eyes were filled. For things—and among them a book in a red binding— as soon as we have perceived them are transformed within us into something immaterial, something of the same nature as all our preoccupations and sensations of that particular time, with which, indissolubly, they blend. A name read long ago in a book contains within its syllables the strong wind and brilliant sunshine that prevailed while we were reading it. And this is why the kind of literature which contents itself with "describing things," with giving of them merely a miserable abstract of lines and surfaces, is in fact, though it calls itself realist, the furthest removed from reality and has more than any other the effect of saddening and impoverishing us, since it abruptly severs all communication of our present self both with the past, the essence of which is preserved in things, and with the future, in which things incite us to enjoy the essence of the past a second time. Yet it is precisely this essence that an art worthy of the name must seek to express; then at least, if it fails, there is a lesson to be drawn from its impotence (whereas from the successes of realism there is nothing to be learnt), the lesson that this essence is, in part, subjective and incommunicable.

Nor is this all. A thing which we saw, a book which we read at a certain period does not merely remain for ever conjoined to what existed then around us; it remains also faithfully united to what we ourselves then were and thereafter it can be handled only by the sensibility, the personality that were then ours. If, even in thought, I pick from the bookshelf *François le Champi*, immediately there rises within me a child who takes my place, who alone has the right to spell out the title *François le Champi*, and who reads it as he read it once before, with the same impression of what the weather was like then in the garden, the same dreams that were then shaping themselves in his mind about the different countries and about life, the same anguish about the next day. Or if I see something which dates from another period, it is a young man who comes to life. So that my personality of to-day may be compared to an abandoned quarry, which supposes everything it contains to be uniform and monotonous, but from which memory, selecting here and there, can, like some Greek sculptor, extract innumerable different statues. And this is true of everything that we see again after a lapse of time, books in this respect behaving just like other things: the way in which the covers of a binding open, the grain of a particular paper, may have preserved in itself as vivid a memory of the fashion in which I once imagined Venice and of the desire that I had to go there as the actual phrases of a book. An even more vivid memory perhaps, for phrases sometimes are an obstruction, just as sometimes when we look at a photograph of a person we recollect him less clearly than we do when we are merely thinking about him. Certainly, there are many books which I read in my childhood, including even, I am sorry to say, some of those of Bergotte himself, which now, if I happen to be tired one evening, I take up merely in the spirit in which I might go for a train journey, with the hope, that is, of resting myself by the sight of objects that I do not see every day and by breathing the atmosphere of an earlier time. But it can happen that this deliberate attempt at evocation is actually thwarted by the prolonged reading of the book. There is, for instance, a book by Bergotte (there was a copy in the Prince's library, with a dedication both sycophantic and platitudinous in the extreme), which I read years ago one winter day when I was unable to see Gilberte and which I now search in vain for the phrases which I then thought wonderful. Certain words almost make me believe that I have found them, but it cannot be so, for of the beauty that I once saw in them there is no trace. But the volume itself still glistens with the snow that covered the Champs-Elysées on the day when I first read it—I open its pages and the scene is before my eyes.

So it is that, if I had been tempted to become a bibliophile like the Prince de Guermantes, I should only have been one in my own peculiar fashion, though I should not have despised that beauty, independent of the intrinsic value of a book, which is attached to it in the eyes of collectors by their knowing the libraries through which it has passed, knowing for instance that it was given by such and such a sovereign, on the occasion of such and such an event, to such and such a famous man, by their having followed it from sale to sale through the course of its life—that beauty, which is in a certain sense the historic beauty of a book, would not be lost upon me. But it is rather in the history of my own life, and not simply as a connoisseur of the past in general, that I should seek this beauty; and I should attach it often not to a particular copy but to the work itself, to *François le Champi*, for instance, first contemplated by me in my little bedroom at Combray, during the night that was perhaps the sweetest and the saddest of my life, when I had alas! (at a time when the Germantes still seemed to me mysterious and inaccessible) won from my parents that first abdication of their authority from which, later, I was to date the decline of my health and my will, and my renunciation, each day disastrously confirmed, of a task that daily became more difficult—and rediscovered by me to-day, in the library of these same Guermantes, on this most wonderful of all days which had suddenly illuminated for me not only the old groping movements of my thought, but even the whole purpose of my life and perhaps of art itself. As for particular copies of books, I should have been able to take an interest in them too, but in a living sense. The first edition of a work would have been more precious in my eyes than any other, but by this term I should have understood the edition in which I read it for the first time. I should seek out original editions, those, that is to say, in which I once received an original impression of a book. For the impressions that one has later are no longer original. In the case of novels I should collect old-fashioned bindings, those of the period when I read my first novels, those that so often heard Papa say to me: "Sit up straight." Like the dress which a woman was wearing when we saw her for the first time, they would help me to rediscover the love that I then had, the beauty on which I have since superimposed so many less and less loved images, they would help me to find that first image again, even though I am no longer the "I" who first beheld it, even though I must make way for the "I" that I then was if that "I" summons the thing that it once knew and that the "I" of to-day does not know.

The library which I should thus assemble would contain volumes of an even greater value; for the books which I read in the past at Combray or in Venice, enriched now by my memory with vast illuminations representing the church of Saint-Hilaire or the gondola moored at the foot of San Giorgio Maggiore and the Grand Canal incrusted with sparkling sapphires, would have become the equals of those ancient "picture books"—illustrated bibles or books of hours—which the collector nowadays opens not to read their text but to savour once more the enchantment of the colours which some rival of Foucquet has added to it and which make these volumes the treasures that they are. And yet, even to open these books for the purpose merely of looking at the pictures with which, when I read them long ago, they were not yet adorned, would seem to me in itself so dangerous that, even in the sense which I have described, which is the only one that I can understand, I should not, I think, be tempted to become a bibliophile. I know very well how easily these images, deposited by the mind, can be effaced by the mind. For the old images it substitutes new ones which no longer have the same power of resurrection. And if I still possessed the *François le Champi* which Mamma unpacked one evening from the parcel of books which my grandmother was to have given me for my birthday, I should never look at it; I should be too afraid that I might gradually insinuate into it my impressions of to-day and smother my original impressions beneath them, that I might see it become so far a thing of the present that, when I asked it to evoke once more the child who spelt out its title in the little bedroom at Combray, the child, not recognising its voice, would no longer reply to its summons and would remain for ever buried in oblivion.

An image presented to us by life brings with it, in a single moment, sensations which are in fact multiple and heterogeneous. The sight, for instance, of the binding of a book once read may weave into the characters of its title the moonlight of a distant summer night. The taste of our breakfast coffee brings with it that vague hope of fine weather which so often long ago, as with the day still intact and full before us, we were drinking it out of a bowl of white porcelain, creamy and fluted and itself looking almost like vitrified milk, suddenly smiled upon us in the pale uncertainty of the dawn. An hour is not merely an hour, it is a vase full of scents and sounds and projects and climates, and what we call reality is a certain connexion between these immediate sensations and the memories which envelop us simultaneously with them—a connexion that is suppressed in a simple cinematographic vision, which just because it professes to confine itself to the truth in fact departs widely from it—a unique connexion which the writer has to rediscover in order to link for ever in his phrase the two sets of phenomena which reality joins together. He can describe a scene by describing one after another the innumerable objects which at a given moment were present at a particular place, but truth will be attained by him only when he takes two different objects, states the connexion between them—a connexion analogous in the world of art to the unique connexion which in the world of science is provided by the law of causality—and encloses them in the necessary links of a well-wrought style; truth—and life too—can be attained by us only when, by comparing a quality common to two sensations, we succeed in extracting their common essence and in reuniting them to each other, liberated from the contingencies of time, within a metaphor. Had not nature herself—if one considered the matter from this point of view—placed me on the path of art, was she not herself a beginning of art, she who, often, had allowed me to become aware of the beauty of one thing only in another thing, of the beauty, for instance, of noon at Combray in the sound of its bells, of that of the mornings at Doncières in the hiccups of our central heating? The link may be uninteresting, the objects trivial, the style bad, but unless this process has taken place the description is worthless.

But my train of thought led me yet further. If reality were indeed a sort of waste product of experience, more or less identical for each one of us, since when we speak of bad weather, a war, a taxi rank, a brightly lit restaurant, a garden full of flowers, everybody knows what we mean, if reality were no more than this, no doubt a sort of cinematograph film of these things would be sufficient and the "style," the "literature" that departed from the simple data that they provide would be superfluous and artificial. But was it true that reality was no more than this? If I tried to understand what actually happens at the moment when a thing makes some particular impression upon one—on the day, for instance, when as I crossed the bridge over the Vivonne the shadow of a cloud upon the water had made me cry: "Gosh!" and jump for joy; or the occasion when, hearing a phrase of Bergotte's, all that I had disengaged from my impression was the not specially relevant remark: "How splendid!"; or the words I had once heard Bloch use in exasperation at some piece of bad behaviour, words quite inappropriate to a very commonplace incident: "I must say that that sort of conduct seems to me absolutely fffantastic!"; or that evening when, flattered at the politeness which the Guermantes had shown to me as their guest and also a little intoxicated by the wines which I had drunk in their house, I could not help saying to myself half aloud as I came away alone: "They really are delightful people and I should be happy to see them every day of my life"—I realised that the words in each case were a long way removed from the impressions that I or Bloch had in fact received. So that the essential, the only true book, though in the ordinary sense of the word it does not have to be "invented" by a great writer—for it exists already in each one of us—has to be translated by him. The function and the task of a writer are those of a translator.

And if in some cases—where we are dealing, for instance, with the inaccurate language of our own vanity—the rectification of an oblique interior discourse (which deviates gradually more and more widely from the first and central impression) until it merges with the straight line which the impression ought to have produced is a laborious undertaking which our idleness would prefer to shirk, there are other circumstances—for example, where love is involved—in which this same process is actually painful. Here all our feigned indifferences, all our indignation at the lies of whoever it is whom we love (lies which are so natural and so like those that we perpetrate ourselves), in a word all that we have not ceased, whenever we are unhappy or betrayed, not only to say to the loved one but, while we are waiting for a meeting with her, to repeat endlessly to ourselves, sometimes aloud in the silence of our room, which we disturb with remarks like: "No, really, this sort of behaviour is intolerable," and: "I have consented to see you once more, for the last time, and I don't deny that it hurts me," all this can only be brought back into conformity with the felt truth from which it has so widely diverged by the abolition of all that we have set most store by, all that in our solitude, in our feverish projects of letters and schemes, has been the substance of our passionate dialogue with ourselves.

Even where the joys of art are concerned, although we seek and value them for the sake of the impression that they give us, we contrive as quickly as possible to set aside, as being inexpressible, precisely that element in them which is the impression that we sought, and we concentrate instead upon that other ingredient in aesthetic emotion which allows us to savour its pleasure without penetrating its essence and lets us suppose that we are sharing it with other art-lovers, with whom we find it possible to converse just because, the personal root of our own impression having been suppressed, we are discussing with them a thing which is the same for them and for us. Even in those moments when we are the most disinterested spectators of nature, or of society or of love or of art itself, since every impression is double and the one half which is sheathed in the object is prolonged in ourselves by another half which we alone can know, we speedily find means to neglect this second half, which is the one on which we ought to concentrate, and to pay attention only to the first half which, as it is external and therefore cannot be intimately explored, will occasion us no fatigue. To try to perceive the little furrow which the sight of a hawthorn bush or of a church has traced in us is a task that we find too difficult. But we play a symphony over and over again, we go back repeatedly to see a church until—in that flight to get away from our own life (which we have not the courage to look at) which goes by the name of erudition—we know them, the symphony and the church, as well as and in the same fashion as the most knowledgeable connoisseur of music or archaeology. And how many art-lovers stop there, without extracting anything from their impression, so that they grow old useless and unsatisfied, like bachelors of Art! They suffer, but their sufferings, like the sufferings of virgins and of lazy people, are of a kind that fecundity or work would cure. They get more excited about works of art than real artists, because for them their excitement is not the object of a laborious and inward-directed study but a force which bursts outwards, which heats their conversations and empurples their cheeks; at concerts they will shout "Bravo, bravo" till they are hoarse at the end of a work they admire and imagine as they do so that they are discharging a duty. But demonstrations of this kind do not oblige them to clarify the nature of their admiration and of this they remain in ignorance. Meanwhile, like a stream which can find no useful channel, their love of art flows over into even their calmest conversations, so that they make wild gestures and grimace and toss their heads whenever they mention the subject. "I was at a concert the other day. They played the first piece and I must say it left me cold. Then they started on the quartet. By Jove, what a difference!" (At this moment the face of the music-lover expresses a sudden anxiety, as if he were thinking: "Don't I see sparks? And I smell burning! Something's on fire.") "It's the most exasperating thing I've ever heard, damn it! It's not exactly a good composition, but it's stunning, it's something quite out of the ordinary." And yet, ludicrous though they may be, such people are not altogether to be despised. They are the first attempts of nature in her struggle to create the artist, experiments as misshapen, as unviable as those first animals that came before the species of to-day and were so constituted that they could not survive for long. And, with their sterile velleities, the art-lovers are as touching to contemplate as those early machines which tried to leave the ground and could not, but which yet held within them, if not the secret, the still to be discovered means, at least the desire of flight. "You know, old boy," goes on the music-lover, as he takes you by the elbow, "this is the eighth time I've heard it, and I promise you it won't be the last." And indeed, since they fail to assimilate what is truly nourishing in art, they need artistic pleasures all the time, they are victims of a morbid hunger which is never satisfied. So they go to concert after concert to applaud the same work and think that they have a duty to put in an appearance whenever it is performed just as other people think they have a duty to attend a board meeting or a funeral. Then presently, whether it be in music or in literature or in painting, other works come along, works that may even be the very opposite of the ones which they supersede. For the ability to launch ideas and systems—and still more of course the ability to assimilate them—has always been much commoner than genuine taste, even among those who themselves produce works of art, and with the multiplication of reviews and literary journals (and with them of factitious vocations as writer or artist) has become very much more widespread. Not so long ago, for instance, the best part of the younger generation, the most intelligent and the most disinterested of them, through a change of fashion admired nothing but works with a lofty moral and sociological, and even religious, significance. This they imagined to be the criterion of a work's value, renewing the old error of David and Chenavard and Brunetière and all those who in the past thought like them. Bergotte, whose prettiest phrases had in fact demanded much deeper reflection on the part of the reader, was rated lower now than writers who seemed more profound simply because they wrote less well. The intricacy of his style was all right for fashionable people but not for anybody else, said democratic critics, paying to fashionable people a tribute which they did not deserve. The truth is that as soon as the reasoning intelligence takes upon itself to judge works of art, nothing is any longer fixed or certain: you can prove anything you wish to prove. Whereas the reality of talent is something universal, whether it be a gift or an acquirement, and the first thing that a reader has to do is to find out whether this reality is present beneath a writer's superficial mannerism of thought and style, it is upon just these superficial mannerisms that criticism seizes when it sets out to classify authors. Because he has a peremptory tone, because he parades his contempt for the school that preceded him, criticism hails as a prophet a writer who in fact has no message that is new. And so frequent are these aberrations of criticism that a writer might almost with reason prefer to be judged by the general public (were not the public incapable even of understanding what an artist has attempted in a realm of discovery which is outside its experience). For there is a closer analogy between the instinctive life of the public and the talent of a great writer, which is simply an instinct religiously listened to in the midst of a silence imposed upon all other voices, an instinct made perfect and understood, than between this same talent and the superficial verbiage and changing criteria of the established judges of literature. From decade to decade their wordy battles are renewed, for it is not only social groups that are kaleidoscopic but ideas too about society and politics and religion; refracted through large bodies they can assume a momentary amplitude but their life-span is the brief one of ideas which owe their success to their novelty and gain the adherence only of such minds as are not particular about proof. So it is that parties and schools follow upon one another's heels, attaching to themselves always the same minds, those men of moderate intelligence who are an easy prey to the successive enthusiasms into which others more scrupulous and less easily satisfied in the matter of proof will decline to plunge. And unfortunately, just because those in the first category are no more than half-minds, they need to buttress themselves in action, with the result that, being more active than the better minds, they draw the crowd after them and create around them not only inflated reputations and victims of undeserved contempt but wars too, both civil and foreign, which a little self-examination of an old-fashioned Jansenist kind might well have prevented.

As for the enjoyment which is derived by a really discerning mind and a truly living heart from a thought beautifully expressed in the writings of a great writer, this is no doubt an entirely wholesome enjoyment, but, precious though the men may be who are truly capable of enjoying this pleasure—and how many of them are there in a generation?—they are nevertheless in the very process reduced to being no more than the full consciousness of another. If, for instance, a man of this type has done everything in his power to make himself loved by a woman who could only have made him unhappy, but has not even succeeded, in spite of efforts redoubled over the years, in persuading her to meet him in private, instead of seeking to express his sufferings and the danger from which he has escaped, he reads over and over again, appending to it "a million words" and the most moving memories of his own life, this observation of La Bruyère: "Men often want to love where they cannot hope to succeed; they seek their own undoing without being able to compass it, and, if I may put it thus, they are forced against their will to remain free." Whether or no this is the meaning that the aphorism had for the man who wrote it (to give it this meaning, which would make it finer, he should have said "to be loved" instead of "to love"), there is no doubt that, with this meaning, the sensitive lover of literature reanimates it and swells it with meaning until it is ready to burst, he cannot repeat it to himself without overflowing with joy, so true and beautiful does he find it—but in spite of all this he has added to it nothing, it remains merely an observation of La Bruyère.

How could the literature of description possibly have any value, when it is only beneath the surface of the little things which such a literature describes that reality has its hidden existence (grandeur, for example, in the distant sound of an aeroplane or the outline of the steeple of Saint-Hilaire, the past in the taste of a madeleine, and so on) and when the things in themselves are without significance until it has been extracted from them? Gradually, thanks to its preservation by our memory, the chain of all those inaccurate expressions in which there survives nothing of what we have really experienced comes to constitute for us our thought, our life, our "reality," and this lie is all that can be reproduced by the art that styles itself "true to life," an art that is as simple as life, without beauty, a mere vain and tedious duplication of what our eyes see and our intellect records, so vain and so tedious that one wonders where the writer who devotes himself to it can have found the joyous and impulsive spark that was capable of setting him in motion and making him advance in his task. The greatness, on the other hand, of true art, of the art which M. de Norpois would have called a dilettante's pastime, lay, I had come to see, elsewhere: we have to rediscover, to reapprehend, to make ourselves fully aware of that reality, remote from our daily preoccupations, from which we separate ourselves by an ever greater gulf as the conventional knowledge which we substitute for it grows thicker and more impermeable, that reality which it is very easy for us to die without ever having known and which is, quite simply, our life. Real life, life at last laid bare and illuminated—the only life in consequence which can be said to be really lived—is literature, and life thus defined is in a sense all the time immanent in ordinary men no less than in the artist. But most men do not see it because they do not seek to shed light upon it. And therefore their past is like a photographic dark-room encumbered with innumerable negatives which remain useless because the intellect has not developed them. But art, if it means awareness of our own life, means also awareness of the lives of other people—for style for the writer, no less than colour for the painter, is a question not of technique but of vision: it is the revelation, which by direct and conscious methods would be impossible, of the qualitative difference, the uniqueness of the fashion in which the world appears to each one of us, a difference which, if there were no art, would remain for ever the secret of every individual. Through art alone are we able to emerge from ourselves, to know what another person sees of a universe which is not the same as our own and of which, without art, the landscapes would remain as unknown to us as those that may exist in the moon. Thanks to art, instead of seeing one world only, our own, we see that world multiply itself and we have at our disposal as many worlds as there are original artists, worlds more different one from the other than those which revolve in infinite space, worlds which, centuries after the extinction of the fire from which their light first emanated, whether it is called Rembrandt or Vermeer, send us still each one its special radiance.

This work of the artist, this struggle to discern beneath matter, beneath experience, beneath words, something that is different from them, is a process exactly the reverse of that which, in those everyday lives which we live with our gaze averted from ourself, is at every moment being accomplished by vanity and passion and the intellect, and habit too, when they smother our true impressions, so as entirely to conceal them from us, beneath a whole heap of verbal concepts and practical goals which we falsely call life. In short, this art which is so complicated is in fact the only living art. It alone expresses for others and renders visible to ourselves that life of ours which cannot effectually observe itself and of which the observable manifestations need to be translated and, often, to be read backwards and laboriously deciphered. Our vanity, our passions, our spirit of imitation, our abstract intelligence, our habits have long been at work, and it is the task of art to undo this work of theirs, making us travel back in the direction from which we have come to the depths where what has really existed lies unknown within us. And surely this was a most tempting prospect, this task of re-creating one's true life, of rejuvenating one's impressions. But it required courage of many kinds, including the courage of one's emotions. For above all it meant the abrogation of one's dearest illusions, it meant giving up one's belief in the objectivity of what one had oneself elaborated, so that now, instead of soothing oneself for the hundredth time with the words: "She was very sweet," one would have to transpose the phrase so that it read: "I experienced pleasure when I kissed her." Certainly, what I had felt in my hours of love is what all men feel. One feels, yes, but what one feels is like a negative which shows only blackness until one has placed it near a special lamp and which must also be looked at in reverse. So with one's feelings: until one has brought them within range of the intellect one does not know what they represent. Then only, when the intellect has shed light upon them, has intellectualised them, does one distinguish, and with what difficulty, the lineaments of what one felt.

But I realised also that the suffering caused by the thought that our love does not belong to the person who inspires it, a suffering which I had first known in connexion with Gilberte, is for two reasons salutary. The first and the less important is that, brief though our life may be, it is only while we are suffering that we see certain things which at other times are hidden from us—we are, as it were, posted at a window, badly placed but looking out over an expanse of sea, and only during a storm, when our thoughts are agitated by perpetually changing movements, do they elevate to a level at which we can see it the whole law-governed immensity which normally, when the calm weather of happiness leaves it smooth, lies beneath our line of vision; perhaps only for a few great geniuses does this movement of thought exist all the time, uncontingent upon the agitations of personal grief, yet can we be sure, when we contemplate the ample and regular development of their joyous creations, that we may not too readily infer from the joyousness of their work that there was joy also in their lives, which perhaps on the contrary were almost continuously unhappy? But the principal reason is that, if our love is not only the love of a Gilberte (and this fact is what we find so painful), the reason is not that it is also the love of an Albertine but that it is a portion of our mind more durable than the various selves which successively die within us and which would, in their egoism, like to keep it to themselves, a portion of our mind which must, however much it hurts us (and the pain may in fact be beneficial), detach itself from individuals so that we can comprehend and restore to it its generality and give this love, the understanding of this love, to all, to the universal spirit, and not merely first to one woman and then to another with whom first one and then another of the selves that we have successively been has desired to be forever united.

I was surrounded by symbols (Guermantes, Albertine, Gilberte, Saint-Loup, Balbec, etc.) and to the least of these I had to restore the meaning which habit had caused them to lose for me. Nor was that all. When we have arrived at reality, we must, to express it and preserve it, prevent the intrusion of all those extraneous elements which at every moment the gathered speed of habit lays at our feet. Above all I should have to be on my guard against those phrases which are chosen rather by the lips than by the mind, those humorous phrases such as we utter in conversation and continue at the end of a long conversation with other people to address, factitiously, to ourselves although they merely fill our mind with lies—those, so to speak, purely physical remarks, which, in the writer who stoops so low as to transcribe them, are accompanied always by, for instance, the little smile, the little grimace which at every turn disfigures the spoken phrase of a Sainte-Beuve, whereas real books should be the offspring not of daylight and casual talk but of darkness and silence. And as art exactly reconstitutes life, around the truths to which we have attained inside ourselves there will always float an atmosphere of poetry, the soft charm of a mystery which is merely a vestige of the shadow which we have had to traverse, the indication, as precise as the markings of an altimeter, of the depth of a work. (For the quality of depth is not inherent in certain subjects, as those novelists believe who are spiritually minded only in a materialistic way: they cannot penetrate beneath the world of appearances and all their noble intentions, like the endless virtuous tirades of certain people who are incapable of the smallest act of kindness, should not blind us to the fact that they have lacked even the strength of mind to rid themselves of those banalities of form which are acquired through imitation.)

As for the truths which the intellectual faculty—even that the greatest minds—gathers in the open, the truths that lie in its path in full daylight, their value may be very great, but they are like drawings with a hard outline and no perspective; they have no depth because no depths have had to be traversed in order to reach them, because they have not been re-created. Yet it happens to many writers that after a certain age, when more mysterious truths no longer emerge from their innermost being, they write only with their intellect, which has grown steadily in strength, and then the books of their riper years will have, for this reason, greater force than those of their youth but not the same bloom.

I felt, however, that these truths which the intellect educes directly from reality were not altogether to be despised, for they might be able to enshrine within a matter less pure indeed but still imbued with mind those impressions which are conveyed to us outside time by the essences that are common to the sensations of the past and of the present, but which, just because they are more precious, are also too rare for a work of art to be constructed exclusively from them. And—capable of being used for this purpose—I felt jostling each other within me a whole host of truths concerning human passions and character and conduct. The perception of these truths caused me joy; and yet I seemed to remember that more than one of them had been discovered by me in suffering, and others in very trivial pleasures (every individual who makes us suffer can be attached by us to a divinity of which he or she is a mere fragmentary reflection, the lowest step in the ascent that leads to it, a divinity or an Idea which, if we turn to contemplate it, immediately gives us joy instead of the pain which we were feeling before—indeed the whole art of living is to make use of the individuals through whom we suffer as a step enabling us to draw nearer to the divine form which they reflect and thus joyously to people our life with divinities). And then a new light, less dazzling, no doubt, than that other illumination which had made me perceive that the work of art was the sole means of rediscovering Lost Time, shone suddenly within me. And I understood that all these materials for a work of literature were simply my past life; I understood that they had come to me, in frivolous pleasures, in indolence, in tenderness, in unhappiness, and that I had stored them up without divining the purpose for which they were destined or even their continued existence any more than a seed does when it forms within itself a reserve of all the nutritious substances from which it will feed a plant. Like the seed, I should be able to die once the plant had developed and I began to perceive that I had lived for the sake of the plant without knowing it, without ever realising that my life needed to come into contact with those books which I had wanted to write and for which, when in the past I had sat down at my table to begin, I had been unable to find a subject. And thus my whole life up to the present day might and yet might not have been summed up under the title: A Vocation. Insofar as literature had played no part in my life the title would not have been accurate. And yet it would have been accurate because this life of mine, the memories of its sadnesses and its joys, formed a reserve which fulfilled the same function as the albumen lodged in the germ-cell of a plant, from which that cell starts to draw the nourishment which will transform it into a seed long before there is any outward sign that the embryo of a plant is developing, though already within the cell there are taking place chemical and respiratory changes, secret but extremely active. In the same way my life was linked to what, eventually, would bring about its maturation, but those who would one day draw nourishment from it would remain ignorant, as most of us do when we eat those grains that are human food, that the rich substances which they contain were made for the nourishment not of mankind but of the grain itself and have had first to nourish its seed and allow it to ripen.

In this context, certain comparisons which are false if we start from them as premises may well be true if we arrive at them as conclusions. The man of letters envies the painter, he would like to take notes and make sketches, but it is disastrous for him to do so. Yet when he writes, there is not a single gesture of his characters, not a trick of behaviour, not a tone of voice which has not been supplied to his inspiration by his memory; beneath the name of every character of his invention he can put sixty names of characters that he has seen, one of whom has posed for the grimaces, another for the monocle, another for the fits of temper, another for the swaggering movement of the arm, etc. And in the end the writer realises that if his dream of being a sort of painter was not in a conscious and intentional manner capable of fulfilment, it has nevertheless been fulfilled and that he too, for his work as a writer, has unconsciously made use of a sketch-book. For, impelled by the instinct that was in him, the writer, long before he thought that he would one day become one, regularly omitted to look at a great many things which other people notice, with the result that he was accused by others of being absent-minded and by himself of not knowing how to listen or look, but all this time he was instructing his eyes and his ears to retain for ever what seemed to others puerile trivialities, the tone of voice with which a certain remark had been made, or the facial expression and the movement of the shoulders which he had seen at a certain moment, many years ago, in somebody of whom perhaps he knows nothing else whatsoever, simply because this tone of voice was one that he had heard before or felt that he might hear again, because it was something renewable, durable. There is a feeling for generality which, in the future writer, itself picks out what is general and can for that reason one day enter into a work of art. And this has made him listen to people only when, stupid or absurd though they may have been, they have turned themselves, by repeating like parrots what other people of similar character are in the habit of saying, into birds of augury, mouthpieces of a psychological law. He remembers only things that are general. By such tones of voice, such variations in the physiognomy, seen perhaps in his earliest childhood, has the life of other people been represented for him and when, later, he becomes a writer, it is from these observations that he composes his human figures, grafting on to a movement of the shoulders common to a number of people—a movement as truthfully delineated as though it had been recorded in an anatomist's note-book, though the truth which he uses it to express is of a psychological order—a movement of the neck made by someone else, each of many individuals having posed for a moment as his model.

(It may be that, for the creation of a work of literature, imagination and sensibility are interchangeable qualities and that the latter may with no great harm be substituted for the former, just as in people whose stomach is incapable of digesting this function is relegated to the intestine. A man born with sensibility but without imagination might, in spite of this deficiency, be able to write admirable novels. For the suffering inflicted upon him by other people, his own efforts to ward it off, the long conflict between his unhappiness and another person's cruelty, all this, interpreted by the intellect, might furnish the material for a book not merely as beautiful as one that was imagined, invented, but also in as great a degree exterior to the day-dreams that the author would have had if he had been left to his own devices and happy, and as astonishing to himself, therefore, and as accidental as a fortuitous caprice of the imagination.)

The stupidest people, in their gestures, their remarks, the sentiments which they involuntarily express, manifest laws which they do not themselves perceive but which the artist surprises in them, and because he makes observations of this kind the writer is popularly believed to be ill-natured. But this belief is false: in an instance of ridiculous behaviour the artist sees a beautiful generality, and he no more condemns on this account the individual in whom he observes it than a surgeon would despise a patient for suffering from some quite common disorder of the circulation; the writer, in fact, is the least inclined of all men to scoff at folly. Unhappily, it cannot also be said that he is not unhappy, for when it comes to his own passions, though he is as well acquainted as other people with the general laws which govern them, he is not so skilful at liberating himself from the personal suffering which they cause. Naturally, when some insolent fellow insults us, we would rather he had paid us a compliment, and *a fortiori*, when a woman whom we adore betrays us, what would we not give for this not to have happened! But were our wish to be granted, the stinging pain of an affront, the anguish of being abandoned would have remained for us lands which we should never have known, lands whose discovery, painful though it may be for the man, is nevertheless invaluable for the artist. And so, though it is neither his wish nor theirs, the ill-natured and the ungrateful find their place in his work. The writer who writes a pamphlet involuntarily associates with his glory the riff-raff whom he castigates in it, and in every work of art one can recognise those whom the artist has most hated and also, alas! those whom he has most loved. They indeed have quite simply been posing for the artist at the very moment when, much against his will, they made him suffer most. When I was in love with Albertine, I had realised very clearly that she did not love me and I had had to resign myself to the thought that through her I could gain nothing more than the experience of what it is to suffer and to love, and even, at the beginning, to be happy.

And when we seek to extract from our grief the generality that lies within it, to write about it, we are perhaps to some extent consoled for yet another reason apart from those that I have mentioned, which is that to think in terms of general truths, to write, is for the writer a wholesome and necessary function the fulfilment of which makes him happy, it does for him what is done for men of a more physical nature by exercise, perspiration, baths. This conclusion, I must admit, I was a little reluctant to accept. I was ready to believe that the supreme truth of life resides in art, and I could see, too, that I was no more capable by an effort of memory of being still in love with Albertine than I was of continuing to mourn my grandmother's death, and yet I asked myself whether a work of art of which they would not be conscious could really for them, for the destiny of these two poor dead creatures, be a fulfilment. My grandmother, whom with so little feeling I had seen agonise and die beside me! I longed that in expiation, when my work should be finished, I might, incurably stricken, suffer for long hours, abandoned by all, and then die! And there were others less dear to me, or for whom I had cared nothing at all, for whom I felt an infinite pity, all those whose sufferings, or merely whose follies, my thought, in its effort to understand their destinies, had used for its own selfish purpose. All those men and women who had revealed some truth to me and who were now no more, appeared again before me, and it seemed as though they had lived a life which had profited only myself, as though they had died for me. Saddening too was the thought that my love, to which I had clung so tenaciously, would in my book be so detached from any individual that different readers would apply it, even in detail, to what they had felt for other women. But had I a right to be shocked at this posthumous infidelity, shocked that strangers should find new and alien objects for my feelings in unknown women, when this infidelity, this division of love between a number of women, had begun in my life-time and even before I had started to write? It was true that I had suffered successively for Gilberte, for Mme de Guermantes, for Albertine. But successively I had also forgotten them, and only the love which I dedicated to different women had been lasting. The profanation of one of my memories by unknown readers was a crime that I had myself committed before them. I felt something near to horror at myself, the self-horror that some nationalist party might come to feel after a long war fought in its name, from which it alone had profited and in which many noble victims had suffered and succumbed without ever knowing (and for my grandmother at least what a recompense this would have been!) what the outcome of the struggle would be. And my only consolation for the thought that she did not know that at last I was getting down to work was (such is the lot of the dead) that, if she could not enjoy my progress, she had at least long ceased to be conscious of my inactivity, of my wasted life, which had been such an unhappiness to her. And certainly there were others besides my grandmother and Albertine, there were many from whom I had been able to assimilate a single phrase or look although as individual human beings I had no recollection of them; a book is a huge cemetery in which on the majority of the tombs the names are effaced and can no longer be read. Sometimes on the other hand we remember a name well enough but do not know whether anything of the individual who bore it survives in our pages. That girl with the very deep-set eyes and the drawling voice, is she here? and if she is, in what part of the ground does she lie? we no longer know, and how are we to find her beneath the flowers? But since we live at a great distance from other human beings, since even our strongest feelings—and in this class had been my love for my grandmother and for Albertine—at the end of a few years have vanished from our hearts and become for us merely a word which we do not understand, since we can talk casually of these dead people with fashionable acquaintances whose houses we still visit with pleasure though all that we loved has died, surely then, if there exists a method by which we can learn to understand these forgotten words once more, is it not our duty to make use of it, even if this means transcribing them first into a language which is universal but which for that very reason will at least be permanent, a language which may make out of those who are no more, in their truest essence, a lasting acquisition for the minds of all mankind? And as for that law of change which made these loved words unintelligible to us, if we succeed at least in explaining it, is not even our infirmity transformed into strength of a new kind?

And so I had to resign myself, since nothing has the power to survive unless it can become general and since the mind's own past is dead to its present consciousness, to the idea that even the people who were once most dear to the writer have in the long run done no more than pose for him like models for a painter.

When we turn to our own future, the work in which our unhappiness has collaborated may be interpreted both as an ominous sign of suffering and as an auspicious sign of consolation. For, when we say that the loves and griefs of a poet have been useful to him, have helped him to construct his work, that the unknown women who had not the least idea what they were doing, have—one through her cruelty to him, another through her mockery—brought each their stone for the building of the monument which they will never see, we do not sufficiently reflect that the life of the writer does not come to an end with this particular work, that the same nature which caused him to have certain sufferings, and which then entered into his work, will continue to live after the work has been concluded and will cause him to love other women in conditions which would be similar, were they not made slightly to differ by the modifications that time brings about in circumstances, in the subject himself, in his appetite for love and in his resistance to pain. And from this point of view this first work of his must be considered simply as an unhappy love which fatally presages others of the kind: his life will resemble his work and in future the poet will scarcely need to write, for he will be able to find in what he has already written the anticipatory outline of what will then be happening. Thus it was that my love for Albertine, however different the two might be, was already inscribed in my love for Gilberte, in the midst of the happy days of which I had for the first time heard the name of Albertine pronounced and her character described by her aunt, without suspecting that this insignificant seed would develop and would one day overshadow the whole of my life.

But from another point of view the work is a promise of happiness, because it shows us that in every love the particular and the general lie side by side and it teaches us to pass from one to the other by a species of gymnastic which fortifies us against unhappiness by making us neglect its particular cause in order to gain a more profound understanding of its essence. Indeed—as I was to experience in the sequel—even at a time when we are in love and suffer, if our vocation has at last been realised, we feel so strongly during the hours in which we are at work that the individual whom we love is being dissolved into a vaster reality that at moments we succeed in forgetting her and we come to suffer from our love merely as we might from some purely physical disease in which the loved one played no part, some kind of malady of the heart. It is true that this only happens at a certain stage of our love and that if the work comes a little later its effect may appear to be the opposite. For when once the women whom we love, through their cruelty or their triviality, have succeeded in spite of us in destroying our illusions, have reduced themselves to nothing and become detached from the amorous chimera which we had fabricated in our imagination—if at this point we set ourselves to work, our mind will exalt them once more and identify them, for the purposes of our self-analysis, with objects of our love, and in this case literature, recommencing the ruined work of amorous illusion, will give a sort of second life to sentiments which have ceased to exist. And certainly we are obliged to re-live our individual suffering, with the courage of the doctor who over and over again practises on his own person some dangerous injection. But at the same time we have to conceptualise it in a general form which will in some measure enable us to escape from its embrace, which will turn all mankind into sharers in our pain, and which is even able to yield us a certain joy. Where life immures, the intelligence cuts a way out, for if there exists no remedy for a love that is not shared, the awareness of a state of suffering is something from which we can extricate ourselves, if only by deducing the consequences which it entails. The intelligence knows nothing of those closed situations of life from which there is no escape.

Sometimes, when a painful passage has remained in an inchoate state, a mere rough draft, a new tenderness and a new suffering come our way which enable us to complete it, to fill it out. And on the score of these great but useful unhappinesses we have little ground for complaint: they are plentiful and we seldom have to wait long for them. (In love, our fortunate rival, which is as much as to say our enemy, is our benefactor. To a woman who previously excited in us a mere paltry physical desire he instantly adds an immense value, foreign to her but confounded by us with her. If we had no rivals, pleasure would not transform itself into love. If we had none, or if we believed that we had none. For it is not necessary that rivals should really exist. The progress of our work requires only that they should have that illusory life which is conferred upon non-existent rivals by our suspicion, our jealousy.) Nevertheless one must make haste to take advantage of them when they come, for they do not last very long: either one consoles oneself or else, when they are too severe, if one's heart is no longer very robust one dies. For if unhappiness develops the forces of the mind, happiness alone is salutary to the body. But unhappiness, even if it did not on every occasion reveal to us some new law, would nevertheless be indispensable, since through its means alone we are brought back time after time to a perception of the truth and forced to take things seriously, tearing up each new crop of the weeds of habit and scepticism and levity and indifference. Yet it is true that truth, which is not compatible with happiness or with physical health, is not always compatible even with life. Unhappiness ends by killing. At every new torment which is too hard to bear we feel yet another vein protrude, to unroll its sinuous and deadly length along our temples or beneath our eyes. And thus gradually are formed those terrible ravaged faces, of the old Rembrandt, the old Beethoven, at whom the whole world mocked. And the pockets under the eyes and the wrinkled forehead would not matter much were there not also the suffering of the heart. But since strength of one kind can change into a strength of another kind, since heat which is stored up can become light and the electricity in a flash of lightning can cause a photograph to be taken, since the dull pain in our heart can hoist above itself like a banner the visible permanence of an image for every new grief, let us accept the physical injury which is done to us for the sake of the spiritual knowledge which grief brings; let us submit to the disintegration of our body, since each new fragment which breaks away from it returns in a luminous and significant form to add itself to our work, to complete it at the price of sufferings of which others more richly endowed have no need, to make our work at least more solid as our life crumbles away beneath the corrosive action of our emotions. Ideas come to us as the successors to griefs, and griefs, at the moment when they change into ideas, lose some part of their power to injure our heart; the transformation itself, even, for an instant, releases suddenly a little joy. But successors only in the order of time, for the primary element, it seems, is the Idea, and grief is merely the mode in which certain ideas make their first entry into us. But within the tribe of ideas there are various families and some of them from the very first moment are joys.

These reflections enabled me to give a stronger and more precise meaning to the truth which I had often dimly perceived, particularly when Mme de Cambremer had expressed surprise that I could give up seeing a remarkable man like Elstir for the sake of Albertine. Even from an intellectual point of view I had felt that she was wrong, but I did not know what it was that she had failed to understand: the nature of the lessons through which one serves one's apprenticeship as a man of letters. In this process the objective value of the arts counts for little; what we have to bring to light and make known to ourselves is our feelings, our passions, that is to say the passions and feelings of all mankind. A woman whom we need and who makes us suffer elicits from us a whole gamut of feelings far more profound and more vital than a man of genius who interests us. It is for us later to decide, according to the plane upon which we are living, whether an infidelity through which some woman has made us suffer is of little or great account beside the truths which it has revealed to us and which the woman who exulted in our suffering would hardly have been able to understand. In any case these infidelities are not likely to be wanting. A writer need have no anxieties on that score when he embarks upon a long labour. Let his intellect begin the work and as he proceeds he will meet with griefs, enough or more than enough, which will undertake to finish it. As for happiness, that is really useful to us in one way only, by making unhappiness possible. It is necessary for us to form in happiness ties of confidence and attachment that are both sweet and strong in order that their rupture may cause us the heart-rending but so valuable agony which is called unhappiness. Had we not been happy, if only in hope, the unhappinesses that befall us would be without cruelty and therefore without fruit.

And more even than the painter, the writer, in order to achieve volume and substance, in order to attain to generality and, so far as literature can, to reality, needs to have seen many churches in order to paint one church and for the portrayal of a single sentiment requires many individuals. For if art is long and life is short, we may on the other hand say that, if inspiration is short, the sentiments which it has to portray are not of much longer duration. It is our passions which draw the outline of our books, the ensuing intervals of repose which write them. And when inspiration is born again, when we are able to resume our work, the woman who was posing for us to illustrate a sentiment no longer has the power to make us feel it. We must continue to paint the sentiment from another model, and if this means infidelity towards the individual, from a literary point of view, thanks to the similarity of our feelings for the two women, which makes a work at the same time a recollection of our past loves and a prophecy of our new ones, there is no great harm in these substitutions. And this is one reason for the futility of those critical essays which try to guess who it is that an author is talking about. A work, even one that is directly autobiographical, is at the very least put together out of several intercalated episodes in the life of the author—earlier episodes which have inspired the work and later ones which resemble it just as much, the later loves being traced after the pattern of the earlier. For to the woman whom we have loved most in our life we are not so faithful as we are to ourself, and sooner or later we forget her in order—since this is one of the characteristics of that self—to be able to begin to love again. At most our faculty of loving has received from this woman whom we so loved a particular stamp, which will cause us to be faithful to her even in our infidelity. We shall need, with the woman who succeeds her, those same morning walks or the same practice of taking her home every evening or giving her a hundred times too much money. (A curious thing, this circulation of the money which we give to women who because of that make us unhappy, that is to say are the cause of our writing books: it almost seems as though a writer's works, like the water in an artesian well, mount to a height which is in proportion to the depth to which suffering has penetrated his heart.) These substitutions add then to our work something that is disinterested and more general and they convey also the austere lesson that it is not to individuals that we should attach ourselves, that it is not individuals who really exist and are, in consequence, capable of being expressed, but ideas. Nevertheless, while we have these models at our disposal we must make haste and lose no time; for those who pose for us as "happiness" can in general spare us only a few sittings, and the same may be true alas!—since grief, yes, grief too passes so quickly—of those who pose as "grief." Yet grief, even when it does not, by revealing it to us, provide the raw material of our writing, is valuable to us as an incitement to work. The imagination, the reflective faculty may be admirable machines in themselves but they may also be inert. Suffering sets them in motion. And then at least the woman who poses for us as grief favours us with an abundance of sittings, in that studio which we enter only in these periods and which lies deep within us. And they are, these periods, like an image of our life with its different griefs. For they too contain different griefs within themselves, and at the very moment when we thought that all had become calm a new one makes its appearance. New in every sense of the word: perhaps because an unforeseen situation forces us to enter more profoundly into contact with ourself, these painful dilemmas which love is constantly putting in our way teach us and reveal to us, layer after layer, the material of which we are made. So when Françoise, seeing that Albertine had the run of the flat and passed in and out of all the rooms like a dog creating disorder everywhere and that she was ruining me and causing me unhappiness of every kind, used to say (for at that time I had already written some articles and done a few translations): "Ah! if only, instead of this girl who makes him waste all his time, Monsieur had got himself a nicely brought up young secretary who could have sorted all Monsieur's paperies for him!", I had perhaps been wrong in thinking that she spoke wisely. By making me waste my time, by causing me unhappiness, Albertine had perhaps been more useful to me, even from a literary point of view, than a secretary who would have arranged my "paperies." But all the same, when a living creature is so faultily constituted (and perhaps, if such a creature exists in nature, it is man) that he cannot love without suffering, and that he has to suffer in order to apprehend truths, the life of such a creature becomes in the end extremely wearisome. The happy years are the lost, the wasted years, one must wait for suffering before one can work. And then the idea of the preliminary suffering becomes associated with the idea of work and one is afraid of each new literary undertaking because one thinks of the pain one will first have to endure in order to imagine it. And once one understands that suffering is the best thing that one can hope to encounter in life, one thinks without terror, and almost as of a deliverance, of death.

If I had had to admit, albeit I found the idea somewhat repugnant, that the writer plays with life and exploits other people for the purpose of his books, I could not fail to observe also that this is sometimes very far from being the case. The history and the circumstances of Werther, the noble Werther, had not alas! been mine. Without for a moment believing in Albertine's love I had twenty times wanted to kill myself for her, I had ruined myself, I had destroyed my health for her. For when it is a question of writing, one is scrupulous, one examines things meticulously, one rejects all that is not truth.

But when it is merely a question of life, one ruins oneself, makes oneself ill, kills oneself all for lies. It is true that these lies are a lode from which, if one has passed the age for writing poetry, one can at least extract a little truth. Sorrows are servants, obscure and detested, against whom one struggles, beneath whose dominion one more and more completely falls, dire and dreadful servants whom it is impossible to replace and who by subterranean paths lead us towards truth and death. Happy are those who have first come face to face with truth, those for whom, near though the one may be to the other, the hour of truth has struck before the hour of death!

When I considered my past life, I understood also that its slightest episodes had contributed towards giving me the lesson in idealism from which I was going to profit to-day. My meetings with M. de Charlus, for instance, had they not, even before his pro-German tendencies taught me the same lesson, demonstrated to me, even better than my love for Mme de Guermantes or for Albertine, or Saint-Loup's love for Rachel, the truth of the axiom that matter is indifferent and that anything can be grafted upon it by thought; an axiom which in the phenomenon, so ill-understood and so needlessly condemned, of sexual inversion is seen to be of even greater scope than in that, in itself so instructive, of love? For love shows us Beauty fleeing from the woman whom we no longer love, and coming to take up her abode in a face which anybody else would find hideous and which to ourselves too might have seemed, as one day it will seem, unpleasing: but even more striking is the spectacle of the goddess, taking with her the reverent homage of a great nobleman who thereupon instantly abandons a beautiful princess, migrating to a new perch beneath the cap of an omnibus conductor. And my astonishment every time I had seen after an interval, in the Champs-Elysées or in the street or on the beach, the face of Gilberte or of Mme de Guermantes or of Albertine, was this not a proof that a memory is prolonged only in a direction which diverges from the impression with which originally it coincided but from which gradually it further and further departs?

The writer must not be indignant if the invert who reads his book gives to his heroines a masculine countenance. For only by the indulgence of this slightly aberrant peculiarity can the invert give to what he is reading its full general import. Racine himself was obliged, as a first step towards giving her a universal validity, for a moment to turn the antique figure of Phèdre into a Jansenist; and if M. de Charlus had not bestowed upon the "traitress" for whom Musset weeps in *La Nuit d'Octobre* or *Le Souvenir* the features of Morel, he would neither have wept nor have understood, since it was only along this path, narrow and indirect, that he had access to the verities of love. For it is only out of habit, a habit contracted from the insincere language of prefaces and dedications, that the writer speaks of "my reader." In reality every reader is, while he is reading, the reader of his own self. The writer's work is merely a kind of optical instrument which he offers to the reader to enable him to discern what, without this book, he would perhaps never have perceived in himself. And the recognition by the reader in his own self of what the book says is the proof of its veracity, the contrary also being true, at least to a certain extent, for the difference between the two texts may sometimes be imputed less to the author than to the reader. Besides, the book may be too learned, too obscure for a simple reader, and may therefore present to him a clouded glass through which he cannot read. And other peculiarities can have the same effect as inversion. In order to read with understanding many readers require to read in their own particular fashion, and the author must not be indignant at this; on the contrary, he must leave the reader all possible liberty, saying to him: "Look for yourself, and try whether you see best with this lens or that one or this other one."

If I had always taken so great an interest in dreams, was this not because, making up for lack of duration by their potency, they help us better to understand the subjective element in, for instance, love through the simple fact that they reproduce—but with miraculous swiftness—the process vulgarly known as getting a woman under one's skin, so effectively that within a sleep of a few minutes we can fall passionately in love with an ugly woman, a thing which in real life could only happen after years of habit and intimacy—as though they were intravenous injections of love discovered by some wonder-working doctor, of love and sometimes also of suffering? With the same speed the amorous suggestions which they have instilled into us are dissipated, and sometimes, when the loving nocturnal visitant has vanished from our sight and reappeared in her familiar shape of an ugly woman, there vanishes with her something more precious, a whole ravishing landscape of feelings of tenderness, of voluptuous pleasure, of vaguely blurred regrets, a whole embarkation for the Cythera of passion, of which we should like to note, for our waking state, the subtle and deliciously lifelike gradations of tone, but which fades away like a discoloured canvas that can no longer be restored. And it was perhaps also because of the extraordinary effects which they achieve with Time that dreams had fascinated me. Have we not often seen in a single night, in a single minute of a night, remote periods, relegated to those enormous distances at which we can no longer distinguish anything of the sentiments which we felt in them, come rushing upon us with almost the speed of light as though they were giant aeroplanes instead of the pale stars which we had supposed them to be, blinding us with their brilliance and bringing back to our vision all that they had once contained for us, giving us the emotion, the shock, the brilliance of their immediate proximity, only, once we are awake, to resume their position on the far side of the gulf which they had miraculously traversed, so that we are tempted to believe—wrongly, however—that they are one of the modes of rediscovering Lost Time?

I had realised before now that it is only a clumsy and erroneous form of perception which places everything in the object, when really everything is in the mind; I had lost my grandmother in reality many months after I had lost her in fact, and I had seen people present various aspects according to the idea that I or others possessed of them, a single individual being several different people for different observers (Swann, for instance, for my family and for his friends in society, the Princesse de Luxembourg for the judge at Balbec and for those who knew her identity) or even for the same observer at different periods over the years (the name of Guermantes, and the different Swanns, for me). I had seen that love places in a person who is loved what exists only in the person who loves, indeed I could hardly have failed to become aware of this when I had seen stretched to its maximum the distance between objective reality and love (in Rachel, for instance, as she appeared to Saint-Loup and to me, in Albertine as she appeared to me and to Saint-Loup, in Morel or the omnibus conductor as they appeared to other people and to M. de Charlus, who in spite of this showered delicate attentions upon them, recited Musset's poems to them, etc.). Finally, to a certain extent, the germanophilia of M. de Charlus (like the expression on the face of Saint-Loup when he had looked at the photograph of Albertine) had helped me to free myself for a moment, if not from my germanophobia, at least from my belief in the pure objectivity of this feeling, had helped to make me think that perhaps what applied to love applied also to hate and that, in the terrible judgment which at this time France passed on Germany—that she was a nation outside the pale of humanity—the most important element was an objectification of feelings as subjective as those which had caused Rachel and Albertine to appear so precious, the one to Saint-Loup and the other to me. What, in fact, made it possible that this perversity was not entirely intrinsic to Germany was that, just as I as an individual had had successive loves and at the end of each one its object had appeared to me valueless, so I had already seen in my country successive hates which had, for example, at one time condemned as traitors—a thousand times worse than the Germans into whose hands they were delivering France—those very Dreyfusards such as Reinach with whom to-day patriotic Frenchmen were collaborating against a race whose every member was of necessity a liar, a savage beast, a madman, excepting only those Germans who, like the King of Rumania, the King of the Belgians, or the Empress of Russia, had embraced the French cause. It is true that the anti-Dreyfusards would have replied to me: "But it is not the same thing." But then it never is the same thing, any more than it is the same person with whom after an interval we fall in love; otherwise, faced with the same phenomenon as before, someone who was a second time taken in by it would have no alternative but to blame his own subjective condition, he could not again believe that the qualities or the defects resided in the object. And so, since the phenomenon, outwardly, is not the same, the intellect has no difficulty in basing upon each set of circumstances a new theory (that it is against nature to have schools directed by the religious orders, as the radicals believe, or that it is impossible for the Jewish race to be assimilated into a nation, or that there exists an undying hatred between the Teutonic and the Latin races, the yellow race having been temporarily rehabilitated). This subjective element in the situation struck one forcibly if one had any conversation with neutrals, since the pro-Germans among them had, for instance, the faculty of ceasing for a moment to understand and even to listen when one spoke to them about the German atrocities in Belgium. (And yet they were real, these atrocities: the subjective element that I had observed to exist in hatred as in vision itself did not imply that an object could not possess real qualities or defects and in no way tended to make reality vanish into pure relativism.) And if, after so many years had slipped away and so much time had been lost, I felt this influence to be dominant even in the sphere of international relations, had I not already had some notion of its existence right at the beginning of my life, when I was reading in the garden at Combray one of those novels by Bergotte which, even to-day, if I chance to turn over a few of its forgotten pages where I see the wiles of some villain described, I cannot put down until I have assured myself, by skipping a hundred pages, that towards the end this same villain is humiliated as he deserves to be and lives long enough to learn that his sinister schemes have failed? For I no longer have any clear recollection of what happened to these characters, though in this respect they are scarcely to be distinguished from the men and women who were present this afternoon at Mme de Guermantes's party and whose past life, in many cases at least, was as vague in my mind as if I had read it in a half-forgotten novel. The Prince d'Agrigente, for instance: had he ended by marrying Mlle X—? Or was it rather the brother of Mlle X— who might have married the sister of the Prince d'Agrigente? Or was I confusing it all with something that I had read long ago or recently dreamed?

Dreams were another of the facts of my life which had always most profoundly impressed me and had done most to convince me of the purely mental character of reality, and in the composition of my work I would not scorn their aid. At a time when I was still living, in a rather less disinterested fashion, for love of one kind or another, a dream would come to me, bringing with it in a sudden strange return to proximity which annihilated vast distances of lost time, perhaps my grandmother, perhaps Albertine, whom briefly I began to love again because in my sleep she had given me a version, highly diluted, of the episode with the laundry-girl in Touraine. And I thought that in the same way dreams would bring sometimes within my grasp truths or impressions which my efforts alone and even the contingencies of nature failed to present to me; that they would re-awaken in me something of the desire, the regret for certain non-existent things which is the necessary condition for working, for freeing oneself from the dominion of habit, for detaching oneself from the concrete. And therefore I would not disdain this second muse, this nocturnal muse who might sometimes do duty for the other one.

I had seen aristocrats turn into vulgar people when their intelligence was vulgar. ("Make yourself at home," for instance the Duc de Guermantes would say, using an expression that Cottard might have used.) I had seen everybody believe, during the Dreyfus affair or during the war, and in medicine too, that truth is a particular piece of knowledge which cabinet ministers and doctors possess, a Yes or No which requires no interpretation, thanks to the possession of which the men in power *knew* whether Dreyfus was guilty or not and *knew*, without having to send Roques to make an inquiry on the spot, whether Sarrail in Salonika had or had not the resources to launch an offensive at the same time as the Russians, in the same way that an X-ray photograph is supposed to indicate without any need for interpretation the exact nature of a patient's disease.

It occurred to me, as I thought about it, that the raw material of my experience, which would also be the raw material of my book, came to me from Swann, not merely because so much of it concerned Swann himself and Gilberte, but because it was Swann who from the days of Combray had inspired in me the wish to go to Balbec, where otherwise my parents would never have had the idea of sending me, and but for this I should never

have known Albertine. Certainly, it was to her face, as I had
seen it for the first time beside the sea, that I traced back certain
things which I should no doubt include in my book. And in a
sense I was right to trace them back to her, for if I had not
walked on the front that day, if I had not got to know her, all
these ideas would never have been developed (unless they had
been developed by some other woman). But I was wrong too,
for this pleasure which generates something within us and
which, retrospectively, we seek to place in a beautiful feminine
face, comes from our senses: but the pages I would write were
something that Albertine, particularly the Albertine of those
days, would quite certainly never have understood. It was,
however, for this very reason (and this shows that we ought
not to live in too intellectual an atmosphere), for the reason
that she was so different from me, that she had fertilised me
through unhappiness and even, at the beginning, through the
simple effort which I had had to make to imagine something
different from myself. Had she been capable of understanding
my pages, she would, for that very reason, not have inspired
them. But Swann had been of primary importance, for had I
not gone to Balbec I should never have known the Guermantes
either, since my grandmother would not have renewed her
friendship with Mme de Villeparisis nor should I have made
the acquaintance of Saint-Loup and M. de Charlus and thus
got to know the Duchesse de Guermantes and through her her
cousin, so that even my presence at this very moment in the
house of the Prince de Guermantes, where out of the blue the
idea for my work had just come to me (and this meant that I
owed to Swann not only the material but also the decision),
came to me from Swann. A rather slender stalk, perhaps, to
support thus the whole development of my life, for the
"Guermantes way" too, on this interpretation, had emanated
from "Swann's way." But often this begetter of all the various
aspects of a man's life is someone very much inferior to Swann,
someone utterly insignificant. Suppose some schoolfriend who
meant nothing to me had described an attractive girl who was
to be enjoyed there (whom probably I should not in fact have
met), would not that have been enough to send me to Balbec?
Often, meeting years later some friend of our youth whom we

never particularly liked, we scarcely trouble to shake hands with him, and yet, did we but think of it, it is from a casual remark which he made to us, "You ought to come to Balbec" or something of the kind, that our whole life and our work have originated. But if it does not occur to us to thank him, this is no proof of ingratitude. For when he uttered those words he had no thought of the huge consequences which they would have for us. It is our sensibility and our intelligence which have exploited the circumstances, which, once he has given them their first impulse, have engendered one another as cause and effect without his having been able to foresee either—to return to my own story—my living with Albertine or the masked ball given by the Guermantes or anything else that had happened. No doubt the impulse that he gave was necessary, and on that account the external form of our life and even the material which we shall use in our work derive from him. Without Swann, as I have said, my parents would never have had the idea of sending me to Balbec. (Yet Swann was not for this reason responsible for the sufferings which he himself had indirectly caused me: they sprang from my weakness, just as his own weakness had made him suffer through Odette.) But whoever it is who has thus determined the course of our life has, in so doing, excluded all the lives which we might have led instead of our actual life. If Swann had not talked to me about Balbec, I should not have known Albertine, the dining-room of the hotel, the Guermantes. I should have gone to some other town, I should have known other people, my memory and my books would be filled with quite different scenes, which I cannot even imagine and the novelty of which, their unknownness, I find so seductive that I almost regret that I was not directed instead towards them and that Albertine and the beach of Balbec and Rivebelle and the Guermantes did not for ever remain unknown to me.

Jealousy is a good recruiting-sergeant who, when there is a gap in our picture, goes out into the street and brings us in the desirable woman who was needed to fill it. Perhaps in our eyes she had ceased to be a beauty? She has become one again, for we are jealous of her and therefore she will fill the gap. Once we are dead, we shall have no joy that our picture was completed in this fashion. But this consideration does not in the least discourage us. We feel merely that life is a little more complicated than it is said to be, and circumstances too. And it is absolutely necessary that we should portray this complexity. The jealousy that is so useful is not necessarily born of a look, or an anecdote, or a retroflexion. It may be found, ready to sting us, between the leaves of a directory—what for Paris is called *Tout-Paris* and for the country the *Annuaire des Châteaux*. We had heard, for instance, but without paying any attention, some beauty to whom we have become indifferent say that she would have to go and see her sister for a few days in the Pas-de-Calais, near Dunkirk; we had also, in the past, but again without paying any attention, thought that perhaps the beauty had formerly been pursued by Monsieur E—, whom she had ceased to see, since she had ceased to go to the bar where she used to meet him. What could her sister be? A housemaid perhaps? Out of tact, we had never asked. And now suddenly, opening the *Annuaire des Châteaux* at random we find that Monsieur E— has his country-house in the Pas-de-Calais, near Dunkirk. At once all is clear: to oblige the beauty he has taken her sister into his employment as a housemaid, and if the beauty no longer sees him in the bar, the reason is that he gets her to come and see him at home, either in Paris, where he lives most of the year, or in the Pas-de-Calais, since he cannot do without her even for the few weeks that he is there. Drunk with rage and love, we paint furiously away at the picture. And yet, suppose we are wrong? May not the truth be that Monsieur E— no longer sees the beauty but, wanting to help her, has recommended her sister to a brother of his who lives all the year round in the Pas-de-Calais? And in that case she is going, perhaps quite by chance, to see her sister at a time when Monsieur E— is not there, for they are no longer interested in each other. And then there is another possibility, that the sister is not a housemaid in the house near Dunkirk or anywhere else, but has relations in the Pas-de-Calais. Our anguish of the first moment gives way before these last hypotheses, which calm our jealousy. But it makes no difference. Jealousy, concealed between the leaves of the *Annuaire des Châteaux*, came at the right moment, and now the space that stood empty in our canvas is filled to abundance. And the whole composition takes shape, thanks to the presence, evoked by jealousy, of the beauty of whom already we are no longer jealous and whom we no longer love.

At this moment the butler came in to tell me that the first piece of music was finished, so that I could leave the library and go into the rooms where the party was taking place. And thereupon I remembered where I was. But I was not in the least disturbed in the train of thought upon which I had embarked by the fact that a fashionable gathering, my return to society, had provided me with that point of departure for a new life which I had been unable to find in solitude. There was nothing extraordinary about this fact, there was no reason why an impression with the power to resuscitate the timeless man within me should be linked to solitude rather than to society (as I had once supposed and as had perhaps once been the case for me, and perhaps ought still to have been the case, had I developed harmoniously instead of going through this long standstill which seemed only now to be coming to an end). For, as this impression of beauty came to me only when, an immediate sensation—no matter how insignificant—having been thrust upon my consciousness by chance, a similar sensation, spontaneously born again within me, somehow in a single moment diffused the first sensation over different periods of my life and succeeded in filling with a general essence the empty space which particular sensations never failed to leave in my mind, as this was how I came to experience beauty I might just as well receive sensations of the appropriate kind in a social as in a natural environment, since they are supplied by chance, aided no doubt by that special kind of excitement which, on the days when we happen to be jolted out of the normal routine of our lives, causes even the simplest things to begin once again to give us those sensations which Habit, in its economical way, ordinarily begrudges our nervous system. Why it was that precisely and uniquely this kind of sensation should lead to the production of a work of art was a question to which I proposed to try and find an objective answer, by following up the thoughts which had come to me, linked in a continuous chain, in the library, and I felt that the impulse given to the intellectual life within me was so vigorous now that I should be able to pursue these thoughts just as well in the drawing-room, in the midst of the guests, as alone in the library; it seemed to me that, from this point of view, even in the midst of a numerous gathering I should be able to maintain my solitude. For just as great events that impinge upon us from without fail to influence the powers of our mind, so that a mediocre writer who lives in a heroic age does not cease to be a mediocre writer, for the same reason, I realised, what is dangerous in social life is merely the social and worldly inclinations with which one approaches it. In itself it can no more turn one into a mediocre writer than an epic war can turn a bad poet into a sublime one. In any case, whether or no it was a good plan, theoretically, for a work of art to be constructed in this fashion, and whatever might be the result of the examination of this point which I intended to make, I could not deny that, so far as I was concerned, whenever genuinely aesthetic impressions had come to me, they had always followed upon sensations of this kind. It is true that such impressions had been rather rare in my life, but they dominated it, and I could still rediscover in the past some of these peaks which I had unwisely lost sight of (a mistake I would be careful not to make again). And already I could say that this characteristic, though it might, in the exclusive importance that it assumed in my thinking, be personal to me, was nevertheless, as I was reassured to find, akin to characteristics, less marked but still perceptible and at bottom not at all dissimilar, of certain well-known writers. Is it not from a sensation of the same species as that of the madeleine that Chateaubriand suspends the loveliest episode in the *Mémoires d'Outre-tombe*: "Yesterday evening I was walking alone . . . I was roused from my reflections by the warbling of a thrush perched upon the highest branch of a birch tree. Instantaneously the magic sound caused my father's estate to re-appear before my eyes; I forgot the catastrophes of which I had recently been the witness and, transported suddenly into the past, I saw again those country scenes in which I had so often heard the fluting notes of the thrush." And of all the lovely sentences in those memoirs are not these some of the loveliest: "A sweet and subtle scent of heliotrope was exhaled by a little patch of beans that were in flower; it was brought to us not by a breeze from our own country but by a wild Newfoundland wind, unrelated to the exiled plant, without sympathy of shared memory or pleasure. In this perfume, not breathed by beauty, not cleansed in her bosom, not scattered where she had walked, in this perfume of a changed sky and tillage and world there was all the diverse melancholy of regret and absence and youth." And in one of the masterpieces of French literature, Gérard de Nerval's *Sylvie*, just as in the book of the *Mémoires d'Outre-tombe* which describes Combourg, there figures a sensation of the same species as the taste of the madeleine and the warbling of the thrush. Above all in Baudelaire, where they are more numerous still, reminiscences of this kind are clearly less fortuitous and therefore, to my mind, unmistakable in their significance. Here the poet himself, with something of a slow and indolent choice, deliberately seeks, in the perfume of a woman, for instance, of her hair and her breast, the analogies which will inspire him and evoke for him

> *l'azur du ciel immense et rond*

and

> *un port rempli de flammes et de mâts.*

I was about to search in my memory for the passages in Baudelaire at the heart of which one may find this kind of transposed sensation, in order once and for all to establish my place in so noble a line of descent and thus to give myself the assurance that the work which I no longer had any hesitation in undertaking was worthy of the pains which I should have to bestow upon it, when, having arrived at the foot of the flight of stairs which led down from the library, I found myself suddenly in the main drawing-room, in the middle of a party which, as I soon discovered, was to seem to me very different from those that I had attended in the past, and was to assume a special character in my eyes and take on a novel significance. In fact, as soon as I entered the crowded room, although I did not falter in the project which I had gone so far towards formulating within me, I was witness of a spectacular and dramatic effect which threatened to raise against my enterprise the gravest of all objections. An objection which I should manage no doubt to surmount, but which, while I continued silently to reflect upon the conditions that are necessary to a work of art, could not fail, by presenting to my gaze in a hundred different forms a consideration more likely than any other to make me hesitate, constantly to interrupt my train of thought.

For a few seconds I did not understand why it was that I had difficulty in recognising the master of the house and the guests and why everyone in the room appeared to have put on a disguise—in most cases a powdered wig—which changed him completely. The Prince himself, as he stood receiving his guests, still had that genial look of a king in a fairy-story which I had remarked in him the first time I had been to his house, but to-day, as though he too felt bound to comply with the rules for fancy dress which he had sent out with the invitations, he had got himself up with a white beard and dragged his feet along the ground as though they were weighted with soles of lead, so that he gave the impression of trying to impersonate one of the "Ages of Man." (His moustaches were white too, as though the hoar-frost of Hop o' My Thumb's forest still lay thick upon them. They seemed to get in the way of his mouth, which he had difficulty in moving, and one felt that having made his effect he ought to have taken them off.) So successful was this disguise that I recognised him only by a process of logical deduction, by inferring from the mere resemblance of certain features the identity of the figure before me. I do not know what young Fezensac had put on his face, but, while others had whitened either half their beard or merely their moustache, he had not bothered to use a dye like the rest but had found some means of covering his features with wrinkles and making his eyebrows sprout with bristles; and all this did not suit him in the least, it had the effect of making his face look hardened, bronzed, rigid and solemn, and aged him to such an extent that one would no longer have said he was a young man at all. Still greater was my surprise when a moment later I heard the name Duc de Châtellerault applied to a little elderly man with the silvery moustaches of an ambassador, in whom, thanks to a tiny fragment which still survived of the look that I remembered, I was just able to recognise the youth whom I had once met at Mme de Villeparisis's tea-party. The first time that I thus succeeded in identifying somebody, by trying to dismiss from my mind the effects of his disguise and building up, through an effort of memory, a whole familiar face round those features which had remained unaltered, my first thought ought to have been—and perhaps for a fraction of a second was—to congratulate him on having made himself up with such wonderful skill that one had initially, before recognising him, that hesitation which a great actor, appearing in a role in which he is unlike himself, can cause an audience to feel when he first comes on to the stage, so that knowing from the programme what to expect, it yet, for a moment, remains silent and puzzled before bursting into applause.

From the point of view of disguise, the most extraordinary of all the guests, the real star turn of the afternoon, was my personal enemy, M. d'Argencourt. Not only had he concealed his real beard, which was hardly even pepper-and-salt in colour, beneath a fantastic bushy growth of a quite improbable whiteness, but altogether (such is the power of small physical changes to shrink or enlarge a human figure and, even more, to alter the apparent character, the personality of an individual) he had turned into a contemptible old beggarman, and the diplomat whose solemn demeanour and starched rigidity were still present to my memory acted his part of old dotard with such verisimilitude that his limbs were all of a tremble and the features of what had once been a haughty countenance were permanently relaxed in an expression of smiling idiocy. Disguise, carried to this extent, ceases to be a mere art, it becomes a total transformation of the personality. And indeed, although certain details assured me that it was really Argencourt who presented this ludicrous and picturesque spectacle, I had to traverse an almost infinite number of successive states of a single face if I wished to rediscover that of the Argencourt whom I had known and who was now, though he had had no other materials than his own body with which to effect the change, so different from himself. Clearly this was the last extremity to which that body could be brought without suffering utter disintegration; already the immobile face and the proudly arched chest were no more than a bundle of rags, twitching and convulsed. With difficulty, by recalling certain smiles with which in the past Argencourt had sometimes for a moment tempered his disdain, was I able to see in the man before me the Argencourt whom I had once known, to understand that this smile of a doddering old-clothes-man existed potentially in the correct gentleman of an earlier day. But even supposing that the same intention lay behind Argencourt's smile now as in the past, because of the prodigious transformation of his face the actual physical matter of the eye through which he had to express this intention was so different that the smile which resulted was entirely new and even appeared to belong to a new person. I was tempted to laugh aloud at the sight of this sublime old gaffer, as senile in his amiable caricature of himself as was, in a more tragic vein, M. de Charlus thunderstruck into humble politeness. M. d'Argencourt, in his impersonation of an aged man in a farce by Regnard rewritten in an exaggerated fashion by Labiche, was as easy of access, as affable as M. de Charlus in the role of King Lear, punctiliously doffing his hat to the most unimportant passer-by. Yet it did not occur to me to tell him how impressed I was by the extraordinary vision which he offered to my eyes. And this was not because of any survival of my old feeling of antipathy, for indeed he had so far become unlike himself that I had the illusion of being in the presence of a different person, as gentle, as kindly, as inoffensive as the other Argencourt had been hostile, overbearing, and dangerous. So far a different person that the sight of this hoary clown with his ludicrous grin, this snow-man looking like General Dourakine[45] in his second childhood, made me think that it must be possible for human personality to undergo metamorphoses as total as those of certain insects. I had the impression that I was looking into a glass-case in a museum of natural history at an instructive example of a later phase in the life-cycle of what had once been the swiftest and surest of predatory insects, and before this flabby chrysalis, more subject to vibration than capable of movement, I could not feel the sentiments which in the past M. d'Argencourt had always inspired in me. However, I was silent, I refrained from congratulating him on presenting a spectacle which seemed to extend the boundaries within which the transformations of the human body can take place.

For whereas at a fancy-dress ball or behind the scenes at a theatre civility leads one, if anything, to exaggerate the difficulty—to talk even of the impossibility—of recognising the person beneath the disguise, here on the contrary an instinct had warned me to do just the contrary; I felt that the success of the disguise was no longer in any way flattering because the transformation was not intentional. And I realised something that I had not suspected when I entered the room a few minutes earlier: that every party, grand or simple, which takes place after a long interval in which one has ceased to go into society, provided that it brings together some of the people whom one knew in the past, gives one the impression of a masquerade, a masquerade which is more successful than any that one has ever been to and at which one is most genuinely "intrigued" by the identity of the other guests, but with the novel feature that the disguises, which were assumed long ago against their wearers' will, cannot, when the party is over, be wiped off with the make-up. Intrigued, did I say, by the identity of the other guests? No more, alas, than they are intrigued by one's own. For the difficulty which I experienced in putting a name to the faces before me was shared evidently by all those who, when they happened to catch sight of mine, paid no more attention to it than if they had never seen it before or else laboriously sought to extract from my present appearance a very different recollection.

In performing this extraordinary "number," this brilliant study in caricature which offered certainly the most striking vision which I was likely to retain of him, M. d'Argencourt might be likened to an actor who at the end of a play makes a final appearance on the stage before the curtain falls for the last time in the midst of a storm of laughter. And if I no longer felt any ill will towards him, it was because in this man who had rediscovered the innocence of childhood there was no longer any recollection of the contemptuous notions which he might once have had of me, no longer any memory of having seen M. de Charlus suddenly drop my arm, either because these sentiments had ceased to exist in him or because in order to

arrive at me they were obliged to pass through physical re-
fractors which so distorted them that in the course of their
journey they completely changed their meaning, so that M.
d'Argencourt appeared to be kind for want of the physical
means of expressing that he was still unkind, from inability to
repress his unfailingly friendly mirth. I have compared him to
an actor, but in fact, unencumbered as he was by any conscious
soul, it was rather as a puppet, a trembling puppet with a beard
of white wool, that I saw him being shakily put through his
paces up and down this drawing-room, in a puppet-show
which was both scientific and philosophical and in which he
served—as though it had been at the same time a funeral
oration and a lecture at the Sorbonne—both as a text for a
sermon on the vanity of all things and as an object lesson in
natural history.

A puppet-show, yes, but one in which, in order to identify
the puppets with the people whom one had known in the past,
it was necessary to read what was written on several planes at
once, planes that lay behind the visible aspect of the puppets
and gave them depth and forced one, as one looked at these
aged marionettes, to make a strenuous intellectual effort; one
was obliged to study them at the same time with one's eyes and
with one's memory. These were puppets bathed in the immaterial colours of the years, puppets which exteriorised Time,
Time which by Habit is made invisible and to become visible
seeks bodies, which wherever it finds it seizes, to display its
magic lantern upon them. As immaterial now as Golo long ago
on the door-handle of my room at Combray, the new, the unrecognisable Argencourt was there before me as the revelation
of Time, which by his agency was rendered partially visible, for
in the new elements which went to compose his face and his
personality one could decipher a number which told one the
years of his age, one could recognise the hieroglyph of life—of
life not as it appears to us, that is to say permanent, but as it
really is: an atmosphere so swiftly changing that at the end of
the day the proud nobleman is portrayed, in caricature, as a
dealer in old clothes.

There were other people in the room in whom these changes,
these veritable alienations seemed to belong rather to the realm

of human psychology than of natural history, so that one was astonished, when one heard certain names, to learn that the same individual could present, not like M. d'Argencourt the characteristics of a new and different species, but the external features of a different personality. From this young girl, for instance, as from M. d'Argencourt, time had extracted possibilities that one could never have suspected, but these possibilities, though it was through her physiognomy or her body that they had expressed themselves, seemed to be of a moral order. The features of the face, if they change, if they group themselves differently, if their oscillations take on a slower rhythm, assume with a different aspect a different significance. In a woman, for instance, whom one had known as stiff and prim, an enlargement out of all recognition of the cheeks, an unpredictable arching of the nose, caused one the same surprise —and often it was an agreeable surprise—as one would have felt at some sensitive and profound remark, some noble and courageous action that one would never have expected of her. On either side of this nose, this new nose, one saw opening out horizons which one would not have dared to hope for. With these cheeks kindness and delicate affection, once out of the question, had become possible. And in the presence of this chin one could utter sentiments that one would never have dreamed of voicing when confronted with its predecessor. All these new features of the face implied new features also of the character; the thin, severe girl had turned into a vast and indulgent dowager. And no longer in a zoological sense, as with M. d'Argencourt, but in a social and moral sense one could say of her that she was a different person.

For all these reasons a party like this at which I found myself was something much more valuable than an image of the past: it offered me as it were all the successive images—which I had never seen—which separated the past from the present, better still it showed me the relationship that existed between the present and the past; it was like an old-fashioned peepshow, but a peepshow of the years, the vision not of a moment but of a person situated in the distorting perspective of Time.

As for the woman whose lover M. d'Argencourt had been, considering the length of time that had elapsed she had not changed very much, that is to say her face was not too utterly demolished for the face of a human being subject, as we all are, to deformation at every moment of her trajectory into the abyss towards which she had been launched, that abyss whose direction we can express only by means of comparisons that are all equally invalid, since we can borrow them only from the world of space and their sole merit, whether we give them the orientation of height, length or depth, is to make us feel that this inconceivable yet apprehensible dimension exists. To find a name for the faces before me I had been obliged, in effect, to follow the course of the years back towards their source, and this forced me, by a necessary consequence, to re-establish, to give their real place to those years whose passage I had hardly noticed. And from this point of view, freeing me from the illusions produced in us by the apparent sameness of space, the totally changed aspect of, for instance, M. d'Argencourt was a striking revelation to me of that chronological reality which under normal conditions is no more than an abstract conception to us, just as the first sight of some strange dwarf tree or giant baobab apprises us that we have arrived in a new latitude.

Life at such moments seems to us like a theatrical pageant in which from one act to another we see the baby turn into a youth and the youth into a mature man, who in the next act totters towards the grave. And as it is through endless small changes that we feel that these beings, who enter our field of vision only at long intervals, can have become so different, we feel that we ourselves must have followed the same law in virtue of which they have been so totally transformed that, without having ceased to exist, indeed just because they have never ceased to exist, they no longer in any way resemble what we observed them to be in the past.

A young woman whom I had known long ago, white-haired now and compressed into a little old witch, seemed to suggest that it is necessary, in the final scene of a theatrical entertainment, for the characters to be disguised beyond all recognition. But her brother was still so straight-backed, so like himself, that one was surprised on his youthful face to see a bristling moustache dyed white. Indeed everywhere the patches of white in beards and moustaches hitherto entirely black lent a note of melancholy to the human landscape of the party, as do the first yellow leaves on the trees when one is still looking forward to a long summer, when before one has begun to enjoy the hot weather one sees that the autumn has arrived. So that at last I, who from childhood had lived from day to day and had received, of myself and of others, impressions which I regarded as definitive, became aware as I had never been before—by an inevitable inference from the metamorphoses which had taken place in all the people around me—of the time which had passed for them, a notion which brought with it the over-whelming revelation that it had passed also for me. And their old age, in itself a matter of indifference to me, froze my blood by announcing to me the approach of my own. At this point, as though to proclaim the lesson aloud and drive it home, there came to my ears at brief intervals a series of remarks which struck them like the trump of the Last Judgment. The first of these was made by the Duchesse de Guermantes; I had just caught sight of her, passing between a double hedge of curious onlookers, who, not fully aware of the marvellous artifices of toilet and aesthetic which evoked these responses within them, yet feeling themselves moved by the sight of this fair, reddish head, this salmon-pink body almost concealed by its fins of black lace and throttled by jewels, gazed at it, with its heredi-tary sinuosity of line, as they might have gazed at some archaic sacred fish, loaded with precious stones, in which was incarnate the protective genius of the Guermantes family. "Ah! how wonderful to see you," she said to me, "you, my oldest friend!" And though the vanity of the sometime young man from Combray who had never for a moment thought that he might become one of her friends, really participating in the real mysterious life that went on in the houses of the Guermantes, with the same title to her friendship as M. de Bréauté or M. de Forestelle or Swann or all those others who were now dead, might well have been flattered by these words, more than anything I was saddened by them. "Her oldest friend!" I said to myself. "Surely she exaggerates. One of the oldest perhaps, but can I really be . . ." At that moment a nephew of the Prince came up to me: "You, as a veteran Parisian . . ." he said to me, and while he was still speaking I was handed a note. Outside the house I had made the acquaintance of a young Létourville, who was related in some way which I had forgotten to the Duchess but who knew at least who I was. He had just left Saint-Cyr, and, telling myself that he would be a nice friend for me, like Saint-Loup, who could initiate me into military matters and explain the changes which had taken place in the army, I had told him that I would see him again at the party and that we might arrange to have dinner together one evening, and for this he had thanked me very civilly. But I had stayed too long lost in thought in the library and the note which he had left for me was to tell me that he had not been able to wait, and to leave me his address. The letter of this imagined comrade ended thus: "With the respectful wishes of your young friend, Létourville." "Young friend!" That was how in the past I had written to men thirty years older than myself, to Legrandin, for example. And now this second lieutenant, whom in my mind's eye I saw as my comrade after the fashion of Saint-Loup, called himself my "young friend"! Since the days of Doncières, it seemed, it was not only military methods that had changed; from this M. de Létourville, with whom I imagined myself sharing the pleasures of a youthful comradeship—and why not, since I appeared to myself to be youthful?—I was separated, it seemed, by an arc traced by an invisible compass whose existence I had not suspected, which removed me so far from the boyish second lieutenant that in the eyes of this "young friend" I was an old gentleman.

Almost immediately afterwards, hearing someone mention the name of Bloch, I asked whether he meant young Bloch or his father (who, though I was not aware of this, had died during the war, from grief, it was said, at seeing France invaded). "I didn't know he had any children," said the Prince, "I didn't even know he was married. But clearly it is the father we are talking about. He is not in the least like a young Bloch," he added with a laugh. "He is quite old enough to have grown-up sons." And I realised that it was my former schoolfriend who was being discussed. A moment later he came into the room. And indeed superimposed upon the features of Bloch I saw the mild but didactic countenance, the frail movements of the head quickly coming to rest like a piece of clockwork, in which I should have recognised the learned weariness of some amiable old man if at the same time I had not recognised my friend standing before me, so that at once my memories animated him with an uninterrupted flow of youthful enthusiasm which he now no longer seemed to possess. For me, who had known him on the threshold of life and had never ceased to see him thus, he was the friend of my boyhood, an adolescent whose youth I measured by the youth which unconsciously, not believing that I had lived since that time, I attributed to myself. I heard someone say that he quite looked his age, and I was astonished to observe on his face some of those signs which are indeed characteristic of men who are old. Then I understood that this was because he was in fact old and that adolescents who survive for a sufficient number of years are the material out of which life makes old men.

Someone, hearing that I had not been well, asked me whether I was not afraid of catching the influenza of which there was an epidemic at that moment, whereupon another well-wisher re-assured me by saying: "Oh! no, it's usually only the young who get it. A man of your age has very little to fear." I was assured also that some of the servants had recognised me. They had whispered my name, and had even, as a lady informed me ("You know the expressions they use"), been heard by her to say: "Look, there's father . . ." (and then my surname), and as I had no children this could only be an allusion to my age.

"What do you mean, did I know the Marshal?" said the Duchess to me. "But I knew figures far more typical of the period: the Duchesse de Galliera, Pauline de Périgord, Monsignor Dupanloup." Hearing her, I naïvely regretted that I had not known what she described as relics of an earlier time. I ought to have reflected that what one calls an earlier time is the period of which one has oneself known only the end: things that we see on the horizon assume a mysterious grandeur and seem to us to be closing over a world which we shall not behold again; but meanwhile we are advancing, and very soon it is we ourselves who are on the horizon for the generations that come after us; all the while the horizon retreats into the distance, and the world, which seemed to be finished, begins again. "I even, when I was a girl," Mme de Guermantes went on, "once saw the Duchesse de Dino. But then, you know I'm no longer a chicken." These last words upset me. "She shouldn't have said that," I thought, "that's the way for an old woman to talk." And immediately I reflected that in fact she was an old woman. "As for you," she continued, "you are always the same, you never seem to change." And this remark I found almost more painful than if she had told me that I had changed, for it proved —if it was so extraordinary that there was so little sign of change in me—that a long time had elapsed. "Yes," she said, "you are astonishing, you look as young as ever," another melancholy remark, which can only mean that in fact, if not in appearance, we have grown old. There was worse to come, for she added: "I have always regretted that you never married. But, who knows, perhaps after all it is fortunate. You would have been old enough to have sons in the war, and if they had been killed, like poor Robert (I still often think of him), sensitive as you are, how would you ever have survived their loss?" And I was able to see myself, as though in the first truthful mirror which I had ever encountered, reflected in the eyes of old people, still young in their own opinion as I in mine, who, when I spoke of "an old man like myself" in the hope of being contradicted, showed in their answering looks, which saw me not as they saw themselves but as I saw them, not a glimmer of protest. For we failed to see our own appearance, our own age, but each one of us, as though it were a mirror that faced him, saw those of the others. And no doubt the discovery that they have grown old causes less sadness to many people than it did to me. But in the first place old age, in this respect, is like death. Some men confront them both with indifference, not because they have more courage than others but because they have less imagination. And then, a man who from his childhood on has aimed at one single idea and who, from idleness and perhaps also because of poor health, has perpetually put off its realisation, every evening striking out as though it had never existed the day that has slipped away and is lost, so that the illness which hastens the ageing of his body retards that of his mind, such a man is more surprised and more appalled to see that all the while he has been living in Time than one who lives little inside himself and, regulating his activities by the calendar, does not in a single horrifying moment discover the total of the years whose mounting sum he has followed day by day. But there was a more serious reason for my distress: I had made the discovery of this destructive action of Time at the very moment when I had conceived the ambition to make visible, to intellectualise in a work of art, realities that were outside Time.

In some of the guests at the party the successive replacement, accomplished in my absence, of each cell by other cells, had brought about a change so complete, a metamorphosis so entire that I could have dined opposite them in a restaurant a hundred times without suspecting that I had known them in the past any more than I would have guessed the royal identity of a sovereign travelling incognito or the hidden vice of a stranger. And even this comparison is hardly adequate to the cases in which I had heard the name of the person before me, for it is perhaps not so extraordinary that a stranger sitting opposite one should be a criminal or a king, but these were people whom I had once known, or rather I had known people who bore the same name and yet were so different that I could not believe that they were the same. Nevertheless, just as I would have tried to introduce into the stranger the idea of royalty or of vice, which in a very short time can give a new face to the unknown person towards whom one might so easily, when one's eyes were still blindfolded, have committed the gaffe of behaving with inappropriate insolence or civility, and in whose unchanged features, once one knows who he is, one discerns traces of distinction or of guilt, so now I set to work to introduce into the face of the unknown, utterly unknown, woman before me the idea that she was, let us say, Mme Sazerat, and I succeeded eventually in restoring the meaning that I had once known to reside in her face, which would, however, have remained for me utterly alienated from its owner—as much the face of another person, wanting in all the human attributes which I had once known it to possess, as that of a man turned back into a monkey—if the name and the affirmation of identity had not, in spite of the arduous nature of the problem, set me on the path of its solution. Sometimes,

however, the old image came to light again in my mind with
such precision that I was able to essay a confrontation; and
then, like a witness brought face to face with a suspect, I was
obliged, so great was the difference, to say: "No, I do not
recognise this person."

But was I right to tell myself that these special characteristics of individuals would die? I had always considered each
one of us to be a sort of multiple organism or polyp, not only
at a given moment of time—so that when a speck of dust passes
it the eye, an associated but independent organ, blinks without
having received an order from the mind, and the intestine, like
an embedded parasite, can fall victim to an infection without
the mind knowing anything about it—but also, similarly,
where the personality is concerned and its duration through
life, I had thought of this as a sequence of juxtaposed but
distinct "I's" which would die one after the other or even come
to life alternately, like those which at Combray took one
another's place within me when evening approached. But I had
seen also that these moral cells of which an individual is composed are more durable than the individual himself. I had seen
the vices and the courage of the Guermantes recur in Saint-
Loup, as also at different times in his life his own strange
and ephemeral defects of character, and as in Swann his
Semitism. And now I could observe the same phenomenon in
Bloch. He had lost his father some years previously, and when
I had written to him at the time, he had at first been unable to
answer my letter, for, quite apart from the strong family sentiments which often exist in Jewish families, the idea that his
father was an altogether exceptional man had imparted to his
affection the character of a cult. He had found his loss unbearable and had had to take refuge in a sanatorium, where he
stayed for nearly a year. To my condolences he replied in a tone
of profound grief which was at the same time almost haughty,
so enviable in his eyes was the privilege which he had enjoyed
of approaching this exceptional man whose very ordinary two-
horse carriage he would have liked to present to some historical
museum. And now, as he sat at table in the midst of his family,
he was animated by the same wrath against his father-in-law as
had animated his own father against M. Nissim Bernard and

even interrupted his meals to deliver the same tirades against him. So that just as, in listening to the conversation of Cottard and Brichot and so many others, I had felt that, through the influence of culture and fashion, a single undulation propagates identical mannerisms of speech and thought through a whole vast extent of space, it seemed to me now that throughout the whole duration of time great cataclysmic waves lift up from the depths of the ages the same rages, the same sadnesses, the same heroisms, the same obsessions, through one superimposed generation after another, and that each geological section cut through several individuals of the same series offers the repetition, as of shadows thrown upon a succession of screens, of a picture as unchanged—though often not so insignificant—as that of Bloch exchanging angry words with his father-in-law, M. Bloch the elder doing the same in the same fashion with M. Nissim Bernard, and many other pairs of disputants whom I had myself never known.

Gilberte de Saint-Loup[46] said to me: "Shall we go and dine together by ourselves in a restaurant?" and I replied: "Yes, if you don't find it compromising to dine alone with a young man." As I said this, I heard everybody round me laugh, and I hastily added: "or rather, with an old man." I felt that the phrase which had made people laugh was one of those which my mother might have used in speaking of me, my mother for whom I was still a child. And I realised that I judged myself from the same point of view as she did. If in the end I had registered, as she had, certain changes which had taken place since my early childhood, these were, nevertheless, changes which were now very remote. I had not advanced beyond the particular one which, long ago, almost before the remark corresponded with the facts, had made people say: "He's almost a grown-up man now." I still thought that that was what I was, but by now the description was absurdly out of date. I did not realise how much I had changed. And indeed, though these people just now had burst out laughing, what was it that made them so sure of the change? I had not a single grey hair, my moustache was black. I should have liked to ask them what the evidence was which revealed the terrible fact.

And now I began to understand what old age was—old age,

which perhaps of all the realities is the one of which we preserve for longest in our life a purely abstract conception, looking at calendars, dating our letters, seeing our friends marry and then in their turn the children of our friends, and yet, either from fear or from sloth, not understanding what all this means, until the day when we behold an unknown silhouette, like that of M. d'Argencourt, which teaches us that we are living in a new world; until the day when a grandson of a woman we once knew, a young man whom instinctively we treat as a contemporary of ours, smiles as though we were making fun of him because to him it seems that we are old enough to be his grandfather—and I began to understand too what death meant and love and the joys of the spiritual life, the usefulness of suffering, a vocation, etc. For if names had lost most of their individuality for me, words on the other hand now began to reveal their full significance. The beauty of images is situated in front of things, that of ideas behind them. So that the first sort of beauty ceases to astonish us as soon as we have reached the things themselves, the second is something that we understand only when we have passed beyond them.

The cruel discovery which I had just made could not fail to be of service to me so far as the actual material of my book was concerned. For I had decided that this could not consist uniquely of the full and plenary impressions that were outside time, and amongst those other truths in which I intended to set, like jewels, those of the first order, the ones relating to Time, to Time in which, as in some transforming fluid, men and societies and nations are immersed, would play an important part. I should pay particular attention to those changes which the aspect of living things undergoes, of which every minute I had fresh examples before me, for, whilst all the while thinking of my work, which I now felt to be launched with such momentum that no passing distractions could check its advance, I continued to greet old acquaintances and to enter into conversation with them. The process of ageing, I found, was not marked in them all by signs of the same sort. I saw someone who was inquiring after my name, and I was told that it was M. de Cambremer. He came up to me and to show that he had recognised me, "Do you still have your fits of breath lessness?" he asked, and, upon my replying in the affirmative, went on: "Well, at least you see that it is no bar to longevity," as if I were already a centenarian. While speaking to him, I fixed my eyes on two or three features which I was able, by an effort of thought, to reintegrate into that complex of my recollections—totally different though it was—which I called his personality. But for a brief moment he turned his head aside. And then I saw that he had been made unrecognisable by the attachment of enormous red pouches to his cheeks, which prevented him from opening his mouth or his eyes completely, and the sight of these startled me into silence, since I did not dare to look at what I took to be some form of anthrax which it seemed more polite not to refer to unless he mentioned it first. However, like a courageous invalid, he made no allusion to his malady but talked and laughed, and I feared to appear lacking in sympathy if I did not ask, no less than in tact if I did ask, what was its nature. "But surely they have become less frequent with age?" he continued, still on the subject of my fits of breathlessness. I replied that they had not. "Oh! but my sister has them much less than she used to," he said, in a tone of contradiction, as though what was true of his sister must also be true of me, and as though age were one of a number of remedies which had helped Mme de Gaucourt and which, therefore, he was quite certain must be beneficial to me. Mme de Cambremer-Legrandin joined us and I became more and more afraid that they must think me callous for failing to deplore the symptoms which I observed on her husband's face, yet still I could not pluck up courage to broach the subject myself. "I expect you're glad to see him again," she said. "Yes, but how is he?" I replied, as though doubtful what answer I should receive. "Why, pretty well, as you can see for yourself." She had not noticed the disfigurement which offended my eyes and which was merely one of the masks in the collection of Time, a mask which Time had fastened to the face of the Marquis, but gradually, adding layer to layer so slowly that his wife had perceived nothing. When M. de Cambremer had finished his questions about my breathlessness, it was my turn to inquire in a low voice of someone standing near whether the Marquis's mother was still alive. And now I was beginning to discover that, in the appreciation of the passage of time, the first step is the hardest. At first one finds it extremely difficult to imagine that so much time has elapsed, later the difficulty is to understand how the lapse can have been so slight. Similarly, when one first suddenly becomes aware of the distance separating the thirteenth century from the present, it is difficult to believe that churches built in that age can still exist—but in fact they are to be found all over France. Within a few minutes I had developed, though very much more rapidly, in the same fashion as those who, after finding it hard to believe that somebody they knew in their youth has reached the age of sixty, are very much more surprised fifteen years later to learn that the same person is still alive and is only seventy-five. Having been assured that M. de Cambremer's mother had not died, I asked him how she was. "She is wonderful still," he said, using to describe her an adjective which in certain families—by contrast with those tribes where aged parents are treated without pity —is applied to old people in whom the continued exercise of the most rudimentary and unspiritual faculties, such as hearing, going to mass on foot, sustaining the demise of their relatives with insensibility, is endowed in the eyes of their children with an extraordinary moral beauty.

If some of the women in the room had acknowledged the arrival of old age by starting to paint their faces, it was also manifested in a contrary fashion by the absence of make-up on the features of certain men, where I had never consciously observed it in the past and who yet seemed to me greatly changed since they had given up the hopeless attempt to please and ceased to use it. One of these was Legrandin. The suppression of the pink, which I had never suspected of being artificial, upon his lips and his cheeks gave to his countenance the greyish tinge and also the sculptural precision of stone, so that with his long-drawn and gloomy features he was like some Egyptian god. Or perhaps less like a god than a ghost. He no longer had the heart either to paint himself or to smile, to make his eyes sparkle, to elaborate his ingenious speeches. One was astonished to see him so pale and so dejected, opening his mouth only at rare intervals to make remarks as trivial as those uttered by the spirits of the dead when we summon them to our presence. One wondered what could be the cause that prevented him from being lively, eloquent, charming, as one does when a medium, putting questions that call for long and fascinating answers to the "double" of a man who in his lifetime was brilliant, elicits from him only the most uninteresting replies. And one told oneself that this cause, which had substituted for a Legrandin of rapid movements and rich colour a pale and melancholy phantom Legrandin, was old age.

There were some people whose hair had not turned white. I recognised for instance, when he came up to say a word to his master, the old valet of the Prince de Guermantes. The coarse hairs which bristled all over his cheeks as well as on his skull were still of a red that verged upon pink, yet one could hardly suspect him of using dye like the Duchesse de Guermantes. Nevertheless, he appeared old. One felt merely that in the human race there exist species, like the mosses and the lichens and a great many others in the vegetable kingdom, which do not change at the approach of winter.

Others again had preserved their faces intact and seemed merely to walk with difficulty; at first one supposed that they had something wrong with their legs; only later did one realise that age had fastened its soles of lead to their feet. A few, of whom the Prince d'Agrigente was one, seemed actually to have been embellished by age. His tall, thin figure, with its lacklustre eye and hair that seemed destined to remain a carroty red for all eternity, had turned, through a metamorphosis more appropriate to an insect, into an entirely different old man, whose red hair, too long exposed to view, had been taken out of service like a table-cloth too long in use and replaced by white. His chest had acquired a new corpulence, robust and almost military, which must have necessitated a positive explosion of the fragile chrysalis that I had known; a conscious gravity flooded his eyes, which were tinged also with a new kindliness which made him bow to right and left. And as, in spite of his altered appearance, a certain resemblance could be detected between the puissant prince before me and the portrait preserved in my memory, I marvelled at the power to renew in fresh forms that is possessed by Time, which can thus, while respecting the unity of the individual and the laws of life, effect a change of scene and introduce bold contrasts into two successive aspects of a single person; for many of these people could be identified immediately, but only as rather bad portraits of themselves hanging side by side in an exhibition in which an inaccurate and spiteful artist has hardened the features of one sitter, robbed another of her fresh complexion and her slender figure, spread a gloom over the countenance of a third. Comparing these effigies with those that the eyes of my memory could show me, I preferred the latter. Just as often, when asked by a friend to choose a photograph, one finds the one he offers less good than some other and would like to refuse it, so to each of these people, presented with the new image which they showed me of themselves, I should have liked to say: "No, not this one, it is not so good of you, it's not really like you." I would not have dared to add: "Instead of your own straight and handsome nose, it has given you your father's crooked nose, which I have never seen in you." And yet this was what had happened: the nose was new, but it was a family nose. If this was a portrait-gallery, Time, the artist, had made of all the sitters portraits that were recognisable; yet they were not likenesses, and this was not because he had flattered them but because he had aged them. He was an artist, moreover, who worked very slowly. That replica of Odette's face, for instance, which I had seen as the merest outline of a sketch in Gilberte's face on the day on which I first met Bergotte, Time had at long last now wrought into the most perfect likeness; he was one of those painters who keep a work by them for half a lifetime, adding to it year after year until it is completed.

In some of the guests I recognised after a while not merely themselves but themselves as they had been in the past. Ski, for instance, was no more altered than a flower or a fruit which had been dried. Aged but still immature, one of those first attempts which nature abandons in the rough, he was a living confirmation of the theory which I had been formulating about the bachelor devotees of art. "Marvellous!" he said, taking me by the arm. "I have heard it eight times. . . ." There were others, too, who had not ripened with age, not only art-lovers like Ski but men who had spent their lives in society. Their faces might be surrounded with a first circle of wrinkles and a sweep of white hair but they were still the same babyish faces, with the naïve enthusiasm of an eighteen-year-old. They were not old men, they were very young men in an advanced stage of withering. The marks of life were not deeply scored here, and death, when it came, would find it as easy to restore to these features their youthfulness as it is to clean a portrait which only a little surface dirt prevents from shining with its original brilliance. These men made me think that we are victims of an illusion when, hearing talk of a celebrated old man, we instantly make up our minds that he is kind and just and gentle; for I felt that, forty years earlier, these elderly men had been ruthless young men and that there was no reason to suppose that they had not preserved their youthful arrogance and their vanity, their duplicity and their guile.

And yet, in complete contrast with these, I had the surprise of talking to men and women whom I remembered as unendurable and who had now, I found, lost almost every one of their defects, possibly because life, by disappointing or by gratifying their desires, had rid them of most of their conceit or their bitterness. A rich marriage, with the consequence that struggle and ostentation had ceased to be necessary, the influence perhaps of the wife herself, the slowly acquired knowledge of values beyond those that had formed the whole creed of a frivolous youth, had allowed them to relax the tensions in their character and to display their good qualities. Growing old, they seemed to have acquired a different personality, like those trees whose essential nature appears to be changed by the autumn which alters their colours; the essential marks of old age were manifested in them, but old age, here, was a moral phenomenon. In others, it was almost entirely physical, and so strange were its effects that a person (Mme d'Arpajon, for instance) seemed to me at the same time unknown and familiar. Unknown, for it was impossible to suspect that it was she and in spite of every effort I could not help showing signs, as I responded to her salutation, of the mental activity which made me hesitate between three or four individuals, not one of whom was Mme d'Arpajon and any one of whom I thought that I might be greeting, and greeting with a fervour which must have astonished her, for, fearing in my uncertainty to appear too

chilly should she turn out to be an old and close friend, I had
made up for the doubtful expression of my eyes by the warmth
of my hand-shake and my smile. And yet, in a way, her new
appearance was not unfamiliar to me. It was the appearance,
often seen by me in the course of my life, of certain stout,
elderly women, of whom at the time I had never suspected that,
many years earlier, they could have looked like Mme d'Arpajon.
So different was she to look at from the woman I had known
that one was tempted to think of her as a creature condemned,
like a character in a pantomime, to appear first as a young girl,
then as a stout matron, with no doubt a final appearance still to
come as a quavering, bent old crone. Like a swimmer in difficulties almost out of sight of the shore, she seemed with
infinite effort scarcely to move through the waves of time
which beat upon her and threatened to submerge her. Yet
gradually, as I studied her face, hesitant and uncertain like a
failing memory which has begun to lose the images of the past,
I succeeded in rediscovering something of the face which I had
known, by playing a little game of eliminating the squares and
the hexagons which age had added to her cheeks. For in her
case the material which the years had superimposed consisted
of geometrical shapes, though on the cheeks of other women it
might be of quite a different character. On those, for instance,
of Mme de Guermantes, in many respects so little changed and
yet composite now like a bar of nougat, I could distinguish
traces here and there of verdigris, a small pink patch of fragmentary shell-work, and a little growth of an indefinable
character, smaller than a mistletoe berry and less transparent
than a glass bead.

Some men walked with a limp, and one was aware that this
was the result not of a motor accident but of a first stroke: they
had already, as the saying is, one foot in the grave. There were
women too whose graves were waiting open to receive them:
half paralysed, they could not quite disentangle their dress
from the tomb-stone in which it had got stuck, so that they
were unable to stand up straight but remained bent towards the
ground, with their head lowered, in a curve which seemed an
apt symbol of their own position on the trajectory from life to
death, with the final vertical plunge not far away. Nothing now

could check the momentum of this parabola upon which they were launched; they trembled all over if they attempted to straighten themselves, and their fingers let fall whatever they tried to grasp.

Certain faces, beneath their hood of white hair, had already the rigidity, the sealed eyelids of those who are about to die, and their lips, shaken by an incessant tremor, seemed to be muttering a last prayer. A countenance of which every line was unchanged needed only the substitution of white hair for black or fair to look totally different, for, as theatrical costumiers know, a powdered wig is in itself an adequate disguise which will make its wearer unrecognisable. The Marquis de Beausergent, whom I had seen, as a young lieutenant, in Mme de Cambremer's box on the day on which Mme de Guermantes had been with her cousin in hers, still had the same perfectly regular features, indeed they had become even more regular, since the pathological rigidity brought about by arteriosclerosis had even further exaggerated the impassive rectitude of his dandy's physiognomy and given to his features the intense hardness of outline, almost grimacing in its immobility, that they might have had in a study by Mantegna or Michelangelo. His complexion, once almost ribaldly red, was now solemnly pale; silvery hair, a slight portliness, the dignity of a Doge, an air of fatigue, even of somnolence, all combined to give him a new and premonitory impression of doomed majesty. The square light brown beard had gone and in its place was a square white beard, of the same trim proportions, which so totally transformed his appearance that, noticing that the second lieutenant whom I remembered now had five bands of braid on his sleeve, my first thought was to congratulate him, not on having been promoted colonel but on looking so well in the part of colonel, a disguise for which he seemed to have borrowed, together with the uniform, the lugubrious gravity of the senior officer that his father had been. But there was another guest whose face, in spite of the substitution of a white for a fair beard, had remained lively, smiling and boyish, so that the change of beard merely made him appear more rubicund and more pugnacious and enhanced the sparkle in his eye, giving to the still youthful man about town the inspired air of a prophet.

The transformations effected, in the women particularly, by white hair and by other new features, would not have held my attention so forcibly had they been merely changes of colour, which can be charming to behold; too often they were changes of personality, registered not by the eye but, disturbingly, by the mind. For to "recognise" someone, and, *a fortiori*, to learn someone's identity after having failed to recognise him, is to predicate two contradictory things of a single subject, it is to admit that what was here, the person whom one remembers, no longer exists, and also that what is now here is a person whom one did not know to exist; and to do this we have to apprehend a mystery almost as disturbing as that of death, of which it is, indeed, as it were the preface and the harbinger. I knew what these changes meant, I knew what they were the prelude to, and that is why the white hair of these women, along with all the other changes, profoundly disquieted me. I was told a name and I was dumbfounded to think that it could be used to describe both the fair-haired girl, the marvellous waltzer, whom I had known in the past, and the massive white-haired lady making her way through the room with elephantine tread. Along with a certain rosiness of complexion, the name was perhaps the only thing common to these two women, the girl in my memory and the lady at the Guermantes party, who were more unlike one another than an *ingénue* and a dowager in a play. To have succeeded in giving to the waltzer this huge body, in encumbering and retarding her movements by the adjustment of an invisible metronome, in substituting—with perhaps as sole common factor the cheeks, larger certainly now than in youth but already in those days blotched with red—for the feather-light fair girl this ventripotent old campaigner, it must have been necessary for life to accomplish a vaster work of dismantlement and reconstruction than is involved in the replacement of a steeple by a dome, and when one considered that this work had been effected not with tractable inorganic matter but with living flesh which can only change impercept-ibly, the overwhelming contrast between the apparition before me and the creature that I remembered pushed back the exist-ence of the latter into a past that was more than remote, that was almost unimaginable. One was terrified, because it made one think of the vast periods which must have elapsed before such a revolution could be accomplished in the geology of a face, to see what erosions had taken place all the way along the nose, what huge alluvial deposits at the edge of the cheeks surrounded the whole face with their opaque and refractory masses. It was difficult to find a link between the two figures, past and present, to think of the two individuals as possessing the same name; for just as one has difficulty in thinking that a dead person was once alive or that a person who was alive is now dead, so one has difficulty, almost as great and of the same kind (for the extinction of youth, the destruction of a person full of energy and high spirits is already a kind of annihilation), in conceiving that she who was once a girl is now an old woman when the juxtaposition of the two appearances, the old and the young, seems so totally to exclude the possibility of their belonging to the same person that alternately it is the old woman and then the girl and then again the old woman who seems to one to be a dream, so that one might well refuse to believe that *this* can ever have been *that*, that the material of *that* has not taken refuge elsewhere but has itself, thanks to the subtle manipulations of Time, turned into *this*, that it is the same matter incorporated in the same body, were it not for the evidence of the similar name and the corroborative testimony of friends, to which an appearance of verisimilitude is given only by the pink upon the cheeks, once a small patch surrounded by the golden corn of fair hair, now a broad expanse beneath the snow.

And often these fair-haired dancers had acquired, along with a wig of white hair, the friendship of duchesses whom in the past they had not known. Nor was this all: having in their youth done nothing but dance, they had been "touched" by art as once a noble lady might have been touched by grace. And as the seventeenth-century lady, when this happened, withdrew into a life of religion, so now her descendant lived in an apartment filled with cubist paintings, a cubist painter worked for her alone and she lived only for him.

As in a snowy landscape, the degree of whiteness attained by a person's hair seemed in general to be an indication of the depth of time through which he or she had lived, just as in a range of mountains the higher peaks, even though they appear to the eye to be on the same level as the rest, nevertheless reveal their greater altitude by the intensity of their snowy whiteness. But there were exceptions to this rule, particularly among the women. Thus the tresses of the Princesse de Guermantes, which, when they were grey and had the lustre of silk, seemed to surround her bulging temples with silver, having in the process of turning white acquired the matness of wool or tow, seemed now on the contrary, for that reason, to be grey, like snow which has become dirty and lost its brilliance.

Some of the old men whose features had changed tried nevertheless to preserve, fixed upon them in a state of permanency, one of those fugitive expressions which one assumes for a second when posing for a photograph, either in order to show off some good point in one's appearance to the best effect or to conceal a deformity; they seemed to have become, once and for all, snapshots of themselves insusceptible of change.

All these people had taken so much time putting on their disguises that generally these passed unobserved by the men and women who saw them every day. Often they had even been granted a reprieve, thanks to which up to a very late hour they were able to remain themselves. But in these cases the disguise, when it finally came, was assumed more rapidly; for disguise, one way or another, was unavoidable. Mme X—, for instance, had never seemed to me to bear any resemblance to her mother, whom I had known only as an old woman, looking like a little hunched Turk. The daughter, on the other hand, I had always known as a charming woman with an upright carriage, and this for many years she had continued to be, for too many years, in fact, for like someone who must not forget, before night falls, to put on his Turkish disguise, she had left things late and had then been obliged precipitately, almost instantaneously, to hunch herself up so as faithfully to reproduce the appearance of an old Turkish woman that had once been presented by her mother.

Someone offered to re-introduce me to a friend of my youth, whom for ten years I had seen almost every day. As I went up to him he said, in a voice which I recognised very well: "How

delightful to see you again after all these years!" But if he was
delighted, I was astonished. The familiar voice seemed to be
emitted by a gramophone more perfect than any I had ever
heard, for, though it was the voice of my friend, it issued from
the mouth of a corpulent gentleman with greying hair whom
I did not know, and I could only suppose that somehow
artificially, by a mechanical device, the voice of my old comrade
had been lodged in the frame of this stout elderly man who
might have been anybody. And yet I knew that this was my
friend; the man who had re-introduced us after all these years
was not someone one could suspect of playing a practical joke.
My friend himself declared that I had not changed, and I
realised that in his own eyes he had not changed. I looked at
him more closely. And in fact, except that he had grown so
much stouter, he had preserved many features of his former
self. And yet I could not take it in that it was he. Then I made
an effort to remember. In his youth he had had blue eyes, always
laughing and perpetually mobile, in search evidently of something the nature of which I had not asked myself, but something no doubt entirely disinterested, Truth perhaps, pursued
in perpetual uncertainty, with a sort of boyish irresponsibility
and yet with a wavering respect for all the friends of his family.
And now that he had become an important politician, able and
masterful, his blue eyes, which in any case had not found what
they were seeking, had lost their mobility, and this gave them
a look of narrow concentration, as though the brow above
them were constantly frowning. His expression was no longer
one of gaiety, innocence and spontaneity but of guile and dis-
simulation. Decidedly, I thought, this must be somebody else,
but then suddenly I heard, evoked by something that I had
said, his laugh, his old loud, unforced laugh, the one that went
with the perpetual gay mobility of his glance. Experienced
concert-goers find that orchestrated by X— the music of Z—
becomes absolutely different, a somewhat subtle distinction
which the ignorant public does not comprehend—but to hear
the wild, choking laugh of a boy emerge from beneath a look
which was as pointed as a well sharpened blue pencil though
set slightly crooked in the face, was more than a mere difference
of orchestration. He stopped laughing; I should have liked to

recognise my friend, but, like Ulysses in the *Odyssey* when he rushes forward to embrace his dead mother, like the spiritualist who tries in vain to elicit from a ghost an answer which will reveal its identity, like the visitor at an exhibition of electricity who cannot believe that the voice which the gramophone restores unaltered to life is not a voice spontaneously emitted by a human being, I was obliged to give up the attempt.

Nobody was exempt from change, but I had to qualify this statement with the observation that for certain people the *tempo* of Time itself may be accelerated or retarded. By chance I had met in the street, some four or five years earlier, the Vicomtesse de Saint-Fiacre (the daughter-in-law of the one who had been a friend of the Guermantes). Her sculptural features seemed to assure her of eternal youth, and indeed she was still young. But I was quite unable to recognise her now, in spite of her smiles and her greetings, in the lady before me whose features were so eroded that the original lines of her face could no longer be restored. For three years she had been taking cocaine and other drugs. Her eyes, deeply ringed with black, were almost frantic, and her mouth opened in a ghastly grin. She spent months on end now, I was told, without leaving her bed or her *chaise longue*, and had got up just for this party. Time has, it seems, special express trains which bring their passengers swiftly to a premature old age. But on the parallel track trains almost as rapid may be moving in the opposite direction. I took M. de Courgivaux for his son, for he looked the younger of the two—though he must have been more than fifty, he seemed younger than he had when he was thirty. He had found an intelligent doctor and given up alcohol and salt, and the result was that he had returned to his early thirties and on this particular day looked even younger still, for the reason that, that very morning, he had had his hair cut.

A curious thing was that the phenomenon of old age seemed, in its different modes, to take into account certain social habits. Thus certain great noblemen, who had always worn the plainest alpaca cloth and on their heads old straw hats which a man of the lower middle class would have refused to put on, had aged in the same fashion as the gardeners and the peasants in whose society they had spent their lives. Patches of brown had begun to spread over their cheeks and their faces had turned yellower and darker like the pages of an old book.

I thought also of all those who were not at the party because they were too weak or too ill to be there, those whom their secretary, seeking to give the illusion of their survival, had excused by one of those telegrams which from time to time were handed to the Princess, those invalids, moribund for years, who no longer leave their beds, no longer move, and even in the midst of the frivolous attentions of visitors, drawn to them by the curiosity of a tourist or the pious hopes of a pilgrim, with their eyes closed and their rosaries clutched in hands which feebly push back the sheet that is already a mortuary shroud, are like monumental figures, carved by illness until the skeleton is barely covered by a flesh which is white and rigid as marble, lying stretched upon a tomb.

There were men in the room whom I knew to be related to each other without it ever having crossed my mind that they had a feature in common. In admiring, for instance, the old hermit with white hair who was Legrandin in a new guise, I suddenly observed, with the satisfaction almost of a zoologist when he makes a scientific discovery, in the transitions between the planes of his cheeks the same construction as in the cheeks of his young nephew, Léonor de Cambremer, who appeared nevertheless to bear no resemblance to him; and to this first common feature I added another which I had never yet noticed in Léonor de Cambremer, and then again others, none of which was included in the youthful synthesis of the nephew which habitually presented itself to me, until soon I had of him a caricature which was truer and more profound for not being a literal representation: his uncle now seemed to me simply a young Cambremer who to amuse himself had assumed the countenance of the old man that he would in fact one day be, so that now it was not merely what had become of the young men of my own youth but what would one day become of those of today that impressed upon me with such force the sensation of Time.

The women sought to remain in contact with whatever had been most individual in their charm, but often the new matter of their face no longer lent itself to this purpose. Those features upon which had been engraved, if not their youth, at least their beauty, had disappeared, and they had endeavoured, with the face that remained to them, to construct a new beauty for themselves. Displacing, if not the centre of gravity, at least the central point of the perspective of their face, and grouping their features around it in a new pattern, they began at the age of fifty to display a beauty of a new type, in the same way that late in life a man may embark on a new profession or a piece of ground which has become useless as a vineyard may be turned over to the production of sugar beet. And in the midst of these new features a second youth was made to bloom. The only women who failed to adjust themselves to this kind of transformation were the ones who were either too beautiful or too ugly. The former were like some block of marble, the lines in which, once it has been carved, are final and admit of no change; ageing, they merely crumbled away like a statue. The others, those who had some deformity of face, actually had certain advantages over the beautiful women. In the first place they were the only women whom one instantly recognised. One knew, for example, that in the whole of Paris there could only be one mouth like *that*, so that at this party, where I failed to recognise almost everybody, I could at least put a name to the possessor of the mouth. And then they did not even appear to have aged. Old age is something human; these were monsters, and they no more seemed to have "changed" than whales.

Others too, both men and women, seemed not to have aged; their figures were just as slim, their faces as young. But if, to speak to them, one approached rather near to the face with the smooth skin and the delicate contours it then appeared quite different, like the surface of a plant or a drop of water or blood when you look at it under a microscope. At close quarters I could distinguish numerous greasy patches on the skin which I had supposed to be smooth and which now, because of these marks, I found repulsive. Nor could the lines of the face stand up to this magnification. That of the nose was seen now to be broken and rounded, its regularity marred by the same oily patches as the rest of the face; and the eyes at short range retreated behind pockets of flesh which destroyed the resemblance of the person before me to the one whom I had known in the past and thought that I had met again. So that these particular guests were young when seen at a distance but their age increased with the enlargement of the face and the possibility of studying its different planes; it was dependent upon the spectator, who to see them as young had to place himself correctly and to view them only with that distant inspection which diminishes its object like the lens selected by an oculist for a long-sighted elderly person; old age here, like the presence of infusoria in a drop of water, was made apparent not so much by the advance of the years as by a greater degree of accuracy in the scale of the observer's vision.

Some women no doubt were still easily recognisable: their faces had remained almost the same and they had merely, out of propriety and in harmony with the season, put on the grey hair which was their autumn attire. But there were others, and there were men too, whose metamorphosis was so complete, their identity so impossible to establish—that old monk, for instance, in a corner of the room and the notorious rake whom one remembered, were they the same person?—that it was of the art not so much of the actor as of certain prodigiously gifted mimes, of whom the supreme example is Fregoli, that these fabulous transformations reminded one. The old woman whose charm had resided in her indefinable and melancholy smile would have liked to weep, at first, when she realised that this smile could no longer break through with its radiance to the surface of the plaster mask with which age had covered her face. Then suddenly, weary of trying to please and finding it more intelligent, more amusing to resign herself to the inevitable, she had started to use it like a mask in the theatre, as a way of making people laugh. But with few exceptions the women strained every nerve in a ceaseless struggle against old age and held out the mirror of their features towards beauty, as it receded, as to a setting sun whose last rays they longed passionately to preserve. To achieve this end some of them tried to plane away all the irregularities of their face, to enlarge its smooth, white surface, renouncing the piquancy of dimples that had not long to live, the archness of a smile condemned and already half disarmed, while others, seeing that beauty had vanished beyond recall and taking refuge perforce in expression,

like an actress whose skill in the art of diction makes up
for the loss of her voice, clung desperately to a pout, to a pretty
crow's-foot, to a dreamy glance, to a smile sometimes which,
because of the incoordination of muscles that no longer obeyed
the brain, made them look as though they were in tears.

Even in the case of the men who had changed very little—
those, for instance, whose moustaches had merely turned white
—one felt that the changes were not strictly speaking material.
One might have been looking at these men through a vapour
which imparted its own colour to them, or through a tinted
optical glass which altered the appearance of their faces and
above all, by making them slightly blurred, showed one that
what it enabled us to see "life-size" was in reality a long way
away, separated from us, it is true, by a distance other than
spatial but from the depths of which, nevertheless, as from a
further shore, we felt that they had as much difficulty in recognising us as we them. Only perhaps Mme de Forcheville, as
though she had been injected with some liquid, some sort of
paraffin with the property of inflating the skin but protecting it
from change, might have been an old-fashioned *cocotte* "stuffed"
for the benefit of posterity. Setting out from the idea that
people have remained unchanged, one finds them old. But once
one starts with the idea that they are old, meeting them again
one does not think that they look too bad. In the case of
Odette one could say much more than this; her appearance,
once one knew her age and expected to see an old woman,
seemed a defiance of the laws of chronology, more miraculous
even than the defiance of the laws of nature by the conservation
of radium. If I failed at first to recognise her, this was, uniquely,
not because she had but because she had not changed. I had
learnt in the last hour to take into account the new items that
are added to people by Time and that had to be subtracted by
me if I wanted to find my friends again as I had known them
in the past, and I now rapidly made this calculation, adding to
the old Odette the number of years which had passed over her;
but the result at which I arrived was a person who could not, it
seemed, be the one before me, precisely because she, the woman
at the party, was so like the Odette of old days. In part, of
course, this effect was achieved by rouge and dye. Beneath her

flat golden hair—a little like the ruffled chignon of a big mechanical doll, above a face with a fixed expression of surprise which might also have belonged to a doll—on top of which rested a straw hat that was also flat, she might well have been "The Exhibition of 1878" (of which she would without a doubt, above all had she then been as old as she was to-day, have been the most fantastic marvel) coming forward on to the stage to speak her two lines in a New Year revue, but the Exhibition of 1878 played by an actress who was still young.

Another figure from the same period, who had been a minister before the era of Boulangism and was now in the government again, passed beside us, wafting to the ladies a tremulous and remote smile, but with the air of being imprisoned in a thousand chains of the past, like a little phantom paraded up and down by an invisible hand or—diminished in stature and altered in substance—a reduced version of himself in pumice stone. This former Prime Minister, now so well received in the Faubourg Saint-Germain, had at one time been the object of criminal proceedings, and had been execrated both by society and by the people. But thanks to the renewal of the individuals who compose these two bodies and to the renewal, within the surviving individuals, of passions and even of memories, nobody now knew this and he was held in high honour. For the fact is that there is no humiliation so great that one should not accept it with unconcern, knowing that at the end of a few years our misdeeds will be no more than an invisible dust buried beneath the smiling and blooming peace of nature. The man whose reputation is momentarily under a cloud will soon find himself, thanks to the balancing mechanism of Time, caught and held between two new social levels which will have for him nothing but deference and admiration. But Time alone will achieve this result and at the moment of his downfall nothing can console him for the fact that the young dairy-maid across the street heard the crowd shout "Bribery and corruption!" at him and saw them shake their fists as he climbed into the Black Maria—for the dairy-maid does not see things in the perspective of Time and does not know that the men who receive the incense of praise from this morning's newspapers were yesterday in disgrace and that the fallen politician, who at this moment feels the shadow of prison bars upon him and yet perhaps, as he thinks of the dairy-maid, cannot find within himself the humble words which might win her sympathy, will one day be extolled by the press and sought after by duchesses. And Time in the same way makes family quarrels recede into the distance. At the Princesse de Guermantes's party, for instance, there was a couple, husband and wife, who were respectively nephew and niece of two men, now dead, who had once come to blows and—worse still—one of them, still further to humiliate the other, had sent him as witnesses his concierge and his butler, indicating that in his judgment gentlemen would have been too good for him. But these stories slumbered in the pages of the newspapers of thirty years ago and nobody now remembered them. And thus the drawing-room of the Princesse de Guermantes—illuminated, oblivious, flowery—was like a peaceful cemetery. Time in this room had done more than decompose the living creatures of a former age, it had rendered possible, had created new associations.

To return to the politician, in spite of his change of physical substance, just as profound as the transformation of the moral ideas which his name now connoted to the public, in spite (to say the same thing more simply) of the lapse of so many years since he had been Prime Minister, he was once again a member of the Cabinet, whose leader had given him a portfolio in the recent re-shuffle rather in the way that a theatrical producer gives a part to an old actress friend long since retired, whom he judges nevertheless to be, even now, better able to interpret a part with subtlety than any of her younger successors and whom he knows, also, to be in financial straits, and who in the event, at the age of nearly eighty, exhibits once more to the public almost the fullness of her talent, with that continued vitality which one is later astonished to have observed up to the very threshold of death.

But if the politician was extraordinary, Mme de Forcheville was so miraculous that one could not even say that she had grown young again—it was more as though, with all her carmines and her russets, she had bloomed for a second time. Even more than the embodiment of the Universal Exhibition of 1878, she might have been the principal rarity and attraction of a flower show of to-day. And indeed, for me she seemed to say, not so much: "I am the Exhibition of 1878" as: "I am the Allée des Acacias of 1892." That was where, it seemed, she still might have been. And just because she had not changed she seemed scarcely to be alive. She looked like a rose that has been sterilised. I greeted her and her eyes travelled for a while over my face, searching for my name as a schoolboy searches on the face of his examiner for the answer that he might more easily have found in his own head. Then I told her who I was and at once, as though the sound of my name had broken a spell and I had lost the look of an arbutus tree or a kangaroo which age no doubt had given me, she recognised me and started to talk to me in that strangely individual voice which people who had admired her acting in some little theatre were astonished, when they were invited to meet her at a luncheon party, to find again, throughout the whole conversation, for as long as they cared to listen, in each one of her remarks. It was a voice that had not changed, exaggeratedly warm, caressing, with a trace of an English accent. And yet, just as her eyes appeared to be looking at me from a distant shore, her voice was sad, almost suppliant, like the voice of the shades in the *Odyssey*. Odette would still have been able to act. I complimented her on her youthfulness. "How nice of you, *my dear*," she said, "thank you," and, as it was difficult for her to express a sentiment, even the most sincere, in a manner that was not rendered artificial by her anxiety to be what she supposed was smart, she repeated several times: "Thank you *so* much, thank you *so* much." I meanwhile, who had once walked miles to see her pass in the Bois, who the first time that I had visited her house had listened to the sound of her voice as it fell from her lips as though it were some priceless treasure, now found the minutes that I was obliged to pass in her company interminable simply because I did not know what on earth to say to her, and I withdrew, thinking to myself that not only had Gilberte's remark, "You take me for my mother" been true,[47] but that the likeness could only be flattering to the daughter.

Gilberte, for that matter, was by no means the only guest at the party in whom family features had become apparent which hitherto had remained as invisible in their faces as the coiled and hidden parts of a seed which one day will burst out into growth in a manner that it is impossible to foresee. Thus, in this woman or that man, at about the age of fifty an enormous maternal hook had arrived to transform a nose which until then had been straight and pure. And the complexion of another woman, a banker's daughter, from being as fresh as that of a milkmaid grew first russet and then coppery and finally assumed as it were a reflection of the gold which her father had so lovingly handled. Some people had even in the end come to resemble the district in which they lived, bearing on their faces a sort of replica of the Rue de l'Arcade or the Avenue du Bois or the Rue de l'Elysée. But most commonly they reproduced the features of their parents.

Alas, Mme de Forcheville's second flowering was not to last for ever. Less than three years later I was to see her at an evening party given by Gilberte, not quite in her dotage but showing signs of senility and grown incapable of concealing beneath a mask of immobility what she was thinking, or rather (for thinking is too elevated a term) what she was passively experiencing, nodding her head, compressing her lips, shaking her shoulders in response to every impression that she felt, like a drunkard or a small child or those poets who, unaware of their surroundings and seized by inspiration, compose verses in the midst of a social occasion and frown and pout as they proceed to the dinner-table with an astonished lady on their arm. The impressions of Mme de Forcheville—save that single sentiment which was the cause of her presence at the party: her tender affection for her beloved daughter and her pride that she should be giving so brilliant a party, a pride which, in the mother, could not disguise the melancholy of being herself now nothing —these impressions were not joyful, their message was merely that she must not relax her defence against the snubs which were showered upon her, a defence, however, as timorous as that of a child. On all sides one heard people say: "I don't know whether Mme de Forcheville recognises me, perhaps I ought to get someone to introduce me to her again." "You may as well spare yourself the trouble," a booming voice would reply, its owner not suspecting that Gilberte's mother could hear every word—or perhaps not caring if she could. "It's quite unnecessary. You wouldn't find her at all amusing! She's best left alone in her corner. She's a bit gaga, you know." Furtively Mme de Forcheville shot a glance from her eyes which had remained so beautiful at the authors of these offensive remarks, then swiftly withdrew it for fear of having been rude, but was distressed nevertheless by the insult, and though she smothered her feeble indignation one saw her head shake and her breast heave until presently another glance was shot at another guest who had expressed himself just as discourteously—yet nothing of all this seemed to surprise her very much, for having felt extremely unwell for several days, she had covertly suggested to her daughter that she should put off her party, but her daughter had refused. Mme de Forcheville did not love her any the less: the sight of all the duchesses entering the room, the admiration of all the guests for the large new house, flooded her heart with joy, and when finally the Marquise de Sabran was announced, who was at that moment the lady at whom one arrived after laboriously ascending the topmost rungs of the social ladder, Mme de Forcheville felt that she had been a good and far-sighted mother and that her maternal task was accomplished. New guests arrived to titter at her and again she shot her glances and spoke to herself, if a mute language expressed only in gesture can be described as speech. Beautiful still, she had become—what she had never been in the past—infinitely pathetic; she who had been unfaithful to Swann and to everybody found now that the entire universe was unfaithful to her, and so weak had she become that, the roles being reversed, she no longer dared to defend herself even against men. And soon she would not defend herself even against death. But we have anticipated, and let us now go back three years, to the afternoon party which is being given by the Princesse de Guermantes.

I had difficulty in recognising my friend Bloch, who was now in fact no longer Bloch since he had adopted, not merely as a pseudonym but as a name, the style of Jacques du Rozier, beneath which it would have needed my grandfather's flair to detect the "sweet vale of Hebron" and those "chains of Israel" which my old schoolmate seemed definitively to have broken.

Indeed an English *chic* had completely transformed his appearance and smoothed away, as with a plane, everything in it that was susceptible of such treatment. The once curly hair, now brushed flat, with a parting in the middle, glistened with brilliantine. His nose remained large and red, but seemed now to owe its tumescence to a sort of permanent cold which served also to explain the nasal intonation with which he languidly delivered his studied sentences, for just as he had found a way of doing his hair which suited his complexion, so he had found a voice which suited his pronunciation and which gave to his old nasal twang the air of a disdainful refusal to articulate that was in keeping with his inflamed nostrils. And thanks to the way in which he brushed his hair, to the suppression of his moustache, to the elegance of his whole figure—thanks, that is to say, to his determination—his Jewish nose was now scarcely more visible than is the deformity of a hunch-backed woman who skilfully arranges her appearance. But above all—and one saw this the moment one set eyes on him—the significance of his physiognomy had been altered by a formidable monocle. By introducing an element of machinery into Bloch's face this monocle absolved it of all those difficult duties which a human face is normally called upon to discharge, such as being beautiful or expressing intelligence or kindliness or effort. The monocle's mere presence even absolved an interlocutor, in the first place, from asking himself whether the face was pleasant to look at or not, just as, when a shop-assistant has told you that some object imported from England is "the last word in *chic*," you no longer dare to ask yourself whether you really like it. In any case, behind the lens of this monocle Bloch was now installed in a position as lofty, as remote and as comfortable as if it had been the glass partition of a limousine and, so that his face should match the smooth hair and the monocle, his features never now expressed anything at all.

Bloch asked me to introduce him to the Prince de Guermantes, and this operation raised for me not a shadow of those difficulties which I had come up against on the day when I went to an evening party at his house for the first time, difficulties which had then seemed to me a part of the natural order whereas now I found it the simplest thing in the world to introduce to the Prince a guest whom he had invited himself and I should even have ventured, without warning, to bring to his party and introduce to him someone whom he had not invited. Was this because, since that distant era, I had become an intimate member, though for a long time now a forgotten one, of that fashionable world in which I had then been so new? Was it, on the contrary, because I did not really belong to that world, so that all the imaginary difficulties which beset people in society no longer existed for me once my shyness had vanished? Was it because, having gradually come to see what lay behind the first (and often the second and even the third) artificial appearance of others, I sensed behind the haughty disdain of the Prince a great human avidity to know people, to make the acquaintance even of those whom he affected to despise? Was it also because the Prince himself had changed, like so many men in whom the arrogance of their youth and of their middle years is tempered by the gentleness of old age—particularly as the new men and the unknown ideas whose progress they had once resisted are now familiar to them, at least by sight, and they see that they are accepted all round them in society—a change which takes place more effectually if old age is assisted in its task by some good quality or some vice in the individual which enlarges the circle of his acquaintance, or by the revolution wrought by a political conversion such as that of the Prince to Dreyfusism?

Bloch started to question me, as years ago, when I first began to go to parties, I had questioned others—a habit which I had not quite lost—about the people whom I had known in society in the old days and who were as remote, as unlike anybody else, as those inhabitants of the world of Combray whom I had often sought to "place" exactly. But Combray for me had a shape so distinctive, so impossible to confuse with anything else, that it might have been a piece of a jig-saw puzzle which I could never succeed in fitting into the map of France. "So the Prince de Guermantes can give me no idea either of Swann or of M. de Charlus?" asked Bloch, whose manner of speaking I had borrowed long ago and who now frequently imitated mine. "None at all." "But what was so different about them?" "To know that, you would have had to hear them talk yourself.

But that is impossible. Swann is dead and M. de Charlus is as good as dead. But the differences were enormous." And seeing Bloch's eyes shine at the thought of what these marvellous personages must have been, I wondered whether I was not exaggerating the pleasure which I had got from their company, since pleasure was something that I had never felt except when I was alone and the real differentiation of impressions takes place only in our imagination. Bloch seemed to guess what I was thinking. "Perhaps you make it out to be more wonderful than it really was," he said; "our hostess to-day, for instance, the Princesse de Guermantes, I know she is no longer young, still it is not so many years since you were telling me about her incomparable charm, her marvellous beauty. Well, I grant you she has a certain splendour, and she certainly has those extraordinary eyes you used to talk about, but I can't say I find her so fantastically beautiful. Of course, one sees that she is a real aristocrat, but still. . . ." I was obliged to tell Bloch that the woman I had described to him was not the one he was talking about. The Princesse de Guermantes had died and the present wife of the Prince, who had been ruined by the collapse of Germany, was the former Mme Verdurin. "That can't be right, I looked in this year's Gotha," Bloch naïvely confessed to me, "and I found the Prince de Guermantes, living at this address where we are now and married to someone of the utmost grandeur, let me try to remember, yes, married to Sidonie, Duchesse de Duras, née des Baux." This was correct. Mme Verdurin, shortly after the death of her husband, had married the aged and impoverished Duc de Duras, who had made her a cousin of the Prince de Guermantes and had died after two years of marriage. He had served as a useful transition for Mme Verdurin, who now, by a third marriage, had become Princesse de Guermantes and occupied in the Faubourg Saint-Germain a lofty position which would have caused much astonishment at Combray, where the ladies of the Rue de l'Oiseau, Mme Goupil's daughter and Mme Sazerat's step-daughter, had during these last years, before she married for the third time, spoken with a sneer of "the Duchesse de Duras" as though this were a role which had been allotted to Mme Verdurin in a play. In fact, the Combray principle of caste requiring that she should die, as she had lived, as Mme Verdurin, her title, which was not deemed to confer upon her any new power in society, did not so much enhance as damage her reputation. For "to make tongues wag," that phrase which in every sphere of life is applied to a woman who has a lover, could be used also in the Faubourg Saint-Germain of women who write books and in the respectable society of Combray of those who make marriages which, for better or for worse, are "unsuitable." After the twice-widowed lady had married the Prince de Guermantes, the only possible comment was that he was a false Guermantes, an impostor. For me, in this purely nominal identity, in the fact that there was once again a Princesse de Guermantes and that she had absolutely nothing in common with the one who had cast her spell upon me, who now no longer existed and had been robbed of name and title like a defenceless woman of her jewels, there was something as profoundly sad as in seeing the material objects which the Princess Hedwige had once possessed—her country house and everything that had been hers—pass into the possession and enjoyment of another woman. The succession of a new individual to a name is melancholy, as is all succession, all usurpation of property; and yet for ever and ever, without interruption, there would come, sweeping on, a flood of new Princesses de Guermantes—or rather, centuries old, replaced from age to age by a series of different women, of different actresses playing the same part and then each in her turn sinking from sight beneath the unvarying and immemorial placidity of the name, one single Princesse de Guermantes, ignorant of death and indifferent to all that changes and wounds our mortal hearts.

Of course, even these external changes in the figures whom I had known were no more than symbols of an internal change which had been effected day by day. Perhaps these people had continued to perform the same actions, but gradually the idea which they entertained both of their own activities and of their acquaintances had slightly altered its shape, so that at the end of a few years, though the names were unchanged, the activities that they enjoyed and the people whom they loved had become different and, as they themselves had become different individuals, it was hardly surprising that they should have new faces.

But there were also guests whom I failed to recognise for the reason that I had never known them, for in this drawing-room, as well as upon individuals the chemistry of Time had been at work upon society. This coterie, within the specific nature of which, delimited as it was by certain affinities that attracted to it all the great princely names of Europe and by forces of an opposite kind which repelled from it anything that was not aristocratic, I had found, I thought, a sort of corporeal refuge for the name of Guermantes, this coterie, which had seemed to confer upon that name its ultimate reality, had itself, in its innermost and as I had thought stable constitution, undergone a profound transformation. The presence of people whom I had seen in quite different social settings and whom I would never have expected to penetrate into this one, astonished me less than the intimate familiarity with which they were now received in it, on Christian name terms; a certain complex of aristocratic prejudices, of snobbery, which in the past automatically maintained a barrier between the name of Guermantes and all that did not harmonise with it, had ceased to function. Enfeebled or broken, the springs of the machine could no longer perform their task of keeping out the crowd; a thousand alien elements made their way in and all homogeneity, all consistency of form and colour was lost. The Faubourg Saint-Germain was like some senile dowager now, who replies only with timid smiles to the insolent servants who invade her drawing-rooms, drink her orangeade, present their mistresses to her. However, the sensation of time having slipped away and of the annihilation of a small part of my own past was conveyed to me less vividly by the destruction of that coherent whole which the Guermantes drawing-room had once been than by the annihilation of even the knowledge of the thousand reasons, the thousand subtle distinctions thanks to which one man who was still to be found in that drawing-room to-day was clearly in his natural and proper place there while another, who rubbed shoulders with him, wore in these surroundings an aspect of dubious novelty. And this ignorance was not merely ignorance of society, but of politics, of everything. For memory was of shorter duration in individuals than life, and besides, the very young, who had never possessed the recollections which had vanished from the minds of their elders, now formed part of society (and with perfect legitimacy, even in the genealogical sense of the word), and the origins of the people whom they saw there being forgotten or unknown, they accepted them at the particular point of their elevation or their fall at which they found them, supposing that things had always been as they were to-day, that the social position of Mme Swann and the Princesse de Guermantes and Bloch had always been very great, that Clemenceau and Viviani had always been conservatives. And as certain facts have a greater power of survival than others, the detested memory of the Dreyfus case persisting vaguely in these young people thanks to what they had heard their fathers say, if one told them that Clemenceau had been a Dreyfusard, they replied: "Impossible, you are making a confusion, he is absolutely on the other side of the fence." Ministers with a tarnished reputation and women who had started life as prostitutes were now held to be paragons of virtue. (Among the guests was a distinguished man who had recently, in a famous lawsuit, made a deposition of which the sole value resided in the lofty moral character of the witness, in the face of which both judge and counsel had bowed their heads, with the result that two people had been convicted. Consequently, when he entered the room there was a stir of curiosity and of deference. This man was Morel. I was perhaps the only person present who knew that he had once been kept by Saint-Loup and at the same time by a friend of Saint-Loup. In spite of these recollections he greeted me with pleasure, though with a certain reserve. He remembered the time when we had seen each other at Balbec, and these recollections had for him the poetry and the melancholy of youth.) Someone having inquired of a young man of the best possible family whether Gilberte's mother had not formerly been the subject of scandal, the young nobleman replied that it was true that in the earlier part of her life she had been married to an adventurer of the name of Swann, but that subsequently she had married one of the most prominent men in society, the Comte de Forcheville. No doubt there were still a few people in the room —the Duchesse de Guermantes was one—who would have smiled at this assertion (which, in its denial of Swann's position as a man of fashion, seemed to me monstrous, although I my-self, long ago at Combray, had shared my great-aunt's belief that Swann could not be acquainted with "princesses"), and others also not in the room, women who might have been there had they not almost ceased to leave their homes, the Duchesses of Montmorency and Mouchy and Sagan, who had been close friends of Swann and had never set eyes on this man Forche-ville, who was not received in society at the time when they went to parties. But it could not be denied that the society of those days, like the faces now drastically altered and the fair hair replaced by white, existed now only in the memories of individuals whose number was diminishing day by day. During the war Bloch had given up going out socially, had ceased to visit the houses which he had once frequented and where he had cut anything but a brilliant figure. On the other hand, he had published a whole series of works full of those absurd sophistical arguments which, so as not to be inhibited by them myself, I was struggling to demolish to-day, works without originality but which gave to young men and to many society women the impression of a rare and lofty intellect, a sort of genius. And so it was after a complete break between his earlier social existence and this later one that he had, in a society itself reconstituted, embarked upon a new phase of his life, honoured and glorious, in which he played the role of a great man. Young people naturally did not know that at his somewhat advanced age he was in fact making his first appearance on the social scene, particularly as, by sprinkling his conversation with the few names which he had retained from his acquaintance with Saint-Loup, he was able to impart to his prestige of the moment a sort of indefinite recession in depth. In any case he was regarded as one of those men of talent who in every epoch have flourished in the highest society, and nobody thought that he had ever frequented any other.

Survivors of the older generation assured me that society had completely changed and now opened its doors to people who in their day would never have been received, and this comment was both true and untrue. On the one hand it was untrue, because those who made it failed to take into account the curve of time which caused the society of the present to see these newly received people at their point of arrival, whilst they, the older generation, remembered them at their point of departure. And this was nothing new, for in the same way, when they themselves had first entered society, there were people in it who had just arrived and whose lowly origins others remembered. In society as it exists to-day a single generation suffices for the change which formerly over a period of centuries transformed a middle-class name like Colbert into an aristocratic one. And yet, from another point of view there was a certain truth in the comments; for, if the social position of individuals is liable to change (like the fortunes and the alliances and the hatreds of nations), so too are the most deeply rooted ideas and customs and among them even the idea that you cannot receive anybody who is not *chic*. Not only does snobbishness change in form, it might one day altogether disappear—like war itself—and radicals and Jews might become members of the Jockey. Some people, who in my own early days in society, giving grand dinner-parties with only such guests as the Princesse de Guermantes, the Duchesse de Guermantes and the Princesse de Parme, and themselves being entertained by these ladies with every show of respect, had been regarded, perhaps correctly, as among the most unimpeachable social figures of the time, had passed away without leaving any trace behind them. Possibly they were foreign diplomats, formerly *en poste* in Paris and now returned to their own countries. Perhaps a scandal, a suicide, an elopement had made it impossible for them to reappear in society; perhaps they were merely Germans. But their name owed its lustre only to their own vanished social position and was no longer borne by anyone in the fashionable world: if I mentioned them nobody knew whom I was talking about, if I spelt out the name the general assumption was that they were some sort of adventurers. People, on the other hand, who according to the social code with which I had been familiar ought not to have been at this party, were now to my great astonishment on terms of close friendship with women of the very best families and the latter had only submitted to the boredom of appearing at the Princess de Guermantes's party for the sake of these new friends. For the most characteristic feature of this new society was the prodigious ease with which individuals moved up or down the social scale.

If in the eyes of the younger generations the Duchesse de Guermantes seemed to be of little account because she was acquainted with actresses and such people, the elder, the now old ladies of her family, still considered her to be an extraordinary personage, partly because they knew and appreciated her birth, her heraldic pre-eminence, her intimate friendships with what Mme de Forcheville would have called *royalties*, but even more because she despised the parties given by the family and was bored at them and her cousins knew that they could never count upon her attendance. Her connexions with the theatrical and political worlds, in any case only vaguely known in the family, merely had the effect of enhancing her rarity and therefore her prestige. So that while in political and artistic society she was regarded as a creature whom it was hard to define, a sort of unfrocked priestess of the Faubourg Saint-Germain who consorted with Under-Secretaries of State and stars of the theatre, in the Faubourg Saint-German itself if one was giving an important evening party one would say: "Is it worth while even asking Oriane? She won't come. Perhaps one should, just for form's sake, but one knows what to expect." And if, at about half past ten, in a dazzling costume and with a hard glint in her eyes which bore witness to her contempt for all her female cousins, Oriane made her entrance, pausing first on the threshold with a sort of majestic disdain, and remained for a whole hour, this was even more of a treat for the old and noble lady who was giving the party than it would have been in the past for a theatrical manager who had obtained a vague promise from Sarah Bernhardt that she would contribute something to a programme, had the great actress, contrary to all expectation, turned up and recited, in the most unaffected and obliging way, not the piece which she had promised but twenty others. For although all the women there were among the smartest in Paris, the presence of this Oriane who was addressed in a condescending manner by Under-Secretaries and continued none the less ("intelligence governs the world") to try to make the acquaintance of more and more of them, had had the effect which nothing could have achieved without her, of placing the dowager's evening party in a class apart from and above all the other dowagers' evening parties of the same *season* (to use another of those English expressions of which Mme de Forcheville was so fond) which she, Oriane, had not taken the trouble to attend.

As soon as I had finished talking to the Prince de Guermantes, Bloch seized hold of me and introduced me to a young woman who had heard a lot about me from the Duchesse de Guermantes and who was one of the most fashionable women of the day. Not only was her name entirely unknown to me, but it appeared that those of the various branches of the Guermantes family could not be very familiar to her, for she inquired of an American woman how it was that Mme de Saint-Loup seemed to be on such intimate terms with all the most aristocratic people in the room. Now the American was married to the Comte de Farcy, an obscure cousin of the Forchevilles, for whom Forcheville was the grandest name in the world. So she replied ingenuously: "Well, isn't she a Forcheville by birth? And what could be grander than that?" But at least Mme de Farcy, though she naïvely believed the name of Forcheville to be superior to that of Saint-Loup, knew something about the latter. But to the charming lady who was a friend of Bloch and the Duchesse de Guermantes it was utterly unknown, and, being somewhat muddleheaded, she replied in all good faith to a young girl who asked her how Mme de Saint-Loup was related to their host, the Prince de Guermantes: "Through the Forchevilles," a piece of information which the girl passed on as if she had known it all her life to one of her friends, a bad-tempered and nervous girl, who turned as red as a turkey cock the first time a gentleman said to her that it was not through the Forchevilles that Gilberte was connected with the Guermantes, with the result that the gentleman supposed that he had made a mistake, adopted the erroneous explanation himself and lost no time in propagating it. For the American woman dinner-parties and fashionable entertainments were a sort of Berlitz School. She heard the names and she repeated them, without having first learnt their precise value and significance. To someone who asked whether Tansonville had come to Gilberte from her father M. de Forcheville I heard the explanation given that, on the contrary, it was a property in her husband's family, that Tansonville was a neighbouring estate to Guermantes and had belonged to Mme de Marsantes, that it had been heavily mortgaged and the mortgage paid off with Gilberte's dowry. And finally, a veteran of the old guard having exchanged memories with me of Swann, friend of the Sagans and the Mouchys, and Bloch's American friend having asked me how I had known Swann, the old man declared that this must have been in the house of Mme de Guermantes, not suspecting that what Swann represented for me was a country neighbour and a young friend of my grandfather. Mistakes of this kind have been made by the most distinguished men and are regarded as particularly serious in any society of a conservative temper. Saint-Simon, wishing to show that Louis XIV was of an ignorance which "sometimes made him fall, in public, into the most gross absurdities," gives of this ignorance only two examples, which are that the King, not knowing either that Renel belonged to the family of Clermont-Gallerande or that Saint-Herem belonged to that of Montmorin, treated these two men as though they were of low extraction. But at least, in so far as concerns Saint-Herem, we have the consolation of knowing that the King did not die in error, for "very late in life" he was disabused by M. de La Rochefoucauld. "Even then," adds Saint-Simon with a touch of pity, "it was necessary to explain to him what these houses were, for their names conveyed nothing to him."

This forgetfulness, which with its vigorous growth covers so rapidly even the most recent past, this encroaching ignorance, creates as its own counter-agent a minor species of erudition, all the more precious for being rare, which is concerned with genealogies, the true social position of people, the reasons of love or money or some other kind for which they have allied or misallied themselves in marriage with this family or that, an erudition which is highly prized in all societies where a conservative spirit rules, which my grandfather possessed in the highest degree with regard to the middle classes of Combray and of Paris and which Saint-Simon valued so highly that when he comes to celebrate the marvellous intelligence of the Prince de Conti, before speaking of the recognised branches of knowledge, or rather as though this were the first of them all, he praises him as "a man of a very fine mind, enlightened, just, exact, wide-ranging; vastly well read and of a retentive memory; skilled in genealogies, their chimeras and their realities; of a politeness variously accommodated to rank and merit, rendering all those courtesies that the princes of the blood owe but no longer render and even explaining why he acted as he did and how the other princes exceeded their rights. The knowledge which he had gained from books and from conversation afforded him material for the most obliging comments possible upon the birth, the offices, etc." In a less exalted sphere, in all that pertained to the bourgeois society of Combray and Paris, my grandfather possessed this same knowledge with no less exactitude and savoured it with no less relish. The epicures, the connoisseurs who knew that Gilberte was not a Forcheville, that Mme de Cambremer had not been born a Méséglise nor her nephew's young wife a Valentinois, were already reduced in number. Reduced in number and perhaps not even recruited from among the highest aristocracy (it is not necessarily among devout believers, or even among Catholics of any kind, that you will find those who are most learned on the subject of the *Golden Legend* or the stained glass of the thirteenth century), but often from a minor aristocracy, whose scions have a keener appetite for the high society which they themselves can seldom approach and which the little time that they spend in it leaves them all the more leisure to study. Still, they meet together from time to time and enjoy making each other's acquaintance and giving succulent corporate dinners, like those of the Society of Bibliophiles or the Friends of Rheims, at which the items on the menu are genealogies. To these feasts wives are not admitted, but the husbands, when they get home, remark: "A most interesting dinner. There was a M. de la Raspelière there who kept us spell-bound with his explanation of how that Mme de Saint-Loup with the pretty daughter is not really a Forcheville at all. It was as good as a novel."

The friend of Bloch and of the Duchesse de Guermantes was not only beautifully dressed and charming, she was also intelligent and conversation with her was agreeable, but for me rendered difficult by the novelty to my ears of the names not only of my interlocutress herself but also of most of the people she talked about, although they were the very people who formed the core of society to-day. The converse also was true: at her request I related various anecdotes of the past, and many of the names which I pronounced meant absolutely nothing to her, they had all sunk into oblivion (all those at least which had shone only with the individual brilliance of a single person and were not the surname, permanent and generic, of some famous aristocratic family, whose exact title even so the young woman seldom knew, having perhaps recently misheard a name at a dinner-party and proceeded to form quite wrong ideas about its pedigree) and she had for the most part never heard them mentioned, having, not merely because she was young but because she had not lived in France for long and when she first arrived had known nobody, only started to go into society some years after I myself had withdrawn from it. So that though for ordinary speech she and I used the same language, when it came to names our vocabularies had nothing in common. The name of Mme Leroi happened to fall from my lips, and by chance, thanks to some elderly admirer, himself an old friend of Mme de Guermantes, my interlocutress had heard of her. But only vaguely and inaccurately, as I saw from the contemptuous tone in which this snobbish young woman replied to me: "Yes, I know who you mean by Mme Leroi, an old friend of Bergotte's, I believe," a tone which barely concealed the comment: "a woman whom I should never have wished to have in my house." I realised at once that the old friend of Mme de Guermantes, as a perfect man of the world imbued with the Guermantes spirit, one of the essential elements of which was not to appear to attach too much importance to aristocratic friendships, had thought it too stupid, too anti-Guermantes to say: "Mme Leroi, who was a friend of every Royalty and Duchess in Paris," and had preferred to say: "She could be quite amusing. Let me tell you the retort she made to Bergotte one day." But for people who are not already in the know information gleaned in this way from conversation is equivalent only to that which is doled out to the masses by the press and which makes them believe alternatively, depending upon the views of their newspaper, either that M. Loubet and M. Reinach are brigands or that they are great patriots. In the eyes of my interlocutress Mme Leroi had been something like Mme Verdurin as she was before her social transformation, but with less brilliance and with a little clan consisting of one member only, Bergotte. But at least this young woman, by pure chance, had heard the name of Mme Leroi, and she is one of the last of whom so much can be said. To-day that name is utterly forgotten, nor is there any good reason why it should be remembered. It does not figure even in the index to the post-humous memoirs of Mme de Villeparisis, whose mind was so much occupied with the lady who bore it. And if the Marquise has omitted to mention Mme Leroi, this is less because in her life-time that lady had been less than friendly towards her than because, once she was dead, no one was likely to take any interest in her, it is a silence dictated less by the social resent-ment of a woman than by the literary tact of an author. My conversation with Bloch's fashionable friend was delightful, for she was an intelligent young woman; but this difference which I have described between our two vocabularies made it at the same time both awkward and instructive. For although we know that the years pass, that youth gives way to old age, that fortunes and thrones crumble (even the most solid among them) and that fame is transitory, the manner in which—by means of a sort of snapshot—we take cognisance of this mov-ing universe whirled along by Time, has the contrary effect of immobilising it. And the result is that we see as always young the men and women whom we have known young, that those whom we have known old we retrospectively endow in the past with the virtues of old age, that we trust unreservedly in the credit of a millionaire and the influence of a reigning monarch, knowing with our reason, though we do not actually believe, that to-morrow both the one and the other may be fugitives stripped of all power. In a more restricted field, one that is purely social—as in a simpler problem which initiates a student into difficulties that are more complex but of the same order—the unintelligibility which, in my conversation with the young woman, resulted from the fact that the two of us had lived in the same world but with an interval of twenty-five years between us, gave me the impression, and might have strengthened within me the sense, of History.

And indeed this ignorance of people's true social position which every ten years causes the new fashionable elect to arise in all the glory of the moment as though the past had never existed, which makes it impossible for an American woman just landed in Europe to see that in an age when Bloch was nobody M. de Charlus was socially supreme in Paris and that Swann, who put himself out to please M. Bontemps, had himself been treated with every mark of friendship by the Prince of Wales, this ignorance, which exists not only in new arrivals but also in those who have always frequented adjacent but distinct regions of society, is itself also invariably an effect—but an effect operative not so much upon a whole social stratum as within individuals—of Time. No doubt we ourselves may change our social habitat and our manner of life and yet our memory, clinging still to the thread of our personal identity, will continue to attach to itself at successive epochs the recollection of the various societies in which, even if it be forty-five years earlier, we have lived. Bloch the guest of the Prince de Guermantes remembered perfectly well the humble Jewish environment in which he had lived at the age of eighteen, and Swann, when he was no longer in love with Mme Swann but with a waitress at that same Colombin's where at one time Mme Swann had thought it smart to go and drink tea (as she did also at the tea-room in the Rue Royale), Swann was very well aware of his own social value—he remembered Twickenham and had no doubt in his mind about the reasons for which he chose to go to Colombin's rather than to call on the Duchesse de Broglie, and he knew also that, had he been a thousand times less "smart" than he was, he would not have become the slightest bit smarter by frequenting Colombin's or the Ritz, since anybody can go to these places who pays. And no doubt the friends, too, of Bloch or of Swann remembered the little Jewish coterie or the invitations to Twickenham and thus, as though they, the friends, were other not very clearly defined "I's" of the two men, made no division in their memories between the fashionable Bloch of to-day and the sordid Bloch of the past, between the Swann who in his latter days could be seen at Colombin's and the Swann of Buckingham Palace. But these friends were to some extent Swann's neighbours in life, their own lives had developed along lines near enough to his own for their memories to be fairly full of him, whereas other men who were more remote from Swann—at a greater distance measured not perhaps socially but in terms of intimacy, which caused their knowledge of him to be vaguer and their meetings with him rarer— possessed of him recollections that were less numerous and in consequence conceptions that were less fixed. And after thirty years a comparative stranger of this kind no longer has any precise recollection with the power to change the value of the person whom he has before his eyes by prolonging him into the past. In the last years of Swann's life I had heard people, even people in society, say when his name was mentioned, as though this had been his title to fame: "You mean the Swann who goes to Colombin's?" And now, with reference to Bloch, even those who ought to have known better might be heard to inquire: "The Guermantes Bloch? The Bloch who is such a friend of the Guermantes?" These errors which split a life in two and, by isolating his present from his past, turn some man whom one is talking about into another, a different man, a creation of yesterday, a man who is no more than the condensation of his current habits (whereas the real man bears within himself an awareness, linking him to the past, of the continuity of his life), these errors, though they too, as I have said, are a result of the passage of Time, are not a social phenomenon but one of memory. And at that very moment I was presented with an example, of a different variety, it is true, but all the more impressive for that, of this forgetfulness which modifies for us our image of a human being. Long ago a young nephew of Mme de Guermantes, the Marquis de Villemandois, had behaved towards me with a persistent insolence which had obliged me to retaliate by adopting an equally insulting attitude towards him, so that tacitly we had become as it were enemies. This man, while I was engaged in my reflections upon Time at the Princesse de Guermantes's party, asked someone to introduce him to me, saying that he thought that I had known some of his family, that he had read articles of mine and wanted to make, or re-make, my acquaintance. Now it is true to say that with age he had become, like many others, serious instead of rude and frivolous and that he had lost much of his former arrogance, and it is also true that I was a good deal talked about now, though on the strength of some very slight articles, in the circles which he frequented. But these motives for his cordiality, for his making advances to me, were only secondary. The principal motive, or at least the one which permitted the others to come into play, was that—either because he had a worse memory than I or because in the past, since I was then for him a much less important personage than he for me, he had paid less attention to my ripostes than I to his attacks—he had completely forgotten our feud. At most my name recalled to him that he must have seen me, or some member of my family, in the house of one of his aunts. And being uncertain whether he was being introduced to me for the first time or whether we were old acquaintances, he made haste to talk to me about the aunt in whose house he was sure that we had met, remembering that my name had often been mentioned there and not remembering our quarrels. A name: that very often is all that remains for us of a human being, not only when he is dead, but sometimes even in his life-time. And our notions about him are so vague or so bizarre and correspond so little to those that he has of us that we have entirely forgotten that we once nearly fought a duel with him but remember that, when he was a child, he used to wear curious yellow gaiters in the Champs-Elysées, where he, on the contrary, in spite of our assurances, has no recollection of ever having played with us.

Bloch had come bounding into the room like a hyena. "He is at home now," I thought, "in drawing-rooms into which twenty years ago he would never have been able to penetrate." But he was also twenty years older. He was nearer to death. What did this profit him? At close quarters, in the translucency of a face in which, at a greater distance or in a bad light, I saw only youthful gaiety (whether because it survived there or because I with my recollections evoked it), I could detect another face, almost frightening, racked with anxiety, the face of an old Shylock, waiting in the wings, with his make-up prepared, for the moment when he would make his entry on to the stage and already reciting his first line under his breath. In ten years, in drawing-rooms like this which their own feebleness of spirit would allow him to dominate, he would enter on crutches to be greeted as "the Master" for whom a visit to the La Trémoïlles was merely a tedious obligation. And what would this profit him?

From changes accomplished in society I was all the better able to extract important truths, worthy of being used as the cement which would hold part of my work together, for the reason that such changes were by no means, as at the first moment I might have been tempted to suppose, peculiar to the epoch in which we lived. At the time when I, myself only just "arrived"—newer even than Bloch at the present day—had made my first entry into the world of the Guermantes, I must have contemplated in the belief that they formed an integral part of that world elements that were in fact utterly foreign to it, recently incorporated and appearing strangely new to older elements from which I failed to distinguish them and which themselves, though regarded by the dukes of the day as members of the Faubourg from time immemorial, had in fact—if not themselves, then their fathers or their grandfathers—been the upstarts of an earlier age. So much so that it was not any inherent quality of "men of the best society" which made this world so brilliant, but rather the fact of being more or less completely assimilated to this world which out of people who fifty years later, in spite of their diverse origins, would all look very much the same, formed "men of the best society." Even in the past into which I pushed back the name of Guermantes in order to give it its full grandeur—and with good reason, for under Louis XIV the Guermantes had been almost royal and had cut a more splendid figure than they did to-day—the phenomenon which I was observing at this moment had not been unknown. The Guermantes of that time had allied themselves, for instance, with the family of Colbert, which to-day, it is true, appears to us in the highest degree aristocratic, since a Colbert bride is thought an excellent match even for a La Rochefoucauld. But it is not because the Colberts, then a purely bourgeois family, were aristocratic that the Guermantes had sought them in a matrimonial alliance, it was because of this

alliance with the Guermantes that the Colberts became aristocratic. If the name of Haussonville should be extinguished with
the present representative of that house, it will perhaps owe its
future renown to the fact that the family to-day is descended
from Mme de Staël, regardless of the fact that before the
Revolution M. d'Haussonville, one of the first noblemen of the
kingdom, found it gratifying to his vanity to be able to tell
M. de Broglie that he was not acquainted with the father of that
lady and was therefore no more in a position to present him at
court than was M. de Broglie himself, neither of the two men
for one moment suspecting that their own grandsons would
later marry one the daughter and the other the grand-daughter
of the authoress of *Corinne*. From the remarks of the Duchesse
de Guermantes I realised that it would have been in my power
to play the role of the fashionable commoner in grand society,
the man whom everybody supposes to have been from his
earliest days affiliated to the aristocracy, a role once played by
Swann and before him by M. Lebrun and M. Ampère and all
those friends of the Duchesse de Broglie who herself at the
beginning of her career had by no means belonged to the best
society. The first few times I had dined with Mme de Guermantes how I must have shocked men like M. de Beauserfeuil,
less by my actual presence than by remarks indicating how
entirely ignorant I was of the memories which constituted his
past and which gave its form to the image that he had of society!
Yet the day would come when Bloch, as a very old man, with
recollections from a now distant past of the Guermantes
drawing-room as it presented itself to his eyes at this moment,
would feel the same astonishment, the same ill-humour in the
presence of certain intrusions and certain displays of ignorance.
And at the same time he would no doubt have developed and
would radiate around him those qualities of tact and discretion
which I had thought were the special prerogative of men like
M. de Norpois but which, when their original avatars have
vanished from the scene, form themselves again for a new
incarnation in those of our acquaintance who seem of all
people the least likely to possess them. It was true that my own
particular case, the experience that I had had of being admitted
to the society of the Guermantes, had appeared to me to be

something exceptional. But as soon as I got outside myself and
the circle of people by whom I was immediately surrounded, I
could see that this was a social phenomenon less rare than I had
at first supposed and that from the single fountain-basin of
Combray in which I had been born there were in fact quite a
number of jets of water which had risen, in symmetry with
myself, above the liquid mass which had fed them. No doubt,
since circumstances have always about them something of the
particular and characters something of the individual, it was in
an entirely different fashion that Legrandin (through his
nephew's strange marriage) had in his turn penetrated into
this exalted world, a fashion quite different to that in which
Odette's daughter had married into it or those in which Swann
long ago and I myself had reached it. Indeed to me, passing by
shut up inside my own life so that I saw it only from within,
Legrandin's life seemed to bear absolutely no resemblance to
my own, the two seemed to have followed widely divergent
paths, and in this respect I was like a stream which from the
bottom of its own deep valley does not see another stream
which proceeds in a different direction and yet, in spite of the
great loops in its course, ends up as a tributary of the same
river. But taking a bird's-eye view, as the statistician does who,
ignoring the reasons of sentiment or the avoidable imprudences which may have led some particular person to his death,
counts merely the total number of those who have died in a
year, I could see that quite a few individuals, starting from the
same social *milieu*, the portrayal of which was attempted in the
first pages of this work, had arrived finally in another *milieu* of
an entirely different kind, and the probability is that, just as
every year in Paris an average number of marriages take place,
so any other rich and cultivated middle-class *milieu* might have
been able to show a roughly equal proportion of men who,
like Swann and Legrandin and myself and Bloch, could be
found at a later stage in their lives flowing into the ocean of
"high society." Moreover, in their new surroundings they
recognised each other, for if the young Comte de Cambremer
won the admiration of society for his distinction, his refinement,
his sober elegance, I myself was able to recognise in these
qualities—and at the same time in his fine eyes and his ardent

craving for social success—characteristics that were already present in his uncle Legrandin, who in spite of his aristocratic elegance of bearing had been no more than a typical middle-class friend of my parents.

Kindness, a simple process of maturation which in the end sweetens characters originally more acid even than that of Bloch, is as widely disseminated as that belief in justice thanks to which, if our cause is good, we feel that we have no more to fear from a hostile judge than from one friendly towards us. And the grandchildren of Bloch would be kind and modest almost from birth. Bloch himself had perhaps not yet reached this stage of development. But I noticed that, whereas once he had pretended to think himself obliged to make a two hours' railway journey in order to visit someone who had scarcely even asked him to come, now that he was flooded with invitations not only to lunch and to dine but to stay for a fortnight here and a fortnight there, he refused many of them and did this without telling people, without bragging that he had received and refused them. Discretion, both in action and in speech, had come to him with social position and with age, with, if one may use the expression, a sort of social longevity. No doubt in the past Bloch had lacked discretion, just as he had been incapable of kindness and devoid of good sense. But certain defects, certain qualities are attached less to this or that individual than to this or that moment of existence considered from the social point of view. One may almost say that they are external to individuals, who merely pass beneath the radiance that they shed as beneath so many solstices, varying in their nature but all pre-existent, general and unavoidable. In the same way a doctor who is trying to find out whether some medicine diminishes or augments the acidity of the stomach, whether it activates or inhibits its secretions, will obtain results which differ not according to the stomach from whose secretions he has removed a small quantity of gastric juice, but according to the more or less advanced stage in the process of ingestion of the drug at which he conducts the experiment.

To return to the name of Guermantes, considered as an agglomeration of all the names which it admitted into itself and into its immediate neighbourhood, at every moment of its duration it suffered losses and recruited fresh ingredients, like a garden in which from week to week flowers scarcely in bud and preparing to take the places of those that have already begun to wither are confounded with the latter in a mass which presents always the same appearance, except to the people who have not seen the newest blooms before and still preserve in their memories a precise image of the ones that are no longer there.

More than one of the men and women who had been brought together by this party, or of whose existence it had reminded me by evoking for me the aspects which he or she had in turn presented as from the midst of different, perhaps opposite circumstances one after another they had risen before me, brought vividly before my mind the varied aspects of my own life and its different perspectives, just as a feature in a landscape, a hill or a large country house, by appearing now on the right hand and now on the left and seeming first to dominate a forest and then to emerge from a valley, reveals to a traveller the changes in direction and the differences in altitude of the road along which he is passing. As I followed the stream of memory back towards its source, I arrived eventually at images of a single person separated from one another by an interval of time so long, preserved within me by "I's" that were so distinct and themselves (the images) fraught with meanings that were so different, that ordinarily when I surveyed (as I supposed) the whole past course of my relations with that particular person I omitted these earliest images and had even ceased to think that the person to whom they referred was the same as the one whom I had later got to know, so that I needed a fortuitous lightning-flash of attention before I could re-attach this latter-day acquaintance, like a word to its etymology, to the original significance which he or she had possessed for me. Mlle Swann, on the other side of the hedge of pink hawthorn, throwing me a look of which, as a matter of fact, I had been obliged retrospectively to re-touch the significance, having learnt that it was a look of desire; Mme Swann's lover—or the man who according to Combray gossip occupied that position—studying me from behind that same hedge with an air of disapproval which, in this case too,

had not the meaning which I had ascribed to it at the time, and
then later so changed that I had quite failed to recognise him
as the gentleman at Balbec examining a poster outside the
Casino, the man of whom, when once every ten years I happened to remember that first image, I would say to myself:
"How strange! That, though I did not know it, was M. de
Charlus!"; Mme de Guermantes at the marriage of Dr Percepied's daughter; Mme Swann in a pink dress in my great-
uncle's study; Mme de Cambremer, Legrandin's sister, so
fashionable that he was terrified that we might ask him to give
us an introduction to her—all these images and many others
associated with Swann, Saint-Loup and others of my friends
were like illustrations which sometimes, when I chanced to
come across them, I amused myself by placing as frontispieces
on the threshold of my relations with these various people, but
always with the feeling that they were no more than images,
not something deposited within me by this particular person,
not something still in any way linked to him. Not only do some
people have good memories and others bad (without going so
far as that perpetual forgetfulness which is the native element
of such creatures as the Turkish Ambassadress, thanks to
which—one piece of news having evaporated by the end of
the week or the next·piece having the power to exorcise its
predecessor—they are always able to find room in their minds
for the news that contradicts what they have previously been
told), we find also that two people with an equal endowment
of memory do not remember the same things. One of two men,
for instance, will have paid little attention to an action for
which the other will long continue to feel great remorse, but
will have seized on the other hand upon some random remark
which his friend let fall almost without thinking and taken it
to be the key to a sympathetic character. Again, the fact that
we prefer not to be proved wrong when we have uttered a
false prophecy cuts short the duration of our memory of such
prophecies and permits us very soon to affirm that we never
uttered them. Finally, preferences of a more profound and
more disinterested kind diversify the memories of different
people, so that a poet, for example, who has almost entirely
forgotten certain facts which someone else is able to recall will,

nevertheless, have retained—what for him is more important—
a fleeting impression. The effect of all these causes is that after
twenty years of absence where one expected to find rancour
one finds often involuntary and unconscious forgiveness, but
sometimes also we stumble upon a bitterness for which (because
we have ourselves forgotten some bad impression that we once
made) we can provide no reasonable explanation. Even where
the people whom we have known best are concerned, we soon
forget the dates of the various episodes in their lives. And
because it was at least twenty years since she had first set eyes
on Bloch, Mme de Guermantes would have sworn that he had
been born in the world to which she herself belonged and had
been dandled on the knees of the Duchesse de Chartres when
he was two years old.

How often had all these people re-appeared before me in the
course of their lives, the diverse circumstances of which seemed
to present the same individuals always, but in forms and for
purposes that were shifting and varied! And the diversity of the
points in my life through which, like so many interwoven
threads, those of each of these personages had passed had in
the end brought into conjunction even those that seemed the
furthest apart from one another, as though for the execution
of infinitely varied patterns life possessed only a limited number of threads. What, for instance, in my various pasts, could
be more widely separated than my visits to my great-uncle
Adolphe, the nephew of Mme de Villeparisis who was herself
a cousin of the Marshal, Legrandin and his sister, and the
former tailor who lived in our courtyard and was a friend of
Françoise? And yet to-day all these different threads had been
woven together to form the fabric, there of the married lives
of Robert and Gilberte Saint-Loup, here of the young Cambremer couple, not to mention Morel and all the others whose
conjunction had played a part in forming a set of circumstances
of such a nature that the circumstances seemed to me to be the
complete unity and each individual actor in them merely a
constituent part of the whole. And by now my life had lasted
so long that not infrequently, when it brought a person to my
notice, I was able, by rummaging in quite different regions of
my memory, to find another person, unlike though with the

same identity, to add to and complete the first. Even to the Elstirs which I saw hanging here in a position which was itself an indication of his glory I was able to add very ancient memories of the Verdurins, the Cottards, my first conversation with the painter in the restaurant at Rivebelle, the tea-party in his studio at which I had been introduced to Albertine, and a host of other memories as well. Thus a connoisseur of painting who is shown one wing of an altar-piece remembers in what church or which museums or whose private collection the other fragments of the same work are dispersed and, in the same way as by studying the catalogues of sales and haunting the shops of the antique-dealers he finds, in the end, some object which is a twin to one he already possesses and makes a pair with it, he is able to reconstruct in his mind the predella and the whole altar as they once were. And just as a bucket being hauled up by a winch swings first against one side of the descending rope and then against the other until it has touched it at every point, so there was scarcely a character, scarcely even a thing which had found a place in my life and had not turn and turn about played in it a whole series of different roles. If after an interval of several years I rediscovered in my memory a mere social acquaintance or even a physical object, I perceived that life all this while had been weaving round person or thing a tissue of diverse threads which ended by covering them with the beautiful and inimitable velvety patina of the years, just as in an old park a simple runnel of water comes with the passage of time to be enveloped in a sheath of emerald.

It was not merely the outward appearance of these people that made one think of them as people in a dream. In their inward experience too life, which already when they were young, when they were in love, had been not far from sleep, had now more and more become a dream. They had forgotten even their resentments, their hatreds, and in order to be certain that the person before them was the one with whom ten years earlier they had not been on speaking terms they would have had to consult some mnemonic register, but one which, unfortunately, was as vague as a dream in which one has been insulted one does not quite know by whom. All these dreams together formed the substance of the apparent contradictions of political life, where one saw as colleagues in a government men who had once accused each other of murder or treason. And this dreamlike existence became as torpid as death in certain old men on the days that followed any day on which they had chanced to make love. During those days it was useless to make any demands on the President of the Republic, he had forgotten everything. Then, if he was left in peace for a day or two, the memory of public affairs slowly returned to him, as haphazard as the memory of a dream.

Sometimes it was not merely in a single vivid image that the stranger so unlike the man or woman whom I had later come to know had first appeared before me. For years I had thought of Bergotte as the sweet bard with the snowy locks, for years my limbs had been paralysed, as though I had seen a ghost, by the apparition of Swann's grey top-hat or his wife's violet cloak, or by the mystery with which, even in a drawing-room, the name of her race enveloped the Duchesse de Guermantes; with all these, and with others too, my relations, which in the sequel were to become so commonplace, had had their origin almost in legend, in a delightful mythology which still at a later date prolonged them into the past as into some Olympian heaven where they shone with the luminous brilliance of a comet's tail. And even those of my acquaintanceships which had not begun in mystery, that for instance with Mme de Souvré, so arid to-day, so purely social in its nature, had preserved among their earliest moments the memory of a first smile calmer and sweeter than anything that was to follow, a smile mellifluously traced in the fullness of an afternoon beside the sea or the close of a spring day in Paris, a day of clattering carriages, of dust rising from the streets and sunny air gently stirring like water. And perhaps Mme de Souvré, had she been removed from this frame, would have been of little significance, like those famous buildings—the Salute, for example—which, without any great beauty of their own, are so well suited to a particular setting that they compel our admiration, but she formed part of a bundle of memories which I valued "all in," as the auctioneers say, at a certain price, without stopping to ask exactly how much of this value appertained to the lady herself.

One thing struck me even more forcibly in all these people than the physical or social changes which they had undergone, and this was the modification in the ideas which they possessed of one another. Legrandin in the past had despised Bloch and never addressed a word to him. Now he went out of his way to be civil. And this was not because of the improvement which had taken place in Bloch's social position—were this the case the fact would scarcely be worthy of mention, for social changes inevitably bring in their train a new pattern of relationships among those who have been affected by them. No: the reason was that people—and in saying "people" I mean "what people are for us"—do not in our memory possess the unvariability of a figure in a painting. Oblivion is at work within us, and according to its arbitrary operation they evolve. Sometimes it even happens that after a time we confuse one person with another. "Bloch? Oh yes, he was someone who used to come to Combray," and when he says Bloch, the speaker is in fact referring to me. Conversely, Mme Sazerat was firmly persuaded that it was I who was the author of a certain historical study of Philip II which was in fact by Bloch. More commonly, you forget after a while how odiously some-one has behaved towards you, you forget his faults of character and your last meeting with him when you parted without shaking hands, and you remember on the other hand an earlier occasion when you got on excellently together. And it was to an earlier occasion of this kind that the manners of Legrandin adverted in his new civility towards Bloch, whether because he had lost the recollection of a particular past or because he thought it was to be deliberately eschewed, from a mixture of forgiveness and forgetfulness and that indifference which is another effect of Time. And then, as we have seen, the memories which two people preserve of each other, even in love, are not the same. I had seen Albertine reproduce with perfect accuracy some remark which I had made to her at one of our first meetings and which I had entirely forgotten. Of some other incident, lodged for ever in my head like a pebble flung with force, she had no recollection. Our life together was like one of those garden walks where, at intervals on either side of the path, vases of flowers are placed symmetrically but not opposite to one another. And if this discrepancy of memories may be observed even in the relation of love, even more understandable is it that when your acquaintance with someone has been slight you should scarcely remember who he is or should remember not what you used to think of him but something different, perhaps something that dates from an earlier epoch or that is suggested by the people in whose midst you have met him again, who may only recently have got to know him and see him therefore endowed with good qualities and a social prestige which in the past he did not possess but which you, having forgotten the past, instantly accept.

No doubt life, by placing each of these people on my path a number of times, had presented them to me in particular circumstances which, enclosing them finally on every side, had restricted the view which I had of them and so prevented me from discovering their essence. For between us and other people there exists a barrier of contingencies, just as in my hours of reading in the garden at Combray I had realised that in all perception there exists a barrier as a result of which there is never absolute contact between reality and our intelligence. Even those Guermantes around whom I had built such a vast fabric of dream had appeared to me, when at last I had first approached two of them, one in the guise of an old friend of my grandmother and the other in that of a gentleman who had looked at me in a most disagreeable manner one morning in the gardens of the Casino. So that it was in each case only in retrospect, by reuniting the individual to the name, that my encounter with them had been an encounter with the Guermantes. And yet perhaps this in itself made life more poetic for me, the thought that the mysterious race with the piercing eyes and the beak of a bird, the unapproachable rose-coloured, golden race, had so often and so naturally, through the effect of blind and varied circumstances, chanced to offer itself to my contemplation, to admit me to the circle of its casual and even of its intimate friends, to such a point that when I had wanted to get to know Mlle de Stermaria or to have dresses made for Albertine, it was to one or another of the Guermantes, as being the most obliging of my friends, that I had appealed for help. Admittedly I was bored when I went to their houses, no less bored than I was in the houses of the other society people whom I had later come to know. And in the case of the Duchesse de Guermantes, as in that of certain pages of Bergotte, even her personal charm was visible to me only at a distance and vanished as soon as I was near her, for the reason that it resided in my memory and my imagination. But still, in spite of everything, the Guermantes—and in this respect Gilberte resembled them—differed from other society people in that they plunged their roots more deeply into my past life, down to a level at which I had dreamed more and had had more belief in individuals. Bored I may have been as I stood talking this afternoon to Gilberte or Mme de Guermantes, but at least as I did so I held within my grasp those of the imaginings of my childhood which I had found most beautiful and thought most inaccessible and, like a shopkeeper who cannot balance his books, I could console myself by forgetting the value of their actual possession and remembering the price which had once been attached to them by my desire. But with other people I had not even this consolation, people however with whom my relations had at one time been swollen to an immense importance by dreams that were even more ardent and formed without hope, dreams into which my life of those days, dedicated entirely to them, had so richly poured itself that I could scarcely understand how their fulfilment could be merely this thin, narrow, colourless ribbon of an indifferent and despised intimacy, in which I could rediscover nothing of what had once been their mystery, their fever and their sweetness.

"What has become of the Marquise d'Arpajon?" inquired Mme de Cambremer. "She died," replied Bloch. "Aren't you confusing her with the Comtesse d'Arpajon, who died last year?" The Princesse d'Agrigente joined in the discussion; as the young widow of an old husband who had been very rich and the bearer of a great name she was much sought in marriage, and this had given her great self-assurance. "The Marquise d'Arpajon is dead too," she said, "she died nearly a year ago." "A year ago!" exclaimed Mme de Cambremer, "that can't be right, I was at a musical evening in her house less than a year ago." Bloch was as incapable as any young man about town of making a useful contribution to the subject under discussion, for all these deaths of elderly people were at too great a distance, from the young men because of the enormous difference in age and from a man like Bloch, because of his recent arrival in an unfamiliar society, by way of an oblique approach, at a moment when it was already declining into a twilight which was for him illumined by no memories of its past. And even for people of the same age and the same social background death had lost its strange significance. Hardly a day passed without their having to send to inquire for news of friends and relations *in articulo mortis*, some of whom, they would be told, had recovered while others had "succumbed," until a point was reached where they no longer very clearly remembered whether this or that person who was no longer seen anywhere had "pulled through" his pneumonia or had expired. In these regions of advanced age death was every- where at work and had at the same time become more in- definite. At this crossroads of two generations and two societies, so ill placed, for different reasons, for distinguishing death that they almost confused it with life, the former of these two conditions had been turned into a social incident, an attribute to be predicated of somebody to a greater or less degree, without the tone of voice in which it was mentioned in any way indicating that for the person in question this "inci- dent" was the end of everything. I heard people say: "But you forget that so and so is dead," exactly as they might have said "he has had a decoration" or "he has been elected to the Academy" or—and these last two happenings had much the same effect as death, since they too prevented a man from going to parties—"he is spending the winter on the Riviera" or "his doctor has sent him to the mountains." Perhaps, where a man was well known, what he left behind him at his death helped others to remember that his existence had come to an end. But in the case of ordinary society people of an advanced age it was easy to make a mistake as to whether or no they were dead, not only because one knew little about their past or had forgotten it but because they were in no way whatever linked to the future. And the difficulty that was universally experienced in these cases in choosing from among the alternatives of illness, absence, retirement to the country and death the one that happened to be correct, sanctioned and confirmed not merely the indifference of the survivors but the insignificance of the departed.

"But if she is still alive, why is it that one never sees her anywhere now, nor her husband either?" asked a spinster who liked to make what she supposed was witty conversation. "For the obvious reason," replied her mother, who in spite of her years never missed a party herself, "that they are old; when you get to that age you stay at home." Before you got to the cemetery, it seemed, there was a whole closed city of the old, where the lamps always glimmered in the fog. Mme de Saint-Euverte cut short the debate by saying that the Comtesse d'Arpajon had died in the previous year after a long illness and that more recently the Marquise d'Arpajon had also died, very rapidly, "in some quite unremarkable way," a death which, in virtue of this latter characteristic, resembled the lives of all these people (its unremarkableness explained too why it had passed unnoticed and excused those who had been in doubt). When she heard that Mme d'Arpajon really had died, the spinster cast an anxious glance at her mother, for she feared that the news of the death of one of her "contemporaries" might "be a blow" to her—indeed she already imagined people talking about her mother's death and explaining it in this way: "Madame d'Arpajon's death had been a *great blow* to her." But the old lady on the contrary, far from justifying her daughter's fears, felt every time someone of her own age "disappeared" that she had gained a victory in a contest against formidable competitors. Their deaths were the only fashion in which she still for a moment became agreeably conscious of her own life. The spinster noticed that her mother, who had seemed not displeased to remark that Mme d'Arpajon was one of those tired old people whose days are spent in homes from which they seldom emerge, had been even less displeased to learn that the Marquise had entered the city of hereafter, the home from which none of us ever emerges at all. This observation of her mother's want of feeling amused the daughter's sarcastic mind. And to make her own "contemporaries" laugh she gave them afterwards a comical account of the gleeful fashion in which her mother had said, rubbing her hands:

"Gracious me, it appears to be true that poor Madame d'Arpajon is dead." Even the people who did not need this death to make them feel any joy in being alive, were rendered happy by it. For every death is for others a simplification of life, it spares them the necessity of showing gratitude, the obligation of paying calls. And yet this was not the manner in which Elstir had received the news of the death of M. Verdurin.

A lady left the room, for she had other afternoon parties to attend, and had also received the commands of two queens to take tea with them. It was the Princesse de Nassau, that great courtesan of the aristocratic world whom I had known in the past. Were it not that she had shrunk in height (which gave her, her head being now situated at a much lower elevation than formerly, an air of having "one foot in the grave"), one could scarcely have said that she had aged. She had remained a Marie-Antoinette with an Austrian nose and an enchanting glance, preserved, one might almost say embalmed, by a thousand cosmetics adorably blended so as to compose for her a face that was the colour of lilac. Over this face there floated that confused and tender expression which I remembered, which was at once an allusion to all the fashionable gatherings where she was expected and an intimation that she was obliged to leave, that she promised sweetly to return, that she would slip away without any fuss. Born almost on the steps of a throne, three times married, richly kept for years at a time by great bankers, not to mention the countless whims in which she had permitted herself to indulge, she bore lightly beneath her gown, mauve like her wonderful round eyes and her painted face, the slightly tangled memories of the innumerable incidents of her life. As she passed near me, making her discreet exit, I bowed to her. She recognised me, took my hand and pressed it, and fixed upon me the round mauve pupils which seemed to say: "How long it is since we have seen each other! We must talk about all that another time." Her pressure of my hand became a squeeze, for she had a vague idea that one evening in her carriage, when she had offered to drop me at my door after a party at the Duchesse de Guermantes's, there might have been an embrace between us. Just to be on the safe side, she seemed to allude to something that had in fact never

happened, but this was hardly difficult for her since a strawberry tart could send her into an ecstasy and whenever she had
to leave a party before the end of a piece of music she put on a
despairing air of tender, yet not final, farewell. But she was
uncertain what had passed between us in the carriage, so she
did not linger long over the furtive pressure of my hand and
said not a word. She merely looked at me in the manner which
I have described, the manner which signified: "How long it is!"
and in which one caught a momentary glimpse of her husbands
and the men who had kept her and two wars, while her stellar
eyes, like an astronomical clock cut in a block of opal, marked
successively all those solemn hours of a so distant past which
she rediscovered every time she wanted to bid you a casual
good-bye which was always also an apology. And then having
left me, she started to trot towards the door, partly so that her
departure should not inconvenience people, partly to show me
that if she had not stopped to talk it was because she was in a
hurry, partly also to recapture the seconds which she had lost
in pressing my hand and so arrive on time at the Queen of
Spain's, where she was to have tea alone with the Queen. I even
thought, when she got near the door, that she was going to
break into a gallop. And indeed she was galloping towards her
grave.

A stout lady came up to me and greeted me, and during the
few moments that she was speaking the most diverse thoughts
jostled each other in my mind. I hesitated an instant to reply
to her, for I was afraid that possibly, recognising people no
better than I did, she might have mistaken my identity, but
then the assurance of her manner caused me on the contrary,
for fear that she might be someone whom I had known extremely well, to exaggerate the amiability of my smile, while
my eyes continued to scan her features for some trace of the
name which eluded me. As a candidate for a degree fixes his
eyes upon the examiner's face in the vain hope of finding there
the answer that he would do better to seek in his own memory,
so, still smiling, I fixed my eyes upon the features of the stout
lady. They seemed to be those of Mme Swann, and there crept
into my smile the appropriate shade of respect, while my indecision began to subside. But a moment later I heard the stout

lady say: "You took me for Mamma, and it's quite true that I'm beginning to look very like her." And I recognised Gilberte.

We had a long talk about Robert, Gilberte speaking of him in an almost reverent tone, as though he had been a superior being whom she was anxious to show me that she had admired and understood. We recalled to one another the ideas which he had expounded in the past upon the art of war (for he had often repeated to her at Tansonville the theories that I had heard him develop at Doncières and elsewhere) and we marvelled how often, and on how many different points, his views had been proved correct by the events of the late war.

"I cannot tell you," I said, "how struck I am now by even the least of the things that I heard him say at Doncières and also during the war. Almost the last remark that he ever made to me, just before we said good-bye for the last time, was that he expected to see Hindenburg, a Napoleonic general, fight one of the types of Napoleonic battle, the one which aims at driving a wedge between two hostile armies—perhaps, he had added, the English and ourselves. Now scarcely a year after Robert was killed, a critic for whom he had a profound admiration and who manifestly exercised a great influence upon his military ideas, M. Henry Bidou, was saying that the Hindenburg offensive of March 1918 was 'the battle of separation fought by a single concentrated army against two armies in extended formation, a manœuvre which the Emperor executed successfully in the Apennines in 1796 but in which he failed in Belgium in 1815.' In the course of the same conversation Robert had compared battles to plays in which it is not always easy to know what the author has intended, in which perhaps the author himself has changed his plan in mid-campaign. Now admittedly, to take this same German offensive of 1918, had Robert interpreted it in this fashion he would not have been in agreement with M. Bidou. But other critics believe that it was Hindenburg's success in the direction of Amiens, followed by his check there, then his success in Flanders and then another check, which, by virtue really of a series of accidents, made first of Amiens and then of Boulogne objectives which he had not fixed upon before the engagement began. And as every critic can refashion a play or a campaign in his own way, there are some who see in this offensive the prelude to a lightning attack upon Paris and others a succession of uncoordinated hammer-blows intended to destroy the English army. And even if the orders actually given by the commander do not fit in with this or that conception of his plan, the critics will always be at liberty to say, as the actor Mounet-Sully said to Coquelin when the latter assured him that *Le Misanthrope* was not the gloomy melodrama that he wanted to make it (for Molière himself, according to the evidence of contemporaries, gave a comical interpretation of the part and played it for laughs): 'Well, Molière was wrong.' "

"And when aeroplanes first started"—it was Gilberte's turn now—"you remember what he used to say (he had such charming expressions): 'Every army will have to be a hundred-eyed Argus'? Alas, he never lived to see his prediction fulfilled!" "Oh! yes, he did," I replied, "he saw the battle of the Somme and he knew that it began with blinding the enemy by gouging out his eyes, by destroying his aeroplanes and his captive balloons." "Yes, that is true. And then," she went on, for now that she "lived only for the mind" she had become a little pedantic, "he maintained that we return always to the methods of the ancients. Well, do you realise that the Mesopotamian campaigns of this war" (she must have read this comparison at the time in Brichot's articles) "constantly recall, almost without alteration, Xenophon's *Anabasis*? And that to get from the Tigris to the Euphrates the English command made use of the *bellam*, the long narrow boat—the gondola of the country—which was already being used by the Chaldeans at the very dawn of history." These words did indeed give me a sense of that stagnation of the past through which in certain parts of the world, by virtue of a sort of specific gravity, it is indefinitely immobilised, so that it can be found after centuries exactly as it was. But I must admit that, because of the books which I had read at Balbec at no great distance from Robert himself, I myself had been more impressed first in the fighting in France to come again upon those "trenches" that were familiar to me from the pages of Mme de Sévigné and then in the Middle East, apropos of the siege of Kut-el-Amara (Kut-of-the-Emir, "just as we say Vaux-le-Vicomte or Bailleau-l'Evêque," as the curé of Combray would have said had he extended his thirst for etymologies to the languages of the East), to see the name of Baghdad once more attended closely by that of Basra, which is the Bassorah so many times mentioned in the *Thousand and One Nights*, the town which, whenever he had left the capital or was returning thither, was used as his port of embarkation or disembarkation, long before the days of General Townshend and General Gorringe, when the Caliphs still reigned, by no less a personage than Sindbad the Sailor.

"There is one aspect of war," I continued, "which I think Robert was beginning to comprehend: war is human, it is something that is lived like a love or a hatred and could be told like the story of a novel, and consequently, if anyone goes about repeating that strategy is a science, it won't help him in the least to understand war, since war is not a matter of strategy. The enemy has no more knowledge of our plans than we have of the objective pursued by the woman whom we love, and perhaps we do not even know what these plans are ourselves. Did the Germans in their offensive of March 1918 aim at capturing Amiens? We simply do not know. Perhaps they did not know themselves, perhaps it was what happened— their advance in the west towards Amiens—that determined the nature of their plan. And even if war were scientific, it would still be right to paint it as Elstir painted the sea, by reversing the real and the apparent, starting from illusions and beliefs which one then slowly brings into line with the truth, which is the manner in which Dostoievsky tells the story of a life. Quite certainly, however, war is not strategic, it might better be described as a pathological condition, because it admits of accidents which even a skilled physician could not have foreseen, such as the Russian Revolution."

Throughout this conversation Gilberte had spoken of Robert with a deference which seemed to be addressed more to my sometime friend than to her late husband. It was as though she were saying to me: "I know how much you admired him. Please believe that I too understood what a wonderful person he was." And yet the love which she assuredly no longer had for his memory was perhaps the remote cause of certain features of her present life. Thus Gilberte now had an inseparable friend in Andrée. And although the latter was beginning, thanks largely to her husband's talent and her own intelligence, to penetrate, if not into the society of the Guermantes, at least into circles infinitely more fashionable than those in which she had formerly moved, people were astonished that the Marquise de Saint-Loup should condescend to be her closest friend. The friendship was taken to be a sign in Gilberte of her penchant for what she supposed was an artistic existence and for what was, unequivocally, a social decline. This explanation may be the true one. But another occurred to me, convinced as I had always been that the images which we see anywhere assembled are generally the reflection, or in some indirect fashion an effect, of a first group of different images—quite unlike the second and at a great distance from it, though the two groups are symmetrical. If night after night one saw Andrée and her husband and Gilberte in each other's company, I wondered whether this was not because, so many years earlier, one might have seen Andrée's future husband first living with Rachel and then leaving her for Andrée. Very likely Gilberte at the time, in the too remote, too exalted world in which she lived, had known nothing of this. But she must have learned of it later, when Andrée had climbed and she herself had descended enough to be aware of each other's existence. And when this happened she must have felt very strongly the prestige of the woman for whom Rachel had been abandoned by the man— the no doubt fascinating man—whom she, Rachel, had preferred to Robert. So perhaps the sight of Andrée recalled to Gilberte the youthful romance that her love for Robert had been, and inspired in her a great respect for Andrée, who even now retained the affections of a man so loved by that Rachel whom Gilberte felt to have been more deeply loved by Saint-Loup than she had been herself. But perhaps on the contrary these recollections played no part in Gilberte's fondness for the artistic couple, and one would have been right to see in her conduct, as many people did, an instance merely of those twin tastes, so often inseparable in society women, for culture and loss of caste. Perhaps Gilberte had forgotten Robert as completely as I had forgotten Albertine, and, even if she knew that Rachel was the woman whom the man of many talents had left for Andrée, never when she saw them thought about this fact which had in no way influenced her liking for them. Whether my alternative explanation was not merely possible but true was a question that could be determined only by appeal to the testimony of the parties themselves, the sole recourse which is open in such a case—or would be if they were able to bring to their confidences both insight and sincerity. But the first of these is rare in the circumstances and the second unknown. Whatever the true explanation of this friendship might be, the sight of Rachel, now a celebrated actress, could not be very agreeable to Gilberte. So I was sorry to hear that she was going to recite some poetry at this party, the programme announced being Musset's *Le Souvenir* and some fables of La Fontaine.

In the background could be heard the Princesse de Guermantes repeating excitedly, in a voice which because of her false teeth was like the rattle of old iron: "Yes, that's it, we will forgather! We will summon the clan! I love this younger generation, so intelligent, so ready to join in! Ah!" (to a young woman) "what a mujishun you are!" And she fixed her great monocle in her round eye, with an expression half of amusement, half of apology for her inability to sustain gaiety for any length of time, though to the very end she was determined to "join in" and "forgather."

"But how do you come to be at a party of this size?" Gilberte asked me. "To find you at a great slaughter of the innocents like this doesn't at all fit in with my picture of you. In fact, I should have expected to see you anywhere rather than at one of my aunt's kettle-drums, because of course she is my aunt," she added meaningly, for having become Mme de Saint-Loup at a slightly earlier date than that of Mme Verdurin's entry into the family, she thought of herself as a Guermantes from the beginning of time and therefore attainted by the misalliance which her uncle had contracted when he married Mme Verdurin, a subject, it is true, on which she had heard a thousand sarcastic remarks made in her presence by members of the family, while naturally it was only behind her back that they discussed the misalliance which Saint-Loup had contracted when he married her. The disdain that she affected for this pinchbeck aunt was not diminished by the fact that the new Princesse de Guermantes, from the sort of perversity which drives intelligent people to behave unconventionally, from the need also to reminisce which is common in old people, and in the hope lastly of conferring a past on her new fashionable status, was fond of saying when the name of Gilberte arose in conversation: "Of course I have known her for donkey's years, I used to see a lot of the child's mother; why, she was a great friend of my cousin Marsantes. And it was in my house that she got to know Gilberte's father. And poor Saint-Loup too, I knew all his family long before he married her, indeed his uncle was one of my dearest friends in the la Raspelière days." "You see," people would say to me, hearing the Princesse de Guermantes talk in this vein, "the Verdurins were not at all bohemian, they had always been friends of Mme de Saint-Loup's family." I was perhaps alone in knowing, through my grandfather, how true it was that the Verdurins were not bohemian. But this was hardly because they had known Odette. However, you can easily dress up stories about a past with which no one is any longer familiar, just as you can about travels in a country where no one has ever been. "But really," Gilberte concluded, "since you sometimes emerge from your ivory tower, wouldn't you prefer little intimate gatherings which I could arrange, with just a few intelligent and sympathetic people? These great formal affairs are not made for you at all. I saw you a moment ago talking to my aunt Oriane, who has all the good qualities in the world, but I don't think one is doing her an injustice, do you, if one says that she scarcely belongs to the aristocracy of the mind."

I was unable to acquaint Gilberte with the thoughts which had been passing through my mind for the last hour, but it occurred to me that, simply on the level of distraction, she might be able to minister to my pleasures, which, as I now foresaw them, would no more be to talk literature with the Duchesse de Guermantes than with Mme de Saint-Loup. Certainly it was my intention to resume next day, but this time with a purpose, a solitary life. So far from going into society, I would not even permit people to come and see me at home during my hours of work, for the duty of writing my book took precedence now over that of being polite or even kind. They would insist no doubt, these friends who had not seen me for years and had now met me again and supposed that I was restored to health, they would want to come when the labour of their day or of their life was finished or interrupted, or at such times as they had the same need of me as I in the past had had of Saint-Loup; for (as I had already observed at Combray when my parents chose to reproach me at those very moments when, though they did not know it, I had just formed the most praiseworthy resolutions) the internal time-pieces which are allotted to different human beings are by no means synchronised: one strikes the hour of rest while another is striking that of work, one, for the judge, that of punishment when already for the criminal that of repentance and self-perfection has long since struck. But I should have the courage to reply to those who came to see me or tried to get me to visit them that I had, for necessary business which required my immediate attention, an urgent, a supremely important appointment with myself. And yet I was aware that, though there exists but little connexion between our veritable self and the other one, nevertheless, because they both go under the same name and share the same body, the abnegation which involves making a sacrifice of easier duties and even of pleasures appears to other people to be egotism.

Was it not, surely, in order to concern myself with them that I was going to live apart from these people who would complain that they did not see me, to concern myself with them in a more fundamental fashion than would have been possible in their presence, to seek to reveal them to themselves, to realise their potentialities? What use would it have been that, for a few more years, I should waste hour after hour at evening parties pursuing the scarce expired echo of other people's remarks with the no less vain and fleeting sound of my own, for the sterile pleasure of a social contact which precluded all penetration beneath the surface? Was it not more worthwhile that I should attempt to describe the graph, to educe the laws, of these gestures that they made, these remarks that they uttered, their very lives and natures? Unfortunately, I should have to struggle against that habit of putting oneself in another person's place which, if it favours the conception of a work of art, is an obstacle to its execution. A habit this is which leads people, through a superior form of politeness, to sacrifice to others not only their pleasure but their duty, since from the standpoint of other people our duty, whatever it may be—and duty for a man who can render no good service at the front may be to remain behind the lines where he is useful—appears illusorily to be our pleasure.

And far from thinking myself wretched—a belief which some of the greatest men have held—because of this life without friends or familiar talk that I should live, I realised that our powers of exaltation are being given a false direction when we expend them in friendship, because they are then diverted from those truths towards which they might have guided us to aim at a particular friendship which can lead to nothing. Still, intervals of rest and society would at times be necessary to me and then, I felt, rather than those intellectual conversations which fashionable people suppose must be useful to writers, a little amorous dalliance with young girls in bloom would be the choice nutriment with which, if with anything, I might indulge my imagination, like the famous horse that was fed on nothing but roses. What suddenly I yearned for once more was what I had dreamed of at Balbec, when, still strangers to me, I had seen Albertine and Andrée and their friends pass across the background of the sea. But alas! I could no longer hope to find again those particular girls for whom at this moment my desire was so strong. The action of the years which had transformed all the individuals whom I had seen to-day, and among them Gilberte herself, had assuredly transformed those of the girls of Balbec who survived, as it would have transformed Albertine had she not been killed, into women too sadly different from what I remembered. And it hurt me to think that I was obliged to look for them within myself, since Time which changes human beings does not alter the image which we have preserved of them. Indeed nothing is more painful than this contrast between the mutability of people and the fixity of memory, when it is borne in upon us that what has preserved so much freshness in our memory can no longer possess any trace of that quality in life, that we cannot now, outside ourselves, approach and behold again what inside our mind seems so beautiful, what excites in us a desire (a desire apparently so individual) to see it again, save by seeking it in a person of the same age, by seeking it, that is to say, in a different person. Often had I had occasion to suspect that what seems to be unique in a person whom we desire does not in fact belong to her. And of this truth the passage of time was now giving me a more complete proof, since after twenty years, spontaneously, my impulse was to seek, not the girls whom I had known in the past, but those who now possessed the youthfulness which the others had then had. (Nor is it only the re-awakening of our old sensual desires which fails to correspond to any reality because it fails to take into account the Time that has been Lost. Sometimes I found myself wishing that, by a miracle, the door might open and through it might enter—not dead, as I had supposed, but still alive—not just Albertine but my grand-mother too. I imagined that I saw them, my heart leapt forward to greet them. But I had forgotten one thing, that, if in fact they had not died, Albertine would now have more or less the appearance that Mme Cottard had presented in the Balbec days and my grandmother, being more than ninety-five years old, would show me nothing of that beautiful calm, smiling face with which I still imagined her, but only by an exercise of the fancy no less arbitrary than that which confers a beard upon God the Father or, in the eighteenth century, regardless of their antiquity, represented the heroes of Homer in all the accoutrements of a gentleman of that age.)

I looked at Gilberte, and I did not think: "I should like to see her again," I said merely, in answer to her offer, that I should always enjoy being invited to meet young girls, poor girls if possible, to whom I could give pleasure by quite small gifts, without expecting anything of them in return save that they should serve to renew within me the dreams and the sad-nesses of my youth and perhaps, one improbable day, a single chaste kiss. Gilberte smiled and then looked as though she were seriously giving her mind to the problem.

Just as Elstir loved to see incarnate before him, in his wife, that Venetian beauty which he had often painted in his works, so I excused myself by saying that there was an aesthetic element in the egotism which attracted me to the beautiful women who had the power to make me suffer, and I had a sentiment almost of idolatry for the future Gilbertes, the future Duchesses de Guermantes, the future Albertines whom I might meet and who might, I thought, inspire me as a sculptor is inspired when he walks through a gallery of noble antique marbles. I ought to have reflected, however, that prior to each of the women whom I had loved there had existed in me a sentiment of the mystery by which she was surrounded and that therefore, rather than ask Gilberte to introduce me to young girls, I should have done better to go to places where there were girls with whom I had not the slightest connexion, those places where between oneself and them one feels an insurmountable barrier, where at a distance of three feet, on the beach, for instance, as they pass one on their way to bathe, one feels separated from them by the impossible. It was in this fashion that a sentiment of mystery had attached itself for me first to Gilberte, then to the Duchesse de Guermantes, then to Albertine and to so many others. (Later no doubt the unknown, the almost unknowable, had become the known, the familiar, perhaps painful, perhaps indifferent, but retaining still from an earlier time a certain charm.) And to tell the truth, as in those calendars which the postman brings us in the hope of a New Year's gift, there was not one of the years of my life that did not have, as a frontispiece, or intercalated between its days, the image of a woman whom I had desired during that year; an image sometimes entirely arbitrary, for the reason that, often, I had never seen the woman in question, whether she were Mme Putbus's maid or Mlle d'Orgeville or some young woman or other whose name had caught my eye on the society page of a newspaper, amongst "the swarm of charming waltzers." I guessed her to be beautiful, I fell in love with her and I constructed for her an ideal body which towered above some landscape in the region of France where I had read in the *Annuaire des Châteaux* that the estates of her family were situated. In cases, however, where I had met and known the woman, the landscape against which I saw her was, at the very least, double. First she rose, each one of these women, at a different point in my life, with the imposing stature of a tutelary local deity, in the midst of one of those landscapes of my dreams which lay side by side like some chequered network over my past, the landscape to which my imagination had sought to attach her; then later I saw her from the angle of memory, surrounded by the places in which I had known her and which she recalled to me, unable to detach herself from them, for if our life is vagabond our memory is sedentary and though we ourselves rush ceaselessly forward our recollections, indissolubly bound to the sites which we have left behind us, continue to lead a placid and sequestered existence among them, like those friends whom a traveller makes for a brief while in some town where he is staying and whom, leaving the town, he is obliged to leave behind him, because it is there that they, who stand on the steps of their house to bid him good-bye, will end their day and their life, regardless of whether he is still with them or not, there beside the church, looking out over the harbour, beneath the trees of the promenade. So that the shadow of, for instance, Gilberte lay not merely outside a church in the Ile de France where I had imagined her, but also upon a gravelled path in a park on the Méséglise way, and the shadow of Mme de Guermantes not only on a road in a watery landscape beside which rose pyramid-shaped clusters of red and purple flowers but also upon the matutinal gold of a pavement in Paris. And this second image, the one born not of desire but of memory, was, for each of these women, not unique. For my friendship with each one had been multiple, I had known her at different times when she had been a different woman for me and I myself had been a different person, steeped in dreams of a different colour. And the law which had governed the dreams of each year polarised around those dreams my recollections of any woman whom I had known during that year: all that related, for instance, to the Duchesse de Guermantes in the time of my childhood was concentrated, by a magnetic force, around Combray, while all that concerned the Duchesse de Guermantes who would presently invite me to lunch was disposed around a quite different centre of sensibility; there existed several Duchesses de Guermantes, just as, beginning with the lady in pink, there had existed several Mme Swanns, separated by the colourless

ether of the years, from one to another of whom it was as
impossible for me to leap as it would have been to leave one
planet and travel across the ether to another. And not merely
separated but different, each one bedecked with the dreams
which I had had at very different periods as with a characteristic
and unique flora which will be found on no other planet; so
much so that, having decided that I would not accept an
invitation to lunch either from Mme de Forcheville or from
Mme de Guermantes, I was only able to say to myself—for in
saying this I was transported into another world—that one of
these ladies was identical with the Duchesse de Guermantes
who was descended from Geneviève de Brabant and the other
with the lady in pink because a well-informed man within me
assured me that this was so, in the same authoritative manner
as a scientist might have told me that a milky way of nebulae
owed its origin to the fragmentation of a single star. Gilberte,
too, whom nevertheless a moment ago I had asked, without
perceiving the analogy, to introduce me to girls who might be
friends for me of the kind that she had been in the past, existed
for me now only as Mme de Saint-Loup. No longer was I
reminded when I saw her of the role which had been played
long ago in my love for her by Bergotte, Bergotte whom she
had forgotten as she had forgotten my love and who for me
had become once more merely the author of his books, without
my ever recalling now (save in rare and entirely unconnected
flashes of memory) the emotion which I had felt when I was
presented to the man, the disillusion, the astonishment wrought
in me by his conversation, in that drawing-room with the
white fur rugs and everywhere bunches of violets, where the
footmen so early in the afternoon placed upon so many different consoles such an array of lamps. In fact all the memories
that went to make up the first Mlle Swann were withdrawn
from the Gilberte of the present day and held at a distance from
her by the forces of attraction of another universe, where,
grouped around a phrase of Bergotte with which they formed
a single whole, they were forever drenched with the scent of
hawthorn.

The fragmentary Gilberte of to-day listened to my request
with a smile and then assumed a serious air as she gave it her

consideration. I was pleased to see this, for it prevented her from paying attention to a group which it could hardly have been agreeable for her to observe. In this group was the Duchesse de Guermantes, deep in conversation with a hideous old woman whom I studied without being able to guess in the least who she was—she seemed to be a complete stranger to me. It was in fact to Rachel, that is to say to the actress, the famous actress now, who was going to recite some poems by Victor Hugo and La Fontaine in the course of this party, that Gilberte's aunt was talking. For the Duchess, too long conscious that she occupied the foremost social position in Paris and failing to realise that a position of this kind exists only in the minds of those who believe in it and that many newcomers to the social scene, if they never saw her anywhere and never read her name in the account of any fashionable entertainment, would suppose that she occupied no position at all, now scarcely saw—save when, as seldom as possible, and then with a yawn, she paid a few calls—the Faubourg Saint-Germain which, she said, bored her to death, and instead did what amused her, which was to lunch with this or that actress whom she declared to be enchanting. In the new circles which she frequented, having remained much more like her old self than she supposed, she continued to think that to be easily bored was a mark of intellectual superiority, but she expressed this sentiment now with a positive violence which turned her voice into a hoarse bellow. When, for instance, I mentioned Brichot, "Tedious man!" she broke in, "how he has bored us all for the last twenty years!", and when Mme de Cambremer was heard to say: "You must re-read what Schopenhauer says about music," the Duchess drew our attention to this phrase by exclaiming: "*Re-read* is pretty rich, I must say. Who does she think she's fooling?" Old M. d'Albon smiled, recognising in this outburst a sample of the Guermantes wit. In Gilberte, who was more modern, it evoked no response. Daughter of Swann though she was, like a duckling hatched by a hen she was more romantically minded than her father. "I find that most touching," she would say, or: "He has a charming sensibility."

I told Mme de Guermantes that I had met M. de Charlus. She found him much more "altered" for the worse than in fact he was, for people in society make distinctions, in the matter of intelligence, not only between different members of their set between whom there is really nothing to choose in this respect, but also, in a single individual, between different phases of his life. Then she went on: "He has always been the image of my mother-in-law, but now the likeness is even more striking." There was nothing very extraordinary in this resemblance: it is well known that women sometimes so to speak project themselves into another human being with the most perfect accuracy, with the sole error of a transposition of sex. This, however, is an error of which one can scarcely say: "*Felix culpa*," for the sex has repercussions upon the personality, so that in a man femininity becomes affectation, reserve touchiness and so on. Nevertheless, in the face, though it may be bearded, in the cheeks, florid as they are beneath their side-whiskers, there are certain lines which might have been traced from some maternal portrait. Almost every aged Charlus is a ruin in which one may recognise with astonishment, beneath all the layers of paint and powder, some fragments of a beautiful woman preserved in eternal youth. While we were talking, Morel came in. The Duchess treated him with a civility which disconcerted me a little. "I never take sides in family quarrels," she said. "Don't you find them boring, family quarrels?"

If in a period of twenty years, like this that had elapsed since my first entry into society, the conglomerations of social groups had disintegrated and re-formed under the magnetic influence of new stars destined themselves also to fade away and then to reappear, the same sequence of crystallisation followed by dissolution and again by a fresh crystallisation might have been observed to take place within the consciousness of individuals. If for me Mme de Guermantes had been many people, for Mme de Guermantes or for Mme Swann there were many individuals who had been a favoured friend in an era that preceded the Dreyfus affair, only to be branded as a fanatic or an imbecile when the supervention of the Affair modified the accepted values of people and brought about a new configuration of parties, itself of brief duration, since later they had again disintegrated and re-formed. And what serves most powerfully to promote this renewal of old friendships, adding its influence to any purely intellectual affinities, is simply the passage of Time, which causes us to forget our antipathies and our disdains and even the reasons which once explained their existence. Had one analysed the fashionableness of the young Mme de Cambremer, one would have found that she was the niece of Jupien, a tradesman who lived in our house, and that the additional circumstance which had launched her on her social ascent was that her uncle had procured men for M. de Charlus. But all this combined had produced effects that were dazzling, while the causes were already remote and not merely unknown to many people but also forgotten by those who had once known them and whose minds now dwelt much more upon her present brilliance than upon the ignominy of her past, since people always accept a name at its current valuation. So that these drawing-room transformations possessed a double interest: they were both a phenomenon of the memory and an effect of Lost Time.

The Duchess still hesitated, for fear of a scene with M. de Guermantes, to make overtures to Balthy and Mistinguett, whom she found adorable, but with Rachel she was definitely on terms of friendship. From this the younger generation concluded that the Duchesse de Guermantes, despite her name, must be some sort of demi-rep who had never quite belonged to the best society. There were, it was true, a few reigning princes (the honour of whose familiar friendship two other great ladies disputed with her) whom Mme de Guermantes still took the trouble to invite to luncheon. But on the one hand kings and queens do not often come to see you and their acquaintances are sometimes people of no social position, and then the Duchess, with the superstitious respect of the Guermantes for old-fashioned protocol (for while well-bred people bored her to tears, she was at the same time horrified by any departure from good manners), would put on her invitation cards: "Her Majesty has commanded the Duchesse de Guermantes," or "has deigned," etc. And newcomers to society, in their ignorance of these formulae, inferred that their use was simply a sign of the Duchess's lowly situation. From the point of view of Mme de Guermantes herself, this intimacy with Rachel signified perhaps that we had been mistaken when we

supposed her to be hypocritical and untruthful in her con-
demnations of a purely fashionable life, when we imagined
that in refusing to go and see Mme de Saint-Euverte she acted
in the name not of intelligence but of snobbery, finding the
Marquise stupid only because, not having yet attained her goal,
she allowed her snobbery to appear on the surface. But the
intimacy with Rachel might also signify that the intelligence of
the Duchess was no more than commonplace, but had remained unsatisfied and at a late hour, when she was tired of
society, had driven her, totally ignorant as she was of the
veritable realities of the intellectual life, to seek for intellectual
fulfilment with a touch of that spirit of fantasy which can cause
perfectly respectable ladies, thinking to themselves: "How
amusing it will be!", to end an evening with a prank which is
in fact deadly dull: you go off and wake up some acquaintance
and then, when you are in his room, you don't know what to
say, so, after standing awkwardly by his bed for a few moments
in your evening clothes and realising how late it is, there is
nothing left to do but go home to bed yourself.

One must add that the antipathy which the changeable
Duchess had recently come to feel for Gilberte may have
caused her to take a certain pleasure in receiving Rachel, a
course of conduct which enabled her also to proclaim aloud
one of the favourite Guermantes maxims, to wit, that the
family was too numerous for its members to have to espouse
one another's quarrels (or even, some might have said, to take
notice of one another's bereavements), an independence, a
spirit of "I can't see that I am obliged" which had been reinforced by the policy that it had been necessary to adopt with
regard to M. de Charlus, who, had you followed him, would
have involved you in hostilities with all your acquaintances.

As for Rachel, if the truth was that she had taken very great
pains to form this friendship with the Duchesse de Guermantes
(pains which the Duchess had failed to detect beneath a mask
of simulated disdain and deliberate incivility, which had put
her on her mettle and given her an exalted idea of an actress so
little susceptible to snobbery), this was no doubt in a general
fashion an effect of the fascination which after a certain time
the world of high society exercises upon even the most har-

dened bohemians, a fascination paralleled by that which the same bohemians themselves exercise upon people in society, flux and reflux which correspond to—in the political order—the reciprocal curiosity, the desire to form a mutual alliance, of two nations which have recently been at war with each other. But Rachel's desire had possibly a more particular cause. It was in Mme de Guermantes's house, it was at the hands of Mme de Guermantes herself, that she had in the past suffered the most terrible humiliation of her life. This snub Rachel had with the passage of time neither forgotten nor forgiven, but the singular prestige which the event had conferred upon the Duchess in her eyes could never be effaced.

The conversation from which I was anxious to divert Gilberte's attention was, in any case, presently interrupted, for the mistress of the house came in search of the actress to tell her that the moment for her recital had arrived. She left the Duchess and a little later appeared upon the platform.

Meanwhile at the other end of Paris there was taking place a spectacle of a very different kind. Mme Berma, as I have said, had invited a number of people to a tea-party in honour of her daughter and her son-in-law. But the guests were in no hurry to arrive. Having learnt that Rachel was to recite poetry at the Princesse de Guermantes's (which utterly scandalised Berma, who from her own lofty position as a great artist looked down on Rachel as still no more than a kept woman who, because Saint-Loup paid for the dresses which she wore on the stage, was allowed to appear in the plays in which she herself, Berma, took the leading roles—and scandalised her all the more because a rumour had run round Paris that, though the invitations were in the name of the Princesse de Guermantes, it was in effect Rachel who was acting as hostess in the Princess's house), Berma had written a second time to certain faithful friends to insist that they should not miss her tea-party, for she was aware that they were also friends of the Princesse de Guermantes, whom they had known when she was Mme Verdurin. And now the hours were passing, and still nobody arrived to visit Berma. Bloch, having been asked whether he meant to

come, had ingenuously replied: "No, I would rather go to the
Princesse de Guermantes's," and this, alas! was what everyone
in his heart of hearts had decided. Berma, who suffered from a
deadly disease which had obliged her to cut down her social
activities to a minimum, had seen her condition deteriorate
when, in order to pay for the luxurious existence which her
daughter demanded and her son-in-law, ailing and idle, was
unable to provide, she had returned to the stage. She knew that
she was shortening her days, but she wanted to give pleasure
to her daughter, to whom she handed over the large sums that
she earned, and to a son-in-law whom she detested but flattered
—for she feared, knowing that his wife adored him, that if she,
Berma, did not do what he wanted, he might, out of spite,
deprive her of the happiness of seeing her child. This child,
with whom secretly the doctor who looked after her husband
was in love, had allowed herself to be persuaded that these performances in Phèdre were not really dangerous for her mother.
She had more or less forced the doctor to tell her this, or
rather of all that he had said to her about her mother's health
she had retained only this in her memory, the truth being that,
in the midst of various objections of which she had taken no
notice, he had remarked that he saw no grave harm in Berma's
appearing on the stage. He had said this because he had sensed
that in so doing he would give pleasure to the young woman
whom he loved, perhaps also from ignorance and also because
he knew that the disease was in any case incurable, since a man
readily consents to cut short the agony of an invalid when the
action that will have this effect will be advantageous to himself
—and perhaps also from the stupid idea that acting made
Berma happy and was therefore likely to do her good, a stupid
idea which had appeared to him to be corroborated when,
having been given a box by Berma's daughter and son-in-law
and having deserted all his patients for the occasion, he had
found her as extraordinarily charged with life on the stage as
she seemed to be moribund if you met her off it. And indeed
our habits enable us to a large degree, enable even the organs
of our bodies, to adapt themselves to an existence which at
first sight would appear to be utterly impossible. Have we not
all seen an elderly riding-master with a weak heart go through

a whole series of acrobatics which one would not have supposed his heart could stand for a single minute? Berma in the same way was an old campaigner of the stage, to the requirements of which her organs had so perfectly adapted themselves that she was able, by deploying her energies with a prudence invisible to the public, to give an illusion of good health troubled only by a purely nervous and imaginary complaint. After the scene in which Phèdre makes her declaration of love to Hippolyte Berma herself might be conscious only of the appalling night which awaited her as a result of her exertions, but her admirers burst into tumultuous applause and said that she was more wonderful than ever. She would go home in terrible pain, happy nevertheless because she brought back to her daughter the blue banknotes which, with the playfulness of a true child of the footlights, she had the habit of squeezing into her stockings, whence she would draw them out with pride, hoping for a smile, a kiss. Unfortunately these banknotes merely made it possible for her son-in-law and her daughter to make new embellishments to their house, which was next door to Berma's own: hence constant hammering, which interrupted the sleep of which the great actress was so desperately in need. According to the latest change in fashion, or to conform to the taste of M. de X— or M. de Y— whom they hoped to attract to their house, they altered every room in it. And Berma, realising that sleep, which alone would have deadened her pain, had gone for good, would resign herself to lying awake, not without a secret contempt for this determination to be smart which was hastening her death and making her last days an agony. That these were its consequences was no doubt in part the reason why she despised this social ambition, contempt being a natural form of revenge upon something that does us harm and that we are powerless to prevent. But there was another reason, which was that, conscious of her own genius and having learnt at a very early age the meaninglessness of all these decrees of Fashion, she for her part had remained faithful to Tradition, which she had always respected and of which she was herself an embodiment, and which caused her to judge things and people as she would have judged them thirty years earlier, to judge Rachel, for example, not as the well-known actress that she was to-day, but as the little tart that she had once been. Berma was, one must add, no better natured than her daughter, for it was from her mother that the young woman had derived, through heredity and through the contagion of an example which an only too natural admiration had rendered more than usually potent, her egotism, her pitiless mockery, her unconscious cruelty. But all this Berma had sacrificed to her daughter and in this way she had liberated herself from it. However, even if Berma's daughter had not incessantly had workmen in her house, she would have tired her mother out just the same, since inevitably youth with its powers of attraction, its ruthless and inconsiderate strength, tires out old age and ill health, which overtax themselves in the effort to keep up with it. Every day there was yet another luncheon party, and Berma would have been condemned as selfish had she deprived her daughter of this pleasure, or even had she refused to be present herself at entertainments where the prestige of the famous mother was counted upon as a means of drawing to the house, not without difficulty, certain recent acquaintances who needed to be coaxed. And even away from home her attendance at a social function might be "promised" to these same acquaintances as a way of doing them a civility. So that the poor mother, seriously engaged in her intimate dialogue with the death that was already installed within her, was compelled to get up early in the morning and drag herself out of the house. Nor was this enough. At about this time Réjane, in the full blaze of her talent, made some appearances on the stage in foreign countries which had an enormous success, and the son-in-law decided that Berma must not allow herself to be put in the shade; determined that his own family should pick up some of the same easily acquired glory, he forced his mother-in-law to set out on tours on which she was obliged to have injections of morphine, which might at any moment have killed her owing to the condition of her kidneys.

This same ambition to be smart, this longing for social prestige, for life, had on the day of the Princesse de Guermantes's reception acted in the manner of a suction-pump, drawing to the latter's house with the irresistible force of some such machine even Berma's loyalest friends, so that at the actress's party there was, in contrast and in consequence, an absolute and deathlike void. One solitary young man had come, thinking that possibly Berma's party might be just as fashionable as the other. When Berma saw the hour pass for which she had issued the invitations and realised that everybody had deserted her, she ordered tea to be served and the four people in the room sat down at the table as though it had been spread for a funeral feast. Nothing now in her face recalled the countenance of which the photograph, one distant New Year's Day, had so disturbed me. Death, as the saying goes, was written all over her face, and she resembled nothing so much as one of the marble figures in the Erechtheum. Her hardened arteries were already almost petrified, so that what appeared to be long sculptural ribbons ran across her cheeks, with the rigidity of a mineral substance. The dying eyes were still relatively alive, by contrast at least with the terrible ossified mask, and glowed feebly like a snake asleep in the midst of a pile of stones. But already the young man, who had sat down only because it would have been rude to do anything else, was incessantly looking at his watch, for he too felt the attraction of the brilliant party in the Guermantes mansion. Berma uttered not a word in reproach of the friends who had deserted her and who were foolish enough to hope that she would not discover that they had been to the Guermantes's. She murmured only: "A Rachel giving a party in the Princesse de Guermantes's house—that is something that could only happen in Paris." And silently and with a solemn slowness she continued to eat the cakes which the doctor had forbidden her, still with the air of playing her part in a funerary rite. The gloom of the tea-party was made more intense by the vile temper of the son-in-law, who was furious that Rachel, whom he and his wife knew very well, had not invited them. To crown his indignation the young man who had come told him that he knew Rachel so well that, if he went off to the Guermantes party straight away, he could even at this eleventh hour ask her to invite the frivolous couple. But Berma's daughter was too well aware of the low level at which her mother placed Rachel, she knew that she would die of despair at the thought of her daughter begging for an invitation from the former prostitute. So she told the young man and her husband that what he suggested was impossible. But she took her revenge as she sat at the tea-table by a series of little grimaces expressive of the desire for pleasure and the annoyance of being deprived of it by her kill-joy mother. The latter pretended not to see her daughter's cross looks and from time to time, in a dying voice, addressed an amiable remark to the solitary guest. But soon the rush of air which was sweeping everything towards the Guermantes mansion, and had swept me thither myself, was too much for him; he got up and said good-bye, leaving Phèdre or death—one scarcely knew which of the two it was—to finish, with her daughter and her son-in-law, devouring the funeral cakes.

My conversation with Gilberte was interrupted by the voice of the actress which now made itself heard. Her style of recitation was intelligent, for it presupposed the existence of the poem whose words she was speaking as a whole which had been in being before she opened her mouth, a whole of which we were hearing merely a fragment, as though for a few moments, as the actress passed along a road, she had happened to be within earshot of us.

The announcement that she was to recite poems with which nearly everybody was familiar had been well received. But when the actress, before beginning to speak, was seen to shoot searching and bewildered glances in every direction, to lift her hands with an air of supplication and then to utter each word as though it were a groan, the general reaction was to feel embarrassed, almost shocked by this display of sentiment. Nobody had said to himself that a recital of poetry could be anything like this. Gradually, however, each member of an audience grows accustomed to what is taking place before him, he forgets his first sensation of discomfort, he picks out what is good in a performance, he mentally compares different ways of reciting and passes judgment: "this is excellent, this is not so good." But for the first few moments, just as when, in a trivial case in a law-court, we see a barrister advance, raise a toga'd arm in the air and start to speak in a threatening tone, we hardly dare look at our neighbours. For our immediate reaction is that this is grotesque—but we cannot be sure that it is not in fact magnificent, so for the present we suspend judgment.

Nevertheless the audience was amazed to see this woman, before she had emitted a single sound, bend her knees, stretch out her arms to cradle an invisible body and then, to recite some very well-known lines of poetry, start to speak in a voice of entreaty. People looked at one another, not knowing what expression to put on their faces: a few bad-mannered young things giggled audibly; everyone glanced at his neighbour with that stealthy glance which at a smart dinner-party, when you find beside your plate an unfamiliar implement, a lobster-fork or sugar-sifter perhaps, of which you know neither what it is for nor how to use it, you cast at some more authoritative guest in the hope that he will pick it up before you and so give you a chance to imitate him—or with which, when someone quotes a line of poetry which you do not know but of which you do not wish to appear ignorant, you turn towards a man better read than yourself and relinquish to him, as though it were a favour, as though you were courteously letting him pass through a door before you, the pleasure of naming the author. With just this same glance, as they listened to the actress, each member of the audience waited, his head lowered but his eyes furtively prying, for others to take the initiative and decide whether to laugh or to criticise, to weep or to applaud. Mme de Forcheville, who had come back specially for the occasion from Guermantes, whence, as we shall see, the Duchess had been almost expelled, had assumed an expression that was attentive, concentrated, almost bad-tempered, either in order to show that she was a connoisseur of the drama and had not come merely for social reasons, or to present a hostile front to people who were less versed in literature and might have talked to her about other things, or from the intensity with which with all her faculties she strove to discover whether she "liked" or "did not like" the performance, or perhaps because, while she found it "interesting," she nevertheless "did not like" the manner in which certain lines were recited. This attitude might, one would have thought, have been more appropriate to the Princesse de Guermantes. But as the recitation was taking place in her house and as, having become as avaricious as she was rich, she had decided that her payment to Rachel would consist of five roses, she chose rather to act as claque and gave the signal for a forced display of enthusiasm by a series of exclamations of delight. And here alone could her Verdurin past be recognised, for she had the air of listening to the poems for her own private enjoyment, of having felt a desire for someone to come and recite them to her alone, so that it seemed to be mere chance that there were in the room five hundred people, her friends, whom she had permitted to come unobtrusively and share in her pleasure.

Meanwhile I observed—without any satisfaction to my vanity, for she was old and ugly—that the actress, in a somewhat restrained fashion, was giving me the glad eye. All the time that she was reciting she allowed to flutter in and out of her eyes a smile that was both repressed and penetrating and that seemed to be the first hint of an acquiescence which she would have liked to see come from me. Certain elderly ladies meanwhile, little accustomed to the recitation of poetry, were saying to their neighbours: "Did you see?", a question which had reference to the solemn, tragic miming of the actress, which they had no words to describe. The Duchesse de Guermantes sensed the slight wavering of opinion and turned the scale of victory with a cry of "Admirable!", ejaculated at a pause in the middle of the poem which perhaps she mistook for the end. More than one guest thought it incumbent upon him to underline this exclamation with a look of approval and an inclination of the head, less perhaps to display his comprehension of the reciter's art than his friendly relations with the Duchess. When the poem was finished, I heard the actress thank Mme de Guermantes, who was standing near her, as I was myself, and at the same time, taking advantage of my presence beside the Duchess, she turned to me and greeted me with charming civility. At this point I realised that she was somebody whom I ought to have known and that, whereas long ago I had mistaken the passionate glances of M. de Vaugoubert for the salutation of someone who was confused as to my identity, to-day on the contrary what I had taken in the actress to be a look of desire was no more than a decorous attempt to make me recognise and greet her. I responded with a smile and a gesture. "I am sure he does not recognise me," said the reciter to the Duchess. "Of course I do," I said confidently, "I recognise you perfectly." "Well then, who am I?" I had not the slightest idea and my position was becoming awkward. But fortunately, if throughout one of La Fontaine's finest poems this woman who was reciting it with such conviction had, whether from good nature or stupidity or embarrassment, thought of nothing but the difficulty of saying good-afternoon to me, throughout this same beautiful poem Bloch had been wondering only how to manoeuvre himself so as to be ready, the moment the poem ended, to leap from his seat like a beleaguered army making a sally and, trampling if not upon the bodies at least upon the feet of his neighbours, arrive and congratulate the reciter, perhaps from an erroneous conception of duty, perhaps merely from a desire to make people look at him. "How curious it is to see Rachel here!" he whispered in my ear. At once the magic name broke the enchantment which had given to the mistress of Saint-Loup the unknown form of this horrible old woman.[48] And once I knew who she was, I did indeed recognise her perfectly. "You were wonderful," Bloch said to Rachel, and having said these simple words, having satisfied his desire, he started on his return journey—but encountered so many obstacles and made so much noise in reaching his place that Rachel had to wait more than five minutes before beginning her second poem. This was *Les Deux Pigeons*, and at the end of it Mme de Morienval came up to Mme de Saint-Loup, whom she knew to be very well read without remembering that she had inherited the oblique and sarcastic wit of her father. "That *is* La Fontaine's fable, isn't it?" she asked, thinking that she had recognised it but not being absolutely certain, since she did not know the fables of La Fontaine at all well and in any case supposed them to be childish things which no one would recite at a fashionable gathering. To have such a success the entertainer had no doubt produced a pastiche of La Fontaine, thought the good lady. Unintentionally Gilberte confirmed her in this idea, for, disliking Rachel and wanting to say that with her style of diction there was nothing left of the fables, she said it in that over-subtle manner which had been her father's and which left simple people in doubt as to the speaker's meaning: "One quarter is the invention of the actress, a second is lunacy, a third is meaningless and the rest is La Fontaine," a remark which encouraged Mme de Morienval to maintain that the poem which had just been recited was not La Fontaine's *Les Deux Pigeons*, but an arrangement of which at most a quarter was by La Fontaine himself. Given the extraordinary ignorance of all these people, this assertion caused no surprise whatever.

Meanwhile, one of his friends having arrived after the recital was over, Bloch had the satisfaction of asking him whether he had ever heard Rachel and of painting for his benefit an extraordinary picture of her art, exaggerating, indeed suddenly discovering, as he described and revealed this modernistic diction to another person, a strange pleasure of which he had felt nothing as he listened to it. Then, with exaggerated emotion, he again congratulated Rachel in a high-pitched voice which proclaimed his sense of her genius and introduced his friend, who declared that his admiration for her was unbounded. To this Rachel, who was now acquainted with ladies of the best society and unwittingly copied them, replied: "Oh! I am most flattered, most honoured by your appreciation." Bloch's friend asked her what she thought of Berma. "Poor woman, it seems that she is living in the most abject poverty. She was once, I won't say not without talent, for what she possessed was not true talent—her taste was appalling—still, one must admit she had merit of a kind: she was more alive on the stage than most actresses, and then she had nice qualities, she was generous, she ruined herself for others. And as it is years now since she has earned a penny, because the public these days loathes the sort of thing she does . . . But of course," she added with a laugh, "I must admit that someone of my generation, naturally, only heard her right at the end of her career, and even then I was really too young to form an opinion." "She didn't recite poetry very well, did she?" hazarded Bloch's friend, to flatter Rachel. "Poetry!" she replied, "she had no idea how to recite a single line. It might have been prose, or Chinese, or Volapük—anything, rather than poetry."

In spite of Rachel's words I was thinking myself that time,

as it passes, does not necessarily bring progress in the arts. And just as some author of the seventeenth century, who knew nothing of the French Revolution, or the discoveries of science, or the War, may be superior to some writer of to-day, just as perhaps Fagon was as great a doctor as du Boulbon (a superiority in genius compensating in this case for an inferiority in knowledge), so Berma was, as the phrase goes, head and shoulders above Rachel, and Time, when simultaneously it turned Rachel into a star and Elstir into a famous painter, had inflated the reputation of a mediocrity as well as consecrated a genius.

It was scarcely surprising that Saint-Loup's former mistress should speak maliciously about Berma. She would have done this when she was young, and even if she would not have done it then, she was bound to now. When a society woman becomes an actress, a woman even of the highest intelligence and the greatest goodness of heart, and in this unfamiliar occupation displays great talent and encounters nothing but success, one will be surprised, meeting her years later, to hear on her lips not her own individual language but that which is common to the theatrical profession, the special brand of obloquy that actresses have for their colleagues, those special qualities which are added to a member of the human race by the passage over him of "thirty years on the stage." These qualities Rachel inevitably had and her origin, as we know, was not in good society.

"You can say what you like, it was a wonderful performance, it had line, it had character, it was intelligent, one has never heard anyone recite poetry like that before," said the Duchess, for fear that Gilberte should make disparaging remarks. Gilberte wandered off towards another group, to avoid an argument with her aunt, whose comments upon Rachel were indeed of the most commonplace kind. But then, since even the best writers cease often, at the approach of old age or after producing too much, to have any talent, society women may well be excused if sooner or later they cease to have any wit. Swann already in the sharp-edged wit of the Duchesse de Guermantes found it difficult to recognise the gentle raillery of the young Princesse des Laumes. And now late in life, wearied by the least effort, Mme de Guermantes said a prodigious number of stupid things. It was true that at any moment, as happened more than once in the course of this party, she could re-become the woman whom I had known in the past and talk wittily on social topics. But alongside these moments there were others, and they were no less frequent, when beneath her beautiful eyes the sparkling conversation which for so many years, from its throne of wit, had held sway over the most distinguished men in Paris, shone, in so far as it still shone at all, in a meaningless way. When the moment came to make a joke, she would check herself for the same number of seconds as in the past, she would appear to hesitate, to have something within her that was struggling to emerge, but the joke, when at last it arrived, was pitifully feeble. But how few of her listeners noticed this! Because the procedure was the same they believed that the wit too had survived intact, like those people who, superstitiously attached to some particular make of confectionery, continue to order their *petits fours* from a certain shop without noticing that they have become almost uneatable. Already during the war the Duchess had shown signs of this decay. If someone pronounced the word "culture," she would stop him, smile, kindle a light in her beautiful eyes and ejaculate: "KKKKultur," which raised a laugh among her friends, who saw in this remark the latest manifestation of the Guermantes wit. And certainly the mould was the same, and the intonation and the smile, the same that had once enchanted Bergotte, who for his part too had preserved the individual rhythm of his phrases, his interjections, his aposiopeses, his epithets, but with all this rhetorical apparatus no longer had anything to say. But newcomers, who did not know her, were surprised and said sometimes, unless they had chanced to encounter her on a day when she was amusing and "at her best": "What a stupid woman this is!"

As her life drew to its close, Mme de Guermantes had felt the quickening within her of new curiosities. Society no longer had anything to teach her. The idea that she occupied the first place in it was as evident to her as the altitude of the blue sky above the earth, and she saw no need to strengthen a position which she deemed to be unshakable. On the other hand she read and she went to the theatre, and enjoying these activities she would have been glad to prolong them; just as in the past, in the little narrow garden where she sipped orangeade with her friends, all that was most choice in the world of grand society would come familiarly, among the scented breezes of the evening and the gusts of pollen, to sustain in her the pleasure that this grand world gave her and her appetite for it, so now a different appetite caused her to want to know the reasons behind this or that literary controversy, to want to meet the authors whose books she had read, to make friends with the actresses whom she had seen on the stage. Her tired mind required a new form of food, and in order to get to know theatrical and literary people she now made herself pleasant to women with whom formerly she would have refused to exchange cards but who, in the hope of getting the Duchess to come to their parties, could boast to her of their great friendship with the editor of some review. The first actress to be invited to her house thought that she was the only one of her kind in an exotic *milieu*, which however appeared more commonplace to the second when she saw that she had a predecessor. The Duchess, because on certain evenings she received reigning monarchs, thought that there was no change in her social position. But the truth was that she who alone could boast of a blood that was absolutely without taint, she who had been born a Guermantes and who when she did not sign herself "La Duchesse de Guermantes" had the right to put "Guermantes-Guermantes," she who even to her husband's sisters seemed to be something more precious than they were themselves, like a Moses saved from the waters or Christ escaped into Egypt or Louis XVII rescued from his prison in the Temple, she the purest of the pure had now, sacrificing no doubt to that hereditary need for spiritual nourishment which had brought about the social decline of Mme de Villeparisis, herself become a Mme de Villeparisis, in whose house snobbish women were afraid of meeting this or that undesirable and of whom the younger generation, observing the *fait accompli* and not knowing what had gone before it, supposed that she was a Guermantes from an inferior cask or of a less good vintage, a Guermantes *déclassée*.

If, however, the Duchess indulged a taste for the society of her inferiors, she was careful to confine this activity within strict limits and not allow it to contaminate those members of her family from whom she derived the gratification of an aristocratic pride. If at the theatre, for instance, in order to fill her role of patroness of the arts, she had invited a minister or a painter and her guest had been so ingenuous as to ask whether her sister-in-law or her husband were not in the audience, the Duchess, with a superb assumption of lofty indifference which concealed her alarm, would haughtily reply: "I have not the slightest idea. As soon as I leave my house, I know nothing of what my family is doing. For politicians, for artists, whoever they may be, I am a widow." In this way she sought to prevent the too eager social climber from drawing upon himself a snub and upon her a reprimand from Mme de Marsantes or from Basin.

"I can't tell you how pleased I am to see you," said the Duchess. "Good heavens, when was it that I saw you last?" "I believe it was at Mme d'Agrigente's—I was paying a call and I found you there, as I often did." "But of course, I was constantly going there, my dear boy, since Basin was in love with her in those days. And calling on Basin's sweetheart of the moment was always where my friends were most likely to find me, because he used to say: 'I shall expect you to visit her without fail.' I must admit that there seemed to me to be a slight impropriety in these 'digestive visits' on which he used to send me to thank the lady for her entertainment of him. But I quite soon grew accustomed to them. The tiresome thing was, however, that I was obliged to continue my relations with his mistress after he had broken off his own. I was always reminded of the line in Victor Hugo:

Emporte le bonheur et laisse-moi *l'ennui.*

Naturally—you remember how the poem goes on—'I entered smiling none the less,' but it really was not fair, he ought to have left me the right to be inconstant, for in the end I accumulated so many of his discards that I had not a single afternoon to myself. Still, compared with the present that epoch now seems to me relatively agreeable. That he has started to be unfaithful again is, of course, something that I can only find flattering, it almost makes me feel younger. But I preferred his old way of doing it. Unfortunately, he was so out of practice that he had forgotten how to set about it. However, in spite of it all we are on excellent terms, we talk to each other, we are even quite fond of each other,"—this the Duchess added because she was afraid that I might think that she and her husband were completely separated, rather as one says apropos of someone who is desperately ill: "But he is still able to speak, I read to him this morning for an hour." "I will tell him you are here," she continued, "he will be delighted to see you." And she went towards the Duke, who was sitting on a sofa in conversation with a lady. I observed with admiration that, except that his hair was whiter, he had scarcely changed, being still as majestic and as handsome as ever. But seeing his wife approach to speak to him he assumed an air of such fury that she had no alternative but to retreat. "I can't interrupt him just now, I don't know what he is doing, we shall see presently," said Mme de Guermantes, preferring to leave me to form my own conclusions.

Bloch now came up to us and on behalf of his American inquired the identity of a young Duchess who was at the party. I replied that she was a niece of M. de Bréauté, which caused Bloch, as this name meant nothing to him, to ask for further explanations. "Bréauté!" the Duchess exclaimed, turning to me. "You remember all that, of course. How ancient it seems now, how far away! Well,"—this to Bloch—"Bréauté was a snob. They were people who lived near my mother-in-law in the country. This couldn't possibly interest you, Monsieur Bloch—though it may amuse this young man, who knew all that world long ago when I was in the midst of it myself." This last remark referred to me, and by it Mme de Guermantes brought home to me in a number of different ways how long was the time that had elapsed. First, her own friendships and opinions had so greatly changed since that period that now, in retrospect, she looked upon her charming Babal as a snob. And then, not only was he now seen at the other end of a great vista of time, but—and of this I had been quite unaware when at my first entry into society I had supposed him to be one of

the quintessential notabilities of Paris, who would for ever
remain associated with its social history as Colbert with the
history of the reign of Louis XIV—he too bore the stamp of a
provincial origin, he was a country neighbour of the old
Duchess and it was as such that the Princesse des Laumes had
made his acquaintance. Moreover this Bréauté, stripped of his
wit and relegated to a distant past for which he himself provided
a date (which proved that between then and now he had been
entirely forgotten by the Duchess) and to the countryside near
Guermantes, was—and this too I would never have thought
possible that first evening at the Opéra, when he had appeared
to me in the guise of a marine deity dwelling in his glaucous
cavern—a link between the Duchess and myself, because she
remembered that I had known him and therefore had been a
friend of hers, if not of the same social origin as herself at any
rate an inhabitant of the same social world for very much
longer than a great many people who were at the party to-day,
she remembered this and yet remembered it so hazily that she
had forgotten certain details which to me on the contrary had
then seemed to be of prime importance, such as that I never
went to Guermantes and at the time when she came to Mlle
Percepied's nuptial mass was merely a boy of a middle-class
Combray family, and that, in spite of all Saint-Loup's entreaties,
throughout the year which followed her apparition at the
Opéra she had never invited me to her house. To me this
seemed to be of supreme importance, for it was precisely
during this brief period that the life of the Duchesse de Guermantes had appeared to me to be a paradise into which I should
never enter. But for her, her life then was merely a part like
any other of her normal, commonplace life, and as from a
certain moment onwards I had dined often at her house and
had also, even before that date, been a friend of her aunt and of
her nephew, she no longer knew exactly at what period our
friendship had begun and was unaware of the grave anachronism that she was perpetrating in supposing that we had become
friends a few years earlier than in fact we had. For this would
have meant that I had known the Mme de Guermantes of the
name of Guermantes, whose essence it was to be unknowable,
that I had been permitted to enter the name of the golden

syllables, had been received into the Faubourg Saint-Germain, whereas in fact I had merely been to dine at the house of a lady who was already nothing more in my eyes than a very ordinary woman and who had occasionally invited me, not to descend into the submarine kingdom of the Nereids, but to spend an evening with her in her cousin's box. "If you want to know anything more about Bréauté," Mme de Guermantes continued, still speaking to Bloch, "though there is no earthly reason why you should, ask our friend here, who is a hundred times more interesting than Bréauté ever was. He must have dined at my house with him fifty times. It was at my house, was it not, that you got to know Bréauté? In any case, it was there that you met Swann." And I was just as surprised that she should imagine that I might have met M. de Bréauté elsewhere than at her house (which could only have happened had I moved in that society before I became acquainted with her) as I was to see that she believed that it was through her that I had met Swann. Less untruthfully than Gilberte, who had been in the habit of saying of Bréauté: "He is an old country neighbour, I so enjoy talking to him about Tansonville," whereas in fact in the past he had never visited the Swanns at Tansonville, I might have said of Swann: "He was a country neighbour who often used to come round and see us in the evening," for indeed the memories which he recalled to my mind had nothing to do with the Guermantes. "I don't know how to describe him," she went on. "He was a man whose only subject of conversation was people with grand titles. He had a whole collection of curious anecdotes about my Guermantes relations and about my mother-in-law and about Mme de Varambon before she became a lady-in-waiting to the Princesse de Parme. But does anybody to-day know who Mme de Varambon was? Our friend here, yes, he knew all those people. But it is all ancient history, they are not even names to-day, and in any case they don't deserve to be remembered." And again it struck me that, in spite of the apparent unity of that thing which we call "society," in which, it is true, social relations reach their maximum of concentration (for all paths meet at the top) and in which there are no barriers to communication, there exist nevertheless within it, or at least there are created within it by Time, separate provinces which after a while change their names and are no longer comprehensible to those who arrive in society only when its pattern has been altered. "Mme de Varambon was a good lady who said things of an incredible stupidity," continued the Duchess, who failed to appreciate that poetry of the incomprehensible which is an effect of Time and chose rather to extract from every situation its element of ironic humour, the element that could be transformed into literature of the type of Meilhac or into the Guermantes brand of wit. "At one moment she had a mania for swallowing a certain kind of lozenge which people used to take in those days for coughs and which was called" (and she laughed as she pronounced a name that was so special, so well known formerly and so unknown to-day to everyone around her) "a Géraudel lozenge. 'Madame de Varambon,' my mother-in-law used to say to her, 'if you don't stop swallowing a Géraudel lozenge every five minutes, you will injure your stomach.' 'But Madame la Duchesse,' replied Mme de Varambon, 'how can they possibly injure the stomach when they go into the bronchial tubes?' And then it was she who made the remark: 'The Duchess has a most beautiful cow, so beautiful that it is always taken for a bull!' " And Mme de Guermantes would gladly have gone on relating anecdotes of Mme de Varambon, of which she and I knew hundreds, but we realised that in the ignorant memory of Bloch this name evoked none of those images which rose up for us as soon as there was mention of her or of M. de Bréauté or of the Prince d'Agrigente, though perhaps for this very reason all these names were endowed in his eyes with a glamour which I knew to be exaggerated but which I found comprehensible—though not because I myself had at one time felt its influence, for it is rarely that our own errors and absurdities, even when we have penetrated to the truth behind them, make us more indulgent to those of others.

The past had been so transformed in the mind of the Duchess (or else the distinctions which existed in my mind had been always so absent from hers that what had been an event for me had gone unnoticed by her) that she was able to suppose that I had first met Swann in her house and M. de Bréauté elsewhere, thus conferring upon me a past as man about town of which she exaggerated the remoteness from the present. For the notion of time elapsed which I had just acquired was something that the Duchess had too, and, whereas my illusion had been to believe the gap between past and present shorter than in fact it was, she on the contrary actually overestimated it, she placed events further back than they really were, a notable consequence of this being her disregard of that supremely important line of demarcation between the epoch when she had been for me first a name and then the object of my love and the utterly different epoch when she had been for me merely a society woman like any other. It was of course only during this second period, when she had become for me a different person, that I had been to her house. But to her own eyes these differences were invisible and she would have seen nothing in the least odd in my going to her house two years earlier, for how was she to know that she had then been a different woman and even her door-mat a different door-mat, since her personality did not present to her that break in continuity which it presented to me?

"All this reminds me," I said to her, "of that first evening when I went to the Princesse de Guermantes's, when I wasn't sure that I had been invited to her party and half expected to be shown the door, and when you wore a red dress and red shoes." "Good heavens, how long ago all that was!" said the Duchesse de Guermantes, accentuating by her words my own impression of time elapsed. She seemed to be gazing into this remote past in a melancholy mood, and yet she laid a particular emphasis upon the red dress. I asked her to describe it to me, which she did most willingly. "One couldn't possibly wear a thing like that now. It was the sort of dress that was worn in those days." "But it was pretty, wasn't it?" I said. She was always afraid of giving away a point in conversation, of saying something that might depreciate her in the eyes of others. "Personally, I found it a charming fashion. If nobody wears those dresses today, it is simply because it isn't done. But they will come back, as fashions always do—in clothes, in music, in painting," she added with vigour, for she supposed there to be a certain originality in this philosophic reflection. Then the

sad thought that she was growing old caused her to resume her
languid manner, which a smile, however, momentarily contradicted: "Are you sure that they were red shoes that I wore?
I thought they were gold." I assured her that I had the most
vivid recollection of the colour of her shoes, though I preferred
not to describe the incident which made me so certain on this
point. "How kind of you to remember that!" she said to me
sweetly, for women call it kindness when you remember their
beauty, just as painters do when you admire their work. And
then, since the past, however remote it may be for a woman
like the Duchess who has more head than heart, may nevertheless chance to have escaped oblivion, "Do you recall," she
said, as though to thank me for remembering her dress and
her shoes, "that Basin and I brought you home in our carriage?
You couldn't come in with us because of some girl who was
coming to see you after midnight. Basin thought it the funniest
thing in the world that you should receive visits at such an
hour." Indeed that was the evening when Albertine had come
to see me after the Princesse de Guermantes's party and I
recalled the fact just as clearly as the Duchess, I to whom
Albertine was now as unimportant as she would have been to
Mme de Guermantes had Mme de Guermantes known that the
girl because of whom I had had to refuse their invitation was
Albertine. (In fact, she was quite in the dark as to the identity
of this girl, had never known it and only referred to the incident because of the circumstances and the singular lateness of
the hour.) Yes, I recalled the fact, for, long after our poor dead
friends have lost their place in our hearts, their unvalued dust
continues to be mingled, like some base alloy, with the circumstances of the past. And though we no longer love them,
it may happen that in speaking of a room, or a walk in a public
park, or a country road where they were present with us on a
certain occasion, we are obliged, so that the place which they
occupied may not be left empty, to make allusion to them,
without, however, regretting them, without even naming them
or permitting others to identify them. Such are the last, the
scarcely desirable vestiges of survival after death.

If the opinions which the Duchess expressed about Rachel
were in themselves commonplace, they interested me for the

reason that they too marked a new hour upon the dial. For Mme de Guermantes had no more completely forgotten than Rachel the terrible evening which the latter had endured in her house, but in the Duchess's mind too this memory had been transformed. "Of course," she said to me, "it interests me all the more to hear her, and to hear her acclaimed, because it was I who discovered her, who saw her worth and praised her and got people to listen when she was quite unknown and everybody thought her ridiculous. Yes, my dear boy, this will surprise you, but the first house in which she recited in public was mine! Yes, while all the so-called *avant-garde*, like my new cousin," she said, pointing ironically towards the Princesse de Guermantes, who for Oriane had remained Mme Verdurin, "would have allowed her to die of hunger rather than condescend to listen to her, I had made up my mind that she was interesting and I offered her a fee to come and act in my house in front of the most distinguished audience that I could muster. I may say, though the word is rather stupid and pretentious— for the truth is that talent needs nobody to help it—that I launched her. But I am not suggesting that she needed me." I made a vague gesture of protest, and I saw that Mme de Guermantes was quite prepared to accept the contrary thesis. "You don't agree? You think that talent needs a support, needs someone to bring it into the light of day? Well, perhaps you are right. Curiously enough, that is exactly what Dumas used to say to me. In this case I am extremely flattered if I have done anything, however little, to promote not of course the talent but the reputation of so fine an artist." Mme de Guermantes preferred to abandon her idea that talent, like an abscess, forces its way to the surface unaided, partly because the alternative hypothesis was more flattering for her, but also because for some time now, mixing with newcomers to the social scene and being herself fatigued, she had become almost humble, questioning others and asking them their opinion before she formed her own. "I don't need to tell you," she went on, "that that intelligent public which calls itself society understood absolutely nothing of her art. They boo'd and they tittered. It was no use my saying: 'This is strange, interesting, something that has never been done before,' nobody believed me, just as nobody has ever believed anything I have said. And it was exactly the same with the piece that she recited, which was a scene from Maeterlinck. Now, of course, it is very well known but in those days people merely thought it ridiculous—not I, however, I admired it. I must say I am surprised, when I think of it, that a mere peasant like myself, with no more education than all the other provincial girls around her, should from the very first moment have felt drawn to these things. Naturally I couldn't have said why, but I liked them, I was moved— indeed, even Basin, who can hardly be called hypersensitive, was struck by the effect that they had on me. 'I won't have you listening to these absurdities,' he said, 'it makes you ill.' And he was right, because although I'm supposed to be a woman without any feeling I'm really a bundle of nerves."

At this moment an unexpected incident occurred. A footman came up to Rachel and told her that the daughter and son-in-law of Berma were asking to speak to her. As we have seen, Berma's daughter had resisted the desire, to which her husband would have yielded, to ask Rachel for an invitation. But after the departure of the solitary guest the irritation of the young pair as they sat with their mother had increased. The thought that other people were enjoying themselves had become a torment to them and presently, profiting from a momentary absence of Berma, who had retired to her room spitting a little blood, they had thrown on some smarter clothes, called for a cab and come, without an invitation, to the Princesse de Guermantes's house. Rachel, guessing what had happened and secretly flattered, put on an arrogant air and told the footman that she could not be disturbed, the visitors must write a line to explain the object of their curious procedure. Soon the footman came back with a card on which Berma's daughter had scribbled a few words to the effect that she and her husband had not been able to resist the desire to hear Rachel—might they have her permission to come in? Rachel smiled at the naïvety of the pretext and at her own triumph. She sent back a reply that she was terribly sorry but she had finished her recital. In the ante-room, where the couple had now been waiting for an embarrassingly long time, the footmen were beginning to jeer at the two rejected petitioners.

But the ignominy of a rebuff, and the thought too of the worthlessness of Rachel in comparison with her mother, drove Berma's daughter to pursue to final victory an enterprise on which she had first embarked merely from an appetite for pleasure. She sent a message to Rachel, asking as a favour that, even if she had missed the privilege of hearing her, she should be allowed to shake her by the hand. Rachel was talking to an Italian prince, said to be not insensible to the attractions of her large fortune, the origin of which was now to some extent disguised by her partial acceptance in the world of society. And here at her feet were the daughter and the son-in-law of the illustrious Berma, a reversal of positions which she was able to savour to the full. After giving a ludicrous account of what had happened to everybody within earshot, she ordered the young couple to be admitted and in they came without waiting to be asked twice, thus at a single stroke ruining Berma's social position just as they had destroyed her health. Rachel had foreseen this; she knew that an amiable condescension on her part would do more than a refusal to win for herself a reputation in society for kindness of heart and for the young couple one for grovelling servility. So she welcomed them with a theatrical gesture of open arms and a few words spoken in the role of an exalted patroness momentarily laying aside her dignity: "Ah! here you are, it is so lovely to see you. The Princess will be delighted." Not knowing that in the world of the theatre it was generally believed that she had sent out the invitations herself, she had feared perhaps that, if she refused to let Berma's daughter and son-in-law come in, they might have doubts as to the extent, not so much of her good nature, which would scarcely have worried her, as of her influence. Instinctively the Duchesse de Guermantes drifted away, for in proportion as anyone betrayed a desire to seek out fashionable society, he or she sank in her esteem. At the moment she was uniquely impressed with Rachel's kindness, and had the daughter and son-in-law been presented to her she would have turned her back on them. Rachel meanwhile was already composing in her head the gracious phrase with which she would annihilate Berma when she saw her the following day backstage: "I was distressed and appalled that your poor daughter should be made to dance attendance on me. If I had only realised! She kept sending me card after card." Her spirits rose as she thought of this blow that she would deal to Berma. Yet perhaps she would have flinched had she known that it would be mortal. We like to have victims, but without putting ourselves clearly in the wrong: we want them to live. Besides, in what way had she done wrong? A few days later she was heard to say, with a laugh: "It's a bit much. I try to be kinder to her children than she ever was to me, and now I'm practically accused of murdering her. The Duchess will be my witness." So died Berma. It seems that the children of actors inherit from their parents all their ugly emotions and all the artificiality of theatrical life, but not, as a by-product of these, the stubborn will to work that their father or mother possessed, and Berma is not the only great tragic actress who has died as the victim of a domestic plot woven around her, repeating in her own person the fate that she so many times suffered in the final act of a play.

In spite of her new interests the life of the Duchess was now very unhappy, for the reason to which she had briefly alluded in her conversation with me, a reason which had, as a further consequence, a parallel degradation of the society which M. de Guermantes frequented. The Duke was still robust, but with the advance of age his desires had grown less imperious and he had long ceased to be unfaithful to Mme de Guermantes, when suddenly, without anyone knowing quite how the liaison had begun, he had fallen in love with Mme de Forcheville. When one considered what her age must now be, this seemed extraordinary. But perhaps she had been very young when she started on her amatory career. And then there are women who, decade after decade, are found in a new incarnation, having new love affairs (sometimes long after one had thought they were dead) and causing the despair of young wives who are abandoned for them by their husbands. In any case, the Duke's liaison with Mme de Forcheville had assumed such proportions that the old man, imitating in this final love the pattern of those that he had had in the past, watched jealously over his mistress in a manner which, if my love for Albertine had, with important variations, repeated the love of Swann for Odette, made that of M. de Guermantes for this same Odette recall my own for Albertine. He insisted that she should lunch with him and dine with him and he was always in her house, so that she was able to show him off to friends who without her would never have made the acquaintance of a Duc de Guermantes and who came there to meet him rather as one might go to the house of a courtesan to meet a king, her lover. It was true that Mme de Forcheville had long ago become a society lady. But starting again late in life to be kept, and to be kept by an old man of such enormous pride who, in spite of the situation, was the important person in her house, she was herself not too proud to wear only those wraps which pleased him, to serve only the dishes that he liked, and to flatter her friends by telling them that she had spoken of them to her new lover just as in the old days she would tell my great-uncle that she had spoken of him to the Grand Duke who sent her cigarettes; in a word, in spite of all that she had accomplished in building up a social position, she was tending under pressure of new circumstances to become once more, as she had first appeared to me in my earliest childhood, the lady in pink. (It was, of course, many years since my uncle Adolphe had died, but the replacement of the old figures around us by new ones does not necessarily prevent us from beginning our old life again.) If Odette had yielded to the pressure of her new circumstances, this was no doubt partly from greed, but also because, having been much sought after in society as the mother of an eligible daughter and then ignored once Gilberte had married Saint-Loup, she foresaw that the Duc de Guermantes, who would have done anything for her, would rally to her side a number of duchesses who would perhaps be delighted to do an ill turn to their friend Oriane; and perhaps too she warmed to the game when she saw how it distressed the Duchess, in whose discomfiture a feminine sentiment of rivalry caused her to rejoice. Even among the Duke's relations she now had her partisans. Saint-Loup up to his death had continued loyally to visit her with his wife. Were not he and Gilberte heirs both to M. de Guermantes and to Odette, who would herself no doubt be the principal beneficiary of the Duke's will? And even Courvoisier nephews with the most exacting standards, even the Princesse

de Trania and Mme de Marsantes, came to her house in the
hope of a legacy, without worrying about the pain that this
might cause the Duchess, of whom Odette, stung by past
affronts, spoke in the most scurrilous fashion. As for the
Duke's own social position, his liaison with Mme de Forcheville—this liaison which was merely a pale copy of earlier affairs
of the same kind—had recently caused him for the second time
in his life to lose his chance of the presidency of the Jockey and
a vacant seat in the Académie des Beaux-Arts, just as the way of
life of M. de Charlus and his public association with Jupien had
cost him the presidency of the Union and that also of the
Société des Amis du Vieux Paris when these were within his
grasp. Thus the two brothers, so different in their tastes, had
lost their reputations from a common indolence and a common
lack of will, qualities already perceptible, but in a more agreeable fashion, in the Duc de Guermantes their grandfather,
member of the Académie Française, but which, re-appearing in
his two grandsons, had permitted a natural taste in the one and
what passes for an unnatural taste in the other to alienate their
possessors from their proper social sphere.

The old Duke no longer went anywhere, for he spent his
days and his evenings with Mme de Forcheville. But to-day, as
he would find her here, he had come for a moment, in spite of
the vexation of having to meet his wife. I had not seen him
and I would certainly have failed to recognise him, had he not
been clearly pointed out to me. He was no more than a ruin
now, a magnificent ruin—or perhaps not even a ruin but a
beautiful and romantic natural object, a rock in a tempest.
Lashed on all sides by the surrounding waves—waves of
suffering, of wrath at being made to suffer, of the rising tide
of death—his face, like a crumbling block of marble, preserved
the style and the poise which I had always admired; it might
have been one of those fine antique heads, eaten away and hopelessly damaged, which you are proud nevertheless to have as
an ornament for your study. In one respect only was it changed:
it seemed to belong to a more ancient epoch than formerly, not
simply because of the now rough and rugged surfaces of what
had once been a more brilliant material, but also because to an
expression of keen and humorous enjoyment had succeeded

one, involuntary and unconscious, built up by illness, by the struggle against death, by passive resistance, by the difficulty of remaining alive. The arteries had lost all suppleness and gave to the once expansive countenance a hard and sculptural quality. And though the Duke had no suspicion of this, there were aspects of his appearance, of his neck and cheeks and forehead, which suggested to the observer that the vital spirit within, compelled to clutch desperately at every passing minute, was buffeted by a great tragic gale, while the white wisps of his still magnificent but now sparse hair lashed with their foam the half submerged promontory of his face. And just as there are strange and unique reflections which only the approach of a supreme all-foundering storm can impart to rocks that hitherto have been of a different colour, so I realised that the leaden grey of the stiff, worn cheeks, the almost white, fleecy grey of the drifting wisps of hair, the feeble light that still shone from the eyes that scarcely saw, were not unreal hues and glimmers —they were only too real but they were fantastic, they were borrowed from the palette and the illumination, inimitable in their terrifying and prophetic sombreness, of old age and the imminence of death.

The Duke stayed only for a few moments, long enough, however, for me to perceive that Odette, reserving her favours for younger wooers, treated him with contempt. But curiously, whereas in the past he had been almost ridiculous when he used to behave like a king in a play, he had now assumed an appearance of true grandeur, rather like his brother, whom old age, stripping him of all unessential qualities, caused him to resemble. And—in this too resembling his brother—he who had once been proud, though not in his brother's fashion, seemed now almost deferential, though again in a different fashion. He had not suffered quite the degradation of M. de Charlus, he was not obliged by the unreliable memory of a sick man to greet with civility people whom he would once have disdained. But he was very old and when, wanting to leave, laboriously he passed through the doorway and down the stairs, one saw that old age, which is after all the most miserable of human conditions, which more than anything else precipitates us from the summit of our fortunes like a king in a Greek tragedy, old age, forcing him to halt in the *via dolorosa* which life must become for us when we are impotent and surrounded by menace, to wipe his perspiring brow, to grope his way forward as his eyes sought the step which eluded them, because for his unsteady feet no less than for his clouded eyes he needed support, old age, giving him without his knowing it the air of gently and timidly beseeching those near him, had made him not only august but, even more, suppliant.

Thus in the Faubourg Saint-Germain three apparently impregnable positions, of the Duc and the Duchesse de Guermantes and of the Baron de Charlus, had lost their inviolability, changing, as all things change in this world, under the action of an inherent principle which had at first attracted nobody's attention: in M. de Charlus his love for Charlie, which had enslaved him to the Verdurins, and then later the advent of senility; in Mme de Guermantes a taste for novelty and for art; in the Duke an exclusive amorous passion, of a kind of which he had had several in the course of his life, but one which now, through the feebleness of age, was more tyrannical than those that had gone before and of which the ignominy was no longer compensated by the opposing, the socially redeeming respectability of the Duchess's *salon*, where the Duke himself no longer appeared and which altogether had almost ceased to function. Thus it is that the pattern of the things of this world changes, that centres of empire, assessments of wealth, letters patent of social prestige, all that seemed to be forever fixed is constantly being re-fashioned, so that the eyes of a man who has lived can contemplate the most total transformation exactly where change would have seemed to him to be most impossible.

Unable to do without Odette, always installed by her fireside in the same armchair, whence age and gout made it difficult for him to rise, M. de Guermantes permitted her to receive friends who were only too pleased to be presented to the Duke, to defer to him in conversation, to listen while he talked about the society of an earlier era, about the Marquise de Villeparisis and the Duc de Chartres. At moments, beneath the gaze of the old masters assembled by Swann in a typical "collector's" arrangement which enhanced the unfashionable and "period"

character of the scene, with this Restoration Duke and this
Second Empire courtesan swathed in one of the wraps which
he liked, the lady in pink would interrupt him with a sprightly
sally: he would stop dead and fix her with a ferocious glance.
Perhaps he had come to see that she too, like the Duchess,
sometimes made stupid remarks; perhaps, suffering from an
old man's delusion, he imagined that it was an ill-timed witticism of Mme de Guermantes that had checked his flow of
reminiscence, imagined that he was still in his own house, like
a wild beast in chains who for a brief second thinks that it is
still free in the deserts of Africa. And brusquely raising his
head, with his little round yellow eyes which themselves had
the glitter of the eyes of a wild animal, he fastened upon her
one of those looks which sometimes in Mme de Guermantes's
drawing-room, when the Duchess talked too much, had made
me tremble. So for a moment the Duke glared at the audacious
lady in pink. But she, unflinching, held him in her gaze, and
after a few seconds which seemed interminable to the spectators, the old tame lion recollecting that he was not free, with
the Duchess beside him, in that Sahara which one entered by
stepping over a door-mat on a landing, but in Mme de Forcheville's domain, in his cage in the Zoological Gardens, he
allowed his head, with its still thick and flowing mane of which
it would have been hard to say whether it was yellow or white,
to slump back between his shoulders and continued his story.
He seemed not to have understood what Mme de Forcheville
was trying to say, and indeed there was seldom any very profound meaning in her remarks. He did not forbid her to have
friends to dinner with him, but, following a habit derived from
his former love-affairs which was hardly likely to surprise
Odette, who had been used to the same thing with Swann, and
which to me seemed touching because it recalled to me my life
with Albertine, he insisted that these guests should take their
leave early so that he might be the last to say good-night to her.
Needless to say, the moment he was out of the house she went
off to meet other people. But of this the Duke had no suspicion
or perhaps preferred her to think that he had no suspicion. The
sight of old men grows dim as their hearing grows less acute,
their insight too becomes clouded and even their vigilance is

relaxed by fatigue, and at a certain age, inevitably, Jupiter himself is transformed into a character in one of Molière's plays, and not even into the Olympian lover of Alcmène but into a ludicrous Géronte. It must be added that Odette was unfaithful to M. de Guermantes in the same fashion that she looked after him, that is to say without charm and without dignity. She was commonplace in this role as she had been in all her others. Not that life had not frequently given her good parts; it had, but she had not known how to play them.

On several occasions after the Guermantes party I attempted to see her again, but each time I was unsuccessful, for M. de Guermantes, in order to satisfy the requirements not only of his jealous nature but also of his medical regime, allowed her to attend social functions only in the day-time and even then placed an embargo upon dances. This seclusion in which she was kept she frankly avowed to me when at last we met, for several reasons. The principal one was that, although I had only written a few articles and published some essays, she imagined me to be a well-known author, an idea which even caused her naïvely to exclaim, recalling the days when I used to go to the Allée des Acacias to see her pass by and later visited her in her home: "Ah! if I had only guessed that he would be a great writer one day!" And having heard that writers seek the society of women as a means of collecting material for their work and like to get them to describe their love-affairs, she now, in order to interest me, reassumed the character of an unashamed tart. She would tell me stories of this sort: "And then once there was a man who was mad about me, and I was desperately in love with him too. We were having a heavenly life together. He had to go to America for some reason, and I was to go with him. The day before we were to leave I decided that, as our love could not always remain at such a pitch of intensity, it was more beautiful not to let it slowly fade to nothing. We had a last evening together —he of course believed that I was coming with him—and then a night of absolute madness, in which I was ecstatically happy in his arms and at the same time in despair because I knew that I should never see him again. A few hours earlier I had gone up to some traveller whom I did not know and given him my ticket. He wanted at least to buy it from me, but I replied: 'No, you are doing me a service by taking it, I don't want any money.' " Here was another: "One day I was in the Champs-Elysées and M. de Bréauté, whom I had only met once, began to stare at me so insistently that I stopped and asked him why he took the liberty of staring at me like that. He replied: 'I am looking at you because you are wearing a ridiculous hat.' This was quite true. It was a little hat with pansies, the fashions were dreadful in those days. But I was furious and said to him: 'I cannot allow you to talk to me like that.' At that moment it started to rain. I said to him: 'I would only forgive you if you had a carriage.' 'But I have one,' he replied, 'and I will accompany you.' 'No, I want your carriage but I don't want you.' I got into the carriage and he walked off in the rain. But the same evening he arrived on my door-step. For two years we were madly in love with each other. Come and have tea with me one day, and I will tell you how I made the acquaintance of M. de Forcheville. The truth is," she went on with a melancholy air, "that I have spent my life in cloistered seclusion because my great loves have all been for men who were horribly jealous. I am not speaking of M. de Forcheville, who was at bottom a commonplace man—and I have never really been able to love anyone who was not intelligent. But M. Swann for one was as jealous as the poor Duke here, for whose sake I renounce all enjoyment, because I know that he is so unhappy in his own home. With M. Swann it was different, I was desperately in love with him and it seems to me only reasonable to sacrifice dancing and society and all the rest of it for a life which will give pleasure to a man who loves you, or will merely prevent him from suffering. Poor Charles, how intelligent he was, how fascinating, just the type of man I liked." And perhaps this was true. There had been a time when she had found Swann attractive, which had coincided with the time when she to him had been "not his type." The truth was that "his type" was something that, even later, she had never been. And yet how he had loved her and with what anguish of mind! Ceasing to love her, he had been puzzled by this contradiction, which really is no contradiction at all, if we consider how large a proportion of the sufferings endured by men in their lives is caused to them by women who are "not their type." Perhaps there are many reasons why this should be so: first, because a woman is "not your type" you let yourself, at the beginning, be loved by her without loving in return, and by doing this you allow your life to be gripped by a habit which would not have taken root in the same way with a woman who was "your type," who, conscious of your desire, would have offered more resistance, would only rarely have consented to see you, would not have installed herself in every hour of your days with that familiarity which means that later, if you come to love her and then suddenly she is not there, because of a quarrel or because of a journey during which you are left without news of her, you are hurt by the severance not of one but of a thousand links. And then this habit, not resting upon the foundation of strong physical desire, is a sentimental one, and once love is born the brain gets much more busily to work: you are plunged into a romance, not plagued by a mere need. We are not wary of women who are "not our type," we let them love us, and if, subsequently, we come to love them we love them a hundred times more than we love other women, without even enjoying in their arms the satisfaction of assuaged desire. For these reasons and for many others the fact that our greatest unhappinesses come to us from women who are "not our type" is not simply an instance of that mockery of fate which never grants us our wishes except in the form which pleases us least. A woman who is "our type" is seldom dangerous, she is not interested in us, she gives us a limited contentment and then quickly leaves us without establishing herself in our life, and what on the contrary, in love, is dangerous and prolific of suffering is not a woman herself but her presence beside us every day and our curiosity about what she is doing every minute: not the beloved woman, but habit.

I was cowardly enough to say that it was kind and generous of her to talk to me in this way, but I knew how little truth there was in my remark, I knew that her frankness was mixed with all sorts of lies. And as she continued to regale me with adventures from her past life, I thought with terror how much there was that Swann had not known—though some of it he had guessed almost to the point of certainty, merely from the look in her eyes when she saw a man or a woman whom she did not know and whom she found attractive—and how much the knowledge of it would have made him suffer, because he had fastened his sensibility to this one individual. And why was she now so outspoken? Simply in order to give me what she believed were subjects for novels. In this belief she was mistaken. It was true that from my earliest years she had supplied my imagination with abundance of material to work on, but in a much more involuntary fashion, through an act which originated with myself when I sought, unbeknown to her, to deduce from my observation of her the laws which governed her life.

M. de Guermantes now reserved his thunderbolts solely for the Duchess, to whose somewhat indiscriminate associations Mme de Forcheville did not fail to draw his wrathful attention. And so Mme de Guermantes was very unhappy. It is true that M. de Charlus, with whom I had once discussed the subject, maintained that the original transgressions had not been on his brother's side and that beneath the legendary purity of the Duchess there in fact lay skilfully concealed an incalculable number of love-affairs. But I had never heard any gossip to this effect. In the eyes of almost all the world Mme de Guermantes was a woman of a very different kind, and the idea that she had always been irreproachable went unchallenged. Which of these two ideas accorded with the truth I was unable to determine, the truth being almost always something that to three people out of four is unknown. I well recalled certain blue and wandering glances, which I had intercepted as they shot from the eyes of the Duchesse de Guermantes down the nave at Combray, but I could not really say that either of the two ideas was disproved by these glances, since both the one and the other could give them meanings which, though different, were equally acceptable. In my foolishness, child as I then was, I had for a moment taken them to be glances of love directed at myself. Later I had realised that they were merely the gracious looks that a sovereign lady, like the one in the stained-glass windows of the church, bestows upon her vassals. Was I now to suppose that my first idea had been correct and that, if in the sequel the Duchess had never spoken to me of love, this was because she had been more afraid to compromise herself with a friend of her nephew and her aunt than with an unknown boy encountered by chance in the church of Saint-Hilaire at Combray?

Perhaps the Duchess had been pleased for a moment to feel that her past had more substance because it had been shared by me, but certain questions which I put to her on the provincialism of M. de Bréauté, whom at the time I had scarcely distinguished from M. de Sagan or M. de Guermantes, caused her to resume the normal point of view of a society woman, the point of view, that is to say, of a woman who affects to despise society. While we were talking, she took me on a tour of the house. In one or two smaller sitting-rooms we came upon special friends of our hostess who had preferred to get away from the crowd in order to listen to the music. One of these was a little room with Empire furniture, where a few men in black evening clothes were sitting about on sofas, listening, while beside a tall mirror supported by a figure of Minerva a *chaise longue*, set at right angles to the wall but with a curved and cradle-like interior which contrasted with the straight lines all round it, disclosed the figure of a young woman lying at full length. The relaxation of her pose, from which she did not even stir when the Duchess entered the room, was set off by the marvellous brilliance of her Empire dress, of a flame-red silk before which even the reddest of fuchsias would have paled and upon whose nacreous texture emblems and flowers seemed to have been imprinted in some distant past, for their patterns were sunk beneath its surface. To acknowledge the presence of the Duchess she made a slight bow with her beautiful, dark head. Although it was broad daylight, she had asked for the curtains to be drawn as an aid to the silence and concentration which the music required and, to prevent people from stumbling over the furniture, an urn had been lit upon a tripod and from it came a faint, iridescent glimmer. I inquired of the Duchess who the young woman was, and she told me that her name was Mme de Saint-Euverte. This led me to inquire further how she was related to the Mme de Saint-Euverte whom I had known. Mme de Guermantes said that she was the wife of one of old Mme de Saint-Euverte's great-

nephews and appeared to think it possible that her maiden
name had been La Rochefoucauld, but denied that she had ever
herself known any Saint-Euvertes. I recalled to her the evening
party (known to me, it is true, only from hearsay) at which,
when she was still Princesse des Laumes, she had unexpectedly
met Swann. Mme de Guermantes assured me that she had
never been at this party. The Duchess had never been very
truthful and now told lies more readily than ever. For her
Mme de Saint-Euverte was a hostess—and one whose reputation, with the passage of time, had sunk very low indeed—
whom she chose to disown. I did not insist. "No, someone
you may perhaps have seen in my house—because at least he
was amusing—is the husband of the woman you are talking
about, but I never had anything to do with his wife." "But
she didn't have a husband." "That is what you imagined,
because they were separated. In fact he was much nicer than
she was." At length it dawned upon me that an enormous man,
of vast height and strength, with snow-white hair, whom I
used to meet in various houses and whose name I had never
known, was the husband of Mme de Saint-Euverte. He had
died in the previous year. As for the great-niece, I do not know
whether it was owing to some malady of the stomach or the
nerves or the veins, or because she was about to have or had
just had a child or perhaps a miscarriage, that she lay flat on
her back to listen to the music and did not budge for anyone.
Very probably she was simply proud of her magnificent red
silks and hoped on her *chaise longue* to look like Mme Récamier.
She could not know that for me she was giving birth to a new
efflorescence of the name of Saint-Euverte, which recurring
thus after so long an interval marked both the distance travelled
by Time and its continuity. Time was the infant that she cradled
in her cockle-shell, where the red fuchsias of her silk dress gave
an autumnal flowering to the name of Saint-Euverte and to the
Empire style. The latter Mme de Guermantes declared that she
had always detested, a remark which meant merely that she
detested it now, which was true, for she followed the fashion,
even if she did not succeed in keeping up with it. To say
nothing of David, whose work she hardly knew, when she was
quite young she had thought M. Ingres the most boring and

academic of painters, then, by a brusque reversal—which caused her also to loathe Delacroix—the most delectable of the masters revered by *art nouveau*. By what gradations she had subsequently passed from this cult to a renewal of her early contempt matters little, since these are shades of taste which the writings of an art critic reflect ten years before the conversation of clever women. After having delivered herself of some strictures upon the Empire style, she apologised for having talked to me about people of as little interest as the Saint-Euvertes and subjects as trivial as the provincial side of Bréauté's character, for she was as far from guessing why these things could interest me as was Mme de Saint-Euverte *née* La Rochefoucauld, seeking in her supine pose the well-being of her stomach or an Ingresque effect, from suspecting that her name—her married name, not the infinitely more distinguished one of her own family—had enchanted me and that I saw her, in this room full of symbolic attributes, as a Nymph cradling the Infant Time.

"But how can I talk to you about this nonsense, how can it possibly interest you?" exclaimed the Duchess. She had uttered these words in an undertone and nobody had been able to hear what she was saying. But a young man (who interested me later when I discovered his name, which had been much more familiar to me at one time than that of Saint-Euverte) got up with an air of exasperation and moved away from us in order to listen undisturbed. For the Kreutzer Sonata was now being played, but having lost his place in the programme the young man thought that it was a piece by Ravel, which he had been told was as beautiful as Palestrina but difficult to understand. In his haste to move to another seat, he bumped violently against an escritoire which he had not seen in the half-dark, and the noise had the effect of slewing round the heads of several people, for whom the trifling physical exertion of looking over their shoulder was a welcome interruption to the torture of listening "religiously" to the Kreutzer Sonata. Mme de Guermantes and I, who had caused this unfortunate little incident, hurriedly left the room. "Yes," she went on, "how can these inanities interest a man of your talent? That is what I asked myself just now, when I saw you talking to Gilberte de Saint-Loup. You should not waste your time on her. For me that woman is quite literally nothing—she is not even a woman, merely the most artificial and *bourgeois* phenomenon that I have ever encountered" (for even when she was defending intellectualism the Duchess did not divest herself of her aristocratic prejudices). "What, in any case, are you doing in a house like this? I can just see that you might want to be here to-day, because there was this recitation by Rachel and naturally that interests you. But wonderful though she was, she does not give of her best before a public like this. You must come and have luncheon alone with her in my house. Then you will see what an extraordinary creature she is. She is worth a hundred times more than all this riff-raff. And after luncheon she will recite Verlaine for you. You will be amazed! But otherwise your coming to a great omnium gatherum like this is something I simply cannot understand. Unless perhaps your interest is professional . . ." she added with a doubtful and mistrustful air and without venturing to follow this speculation too far, for she had no very precise ideas as to the nature of the improbable operations to which she alluded. She went on to tempt me with the glittering prospect of her "afternoons": every day after luncheon there was X— and there was Y—, and I found that her views on these matters were now those of all women who preside over a *salon*, those women whom in the past (though she denied it today) she had despised and whose great superiority, whose sign of election lay, according to her present mode of thinking, in getting "all the men" to come to them. If I happened to say that some great lady with a *salon* had spoken with malice of Mme Howland when she was alive, the Duchess burst out laughing at my simplicity: "But of course, she had all the men and Mme Howland was trying to get them away from her."

"Don't you think," I said to the Duchess, "that it must be painful for Mme de Saint-Loup to have to listen, as she has just been doing, to a woman who was once her husband's mistress?" I saw form in Mme de Guermantes's face one of those oblique bars which indicate that a train of thought is linking something a person has just heard to some disagreeable subject of reflection. A train of thought, it is true, which usually remains unexpressed, for seldom if ever do we receive any answer to the unpleasant things that we say or write. Only a fool begs vainly ten times in succession for a reply to a letter which was a blunder and which he ought never to have written, for the only reply ever vouchsafed to this sort of letter is in the form of action: the lady whom you suppose to be merely an unpunctual correspondent addresses you as "Monsieur" when she next meets you instead of calling you by your Christian name. My reference to Saint-Loup's liaison with Rachel was, however, not seriously unpleasant and could only cause Mme de Guermantes a moment's annoyance by reminding her that I had been Robert's closest friend and that he had perhaps confided in me on the subject of the snubs which Rachel had suffered when she gave her performance at the Duchess's party. But Mme de Guermantes did not persist in these reflections, the stormy bar faded from her face and she replied to my question concerning Mme de Saint-Loup: "Frankly, it is my belief that it can matter very little to Gilberte, since she never loved her husband. She is a quite dreadful young woman. She loved the social position and the name and being my niece and getting away from the slime where she belonged, but then having done this her one idea was to return to it. I don't mind telling you that I suffered a great deal for poor Robert, because, though he was no genius, he saw this perfectly well, and a lot of other things too. Perhaps I shouldn't say it, because after all she is my niece and I have no absolute proof that she was unfaithful to him, but there were any number of stories. Oh! yes, there were, and I know for a fact there was something between her and an officer at Méséglise. Robert wanted to challenge him. It was because of all this that Robert joined up —the war came to him as a deliverance from the misery of his family life: if you want my opinion, he wasn't killed, he got himself killed. Do you think she felt any grief? Not a scrap, she even astonished me by the extraordinary cynicism with which she displayed her indifference, and this distressed me very much, because I was really extremely fond of poor Robert. Perhaps this will surprise you, because people have a wrong idea of my character, but even now I still think of him sometimes—I never forget anybody. He never said a word to me, but he saw very clearly that I guessed everything. Do you suppose, if she had loved her husband the least little bit, that she could stoically endure like this to be in the same drawing-room as the woman with whom he was desperately in love for so many years—indeed one may say 'always,' for I am quite certain that he never gave her up, even during the war. Why, she would fly at her throat!" exclaimed the Duchess, forgetting that she herself, in arranging for Rachel to be invited and so setting the stage for the drama which she judged to be inevitable if it were true that Gilberte had loved Robert, had perhaps acted cruelly. "No, in my opinion," the Duchess concluded, "she is a bitch." Such an expression on the lips of the Duchesse de Guermantes was rendered possible by the downward path which she was following, from the polished society of the Guermantes to that of her new actress friends, and came to her all the more easily because she grafted it on to an eighteenth-century mode of speech which she thought of as broad and racy—and then had she not always believed that to her all things were permitted? But the actual choice of the word was dictated by the hatred which she felt for Gilberte, by an irresistible wish to strike her at least in effigy if she could not attack her with physical blows. And at the same time the Duchess thought that somehow the word justified the whole manner in which she conducted herself towards Gilberte, or rather conducted hostilities against Gilberte, in society and in the family and even where pecuniary interests were concerned such as the succession to Robert's estate.

This savage attack on Gilberte struck me as quite unwarranted, but sometimes we pronounce a judgment which receives later from facts of which we were ignorant and which we could not have guessed an apparent justification, and Mme de Guermantes's tirade perhaps belonged to this category. For Gilberte, who had no doubt inherited certain family characteristics from her mother (and I had perhaps unconsciously anticipated some such laxness of principle in her when I had asked her to introduce me to young girls), had now had time to reflect upon my request and, anxious no doubt that the profit should stay in the family, had reached a decision bolder than any that I would have thought possible. "Let me fetch my

daughter for you," she said, "I should so like to introduce her
to you. She is over there, talking to young Mortemart and
other babes in arms who can be of no possible interest. I am
sure that she will be a charming little friend for you." I asked
whether Robert had been pleased to have a daughter. "Oh!
yes," she replied, "he was very proud of her. But naturally,"
she went on, with a certain naïvety, "I think that nevertheless,
his tastes being what they were, he would have preferred a
son." Years later, this daughter, whose name and fortune gave
her mother the right to hope that she would crown the whole
work of social ascent of Swann and his wife by marrying a
royal prince, happening to be entirely without snobbery chose
for her husband an obscure man of letters. Thus it came about
that the family sank once more, below even the level from
which it had started its ascent, and a new generation could only
with the greatest difficulty be persuaded that the parents of the
obscure couple had enjoyed a splendid social position. The
names of Swann and Odette de Crécy came miraculously to life
whenever anyone wanted to explain to you that you were
wrong, that there had been nothing so very wonderful about
the family, and it was generally supposed that Mme de Saint-
Loup had really made as good a match for her daughter as
could be expected and that the marriage of this daughter's
grandfather to Mme de Crécy had been no more than an unsuccessful attempt to rise to a higher sphere—a view of Swann's
marriage which would have astonished his fashionable friends,
in whose eyes it had been rather the product of an idealistic
theory like those which in the eighteenth century drove
aristocratic disciples of Rousseau and other precursors of the
Revolution to abandon their privileges and live according to
nature.

My surprise at Gilberte's words and the pleasure that they
caused me were soon replaced, while Mme de Saint-Loup left
me and made her way into another drawing-room, by that idea
of Time past which was brought home to me once again, in
yet another fashion and without my even having seen her, by
Mlle de Saint-Loup. Was she not—are not, indeed, the majority
of human beings?—like one of those star-shaped cross-roads
in a forest where roads converge that have come, in the forest

as in our lives, from the most diverse quarters? Numerous for me were the roads which led to Mlle de Saint-Loup and which radiated around her. Firstly the two great "ways" themselves, where on my many walks I had dreamed so many dreams, both led to her: through her father Robert de Saint-Loup the Guermantes way; through Gilberte, her mother, the Méséglise way which was also "Swann's way." One of them took me, by way of this girl's mother and the Champs-Elysées, to Swann, to my evenings at Combray, to Méséglise itself; the other, by way of her father, to those afternoons at Balbec where even now I saw him again near the sun-bright sea. And then between these two high roads a network of transversals was set up. Balbec, for example, the real Balbec where I had met Saint-Loup, was a place that I had longed to go to very largely because of what Swann had told me about the churches in its neighbourhood, and especially about its own church in the Persian style, and yet Robert de Saint-Loup was the nephew of the Duchesse de Guermantes, and through him I arrived at Combray again, at the Guermantes way. And there were many other points in my life to which I was led by starting from Mlle de Saint-Loup, to the lady in pink, for instance, who was her grandmother and whom I had seen in the house of my great-uncle. And here there was a new transversal, for this great-uncle's man-servant, who had opened the door to me that day and who later, by the gift of a photograph, had enabled me to identify the lady in pink, was the father of the young man with whom not only M. de Charlus but also Mlle de Saint-Loup's father had been in love, the young man on whose account he had made her mother unhappy. And was it not Swann, the grandfather of Mlle de Saint-Loup, who had first spoken to me of the music of Vinteuil, just as it was Gilberte who had first spoken to me of Albertine? Yet it was in speaking of this same music of Vinteuil to Albertine that I had discovered the identity of her great friend and it was with this discovery that that part of our lives had commenced which had led her to her death and caused me such terrible sufferings. And it was also Mlle de Saint-Loup's father who had gone off to try and bring Albertine back. And indeed my whole social life, both in the drawing-rooms of the Swanns and the Guermantes in Paris and also that very different life which I had led with the Verdurins in the country, was in some sense a prolongation of the two ways of Combray, a prolongation which brought into line with one way or the other places as far apart as the Champs-Elysées and the beautiful terrace of la Raspelière. Are there in fact among all our acquaintances any who, if we are to tell the story of our friendship with them, do not constrain us to place them successively in all the most different settings of our own lives? A life of Saint-Loup painted by me would have as its background the various scenes of my own life, would be related to every part of that life, even those to which it was apparently most foreign, such as my grandmother and Albertine. And the Verdurins, though they might be diametrically opposed to these other characters, were yet linked to Odette through her past and to Robert de Saint-Loup through Charlie—and in the Verdurins' house too what a role, what an all-important role had not the music of Vinteuil played! And then Swann had been in love with Legrandin's sister, and Legrandin had known M. de Charlus, whose ward Legrandin's nephew, young Cambremer, had married. Certainly, if he was thinking purely of the human heart, the poet was right when he spoke of the "mysterious threads" which are broken by life. But the truth, even more, is that life is perpetually weaving fresh threads which link one individual and one event to another, and that these threads are crossed and recrossed, doubled and redoubled to thicken the web, so that between any slightest point of our past and all the others a rich network of memories gives us an almost infinite variety of communicating paths to choose from.

At every moment of our lives we are surrounded by things and people which once were endowed with a rich emotional significance that they no longer possess. But let us cease to make use of them in an unconscious way, let us try to recall what they once were in our eyes, and how often do we not find that a thing later transformed into, as it were, mere raw material for our industrial use was once alive, and alive for us with a personal life of its own. All round me on the walls were paintings by Elstir, that Elstir who had first introduced me to Albertine. And it was in the house of Mme Verdurin that I was about to be presented to Mlle de Saint-Loup whom I was going to ask to be Albertine's successor in my life, in the house of that very Mme Verdurin whom I had so often visited with Albertine—and how enchanting they seemed in my memory, all those journeys that we had made together in the little train on the way to Douville and la Raspelière—and who had also schemed first to promote and then to break not only my own love for Albertine but, long before it, that of the grandfather and the grandmother of this same Mlle de Saint-Loup. And to complete the process by which all my various pasts were fused into a single mass Mme Verdurin, like Gilberte, had married a Guermantes.

I have said that it would be impossible to depict our relationship with anyone whom we have even slightly known without passing in review, one after another, the most different settings of our life. Each individual therefore—and I was myself one of these individuals—was a measure of duration for me, in virtue of the revolutions which like some heavenly body he had accomplished not only on his own axis but also around other bodies, in virtue, above all, of the successive positions which he had occupied in relation to myself. And surely the awareness of all these different planes within which, since in this last hour, at this party, I had recaptured it, Time seemed to dispose the different elements of my life, had, by making me reflect that in a book which tried to tell the story of a life it would be necessary to use not the two-dimensional psychology which we normally use but a quite different sort of three-dimensional psychology, added a new beauty to those resurrections of the past which my memory had effected while I was following my thoughts alone in the library, since memory by itself, when it introduces the past, unmodified, into the present —the past just as it was at the moment when it was itself the present—suppresses the mighty dimension of Time which is the dimension in which life is lived.

I saw Gilberte coming across the room towards me. For me the marriage of Saint-Loup and the thoughts which filled my mind at that date—and which were still there, unchanged, this very morning—might have belonged to yesterday, so that I was astonished to see at her side a girl of about sixteen, whose tall figure was a measure of that distance which I had been reluctant to see. Time, colourless and inapprehensible Time, so that I was almost able to see it and touch it, had materialised itself in this girl, moulding her into a masterpiece, while correspondingly, on me, alas! it had merely done its work. And now Mlle de Saint-Loup was standing in front of me. She had deep-set piercing eyes, and a charming nose thrust slightly forward in the form of a beak and curved, perhaps not in the least like that of Swann but like Saint-Loup's. The soul of that particular Guermantes had fluttered away, but his charming head, as of a bird in flight, with its piercing eyes, had settled momentarily upon the shoulders of Mlle de Saint-Loup and the sight of it there aroused a train of memories and dreams in those who had known her father. I was struck too by the way in which her nose, imitating in this the model of her mother's nose and her grandmother's, was cut off by just that absolutely horizontal line at its base, that same brilliant if slightly tardy stroke of design—a feature so individual that with its help, even without seeing anything else of a head, one could have recognised it out of thousands—and it seemed to me wonderful that at the critical moment nature should have returned, like a great and original sculptor, to give to the granddaughter, as she had given to her mother and her grandmother, that significant and decisive touch of the chisel. I thought her very beautiful: still rich in hopes, full of laughter, formed from those very years which I myself had lost, she was like my own youth.

The idea of Time was of value to me for yet another reason: it was a spur, it told me that it was time to begin if I wished to attain to what I had sometimes perceived in the course of my life, in brief lightning-flashes, on the Guermantes way and in my drives in the carriage of Mme de Villeparisis, at those moments of perception which had made me think that life was worth living. How much more worth living did it appear to me now, now that I seemed to see that this life that we live in half-darkness can be illumined, this life that at every moment we distort can be restored to its true pristine shape, that a life, in short, can be realised within the confines of a book! How happy would he be, I thought, the man who had the power to write such a book! What a task awaited him! To give some idea of this task one would have to borrow comparisons from the loftiest and the most varied arts; for this writer—who, moreover, to indicate the mass, the solidity of each one of his characters must find means to display that character's most opposite facets—would have to prepare his book with meticulous care, perpetually regrouping his forces like a general conducting an offensive, and he would have also to endure his book like a form of fatigue, to accept it like a discipline, build it up like a church, follow it like a medical regime, vanquish it like an obstacle, win it like a friendship, cosset it like a little child, create it like a new world without neglecting those mysteries whose explanation is to be found probably only in worlds other than our own and the presentiment of which is the thing that moves us most deeply in life and in art. In long books of this kind there are parts which there has been time only to sketch, parts which, because of the very amplitude of the architect's plan, will no doubt never be completed. How many great cathedrals remain unfinished! The writer feeds his book, he strengthens the parts of it which are weak, he protects it, but afterwards it is the book that grows, that designates its author's tomb and defends it against the world's clamour and for a while against oblivion. But to return to my own case, I thought more modestly of my book and it would be inaccurate even to say that I thought of those who would read it as "my" readers. For it seemed to me that they would not be "my" readers but the readers of their own selves, my book being merely a sort of magnifying glass like those which the optician at Combray used to offer his customers—it would be my book, but with its help I would furnish them with the means of reading what lay inside themselves. So that I should not ask them to praise me or to censure me, but simply to tell me whether "it really is like that," I should ask them whether the words that they read within themselves are the same as those which I have written (though a discrepancy in this respect need not always be the consequence of an error on my part, since the explanation could also be that the reader had eyes for which my book was not a suitable instrument). And—for at every moment the metaphor uppermost in my mind changed as I began to represent to myself more clearly and in a more material shape the task upon which I was about to embark—I thought that at my big deal table, under the eyes of Françoise, who like all unpretentious people who live at close quarters with us would have a certain insight into the nature of my labours (and I had sufficiently forgotten Albertine to have forgiven Françoise anything that she might have done to injure her), I should work beside her and in a way almost as she worked herself (or at least as she had worked in the past, for now, with the onset of old age, she had almost lost her sight) and, pinning here and there an extra page, I should construct my book, I dare not say ambitiously like a cathedral, but quite simply like a dress. Whenever I had not all my "paperies" near me, as Françoise called them, and just the one that I needed was missing, Françoise would understand how this upset me, she who always said that she could not sew if she had not the right size of thread and the proper buttons. And then through sharing my life with me had she not acquired a sort of instinctive comprehension of literary work, more accurate than that possessed by many intelligent people, not to mention fools? Already years ago, when I had written my article for *Le Figaro*, while our old butler, with that sort of commiseration which always slightly exaggerates the laboriousness of an occupation which the sympathiser does not practise himself and does not even clearly visualise—or even of a habit which he does not have himself, like the people who say to you: "How tiring you must find it to sneeze like that!"—expressed his quite sincere pity for writers in the words: "That's a head-splitting job you've got there," Françoise on the contrary both divined my happiness and respected my toil. The only thing that annoyed her was my speaking about the article to Bloch before it appeared, for she was afraid that he might forestall me. "You're too trustful," she would say, "all those people are nothing but copiators." And it was true that, whenever I had outlined to Bloch something that I had written and that he admired, he would provide a retrospective alibi for himself by saying: "Why, isn't that curious, I have written something very similar myself, I must read it to you one day," from which I inferred that he intended to sit down and write it that very evening.

These "paperies," as Françoise called the pages of my writing, it was my habit to stick together with paste, and sometimes in this process they became torn. But Françoise then would be able to come to my help, by consolidating them just as she stitched patches on to the worn parts of her dresses or as, on the kitchen window, while waiting for the glazier as I was waiting for the printer, she used to paste a piece of newspaper where a pane of glass had been broken. And she would say to me, pointing to my note-books as though they were worm-eaten wood or a piece of stuff which the moth had got into: "Look, it's all eaten away, isn't that dreadful! There's nothing left of this bit of page, it's been torn to ribbons," and examining it with a tailor's eye she would go on: "I don't think I shall be able to mend this one, it's finished and done for. A pity, perhaps it has your best ideas. You know what they say at Combray: there isn't a furrier who knows as much about furs as the moth, they always get into the best ones."

And in yet another way my work would resemble that of Françoise: in a book individual characters, whether human or of some other kind, are made up of numerous impressions derived from many girls, many churches, many sonatas and combined to form a single sonata, a single church, a single girl, so that I should be making my book in the same way that Françoise made that *bœuf à la mode* which M. de Norpois had found so delicious, just because she had enriched its jelly with so many carefully chosen pieces of meat.

Thus it was that I envisaged the task before me, a task which would not end until I had achieved what I had so ardently desired in my walks on the Guermantes way and thought to be impossible, just as I had thought it impossible, as I came home at the end of those walks, that I should ever get used to going to bed without kissing my mother or, later, to the idea that Albertine loved women, though in the end I had grown to live with this idea without even being aware of its presence; for neither our greatest fears nor our greatest hopes are beyond the limits of our strength—we are able in the end both to dominate the first and to achieve the second.

Yes, upon this task the idea of Time which I had formed to-day told me that it was time to set to work. It was high time.

But—and this was the reason for the anxiety which had gripped me as soon as I entered the drawing-room, when the theatrical disguises of the faces around me had first given me the notion of Lost Time—was there still time and was I still in a fit condition to undertake the task? For one thing, a necessary condition of my work as I had conceived it just now in the library was a profound study of impressions which had first to be re-created through the memory. But my memory was old and tired. The mind has landscapes which it is allowed to contemplate only for a certain space of time. In my life I had been like a painter climbing a road high above a lake, a view of which is denied to him by a curtain of rocks and trees. Suddenly through a gap in the curtain he sees the lake, its whole expanse is before him, he takes up his brushes. But already the night is at hand, the night which will put an end to his painting and which no dawn will follow. How could I not be anxious, seeing that nothing was yet begun and that though on the ground of age I could still hope that I had some years to live, my hour might on the other hand strike almost at once? For the fundamental fact was that I had a body, and this meant that I was perpetually threatened by a double danger, internal and external, though to speak thus was merely a matter of linguistic convenience, the truth being that the internal danger —the risk, for instance, of a cerebral haemorrhage—is also external, since it is the body that it threatens. Indeed it is the possession of a body that is the great danger to the mind, to our human and thinking life, which it is surely less correct to describe as a miraculous entelechy of animal and physical life than as an imperfect essay—as rudimentary in this sphere as the communal existence of protozoa attached to their polyparies or as the body of the whale—in the organisation of the spiritual life. The body immures the mind within a fortress; presently on all sides the fortress is besieged and in the end, inevitably, the mind has to surrender.

But—to accept provisionally the distinction which I have just made between the two sorts of danger that threaten the mind, and to begin with that which is in the fullest sense external—I recalled that it had often happened to me in the course of my life, in moments of intellectual excitement which coincided with a complete suspension of physical activity, as for example on those evenings when, half drunk, I had left the restaurant at Rivebelle in a carriage to go to some neighbouring casino, to feel very clearly within me the present object of my thought and at the same time to realise how much at the mercy of chance this intellectual activity was: how fortuitous it was that this particular thought had not entered my mind before, and how easily, through an accident to the carriage which was hurtling through the darkness, it might, along with my body, be annihilated. At the time this did not worry me. My high spirits knew neither forethought nor anxiety. The possibility that this joy might end in a second and turn into nothingness mattered to me scarcely at all. How different was my attitude now! The happiness which I was feeling was the product not of a purely subjective tension of the nerves which isolated me from the past, but on the contrary of an enlargement of my mind, within which the past was re-forming and actualising itself, giving me—but alas! only momentarily—something whose value was eternal. This I should have liked to bequeath to those who might have been enriched by my treasure. Admittedly, what I had experienced in the library and what I was seeking to protect was pleasure still, but no longer pleasure of an egotistical kind, or if there was egotism in it (for all the fruitful altruisms of nature develop in an egotistical manner and any human altruism which is without egotism is sterile, like that of the writer who interrupts his work to receive a friend in distress or to accept some public function or to write propaganda articles) it was an egotism which could be put to work for the benefit of other people. No longer was I indifferent to my fate as I had been on those drives back from Rivebelle; I felt myself enhanced by this work which I bore within me as by something fragile and precious which had been entrusted to me and which I should have liked to deliver intact into the hands of those for whom it was intended, hands which were not my own. And this feeling that I was the bearer of a work made me think in a changed way of an accident in which I might meet with death, as of something much more greatly to be feared and at the same time, to the extent to which this work of mine seemed to me necessary and durable, absurd because in contradiction with my desire, with the flight of my thought, yet none the less possible for that, since accidents, being produced by material causes, can perfectly well take place at the very moment when wishes of a quite different order, which they destroy without being aware of their existence, render them most bitterly regrettable (at a trivial level of existence such accidents happen every day: at the very moment, for instance, when you are trying your hardest not to make a noise because of a friend who is asleep, a carafe placed too near the edge of his table falls to the ground and awakens him). I knew that my brain was like a mountain landscape rich in minerals, wherein lay vast and varied ores of great price. But should I have time to exploit them? For two reasons I was the only person who could do this: with my death would disappear the one and only engineer who possessed the skill to extract these minerals and—more than that—the geological formation itself. Yet presently, when I left this party to go home, it only needed a chance collision between the taxi which I should take and another car for my body to be destroyed, thus forcing my mind, from which life instantly would ebb away, forever to abandon the new ideas which at this moment, not yet having had time to place them within the safety of a book, it anxiously embraced with the fragile protection of its own pulpy and quivering substance.

But by a strange coincidence, this rational fear of danger was taking shape in my mind at a moment when I had finally become indifferent to the idea of death. In the past the fear of being no longer myself was something that had terrified me, and this had made me dread the end of each new love that I had experienced (for Gilberte, for Albertine), because I could not bear the idea that the "I" who loved them would one day cease to exist, since this in itself would be a kind of death. But by dint of repetition this fear had gradually been transformed into a calm confidence. So that if in those early days, as we have seen, the idea of death had cast a shadow over my loves, for a long time now the remembrance of love had helped me not to fear death. For I realised that dying was not something new, but that on the contrary since my childhood I had already died many times. To take a comparatively recent period, had I

not clung to Albertine more tenaciously than to my own life?
Could I at the time when I loved her conceive my personality
without the continued existence within it of my love for her?
Yet now I no longer loved her, I was no longer the person
who loved her but a different person who did not love her, and
it was when I had become a new person that I had ceased to
love her. And yet I did not suffer from having become this
new person, from no longer loving Albertine, and surely the
prospect of one day no longer having a body could not from
any point of view seem to me as sad as had then seemed to me
that of one day no longer loving Albertine, that prospect which
now was a fact and one which left me quite unmoved. These
successive deaths, so feared by the self which they were destined to annihilate, so painless, so unimportant once they were
accomplished and the self that feared them was no longer there
to feel them, had taught me by now that it would be the merest
folly to be frightened of death. Yet it was precisely when the
thought of death had become a matter of indifference to me
that I was beginning once more to fear death, under another
form, it is true, as a threat not to myself but to my book, since
for my book's incubation this life that so many dangers
threatened was for a while at least indispensable. Victor Hugo
says:

Il faut que l'herbe pousse et que les enfants meurent.

To me it seems more correct to say that the cruel law of art is
that people die and we ourselves die after exhausting every
form of suffering, so that over our heads may grow the grass
not of oblivion but of eternal life, the vigorous and luxuriant
growth of a true work of art, and so that thither, gaily and
without a thought for those who are sleeping beneath them,
future generations may come to enjoy their *déjeuner sur l'herbe*.

So much for the dangers from without; there were others,
as I have said, that threatened me from within. Supposing that
I were preserved from all accidents of an external kind, might I
not nevertheless be robbed of the fruits of this good fortune
by some accident occurring within myself, some internal
catastrophe assailing me before the necessary months had
passed and I had had time to write my book? When presently

I made my way home through the Champs-Elysées, who was to say that I might not be struck down by that malady which had struck my grandmother one afternoon when she had gone there with me for a walk which, though of this she had no suspicion, was destined to be her last—so ignorant are we, as ignorant as the hand of a clock when it arrives at the point upon its dial where a spring will be released within the mechanism which will cause the hour to strike. And indeed perhaps the fear that I might already have traversed almost the whole of that last minute which precedes the first stroke of the hour, that minute during which the stroke is already preparing itself, perhaps the fear of the stroke that might already be moving into action within my brain was itself a sort of obscure awareness of something that was soon to happen, a sort of reflection in the conscious mind of the precarious state of the brain whose arteries are about to give way, a phenomenon no more impossible than that sudden acceptance of death that comes to wounded men who, though the doctor and their own desire to live try to deceive them, say, realising the truth: "I am going to die, I am ready," and write their farewells to their wives.

Nor was anything so grave as a cerebral haemorrhage needed to hinder me in the execution of my task. Already the premonitory symptoms of the same malady, perceptible to me in a certain emptiness in the head and a tendency to forgetfulness thanks to which I now merely stumbled upon things in my memory by chance in the way in which, when you are tidying your belongings, you find objects which you had forgotten even that you had to look for, were making me resemble a miser whose strong-box has burst open and whose treasures little by little are disappearing. For a while there existed within me a self which deplored the loss of these treasures, then I perceived that memory, as it withdrew from me, carried away with it this self too.

And something not unlike my grandmother's illness itself happened to me shortly afterwards, when I still had not started to work on my book, in a strange fashion which I should never have anticipated. I went out to see some friends one evening and was told that I had never looked so well, and how wonderful it was that I had not a single grey hair. But at the end of

the visit, coming downstairs, three times I nearly fell. I had
left my home only two hours earlier; but when I got back, I
felt that I no longer possessed either memory or the power of
thought or strength or existence of any kind. People could
have come to call on me or to proclaim me king, to lay violent
hands on me or arrest me, and I should passively have submitted, neither opening my eyes nor uttering a word, like
those travellers of whom we read who, crossing the Caspian
Sea in a small boat, are so utterly prostrated by seasickness that
they offer not even a show of resistance when they are told
that they are going to be thrown into the sea. I had, strictly
speaking, no illness, but I felt myself no longer capable of
anything, I was in the condition of those old men who one day
are in full possession of their faculties and the next, having
fractured a thigh or had an attack of indigestion, can only drag
on for a while in their bed an existence which has become
nothing more than a preparation, longer or shorter, for a now
ineluctable death. One of my selves, the one which in the past
had been in the habit of going to those barbarian festivals that
we call dinner-parties, at which, for the men in white shirt-
fronts and the half-naked women beneath feathered plumes,
values have been so reversed that a man who does not turn up
after having accepted the invitation—or merely arrives after
the roast has been served—is deemed to have committed an
act more culpable than any of those immoral actions which,
along with the latest deaths, are so lightly discussed at this
feast which nothing but death or a serious illness is an acceptable excuse for failing to attend—and then only provided that
one has given notice in good time of one's intention to die, so
that there may be no danger for the other guests of sitting
down thirteen to table—this one of my selves had retained its
scruples and lost its memory. The other self, the one which
had had a glimpse of the task that lay before it, on the contrary
still remembered. I had received an invitation from Mme Molé
and I had learnt that Mme Sazerat's son had died. I determined
therefore to employ one of those few hours after which I could
not hope even to pronounce another word or to swallow a
mouthful of milk, since my tongue would be tied as my grandmother's had been during her agony, in addressing my excuses

to the one lady and my condolences to the other. But a moment
or two later I had forgotten that I had these things to do—most
happily forgotten, for the memory of my real work did not
slumber but proposed to employ the hour of reprieve which
was granted me in laying my first foundations. Unfortunately,
as I took up a note-book to write, Mme Molé's invitation card
slipped out in front of my eyes. Immediately the forgetful self,
which nevertheless was able to dominate the other—is this not
always the case with those scrupulous barbarians who have
learnt the lore of the dinner-party?—pushed away the note-
book and wrote to Mme Molé (whose esteem for me would no
doubt have been great had she known that I had allowed my
reply to her invitation to take precedence over my labours as
an architect). Then suddenly a word in my letter reminded me
that Mme Sazerat had lost her son and I wrote to her as well,
after which, having sacrificed a real duty to the factitious
obligation to appear polite and sympathetic, I fell back exhausted and closed my eyes, not to emerge from a purely vegetal
existence before a week had elapsed. During this time, however, if all my unnecessary duties, to which I was willing to
sacrifice my true duty, vanished after a few moments from my
head, the idea of the edifice that I had to construct did not
leave me for an instant. Whether it would be a church where
little by little a group of faithful would succeed in apprehending
verities and discovering harmonies or perhaps even a grand
general plan, or whether it would remain, like a druidic monument on a rocky isle, something for ever unfrequented, I could
not tell. But I was resolved to devote to it all my strength,
which ebbed, as it seemed, reluctantly and as though to leave
me time to complete the periphery of my walls and close "the
funeral gate." Before very long I was able to show a few
sketches. No one understood anything of them. Even those
who commended my perception of the truths which I wanted
eventually to engrave within the temple, congratulated me on
having discovered them "with a microscope," when on the
contrary it was a telescope that I had used to observe things
which were indeed very small to the naked eye, but only
because they were situated at a great distance, and which were
each one of them in itself a world. Those passages in which I

was trying to arrive at general laws were described as so much pedantic investigation of detail. What, in any case, was I hoping to achieve? In my youth I had had a certain facility, and Bergotte had praised as "admirable" the pages which I wrote while still at school. But instead of working I had lived a life of idleness, of pleasures and distractions, of ill health and cosseting and eccentricities, and I was embarking upon my labour of construction almost at the point of death, without knowing anything of my trade. I felt that I no longer possessed the strength to carry out my obligations to people or my duties to my thoughts and my work, still less to satisfy both of these claims. As for the first, my forgetfulness of the letters I had to write and of the other things I had to do, to some extent simplified my task. But suddenly, at the end of a month, the association of ideas brought back the painful recollection of these duties and I was momentarily overwhelmed by the thought of my impotence. To my astonishment I found that I did not mind, the truth being that, since the day when my legs had trembled so violently as I was going downstairs, I had become indifferent to everything, I longed only for rest, while waiting for the great rest which would come in the end. Amongst other things I was indifferent to the verdict which might be passed on my work by the best minds of my age, and this not because I relegated to some future after my death the admiration which it seemed to me that my work ought to receive. The best minds of posterity might think what they chose, their opinions mattered to me no more than those of my contemporaries. The truth was that, if I thought of my work and not of the letters which I ought to answer, this was not because I attached to these two things, as I had during my years of idleness and later, in that brief interval between the conception of my book and the day when I had had to cling to the banister, very different degrees of importance. The organisation of my memory, of the preoccupations that filled my mind, was indeed linked to my work, but perhaps simply because, while the letters which I received were forgotten a moment later, the idea of my work was inside my head, always the same, perpetually in process of becoming. But even my work had become for me a tiresome obligation, like a son for a dying mother who still, between her injections and her blood-lettings, has to make the exhausting effort of constantly looking after him. Perhaps she still loves him, but it is only in the form of a duty too great for her strength that she is aware of her affection. In me, in the same way, the powers of the writer were no longer equal to the egotistical demands of the work. Since the day of the staircase, nothing in the world, no happiness, whether it came from friendship or the progress of my book or the hope of fame, reached me save as a sunshine unclouded but so pale that it no longer had the virtue to warm me, to make me live, to instil in me any desire; and yet, faint though it was, it was still too dazzling for my eyes, I closed them and turned my face to the wall. When a lady wrote to me: "I have been *very surprised* not to receive an answer to my letter," I must, it seemed, to judge from the sensation of movement in my lips, have twisted an infinitesimal corner of my mouth into a little smile. Nevertheless, I was reminded of her unanswered letter and I wrote her a reply. Not wishing to be thought ungrateful, I tried hard to raise my tardy civilities to the level of those which I supposed that other people, though I had forgotten it, had shown to me. And I was crushed by the effort to impose upon my moribund existence the superhuman fatigues of life. The loss of my memory helped me a little by creating gaps in my obligations; they were more than made good by the claims of my work.

The idea of death took up permanent residence within me in the way that love sometimes does. Not that I loved death, I abhorred it. But after a preliminary stage in which, no doubt, I thought about it from time to time as one does about a woman with whom one is not yet in love, its image adhered now to the most profound layer of my mind, so completely that I could not give my attention to anything without that thing first traversing the idea of death, and even if no object occupied my attention and I remained in a state of complete repose, the idea of death still kept me company as faithfully as the idea of my self. And, on that day on which I had become a half-dead man, I do not think that it was the accidents characterising this condition—my inability to walk down-stairs, to remember a name, to get up from a chair—that had, even by an unconscious train of thought, given rise to this idea of death, this conviction that I was already almost dead, it seems to me rather that the idea had come simultaneously with the symptoms, that inevitably the mind, great mirror that it is, reflected a new reality. Yet still I did not see how from my present ailments one could pass, without warning of what was to come, to total death. Then, however, I thought of other people, of the countless people who die every day without the gap between their illness and their death seeming to us extraordinary. I thought also that it was only because I saw them from within—rather than because I saw them in the deceptive colours of hope—that certain of my ailments, taken singly, did not seem to me to be fatal although I believed that I would soon die, just as those who are most convinced that their hour has come are, nevertheless, easily persuaded that if they are unable to pronounce certain words, this is nothing so serious as aphasia or a stroke, but a symptom merely of a local fatigue of the tongue, or a nervous condition analogous to a stutter, or the lassitude which follows indigestion.

No doubt my books too, like my fleshly being, would in the end one day die. But death is a thing that we must resign ourselves to. We accept the thought that in ten years we ourselves, in a hundred years our books, will have ceased to exist. Eternal duration is promised no more to men's works than to men.

In my awareness of the approach of death I resembled a dying soldier, and like him too, before I died, I had something to write. But my task was longer than his, my words had to reach more than a single person. My task was long. By day, the most I could hope for was to try to sleep. If I worked, it would be only at night. But I should need many nights, a hundred perhaps, or even a thousand. And I should live in the anxiety of not knowing whether the master of my destiny might not prove less indulgent than the Sultan Shahriyar, whether in the morning, when I broke off my story, he would consent to a further reprieve and permit me to resume my narrative the following evening. Not that I had the slightest pretension to be writing a new version, in any way, of the *Thousand and One Nights*, or of that other book written by night, Saint-Simon's

Memoirs, or of any of those books which I had loved with a child's simplicity and to which I had been as superstitiously attached as later to my loves, so that I could not imagine without horror any work which should be unlike them. But— as Elstir had found with Chardin—you can make a new version of what you love only by first renouncing it. So my book, though it might be as long as the *Thousand and One Nights,* would be entirely different. True, when you are in love with some particular book, you would like yourself to write something that closely resembles it, but this love of the moment must be sacrificed, you must think not of your own taste but of a truth which far from asking you what your preferences are forbids you to pay attention to them. And only if you faithfully follow this truth will you sometimes find that you have stumbled again upon what you renounced, find that, by forgetting these works themselves, you have written the *Thousand and One Nights* or the *Memoirs* of Saint-Simon of another age. But for me was there still time? Was it not too late?

And I had to ask myself not only: "Is there still time?" but also: "Am I well enough?" Ill health, which by compelling me, like a severe director of conscience, to die to the world, had rendered me good service ("for unless the grain of wheat dies after it has been sown, it will abide alone; but if it dies, it will bring forth much fruit"), and which, after idleness had preserved me from the dangers of facility, was perhaps going to protect me from idleness, that same ill health had consumed my strength and as I had first noticed long ago, particularly when I had ceased to love Albertine, the strength of my memory. But was not the re-creation by the memory of impressions which had then to be deepened, illumined, transformed into equivalents of understanding, was not this process one of the conditions, almost the very essence of the work of art as I had just now in the library conceived it? Ah! if only I now possessed the strength which had still been intact on that evening brought back to my mind by the sight of *François le Champi*! Was not that the evening when my mother had abdicated her authority, the evening from which dated, together with the slow death of my grandmother, the decline of my health and my will? All these things had been decided in that moment when, no longer able to bear the prospect of waiting till morning to place my lips upon my mother's face, I had made up my mind, jumped out of bed and gone in my night-shirt to post myself at the window through which the moonlight entered my room until I should hear the sounds of M. Swann's departure. My parents had gone with him to the door, I had heard the garden gate open, give a peal of its bell, and close. . . .

While I was asking myself these questions, it occurred to me suddenly that, if I still had the strength to accomplish my work, this afternoon—like certain days long ago at Combray which had influenced me—which in its brief compass had given me both the idea of my work and the fear of being unable to bring it to fruition, would certainly impress upon it that form of which as a child I had had a presentiment in the church at Combray but which ordinarily, throughout our lives, is invisible to us: the form of Time. Many errors, it is true, there are, as the reader will have seen that various episodes in this story had proved to me, by which our senses falsify for us the real nature of the world. Some of these, however, it would be possible for me to avoid by the efforts which I should make to give a more exact transcription of things. In the case of sounds, for instance, I should be able to refrain from altering their place of origin, from detaching them from their cause, beside which our intelligence only succeeds in locating them after they have reached our ears—though to make the rain sing softly in the middle of one's room or, contrarily, to make the quiet boiling of one's *tisane* sound like a deluge in the courtyard outside should not really be more misleading than what is so often done by painters when they paint a sail or the peak of a mountain in such a way that, according to the laws of perspective, the intensity of the colours and the illusion of our first glance, they appear to us either very near or very far away, through an error which the reasoning mind subsequently corrects by, sometimes, a very large displacement. Other errors, though of a more serious kind, I might continue to commit, placing features, for instance, as we all do, upon the face of a woman seen in the street, when instead of nose, cheeks and chin there ought to be merely an empty space with nothing more upon it than a flickering reflection of our desires. But at least, even if I had not the leisure to prepare—and here was a much more important matter—the hundred different masks which ought properly to be attached to a single face, if only because of the different eyes which look at it and the different meanings which they read into its features, not to mention, for the same eyes, the different emotions of hope and fear or on the contrary love and habit which for thirty years can conceal the changes brought about by age, and even if I did not attempt—though my love-affair with Albertine was sufficient proof to me that any other kind of representation must be artificial and untruthful—to represent some of my characters as existing not outside but within ourselves, where their slightest action can bring fatal disturbances in its train, and to vary also the light of the moral sky which illumines them in accordance with the variations in pressure in our own sensibility (for an object which was so small beneath the clear sky of our certainty can be suddenly magnified many times over on the appearance of a tiny cloud of danger)—if, in my attempt to transcribe a universe which had to be totally redrawn, I could not convey these changes and many others, the needfulness of which, if one is to depict reality, has been made manifest in the course of my narrative, at least I should not fail to portray man, in this universe, as endowed with the length not of his body but of his years and as obliged—a task more and more enormous and in the end too great for his strength—to drag them with him wherever he goes.

Not that there was anything new in the idea that we occupy a place in Time which is perpetually being augmented. Everyone feels this, and the universality of the idea could not but rejoice me, since it was the truth, the truth dimly apprehended by each one of us, that I was to attempt to elucidate. And not only does everyone have this feeling that we occupy a place in Time, but this "place" is something that the simplest among us habitually measures in an approximate fashion, as he might measure with his eye the place which we occupy in space. People with no special perspicacity, seeing two men whom they do not know, both perhaps with black moustaches or both clean-shaven, will say that of the two one is about twenty and the other about forty years old, for the face of a young man cannot possibly be confused with that of a man of middle age, which in the eyes even of the most ignorant beholder is veiled by a sort of mist of seriousness. Of course, this evaluation of age that we make is often inaccurate, but the mere fact that we think ourselves able to make it indicates that we conceive of age as an entity which is measurable. And the second of the two men with black moustaches has, in effect, had twenty years added to his stature.

This notion of Time embodied, of years past but not separated from us, it was now my intention to emphasise as strongly as possible in my work. And at this very moment, in the house of the Prince de Guermantes, as though to strengthen me in my resolve, the noise of my parents' footsteps as they accompanied M. Swann to the door and the peal—resilient, ferruginous, interminable, fresh and shrill—of the bell on the garden gate which informed me that at last he had gone and that Mamma would presently come upstairs, these sounds rang again in my ears, yes, unmistakably I heard these very sounds, situated though they were in a remote past. And as I cast my mind over all the events which were ranged in an unbroken series between the moment of my childhood when I had first heard its sound and the Guermantes party, I was terrified to think that it was indeed this same bell which rang within me and that nothing that I could do would alter its jangling notes. On the contrary, having forgotten the exact manner in which they faded away and wanting to re-learn this, to hear them properly again, I was obliged to block my ears to the conversations which were proceeding between the masked figures all round me, for in order to get nearer to the sound of the bell and to hear it better it was into my own depths that I had to re-descend. And this could only be because its peal had always been there, inside me, and not this sound only but also, between that distant moment and the present one, unrolled in all its vast length, the whole of that past which I was not aware that I carried about within me. When the bell of the garden gate had pealed, I already existed and from that moment onwards, for me still to be able to hear that peal, there must have been no break in continuity, no single second at which I had ceased or rested from existing, from thinking, from being conscious of

myself, since that moment from long ago still adhered to me
and I could still find it again, could retrace my steps to it
merely by descending to a greater depth within myself. And
it is because they contain thus within themselves the hours of
the past that human bodies have the power to hurt so terribly
those who love them, because they contain the memories of so
many joys and desires already effaced for them, but still cruel
for the lover who contemplates and prolongs in the dimension
of Time the beloved body of which he is jealous, so jealous
that he may even wish for its destruction. For after death Time
withdraws from the body, and the memories, so indifferent,
grown so pale, are effaced in her who no longer exists, as they
soon will be in the lover whom for a while they continue to
torment but in whom before long they will perish, once the
desire that owed its inspiration to a living body is no longer
there to sustain them.

In this vast dimension which I had not known myself to
possess, the date on which I had heard the noise of the garden
bell at Combray—that far-distant noise which nevertheless was
within me—was a point from which I might start to make
measurements. And I felt, as I say, a sensation of weariness and
almost of terror at the thought that all this length of Time had
not only, without interruption, been lived, experienced, secreted by me, that it was my life, was in fact me, but also that I was
compelled so long as I was alive to keep it attached to me, that
it supported me and that, perched on its giddy summit, I could
not myself make a movement without displacing it. A feeling
of vertigo seized me as I looked down beneath me, yet within
me, as though from a height, which was my own height, of
many leagues, at the long series of the years.

I understood now why it was that the Duc de Guermantes,
who to my surprise, when I had seen him sitting on a chair,
had seemed to me so little aged although he had so many more
years beneath him than I had, had presently, when he rose to
his feet and tried to stand firm upon them, swayed backwards
and forwards upon legs as tottery as those of some old arch-
bishop with nothing solid about his person but his metal
crucifix, to whose support there rushes a mob of sturdy young
seminarists, and had advanced with difficulty, trembling like a

leaf, upon the almost unmanageable summit of his eighty-three years, as though men spend their lives perched upon living stilts which never cease to grow until sometimes they become taller than church steeples, making it in the end both difficult and perilous for them to walk and raising them to an eminence from which suddenly they fall. And I was terrified by the thought that the stilts beneath my own feet might already have reached that height; it seemed to me that quite soon now I might be too weak to maintain my hold upon a past which already went down so far. But at least, if strength were granted me for long enough to accomplish my work, I should not fail, even if the results were to make them resemble monsters, to describe men first and foremost as occupying a place, a very considerable place compared with the restricted one which is allotted to them in space, a place on the contrary prolonged past measure—for simultaneously, like giants plunged into the years, they touch epochs that are immensely far apart, separated by the slow accretion of many, many days—in the dimension of Time.

NOTES

1 (p. 10) From Racine's *Esther*, Act I, Scene 3.

2 (p. 67) Two famous Siamese twins who appeared in music halls and had a *succès de curiosité* at the 1900 World's Fair.

3 (p. 113) These words appear neither in the libretto of *Pelléas et Mélisande* nor in any of Rameau's operas, but in Gluck's *Armide* in this form: "*Ah, si la liberté me doit être ravie, est-ce à toi d'être mon vainqueur?*" Similarly, one or two of the phrases attributed to Arkel and Golaud in the next paragraph are a little fanciful: Proust invariably quoted from memory.

4 (p. 122) *Maquereau*=pimp.

5 (p. 129) Clarification of this expression can be found in an essay of Proust's entitled *En mémoire des églises assassinées*, in which, during a drive through Normandy, he compares his chauffeur with his steering-wheel to the statues of apostles and martyrs in mediaeval cathedrals holding symbolic objects representing the arts which they practised in their lifetimes or the instruments of their martyrdom—in this case a stylised wheel: a circle enclosing a cross. Cf. Vol. Two p. 1061.

6 (p. 156) Comic opera by Adolphe Adam (1836).

7 (p. 161) *Grue* means "crane" (in both the ornithological and the mechanical sense) and also, by analogy, "prostitute." *Faire le pied de grue*="to kick one's heels," "to stand around for a long time"—like a crane standing on one leg, or a street-walker in search of custom. Morel's use of the term is grammatically nonsensical.

8 (p. 188) Claude-Philibert Berthelot, Baron de Rambuteau: politician and administrator, *préfet* of the Seine in 1833, introduced public urinals with individual compartments.

9 (p. 208) Famous nineteenth-century tragedian.

10 (p. 218) This passage was obviously written before Proust composed his account of Bergotte's death and inserted it at an earlier point in this volume.

11 (p. 235) Mme Pipelet is the concierge in Eugène Sue's *Les Mystères de Paris*. Mme Gibout and Mme Prudhomme

are characters in Henri Monnier's *Scènes populaires* and *Les Mémoires de Joseph Prudhomme*.

12 (p. 237) Famous Parisian caterers.

13 (p. 242) Cottard will nevertheless reappear—indeed at this same soirée (see p. 281)—to die during the Great War, in *Time Regained*.

14 (p. 278) The French has a play on the words *allegro* and *allègre*.

15 (p. 280) Mme Verdurin uses here the word *tapette*, no doubt unaware of its popular meaning (see Vol. Two note 49 to p. 1071).

16 (p. 289) The heroine of Victor Hugo's *Hernani*: the reference is to the final scene, which ends with Hernani's enforced suicide after the nuptial feast.

17 (p. 289) Thomas Couture, nineteenth-century French painter. The allusion is to his picture, *Les Romains de la Décadence*, shown in the Salon of 1847.

18 (p. 292) Auguste Vacquerie and Paul Meurice were two devoted disciples of Victor Hugo.

19 (p. 296) Mme de Villeparisis will reappear, extremely aged but very much alive, in *The Fugitive*.

20 (p. 307) There is a marginal note by Proust in the manuscript at this point: "Stress the fact that homosexuality has never precluded bravery, from Caesar to Kitchener."

21 (p. 333) The *blancs d'Espagne* were a group of extreme legitimists who held that the true heirs to the French throne were the Spanish Bourbons who were descended in direct line from Louis XIV through his grandson Philip V of Spain.

22 (p. 345) Slang for anus. What Albertine had been about to say was "me faire casser le pot," an obscene slang expression meaning to have anal intercourse (passive).

23 (p. 385) There is a gap in Proust's manuscript at this point. For an illustration of the narrator's point, see Vol. One p. 703.

24 (p. 419) Racine's *Esther* again.

25 (p. 446) "*Notre mal ne vaut pas un seul de ses regards*"—the line is from one of Ronsard's *Sonnets pour Hélène* (cf. Vol. Two p. 1183).

26 (p. 464) Again, in quoting by heart, Proust has got it slightly wrong. The Pléiade editors (whom we have followed here) reproduce his inaccuracies except in one point, replacing his "que mourir" by "comme mourir" in the penultimate line to avoid a false quantity.

27 (p. 553) Albert, Duc de Broglie, the grandson of Mme de
Staël, was exiled by Napoleon I and retired to
Chaumont-sur-Loire—whence the association of ideas.

28 (p. 581) *Le chancelier* Pasquier, friend of Mme de Boigne, who
ran a famous salon under the July Monarchy and
whose *Mémoires* (published in 1907) suggested those of
Mme de Beausergent which the narrator's grandmother
loved to read. The Duc de Noailles was a friend and
patron of Sainte-Beuve. Mme d'Arbouville was the
latter's mistress.

29 (p. 597) Mme de Guermantes has told this story before, at the
expense of the Prince de Léon (see p. 29).

30 (p. 611) These lines are from Musset's *La Nuit d'Octobre*, and
the lines beginning *Tu les feras pleurer* from Sully-
Prudhomme's *Aux Tuileries*.

31 (p. 659) The reference is to *Phèdre*, Act II, Scene 5, in which
Phèdre declares her love for Hippolyte in cryptic
terms: she loves Thésée *"non point tel que l'ont vu les
enfers . . . mais fidèle, mais fier, et même un peu farouche."*

32 (p. 663) Roland Garros: famous French aviator.

33 (p. 673) An illegitimate daughter of the Duc de Berry, son of
Charles X, married a Lucinge-Faucigny.

34 (p. 678) *Sous-maîtresse*: euphemism for a brothel-keeper or
"madam."

35 (p. 685) This passage is a little confusing. Proust never got
round to marrying Gilberte to the Duc de Guermantes.
In *Time Regained* she reappears as Saint-Loup's widow
while Oriane is still alive and married to the aged
Duke.

36 (p. 685) Agamemnon in Offenbach's *La Belle Hélène*.

37 (p. 695) This signature can be explained by the fact that Charles
Morel was Bobby Santois in Proust's original manuscript.

38 (p. 698) The widowed Gilberte, in *Time Regained*, appears to be
the mother of an only daughter.

39 (p. 715) Proust's manuscript adds at this point: "Cruelty on the
death of her father (copy from the note-book where
it is described)."

40 (p. 717) Legrandin has earlier been described in almost identical
terms (see p. 683).

41 (p. 719) Another chronological inconsistency. Bergotte's death
was reported long before the marriage of Gilberte and
Saint-Loup.

42 (p. 737) From Victor Hugo's *Les Contemplations*.

43 (p. 782) Quotation from Baudelaire's *Le Balcon*.

44 (p. 819) "Le moi est haïssable" (Pascal).

45 (p. 962) Eponymous hero of a novel by the Comtesse de Ségur.

46 (p. 973) And yet the narrator does not meet her until 50 pages later, failing to recognise her at first (see pp. 1028-1029).

47 (p. 993) The remark occurs later: see preceding note.

48 (p. 1053) This passage is also rather surprising, since Rachel has been identified several pages before. All such inconsistencies are attributable to Proust's endless additions to his original text. He died before he had time to resolve the resulting confusions.

ADDENDA

Page 95.   *There is a brief passage inserted here in Proust's manuscript which interrupts the thread of the narrative:—*

Lying is a very small matter; we live in the midst of it without giving it more than a smile, we practise it without meaning to harm anyone, but jealousy suffers because of it and sees more in it than it conceals (often one's mistress refuses to spend the evening with one and goes to the theatre simply to prevent us from seeing that she is not looking her best), just as it often remains blind to what the truth conceals. But it can elicit nothing, for women who swear that they are not lying would refuse even with a knife at their throats to confess their true character.

Page 98.   *The Pléiade editors have relegated to their "Notes and Variants" the following isolated passage which the original editors inserted, somewhat arbitrarily, after "for so long."*

The curious thing is that, a few days before this quarrel with Albertine, I had already had one with her in Andrée's presence. Now Andrée, in giving Albertine good advice, always appeared to be insinuating bad. "Come, don't talk like that, hold your tongue," she said, as though she were at the peak of happiness. Her face assumed the dry raspberry hue of those pious housekeepers who get all the servants sacked one by one. While I was heaping unjustified reproaches upon Albertine, Andrée looked as though she were sucking a lump of barley sugar with keen enjoyment. At length she was unable to restrain an affectionate laugh. "Come with me, Titine. You know I'm your dear little sister."

I was not merely exasperated by this rather sickly exhibition; I wondered whether Andrée really felt the affection for Albertine that she pretended to feel. Seeing that Albertine, who knew Andrée far better than I did, always shrugged her shoulders when I asked her whether she was quite certain of Andrée's affection, and always answered that nobody in the world cared for her more, I am convinced even now that Andrée's affection was sincere. Possibly, in her wealthy but provincial family, one might find the equivalent in some of the shops in the Cathedral square, where certain sweetmeats are declared to be "the best going." But I know that, for my part, even if I had invariably come to the opposite conclusion, I had so strong an impression that Andrée was trying to rap Albertine over the knuckles that my mistress at once regained my affection and my anger subsided.

Page 116. *In the place of this passage, the manuscript contains the following:*—

"What? You wouldn't kill yourself after all?" she said with a laugh.

"No, but it would be the greatest sorrow that I could possibly imagine." And since, although living exclusively with me, and having become extremely intelligent, she none the less remained mysteriously in tune with the atmosphere of the world outside— as the roses in her bedroom flowered again in the spring—and followed as though by a pre-established accord (for she spoke to almost no one) the charmingly idiotic fashions of feminine speech, she said to me: "Is it really true, that great big fib?" And indeed she must, if not love me more than I loved her, at least infer from my niceness to her that my tenderness was deeper than it was in reality, for she added: "You're very sweet. I don't doubt it at all, I know you're fond of me." And she went on: "Ah, well, perhaps it's my destiny to die in a riding accident. I've often had a presentiment of it, but I don't care a fig. I accept whatever fate has in store for me."

I believe that, on the contrary, she had neither a presentiment of nor a contempt for death, and that her words were lacking in sincerity. I am sure in any case that there was no sincerity in mine, as to the greatest sorrow I could imagine. For, feeling that Albertine could henceforth only deprive me of pleasures or cause me sorrows, that I would be ruining my life for her sake, I remembered the wish that Swann had once formed apropos of Odette, and without daring to wish for Albertine's death, I told myself that it would have restored to me, in the words of the Sultan, my peace of mind and freedom of action.

Page 267. *There is an additional passage here, isolated by the Pléiade editors at the foot of the page. Saniette reappears further on (pp. 329-331).*

"Pretty well played, what!" said M. Verdurin to Saniette. "My only fear," the latter replied, stuttering, "is that Morel's very virtuosity may somewhat offend against the general spirit of the work." "Offend? What do you mean?" roared M. Verdurin while a number of the guests gathered round like lions ready to devour a man who has been laid low. "Oh, I'm not aiming at him alone . . ." "But the man doesn't know what he's talking about. Aiming at what?" "I . . . shall have . . . to listen to it. . . once again to form a judgment *à la rigueur*." "*A la rigueur*! the man's mad!" said M. Verdurin, clutching his head between his hands, "he ought to be put away." "The term means 'with exactitude.' You . . . sssay 'with rigorous exactitude,' after all. I'm saying that I can't judge *à la rigueur*." "And I'm telling you to go away," M. Verdurin shouted, intoxicated by his own rage, and pointing to the door with blazing eyes. "I will not allow people to talk like that in my house!"

Saniette went off zigzagging like a drunken man. Some of the guests, seeing him thus ejected, assumed that he had not been invited. And a lady who had been extremely friendly with him hitherto, and to whom he had lent a precious book the day before, sent it back to him next day without a word, scarcely even wrapped in some paper on which she had her butler simply put Saniette's address. She did not wish to be in any way "indebted" to someone who was obviously far from being in the good graces of the little clan. Saniette, as it happened, was never to know of this piece of rudeness. For scarcely five minutes had passed after M. Verdurin's outburst when a footman came to inform the latter that M. Saniette had had a stroke in the courtyard. But the evening was not yet over. "Have him taken home; I'm sure it won't be serious," said M. Verdurin, whose *hôtel particulier*, as the manager of the hotel at Balbec would have said, thus became assimilated to those grand hotels where the management hasten to conceal sudden deaths in order not to frighten off their customers, and where the deceased is temporarily hidden in a meat-safe until the moment when, even if he has been in his lifetime the most distinguished and the most generous of men, he is clandestinely evacuated by the door reserved for the dishwashers and sauce chefs. In fact Saniette was not quite dead. He lived for another few weeks, but only intermittently regaining consciousness.

Page 475.   *The Pléiade editors have inserted here as a footnote an additional passage which Proust placed a few pages later (clearly in error):—*

I was going to buy, in addition to the motor-cars, the finest yacht which then existed. It was for sale, but at so high a price that no buyer could be found. Moreover, once bought, even if we confined ourselves to four-month cruises, it would cost two hundred thousand francs a year in upkeep. We should be living at the rate of half a million francs a year. Would I be able to sustain it for more than seven or eight years? But never mind; when I had only an income of fifty thousand francs left, I could leave it to Albertine and kill myself. This was the decision I made. It made me think of *myself*. Now, since one's ego lives by thinking incessantly of all sorts of things, since it is no more than the thought of those things, if by chance, instead of being preoccupied with those things, it suddenly thinks of itself, it finds only an empty apparatus, something which it does not recognise and to which, in order to give it some reality, it adds the memory of a face seen in a mirror. That peculiar smile, that untidy moustache—they are what would disappear from the face of the earth. When I killed myself five years hence, I would no longer be able to think all those things which passed through my mind unceasingly, I would no longer exist on the face of the earth and would never come back to it; my thought would stop forever. And my ego seemed to me even more null when I saw it as something that no longer exists. How could it be difficult to sacrifice, for the sake of the person to whom one's thought is constantly straining (the person we love), that other person of whom we never think: ourselves? Accordingly, this thought of my death, like the notion of my ego, seemed to me most strange, but I did not find it at all disagreeable. Then suddenly it struck me as being terribly sad; this was because, reflecting that if I did not have more money at my disposal it was because my parents were still alive, I suddenly thought of my mother. And I could not bear the idea of what she would suffer after my death.

Page 654. *Proust's manuscript has a different version of the Norpois-Villeparisis episode which the Pléiade editors print as an appendix. Passages that have become illegible are indicated by square brackets:—*

Several of the palaces on the Grand Canal were transformed into hotels, and by way of a change from the one at which we were staying, we decided one evening to dine in another where the food was said to be better. While my mother was paying the gondolier, I entered a vast marble-pillared hall that had once been entirely covered with frescoes, [. . .].

One of the waiters asked if the "old couple" [. . .] were coming down [. . .], that they never gave any warning, and that it was most tiresome. Then he saw the lady appear. It was in fact Mme de Villeparisis [. . .] but bent towards the ground, with that air of dejection and bemusement produced by extreme fatigue and the weight of years. We happened by chance to be given a table

immediately behind hers, up against the splendid marble walls of
the palace, and fortunately, since my mother was tired and wanted
to avoid introductions, we had our backs to the Marquise and
could not be seen by her, and were moreover protected by the
relief of a massive column with a [. . .] capital. Meanwhile I was
wondering which of her relations was being referred to as M. de
Villeparisis, when a few minutes later I saw her old lover, M. de
Norpois, even more bent than she, sit down at her table, having
just come down from their room. They still loved each other, and,
now that he had given up his functions at the Ministry, as soon as
the relative incognito which one enjoys abroad permitted, they
lived together completely. In order to allow his old mistress a degree
of respectability, he was careful not to give his name in hotels, and
the waiters, ignorant at this distance of celebrated Parisian liaisons,
and moreover seeing this old gentleman, even when he had gone
out without her, invariably coming back to dine alone with the old
lady, assumed that they were M. and Mme de Villeparisis. The
matrimonial character of their relationship, which had been greatly
accentuated by the carelessness of old age and travel, manifested
itself at once in the fact that on sitting down to table M. de Norpois
evinced none of those courtesies one shows towards a woman who
is not one's wife, any more than she herself made any effort for
him. More lively than Mme de Villeparisis, he related to her with a
familiarity that surprised me what he had learned that day from a
foreign ambassador he had been to see. She let a fair proportion
of his words go by without answering, either from fatigue, or lack
of interest, or deafness and a desire to conceal it. From time to time
she addressed a few words to him in a faint voice, as though
overcome with exhaustion. It was obvious that she now lived
almost exclusively for him, and had long since lost touch with the
social world—from which, with considerable volubility and in a
rather loud voice (perhaps to enable her to hear him), he brought
her the latest news—for she put to him, in a low-pitched, weary
voice, questions that seemed strange on the lips of a person who,
even though excluded from it for a long time, nevertheless belonged
to the highest society. After a long silence [. . .] asked: "So this
Bisaccia you [. . .] this afternoon, is he one of Sosthène's sons?"
"Yes, of course, he's the one who became Duc de Bisaccia when
Arnaud took the name Doudeauville. He's charming; he's a bit
like Carnot's youngest son, only better-looking." And once more
there was silence. What seemed most of all to be preoccupying the
old woman, whose charming eyes in that ruined face no one could
have identified through the mists which the distance from Paris

and the remoteness of age accumulated round her, was a war over Morocco. In spite of what the foreign ambassador had said to M. de Norpois, she did not seem reassured. "Ah, but you always see the black side," said M. de Norpois with some asperity. "I admit that Emperor William is often unfortunate in his choice of words and gestures. But the fact that certain things must be taken seriously doesn't mean that they should be taken tragically. It would be a case of Jupiter making mad those he wishes to destroy; for war is in nobody's interest, least of all Germany's. They're perfectly aware in the Wilhelmstrasse that Morocco isn't worth the blood of a single Pomeranian grenadier. You're alarming yourself about trifles." And again there was silence, prolonged indefinitely by Mme de Villeparisis, whose beauty, which was said to have been so striking, had been as thoroughly effaced as the frescoes that had decorated the ceiling of this magnificent hall with its broad red pillars, and whose personality was as well concealed, if not from the eyes of Parisians who might perhaps have identified her, at least from the hotel's Venetian staff, as if she had been wearing a carnival mask as in the old days in Venice. M. de Norpois addressed an occasional reproof to a waiter who had failed to bring something he had ordered. I noticed that he enjoyed good food as much as at the time when he used to dine with my family, and Mme de Villeparisis was as finicky as she had been at Balbec. "No no, don't ask them for a soufflé," M. de Norpois said, "they've no idea what it is. They'll bring you something that bears not the slightest resemblance to a soufflé. In any case it's your own fault, since you won't hear of Italian cooking." Mme de Villeparisis did not answer; then after a while, in a plaintive voice, as sad and faint as the murmur of the wind, she wailed: "No one knows how to make anything any more. I don't know whether you remember, in the old days at my mother's house, they used to bring off to perfection a dish called a *crème renversée*. Perhaps we could ask for one of those." "In fact it hadn't yet come to be called a *crème renversée*; it was called," said M. de Norpois, putting the phrase in inverted commas, " 'creamed eggs.' What they give you here won't be up to much. Creamed eggs were so smooth and succulent, do you remember?" But, whether because she did not in fact remember, or because she had talked enough, Mme de Villeparisis said nothing. She relapsed into a long silence which did not offend M. de Norpois, presumably because it did not surprise him and because it must have been one of the characteristics, perhaps one of the charms, of his life with her. And while she laboriously cut up her beans, he went back to telling her how interesting, and on the whole optimistic, the foreign ambassador had been, meanwhile keeping an eye out for a waiter from whom he could order their dessert. Before this had been served, my mother and I rose from the table, and, while keeping my head turned away so as not to attract their attention, I could nevertheless still see the two aged lovers, seemingly indifferent to one another, but in reality bent by time like two branches which have developed the same tilt, which have drawn so close to each other that they almost touch, and which nothing will ever either straighten up or separate again.

This was perhaps what might have happened to me in the long run if Albertine had lived. And yet, comforting though it must after all be, since worldly men and women sacrifice social life and ambition for it, I felt no regret that what might have been had failed to come about, so impervious had I become to the memory of Albertine. I cannot however say that sometimes in the evening, when we returned to our hotel (for, since our encounter with the old Villeparisis-Norpois couple, my mother had decided against our dining elsewhere), I did not feel, in the nervous restlessness of nightfall, that the Albertine of old, invisible to myself . . . (*cf. p. 654, line 10.*)

SYNOPSIS

THE CAPTIVE

Life with Albertine. Street sounds (1). Albertine and I under the same roof (2). My mother's disapproval (5). My irregular sleeping habits (7). Françoise's respect for tradition (8). Intellectual development and physical change in Albertine (9). I advise against a trip with Andrée to the Buttes-Chaumont (11). My confidence in Andrée (12). I no longer love Albertine, but my jealousy subsists (13). Ubiquity of Gomorrah (15). The virtues of solitude (17). I long to be free of Albertine (20). Jealousy, a spasmodic disease (22).

Visits to the Duchesse de Guermantes (23). What survives of the magic of her name (24; cf. Vol. Two p. 23). The Fortuny dresses (26). Attraction of the Duchess's conversation (26-29). Mme de Chaussepierre (32; cf. Vol. Two p. 697). Digression about the Dreyfus Case (33).

M. de Charlus and Morel *chez* Jupien (37). "Stand you a tea" (37). M. de Charlus receives a note from a club doorman (38). Natural distinction of Jupien's niece (41). M. de Charlus delighted at the prospect of her marriage with Morel (42). Morel's capricious sentiments and pathological irritability (45).

The syringa incident (48; cf. 613). Waiting for Albertine's return: pleasures of art (50). Change in her since she has sensed my jealousy (50). Andrée's defects; her calumnies about "I'm a wash-out" (53; cf. 617). Reports on her outings with Albertine (54). Albertine's taste and elegance (57). Variability of the nature of girls (58). Persistence of my desire for the fleeting image of Albertine at Balbec (61). Albertine asleep (63). Watching her sleeping (65), and waking (68). The soothing power of her kiss, comparable to that of my mother at Combray (71). My increasing resemblance to all my relations (72).

Changes of weather; their effect on my indolence (76) and on my jealous suspicions (79). Bloch's cousin Esther (80). Albertine's plan to visit Mme Verdurin (83). I suggest other expeditions (86). A "fugitive being" (87-90). Françoise's hostile prophecies about Albertine (93). Telephone call to Andrée about Albertine's visit to the Verdurins (95). But can I trust Andrée? (97). Albertine tries to dissuade me from accompanying her to the Verdurins' (99). I advise her to go to the Trocadéro instead (102). The anguish of being deprived of her customary good-night kiss (107). Her sleep again (108-110) and her charming awakening (111).

Spring morning (111). Street sounds; the musical cries of the street-vendors (112-115). Reflections on different kinds of sleep (116-121). Albertine's enthusiasm for the cries of Paris and the foodstuffs they offer (122); her eloquent disquisition on the subject of ices (125).

The chauffeur and the expedition to Versailles (127). Alone at the window, I listen to the sounds of Paris (132). Nostalgia for little girls (134). Françoise sends me one to do an errand: a pretty dairy-maid whom I had noticed (136), but whose glamour quickly evaporates when she is in my presence (138). Léa is to perform at the Trocadéro (141). How to prevent Albertine from meeting her? (142). I send Françoise to fetch her (148). Deterioration in Françoise's speech (151); her inability to tell the right time (152). Awaiting Albertine's return, I play Vinteuil's Sonata (155). Music and introspection (156). Reflections on the attitude to their work of nineteenth-century artists (157). Morel's mysterious occupations (159). His outburst against Jupien's niece: *grand pied de grue* (161). Drive to the Bois with Albertine (163). Similarities between desire and travel (168). Alternations of boredom and desire (171). Our shadows in the Bois (172). My servitude and hers (175). A meeting with Gisèle (175). The lies of the little band fit together exactly (176). Albertine admits a lie (178).

I learn of Bergotte's death (180). His illness, prolonged by medical treatment (181). At the Vermeer exhibition: the little patch of yellow wall. Dead forever? (185). Albertine's lie about meeting Bergotte (186). Her technique of lying (187, 190).

The Verdurins quarrel with M. de Charlus. I set off for the Verdurins' in secret (191). Encounter with a repentant Morel (192; cf. 161). His capriciousness and cynicism (194), and his rancour towards those to whom he causes pain (196). Meeting with Brichot (197). The death of Swann (197). Brichot evokes the Verdurin salon of old (200). Arrival of M. de Charlus, greatly changed (203). Brichot's attitude towards him (203). Homosexuality and the refinement of artistic tastes (205). M. de Charlus's conjugal behaviour with Morel (209). His detachment from social constraints (210). Morel's letter from Léa (211). M. de Charlus admires Morel's successes with women (213); and meanwhile tries to seduce other young men, in particular Bloch (216).

Arrival at the Verdurins' house (226). M. de Charlus and the footman (227). Saniette snubbed by M. Verdurin for announcing

three-day trip to Balbec (339). A mysterious and horrible Albertine reveals herself ("casser le pot") (343). My mendacious proposal that we should separate (347). Esther's photograph (348; cf. 80). Albertine and Léa (351). I am intoxicated by my grief (359), which I suddenly bring to an end by "a renewal of the lease" (365). Albertine's sleeping body: a mysterious allegory (366). A letter from my mother (370). Curiosity and sagacity of Françoise (372). Albertine's artistic tastes (375). The Fortuny gowns (376). Albertine plays me some music (378). The profound truth of Vinteuil's music (380). Reflections on genius (381). Key phrases (382); the example of Dostoievsky (384).

Return of spring; vain resolution to change my way of life (395). Mme Bontemps' revelations about the Buttes-Chaumont and Albertine's readiness to leave Balbec with me (396). Two character traits: the multiple utilisation of a single action (397; cf. Vol. One p. 1000) and the incapacity to resist the tempation of a pleasure (398). My outburst of anger (401). Interrogation of Albertine about her relations with Andrée (404). Reconciliation, but no good-night kiss (406). A presentiment of death (408). The noise of a window being opened in the silence of the night (409).

We go out together (411). The aeroplane (413; cf. Vol. Two p. 1062). Albertine and the pastry-cook (416). Sounds and scents of spring (417); thirst for Venice (419). I resolve to leave Albertine immediately (420). Françoise informs me that she has just left (422).

THE FUGITIVE

Grief and Forgetting. "Mlle Albertine has gone" (425). Albertine's letter (427). Hypotheses about the reasons for her departure (428). All my different "selves" must learn to live with my suffering (437). Albertine in Touraine (438). The little poor girl in my room (440). Saint-Loup's mission to Touraine (443). His astonishment on seeing Albertine's photograph (445). Bloch's indiscretion and my anger (450). Summons from the Sûreté (451). First furtive hint of forgetting (455). My sleep is full of Albertine (456). First telegram from Saint-Loup: mission delayed (456); second telegram: Albertine has seen him (459). Furious, I cable to him telling him to return (461). A letter from Albertine (461). My mendacious reply (462). The declaration scene in *Phèdre* (467). The mystery of Albertine's rings (471; cf. 162). Another letter from Albertine (477). I ask Andrée to come and live with me, and tell Albertine (478). Saint-Loup's return; an overheard conversation shows him in a new light (479). His report on his mission (480).

A telegram from Mme Bontemps: Albertine's death in a riding accident (485). New and unprecedented suffering (485). Proliferation of memories (487-489). The baths at Balbec (501). Aimé's mission of inquiry (502). Alternation of odious suspicions and tender memories (503). Analogy between my love for Gilberte and my love for Albertine (511). Our mistresses are the daughters of our anguish (515). Lying words become prophetic truths (517). Aimé's letter confirming my suspicions (525). His mission to Touraine (534). Albertine and the laundry-girl (535); evocation of an Elstir painting (537). Revival in my memory of a sweet, kind and innocent Albertine (540).

Beginnings of recovery (544). I grow accustomed to the idea of Albertine's death (544). Intermittent revival of my love and my suffering (547 sqq.). Andrée confesses her taste for women, but denies having had relations with Albertine (556). Renewal of desire for other women (564). The power of oblivion (568).

Mlle de Forcheville. Three stages on the road to indifference (570). A walk in the Bois on All Saints' Day (570). The three girls (573). Some days later, one of them gives me a look which rouses my passion (574). I identify her with Mlle d'Eporcheville, whom Robert had met in a house of assignation (574; cf. Vol. Two p. 719). Robert, in reply to a cable from me, tells me it is the wrong girl (578). My article in the *Figaro* (579-583). Visit to the Guermantes's (584). The blonde girl: Mlle de Forcheville (584), in other words Gilberte (586). Mme de Guermantes's changed attitude towards Swann's wife and daughter after his death (589); she entertains Gilberte and talks to her about her father (592). The Duke reads my article (596). Gilberte's snobbery (597). Two congratulatory letters (602). Gilberte helps to bury the memory of her father (604) and hastens the process of forgetting in me as regards Albertine (605). A new social self replaces the one that loved Albertine (607).

Second stage on the road towards indifference: second conversation with Andrée (609); her relations with Albertine (612); Albertine and Morel (612); the evening of the syringas (613; cf. 48). Andrée's different natures (616); her engagement to the Verdurins' nephew, "I'm a wash-out" (617), an artist of genius underneath his crude and frivolous exterior (618). The Princesse de Parme's visit to my mother (626). Third visit from Andrée (627); a new explanation for Albertine's departure (627). Albertine and "I'm a wash-out" (629). His attitude towards me (635).

Third stage towards indifference: a trip to Venice (637). Venice and Combray (637). Mme de Villeparisis and M. de Norpois, greatly aged (644-654). A telegram from Albertine telling me she is alive; it gives me no joy (656). The self that loved Albertine is dead (657). My outings in Venice, alone or with my mother (660). The Giotto chapel at Padua (662). Evening walks in Venice (665).

I ask my mother to postpone our departure (666); she refuses, and I decide to stay (667). Solitude, misery, *O sole mio* (667). The train (670). A letter from Gilberte announcing her engagement to Robert de Saint-Loup (670); the recent telegram was from her (671).

A new aspect of Saint-Loup. My mother tells me of another marriage, that of the Cambremers' son and Mlle d'Oloron, Jupien's niece (672). My mother's reflections on the news, and thoughts of my grandmother (672). Ups and downs of Saint-Loup's engagement plans (676). Disapproval from Combray (677). Reactions of society people (678). Opposite effects of the same vice in Charlus and Legrandin (681). Roles of the Princesse de Parme, Charlus and Legrandin in Mlle d'Oloron's marriage (682). Change in Legrandin (683). Gilberte, at first happy in her new social position (684), becomes indifferent to it (686). Mlle d'Oloron's death (688). The Muse of History (692).

A visit to Tansonville (694). Saint-Loup's infidelity; his relations with Morel (695). Retrospective analysis of Robert's sexual tastes (696-699). Robert and Mme de Forcheville (701). My tarnished friendship (705).

TIME REGAINED

Tansonville. Walks with Gilberte (709). Disenchantment with the scenes of my childhood (710). Gilberte shows me that the Guermantes and the Méséglise ways are not irreconcilable (711; cf. Vol. One p. 146) and reveals the meaning of the sign she made to me years ago (694).

Scene from the window of my room at Tansonville (715). Effects of Saint-Loup's vice on his behaviour (717). His lies (718). Françoise's esteem for him (719). His feelings towards Gilberte (720). The Guermantes type in Robert (722). The Guermantes' amatory tastes (723). Conversation with Gilberte about Albertine (725-727).

The Goncourt journals (728). Their description of the Verdurin salon (728-736). My lack of a bent for literature (737).

M. de Charlus during the war. My return to Paris in 1916 (743). War-time Paris: changes in fashions and in Society (743-749). News of the war in the Verdurin salon (750). The new "faithful"; Morel, a deserter, and "I'm a wash-out," Andrée's husband (751). Mme Verdurin's overtures to Odette (753).

Aircraft in the sky at nightfall (755). Walks in night-time Paris, reminiscent of Combray (756).

Meeting with Saint-Loup in 1914 (758); his secret efforts to get to the front (759). Bloch passed fit for military service (761). Bloch and Saint-Loup (762). Ideal of virility among homosexuals (766-769). The manager of the Grand Hotel and the lift-boy (769). Françoise and the war (770); tormented by the butler (771-773).

Return to the sanatorium (773). A letter from Gilberte: German occupation of Tansonville (773). A letter from Robert (774).

Second return to Paris: another letter from Gilberte, with news of the fighting round Combray (777). A visit from Saint-Loup, in Paris on leave (779). Beauty of nocturnal air-raids (780); reflections on strategy (782).

Beauty of night-time Paris (785). Meeting with M. de Charlus (787); Mme Verdurin's malevolence towards him (788); Morel's ingratitude and scurrilous articles in the press (790). Mme Verdurin's croissant and the *Lusitania* (797). M. de Charlus's pro-Germanism (797-802). His sarcasm about Brichot's articles (803). Morel and women (805). Norpois's articles (807). Odette's remarks about the war (815). Brichot falls out of favour with the Verdurins (816). M. de Charlus's defeatist harangue on the boulevards (820-826). Aeroplanes in the night sky (828). M. de Charlus and Morel (831-833). Paris and Pompeii (834). M. de Charlus's admiration for Allied and German soldiers (835). His hand-clasp (836).

I look for a hotel (837) and find one open from which a familiar figure (Saint-Loup?) emerges (838). Conversation between soldiers and workers (839). The *patron* comes in with some chains (842). I see M. de Charlus being thrashed by a soldier (843). Jupien appears (843). Other clients of the hotel (844). The lost *croix de guerre* (849; cf. 871). M. de Charlus in the midst of the harem (853-857). Jupien's explanations (858-862).

An air-raid (863). Pompeians in the Métro or in Jupien's establishment (864). Reflections on morality, on Jupien, on M. de Charlus and his aberrations (867). Françoise and the butler (871). The Larivières (876).

Saint-Loup's death (877). Recollections of his friendship (878). Parallel with Albertine (879). Françoise in the role of mourner (879). The Duchesse de Guermantes's unexpected grief (882).

Morel's arrest as a deserter (883); his revelations cause the arrest of M. de Charlus and M. d'Argencourt (884). If Saint-Loup had survived . . . (884).

Reception at the Princesse de Guermantes's. Return to Paris many years later (885). Train stops in the middle of the countryside (886). My incurable lack of literary talent (886). Invitation to the Princesse de Guermantes's musical afternoon (887). Cab-drive towards the Champs-Elysées (888); the silent heights of memory (890). Meeting with a greatly aged Charlus (891). His greeting to Mme de Saint-Euverte (891). His roll-call of dead friends and relations (894). The Duchesse de Létourville, shocked by his mumbling voice (895). Jupien speaks of the Baron's health, his Germanophilia, his persistent randiness (896).

The uneven paving-stones in the Guermantes courtyard (898); sensation of felicity similar to that of the madeleine, etc. (899); resurrection of Venice (900). Further exhilarating sensations (900). "The true paradises are the paradises one has lost" (903). Impressions "outside time" (904). Reflections on time, reality, memory, artistic creation (905 sqq.). Futility of literary theories (915). Absurdity of popular art or patriotic art (917). *François le Champi* (918). Bibliophilia (922). Celibates of art (927). Aberrations of literary criticism (929).

Further reflections on literary and artistic creation (931 sqq.). The raw material for literature: my past life (935). A vocation? (936). The importance of dreams (949). The influence of Swann (953). The role of jealousy (955). Chateaubriand, Nerval and Baudelaire (958).

Back to the Guermantes reception: a *coup de théâtre* (960). M. d'Argencourt as an old beggar (961). Bloch (968). The Duchesse de Guermantes (969). The meaning of old age (973). M. de Cambremer (974). Legrandin (976). The Prince d'Agrigente (977). Various effects of Time (981). Odette: a challenge to the laws of chronology (990); "a sterilised rose" (993). Bloch's English *chic* (995); I introduce him to the Prince de Guermantes (996). Mme Verdurin has become the Princesse de Guermantes (998). Society and the chemistry of Time (1000 sqq.). Following the stream of memory back to its source (1017 sqq.). "Who's dead?" (1024-1027).

The Princesse de Nassau (1027). Gilberte: "You took me for Mamma" (1028). Conversation about Robert (1029) and the art of war (1030). Her friendship with Andrée (1032). My determination to avoid social life (1034). The Duchesse de Guermantes and Rachel (1041).

Berma's tea-party (1045). Her daughter and son-in-law (1046). Rachel's performance (1050). She runs down Berma (1054). Mme de Guermantes in old age: her social decline (1056). Berma's daughter and son-in-law received by Rachel (1066).

The Duke's liaison with Odette (1068). "A magnificent ruin"